C0-AMY-442

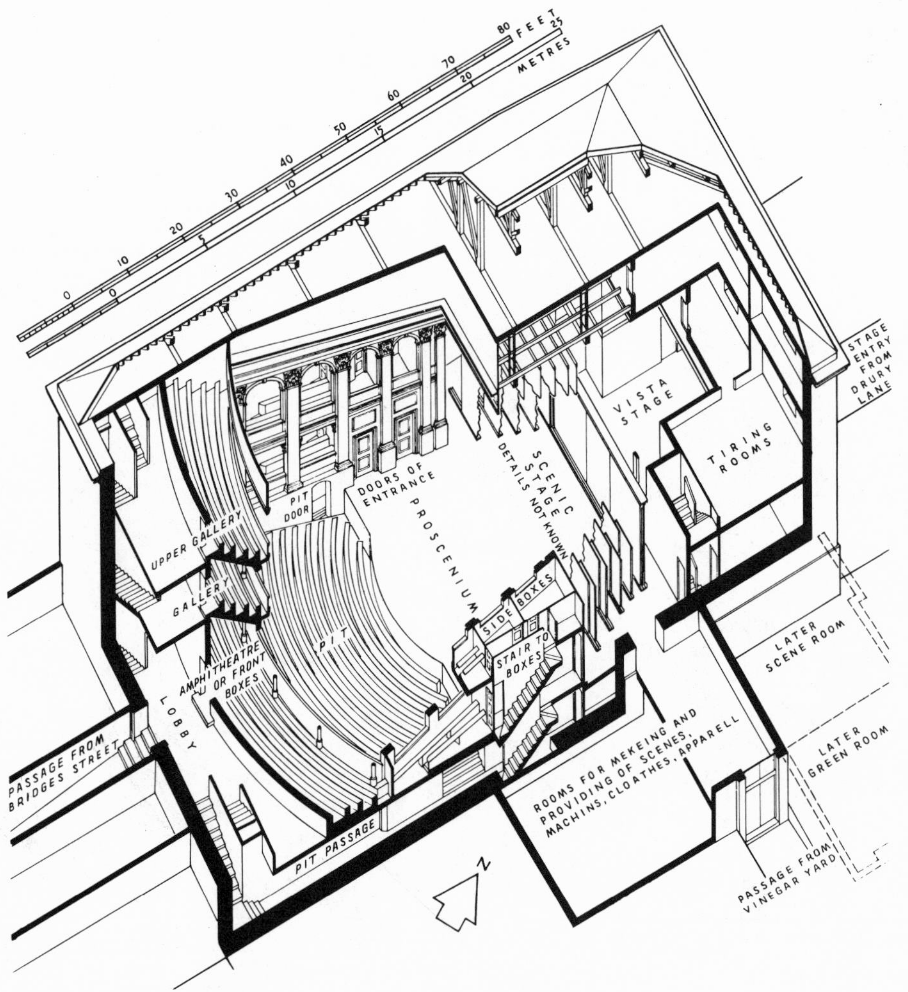

Edward A. Langhans

Conjectural reconstruction by Richard Leacroft of the Drury Lane Theatre in 1674, from his *Development of the English Playhouse*. By kind permission of Mr. Leacroft and Eyre Methuen Ltd.

RESTORATION PROMPTBOOKS

Southern Illinois University Press
Carbondale and Edwardsville

Printed in the United States of America
Designed by Design for Publishing

Library of Congress Cataloging in Publication Data

Main entry under title:

Restoration promptbooks.

Bibliography: p.
Includes index.
1. Theater—England—London—History.
2. Promptbooks. I. Langhans, Edward A.
PN2592.R47 792'.09421 80-15626
ISBN 0-8093-0885-1

To my good friends and colleagues

Philip H. Highfill
and
Kalman A. Burnim

Contents

Acting Companies and Their Promptbooks

Facsimiles of Complete Promptbooks

Illustrations

Acknowledgments

I am deeply grateful to the many libraries and librarians in America, England, and Australia who have aided me in my search for Restoration promptbooks and related documents. I especially wish to thank the Baillieu Library at the University of Melbourne, the Bodleian Library at Oxford University, the Harvard Theatre Collection, the Folger Shakespeare Library in Washington, D.C., the Pennsylvania State University Libraries, and the University of Illinois Library for granting me permission to present here facsimile reproductions of promptbooks in their collections. My thanks go out to the splendid staffs at those libraries and at the Beinecke, Clark, Huntington, and Newberry research libraries; the British Library, Victoria and Albert Museum, National Library of Scotland, Boston Public Library, New York Public Library, and the Library of Congress; the Worcester College Library, Oxford; and the libraries at the universities of Edinburgh, London, and Texas.

Many friends and colleagues have given me direct or indirect help and encouragement along the way. I extend my gratitude to Kalman A. Burnim, Diana De Luca, David Dyregrov, Gwynne Blakemore Evans, Philip H. Highfill, Leo Hughes, Robert D. Hume (who courageously read my manuscript and offered many helpful suggestions), Shirley Strum Kenny, Kathleen Lesko, Richard Leacroft, Lilly Lievsay, James G. McManaway, Judith Milhous, Donald C. Mullin, Alois M. Nagler, Elizabeth Niemyer, Jeanne T. Newlin, James P. O'Donnell, Marvin Rosenberg, Sybil Rosenfeld, Arthur H. Scouten, Charles H. Shattuck, Richard Southern, and Laetitia Yeandle. I am also indebted to the late Emmett L. Avery, John Crow, Una Ellis Fermor, and William Van Lennep. The research of many scholars, including some of the above, has helped me in a variety of ways, and I have tried to credit their works in the bibliography or in the headnotes to each item presented on the following pages.

The late Vernon Sternberg of Southern Illinois University Press, so great a friend of Restoration and eighteenth-century scholars, first encouraged the publication of this book and assigned Beatrice Moore as my editor. I am immensely indebted to her for her great patience and meticulous handling of my manuscript.

Honolulu, Hawaii
12 February 1980

EDWARD A. LANGHANS

Introduction

> Promptbooks are tricky, secretive, stubborn informants. They chatter and exclaim about what we hardly need to know: that certain characters are being readied by the callboy to make their entrances; that the scene is about to change or the curtain to drop; that the orchestra is about to play at the act-end. They fall blackly silent just when we most hope to be told where the actor stood or how he looked or what he did. Rarely do they give us a hint of voice or temper or histrionic manner.
>
> Charles Shattuck, *The Shakespeare Promptbooks*

And yet promptbooks are among the most precious theatrical raw materials we have, even when they are incomplete or fail to tell us all we wish to know, and until they have been gathered and studied the history of the English-speaking theatre will be incomplete. Most of the Shakespeare promptbooks catalogued in Shattuck's invaluable work belong to the eighteenth century or later, and those studied by G. Blakemore Evans in his splendid *Shakespearean Prompt-Books of the Seventeenth Century* are mostly pre-Restoration or Irish.[1]

What I have done here is to bring together for examination the promptbooks of the professional theatres in London from 1660 to 1700, a period for which such materials have never been gathered and are extremely rare. Most have not received detailed examinations before, and many are presented here for the first time. In 1936 only one promptbook had been found for the London theatres of the Restoration period: *The Sisters*, then at Sion College Library. In 1956 in *The Theatre Annual* I was able to say that we then knew of six promptbooks. Now I can provide facsimiles of eleven (plus one from Dublin for purposes of comparison), and I have transcribed the prompt notes from an additional nine less heavily annotated London promptbooks and the traces of prompt copy in thirty printed plays. That seems like a wealth of material, but only in comparison with what had been discovered years ago. There are surely more promptbooks from the 1660 to 1700 period to be found, but the number of documents presented here is sufficient, I think, to provide us with much new and useful information about production practices in the theatres of the time.

The focus here is theatrical, not literary: no attempt has been made to

1. To avoid excessive footnoting, I have given brief citations in the text, with page number where necessary; full citations of all sources can be found in the Bibliography.

provide bibliographical descriptions of the documents, to gloss obscure passages or topical allusions in the texts of the plays, to collate manuscript plays with printed texts, or to supply author biographies, stage histories, social and historical backgrounds to the plays, and so on. I have not provided critical editions of plays but rather facsimiles and transcriptions and comments on them.

I have concentrated my attention on London from 1660 to 1700 but have strayed outside my limits, chiefly in the appendices, to provide for purposes of comparison information on related London materials and on promptbooks from Dublin. Excluded or given only passing attention are plays with notes that may not be theatrical in origin. When the only manuscript markings in a copy are deletions of words, phrases, speeches, or scenes, one is hard put to determine the date of the marks even if they seem to have been made by someone with play production in mind. Such borderline cases I have included in the appendices, if only for a brief notice, hoping that future scholars may pin down dates and sources.

Promptbooks

What qualifies as a promptbook? I am encouraged by Professor Shattuck to use the term loosely and include all marked copies of plays prepared for use in professional theatrical productions in London during my period. Some of these, as will be seen, are incomplete or contain only one or two kinds of notes. A complete promptbook from the late seventeenth century normally included warnings and cues for entrances, sound, music, and special effects; notes on large and small properties; descriptions of stage settings; warnings and cues for scene shifts; and indications of lines to be omitted in performance. The manuscript notes concerning these matters are usually found in more than one hand—there are at least six theatrical hands in *The Change of Crownes*. The prompter (or book holder, bookkeeper) and his assistants were chiefly concerned with warnings and cues for actors and sound, and with cuts and emendations, while the machinist (or stage keeper; our modern technical director is a parallel) and his helpers were responsible for scenery, properties, special effects, and the like. But to determine who wrote what in Restoration promptbooks is nearly impossible.

Of the promptbooks gathered here none is as rich as the best of those from a century later, but several are very full by Restoration standards: *The Change of Crownes*, *The Sisters*, *The Maides Revenge*, *Aglaura*, *Brennoralt*, and *The Wittie Faire One*. Others vary considerably in their contents. *The Cheats*, for example, is very complete as far as it goes, but after a few pages the prompter apparently abandoned the copy in favor of a cleaner one. In a few cases it seems clear that what we have is not *the* promptbook for a production but *a* promptbook: in *Romeo and Juliet* we find only music and deletion notes; *Tyrannick Love* has mostly technical notes; *The Lady-Errant* markings are chiefly cuts and emendations. There were probably for these plays other partial books plus a relatively full one for the prompter. But for sake of convenience one can use the term promptbook for all such documents.

One supposes that for every play produced during the Restoration period—and there were hundreds of them—a full promptbook once existed. In addition to the few that have been found, we have hints of a number more in printed plays containing traces of prompt copy. In 1936, when only one London promptbook for our period had been discovered, traces of prompt copy excited the interest of the late William Smith Clark II, who listed eighteen editions with traces in "Restoration Prompt Notes and Stage Practices." We now know of thirty. Traces of prompt copy in printed plays come about through the negligence of compositors in printing shops. Traces often occur in clusters—all within a few pages or confined to one or two gatherings. In the fascinating case of *Guzman*, where in some sections of the text every one of the prompt notes seems to have ended up in print, three compositors may have set the type: one remarkably careful, one rather negligent, and a third who, luckily for us, was either irresponsible or simply did not understand much about promptbooks.

Careful printers may well have produced many editions based on promptbooks without allowing any discernible traces of prompt notes to appear in print. I say discernible, because today we may mistakenly read a trace of prompt copy as a stage direction written by the author. Thus there may be many editions of plays published during the Restoration period which were set from prompt copy but in which we cannot distinguish the traces.

In a printed play it is indeed difficult to separate authors' stage directions from traces of prompt notes unless such clear prompter's words as "Call" or "Ready" are found. In *The Revenge*, for instance, an actor's name turned up in a list of characters; in the manuscript from which the printer worked, the author may have jotted down the name of the player best suited for the role, but such a note is more likely to have been made by someone at the theatre who was concerned with casting. One guesses, then, that in this case the copy used by the printer came from the playhouse; thus when we find in the first quarto of that play a stage direction saying, "*Two Chairs, a Table*," we might conclude that the note was written by the prompter or machinist. In *Tom Essence* we find "*(Call* Luce" printed about twenty-five lines before the entrance of that character; that is proof positive that the printed edition was set from prompt copy. Later in the play we read, "*(A Candle set in the Window*." It is even printed the same way as the clear trace, and one is certainly tempted to assign it to someone backstage rather than to the author. But without the original manuscript promptbooks we have no way of being sure. And we want to be sure, for what we hope to learn, in addition to information on stage practices, is how the acting companies treated the plays they produced. What did they add or subtract, what wishes of an author did they respect, and what did they ignore? What they did or did not do can tell us a great deal about the taste of the times and how the players, willingly or unwillingly, wittingly or unwittingly, catered to it.

Fortunately, we have a sufficient number of actual promptbooks from the period to provide us with examples of just what kinds of notes were written by the various backstage personnel and what their notes looked like. An example of this is in the promptbook for *The Wittie Faire One*, where we see manuscript notes reading *SCENE GARD[EN]* and *CHAMBER*, in that kind of lettering. In *The Villain*, which contains a clear trace of prompt copy and was certainly set from a promptbook, we find "TOWN" and "[H]ALL." Same company of actors, same theatre, same decade, and a compositor matching in typography what he found in the manuscript notes: we can be sure that those setting descriptions in *The Villain* were written by someone at the playhouse and not by the author. But this is treacherous territory, and I have tried my best to indicate when I am not certain about matters of attribution.

We can understand more easily why some printers could not keep traces of prompt copy out of printed plays when we see what manuscript promptbooks looked like. *The Change of Crownes* is our best example. One wonders how a prompter could have run a performance from this chaotic and, in places, incorrect, promptbook, but he evidently did. A printer setting type from such copy would have his work cut out for him even if he was familiar with playhouse practices, and the possibility of some of the prompt notes ending up in print would be high. *The Change of Crownes* was not published in Restoration times, and, alas, we have no example of a promptbook and a printed edition set from it.

The disposition of a promptbook after a play completed its run is not fully known. Some were clearly given to printers and served as the bases for editions of plays. Would such manuscripts have served again in the theatre after passing through the hands of the printing-shop workers? I seriously doubt it, not just because of the mauling they might get in the shop, but because I cannot imagine that the players would want a promptbook back if it had not been important enough to keep in the first place. Further, if a company revived a play a few months or a few years later, a new promptbook using a printed copy of the text would be superior to a manuscript—as can be seen from those that have been discovered. But the majority of plays struggled through three performances (for the sake of the author, who received the profits of the third day's presentation) and then died unlamented. In such cases the promptbooks would have been of little further use to the players, though the author might have been anxious to salvage whatever he could through publication; the promptbook would have been the logical text from which to set a printed edition, since it was the final version of the play and could be puffed "as performed in the theatre."

On the other hand, a play that "took," as the prompter John Downes said, might remain popular for several seasons, and the promptbook for it would have been a valuable property—too valuable to be loaned to a printer. The 1676 quarto of *Hamlet*, for example, is a full text, based on the 1637 quarto, with Restoration playhouse omissions set within quotation marks:

> To the Reader.
>
> This Play being too long to be conveniently Acted, such Places as might be least prejudicial to the Plot or Sense, are left out upon the Stage: but that we may no way wrong the incomparable Author, are here inserted according to the Original Copy with this Mark " [A2]

What was *not* omitted was what, presumably, Thomas Betterton acted. Would the players have allowed their promptbook (containing not only the indications of cuts but all the other prompt notes as well) to be used by the printer for setting the 1676 edition? I think not. That promptbook was probably a copy of the 1637 quarto with manuscript prompt notes. It would have been safer for the players to give the printer another copy of that quarto, in which the playhouse omissions were marked. Significantly, the 1676 edition shows no evidence of having been set from prompt copy.

When a promptbook for such a popular play as *Hamlet* wore out or became obsolete because of changes in company personnel or taste, probably a new one would be made up and the old one destroyed. Players then, as now (except the academic types or historically minded), saved costumes, promptbooks, scenery, properties, and the like only as long as they were useful. In their tiny Restoration playhouses the acting companies could ill afford saving something for the sake of saving something. And who would ever find a promptbook of interest after the play had dropped from the repertoire or after a printed edition based on the promptbook appeared? We would, but they were not thinking of us.

Most of the London promptbooks that have been discovered for the Restoration period date from the 1660s and 1670s; evidence from the 1680s and 1690s comes chiefly from printed plays with traces of prompt copy. Did the players in the last two decades of the century guard their promptbooks more carefully and retrieve them from printers more consistently? It is not possible to say, but it is certainly curious that so many have survived from the early years and so few from the later ones.

Significantly, most of the promptbooks that have survived are for plays that did not catch the fancy of the fickle Restoration public. One needs only to run his eyes down my table of contents to see how many forgettable plays are represented by surviving promptbooks or printed plays with traces of prompt copy.

More care was taken to save promptbooks in the eighteenth century and later. Theatres grew in size, staffs increased, productions became more complicated, scenery and costumes were more historically authentic, and more interest was shown in saving things. Professor Shattuck's catalogue, though it concerns only Shakespearean promptbooks, shows vividly the growing interest in preserving such theatrical documents. We have inherited that tradition of keeping archives, flattering ourselves that three hundred years from now someone will care what *we* did in the theatre. The Restoration players seem not to have been that vain.

Audiences

The documents on the period gathered by Alois M. Nagler in *Sources of Theatrical History* show how casual and indifferent—by our standards—Restoration audiences sometimes were. Samuel Pepys complained to his *Diary*, but not too bitterly, about byplay in the auditorium that caused him to lose a play completely. In *The Humours and Conversations of the Town* in 1693 James Wright may not have been exaggerating too much when he asked:

> What wou'd you go to the Play for? . . . to be dun'd all round with the impertinent Discourse of Beardless Fops to the Orange-Wenches, with Commodes an Ell high; and to the Vizor-Masks: of the Rake-Hells, talking loud to one another; or the perpetual Chat of the Noisy Coquets, that come there to get Cullies, and to disturb, not mind the Play. Or to what effect has all the Plays upon you? Are not your Fops in the Pit and Boxes incorrigible to all the Endeavours of your Writers, in their Prologues and Epilogues, or the variety of Characters that have been made to reform them? Tho a Play be an generous Diversion, yet 'tis better to read than see, unless one cou'd see it without these Inconveniences. (Pp. 105–6)

That unruly audience could sometimes be galvanized into attention by such an actor as Thomas Betterton (so Colley Cibber tells us in his *Apology*), but theatre was a social occasion for many if not most of the playgoers. If in a performance of *Aglaura* the same setting was used to represent both the Queen's Chamber and Aglaura's Chamber, the spectators may not have noticed it; a Chamber was a Chamber, and theatre was theatre, not real life. Times have changed, and modern audiences prefer a stage production of a realistic play to be logical and believable, with nothing to shatter the illusion or remind us (until intermission) that we are witnessing a theatrical performance. Similarly, we may be bothered because the plot of such a play as *The Way of the World* is too complicated for anyone, even the characters, to follow, forgetting that following the plot may not have been of primary interest to Congreve's audience or, indeed, to Congreve himself.

Pepys sometimes said he went to "hear" a play. We go to see one. The difference in terminology is significant. Though we tend to associate

Baroque theatre with scenic splendor—something to see—typical Restoration productions may not have had much visual emphasis. Had stage spectacle been of great importance to playgoers of Restoration London I think we would have had more pictorial evidence of it. There are dozens of prints of late seventeenth-century continental scene designs for public and court productions; there are hardly any English. Except for occasional spectacular shows, the Restoration public theatre may still have been something like Shakespeare's: not a place of scenes and machines, as at court, but a place for playwrights and actors. Not until the eighteenth century did pantomime and Italian opera, bourgeois and aristocratic spectacles respectively, really begin to compete with what we now call legitimate theatre. Those often disreputable Restoration audiences had not lost their taste for poetry completely, had certainly not abandoned wit, and could be struck dumb by a Charles Hart or an Anne Bracegirdle delivering a well-turned line.

A typical Restoration auditorium had rows of backless benches in the pit, one or two levels of boxes forming a U around the pit, and a U-shaped open gallery. The royal box was (or should have been) at the point of distance in the house, a spot corresponding to the vanishing point for the perspective scenery. Both the auditorium and the stage were illuminated throughout the performance by chandeliers, a factor which contributed to the sometimes noisy behavior of the audience. Though many of the spectators were from the upper class, Pepys noted that by 1 January 1668 a considerable number of "citizens, 'prentices, and others" attended the theatre.

Playhouses

With the exception of the tiny converted tennis court theatre in Vere Street, which evidently opened with no facilities for changeable scenery, most of the Restoration playhouses probably had similar, but certainly not identical, stage arrangements and equipment, based partly on the court, private, and public theatres of pre-Commonwealth London and partly on continental models. In front of the main curtain was a forestage or apron, sometimes more than 15′ deep, flanked by proscenium doors, at least one if not two on each side of the stage. The forestage and proscenium doors were descendants of the platform and entrance doors in the public and so-called private theatres of Shakespeare's day. The forestage was a most important acting area, especially for heroic tragedies or high comedies or any play in which the spoken word took precedence over physical action. Farces and spectacle pieces seem to have made more use of the scenic area. The choice of that area or of the forestage apparently depended on whether a play encouraged the characters to relate physically to their scenic environment or to use the scenery as a decorative background. The width of the forestage varied from theatre to theatre, being perhaps as little as 15′ to 20′ in the smaller playhouses but not much wider than 30′ to 35′ in the larger ones. The stage floor was raked, rising gradually from the front edge toward the back, aiding the perspective effect of the scenery and giving us the upstage-downstage terms we still use today.

There has been some argument about the placement of the wings and shutters on Restoration stages, but I believe the standard layout was that which is depicted in most plans of English and continental theatres from the 1640s to the middle of the eighteenth century: a series of wings on each side of the stage, painted in perspective and standing in grooves (or, as we shall see, possibly attached to poles rising through slots in the stage floor); then shutters, similarly painted, about halfway upstage, capable of closing off the deeper reaches of the scenic area by meeting at the center line; then perhaps another set of wings on each side; then a deeper set of shutters; and finally a backscene or final prospect.

Though a few theatre plans from the seventeenth century show packs of several wings and shutters at each position (Inigo Jones's plan for *Salmacida Spolia* in 1640 is an example), such an arrangement used up stage depth, which in early Restoration playhouses was at a premium. In any case, no more than two grooves (on the stage floor and suspended from above) at each wing and shutter position would have been necessary. Conjecturally, setting #1, painted on wings and shutters, would stand in the first grooves at each position; directly behind, in the second grooves at each position, would stand setting #2. At the sound of a whistle, as *The Change of Crownes* promptbook shows, stagehands at each wing and shutter post would slide off all the units in the first grooves, revealing setting #2. While the first scene was playing, setting #1, if it was not to be used at the next scene change, could be drawn completely out of the first grooves, to be replaced at each position by wings and shutters for setting #3. And so on. Any number of different settings could thus be used in a play. Between each wing position was enough space—two to three feet on most plans—to permit entrances by performers. For most members of the audience, the arrangement of wings also served to mask the backstage area from their view.

Masking from the spectators' eyes the area above the stage—the "flies"—were borders: horizontal strips of scenery hanging over each wing and shutter position and capable of being raised and lowered as a scene change occurred. Again, no more than two borders at each position would have been necessary, for stagehands on catwalks over the stage could take a border from its batten and replace it with another or, if several borders were hung on the same batten, flip the first one back to reveal the next. One set of borders—sky borders, for example—could be used with a number of different settings, so the borders did not have to change as often as the wings and shutters.

I have suggested that in Restoration playhouses there were two shutter positions, the first about halfway upstage and the second a few feet upstage of that. We have no evidence for two shutter positions in English theatre plans of the late seventeenth century, but the demands made by the playwrights in their stage directions would seem to require two, and a number of seventeenth-century continental plans show such, or similar, arrangements. The clearest examples are the Teatro SS. Giovanni e Paolo, Venice (1639); the Teatro della Pergola, Florence (1656); the Komödienhaus, Dresden (1667); the Teatro degli Intronati, Siena (1670); the Teatro della Fortuna, Fano (1677); and the Théâtre Français, Paris (1689). Reproductions of those plans may be found in Donald Mullin's *The Development of the Playhouse* and Allardyce Nicoll's *The Development of the Theatre*.

The need for two shutter positions can be seen in the frequent requests by English playwrights for "discovered" scenes, sometimes two in succession; the area between the two shutter positions served as an inner stage or discovery area, and the space upstage of the deeper shutters became a second such inner stage. Actors and properties could be prearranged behind closed shutters and revealed when the shutters were drawn off. A second discovered scene could be staged in the deeper reaches of the stage, behind the upstage shutters. Alternatively, as a stage direction in Aphra Behn's *Sir Patient Fancy* shows, the first inner stage could be closed over, a new tableau set up, and the shutters reopened.[2]

Within the scenic area and on the forestage of a typical Restoration playhouse must have been trap doors, since numerous plays of the time require their usage. Stage directions in several plays (Dryden's *Albion and Albanius* especially) suggest that such theatres as Dorset Garden had rigging systems capable of flying objects and people up, down, forward, back, and perhaps across the stage. The discovered promptbooks for the London theatres of the Restoration reveal very little about traps and flying machinery, though the Dublin promptbook for *Belphegor* contains some special effects.

The position of the music room varied from one theatre and time to another. The one at Dorset Garden Theatre, pictured in the prints illustrating Settle's *The Empress of Morocco* in 1673, was above the proscenium arch, perhaps in imitation of the music room in some Elizabethan public playhouses. Pepys complained about the location of the musicians at the Bridges Street Theatre on 8 May 1663: "the musique being below, and most of it sounding under the very stage, there is no hearing of the bases at all, nor very well of the trebles, which surely must be mended." Apparently Pepys was used to hearing the music come from a side box on an upper level. Musicians sometimes had to get from the music room to a position in the wings or perhaps onstage, and the prompter needed to warn them in time, as can be seen in the

2. Richard Southern in *Changeable Scenery* (pp. 146–52), using *Sir Patient Fancy*, argues in favor of a dispersed shutter arrangement, with grooves for shutters at several planes of the stage, beginning downstage, behind the curtain line, at the first wing position. It is an interesting conjecture but not, I think, feasible in view of the narrowness of Restoration playhouses, the widest of which measured only 59′ (outside dimension). Because of the use of perspective in seventeenth-century scene painting, the distance across the stage between pairs of wings diminished as one moved upstage. Thus, if the proscenium opening was, say, 30′ wide, the first pair of wings might be 28′ apart, the second pair 26′ apart, and so on; halfway upstage, at the first shutter position in the plan I have just described, the visible stage width would have narrowed to perhaps 20′. A pair of shutters, in order to close that 20′ opening, would have to be 10′ wide each; to accommodate them offstage, each side of the stage would need 10′ of width plus about 3′ for passageway. Added up, that consumes 46′ of stage width to accommodate shutters at mid-stage. In a building 59′ wide outside, with walls about 3′ thick (as the Wren section view shows), that arrangement would work.

But if one follows Southern's plan and has shutters closing off the prospect downstage, near the first wing positions, the shutters would have to be wider, and more offstage space would be needed. To fill a 28′ width each shutter would have to be 14′ wide and the total inside building width would have to be 56′ plus passageways. In a theatre quite capable of having a proscenium opening 30′ wide it would seem pointless to limit it unnecessarily to 22′. In the smaller Restoration playhouses, with total building widths of 25′ to 30′, Southern's plan would narrow the proscenium opening unacceptably.

In addition, Southern's plan is not really necessary, since the most complicated scene changes in Restoration plays can be accomplished without resorting to the dispersed shutter layout and the problems it creates. If a theatre had two shutter positions, as described earlier, it could handle two discovered scenes in succession—and hardly any Restoration plays call for more. Significantly, Southern does not mention his dispersed shutter theory in his chapter on theatre and scenery in the fifth volume of *The Revels History of Drama in English*.

traces of prompt copy in *The Careless Lovers*. The musicians played before a play and probably after it, though the promptbooks take little notice of those entertainments; warning and cuing entr'acte music, however, was a concern of the prompter, as several books prove.

Tiring rooms—or backstage rooms of various sorts—are shown in Sir Christopher Wren's section view of a Restoration playhouse (probably a preliminary plan for Drury Lane Theatre); he clustered them at the rear of the stage area and partly around it on the upper levels. Each theatre must have had its own arrangement of dressing rooms and the equivalent of an actors' lounge. On 5 October 1667 Pepys helped his actress friend Mrs. Knepp with her lines in what he called the scene room: ". . . and so walked all up and down the House above, and then below into the Scene-room, and there sat down and she gave us fruit; and here I read the Qu's to Knepp while she answered me, through all her part of *Flora's Figarys*, which was acted today." They must have been in what was later called the "Green Room," and not, as the editors of the new Bell-California edition of Pepys's *Diary* state, in the scenic area of the stage. Presumably the warnings to actors, found in many promptbooks, were carried to the performers in the tiring rooms or scene room by a prompter's assistant—a callboy, one supposes, though I have not found that term used in Restoration theatre documents.

The Prompter

The only firsthand description we have of the Restoration prompter and his responsibilities is the general statement by the veteran prompter John Downes prefacing his *Roscius Anglicanus* of 1708:

> The Editor of the ensuing Relation, being long Conversant with the Plays and Actors of the Original Company, under the Patent of Sir William Davenant, at his Theatre in Lincolns-Inn-Fields, Open'd there 1662. And as Book-keeper and Prompter, continu'd so, till October 1706. He Writing out all the Parts in each Play; and Attending every Morning the Actors Rehearsals, and their Performances in Afternoons; Emboldens him to affirm, he is not very Erronious in his Relation. (A2–A2^{v})

Of his other duties and of the duties of his backstage colleagues Downes said nothing.

One needs only to compare the fairly primitive promptbooks of the late seventeenth century with the much more complex ones of the first quarter of the following century to see how stage production grew more sophisticated over the years. (Descriptions of some eighteenth-century books may be found in Appendix D.) The prompter's job must have increased in complexity too, so we cannot tell how germane to Restoration prompting is Aaron Hill's description in the initial issue of *The Prompter* on 12 November 1734. But theatrical traditions die hard, so part of what he said may have been true of prompters fifty years earlier. In his first essay Hill explained to his readers why he had chosen to call himself "The Prompter"—and one must read his piece in that context as well as for the theatrical information it contains. On one of his visits behind the scenes at the theatre, evidently Drury Lane, he

> . . . observed an humble but useful officer standing in a corner and attentively perusing a book which lay before him. He never forsook his post but, like a general in the field, had many *aides de camp* about him, whom he dispatched with his orders, and I could perceive that though he seemed not to command, yet all his instructions were punctually complied with, and that in the modest character of an adviser he had the whole management and direction of that little commonwealth. I enquired into his name and office and was informed that he was THE PROMPTER.
>
> . . . .
>
> To proceed then. He stands in a corner, unseen and unobserved by the audience, but diligently attended to by everyone who plays a part; yet, tho' he finds them all very observant of him, he presumes nothing upon his own capacity; he has a book before him, from which he delivers his advice and instructions. . . .
>
> He takes particular care not only to supply those that are *out* in their parts with hints and directions proper to set them right, but also, by way of caution, drops words to those who are perfect, with an intention to keep them from going wrong. I have often observed the most expert and courageous generals tremble thro' fear of missing his instructions, and the wisest of monarchs lend him an attentive ear. I have seen the merriest of mortals not dare to crack a joke till [he] gave them the cue, and the most despairing of lovers refrain from sighs and tears till they had his permission to be miserable. I have seen a discontented statesman hush sedition at his nod, and a very habile prime minister not able to pay pensions without his advice and concurrence. In short, I have seen so much, that I shall not hesitate to pronounce him a Director of the Ignorant, a Comforter of the Afflicted, a Terror to the evil Actor, and a Counsellor to the Counsellors of Kings.

> I have already taken notice of the scouts and messengers which attend him. By dispatching one of these he can, at a minute's warning, bring the greatest characters of antiquity, or the pleasantest of the present times, upon the stage, for the improvement or diversion of the audience. . . .
>
> Among his *Instrumenta Regni*, his implements of government, I have taken particular notice of a little bell which hangs over his arm. By the tinkling of this bell, if a lady in Tragedy be in the spleen for the absence of her lover, or a hero in the dumps for the loss of a battle, he can conjure up soft music to soothe their distress. Nay, if a wedding happens in a Comedy, he can summon up the fiddlers to dispel care by a country dance. . . .
>
> Another tool of his authority is a whistle which hangs about his neck. This is an instrument of great use and significance. I won't say but the sound of a boatswain's whistle may be sometimes more terrible, but I am sure it cannot be more punctually obeyed. Dr. Faustus' celebrated wand has not a more arbitrary and extensive power than this musical machine. At the least blast of it I have seen houses move as it were upon wings, cities turned into forests, and dreary deserts converted into superb palaces. I have seen an audience removed in a moment from Britain to Japan, and the frozen mountains of Zembla resembling the sunny vales of Arabic Felix. I have seen Heaven and Earth pass away and Chaos ensue, and from thence a new Creation arise, fair and blooming as the poet's fancy, and all by the powerful magic influence of this wonder-working whistle. Nobody will be surprised, after this, to hear that I have made use of all my interest to procure from the ingenious Mr. Chetwood [the prompter at Drury Lane] an attested copy of this marvellous instrument, by virtue of which, and some directions from that eminent adept, I shall be able to present my readers with a never-failing variety of objects.

The Restoration promptbooks confirm the use of the bell and whistle as cues and the importance of the prompter in regulating the performance of a play. In Hill's day, if not earlier, the prompter was evidently a combination of a modern prompter (who just prompts) and a modern stage manager (who runs the show).

The emphasis on the spoken word in the Restoration theatre suggests that the prompter's primary responsibility was helping the actors and that the cuing of scenes and machines was probably delegated to the machinist. In his picture of the prompter at work Hill placed him, rather vaguely, "in a corner." We imagine him to have been offstage left or right (the actor's left or right when facing the audience). But where could he have best positioned himself? To be of most help to the performers he needed to be where he could hear them and they could hear him; behind one of the proscenium doors he would have been blind and unable to hear well enough, while a position between the wings would have interfered with scene keepers shifting the settings and players making entrances. Given the extensive forestage in Restoration theatres, there was really no good spot backstage for the prompter. The best place would have been at the curtain line, for once the curtain was raised—and it usually remained up throughout a performance—there would have been a gap between the back of the proscenium wall and the first wing position. But the actors on the forestage would then have had their backs to the prompter much of the time. In any case, whichever side he worked on would have been called prompt side; the logical side for him would have been the one where the curtain pull was located, the "working" side of the stage. Prompt side probably varied from theatre to theatre, since some playhouses were built on odd-shaped sites and may not have had symmetrical backstage arrangements.

But no discovered Restoration promptbook mentions prompt side (PS) or opposite prompt (OP), though those terms are found in many books dating from the eighteenth century. If the Restoration promptbooks do not refer to PS or OP, perhaps the prompter was not stationed backstage at all. The promptbook for *Belphegor*, from the Smock Alley Theatre in Dublin (in Appendix B), suggests that the prompter there was in something like an opera-house prompter's box, downstage center, where he would have had a splendid view and where he would have had no trouble prompting actors.

The possibility that some London prompters may also have worked from a box at the front of the stage is intriguing, and evidence in the London promptbooks, at least those for the Duke's Company, supports it. The Duke's players' books contain warnings for actors but no entrance cues, which argues that the actors in that troupe may have been expected to look after their own entrances. No Restoration London promptbooks record from which side of the stage actors were supposed to enter; again, players may have been asked to memorize such information. We might suppose that whatever they had to memorize was something the prompter, because of the location of his station, could not help them with. The King's Company books, on the other hand, are replete with entrance cue marks, and there would have been no point in the prompter having those cues in his book if he was not able to cue the entrances. There is a possibility, then, that the Duke's prompter was in a box at the front of the stage, while his King's Company counterpart was stationed backstage.

This is speculation, not too idle, I hope. The fact is that we do not know where Restoration London prompters operated, and because we have no certain evidence, I have arbitrarily assumed in my comments on the plays and their prompt notes that the prompters worked backstage.

The commonest kind of prompt note we find is the warning for an actor's entrance. It comes from one half to two or three pages in advance. When the prompters began marking their copies, they sometimes worked mechanically, stating in the warning what they found in the author's coming stage direction. In some instances they did not take into account that they were warning an actor who was already onstage and would soon exit. At the point of entrance the King's Company prompter (or his assistant) drew a distinctive cross-hatch mark: –/////////////–. In other promptbooks entrances are sometimes cued with *X* or # or not cued at all. Some prompters may have kept an entrance cue sheet separate from their promptbook, or they may have delegated warning and cuing to an assistant. The players sometimes would have needed help, for they worked in a repertory system that required them to carry perhaps two dozen or more roles in their heads at any given time, and the parts or "sides" they worked from, as the sample in Appendix E shows, gave them almost no notion of what was going on in a play.

Could a Restoration prompter have been able to work effectively from a manuscript promptbook as messy and inaccurate as that, say, for *The Change of Crownes*? We should consider the possibility that he sometimes found the task impossible and made up a cleaner book. *The Cheats* promptbook is evidence that a prompter might abandon a copy that was too difficult to follow. Yet he and his colleagues found the manuscript of *The Change of Crownes* suitable enough to fill it throughout with copious notes. A performance could have been run from this promptbook if (a) the prompter knew the play well enough, and (b) the machinist had a corrected set of technical notes and could allow the incorrect ones in the promptbook to stand. Both of those conditions were probably met. Downes tells us that the prompter was responsible for copying out the actors' parts, and that task would certainly have made him thoroughly familiar with the script. The machinist must have had not only a corrected set of the technical notes that appear in the promptbook but a scene plot showing which grooves should be used for the various settings. Without such information the show could hardly have been run.

The Machinist and Scenery

Hill described the prompter's task as including the cuing of scene shifts and special effects as well as actor entrances, but the Restoration promptbooks suggest that a technician—the machinist, or stage keeper—probably handled the technical cues and allowed the prompter to concentrate on the actors and sound effects. Perhaps we shall one day find a Restoration machinist's papers; there surely must once have been inventories of scenery and machinery, scene plots for each production, cue sheets, and the like. Lacking any of those, we must depend on stage directions in plays and technical notes in promptbooks to tell us about Restoration stagecraft.

Scene shifts were evidently cued with a whistle, which could be heard by the scene keepers stationed at the wings, shutters, and borders—and which surely could be heard by the audience as well. There are no indications in Restoration promptbooks of quiet signals, as there are in books from the nineteenth century, when realism was an aim. Audiences in the late seventeenth century would probably not have been upset at being able to hear the bell and whistle cues; these and the *a vista* scene changes were part of the show, like the clacks used in Kabuki performances in Japan as rhythmic accompaniments to curtain openings and peak emotional moments.

The Restoration machinist's chief worry must have been to train his crew to move the right scenic units at the right time. The clever Italians by mid-century had developed the mechanical pole and carriage system of scene shifting; it involved two slots in the stage floor at each wing position, through which poles or ladders thrust up from carriages riding on tracks in the substage. By an intricate system of connecting ropes and the turning of a central cylinder in the substage, all #1 poles moved off as all #2 poles moved on, carrying with them their attached wings. Though there was the chance that a negligent scene keeper might attach the wrong wing to a pole, there was perfect coordination in the movement and much less physical effort. The Restoration promptbooks give no indication that the system was adopted in London, and some historians have assumed that the stubborn English resisted that particular foreign influence until the eighteenth century and even then did not use it in many playhouses. Two pieces of evidence, however, argue otherwise.

The first is a proclamation issued by Charles II in 1673 (just when big spectacles began being presented at Dorset Garden Theatre) and reprinted almost unchanged in later years. It admonished those rude playgoers who bullied their way into theatres without paying, and then it said:

> And forasmuch as 'tis impossible to command those vast Engines (which move the Scenes and Machines) and to order such a number of Persons as must be employed in Works of that nature, if any but such as belong thereunto, be suffer'd to press in amongst them; Our Will and Command is, That no Person of what Quality soever, presume to stand or sit on the Stage, or to come within any part of the Scenes, before the Play begins, While 'tis Acting, or after 'tis ended. . . . (Lord Chamberlain's accounts, LC 7/3)

What I find significant is that similar proclamations of earlier years did not mention the "vast Engines (which move the Scenes and Machines)." The wording is a bit odd, to be sure; I am not sure I understand the difference between engines and machines. But there is certainly a hint there of some kind of mechanical shifting of scenery.

The second piece of evidence is much more convincing, though it dates from a bit later than our period. Folger Shakespeare Library MS Wb 110 is a collection of various Drury Lane Theatre bills and accounts, among which is the following, dated 26 February 1713/14:

For 6 pounds of new Rope for the Scen[e]	ll s d
frames in the celer att 8 p pound - -	0=4—0

That must refer to a pole and carriage system. How long Drury Lane had had it, there is no way of telling. Judging by the number of spectacle productions at Dorset Garden Theatre from 1673 on—*Macbeth* and *The Empress of Morocco* in 1673, the Shadwell version of *The Tempest* in 1674, *Psyche* in 1675—perhaps when that playhouse opened in 1671 it had a pole and carriage system, and when the King's Company opened their new Drury Lane playhouse in 1674 they may have followed suit.

The technical notes in *The Change of Crownes* promptbook, though not as full as might be needed to run a performance effectively, still provide much information about staging methods. For example, at least at the Bridges Street playhouse in the 1660s, scene keepers could tell from the whistle number which scene shift it was: first whistle, first shift; second whistle, second shift; and so on. One imagines that the machinist and a helper, standing upstage on each side, could with hand signals advise the scene keepers which whistle number was forthcoming. Just one whistle blast as a cue would have been sufficient. The individual technical employees may have had their own scene plots to indicate that Act II, whistle 3 meant the forest setting, and so on. In some way, at any rate, the whistle numbers and the settings to be used were connected.

Other promptbooks give us further information about scenic matters in the Restoration playhouses, though from single examples we cannot tell how widespread the practices were. Scholars have said that in the Restoration theatre it was sometimes the practice to change the shutters but not the wings; the drawings by John Webb for *The Siege of Rhodes* at Rutland House in 1656 appear to be the chief evidence for that assumption, but that was a rather special production in a theatre set up inside a house. More solid evidence can be seen in the prompt notes for *Guzman*, *The Sisters*, and *The Careless Lovers*. The practice was a sensible one; it would have been expensive (and created a storage problem) to have a pair of shutters for every set of wings. Combinations of wings from one setting and shutters from another, and the practice of sometimes changing the shutters but letting the wings stand, or vice versa, would allow a company almost to double the utility of its stock. (It would not have been possible, however, to interchange wings from one position to another or to use mid-stage shutters in the upstage shutter grooves, since the perspective effect would be ruined. In fact, such mixing was impossible, because the heights of the wings and shutters decreased from downstage to upstage, in keeping with the perspective painting, as the Wren section view shows.)

From the traces of prompt copy in *The Injured Princess* we find a related expedient: the use of double-faced scenic units. If all the wings and shutters a company owned were reversible, there would have been a great saving in storage space. The initial cost of constructing wings and shutters that could be covered and painted on both sides would have been high, for the carpentry must have involved mortise-and-tenon or halve joints, but the saving in the long run would have been considerable.

Even if Restoration managers were economical about scenery, they were aware that scenic spectacle occasionally had its place in the theatre. Of the full promptbooks that have been found none is for a play with a heavy emphasis on scenery, but in *The Change of Crownes* there is a stage direction suggesting that the Bridges Street Theatre may have had split-level shutters similar to those Inigo Jones used in the court theatre production of *Salmacida Spolia* in 1640. The shutters were divided horizontally so that they could be opened either above or below. To accomplish that there must have been grooves on the floor, suspended grooves running across the stage in mid-air (probably just above head-level), and suspended grooves yet higher, to steady the tops of the upper shutters. In the fifth volume of *The Revels History of Drama in English* (p. 109), Richard Southern observes that Wren's section view appears to show upper shutters.

The promptbooks are sometimes helpful in showing us how the stage technicians responded to requests made by authors in their stage directions. Scholars have depended heavily on printed stage directions in their reconstructions of the staging of Restoration plays, as Southern did in *Changeable Scenery*, Lee Martin in "From Forestage to Proscenium," and Colin Visser in "The Anatomy of the Early Restoration Stage." There is nothing in the promptbooks to prove their conjectural reconstructions incorrect, yet there is evidence to caution us that what appears in printed plays and what was actually done on stage may have been quite different. The traces of prompt copy in *Guzman*, for instance, show that though the author wanted "*a Field with Trees*" for III, iv and "*a Grove of Trees*" for IV, v, he was given "the Forest" for both. And the machinist changed the shutters but not the wings of the forest setting and let that serve for "*a Garden*" the author asked for in IV, vi. Shadwell wanted some footmen to enter with flambeaux near the end of Act II of *The Woman-Captain*; the company gave him only a "*Boy with a Flambeaux*." Sampson asked for an onstage hanging in *The Vow-Breaker*, but the effect could not be managed and the victim had to go offstage and be hanged.

Properties receive some attention in the promptbooks but not as much as one might expect. In several copies there are properties clearly needed for the action of the play and mentioned by the playwright in the dialogue or stage directions but ignored by the machinist and prompter. *The Ordinary* and *The Lady-Errant*, both of which contain detailed property lists in the prompt notes, are still missing some items. That can only mean, I believe, that it was not essential to have a full property list in the prompter's book; more complete and precise property plots must have been kept elsewhere, just as were, I feel sure, details about scenery.

The Actors

Almost all of the promptbooks contain playhouse cuts or emendations, some slight but many considerable. These indicate how a playwright's original intentions were on occasion of less concern to the players than (a) keeping a play down to a reasonable running time—see, for example, *The Wise-Woman of Hogsdon*—or (b) satisfying the censor—see *The Lady-Errant* and *The Ordinary*. The 1676 quarto of *Hamlet*, with its numerous omissions, is a different example of the same sort of thing. *Hamlet* as Betterton played it was apparently swift-moving, with plenty of opportunities for histrionics and melodrama but with much of the depth of characterization and thought omitted. Many of the Dublin Shakespeare promptbooks listed in Appendix A also show how cavalier the players were with the texts of our favorite playwright. We still do not give playwrights what they ask for: Tennessee Williams did not get his original third act of *Cat on a Hot Tin Roof* performed, because his director preferred a different version. The playwright's only recourse was to publish the play with both third acts, to show readers what he had wanted and what was presented. One can almost understand the literary critics who would rather read a play than see it mangled in production. But, of course, the players did not and do not always mangle a play: they often know better than playwrights what will and what will not work in performance. And a Betterton, Garrick, Siddons, or Olivier can give a play a kind of life on stage it may never have on the printed page, even in a reader's most vivid imagination. Theatre often corrupts dramatic literature at the same time that it brings it to life.

Restoration promptbooks make little or no mention of costumes, stage movement, or line interpretation. Something can perhaps come of nothing if we consider the implications. For example, once an actor was warned for an entrance, came from wherever he was to the stage, was shown (if he was) where he should enter, and was given (if he was) his cue to go onstage, he seems to have been left to his own devices. As with notes on technical matters that may have been kept by the machinist, so actors perhaps made notes—in their parts, one would guess, though the only discovered part has no marginalia. But we may be wrong in supposing that the actors took notes. Under the twentieth-century influence of the Stanislavski system perhaps we assume incorrectly that players three hundred years ago went to great pains to develop a character and that precise blocking of stage movement was worked out for all the characters in a series of rehearsals lasting over a period of weeks.

That is all quite possible today, even in repertory companies, partly because troupes now seldom carry more than a half-dozen plays in their active repertoire; Restoration companies, judging by some of the calendar records we have for the early years of the period, might perform fifteen or more different plays within a month and keep adding other productions as the season wore on. Today even a production that fails may be kept in the repertoire and given a number of performances—until another show is prepared to replace it; back then some plays were lucky to receive more than one or two performances, and a flop could be replaced with something else in a day's time.

We sometimes forget, too, that the modern notion of finding a new approach to old plays—of never doing *Hamlet*, say, as it was successfully done by someone else—was not the Restoration way. They had a tradition of imitation, about which the prompter Downes wrote admiringly. Of Sir William Davenant's production of *Henry VIII* he said, "The part of the King was so right and justly done by Mr. *Betterton*, he being Instructed in it by Sir *William*, who had it from old Mr. *Lowen*, that had his Instructions from Mr. *Shakespear* himself . . ." (p. 24). The same approach was used for *Hamlet*: the tradition (said Downes, his genealogy a bit off) went from Shakespeare to Taylor, who was seen by Davenant, who coached Betterton "in every Particle of it . . ." (p. 21). That is perhaps why Restoration promptbooks do not tell us anything about stage movement, line interpretation, characterization, gestures, and stage business. The tradition for revived plays was oral, from master to student.

Japanese Kabuki actors today do not tamper with the interpretations that have come down through the centuries and are theirs to be guarded, preserved, and passed on to the next generation—unless they have reached the top of their profession and can risk adding a touch or two which will then become part of the tradition.[3]

Arthur Colby Sprague studied stage traditions in *Shakespeare and the Actors*, *Shakespearean Players and Performances*, and *The Stage Business in Shakespeare's Plays*; what a pity that today we must read about these rather than witness them. Years ago the training of actors changed from a master teaching his apprentice how to play the roles *he* played to general training in how to act: how to use the voice and body, how to interpret scripts, how to create characters. Presumably all those aspects of acting were also a part of a master's training of his apprentice.

What kinds of conventions might Restoration actors have had? For example, the prompter seems to have been concerned with getting actors onstage but not with getting them off. Nothing in the promptbooks suggests that actors were coached on their exits—when to exit, which side, which door, or between which wings. Were the players required to memorize their exit cues but at liberty to exit whichever side of the stage suited their fancy? Or perhaps there was an unwritten rule governing exits and entrances. In Peking Opera, at the back of the stage are two doorways; the stage right one is for all entrances, the stage left one for all exits. Commedia dell'Arte troupes, according to Andrea Perucci's *Dell'arte rappresentativa* in 1699, had a similar tradition: "characters should take care not to run into each other when they enter, which can more easily happen in improvised than in premeditated plays . . . though to leave the scene upstage and to enter it down-stage is an infallible rule, unless it is changed by some necessity" (quoted in Nagler, p. 258; translation by Salvatore Castiglione).

I suspect that Restoration players may have had a number of simple conventions of like nature that governed many of the things about which the promptbooks are silent. It may have been understood, for example, that unless the script required otherwise, whichever side of the stage an actor used for an entrance became the side to which he would restrict his movements during the ensuing scene. Or maybe it was standard practice to keep movements to a minimum and simply take a stand and start spouting. Whatever conventions the players had must not have varied too much from company to company, for there was a fair amount of interchange between companies in London and between London and Dublin.

If we find no prompt notes about costumes, that may mean, again, that such information was kept elsewhere or that costumes, too, were conventional: special garb for such characters as the Ghost in *Hamlet*, the Witches in *Macbeth*, or Beelzebub in *Belphegor*, and correct modern dress, according to class and the special qualities of a character, for everyone else. Hamlet is a gentleman, but a mad gentleman, so, as we see in the frontispiece to Rowe's *Hamlet* of 1709, Betterton (probably fol-

3. Asians have a general tendency to cling to old forms and, instead of replacing them with new ones, add new forms that can exist side by side with the old. Had the Restoration acting companies followed that sensible notion and revived the Shakespearean public theatre form along with the court theatre form, we might today have Shakespeare still being performed his way in his kind of theatre, Congreve his way, and so on.

lowing a tradition handed down to him) wore the fashionable gentleman's dress of the time but let a stocking droop—to show he was mad. Restoration audiences would not have been upset, one guesses, to see Anne Bracegirdle wear the same dress for Cordelia, Ophelia, and Desdemona, since they are similar character types. The notion of historical authenticity in costuming and of specially designed costumes for each play surely would have struck Restoration players as unnecessarily extravagant. Stock scenery, stock costumes, stock plays, stock characters, and stock characterizations were a part of theatre for twenty-five hundred years; only in the last one hundred have we tried to alter that tradition.

The Further Search for Restoration Theatrical Materials

One dreams of finding, somewhere, a magnificent cache: perhaps all the old Duke's Company promptbooks that John Downes prepared and from which, one might guess, he culled his odds and ends of facts about the history of the Restoration theatre companies for his *Roscius Anglicanus*. Or were they all destroyed? More promptbooks and other primary source materials must exist, and if we continue searching perhaps an annotated player's part will turn up, or a scene plot of some kind, or an inventory of a Restoration company's stock of properties, or some stage plans, or scene designs—the raw materials which are plentiful for the continental theatre of the time and for the eighteenth-century theatre in England.

But on the basis of the evidence we now have, the prospects seem dim of finding promptbooks that will tell us much more than what we can glean from those presented here. It became fashionable in later years to prepare and preserve elaborate production books just for the record, not as working promptbooks to be used in performance. Not so in Restoration London. For the public theatre of Betterton's time we have, aside from the plays themselves, almost nothing. The handful of scene designs by John Webb were done for the tiny pre-Restoration Rutland House stage or for the court theatre; Wren's section view is the only detailed theatre design we have, and it was apparently only a preliminary one; the *Ariadne* and *Empress of Morocco* illustrations are the only discovered pictures of Restoration stages, and they do not reveal much. The paucity of such documents makes the promptbooks we have even more valuable to us.

Remarkably, promptbooks are even rarer for the continental theatres of the seventeenth century, but there is a wealth of other theatrical material. We have the Sabbattini and Furttenbach stagecraft books from Italy and Germany; the invaluable *Memoire* of the scene designer Mahelot and his colleagues from France; many plans for playhouses in Italy, France, Germany, Holland, and Spain; dozens of scene designs by Torelli, Santurini, the Vigaranis, Bérain, Burnacini, Bernini, and others; drawings of stage machinery; and detailed descriptions of company operations and staging conventions. Did the London players go out of their way to keep the inner workings of their profession a secret, while their continental counterparts did just the opposite?

English theatre technicians were not much interested in copying their fellows on the Continent. The resistance to foreign technical developments is perhaps best illustrated by the fact that Inigo Jones in the early seventeenth century introduced the proscenium arch and the notion of the picture-frame stage to England one hundred years after it had been first used in Italy. Combine that resistance with the traditional English interest in the written and spoken word rather than the pictorial image. If they went to the theatre to hear a play, then they would have been more interested in preserving play texts than scene designs or theatre plans. And so most of the materials we have for the Restoration theatre are textual—hundreds of printed plays, dozens of manuscript plays, and these precious promptbooks.

Searching for promptbooks is a tedious business, but for those who would like to join the party I should set down briefly the procedures I followed. I began in 1955 at the British Library (then called the British Museum) examining every copy of every edition through 1700 of every play that might possibly have been performed in London between 1660 and the end of the century—pre-Restoration plays, Restoration plays, closet dramas, anything that might contain manuscript markings or traces of prompt copy. I explored the ten years before my period and the ten years after, but with less thoroughness. Then I did the same thing with manuscript plays. Though I turned up numerous items containing manuscript dates or casts and several works with non-theatrical marginalia, I found only one actual promptbook, that for *The Scornful Ladie*, and several plays with traces of prompt copy. Something like that method needs to be followed in any library where the catalogue does not indicate whether or not a play contains manuscript markings. The Folger Shakespeare Library, for example, has a separate promptbook catalogue, but the Library of Congress rare books catalogue does not alert a reader to copies with notes. Since one has but one life to live, full searches of all libraries are not always possible; after going through half of the collection at the Library of Congress and finding nothing, I abandoned my search, but Yale, Harvard, and the Huntington seemed to me to deserve the full treatment. Yet except for some manuscript casts and dates, the yield at those four collections was disappointing. A systematic search, I have found, is clearly the sensible, scholarly thing to do; unfortunately, it is not a very good way to find promptbooks. Serendipity, scholarly reports, and tips from friends led me to most of the copies studied here. Elizabeth Niemyer of the Folger Shakespeare Library told me she saw a promptbook advertised in a sale catalogue; it turned out to be *The Maides Revenge*, which Harvard recently acquired. At the Bodleian in 1964 I was studying *The Wittie Faire One* promptbook which Bertram Joseph had written up, and I found the promptbook for *The Ball* in the same volume. My friend Robert Hume of Pennsylvania State University wrote me that James O'Donnell had found three Beaumont and Fletcher promptbooks at the library there. The research of other scholars has, of course, been invaluable; the work of Evans and Shattuck has done much to alert nontheatrical scholars to the value of promptbooks, and items are now being reported that were in earlier years passed over as of no interest.

There are places I have not been able to check thoroughly for various reasons, and I would urge interested parties to explore further the Boston Public Library, the Clark, the National Library of Scotland, and the Victoria and Albert Museum. I made no attempt to look at private collections, and I am still not sure where one might begin. "Undiscovered" promptbooks and related materials are not really undiscovered; they have been seen, but by eyes that were not looking for theatrical documents. I feel that my work will have been more than justified if it stimulates those who have seen promptbooks to bring them to the attention of theatre scholars.

Modus Operandi

Would that I could offer here a promptbook for some great Restoration production—for Betterton's *Hamlet*, for instance, or for the original presentation of *The Country Wife*, or for a spectacular "machine" play or opera. Sorry. The discovered promptbooks for the period are almost all for plays of no great literary distinction, and none is for a work calling for really elaborate scenes and machines. I present here a combination of (a) full facsimiles of the twelve richest promptbooks, including one from Dublin, (b) transcriptions of the manuscript prompt notes in nine others, (c) quotations of all the certain and possible traces of prompt copy in thirty printed plays, and (d) a number of reproductions of interesting pages. The documents are arranged chronologically by acting company, though to solve production problems, the facsimiles are grouped together in the second part of the book. Headnotes provide information on the dates of the documents, dates (not necessarily premieres) and places of stage productions most likely to have been related to the promptbooks, the present location of unique documents if known, and citations of relevant books and articles. I have relegated to the Bibliography modern editions of the plays by editors who show no awareness of the promptbooks. Then follows, for each item, whatever prefatory notes might be pertinent, the presentation of the material itself with accompanying explanatory notes, and, in a commentary section, a discussion where appropriate of casting, staging, or whatever else of special interest the promptbook contains. I have provided the most complete notes and commentaries for the first few items in my collection, on the supposition that the reader may need more explanations at first but can manage with fewer after becoming familiar with the characteristics of these documents.

Line numbering has been supplied in all facsimiles, but since most of the texts contain cuts and emendations which alter the versification, every line of dialogue has been counted, regardless of length. I have added scene numbers in brackets whenever the author did not supply them but where a locale change is indicated in either the stage directions or the prompt notes.

In a few promptbooks it is fairly easy to distinguish the different hands at work; in some books all the notes are in the same hand. But *The Change of Crownes*, a manuscript promptbook, contains, according to its editor Frederick Boas, at least eight hands, six of them theatrical. If the hands in these promptbooks could actually be identified by a person's name or theatrical position, the painstaking work of trying to distinguish different hands would certainly be well worthwhile. But even in cases where we can say with confidence that Hand A wrote the actor warnings and Hand B made the entrance cue marks, we have learned very little, since we do not know who A and B were. If we were sure that A was the prompter, B the underprompter, C the machinist, and so on, the distinguishing of hands in the manuscript notes would be extremely valuable. But we cannot do that. We know that John Downes was the prompter for the Duke's Company, then the United Company, and finally Betterton's Company; at the Folger Shakespeare Library is a sample of *a* John Downes's handwriting—but there is no assurance that it is the handwriting of the theatrical John Downes, and it does not match any of the hands found in discovered Restoration promptbooks. But even that means little, for a troupe's promptbooks could have been prepared under the prompter's supervision without his hand appearing in any of them. Downes said that Charles Booth was the prompter for the King's Company, but we do not know when Booth worked with that troupe, and we have no example of his handwriting. We know the names of several of the backstage personnel in Restoration companies, but we have none of their autographs. To what purpose, then, should we seek to distinguish the hands in the manuscript prompt notes? It is of academic interest but of little practical value. Yet I have tried to indicate how many hands seem to be at work in each promptbook and to suggest with what kinds of notes each hand was concerned. These identifications should be taken as highly conjectural, for prompt notes consist not only of written words but of marks—brackets, boxing, slashes, symbols, and the like—and in some instances to tell which of several scribal hands made which marks is nearly impossible.

Some copies contain marginalia that are not theatrical in origin, such as doodles, glosses, or notes made before or after a book's use in the theatre. I have identified these as by a nontheatrical hand.

In the appendices, for purposes of comparison, are the contemporaneous Dublin promptbook for Wilson's *Belphegor*, an excerpt from the only discovered Restoration actor's part, brief descriptions of some pre-Restoration and early eighteenth-century promptbooks, and a few notes on some marked play texts that may or may not have been connected with Restoration theatrical productions.

In the transcriptions of manuscript notes or traces of them, I have used the left margin for page numbers or signatures. In the side margins of the facsimiles in the second part of this book are line numberings, act and scene numbers (when they are not indicated in the original), and clarifications of cropped or illegible individual words or short phrases. Footnotes contain clarifications of groups of cropped or illegible words, comments on the prompter's work, and discussions of unusual prompt notes.

Promptbook Symbols and Signals

–++++++++– or –+++–––––– The cross-hatch symbol was used to cue actor entrances and, sometimes, music and sound effects.

⊙ The circle-and-dot symbol was a cue for a scene shift. Since the cue itself was a whistle, perhaps the symbol was intended to picture the end of a whistle, but the symbol may have been borrowed from astronomy, as are some eighteenth-century promptbook symbols.

X and *#* These marks were also used as cues.

Whistle The *Whistle* note was usually used as a warning for a coming scene shift; at the actual shift the whistle was blown.

Call Usually found in connection with actor warnings, this was a note for the callboy (or someone) to fetch an actor for an entrance. The accompanying note sometimes named the actual players (usually minor members of the company) and sometimes the characters. *Call* was often omitted, leaving only the list of people to be summoned. The term was occasionally used for warnings for music and other effects.

Ready or *be ready* Sometimes actors were warned with this note, as in the Rhodes Company books, but usually *Ready* was used as a warning for a sound or special effect.

Act or *Act Ready* These notes usually served as a warning for scene shifts, actor entrances, and entr'acte music.

Ring *Ring* was a cue for act endings and was connected with the *Act* and *Act Ready* warnings. Dublin prompters sometimes used *Ring* as a cue for special effects, such as risings and sinkings via trap doors.

Acting Companies and Their Promptbooks

1 / John Rhodes's Company (1660)

For a brief time in 1660, before the formation of the two main Restoration acting companies, a group of young players under the leadership of John Rhodes performed at the Cockpit (or Phoenix) in Drury Lane. In his *Roscius Anglicanus* in 1708 the prompter John Downes remembered the troupe:

Mr. *Rhodes* a Bookseller being Wardrobe-Keeper formerly (as I am inform'd) to King *Charles* the First's, Company of Comedians in *Black-Friars*; getting a License from the then Governing State, fitted up a House then for Acting call'd the *Cock-Pit* in *Drury-Lane*, and in a short time Compleated his Company.

Their Names were, *viz.*

Mr. *Betterton.*
Mr. *Sheppy.*
Mr. Lovel.
Mr. Lilliston.
Mr. Underhill.
Mr. Turner.
Mr. Dixon.
Robert Nokes.

Note, These six commonly Acted Women's Parts.
Mr. Kynaston.
James Nokes.
Mr. Angel.
William Betterton.
Mr. Mosely.
Mr. Floid.

The Plays there Acted were,

The Loyal Subject.
*M*aid in the *M*ill.
Rule a Wife and have a Wife.
The *Tamer* Tam'd.
The Wild Goose Chase.
The *Spanish* Curate.
The *M*ad Lover.
Pericles, Prince of *Tyre.*
A Wife for a *M*onth.
The Unfortunate Lovers.
Aglaura.
Changling.
Bondman. *With divers others.*

(Pp. 17–18)

Several of the plays on the list had belonged to the pre-Restoration King's Company, of which an earlier John Rhodes (not, as Downes thought, the Restoration manager) had been a member.

Rhodes and his group may have begun performing by 4 February 1660, for Thomas Lilleston, one of the actors associated with him, was summoned before the Middlesex Sessions for acting a play on that date. Rhodes had to pay a fine for each day his troupe had performed at the Cockpit before 28 July 1660, according to John Parton's *Some Account of the Hospital and Parish of St. Giles in the Fields* (p. 236). In *The Commonwealth and Restoration Stage* (p. 198) Leslie Hotson estimates that the total fine, £4 6*d.*, probably represented forty-three acting days in the spring of 1660. Sir Henry Herbert's *Dramatic Records* (pp. 83–84) show that the Cockpit troupe was one of three performing in London as of 7 August 1660, and from the diarist Samuel Pepys we know that Fletcher's *The Loyal Subject* was presented at the Cockpit on 18 August—the only dated performance we know of for Rhodes's actors. By early October Rhodes had leased the Cockpit to the new King's Company, and his players had attached themselves to the Duke's Company under Sir William Davenant or the King's under Thomas Killigrew.

Two scholars have demonstrated that some drawings by Inigo Jones, I/7B and 7C at Worcester College, Oxford, are of the Cockpit in Drury Lane: Iain Mackintosh in the September 1973 issue of *Tabs* and John Orrell in *Shakespeare Survey 30*. They have shown that the Cockpit was basically a sceneryless "private" theatre, like the Blackfriars, but it was cleverly adaptable and could handle scenery when needed.

James O'Donnell found in a 1647 Beaumont and Fletcher folio at Pennsylvania State University three plays with manuscript prompt notes: *The Loyal Subject*, *The Spanish Curate*, and *A Wife for a Moneth*. All three were in Rhodes's repertoire, and it seems most likely that the promptbooks were prepared for Cockpit productions in 1660, though the notes in *A Wife for a Moneth* are incomplete, and production plans may have been abandoned. The three promptbooks make no mention of scenery, so one may guess that Rhodes and his players economized by operating the flexible playhouse as a sceneryless theatre, just as they followed the Elizabethan tradition of using boys to play female roles.

Since the single hand appearing in all three promptbooks resembles that to be seen in several King's Company books, there is a possibility that the annotated Beaumont and Fletcher copy belonged to that troupe and not to Rhodes. Indeed, after the Rhodes Company disbanded in the fall of 1660 *The Loyal Subject* and *The Spanish Curate*, after being assigned to Sir William Davenant's Duke's Company at Salisbury Court for a brief period in the winter of 1660–61, were presented at the Vere Street Theatre by the King's Company in the spring of 1661 and winter of 1661–62 respectively. *A Wife for a Moneth* was also presented by the King's Company in the spring of 1661. But I am inclined to assign these three promptbooks to Rhodes's company. The annotations appear to have been made by a prompter new to his job; they are simple and rather mechanical. Further, all three promptbooks are remarkably clean, suggesting little usage in performance; that could mean that they never saw production use, or it could mean that they were used by a troupe that was not in business very long.

In any case, these are probably the three earliest Restoration promptbooks to come to light, and O'Donnell's discovery is a most important one. In the presentation that follows I have taken the plays alphabetically by title, providing for *The Loyal Subject* a full facsimile in chapter 9. *A Wife for a Moneth*, though incomplete, may have been the last one prepared; toward the end of it the annotations seem to me slightly more sophisticated—the dropping of the imperative and the simple listing of the characters to be warned.

The Loyal Subject *by John Fletcher*

In a 1647 Beaumont and Fletcher folio with fairly complete manuscript prompt notes probably for the Rhodes Company production at the Cockpit in Drury Lane on 18 August 1660; at Pennsylvania State University. Discussed by James P. O'Donnell in "Some Beaumont and Fletcher Prompt Annotations," *The Papers of the Bibliographical Society of America*, 73 (1979), 334–37. Reproduced here in chapter 9 by permission of the Pennsylvania State University Libraries.

Samuel Pepys saw *The Loyal Subject* on 18 August 1660.

> . . . Captain Ferrerrs, my Lord's Cornett, comes to us—who after dinner took me and Creed to the Cockepitt play, the first that I have had time to see since my coming from sea, *The Loyall Subject*, where one Kinaston, a boy, acted the Dukes sister [Olimpia] but made the loveliest lady that ever I saw in my life—only her voice not very good.

John Downes tells us that Thomas Betterton played the title role, Archas, and Thomas Sheppy was Theodore. Though *The Loyal Subject* ultimately became a King's Company play after Rhodes gave up his venture at the Cockpit, on 12 December 1660 the rival Duke's Company was granted permission to perform it for two months. There is no evidence that they exercised their option. The play is known to have been presented by the King's Company at the Vere Street Theatre between February and April 1661 and probably by the United Company at Drury Lane in 1684–85.

Most of the annotations are warnings and cues. The prompter entered his warnings, usually, in the imperative: *be ready*, instead of the more common *call* or *ready* found in other Restoration promptbooks. In his *Shakespearean Prompt-Books of the Seventeenth Century* G. Blakemore Evans, in commenting on the "Bee ready" warnings found in the pre-Restoration Padua promptbook of *Measure for Measure*, said he had seen "no cases of this particular imperative in Restoration promptbooks." But he was writing before O'Donnell's discovery of these

Pennsylvania State books. The imperative warning may have been used at this early date because the troupe had just been organized and consisted of a number of players (like Betterton) with little or no acting experience. Perhaps as the acting companies matured the prompters found that all the callboy really needed was a list of actors' or characters' names marginally noted in advance of an entrance.

The prompter made cue marks for sound effects and for entrances (except those at the beginnings of acts): *–+++––––––*. Sometimes he used a mark in each margin (to point out entrances that had been missed in rehearsal?), and in *The Spanish Curate* and *A Wife for a Moneth* he occasionally varied the size or appearance of the symbol. In King's Company books in later years the cue mark became: *–++++++++–*.

The prompt notes, when cropped or difficult to make out, are easily reconstructed, since in almost every case the prompter simply took what he found in the printed stage direction for an entrance and wrote it in the margin in advance. His warnings were sometimes short when he had an entrance cue to attend to; after cuing an entrance he would turn his attention to warning the next entrance, even if it was only a few lines away and could have been warned earlier. The shortest warning—an almost useless one—is on page 45 of the facsimile, where a Gentleman is given only a two-line warning. Similarly, on page 48 a group is given only a three-line warning. The prompter seemed reluctant to do the obvious: combine warnings for two or more entrances and provide sufficient lead time.

O'Donnell feels that *The Loyal Subject* promptbook (and the other two promptbooks in the Pennsylvania State Beaumont and Fletcher folio) may have been the beginning of a prompt copy that was never completed. That could be true, for the prompter missed several warnings and cues, and there are no notes on properties or music beyond what the stage directions supply. But as will be seen in later promptbooks which seem clearly to have been used in performance, prompter's copies often contained errors of omission and commission. On the other hand, the copy is remarkably clean and contains no textual emendations, such as cuts. Most promptbooks are messier, reveal numerous cuts and changes, and contain notes by more than one hand. Those might be better reasons for arguing that the promptbook we have never saw use in the theatre. Yet the Rhodes Company was a neophyte group and in business only for a few months; their prompter may have had little experience, and Rhodes may have found it simpler to produce plays uncut rather than go through the difficult process of pruning.

The text of *The Loyal Subject* was set from prompt copy, as can be seen on page 33: "*Little Trunke ready*." That note may have been made by the prompter of the old King's Company, which presented the play in the 1630s. Similar traces may be seen in *The Spanish Curate*.

The Spanish Curate
by John Fletcher and Philip Massinger

In a 1647 Beaumont and Fletcher folio with fairly complete manuscript prompt notes, probably for a production by the Rhodes Company at the Cockpit in Drury Lane in 1660; at Pennsylvania State University. Discussed by James P. O'Donnell in "Some Beaumont and Fletcher Prompt Annotations," *The Papers of the Bibliographical Society of America*, 73 (1979), 334–37.

The second of the three annotated plays at Pennsylvania State was prepared for production by the same person who worked on *The Loyal Subject* and *A Wife for a Moneth*. The prompter's practices are repeated: warnings usually employing the imperative *be ready*, cross-hatch marks for cues, and occasional missed warnings and cues. In addition, the prompter here warned the endings of acts III and IV with the word *Act*; he did not cue the act-endings, however, with the *ring* found in other promptbooks. Entrances at act-openings are not warned—nor are they in the other Fletcher books. The prompter corrected an error on page 28, moving Henrique's entrance down ten lines, where it should be. On page 33 one can see the prompter again giving short warnings because of a sequence of entrances not many lines apart, as in *The Loyal Subject*. The printed text was set from prompt copy probably belonging to the pre-Restoration King's Company; certain and possible traces of those notes have been recorded here along with the manuscript annotations.

The Spanish Curate, according to the prompter John Downes, was presented by John Rhodes and his troupe, though no specific performance dates are known. In *The Life of Mr. Thomas Betterton* in 1710 Charles Gildon claimed that Thomas Betterton gained much applause acting in the play in 1660, presumably in the title role of Lopez. On 12 December 1660, after Rhodes's troupe had dispersed, *The Spanish Curate* was assigned for two months to the new Duke's Company under Sir William Davenant, and Pepys tells us that he saw their production of the play on 16 March 1661 at the Salisbury Court Theatre. He did not name Betterton as acting in it but said only that the play gave him "no great content." The work then became the property of the rival King's Company at the Vere Street Theatre. It was presented there on 20 December 1661, and Pepys saw it on 1 January 1662:

[S]eeing that *The Spanish Curate* was acted to-day, I . . . home again and sent to young Mr. Pen and his sister to go anon with my wife and I to the Theatre [Pepys's name for Vere Street]. . . . [W]e went by coach to the play, and there saw it well acted, and a good play it is. Only, Diego the Sexton did overdo his part too much.

The play was officially assigned to the King's Company on 12 January 1669. It was revived the following May and periodically thereafter. Transcriptions of the prompt notes in the Pennsylvania State copy follow, with pertinent explanatory notes. Readex microcards of the original will help to set the promptnotes in context—and so too for the other plays for which facsimile reproductions are not provided.

Act I, Scene i

P. 25 *Jamy Leander & / ascanio be ready* actor warning c.22 lines before entrance.

–⧺+–––––– entrance cue for Jamy, Leandro, and Ascanio.

P. [26] The page is misnumbered 28.

Henrique be ready actor warning 40 lines before entrance.

The printed text has Henrique enter after line 148; the prompter made an entrance cue mark (*–⧺+––––––*) at that point but then canceled it and moved the entrance to line 158 and made another cue mark.

P. [27] The page is misnumbered 29.

P. 28 *Octavio & Jacinta / be ready* actor warning 21 lines before entrance.

Act I, Scene ii

–⧺+–––––– entrance cue for Octavio and Jacinta at the opening of I, ii.

ascanio be / ready actor warning c.23 lines before entrance.

––––––⧺+– and *–⧺+––––––* entrance cues in each margin for Ascanio.

Hen: & Viol: be / ready actor warning c.13 lines before entrance.

Act I, Scene iii

–⧺+–––––– entrance cue for Henrique and Violante at the opening of I, iii.

Act II, Scene i

P. 29 *Lop: & Diegoe / be ready* actor warning c.29 lines before entrance.

–⧺+–––––– entrance cue for Lopez and Diego.

P. 31 *Bar: & Ama: / be ready* actor warning 32 lines before entrance.

Act II, Scene ii

–⧺+–––––– entrance cue for Bartolus and Amaranta at the opening of II, ii.

moore be rea[dy] actor warning 30 lines before entrance.

P. 32 *–⧺+––––––* entrance cue for a "*Woman-Moore*."

lop: lean: / Diego / be redy actor warning c.26 lines before entrance.

––––––⧺+– entrance cue for Lopez, Leandro, and Diego.

P. 33 *Jamy Mill: arse, be / ready* actor warning 29 lines before entrance.

Act II, Scene iii

–⧺+–––––– entrance cue for Jamy, Millanes, and Arsenio at the opening of II, iii.

Seruant / be ready actor warning c.13 lines before entrance.

bar: & Ama / be incomplete actor warning c.20 lines before entrance.

–++––––––– entrance cue for the Servant.

There is an indecipherable word in the right column margin at line 19.

Act II, Scene iv

–⧺+–––––– entrance cue for Bartolus and Amaranta at the opening of II, iv.

Ser: be ready actor warning 23 lines before entrance.

Amaranta be / ready actor warning c.16 lines before entrance, but Amaranta is on stage at this point. She exits, apparently at line 35, though no stage direction takes her off; then she reenters at line 44.

–*+++*------ sound effect (knock) and entrance cue for the Servant, two lines before the printed stage direction bringing him on.

Lean[dro] / be re[ady] actor warning c. 7 lines before offstage line of dialogue and c. 15 lines before entrance.

-------*+++*– and –*+++*------ cues for Leandro's offstage line and for Amaranta's entrance, in each margin.

–*+++*------ entrance cue for Leandro.

Amaran[ta] / be read[y] actor warning c. 7 lines before entrance; Amaranta is just leaving the stage at this point and reenters after a few lines.

-------*+++*– and –*+++*------ cues for Amaranta's entrance and for "*Lute and Song*," respectively, in each margin. The lute and song were not warned.

Leandro's "*peeping*" entrance was neither warned nor cued, but he left the stage only 4 lines before and probably needed no prompting.

P. 34 A "*noise / within*" called for by the author was neither warned nor cued.

Act III, Scene ii

The entrance of Lopez, Diego, and four Parishioners and Singers at the opening of III, ii, was neither warned nor cued.

"*Two chaires set out*" at line 13 is probably a trace of prompt copy.

P. 35 *Arseno & Millanes be ready* actor warning 17 lines before entrance.

There is a partly faded manuscript note in the top margin which apparently reads *[Bar & Book] / ready on ye / table*.

Dance be ready warning 9 lines in advance. This and the following probably concerned both dancers and musicians.

Dance –*+++*------ cue at line 120.

–*+++*------ entrance cue for Arsenio and Millanes.

"*The Bar & Book ready on a / (Table*." Trace of prompt copy.

octa: Jacin & Ascani[o] / be ready actor warning c. 24 lines before entrance.

Act III, Scene iii

P. 36 –*+++*------ entrance cue for Octavio, Jacinta, and Ascanio at the opening of III, iii.

"*A Bar. Table-booke, / 2 chairs, & paper standish / (set out*." Trace of prompt copy.

Jamy & bar: / be ready actor warning c. 21 lines before entrance.

–*+++*------ entrance cue for Jamy and Bartolus.

The entrance of the Assistant, Henrique, an Officer, and Witnesses was neither warned nor cued.

P. 37 "*Chess-boord and / men set ready*." Trace of prompt copy.

P. 38 *Bar: be ready* actor warning 27 lines before entrance. See illustration.

Act III, Scene iv

–*+++*------ entrance cue for Bartolus at the opening of III, iv.

Amar / be ready actor warning 13 lines before entrance.

–*+*----*+++*– cue for offstage line of dialogue by Leandro. This was not warned. The variant form of the cue symbol here and elsewhere does not appear to have any special significance.

–*+++*------ entrance cue for Amaranta.

moore with / a Chese bor[d] actor and property warning 9 lines before entrance; the warning could have been placed earlier.

The entrance of the Moor with the chessboard was not cued.

–*+++*------ entrance cue for Leandro.

moore / be ready actor warning c. 11 lines before entrance. After bringing on the chessboard the Moor apparently left the stage, but no stage direction took him off, and the prompter did not correct the error.

–*+*-------- sound effect (knock) cue; this was not warned.

–*+*– sound effect (knock) cue; this was not warned.

–*+++*------ entrance cue for the Moor.

---*++*--- sound effect (knock) cue; this was not warned.

P. 39 *bartolus be / ready* actor warning 26 lines before entrance.

–*+++*------ entrance cue for Bartolus.

Act warning for act ending c. 21 lines in advance. Perhaps music was played between the acts, necessitating this warning. But the end of the act was not cued (*ring* was the cue used in later promptbooks).

Act IV, Scene i

P. 40 *Lo: Mil: ar:* actor warning c. 30 lines before entrance.

"*Bed ready wine, / tableStandish & / Paper*." Trace of prompt copy.

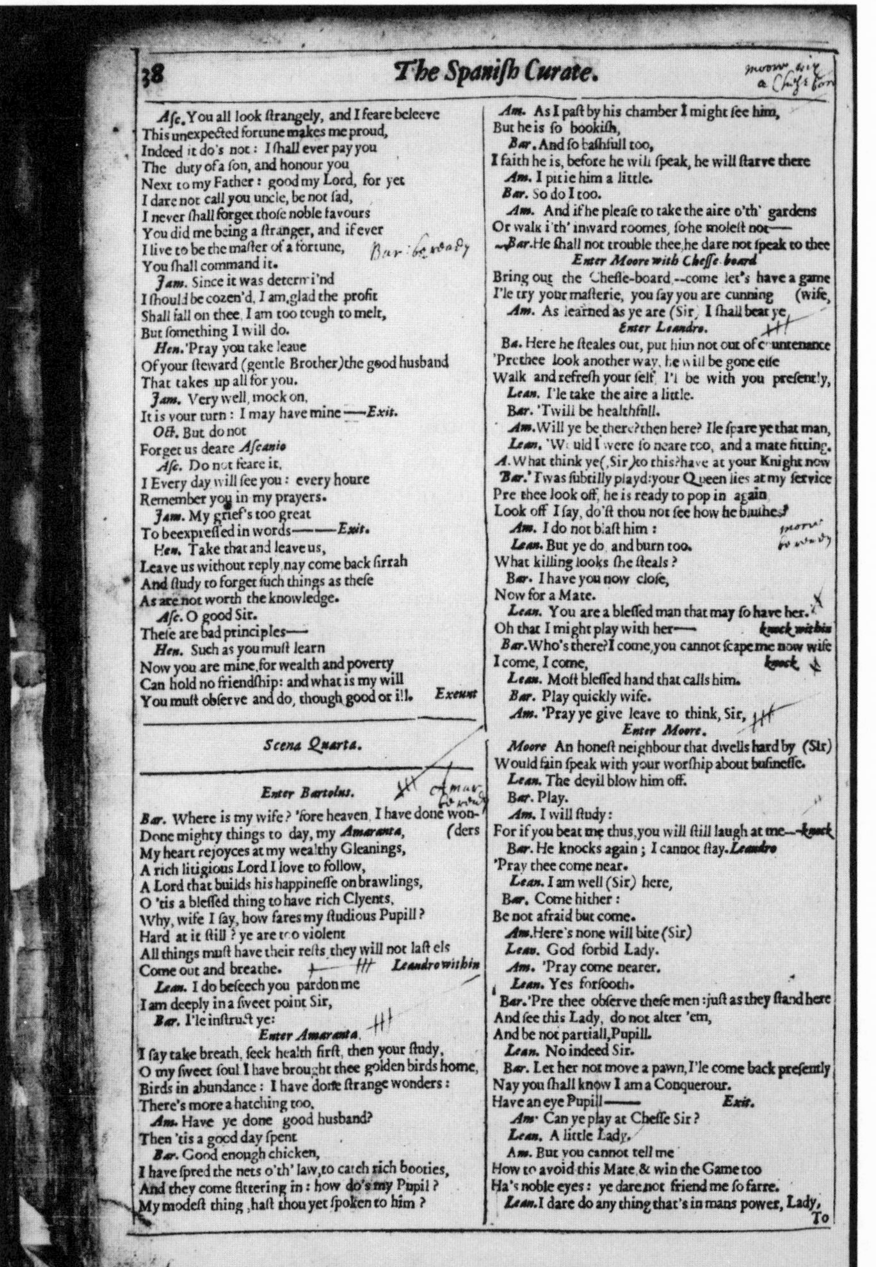

38 *The Spaniſh Curate.*

Aſc. You all look ſtrangely, and I feare beleeve
This unexpected fortune makes me proud,
Indeed it do's not: I ſhall ever pay you
The duty of a ſon, and honour you
Next to my Father: good my Lord, for yet
I dare not call you uncle, be not ſad,
I never ſhall forget thoſe noble favours
You did me being a ſtranger, and if ever
I live to be the maſter of a fortune,
You ſhall command it.
Jam. Since it was determ'i'nd
I ſhould be cozen'd, I am glad the profit
Shall fall on thee, I am too tough to melt,
But ſomething I will do.
Hen. 'Pray you take leaue
Of your ſteward (gentle Brother) the good husband
That takes up all for you.
Jam. Very well, mock on,
It is your turn: I may have mine —*Exit.*
Oct. But do not
Forget us deare *Aſcanio*
Aſc. Do not feare it,
I Every day will ſee you: every houre
Remember you in my prayers.
Jam. My grief's too great
To be expreſſed in words——*Exit.*
Hen. Take that and leave us,
Leave us without reply, nay come back ſirrah
And ſtudy to forget ſuch things as theſe
As are not worth the knowledge.
Aſc. O good Sir.
Theſe are bad principles—
Hen. Such as you muſt learn
Now you are mine, for wealth and poverty
Can hold no friendſhip: and what is my will
You muſt obſerve and do, though good or ill. *Exeunt*

Scena Quarta.

Enter Bartolus.

Bar. Where is my wife? 'fore heaven, I have done won-
Done mighty things to day, my *Amaranta,* (ders
My heart rejoyces at my wealthy Gleanings,
A rich litigious Lord I love to follow,
A Lord that builds his happineſſe on brawlings,
O 'tis a bleſſed thing to have rich Clyents,
Why, wife I ſay, how fares my ſtudious Pupill?
Hard at it ſtill? ye are too violent
All things muſt have their reſts, they will not laſt els
Come out and breathe. *Leandro within*
Lean. I do beſeech you pardon me
I am deeply in a ſweet point Sir,
Bar. I'le inſtruct ye:
Enter Amaranta.
I ſay take breath, ſeek health firſt, then your ſtudy,
O my ſweet ſoul I have brought thee golden birds home,
Birds in abundance: I have done ſtrange wonders:
There's more a hatching too,
Am. Have ye done good husband?
Then 'tis a good day ſpent
Bar. Good enough chicken,
I have ſpred the nets o'th' law, to catch rich booties,
And they come fluttering in: how do's my Pupil?
My modeſt thing, haſt thou yet ſpoken to him?

Am. As I paſt by his chamber I might ſee him,
But he is ſo bookiſh,
Bar. And ſo baſhfull too,
I faith he is, before he will ſpeak, he will ſtarve there
Am. I pitie him a little.
Bar. So do I too.
Am. And if he pleaſe to take the aire o'th' gardens
Or walk i'th' inward roomes, ſo he moleſt not—
Bar. He ſhall not trouble thee, he dare not ſpeak to thee
Enter Moore with Cheſſe board
Bring out the Cheſſe-board,--come let's have a game
I'le try your maſterie, you ſay you are cunning (wife,
Am. As learned as ye are (Sir) I ſhall beat ye,
Enter Leandro.
Ba. Here he ſteales out, put him not out of countenance
'Prethee look another way, he will be gone elſe
Walk and refreſh your ſelf, I'l be with you preſently,
Lean. I'le take the aire a little.
Bar. 'Twill be healthfull.
Am. Will ye be there? then here? Ile ſpare ye that man,
Lean. 'Would I were ſo neare too, and a mate fitting.
A. What think ye (Sir) to this? have at your Knight now
Bar. 'Twas ſubtilly playd: your Queen lies at my ſervice
Pre thee look off, he is ready to pop in again
Look off I ſay, do'ſt thou not ſee how he bluſhes?
Am. I do not blaſt him:
Lean. But ye do, and burn too.
What killing looks ſhe ſteals?
Bar. I have you now cloſe,
Now for a Mate.
Lean. You are a bleſſed man that may ſo have her.
Oh that I might play with her— *knock within*
Bar. Who's there? I come, you cannot ſcape me now wife
I come, I come, *knock*
Lean. Moſt bleſſed hand that calls him.
Bar. Play quickly wife.
Am. 'Pray ye give leave to think, Sir,
Enter Moore.
Moore An honeſt neighbour that dwells hard by (Sir)
Would fain ſpeak with your worſhip about buſineſſe.
Lean. The devil blow him off.
Bar. Play.
Am. I will ſtudy:
For if you beat me thus, you will ſtill laugh at me—*knock*
Bar. He knocks again; I cannot ſtay. *Leandro*
'Pray thee come near.
Lean. I am well (Sir) here,
Bar. Come hither:
Be not afraid but come.
Am. Here's none will bite (Sir)
Lean. God forbid Lady.
Am. 'Pray come nearer.
Lean. Yes forſooth.
Bar. 'Pre thee obſerve theſe men: juſt as they ſtand here
And ſee this Lady, do not alter 'em,
And be not partiall, Pupill.
Lean. No indeed Sir.
Bar. Let her not move a pawn, I'le come back preſently
Nay you ſhall know I am a Conquerour.
Have an eye Pupill—— *Exit.*
Am. Can ye play at Cheſſe Sir?
Lean. A little Lady.
Am. But you cannot tell me
How to avoid this Mate, & win the Game too
Ha's noble eyes: ye dare not friend me ſo farre.
Lean. I dare do any thing that's in mans power, Lady,
To

From Fletcher and Massinger's *The Spanish Curate.* By kind permission of The Pennsylvania State University Libraries.

Act IV, Scene ii

–*ǂǂǂ*–––––– entrance cue for Lopez, Millanes, and Arsenio at the opening of IV, ii.

Act IV, Scene iii

P. 41 The entrance of Amaranta and the Moor at the opening of IV, iii, was neither warned nor cued.

Act IV, Scene iv

The entrance of Octavio and Jacinta at the opening of IV, iv, was neither warned nor cued.

Jai: & asca: be / ready actor warning c.18 lines before entrance.

–*ǂǂǂ*–––––– entrance cue for Jamy and Ascanio.

–*ǂǂǂ*–––––– entrance cue for a Servant; the entrance was not warned.

Lopez & bartolus / be ready actor warning c.15 lines before entrance.

Act IV, Scene v

–*ǂǂǂ*–––––– entrance cue for Lopez and Bartolus at the opening of IV, v.

–*ǂǂǂ*–––––– cue mark calling attention to a trace of prompt copy: "*Diego ready in Bed, wine, cup.*" The trace is 47 lines before Diego's appearance.

"*Table out Stan- / dish paper, stools.*" Trace of prompt copy.

P. 42 *arsenio & parishoners* actor warning 28 lines before entrance. This note is in the top margin; just above it, almost completely cropped, is the first part of the warning, which presumably named Diego and Millanes.

––––––*ǂǂǂ*– and –––*ǂǂǂ*–––– entrance cues in each margin for Diego (in a bed), Millanes, Arsenio, and the Parishioners. Three lines after the stage direction bringing on this group is another stage direction (or trace of prompt copy?): "*Bed thrust out.*" From the dialogue it is clear that Diego actually appeared at this point.

P. 43 *Amarant & / Leandro be / ready* actor warning c.23 lines before entrance.

Act IV, Scene vi

–+++–––––– entrance cue for Amaranta and Leandro at the opening of IV, vi.

––+++–– cue mark (warning, actually) following a trace of prompt copy: "P*ewter ready / for noyse*." The noise comes 44 lines later.

bartolus be / ready actor warning c.16 lines before entrance.

Act IV, Scene vii

–+++–––––– entrance cue for Bartolus at the opening of IV, vii.

P. 44 *Lo: Ar: Mill: Diego / be ready* actor warning 12 lines before entrance.

–––––+++– and –+++–––––– entrance cues in each margin for Lopez, Arsenio, Millanes, and Diego.

The "*great noyse within*" at line 22, which was warned on the previous page, was not cued.

bar: / be ready actor warning c.12 lines before entrance.

––––––+++– entrance cue for Diego; this entrance was not warned, since Diego left the stage just 2 lines before.

Ama / Leandro / be ready actor warning c.13 lines before entrance.

"*Noyse still*" was not cued.

––––––+++– entrance cue for Bartolus.

––––––+++– entrance cue for Amaranta and Leandro.

P. 45 *Act* warning for act-end c.27 lines in advance. Perhaps music was played between the acts, but the end of the act was not cued.

Act V, Scene i

Jamy & / seruant actor warning 11 lines before entrance.

"Chaire and stooles out." Possible trace of prompt copy at the opening of V, i.

–+++–––––– entrance cue for Jamy and the Servant.

"*A Table ready co- / vered with Cloath / Napkins Salt / Trenchers and / Bread.*" Trace of prompt copy.

P. 46 "*Dishes cove- / red with pa- / pers in each / ready*." Trace of prompt copy.

be ready actor warning for Bartolus and others 25 lines before entrance; why did the prompter not name the characters?

Act V, Scene ii

–+++–––––– entrance cue for Bartolus, Algazeirs, and a Paratour at the opening of V, ii.

Mitt / be rea[dy] actor warning at the opening of V, ii, for Millanes and three other characters 12 lines before entrance.

"*The Table set out and stooles.*" Possible trace of prompt copy at the opening of V, ii.

The entrance of Millanes, Arsenio, Lopez, and Diego, though warned, was not cued.

P. 47 *Ama: & lean: / be ready* actor warning c.20 lines before entrance.

–+++–––––– entrance cue for Amaranta and Leandro.

Algazeers / with dishes / ready actor and property warning c.15 lines before entrance.

–+++–––––– entrance cue for Algazeirs with dishes.

P. 48 The entrance of Jamy and the Assistant was neither warned nor cued.

octa: Ja: ascanio / be ready actor warning c.24 lines before entrance.

Act V, Scene iii

–+++–––––– entrance cue for Octavio, Jacinta, and Ascanio at the opening of V, iii.

Henry & Jami / be ready actor warning c.10 lines before entrance.

–+++–––––– entrance cue for Henrique and Jamy.

Le: Mill: ar: Bar / be ready actor warning c.25 lines before entrance of Leandro and at least nine others.

–+++–––––– entrance cue for Leandro, Millanes, Arsenio, Bartolus, Lopez, Diego, Octavio, Jacinta, Ascanio, and Servants.

P. 49 *violante be / ready* actor warning c.21 lines before entrance.

–+++–––––– entrance cue for Violante.

assistant / & officers / be ready actor warning c.9 lines before entrance.

–+++–––––– entrance cue for the Assistant and Officers.

A Wife for a Moneth by *John Fletcher*

In a 1647 Beaumont and Fletcher folio with incomplete manuscript prompt notes, possibly for an intended production by the Rhodes Company at the Cockpit in Drury Lane in 1660; at Pennsylvania State University. Discussed by James P. O'Donnell in "Some Beaumont and Fletcher Prompt Annotations," *The Papers of the Bibliographical Society of America*, 73 (1979), 334–37.

The prompter who prepared the relatively complete notes for *The Loyal Subject* and *The Spanish Curate* annotated *A Wife for a Moneth* as well, but here the manuscript notes do not begin until well into the first act and trail off before the end of Act V. Perhaps a production was contemplated and then abandoned, or perhaps another promptbook was prepared. According to *The Dramatic Records of Sir Henry Herbert* the work was acted by the King's Company at the Vere Street Theatre, probably in April 1661 (thinks Robert Hume; *The London Stage* dates it May 1661). The play was one of many officially assigned to the King's Company at the Bridges Street Theatre on 12 January 1669. *A Wife for a Moneth* had been the property of the old King's Company in pre-Restoration days; if the printed text was set from prompt copy, as *The Loyal Subject* and *The Spanish Curate* certainly were, no traces crept into print.

The play begins on page 47. After the prompter began his annotations at the top of page 50 he followed the practices used in *The Loyal Subject* and *The Spanish Curate*. Entrances at act openings are not warned, nor are act endings. No scenery is indicated. This is the only one of the three promptbooks containing indications of textual emendations.

Act I, Scene i

P. 50 *Euanthe & Cassandra / be ready* actor warning 23 lines before entrance.

---------+++- entrance cue for Evanthe and Cassandra.

Vale: & Podra / be ready actor warning c.30 lines before entrance.

---------+++- and *-+++-* entrance cues in each margin for Valerio and Podrano. The variation in the appearance of the cue symbol seems to have no significance.

P. 51 *Tony with / a urinall* actor and property warning c.14 lines before entrance.

Act II, Scene i

-+++------ entrance cue for Tony with urinal.

Queene & / euanthe / be ready actor warning c.30 lines before entrance.

------+++- and *-+++------* entrance cues in each margin for the Queen and Evanthe.

P. 52 *ffred: & so: / be ready* actor warning c.36 lines before entrance.

-+++------ entrance cue for Frederick and Sorano.

Tony 3 Citi: / there wifes / be ready actor warning c.37 lines before entrance.

-+++----+++- entrance cue for Tony, three Citizens, and three Wives.

P. 53 *ffrederik / be ready* actor warning 17 lines before entrance.

-+++------ entrance cue for Frederick.

Cas & a / old Lady / be re actor warning c.13 lines before entrance.

---+++---- entrance cue for Cassandra and an Old Lady passing over the stage.

Val: Cam: Cle: / menella & actor warning c.19 lines before entrance.

-+++------ entrance cue for Valerio, Camillo, Cleanthes, and Menallo; Servants were included in the stage direction for the entrance, but they were not warned, and the intention may have been to omit them.

2 Seruants b[e] / ready actor warning c.35 lines before entrance.

Knockin[g] / be ready sound effect warning c.18 lines in advance of stage direction calling for knocking within.

A stage direction asking for "*Musick*" 7 lines before the two Servants enter was neither warned nor cued; it should have been, since Valerio speaks of hearing music.

The knocking, which was warned, was not cued.

-+++------ entrance cue for the two Servants.

-+++------ entrance cue for Camillo, Cleanthes, Menallo, Tony, and a Fool; the entrance was not warned.

P. 54 A stage direction calling for "*Knocks within*" was neither warned nor cued.

-+++------ cue for drawing a curtain to discover the King and others gathered to witness a masque. The discovery was not warned.

The descent of Cupid was neither warned nor cued.

A wavy vertical line to the right of Cupid's first speech in the masque may indicate that the speech was to be omitted.

The entrance of the masquers was neither warned nor cued. In view of the above, perhaps the whole masque was to be omitted in performance.

Act III, Scene i

Valerio be / ready actor warning c.15 lines before entrance.

–+++––––––– entrance cue for Valerio.

Sorano / be / ready actor warning c.10 lines before entrance.

P. 55 ––––––+++– and –+++–––––– entrance cues in each margin for Sorano.

ffred be / ready actor warning c.36 lines before entrance.

–+++––––––– entrance cue for Frederick.

P. 56 *Vale: Cam: Clean: Menello, / be ready* actor warning c.32 lines before entrance.

–++–––+++– and –+++–––––– entrance cues in each margin for Valerio, Camillo, Cleanthes, and Menallo.

Quee Euanthy / & ladyes / be ready actor warning c.24 lines before entrance.

–––+++–––– and –+++–––––– entrance cues in each margin for the Queen, Evanthe, and Ladies. The stage direction also has the Fool enter, but he was left out of the warning; the intention may have been to omit him, since he has no lines.

Act IV, Scene i

P. 59 *ffre: & po:* actor warning 23 lines before entrance. See illustration.

Cassand / be ready actor warning c.21 lines before entrance.

–+++––––––– entrance cue for Frederick and Podrano.

–++++––––– entrance cue for Cassandra. Immediately following Cassandra's entrance and for the following c.44 lines, wavy vertical lines in the right margin may indicate the omission of some or all of those lines or may be a direction to place Cassandra's entrance later, where, in fact, it should be. Within the marked section is an entrance for Valerio which was neither warned nor cued, and shortly after the marked section Valerio must make an exit, though no stage direction takes him off. He reenters a bit later but was neither warned nor cued.

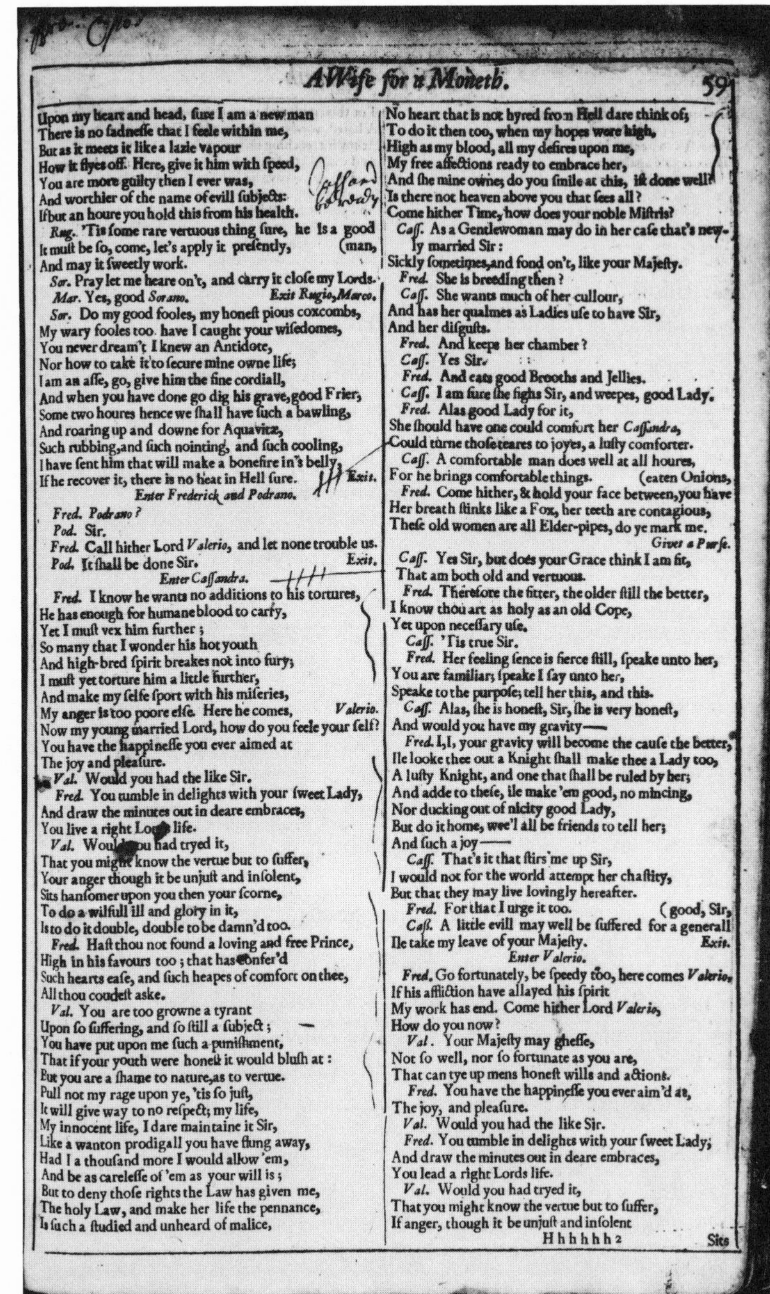

A Wife for a Moneth. 59

Upon my heart and head, ſure I am a new man
There is no ſadneſſe that I feele within me,
But as it meets it like a lazie vapour
How it flyes off. Here, give it him with ſpeed,
You are more guilty then I ever was,
And worthier of the name of evill ſubjects:
If but an houre you hold this from his health.
Rug. 'Tis ſome rare vertuous thing ſure, he is a good (man,
It muſt be ſo, come, let's apply it preſently,
And may it ſweetly work.
Sor. Pray let me heare on't, and carry it cloſe my Lords.
Mar. Yes, good *Sorano.* *Exit Rugio, Marco.*
Sor. Do my good fooles, my honeſt pious coxcombs,
My wary fooles too. have I caught your wiſedomes,
You never dream't I knew an Antidote,
Nor how to take it to ſecure mine owne life;
I am an aſſe, go, give him the fine cordiall,
And when you have done go dig his grave, good Frier,
Some two houres hence we ſhall have ſuch a bawling,
And roaring up and downe for Aquavitæ,
Such rubbing, and ſuch nointing, and ſuch cooling,
I have ſent him that will make a bonefire in's belly,
If he recover it, there is no heat in Hell ſure. *Exit.*
Enter Frederick and Podrano.
Fred. Podrano?
Pod. Sir.
Fred. Call hither Lord *Valerio,* and let none trouble us.
Pod. It ſhall be done Sir. *Exit.*
Enter Caſſandra.
Fred. I know he wants no additions to his tortures,
He has enough for humane blood to carry,
Yet I muſt vex him further;
So many that I wonder his hot youth
And high-bred ſpirit breakes not into fury;
I muſt yet torture him a little further,
And make my ſelfe ſport with his miſeries,
My anger is too poore elſe. Here he comes, *Valerio.*
Now my young married Lord, how do you feele your ſelf?
You have the happineſſe you ever aimed at
The joy and pleaſure.
Val. Would you had the like Sir.
Fred. You tumble in delights with your ſweet Lady,
And draw the minutes out in deare embraces,
You live a right Lo[illegible] life.
Val. Woul[illegible]ou had tryed it,
That you mig[illegible] know the vertue but to ſuffer,
Your anger though it be unjuſt and inſolent,
Sits hanſomer upon you then your ſcorne,
To do a wilfull ill and glory in it,
Is to do it double, double to be damn'd too.
Fred. Haſt thou not found a loving and free Prince,
High in his favours too; that has confer'd
Such hearts eaſe, and ſuch heapes of comfort on thee,
All thou coudeſt aske.
Val. You are too growne a tyrant
Upon ſo ſuffering, and ſo ſtill a ſubject;
You have put upon me ſuch a puniſhment,
That if your youth were honeſt it would bluſh at:
But you are a ſhame to nature, as to vertue.
Pull not my rage upon ye, 'tis ſo juſt,
It will give way to no reſpect; my life,
My innocent life, I dare maintaine it Sir,
Like a wanton prodigall you have flung away,
Had I a thouſand more I would allow 'em,
And be as careleſſe of 'em as your will is;
But to deny thoſe rights the Law has given me,
The holy Law, and make her life the pennance,
Is ſuch a ſtudied and unheard of malice,
No heart that is not hyred from Hell dare think of;
To do it then too, when my hopes were high,
High as my blood, all my deſires upon me,
My free affections ready to embrace her,
And ſhe mine owne; do you ſmile at this, iſt done well?
Is there not heaven above you that ſees all?
Come hither Time, how does your noble Miſtris?
Caſſ. As a Gentlewoman may do in her caſe that's newly married Sir:
Sickly ſometimes, and fond on't, like your Majeſty.
Fred. She is breeding then?
Caſſ. She wants much of her cullour,
And has her qualmes as Ladies uſe to have Sir,
And her diſguſts.
Fred. And keeps her chamber?
Caſſ. Yes Sir.
Fred. And eats good Brooths and Jellies.
Caſſ. I am ſure ſhe ſighs Sir, and weepes, good Lady.
Fred. Alas good Lady for it,
She ſhould have one could comfort her *Caſſandra,*
Could turne thoſe teares to joyes, a luſty comforter.
Caſſ. A comfortable man does well at all houres,
For he brings comfortable things. (eaten Onions,
Fred. Come hither, & hold your face between, you have
Her breath ſtinks like a Fox, her teeth are contagious,
Theſe old women are all Elder-pipes, do ye mark me.
Gives a Purſe.
Caſſ. Yes Sir, but does your Grace think I am fit,
That am both old and vertuous.
Fred. Therefore the fitter, the older ſtill the better,
I know thou art as holy as an old Cope,
Yet upon neceſſary uſe.
Caſſ. 'Tis true Sir.
Fred. Her feeling ſence is fierce ſtill, ſpeake unto her,
You are familiar; ſpeake I ſay unto her,
Speake to the purpoſe; tell her this, and this.
Caſſ. Alas, ſhe is honeſt, Sir, ſhe is very honeſt,
And would you have my gravity——
Fred. I, I, your gravity will become the cauſe the better,
Ile looke thee out a Knight ſhall make thee a Lady too,
A luſty Knight, and one that ſhall be ruled by her;
And adde to theſe, ile make 'em good, no mincing,
Nor ducking out of nicity good Lady,
But do it home, wee'l all be friends to tell her;
And ſuch a joy——
Caſſ. That's it that ſtirs me up Sir,
I would not for the world attempt her chaſtity,
But that they may live lovingly hereafter.
Fred. For that I urge it too. (good, Sir,
Caſſ. A little evill may well be ſuffered for a generall
Ile take my leave of your Majeſty. *Exit.*
Enter Valerio.
Fred. Go fortunately, be ſpeedy too, here comes *Valerio,*
If his affliction have allayed his ſpirit
My work has end. Come hither Lord *Valerio,*
How do you now?
Val. Your Majeſty may gheſſe,
Not ſo well, nor ſo fortunate as you are,
That can tye up mens honeſt wills and actions.
Fred. You have the happineſſe you ever aim'd at,
The joy, and pleaſure.
Val. Would you had the like Sir.
Fred. You tumble in delights with your ſweet Lady;
And draw the minutes out in deare embraces,
You lead a right Lords life.
Val. Would you had tryed it,
That you might know the vertue but to ſuffer,
If anger, though it be unjuſt and inſolent
Hhhhhh2 Sits

From Fletcher's *A Wife for a Moneth.* By kind permission of The Pennsylvania State University Libraries.

P. 60 *Euanthe & Cassan / be ready* actor warning 28 lines before entrance.
------+++- and -+++------ entrance cues in each margin for Evanthe and Cassandra.

P. 61 *fred: be / ready* actor warning c.55 lines before entrance; there seems to be no reason for the unusually long warning.
------+++- and ---+++---- entrance cues in each margin for Frederick.

P. 62 The entrance of Rugio and Friar Marco was neither warned nor cued, nor was the entrance of Alphonso and two Friars.

P. 63 *Valerio & Euanthe / be ready* actor warning c.39 lines before entrance.
-+++------ entrance cue for Valerio and Evanthe.

P. 64 *Castruchio wi[th] a guard* actor warning c.24 lines before entrance.
-+++------ entrance cue for Castruchio and Guard.

Act V, Scene i

Castr: be / ready actor warning c.11 lines before entrance; the warning could have been placed earlier.
Alpon / fryers actor warning c.10 lines before entrance; the warning could have been placed earlier.
-------++- and -+++------ entrance cues in each margin for Castruchio.
------+++- and -+++------ entrance cues in each margin for Alphonso and the Friars.
ffoole & podrano actor warning 27 lines before entrance.

P. 65 -+++------ entrance cue for the Fool and Podrano.
The entrance of Camillo, Menallo, Cleanthes, and Castruchio was neither warned nor cued, nor was the entrance of Frederick and Sorano.
-+++------ entrance cue for Evanthe, Camillo, Cleanthes, Menallo, the Fool, and Castruchio; the entrance was not warned.

P. 66 The entrance of the Lawyer, Physician, and Captain Cutpurse was neither warned nor cued.
Valerio to disgus actor warning 42 lines before entrance.
-+++------ entrance cue for Valerio "*disguis'd*."

P. 67 The entrance of Alphonso, Rugio, Marco, Castruchio, the Queen, and a Guard was neither warned nor cued.

2 / The King's Company (1660–1682)

The King's Company, managed under a royal patent by the courtier Thomas Killigrew, began acting on 8 November 1660 at a tiny converted tennis court in Vere Street, Clare Market, the house they used until 1663. The troupe was able to begin performing sooner than the rival Duke's Company, partly because, so far as we can tell from available evidence, they chose to present plays without the embellishment of changeable scenery. Precisely what the inside of the Vere Street playhouse looked like we do not know, but judging from the plays performed there it seems probable that the stage arrangement, within an oblong, roofed tennis court building measuring perhaps as little as 23′ by 64′, was something like that found in the private theatres of Shakespeare's time: an apron stage, doors opening onto it on each side toward the back, either curtained inner stages on two levels or a pavilion arrangement to cope with discovered scenes, and balcony acting areas over the entrance doors. The players, many of whom, like Killigrew, were old enough to have been a part of the theatre world before 1642, when the playhouses were officially closed, might well have converted their tennis court into something like what we believe the old Blackfriars private theatre was like. In any case, they seem to have worked without scenery, at least in the beginning, and part of our reason for thinking so is the lack of any scenic notes in the promptbooks for plays presented at Vere Street. Confirmation comes from Pepys, who commented favorably on the use of scenery at the rival Duke's house and made no mention of scenery at Vere Street.

The Duke's Company began acting, with scenery, on 28 June 1661; on the following 20 December the King's players purchased some property and began planning a new playhouse, one to be built from the ground up and equipped with changeable scenery. The site they chose was in Bridges Street, Covent Garden, where part of Drury Lane Theatre now stands. They began acting there on 7 May 1663. Exterior views of the Bridges Street house show it to have had a dome of considerable size near the center of the peaked roof. We have no certain evidence about the interior, though two intriguing sketches among Sir Christopher Wren's papers at All Souls College, Oxford, may pertain to it (or to the Hall Theatre at Court). If the plans are for Bridges Street, within the rectangular building the company had a seating arrangement based on a semicircular plan, a forestage flanked by openings in which may have been set periaktoi (three-sided revolving scenic units developed by the Greeks in the fifth century B.C.), a proscenium arch, and a scenic area with conventional wings, borders, and shutters. Since the promptbooks prepared for the Bridges Street Theatre clearly reveal the use of changeable scenery but contain no evidence of periaktoi (or, alternatively, multiple proscenium doors), the final form of the Bridges Street forestage area may have been conventional. Donald

Mullin discussed the building in "The Theatre Royal, Bridges Street: A Conjectural Reconstruction" and "The Theatre Royal, Bridges Street: An Architectural Puzzle." But see also Graham Barlow's article on Drury Lane in *The Eighteenth-Century English Stage* and volume 35 of *Survey of London*.

The playhouse burned on 25 January 1672, and for a period of two years the King's Company used the tennis court theatre in Lincoln's Inn Fields that had for ten years been the home of the rival Duke's Company. The Duke's players had moved in 1671 to their new Dorset Garden Theatre, a playhouse so grand that the scenery constructed for the small 30′ by 75′ Lincoln's Inn Fields Theatre could not have been useable. If they left their scenery behind, the King's Company probably had a proper theatre to move into, as Colin Visser believes in his study of Dryden's *Amboyna* at Lincoln's Inn Fields in May 1673 in *Restoration and 18th Century Theatre Research*. The promptbook for *Tyrannick Love*, if it was in fact prepared for use at Lincoln's Inn Fields during the King's Company's stay there, suggests simplified staging. Since the players almost immediately laid plans for a new theatre on their old site in Bridges Street, I cannot imagine that they would have laid out much money for new scenery or elaborate staging at Lincoln's Inn Fields.

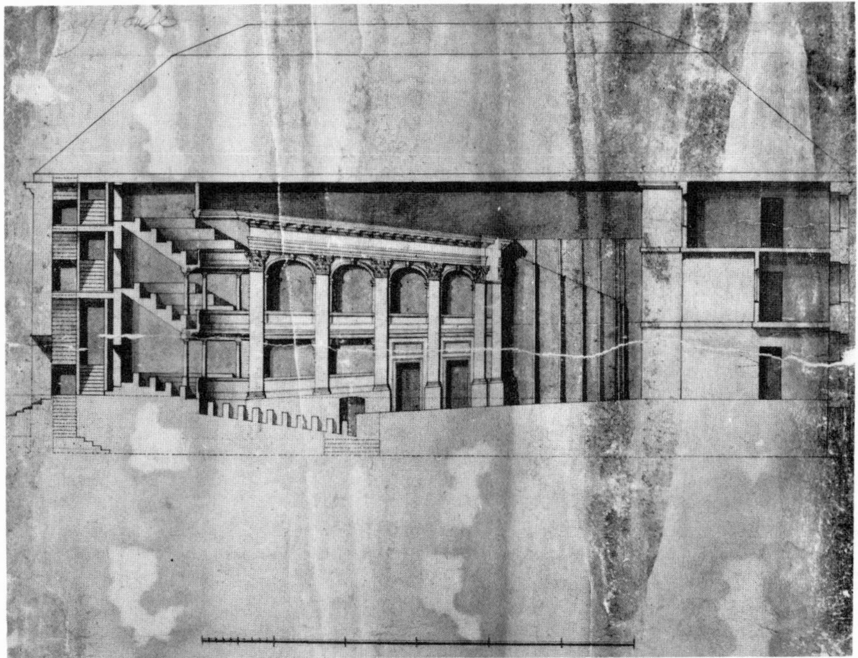

Sir Christopher Wren's section view of a playhouse, c.1672–1674. By kind permission of The Warden and Fellows of All Souls College, Oxford.

The new King's Company playhouse, Drury Lane, probably looked something like the section view of a Restoration theatre by Sir Christopher Wren. That drawing might not have survived had it been the final plan for the building; it was torn up, so we cannot be sure just what the final form of the 1674 Drury Lane was. The section view shows conventional pit, box, and gallery seating; an extensive forestage with two proscenium doors opening onto it on each side; a proscenium arch; a raked stage; and a scenic area laid out with the usual wings, borders, and shutters. Half of the thirty-fifth volume of *Survey of London* is devoted to Drury Lane.

The King's Company, plagued by mismanagement in the late 1670s, struggled on until 1682, when it merged with (or, more correctly, was absorbed by) the stronger Duke's Company. Drury Lane became the new United Company's main theatre.

Nine of the King's Company's promptbooks have been found, four of which are presented here in facsimile. Seven other promptbooks belonging to the troupe are known through traces of manuscript notes that appeared in printed plays.

The Scornful Ladie
by Francis Beaumont and John Fletcher

1616 quarto with fairly complete manuscript prompt notes probably for the King's Company production in 1660–61 at the Vere Street Theatre; British Library copy C 34 c 5.

To determine the exact date of this promptbook and relate it to a particular playhouse is difficult. We know of performances of the play at the Vere Street Theatre on 27 November 1660 and 4 and 25 January and 12 February 1661, at court during the early 1660s, at the Bridges Street Theatre in the late 1660s, and at Drury Lane Theatre in the 1680s and 1690s. But the lack of scenic notes in this copy would argue for an early date and suggest that, like the promptbook for Wilson's *The Cheats*, this one was prepared for the sceneryless (we think) Vere Street playhouse. We should still not rule out the possibility of the promptbook having been made up for use in a Jacobean or Caroline production, though the single prompter's hand would seem to match that in other King's Company promptbooks of the 1660s.

Some reconstructions have been necessary in the transcriptions of the notes, for cropping has deprived us of portions of the valuable marginalia.

Act I, Scene i

B1 *Abigale* actor warning c.19 lines before entrance.

B1^{v} *Lady & / Abigale* actor warning c.26 lines before entrance. Abigale is onstage at this point and exits some nine lines after this warning, so the warning for her is pointless. But, as will be seen in many promptbooks, when the prompter (?) wrote down actor warnings he often was quite mechanical: for every entrance there was to be a warning a page or half page in advance.

B3 *[Young Loveless, and] / Savill* actor warning, badly cropped, c.37 lines before entrance.

for appears twice in the right margin in a nontheatrical hand.

B3^{v} *Abigale* actor warning c.27 lines before entrance.

B4 *Welfor[d]* actor warning c.23 lines before entrance.

B4^{v} *Roger* actor warning c.30 lines before entrance. As one can see, the warnings for the actors are given here by character name; in some promptbooks minor characters are warned by the name of the player.

C1 *Roger* actor warning 8 lines before entrance. No earlier warning was possible, since Roger just made an exit. In this case the prompter was more careful than on B1^{v}.

Yo: Lovelesse Savill actor warning c.26 lines before entrance. A property "writing" which Young Lovelesse and Savill bring onstage when they enter should have been warned here but was not.

C2 *Comrades* actor warning c.30 lines before entrance.

Act II, Scene i

C4 *Martha Abigale with / posset* actor and property warning c.32 lines before entrance.

D1 *Yo: Lovelesse & Comrade[s] / fidlers & / wenches* actor warning c.54 lines before entrance. A cut of c.40 lines on this and the following page reduced this warning to c.14 lines before the entrance, a rather short warning for a large group entrance. The cut runs from Welford's "Why how now, shall we haue an Antique" on D1 through his "Ile heare no more. *Exeunt*" on D1^{v}. This cut eliminates the entrance and lines of a Servant and was apparently made before the actor warnings were entered in the promptbook, for the Servant is not warned. The logical sequence in preparing a promptbook would be to go through the play and make whatever cuts or emendations might be necessary, then to go through again entering actor, property, music, sound effect, and other warnings, and finally to hand the book over to the machinist or technician (or whatever he was called) and let him enter whatever technical notes might be required. There are no technical notes in this copy, which suggests that the play may have been done in a theatre with no scenery.

D1^{v} *Savill* actor warning c.15 lines before entrance. This is a rather short warning; the prompter could have placed it on D1 before the cut.

D2 *El: Lovelesse / disguis'd* actor warning c.28 lines before entrance.

D3^{v} *Moorcraft / & widdow* actor warning c.16 lines before entrance.

D4 *Savill* actor warning c.25 lines before entrance.

D4^{v} In the Widow's speech "feede ill" and "and gave way . . . Sir so little" are underlined—but to what purpose?

Yo. Lovelesse & / Comrades actor warning c.20 lines before entrance.

Act III, Scene i

E2 *Welford* actor warning 2 lines before entrance. No earlier warning would have been needed, since this is the opening of an act; presumably an interval between the acts was taken, perhaps with music playing, providing the prompter with time enough to see that all actors were in their places before the new act commenced. Abigale, who enters at the opening of the act, is not warned, though Welford, who comes on almost immediately after her, is.

El: Lovelesse / disguis'd actor warning c.16 lines before entrance.

E3 *Lady* actor warning c.17 lines before entrance.

F1 *Welford* actor warning c.17 lines before entrance.

F1^{v} *[Welford]* actor warning, cropped, c.21 lines before entrance. Only the bottom half of the name is left.

for in upper left margin, in a different, nontheatrical hand.

Abigale actor warning c.20 lines before entrance.

F2 *Yo: Lovelesse Comrade[s] / Moorecraft / widdow / Savill* actor warning c.34 lines before entrance. The prompter provided more time for assembling this group for their entrance, as he probably should have with the warning on D1 (though the cut seems to have thrown him off there). He probably judged how much time was needed on the basis of costume changes, from which side of the stage an actor would enter, and other prompting duties demanding his attention.

F3 This page (see illustration) contains what may be merely doodles, for they seem to be unrelated to the action of the play. In the upper right margin is a note that appears to read: *R3071∅*. In the middle of the page, just before Young Lovelesse's speech beginning "Drinke M^r. Moorecraft . . ." is a series of marks that appear to be: *3 3 3 3 3 3 3*. Similar *3 3* marks appear again on B3 of James Shirley's *A Contention for Honour and Riches*, 1633, in Bodleian copy Malone 253 (1). The hand that made the markings was probably the one that wrote *for* on F1^v above; the ink is different and the hand nontheatrical.

F3^v *El: Lovelesse* actor warning c.15 lines before entrance.

F4 *–++++++++++–* entrance cue for Elder Lovelesse. This is the only use in the copy of the common cross-hatch symbol. In several Restoration promptbooks (but not in Duke's Company books) most or all entrances and sound effects are cued in this manner. But why did the prompter cue only this particular entrance? The answer may be that the prompter did not make the mark. The ink looks more like the nontheatrical marks on F3.

There are some indecipherable, nontheatrical, marks in the right margin.

Act IV, Scene i

G1^v Roger's entrance on this page was not warned.

G2 *Lady. Martha* actor warning c.32 lines before entrance.
El: Lovelesse actor warning c.24 lines before entrance.

H1^v *Abigale* actor warning c.4 lines before entrance. No earlier warning was possible, since Abigale just made an exit.

There is a cut of 88 lines, from "*Musicke. Enter young Louelesse and Widdow* . . ." on H1^v through the end of Act IV on H2^v.

Act V, Scene i

H2^v *Servant / Welford* actor warning c.15 lines (for the Servant) and c.17 lines (for Welford) before entrances.

and this ſhall ſerue for witneſſe. And widdow, ſince y'are come ſo happily, you ſhall deliuer vp the keys, and free poſſeſſion of this houſe; whilſt I ſtand by to ratifie.

Wi. I had rather giue it back againe beleeue me,
'Tis a miſery to ſay you had it. Take heede.

Yo. Lo. 'Tis paſt that widowe, come, ſit downe; ſome wine there: there is a ſcuruy banquet if we had it. All this faire houſe is yours Sir. *Sauill.* *Sa.* Yes Sir.

Yo. Lo. Are your keys ready, I muſt eaſe your burden.

Sa. I am ready Sir to be vndone, when you ſhall call me to't.

Yo. Lo. Come come, thou ſhalt liue better.

Sa. I ſhall haue leſſe to doe, thats all, ther's halfe a dozen of my friends ith fields, ſunning againſt a banke, with halfe a breech among vm, I ſhall bee with vm ſhortly. The care and continuall vexation of being rich eate vp this raſcall. What ſhall become of my poore familie? they are no ſheepe, and they muſt keepe themſelues.

Yo. Lo. Drinke M^r. *Moorecraft*, pray be merry all:
Nay and you willl not drinke ther's no ſociety.
Captaine ſpeake lowd, and drinke: widdow a word.

Cap. Expound her throughly Knight. Here God a gold, here's to thy faire poſſeſſions: Bee a Barron, and a bolde one: leaue off your tickling of young heires like trouts, and let thy chimneys ſmoke. Feede men of war, liue and bee honeſt, and be ſaued yet.

Mo. I thanke you worthy Captain for your counſell. You keep your chimneys ſmoking there, your noſtrels, and when you can, you feede a man of war: this makes not you a Barron, but a bare one: and how or when you ſhall be ſaued, let the clarke o'th company (you haue commanded) haue a iuſt care of.

Poet. The man is much moued. Be not angry Sir, but as the Poet ſings; Let your diſpleaſure be a ſhort furie, and goe out. You haue ſpoke home, and bitterly, to me Sir? Captain take truce, the Miſer is a tart and a witty whorſon.

Cap. Poet you faine perdie, the wit of this man lies in his fingers ends, he muſt tell al: his tongue fils but his mouth like a neats tongue, and onely ſerues to lick his hungry chaps after a purchaſe: his braines and brimſtone are the Diuels diet to a fat vſerers head. To her Knight, to her: clap her abourd and ſtow her. Where's the braue Steward?

F 3 *Sa.*

From Beaumont and Fletcher's *The Scornful Ladie*. By kind permission of the British Library.

H3ᵛ *Servant* actor warning c. 11 lines before entrance. The prompter failed to correct an error in the printed text. The Servant must have made an exit shortly after his entrance on H3, but there is no stage direction taking him off. He reenters on H3ᵛ.

Abigale actor warning c. 16 lines before entrance.

H4 *Lady* actor warning c. 30 lines before entrance.

Abigale actor warning c. 15 lines before entrance, but there is a cut of about 6 lines on this and the following page, leaving Abigale a warning of only about 9 lines. This cut may therefore have been made after the warning note was entered; the prompter should have advanced the warning. The cut is within the Lady's speech, from "I know 'tis like a man . . ." on H4 through ". . . to mine owne ruine" on H4ᵛ.

H4ᵛ *El: Lovelesse Welford as A / woma[n]* actor warning c. 24 lines before entrance.

I1 Martha's entrance on this page was not warned.

I3 *Yo: Lovelesse / Savill* actor warning c. 24 lines before entrance.

I3ᵛ *Moorecraft* actor warning c. 29 lines before entrance.

I4 *El: Lovelesse / & Lady* actor warning placed directly opposite their entrance. The warning should have been c. 20 lines earlier. One wonders why this error was not caught either during rehearsals or performances. Two possibilities suggest themselves: either the entrance never gave the prompter trouble, so he simply did not notice the mistake; or actor warnings were not as important to him as following the dialogue, so a prompt could be given if necessary. The actors may have marked their parts and taken care of their own warnings and entrances; if so, the warnings and entrance cues in promptbooks were safeguards. This would help explain why it seems not to have mattered that some entrances were not warned at all.

I4ᵛ *Welford [&] Martha* actor warning c. 18 lines before entrance.

K1 *Yo: Lovelesse widdow / Moorecraft, Savill / & Servingmen* actor warning c. 29 lines before entrance.

K2 *Roger, Abigale* actor warning c. 28 lines before entrance.

Not recorded in the transcriptions above is another type of manuscript notation appearing throughout the copy. The mark looks very like a 6 but in some places appears to be a script *E*. It occurs fifty-three times in the outer margins, usually at the beginning of some character's speech. Perhaps it was a mark made by the prompter to signal speeches that gave the actors trouble during rehearsals, yet the marks sometime appear within passages marked for cutting. Possibly they were random doodles by some reader, but the ink looks like that in the actor warnings.

The cuts indicated in the copy shorten the play only a little and seem to have been made primarily to delete extraneous material and some bawdry. For example, the cut on H1ᵛ that continues to the end of the act has some obscene innuendoes by the Comrades concerning Young Lovelesse's coming marriage to the Widow. But in the final scene, when Young Lovelesse comes on with his supposed bride, no mention is made of the marriage and she, indeed, has no lines. The cut scene does no damage to the play.

Since this promptbook stresses actor warnings and cuts and contains only one property note (and that a mere copy of a printed stage direction), only one entrance cue, no music or sound notes, and no technical notes, perhaps it was a book prepared for the use of the callboy rather than the prompter himself. As will be seen, there is other evidence that more than one book may have been prepared for Restoration productions, each with specialized notes.

The Cheats *by John Wilson*

Manuscript play, 1663, with incomplete manuscript prompt notes related to the King's Company production at the Vere Street Theatre c. 16 (?) March 1663; in the Worcester College Library, Oxford. Manuscript edited by Milton Nahm (Oxford: B. Blackwell, 1935).

Though the prompter's notes in the manuscript of Wilson's comedy are incomplete, we can nevertheless reconstruct the probable history of the book. Wilson had his play copied by a scribe, as did many playwrights of the time, apparently, and the scribe's copy was turned over to the King's Company prompter (Charles Booth?). The copy was, to say the least, a poor one: the spelling is more than usually erratic, abbreviations and corrections clutter the manuscript in many places, and the copyist often misunderstood Wilson's original papers and transcribed lines inaccurately. The prompter (or someone under his command) went through the entire copy making textual emendations; after having done that—or perhaps while doing it—he inserted some of the necessary prompt notes. After the third scene of Act I—that is, after page nine of the eighty-eight-page manuscript—his rather careful prompt notes stop. He probably abandoned the copy for a cleaner one, for the worst part of the manuscript is the latter half.

At any rate, the prompter seems to have made textual emendations throughout but production notes only for a few pages, and the manuscript could not have served as the actual promptbook during performances. *The Cheats* was licensed on 6 March 1663. Montague Summers in *The Playhouse of Pepys* (p. 272) says that the play was first presented about 16 March, but, typically, Summers does not reveal his source. *The Cheats* was banned on the twenty-second, perhaps revived in May 1671, again possibly revived in 1683–84, and certainly revived in 1692–93. Clues to the revivals are the editions of 1671, 1684, and 1693 (two issues). The play was edited by Maidment and Logan in their edition of Wilson's *Dramatic Works* in 1874, but they were evidently unaware of the existence of the manuscript. Nahm in his modern edition footnotes all of the prompter's notes. Kathleen Lesko of George Washington University has edited Wilson's plays for her doctoral dissertation; she has included a study of the manuscript.

Though incomplete as a promptbook, *The Cheats* manuscript still has considerable theatrical value as one of the earliest Restoration records of prompter's notations. Most of the notes in the copy can be found in later promptbooks: actor warnings by actor or character names (either would apparently do; here both are used), cross-hatch marks for entrances, reminders about necessary properties, and cues for sound effects. In the following transcriptions of the prompt notes, page numbers have been assigned; the original manuscript is not paginated.

Act I, Scene i

[P. 1] *Mr Shotterell / Mr Clunn / –+++++++++–* entrance cue at the opening of I, i for the actors playing Bilboe and Titere Tu. Entrances at the beginnings of acts are not normally marked in Restoration promptbooks, since, one supposes, there was ample time to see that everything and everyone was ready.

[P. 3] *D. Dilligene / & wife / Mr Loveday / M^ris Marshall / ––++––y.––++––* actor warning c.25 lines before entrance. Naming both the characters and the actors rather than one or the other is uncommon, and the odd symbol—similar to the cross-hatch entrance cue mark—is unique. It evidently was used to call attention to the warning. The significance of the *y.* remains a mystery.

–+++++++++++– entrance cue for Double-Diligence and his wife.

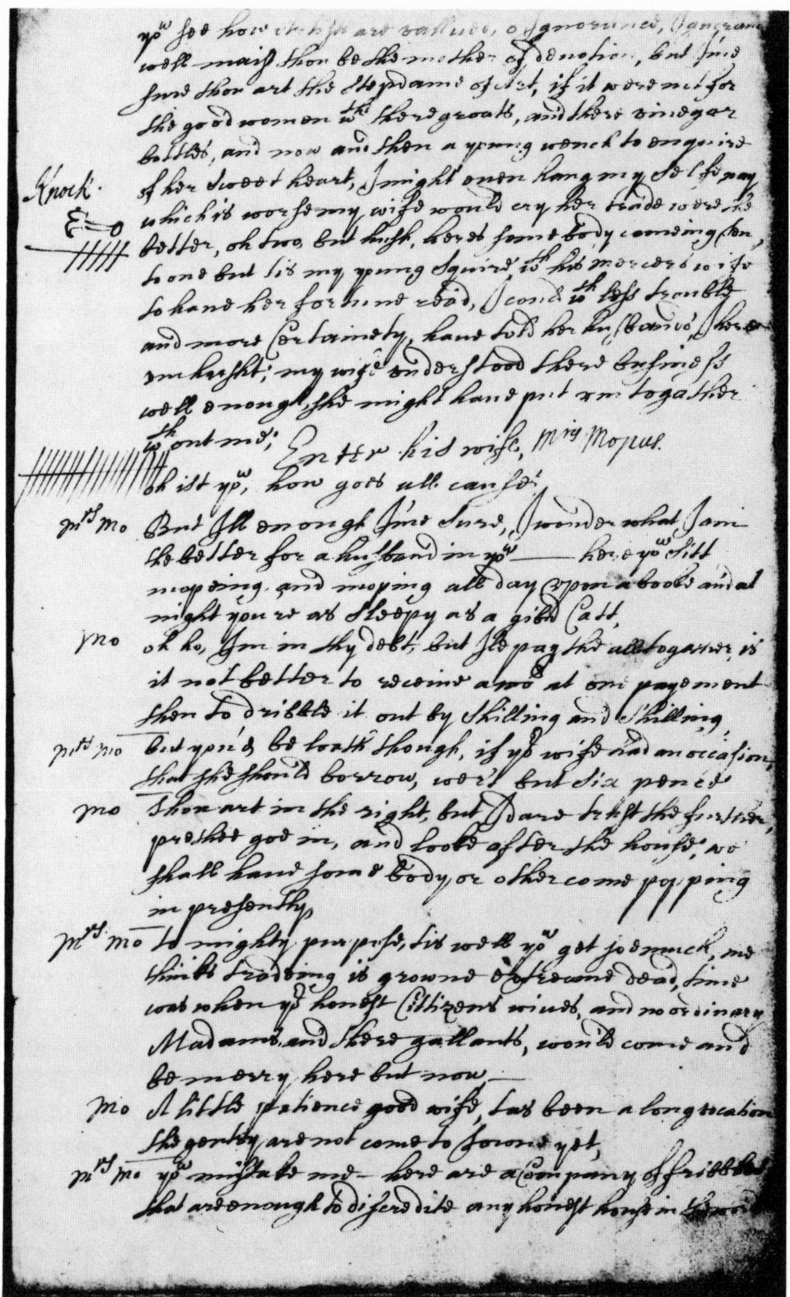

From Wilson's *The Cheats*. By kind permission of the Provost and Fellows of Worcester College, Oxford.

[P. 4] *Mr Hart / ––+–––––––+–– / Mr Burt / Jolly & / Afterwitt* actor warning c.22 lines before entrance.

Act I, Scene ii

[P. 5] *–++++++++++++–* entrance cue for Jolly and Afterwitt.

[P. 7] *Mopus & / Role* actor and property (roll; i.e. almanack) warning c.25 lines before entrance. The actor playing Mopus was Michael Mohun, according to the 1693 edition of the play.

Enter over leaffe /–+++++++++– advance entrance cue for Mopus at the bottom of the page, for an entrance at the top of the next. The prompter was being unusually careful in preparing his book. All of the notes thus far have been very thorough.

Act I, Scene iii

[P. 8] *–+++++++++++–* entrance cue for Mopus at the top of the page, 2 lines before his entrance.

M[ris] Mopus / M[ris] Marg[t]. actor warning c.29 lines before entrance. The actress cited was probably Margaret Rutter or possibly Margaret Hughes.

[P. 9] *Knock / E=o / –+++++++++–* sound effect cue, using the cross-hatch symbol as a signal. The meaning of the unique *E=o* is unclear, unless it means something like "enter opposite"—that is, the knock should be made opposite the prompter's side of the stage. See illustration.

–+++++++++++– entrance cue for Mrs. Mopus. The prompter also added *m[ris] Mopus* to the stage direction, which reads only, "Enter his wife."

The prompt notes end at that point, though textual emendations continue to the end of the manuscript.

At the end of the text of the play is Herbert's statement: *"This Comedy of the Cheates may be Acted as Allowed for the / [st]age, the reformations strictly observed, to the Kings Company of / Actors by Henry Herbert. Master of the Revells. / [March] 6.th / [1663]"* (the manuscript is badly deteriorated, and some of the statement is indecipherable).

Missing from the prompt notes in *The Cheats* are technical notes on scenery, which is one of the arguments for the Vere Street Theatre, where we know the play was produced, having little or no scenery, after the Elizabethan manner.

The Ball *by James Shirley*

1639 first quarto with fairly complete manuscript prompt notes dating after 1663 for a King's Company production at the Bridges Street Theatre, Lincoln's Inn Fields Theatre, or Drury Lane Theatre in the 1660s or 1670s; in Bodleian copy Malone 253 (9). Discussed by Dana McKinnen in "A Description of a Restoration Promptbook of Shirley's *The Ball*," *Restoration and 18th Century Theatre Research*, 10 (May 1971), 25–28.

The title page of *The Ball* lists George Chapman as co-author, though G. E. Bentley in *The Jacobean and Caroline Stage* (vol. 5, p. 1078), believes the play was Shirley's alone. There is no record of a Restoration production of *The Ball* under its main title, but the alternate title was *The French Dancing Master*, and Samuel Pepys saw a play of that name at the King's Company's Vere Street Theatre on 21 May 1662. The promptbook contains notes on scenery, which we assume the Vere Street playhouse did not have, so I would conclude that the play was not prepared for that house. (And we cannot be certain that the play Pepys saw was Shirley's *The Ball*; he may have seen a droll based on Cavendish's *The Variety*.) Since the hands found in the prompt notes match those in other King's Company promptbooks, it is likely that the troupe revived the play at one of their theatres that had scenic facilities—Bridges Street, Lincoln's Inn Fields, or Drury Lane. McKinnen sees two theatrical hands in the copy; a later, nontheatrical, hand wrote some explanatory notes on H4 and I1. But I believe all the theatrical notes were written by the same person, who usually used a pen but sometimes a pencil.

The 1639 quarto of *The Ball* was set from prompt copy, as a trace in Act IV proves. That trace and a stage direction in Act V indicate that three of the characters had different names in the original production of the play: Loveall for Coronell, Stephen for Marmaduke, and Lionell for Ambrose. In his edition of Shirley's *Dramatic Works* William Gifford, assuming that the play was a collaboration, supposed that the double names came about because the two playwrights failed to communicate clearly to one another.

Act I

A2 *Town* setting for Act I. The printed stage direction gives no locale.

A2^v *[Am]brose* actor warning c.31 lines before entrance. This, and many other marginal notes, are cropped. Entrances throughout the copy were warned but not cued.

A3 *Solo[mon]* actor warning c.28 lines before entrance.

A3^v *[Corone]ll* actor warning c.30 lines before entrance. See also the next note.
[Coro]nell actor warning c.10 lines before entrance, in pencil. This repeats the warning in the previous note, for no evident reason.
[Fres]hwatter / & / [La F]risk—actor warning c.29 lines before entrance.
[Gud]geon: actor warning. No stage direction brings this character onstage, though he has lines two pages hence and probably enters with Freshwater and La Friske on A4; if so, this warning is c.27 lines before his entrance. This note closely follows the previous one but is divided from it by a horizontal line.

A4^v *[Ra]inbow / [&] / [Bar]ker* actor warning c.36 lines before entrance.

B1 *Rosamo[nd] / Honor[ia]* actor warning in a brace c.25 lines before entrance. McKinnen suggests that I, ii begins on this page, though no prompt note is visible; it may have been cropped, as McKinnen suggests. But a new scene, if it was intended, would probably begin on B1^v at the entrance of Rosamond and Honoria. In any case, in the matter of numbering scenes within acts, I have shown a new scene number only when the author has or when a scene shift is clearly indicated.

B1^v *[Ra]inbow* actor warning c.32 lines before entrance.

B3 *[Act ready]* warning for act ending, c.98 lines in advance. This note is extremely faint and appears to have been rubbed out; perhaps it was a mistake, since it is set unusually far in advance. No later warning for the end of the act is visible, but cropping may have lost it to us. The warning would have served to prepare musicians for entr'acte music (if there was any), actors for entrances, and stagehands for a scene shift (if there was one).

Act II, [Scene i]

B4 *Tow[n]* setting for the opening of Act II. The stage direction gives no locale. The note is hardly necessary, since the locale is the same as for Act I.

C1 *L^d R[ainbow]* actor warning c.33 lines before entrance.
Coron[ell] actor warning c.30 lines before entrance.

C1^v *[Scut]illa / [So]lomon* actor warning in a brace c.26 lines before entrance. See illustration.
[La Fri]sk / [Rosa]mond / [Luci]na / [Hon]oria actor warning in a brace c.20 lines before entrance.
[Scut]illa actor warning? This cannot be an entrance warning, for Scutilla has already been warned; perhaps it has something to do with the stage direction on C2 that reads: "*Another Lady dances.*" That direction comes c.20 lines after this warning. McKinnen suggests that Scutilla was added to the entrance on C2 which names a Dancer plus Rosamond, Lucina, and Honoria, but that cannot be, for Scutilla enters with Solomon four speeches before those ladies enter.

Act II, [Scene ii]

C2 *Cha[mber] / Cha[mber] / Da[nce]* setting and cue for II, [ii]. The stage direction gives no locale. The manuscript note is very faint and in pencil.
rea[dy] dance warning c.26 lines in advance of a stage direction on C2^v that reads: "*They dance a new Country Dance.*" Cropping may have lost the word *Dance* in this warning.

C2^v *[Solo]mon / [Coron]ell* actor warning in a brace c.19 lines before entrance.
[Da]nce cue for the country dance warned above.
[Lucin]a: actor warning c.13 lines before entrance. Since Lucina has just made an exit, this warning for her reentrance could not have been placed much earlier.

C3 *Sr Marmaduk[e]* actor warning c.20 lines before entrance. The entrance of Solomon on this page was not warned; on the other hand, after his entrance with Coronell on C2^v Solomon was not given an exit. He is a servant, used chiefly to announce visitors; in this section of the text Solomon has three entrances and a few lines but no designated exits. The prompter could have corrected those errors, but, as can be seen in many promptbooks, his notes concerned warnings and entrances, not exits.

C3^v *[Am]bros: / [Solo]mon* actor warning c.24 lines before entrance.

C4^v *[Bos]tock* actor warning c.22 lines before entrance.

D1^v *[Coron]ell* actor warning c.35 lines before entrance.

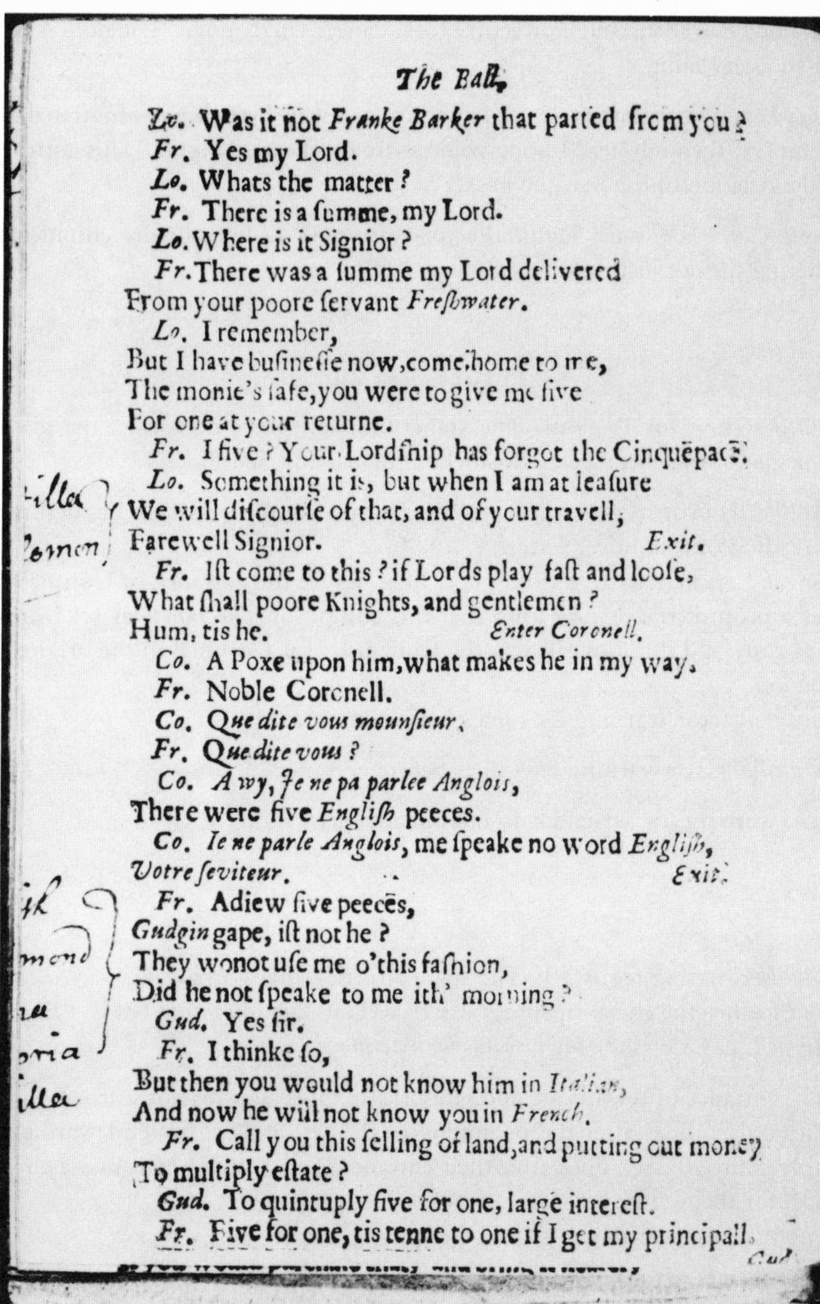

The Ball.

Lo. Was it not *Franke Barker* that parted from you?
Fr. Yes my Lord.
Lo. Whats the matter?
Fr. There is a ſumme, my Lord.
Lo. Where is it Signior?
Fr. There was a ſumme my Lord delivered
From your poore ſervant *Freſhwater.*
Lo. I remember,
But I have buſineſſe now, come home to me,
The monie's ſafe, you were to give me five
For one at your returne.
Fr. I five? Your Lordſhip has forgot the Cinquepace.
Lo. Something it is, but when I am at leaſure
We will diſcourſe of that, and of your travell,
Farewell Signior. *Exit.*
Fr. Iſt come to this? if Lords play faſt and looſe,
What ſhall poore Knights, and gentlemen?
Hum, tis he. *Enter Coronell.*
Co. A Poxe upon him, what makes he in my way.
Fr. Noble Coronell.
Co. *Que dite vous mounſieur.*
Fr. *Que dite vous?*
Co. *A wy, Je ne pa parlee Anglois,*
There were five *Engliſh* peeces.
Co. *Je ne parle Anglois,* me ſpeake no word *Engliſh,*
Votre ſeviteur. *Exit.*
Fr. Adiew five peeces,
Gudgin gape, iſt not he?
They wonot uſe me o'this faſhion,
Did he not ſpeake to me ith' morning?
Gud. Yes ſir.
Fr. I thinke ſo,
But then you would not know him in *Italian,*
And now he will not know you in *French.*
Fr. Call you this ſelling of land, and putting out money
To multiply eſtate?
Gud. To quintuply five for one, large intereſt.
Fr. Five for one, tis tenne to one if I get my principall.

From Shirley's *The Ball.* By kind permission of the Bodleian Library, Oxford.

D2 *Ac[t]* warning for act-end c.43 lines in advance. The word *ready* may have been cropped from this note, though in some promptbooks just the word Act serves as a warning.

Act III, [Scene i]

D2ᵛ *[~~Cha]mber~~ Court* setting for III, [i]. The first word is in ink, deleted in pencil; *Court* is in pencil. The stage direction gives no locale.

D3 *La friske* actor warning c.27 lines before entrance.

D3ᵛ *[Bo]stock* actor warning c.29 lines before entrance.
[A]mbros actor warning c.29 lines before entrance.

D4 *S^r Ma[rmaduke]* actor warning c.31 lines before entrance.
Coron[ell] actor warning c.26 lines before entrance. In pencil, apparently, under that ink warning, is a similar cue: *Coro[nell].*

Act III, [Scene ii]

Tow[n] setting for III, [ii]. The stage direction gives no indication of a scene change. The new scene begins at the entrance of Bostocke.

There is a very faint, indecipherable pencil note at the entrance of Sir Marmaduke. It may be: ~~*Court.*~~

D4ᵛ *enter Coronell* actor entrance cue following Marmaduke's line that ends ". . . Noble sir how ist?" No stage direction brings Coronell on, but the prompter caught the mistake. The note is partly smudged.

E1 *ffreshwa[ter] / Gudgeo[n] / Sollom[on]* actor warning c.46 lines before entrance.

Act III, [Scene iii]

E1ᵛ *[Cham]ber* setting for III, [iii]. The note is badly cropped and in faint pencil. The shift comes at the entrance of Freshwater, Gudgeon, and Solomon. No scene change is indicated in the stage direction.

E2 *freshwa[ter] / Rosam[ond]* actor warning c.27 lines before entrance.

E2ᵛ *[Bar]ker / [Hon]oria* actor warning c.22 lines before entrance.

E3ᵛ *[Luci]na / [Scut]illa* actor warning c.26 lines before entrance.

[Solo]mon actor warning c.22 lines before entrance.

[Bosto]ck / [Am]bros / [Lamo]unt: / [Coron]ell: in a brace; then: *[Ma]rma* actor warning c.19 lines before entrance. Ambrose *is* Lamount.

The entrance of Honoria on this page was not warned, since she made her exit only 4 lines before her reentrance.

Act III, [Scene iv]

E4 *Cou[rt]* setting for III, [iv]. This note is in pencil and barely visible. The scene shift comes at the entrance of Lucina and Scutilla.

E4^{v} McKinnen cites an indecipherable manuscript note on this page; I found none.

F2 *Act* warning for act-end c.32 lines in advance.

Act IV, [Scene i]

F2^{v} *[Cou]rt* (?) setting for IV, i. This note is badly cropped and the word may be something other than Court. Neither the stage direction nor the dialogue indicates the locale.

[Bark]er actor warning c.18 lines before entrance.

F4 *Sr Ambrose / Sr Marma[duke]* actor warning c.32 lines before entrance.

G1 *[Rosa]mond / [Ma]rmaduk / [Am]brose* actor warning c.36 lines before entrance. Honoria should have been included in this warning.

G1^{v}–G2 A very faint pencil line in the margin indicates a cut from Lord Rainbow's line, ". . . and the Coronell . . ." in his last speech on G1^{v} through "Our staine . . ." in the same speech at the top of G2. The cut would make the speech less windy.

Act IV, [Scene ii]

G2 *Chamb[er]* setting for IV, [ii]. The stage direction gives no locale; the new scene begins at the entrance of Rosamond, Honoria, Marmaduke, and Ambrose.

G3 *Lafris[k]* actor warning c.25 lines before entrance.

ready dance warning c.38 lines in advance of a stage direction on G3^{v} that reads: "*They Dance*."

G3^{v} *[Dan]ce* cue at the stage direction for a dance, cited above. The note is in pencil and very faint.

G3^{v}–G4 Pencil lines indicate a cut from Honoria's "A French *Cupid*" after the dance on G3^{v} through her "I hope youle spare our hearts" on G4. This anticipates the deletion of the masque in Act V.

G4 *Bost[ocke] / Luci[na] / Scut[illa]* actor warning c.14 lines before entrance, considering the cut just described.

Act IV, [Scene iii]

Cour[t] setting for IV, [iii]. The stage direction gives no locale; the new scene begins at the entrance of Bostocke, Lucina, and Scutilla.

G4^{v} *[Lett]er* (?) property warning in very faint pencil in the margin beside Lucina's reading of Rainbow's letter.

"*Loveall*" printed actor warning c.33 lines before the entrance of Coronell. This is a prompt trace, indicating that this edition of *The Ball* was set from prompt copy and that Loveall was the name used for Coronell in the original production.

[Coron]ell actor warning c.25 lines before entrance.

H2 *Scutti[lla]* actor warning c.25 lines before entrance.

H3 *Ac[t]* warning for act-end c.30 lines in advance.

Act V

Cham[ber] setting for Act V. The stage direction gives no locale.

frisk / fresh actor cue at opening of Act V. The stage direction reads: "*Enter Mounsieur* [i.e. La Friske] *and servants with perfumes*."

H3^{v} The entrance of Rosamond and Honoria on this page was not warned, but it comes only 6 lines after the beginning of the act, and the act-end warning probably sufficed. Two lines after their entrance is an *X* in the margin—a cue, perhaps, for their entry.

Rainbow actor warning c.22 lines before entrance.

H4 The words "Martheme, / In *London*" in Freshwater's speech about the middle of the page are underlined, and in the margin is a faint pencil note by some later annotator: *Match me / in London / Dekker*—a reference to Dekker's play of c. 1611–12. See also the similar gloss on I1.

H4^{v} McKinnen cites an indecipherable manuscript note on this page, but it is an ink blot transferred from a marginal note on the facing page, I1.

I1 Following Honoria's speech that ends, "She that found her wedding ring in the / Haddocks belly" is a very faint pencil gloss. It is partly indecipherable, but it concludes with *to show boys this A new / Wonder* —a reference to Rowley's play of 1632.

Monsi[eur] / Lefr[iske] actor warning c.23 lines before entrance.

I2 *Ld Ran[bow] / Coronel[l] / Bosto[cke]* actor warning c.32 lines before entrance. Then, in pencil: *Luci[na]*, who is forgotten in the entrance on I2^{v}.

Lo speech ascription added in pencil in the left margin before Lord Rainbow's line, "You cannot otherwise be reconcil'd." The compositor forgot the ascription, thus giving the line to Honoria; someone, not the prompter, whose hand is distinctly different, made the correction.

I2^{v} *[Barke]r / [as] a Satyr* actor warning c.20 lines before entrance, taking into account the cut noted below.

A stage direction reads, "*Enter ~~Rainbow,~~ Coronell, Bostoke.*" Rainbow is crossed out in pencil. Lucina should have been included but was not.

I2^{v}–I3^{v} The entire scene involving Venus, Diana, and Cupid is marked for cutting. It begins with the stage direction, "A golden Ball descends . . ." on I2^{v} and ends with "*A Dance*" on I3^{v}. Perhaps the brief masque too difficult to stage.

I3^{v} ~~*[Step]hen / [Lion]ell*~~ actor warning in a brace, canceled, c.32 lines before the entrance on I4 of Sir Stephen and Sir Lionell—two characters who are not in the dramatis personae but who must have been the originals of Marmaduke and Ambrose in the first production. The prompter made a warning note automatically, discovered the error (the characters should be Sir Marmaduke and Sir Ambrose), canceled the incorrect warning, wrote a new one (see the next note), and corrected the stage direction on I4.

[Mar]maduke / [Am]brose actor warning in a brace, correcting the warning above, c.27 lines before entrance.

I4 *Sr Marmaduke* ——— *Sr Ambrose* written above the stage direction, "*Enter* Sir ~~*Stephen*~~, *and* Sir ~~*Lionell*~~." This corrects the error noted above.

"*Co*. Then lets tosse the Ball" marked faintly in pencil for deletion, since the masque, involving the tossing of the golden ball, was omitted.

Act warning for act-end c.31 lines in advance.

I4^{v} There is no warning for the dance that takes place 5 lines before the end of the play, though perhaps the act-end warning was considered sufficient. Indeed, in promptbooks containing warnings for the ends of acts, a warning for the end of Act V is usually omitted.

The Change of Crownes *by Edward Howard*

Manuscript play, 1667, with very complete manuscript prompt notes for the King's Company production at the Bridges Street Theatre on 15 April 1667; formerly in the possession of R. A. Austen-Leigh. Edited by Frederick S. Boas (London: Oxford University Press for the Royal Society of Literature, 1949). Staging discussed in Richard Southern's "The Scene Plot of *The Change of Crownes*," *Theatre Notebook*, 4 (April–June 1950), 65–68. Reproduced here in chapter 10.

This is the richest of the Restoration promptbooks and a theatrical document of the first importance. The promptbook is a scribe's copy with manuscript notes in at least eight different hands. Boas distinguished them as follows: "A, the original script; B, additional textual corrections; C, the book-keeper's [prompter's] cues and other annotations; D, additional scene-headings [by the machinist]; E and F, the inserted actors' names [by the prompter's assistant?]; G, the herring-bone diagrams, except in folios 8–10; H, the herring-bone diagrams and some marginal notes in folios 8–10. . . . With so many factors involved some of the attributions are to be considered tentative and provisional . . ." (p. 91).

Boas, being chiefly interested in the literary and historical aspects of the play, omitted many of the theatrical notes in the copy, feeling that, "While these served their purpose during the performance they duplicate the original stage-directions that follow in the MS. and would be confusing to readers of the play" (p. 6). The fact is that the prompt notes do not always duplicate the stage directions, and, instead of keeping his readers unconfused, Boas led at least one into confusion. Richard Southern in his analysis of the scene plot of *The Change of Crownes* had to depend on what Boas had printed; Southern concluded incorrectly that Act II had three scenes, and he mistook some of the author's stage directions for prompt notes.

The Royal Society of Literature was not able to locate the manuscript for me, nor have I been able to contact Mr. R. A. Austen-Leigh, in whose hands the document was in the 1940s. Queries in the *Times Lit-*

erary Supplement and *Theatre Notebook* and searches in a number of libraries have yielded no results. Perhaps the facsimile presented here will stimulate interest in the manuscript and help us find it.

The following commentary discusses the cast and staging. Footnotes to the facsimile, which deal with specific problems, are more complete here than they will be later, since this is the richest promptbook presented.

Cast

The cast of *The Change of Crownes* can only be reconstructed in part. Pepys saw the premiere on 15 April 1667 and commented on John Lacy's portrayal of "the country-gentleman come up to Court"—that is, Asinello—which so aggravated Charles II that the play was banned. Some prompt notes in the manuscript indicate that William Hughes played a Messenger (see IV, iii, 39–40 and V, iv, 139–40), Thomas Gradwell acted the mute role of a General (IV, iii, 56), William Harris apparently played a Gentleman (IV, i, 24–25 and 45), and a little-known actor named John Benion (or Binion) seems to have played a Captain (IV, ii, 53). Also in the cast were Edward Lydall, Thomas Hancock, and either Robert or Edward Shatterell (II, i, 209–11). Assigning those actors specific roles is difficult, for their names do not seem to be clearly connected with an entrance for three characters. The trio may have played Alberto, Andrugio, and Castruchio, who make their first entrance in the play at the opening of IV, iii—long after the marginal warning note near the end of II, i; but it could be that the actors playing those parts were not required to be at the theatre until the performance began but would have to be present by the middle of the second act.

Staging

The scene plot for the production can be reconstructed with more ease.

Act & Scene	*Author's Description*	*Machinist's Description*
I, i	None	Description deleted; could be ~~*first Court Scene*~~
I, ii	"Courtiers, and Statesmen before the Queene under a Canopy . . ."	*State Scene* and *Canopie Gauz'd* (the latter is in the warning for the Queen's entrance)
II, i	None	*outside of ye Court*

Boas begins a new scene after line 138 and the entrance of Leonidas and Barsanes, but there is no indication in either the text or the prompt notes of any scene change; in the facsimile of the manuscript I have continued the line numbering until the scene change at line 244.

II, ii	None	*State cham / ber*

Southern divides Act II into three scenes, but the manuscript shows only two; he was, I believe, misled by Boas.

III, i	None	None; the scene presumably did not change
III, ii	None	*outside of the / Court*

This entire scene is boxed for cutting, yet the boxing does not include the opening stage direction for Antonio and Asinello's entrance or the machinist's description of the setting to be used.

III, iii	"a Monastery wherein Nunns are Discoverd in the Quire singing, at the Ringing of ~~the~~ a Bell, the Quire is closed"	*Scene Nunnery / A lamp / burning*
IV, i	None	*state Scene / 2^{d} 1st Scene of the Court / or Presence / Chamber*
IV, ii	None	*1st Court / outside*
IV, iii	"a Camp, a Pavillyon Royall"	*A Camp Scene*
V, i	None	*out side of the / Court Scene*
V, ii	None	*A Red Canopy Chamb[er]*

Act & Scene	*Author's Description*	*Machinist's Description*
V, iii	None	*Scene outside / of the Court*
V, iv	None	*State Scene of the / Court*

The wording of the scene descriptions by the machinist—or whoever wrote them—is sometimes confusing, but the production seems to have called for six, or possibly seven, different settings:

Court. I, i; but the description was canceled, and perhaps the Outside Court scene was used.

State. I, ii; II, ii; IV, i; and V, iv. Though the descriptions vary, a single setting may have served for all four scenes; alternatively, two settings may have been used—a state scene and a presence chamber scene.

Outside Court. II, i; III, ii; IV, ii; V, i; and V, iii.

Nunnery. III, iii. The stage direction for the opening of the scene indicates that the choir of the nunnery is first shown, a song is sung, the "Quire" is closed, and the scene proceeds. If the choir was above, that would suggest the use of shutters split horizontally as well as vertically, so that the upper pair could open while the lower remained closed, a system known to have been used by Inigo Jones in Caroline times. Dryden seems to have asked for such an effect in Act II of *Albion and Albanius* in 1685.

Camp. IV, iii.

Chamber. V, ii. This would seem to differ from the presence chamber, which I have put under the State setting. The machinist's description, *A red Canopy Chamb[er]*, suggests that the company had at least one other similar setting, perhaps with a canopy of a different color.

The shifting of the scenery is indicated in greater detail in *The Change of Crownes* manuscript than in any other known Restoration promptbook. There are whistle warnings in advance of the shifts at scene endings within acts, act-ready warnings near the ends of acts for entr'acte shifts, and whistle signals at the points where the shifts actually take place. The notes made by the machinist are not always correct, and perhaps there was a separate, carefully prepared scene plot posted backstage containing all warnings, cues, and setting labels. What appears in the prompter's book may be only those technical notes that in some way affected the prompter's work.

Since the technical cues are scattered throughout the manuscript, perhaps it will be useful to gather them here and discuss some of the problems they raise:

No warnings or cues occur at the opening of the play, since the stage would have been set well in advance of curtain time. We know that as a rule the curtain was down when the audience arrived and did not rise until the first act was ready to begin; interestingly, only one Restoration promptbook has notes on the curtain. Its use was probably so traditional that no notes were needed: as soon as the speaker of the prologue made his exit from the forestage, the curtain went up and the play began. The promptbook would not need to contain any cues or even a description of the first setting. The first technical cue is:

Thirty-four lines before the end of I, i: *i[st] whistle / ready*

At the opening of I, ii: ⊙

The scenemen were warned to get to their positions in the wings and flies; the circle-and-dot symbol cued the blowing of the whistle for the first shift in the act. All scenemen—indeed, everyone backstage and many of the playgoers in the house—could have heard the signal. Assuming that all the scenemen were alert, all scenic pieces to be shifted—wings, shutters, borders, etc.—would have moved simultaneously.

Forty-eight lines before the end of I, ii: *Act / Ready*

This warning would substitute, before act endings (as opposed to scene endings within acts), for a whistle warning. In addition to the scenemen, musicians and actors would have required a warning, hence the use of a more general note.

At the opening of II, i: ⊙

Twenty-eight lines before the end of II, i: *2[d] whistle / Ready*

This is a warning for the second shift in the act, the first one having been at the beginning of the act. The numbering of the whistle warnings implies that one blast cued the first shift, two the second, and so on. But a stagehand would have needed to know at the warning, not the cue, which setting was to be shifted, so the warning may have been a hand signal indicating what the whistle number (and, consequently, the correct setting) was. One blast on cue would have been sufficient to start the shift.

At the opening of II, ii: ⊙

Thirty-three lines before the end of II, ii: *Act Ready*

The act-ready warning would not have affected the scenemen in this case, since Act III begins without a scene shift; however, musicians and actors would have needed this warning. In several other promptbooks the cue for a new act is the ringing of a bell at the conclusion of the previous act, but *The Change of Crownes* promptbook contains no ring cues. There is no whistle warning before the end of III, i; either the prompter or machinist forgot to enter a warning in the promptbook, or it was purposely omitted, or perhaps the omission was caused by changes in the script following the banning of the play. A note at III, i, 247 calling for a second promptbook to be ready is canceled. The prompter certainly had at one point two or more books prepared, and the errors in this one may have been corrected in another. He apparently prepared a second book (and a third?) for use at two points in the play: at the beginning of III, ii and the beginning of IV, ii. Both scenes contain material offensive to Charles II and were severely cut. Boas quotes T. C. Skeat on a related matter:

> An important detail in the make-up of the MS. remains to be discussed. Folios 8–10 [Act I, ii, 273–II, ii, 20 (*recte*: II, i, 159)] are a later insertion, replacing two leaves cut out of the original MS., the stubs of which are still visible. There are in fact other reasons for postulating an insertion at this point: (*a*) the ink on ff. 8–10 is greyer than usual, (*b*) the watermark of ff. 8–10 differs from that of the adjoining pages, and (*c*) ff. 8–10 contain only 188 lines of text, an average of 31 lines to the page, as against the scribe's normal average of 39–42.
>
> The wider spacing in ff. 8–10 is readily explained: 188 lines in the scribe's normal spacing would occupy 4 1/2–4 2/3 pages, and the scribe, faced with the alternative of compressing this into two folios (four pages) or spreading it out over three (six pages), chose the latter course.
>
> The two original excised folios must have contained about 160 lines, *i.e.* about 28 lines less than the existing text. The few remnants of writing on the stubs suggest that the revision did not involve radical changes in the action, and alterations may therefore have been confined to the text.
>
> While it would be rash to assign a reason for the insertion of these leaves, it is worthy of note that the stubs show traces of the encircling lines which elsewhere in the MS. surround passages which are known to have given offence. Possibly, therefore, the insertion represents an attempt, after the first production, to re-write the offending passages. But if so, the work was certainly not completed, as subsequent passages similarly marked by encircling lines have been left untouched. (P. 5)

The banning of the play, then, seems to have caused the players to make alterations in the text and to prepare one or two alternate books. The other book referred to at III, i, 247 probably contained rewritten scenes, prepared after the premiere and the banning of the play. But if so, the revised portions of the play must have been abandoned, since the prompter deleted both references to the use of the other book (or books). In any case, even the confusion caused by the preparation of an alternate promptbook would not explain why the whistle warning before the end of III, i was omitted. See the further confusion following.

At the opening of III, ii: ⊙

Fifty-nine lines before the end of III, ii:
ffirst whistle ready

If the whistle cue at the opening of III, ii (the one that was not warned) was the first one in the act, then this warning should have been for the second whistle. But, as will be seen below, this is apparently the beginning of a new whistle sequence, and some whistle notes were not properly renumbered. Act III, ii may actually have become the opening scene in Act IV.

At the opening of III, iii: ⊙

Thirty-six lines before the end of III, iii: *Act / Ready*

At the opening of IV, i:
ffirst whistle and *i*st *whistle Co*^{rt}. ⊙ but then: ⊙ *2d*

There is much confusion here, for the notes twice emphasize the use of the first whistle, yet ⊙ *2d* implies (correctly) second whistle. There seems also to have been confusion over which setting was to be used, the first scene or the state scene of the court or presence chamber. Further, this is one of the two places in the manuscript where a whistle note, in addition to the circle-and-dot whistle cue symbol, are used together, the second occurrence being at the beginning of Act V; usually the word whistle serves as a warning and the symbol as a cue. I suspect that the confusion over which setting was to be used caused the machinist to emphasize the whistle signal. In the process, however, he forgot to delete the references to the first whistle.

Thirty-four lines before the end of IV, i:
3^d whistle / Ready

At the opening of IV, ii: ⊙

Fifteen lines before the end of IV, ii:
3^d whistle / 4 Ready

In the last note, the *3^d* should have been canceled when the *4* was added. This clears up the sequence of apparent errors in whistle numbers noted above. Apparently the scene marked IV, i did not, in fact, begin the act, and perhaps the prompter should have renumbered as necessary. The fact that he did not and that some of the technical warnings and cues are confusing suggests that the errors we see in the promptbook did not matter; that is, they may not have affected the running of a performance. After all, the division of a play into acts and scenes in Restoration times, when playgoers did not have programs to indicate such divisions, may have been of concern only to playwrights, readers, and critics. Spectators at most performances would only have been aware of a sequence of scenes, not of formal structural divisions in the script. Backstage, as long as everything happened when it was supposed to, act and scene numbers may have been of little importance. Other promptbooks demonstrate this: what mattered to the performers and crews were warnings and cues.

At the opening of IV, iii: ⊙

Forty lines before the end of IV, iii: *Act Ready*

At the opening of V, i: *ffirst Whistle* and ⊙

This is the second instance of a whistle cue in addition to a whistle note at an act opening, the first being at the beginning of IV, i. Act III, i did not need such a note, since it did not open with a shift; II, i should have had a whistle note.

Forty-one lines before the end of V, i: *2^d whistle ready*

At the opening of V, ii: *2^d* ⊙

That last note confirms the use of a circle-and-dot whistle cue symbol along with a number at the opening of IV, i. Indeed, one would expect that throughout the manuscript numbers would be attached to both warnings and cues for whistles, but the machinist was not consistent.

Twenty-eight lines before the end of V, ii:
3^d whistle / ready

At the opening of V, iii: ⊙

Twenty-two lines before the end of V, iii:
4th whistle / Ready

That last warning probably should have been deleted, since V, iii was cut, presumably after the play was banned. But there would have been no serious problem: the third whistle would become a warning for V, iv instead of V, iii.

At the opening of V, iv: ⊙

Twenty-eight lines before the end of V, iv: *Act Ready*

The warning for the end of the last act is unusual, and most promptbooks that contain act warnings do not have one for the closing act. All that the warning could concern, one guesses, was the epilogue and fall of the curtain.

Though *The Change of Crownes* promptbook contains some errors, it is remarkably complete, and the errors can be attributed to the fact that the play was presented, banned, cut, and then perhaps revised for a contemplated revival. Only one entrance is not warned, all entrances are cued; careful attention is given to such details as properties, sound effects, and irregularities in the lines. Virtually all of the errors pertain to scene-shift warnings. The book is without question one of the most valuable surviving sources of information on Restoration production practices.

The Mulberry Garden *by Sir Charles Sedley*

1668 first quarto containing a few traces of prompt copy related to the King's Company production at the Bridges Street Theatre on 18 May 1668. Copy studied: British Library 644 c 4.

The text contains only one certain trace of prompt copy (the second quotation given below), but since that proves that the edition was set from prompt copy, the other two notes quoted here may well have been made by the prompter rather than the author.

P. 1 "*Sir* John Everyoungs *House stands*" setting note at the opening of I, i. The use of "stands" in the description of the setting suggests a theatrical source—the machinist or prompter; there is a similar example in *The Sisters*: A wood stands—which was certainly written by someone at the theatre and not by the author.

P. 16 "*Ring*" act-end cue for entr'acte music (and whatever else needed preparation for the beginning of Act II) at the conclusion of Act I, placed just after the last line of dialogue but before the exeunt. Perhaps the music accompanied the departure of Diana and Althea "*severally*."

P. 32 "[*A Song*" in the margin near the end of Act II, 14 lines before a dance, with which the song may have been connected. There is no indication of a song in either the dialogue or the stage directions. Probably the song was added to the play in rehearsal.

The Dumb Lady *by John Lacy*

1672 first quarto containing a few traces of prompt copy related to the King's Company production at the Bridges Street Theatre about 1669. Copy studied: British Library 644 c 58.

All of the traces of prompt copy that crept into the printed edition of Lacy's comedy concern act endings.

P. 14 "[*Act ready*" act-end warning c.19 lines in advance of the end of Act I.

P. 15 "[*Ring*" act-end cue following the last line in Act I.

P. 29 "[*Ring*" act-end cue following the penultimate line in Act II. The variation in placement probably has no significance.

P. 46 "[*Act ready*" act-end warning 34 lines in advance of the end of Act III.

Most, if not all, of the acts in the play were probably similarly warned and cued. If the copy used by the printer contained only notes concerned with act endings, perhaps the copy was one prepared for the use of the musicians (see the *Romeo and Juliet* promptbook in the Duke's Company collection). The musicians needed warnings and cues for entr'acte music.

The Sisters *by James Shirley*

1652 first edition in *Six New Playes* (octavo 1653) with very complete manuscript prompt notes for a King's Company production at the Bridges Street Theatre in 1669–70; in a copy formerly at Sion College Library and now at the Folger Shakespeare Library. Discussed by Montague Summers in "A Restoration Prompt-Book," *Times Literary Supplement*, 24 June 1920, p. 400, reprinted in his *Essays in Petto* (London: Fortune Press, n.d. [1928]), pp. 103–10, and by Edward A. Langhans in "The Restoration Promptbook of Shirley's *The Sisters*," *The Theatre Annual*, 14 (1956), 51–65. Reproduced here in chapter 11 by permission of the Folger Shakespeare Library, Washington, D.C.

Though there is no recorded Restoration performance of *The Sisters*, the play was assigned to the King's Company about 12 January 1669, according to the Lord Chamberlain's accounts at the Public Record Office (LC 5/12, p. 212), and this promptbook is evidence that it was indeed performed, almost certainly in the 1669–70 season, when the personnel referred to in the marginal notes could have been gathered. The absence among the players mentioned of such leading actors as Hart, Mohun, Lacy, Kynaston, Mrs. Corey, the Marshall sisters, and Mrs. Rutter suggests that the promptbook was prepared for a Lenten or summer production by the younger players in the troupe. Since specific performers are so frequently mentioned in the notes, the promptbook could hardly have been useful in later performances with different players without revision, and I would guess that the play was not kept in the active repertoire. Charles Booth, the King's Company prompter at some point (according to the rival Duke's prompter, John Downes), may have supervised the preparation of the book, which is remarkably complete. The main prompt hand in the copy can be seen in several other King's Company promptbooks and in one prepared for a Nursery or touring production (*The Wise-Woman of Hogsdon*). That hand was responsible for the warnings and cues, while a second hand, that of the machinist or one of his assistants, provided the technical cues. Throughout the text a third hand has made strokes beside nearly all of

Paulina's speeches, which suggests that the book may have belonged to Samuel Pepys's friend Mrs. Knepp, who played the role.

In the University of Chicago Library is a copy of the 1652 edition of the play with all the prompt notes from this copy transcribed. In addition, the Chicago copy contains extensive editorial notes and was evidently used by William Gifford when he was preparing *The Dramatic Works and Poems of James Shirley*. Gifford studied the promptbook:

> While I was engaged on this Play, the Librarian of Sion College obligingly informed me that they possessed a copy of *the Sisters*, with ms. variations of an early period. On examining the Play, however, it turned out to be merely the prompter's copy. The book appears to have belonged to Davenant's [*recte* Killigrew's] Company, in Drury Lane, and must, from the names, have been in use about 1666 [*recte* 1669–70]. It is piteously scrawled; and there are characters dispersed along the margin, *interiore note*, and such as the initiated alone probably understand. (V, 354)

So much for Restoration promptbooks!

Cast

Though the printed dramatis personae does not contain a cast list, the prompt notes in the copy permit an almost complete reconstruction.

Farnese	George Beeston
Contarini	William Harris
Antonio	William Cartwright
Frapolo	Richard Bell
Longino	Mr. Graydon
Strozzo	Thomas Reeves
Rangino	
Pacheco	
Lucio	Marmaduke Watson
Giovanni	Edward Lydall
Stephanio	John Littlewood
Fabio	
Piperollo	Joseph Haines
Countrymen	
Citizens	
Petitioners	
Scholar	John Littlewood
Servant	Edward Lydall
Pulcheria (Vergerio)	Nell Gwyn
Paulina	Mrs. Knepp
Angellina	Margaret Hughes
Morulla	
Francescina	Elizabeth Youckney
Gentlewomen	

Lydall and Littlewood played two roles each; the character of Francescina is not listed in the printed dramatis personae. The manuscript notes contain some variations in spelling, as might be expected, and the Jack Haines mentioned on page 3 was probably the popular actor Joseph Haines. The manuscript *d* marks on the cast page are very likely check marks, made, perhaps, by someone concerned with the casting of the roles. In the printed cast Piperollo, an important character, is crossed out, but the reason for the deletion is not clear.

Staging

The scene plot for *The Sisters* is not a complicated one. As in the promptbook for *The Change of Crownes*, descriptions of settings were entered by someone other than the prompter, probably the machinist. (Shirley's text, as might be expected of a pre-Restoration play, contains no author's descriptions of settings in the stage directions.)

I, i *A wood stands*

I, ii *Castle*

II, i *fabios / house & Landchape*

That sounds very like a combination of wings from one stock setting and shutters from another.

II, ii *Balcony ~~presence~~*

The action of the scene suggests a presence chamber of some kind. Though some characters may have appeared in one of the balconies over a proscenium door, the term may have been used by the machinist merely to indicate a setting with balconies represented.

III, i *A Roome in / ye castle*

III, ii (no description)

The scene seems to take place in another room in the castle.

IV, i *wood*

IV, ii *Angellinas / Chamber*

IV, iii *Court or / Chamber*

The vagueness of the description supports the argument that a more precise scene plot was kept elsewhere and that the technical notes in the promptbook were not final.

IV, iv *Chamber*

This is a strange designation; at the end of the scene Angellina says, "We are now arriv'd the Castle"—as though the scene had been an exterior. Within this scene, at IV, iv, 55, the circle-and-dot symbol was entered and then deleted; a new scene was apparently contemplated and then decided against, and it would certainly have been an exterior. The chamber description for IV, iv is probably an error—a note that was correct when the scene was split into two parts with different settings. It should have been altered to "outside the castle" when the scene sequence was finally settled.

V, i *A chamber*

V, ii *Court*

At least eight settings seem to have been used, but there is vagueness in some of the notes, and they should probably not be taken too literally. I would suggest the following as a possible scene plot:

Wood. I, i; partial use in II, i; IV, i.
Court. I, ii; IV, iii; V, ii.
House exterior. II, i, using part of the Wood setting.
Balcony. II, ii, though the action suggests a court setting.
Room. III, i.
Another room. III, ii, though the room here could as easily have been the same as in III, i; the notes show a scene shift but give no setting description.
Chamber. IV, ii; and possibly V, i.
Castle exterior. IV, iv, though the notes specify a chamber.

Circle symbols, sometimes with and sometimes without dots in the middle, are regularly used to indicate scene shifts. There are no whistle notes, as in *The Change of Crownes* promptbook, though that would not necessarily argue that whistles were not used for cues.

The signal *Ring* appears at the end of each act; presumably a bell was rung at these points—even at the end of the play—to cue music and scene shifts. Warnings for the ring cues, *Act Ready*, appear, but not for the ends of acts III, and V. If the ring cue was entered, why not the warning? Possibly the lack of a ring warning before the end of Act III meant that an interval was taken and that the ring came not at the end of that act but, after the interval, at the opening of Act IV.

The prompter was quite meticulous about preparing the warnings and cues for actors, properties, and sound effects, and he also corrected most but not all of the printing errors in the text. The cuts in the play are clearly indicated and seem to have been made more for the purpose of reducing the length of the play and the size of the cast than for prudish reasons. There is no indication that the Master of the Revels did any of the cutting, but some occasional bawdry is deleted.

Aglaura *by Sir John Suckling*

1658 (in *Fragmenta Aurea*, third edition, octavo 1658) with very complete manuscript prompt notes for a King's Company production at either the Bridges Street Theatre, Lincoln's Inn Fields Theatre, or Drury Lane Theatre in the 1670s; in Bodleian copy Vet. A3. F824. Discussed briefly by L. A. Beaurline in *The Works of Sir John Suckling* (Oxford: Clarendon Press, 1971), II, 262. Reproduced here in chapter 12 by permission of the Bodleian Library, Oxford.

The Bodleian copy of *Fragmenta Aurea* containing the promptbook for *Aglaura* also has in it the promptbook for Suckling's *Brennoralt*, prepared by the same hands. While the *Brennoralt* book is unusual in having occasional circle-and-dot shift symbols but no descriptions of the settings, the *Aglaura* promptbook, like that for *The Sisters*, is fully annotated. On the other hand, the prompter named most of the actors in the *Brennoralt* production, while the *Aglaura* promptbook contains the names of only two people: *M^r: Moone* (Michael Mohun, who played Zorannes/Ziriff) and *Fitz* (probably Theophilus Fitz, who apparently played the violin accompaniment to a song). The prompter used character names for all other warnings. Two annotators appear to have been at work here: one wrote actor warnings and cues and act-end warnings and cues; the other drew the circle-and-dot scene shift cues and wrote the descriptions of settings to be used. There are no manuscript notes in the happy-ending version of *Aglaura*.

Staging

The scene plot for *Aglaura* is fairly straightforward, but it contains what appears to be evidence showing that the same setting was used for two different locales. Suckling's stage directions, having been written before changeable scenery became a standard feature of the public theatre in England, do not contain descriptions of settings, but in some instances the dialogue and action make the locale clear.

Act & Scene	*Author's Description*	*Machinist's Description*
I,i	None	*court stands*
I, ii	None; action is a hunt	*wood*
I, iii	None	*Court*
I, iv	None; Aglaura undressing	*Chamber* (Aglaura's)
II, i	None	*Court*
II, ii	None	*Chamber* (Queen's)

Perhaps a different setting was used, but the manuscript note does not differentiate between the two locales. Maybe a separate scene plot kept by the machinist showed two similar but different chamber settings.

Act & Scene	*Author's Description*	*Machinist's Description*
II, iii	None	*Court*
III, i	None	*wood*
III, ii	None, but clearly Aglaura's chamber	*Chamber* (Aglaura's)
III, iii	None	*wood*
IV, i	None	*Court*
IV, ii	None	*Garden*
IV, iii	None	*Chamber* (Aglaura's)
IV, iv	None	*Court*
V, i	None; a cave entrance	*wood*
V, ii	None	*Chamber* (Aglaura's)
V, iii	None	*court*
V, iv	None	*Chamber* (Queen's?)

The simplicity of the staging—the use of so few different settings—might argue for the production having been presented at the Lincoln's Inn Fields Theatre, where the King's Company was temporarily housed from early 1672, when their Bridges Street Theatre burned, to early 1674, when Drury Lane opened. We do not know how much scenery the troupe had at Lincoln's Inn Fields, but perhaps at first they had to make do with very little.

Act endings in the *Aglaura* promptbook are warned and cued as follows: acts I, II, and III are warned and cued; Act IV is warned but not cued; Act V is neither warned nor cued, but about one hundred lines from the end of the play the prompter noted *The last / scene*.

Tyrannick Love *by John Dryden*

1672 second quarto containing manuscript prompt notes, mostly technical, possibly related to a King's Company production at Lincoln's Inn Fields Theatre about 1672; Folger copy Prompt T 40. Discussed by Henry Hitch Adams in "A Prompt Copy of Dryden's *Tyrannick Love*," *Studies in Bibliography*, 4 (1951–52), 170–74.

There are no manuscript notes in this copy to identify it as a London promptbook, let alone a King's Company promptbook, or to date it in the 1670s. The phrasing of some of the notes, such as the use of "call" rather than "ready," does not match other King's Company books, and the handwriting may be later than the seventeenth century. In *Restora-*

tion and 18th Century Theatre Research in May 1966 I said the notes were probably post-1710. And yet I am reluctant to omit the copy from this study. Adams presents a good argument for this being a promptbook prepared by the King's Company after the Bridges Street fire on 25 January 1672. They would have lost their stock of scenery, properties, costumes, and, presumably, promptbooks, and for productions at Lincoln's Inn Fields Theatre, to which they removed, they may have been forced by circumstances to prepare new books for less elaborate productions. Their original *Tyrannick Love* promptbook having been lost, argues Adams, the troupe equipped itself with a copy of the second quarto (which contained some revisions by Dryden) and used it as the basis for a new promptbook. The copy later passed out of the hands of the company, and there are a number of marginal notes in English and Latin and some practice scribblings, all nontheatrical, in later hands.

The theatrical notes in the copy are not in the prompt hand one finds in other King's Company books, but since they pertain almost exclusively to sound and technical matters, they were probably written by someone other than the prompter. A second hand wrote *Enter Valeria* on page 62. This is not *the* promptbook for *Tyrannick Love* but *a* promptbook for that play. The scanty performance records for the Restoration period show no presentation of the play between 24 June 1669 at Bridges Street and 18 May 1676 at Drury Lane. It was a popular work, however, as is indicated by new editions that appeared in 1672, 1677, 1686, 1694 (reissued in 1695), and 1702. A new edition was often inspired by a revival of a play.

Act I, Scene i

P. 1 *The Curten drawes & Discouers* note at the opening of I, i, written just above the stage direction naming the characters in the opening tableau. The wording of the prompt note suggests a main traverse curtain, though drop curtains were more common.

P. 4 *Flourish / very short* sound effect cue just before Charinus's line, "I hear the sound of Trumpets from afar."

to ye staires actor direction for the exit of Albinus, which follows immediately upon the flourish.

Flourish agen sound effect cue just before the reentrance of Albinus.

P. 5 *Floushish* sound effect cue after Charinus's line that ends, ". . . in the dire Visions scorn."

Flourish agen / at ye Greate / Dore sound effect cue just before the entrance of Porphyrius.

P. 7. *Dead March / at Greate / Dore* sound effect cue just before the stage direction calling for "A Dead March within, and Trumpets." The references to the great door are presumably to a door depicted in the scenery, perhaps on the shutters upstage, which could be drawn to suggest the opening of the door.

agen / Dead March / Dead Marc sound effect cue just before and apparently during the entrance of Albinus. Adams incorrectly cites these prompt notes on page 7 as being on page 6.

P. 11 *Call ye Musique* at the end of Act I. Though worded as a warning this note is not anticipatory and must have been a cue. In some promptbooks the interval music was cued by the ringing of a bell.

Act II, Scene i

P. 19 *Musique* cue at the end of Act II.

Act III, Scene i

P. 28 *Musique* cue at the end of Act III.

Act IV, Scene i

P. 29 *The bl Curten* setting for IV, i. The stage direction describes the locale as an "*Indian Cave.*" This is the first of two references to the use of a black curtain; it was apparently not the theatre's main curtain. Adams suggests that this black curtain was used in lieu of painted scenery which, because of the Bridges Street fire, the company had lost.

Call ye Thunde[r] sound effect warning just after Placidius's line ending, ". . . Remember you oblige an Emperour." The exact cue for the thunder is not indicated, but it apparently came 4 lines later.

the rest is left / out. This marginal note refers to a cut of 184 lines, including song lyrics, beginning with Nigrinus's line, "Not in their Natures simply good or ill . . ." and continuing through his line at the top of page 35, "No Charms prevail against the Christians God." This cut would have omitted the complicated "Elizium" or St. Catharine scene which Isaac Fuller painted for the original production of the play and over which there was a great deal of litigation—discussed by Leslie Hotson in *The Commonwealth and Restoration Stage* (pp.

250–53). Such a cut in the text would have been reasonable had the company lost their scenes and machines for the play and had to revive it with less elaborate staging.

After y^e / Thunder ca[ll] / for ye Song. This note comes immediately after the previous one concerning the cut. Adams supposes that despite the cut some portion of the deleted St. Catharine scene was staged—probably one of the songs essential to an understanding of the plot.

Exeunt actor direction at the bottom of page 29, intended to get Placidius and Nigrinus off the stage before the cut. The copy contains no notes to clarify what happened next in the staging, but there was evidently a scene change of some sort. Before the cut, the black curtain set the scene, and after it, the same black curtain was lowered, so another setting must have been used in between. Adams guesses that a portion of the temptation of St. Catharine scene was played "against a drop of some color other than black." If this promptbook was prepared for a production in the 1670s, shutters rather than a drop probably would have been used (drops seem not to have been employed until the 1690s)—or a curtain. In any case, it is clear that the black curtain was taken up, and something else was displayed. Then:

P. 35 *before Placid [enters lower y^e] / Black & sett vp ye State.* This setting note in the top margin is badly cropped. Adams reads a conjectural "shut" instead of "lower," but the visible bottoms of some of the letters suggest to me the latter. If one takes this note literally—and for coming notes to make sense I believe one must—the black curtain was lowered and the state set up *before* Placidius enters, not while the rest of the act was playing. The *State* is needed for the Emperor Maximin, who enters 4 lines after Placidius. So I infer that the black curtain was lowered, the state scene was set up, and the curtain was raised. Then:

Enter Placid actor direction at the end of the deleted scene, just before Placidius's line, "How doubtfully these Specters Fate foretell . . ." —a further indication that some part of the temptation scene had just been presented.

P. 48 *Musique* cue at the end of Act IV. See illustration.

Act V, Scene i

Drawe y^e / Curten & / Sett vp y^e / wheele. Note at the opening of V, i.

U y^e ~~Chy~~ / Chayre / at ye End / of ye Stage. Note at the opening of V, i. The first note is to the left of the act designation, the second to the right. I believe the curtain used here was the theatre's main one (see the prompt note at the beginning of I, i, where *The Curten drawes*); the black curtain, so far as I can

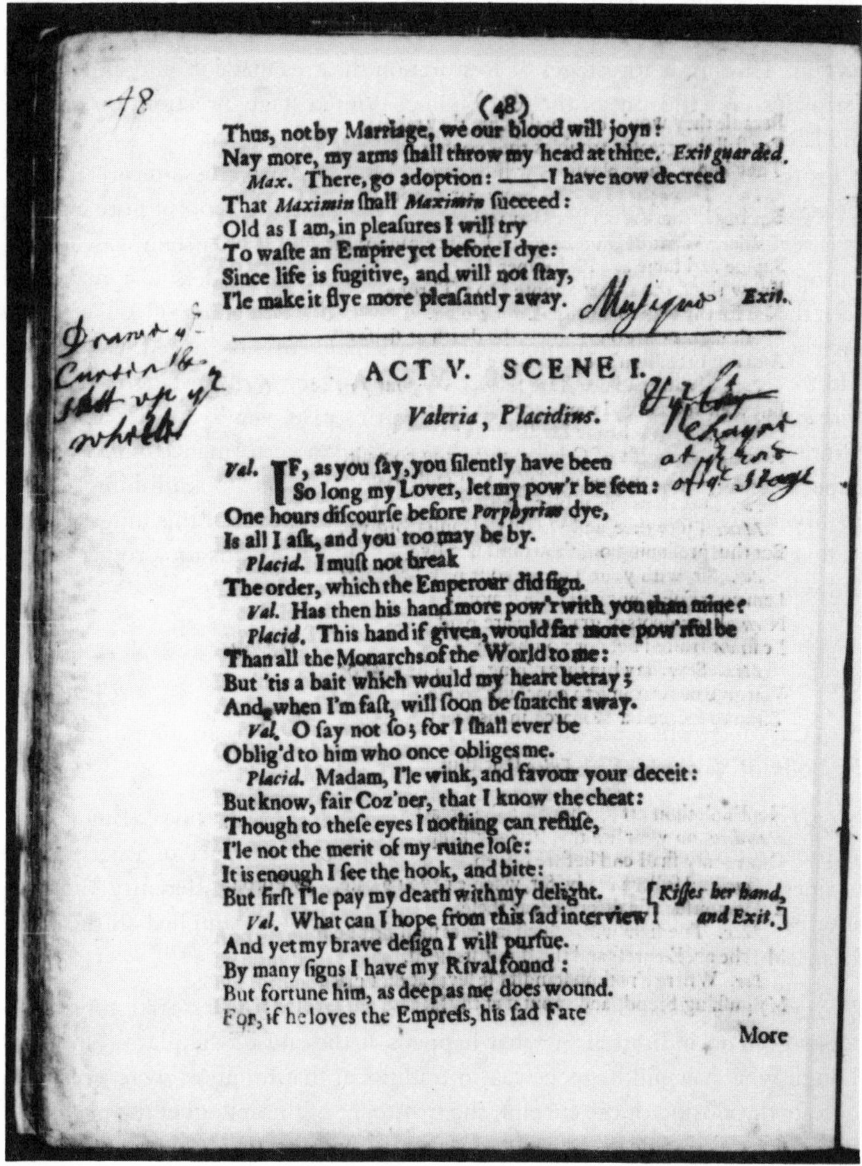

(48)

Thus, not by Marriage, we our blood will joyn:
Nay more, my arms ſhall throw my head at thine. *Exit guarded.*
Max. There, go adoption: ——I have now decreed
That *Maximin* ſhall *Maximin* ſucceed:
Old as I am, in pleaſures I will try
To waſte an Empire yet before I dye:
Since life is fugitive, and will not ſtay,
I'le make it flye more pleaſantly away. *Exit.*

ACT V. SCENE I.

Valeria, Placidius.

Val. IF, as you ſay, you ſilently have been
So long my Lover, let my pow'r be ſeen:
One hours diſcourſe before *Porphyrius* dye,
Is all I aſk, and you too may be by.
Placid. I muſt not break
The order, which the Emperour did ſign.
Val. Has then his hand more pow'r with you than mine?
Placid. This hand if given, would far more pow'rful be
Than all the Monarchs of the World to me:
But 'tis a bait which would my heart betray;
And, when I'm faſt, will ſoon be ſnatcht away.
Val. O ſay not ſo; for I ſhall ever be
Oblig'd to him who once obliges me.
Placid. Madam, I'le wink, and favour your deceit:
But know, fair Coz'ner, that I know the cheat:
Though to theſe eyes I nothing can refuſe,
I'le not the merit of my ruine loſe:
It is enough I ſee the hook, and bite:
But firſt I'le pay my death with my delight. [*Kiſſes her hand,*
Val. What can I hope from this ſad interview! *and Exit.*]
And yet my brave deſign I will purſue.
By many ſigns I have my Rival found:
But fortune him, as deep as me does wound.
For, if he loves the Empreſs, his ſad Fate

More

From Dryden's *Tyrannick Love.* By kind permission of the Folger Shakespeare Library, Washington, D.C.

tell, was a drop curtain. The *wheele* to be set up is used eight pages hence, and Adams suggests that the chair was for the Emperor (though he reads "head" rather than "End" of the stage; in either case, since the wheel is certainly to be revealed upstage, the Emperor's chair must surely have been positioned at one side of the stage). The first scene in the act must have played while the stage-hands were arranging the wheel (and its scaffolding, presumably) behind the curtain. The ample forestages of Restoration theatres made it quite possible to perform scenes in front of the curtain line. Printed stage directions on page 55 and later provide for the showing of the wheel.

Professor Colin Visser has suggested to me an alternative interpretation of the evidence about curtains in *Tyrannick Love*. Since the prompt note on page 35 is severely cropped, we cannot be certain that the black curtain was, in fact, a drop curtain rather than a traverse curtain. Visser wonders if it may have been the latter; if it was, then the curtain drawn at the opening of Act V would have been the black curtain, not the theatre's main curtain. Indeed, it would be odd to close the main curtain to set up a discovery well upstage if a curtain within the scenic area (the black curtain in this case) was available. The main curtain was normally closed during the course of a performance only when an elaborate tableau needed to be set up; the wheel and its scaffolding hardly qualify as an elaborate discovery. The interpretation of all of this hinges on the badly cropped word which I read as "lower," which Adams took to be "shut," and which Visser suggests might have been "drawe."

Act V, [Scene iv]

P. 59 *Caryded / out* actor direction at the end of V, iv; this arranges for getting the body of Valerius off the stage.

P. 62 *Enter Valeria* actor direction following Porphyrius's line, "But yet remember me when you are dead." This advances the entrance of Valeria about 17 lines and allows her to overhear the dialogue between Berenice and Porphyrius. This note was not written by the person who supplied all the other theatrical notes in the copy.

P. 67 *Musique* cue at the end of Act V. This is rare. Most Restoration promptbooks give no indication of what happens at the end of the play—almost as though whatever did happen was so traditional that no notes were needed to indicate the closing of the curtain, the treatment of the epilogue, the playing of music, the announcing of the next day's play, and so forth.

The Mall *by J[ohn] D[over]*(?)

1674 first quarto containing two possible traces of prompt copy related to the King's Company production at Lincoln's Inn Fields Theatre about January 1674. Copy studied: Folger D2305.

The authorship of *The Mall* is in doubt; the dedication is signed "*J. D.*"

P. 34 "*Scene a Bed-chamber, a Table out, and a Chair*" setting for III, [ii]. This may be the author's note, but it is printed apart from the opening stage direction in the scene, and the terminology "*Table out*" sounds more theatrical than literary.

P. 47 "Scene Second, Chairs set out" setting for IV, ii. This, again, may have been written by the author but reads like a prompt note, especially the second half.

The Mistaken Husband *by Richard Brome*(?)

1675 first quarto containing a few traces of prompt copy perhaps related to the King's Company production at Lincoln's Inn Fields Theatre about March 1674. Copy studied: British Library 643 d 32.

Dryden may have written a scene of this play, which Alfred Harbage in *Modern Language Review* (pp. 306–7) thinks was probably the work of Richard Brome. *The Mistaken Husband* may have been produced at the new Drury Lane Theatre shortly after it opened on 26 March 1674 rather than at the company's temporary home in Lincoln's Inn Fields, but most evidence points to an earlier premiere. The handful of prompt traces in the text are valuable even if details of the authorship and place of production are not certainly known.

P. 2 "*A Drawer / Jack*" actor warning 27 lines before entrance in I, i (see illustration). This note seems to warn both the character and the actor. I know of no King's Company performer for the 1673–74 season called Jack, though there were several Johns: Chudleigh, Coysh, Lacy, and the machinist Guip-

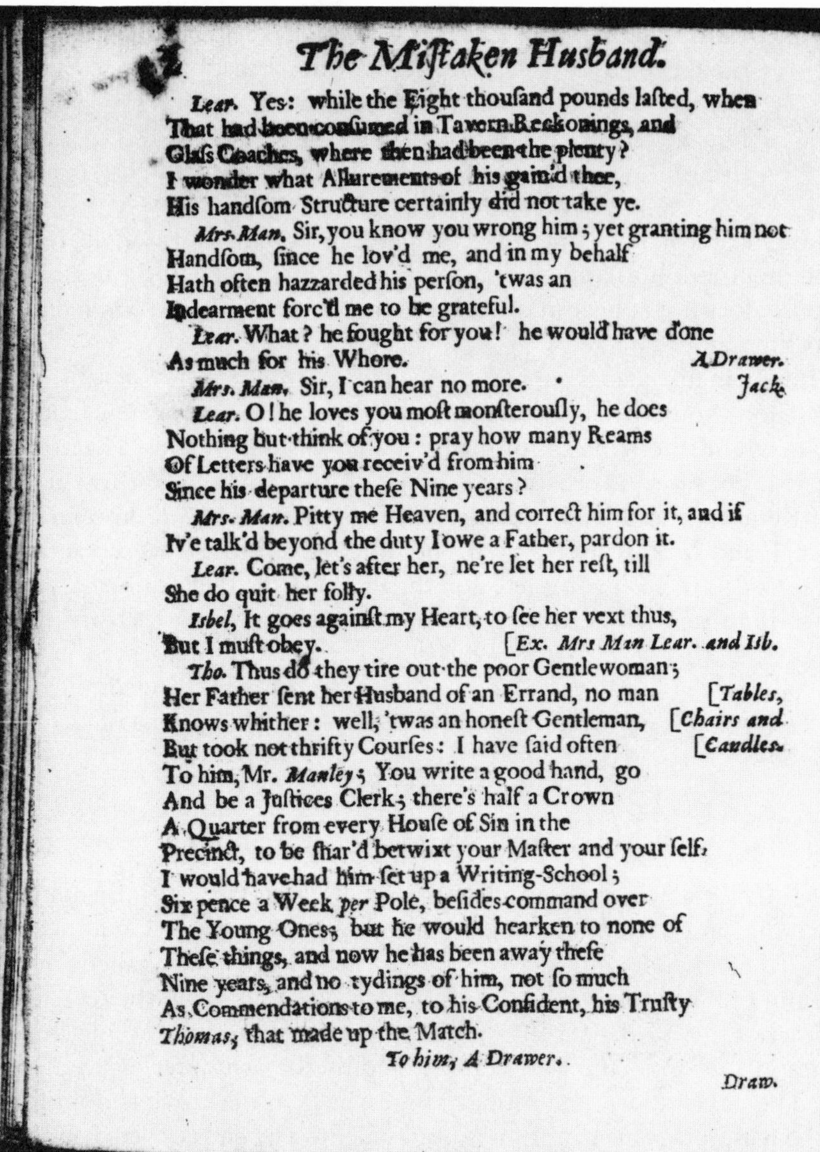

The Miſtaken Husband.

Lear. Yes: while the Eight thouſand pounds laſted, when
That had been conſumed in Tavern Reckonings, and
Glaſs Coaches, where then had been the plenty?
I wonder what Allurements of his gain'd thee,
His handſom Structure certainly did not take ye.

Mrs. Man. Sir, you know you wrong him; yet granting him not
Handſom, ſince he lov'd me, and in my behalf
Hath often hazzarded his perſon, 'twas an
Indearment forc'd me to be grateful.

Lear. What? he fought for you! he would have done
As much for his Whore. *A Drawer.*

Mrs. Man. Sir, I can hear no more. *Jack.*

Lear. O! he loves you moſt monſterouſly, he does
Nothing but think of you: pray how many Reams
Of Letters have you receiv'd from him
Since his departure theſe Nine years?

Mrs. Man. Pitty me Heaven, and correct him for it, and if
Iv'e talk'd beyond the duty I owe a Father, pardon it.

Lear. Come, let's after her, ne're let her reſt, till
She do quit her folly.

Isbel, It goes againſt my Heart, to ſee her vext thus,
But I muſt obey. *[Ex. Mrs Man Lear. and Isb.*

Tho. Thus do they tire out the poor Gentlewoman;
Her Father ſent her Husband of an Errand, no man *[Tables,*
Knows whither: well; 'twas an honeſt Gentleman, *[Chairs and*
But took not thrifty Courſes: I have ſaid often *[Candles.*
To him, Mr. *Manley*; You write a good hand, go
And be a Juſtices Clerk; there's half a Crown
A Quarter from every Houſe of Sin in the
Precinct, to be ſhar'd betwixt your Maſter and your ſelf,
I would have had him ſet up a Writing-School;
Six pence a Week *per* Pole, beſides command over
The Young Ones; but he would hearken to none of
Theſe things, and now he has been away theſe
Nine years, and no tydings of him, not ſo much
As Commendations to me, to his Confident, his Truſty
Thomas; that made up the Match.

To him, A Drawer.

Draw.

From Brome's (?) *The Mistaken Husband.* By kind permission of the British Library.

poni. Chudleigh and Coysh, both secondary actors, are the most likely candidates.

"[*Tables*, / [*Chairs and* / [*Candles*" property warning c.21 lines in advance in I, i.

P. 3 "[*Table out*" property cue in I, i. There is a scene shift at this point (the entrance of Hazzard, Underwit, and the Drawer) from the exterior to the interior of a tavern, though no stage direction calls for it. The needed table would have been brought onstage by stagehands or actors dressed as servants.

P. 26 "[Between the Scenes" note in II, i. This is perhaps a stage direction by the author, or the prompter may have written it. At this point in the scene Hazzard is pointing the way for Mrs. Manley's exit "down Into the Garden."

P. 53 "*Learcut*, and the *Boatswain*, Duke *Watson*" entrance cue containing an actor's name, at the opening of V, i. Though the text is rather obscure on the matter, Marmaduke Watson apparently played Captain Salteel. If the author wrote that part with Watson in mind, the note may have been written by him; if not, the prompter probably wrote the note.

The Maides Revenge *by James Shirley*

1639 first quarto with extensive manuscript prompt notes, probably for a King's Company production at Lincoln's Inn Fields Theatre early in the 1673–74 season; in Harvard copy STC 22450[A]. Reproduced here in chapter 13 by permission of the Harvard Theatre Collection.

This promptbook only recently came to light, and though dating the notes is difficult, they seem to come from the early 1670s. The paucity of scenic notes would argue for a production at Lincoln's Inn Fields playhouse, where the troupe acted while their Drury Lane Theatre was under construction. The play is not otherwise known to have been performed during the Restoration period, and the prompt notes cite three actors whose names are new: [Broad?], Jenning[s?], and Bogr[?]. Severe cropping in the copy makes it impossible to tell whether the first and last are full or partial names. Jenning (or Jennings) was possibly related to the Mrs. Jennings who performed with the Duke's Company in the 1660s.

The main hand in the copy is that found in several other King's Company promptbooks. A second hand made some textual emendations, and a third, apparently nontheatrical, made some notes on the title and cast pages. All but one of the speeches assigned to Berinthia are marked with slanted lines in the margin, which suggests that the copy may have belonged to Mrs. Marshall, who played the role, before it was annotated by the prompter and his colleagues.

The 1639 quarto of *The Maides Revenge* was evidently printed in haste, for it is full of typographical errors and garbled passages, none of which the prompter corrected. A number of cuts were made in the text, most of them designed to shorten the play and delete some of the flowery language.

Cast

The most valuable information in *The Maides Revenge* promptbook is found in the actor warnings, most of which name the players. Not only do we now have new roles for many of the known King's Company performers, but we have the names (or rather, thanks to the villain who cropped the copy, partial names) of at least three minor actors otherwise unknown.

Vilarezo .... William Cartwright
Sebastiano .... Michael Mohun
Antonio .... Edward Kynaston
Villandras .... Edward Lydall
Sforza .... Marmaduke Watson
Valasco .... Nicholas Burt
Count de Monte Nigro .... Robert Shatterell
Diego .... William Harris
Signior Sharkino ....
Scarabeo .... [Martin Powell?]
Vilarezo's servant .... Nathaniel Kew
[Servingmen] .... Thomas Hancock, Theophilus Bird Jr
[Friends of Valasco] .... Thomas Hancock, [Mr. Broad?]
Servants ... Matthew Kempton, Mr. Jenning[s?], Abraham [Ivory?], Martin Powell, John Coysh, Mr. Bogr[?]
Catalina .... Margaret Rutter
Berinthia .... Rebecca Marshall
Castabella .... Elizabeth Bowtell
Ansilva .... Katherine Corey
Nurse ....
[Maid] .... [Susanna Uphill?]

One of the Eastlands, probably Edward, was named in III, iii for a servingman, but his name was deleted. The Nurse cited in the dramatis personae does not appear in the play; perhaps the Maid who enters in II, ii was the same character.

With so many players mentioned in the prompt notes, dating the production should be easy, but it is not. Most of the performers named were active in the King's Company at Lincoln's Inn Fields Theatre in 1672–73, but no roles are known that season for Shatterell, Bird, Eastland, Kempton, and Mrs. Rutter. In 1673–74 no roles are known for Hancock and Mrs. Rutter, but all the others seem to have been active. The records are so incomplete for the early 1670s that if no roles are known for a performer, that is not proof that he was not performing. My guess is that *The Maides Revenge* was probably performed in the early part of the 1673–74 season, before the company moved into the new Drury Lane Theatre.

Staging

The Maides Revenge promptbook contains only scanty information on staging, unless some technical notes were cropped. A *Great Scene* was used at the opening of Act I and a *Castle* setting was called for in IV, i and iii. Scene changes are indicated at other points in the text, but no descriptions of the settings were provided. The three scenic notes are not in a second hand but were entered by the prompter or his assistant. The circle-and-dot symbol changes; at II, ii the circle is doubled, but the reason for this variation is not evident. The ends of acts I, II, III, and IV are warned in the usual fashion with *act ready* notes, and the first three acts end with a *Ring*. Perhaps Act IV had a similar cue that was cropped.

Brennoralt *by Sir John Suckling*

1658 (in *Fragmenta Aurea*, third edition, octavo 1658) with very complete manuscript promptnotes for a King's Company production at Lincoln's Inn Fields Theatre or, more likely, Drury Lane Theatre about 1673–1675; in Bodleian copy Vet. A3. F824. Discussed briefly by L. A. Beaurline in *The Works of Sir John Suckling* (Oxford: Clarendon Press, 1971), II, 293–94. Reproduced here in chapter 14 by permission of the Bodleian Library, Oxford.

Though the prompt notes in this copy of *Brennoralt* are complete in many ways—the warnings and cues for actors, for instance—they are strangely incomplete in others, especially technical notes. There are circle-and-dot scene shift symbols but no accompanying descriptions of the settings to be used. Thus, as will be seen, the cast can be reconstructed almost completely but the staging can not.

The Bodleian copy contains a number of typographical errors, such as inverted type or the substitution of n for u, and shows a modern reader just what kind of text a prompter worked with and what corrections he did or did not make in it. Beaurline's edition shows scene breaks whenever the locale seems to have changed, but in the facsimile a new scene number is given only when a circle-and-dot symbol clearly indicates a scene shift. One hand appears to have been responsible for all notes and markings except the circle-and-dot symbol on T2.

Cast

The prompter used actors' names so frequently in warnings that an almost complete reconstruction of the cast is possible. This is unusual, for in most promptbooks, if actors' names are used, they refer only to minor players in nameless roles. In the following reconstruction I differ from Suckling's editor, Beaurline, in two instances: *Abram* was surely Abraham Ivory the actor, and if the play was performed in the mid-1670s, the Harris playing Marinell must have been William, not Joseph.

Role	Actor
Sigismond, King of Poland	William Cartwright or Marmaduke Watson
Miesla	William Cartwright or Marmaduke Watson
Melidor	William Wintershall
A Lord	
Brennoralt	Michael Mohun
Doran	Edward Kynaston
Villanor	Robert Shatterell
Grainevert	John Lacy
Marinel[l]	William Harris
Stratheman	Thomas Hancock
Fresolin	Martin Powell
Iphigene	Margaret Rutter
Palatine of Mensecke	Mr. Vener or George Beeston
Palatine of Trocke	Mr. Vener or George Beeston
Almerin	Charles Hart
Morat	John Coysh
Francelia	Rebecca Marshall
Orilla	Anne Reeves
Raguelin	Theophilus Bird Jr
Jaylor	John Coysh
Guard	George Morris
Soldiers	John Coysh, Nathaniel Kew, George Morris, Abraham Ivory
[General]	Edward Lydall
[Servant]	George Morris

Suckling omitted the last two characters from his dramatis personae, unless the Lord and the General should be considered the same character.

Staging

The scene plot for *Brennoralt* cannot be reconstructed on the basis of the confusing and incomplete technical notes in the promptbook. As can be seen below, sometimes a circle and dot indicates a shift, but there is no author's or machinist's description of the setting; sometimes a stage direction clearly indicates a shift, but there is no shift cue symbol. The technical crew could not have run a performance on the basis of the notes here, so a second scene plot must have been made up.

Act & Scene	*Author's Description*	*Machinist's description*
I, i	None	None, but: ⊙
I, [ii]	"*Iphigene, Almerin* (as in prison.)"	None, but: ⊙
II, i	"*Almerin* (in prison.)"	None; no change
III, i	"*Iphigene (as in a Garden)*"	None; no circle and dot
III, [ii]	"*Francelia (as in a Bed)*"	None, but: ⊙
IV, i	None	None; no circle and dot
V, i	None	None; no circle and dot
V, [ii]	None	None, but: ⊙ and *a chair*

At other points in the text, as at III, i, 251, a scene change was certainly needed, but the machinist indicated none. Suckling did not help matters by indicating at the beginning of every act a first scene, and never noting a second.

The prompt notes regarding music, sound effects, properties, and actor entrances are much more carefully handled.

The Mock-Duellist *by P[eter] B[ellon]*

1675 first quarto containing a few possible traces of prompt copy related to the King's Company production at Drury Lane Theatre about February or March 1675. Copy studied: Folger B 1854.

None of the quotations below can be identified with certainty as traces of prompt copy, but some may have been written by the prompter.

P. 30 "*Noise here*" sound effect cue in III, ii.

P. 31 "Two Chairs" property note following the stage direction reading, "*Lovewealth*'s house" at the opening of III, iii.

P. 43 "Two Chairs out" property note following the stage direction reading, "*Lovewealth*'s house" at the opening of IV, iii. The use of "out" (that is, to be set out on the stage) can be seen in other King's Company promptbooks of this period.

Sir Barnaby Whigg *by Thomas D'Urfey*

1681 first quarto containing two probable traces of prompt copy related to the King's Company production at Drury Lane Theatre in the summer of 1681. Copy studied: British Library 81 c 4.

P. 1 "*A Table, Bottles and Cards ready*" property note at the opening of I, i. This seems to be a note on the initial property arrangement for the scene, though it is written like a warning.

P. 27 "*A Table and Musicians*" property note for III, ii. This may have been written by the author, but it reads like a prompt note and is printed apart from the opening stage direction for the scene, which "Discovers the Captain . . ."

The Injured Princess *by Thomas D'Urfey*

1682 first quarto containing a few traces of prompt copy related to the King's Company production at Drury Lane Theatre in February or March 1682. Copy studied: British Library 644 h 14.

Though few in number, the traces of prompt copy in D'Urfey's alteration of *Cymbeline* are most curious.

P. 11 "*Enter behind* Cymbeline, Queen, *a Purse*, Pisanio, Doctor *and* / Guards *a Viol, Mrs.* Holten, Sue" opening stage direction in Act II. This is a weird combination of characters' names, actors' names, and properties. The original manuscript probably contained a fairly normal author's stage direction for the entrance of Cymbeline, the Queen, Pisanio, the Doctor, some Guards, and others, to which the prompter added two notes on properties and the names of two actresses playing small roles. The "*Viol*" referred to was a phial; Mrs. Holten's name is otherwise unknown, unless this was a mistake for the Mrs. Dalton who performed for the King's Company in the 1660s; and Sue may have been Susanna Percival, later Mrs. William Mountfort. (In *The Restoration*

Theatre, p. 145, Montague Summers took Mrs. Holten to be Mrs. Holden, who acted for the rival Duke's Company in the early 1660s.)

P. 19 "*A Viol*" property note following the stage direction for the entrance of the Queen, Pisanio, and Attendants in II, ii. This note may have been written by the author, but it appears to have been tacked onto the end of the stage direction. So too, the next note.

P. 20 "a Table-book" property note following the stage direction for Shattillion's entrance out of a chest in II, iv (*recte*, II, iii).

P. 42 "[*Cry within*" sound effect cue shortly after Arviragus's second entrance in IV, iv. This, too, is printed like a prompt note but may have been written by the author.

P. 46 "[*Shout here*" sound effect cue just before the battle begins in V, i. Again, this may have been the author's note.

P. 47 "[Shout within" sound effect cue just before Lucius's line, "Hark, they pursue us . . ." in V, i. Another possible author's note.

P. 51 "*Palace backward*" setting for V, "iii" (though no V, ii is indicated in the text). This is surely a prompter's or machinist's note. It appears to signify a stock palace setting turned around to show its rear face, a pretty piece of economy. Double-sided wings and shutters would have been more expensive to build, and they would have had to be handled carefully so as not to finger mark the painted surfaces, but the saving in storage space would have been considerable.

3 / The Duke's Company (1660–1682)

Sir William Davenant formed the Duke's Company under a royal patent and with the protection of the King's brother, the Duke of York. The new Duke's Company was not able to go into full operation until June 1661, several months after the King's Company began playing regularly, probably because Davenant chose to use a theatre with changeable scenery. The Duke's players acquired the little tennis court in Lincoln's Inn Fields and converted it into a playhouse, acting temporarily in 1660–61 at the sceneryless Salisbury Court Theatre.

We have no pictures of the interior of the Lincoln's Inn Fields house, and though pictures exist of the exterior, they do not tell us much beyond the apparent size of the building and its location. Leslie Hotson in *The Commonwealth and Restoration Stage* (p. 123) estimates the outside dimensions at 30′ by 75′; I take the building to have been about 20′ to 30′ high. On the basis of stage directions and dialogue in plays performed at Lincoln's Inn Fields, and from descriptions by contemporary playgoers, a partial reconstruction is possible. Working at approximately the same time but separately, the late Elizabeth Scanlan and I arrived at remarkably similar reconstructions, our chief differences being of no great importance: I guessed (in *Theatre Notebook*, 10) that Davenant could have squeezed three levels of seating into the space he had; Ms. Scanlan (in the same volume) thought only two; I conjectured two proscenium doors on each side of the forestage; she thought one on each side. In most other respects we were in agreement: the auditorium had a pit, squared-off U-shaped box and gallery seating, a forestage and proscenium doors in front of a proscenium arch, and a full complement of wings, borders, and shutters. One wonders how Davenant had the audacity to try to fit within so tiny a building a stage with changeable scenery, but he managed to do it and still accommodate an audience of perhaps as many as 570 people.

The Duke's Company used the Lincoln's Inn Fields Theatre until 1671, when they moved into their new playhouse in Dorset Garden, a structure twice the size of their old building but probably laid out in a similar fashion. It measured approximately 148′ by 57′ and faced the Thames at Dorset Stairs, not far from where the old Salisbury Court playhouse must have stood. On the basis of the plays written specifically for Dorset Garden, I believe the theatre had one proscenium door on each side of the forestage.[1] The illustrations for *The Empress of Morocco* in 1673 show a hint of the doors and reveal that the music room was situated over the proscenium arch rather than, as at Lincoln's Inn Fields, in a side box near the stage on the second (?) level. The new theatre had a capacity of about twelve hundred and was evidently the

1. In his chapter on theatres and scenery in the fifth volume of *The Revels History of Drama in English* Richard Southern suggests four proscenium doors at Dorset Garden Theatre, but his evidence for more than two doors does not come from plays written for that house.

best house in London for spectacle shows.[2] When the Duke's and King's troupes joined in 1682, Drury Lane became the home theatre, but Dorset Garden continued to be used from time to time for "machine" plays.

Romeo and Juliet *by William Shakespeare*

1599 second quarto containing a few manuscript prompt notes, cuts, and other marginalia, possibly related to the Duke's Company production at Lincoln's Inn Fields Theatre on 1 March 1662; in a copy at the Elizabethan Club, Yale University. Reported by Charles Shattuck in *The Shakespeare Promptbooks* (Urbana: University of Illinois Press, 1965), p. 411.

The second quarto of *Romeo and Juliet* contains no act and scene divisions, but since several of the manuscript notes in the Elizabethan Club copy concern such divisions, I have indicated in parentheses after each note the location of it in most modern texts.

C1 *ffinis Act [I] / musicke / 2* at the entrance of Romeo and others (I, iv, 10). The *2* I take to refer to the new act, not a designation of the music to be played.

C2ᵛ–C3 "*Ser.* Wheres Potpan . . . the longer liuer take all" is bracketed for cutting (I, v, 1–16). That would omit the brief servants' scene before the entrance of the guests.

D1 *play musick* at the beginning of the speech by the Chorus (II, Prologue). The entire prologue speech is bracketed, not for cutting, apparently, but to indicate that the "mood" music should play throughout.

D4ᵛ *Rom:* speech ascription added before the line "Parting is such sweete sorrow . . ." (II, ii, 186), correcting an error in the quarto. See illustration.

The lines "The grey-eyde morne . . . *Tytans* wheele" in Romeo's exit speech are boxed and crossed out (II, iii, 1–4), since they are the Friar's lines and are repeated in his opening speech that follows.

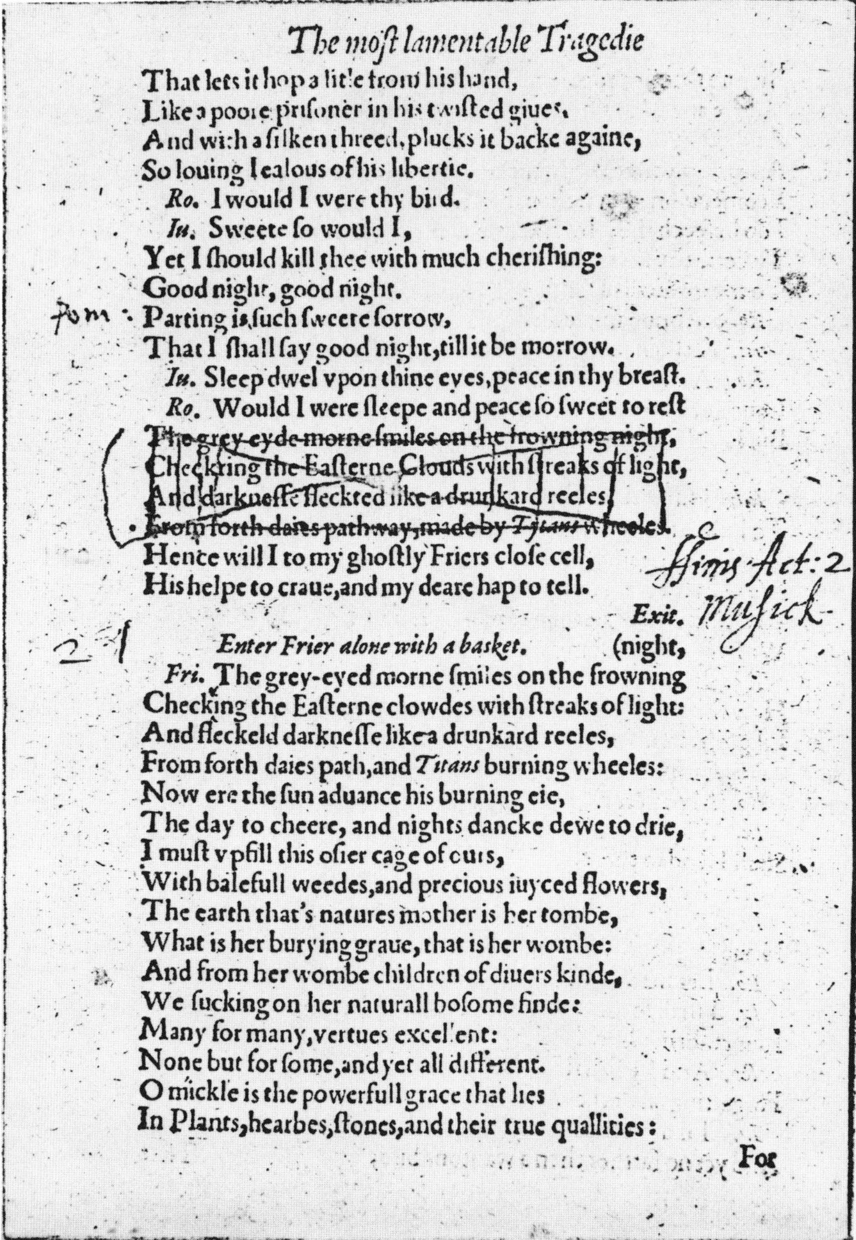

The most lamentable Tragedie

That lets it hop a litle from his hand,
Like a poore prisoner in his twisted giues,
And with a silken threed, plucks it backe againe,
So louing Iealous of his libertie.
Ro. I would I were thy bird.
Iu. Sweete so would I,
Yet I should kill thee with much cherishing:
Good night, good night.
Rom · Parting is such sweete sorrow,
That I shall say good night, till it be morrow.
Iu. Sleep dwel vpon thine eyes, peace in thy breast.
Ro. Would I were sleepe and peace so sweet to rest
The grey eyde morne smiles on the frowning night,
Checking the Easterne Clouds with streaks of light,
And darknesse fleckted like a drunkard reeles,
From forth daies pathway, made by *Tytans* wheeles.
Hence will I to my ghostly Friers close cell,
His helpe to craue, and my deare hap to tell.
Exit. ffinis Act: 2 Musick
2 *Enter Frier alone with a basket.* (night,
Fri. The grey-eyed morne smiles on the frowning
Checking the Easterne clowdes with streaks of light:
And fleckeld darknesse like a drunkard reeles,
From forth daies path, and *Titans* burning wheeles:
Now ere the sun aduance his burning eie,
The day to cheere, and nights dancke dewe to drie,
I must vpfill this osier cage of ours,
With balefull weedes, and precious iuyced flowers,
The earth that's natures mother is her tombe,
What is her burying graue, that is her wombe:
And from her wombe children of diuers kinde,
We sucking on her naturall bosome finde:
Many for many, vertues excellent:
None but for some, and yet all different.
O mickle is the powerfull grace that lies
In Plants, hearbes, stones, and their true qualities:
For

From Shakespeare's *Romeo and Juliet*. By kind permission of The Elizabethan Club of Yale University.

2. The capacity was estimated by W. J. Lawrence in a letter quoted in Montague Summers's *Restoration Theatre*, p. 64. In my reconstruction of the playhouse I arrived independently at approximately the same figure; see *Theatre Survey*, 13 (November 1972), 92.

ffinis Act: 2 / Musick at the exit of Romeo at the end of the balcony scene (II, ii, 191).

2 | at the entrance of the Friar with his basket (II, iii, 1). I cannot decipher this note; it certainly could not mean Act II, since the previous note indicated that Act III would begin with the Friar's entrance.

G3^v *ffinis Act : 3· / Musick·Act: 4·* just before the entrance of the Friar and Romeo (III, iii, 1).

K3^v–K4 The entire scene between Peter and the musicians is bracketed for cutting (IV, v, 102–49). Within the bracketed section is an Elizabethan trace of prompt copy (or an author's slip): instead of "*Enter Peter*" the opening stage direction reads "*Enter Will Kemp.*"

L1^v *ffinis Act: 4· / Act. 5.* at the entrance of Paris and his Page (V, iii, 1). In this instance no music is called for between the acts.

L4^v The stage direction "Enter Capulet and his wife" is crossed out (V, iii, before 202), correcting an error in the printed text, since the Capulets are already onstage.

This copy could not have served as *the* promptbook, since it is too incomplete to be useful. It may, however, have been prepared for the musicians. Most of the notes in the copy would have concerned the men in the music room: they would have needed to know what cuts had been made in the text and where their music cues were. The copy contains little else. The manuscript note between Act IV and Act V would have been useful to the musicians as an indication that in that instance no entr'acte music was to be played.

In addition to the theatrical notes transcribed above, the copy contains occasional manuscript notes—scraps of poetry, an anagram—by a reader.

The Villain *by Thomas Porter*

1663 first quarto containing a few traces of prompt copy related to the Duke's Company production at Lincoln's Inn Fields Theatre on 18 October 1662. Copy studied: British Library 644 c 6.

The pagination in the 1663 edition is erratic; there are two pages numbered 56 and two numbered 57. In the transcription below the original pagination has been used, but a corrected page number has been supplied in brackets where necessary. The traces of prompt copy begin near the conclusion of Act III.

P. 57 "TOWN" in right margin opposite a stage direction for the entrances of D'elpech and others near the end of Act III. Though the dialogue does not suggest a scene change at this point, it does imply an exterior. Indications of locale in the stage directions are very scarce in this text. "TOWN" was probably a manuscript setting note similar to that found in *The Wittie Faire One*, Act IV, Scene i (see chapter 15).

P. 56 [58] "[T]he new / [S]cene of the / [H]ALL" setting for IV, i, printed opposite the opening stage direction; no locale was indicated by the author. (Partly cropped in this copy; checked against Folger copy P2995.)

P. 70 [72] "*A Hearse / set out on a / Table*" at the entrance of D'orvile, La Barr, and Attendants for the last scene in Act IV (the scenes within the acts are not numbered). This may have been a note written by the author, but it reads like a promptnote, and the author was very sparing with indications of scenery and properties.

P. 87 [89] "*Boutefeu*" actor warning 78 lines before entrance in Act V. Boutefeu made an exit a page before this note, and the actor playing the part would now be changing into a friar's costume—hence the ample warning.

P. 93 [95] "[*Noise here*" sound effect cue just before the entrance of D'orvile, D'elpech, La'March, La Barr, and Attendants near the end of Act V. This may have been written by the author or by the prompter.

These traces of prompt copy are all repeated in the 1670 edition of the play. In that edition the second and third notes quoted above were reset and moved from the margin to the center of the page; the compositor probably could not understand why they had not been set there in the first place.

The Wittie Faire One *by James Shirley*

1633 quarto with fairly complete manuscript prompt notes for a Duke's Company production at Lincoln's Inn Fields Theatre about 1666–67; in

Bodleian copy Malone 253 (2), which is lacking signatures F2 and F3. Briefly discussed by Bertram Joseph in "Stage-Directions in a 17th Cent. Copy of Shirley," *Theatre Notebook*, 3 (1949), 66–67. Reproduced here in chapter 15 by permission of the Bodleian Library, Oxford.

The Duke's Company prompter and author of *Roscius Anglicanus* (1708), John Downes, may have prepared—with the help of his backstage colleagues—this promptbook of Shirley's comedy. Most of the notes are in pencil and are very faint, but some that deal with scenery are in ink and in two different hands. One would guess that the prompter or his assistant entered the pencil notes that deal with actors, while the machinist and his helper wrote the designations of scenery to be used. Severe cropping by someone who valued the book's form more than its content, plus the faintness of some of the notes, make reading and interpreting extremely difficult. The date of the notes is also uncertain. Downes indicated a revival of the play after the plague and fire. Joseph takes the marginalia to be from the last third of the seventeenth century; following Downes, I would guess the production took place about 1666–67.

The prompter here was generally careful and complete in his notes, as was the machinist (or whoever entered the scenic notes). Inconsistencies in the printed text, however, were not corrected. The crosshatch sign for cues, common in King's Company promptbooks of the time, is not used here. The Duke's Company prompter either did not concern himself with actor entrances, or entrance cues were taken care of in some way not shown by the promptbook.

Something needs to be said about the brief analysis of this promptbook by Bertram Joseph. Some of his comments are misleading: he speaks of cues for songs, for instance, and there are none; he mistook actor warnings for song cues, so far as I can tell; and his identification of signatures is not always correct. At one point he comments on a cut on F4[v] that alters a servant's entrance in Act IV, Scene i, but there is no anonymous servant in Act IV, and cuts in the play do not change any character's entrance "from the end to the beginning of another character's speech." Joseph evidently mistook the warning *Sen* as a speech ascription for the chambermaid Sensible; but *Sen* is a warning for the scene change on the following page. What is most surprising, however, is that the volume of Shirley plays in which Joseph found *The Wittie Faire One* promptbook also contains a second promptbook which he apparently did not notice, *The Ball*.

Cast

The Wittie Faire One promptbook contains no mention of actors' names, a characteristic of Duke's Company books. Though this is frustrating to a modern scholar trying to date a promptbook, it is not unexpected. There is no reason why a warning for an actor should name him rather than the character, since a promptbook should be prepared on the assumption that it might serve the troupe for several years, during which time there would be changes in company personnel.

Staging

As might be expected with a play written in pre-Restoration times, the printed text provides no descriptions of settings in the stage directions (though at I, i, 202 Violetta comes from "the Arbor"). The promptbook, on the other hand, provides technical notes on scenery for the full play:

I, i	*SCENE GARD[EN]*
II, i	*Cham[ber]*
II, ii	*Gard[en]*
III, i	*CHAMBER*
III, ii	*Tow[n]*
III, iii	*[C]ham- / [b]er / wth a bed*
IV, i	*Towne*
IV, ii	*Chamber*
IV, iii	*Garden*
IV, iv	*[Ch]amber*
IV, v	*Tow[n]*
V, i	*Garden*
V, ii	*Town[e]*
V, iii	*Chamber / [&] hearse*

Scene shifts are warned by the word *Scene* (or some variant spelling) placed in advance of the shift if the change takes place within an act. If the change comes at the end of an act, the warning is the standard one in many Restoration promptbooks: *Act*, written in the margin in advance of the scene shift. *Act* would serve, as in other books, as a warning for scene shifters, actors, and, usually, musicians. For example, at the opening of III, i the stage direction indicates that the first entrance in the new act and new setting is made while the music is playing. In some promptbooks act warnings appear before the ends of some but not all acts; in *The Wittie Faire One* book they appear before all act endings. This may mean that no intervals were taken.

The manuscript notes and stage directions call for several properties: a letter for Sensible in II, ii is cited in the notes but is not mentioned in the stage direction; on the other hand, the letter for Braines at the opening of III, i is cited by the author but not mentioned in the notes; the poem the Tutor brings in at III, i, 25 is not mentioned in either the stage direction or the notes, nor is the poem Sir Nicholas reads in the same scene; the letter Aimwell brings on at the opening of II, ii is properly warned; the bed needed in III, iii is mentioned in the prompt notes but not in the stage directions; the light brought on by Winifred at IV, iv, 121 seems to be included in the warning for her, though the note is hard to decipher; the hearse at the opening of V, iii is warned, but the tapers mentioned in the stage direction are not cited in the notes and thus may not have been used; and the poems read in the middle of V, iii are not mentioned in the notes.

There are only two sound effect cues in the play: a knock at III, iii, 20, which is cued but not warned, and music accompanying the song at IV, iii, 8, which is warned but not cued.

The bulk of the manuscript notes in the copy are warnings for actors, and they are very carefully handled, even though many are now, but presumably not then, difficult to read. Violetta's entrance from the arbor (between the wings, presumably) at I, i, 202 was not warned; Braines's entrance at II, ii, 105 was not warned, but it is a reentrance shortly after an exit, as the note indicates; Winifred is even warned just before her entrance at IV, iii, 27 that she has another entrance at IV, iv, 8; and the Tutor's entrance at the opening of IV, v seems not to have been warned, though there is a note too faint to read just before IV, iv, 147. The prompter was careful about warnings, but he supplied no entrance cues—unless he simply relied on the printed stage directions and needed no mark to catch his eye. As I suggested in the Introduction, there is a possibility that he was stationed in a prompter's box at the front of the stage, where he could not give entrance cues.

The markings in the margin beside the character names listed in the dramatis personae I cannot interpret.

Guzman *by Roger Boyle, Earl of Orrery*

1693 first edition (in folio) with extensive traces of prompt copy probably related to the Duke's Company production at Lincoln's Inn Fields Theatre on 15 April 1669. Edited by William Smith Clark II, in *The Dramatic Works of Roger Boyle Earl of Orrery* (Cambridge, Mass.: Harvard University Press, 1937), vol. 1, 437–513 text and vol. 2, 800–806 and 891–901 commentary; discussed by Clark in "Restoration Prompt Notes and Stage Practices," *Modern Language Notes*, 51 (April 1936), 226–30, and by Richard Southern in *Changeable Scenery* (London: Faber and Faber, 1952), pp. 142–45. Copy studied: British Library 644 k 13.

This is one of the most remarkable Restoration theatrical documents that has come down to us. It is an edition printed long after the play's premiere, but the traces of prompt notes surely relate to the original production, as will be seen from references to scenery from other plays of the 1660s. The play is not known to have been revived between 1669 and the appearance of the first edition in 1693. It may have been produced in the early 1690s, prompting the publication. Clark's edition of the play prints the traces of prompt copy in their proper places in the text, but they have never been gathered, as here, and discussed in detail.

The traces begin at the opening of Act II. A compositor struggled through Act I, separating the prompt notes from the author's stage directions, and then either gave up the task as hopelessly time-consuming or, more likely, was replaced by a second, less capable, compositor. A discussion of the staging follows the transcriptions of the traces.

Act II, [Scene i]

P. 10 "*The Scene with the Chimny in it*" setting for II, [i]. The author did not describe the locale.

"[*with a Paper*" property note following the stage direction for the entrance of Guzman and Francisco. This may have been an author's note, and Clark so prints it, but the use of the bracket, which Clark omits, suggests a prompt note. Brackets are used in a number of prompt traces below.

"[*Two ready*" actor warning for offstage lines by Guivarro and Alvares c.22 lines in advance.

"[*Knocking / prepar'd*" sound effect warning c.12 lines in advance. The wording suggests that the knocking was done by stagehands rather than the actors playing Guivarro and Alvares.

"*Guiv*. Two without say———" This is printed as an interrupted speech by Guivarro, but it was probably a stage direction or prompt note in the original. It appears at about the point when Guivarro and Alvares are supposed to issue an offstage challenge.

P. 11 "*Guzman*'s ready" actor warning for offstage dialogue 6 lines in advance. No earlier warning was possible, since Guzman just made his exit.

The entrance of Guivarro and Alvares on this page was not warned (or the prompt note was not picked up by the compositor); if they were not warned, perhaps it was because their offstage speeches' warning was considered sufficient.

Act II, [Scene ii]

"A Table and Two Swords" property note at the opening of II, [ii].

P. 12 The entrance of Oviedo and Piracco at the opening of II, [ii] was not warned.

"[*A flat Scene of a Chamber*" setting for II, [ii]. The stage direction indicates only ". . . Piracco *in his Chamber*."

"*Leon. Pastra. / Anton.*" actor warning c.18 lines before entrance, printed, in error, as a speech ascription.

Act II, [Scene iii]

"[*The Q. of* Hungary's *Chamber*" setting for II, [iii]. The stage direction gives no locale. This setting is one which was used in 1665, five years before the *Guzman* premiere, for another Boyle play, *Mustapha*; there is no Queen of Hungary in *Guzman*.

P. 13 The entrance of Julia on this page was not warned.

"*Maria, Lucia, Sala. / Ferd.*" actor warning for "four Boys" c.13 lines before entrance. The actors of the four characters named, since they were not needed in this scene in those characters, doubled as the boys who caper about as hobgoblins in fantastic costumes.

"*A little Bell ready*" sound effect warning c.10 lines in advance.

"*Guzm.* ready" actor warning c.6 lines before entrance; the prompter could have provided a more ample warning.

Act II, [Scene iv]

"*The new Black Scene*" setting for II, [iv]. The stage direction describes the locale as Alcanzar's "Closet painted about with Mathematical Instruments and Grotesque Figures . . ." The prompt note implies that the setting was created especially for *Guzman*. It was probably used for other productions after that and called the "Black Scene."

"[*Flashes of / Fire ready*" special effect warning c.19 lines in advance.

"[*Tripos*" property note at opening of II, [iv].

Francisco's entrance at the opening of II, [iv] was not warned.

"[*Bell Rings here*" sound cue at the end of the first speech in II, [iv]. This is probably the prompter's, not the author's, note.

P. 14 "[*When* Fran. *rises flashes of Fire*" special effect cue. This, too, is probably a cue by the prompter, not the author.

P. 15 The entrance of the four boys on this page was not warned.

"[*Dance here*" music cue, repeating information in a stage direction: "They Dance about Guzm. . . ." This was not warned.

Act III, [Scene i]

P. 17 "A little Bell read[y]" sound effect warning c.16 lines in advance. See illustration.

"[Flashes of Fire ready" special effect warning c.40 lines in advance.

"[*Leonora, Anto. / Pastra. Jul.*" actor warning c.19 lines before entrance.

All three of the above notes come at the opening of III, [i]; there is no trace of a prompt note describing the setting for the scene, but the stage direction calls for "Alcanzar's *Astrological Cabinet*"—presumably the "new Black Scene" used in II, [iv]. The setting would not have changed.

The entrance of Francisco (disguised as Alcanzar), Maria, and Lucia at the opening of III, [i] was not warned; Francisco could not have been warned, since he made an exit at the end of the previous scene.

"[*Bell Rings here*" sound effect cue just before the entrance of Leonora and the others.

P. 18 "[*Flashes of Fire here*" special effect cue.

The entrance of a Boy on this page was not warned.

"[*Trampling*" sound effect warning c.21 lines in advance.

P. 19 "[*A Trampling with- / out*" sound effect cue, probably written by the

GUZMAN 17

For now, who e'er my Fury does provoke,
Shall find his Deſtiny in Fire and Smoke.

[*Ex. Strutting.*

Fran. If he were as well Charm'd as he is Fool'd; he would be Invulnerable indeed. [*Ex.*

ACT III.

The Scene is Alcanzar's *Aſtrological Cabinet.*

[A little Bell read.
[Flaſhes of Fire ready.

Alcanzar *in his Conjuring-habit, with* Maria *and* Lucia, *dreſt like good Spirits.* [*Leonora, Anto. Paſtra. Jul.*

Fran. JUlia has aſſured me, that *Leonora* and her two Fair Daughters, the Rich Heireſſes, will be here by Four a Clock; they cannot long be abſent; ſhe has inform'd me too of all the Secrets of the Family. *Maria*, you know your Part: After you and *Lucia*, with your Maids, have danc'd, you muſt mount on yonder *Tripos*, and diſtinctly Pronounce the firſt Oracle; and perform all thoſe other things I have already directed.

Mar. Well, if ever *Delphian Virgin* e'er declar'd Oracle with more Authentick Gravity than I, (bating the Convulſion of the Eyes, and twiſting of the Neck) ne'er take my Word again.

Fran. And you, *Lucia*, muſt ſpeak the ſecond Oracle, I gave you, with the Gravity of a *Sybil.*

Luci. If you can give me, Mr. Conjurer, but a Spell to prevent Laughing, doubt not but they ſhall take me at leaſt for *Sybilla Cumea.*

Fran. 'Slight, if you Laugh, we are all undone.

Luci. I hope, I ſhall have the Retentive Faculty for once, to contain; I muſt pinch my ſelf worſe than the Fairies do the drowſie Maids. [*Bell Rings here.*

Fran. Julia has ſo finely fool'd them; that whatever they hear from from me, will be believ'd as zealouſly as an old dying *Turk* does the *Alcoran.* I hear them; away, away———— [*Ex. Mar. Lucia.*

Enter Leonora, Antonia, Paſtrana *and* Julia. (*all vail'd but* Julia.)

Jul. Madam, I'll be your Guide; this is the Aſtrological Cabinet; and I ſee the Great *Alcanzar* in his Chair.

Fran. riſing. Ladies, why do you thus come in Maſquerade? Can you believe that I can tell Future Events, and yet think a little Crape can hide things preſent from my knowledge? Though your ſcrupulous Maid would not tell me who you were, yet by my Art, I know you are the Beautiful *Leonora*, Mother to the fair *Antonia* and *Paſtrana*, who attend you now to learn your Fates, from my all-knowing Skill: Come, Unvail, unvail——— [*They all Unvail.*

Leon. We find, Sir, 'tis in vain to hide our ſelves, for you know who we are, and what we come to learn: But Sir, I beſeech you, be not offended at *Julia*, ſhe did but Obey my Orders.

Fran. He, who commands the Spirits of the Air, and thoſe black Fiends which dwell in Flames of Sulphur, muſt not be trifled with; I ne'er receiv'd Affront, but I re-paid it with a quick Revenge.

Julia, Kneeling.——O, Sir! Forgive me.

Leon. Great *Alcanzar*, I beg you for her.

Anton. Paſtra. We both join in the ſame Requeſt.

F *Fran.*

From Boyle's *Guzman.* By kind permission of the British Library.

prompter, judging from the use of brackets, though Clark transcribes this as an author's stage direction.

"[*A Purse*" property note following the stage direction for Guzman's entrance, which was not warned.

"[Maria, Lucia / [Julia" actor warning for offstage noise c.20 lines in advance. This is an error, for Julia is onstage during the scene, and the stage direction for the noise mentions only Maria and Lucia.

"(Boy ready" actor warning c.21 lines before entrance.

"None here" sound effect cue for offstage noise; it should read "Noise here."

P. 20 "Song here.*)* / Then Dance. / Soft Musick / here" music cues, repeating information in a stage direction.

P. 21 "*Maria, Lucia / ready*" actor warning c.28 lines before entrance.

"[*Guzman*" actor warning c.23 lines before entrance.

"[*Servant*" actor warning c.19 lines before entrance.

Act III, [Scene ii]

P. 22 "[*A Flat Scene of a Chamber*" setting for III, [ii]. The stage direction gives no indication of a scene change at this point; the scene begins at Guzman's entrance.

"[T*wo Letters*" property note for Guivarro and Alvares at their entrance, which was not warned.

P. 23 "[*Sala. Fern. Ma- / ria and Luc.*" actor warning c.22 lines before entrance.

Act III, [Scene iii]

"[The new flat Scene" setting for III, [iii]. The stage direction describes the locale as "*the* Piazzo."

P. 24 "[*Ovie. Pirac.*" actor warning c.18 lines before entrance.

"[Guz. *and* Fran. / *ready*" actor warning c.23 lines before entrance.

Act III, [Scene iv]

P. 25 "[The Forest" setting for III, [iv]. The stage direction describes the locale as "*a Field with Trees.*"

"[*Trampling ready*" sound effect warning c.23 lines in advance.

"[*Messenger*" actor warning c.20 lines before entrance.

P. 26 "[*Trampling without*" sound effect cue, possibly written by the prompter, though Clark transcribes this as a stage direction.

"[*Call* Mar. Lucia" actor warning c.29 lines before entrance.

Act IV, [Scene i]

P. 27 "*The New Flat Scene*" setting for IV, [i]. The stage direction gives no locale but only the entrance of Maria and Lucia. The "*New Flat Scene*" was previously used to satisfy the author's request for a scene showing the "Piazzo."

"[*Ovie. Pastra. Pir. Anto. Jul.*" actor warning c.22 lines before entrance.

Act IV, [Scene ii]

P. 28 "[*Q. of* Hungary'*s / Chamber*" setting for IV, [ii]. The stage direction gives no indication of a scene change at this point but only the group entrance warned above.

"[*Call* Julia" actor warning c.23 lines before entrance; this is a pointless note, since Julia is onstage at this moment and does not exit until two lines before her reentrance.

The entrance of Guzman on this page was not warned.

P. 30 "[Leon *ready within*" actor warning, but Leonora has no entrance for several pages; this note is probably an error and should be a warning for Guivarro, Alvares, and Francisco c.12 lines hence.

Act IV, [Scene iii]

"[The Chamber with / the Chimney in't" setting for IV, [iii]. The stage direction describes the locale as "Francisco's *House*."

The entrance of Guivarro, Alvares, and Francisco at the opening of IV, [iii] was not warned; see the erroneous warning for Leonora above.

P. 31 The entrances of Julia and Guzman on this page were not warned.

P. 33 "[*Alva. Guiv. Jul.*" actor warning c.30 lines before entrance.

Act IV, [Scene iv]

P. 34 "*The New Flat Scene*" setting for IV, [iv]. The stage direction gives no indication of a scene change at this point but only the entrance of Salazar and Fernando, which was not warned.

Act IV, [Scene v]

P. 35 "[The Forest" setting for IV, [v]. The stage direction describes the locale as "*a Grove of Trees.*" The author asked for but did not get a setting different from III, [iv].

Pp. 35–36 None of the five entrances in this scene was warned.

Act IV, [Scene vi]

P. 37 "[The Garden in *Tryphon* / as a Back Scene" setting for IV, [vi]. The stage direction describes the locale as "a *Garden.*" *Tryphon* was another Boyle play, performed a year before *Guzman.* The wording here indicates that the side wings from the previous forest setting remained in place, while the upstage shutters changed. This was evidently a common practice in Restoration productions, beginning with *The Siege of Rhodes* at Rutland House in 1656.

Pp. 37–40 None of the four entrances in this scene was warned. Perhaps the compositor finally decided that the actor warnings in the promptbook did not belong in the printed text, for the text contains none from IV, [v] to the end of the play. But more likely there had been a change of compositors.

Act IV, [Scene vii]

P. 42 "[The New Flat Scene" setting for IV, [vii]. The stage direction describes the locale, again, as "*the Piazzo.*"

Act IV, [Scene viii]

P. 43 "[The new black Scene" setting for IV, [viii]. The stage direction describes the locale as "*the Astrological Cabinet.*"

"[*Rapping ready*" sound effect warning c.10 lines in advance; the warning could not have been placed earlier, since this is at the opening of IV, [viii]. The prompter apparently did not wish to place the warning within the previous scene, though he did just that with a number of actor warnings.

P. 44 "[*Rapping ready*" sound effect warning c.23 lines in advance.

P. 45 The offstage lines of the Boy were not warned.

Act V, [Scene i]

P. 46 "*The New Flat Scene*" setting for V, [i]. The stage direction gives no indication of a scene change at this point, only a group entrance at the opening of the act. This setting was previously used for Piazza scenes.

Act V, [Scene ii]

P. 47 "*Queen of* Hungary'*s Chamber*" setting for V, [ii]. The stage direction gives no indication of a scene change at this point, only a group entrance at the opening of the scene. The locale seems to be Leonora's house.

"[A Periwig for *Francisco*" property note at the opening of V, [ii]; the periwig is carried on by Francisco, not worn, and thus is a property and not a costume—a nice theatrical distinction.

"[A Paper like a Bond" property note at the opening of V, [ii]; the paper is brought on by Francisco.

P. 50 "[*Clashing of Swords ready*" sound effect warning c.26 lines in advance of "A great Noise without."

P. 51 "*Noise with Swords*" sound effect cue, repeating some of the information in the stage direction just quoted.

Guzman is most unusual in containing so many traces of prompt copy; only one other printed book of the period (actually a bit later), the 1714(?) edition of Banks's *The Albion Queens*, is so rich in traces. Printers ordinarily made an effort to weed out prompt notes from printed editions, and the few that creep into some texts are errors on the part of a compositor. In *Guzman*, acts II and III contain so many traces that it is evident that the compositor simply made little effort to omit them. Act I contains none, and acts IV and V contain numerous traces but not many entrance warnings. Perhaps three compositors were at work, going about their tasks with different degrees of care. If that was so, I would suggest that signatures A–C (pp. 1–8) were set by one compositor, D–H (pp. 9–28) by another, and I–O (pp. 29–52) by a third. But who did what does not really matter so far as the present study is concerned; we should be grateful that the printer did such a poor job, for he preserved for us a mass of useful theatrical information.

Though we should assume that a great number of prompt notes in the original manuscript of *Guzman* did not get into print, some sections of the printed edition are complete enough for us to judge what kind of notes the manuscript contained and to reconstruct the scene plot for the production. The notes that made their way into the printed text cover warnings and cues for sound and special effects, warnings for actor entrances, labels for settings, and occasional notes on properties. There are no warnings for scene shifts or act-endings, nor, understandably, symbols to cue actor entrances and scene shifts (those symbols are not to be found in any Duke's Company promptbook studied here). Actor warnings are by character name, so the traces are of no help in reconstructing the cast. The terminology used by the Duke's Company prompter and his associates is similar to that found in many other promptbooks throughout the period, though the *Guzman* scenery labels are unusually specific, and the normal warning here is "ready" rather than "call."

Staging

The scene plot for *Guzman* can be almost completely reconstructed.

Act & Scene	*Author's Description*	*Machinist's Description*
I, i	"*a Piazza, with Walks of Trees, and Houses round about it.*"	None. Presumably "*The New Flat Scene*" was used.
II, i	None. The locale seems to be Guzman's house.	"*The Scene with the Chimny in it.*"
II, ii	Piracco's "*Chamber.*"	"[*A flat Scene of a Chamber.*"
II, iii	None. The locale seems to be Leonora's house.	"[*The Q. of* Hungary's *Chamber.*"
II, iv	Alcanzar's "Closet painted about with Mathematical Instruments and Grotesque Figures . . ."	"*The new Black Scene.*"
III, i	"Alcanzar's *Astrological Cabinet.*"	None, since the locale does not change.
III, ii	None. The locale seems to be Guzman's house.	"[*A Flat Scene of a Chamber.*"

Act & Scene	*Author's Description*	*Machinist's Description*
III, iii	"the Piazzo."	"[The new flat Scene."
III, iv	"*a Field with Trees.*"	"[The Forest."
IV, i	None. The locale seems to be the Piazza.	"*The New Flat Scene.*"
IV, ii	None. The locale seems to be Leonora's house.	"*Q. of* Hungary'*s* / *Chamber.*"
IV, iii	"Francisco's *House.*"	"[The Chamber with / the Chimney in't."
IV, iv	None. The locale seems to be the Piazza.	"*The New Flat Scene.*"
IV, v	"*a Grove of Trees.*"	"[The Forest."
IV, vi	"*a Garden.*"	"[The Garden in *Tryphon* / as a Back Scene."
IV, vii	"*the Piazzo.*"	"[The New Flat Scene"
IV, viii	"*the Astrological Cabinet.*"	"[The new black Scene."
V, i	None. The locale seems to be the Piazza.	"*The New Flat Scene.*"
V, ii	None. The scene seems to be Leonora's house.	"*Queen of* Hungary'*s* *Chamber.*"

When these descriptions by the author on the one hand and the theatre machinist on the other are sorted out and rearranged one sees some peculiar inconsistencies (brackets below indicate conjectural reconstructions of what settings were probably used for scenes with no designated settings).

Piazza	The new flat scene ([I, i]; III, iii; IV, i; IV, iv; IV, vii; V, i)
Guzman's house	The scene with the chimney in it (II, i)
Guzman's house	A flat scene of a chamber (III, ii)
Piracco's chamber	A flat scene of a chamber (II, ii)
Leonora's house	The Queen of Hungary's chamber (II, iii; IV, ii; V, ii)
Alcanzar's cabinet	The new black scene (II, iv; [III, i]; IV, viii)
Field with trees	The forest (III, iv)
Francisco's house	The chamber with the chimney in it (IV, iii)
A grove of trees	The forest (IV, v)
A garden	The garden in *Tryphon* as a back scene (IV, vi)

Guzman's house is represented by two different settings, which is reasonable enough, since two different rooms in his house may have been shown. But each of those two settings may also have been used to represent two other locales: Piracco's chamber and Francisco's house. Clark suggests that this was an example of economy and variety, which may be true, but economy is better demonstrated here by the company's use of the forest setting for both the field with trees and the grove of trees and by what appears to be the use of wings from the forest setting with shutters from the old *Tryphon* garden setting to create a new garden scene. The odd mixing of two different interior settings for three different locales, however, seems too confusing, and I would wager that either the traces of prompt copy contain some errors or, during the actual production of *Guzman*, the inconsistencies were corrected in some way that the traces of prompt copy do not reveal. Part of the problem would be solved if we took the labels on the settings quite literally and supposed that the *chamber* with the chimney in it was a different setting from the *scene* with the chimney in it.

My conjectural reconstruction of the *Guzman* scenic arrangement is relatively simple. For I, i, the Piazza, "*The New Flat Scene,*" would have been in position at the opening of the play; it would have consisted of a series of side wings and a pair of shutters standing in the first set of grooves at each position. Standing behind that setting, waiting for use in II, i, would have been "*The Scene with the Chimny in it*" in the second set of grooves at each position. At the end of Act I the wings and shutters of the Piazza setting would have been drawn off simultaneously and taken out of the first set of grooves, revealing the new scene, Guzman's house. While that scene was playing, the wings and shutters for the next scene, "*A flat Scene of a Chamber*" depicting Piracco's house in II, ii, would have been placed in the first set of grooves, but out of sight, offstage. At the end of II, i, this setting would have been slid onstage to cover the previous one, and the Guzman setting would have been drawn off and out of the grooves to make way for the next setting, Leonora's house. And so on throughout the performance.

The set-up described above differs from the one suggested by Clark, which would have all the wings and shutters for all the settings needed in the play standing in grooves throughout the play, ready to be slid on. In the Introduction I explained why I think such a luxurious arrangement would not have been used even in Restoration theatres with plenty of stage depth (which Lincoln's Inn Fields did not have). Clark and Southern imagine a dispersed shutter arrangement, with shutters at each wing position, and I have set forth my arguments against that in the Introduction as well; shutters downstage would have been too wide to leave offstage passage space from downstage to upstage.

Juliana *by John Crowne*

1671 first quarto containing a trace of prompt copy related to the Duke's Company production at Lincoln's Inn Fields Theatre in late June 1671. Copy studied: British Library 644 g 35.

Though there are many stage directions in Crowne's play that may have been prompt notes in the original manuscript, only one certain trace can be cited.

P. 38 "*Call* Off. Dem. Bat. *bound*" actor warning near the beginning of IV, ii, c.20 lines before the stage direction "(*Enter* Offolimsky *and* Guard, with Demetrius, *and* Battista *bound*."

Since one certain trace is in the edition, we can be sure the printer worked from prompt copy, and the temptation is great to see traces everywhere. But I think the printer in this case managed to weed out all but that one trace.

The Ordinary *by William Cartwright*

1651 first edition (in *Comedies Tragi-Comedies, With other Poems*, octavo 1651) with some manuscript prompt notes and many textual emendations for a Duke's Company production at Dorset Garden Theatre probably soon after 15 January 1672; in T. W. Baldwin's copy at the University of Illinois Library (Baldwin 2920a). Reported in *The London Stage*, Part 1, p. 179 as 15 January 1671 (a Sunday) with a note suggesting that 1672 may have been meant and making no mention of the copy being a promptbook. Collated and discussed by G. Blakemore Evans in *The Plays and Poems of William Cartwright* (Madison: University of Wisconsin Press, 1951). Reproduced here in chapter 16 by permission of the University of Illinois Library.

The Master of the Revels, Sir Henry Herbert, signed the copy on 15 January 1671 (that is, 1671/72) with the caution that it could be acted if the "Reformations" were observed, so some of the cuts and changes in the copy are his. He gave a similar license to Cartwright's *The Lady-Errant* two months later but found no need to caution the players. We have no other record of *The Ordinary* having been performed during the Restoration period, but this copy and the license date make it almost certain that the work was presented by the Duke's players shortly after 15 January 1672. The text of *The Ordinary* is not as severely cut as that of *The Lady-Errant*, but there are more technical notes. There is one actor warning, and either this copy served only as a basis for another, more completely annotated book, or this one served chiefly as a technical copy to aid the backstage crews. Further, the copy is imperfect, lacking pages 11–15 and 27–30.

Evans describes the copy as containing two hands, one that of Sir Henry Herbert and the other that of the playhouse annotator and reviser. I think there may have been two people from the theatre at work on the copy, one who wrote the technical notes and may have been responsible for the cuts and a second who made a few textual emendations.

The editions of *The Ordinary* and *The Lady-Errant* by Evans are not of the promptbooks, though he records all the prompt notes, cuts, and alterations in his textual notes.

The cast of *The Ordinary* is not known. The promptbook does not name any actors, and the single actor-warning, at IV, iii, 136, is there chiefly because IV, iv is completely cut and special care needed to be taken to see that the actors playing Rimewell, Bagshot, Sir Christopher, and Catchmey were ready for their entrance at the opening of IV, v. But V, i is also cut, and no attempt was made to warn the actors or, indeed, to adjust the entrances of Sir Thomas and Jane, who needed to be onstage at the opening of V, ii. The prompter must have used a more complete book than this during performances. On the other hand, there are four entrances cued in the copy: # marks the entrance of Hearsay at I, ii, 9; of Slicer at I, ii, 54; and of Jane at IV, iii, 36; and *X* cues the entrance of Meanwell and Sir Thomas "above" at V, iii, 6.

Staging

Cartwright used French scene divisions—a new scene begins whenever a new character enters—so that a new scene number does not necessarily indicate a change of locale in the following scene plot. Rarely did the author provide any indication of the locale.

Act & Scene	*Author's Description*	*Machinist's Description*
I, i	None	*New hall*
I, ii	None	*new / ordnary*
I, iii	None	None; no change
I, iv	(Beginning of scene is on missing page.)	
I, v	None	None; no change
II, i	None	*Coven Garden*
II, ii	None	None; no change
II, iii	None	*New / ordinary*
II, iv	None	*ordin: Continues* and ~~*Coven Garden*~~
II, v	None	None; no change
III, i	None	None; no change
III, ii	None	~~*Coven G*~~ *Red-Lyon feilds* and ~~*New hall*~~
III, iii	None	*New hall*
III, iv	Characters "as to the Ordinary"	*Coven-Garden*
III, v	None	*ordinary* with *Table And 4 Chaires*
III, vi	None	*Hall*
IV, i	None	*ordin:*
IV, ii	None	*Red Lyon feilds* ~~*ffeild*~~
IV, iii	None	*Hall*
IV, iv	(Scene marked for omission.)	
IV, v	Characters "at a window"	*Coven Garde*^{n}
V, i	(Scene marked for omission.)	
V, ii	None	*Hall*
V, iii	None	*Ordinary* with a *Table & 4 Chaires*
V, iv	None	None; no change
V, v	None	None; no change

To tell whether there were two hall and two ordinary settings is difficult; I suspect there was only one of each but that each was either a new setting or a setting with that label. If the play was presented at Dorset Garden Theatre in 1672, most, if not all, of the scenery must have been fairly new, for the playhouse was much larger than the company's old Lincoln's Inn Fields playhouse, and scenery built for that theatre would not have been suitable for the new one. Thus I would count the different settings in *The Ordinary* as follows: a hall, the ordinary, Covent Garden (probably a view of the piazza), and Red Lion Fields. Is it significant that the scenic requirements of this play and of *The Lady-Errant* were simple? The troupe had just spent an enormous sum (£9,000) on the new Dorset Garden playhouse, and for a while they may well have avoided plays requiring many settings.

The property plot for *The Ordinary* is also simple, like that for *The Lady-Errant*:

I, ii opening *A purse / for Hearsay*

III, v *Table And 4 Chaires* and Sir Christopher w^{th} *a Letter*.

At line 69 a Servant passes by w^{th} *a / Lette[r]*.

At line 183 the stage direction reads: "[Ba. *draws his Inkhorn and* Ri. *catcheth off Sr* Chr. *hat and spectacles*]." The manuscript notes contain nothing about that business; the inkhorn, if not the hat and spectacles, was a property.

At line 197 a Servant enters with beer; the notes do not mention that property.

III, vi A letter for Meanwell is mentioned in the stage direction but not in the manuscript notes.

V, iii a *Table & 4 Chaires* as in III, v. One supposes that in the other scenes in the ordinary the table and chairs were not needed and thus not brought on. Scenes were changed *a vista*, and heavy properties were probably carried on only if they were to be used by the actors.

The Lady-Errant *by William Cartwright*

1651 first edition (in *Comedies Tragi-Comedies, With other Poems*, octavo 1651) with some manuscript prompt notes and many textual emendations for a Duke's Company production at Dorset Garden Theatre probably soon after 9 March 1672 and very likely on 13 March; in T. W. Baldwin's copy at the University of Illinois Library (Baldwin 2920a). Reported in *The London Stage*, Part 1, pp. 181 and 193 as either 1670–71 or 1671–72 but not cited as a promptbook. Collated and discussed by G. Blakemore Evans in *The Plays and Poems of William Cartwright* (Madison: University of Wisconsin Press, 1951). Performance discussed in Judith Milhous and Robert D. Hume's "Lost English Plays, 1660–1700," *Harvard Library Bulletin*, 25 (January 1977), 18. Reproduced here in chapter 17 by permission of the University of Illinois Library.

Sir Henry Herbert's licensing date on the last page of *The Lady-Errant* is "March: 9: 1671"—that is, 1671/72. There is no record of a specific performance, but the work was probably presented soon after the license date, and Milhous and Hume show that *The Romantic Lady*, given by the Duke's Company on 13 March 1672, was almost certainly *The Lady-Errant*. The copy is generously annotated, though most of the manuscript notes are cuts and textual emendations. There are some prompt notes dealing with properties, scenery, sound effects, and actors, but these do not seem to be complete enough for effective use during a performance—unless cropping has lost us some marginalia. Since the copy is very cluttered with notes at some points, the prompter may have prepared a second, cleaner copy for his use, transferring the notes in this copy and adding others.

In addition to the censor's marks I see two different theatrical hands in the prompt notes. The main hand wrote, I believe, all of the actual prompt notes and most of the textual emendations.

Cast

Only three performers are named in the prompt notes, and they are minor players brought on for a dance in II, ii. They are warned at line 50, but severe cropping has lost us the full names; the men called seem to have been Sherwood, Burford, and Bampfield.

Staging

Though the promptbook contains a few technical notes, nothing much can be done in the way of reconstruction of the staging. The author's stage directions rarely describe locales: I, i—"Myrtle Grove"; III, i—"in the Grove"; IV, i—several characters "sate as at Parliament." Descriptions by the machinist are less rare: II, i—*Hall*; II, vi—*Grove*; III, iv—*grove / Continu[es]*; IV, i—*a Table and 10 / Chaires with / ye great*; V, ii—*Pallace / for Church [to?] / be read[y]*. If the technical notes, though few in number, are complete, then four different settings seem to have sufficed for the production: a hall, a grove, a great (hall?), and a palace to serve as a church setting (to be used, apparently, for V, iii). The notes do not include shift warnings or cue symbols.

The prompt notes seem more concerned with properties than actor warnings or scenery notes, and perhaps this book began as the prompter's copy but ended up serving chiefly as a property plot. Each of the first four acts contains property needs, and the annotator listed them all on the first page:

Act I: *a Roll: for Cosmeta* (used at I, i, 41)
a Letter for / olind: in lst act. (used at I, v, 9)

Act II: *a Letter for / Eumela in 2 A[ct]* (used at II, iv, 2)

Act III: *2 Napkins / in 3 Act* (used by Philaenis at opening of III, v)

Act IV: *particular for / Cosmeta in 4 Act* (used at IV, i, 116)

Not listed at the opening of Act I are heavy properties, such as the table and ten chairs called for in the notes at the opening of Act IV or the bench or seats on which, the stage direction says, Florina and Malthora are "sate in the Grove" at the opening of I, iv. Also missing from the list at the opening of the play is a particular brought on (according to the manuscript notes) by Cosmeta at the opening of II, i—but it is not used. At IV, i, 148 Pandena reads from a list of particulars, and since that particular is not mentioned in the notes, perhaps it is the same one Cosmeta reads from at IV, i, 116.

In the text of the play are many references to such costume accessories as swords, myrtle wreaths, helmets, a falchion, and a lance. These were not considered properties and were evidently the responsibility of the actors, not the prompter and his helpers. Similarly, a lute mentioned in I, iv is not cited in a prompt note, so the musician who used it to accompany a song was evidently responsible for it.

The Careless Lovers *by Edward Ravenscroft*

1673 first quarto containing many traces of prompt copy related to the Duke's Company production at Dorset Garden Theatre on 12 March 1673. Discussed by James G. McManaway in "The Copy for *The Careless Lovers*," *Modern Language Notes*, 46 (June 1931), 406–9, and briefly by Montague Summers in *The Restoration Theatre* (London: Kegan Paul, Trench, Trubner, 1934), pp. 147–48. Copy studied: British Library 1346 e 11.

Though not as rich in traces of prompt copy as the first edition of Boyle's *Guzman*, the edition of Ravenscroft's comedy contains a great many printed prompt notes. The Duke's Company production was presented during Lent by the younger actors in the troupe.

Act II

P. 15 "*Ready to shut / the Boult*" warning, probably for the actor playing Toby as well as a stagehand on the offstage side of the door, c.22 lines in advance of the author's stage direction, "[*Shut the Boult*."

P. 19 "*All* Much. / Jacinta" actor warning 29 lines before Muchworth's entrance and 33 lines before Jacinta's entrance. The note should read, of course, "Call."

P. 21 "[*Pass*" possible actor cue (for passing over the stage) and so interpreted by Summers, but this may have been a direction by the author.

[P. 29] "[D. Boast. *with a Letter*" actor and property warning 37 lines before entrance. The page is incorrectly numbered 37.

P. 33 "[*Call* Beatrice" actor warning 17 lines before entrance.

"[*Bring Napkins and stop their Mouths*.]" This curious note may have been written by either the author or the prompter; Summers and McManaway take it to be a prompt note. But it reads like a speech, and I would be inclined to treat it as such and assign it to De Boastado or, possibly, Muchworth. It is placed just after the entrance of Beatrice and is centered on the page. I think the compositor simply mistook it for a stage direction.

Act IV, [Scene i]

P. 37 "[*Hall continues*" setting for IV, [i] and apparently for all of Act III. The stage direction at this point indicates an entrance but does not describe the locale.

P. 39 "*A Bottle of Sack, / and Glass ready / for* Beatrice" property warning c.73 lines in advance. This is a much more ample warning than normal; perhaps a portion of the ensuing scene was cut in performance, bringing the warning and cue closer together.

P. 40 "[*Knock ready*" sound effect warning 36 lines in advance. Again, this is a very ample warning, and there may have been a cut following it.

P. 41 "*Knocking at the Door*]" and "*Knocking within*" sound effect cues. The first is probably the author's stage direction and the second a note by the prompter; the notes appear at opposite ends of the same printed line, just before Beatrice's entrance.

P. 43 "*Knock / here*" and "[*Knocking at Door*" sound effect cues. The first is probably a note by the prompter and the second the author's original stage direction; again, they are at opposite ends of the same printed line, just before the entrance of Clappam and Tommie.

Act IV, [Scene ii]

P. 45 "*Coven-garden*]" and "[Muchw. *House*" setting for IV, [ii]. The stage direction at this point indicates an entrance for Careless and Lovell but no locale. One of these two notes, which are printed at opposite ends of the same line, may have been written by the author and the other by the prompter or machinist—or theatre personnel may have written both. I would guess "Muchw. *House*" to be by the author, since it mentions a character; then the prompter or machinist indicated what setting would be used—one called Covent Garden, probably showing the piazza and probably the same setting (or part of the same setting) used in Cartwright's *The Ordinary*. These notes may indicate that the wings showed Muchworth's house and the shutters a prospect of Covent Garden, or vice versa. Or the wings may have shown a tavern on one side and a house on the other, with the piazza seen in the distance. Such combinations were quite possible. In any case, the dialogue makes it clear that the scene is an exterior; a door to a tavern is mentioned.

"[*Call* D. Boastado" actor warning 30 lines before entrance.

P. 48 "[*Ex.* [*To the Tavern*" This exit refers to Clappam and Mrs. Breeder; the author may have written the whole note, but I would guess he wrote "[*Ex.*" and left the prompter to indicate where. Stage movement and exit sides are not usually indicated in Restoration promptbooks, but if, as suggested above, the two sides of the stage represented different sides of the street, the prompter may have needed to jot down a clarifying note about the exit. See illustration.

Act IV, [Scene iii]

"*Tables, Chairs,*) / *Candles, Bottles*)" property cue at the opening of what is clearly indicated in the action as a new scene inside the tavern. The original promptbook probably described the setting and called for a scene shift.

P. 50 "[*Musick ready* / (*below*" sound effect and musicians' warning c.35 lines in advance. We may guess from this that it would have taken the musicians at Dorset Garden Theatre (where the music room was located over the proscenium arch) about 35 lines, or roughly a minute to a minute and a half, to get from their room to stage level.

P. 51 "[*Musicke playes*" sound effect cue. This is probably an author's direction, but it may have been written by the prompter.

"[*A Dance here of four*" dance cue. Again, this could be either a stage direction or a prompt note.

Act V, [Scene i]

P. 56 "Covent Garden" setting for V, [i]. Though this reads like a stage direction by the author and is printed as one, I take it to be a prompter's or machinist's note, since Ravenscroft left out locale descriptions elsewhere in the play. Indeed, in his Epistle to the Reader he commented on the haste with which the play was written (three days for the first three acts and a week for acts IV and V), so it is no wonder that details of locale were omitted. The printer was just

48 *The Careleſs Lovers.*

Beat. The Cry comes this way—— Follow me with all the haſt you can, that they not come within view of us. [*Ex.* D. Boaſt. Beatrice.

Enter Mrs. Breeder *and* Clappam.

Breed. So, now the Children are ſent home, let's to the place of Rendezvous.

Clap. Here's the Tavern; Enter—— [*Ex.* [*To the Tavern.*

Lovel *and* Careleſs *appear.*

Carel. Come *Lovel*, they are gone to the Tavern to look for us.

Lov. I am the worſt man i'th world, to Converſe with this ſort of Cattle.

Carel. Thou ought'ſt to be civil to e'm upon Account of the Kindneſs they have done for thee at my Requeſt.

Lov. Will not my Money excuſe my Company.

Carel. Did not I condeſcend to viſit a Pair of Honeſt women at your requeſt? Aye, and viſit them a ſecond time; and can you in Conſcience refuſe to Accompany me now——?

Lov. Your firſt Viſit was made by my perſwaſions; but the ſecond, was the Effect of your own Inclinations.

Carel. Well; but come along, if you like not your Company, be gone aſſoon as you will. [*Ex.* Lov. Carel.

Enter Hilaria, *and* Jacinta.

Hil. 'Tis e'en ſo; your Lover and my Gallant are gone in after e'm: We'l put off our Frollique of going to the Nurſery, and I'le adventure into the Tavern, to ſee after what manner they Treat e'm.

Jac. But ſhou'd they know you——

Hil. They know you: they can't in this Diſguiſe; but if they do, 'twill paſs for a Frolique—— [*Exeunt.*

Tables, Chairs,) *Candles, Bottles.*) *Enter Mrs.* Breeder, Clappam, *Drawer in Tavern.*

Draw. What Wine do you pleaſe to drink, Ladies?

Breed. Sack and Claret; Is it good?

Draw. We have as good as any is in *England.*

Clap.

From Ravenscroft's *The Careless Lovers.* By kind permission of the British Library.

as hasty producing the first edition, fortunately for us, or the prompt notes might have been weeded out.

P. 58 "*Call* Lovel, / Careless" actor warning c.41 lines before entrance.

"*Call* Hilaria" actor warning 59 lines before entrance, an unusually ample warning. The text shows two entrances for Hilaria, one on page 60 and another on page 61, with no exit in between. This warning may refer to the second entrance, for the first seems to be a mistake.

P. 62 "*Call* Careless, *Musick* / Breed. Clap" actor and musician warning c.42 lines before entrance, written with no concern about the quaint juxtaposition of the words.

P. 64 "[Beat. *on the Beir ready*" actor and property warning c.51 lines in advance. Since this had to be set up, an ample warning was needed.

P. 67 "*Musick / ready*" musicians' warning c.38 lines in advance. No stage direction indicates the entrance of the musicians (on p. 68), but the lines reveal when they should enter.

Act V, [Scene ii]

"*Hall-Table and / Candles, 4 Chaires*" property note at the opening of V, [ii]. The stage direction at this point reads: "*Enter* Lovel, Jacinta, *the Scene changes, / and a Room in* Muchworth's House."

Tom Essence *by Thomas Rawlins*

1677 first quarto containing a few traces of prompt copy related to the Duke's Company production at Dorset Garden Theatre in late August 1676. Copy studied: British Library 643 i 21 (2).

P. 2 "*Mrs.* Essence / *ready above*" actor warning c.39 lines before balcony entrance in I, i. The entrance stage direction on page 3 reads: "*Mrs.* Essence *discover'd at a VVindow.*"

P. 8 "*Noise*" sound effect cue just after Laurence's line, ". . . I hear somebody comeing . . ." in I, [ii]. This may be the author's note, but it is not printed like other stage directions in this section of the text.

P. 11 "*(Call* Luce" actor warning c.25 lines before entrance in I, [ii].

P. 12 "(*Noise of a Door shutting*" sound effect cue just before Loveall's line, ". . . *I hear a Door shut* . . ." in I, [ii]. This may be the author's note.

P. 15 "*(A Candle set in the Window*" property note following Stanly's line, ". . . The Candle's brought" in I, [ii]. This may be the author's note.

Madam Fickle (1677) *by Thomas D'Urfey*

1677 first quarto containing a few traces of prompt copy related to the Duke's Company production at Dorset Garden Theatre on 4 November 1676. Copy studied: British Library 644 h 9.

Some, but not all, of the traces of prompt copy in this 1677 quarto of *Madam Fickle* were repeated in the 1682 quarto, and the British Library copy of the latter (discussed below under the United Company promptbooks) contains, in addition, some manuscript prompt notes. There seems to be no relationship between the two productions, however. The probable history of the *Madam Fickle* promptbook is discussed under the 1682 edition. The traces of prompt copy in the first quarto are:

P. 19 "[*a Ring*" property note following Manley's line, "Wear this Sweet Creature, and / remember me—" in II, ii. This may be a note by the author, but it is printed like a prompt note. Repeated in the 1682 quarto.

P. 25 "[*A Table with Scull, Sword, Vial, Shooing-horn, / Box and Picktooth*, cum caeteris" property note at the opening of III, i. This, too, may have been written by the author. Repeated in the 1682 quarto.

P. 26 "[*Call Servant*" actor warning c.23 lines before entrance in III, i. Not repeated in the 1682 quarto, perhaps because it is clearly a trace of prompt copy.

P. 29 "*Call* Jollyman" actor warning c.16 lines before entrance in III, i. Not repeated in the 1682 quarto.

P. 31 "*Letter*" property note following the stage direction at the opening of III, ii, reading, "Scene 2. *Covent-Garden.*" This may be the author's note. Repeated in the 1682 quarto.

P. 37 "[*Call* Bellmore *Footman*" actor warning c.19 lines before entrance in III, ii. Not repeated in the 1682 quarto.

The three certain traces of prompt copy were omitted from the 1682 quarto, which suggests that the 1682 printer knew which notes were made by the prompter and which by the author.

The British Library copy of the 1677 quarto also contains many manuscript markings. Occasional sentences in speeches are underlined and sometimes marked with double vertical lines in the margin as well. A few speeches are given sketchy marginal brackets. *Bell* (for Bellamore) is written in front of the portion of Madam Fickle's speech on page 34 reading, "*Jack Manly*, thine, Dear Rogue!" That seems to correct a printer's omission of a speech ascription. On the cast page the spelling of Mrs. Barry's name is altered from "*Barrer*" to "*Barrey*." These are perhaps some reader's markings, but the reader may have been someone in the Duke's Company.

Sir Patient Fancy *by Aphra Behn*

1678 first quarto containing a few possible traces of prompt copy related to the Duke's Company production at Dorset Garden Theatre on 17 January 1678. Copy studied: British Library 643 h 9 (4).

Mrs. Behn's plays are often full of detailed stage directions and very specific instructions on scene changes, so it is especially difficult to tell whether the notes below were made by her or by the prompter or property man. They are printed differently from the regular stage directions, however.

P. 5 "*A Chair and / a Table*" property note added to the stage direction for the entrance of Sir Credulous and Curry at the opening of I, [ii].

P. 54 "*A Table and Chairs*" property note at the opening of IV, ii.

P. 63 "*A Table, Sword, and Hatt*" property note at the opening of IV, [iv]. In this instance the note is printed as a second sentence in the opening stage direction describing Lady Fancy and Wittmore discovered in her bedchamber.

P. 69 "*A Table, and Six Chairs*" property note at the opening of V, i.

Squire Oldsapp *by Thomas D'Urfey*

1679 first quarto containing a few possible traces of prompt copy related to the Duke's Company production at Dorset Garden Theatre in June 1678. Copy studied: Folger D2786.

None of the notes quoted below can be certainly identified as traces of prompt copy, but some may have been written by the prompter or property man.

P. 20 "[*A snuff Box*" property note opposite Sir Frederick's line, ". . . dost thou see this here———" in II, ii.

P. 38 "*Table, Chairs, and Wine*" property note at the opening of IV, ii. No setting is described, and it would be odd for an author to list properties and nothing else.

P. 58 "*Table, Chairs, and Bottles of Wine*" property note at the opening of V, iii. No setting is described.

The Woman-Captain *by Thomas Shadwell*

1680 first quarto containing two traces of prompt copy related to the Duke's Company production at Dorset Garden Theatre about September 1679. Copy studied: British Library 644 i 35.

P. 25 "[*Boy with a Flambeaux ready*" actor and property warning c.40 lines before entrance near the end of Act II. The stage direction for the entrance reads, "*Enter Footmen / with Flambeaux*."

P. 38 "Gripe *and* Richard" actor warning c.4 lines before entrance near the end of Act III. This note is added to a stage direction bringing the High Constable and the Watch onstage. After a few lines of dialogue there is a scuffle which ends with Gripe and Richard being brought on as prisoners. The warning should have been placed earlier.

The Virtuous Wife *by Thomas D'Urfey*

1680 first quarto containing a possible trace of prompt copy related to the Duke's Company production at Dorset Garden Theatre in September 1679. Copy studied: Folger D2790.

The single possible trace of prompt copy is in II, [i] and is set apart from the stage direction for the entrance of Lady Beardly and others.

P. 16 "*A Chair / set on.*" The note may have been written by the author.

The Revenge *by Aphra Behn(?)*

1680 first quarto containing a few possible traces of prompt copy related to the Duke's Company production at Dorset Garden Theatre between January and April 1680. Copy studied: British Library 643 d 55.

The authorship of this alteration of Marston's *The Dutch Courtezan* is in doubt; a Luttrell manuscript note attributes it to Mrs. Behn, but *A Comparison Between the Two Stages* (1702) gives it to Thomas Betterton. Judith Milhous argues against the Betterton attribution in the *Bulletin of the New York Public Library* (p. 380). All the possible traces in the copy are clustered within signatures H and I.

P. 49 "*Table* and *Lights*" property note following the stage direction, "ACT the Fifth. / SCENE the First. *Corina's House.*"

P. 53 "*Two Chairs, a Table*" property note following the stage direction, "SCENE [i.e. V, ii] *Sir Lyonel*'s House."

P. 57 "*Great-gate*" setting for V, [iii], printed just before the stage direction, "SCENE changes to the Front of *New-gate* at / the Grate two or three Prisoners, one a beging, a Box / hangs out." "*Great-gate*" is almost certainly a prompter's note augmenting the author's stage direction, and this suggests that the two previous notes may also be traces of prompt copy, since they were set in print the same way.

In addition to the possible traces of prompt copy in the text there are some curious listings on the cast page that may have been prompter's notes. The cast is arranged in three columns, the first naming the actors, the second the characters, and the third providing character descriptions. This is done consistently except for three minor characters, who are listed as follows:

Captain,	Jervice,	*His man.*
A Boy,	Sam,	Dashit'*s man,*
Mumford,	Jack,	*The Barber's man.*

The "*Captain*" applied to the servant Jervice in the cast list is not used for that character in the text; "*Mumford*" is the actor William Mountfort. This might suggest that some actor called Captain played Jervice. Among the women's names on the cast page, "*Any-body*" is listed to play the servingwoman Ample. That may also have been a prompter's note.

Theodosius *by Nathaniel Lee*

1680 first quarto containing two traces of prompt copy related to the Duke's Company production at Dorset Garden Theatre, perhaps in the early summer of 1680. Copy studied: British Library 841 f 50.

The first example below is a certain trace of prompt copy; the second may have been written by the author, though it is printed very like the first.

P. 4 "[*Recorders ready to flourish*" sound effect warning 31 lines in advance, in I, i.

"[*Recorders flourish*" sound effect cue in I, i, following Varanes's line, "Retire, my Fair."

The City Heiress *by Aphra Behn*

1682 first quarto containing a possible trace of prompt copy related to the Duke's Company production at Dorset Garden Theatre in late April 1682. Copy studied: Folger B1719.

P. 28 "[*Enter Bottles and Glasses*" property cue in III, i. This is a quaint way of cuing an actor and his properties and the printer may have left out "Servant" or some other words. But prompt notes do not usually use the term "Enter," so this note may have derived from the author's stage direction. .

4 / The United Company (1682–1694)

In 1682 the two patent companies, the Duke's and the King's, merged, forming the United Company. Drury Lane Theatre was the troupe's main house, though the scanty records show that the players used the Dorset Garden playhouse on occasion for spectacle productions. The two theatres evidently remained unchanged during the life of the United Company. By the end of 1693 control of the troupe had passed out of the hands of the Davenant and Killigrew families and into those of the wily lawyer Christopher Rich and his partner Sir Thomas Skipwith. Rich's tyrannical ways so irked the older players that, led by Thomas Betterton, most of them rebelled and asked the Lord Chamberlain for a license to operate their own company. Their plea was granted, and they set themselves up at the Lincoln's Inn Fields playhouse in 1695.

Constantine the Great *by Nathaniel Lee*

1684 first quarto containing a few traces of prompt copy related to the United Company production at Drury Lane Theatre on 12 November 1683. Copy studied: British Library 644 h 60.

P. 12 "*Ready Trumpets, a / March at Distance*" sound effect warning 23 lines in advance in II, [i].

"*Call Serena*" actor warning 37 lines before entrance in II, [i].

P. 14 "*Ready Trumpets / for a Call*" sound effect warning c.28 lines in advance in II, [i]. No stage direction cues this effect, but it should come on page 15 just before Fausta says, "Your Fathers Trumpets call you." There may have been a cue (possibly the common cross-hatch mark) in the original promptbook.

P. 16 "*Trumpets ready for a Call*" sound effect warning 26 lines in advance in II, [i].

P. 18 "*Call* Dalmatius, Crispus, / *all Attendants*" actor warning 31 lines before entrance in II, [i]. The stage direction bringing these characters on does not mention the attendants.

P. 51 "*The Scene a Bedchamber. / A Bowl and a Dagger on the Table*" setting for V, ii. This reads like a stage direction written by the author, but it is printed and worded differently from the two other locale descriptions in the text (I, ii: "*ROME. Constantines Palace*" and II, [i]: "*ROME*") and thus may have been written by the prompter or machinist. Most of the scenes in the play do not have locale descriptions.

Valentinian *by John Wilmot, Earl of Rochester*

1685 first quarto containing a few traces of prompt copy related to the United Company production at court (and at Drury Lane Theatre); the court performance took place on 11 February 1684. Copy studied: British Library 644 f 83.

Rochester's alteration of Fletcher's play is known to have been presented at court, and though we have no dates for performances at Drury Lane, the title page of the first quarto contains the fairly standard puff: ". . . Acted at the / Theatre-Royal." There is no way of telling whether the original promptbook was prepared for the court performance or for Drury Lane; a single promptbook may have served for both. Indeed, a promptbook containing special notes applicable only to a performance at court would hardly be useful at the company's theatre, where the play would be performed much more frequently. In any case, the traces of prompt copy are few in number.

P. 33 "*A Ring!*" property note in the margin opposite the stage direction for Lycias' entrance in III, iii. The ring will be needed in two and a half pages. The exclamation mark may have been the prompter's way of indicating that the ring had been forgotten in one of the rehearsals.

P. 43 "[*Call Emperor behind*" actor warning 30 lines before entrance in IV, ii. The stage direction on page 44 for the Emperor's entrance does not say where he enters, but this note by the prompter would indicate an upstage entrance, perhaps between the wings or from the shutter area.

P. 44 "*Ring*" possibly a property note, following the stage direction for the entrance of the Emperor and Lucina in IV, ii. The note seems to concern the ring Lucina is now wearing, though there are no references to it in the dialogue; nothing in the text would suggest that the note refers to a sound effect or bell cue. But Chylax has just said, "Hark, I hear 'em"—referring to their footsteps; could the prompter have used a bell cue for the offstage steps?

P. 58 "A Letter" property note at the opening of V, i, printed after the stage direction, "*Æcius Solus.*" This may be the author's note.

P. 66 "[Aretus *here*" marginal note following Pontius' line, "He did me / All the disgrace he could" in V, iii. This note may be a trace of a warning for the entrance of Phidius, Aretus, and Æcius c.23 lines hence, at the opening of V, iv, but the dialogue in V, iv suggests that Aretus eavesdropped during V, iii, so I take this note to be his cue, written by the prompter or perhaps by the author.

A Fool's Preferment *by Thomas D'Urfey*

1688 first quarto containing a few traces of prompt copy related to the United Company production at Dorset Garden Theatre about April 1688. Noted in Robert Forsythe's *A Study of the Plays of Thomas D'Urfey* (Cleveland: Western Reserve University Press, 1916). Copy studied: British Library 644 h 20.

D'Urfey's adaptation of Fletcher's *Noble Gentleman* contains a handful of prompt traces.

P. 53 "Lyonel, Toby *go above*" actor note just before the entrance of Celia and the Doctor in IV, i. This may be the author's note.

P. 56 "*Call* Longo, / Bewford" actor warning 11 lines before entrance in IV, i.

P. 75 "*(Call* Maria" actor warning 30 lines before entrance in V, i.

Forsythe cites only the second and third examples above as traces of prompt copy.

The British Library copy studied contains numerous very faint markings, possibly theatrical in origin, consisting chiefly of brackets and boxing, possibly for intended cuts. These marks seem to be restricted to pages 10–19, 40, and 48–51. There is one very faint word, *beg[in?]*, in the margin opposite the entrance of Cockle-brain and Toby in I, i.

The Treacherous Brothers *by George Powell*

1690 first quarto containing a trace of prompt copy related to the United Company production at Drury Lane Theatre about January 1690. Copy studied: British Library 1346 e 13.

George Powell was an actor and probably wrote most of the many stage directions in the text dealing with stage business, properties, scenery, sound effects, and the like. Yet some notes in the original manuscript may have been made by the prompter. The one almost certain trace of prompt copy is unusual.

P. 61 "[*Enter Mr.* Harris]" actor entrance cue just before the scene changes to show the executed men being thrown from the battlements, at the end of V, v. The Harris in question was Joseph, and the role he played was apparently Bassanes, a character not listed in the dramatis personae. The author did not give Bassanes an entrance at this point, but he should have. A prompter's note such as this one, naming an actor, is common in warnings but rare in entrance cues.

Bussy D'Ambois *by Thomas D'Urfey*

1691 first quarto containing a few traces of prompt copy related to the United Company production at Drury Lane Theatre about March 1691. Noted in Robert Forsythe's *A Study of the Plays of Thomas D'Urfey* (Cleveland: Western Reserve University Press, 1916). Copy studied: British Library 644 g 32.

The traces of prompt copy in D'Urfey's alteration of Chapman's play are all warnings, and all of the traces appear between pages 26 and 39 (gatherings E and F); one of the compositors was careless, for which we thank him very much.

P. 26 "[*Call Page*, Maff." actor warning 22 lines before entrance in III, [iii]. (The scene is misnumbered III, ii in the text.)

P. 27 "[*Call* Dambo." actor warning 28 lines before entrance in III, [iii].

P. 32 "[*Call* Tamira, Charlot" actor warning 20 lines before entrance in IV, i.

P. 38 "[*Call* Mountsurry, Monsieur, *and* Guise" actor warning 36 lines before entrance (but 21 lines before Monsurry's offstage speech) in IV, iii.

P. 39 "[*Call* Charlot *Letter*" actor and property warning 16 lines before entrance in IV, iii.

The British Library copy studied contains occasional manuscript underlinings and the words *Sapless Dyet* (on p. 35), but these seem to be nontheatrical.

Madam Fickle (1682) *by Thomas D'Urfey*

1682 second quarto with a few manuscript prompt notes and three manuscript cast lists, plus some possible traces of prompt copy carried over from the 1677 edition; the manuscript notes are probably related to a production of the play by the United Company at Drury Lane Theatre or Dorset Garden Theatre about spring or summer 1691; in British Library copy 18953 (2). Casts and dating discussed by Edward A. Langhans in "New Restoration Manuscript Casts," *Theatre Notebook*, 27 (Summer 1973), 149–57.

Though far from a complete promptbook, this copy of *Madam Fickle* contains much useful information. The play was performed at Dorset Garden Theatre by the Duke's Company by 4 November 1676; the first quarto appeared the following year with a license date of 20 November 1676, and it contains some traces of prompt copy (transcribed in chapter 3). The second quarto of 1682, in which some but not all of the possible traces of prompt copy in the 1677 edition were dropped, was used as a basis for a new promptbook, probably for a production by the United Company. Thus, the old Duke's Company promptbook of 1676 was by 1682 considered inadequate, and a new book was prepared, or at least partly prepared. The prompter, after entering only a few notes here and there in the first three acts, seems to have abandoned the copy. Maybe he decided to continue using the old 1676 promptbook after all, altering it to suit a production with different actors in, perhaps, a different playhouse.

P. 1 *–++++++++++++–* entrance cue for Jollyman and Henry at the opening of Act I.

P. 2 *[Di]ck Barnes* opposite a song in I, i. Jollyman has speeches before and after the song and would be the logical character to sing it. The naming of the actor Richard Barnes probably means that Barnes was brought on to sing the song in lieu of the actor playing Jollyman, who either could not or would not sing it.

Lord *Bellamore.*	Mr. *Betterton.*
Manley Friend to *Bellam.*	Mr. *Smith.*
Sir Arthur Oldlove, an Antiquary.	Mr. *Sandford.*
Captain *Tilbury,* an old faſhion'd blunt Fellow.	Mr. *Medbourn.*
Zechiel. Sons to *Tilbury.*	Mr. *Anthony Leigh.*
Toby.	Mr. *James Nokes.*
Old *Jollyman.*	Mr. *Underhill.*
Harry, Son to *Jollyman.*	Mr. *Jevan.*
Flaile, Servant to *Tilbury.*	Mr. *Richards.*
Dorrel, alias *Friendlove.*	Mr. *Norrice.*
WOMEN.	
Madam Fickle.	Mrs. *Mary Lee.*
Conſtantia, Daughter to *Sir Arthur.*	Mrs. *Barrer.*
Arbella.	Mr. *Gibbs.*
Silvia Attendant to *Fickle.*	Mrs. *Napper.*
Three Wenches.	
Conſtable, Watch, Footmen, Maskers, Muſitioners, and Attendants.	

SCENE
Covent-Garden.

From D'Urfey's *Madam Fickle* (1682). By kind permission of the British Library.

P. 15 *what* inserted to replace a deleted "with" in the sixth line of Silvia's song in II, ii; this note is not in the prompter's hand and may have been a correction made by an owner of the copy.

P. 19 *Act R[eady]* warning for the end of Act II, c.30 lines in advance. This note, like others in the copy, is badly cropped. Also on this page is what may be a trace of earlier prompt copy: "[*A Ring*" refers to a costume accessory which Manly gives to Madam Fickle. This printed note appeared in the 1677 edition of the play.

P. 20 Another possible trace of prompt copy, also carried over from the 1677 edition, is a printed note following the opening stage direction in II, i: "[*A Table with Scull, Sword, Vial, Shooing-horn, / Box and Picktooth,* cum caeteris."

P. 26 *[Har]ry & Manly:* at the opening of III, ii. The printed stage direction failed to indicate their entrance, so the prompter supplied their names. He did not make a cross-hatch entrance cue sign. In the printed stage direction at this point is yet another possible trace of prompt copy, again carried over from the 1677 edition; the full direction reads: "Scene 2. *Covent-Garden, Letter.*" Authors sometimes mentioned properties, but the wording here is typical of prompt notes.

The only other manuscript notes within the text of the play appear on page 40 and may be doodles, perhaps by a reader. Cropping has lost us some of the scribbling, but what is left happens to spell out a name. Along the left edge of the page are the following letters:

S
Ch
n
g
G
e
o
r
g
e

These letters seem to have no connection with the action of the play.

The manuscript cast lists in the copy (see illustration) are badly cropped, and several entries are canceled, blotted, or scribbled over:

Dramatis Personae.

Pow:[11]	Lord *Bellamore*. ——	Mr. *Betterton*.	Mr Alexand^r ~~M~~
[A]lex:	*Manley* Friend to *Bellam*. —	Mr. *Smith*.	M^r: powell. ~~M^r~~
	Sir Arthur Oldlove, an Antiquary. —	Mr. *Sandford*.	Mr Sandford.
[F]reeman	Captain *Tilbury*, an old fashion'd blunt Fellow. —	Mr. Medbourn.	Mr Cudworth ~~M^r~~
[B]owen	*Zechiel*. } Sons to *Tilbury*. ——	Mr. *Anthony Leigh*.	M^r powell ~~M^r~~
~~Bright~~	*Toby*. } trefusis ——	Mr. *James Nokes*.	Mr Trefusis ~~M^r~~
~~Baker~~	Old *Jollyman*. [~~Bri~~]ght ——	Mr. *Underhill*.	Mr Bright. ~~M^r~~
Hodgson	*Harry*, Son to *Jollyman*. ——	Mr. *Jevan*.	~~M^r~~
Chappell	*Flaile*, Servant to *Tilbury*. —	Mr. *Richards*.	~~M^r~~
Harris	*Dorrel*, alias *Friendlove*. ——	Mr. *Norrice*.	~~M^r L~~

Women.

Correr	*Madam Fickle*. ——	Mrs. *Mary Lee*.	Mrs Momfort ~~M^{rs}~~
k^t:	*Constantia*, Daughter to *Sir Arthur*. ——	Mrs. *Barrer*.	~~M^{rs} C~~
Cockey	*Arbella*. ——	Mr. *Gibbs*.	~~M^{rs}~~
Davis	*Silvia* Attendant to *Fickle*. —	Mrs. *Napper*.	~~M^{rs}~~

Three Wenches.

Trefusis. *Constable, Watch, Footmen, Maskers, Musitioners, and Attendants.*

SCENE

Covent-Garden.

To make much of the third list is impossible, but the first two, with some guesswork, can be reconstructed:

George Powell	*Lord Bellamore*	Mr. Alexander
Mr. Alexander	*Manley*	George Powell
	Sir Arthur Oldlove	Samuel Sandford
John Freeman	*Captain Tilbury*	Mr. Cudworth
William Bowen	*Zechiel*	Martin Powell
George Bright [canceled]	*Toby*	Joseph Trefusis
Joseph Trefusis		
Francis Baker [canceled]	*Old Jollyman*	George Bright
George Bright		
John Hodgson	*Harry*	
Mr. Chappell	*Flaile*	
Joseph Harris	*Dorrel*	
Elizabeth Currer	*Madam Fickle*	Susanna Mountfort
Frances Maria Knight [?]	*Constantia*	
Mrs. Cockye	*Arbella*	
Katherine Davis	*Silvia*	
	Three Wenches	
Joseph Trefusis	*Constable, Watch, Footmen, Maskers, Musitioners, and Attendants.*	

In the above lists, Alexander may be John Verbruggen, for he is said to have acted under that name until 1695; however, Montague Summers in his edition of Congreve's *The Old Bachelor* has an explanatory note (I, 246–47) observing that there may have been another actor named Alexander in the United Company. The Harris named is certainly Joseph (*The London Stage* under 1689–90 questions the Christian name, but it is correct). Mr. Chappell is an actor not named in other Restoration documents. My conjecture of Mrs. Knight for the role of Constantia is perhaps far-fetched; the manuscript note, like all those for the first cast, runs into the gutter of the copy. The note seems to be k^t or h^t and is an abbreviation rather than the tail end of a name. Mrs. Knight's name is the only one that seems to come close to matching. Listed beside the Constable and other minor roles is the ubiquitous Joseph Trefusis. He could not have played both Toby and the Constable, for they are onstage together at one point; he apparently played Toby and some other small part, of which there are several in the play not listed on the cast page.

The two lists may have been for two different productions, since they are in different hands, but they might also be preliminary and final casts for the same production, jotted down by two different people. In any case, all of the actors listed were working together in the United Company between 1689 and 1695, as was Dick Barnes, whose name is mentioned in the prompt notes. About spring or summer 1691 seems the likeliest time for both lists and for the promptbook. The play was reprinted the following fall—a good indication of a recent revival. Since some of the more famous actors in the troupe—Thomas Betterton and Elizabeth Barry, for instance, who had created major roles in *Madam Fickle* when it was originally produced—are not included in the manuscript casts, a Lenten or summer production seems indicated. The printed cast in the 1682 quarto incidentally, is simply a reprint of the names listed in the 1677 first edition but with a typographical error that turned Mrs. Gibbs into a man.

The Richmond Heiress *by Thomas D'Urfey*

1693 first quarto containing a few traces of prompt copy related to the United Company production at Drury Lane Theatre about mid-April 1693. One trace cited in Robert Forsythe's *A Study of the Plays of Thomas D'Urfey* (Cleveland: Western Reserve University Press, 1916). Copy studied: British Library 644 h 23.

Some misnumbering in the 1693 edition has been corrected below.

[P. 33] "*Exit Sir* Quib. *and* Dog." actor exit note in III, iii containing an actor's name (Thomas Doggett) instead of the name of the character he played (Quickwit). This may have been the author's slip if D'Urfey wrote the part with Doggett in mind; there are similar errors elsewhere in the text. The prompter would not normally insert exit notes in the promptbook unless the author had forgotten them. The pagination is off in the first edition; this page is incorrectly numbered 29.

[P. 40] "(*Exit* Dogget *and* Marm." actor exit note in IV, i containing an actor's name, as in the previous example. This page is incorrectly numbered 36.

P. 41 "[*Call Quickwitt*" actor warning 8 lines before entrance in IV, i. No earlier warning was possible, since Quickwit has just made an exit (though no stage direction for it was provided) and will reenter shortly. The text at this point contains several errors: the catchword at the bottom of [p. 40] does not match the first word on page 41; no stage direction brings Quickwit onstage for his soliloquy at the top of page 41; no stage direction takes him off after it; and the direction on page 41 for Marmalet should include Cunning. There is little wonder that the trace of prompt copy got into print. The call for Quickwit is cited by Forsythe.

P. 48 "*Enter Sir* Quibble, Fulvia, Dogget *and* Marmalett" actor entrance cue at the opening of IV, iv containing an actor's name.

P. 49 "[*Sir* Charles. T. Romance, Shink. Guiac. *Constable*" actor warning 18 lines before entrance in IV, iv. The stage direction for the entrance also includes Sophronia and the Watch; they have no lines and may have been omitted from the scene when the play was acted.

P. 50 "[*to* Doggett" actor note following Marmalet's speech near the beginning of V, i which begins, "I'm sure my loss . . ."

The British Library copy studied also contains, as did the copies of D'Urfey's *A Fool's Preferment* and *Madam Fickle* (1677 quarto), occasional faint manuscript marks: vertical lines in the margin opposite some speeches, brackets opposite others, double diagonal or horizontal lines opposite still others, and, most curiously, *Cunning* at the top of page 41, where the stage direction omits an entrance for that character. Perhaps these markings were theatrical in origin, but most do not seem to be notes a prompter or his colleagues would make. Did these copies belong to actors, perhaps?

5 / Christopher Rich's Company (1695–1709)

In December 1694 some of the older players in the United Company petitioned against the harsh management of Christopher Rich and Sir Thomas Skipwith, and in March 1695 the rebels were granted a license to set up a new company led by Thomas Betterton. Most of the performers who stayed with Rich were less experienced, and the troupe could not match their rivals in quality. But Rich (with Skipwith as a relatively silent partner) had Drury Lane Theatre and, when needed for lavish machine plays, the playhouse in Dorset Garden, both of which were finer theatres than Betterton's refurbished house in Lincoln's Inn Fields. But by 1698–99 Dorset Garden was little-used by Rich's company, and in 1699–1700 the venerable theatre was rented to the Kentish Strong Man William Joy for his displays of physical prowess. It was used from time to time in the early years of the eighteenth century, and in 1709 it was torn down. (In 1709, too, Rich lost control of his company.)

Drury Lane, on the other hand, remained busy to the end of the seventeenth century and, though remodeled several times in the following century, was not completely reconstructed until 1791. Rich made a significant alteration in 1696, shortly after Betterton's rebellion. According to Colley Cibber in his *Apology*, Rich cut back the forestage four feet and replaced the downstage proscenium doors with boxes. Rich thereby gained some seating capacity and the players, lamented Cibber, were drawn further upstage. Cibber described Rich as constantly busy creating nooks and crannies around the playhouse, but we have no way of knowing if any of those alterations affected the staging of plays as, clearly, the cutting back of the forestage did. Cibber did not like being so far away from the middle of the auditorium: ". . . the Voice was then [before the alteration] more in the Centre of the House, so that the most distant Ear had scarce the least doubt, or Difficulty in hearing what fell from the weakest Utterance . . ." (II, 85). The gradual withdrawal of the actor into the scenic area had begun.

Since no promptbooks have been found for productions by Rich's Company in the last five years of the seventeenth century, I have gone slightly beyond my date limits to include *The Albion Queens*, a play printed about 1714 with copious and interesting traces of prompt copy probably belonging to the Drury Lane production of the work in 1704.

Neglected Virtue

1696 first quarto containing a few traces of prompt copy related to the Rich Company production at Drury Lane Theatre about mid-February 1696. Copy studied: British Library 643 d 67.

The authorship of this play is in doubt; the dedication was signed by the actor Hildebrand Horden, under whose name the British Library catalogues the play, but he did not claim the work as his. If Horden had a hand in the writing of *Neglected Virtue* the wording used in the second and third traces cited below may have been his.

P. 28 "*Enter* Simpson" actor entrance cue naming the actor (Thomas Simpson) instead of the character (Curio) in IV, i. Perhaps this was the author's slip if the role was intended for Simpson, but Curio is a very small part, so that seems unlikely. I take the note to have been written by the prompter, possibly because the author omitted a stage direction.

P. 39 "SCENE, *Flat-Palace*" setting designation for V, [ii]. This would be a most unusual way for an author to describe a locale unless he was very familiar with stage terminology. Horden, for example, might have used such a term. But it is just as likely that this was a note by the prompter or machinist.

P. 43 "*Town, a Scaffold behind the Flat-Palace. The Scene opens, and discovers /* Artaban *led away by a Procession of Guards, bound to a Scaffold, as he is / going,*—" setting description for V, iii. This is the complete stage direction, though it appears broken off. The terminology again would seem to come from someone familiar with scenery labels (see, for comparison, the references to flat scenes in the prompt traces in *Guzman* at the Duke's Company playhouse in 1669). The term "Flat-Palace" would seem to refer to a pair of shutters, behind which a scaffold was set. The first sentence of this note may have been written by the prompter or machinist to explain the setting to be used. The second sentence may have been written by the author.

The Albion Queens *by John Banks*

Undated first quarto (c. 1714) containing extensive traces of prompt copy probably related to the Rich Company production at Drury Lane Theatre on 6 March 1704. Discussed by Montague Summers in *The Restoration Theatre* (London: Kegan Paul, Trench, Trubner, 1934), pp. 141–42; cast and date studied by James J. Devlin in "The Dramatis Personae and the Dating of John Banks's 'The Albion Queens,'" *Notes and Queries*, 208 (June 1963), 213–15. Copy studied: British Library 644 g 3.

Banks's alteration of his own *The Island Queens* (banned in 1684) dates just outside the period covered by this study, but so many interesting prompt notes found their way into the c. 1714 edition that I trust no one will object if I provide transcriptions of all the traces. Further, we have so little evidence relating to Rich's troupe that *The Albion Queens* is much needed to show us staging at the end of the Restoration period.

The traces of prompt copy here are not only extensive, they differ greatly from those found in earlier books. For example, the use of proscenium doors—which one to use, which side to enter—seems in early days to have been left to the actors or recorded in some book other than the prompter's. In Appendix B there is a facsimile of the Dublin promptbook for *Belphegor*, which shows that the Dubliners early on developed a system of identifying entranceways. If their London counterparts had such a system, there is no evidence of it in promptbooks. But the system revealed in *The Albion Queens* may well have been used long before 1704. It is found in many promptbooks of the early eighteenth century. The following abbreviations are used to indicate entrances:

LDOP	lower door, opposite prompt
MDOP	middle door, opposite prompt
UDOP	upper door, opposite prompt
LDPS	lower door, prompt side
MDPS	middle door, prompt side
UDPS	upper door, prompt side

Not all promptbooks use all of those designations; in *The Albion Queens* there are no references to middle doors. Since Drury Lane after 1696 had only one proscenium door on each side of the forestage, the references to upper doors must have been to entranceways between the wings or doors in wing units. (See the comments in Appendix D on notes in early eighteenth-century promptbooks concerning entrance doors.)

If these entrance designations were set down in the promptbooks of the eighteenth century, perhaps Restoration prompters or actors used similar abbreviations but recorded them elsewhere. Players working in a repertory system, with many plays in their heads simultaneously, must not have wanted to trust their memories about entrance positions. Perhaps Restoration entrance plots were posted backstage.

Act I, Scene i

P. 2 "A LETTER for Mr. *Wilks*" property and actor warning 38 lines before the entrance of Norfolk. This note is oddly printed: it interrupts the dialogue completely, and the printer treated it as though it were a scene heading, complete with a horizontal rule dividing it from the speech before it.

P. 3 "*V.D.O.P.*" door indication for Norfolk's entrance. The note serves both to indicate which entrance to use and to cue the actor to go onstage.

P. 5 "Mrs. *Knight*, Mr. *Mills*, Mr. *Williams*, Ladies, Gentlemen, Guards / Behind" actor warning 45 lines before the entrance of "Queen *Eliz. Morton, Davison*, Women, Gent. Guards, all discover'd / at the Throne." The "Behind" in the warning indicates that the group formed a tableau behind closed shutters or a drop upstage.

"A LETTER for Mr. *Mills*" property warning 39 lines in advance. Again the printer treated the note as a scene heading.

Act II, Scene i

P. 13 "V.D.P.S." door indication for Norfolk's entrance at the opening of II, i. See illustration.

"*V.D.O.P.*" door indication for Morton's entrance.

P. 15 "Mrs. *Knight*, Capt. *Griffin*, Ladies, Gentlemen, Guards" actor warning 44 lines before the entrance of "Q. Eliz. Cecil, *Attendants and Guards.*"

P. 16 "V.D.P.S." door indication for the entrance of the above group. In *The Rover* promptbook (see Appendix D) the door indications are placed, more sensibly, with the warnings rather than the entrances.

"*V.D.P.S.*" door indication for Davison's entrance.

P. 18 "[*Shout here*" sound effect cue. This note, which may have been written by the author rather than the prompter, appears three times on this page.

P. 19 "V.D.P.S." door indication for the entrance of Queen Mary, Dowglass, two gentlemen, and four ladies. Perhaps the numbers of the supernumeraries in this stage direction were added by the prompter.

P. 21 "*L.D.O.P.*" door indication for Norfolk's entrance.

Mary *Queen of* Scotts. 13

ACTUS SECUNDUS,
Scœna Prima.
Norfolk Solus. V. D. P. S.

Nor. SHout the Loud world, ſound all the vaſt Creation,
Let proud *Auguſta* clad in Robes of Triumph,
Thro' her glad Streets, with Golden Trumpets ſound,
And Ecchoe to the Ocean that She comes;
Maria comes proclaim it to the clouds,
Let the four winds from diſtant corners meet,
And on their wings, firſt bear it into *France*,
Then back agen to *Edina*'s proud walls,
Till Victim to the ſound th' aſpiring city falls.

Enter Morton. *V. D. O. P.*

Mor. My Lord, I came to find you.
Nor. Pardon me,
The mighty Joy that has ſince fill'd my Breaſt,
And left no Room for other Thoughts, has made me
Forget that you and I were angry.
Mor. And I. My Lord—
Brave Spirits ſhou'd be ſtirr'd to wrath,
As ſeldom as the Center is with Earth-quakes,
Not like the Sea diſturb'd with every blaſt;
I came to ſpeak with you, but as a friend.
Laſt night when laid to reſt, prepar'd for ſlumber,
That gives ſoft eaſe to all but ſorrowful
And guilty mind, a ſudden dread aſſail'd me——
Inſpir'd by ſome ſuperiour Power that aw'd
And ſtole quick Paſſage to my cruel boſom.
My barb'rous *Z*eal, for a more barb'rous cauſe,
Began to ſlack, whilſt true Remorſe and Pity
Surpriz'd my Soul, and held it for the Queen.

Nor. O

From Banks's *The Albion Queens*. By kind permission of the British Library.

P. 24 *"L.D.P.S."* door indication for the entrance of Davison and Guards.

Act III, Scene i

P. 25 "O.P.P.S." side indication for the entrances of Morton and Davison, simultaneously and from opposite sides of the stage, at the opening of III, i. Why did the prompter not indicate which door—or plane of the stage—the actors should use? Perhaps it was understood that when no specific indication was given, the furthest downstage entrance (or furthest upstage, or whatever) should be used.

P. 27 "*V.D.O.P.*" door indication for Gifford's entrance, meeting Davison as he exits.

P. 31 "*V.D.P.S.*" door indication for the entrance of Norfolk and Morton.

Act IV, Scene i

P. 38 "*V.D.P.S.*" door indication for the entrance of Norfolk and two Guards. The number of guards may have been added to the original stage direction by the prompter.

P. 39 "*V.D.P.S.*" door indication for the entrance of Queen Elizabeth, Morton, gentlemen, guards, and ladies.

P. 40 "*V.D.O.P.*" door indication for Gifford's entrance.

P. 44 "*L.D.P.S.*" door indication for the entrance of Queen Mary, Dowglass, ladies, and gentlemen.

Act V, [Scene ii]

P. 52 "[Alcove *with a Table, Pen, Ink and Paper, and Chairs*]" setting and properties for V, [ii]. This may have been written by the author, but it is worded and printed like a prompt note.

P. 57 "[*Soft Musick ready with Flutes*]" sound effect warning 22 lines in advance.

P. 58 "*Soft Musick here*" sound effect cue. This may have been written by the author. The printer put brackets around some notes and centered them on the page, indicating, perhaps, a different hand in the manuscript. But not in this case.

Act V, [Scene iii]

"[*A Table, at the upper End of the Stage*]" property note at the opening of V, [iii].

6 / Thomas Betterton's Company (1695–1706)

Thomas Betterton, who began his acting career at the Restoration under Sir William Davenant, rebelled in December 1694 against the management of Christopher Rich at the Drury Lane and Dorset Garden theatres. The petition Betterton submitted to the Lord Chamberlain was signed by many of the older players, foremost among whom were Betterton's two brilliant leading ladies, Elizabeth Barry and Anne Bracegirdle. On 25 March 1695 the rebel group was granted a license to set up a new company, and on 30 April they opened with Congreve's *Love for Love* at the theatre in Lincoln's Inn Fields. There they performed for over ten years.

No one has attempted a reconstruction of the Lincoln's Inn Fields playhouse of the 1690s. It was the third use of that name: the Duke's Company had originally converted the tennis court in Lincoln's Inn Fields and used it as a playhouse from 1661 to 1671; the King's Company occupied it from 1672 to 1674; and Betterton set up his troupe in the (same?) building in 1695. The old theatre had been reconverted to a tennis court by 1676, and whether Betterton turned that building or one near it to theatrical use we can not be certain; pictures on maps seem to suggest an altered or different structure. In any case, he was able to have his troupe in operation a month after receiving his license, so whatever building he occupied was easily convertible to use as a playhouse.

Unfortunately, no promptbooks have been found for Betterton's Company. The *Measure for Measure* promptbook listed in Shattuck's catalogue as for the Betterton Company has notes in the same hand as that found in the Dublin *Belphegor* promptbook and was presumably prepared for an Irish production; it is discussed in Appendix A. The two play texts revealing traces of Betterton Company prompt copy do not contain enough information to allow useful conjectures about the features of the third Lincoln's Inn Fields Theatre, but one supposes that the stage was arranged pretty much like others of the Restoration period.

She Ventures, and He Wins

1696 first quarto containing a few traces of prompt copy related to the Betterton Company production in mid-September 1695 at Lincoln's Inn Fields Theatre. Date discussed in Maximillian E. Novak's "The Closing of Lincoln's Inn Fields Theatre in 1695," *Restoration and 18th Century Theatre Research*, 14 (May 1975), 51–52. Copy studied: British Library 643 d 60.

This anonymous play, according to the title page, was "Written by Young Lady"; the British Library catalogue lists the work under

26 *She Ventures,*

Love. Ha! What ſhould be the meaning of this! [*Opens, and reads.*

——Diſpoſe of your ſelf as your Humour ſerves you, when you have done with the Employment I left you; for you will meet at this time with no other Entertainment from your Bride. [*Drawer ready.*

Death, Hell, and Furies! what can this mean! Am I thus Jilted at laſt by ſome lewd Woman! O Sot! that I could think one of *Charlot*'s Birth and Fortune would marry at that wild Rate. She only took up that Name to gull the eaſy Coxcomb, unthinkful Fool; I could curſe my ſelf, her, the Sex, and all the World. What ſhall I do, O dear damn'd Impoſtor! By Heaven I love her ſo, I can ſcarce repent I have made her mine; were ſhe but Honeſt, which much I fear, I would not change her for the Worlds Empreſs. But why do I flatter thus a ſenſeleſs Paſſion? This Toad, for ought I know, a leud Proſtitute, who only has drawn me in to go to Goal for her. O there it is! Some falſe fair Devil, forſaken by her Keeper, that wanted only a Husband for that uſe, or elſe to Father ſome Body's Child: But however, ſhe is no very poor Whore. [*Shews the Purſe.*

But this is no Place to Expoſtulate in. Here Drawer.

Drawer. Did you call, Sir?

Enter Dubois.

Love. Ay, what's to pay?

Drawer. All's paid, Sir, by the Ladies? [*Exit Drawer.*

Love. So that's ſome Comfort ſtill; come chear thy Heart, *Lovewell*; all yet may be well: They're Jilts of Quality however. I believe it is e'en ſome Lady errant that's run mad reading of *Don Quixot*; but hang't, jeſting is a little Unſavory at this time. I'll ſee if I can find out Sir *Roger Marwood*, who may tell me ſome Tidings of the true *Charlot*, though not of my fair damn'd Devil; O curſe of my Credulity.

Well; ſince this damn'd Jilt is gone,
I am fairly rid of all the Sex in one. [*Exit* Lovewell.

The end of the Third Act.

ACT IV. SCENE I.

Enter Lovewell, *and Drawer.*

Love. IS Sir *Roger Marwood* here?

Draw. Yes, Sir.

Love. Who's with him?

Draw. Only Sir *Charles Frankford.*

Love.

From *She Ventures, and He Wins.* By kind permission of the British Library.

"Ariadne." The piece failed, as Novak notes, and Betterton temporarily closed down the theatre.

P. 25 "*Enter* Frank *with a Note*" actor entrance cue in III, v, printed beside a stage direction reading, "*Enter Waiter with a Letter.*" "Frank" could be either an actor's or a character's name; I cannot find Frank mentioned elsewhere in the text, but see below.

P. 26 "[*Drawer ready*" actor warning c.13 lines before entrance in III, v, though no stage direction brings him on. See illustration.

"*Enter* Dubois" actor entrance cue in III, v. There is no Dubois in the dramatis personae, nor does *The London Stage* cite an actor of that name. I believe the author wrote dialogue and action involving a Drawer but forgot to provide him with an entrance; the prompter inserted an entrance warning ("[*Drawer ready*") and an entrance cue ("*Enter* Dubois"). Putting this together with the trace of prompt copy on page 25 we discover the name of an otherwise unknown actor: Frank Dubois. This was reported, but without details, in the fourth volume of the Highfill, Burnim, and Langhans *Biographical Dictionary of Actors*.

P. 27 "Call Drawer" actor warning c.18 lines before entrance in IV, i, printed, in error, as an aside by Lovewell, just before his exit with Sir Roger.

"Glasses and Bottles" property note added to a stage direction reading, "*Scene draws, discovers Sir* Charles Frankford writing at a Table." All of this may have been written by the author, but the wording "Glasses and Bottles" is similar to many prompt notes concerning properties. (The new scene should have been numbered IV, ii but was not.)

As in some other promptbooks, the traces of prompt copy in *She Ventures, and He Wins* appear in a cluster, suggesting that one compositor was less careful than the others. Here the traces are all on E1 and E2.

The Life and Death of Doctor Faustus
by William Mountfort

1697 first quarto containing a few traces of prompt copy probably related to the Betterton Company production at Lincoln's Inn Fields Theatre on 13 March 1697 (or possibly to the production by the United Company at Dorset Garden Theatre in the spring of 1688). Briefly discussed in W. S. Clark II's "Restoration Prompt Notes and Stage Practices," *Modern Lan-*

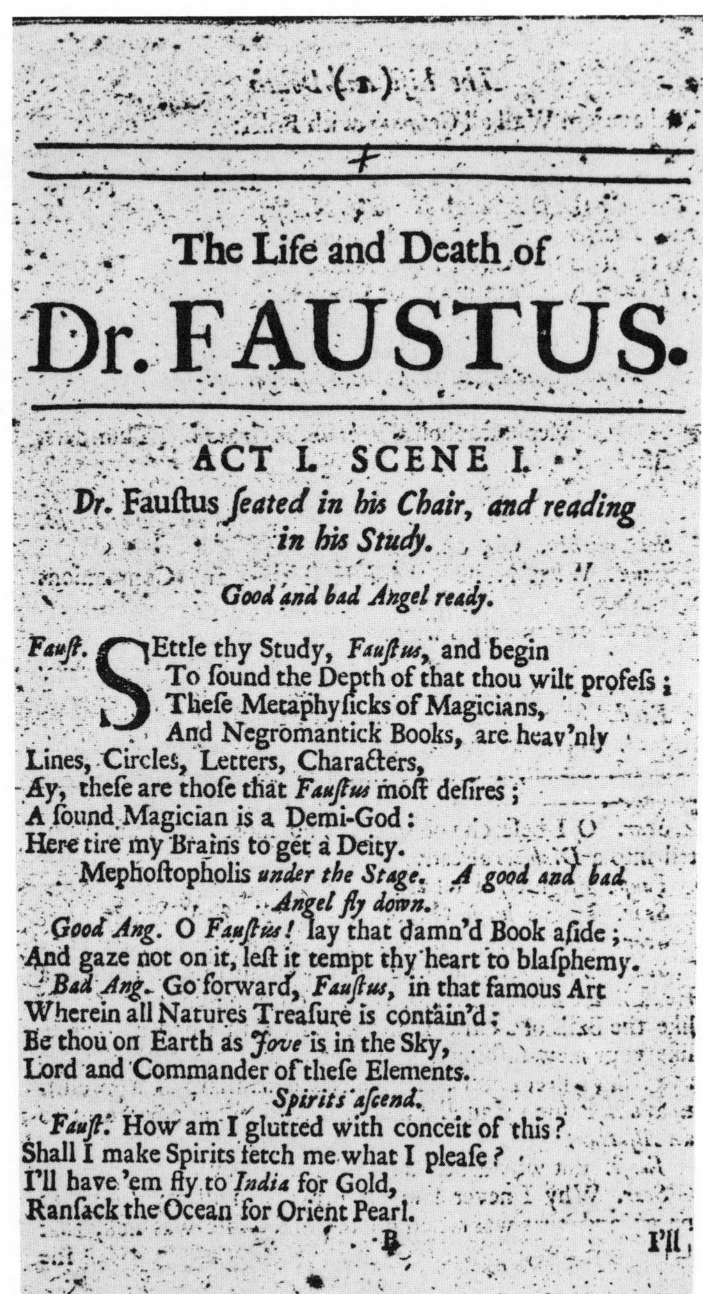

(1)

The Life and Death of

Dr. FAUSTUS.

ACT I. SCENE I.

Dr. Fauſtus *ſeated in his Chair, and reading in his Study.*

Good and bad Angel ready.

Fauſt. SEttle thy Study, *Fauſtus*, and begin
To ſound the Depth of that thou wilt profeſs;
Theſe Metaphyſicks of Magicians,
And Negromantick Books, are heav'nly
Lines, Circles, Letters, Characters,
Ay, theſe are thoſe that *Fauſtus* moſt deſires;
A ſound Magician is a Demi-God:
Here tire my Brains to get a Deity.

Mephoſtopholis *under the Stage. A good and bad Angel fly down.*

Good Ang. O *Fauſtus!* lay that damn'd Book aſide;
And gaze not on it, leſt it tempt thy heart to blaſphemy.
Bad Ang. Go forward, *Fauſtus*, in that famous Art
Wherein all Natures Treaſure is contain'd:
Be thou on Earth as *Jove* is in the Sky,
Lord and Commander of theſe Elements.

Spirits aſcend.

Fauſt. How am I glutted with conceit of this?
Shall I make Spirits fetch me what I pleaſe?
I'll have 'em fly to *India* for Gold,
Ranſack the Ocean for Orient Pearl.

B I'll

From Mountfort's *The Life and Death of Doctor Faustus*. By kind permission of the British Library.

guage Notes, 41 (April 1936), 226–30. Date discussed in Robert D. Hume's "The Date of Mountfort's *The Life and Death of Doctor Faustus*," *Archiv für das Studium der neueren Sprachen und Literaturen*, 213 (1976), 109–11. Copy studied: British Library 644 h 70.

Mountfort's farcical version of the Faustus story was not printed until some ten years after its first production, and there is no way of determining for certain whether the handful of prompt-copy traces in the first quarto pertain to the premiere or to the revival in 1697. I incline toward the revival, since the promptbook used by Betterton's Company was probably the copy given to the publisher. The text contains a great many stage directions calling for special effects, but since Mountfort was an actor familiar with stage terminology, most such notes could well have been written by him. Only three can clearly be credited to the prompter.

P. 1 "*Good and bad Angel ready*" actor warning 8 lines before entrance. No earlier warning could have been given, since this note comes at the opening of I, i. See illustration.

"Mephostopholis *under the Stage*" actor warning 17 lines before entrance in I, i, printed as part of a stage direction bringing the good and bad Angels down from above the stage.

P. 7 "[*Ring. Good and bad descend*" technical cue for the flymen to lower two actors from above the stage in I, i. The use of "*Ring*" here is unusual for London promptbooks but can be found in the Dublin *Belphegor* book, where it signaled special effects. London prompters usually reserved the ringing of a bell for act endings and entr'acte music. A signal that could be clearly heard by the flymen working the rigging system above the stage was certainly necessary; the use of a whistle might have confused the scene shifters.

7 / Nursery, Touring, and Summer Fair Productions (1660–1700)

In the spring of 1667 a "Nursery" or training theatre for young players was set up in Hatton Garden, jointly operated by the King's and Duke's companies and managed by Edward Bedford. The promptbook for *The Wise-Woman of Hogsdon*, a Nursery or possibly touring play, appears to have been prepared by the King's Company prompter or his helpers. According to Leslie Hotson in *The Commonwealth and Restoration Stage*, pages 187–91, the Nursery moved in 1668–69 to the Vere Street Theatre, which had been abandoned in 1663 by the King's players. John Perin had a 40′ by 60′ Nursery in Finsbury Fields (Bunhill) in 1671, and late that year Lady Davenant, Sir William's widow, established another Nursery in the Barbican. Though the nurseries did not flourish much beyond Dryden's mention of the Barbican house in *MacFlecknoe* in 1682, the idea was a good one, and a number of young actors (Joe Haines was one of the most successful) were provided with theatre training.

Of the physical features of the Vere Street Theatre we have some information (discussed under the King's Company), but what the other nurseries looked like we do not know. If the Vere Street house was considered serviceable, perhaps some or all of the others were simple, sceneryless, theatres. The promptbook for *The Wise-Woman of Hogsdon* contains no notes on scenery.

Among the players who saw service at the nurseries was John Coysh, who was also involved in tours to the provinces. Since performances were probably kept simple for both Nursery and provincial audiences, a promptbook such as that for *The Wise-Woman of Hogsdon* may have been prepared for one or the other or both. Coysh led a band of strolling players to Cambridge in 1667 and probably managed the Duke of Monmouth's Company at Norwich in 1672. Some of his plays and personnel in the latter year were the same as those at the Nursery (in the Barbican, one supposes). The copy of *A Midsummer Night's Dream* (discussed under Related Documents in Appendix F) seems to have been made up for a Nursery production that never materialized. In his *Shakespearean Prompt-Books* Professor Evans supposes that any Nursery productions about 1672 took place at Hatton Garden, but I am not certain Hatton Garden was still in use at that date; the Barbican house certainly was.

Of the staging of plays at the theatrical "booths" at Bartholomew and Southwark fairs in August and September each year we know even less, which makes the discovery by Philip Ayres of the promptbook for *The Vow-Breaker* especially important. The book was clearly intended to serve for a production sometime after the introduction of scenery on the English public stage in 1660–61, but we do not know when or where. Perhaps it was for a performance at one of the fairs. Virtually all the written and pictorial material concerning fair booths dates from after 1700, so we cannot tell how much the early booths resembled those of the eighteenth century. Sybil Rosenfeld in *The Theatre of the*

London Fairs, page 150, notes that in the 1670s some showmen rented 40′ to 50′ of ground for their booths. That would suggest that some booths were fairly sizeable, though not as large as the Vere Street Theatre (the smallest of the regular Restoration houses). In the eighteenth century, Ms. Rosenfeld tells us, the booths "were not, as one might expect, tents but barn-like buildings constructed of wooden boards, tall and narrow in shape" (p. 151). Some managers set up their theatres inside inns or built booths in innyards. By the end of the first quarter of the eighteenth century showmen had theatres with pits and boxes, like the major London playhouses, and put on plays requiring elaborate scenes and machines. Seventeenth-century booths may not have been so fancy.

The Wise-Woman of Hogsdon
by Thomas Heywood

1638 first quarto with manuscript prompt notes for a Barbican Nursery or perhaps provincial production by young London players about 1671–72; Folger STC 13370, copy 3. Discussed by Sandra Burner in "A Provincial Strolling Company of the 1670's," *Theatre Notebook*, 20 (Winter 1965/66), 74–78. Reproduced here in chapter 18 by permission of the Folger Shakespeare Library, Washington, D.C.

This edition of Heywood's play was carelessly printed and contains many typographical errors. The copy is marked for heavy cutting and has a number of notes similar to those found in promptbooks prepared for the King's Company and, indeed, in the same hands. From these notes and from the fact that most of the players named were associated with the King's troupe, it seems clear that the Nursery in the Barbican, though established by Lady Davenant and the Duke's Company, was chiefly the concern of Thomas Killigrew and his troupe. The heavy cutting argues for a scaled-down production suitable for either the Nursery or for a strolling company in the provinces.

Sandra Burner observes in her article that the cast as indicated in the notes may well have been Nursery actors in John Coysh's troupe that played in Norwich in the summer of 1672. The promptbook could have served the players either in London or on tour.

The copy contains some faint, indecipherable marginalia here and there, apparently of a nontheatrical nature. There seem to be two theatrical hands in the copy: one made most if not all of the cuts and the other wrote the warnings and cues and may have made some of the deletions.

Cast

The cast can be partly reconstructed from the notes in the copy.

Young Chartley	Thomas Disney
Boyster	Nathaniel Kew
Sencer	John Coysh
Haringfield	(part omitted)
Luce	Mrs. Chock
Luce's Father	Mr. Wingfield
Joseph	William Wall
Old Master Chartley	John Biggs
Young Chartley's Man	
Old Chartley's Man	
Sir Harry	Mr. Taddy
Gratiana	Mrs. John Coysh
Taber	J. Wall
Sir Boniface	Mr. James
The Wise-Woman	Mrs. Wall
A Countryman	
A Kitchen Maid	
Two Citizen's Wives	
[Second Luce]	Sarah Cook

Young Chartley's Man, who has no lines, was probably omitted; Old Chartley's Man, called Gyles in the text, was kept and probably did duty as the "three or foure serving men . . ."

The cuts indicated in the copy are extensive, but sometimes the marginal lines or boxing seem incomplete, and it is difficult in some cases to tell precisely what was intended for omission. The players apparently cut all of I, i (161 lines); almost 60 lines from Act II; about 224 lines from Act III (roughly half the act); about 154 lines from Act IV (about a quarter of the act); and about eight lines from Act V. The character of Haringfield, which is crossed out on the cast page, was certainly omitted, though the prompter failed to cut or reassign all of his lines (for an example see IV, i, 50). Most promptbooks indicate some cuts, but the intention here was to shorten the play considerably and reduce the cast somewhat. Length was of more concern than size of cast, for the clients of the Wise-Woman, who appear only in II, i, could easily have been dropped; three are women and the actresses playing them could not have been used for any doubling. The one male client was probably played by the actor who was Gyles, Old Chartley's servant. But the superfluous scene was kept, probably because it is funny, while I, i was cut, perhaps because it is not. If the promptbook was, in fact, prepared for a touring group, one would expect to see more efforts to reduce the number of personnel needed.

Staging

Act endings for I, II, III, and IV are warned and cued as in King's Company promptbooks. There are no sound, music, or special effect cues, and the notes mention only one property—a beer. Actors are regularly warned and cued. The absence of any notes on scenery—no descriptions of settings, no shift cues, no whistle warnings, no technical notes—certainly suggests a production planned for a simple, sceneryless stage. The Nursery in the Barbican may have had such a stage, just as players on tour would very likely take no scenery with them and play in fairly simple theatres. If they were lucky enough to perform in a provincial playhouse that had some scenery, they doubtless used it, but not knowing what they might encounter, they probably would have left technical notes out of their promptbooks.

The Comedie of Errors
by William Shakespeare

Text excerpted from a 1623 folio, containing extensive manuscript prompt notes for a production at the Barbican Nursery or perhaps for a touring company from the Nursery about 1672; at the Edinburgh University Library. Studied in detail, with a facsimile reproduction of the copy, in G. Blakemore Evans, ed. *Shakespearean Prompt-Books of the Seventeenth Century*, Vol. III (Charlottesville: Bibliographical Society of the University of Virginia, 1964); briefly discussed by Sandra Burner in "A

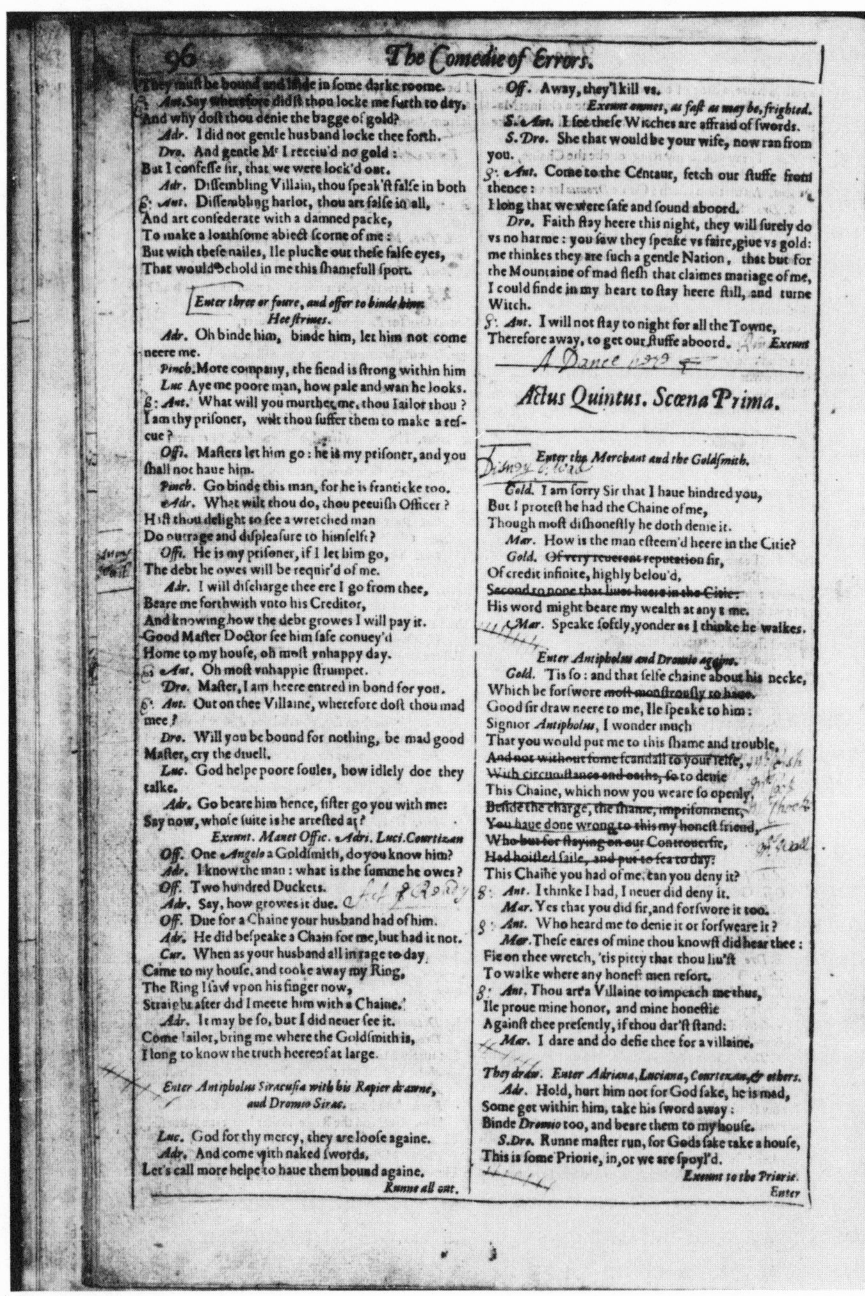

96 The Comedie of Errors.

They must be bound and laide in some darke roome.
Ant. Say wherefore didst thou locke me forth to day,
And why dost thou denie the bagge of gold?
Adr. I did not gentle husband locke thee forth.
Dro. And gentle Mr I receiu'd no gold:
But I confesse sir, that we were lock'd out.
Adr. Dissembling Villain, thou speak'st false in both
Ant. Dissembling harlot, thou art false in all,
And art confederate with a damned packe,
To make a loathsome abiect scorne of me:
But with these nailes, Ile plucke out these false eyes,
That would behold in me this shamefull sport.

Enter three or foure, and offer to binde him. Hee striues.

Adr. Oh binde him, binde him, let him not come neere me.
Pinch. More company, the fiend is strong within him
Luc Aye me poore man, how pale and wan he looks.
Ant. What will you murther me, thou Iailor thou?
I am thy prisoner, wilt thou suffer them to make a rescue?
Offi. Masters let him go: he is my prisoner, and you shall not haue him.
Pinch. Go binde this man, for he is franticke too.
Adr. What wilt thou do, thou peeuish Officer?
Hast thou delight to see a wretched man
Do outrage and displeasure to himselfe?
Offi. He is my prisoner, if I let him go,
The debt he owes will be requir'd of me.
Adr. I will discharge thee ere I go from thee,
Beare me forthwith vnto his Creditor,
And knowing how the debt growes I will pay it.
Good Master Doctor see him safe conuey'd
Home to my house, oh most vnhappy day.
Ant. Oh most vnhappie strumpet.
Dro. Master, I am heere entred in bond for you.
Ant. Out on thee Villaine, wherefore dost thou mad mee?
Dro. Will you be bound for nothing, be mad good Master, cry the diuell.
Luc. God helpe poore soules, how idlely doe they talke.
Adr. Go beare him hence, sister go you with me:
Say now, whose suite is he arrested at?

Exeunt. Manet Offic. Adri. Luci. Courtizan

Off. One *Angelo* a Goldsmith, do you know him?
Adr. I know the man: what is the summe he owes?
Off. Two hundred Duckets.
Adr. Say, how growes it due.
Off. Due for a Chaine your husband had of him.
Adr. He did bespeake a Chain for me, but had it not.
Cur. When as your husband all in rage to day
Came to my house, and tooke away my Ring,
The Ring I saw vpon his finger now,
Straight after did I meete him with a Chaine.
Adr. It may be so, but I did neuer see it.
Come Iailor, bring me where the Goldsmith is,
I long to know the truth heereof at large.

Enter Antipholus Siracusia with his Rapier drawne, and Dromio Sirac.

Luc. God for thy mercy, they are loose againe.
Adr. And come with naked swords,
Let's call more helpe to haue them bound againe.

Runne all out.

Off. Away, they'l kill vs.

Exeunt omnes, as fast as may be, frighted.

S. Ant. I see these Witches are affraid of swords.
S. Dro. She that would be your wife, now ran from you.
Ant. Come to the Centaur, fetch our stuffe from thence:
I long that we were safe and sound aboord.
Dro. Faith stay heere this night, they will surely do vs no harme: you saw they speake vs faire, giue vs gold: me thinkes they are such a gentle Nation, that but for the Mountaine of mad flesh that claimes mariage of me, I could finde in my heart to stay heere still, and turne Witch.
Ant. I will not stay to night for all the Towne,
Therefore away, to get our stuffe aboord. *Exeunt*

Actus Quintus. Scœna Prima.

Enter the Merchant and the Goldsmith.

Gold. I am sorry Sir that I haue hindred you,
But I protest he had the Chaine of me,
Though most dishonestly he doth denie it.
Mar. How is the man esteem'd heere in the Citie?
Gold. Of very reuerent reputation sir,
Of credit infinite, highly belou'd,
Second to none that liues heere in the Citie:
His word might beare my wealth at any time.
Mar. Speake softly, yonder as I thinke he walkes.

Enter Antipholus and Dromio againe.

Gold. 'Tis so: and that selfe chaine about his necke,
Which he forswore most monstrously to haue.
Good sir draw neere to me, Ile speake to him:
Signior *Antipholus*, I wonder much
That you would put me to this shame and trouble,
And not without some scandall to your selfe,
With circumstance and oaths, so to denie
This Chaine, which now you weare so openly,
Beside the charge, the shame, imprisonment,
You haue done wrong to this my honest friend,
Who but for staying on our Controuersie,
Had hoisted saile, and put to sea to day:
This Chaine you had of me, can you deny it?
Ant. I thinke I had, I neuer did deny it.
Mar. Yes that you did sir, and forswore it too.
Ant. Who heard me to denie it or forsweare it?
Mar. These eares of mine thou knowst did hear thee:
Fie on thee wretch, 'tis pitty that thou liu'st
To walke where any honest men resort.
Ant. Thou art a Villaine to impeach me thus,
Ile proue mine honor, and mine honestie
Against thee presently, if thou dar'st stand:
Mar. I dare and do defie thee for a villaine.

They draw. Enter Adriana, Luciana, Courtezan, & others.

Adr. Hold, hurt him not for God sake, he is mad,
Some get within him, take his sword away:
Binde *Dromio* too, and beare them to my house.
S. Dro. Runne master run, for Gods sake take a house,
This is some Priorie, in, or we are spoyl'd.

Exeunt to the Priorie.

Enter

From Shakespeare's *The Comedie of Errors*. By kind permission of the Edinburgh University Library.

Provincial Strolling Company of the 1670's," *Theatre Notebook*, 20 (Winter 1965/66), 74–78.

The splendid study of this promptbook by Professor Evans makes more than a general comment here unnecessary. Evans makes a convincing case for the book having been prepared for a production by neophyte performers at the Nursery (in Hatton Garden, he implies, but I take it to have been the one in the Barbican, which opened in 1671 and was in use throughout the 1670s). Alternatively, the promptbook may have been prepared for John Coysh's touring group or, less likely, for the King's Company. Personnel from the King's Company clearly had a hand in the book's preparation, for some of the notes are in a hand that can be found in some of that troupe's prompt copies. Possibly someone from the Nursery worked as an assistant to the prompter at the Theatre Royal.

The promptbook is very complete (see illustration), though the last leaf of the separately bound copy is missing (it was restored from another copy). On the basis of the remainder one can guess that about four hundred lines in the complete copy were marked for cutting. The manuscript notes give no indication of the use of scenery, which matches the promptbook for *The Wise-Woman of Hogsdon*. Other prompt notes similar to those found in King's Company books are in evidence: cross-hatch signs for entrances, actor warnings (usually by the actor's name), act-end warnings and cues, and indications of added songs and dances.

The London Stage, Part 1, pages 186–87, cites this copy, gives the cast as reconstructed by Evans, argues for the production being by a touring company, and places it in the 1671–72 season.

The Vow-Breaker *by William Sampson*

1636 quarto with numerous manuscript prompt notes and emendations, apparently dating from the Restoration period and suggesting a production between 1660 and 1700, perhaps at one of the late summer fairs; in a copy in the R. C. Bald Collection at Baillieu Library, University of Melbourne. Discussed by Philip Ayres in "Production and Adaptation of William Sampson's *The Vow-Breaker* (1636) in the Restoration," *Theatre Notebook*, 27 (Summer 1973), 145–49. Reproduced here in chapter 19 by permission of the University of Melbourne Library.

The copy is imperfect, lacking signatures A through A3 and I3 through K2. Nor are the prompt notes complete; a performance could hardly have been run from this copy. Yet it contains a number of whistle cues, presumably for scene changes, as in *The Change of Crownes* promptbook, act-end ring cues, and some interesting information on the solution of difficult staging problems. Ayres believes that the hand that entered the prompt notes was also responsible for the vast number of spelling emendations in the copy. The changes are in the direction of modernization, usually the canceling or rubbing out of the final e in many words (thinke, deepe, owne, goe, and so forth). Why a prompter should have concerned himself with such matters is beyond me. In most other Restoration promptbooks we find prompters ignoring typographical errors and incorrect or old-fashioned spelling. In any case, whoever made the editorial emendations did so only sporadically; some pages he left untouched. His time would have been better spent correcting the numerous printing mistakes in the edition.

The play must have been printed in great haste, for in addition to many typographical errors, the spacing between words and between punctuation marks and words is very erratic throughout. I have indicated scene divisions only when the author began a new act or the prompter called for a scene change.

The many spelling emendations in the text, even if made by someone in the theatre, are of no theatrical significance so far as I can determine. Many of the marks the emender made—the striking out of final e's, for instance—bled through one page to its verso, creating what appear to be many exclamation points. Occasionally, as on signature B1, some sentences seem to be concluded by points when they are not. That makes for confusion, because sometimes—at the opening of I, i, for example—the emender actually did add exclamation points. Sometimes he provided punctuation the author (or printer) neglected, punctuation an actor might need (as in I, i, 12, "pray thee no more*!*" where the original had no emphasis).

Staging

The theatrical notes in the copy are of several sorts: *X* marks, often at entrances and perhaps serving as cue signs in place of the more common cross-hatch symbol; textual emendations affecting entrances, exits, speech ascriptions, and stage action; *Ring* warnings and cues for the ends of acts (which may, as in other promptbooks, have concerned some shifts, entr'acte music, and actor entrances); and *Whistle* cues, apparently for scene changes—though no settings are described. There are no properties mentioned in the prompt notes, though the printed stage directions make occasional mention of such things as a bed or picture. There are no warnings for actors; there are no printed descriptions of locales, even though scene changes seem to be indicated in the manuscript notes, and the action of the play clearly moves from place to place.

The use of *X* as a cue (apparently) is not consistent, and perhaps the prompter marked only those entrances which had presented problems during rehearsals or which took place opposite prompt side. The marks appear several times in Act I, for instance, but not for all entrances; when the mark does appear at an entrance, it is always followed or preceded by a second *X* (at I, i, 180 the cue is followed by two *X* marks, one of them in a circle, which seems to relate them to the more common circle-and-dot symbol used for scene shifts). Act II contains only one such cue; Act III has several, two of which are single *X* marks and one of which, at III, ii, 74, is a trumpet cue. The single *X* is used again in Act IV for a trumpet cue and one entrance cue. The mark is not found at all in Act V. The *X* seems clearly to have served the prompter as a cue, but it is hard to see the significance of two marks instead of one, and there is no evident reason for some things being cued and others not.

Several of the textual emendations affecting entrances, exits, speech ascriptions, and stage action are commented on in the notes to the facsimiles, but a few deserve consideration here. On E2^{v} is a note: *Exit, & when / the Scene Chan[ges] / Returns*. This and the whistle note proves that scene changes were used in the production, and perhaps descriptions of the settings—along with more complete warnings and cues—were recorded in a separate document, leaving the promptbook to cover only those technical cues of direct concern to the prompter. In this case, an exit and quick reentrance is involved, which the prompter would have needed to know about.

The most interesting manuscript note concerns the hanging of Young Bateman. The author specified that he should hang himself in full view of the audience. That stage trick can be managed if there are several characters in the scene, some of whom can mask the business of hooking the victim's girdle to a tree trunk or wall before the simulated hanging. To stage a solo hanging would be difficult. The problem was solved here by simply striking out "*Falls, hangs*" from the printed stage direction and having Young Bateman exit. The deleted notes indicating that Act II should end at that point may have been made before the producers decided how to manage the hanging scene; having found a solution, perhaps they decided there was no need to end the act early.

The *Ring* notes found in *The Vow-Breaker* promptbook are very like those appearing in other Restoration promptbooks, with a slight variation. At the end of Act I the prompter, instead of writing the usual "Act" or "Act Ready" warning simply wrote *Ring* sixteen lines before the end of the act; then he repeated the word as a cue to signal whatever else took place between the acts. He did the same at the end of Act II, correctly placing the warning and cue to account for the deleted lines at the end of the act, and at the end of Act III. He cued the end of Act IV but forgot to enter a warning. Since the copy is imperfect, we do not know how he handled the end of Act V.

We can suppose that all whistle cues, whatever else they may have involved, signaled scene changes. The text clearly indicates changes of locales (Act I, for example, needs at least one scene shift, but no change is indicated in the manuscript notes). The first *Whistle* note comes on D2 at the entrance of Ursula. A scene change is clearly needed here, and the whistle seems definitely to have been the cue for the scenemen to coordinate their efforts at the wings, shutters, and borders—or whatever scenic pieces were used in the production—just as in *The Change of Crownes* promptbook. There is no whistle cue on E2^{v}, though the prompt note concerning old Bateman's exit and reentrance clearly states that a change occurs. The next whistle comes on F2, and the subsequent uses of the cue bring about scene shifts at points where they logically should have been.

An effect noted by the prompter but not indicated by the author in his stage directions is on H3: *Sinks with Ghost*—the use of a trap door, probably upstage in the scenic area near the indicated bed.

8 / The Contents of the Promptbooks

The materials gathered here provide us with a remarkable amount of information about the Restoration theatre—from the fact that the companies saved money by double-facing their scenic units so they could be reversible, to the cavalier manner in which playwrights' wishes were sometimes treated; from the clout that the censor Sir Henry Herbert had, to the system of whistle cues the machinists developed for signaling scene changes; from the significant absence in promptbooks of information concerning such important matters as portraying characters, to the equally significant practical concern with getting actors and music properly warned and cued; from the implication that in addition to promptbooks the Restoration theatre personnel must have kept separate scene and property plots, to the certain fact that companies mixed settings from one play with settings from another; from the evidence that the joint Nursery project that the Duke's and King's companies supported was probably dominated by the King's troupe, to the differences and similarities between London and Dublin staging practices; from the encouraging fact that we now know of seventeen times as many promptbooks for the Restoration period as we did forty years ago, to the discouraging news that recent discoveries suggest we are not likely to find in the future much new information; from the clearer picture we now have of printing house practices and the disposition of promptbooks, to the useful evidence in some copies that one should not take stage directions in printed plays as proof of actual production practices; from the discovery in prompt notes of the names of actors not hitherto known, to tantalizing hints about acting conventions. And on and on.

Of the handwriting in the promptbooks one dares not say much more than that certain hands appear to be common to several books. I believe I see one hand in seven of the King's Company promptbooks (*The Scornful Ladie*, *The Ball*, *The Change of Crownes*, *The Sisters*, *Aglaura*, *The Maides Revenge*, and *Brennoralt*) as well as in the Nursery or strolling promptbooks for *The Wise-Woman of Hogsdon* and *The Comedie of Errors*. We have no way of knowing if that hand belonged to the prompter Charles Booth. It does not appear in *The Cheats* or *Tyrannick Love*. A different hand, possibly that of John Downes, appears in both *The Lady-Errant* and *The Ordinary*—Duke's Company plays of about 1672. One of the notes in *Romeo and Juliet* may be in that same hand, but I find no trace of it in *The Wittie Faire One*. The manuscript notes in the United Company prompt copy of *Madam Fickle* (1682) do not seem to be in a hand found in any of the other books, and the hand in *The Vow-Breaker* seems also to be unique. The prompt hand in the Dublin *Belphegor* matches that in *Measure for Measure*.

Summing up the information collected here can perhaps best be done with charts that can do double duty as finding lists. The charts on the following pages display the features of sixteen of the relatively complete promptbooks and three printed plays with copious traces of prompt copy. I have tried to give some indication of the frequency with which some of the terms and symbols were used, and at the end I have provided capsule summaries of unusual features in each book. Abbreviations for the various theatres are C for the Cockpit in Drury Lane, V for Vere Street, B for Bridges Street, DL for Drury Lane, LIF for Lincoln's Inn Fields, DG for Dorset Garden, and SA for Smock Alley (for which, see Appendix A). Following the charts is a finding list of supporting evidence in the rest of the Restoration promptbooks dealt with in this study.

		"Call"	"Ready"	Warn by character	Warn by person	–++++++++– as cue
Rhodes's	*Loyal Subject* (C) 1 theatrical hand		"be ready" many, for actors, sound	all		–+++–––––– or ––––––––+++– regularly
Rhodes's	*Spanish Curate* (C) 1 theatrical hand		"be ready" many, for actors, dance, props	all		–+++–––––– or ––––––+++– regularly
King's	*Scornful Ladie* (V) 1 theatrical hand			all		once
King's	*Ball* (B, LIF, or DL) 1 theatrical hand		3, for dance & Act	all		
King's	*Change of Crownes* (B) 6 theatrical hands		many, for whistle, sound, Act	some	some	regularly
King's	*Sisters* (B) 3 theatrical hands		many, for sound, Act, actors	some	most	regularly
King's	*Aglaura* (B, LIF, or DL) 2 theatrical hands			most	a few	
King's	*Tyrannick Love* (LIF?) 2 theatrical hands	2, for music & sound				
King's	*Maides Revenge* (LIF) 3 theatrical hands		a few, for actors, Act	some	most	regularly
King's	*Brennoralt* (LIF or DL) 2 theatrical hands		many, for sound, Act	some	most	regularly

		"Call"	"Ready"	Warn by character	Warn by person	–++++++++– as cue
Duke's	*Wittie Faire One* (LIF) 3 theatrical hands			all		
Duke's	*Guzman* (LIF) traces	a few, for actors	a few, for actors, sound, effects	all		N/A
Duke's	*Ordinary* (DG) 2 theatrical hands (?)	1, for actors				
Duke's	*Lady-Errant* (DG) 2 theatrical hands (?)	1, for actors	1, for sound			
Duke's	*Careless Lovers* (DG) traces	many, for actors	a few, for actors, sound			N/A
Rich	*Albion Queens* (DL) traces			some	some	N/A
Nursery/Fair	*Wise-Woman* (Nursery?) 2 theatrical hands		4, for Act		all	regularly
Nursery/Fair	*Vow-Breaker* (Fair?) 1 theatrical hand	1, for actors		once	once	
Dublin	*Belphegor* (SA) 4 theatrical hands (?)	many, for actors	a few, for effects, sound, traps	most	some	

		# or X as cue	Scene shift warning	⊙ shift cue	Whistle notes	Setting descriptions
Rhodes's	*Loyal Subject* (C) 1 theatrical hand					
Rhodes's	*Spanish Curate* (C) 1 theatrical hand					

		# or X as cue	Scene shift warning	⊙ shift cue	Whistle notes	Setting descriptions
King's	*Scornful Ladie* (V) 1 theatrical hand					
King's	*Ball* (B, LIF, or DL) 1 theatrical hand					regularly
King's	*Change of Crownes* (B) 6 theatrical hands	1 X for sound	"whistle ready"	regularly	yes, numbered	regularly
King's, continued	*Sisters* (B) 3 theatrical hands			regularly		regularly
King's, continued	*Aglaura* (B, LIF, or DL) 2 theatrical hands			regularly		regularly
King's, continued	*Tyrannick Love* (LIF?) 2 theatrical hands					
King's, continued	*Maides Revenge* (LIF) 3 theatrical hands	Xs for sound		regularly		sometimes
King's, continued	*Brennoralt* (LIF or DL) 2 theatrical hands			sometimes		
Duke's	*Wittie Faire One* (LIF) 3 theatrical hands		"Scene"			regularly
Duke's	*Guzman* (LIF) traces	N/A		N/A		regularly
Duke's	*Ordinary* (DG) 2 theatrical hands (?)	# for some entrances				regularly
Duke's	*Lady-Errant* (DG) 2 theatrical hands (?)	# for sound				sometimes
Duke's	*Careless Lovers* (DG) traces	N/A		N/A		regularly
Rich	*Albion Queens* (DL) traces	N/A		N/A		
Nursery/Fair	*Wise-Woman* (Nursery?) 2 theatrical hands					
Nursery/Fair	*Vow-Breaker* (Fair?) 1 theatrical hand	X for some entrances			a few	
Dublin	*Belphegor* (SA) 4 theatrical hands (?)				one	sometimes

		Act-end warnings	Act-end cues	Props cited	Music, sound notes	Curtain cited
Rhodes's	*Loyal Subject* (C) 1 theatrical hand			one	five	
Rhodes's	*Spanish Curate* (C) 1 theatrical hand	Act; III, iv		three		
King's	*Scornful Ladie* (V) 1 theatrical hand			one		
King's, continued	*Ball* (B, LIF, or DL) 1 theatrical hand	Act or Act ready; I, II, III, IV, V		one		
King's, continued	*Change of Crownes* (B) 6 theatrical hands	Act ready; I, II, III, IV, V		a few	two	
King's, continued	*Sisters* (B) 3 theatrical hands	Act ready; I, II, IV	Ring; I, II, III, IV, V	a few	several	
King's, continued	*Aglaura* (B, LIF, or DL) 2 theatrical hands	Act ready; I, II, III, IV	Ring; I, II, III	a few	a few	
King's, continued	*Tyrannick Love* (LIF?) 2 theatrical hands		Musique; I, II, III, IV, V		several	draw and drop
King's, continued	*Maides Revenge* (LIF) 3 theatrical hands	Act ready; I, II, III, IV	Ring; I, II, IV (cropping)	a few		
King's, continued	*Brennoralt* (LIF or DL) 2 theatrical hands	Act ready; I, II, III, IV	Ring; I, II, IV, V	a few	a few	
Duke's	*Wittie Faire One* (LIF) 3 theatrical hands	Act; I, II, III, IV, V		several	several	
Duke's	*Guzman* (LIF) traces			a few	a few	
Duke's	*Ordinary* (DG) 2 theatrical hands (?)			a few		
Duke's	*Lady-Errant* (DG) 2 theatrical hands (?)			several		
Duke's	*Careless Lovers* (DG) traces			a few	a few	
Rich	*Albion Queens* (DL) traces			a few	a few	

		Act-end warnings	Act-end cues	Props cited	Music, sound notes	Curtain cited
Nursery/Fair	*Wise-Woman* (Nursery?) 2 theatrical hands	Act ready; I, II, III, IV	Ring; I, II, III, IV	one		
	Vow-Breaker (Fair?) 1 theatrical hand	Ring; I, II, III (text incomplete)	Ring; I, II, III, IV (incomplete)		a few	
Dublin	*Belphegor* (SA) 4 theatrical hands (?)	Act ready; I, II, III	Whistle; I	many	several	

		Traps cited	Entrance doors cited	Dance notes	Special effects notes	Musicians cited
Rhodes's	*Loyal Subject* (C) 1 theatrical hand					one
	Spanish Curate (C) 1 theatrical hand			two		
King's	*Scornful Ladie* (V) 1 theatrical hand					once
	Ball (B, LIF, or DL) 1 theatrical hand			one		
	Change of Crownes (B) 6 theatrical hands			one		
	Sisters (B) 3 theatrical hands					
	Aglaura (B, LIF, or DL) 2 theatrical hands					one: Fitz
	Tyrannick Love (LIF?) 2 theatrical hands					
	Maides Revenge (LIF) 3 theatrical hands					
	Brennoralt (LIF or DL) 2 theatrical hands					
Duke's	*Wittie Faire One* (LIF) 3 theatrical hands					
	Guzman (LIF) traces			one	a few	
	Ordinary (DG) 2 theatrical hands (?)					
	Lady-Errant (DG) 2 theatrical hands (?)			three		
	Careless Lovers (DG) traces			one		twice
Rich	*Albion Queens* (DL) traces		OP, PS, LDOP, UDOP, LDPS, UDPS			
Nursery/Fair	*Wise-Woman* (Nursery?) 2 theatrical hands					
	Vow-Breaker (Fair?) 1 theatrical hand	once				
Dublin	*Belphegor* (SA) 4 theatrical hands (?)	frequently; cue: Ring	E or W, U or L	two	several	once

		Cuts	Additions	Line changes
Rhodes's	*Loyal Subject* (C) 1 theatrical hand			
	Spanish Curate (C) 1 theatrical hand			

Company	Play	Cuts	Additions	Line changes	Other
Rhodes's	*Loyal Subject* (C) 1 theatrical hand				
Rhodes's	*Spanish Curate* (C) 1 theatrical hand				
King's	*Scornful Ladie* (V) 1 theatrical hand	a few			Doodles; marks beside some speeches
King's	*Ball* (B, LIF, or DL) 1 theatrical hand	several			Some nontheatrical glosses
King's	*Change of Crownes* (B) 6 theatrical hands	several, some large		a few	Canceled reference to second promptbook; Sir Henry Herbert's license
King's	*Sisters* (B) 3 theatrical hands	several, small	a few	two	Many of Paulina's (Mrs Knepp's) speeches marked; mixed wings and shutters
King's	*Aglaura* (B, LIF, or DL) 2 theatrical hands				"The last scene" two and a half pages before end; alternate Act V not marked; same set for two different locales
King's	*Tyrannick Love* (LIF?) 2 theatrical hands				References to a black curtain
King's	*Maides Revenge* (LIF) 3 theatrical hands	several			Xs on cast page; names of three hitherto unknown actors; marks by Berinthia's (Mrs Marshall's) speeches
King's	*Brennoralt* (LIF or DL) 2 theatrical hands	a few			"The last scene" two and a half pages before end; prompter, not machinist, made two ⊙ symbols
Duke's	*Wittie Faire One* (LIF) 3 theatrical hands	a few			"Knocking Prepar'd" warning; some notes in ink, some in pencil; Sir Henry Herbert's license, 1632
Duke's	*Guzman* (LIF) traces	N/A	N/A	N/A	Unusual setting labels; references to scenery made for other plays by same author; mixed wings & shutters
Duke's	*Ordinary* (DG) 2 theatrical hands (?)	many		a few	Sir Henry Herbert's license
Duke's	*Lady-Errant* (DG) 2 theatrical hands (?)	many		several	Sir Henry Herbert's license; Xs on cast page
Duke's	*Careless Lovers* (DG) traces	N/A	N/A	N/A	Use of mixed wings and shutters
Rich	*Albion Queens* (DL) traces	N/A	N/A	N/A	
Nursery/ Fair	*Wise-Woman* (Nursery?) 2 theatrical hands	many	a few		Xs on cast page
Nursery/ Fair	*Vow-Breaker* (Fair?) 1 theatrical hand	a few		a few	References to stage business; sporadic modernization of spelling
Dublin	*Belphegor* (SA) 4 theatrical hands (?)	many		many, by author	Textual emendations in author's hand

To complete the picture shown in the charts, evidence from the rest of the promptbooks and printed books with traces of prompt copy must be considered. Listed below are those categories used in the charts for which supporting evidence can be found in the rest of the Restoration documents studied.

"Call"	Duke's Company: *Juliana, Madam Fickle* (1677), *Tom Essence.* United Company: *Fool's Preferment, Constantine, Valentinian, Bussy D'Ambois, Richmond Heiress.* Betterton's Company: *She Ventures, and He Wins.*
"Ready"	Rhodes's Company: *Wife for a Moneth* ("be ready"). King's Company: *Dumb Lady.* United Company: *Madam Fickle* (1682), *Constantine.* Betterton's Company: *She Ventures, Doctor Faustus.*
Warn by character	Rhodes's Company: *Wife for a Moneth.* King's Company: *Cheats, Injured Princess.* Duke's Company: *Villain, Juliana, Madam Fickle* (1677), *Tom Essence, Woman-Captain.* United Company: *Fool's Preferment, Constantine, Valentinian, Bussy D'Ambois, Richmond Heiress.* Betterton's Company: *She Ventures, Doctor Faustus.*
Warn by person	King's Company: *Cheats, Mistaken Husband, Injured Princess.*
Setting descriptions	King's Company: *Mulberry Garden, Injured Princess.* Duke's Company: *Villain, Revenge.* Rich's Company: *Neglected Virtue.*
Act-end warnings	King's Company: *Dumb Lady.* United Company: *Madam Fickle* (1682).
Act-end cues	King's Company: *Mulberry Garden, Dumb Lady.* Duke's Company: *Romeo and Juliet.*
Props cited	Rhodes's Company: *Wife for a Moneth.* King's Company: *Cheats, Mistaken Husband, Mall, Mock-Duellist, Sir Barnaby Whigg, Injured Princess.* Duke's Company: *Villain, Madam Fickle* (1677), *Tom Essence, Sir Patient Fancy, Squire Oldsapp, Virtuous Wife, Revenge, Woman-Captain, City Heiress.* United Company: *Madam Fickle* (1682), *Constantine.* Betterton's Company: *She Ventures, and He Wins.*
Music, sound notes	King's Company: *Mulberry Garden, Mock-Duellist, Injured Princess.* Duke's Company: *Romeo and Juliet, Villain, Tom Essence, Theodosius.* United Company: *Constantine.*

Much more can be done with the information gathered here than I have tried to do, since my intention was to bring these materials together and make them available for study. I hope others will now be encouraged not only to search for more raw materials like these promptbooks but to explore the relationship of the promptbooks to later printed editions of the plays; to reassess staging practices in the light of the information these promptbooks give us; to investigate further the cuts and emendations in the promptbooks for what they can reveal about censorship, audience tastes, and company attitudes toward the scripts they produced; to comb the prompt copies for what they can tell us about stock properties and scenery kept by Restoration companies; to reconsider conjectural reconstructions of Restoration playhouses in view of the evidence contained in the promptbooks; to study the stage histories of the plays collected here to see what traditions in later years may have begun in these late seventeenth-century productions; to use these prompt copies to reconstruct Restoration performances; to compare in much greater detail these promptbooks with those of earlier and later times; to search for evidence that may help date more precisely the copies that are now only loosely assigned a time and place; and so on. I trust that anyone who has been courageous enough to come this far with me can see the many possibilities for future work.

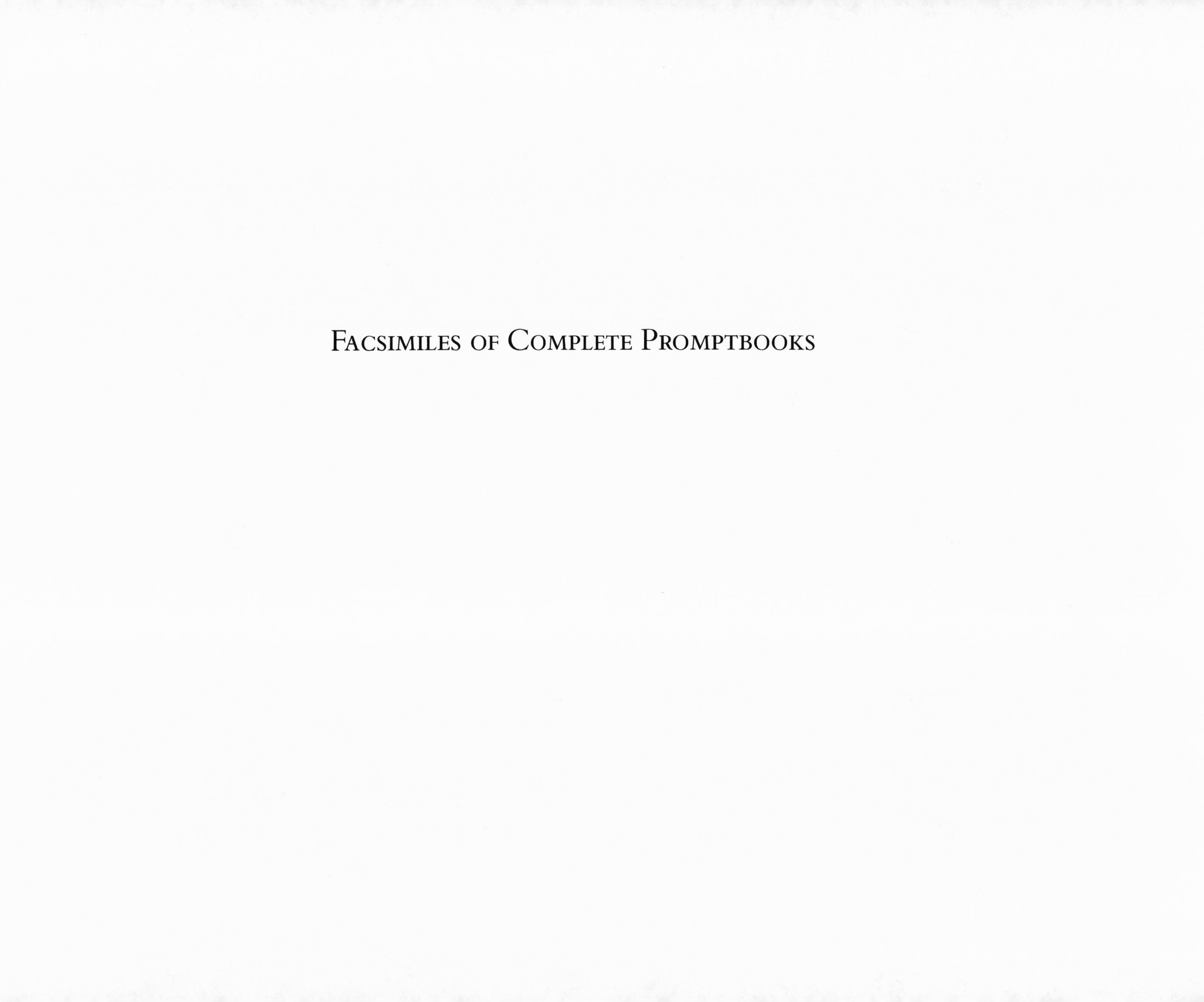

Facsimiles of Complete Promptbooks

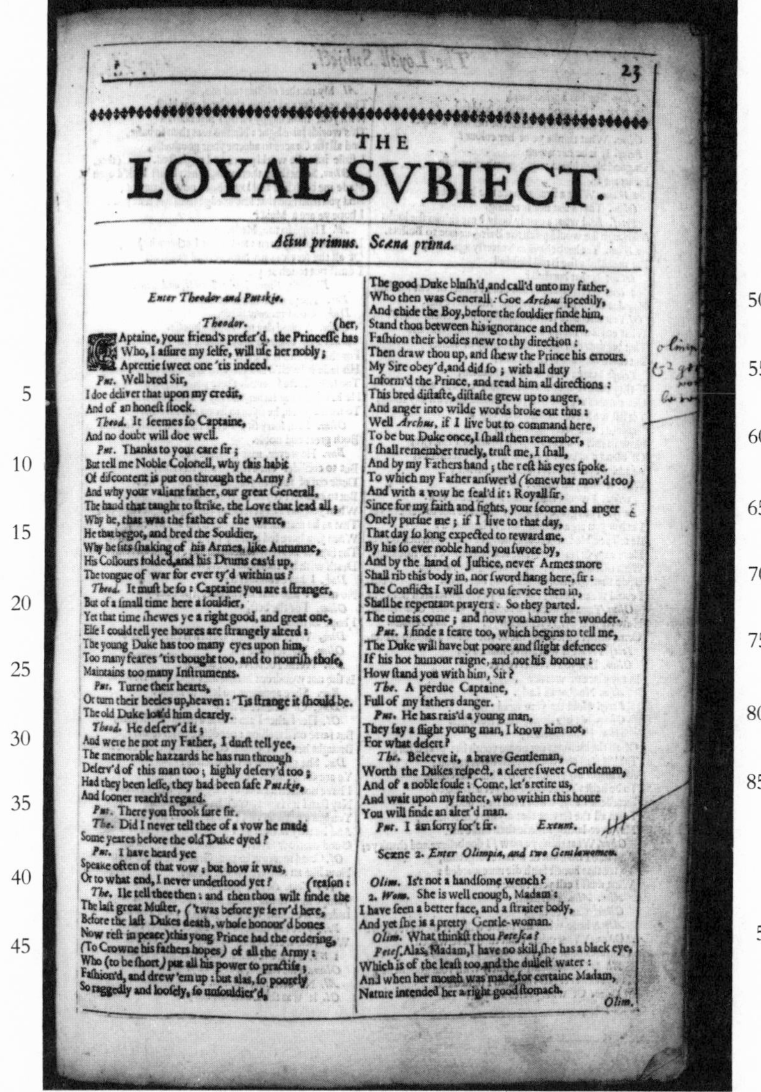

23

THE LOYAL SVBIECT.

Actus primus. Scæna prima.

Enter Theodor and Putskie.

Theodor. (her,
CAptaine, your friend's prefer'd, the Princeſſe has
Who, I aſſure my ſelfe, will uſe her nobly;
A prettie ſweet one 'tis indeed.
Put. Well bred Sir,
I doe deliver that upon my credit,
And of an honeſt ſtock.
Theod. It ſeemes ſo Captaine,
And no doubt will doe well.
Put. Thanks to your care ſir;
But tell me Noble Colonell, why this habit
Of diſcontent is put on through the Army?
And why your valiant father, our great Generall,
The hand that taught to ſtrike, the Love that lead all;
Why he, that was the father of the warre,
He that begot, and bred the Souldier,
Why he ſits ſhaking of his Armes, like Autumne,
His Collours folded, and his Drums cas'd up,
The tongue of war for ever ty'd within us?
Theod. It muſt be ſo: Captaine you are a ſtranger,
But of a ſmall time here a ſouldier,
Yet that time ſhewes ye a right good, and great one,
Elſe I could tell yee houres are ſtrangely alterd:
The young Duke has too many eyes upon him,
Too many feares 'tis thought too, and to nouriſh thoſe,
Maintains too many Inſtruments.
Put. Turne their hearts,
Or turn their heeles up, heaven: 'Tis ſtrange it ſhould be.
The old Duke lov'd him dearely.
Theod. He deſerv'd it;
And were he not my Father, I durſt tell yee,
The memorable hazzards he has run through
Deſerv'd of this man too; highly deſerv'd too;
Had they been leſſe, they had been ſafe *Putskie*,
And ſooner reach'd regard.
Put. There you ſtrook ſure ſir.
The. Did I never tell thee of a vow he made
Some yeares before the old Duke dyed?
Put. I have heard yee
Speake often of that vow; but how it was,
Or to what end, I never underſtood yet? (reaſon:
The. Ile tell thee then: and then thou wilt finde the
The laſt great Muſter, ('twas before ye ſerv'd here,
Before the laſt Dukes death, whoſe honour'd bones
Now reſt in peace) this yong Prince had the ordering,
(To Crowne his fathers hopes) of all the Army:
Who (to be ſhort) put all his power to practiſe;
Faſhion'd, and drew 'em up: but alas, ſo poorely
So raggedly and looſely, ſo unſouldier'd,
The good Duke bluſh'd, and call'd unto my father,
Who then was Generall: Goe *Archus* ſpeedily,
And chide the Boy, before the ſouldier finde him,
Stand thou between his ignorance and them,
Faſhion their bodies new to thy direction;
Then draw thou up, and ſhew the Prince his errours.
My Sire obey'd, and did ſo; with all duty
Inform'd the Prince, and read him all directions:
This bred diſtaſte, diſtaſte grew up to anger,
And anger into wilde words broke out thus:
Well *Archus*, if I live but to command here,
To be but Duke once, I ſhall then remember,
I ſhall remember truely, truſt me, I ſhall,
And by my Fathers hand; the reſt his eyes ſpoke.
To which my Father anſwer'd (ſomewhat mov'd too)
And with a vow he ſeal'd it: Royall ſir,
Since for my faith and fights, your ſcorne and anger
Onely purſue me; if I live to that day,
That day ſo long expected to reward me,
By his ſo ever noble hand you ſwore by,
And by the hand of Juſtice, never Armes more
Shall rib this body in, nor ſword hang here, ſir:
The Conflicts I will doe you ſervice then in,
Shall be repentant prayers. So they parted.
The time is come; and now you know the wonder.
Put. I finde a feare too, which begins to tell me,
The Duke will have but poore and ſlight defences
If his hot humour raigne, and not his honour:
How ſtand you with him, Sir?
The. A perdue Captaine,
Full of my fathers danger.
Put. He has rais'd a young man,
They ſay a ſlight young man, I know him not,
For what deſert?
The. Beleeve it, a brave Gentleman,
Worth the Dukes reſpect, a cleere ſweet Gentleman,
And of a noble ſoule: Come, let's retire us,
And wait upon my father, who within this houre
You will finde an alter'd man.
Put. I am ſorry for't ſir. *Exeunt.*

Scæne 2. *Enter Olimpia, and two Gentlewomen.*

Olim. Is't not a handſome wench?
2. *Wom.* She is well enough, Madam:
I have ſeen a better face, and a ſtraiter body,
And yet ſhe is a pretty Gentle-woman.
Olim. What thinkſt thou *Peteſca*?
Peteſ. Alas, Madam, I have no skill, ſhe has a black eye,
Which is of the leaſt too, and the dulleſt water:
And when her mouth was made, for certaine Madam,
Nature intended her a right good ſtomach.
Olim.

olimp[ia]
& 2 gen[tle]
wom[en]
re[ady]

The Loyal Subject by John Fletcher. Reproduced by permission of The Pennsylvania State University Libraries.

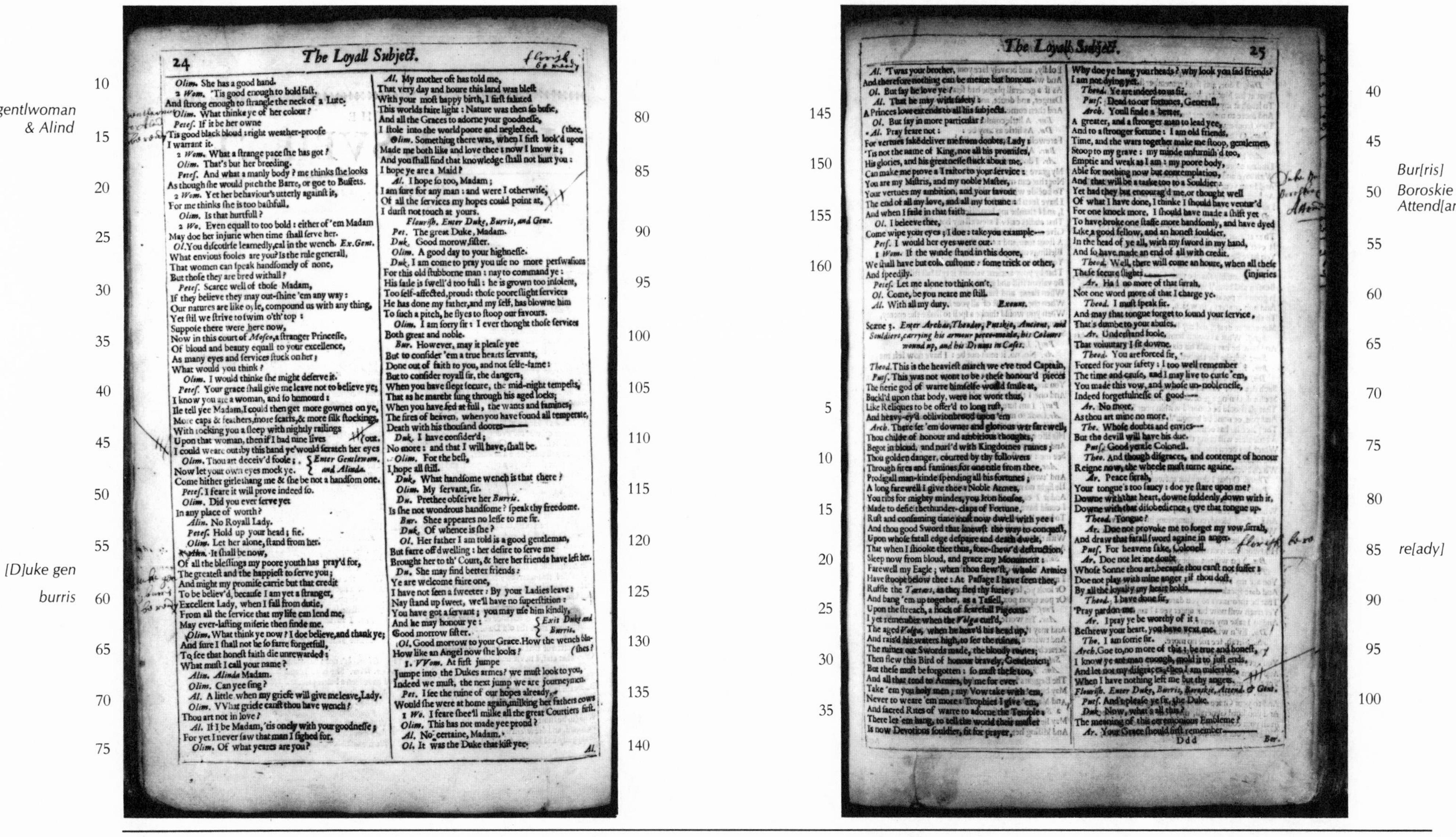

24 *The Loyall Subject.*

Olim. She has a good hand.
2 Wom. 'Tis good enough to hold faſt,
And ſtrong enough to ſtrangle the neck of a Lute.
Olim. What thinke ye of her colour?
Peteſ. If it be her owne
'Tis good black bloud: right weather-proofe
I warrant it.
2 Wom. What a ſtrange pace ſhe has got?
Olim. That's but her breeding.
Peteſ. And what a manly body? me thinks ſhe looks
As though ſhe would pitch the Barre, or goe to Buffets.
2 Wom. Yet her behaviour's utterly againſt it,
For me thinks ſhe is too baſhfull.
Olim. Is that hurtfull?
2 Wo. Even equall to too bold: either of 'em Madam
May doe her injurie when time ſhall ſerve her.
Ol. You diſcourſe learnedly, cal in the wench. *Ex. Gent.*
What envious fooles are you? Is the rule generall,
That women can ſpeak handſomely of none,
But thoſe they are bred withall?
Peteſ. Scarce well of thoſe Madam,
If they believe they may out-ſhine 'em any way:
Our natures are like oyle, compound us with any thing,
Yet ſtil we ſtrive to ſwim o'th' top:
Suppoſe there were here now,
Now in this court of *Moſco*, a ſtranger Princeſſe,
Of bloud and beauty equall to your excellence,
As many eyes and ſervices ſtuck on her;
What would you think?
Olim. I would thinke ſhe might deſerve it.
Peteſ. Your grace ſhall give me leave not to believe ye;
I know you are a woman, and ſo humour'd:
Ile tell yee Madam, I could then get more gownes on ye,
More caps & feathers, more ſcarfs, & more ſilk ſtockings,
With rocking you a ſleep with nightly railings
Upon that woman, then if I had nine lives (out.
I could weare out: by this hand ye'would ſcratch her eyes
Olim. Thou art deceiv'd foole; { *Enter Gentlewom. and Alinda.*
Now let your own eyes mock ye.
Come hither girle: hang me & ſhe be not a handſom one.
Peteſ. I feare it will prove indeed ſo.
Olim. Did you ever ſerve yet
In any place of worth?
Alin. No Royall Lady.
Peteſ. Hold up your head; fie.
Olim. Let her alone, ſtand from her.
Alin. It ſhall be now,
Of all the bleſſings my poore youth has pray'd for,
The greateſt and the happieſt to ſerve you;
And might my promiſe carrie but that credit
To be believ'd, becauſe I am yet a ſtranger,
Excellent Lady, when I fall from dutie,
From all the ſervice that my life can lend me,
May ever-laſting miſerie then finde me.
Olim. What think ye now? I doe believe, and thank ye;
And ſure I ſhall not be ſo farre forgetfull,
To ſee that honeſt faith die unrewarded:
What muſt I call your name?
Alin. *Alinda* Madam.
Olim. Can yee ſing?
Al. A little when my griefe will give me leave, Lady.
Olim. VVhat griefe canſt thou have wench?
Thou art not in love?
Al. If I be Madam, 'tis onely with your goodneſſe;
For yet I never ſaw that man I ſighed for.
Olim. Of what yeares are you?
Al. My mother oft has told me,
That very day and houre this land was bleſt
With your moſt happy birth, I firſt ſaluted
This worlds faire light: Nature was then ſo buſie,
And all the Graces to adorne your goodneſſe,
I ſtole into the world poore and neglected. (thee,
Olim. Something there was, when I firſt look'd upon
Made me both like and love thee: now I know it;
And you ſhall find that knowledge ſhall not hurt you:
I hope ye are a Maid?
Al. I hope ſo too, Madam;
I am ſure for any man: and were I otherwiſe,
Of all the ſervices my hopes could point at,
I durſt not touch at yours.
Flouriſh. Enter Duke, Burris, and Gent.
Pet. The great Duke, Madam.
Duk. Good morow ſiſter.
Olim. A good day to your highneſſe.
Duk. I am come to pray you uſe no more perſwaſions
For this old ſtubborne man: nay to command ye:
His ſaile is ſwell'd too full: he is grown too inſolent,
Too ſelf-affected, proud: thoſe poore ſlight ſervices
He has done my father, and my ſelf, has blowne him
To ſuch a pitch, he flyes to ſtoop our favours.
Olim. I am ſorry ſir: I ever thought thoſe ſervices
Both great and noble.
Bur. However, may it pleaſe yee
But to conſider 'em a true hearts ſervants,
Done out of faith to you, and not ſelfe-fame:
But to conſider royall ſir, the dangers,
When you have ſlept ſecure, the mid-night tempeſts,
That as he marcht ſung through his aged locks;
When you have fed at full, the wants and famines;
The fires of heaven, when you have found all temperate,
Death with his thouſand doores——
Duk. I have conſider'd;
No more: and that I will have, ſhall be.
Olim. For the beſt,
I hope all ſtill.
Duk. What handſome wench is that there?
Olim. My ſervant, ſir.
Du. Prethee obſerve her *Burris.*
Is ſhe not wondrous handſome? ſpeak thy freedome.
Bur. Shee appeares no leſſe to me ſir.
Duk. Of whence is ſhe?
Ol. Her father I am told is a good gentleman,
But farre off dwelling: her deſire to ſerve me
Brought her to th' Court, & here her friends have left her.
Du. She may find better friends:
Ye are welcome faire one,
I have not ſeen a ſweeter: By your Ladies leave:
Nay ſtand up ſweet, we'll have no ſuperſtition:
You have got a ſervant; you may uſe him kindly,
And he may honour ye: { *Exit Duke and Burris.*
Good morrow ſiſter.
Ol. Good morrow to your Grace. How the wench bluſhes?
How like an Angel now ſhe looks?
1. VVom. At firſt jumpe
Jumpe into the Dukes armes? we muſt look to you,
Indeed we muſt, the next jump we are journeymen.
Pet. I ſee the ruine of our hopes already,
Would ſhe were at home again, milking her fathers cows
1 Wo. I feare ſhee'll milke all the great Courtiers firſt.
Olim. This has not made yee proud?
Al. No certaine, Madam.
Ol. It was the Duke that kiſt yee.
Al.

The Loyall Subject. 25

Al. 'Twas your brother,
And therefore nothing can be meant but honour.
Ol. But ſay he love ye?
Al. That he may with ſafety:
A Princes love extends to all his ſubjects.
Ol. But ſay in more particular?
Al. Pray feare not:
For vertues ſake deliver me from doubts, Lady:
'Tis not the name of King, nor all his promiſes,
His glories, and his greatneſſe ſtuck about me,
Can make me prove a Traitor to your ſervice:
You are my Miſtris, and my noble Maſter,
Your vertues my ambition, and your favour
The end of all my love, and all my fortune:
And when I faile in that faith——
Ol. I beleeve thee,
Come wipe your eyes; I doe: take you example——
Petſ. I would her eyes were out.
1 Wom. If the winde ſtand in this doore,
We ſhall have but cold cuſtome: ſome trick or other,
And ſpeedily.
Peteſ. Let me alone to think on't,
Ol. Come, be you neare me ſtill.
Al. With all my duty. *Exeunt.*

Scæne 3. *Enter Archas, Theodor, Putskie, Ancient, and Souldiers, carrying his armour peece-meale, his Colours wound up, and his Drums in Caſes.*

Theod. This is the heavieſt march we e're trod Captain,
Putſ. This was not wont to be; theſe honour'd pieces
The fierie god of warre himſelfe would ſmile at,
Buckl'd upon that body, were not wont thus,
Like Reliques to be offer'd to long ruſt,
And heavy-ey'd oblivion brood upon 'em
Arch. There ſet 'em downe: and glorious warre farewell,
Thou childe of honour and ambitious thoughts,
Begot in bloud, and nurſ'd with Kingdomes ruines;
Thou golden danger, courted by thy followers
Through fires and famines, for one title from thee,
Prodigall man-kinde ſpending all his fortunes;
A long farewell I give thee: Noble Armes,
You ribs for mighty mindes, you Iron houſes,
Made to defie the thunder-claps of Fortune,
Ruſt and conſuming time muſt now dwell with yee:
And thou good Sword that knowſt the way to conqueſt,
Upon whoſe fatall edge deſpaire and death dwelt,
That when I ſhooke thee thus, fore-ſhew'd deſtruction,
Sleep now from bloud, and grace my Monument:
Farewell my Eagle; when thou flew'ſt, whole Armies
Have ſtoopt below thee: At Paſſage I have ſeen thee,
Ruffle the *Tartars*, as they fled thy furie;
And bang 'em up together, as a Taſſell,
Upon the ſtreach, a flock of fearefull Pigeons.
I yet remember when the *Volga* curl'd,
The aged *Volga*, when he heav'd his head up,
And rais'd his waters high, to ſee the ruines,
The ruines our Swords made, the bloudy ruines;
Then flew this Bird of honour bravely, Gentlemen;
But theſe muſt be forgotten: ſo muſt theſe too,
And all that tend to Armes, by me for ever.
Take 'em you holy men; my Vow take with 'em,
Never to weare 'em more: Trophies I give 'em,
And ſacred Rites of warre to adorne the Temple:
There let 'em hang, to tell the world their maſter
Is now Devotions ſouldier, fit for prayer,
Why doe ye hang your heads? why look you ſad friends?
I am not dying yet.
Theod. Ye are indeed to us ſir.
Putſ. Dead to our fortunes, Generall.
Arch. Youll finde a better,
A greater, and a ſtronger man to lead yee,
And to a ſtronger fortune: I am old friends,
Time, and the wars together make me ſtoop, gentlemen,
Stoop to my grave: my minde unfurniſh'd too,
Emptie and weak as I am: my poore body,
Able for nothing now but contemplation,
And that will be a taske too to a Souldier:
Yet had they but encourag'd me, or thought well
Of what I have done, I thinke I ſhould have ventur'd
For one knock more, I ſhould have made a ſhift yet
To have broke one ſtaffe more handſomly, and have dyed
Like a good fellow, and an honeſt ſouldier,
In the head of ye all, with my ſword in my hand,
And ſo have made an end of all with credit.
Theod. Well, there will come an houre, when all theſe (injuries
Theſe ſecure ſlights——
Ar. Ha! no more of that ſirrah,
Not one word more of that I charge ye.
Theod. I muſt ſpeak ſir.
And may that tongue forget to ſound your ſervice,
That's dumbe to your abuſes.
Ar. Underſtand foole,
That voluntary I ſit downe.
Theod. You are forced ſir,
Forced for your ſafety: I too well remember
The time and cauſe, and I may live to curſe 'em,
You made this vow, and whoſe un-nobleneſſe,
Indeed forgetfulneſſe of good——
Ar. No more,
As thou art mine no more.
The. Whoſe doubts and envies——
But the devill will have his due.
Putſ. Good gentle Colonell.
Theo. And though diſgraces, and contempt of honour
Reigne now, the wheele muſt turne againe.
Ar. Peace ſirrah,
Your tongue's too ſaucy: doe ye ſtare upon me?
Downe with that heart, downe ſuddenly, down with it,
Downe with that diſobedience; tye that tongue up.
Theod. Tongue?
Ar. Doe not provoke me to forget my vow ſirrah,
And draw that fatall ſword againe in anger.
Putſ. For heavens ſake, Colonell.
Ar. Doe not let me doubt
Whoſe Sonne thou art, becauſe thou canſt not ſuffer:
Doe not play with mine anger; if thou doſt,
By all the loyalty my heart holds——
Theod. I have done ſir,
'Pray pardon me.
Ar. I pray ye be worthy of it:
Beſhrew your heart, you have vext me.
The. I am ſorrie ſir.
Arch. Goe to, no more of this: be true and honeſt,
I know ye are man enough, mold it to juſt ends,
And let not my diſgraces, then I am miſerable,
When I have nothing left me but thy anger.
Flouriſh. Enter Duke, Burris, Boroskie, Attend. & Gent.
Putſ. And't pleaſe ye ſir, the Duke.
Duk. Now, what's all this?
The meaning of this ceremonious Embleme?
Ar. Your Grace ſhould firſt remember——
Ddd *Bur.*

I, iii, opening. The entrance of Archas and others was neither warned nor cued; normally, the prompter warned and cued all entrances except those at the openings of acts.

I, iii, 86–98. A dotted line appears to connect the flourish warning and cue.

I, iii, 98. The stage direction includes some Gentlemen, but since they were not named in the warning, perhaps they were omitted from the scene. The company may well have been operating with as few personnel as possible.

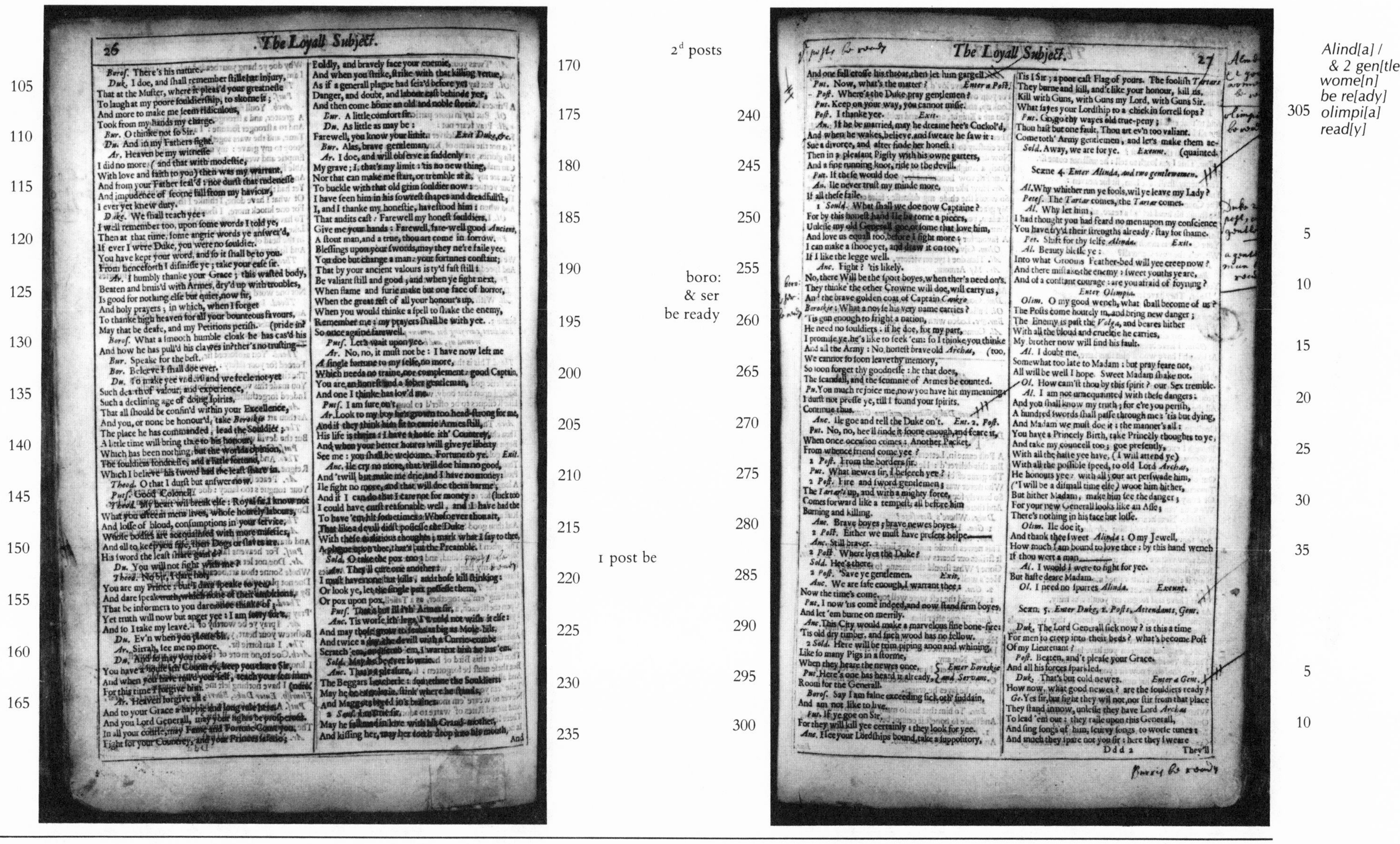

I, iii, 293. The entrance of Boroskie and a Servant was not cued.

I, iii, following 301. The warning for Alinda and the Gentlewomen could easily have been placed earlier.

I, iv, following 10. The entrance of Olimpia was not cued.

I, v, opening. The Attendants mentioned in the entrance stage direction seem not to have been warned and may have been omitted from the scene.

I, v, following 12. The warning for Burris could have been placed earlier.

Archas, olim: / & alinda, be ready

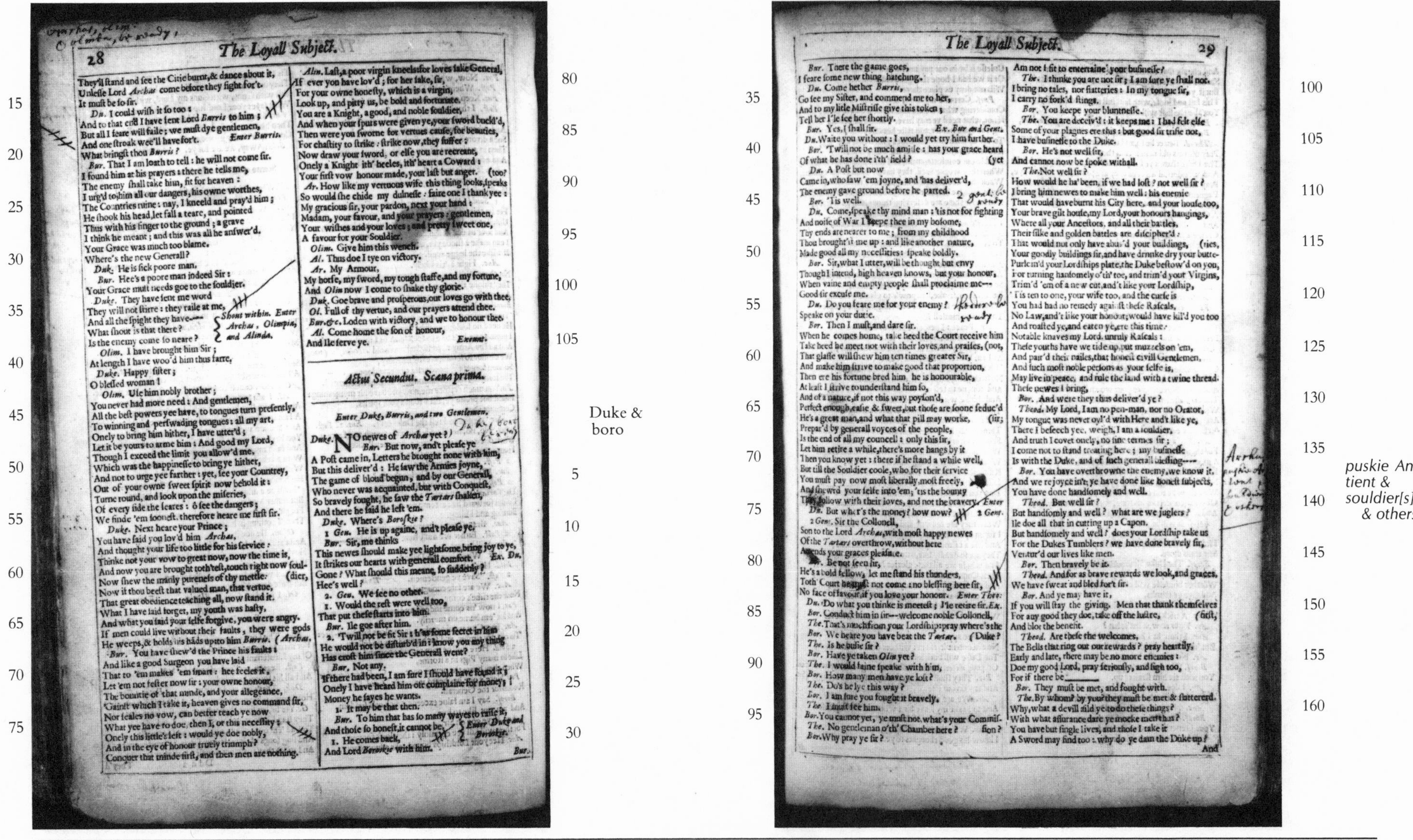
28 The Loyall Subject.

They'll stand and see the Citie burnt, & dance about it,
Unlesse Lord *Archas* come before they fight for't.
It must be so sir.
Du. I could wish it so too:
And to that end I have sent Lord *Burris* to him;
But all I feare will faile; we must dye gentlemen,
And one stroak wee'll have for't. *Enter Burris.*
What bringst thou *Burris*?
Bur. That I am loath to tell: he will not come sir.
I found him at his prayers: there he tells me,
The enemy shall take him, fit for heaven:
I urg'd to him all our dangers, his owne worthes,
The Countries ruine: nay, I kneeld and pray'd him;
He shook his head, let fall a teare, and pointed
Thus with his finger to the ground; a grave
I think he meant; and this was all he answer'd.
Your Grace was much too blame.
Where's the new Generall?
Duk. He is sick poore man.
Bur. Hee's a poore man indeed Sir:
Your Grace must needs goe to the souldier.
Duke. They have sent me word
They will not stirre: they raile at me,
And all the spight they have—— *Shout within. Enter Archas, Olimpia, and Alinda.*
What shout is that there?
Is the enemy come so neare?
Olim. I have brought him Sir;
At length I have woo'd him thus farre,
Duke. Happy sister;
O blessed woman!
Olim. Use him nobly brother;
You never had more need: And gentlemen,
All the best powers yee have, to tongues turn presently,
To winning and perswading tongues: all my art,
Onely to bring him hither, I have utter'd;
Let it be yours to arme him: And good my Lord,
Though I exceed the limit you allow'd me,
Which was the happinesse to bring ye hither,
And not to urge ye farther: yet, see your Countrey,
Out of your owne sweet spirit now behold it:
Turne round, and look upon the miseries,
Of every side the feares: see the dangers;
We finde 'em soonest, therefore heare me first sir.
Duke. Next heare your Prince;
You have said you lov'd him *Archas*,
And thought your life too little for his service:
Thinke not your vow to great now, now the time is,
And now you are brought toth'test, touch right now soul-(dier,
Now shew the mainly purenesse of thy mettle:
Now if thou beest that valued man, that vertue,
That great obedience teaching all, now stand it.
What I have said forget, my youth was hasty,
And what you said your selfe forgive, you were angry.
If men could live without their faults, they were gods
He weeps, & holds his hāds up to him *Burris.* (*Archas,*
Bur. You have shew'd the Prince his faults:
And like a good Surgeon you have laid
That to 'em makes 'em smart: hee feeles it,
Let 'em not fester now sir: your owne honour,
The bountie of that minde, and your allegeance,
'Gainst which I take it, heaven gives no command sir,
Nor seales no vow, can better teach ye now
What yee have to doe; then I, or this necessity;
Onely this little's left: would ye doe nobly,
And in the eye of honour truely triumph?
Conquer that minde first, and then men are nothing.

Alin. Last, a poore virgin kneels for loves sake General,
If ever you have lov'd; for her sake, sir,
For your owne honesty, which is a virgin,
Look up, and pitty us, be bold and fortunate.
You are a Knight, a good, and noble souldier,
And when your spurs were given ye, your sword buckl'd,
Then were you sworne for vertues cause, for beauties,
For chastity to strike: strike now, they suffer:
Now draw your sword, or else you are recreant,
Onely a Knight ith' heeles, ith' heart a Coward:
Your first vow honour made, your last but anger. (too?
Ar. How like my vertuous wife this thing looks, speaks
So would she chide my dulnesse: faire one I thank yee:
My gracious sir, your pardon, next your hand:
Madam, your favour, and your prayers: gentlemen,
Your wishes and your loves; and pretty sweet one,
A favour for your Souldier.
Olim. Give him this wench.
Al. Thus doe I tye on victory.
Ar. My Armour,
My horse, my sword, my tough staffe, and my fortune,
And *Olin* now I come to shake thy glorie.
Duk. Goe brave and prosperous, our loves go with thee.
Ol. Full of thy vertue, and our prayers attend thee.
Bur. &c. Loden with victory, and we to honour thee.
Al. Come home the son of honour,
And Ile serve ye. *Exeunt.*

Actus Secundus. Scæna prima.

Enter Duke, Burris, and two Gentlemen.

Duke. No newes of *Archas* yet?
Bur. But now, an't please ye
A Post came in, Letters he brought none with him,
But this deliver'd: He saw the Armies joyne,
The game of bloud begun, and by our Generall,
Who never was acquainted, but with Conquest,
So bravely fought, he saw the *Tartars* shaken,
And there he said he left 'em.
Duke. Where's *Boroskie*?
1 *Gen.* He is up againe, an't please ye.
Bur. Sir, me thinks
This newes should make yee lightsome, bring joy to ye,
It strikes our hearts with generall comfort. *Ex. Du.*
Gone? What should this meane, so suddenly?
Hee's well?
2. *Gen.* We see no other.
1. Would the rest were well too,
That put these starts into him.
Bur. Ile goe after him.
2. 'Twill not be fit Sir: h'as some secret in him
He would not be disturb'd in: know you any thing
Has crost him since the Generall went?
Bur. Not any.
If there had been, I am sure I should have found it;
Onely I have heard him oft complaine for money;
Money he sayes he wants.
1. It may be that then.
Bur. To him that has so many wayes to raise it,
And those so honest, it cannot be. *Enter Duke and Boroskie.*
1. He comes back,
And Lord *Boroskie* with him. Bur.

The Loyall Subject. 29

Bur. There the game goes,
I feare some new thing hatching.
Du. Come hether *Burris*,
Goe see my Sister, and commend me to her,
And to my litle Mistrisse give this token;
Tell her I'le see her shortly.
Bur. Yes, I shall sir. *Ex. Bur and Gent.*
Du. Waite you without: I would yet try him further.
Bor. 'Twill not be much amisse: has your grace heard
Of what he has done i'th' field? (yet
Du. A Post but now
Came in, who saw 'em joyne, and has deliver'd,
The enemy gave ground before he parted.
Bor. 'Tis well.
Du. Come, speake thy mind man: 'tis not for fighting
And noise of War I keepe thee in my bosome,
Thy ends are nearer to me; from my childhood
Thou brought'st me up: and like another nature,
Made good all my necessities: speake boldly.
Bor. Sir, what I utter, will be thought but envy
Though I intend, high heaven knows, but your honour,
When vaine and empty people shall proclaime me—
Good sir excuse me.
Du. Do you feare me for your enemy?
Speake on your duty.
Bor. Then I must, and dare sir.
When he comes home, take heed the Court receive him
Take heed he meet not with their loves, and praises, (not,
That glasse will shew him ten times greater Sir,
And make him strive to make good that proportion,
Then ere his fortune bred him: he is honourable,
At least I strive to understand him so,
And of a nature, if not this way poyson'd,
Perfect enough, easie & sweet, but those are soone seduc'd
He's a great man, and what that pill may worke, (sir;
Prepar'd by generall voyces of the people,
Is the end of all my feare: only this sir,
Let him retire a while, there's more hangs by it
Then you know yet: there if he stand a while well,
But till the Souldier coole, who for their service
You must pay now most liberally, most freely,
And shewrd your selfe into 'em; 'tis the bounty
They follow with their loves, and not the bravery. *Enter*
Du. But what's the money? how now? *2 Gent.*
2 *Gen.* Sir the Collonell,
Son to the Lord *Archas*, with most happy newes
Of the *Tartars* overthrow, without here
Attends your graces pleasure.
Bo. Be not seen sir,
He's a bold fellow, let me stand his thunders,
Toth' Court he shall not come: no blessing here sir,
No face of favour, if you love your honour. *Enter Theo.*
Du. Do what you thinke is meetest; I'le retire sir. *Ex.*
Bor. Conduct him in sir—welcome noble Collonell,
The. That's much from your Lordship: pray where's the
Bor. We heare you have beat the *Tartar*. (Duke?
The. Is he busie sir?
Bor. Have ye taken *Olin* yet?
The. I would faine speake with him,
Bor. How many men have ye lost?
The. Do's he lye this way?
Bor. I am sure you fought it bravely.
The. I must see him.
Bor. You cannot yet, ye must not: what's your Commis-
The. No gentleman o'th' Chamber here? (sion?
Bor. Why pray ye sir?

Am not I fit to entertaine your businesse?
The. I thinke you are not sir; I am sure ye shall not.
I bring no tales, nor flatteries: In my tongue sir,
I carry no fork'd stings.
Bor. You keepe your bluntnesse.
The. You are deceiv'd: it keeps me: I had felt else
Some of your plagues ere this: but good sir trifle not,
I have businesse to the Duke.
Bor. He's not well sir,
And cannot now be spoke withall.
The. Not well sir?
How would he ha' been, if we had lost? not well sir?
I bring him newes to make him well: his enemie
That would have burnt his City here, and your house too,
Your brave gilt house, my Lord, your honours hangings,
Where all your Ancestors, and all their battles,
Their silke and golden battles are decipher'd:
That would not only have abus'd your buildings, (ties,
Your goodly buildings sir, and have drunke dry your butte-
Purloin'd your Lordships plate, the Duke bestow'd on you,
For turning handsomely o'th' toe, and trim'd your Virgins,
Trim'd 'em of a new cut, and't like your Lordship,
'Tis ten to one, your wife too, and the curse is
You had had no remedy against these Rascals,
No Law, and't like your honour, would have kill'd you too
And roasted ye, and eaten ye, ere this time:
Notable knaves my Lord, unruly Rascals:
These youths have we tide up, put muzzels on 'em,
And par'd their nailes, that honest civill Gentlemen,
And such most noble persons as your selfe is,
May live in peace, and rule the land with a twine thread.
These newes I bring,
Bor. And were they thus deliver'd ye?
Theod. My Lord, I am no pen-man, nor no Orator,
My tongue was never oyl'd with Here and't like ye,
There I beseech yee, weigh, I am a souldier,
And truth I covet onely, no fine termes sir;
I come not to stand treating here; my businesse
Is with the Duke, and of such generall blessing—
Bor. You have overthrowne the enemy, we know it,
And we rejoyce in't; ye have done like honest subjects,
You have done handsomely and well.
Theod. But well sir?
But handsomly and well? what are we juglers?
Ile doe all that in cutting up a Capon.
But handsomly and well? does your Lordship take us
For the Dukes Tumblers? we have done bravely sir,
Ventur'd our lives like men.
Bor. Then bravely be it.
Theod. And for as brave rewards we look, and graces,
We have sweat and bled for't sir.
Bor. And ye may have it,
If you will stay the giving. Men that thank themselves
For any good they doe, take off the lustre, (first,
And blot the benefit.
Theod. Are these the welcomes,
The Bells that ring out our rewards? pray heartily,
Early and late, there may be no more enemies:
Doe my good Lord, pray seriously, and sigh too,
For if there be______
Bor. They must be met, and fought with.
The. By whom? by you they must be met & flattered.
Why, what a devill aild ye to doe these things?
With what assurance dare ye mocke men thus?
You have but single lives, and those I take it
A Sword may find too: why do ye dam the Duke up?
And

Duke & boro

puskie Antient & souldier[s] & others

I, v, 36. The *"Shout within"* was not warned and may have been omitted, though lines refer to it.

30 The Loyall Subject.

And choake that course of love that like a River
Should fill our empty veines againe with comforts?
But if ye use these knick knacks,
This fast and loose, with faithfull men and honest,
You'l be the first will find it.
Enter Archas, Souldiers, Putskey, Ancient, and others,
Boros. You are too untemperate.
Theod. Better be so, and thecse too, then unthankfull:
Pray use this old man so, and then we are paid all.
The Duke thanks ye for your service, & the Court thanks
And wonderfull desirous they are to see ye; (ye,
Pray heaven we have roome enough to march for May-
Pageants, & bonfires for your welcome home Sir, (games,
Here your most noble friend the Lord *Boroskey*,
A Gentleman too tender of your credit,
And ever in the Dukes eare, for your good Sir,
Crazie and sickly, yet to be your servant,
Has leapt into the open aire to meet ye. (come home Sir.
Bor. The best is your words wound not. you are wel-
Hartily welcome home, and for your service.
The noble overthrow you gave the Enemy,
The Duke salutes ye too with all his thanks Sir.
Anc. Sure they will now regard us.
Puts. There's a reason:
But by the changing of the Colonels countenance,
The rolling of his eyes like angry billowes;
I feare the wind's not downe yet, *Ancient*.
Arch. Is the Duke well Sir?
Boros. Not much unhealthy,
Only a little grudging of an ague,
Which cannot last: he has heard, which makes him fearfull,
And loath as yet to give your worth due welcome,
The sicknesse hath been somewhat hot i'th' Army,
Which happily may prove more doubt, then danger,
And more his feare then fate: yet howsoever,
An honest care.——
Ar. Ye say right, and it shall be;
For though upon my life 'tis but a rumor,
A meere opinion, without faith or feare in't;
For Sir, I thanke heaven, we never stood more healthy,
Never more high and lusty; yet to satisfie,
We cannot be too curious, or too carefull
Of what concernes his state, wee'l draw away Sir,
And lodge at further distance, and lesse danger.
Boros. It will be well.
Anc. It will be very scurvy.
I smell it out, it stinks abominably,
Stir it no more.
Boros. The Duke Sir would have you too,
For a short day or two, retyre to your owne house,
Whither himselfe will come to visit ye,
And give ye thanks.
Arch. I shall attend his pleasure.
Anc. A trick, a lowsie trick: so ho, a trick boyes.
Ar. How now, what's that?
Anc. I thought I had found a Hare Sir,
But 'tis a Fox, an old Fox, shall we hunt him?
Ar. No more such words.
Boros. The souldier's growne too sawcy,
You must tie him straiter up.
Ar. I doe my best Sir;
But men of free-born minds sometimes will flie out.
Anc. May not we see the Duke?
Boros. Not at this time Gentlemen,
Your Generall knowes the cause.
Anc. We have no plague Sir,
Unlesse it be in our pay, nor no pox neither;
Or if we had, I hope that good old Courtier
Will not deny us place there.
Puts. Certaine my Lord,
Considering what we are and what we have done;
If not, what need ye may have, 'twould be better,
A great deale nobler, and taste honester
To use us with more sweetnes; men that dig
And lash away their lives at the Carts taile,
Double our comforts, meat, and their Masters thanks too,
When they worke well, they have: Men of our qualitie,
When they doe well, and venture for't with valor,
Fight hard, lye hard, feed hard, when they come home Sir,
And know these are deserving things, things worthy,
Can you then blame 'em if their minds a little
Be stirr'd with glory? 'tis a pride becomes 'em,
A little season'd with ambition,
To be respected, reckon'd well, and honour'd
For what they have done: when to come home thus poorly,
And met with such unjointed joy, so looked on,
As if we had done no more but drest a horse well;
So entertain'd, as if I thank ye Gentlemen,
Take that to drinke, had pow'r to please a souldier?
Where be the shouts, the bels rung out, the people?
The Prince himself?
Ar. Peace: I perceive your eye Sir
Is fixt upon this Captaine for his freedome,
And happily you find his tongue too forward;
As I am Master of the place, I carry,
'Tis fit I thinke so too; but were I this man,
No stronger tye upon me, then the truth
And tongue to tell it, I should speake as he do's,
And thinke with modestie enough, such Saints
That daily thrust their loves & lives through hazards,
And fearelesse for their Countries peace, march hourely
Through all the doores of death, and know the darkest,
Should better be canoniz'd for their service:
What labour would these men neglect, what danger
Where honour is, though seated in a billow,
Rising as high as heaven, would not these souldiers,
Like to so many Sea-gods charge up to it?
Doe you see these swords? times Sithe was ne're so sharp
Nor ever at one harvest mow'd such handfuls: (Sir;
Thoughts ne're so sudden, nor beliefe so sure,
When they are drawne, and were it not sometimes,
I swim upon their angers to allay 'em,
And like a calme depresse their fell intentions;
They are so deadly sure, nature would suffer——
And whose are all these glories? why their Princes,
Their Countries, and their friends? Alas, of all these,
And all the happy ends they bring, the blessings,
They only share the labors, a little joy then,
And outside of a welcome at an upshot
Would not have done amisse Sir; But howsoever
Between me and my duty, no crack Sir
Shall dare appeare: I hope by my example
No discontent in them: without doubt Gentlemen,
The Duke will both looke suddenly and truly
On your deserts: Methinks 'twere good they were paid
Bor. They shall be immediately; I stay for mony; (Sir.
And any favour else——
Ar. We are all bound to ye;
And so I take my leave Sir; when the Duke pleases
To make me worthy of his eyes.——
Bor. Which will be suddenly,
I know his good thoughts to ye.
Ar.

The Loyall Subject. 31

Ar. With all duty.
And all humility, I shall attend Sir.
Bor. Once more you are welcome home: these shall be
The. Be sure we be: and hansomely. (satisfied.
Ar. Waite you on me sir.
The. And honestly: no jugling.
Ar. Will ye come sir? *Exit.*
Bor. Pray do not doubt.
Theo. We are no Boyes. *Exit. Enter a Gent. and 2 or 3 with money.*
Bor, Well sir.
Gent. Here's money from the Duke, and't please your
Bor. 'Tis well. (Lordship.
Gent. How sowre the Souldiers looke?
Bor. Is't told?
Gent. Yes; and for every company a double pay,
And the Dukes love to all.
Anc. That's worth a ducket.
Bor. You that be Officers, see it discharg'd then,
Why do not ye take it up?
Anc. 'Tis too heavy:
'Body o'me, I have strain'd mine arme.
Bor. Do ye scorne it?
Anc. Has your Lordship any dice about ye? sit round
And come on seaven for my share. (Gentlemen.
Put. Do you thinke sir,
This is the end we fight? can this durt draw us
To such a stupid tamenesse, that our service
Neglected, and look'd lamely on, and skewd at
With a few honourable words, and this, is righted?
Have not we eyes and eares, to heare and see Sir,
And minds to understand the slights we carry?
I come home old, and full of hurts, men looke on me
As if I had got 'em from a whore, and shun me;
I tell my griefes, and feare my wants, I am answer'd,
Alas 'tis pity! pray dine with me on Sunday:
These are the sores we are sicke of, the minds malladies,
And can this cure 'em? you should have us'd us nobly,
And for our doing well, as well proclam'd us,
To the worlds eye, have shew'd and sainted us,
Then ye had paid us bravely: then we had shin'd sir,
Not in this gilded stuffe but in our glory:
You may take backe your money.
Gent. This I fear'd still.
Bor. Consider better Gentlemen.
Anc. Thanke your Lordship:
And now I'l put on my considering cap:
My Lord, that I am no Courtier, you may guesse it
By having no sute to you for this money:
For though I want, I want not this, nor shall not,
Whilst you want that civility to ranke it
With those rights we expected; money growes sir,
And men must gather it, all is not put in one purse.
And that I am no Carter, I could never whistle yet:
But that I am a Souldier, and a Gentleman,
And a fine Gentleman, and't like your honour,
And a most pleasant companion: all you that are witty,
Come list to my ditty: come set in boyes,
With your Lordships patience. *Song.*
How do you like my Song, my Lord?
Bor. Even as I like your self, but 'twould be a great deale (better,
You would prove a great deale wiser, and take this mony,
In your owne phrase I speake now sir, and 'tis very well:
You have learn'd to sing; for since you prove so liberall,
To refuse such meanes as this, maintaine your voice still,
'Twill prove your best friend.
Anc. 'Tis a singing age sir,
A merry moone here now: I'le follow it:
Fidling, and fooling now, gaines more then fighting.
Bor. What is't you blench at? what would you aske? speak
Sol. And so we dare: a triumph for the Generall. (freely.
Put. And then an honour speciall to his vertue.
Anc. That we may be prefer'd that have serv'd for it, Duke be
And cramm'd up into favour like the worshipfull,
At least upon the Cities charge made drunke
For one whole year; we have done 'em ten yeares service;
That we may enjoy our lechery without grudging,
And mine, or thine be nothing, all things equall,
And catch as catch may be proclamed: that when we
And have no will to pay againe, no Law (borrow,
Lay hold upon us, nor no Court controule us.
Bor. Some of these may come to passe; the Duke may
And no doubt will: the Generall will find too, (do 'em,
And so will you, if you but stay with patience: I have no
Put. Nor will: come fellow Souldiers, (power.
Bor. Pray be not so distrustfull.
Put. There are waies yet,
And honest waies; we are not brought up Statues.
Anc. If your Lordship
Have any silke stockings, that have holes i'th' heeles,
Or ever an honourable Cassock that wants buttons,
I could have cur'd such malladies: your Lordships custome
And my good Ladies, if the bones want setting
In her old bodies.——
Bor. This is disobedience.
Anc. Eight pence a day, and hard Eggs.
Put. Troop off Gentlemen,
Some Coine we have, whilst this lasts, or our credits,
Wee'll never sell our Generalls worth for six-pence.
Ye are beholding to us.
Anc. Fare ye well Sir,
And buy a pipe with that: doe ye see this skarfe sir?
By this hand Ile cry Brooms in't, birchen Brooms sir,
Before I eate one bit from your benevolence.
Now to our old occupations againe.
By your leave Lord. *Exit.*
Bor. You will bite when ye are sharper; take up the
This love I must remove, this fondnes to him, (money.
This tendernesse of heart; I have lost my way else.
There is no lending man, they will not take it,
They are yet too full of pillage,
They'll dance for't ere't be long:
Come, bring it after. *Enter Duke.*
Duke How now, refus'd their money?
Bor. Very bravely,
And stand upon such termes 'tis terrible.
Du. Where's *Archas*? rea[dy]
Bor. Hee's retir'd Sir, to his house,
According to your pleasure, full of dutie
To outward shew; but what within.——
Duk. Refuse it?
Bor. Most confidently: 'tis not your revenewes
Can feed them sir, and yet they have found a Generall
That knowes no ebbe of bountie: there they eate Sir,
And loath your invitations.
Du. 'Tis not possible,
Hee's poor as they.
Bor. You'll find it otherwise.
Pray make your journey thither presently,
And as ye goe Ile open yee a wonder.
Good sir this morning.
Duke. Follow me, Ile doe it.
Exeunt.
Scene

Scæn. 2. *Enter Olimpia, Alinda, Burris, and Gentlewomen.*

Olim. But doe you thinke my brother loves her.
Bur. Certaine Madam,
He speaks much of her, and sometimes with wonder,
Oft wishes she were nobler borne.
Olim. Doe you thinke him honest?
Bur. Your Grace is nearer to his heart, then I am,
Upon my life I hold him so.
Olim. 'Tis a poore wench,
I would not have her wrong'd: methinks my Brother—
But I must not give rules to his affections;
Yet if he weigh her worth——
Bur. You need not feare Madam.
Olim. I hope I shall not: Lord *Burris*
I love her well; I know not, there is something
Makes me bestow more then a care upon her:
I doe not like that ring, from him to her;
I meane to women of her way, such tokens
Rather appeare as baits, then royall bounties:
I would not have it so.
Bur. You will not find it,
Upon my troth I thinke his most ambition
Is but to let the world know 'has a hansome Mistris:
Will your Grace command me any service to him?
Olim. Remember all my duty.
Bur. Blessings crowne ye:
What's your will Lady?
Al. Any thing that's honest;
And if you thinke it fits so poore a service,
Clad in a ragged vertue, may reach him,
I doe beseech your Lordship speake it humbly.
Bur. Faire one I will: in the best phrase I have too,
And so I kisse your hand *Exit.*
Al. Your Lordships servant.
Olim. Come hither wench, what art thou doing with (that Ring.
Al. I am looking on the posie, Madam.
Olim. What is't?
Al. The Jewels set within.
Olim. But where the joy wench,
When that invisible Jewel's lost? why dost thou smile so?
What unhappy meaning hast thou?
Al. Nothing Madam,
But only thinking what strange spels these Rings have,
And how they worke with some.
Pet. I feare with you too.
Al. This could not cost above a Crowne.
Pet. 'Twill cost you
The shaving of your crowne, if not the washing.
Olim. But he that sent it, makes the vertue greater.
Al. I and the vice too Madam: goodnes blesse me:
How fit 'tis for my finger.
2 W. No doubt you'l find too
A finger fit for you.
Al. Sirrah, *Petesea*,
What wilt thou give me for the good that followes this?
But thou hast Rings enough, thou art provided:
Heigh ho, what must I doe now?
Pet. You'l be taught that,
The easiest part that e're you learn't, I warrant you.
Al. Ay me, ay me.
Pet. You will divide too, shortly,
Your voice comes finely forward.
Olim. Come hither wanton,
Thou art not surely as thou saist.
Al. I would not:
But sure there is a witchcraft in this Ring, Lady,
Lord how my heart leaps.
Pet. 'Twill goe pit a pat shortly.
Al. And now methinks a thousand of the Dukes shapes.
2 W. Will no lesse serve ye?
Al. In ten thousand smiles.
Olim. Heaven blesse the wench.
Al. With eyes that will not be denide to enter;
And such soft sweet embraces; take it from me,
I am undone else Madam: I'm lost else.
Olim. What ailes the girle?
Al. How suddenly I'm alter'd?
And growne my selfe againe? doe not you feele it?
Olim. Weare that, and I'le weare this:
I'le try the strength on't.
Al. How cold my bloud growes now?
Here's sacred vertue:
When I leave to honour this,
Every houre to pay a kisse,
When each morning I arise,
Or I forget a sacrifice:
When this figure in my faith,
And the purenes that it hath,
I pursue not with my will,
Nearer to arrive at still:
When I lose, or change this Jewell,
Flie me faith, and heaven be cruell.
Olim. You have halfe confirm'd me,
Keep but that way sure,
And what this charme can doe, let me endure. *Exeunt.*

2 da: Ho: & Viola

Scæne 3. *Enter Archas, Theodore, 2 Daughters. Honora and Viola.*

Ar. Carry your selfe discreetly, it concernes me;
The Duke's come in, none of your froward passions,
Nor no distastes to any: Prethee *Theodor*,
By my life, boy, 'twill ruine me.
The. I have done Sir,
So there be no foule play he brings along with him.
Ar. What's that to you?
Let him bring what please him,
And whom, and how.
The. So they meane well——
Ar. Is't fit you be a Judge firrah,
The. 'Tis fit I feele Sir.
Ar. Get a banquet ready,
And trim your selves up hansomly.
The. To what end?
Doe you meane to make 'em whores?
Hang up a signe then,
And set 'em out to Livery.
Ar. Whose sonne art thou?
The. Yours Sir, I hope: but not of your disgraces.
Ar. Full twenty thousand men I have commanded,
And all their minds with this, calm'd all their angers;
And shall a boy of mine owne breed too, of mine owne (bloud,
One crooked stick——
The. Pray take your way, and thrive in't,
I'le quit your house; if taint or black dishonour
Light on ye, 'tis your owne, I have no share in't.
Yet if it doe fall out so, as I feare it,
And partly find it too——
Ar. Hast thou no reverence?
No

Duke Ar: [Bor]

No dutie in thee?
The. This shall shew I obey ye:
I dare not stay: I would have shew'd my love too,
And that you aske as duty, with my life sir,
Had you but thought me worthy of your hazzards,
Which heaven preserve ye from, and keep the Duke too:
And there's an end of my wishes, God be with ye. *Exit.*
Ar. Stubborne, yet full of that we all love, honesty,
Lord *Burris*, where's the Duke? *Enter Burris.*
Bur. In the great chamber Sir,
And there stayes till he see you: ye 'have a fine house here.
Ar. A poore contented lodge, unfit for his presence,
Yet all the joy it hath.
Bur. I hope a great one, and for your good, brave Sir.
Ar. I thanke ye Lord:
And now my service to the Duke.
Bur. I'le wait on ye. *Exeunt.*
Enter Duke, Boroskey, Gent. and Attendants.
Du. May this be credited?
Bor. Disgrace me else,
And never more with favour looke upon me.
Du. It seemes impossible.
Bor. It cannot chuse Sir,
Till your owne eies behold it; but that it is so.
And that by this meanes the too haughtie souldier
Has been so cramm'd and fed, he cares not for ye;
Beleeve, or let me perish: Let your eyes
As you observe the house, but where I point it,
Make stay, and take a view, and then you have found it.

& Anti:

Enter Archas, Burris, 2 Daughters and Servant.
Du. I'le follow your direction: welcome *Archas*,
You are welcome home brave Lord, we are come to visit (ye,
And thanke ye for your service.
Ar. 'Twas so poore Sir,
In true respect of what I owe your Highnesse,
It merits nothing.
Du. Are these faire ones yours Lord?
Ar. Their Mother made me thinke so Sir.
Du. Stand up Ladies:
Beshrew my heart they are faire ones; methinks fitter
The lustre of the Court, then thus live darken'd:
I would see your house Lord *Archas*, it appeares to me,
A hansome pile.
Ar. 'Tis neate but no great structure;
I'le be your Graces guide, give me the keyes there.
Du. Lead on, wee'l follow ye: begin with the Gallery,
I think that's one.
Ar. 'Tis so, and't please ye Sir,
The rest above are lodgings all.
Du. Goe on Sir. *Exeunt.*

Scæne 4. *Enter Theodore, Putskey, and Ancient.*

Put. The Duke gone thither, doe you say?
The. Yes marry doe I,
And all the ducklings too: but what they'l doe there.——
Put. I hope they'l crowne his service.
The. With a Custard;
This is no weather for rewards, they crowne his service?
Rather, they goe to shave his crowne: I was rated,
As if I had been a dog had worried sheep, out of doores,
For making but a doubt.
Put. They must now grace him.
The. Marke but the end.
Anc. I am sure they should reward him, they cannot want (him
The. They that want honesty, want any thing.
Put. The Duke is so noble in his owne thoughts.
The. That I grant ye,
If those might only sway him: but 'tis most certaine,
So many new borne flyes, his light gave life too,
Buzze in his beames, flesh flies, and Butterflies,
Hornets, and humming Scarrabs, that not one honey Bee
That's loden with true labour, and brings home
Encreale, and credit, can scape rifling,
And what she sucks for sweet, they turne to bitternesse.
An. Shall we go see what they do, & talke our minds to
P. That we have done too much, & to no purpose. ('em?
Anc. Shall we be hang'd for him?
I have a great mind to be hangd now
For doing some brave thing for him; a worse end will
And for an action of no worth, not honour him? (take me
Upon my conscience even the devill, the very devill
(Not to belye him) thinkes him an honest man,
I am sure he has sent him soules any times these twenty
Able to furnish all his fishmarket. (yeares,
The. Leave thy talking
And come, let's go to dinner and drinke to him,
We shall heare more ere supper time: if he be honour'd,
He has deserv'd it well, and we shall fight for't:
If he be ruin'd so, we know the worst then,
And for my selfe I'le meet it.
Put. I ne're feare it. *Exeunt.*

Scæne 5. *Enter Duke, Archas, Boroskey, Burris, Gentlemen, and Attendants.*

Du. They are handsome roomes all, well contriv'd and (fitted,
Full of covenience, the prospects excellent.
Ar. Now will your Grace passe downe, and do me but (the honour
To taste a Country banket?
Du. What roome's that?
I would see all now; what conveyance has it?
I see you have kept the best part yet; pray open it.
Ar. Ha? I misdoubted this: 'tis of no receipte sir,
For your eyes most unfit——
Du. I long to see it, (lent paintings,
Because I would judge of the whole peece: some excel-
Or some rare spoiles you would keep to entertaine me
An other time, I know.
Ar. In troth there is not,
Nor any thing worth your sight: below I have
Some fountaines, and some ponds.
Du. I would see this now.
Ar. *Borosky*, thou art a knave; It containes nothing
But rubbish from the other roomes and unnecessaries:
Wil't please you see a strange Clocke?
Du. This, or nothing: *Little Trunke*
Why should you barre it up thus with defences *ready.*
Above the rest, unlesse it contain'd something
More excellent, and curious of keeping:
Open't, for I will see't.
Ar. The keyes are lost sir;
Do's your grace thinke if it were fit for you,
I could be so unmannerly?
Du. I will see it, and either shew it——
Ar. Good sir——
Du. Thanke ye *Archas*,
You shew your love abundantly,
Do I use to entreat thus? force it open,
Bur. That were inhospitable: you are his guest sir,
And with his greatest joy, to entertaine ye.
Du. Hold thy peace foole; will ye open it?
Ar. Sir, I cannot.
Eee Duk,

II, ii, opening. Since the Gentlewomen were not warned, perhaps they were omitted from the scene.

II, iii, opening. The entrance of Archas and the others was not cued.

II, iii, 45. The prompter wrote *Enter* two lines in advance of the entrance of the Duke and others. Perhaps he intended advancing the entrance, though he made the cue sign at the printed stage direction.

II, iii, 47–78. The prompter here had a sequence of entrances close together, but he preferred not to warn one entrance before another had been cued.

II, v, 21. "*Little Trunke / ready*" is a trace of earlier prompt copy c.82 lines before the trunk is needed.

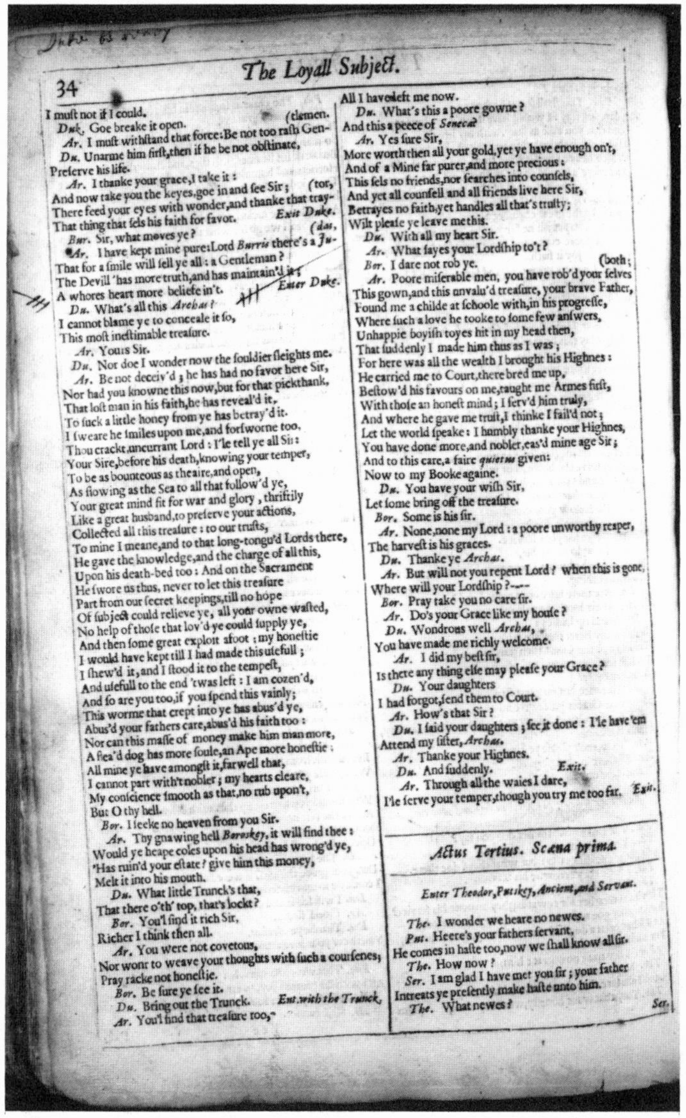

34 *The Loyall Subject.*

I muſt not if I could. (tlemen.
Duk. Goe breake it open.
Ar. I muſt withſtand that force: Be not too raſh Gen-
Du. Unarme him firſt, then if he be not obſtinate,
Preſerve his life.
Ar. I thanke your grace, I take it: (tor,
And now take you the keyes, goe in and ſee Sir;
There feed your eyes with wonder, and thanke that tray-
That thing that ſels his faith for favor. *Exit Duke.*
Bur. Sir, what moves ye? (das,
Ar. I have kept mine pure: Lord *Burris* there's a *Ju-*
That for a ſmile will ſell ye all: a Gentleman?
The Devill 'has more truth, and has maintain'd it;
A whores heart more beliefe in't. *Enter Duke.*
Du. What's all this *Archas*?
I cannot blame ye to conceale it ſo,
This moſt ineſtimable treaſure.
Ar. Yours Sir.
Du. Nor doe I wonder now the ſouldier ſleights me.
Ar. Be not deceiv'd; he has had no favor here Sir,
Nor had you knowne this now, but for that pickthank,
That loſt man in his faith, he has reveal'd it,
To ſuck a little honey from ye has betray'd it.
I ſweare he ſmiles upon me, and forſworne too.
Thou crackt, uncurrant Lord: I'le tell ye all Sir:
Your Sire, before his death, knowing your temper,
To be as bounteous as the aire, and open,
As flowing as the Sea to all that follow'd ye,
Your great mind fit for war and glory, thriftily
Like a great husband, to preſerve your actions,
Collected all this treaſure: to our truſts,
To mine I meane, and to that long-tongu'd Lords there,
He gave the knowledge, and the charge of all this,
Upon his death-bed too: And on the Sacrament
He ſwore us thus, never to let this treaſure
Part from our ſecret keepings, till no hope
Of ſubject could relieve ye, all your owne waſted,
No help of thoſe that lov'd ye could ſupply ye,
And then ſome great exploit afoot; my honeſtie
I would have kept till I had made this uſefull;
I ſhew'd it, and I ſtood it to the tempeſt,
And uſefull to the end 'twas left: I am cozen'd,
And ſo are you too, if you ſpend this vainly;
This worme that crept into ye has abus'd ye,
Abus'd your fathers care, abus'd his faith too:
Nor can this maſſe of money make him man more,
A flea'd dog has more ſoule, an Ape more honeſtie:
All mine ye have amongſt it, farwell that,
I cannot part with't nobler; my hearts cleare,
My conſcience ſmooth as that, no rub upon't,
But O thy hell.
Bor. I ſeeke no heaven from you Sir.
Ar. Thy gnawing hell *Boroskey*, it will find thee:
Would ye heape coles upon his head has wrong'd ye,
'Has ruin'd your eſtate? give him this money,
Melt it into his mouth.
Du. What little Trunck's that,
That there o'th' top, that's lockt?
Bor. You'l find it rich Sir,
Richer I think then all.
Ar. You were not covetous,
Nor wont to weave your thoughts with ſuch a courſenes;
Pray racke not honeſtie.
Bor. Be ſure ye ſee it.
Du. Bring out the Trunck. *Ent. with the Trunck.*
Ar. You'l find that treaſure too,
All I have left me now.
Du. What's this a poore gowne?
And this a peece of *Seneca*?
Ar. Yes ſure Sir,
More worth then all your gold, yet ye have enough on't,
And of a Mine far purer, and more precious:
This ſels no friends, nor ſearches into counſels,
And yet all counſell and all friends live here Sir,
Betrayes no faith, yet handles all that's truſty;
Wilt pleaſe ye leave me this.
Du. With all my heart Sir.
Ar. What ſayes your Lordſhip to't?
Bor. I dare not rob ye. (both;
Ar. Poore miſerable men, you have rob'd your ſelves
This gown, and this unvalu'd treaſure, your brave Father,
Found me a childe at ſchoole with, in his progreſſe,
Where ſuch a love he tooke to ſome few anſwers,
Unhappie boyiſh toyes hit in my head then,
That ſuddenly I made him thus as I was;
For here was all the wealth I brought his Highnes:
He carried me to Court, there bred me up,
Beſtow'd his favours on me, taught me Armes firſt,
With thoſe an honeſt mind; I ſerv'd him truly,
And where he gave me truſt, I thinke I fail'd not;
Let the world ſpeake: I humbly thanke your Highnes,
You have done more, and nobler, eas'd mine age Sir;
And to this care, a faire *quietus* given:
Now to my Booke againe.
Du. You have your wiſh Sir,
Let ſome bring off the treaſure.
Bor. Some is his ſir.
Ar. None, none my Lord: a poore unworthy reaper,
The harveſt is his graces.
Du. Thanke ye *Archas*.
Ar. But will not you repent Lord? when this is gone,
Where will your Lordſhip?——
Bor. Pray take you no care ſir.
Ar. Do's your Grace like my houſe?
Du. Wondrous well *Archas*,
You have made me richly welcome.
Ar. I did my beſt ſir,
Is there any thing elſe may pleaſe your Grace?
Du. Your daughters
I had forgot, ſend them to Court.
Ar. How's that Sir?
Du. I ſaid your daughters; ſee it done: I'le have 'em
Attend my ſiſter, *Archas*.
Ar. Thanke your Highnes.
Du. And ſuddenly. *Exit.*
Ar. Through all the waies I dare,
I'le ſerve your temper, though you try me too far. *Exit.*

Actus Tertius. Scæna prima.

Enter Theodor, Putskey, Ancient, and Servant.

The. I wonder we heare no newes.
Put. Heere's your fathers ſervant,
He comes in haſte too, now we ſhall know all ſir.
The. How now?
Ser. I am glad I have met you ſir; your father
Intreats ye preſently make haſte unto him.
The. What newes? *Ser.*

Archas
Hono.
& viola

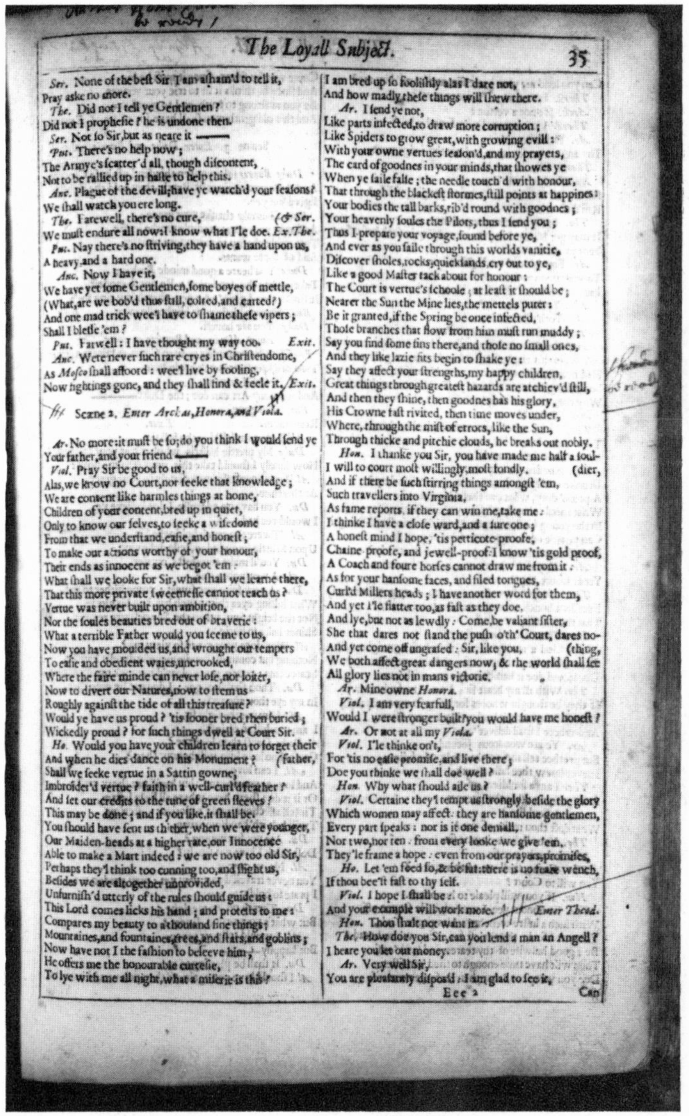

The Loyall Subject. 35

Ser. None of the beſt Sir I am aſham'd to tell it,
Pray aske no more.
The. Did not I tell ye Gentlemen?
Did not I propheſie? he is undone then.
Ser. Not ſo Sir, but as neare it ——
Put. There's no help now;
The Armye's ſcatter'd all, though diſcontent,
Not to be rallied up in haſte to help this.
Anc. Plague of the devill; have ye watch'd your ſeaſons?
We ſhall watch you ere long.
The. Farewell, there's no cure, (& Ser.
We muſt endure all now: I know what I'le doe. *Ex. The.*
Put. Nay there's no ſtriving, they have a hand upon us,
A heavy and a hard one.
Anc. Now I have it,
We have yet ſome Gentlemen, ſome boyes of mettle,
(What, are we bob'd thus ſtill, colted, and carted?)
And one mad trick wee'l have to ſhame theſe vipers;
Shall I bleſſe 'em?
Put. Farwell: I have thought my way too. *Exit.*
Anc. Were never ſuch rare cryes in Chriſtendome,
As *Moſco* ſhall affoord: wee'l live by fooling,
Now fightings gone, and they ſhall find & feele it. *Exit.*

Scæne 2. *Enter Archas, Honora, and Viola.*

Ar. No more: it muſt be ſo; do you think I would ſend ye
Your father, and your friend ——
Viol. Pray Sir be good to us,
Alas, we know no Court, nor ſeeke that knowledge;
We are content like harmles things at home,
Children of your content, bred up in quiet,
Only to know our ſelves, to ſeeke a wiſedome
From that we underſtand, eaſie, and honeſt;
To make our actions worthy of your honour,
Their ends as innocent as we begot 'em:
What ſhall we looke for Sir, what ſhall we learne there,
That this more private ſweetneſſe cannot teach us?
Vertue was never built upon ambition,
Nor the ſoules beauties bred out of braverie:
What a terrible Father would you ſeeme to us,
Now you have moulded us, and wrought our tempers
To eaſie and obedient waies, uncrooked,
Where the faire minde can never loſe, nor loiter,
Now to divert our Natures, now to ſtem us
Roughly againſt the tide of all this treaſure?
Would ye have us proud? 'tis ſooner bred then buried;
Wickedly proud? for ſuch things dwell at Court Sir.
Ho. Would you have your children learn to forget their
And when he dies dance on his Monument? (father,
Shall we ſeeke vertue in a Sattin gowne,
Imbroider'd vertue? faith in a well-curl'd feather?
And ſet our credits to the tune of green ſleeves?
This may be done; and if you like, it ſhall be.
You ſhould have ſent us thither, when we were younger,
Our Maiden-heads at a higher rate, our Innocence
Able to make a Mart indeed: we are now too old Sir,
Perhaps they'l think too cunning too, and ſlight us,
Beſides we are altogether unprovided,
Unfurniſh'd utterly of the rules ſhould guide us:
This Lord comes licks his hand; and proteſts to me:
Compares my beauty to a thouſand fine things;
Mountaines, and fountaines, trees, and ſtars, and goblins;
Now have not I the faſhion to beleeve him,
He offers me the honourable curteſie,
To lye with me all night, what a miſerie is this?
I am bred up ſo fooliſhly alas I dare not,
And how madly theſe things will ſhew there.
Ar. I ſend ye not,
Like parts infected, to draw more corruption;
Like Spiders to grow great, with growing evill:
With your owne vertues ſeaſon'd, and my prayers,
The card of goodnes in your minds, that ſhowes ye
When ye ſaile falſe; the needle touch'd with honour,
That through the blackeſt ſtormes, ſtill points at happines:
Your bodies the tall barks, rib'd round with goodnes;
Your heavenly ſoules the Pilots, thus I ſend you;
Thus I prepare your voyage, ſound before ye,
And ever as you ſaile through this worlds vanitie,
Diſcover ſholes, rocks, quickſands, cry out to ye,
Like a good Maſter tack about for honour:
The Court is vertue's ſchoole; at leaſt it ſhould be;
Nearer the Sun the Mine lies, the mettels purer:
Be it granted, if the Spring be once infected,
Thoſe branches that flow from him muſt run muddy;
Say you find ſome ſins there, and thoſe no ſmall ones,
And they like lazie fits begin to ſhake ye:
Say they affect your ſtrengths, my happy children,
Great things through greateſt hazards are atchiev'd ſtill,
And then they ſhine, then goodnes has his glory,
His Crowne faſt rivited, then time moves under,
Where, through the miſt of errors, like the Sun,
Through thicke and pitchie clouds, he breaks out nobly.
Hon. I thanke you Sir, you have made me half a ſoul-
I will to court moſt willingly, moſt fondly. (dier,
And if there be ſuch ſtirring things amongſt 'em,
Such travellers into Virginia,
As fame reports, if they can win me, take me:
I thinke I have a cloſe ward, and a ſure one;
A honeſt mind I hope, 'tis petticote-proofe,
Chaine-proofe, and jewell-proof: I know 'tis gold proof,
A Coach and foure horſes cannot draw me from it:
As for your hanſome faces, and filed tongues,
Curl'd Millers heads; I have another word for them,
And yet I'le flatter too, as faſt as they doe,
And lye, but not as lewdly: Come, be valiant ſiſter,
She that dares not ſtand the puſh o'th' Court, dares no-
And yet come off ungrafed: Sir, like you, (thing,
We both affect great dangers now; & the world ſhall ſee
All glory lies not in mans victorie.
Ar. Mine owne *Honora*.
Viol. I am very fearfull,
Would I were ſtronger built? you would have me honeſt?
Ar. Or not at all my *Viola*.
Viol. I'le thinke on't,
For 'tis no eaſie promiſe, and live there;
Doe you thinke we ſhall doe well?
Hon. Why what ſhould aile us?
Viol. Certaine they'l tempt us ſtrongly: beſide the glory
Which women may affect: they are hanſome gentlemen,
Every part ſpeaks: nor is it one deniall,
Nor two, nor ten: from every looke we give 'em,
They'le frame a hope: even from our prayers, promiſes,
Ho. Let 'em feed ſo, & be fat: there is no fear wench,
If thou bee'ſt faſt to thy ſelf.
Viol. I hope I ſhall be:
And your example will work more. *Enter Theod.*
Hon. Thou ſhalt not want it.
The. How doe you Sir, can you lend a man an Angell?
I heare you let out money.
Ar. Very well Sir,
You are pleaſantly diſpos'd: I am glad to ſee it,
Eee 2 Can

theodor[e]

Can you lend me your patience, and be rul'd by me?
Theod. Is't come to Patience now?
Arch. Is't not a vertue?
Theod. I know not. I ne're found it ſo.
Ar. That's becauſe
Thy anger ever knowes, and not thy judgement.
Theod. I know you have been rifl'd.
Ar. Nothing leſſe boy:
Lord what opinions theſe vaine people publiſh!
Rifl'd of what?
The. Study your vertue patience,
It may get Muſtard to your meat. Why in ſuch haſte ſir,
Sent ye for me?
Ar. For this end onely, *Theodore*,
To wait upon your ſiſters to the Court;
I am commanded they live there.
The. Toth' Court ſir?
Ar. Toth' Court I ſay.
The. And muſt I wait upon 'em?
Ar. Yes, 'tis moſt fit yee ſhould, ye are their brother.
The. Is this the buſineſſe? I had thought your mind ſir
Had been ſet forward on ſome noble action,
Something had truely ſtirr'd ye. Toth' Court with theſe?
Why they are your daughters ſir.
Ar. All this I know ſir.
The. The good old woman on a bed he threw.
Toth' Court?
Ar. Thou art not mad.
The. Nor drunke as you are:
Drunke with your duty ſir: doe you call it duty?
A pox o' duty, what can theſe doe there?
What ſhould they doe? Can ye look Babies ſiſters
In the young Gallants eyes, & twirle their Band-ſtrings?
Can ye ride out to ayre your ſelves? pray ſir,
Be ſerious with me: doe you ſpeake this truely?
Ar. Why didſt thou never heare of women
Yet at Court boy?
The. Yes, and good women too, very good women,
Excellent honeſt women: but are you ſure ſir,
That theſe will prove ſo?
Hon. There's the danger brother.
The. God a mercy wench, thou haſt a grudging of it.
Ar. Now be you ſerious ſir, and obſerve what I ſay,
Doe it, and doe it handſomely: goe with 'em.
The. With all my heart ſir; I am in no fault now;
If they be thought whores for being in my company,
Pray write upon their backs, they are my ſiſters,
And where I ſhall deliver 'em.
Ar. Ye are wondrous jocund,
But prethee tell me, art thou ſo lewd a fellow,
I never knew thee faile a truth.
The. I am a ſouldier,
And ſpell you what that meanes.
Ar. A Souldier?
What doſt thou make of me?
The. Your Pallat's downe ſir.
Ar. I thanke yee ſir.
The. Come, ſhall we to this matter?
You will to Court?
Hon. If you will pleaſe to honour us.
The. Ile honour yee, I warrant: Ile ſet yee off
With ſuch a luſtre wenches: Alas poore *Viola*,
Thou art a foole, thou crieſt for eating white-bread:
Be a good huſwife of thy teares, and ſave 'em,
Thou wilt have time enough to ſhed 'em ſiſter.
Doe you weep too? nay then Ile foole no more.

Come worthy ſiſters, ſince it muſt be ſo,
And ſince he thinks it fit to trie your vertues,
Be you as ſtrong to truth, as I to guard yee,
And this old gentleman ſhall have joy of ye. *Exeunt.*

Scæne 3. *Enter Duke and Burris.*

Duke *Burris* take you ten thouſand of thoſe Crowns,
And thoſe two chaines of Pearle they hold the richeſt,
I give 'em yee.
Bur. I humbly thanke your grace;
And may your great example worke in me
That noble charity to men more worthy,
And of more wants.
Duke You beare a good minde *Burris*;
Take twenty thouſand now: Be not ſo modeſt,
It ſhall be ſo, I give 'em: goe, there's my ring for't.
Bur. Heaven bleſſe your Highneſſe ever. *Exit.*
Duke You are honeſt.
Enter Alinda, and Putskie at doore.
Putſ. They're comming now to Court, as faire as vertue:
Two brighter ſtarres ne're roſe here.
Al. Peace, I have it,
And what my Art can doe; the Duke.——
Put. I am gone,
Remember. *Exit.*
Al. I am counſell'd to the full ſir.
Duke My prettie Miſtris, whither lyes your buſineſſe?
How kindly I ſhould take this, were it to me now?
Al. I muſt confeſſe immediately to your grace,
At this time.
Du. You have no addreſſe, I doe believe ye,
I would yee had.
Al 'Twere too much boldneſſe Sir,
Upon ſo little knowledge, leſſe deſerving.
Du. You'll make a perfect Courtier.
Al. A very poore one.
Du. A very faire one ſweet: come hither to me.
What killing eyes this wench has? in his glorie
Not the bright Sun, when the *Sirian* ſtarre reignes,
Shines halfe ſo fierie.
Al. Why does your grace ſo view me?
Nothing but common handſomeneſſe dwells here ſir,
Scarce that: your grace is pleas'd to mock my meanneſs.
Du. Thou ſhalt not goe: I doe not lie unto thee,
In my eye thou appear'ſt——
Al. Dim not the ſight ſir,
I am too dull an object.
Duke Canſt thou love me?
Canſt thou love him will honour thee?
Al. I can love,
And love as you doe too: but 'twill not ſhew well:
Or if it doe ſhew here where all light luſtres,
Tinſell affections, make a glorious gliſtering,
'Twill halt ith' handſome way.
Du. Are yee ſo cunning?
Doſt think I love not truely?
Al. No, ye cannot,
You never travell'd that way yet: pray pardon me,
I prate ſo boldly to you.
Du. There's no harme done:
But what's your reaſon, ſweet?
Al. I would tell your grace,
But happily——
Du. It ſhall be pleaſing to me.
Al. I ſhould love you again, & then you would hate me.
With

With all my ſervice I ſhould follow yee,
And through all dangers.
Du This would more provoke me,
More make me ſee thy worthes,
More make me meet 'em.
Al. You ſhould doe ſo, if yee did well and truely.
But though yee be a Prince, and have power in ye,
Power of example too, ye have fail'd and falter'd.
Du. Give me example where?
Al. You had a Miſtris,
Oh heaven, ſo bright, ſo brave a dame, ſo lovely,
In all her life ſo true.
Du. A Miſtris?
Al. That ſerv'd yee with that conſtancy, that care,
That lov'd your will, and woo'd it too.
Du. What Miſtris?
Al. That nus'rd your honour up, held faſt your vertue,
And when ſhe kiſt encreas'd, not ſtole your goodneſſe.
Du. And I neglected her?
Al. Loſt her, forſook her,
Wantonly flung her off.
Du. What was her name?
Al. Her name as lovely as her ſelfe, as noble,
And in it all that's excellent.
Du. What was it?
Al. Her name was *Beau-deſert*:

olim: & petesca
priuately

Doe you know her now ſir?
Du. *Beau-deſert*? I not remember.——
Al. I know you doe not:
Yet ſhe has a plainer name; Lord *Archas* ſervice;
Do you yet remember her? there was a Miſtris
Fairer then women, far fonder to you ſir,
Then Mothers to their firſt-borne joyes: Can you love?
Dare you profeſſe that truth to me a ſtranger,
A thing of no regard, no name, no luſtre,
When your moſt noble love you have neglected,
A beautie all the world would wooe and honour?
Would you have me credit this? thinke ye can love me,
And hold ye conſtant, when I have read this ſtorie?
Is't poſſible you ſhould ever favour me,
To a ſlight pleaſure prove a friend, and faſt too,
When, where you were moſt ty'd, moſt bound to benefit,
Bound by the chaines of honeſty and honour,
You have broke and boldly too? I am a weak one,
Arm'd onely with my feares: I beſeech your Grace
Tempt me no further.
Du. Who taught you this Leſſon?
Al. Woefull experience Sir: if you ſeek a faire one,
Worthy your love, if yet you have that perfect,
Two daughters of his ruin'd vertue now
Arive at Court, excellent faire indeed ſir,
But this will be the plague on't, they'r excellent honeſt.
Enter Olimpia and Peteſca privately.
Duk. I love thy face.
Al. Upon my life yee cannot.
I doe not love it my ſelfe Sir, 'tis a lewd one,
So truely ill Art cannot mend it; 'lod if 'twere handſome,
At leaſt if I thought ſo, you ſhould heare me talke ſir
In a new ſtraine; and though ye are a Prince,
Make ye Petition to me too, and wait my anſwers;
Yet o' my conſcience I ſhould pitty yee,
After ſome ten yeares ſiege.
Du. Prethee doe now.
Al. What would ye doe?
Du. Why I would lye with yee.
Al. I doe not think yee would.

Du. Introth I would wench.
Here, take this Jewell.
Al. Out upon't that's ſcurvee.
Nay, if we doe, ſure wee'll doe for good fellowſhip,
For pure love, or nothing: thus you ſhall be ſure ſir
You ſhall not pay too deare for't.
Duke Sure I cannot.
Alin. By'r Lady but yee may: when ye have found me
To doe your work well, ye may pay my wages. (able,
Pet. Why does your Grace ſtart back?
Olim. I ha' ſeen that ſhakes me:
Chills all my bloud: O where is faith or goodneſſe?
Alinda thou art falſe, falſe, falſe thou faire one,
Wickedly falſe; and (woe is me) I ſee it.
For ever falſe.
Pet. I am glad 't has taken thus right. *Exit.*
Alin. Ile goe aske my Lady, ſir.
Du. What? (willing——r
Al. Whether I ſhall lye with ye, or no: If I find he-
For look ye ſir, I have ſworn, while I am in her ſervice——
('Twas a raſh oath I muſt confeſſe.)
Duke Thou mockſt me.
Al. Why, would yee lye with me, if I were willing?
Would you abuſe my weakneſſe?
Du. I would peece it,
And make it ſtronger.
Al. I humbly thank your highneſſe,
When you piece me, you muſt piece me to my Coffin:
When you have got my Maiden-head, I take it,
'Tis not an inch of an Apes taile will reſtore it;
I love ye, and I honour yee, but this way
Ile neither love nor ſerve yee:
Heaven change your minde ſir. *Exit.*
Duke And thine too:
For it muſt be chang'd, it ſhall be. *Exit.*

Scæne 4. *Enter Boroskie, Burris, Theodore, Viola, and Honora.*

Bor. They are goodly gentlewomen.
Bur. They are,
Wondrous ſweet women both.
The. Does your Lordſhid like 'em?
They are my ſiſters ſir; good luſty Laſſes,
They'll doe their labour well, I warrant yee
You'll finde no bed-ſtraw here ſir.
Hon. Thanke yee brother.
The. This is not ſo ſtrongly built: but ſhe is good mettle,
Of a good ſtirring ſtraine too: ſhe goes tith ſir. *Enter 2. Gent.*
Here they be gentlemen muſt make ye merry,
The toyes you wot of: doe you like their complexions?
They be no Moors: what think ye of this hand gentlemen?
Here's a white Altar for your ſacrifice:
A thouſand kiſſes here. Nay, keep off yet gentlemen,
Let's ſtart firſt, & have fair play: what would ye give now
To turne the globe up, and finde the rich *Moluccas*?
To paſſe the ſtraights? here (doe ye itch) by St. *Nicolas*,
Here's that will make ye ſcratch and claw,
Claw my fine Gentlemen, move ye in divers ſorts:
Pray ye let me requeſt yee, to forget
To ſay your prayers, whilſt theſe are Courtiers;
Or if yee needs will thinke of heaven, let it be no higher
Then their eyes?
Bor. How will ye have 'em beſtow'd ſir?
Theo. Even how your Lordſhip pleaſe,
So you doe not bake 'em.
Bor.

boro: hono
Viola

[Se]ruant

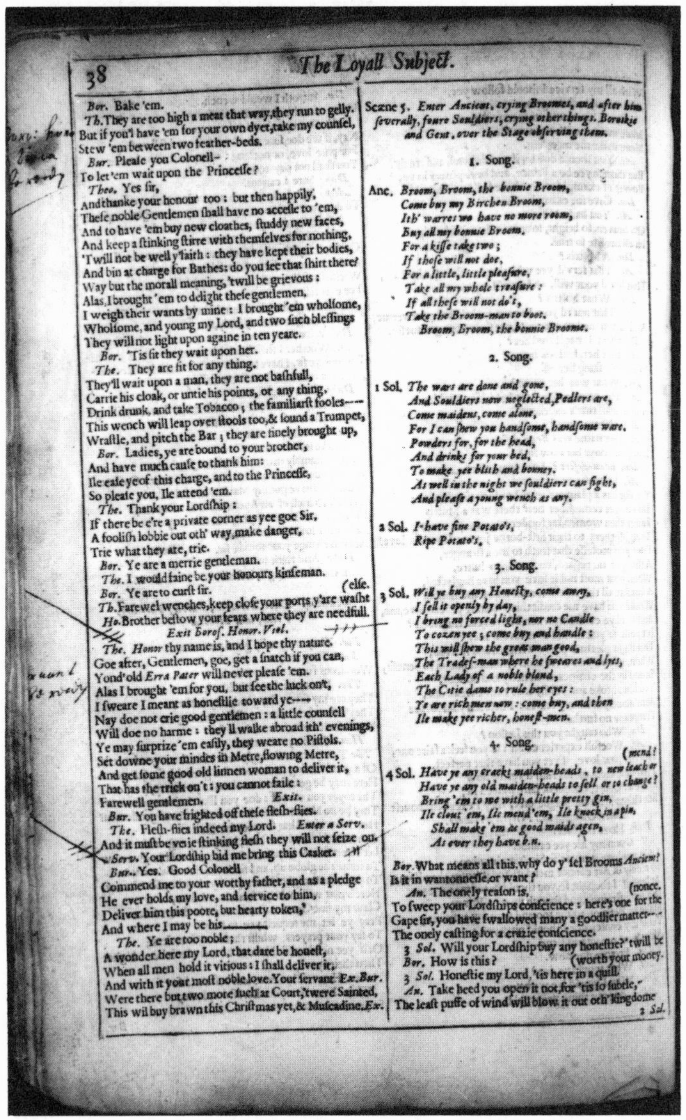

38 *The Loyall Subject.*

Bor. Bake 'em.
Th. They are too high a meat that way, they run to gelly.
But if you'l have 'em for your own dyet, take my counſel,
Stew 'em between two feather-beds.
Bur. Pleaſe you Colonell—
To let 'em wait upon the Princeſſe?
Theo. Yes ſir,
And thanke your honour too: but then happily,
Theſe noble Gentlemen ſhall have no acceſſe to 'em,
And to have 'em buy new cloathes, ſtuddy new faces,
And keep a ſtinking ſtirre with themſelves for nothing,
'Twill not be well y'faith: they have kept their bodies,
And bin at charge for Bathes: do you ſee that ſhirt there?
Way but the morall meaning, 'twill be grievous:
Alas, I brought 'em to delight theſe gentlemen,
I weigh their wants by mine: I brought 'em wholſome,
Wholſome, and young my Lord, and two ſuch bleſſings
They will not light upon againe in ten yeare.
Bor. 'Tis fit they wait upon her.
The. They are fit for any thing.
They'll wait upon a man, they are not baſhfull,
Carrie his cloak, or untie his points, or any thing,
Drink drunk, and take Tobacco; the familiarſt fooles——
This wench will leap over ſtools too, & ſound a Trumpet,
Wraſtle, and pitch the Bar; they are finely brought up,
Bor. Ladies, ye are bound to your brother,
And have much cauſe to thank him:
Ile eaſe ye of this charge, and to the Princeſſe,
So pleaſe you, Ile attend 'em.
The. Thank your Lordſhip:
If there be e're a private corner as yee goe Sir,
A fooliſh lobbie out oth' way, make danger,
Trie what they are, trie.
Bor. Ye are a merrie gentleman.
The. I would faine be your honours kinſeman.
Bor. Ye are to curſt ſir.
Th. Farewel wenches, keep cloſe your ports y'are waſht (elſe.
Ho. Brother beſtow your fears where they are needfull.
Exit Boroſ. Honor. Viol.
The. *Honor* thy name is, and I hope thy nature.
Goe after, Gentlemen, goe, get a ſnatch if you can,
Yond' old *Erra Pater* will never pleaſe 'em.
Alas I brought 'em for you, but ſee the luck on't,
I ſweare I meant as honeſtlie toward ye——
Nay doe not crie good gentlemen: a little counſell
Will doe no harme: they'll walke abroad ith' evenings,
Ye may ſurprize 'em eaſily, they weare no Piſtols.
Set downe your mindes in Metre, flowing Metre,
And get ſome good old linnen woman to deliver it,
That has the trick on't: you cannot faile:
Farewell gentlemen. *Exit.*
Bur. You have frighted off theſe fleſh-flies.
The. Fleſh-flies indeed my Lord. *Enter a Serv.*
And it muſt be verie ſtinking fleſh they will not ſeize on.
Serv. Your Lordſhip bid me bring this Casket.
Bur. Yes. Good Colonell
Commend me to your worthy father, and as a pledge
He ever holds my love, and ſervice to him,
Deliver him this poore, but hearty token,
And where I may be his——
The. Ye are too noble;
A wonder here my Lord, that dare be honeſt,
When all men hold it vitious: I ſhall deliver it,
And with it your moſt noble love. Your ſervant. *Ex. Bur.*
Were there but two more ſuch at Court, 'twere Sainted,
This wil buy brawn this Chriſtmas yet, & Muſcadine. *Ex.*

Scæne 5. *Enter Ancient, crying Broomes, and after him ſeverally, foure Souldiers, crying other things. Boroskie and Gent, over the Stage obſerving them.*

1. Song.

Anc. *Broom, Broom, the bonnie Broom,*
Come buy my Birchen Broom,
Ith' warres we have no more room,
Buy all my bonnie Broom.
For a kiſſe take two;
If thoſe will not doe,
For a little, little pleaſure,
Take all my whole treaſure:
If all theſe will not do't,
Take the Broom-man to boot.
Broom, Broom, the bonnie Broome.

2. Song.

1 Sol. *The wars are done and gone,*
And Souldiers now neglected, Pedlers are,
Come maidens, come alone,
For I can ſhew you handſome, handſome ware.
Powders for, for the head,
And drinks for your bed,
To make yee blith and bonny.
As well in the night we ſouldiers can fight,
And pleaſe a young wench as any.

2 Sol. *I have fine Potato's,*
Ripe Potato's,

3. Song.

3 Sol. *Will ye buy any Honeſty, come away,*
I ſell it openly by day,
I bring no forced light, nor no Candle
To cozen yee; come buy and handle:
This will ſhew the great man good,
The Tradeſ-man where he ſweares and lyes,
Each Lady of a noble blood,
The Citie dame to rule her eyes:
Ye are rich men now: come buy, and then
Ile make yee richer, honeſt-men.

4. Song.

4 Sol. *Have ye any crackt maiden-heads, to new leach or* (mend?
Have ye any old maiden-heads to ſell or to change?
Bring 'em to me with a little pretty gin,
Ile clout 'em, Ile mend 'em, Ile knock in a pin,
Shall make 'em as good maids agen,
As ever they have bin.

Bor. What means all this, why do y' ſel Brooms *Ancient?*
Is it in wantonneſſe, or want?
An. The onely reaſon is, (nonce.
To ſweep your Lordſhips conſcience: here's one for the
Gape ſir, you have ſwallowed many a goodlier matter——
The onely caſting for a crazie conſcience.
3 *Sol.* Will your Lordſhip buy any honeſtie? 'twill be
Bor. How is this? (worth your money.
3 *Sol.* Honeſtie my Lord, 'tis here in a quill.
An. Take heed you open it not, for 'tis ſo ſubtle,
The leaſt puffe of wind will blow it out oth' kingdome.

2 *Sol.*

& viola

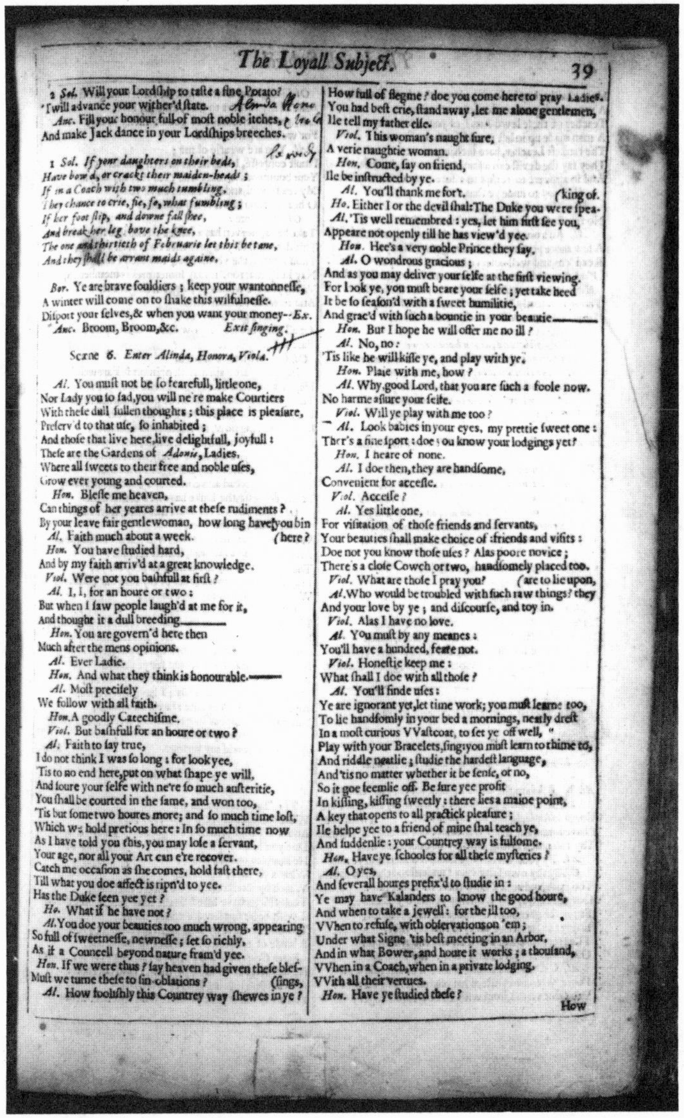

The Loyall Subject. 39

2 *Sol.* Will your Lordſhip to taſte a fine Potato?
'Twill advance your wither'd ſtate.
Anc. Fill your honour full of moſt noble itches,
And make Jack dance in your Lordſhips breeches.

1 *Sol.* *If your daughters on their beds,*
Have bow'd, or crackt their maiden-heads;
If in a Coach with two much tumbling,
They chance to crie, fie, fo, what fumbling;
If her foot ſlip, and downe fall ſhee,
And break her leg 'bove the knee,
The one and thirtieth of Februarie let this be tane,
And they ſhall be arrant maids againe.

Bor. Ye are brave ſouldiers; keep your wantonneſſe,
A winter will come on to ſhake this wilfulneſſe.
Diſport your ſelves, & when you want your money—*Ex.*
Anc. Broom, Broom, &c. *Exit ſinging.*

Scæne 6. *Enter Alinda, Honora, Viola.*

Al. You muſt not be ſo fearefull, little one,
Nor Lady you ſo ſad, you will ne're make Courtiers
With theſe dull ſullen thoughts; this place is pleaſure,
Preſerv'd to that uſe, ſo inhabited;
And thoſe that live here, live delightfull, joyfull:
Theſe are the Gardens of *Adonis*, Ladies,
Where all ſweets to their free and noble uſes,
Grow ever young and courted.
Hon. Bleſſe me heaven,
Can things of her yeares arrive at theſe rudiments?
By your leave fair gentlewoman, how long have you bin (here?
Al. Faith much about a week.
Hon. You have ſtudied hard,
And by my faith arriv'd at a great knowledge.
Viol. Were not you baſhfull at firſt?
Al. I, I, for an houre or two:
But when I ſaw people laugh'd at me for it,
And thought it a dull breeding——
Hon. You are govern'd here then
Much after the mens opinions.
Al. Ever Ladie.
Hon. And what they think is honourable——
Al. Moſt preciſely
We follow with all faith.
Hon. A goodly Catechiſme.
Viol. But baſhfull for an houre or two?
Al. Faith to ſay true,
I do not think I was ſo long: for look yee,
'Tis to no end here, put on what ſhape ye will,
And ſoure your ſelfe with ne're ſo much auſteritie,
You ſhall be courted in the ſame, and won too,
'Tis but ſome two houres more; and ſo much time loſt,
Which we hold pretious here: In ſo much time now
As I have told you this, you may loſe a ſervant,
Your age, nor all your Art can e're recover.
Catch me occaſion as ſhe comes, hold faſt there,
Till what you doe affect is ripn'd to yee.
Has the Duke ſeen yee yet?
Ho. What if he have not?
Al. You doe your beauties too much wrong, appearing
So full of ſweetneſſe, newneſſe; ſet ſo richly,
As if a Councell beyond nature fram'd yee.
Hon. If we were thus? ſay heaven had given theſe bleſ-
Muſt we turne theſe to ſin-oblations? (ſings,
Al. How fooliſhly this Countrey way ſhewes in ye?
How full of flegme? doe you come here to pray Ladies.
You had beſt crie, ſtand away, let me alone gentlemen,
Ile tell my father elſe.
Viol. This woman's naught ſure,
A verie naughtie woman.
Hon. Come, ſay on friend,
Ile be inſtructed by ye.
Al. You'll thank me for't.
Ho. Either I or the devil ſhal: The Duke you were ſpea- (king of.
Al. 'Tis well remembred: yes, let him firſt ſee you,
Appeare not openly till he has view'd yee.
Hon. Hee's a very noble Prince they ſay.
Al. O wondrous gracious;
And as you may deliver your ſelfe at the firſt viewing,
For look ye, you muſt beare your ſelfe; yet take heed
It be ſo ſeaſon'd with a ſweet humilitie,
And grac'd with ſuch a bountie in your beautie——
Hon. But I hope he will offer me no ill?
Al. No, no:
'Tis like he will kiſſe ye, and play with ye.
Hon. Plaie with me, how?
Al. Why, good Lord, that you are ſuch a foole now.
No harme aſſure your ſelfe.
Viol. Will ye play with me too?
Al. Look babies in your eyes, my prettie ſweet one:
Ther's a fine ſport: doe you know your lodgings yet?
Hon. I heare of none.
Al. I doe then, they are handſome,
Convenient for acceſſe.
Viol. Acceſſe?
Al. Yes little one,
For viſitation of thoſe friends and ſervants,
Your beauties ſhall make choice of: friends and viſits:
Doe not you know thoſe uſes? Alas poore novice;
There's a cloſe Cowch or two, handſomely placed too.
Viol. What are thoſe I pray you?
Al. Who would be troubled with ſuch raw things? they (are to lie upon,
And your love by ye; and diſcourſe, and toy in.
Viol. Alas I have no love.
Al. You muſt by any meanes:
You'll have a hundred, feare not.
Viol. Honeſtie keep me:
What ſhall I doe with all thoſe?
Al. You'll finde uſes:
Ye are ignorant yet, let time work; you muſt learne too,
To lie handſomly in your bed a mornings, neatly dreſt
In a moſt curious VVaſtcoat, to ſet ye off well,
Play with your Bracelets, ſing: you muſt learn to rhime to,
And riddle neatlie; ſtudie the hardeſt language,
And 'tis no matter whether it be ſenſe, or no,
So it goe ſeemlie off. Be ſure yee profit
In kiſſing, kiſſing ſweetly: there lies a maine point,
A key that opens to all practick pleaſure;
Ile helpe yee to a friend of mine ſhal teach ye,
And ſuddenlie: your Countrey way is fulſome.
Hon. Have ye ſchooles for all theſe myſteries?
Al. O yes,
And ſeverall houres prefix'd to ſtudie in:
Ye may have Kalanders to know the good houre,
And when to take a jewell: for the ill too,
VVhen to refuſe, with obſervations on 'em;
Under what Signe 'tis beſt meeting in an Arbor,
And in what Bower, and houre it works; a thouſand,
VVhen in a Coach, when in a private lodging,
VVith all their vertues.
Hon. Have ye ſtudied theſe?

How

III, iv, 30, 65. The prompter warned Boroskie, Honora, and Viola at line 30 for what he mistook as an entrance at line 65. But the stage direction at line 65, though centered like an entrance, is for an exit. Since the prompter did not bother to correct his error, perhaps it did no harm to let it stand.

III, v, opening. The entrance of the Ancient and others was neither warned nor cued.

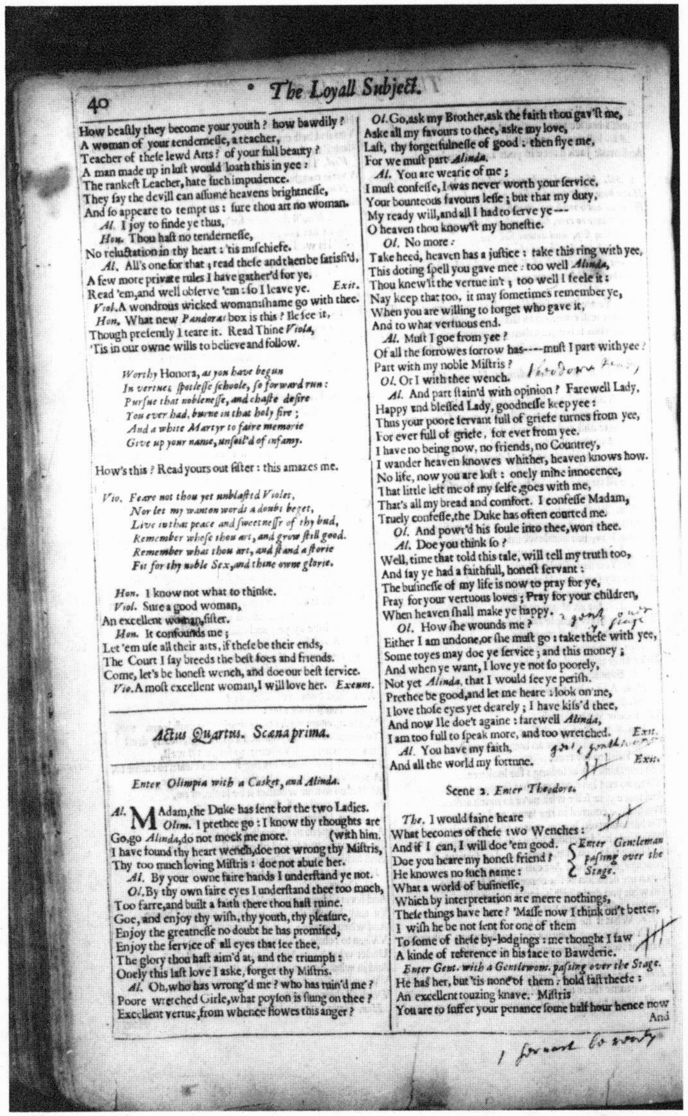

40 The Loyall Subject.

…

Actus Quartus. Scæna prima.

Enter Olimpia with a Casket, and Alinda.

Scene 2. Enter Theodore.

Enter Gentleman passing over the Stage.

Enter Gent. with a Gentlewom. passing over the Stage.

a gent ouer ye stage

gent & gentlewoma[n]

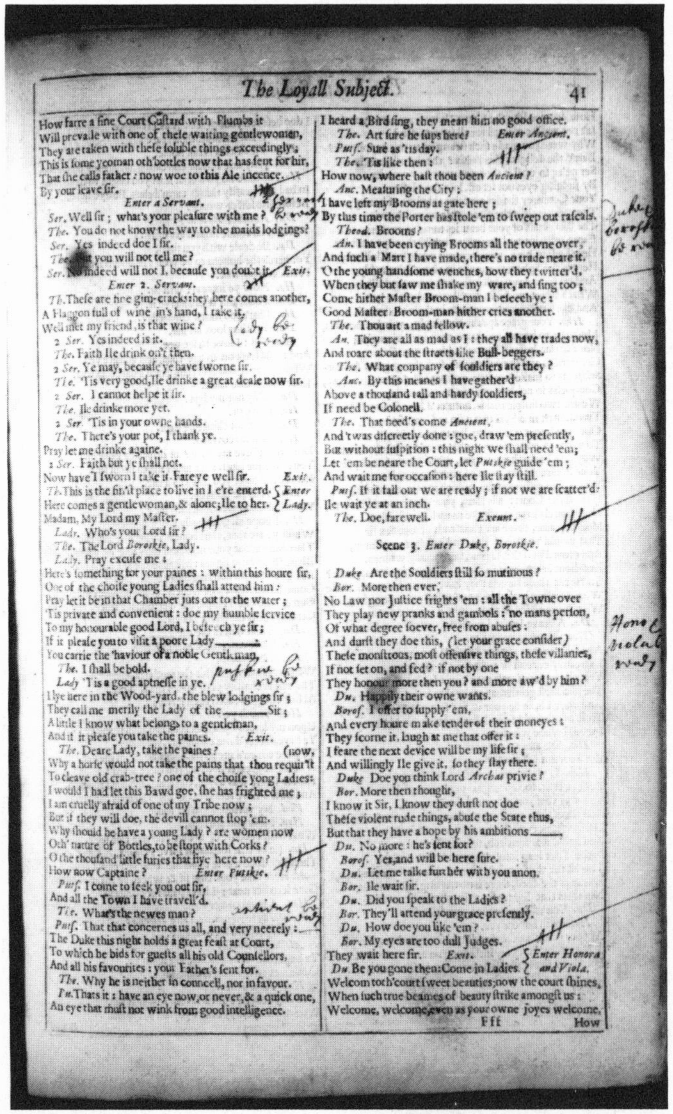

The Loyall Subject. 41

Enter a Servant.

Enter 2. Servant.

Scene 3. Enter Duke, Burorskie.

Enter Honora and Viola.

How doe you like the Court? how ſeems it to you?
Is't not a place created for all ſweetneſſe?
Why were you made ſuch ſtrangers to this happineſſe?
Barr'd the delights this holds? the richeſt jewels
Set ne're ſo well, if then not worne to wonder,
By judging eyes not ſet off, loſe their luſtre:
Your Countrey ſhades are faint; blaſters of beauty;
The manners like the place, obſcure and heavie;
The Roſe buds of your beauties turne to cankers,
Eaten with inward thoughts: whilſt there ye wander.
Here Ladies, here, you were not made for Cloiſters,
Here is the Sphere you move in: here ſhine nobly,
And by your powerfull influence command all:
What a ſweet modeſtie dwells round about 'em,
And like a nipping morne pulls in their bloſſoms?

Hon. Your grace ſpeaks cunningly, you doe not this,
I hope ſir, to betray us; wee are poore triumphs;
Nor can our loſſe of honour adde to you ſir:
Great men, and great thoughts, ſeek things great & wor-
Subjects to make 'em live, and not to loſe 'em; (thy,
Conqueſts ſo nobly won, can never periſh;
We are two ſimple maids, untutor'd here ſir;
Two honeſt maids, is that a ſin at Court ſir?
Our breeding is obedience, but to good things,
To vertuous and to faire: what wou'd you win on us?
Why doe I aske that queſtion, when I have found yee?
Your Preamble has pow'rd your heart out to us;
You would diſhonour us; which in your tranſlation
Here at the Court reads thus, your grace would love us,
Moſt dearely love us: ſticke us up for miſtreſſes:
Moſt certaine, there are thouſands of our Sex ſir
That would be glad of this, and handſome women,
And crowd into this favour, faire young women,
Excellent beauties ſir: when ye have enjoyd 'em, (then?
And ſuckt thoſe ſweets they have, what Saints are theſe
What worſhip have they won? what name you gheſſe ſir,
What ſtorie added to their time, a ſweet one?

Du. A brave ſpirited wench.

Hon. Ile tell your grace,
And tell yee true: ye are deceiv'd in us two,
Extreamly cozend ſir: And yet in my eye
You are the handſomſt man I ever lookt on,
The goodlieſt gentleman; take that hope with yee;
And were I fit to be your wife (ſo much I honour yee)
Truſt me I would ſcratch for ye but I would have yee.
I would wooe you then.

Du. She amazes me:
But how am I deceiv'd?

Hon. O we are too honeſt,
Believe it ſir, too honeſt, far too honeſt,
The way that you propound too ignorant,
And there is no medling with us; for we are fooles too,
Obſtinate, peeviſh fooles: if I would be ill,
And had a wanton itch, to kick my heeles up,
I would not leap intoth' Sun, and doe't there,
That all the world might ſee me: an obſcure ſhade ſir,
Darke as the deed, there is no truſting light with it,
Nor thats that lighter far, vain-glorious greatneſſe.

Du. You will love me as your friend?

Ho. I will honour yee,
As your poore humble handmaid ſerve, and pray for ye.

Du. What ſayes my little one; you are not ſo obſtinate?
Lord how ſhe bluſhes: here are truely faire ſoules:
Come you will be my love?

Viol. Good ſir be good to me,
Indeed Ile doe the beſt I can to pleaſe yee;
I doe beſeech your grace: Alas I feare ye.

Du. What ſhouldſt thou feare?

Hon. Fie ſir, this is not noble.

Du. Why doe I ſtand entreating, where my power—

Ho. You have no power, at leaſt you ought to have none
In bad and beaſtly things: arm'd thus, Ile dye here,
Before ſhe ſuffer wrong.

Du. Another *Archas*?

Ho. His childe ſir, and his ſpirit.

Du. Ile deale with you then,
For here's the honour to be won: ſit down ſwe[et]
Prethee *Honora* ſit.

Ho. Now ye intreat I will ſir.

Du. I doe, and will deſerve it.

Ho. That's too much kindneſſe.

Du. Prethee look on me.

Ho. Yes: I love to ſee yee,
And could look on an age thus, and admire ye:
Whilſt ye are good and temperate I dare touch ye,
Kiſſe your white hand.

Du. Why not my lips?

Ho. I dare ſir.

Du. I doe not thinke ye dare.

Ho. I am no coward.
Doe you believe me now? or now? or now ſir?
You make me bluſh: but ſure I mean no ill ſir:
It had been fitter you had kiſs'd me.

Du. That Ile doe too.
What haſt thou wrought into me?

Ho. I hope all goodneſſe:
Whilſt ye are thus, thus honeſt, I dare doe any thing,
Thus hang about your neck, and thus doat on yee;
Bleſſe thoſe faire lights: hell take me if I durſt not---
But good Sir pardon me. Siſter come hither,
Come hither, feare not wench: come hither, bluſh not,
Come kiſſe the Prince, the vertuous Prince, the good
Certaine he is excellent honeſt. (Prince:

Du. Thou wilt make me ——

Ho. Sit downe, and hug him ſoftly.

Du. Fie *Honora*,
Wanton *Honora*; is this the modeſty,
The noble chaſtity your on-ſet ſhew'd me,
At firſt charge beaten back? Away.

Hon. Thank ye:
Upon my knees I pray, heaven too may thank ye;
Ye have deceiv'd me cunningly, yet nobly
Ye have cozen'd me: In all your hopefull life yet,
A Scene of greater honour, you ne're acted:
I knew Fame was a lyar, too long, and loud tongu'd,
And now I have found it: O my vertuous Maſter.

Viol. My vertuous Maſter too.

Hon. Now you are thus,
What ſhall become of me let Fortune caſt for't.

Du. Ile be that fortune, if I live *Honora*. *Enter Alin.*
Thou haſt done a cure upon me, counſell could not.

Al. Here take your ring ſir, & whom ye mean to ruine,
Give it to her next; I have paid for't dearely.

Hon. A Ring to her?

Du. Why frownes my faire *Alinda*?
I have forgot both theſe againe.

Al. Stand ſtill ſir,
Ye have that violent killing fire upon ye,
Conſumes all honour, credit, faith.

Hon. How's this?

Al. My Royall Miſtris favour towards me,
Woe-worth ye ſir, ye have poyſon'd, blaſted.

Duke.

Duke I ſweet?

Al. You have taken that unmanly liberty,
Which in a worſe man, is vaine-glorious feigning,
And kild my truth.

Du. Upon my life 'tis falſe wench.

Al. Ladies,
Take heed, ye have a cunning gamſter,
A handſome, and a high; come ſtoar'd with Antidotes,
He has infections elſe will fire your bloods.

Du. Prethee *Alinda* heare me.

Al. Words ſteept in honey,
That will ſo melt into your mindes, buy Chaſtity,
A thouſand wayes, a thouſand knots to tie ye;
And when he has bound ye his, a thouſand ruines.
A poore loſt woman ye have made me.

Du. Ile maintaine thee,
And nobly too.

Al. That Gin's too weak to take me:
Take heed, take heed young Ladies: ſtill take heed,
Take heed of promiſes, take heed of gifts,
Of forced feigned ſorrowes, ſighes, take heed.

Du. By all that's mine, *Alinda* ——

Al. Sweare
By your miſchiefes:
O whither ſhall I goe?

Du. Goe back againe,
Ile force her take thee, love thee.

Al. Fare ye well Sir,
I will not curſe ye; onely this dwell with ye,
When ever you love, a falſe beliefe light on ye. *Exit.*

Hon. Wee'll take our leaves too ſir.

Duk. Part all the world now,
Since ſhe is gone.

Hon. You are crooked yet, deare Maſter,
And ſtill I feare —— *Exeunt.*

Duke I am vext,
And ſome ſhall finde it. *Exit.*

Scæne 4. *Enter Archas and a Servant.*

Ar. 'Tis ſtrange
To me to ſee the Court, and welcome:
O royall place, how have I lov'd and ſerv'd thee?
Who lies on this ſide, know'ſt thou?

Ser. The Lord *Burris*.

Ar. Thou haſt nam'd a gentleman
I ſtand much bound to.
I think he ſent the Casket ſir?

Ser. The ſame Sir.

Ar. An honeſt minded man, a noble Courtier:
The Duke made perfect choice when he took him.
Goe you home, I ſhall hit the way
Without a guide now.

Ser. You may want ſomething ſir.

Ar. Onely my horſes,
Which after Supper let the Groom wait with:
Ile have no more attendance here.

Ser. Your will ſir? *Exit.*

Enter Theodore.

Theod. You are well met here ſir.

Ar. How now boy,
How do'ſt thou?

The. I ſhould aske
You that queſtion: how doe you ſir?
How doe you feele your ſelfe?

Ar. Why well, and luſtie.

The. What doe you here then?

Ar. Why I am ſent for
To Supper with the Duke.

The. Have you no meat at home?
Or doe you long to feed as hunted Deere doe,
In doubt and feare?

Ar. I have an excellent ſtomach,
And can I uſe it better
Then among my friends boy?
How doe the wenches?

The. They doe well enough ſir,
They know the worſt by this time: pray be rul'd ſir,
Goe home againe, and if ye have a Supper
Eate it in quiet there: this is no place for ye,
Eſpecially at this time,
Take my word for't.

Ar. May be they'll drink hard;
I could have drunk my ſhare Boy.
Though I am old, I will not out.

The. I hope you will.
Hark in your eare: the Court's
Too quick of hearing.

Ar. Not mean me wel?
Thou art abus'd and cozen'd.
Away, away.

The. To that end ſir I tell ye.
Away, if ye love your ſelfe.

Ar. Who dare doe theſe things,
That ever heard of honeſty?

The. Old Gentleman,
Take a fooles counſell.

Ar. 'Tis a fooles indeed;
A very fooles: thou haſt more of
Theſe flams in thee, theſe muſty doubts:
Is't fit the Duke ſend for me,
And honour me to eate within his preſence,
And I, like a tal fellow, play at bo-peep
With his pleaſure?

The. Take heed
Of bo-peep with your pate, your pate ſir,
I ſpeak plain language now.

Ar. If 'twere not here,
Where reverence bids me hold,
I would ſo ſwinge thee, thou rude,
Unmanner'd knave, take from his bounty,
His honour that he gives me, to beget
Sawcy, and ſullen feares?

The. You are not mad ſure:
By this faire light, I ſpeak
But what is whiſper'd,
And whiſper'd for a truth.

Ar. A dog: drunken people,
That in their Pot ſee viſions,
And turne ſtates, mad-men and children;
Prethee doe not follow me;
I tell thee I am angrie:
Doe not follow me.

The. I am as angrie
As you for your heart.
I and as wilfull too: goe, like a Wood-cock,
And thruſt your neck ith' nooſe.

Ar. Ile kill thee.

Fff 2 And

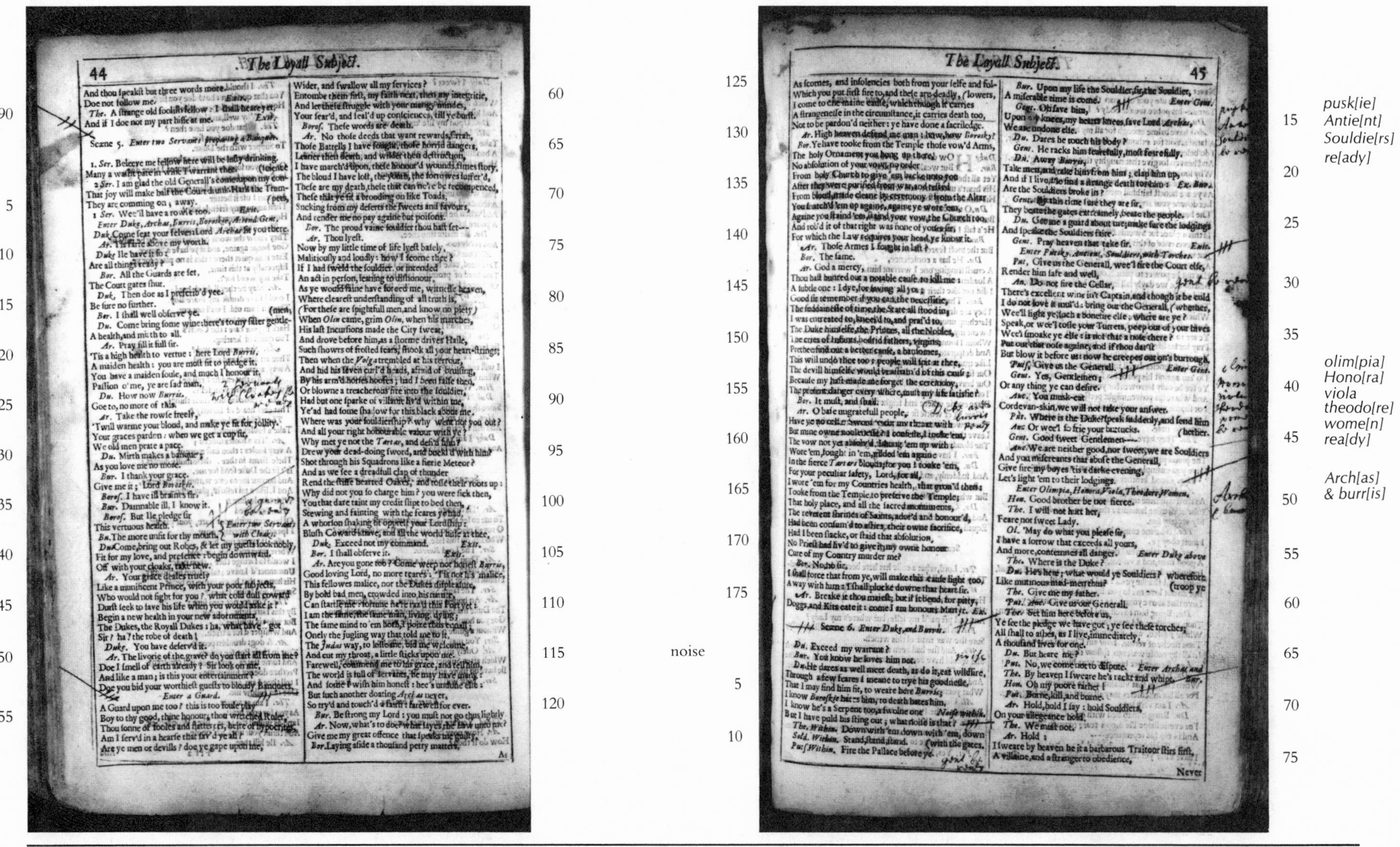

IV, v, 6. The entrance of the Duke and others was neither warned nor cued.

IV, vi, following 27. The torches mentioned in the stage direction were not included in the warning and may have been omitted, though the dialogue mentions them.

IV, vi, 55. The appearance of the Duke "*above*" was neither warned nor cued; the text contains no exit for him prior to this reentrance, but the prompter did not correct the error. As other promptbooks make clear, prompters rarely concerned themselves with exits.

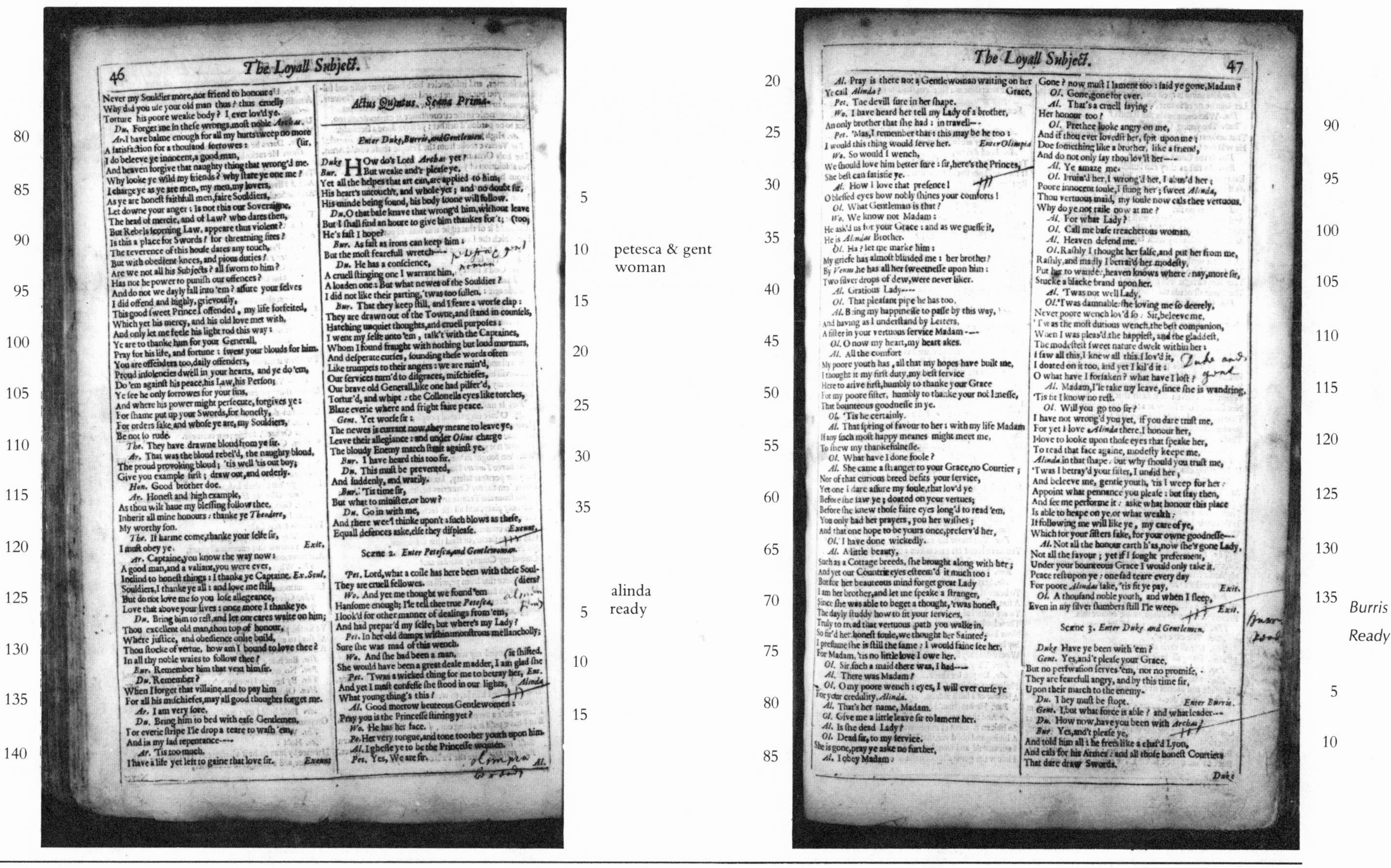

46 *The Loyall Subject.*

Never my Souldier more,nor friend to honour:
Why did you use your old man thus? thus cruelly
Torture his poore weake body? I ever lov'd ye.
Du. Forget me in these wrongs,most noble *Archas*.
Ar. I have balme enough for all my hurts:weep no more (sir,
A satisfaction for a thousand sorrowes:
I do beleeve ye innocent,a good man,
And heaven forgive that naughty thing that wrong'd me.
Why looke ye wild my friends? why stare ye one me?
I charge ye as ye are men, my men,my lovers,
As ye are honest faithfull men,faire Souldiers,
Let downe your anger: Is not this our Soveraigne,
The head of mercie, and of Law? who dares then,
But Rebels scorning Law, appeare thus violent?
Is this a place for Swords? for threatning fires?
The reverence of this house dares any touch,
But with obedient knees, and pious duties?
Are we not all his Subjects? all sworn to him?
Has not he power to punish our offences?
And do not we dayly fall into 'em? assure your selves
I did offend and highly, grievously,
This good sweet Prince I offended, my life forfeited,
Which yet his mercy, and his old love met with,
And only let me feele his light rod this way:
Ye are to thanke him for your Generall,
Pray for his life, and fortune: sweat your bloods for him.
You are offenders too,daily offenders,
Proud insolencies dwell in your hearts, and ye do 'em,
Do 'em against his peace,his Law,his Person;
Ye see he only sorrowes for your sins,
And where his power might persecute, forgives ye:
For shame put up your Swords,for honesty,
For orders sake,and whose ye are, my Souldiers,
Be not so rude.
The. They have drawne bloud from ye sir.
Ar. That was the bloud rebel'd, the naughty blood,
The proud provoking bloud; 'tis well 'tis out boy;
Give you example first; draw out,and orderly.
Hon. Good brother doe.
Ar. Honest and high example,
As thou wilt have my blessing follow thee,
Inherit all mine honours: thanke ye *Theodore*,
My worthy son.
The. If harme come,thanke your selfe sir,
I must obey ye. *Exit.*
Ar. Captaine,you know the way now:
A good man,and a valiant,you were ever,
Inclin'd to honest things: I thanke ye Captaine. *Ex.Soul.*
Souldiers,I thanke ye all: and love me still,
But do not love me so you lose allegeance,
Love that above your lives: once more I thanke ye.
Du. Bring him to rest,and let our cares waite on him;
Thou excellent old man,thou top of honour,
Where justice, and obedience onlie build,
Thou stocke of vertue, how am I bound to love thee?
In all thy noble waies to follow thee?
Bur. Remember him that vext him sir.
Du. Remember?
When I forget that villaine,and to pay him
For all his mischiefes,may all good thoughts forget me.
Ar. I am very sore.
Du. Bring him to bed with ease Gentlemen,
For everie stripe I'le drop a teare to wash 'em,
And in my sad repentance----
Ar. 'Tis too much.
I have a life yet left to gaine that love sir. *Exeunt*

Actus Quintus. Scena Prima.

Enter Duke,Burris,and Gentlemen.

Duke How do's Lord *Archas* yet?
Bur. But weake and't please ye,
Yet all the helpes that art can,are applied to him;
His heart's untouch't, and whole yet; and no doubt sir,
His minde being sound, his body soone will follow.
Du. O that base knave that wrong'd him,without leave
But I shall find an houre to give him thankes for't; (too;
He's fast I hope?
Bur. As fast as irons can keep him:
But the most fearefull wretch----
Du. He has a conscience,
A cruell stinging one I warrant him,
A loaden one: But what newes of the Souldier?
I did not like their parting,'twas too sullen.
Bur. That they keep still, and I feare a worse clap:
They are drawn out of the Towne,and stand in counsels,
Hatching unquiet thoughts,and cruell purposes:
I went my selfe unto 'em, talk't with the Captaines,
Whom I found fraught with nothing but loud murmurs,
And desperate curses, sounding these words often
Like trumpets to their angers: we are ruin'd,
Our services turn'd to disgraces, mischiefes,
Our brave old Generall,like one had pilfer'd,
Tortur'd, and whipt: the Collonells eyes like torches,
Blaze everie where and fright faire peace.
Gent. Yet worse sir:
The newes is currant now,they meane to leave ye,
Leave their allegiance: and under *Olins* charge
The bloudy Enemy march straight against ye.
Bur. I have heard this too sir.
Du. This must be prevented,
And suddenly, and warily.
Bur. 'Tis time sir,
But what to minister,or how?
Du. Go in with me,
And there wee'l thinke upon't: such blows as these,
Equall defences aske,else they displease. *Exeunt.*

petesca & gent woman

Scæne 2. *Enter Petesca,and Gentlewoman.*

Pet. Lord,what a coile has here been with these Soul-
They are cruell fellowes. (diers!
Wo. And yet me thought we found 'em
Hansome enough; I'le tell thee true *Petesca*,
I look'd for other manner of dealings from 'em,
And had prepar'd my selfe; but where's my Lady?
Pet. In her old dumps within:monstrous mellancholly;
Sure she was mad of this wench.
Wo. And she had been a man, (is shifted.
She would have been a great deale madder, I am glad she
Pet. 'Twas a wicked thing for me to betray her, *Ent.*
And yet I must confesse she stood in our lights, *Alinda*
What young thing's this?
Al. Good morrow beuteous Gentlewomen:
Pray you is the Princesse stirring yet?
Wo. He has her face.
Pe. Her very tongue,and tone too:her youth upon him.
Al. I ghesse ye to be the Princesse women.
Pet. Yes, We are sir. *Al.*

alinda ready

The Loyall Subject. 47

Al. Pray is there not a Gentlewoman waiting on her
Ye call *Alinda*? Grace,
Pet. The devill sure in her shape.
Wo. I have heard her tell my Lady of a brother,
An only brother that she had: in travell--
Pet. 'Mas,I remember that: this may be he too:
I would this thing would serve her. *Enter Olimpia*
Wo. So would I wench,
We should love him better sure: sir,here's the Princes,
She best can satisfie ye.
Al. How I love that presence!
O blessed eyes how nobly shines your comforts!
Ol. What Gentleman is that?
Wo. We know not Madam:
He ask'd us for your Grace: and as we guesse it,
He is *Alindas* Brother.
Ol. Ha? let me marke him:
My griefe has almost blinded me: her brother?
By *Venus* he has all her sweetnesse upon him:
Two silver drops of dew,were never liker.
Al. Gratious Lady----
Ol. That pleasant pipe he has too.
Al. Being my happinesse to passe by this way,
And having as I understand by Letters,
A sister in your vertuous service Madam----
Ol. O now my heart,my heart akes.
Al. All the comfort
My poore youth has, all that my hopes have built me,
I thought it my first duty,my best service
Here to arive first,humbly to thanke your Grace
For my poore sister, humbly to thanke your noblenesse,
That bounteous goodnesse in ye.
Ol. 'Tis he certainly.
Al. That spring of favour to her: with my life Madam
If any such most happy meanes might meet me,
To shew my thankefulnesse.
Ol. What have I done foole?
Al. She came a stranger to your Grace,no Courtier;
Nor of that curious breed befits your service,
Yet one I dare assure my soule,that lov'd ye
Before she saw ye; doated on your vertues;
Before she knew those faire eyes long'd to read 'em,
You only had her prayers, you her wishes;
And that one hope to be yours once,preserv'd her,
Ol. I have done wickedly.
Al. A little beauty,
Such as a Cottage breeds, she brought along with her;
And yet our Countrie eyes esteem'd it much too:
But for her beauteous mind forget great Lady
I am her brother,and let me speake a stranger,
Since she was able to beget a thought, 'twas honest,
The dayly study how to fit your services,
Truly to tread that vertuous path you walke in,
So fir'd her honest soule,we thought her Sainted;
I presume she is still the same: I would faine see her,
For Madam, 'tis no little love I owe her.
Ol. Sir,such a maid there was, I had----
Al. There was Madam?
Ol. O my poore wench: eyes, I will ever curse ye
For your credulity, *Alinda*.
Al. That's her name, Madam.
Ol. Give me a little leave sir to lament her.
Al. Is she dead Lady?
Ol. Dead sir, to my service.
She is gone,pray ye aske no further,
Al. I obey Madam:
Gone? now must I lament too: said ye gone,Madam?
Ol. Gone,gone for ever.
Al. That's a cruell saying:
Her honour too?
Ol. Prethee looke angry on me,
And if thou ever lovedst her, spit upon me;
Doe something like a brother, like a friend,
And do not only say thou lov'st her----
Al. Ye amaze me.
Ol. I ruin'd her,I wrong'd her, I abus'd her;
Poore innocent soule,I flung her; sweet *Alinda*,
Thou vertuous maid, my soule now cals thee vertuous.
Why do ye not raile now at me?
Al. For what Lady?
Ol. Call me base treacherous woman.
Al. Heaven defend me.
Ol. Rashly I thought her false,and put her from me,
Rashly,and madly I betraid her modesty,
Put her to wander,heaven knows where: nay,more sir,
Stucke a blacke brand upon her.
Al. 'Twas not well Lady.
Ol. 'Twas damnable: she loving me so deerely,
Never poore wench lov'd so: Sir,beleeve me,
'Twas the most dutious wench,the best companion,
When I was pleas'd,the happiest, and the gladdest,
The modestest sweet nature dwelt within her:
I saw all this,I knew all this,I lov'd it,
I doated on it too, and yet I kil'd it:
O what have I forsaken? what have I lost?
Al. Madam,I'le take my leave, since she is wandring,
'Tis fit I know no rest.
Ol. Will you go too sir?
I have not wrong'd you yet, if you dare trust me,
For yet I love *Alinda* there,I honour her,
I love to looke upon those eyes that speake her,
To read that face againe, modesty keepe me,
Alinda in that shape: but why should you trust me,
'Twas I betray'd your sister, I undid her,
And beleeve me, gentle youth, 'tis I weep for her:
Appoint what pennance you please: but stay then,
And see me performe it: aske what honour this place
Is able to heape on ye,or what wealth:
If following me will like ye, my care of ye,
Which for your sisters sake, for your owne goodnesse---
Al. Not all the honour earth h'as,now she's gone Lady,
Not all the favour; yet if I sought preferment,
Under your bounteous Grace I would only take it.
Peace rest upon ye: one sad teare every day
For poore *Alindas* sake, 'tis fit ye pay, *Exit.*
Ol. A thousand noble youth, and when I sleep,
Even in my silver slumbers still I'le weep. *Exit.*

Burris
Ready

Scæne 3. *Enter Duke and Gentlemen.*

Duke Have ye been with 'em?
Gent. Yes,and't please your Grace,
But no perswasion serves 'em, nor no promise,
They are fearfull angry, and by this time sir,
Upon their march to the enemy.
Du. They must be stopt. *Enter Burris.*
Gent. I,but what force is able? and what leader---
Du. How now,have you been with *Archas*?
Bur. Yes,and't please ye,
And told him all: he frets like a chaf'd Lyon,
And cals for his Armes: and all those honest Courtiers
That dare draw Swords.
Duke

V, ii, 30. The prompter placed the entrance cue for Olimpia 4 lines after the stage direction bringing her on, correcting an error in the printed text.

V, iii, 9. The prompter placed the entrance cue for Burris 4 lines after the stage direction bringing him on, for no apparent reason.

Theodore puskie
Antient
/ souldiers
Drummer &
Coullers

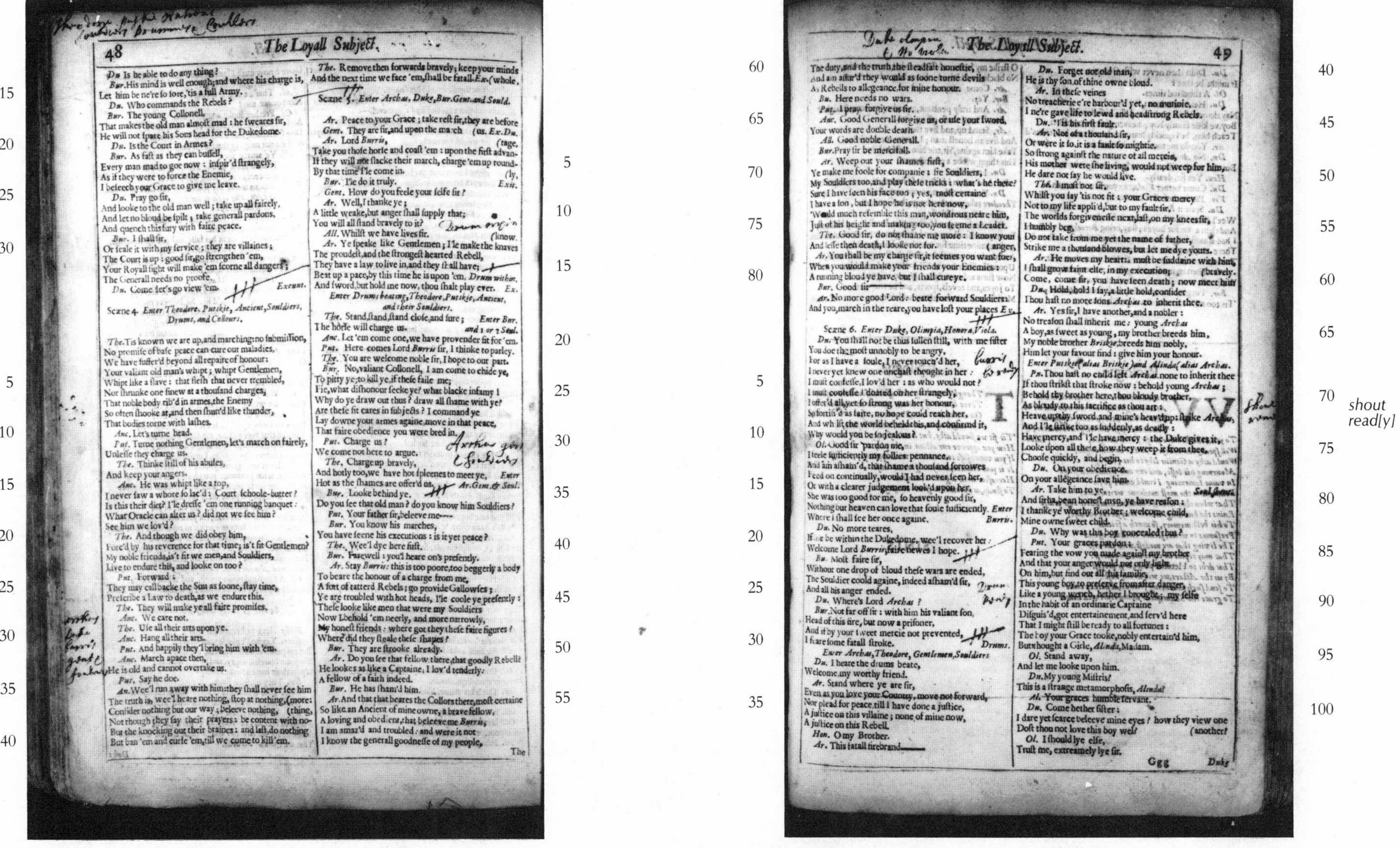

48 *The Loyall Subject.*

Du. Is he able to do any thing?
Bur. His mind is well enough; and where his charge is,
Let him be ne're so sore, 'tis a full Army.
Du. Who commands the Rebels?
Bur. The young Collonell,
That makes the old man almost mad: he sweares sir,
He will not spare his Sons head for the Dukedome.
Du. Is the Court in Armes?
Bur. As fast as they can bussell,
Every man mad to goe now: inspir'd strangely,
As if they were to force the Enemie,
I beseech your Grace to give me leave.
Du. Pray go sir,
And looke to the old man well; take up all fairely,
And let no bloud be spilt; take generall pardons,
And quench this fury with faire peace.
Bur. I shall sir,
Or seale it with my service; they are villaines;
The Court is up: good sir, go strengthen 'em,
Your Royall sight will make 'em scorne all dangers;
The Generall needs no proofe.
Du. Come let's go view 'em. *Exeunt.*

Scæne 4. *Enter Theodore, Putskie, Ancient, Souldiers, Drums, and Collours.*

The. Tis known we are up, and marching: no submission,
No promise of base peace can cure our maladies,
We have suffer'd beyond all repaire of honour:
Your valiant old man's whipt; whipt Gentlemen,
Whipt like a slave: that flesh that never trembled,
Nor shrunke one sinew at a thousand charges,
That noble body rib'd in armes, the Enemy
So often shooke at, and then shun'd like thunder,
That bodies torne with lashes.
Anc. Let's turne head.
Put. Turne nothing Gentlemen, let's march on fairely,
Unlesse they charge us.
The. Thinke still of his abuses,
And keep your angers.
Anc. He was whipt like a top,
I never saw a whore so lac'd: Court schoole-butter?
Is this their diet? I'le dresse 'em one running banquet:
What Oracle can alter us? did not we see him?
See him we lov'd?
The. And though we did obey him,
Forc'd by his reverence for that time; is't fit Gentlemen?
My noble friends, is't fit we men, and Souldiers,
Live to endure this, and looke on too?
Put. Forward:
They may call backe the Sun as soone, stay time,
Prescribe a Law to death, as we endure this.
The. They will make ye all faire promises.
Anc. We care not.
The. Use all their arts upon ye.
Anc. Hang all their arts.
Put. And happily they'l bring him with 'em.
Anc. March apace then,
He is old and cannot overtake us.
Put. Say he doe.
An. Wee'l run away with him: they shall never see him
The truth is, wee'l heare nothing, stop at nothing, (more:
Consider nothing but our way; beleeve nothing, (thing,
Not though they say their prayers: be content with no-
But the knocking out their braines: and last, do nothing
But ban 'em and curse 'em, till we come to kill 'em.

The. Remove then forwards bravely; keep your minds
And the next time we face 'em, shall be fatall. *Ex.* (whole,

Scæne 5. *Enter Archas, Duke, Bur. Gent. and Sould.*

Ar. Peace to your Grace; take rest sir, they are before
Gent. They are sir, and upon the march (us. *Ex. Du.*
Ar. Lord *Burris*, (tage,
Take you those horse and coast 'em: upon the first advan-
If they will not slacke their march, charge 'em up round-
By that time I'le come in. (ly,
Bur. I'le do it truly. *Exit.*
Gent. How do you feele your selfe sir?
Ar. Well, I thanke ye;
A little weake, but anger shall supply that;
You will all stand bravely to it?
All. Whilst we have lives sir. (know.
Ar. Ye speake like Gentlemen; I'le make the knaves
The proudest, and the strongest hearted Rebell,
They have a law to live in, and they shall have;
Beat up a pace, by this time he is upon 'em. *Drum within.*
And sword, but hold me now, thou shalt play ever. *Ex.*
Enter Drums beating, Theodore, Putskie, Ancient, and their Souldiers.
The. Stand, stand, stand close, and sure; *Enter Bur.*
The horse will charge us. *and 1 or 2 Soul.*
Anc. Let 'em come one, we have provender fit for 'em.
Put. Here comes Lord *Burris* sir, I thinke to parley.
The. You are welcome noble sir, I hope to our part.
Bur. No, valiant Collonell, I am come to chide ye,
To pitty ye; to kill ye, if these faile me;
Fie, what dishonour seeke ye? what blacke infamy!
Why do ye draw out thus? draw all shame with ye?
Are these fit cares in subjects? I command ye
Lay downe your armes againe, move in that peace,
That faire obedience you were bred in.
Put. Charge us?
We come not here to argue.
The. Charge up bravely,
And hotly too, we have hot spleenes to meet ye, *Enter*
Hot as the shames are offer'd us. *Ar. Gent. & Soul.*
Bur. Looke behind ye.
Do you see that old man? do you know him Souldiers?
Put. Your father sir, beleeve me——
Bur. You know his marches,
You have seene his executions: is it yet peace?
The. Wee'l dye here first.
Bur. Farewell: you'l heare on's presently.
Ar. Stay *Burris*: this is too poore, too beggerly a body
To beare the honour of a charge from me,
A sort of tatterd Rebels; go provide Gallowses;
Ye are troubled with hot heads, I'le coole ye presently:
These looke like men that were my Souldiers
Now I behold 'em neerly, and more narrowly,
My honest friends: where got they these faire figures?
Where did they steale these shapes?
Bur. They are strooke already.
Ar. Do you see that fellow there, that goodly Rebell?
He lookes as like a Captaine, I lov'd tenderly:
A fellow of a faith indeed.
Bur. He has sham'd him.
Ar. And that that beares the Collors there, most certaine
So like an Ancient of mine owne, a brave fellow,
A loving and obedient, that beleeve me *Burris*,
I am amaz'd and troubled: and were it not
I know the generall goodnesse of my people,
The

The Loyall Subject. 49

The duty, and the truth, the stedfast honestie,
And a man assur'd they would as soone turne devils
As Rebells to allegeance, for mine honour.
Bu. Here needs no wars.
Put. I pray forgive us sir.
Anc. Good Generall forgive us, or use your sword.
Your words are double death.
All. Good noble Generall.
Bur. Pray sir be mercifull.
Ar. Weep out your shames first;
Ye make me foole for companie: fie Souldiers,
My Souldiers too, and play these tricks: what's he there?
Sure I have seen his face too; yes, most certaine
I have a son, but I hope he is not here now,
Would much resemble this man, wondrous neare him,
Just of his height and making too, you seeme a Leader.
The. Good sir, do not shame me more: I know your
And lesse then death, I looke not for. (anger,
Ar. You shall be my charge sir, it seemes you want foes,
When you would make your friends your Enemies:
A running bloud ye have, but I shall cure ye.
Bur. Good sir
Ar. No more good Lord: beate forward Souldiers:
And you, march in the reare, you have lost your places *Ex.*

Scæne 6. *Enter Duke, Olimpia, Honora, Viola.*

Du. You shall not be thus sullen still, with me sister
You doe the most unnobly to be angry.
For as I have a soule, I never touch'd her,
I never yet knew one unchast thought in her:
I must confesse, I lov'd her: as who would not?
I must confesse I doated on her strangely,
I offer'd all, yet so strong was her honour,
So fortifi'd as faire, no hope could reach her,
And while the world beheld this, and confirm'd it,
Why would you be so jealous?
Ol. Good sir pardon me,
I feele sufficiently my follies pennance,
And am asham'd, that shame a thousand sorrowes
Feed on continually, would I had never seen her,
Or with a clearer judgement look'd upon her,
She was too good for me, so heavenly good sir,
Nothing but heaven can love that soule sufficiently. *Enter*
Where I shall see her once againe. *Burris.*
Du. No more teares,
If she be within the Dukedome, wee'l recover her:
Welcome Lord *Burris*, faire newes I hope.
Bu. Most faire sir,
Without one drop of bloud these wars are ended,
The Souldier could againe, indeed asham'd sir,
And all his anger ended.
Du. Where's Lord *Archas*?
Bur. Not far off sir: with him his valiant son,
Head of this fire, but now a prisoner,
And in by your sweet mercie not prevented,
I feare some fatall stroke. *Drums.*
Enter Archas, Theodore, Gentlemen, Souldiers
Du. I heare the drums beate,
Welcome my worthy friend.
Ar. Stand where ye are sir,
Even as you love your Countrey, move not forward,
Nor plead for peace, till I have done a justice,
A justice on this villaine; none of mine now,
A justice on this Rebell.
Hon. O my Brother.
Ar. This fatall firebrand——

Du. Forget not old man,
He is thy son, of thine owne bloud.
Ar. In these veines
No treacherie e're harbour'd yet, no mutinie,
I ne're gave life to lewd and headstrong Rebels.
Du. 'Tis his first fault.
Ar. Not of a thousand sir,
Or were it so, it is a fault so mightie,
So strong against the nature of all mercie,
His mother were she living, would not weep for him,
He dare not say he would live.
The. I must not sir,
Whilst you say 'tis not fit: your Graces mercy
Not to my life appli'd, but to my fault sir,
The worlds forgivenesse next, last, on my knees sir,
I humbly beg,
Do not take from me yet the name of father,
Strike me a thousand blowes, but let me dye yours.
Ar. He moves my heart: I must be suddaine with him,
I shall grow faint else, in my execution; (bravely.
Come, come sir, you have seen death; now meet him
Du. Hold, hold I say, a little hold, consider
Thou hast no more sons *Archas* to inherit thee.
Ar. Yes sir, I have another, and a nobler:
No treason shall inherit me: young *Archas*
A boy, as sweet as young, my brother breeds him,
My noble brother *Briskie*, breeds him nobly,
Him let your favour find: give him your honour.
Enter Putskie (alias Briskie) and Alinda (alias Archas.
Pu. Thou hast no child left *Archas* none to inherit thee
If thou strikst that stroke now: behold young *Archas*;
Behold thy brother here, thou bloudy brother,
As bloudy to this sacrifice as thou art:
Heave up thy sword, and mine's heav'd up: strike *Archas*,
And I'le strike too as suddenly, as deadly:
Have mercy, and I'le have mercy: the Duke gives it,
Looke upon all these, how they weep it from thee,
Choose quickly, and begin.
Du. On your obedience,
On your allegeance save him.
Ar. Take him to ye. *Soul. shout.*
And sirha, be an honest man, ye have reason:
I thanke ye worthy Brother; welcome child,
Mine owne sweet child.
Du. Why was this boy concealed thus?
Put. Your graces pardon:
Fearing the vow you made against my brother
And that your anger would not only light
On him, but find out all his familie,
This young boy, to preserve from after danger,
Like a young wench, hether I brought; my selfe
In the habit of an ordinarie Captaine
Disguis'd, got entertainement, and serv'd here
That I might still be ready to all fortunes:
The boy your Grace tooke, nobly entertain'd him,
But thought a Girle, *Alinda*, Madam.
Ol. Stand away,
And let me looke upon him.
Du. My young Mistris!
This is a strange metamorphosis, *Alinda*!
Al. Your graces humble servant.
Du. Come hether sister:
I dare yet scarce beleeve mine eyes! how they view one
Dost thou not love this boy well? (another?
Ol. I should lye else,
Trust me, extreamely lye sir.
Ggg *Duke*

shout
read[y]

V, v, following 17. The entrance of Theodore and others was neither warned nor cued; the group left the stage 17 lines earlier and may not have needed the prompter's help at their re-entrance. Similarly, the entrance of Burris and some soldiers was neither warned nor cued, since they left the stage 12 lines earlier.

V, vi, 22. The prompter moved the entrance of Burris 5 lines later, correcting an error in the printed text.

V, vi, 30. The combination drum cue and entrance cue was not warned.

V, vi, following 67. The entrance of Putskie and Alinda disguised was neither warned nor cued.

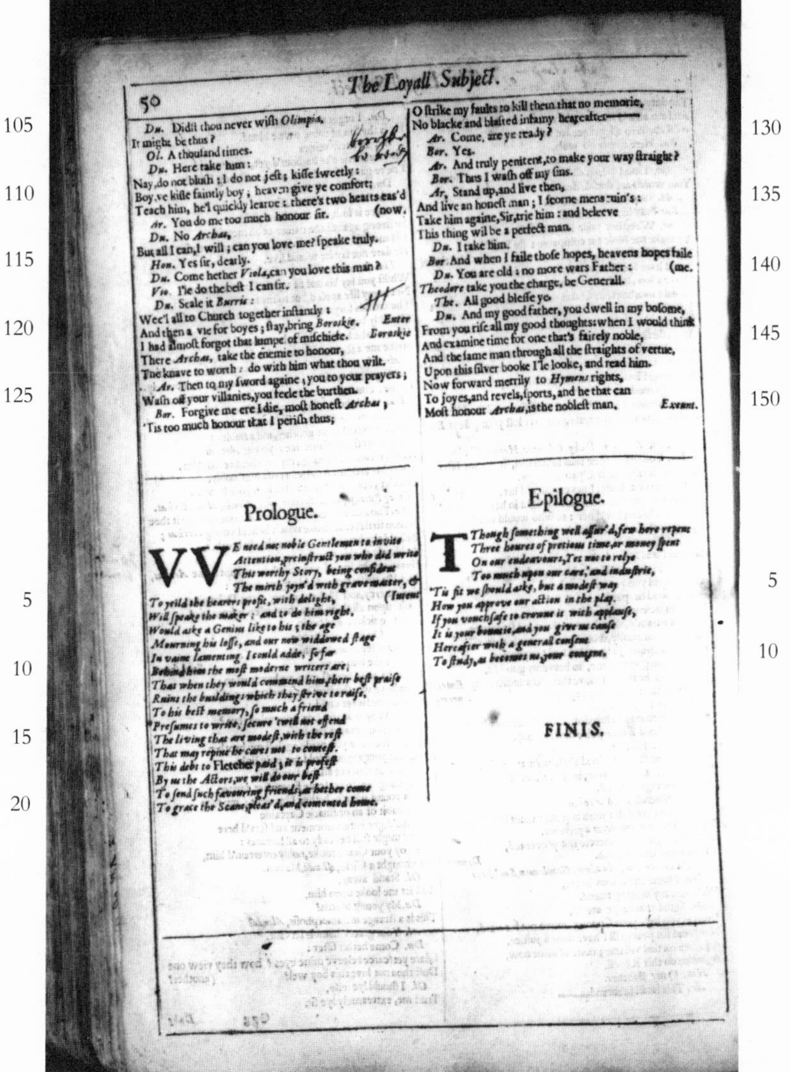

50 The Loyall Subject.

Du. Didſt thou never wiſh *Olimpia*,
It might be thus?
Ol. A thouſand times.
Du. Here take him:
Nay, do not bluſh; I do not jeſt; kiſſe ſweetly:
Boy, ye kiſſe faintly boy; heaven give ye comfort;
Teach him, he'l quickly learne: there's two hearts eas'd (now.
Ar. You do me too much honour ſir.
Du. No *Archas*,
But all I can, I will; can you love me? ſpeake truly.
Hon. Yes ſir, dearly.
Du. Come hether *Viola*, can you love this man?
Vio. I'le do the beſt I can ſir.
Du. Seale it *Burris*:
Wee'l all to Church together inſtantly:
And then a vie for boyes; ſtay, bring *Boroskie*. *Enter Boroskie*
I had almoſt forgot that lumpe of miſchiefe.
There *Archas*, take the enemie to honour,
The knave to worth: do with him what thou wilt.
Ar. Then to my ſword againe; you to your prayers;
Waſh off your villanies, you feele the burthen.
Bor. Forgive me ere I die, moſt honeſt *Archas*;
'Tis too much honour that I periſh thus;
O ſtrike my faults to kill them that no memorie,
No blacke and blaſted infamy hereafter——
Ar. Come, are ye ready?
Bor. Yes.
Ar. And truly penitent, to make your way ſtraight?
Bor. Thus I waſh off my ſins.
Ar. Stand up, and live then,
And live an honeſt man; I ſcorne mens ruin's:
Take him againe, Sir, trie him: and beleeve
This thing wil be a perfect man.
Du. I take him.
Bor. And when I faile thoſe hopes, heavens hopes faile (me.
Du. You are old: no more wars Father:
Theodore take you the charge, be Generall.
The. All good bleſſe ye.
Du. And my good father, you dwell in my boſome,
From you riſe all my good thoughts: when I would think
And examine time for one that's fairely noble,
And the ſame man through all the ſtraights of vertue,
Upon this ſilver booke I'le looke, and read him.
Now forward merrily to *Hymens* rights,
To joyes, and revels, ſports, and he that can
Moſt honour *Archas*, is the nobleſt man. *Exeunt.*

Prologue.

WE need not noble Gentlemen to invite
Attention, preinſtruct you who did write
This worthy Story, being confident
The mirth joyn'd with grave matter, & (Intent
To yeild the hearers profit, with delight,
Will ſpeake the maker; and to do him right,
Would aske a Genius like to his; the age
Mourning his loſſe, and our new widdowed ſtage
In vaine lamenting. I could adde, ſo far
Behind him the moſt moderne writers are;
That when they would commend him, their beſt praiſe
Ruins the buildings which they ſtrive to raiſe,
To his beſt memory, ſo much a friend
Preſumes to write, ſecure 'twill not offend
The living that are modeſt, with the reſt
That may repine he cares not to conteſt.
This debt to Fletcher *paid; it is profeſt*
By us the Actors, we will do our beſt
To ſend ſuch favouring friends, as hether come
To grace the Scane, pleas'd, and contented home.

Epilogue.

THough ſomething well aſſur'd, few here repent
Three houres of pretious time, or money ſpent
On our endeavours, Yet not to relye
Too much upon our care, and induſtrie,
'Tis fit we ſhould aske, but a modeſt way
How you approve our action in the play.
If you vouchſafe to crowne it with applauſe,
It is your bountie, and you give us cauſe
Hereafter with a generall conſent
To ſtudy, as becomes us, your content.

FINIS.

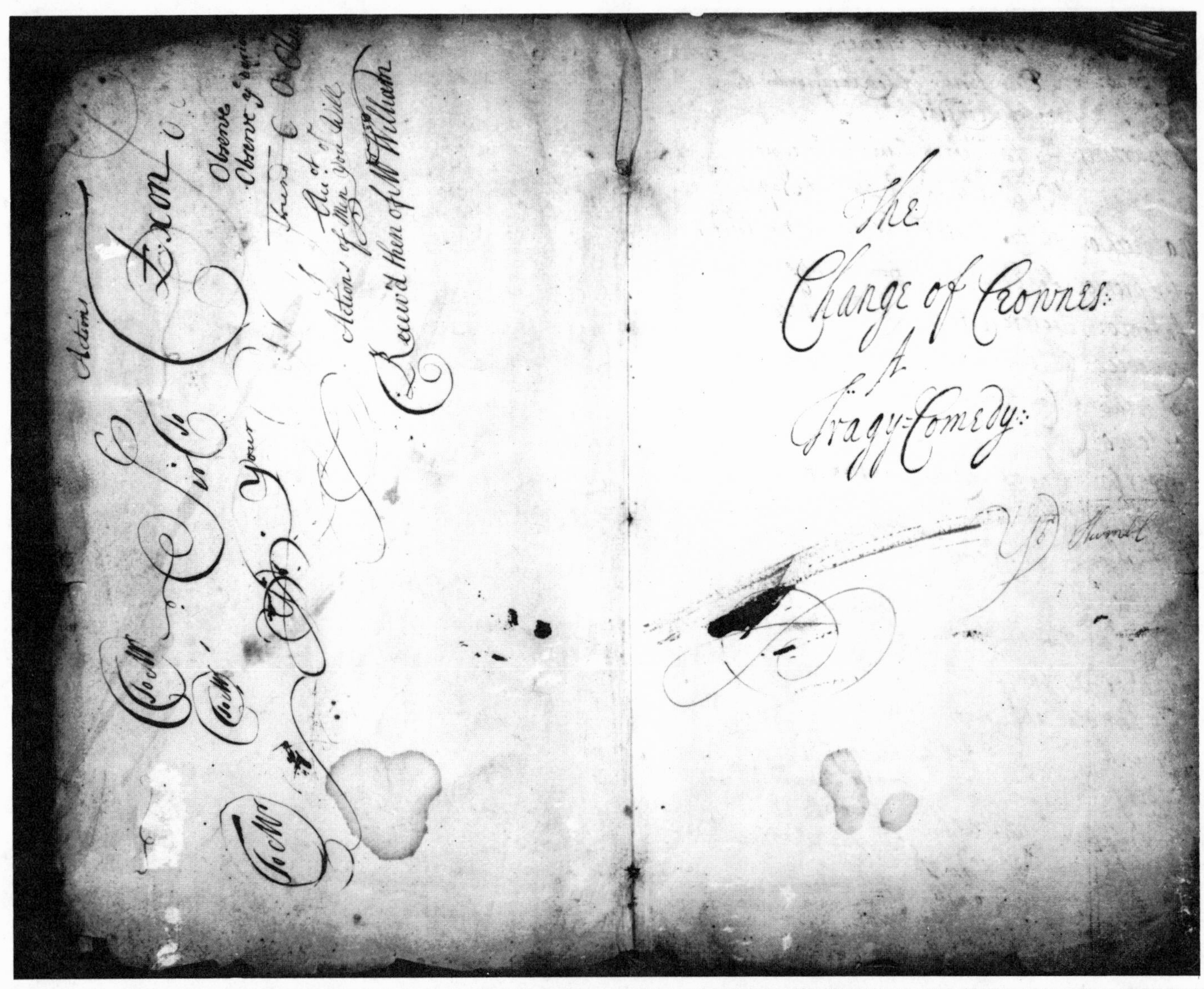

The Change of Crownes by Edward Howard. Present owner not known.

The Persons Names:

Carolo: The Elder Brother of Lombardy, under the Name of Leonidas:
Barsanes: His Confident, & father to Andrugio.
Guarini: A Duke of the Royal Blood of Naples.
Malvecchio: The Cheife minister of State & ye Dukes Creature.
Sempronio: An Embassador from the King of Lombardy:
Antonio: Secretary, to the Lord Malvecchio:
Lodovico: / Fiorelli: / Octavio: { Courtiers.
Alberto: King of Lombardy, but younger Brother to Carolo:
Andrugio: / Castruchio: / Valerio: { His officers:
Asinello: The Humerist:
A Capt of the Guard.
Two Porters of the Court:
A Guard:
Messengers & Attendants:
Artemia: the present Queene, but younger Sister in Love with Carolo:
Ariana: The Elder Sister:
A Lady Abbesse
Two Nunnes
Ladies Attendants:

The Scene Naples:

Act ye first.
Scene ye first.
Enter Fiorelli & Lodovico Courtiers.

Flo: I am glad the Queene hath throwne off mourning, this is her first Day of State.
Lodo: Even what shee pleases. but I wish still, that her Ascent to th' Throne had been more natural.
Flo: Take heed, ith' Court Are many Eares.
Lodo: There's an elder Sister, is that Treason?
Flo: Shee went before to th' Nunnery.
Lodo: A Crowne should Tempt weake flesh and Blood, shee's but In her Probation yet, though shee had been Profest, there have been Dispensations— but shee was not Consulted.
Flo: Malvecchio, our great minister of State, was Active for Artemia.
Lodo: yes, and the Duke Guarini too.
Flo: I expected rather, He being a Prince of the Blood, and a man Popular, would at this nick of tyme, putt in a Tytle—
Lodo: And Leap'd into the Throne himselfe;
Flo: but he has taken a more easy way to that Advancement, if wee may presage from the Queenes favours, by whose choice of him (as the present streame inclynes her) he may Rise to a King without this Trouble of Appearing Ambitious for it.
Lodo: oh the Court Politiques! there is not so much Juggling in Cards,
Flo: there must be Knaves in Both.
Enter Octavio.
You come from the Presence, is the Queene come forth?
Oct: Not yet, but Persons are flowing from all parts;

Octavio.

Duke Malvecchio

I, i, 29. The warning for the Duke and Malvecchio is only 12 lines before their entry; it could have been placed earlier. There are occasional other short warnings in the promptbook, though in most cases the prompter placed his warnings 20 to 30 lines in advance. Short warnings may have been those for entrances on prompt side.

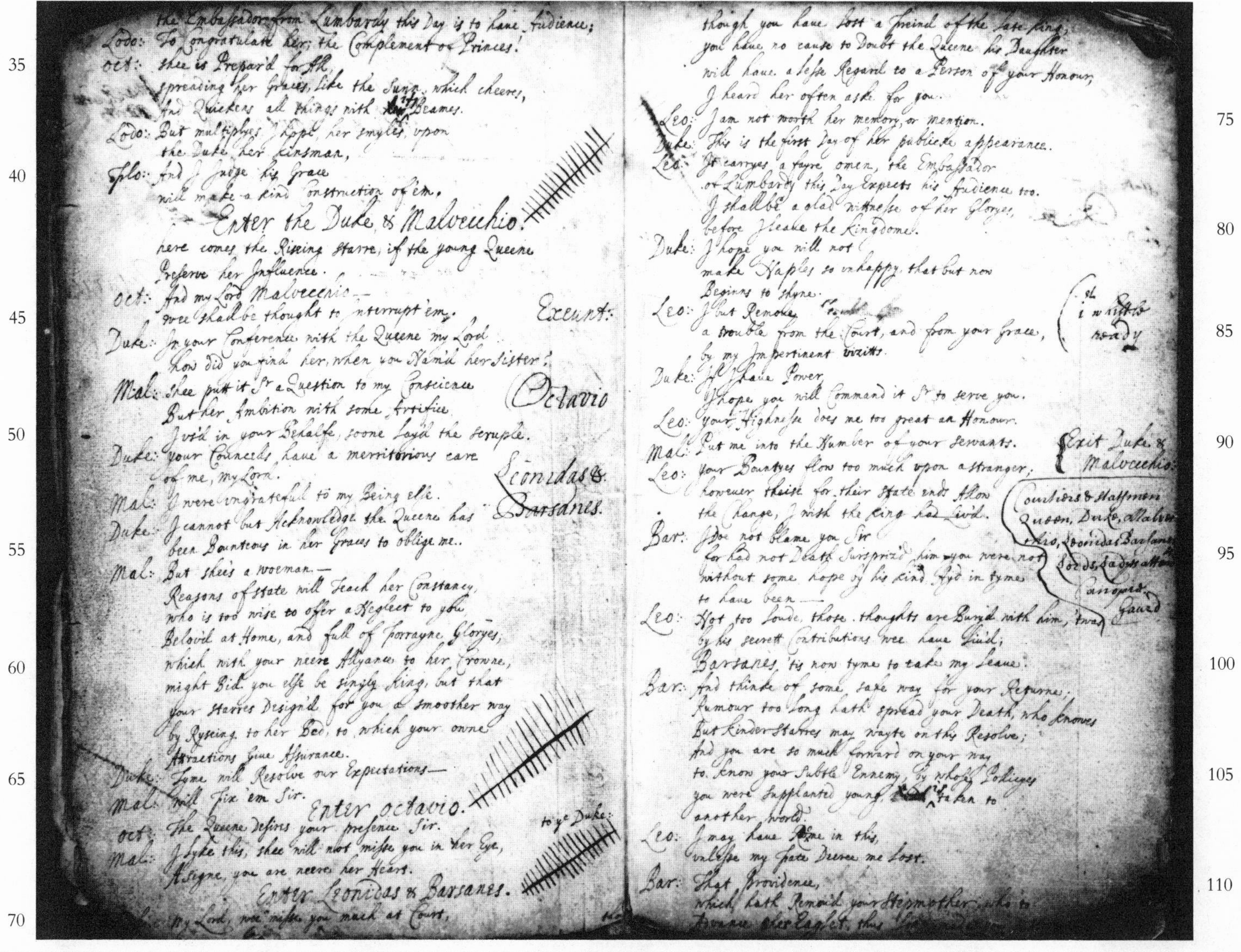

the Embassador from Lumbardy this Day is to have Audience;
Lodo: To Congratulate her; the Complement of Princes!
oct: shee is Prepar'd for All,
spreading her Graces, like the Sunn, which cheeres,
And Quickens all things with its Beames.
Lodo: But multiplyes I hope, her smyles, upon
the Duke her Kinsman,
Flo: And I Judge his Grace
will make a kind Construction of 'em.
Enter the Duke, & Malvecchio.
here comes the Rising Starre, if the young Queene
Preserve her Influence.
oct: And my Lord Malvecchio—
wee shallbe thought to Interrupt 'em. Exeunt:
Duke: In your Conference with the Queene my Lord
How did you find her, when you Nam'd her Sister?
Mal: Shee putt it Sr a Question to my Conscience Octavio
But her Ambition with some Artifice
Us'd in your Behalfe, soone Layd the scruple.
Duke: your Councells have a merritorious care
of me, my Lord. Leonidas &
Mal: I were ingratefull to my Being else. Barsanes.
Duke: I cannot but Acknowledge the Queene has
been Bounteous in her Graces to oblige me..
Mal: But shee's a woeman—
Reasons of State will Teach her Constancy,
who is too wise to offer a Neglect to you,
Belov'd at Home, and full of Forrayne Gloryes,
which with your neere Allyance to her Crowne,
might Bid you else be singly King, but that
your Starres Design'd for you a smoother way
by Ryseing to her Bed, to which your owne
Attractions give Assurance.
Duke: Tyme will Resolve our Expectations—
Mal: will Fix 'em Sir. Enter octavio.
oct: The Queene Desires your presence Sir. to ye Duke:
Mal: I lyke this, shee will not misse you in her Eye,
A signe, you are neere her Heart.
Enter Leonidas & Barsanes.
My Lord, wee misse you much at Court,

though you have lost a Freind of the late King,
you have no cause to Doubt the Queene his Daughter
will have a lesse Regard to a Person of your Honour,
I heard her often aske for you.
Leo: I am not worth her memory, or mention.
Duke: This is the first Day of her publicke appearance.
Leo: It carryes a fayre omen, the Embassador
of Lumbardy this Day Expects his Audience too.
I shallbe a glad witnesse of her Gloryes,
before I leave the Kingdome.
Duke: I hope you will not
make Naples so unhappy, that but now
Begins to shyne.
Leo: I but Remove a trouble from the Court, and from your Grace, (St i with the ready
by my Impertinent vizitts.
Duke: If I have Power,
I hope you will Command it Sr to serve you.
Leo: your Highnesse does me too great an Honour.
Mal: Put me into the Number of your Servants. Exit Duke & Malvecchio:
Leo: your Bountyes flow too much upon a Stranger,
however theise for their State ends Allow
the Change, I wish the King had Liv'd. (Courtiers & Waytmen Queen, Duke, Malvecchio, Leonidas Barsanes Lords, Ladys atten Canopied Guard
Bar: I doe not blame you Sir
for had not Death Surpriz'd him you were not
without some hope by his kind Ayd in tyme
to have been—
Leo: Not too loude, those thoughts are Bury'd with him, 'twas
by his secrett Contributions wee have Liv'd;
Barsanes, 'tis now tyme to take my leave.
Bar: And thinke of some safe way for your Returne,
Rumour too long hath spread your Death, who knowes
But Kinder Starres may wayte on this Resolve;
And you are so much forward on your way
to know your Subtle Ennemy, by whose Policyes
you were Supplanted young, & taken to
another world.
Leo: I may have Tyme in this,
unlesse my Fate Decree me lost.
Bar: That Providence,
which hath Remov'd your Stepmother, who to
Avance her Eaglet, thus [illegible]

I, i, 92–97. This group warning, like others in the manuscript, is a repeat of the author's stage direction at the point of entrance. Perhaps prompt notes such as this one, made up before rehearsals began, were not adhered to exactly in practice. The prompter, preparing his book in advance, would probably match his warnings to the author's directions; if changes were made in rehearsals, he would alter the warnings—if he was alert. But see the warning at I, ii, 105–6.

[I, ii]

Queene:· Be it your

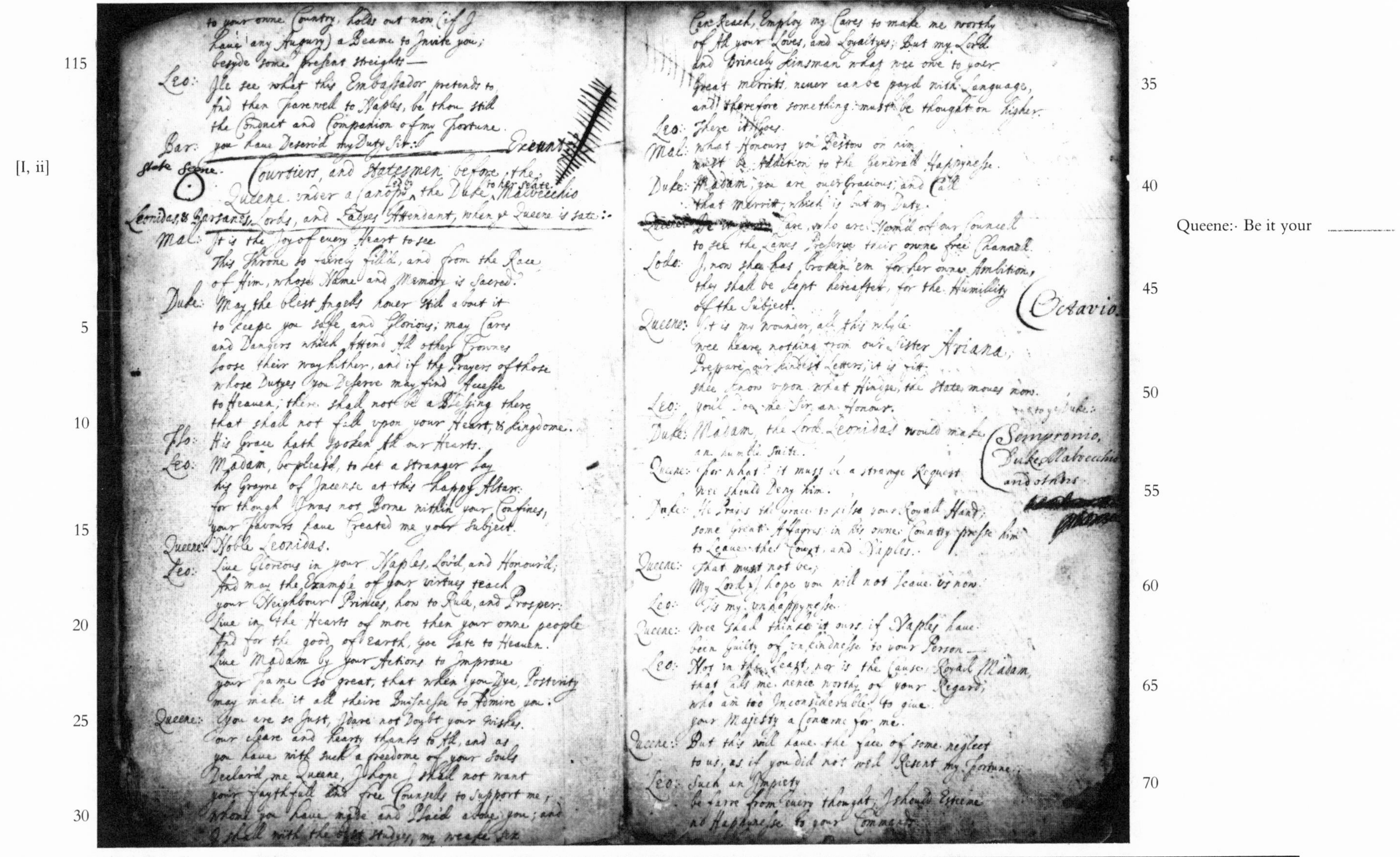

to your owne Country holds out now (if I
have any Augury) a Beame to Invite you;
besyde some present streights—
Leo: Ile see what this Embassador pretends to,
And then farewell to Naples, be thou still
the Conduct and Companion of my Fortune.
Bar: you have Deserv'd my Duty Sir:· Exeunt
State Scene. Courtiers, and Statesmen before, the
Queene under a Canopy, the Duke Malvecchio to her seate.
Leonidas & Barsanes Lords, and Ladyes Attendant, when ye Queene is sate:·
Mal: It is the Joy of every Heart to see
This Throne so rarely fill'd, and from the Race
of Him, whose Name and Memory is sacred.
Duke: May the blest Angels hover still about it
to keepe you safe, and Glorious; may Cares
and Dangers which attend All other Crownes
loose their way hither, and if the Prayers of those
whose Dutyes you Deserve may find Accesse
to Heaven, there shall not be a Blessing there
that shall not fall upon your Heart, & kingdome.
Flo: His Grace hath spoken All our Hearts.
Leo: Madam, be pleas'd, to let a stranger lay
his Grayne of Incense at this happy Altar.
for though I was not Borne within your Confines,
your Favours have Created me your Subject.
Queene: Noble Leonidas.
Leo: Live Glorious in your Naples, Lov'd, and Honour'd;
And may the Example of your virtues teach
your Neighbour Princes, how to Rule, and Prosper.
Live in the Hearts of more then your owne people
And for the good of Earth, goe Late to Heaven.
Live Madam by your Actions to Improve
your Fame so great, that when you Dye, Posterity
may make it all theire Businesse to Admire you.
Queene: You are so Just, I dare not Doubt your wishes.
our cleare and hearty thanks to All, and as
you have with such a freedome of your Souls
Declar'd me Queene, I hope I shall not want
your Faythfull and free Counsells to Support me,
whom you have made and Plac'd above you; and
I shall with the best studyes, my weake sex

Can Reach, Employ my Cares to make me worthy
of All your Loves, and Loyaltyes; But my Lord
and Princely Kinsman what wee owe to your
great merritts never can be payd with Language,
and therefore something must be thought on higher.
Leo: There it goes.
Mal: What Honours you Bestow on him
must be Addition to the Generall Happynesse.
Duke: Madam, you are over Gracious; and Call
that merrit, which is but my Duty.
[struck through] Care, who are Nam'd of our Councell
to see the Lawes Preserve their owne free Channell.
Lodo: I, now shee has broken 'em for her owne Ambition,
they shall be kept hereafter, for the Humility
of the Subject.
Queene: It is my wonder, all this while
wee heare nothing from our sister Ariana,
Prepare our kindest Letters, it is fitt
shee know upon what Hinges, the State moves now.
Leo: you'l doe me Sir, an Honour. to ye Duke:·
Duke: Madam, the Lord Leonidas would make
an humble suite.
Queene: for what? it must be a strange Request
wee should Deny him.
Duke: He prays the grace to kisse your Royall Hand;
some great Affayres in his owne Country presse him
to Leave the Court, and Naples.
Queene: That must not be;
My Lord, I hope you will not leave us now.
Leo: Tis my unhappynesse.
Queene: Wee shall thinke it ours if Naples have
been guilty of unkindnesse to your Person—
Leo: Not in the least, nor is the Cause, Royall Madam,
that calls me hence worthy of your Regard;
who am too Inconsiderable to give
your Majesty a Concerne for me.
Queene: But this will have the face of some neglect
to us, as if you did not well Resent my Fortune.
Leo: Such an Impiety
be farre from every thought, I should Esteeme
it Happynesse to your Command.

Octavio.
Sempronio, Duke Malvecchio and others.

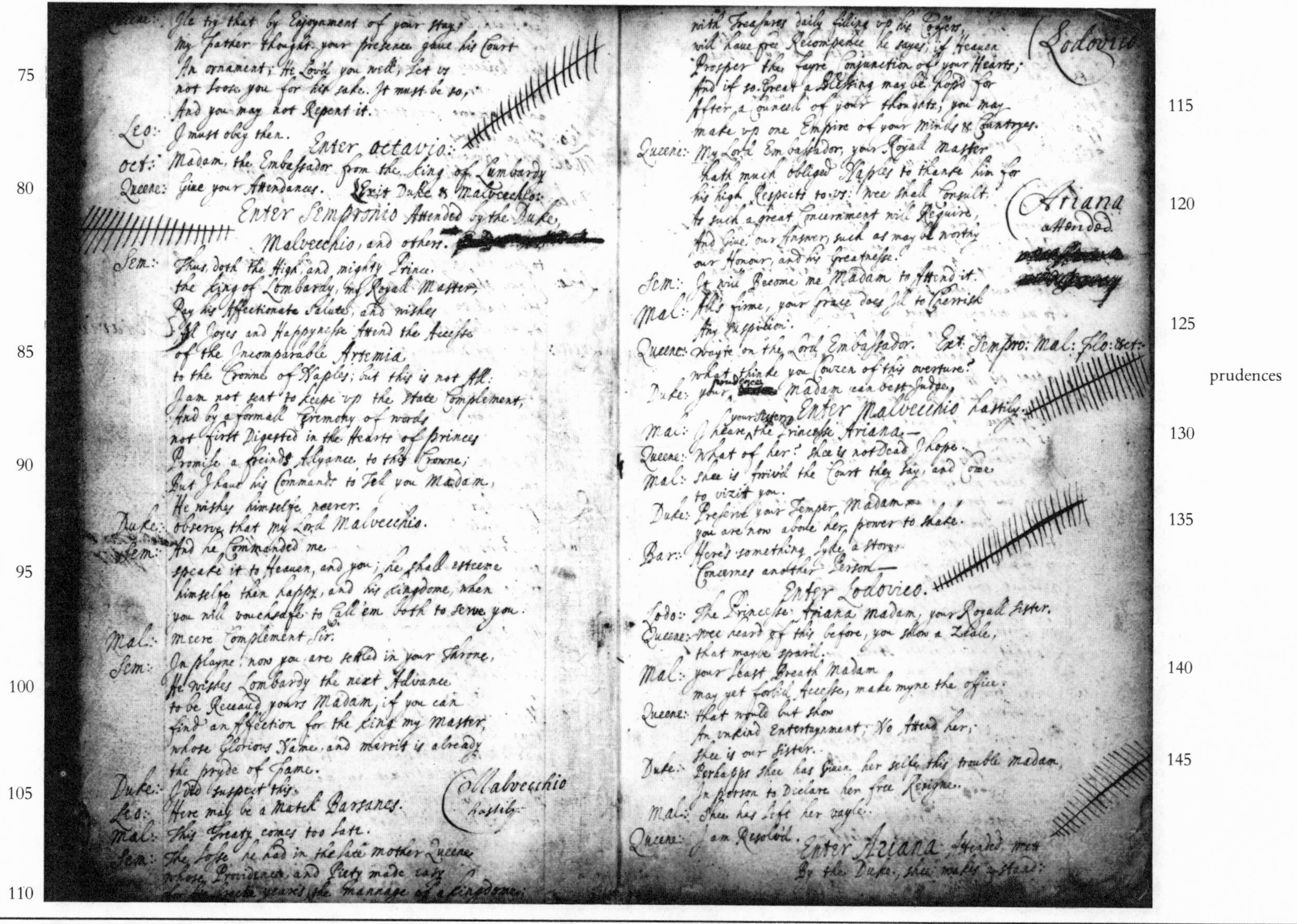

prudences

I, ii, 105–6. This warning for Malvecchio is pointless: he is onstage at the moment and will only be off for two lines before reentering for the cue here warned. The prompter, making his notes well in advance of production, dutifully picked up the author's stage direction without concerning himself with the practical value of the warning. Once in rehearsal he probably should have canceled the warning, but leaving it did no harm.

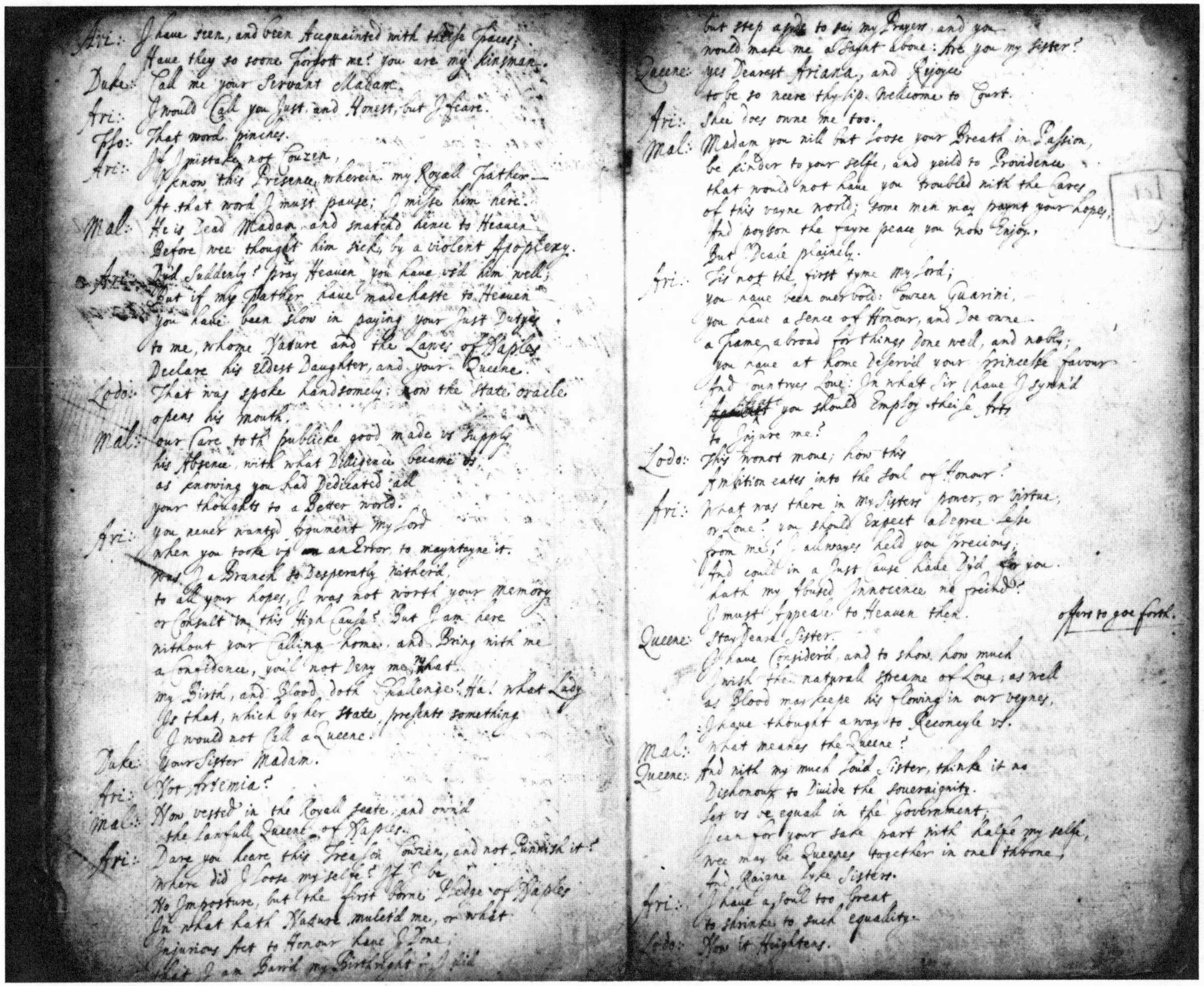

Ari: I have seen, and been Acquainted with these Faces;
Have they so soone forgott me? You are my Kinsman.
Duke: Call me your Servant Madam.
Ari: I would Call you Just, and Honest, but I feare.
Theo: That word pinches.
Ari: If I mistake not Couzen,
I know this Presence, wherein my Royall Father —
At that word I must pause; I misse him here.
Mal: He is Dead Madam, and snatch'd hence to Heaven
Before wee thought him sick, by a violent Apoplexy.
Ari: Dyd Suddenly? pray Heaven you have us'd him well;
but if my Father have made haste to Heaven
you have been slow in paying your Just Dutyes
to me, whome Nature and the Lawes of Naples
Declare his eldest Daughter, and your Queene.
Lodo: That was spoke handsomely; now the State oracle
opens his mouth.
Mal: our Care to th' publicke good made us happy
his Absence with what Dilligence became us
as knowing you had Dedicated all
your thoughts to a Better world.
Ari: you never wanted Ornament my Lord
when you tooke up ~~an~~ an Error to mayntayne it.
was I a Branch so desperately witherd
to all your hopes, I was not worth your memory
or Consult in this High Cause? But I am here
without your Calling home, and Bring with me
a Providence, you'l not Deny me, what
my Birth, and Blood doth Challenge. Ha! what Lady
Is that, which by her State, presents something
I would not Call a Queene.
Duke: Your Sister Madam.
Ari: Not Artemia?
Mal: Now vested in the Royall seate, and own'd
the Lawfull Queene of Naples.
Ari: Dare you heare this Treason Couzen, and not Punish it?
Where did I loose my selfe? If I be
No Imposture, but the first borne Pledge of Naples
In what hath Nature mulct'd me, or what
injurious Act to Honour have I Done
that I am Bar'd my Birthright? I did
but step aside to say my Prayers, and you
would make me a Saynt above: Are you my Sister?
Queene: yes Dearest Ariana, and Rejoyce
to be so neere thy lip. welcome to Court.
Ari: Shee does owne me too.
Mal: Madam you will but loose your Breath in Passion,
be kinder to your selfe, and yeild to Providence
that would not have you troubled with the Cares
of this vayne world; some men may taynt your hopes,
And poyson the fayre peace you now Enjoy,
But I speake playnely.
Ari: Tis not the first tyme my Lord;
you have been over bold: Couzen Guarini,
you have a sence of Honour, and Doe owne
a fame abroad for things Done well, and nobly;
you have at home deserv'd your Princesse favour
And our true Love: In what Sir have I synn'd
~~Against~~ that you should Employ these Arts
to Injure me?
Lodo: This wonnot move; how this
Ambition eates into the Soul of Honour!
Ari: What was there in my Sisters power, or Virtue,
or Love? you should Expect a Degree lesse
from me; I allwayes held you precious,
And could in a Just cause have Dyd for you.
Hath my Abused Innocence no freind?
I must Appeale to Heaven then. offers to goe forth.
Queene: Stay Deare Sister.
I have Considerd, and to show how much
I wish the naturall streame of Love, as well
as Blood may keepe his flowing in our veynes,
I have thought a way to Reconcyle us.
Mal: What meanes the Queene?
Queene: And with my much lov'd Sister, think it no
Dishonour to Divide the Soveraignity.
Let us be equall in the Government,
I can for your sake part with halfe my selfe,
wee may be Queenes together in one throne,
And Raigne like Sisters.
Ari: I have a soul too great
to shrinke to such equality.
Lodo: How it Frighters.

that [instead of] Against

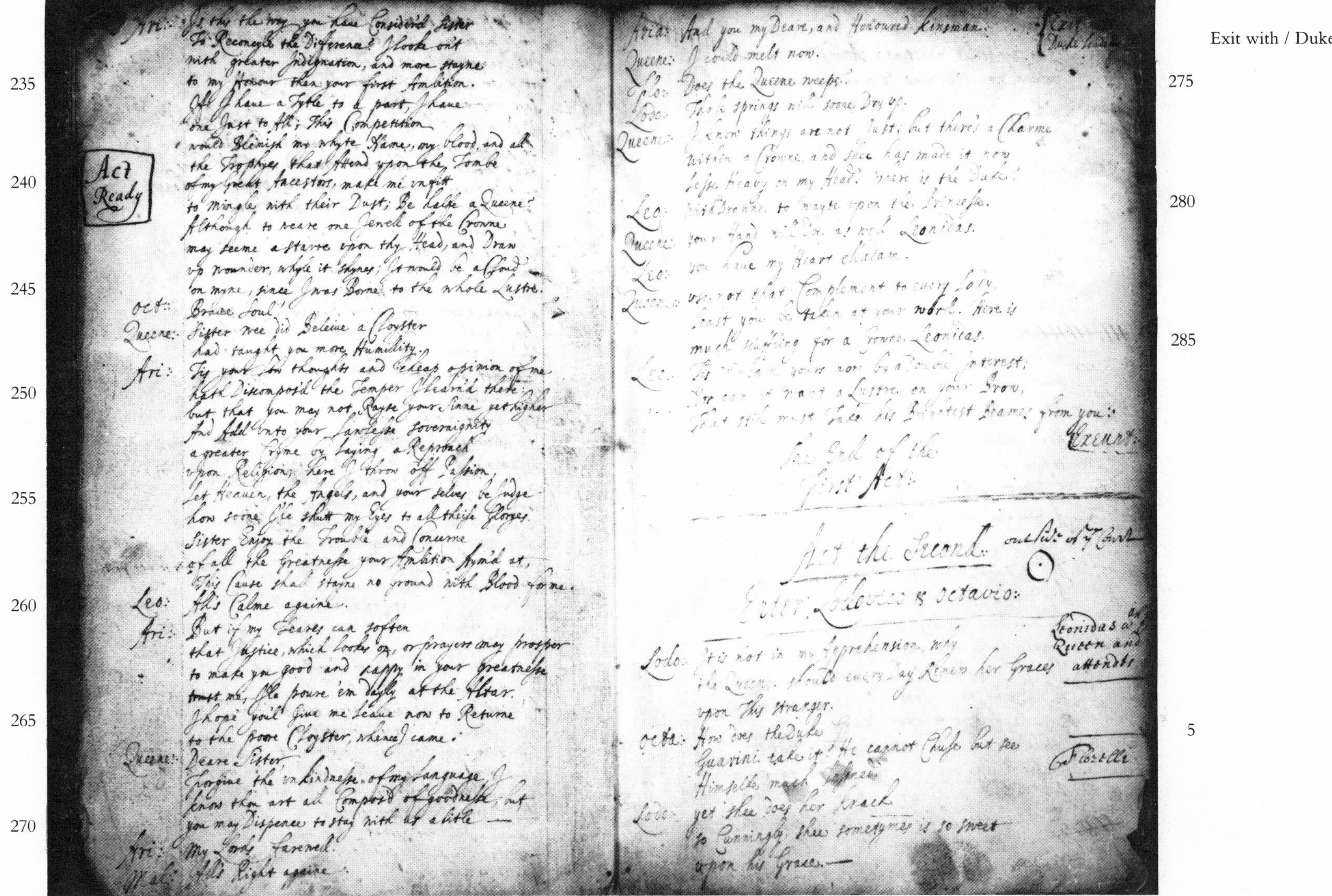

Act Ready

Ari: Is this the way you have Considered Sister
To Reconcyle the Differences? I looke on't
with greater Indignation, and more stayne
to my Honour then your first Ambition.
Iff I have a Tytle to a part, I have
one Just to all; This Competition
would Blemish my whyte Name, my blood, and all
the Trophyes that attend upon the Tombe
of my great Ancestors, make me unfitt
to Mingle with their Dust; Be halfe a Queene?
Although to weare one Jewell of the Crowne
may seeme a Starre upon thy Head, and Draw
up wonder, whyle it shynes; It would be a Cloud
on myne, since I was borne to the whole Lustre.
Oct: Brave Soul!
Queene: Sister wee did beleive a Cloyster
had taught you more Humility.
Ari: Ty your low thoughts and cheap opinion of me
hath Discompos'd the Temper I bear'd there
but that you may not Rayse your Sinne yet higher
And Add unto your Lawlesse Soveraignity
a greater Cryme by Laying a Reproach
upon Religion, here I throw off Passion;
Let Heaven, the Angels, and your selves be Judge
how soone I'le shutt my Eyes to all theise Glories.
Sister Enjoy the Trouble and Concerne
of all the Greatnesse your Ambition Aym'd at,
This Cause shall stayne no ground with Blood for me.
Leo: All's Calme againe.
Ari: But if my Teares can soften
that Justice, which looks on, or prayers may prosper
to make you good and happy in your Greatnesse
trust me, I'le poure 'em dayly at the Altar.
I hope you'll give me leave now to Returne
to the poore Cloyster, whence I came.
Queene: Deare Sister
Forgive the unkindnesse of my language; I
know thou art all Compos'd of Goodnesse, but
you may Dispence to stay with us a litle —
Ari: My Lords farewell.
Wal: All's Right againe.

Aria: And you my Deare, and Honoured Kinsman. Exit / Duke leading
Queene: I could melt now.
Olo: Does the Queene weepe?
Lodo: Those springs will soone Dry up.
Queene: I know things are not Just, but there's a Charme
within a Crowne, and shee has made it now
lesse heavy on my Head. Where is the Duke?
Leo: Withdrawne to wayte upon the Princesse.
Queene: Your hand, will you, as well Leonidas.
Leo: You have my Heart, Madam.
Queene: Use not that Complement to every Lady,
Least you be taken at your word. Here is
much suffring for a Crowne, Leonidas.
Leo: Tis [illegible] yours now by a double interest,
[illegible] it want a Lustre on your Brow,
That still must take his Brightest Beames from you:
Exeunt.

The End of the First Act.

Act the Second. outside of ye Court

Enter Lodovico & Octavio.

Leonidas and Queen and attendts

Lodo: 'Tis not in my Apprehension why
the Queene should every day Renew her Graces
upon this Stranger.
Octa: How does the Duke
Guarini take it? He cannot Chuse but see
Himselfe much lessen'd
Lodo: yet shee does her Grace
so Cunningly, shee sometymes is so sweet
upon his Grace —

Fiorelli

Exit with / Duke leading

Octa: when the other's Absent.
Lodo: But wee that constantly Attend can see
which way the wind blowes fayrest: shee's here.
Enter Leonidas with the Queene
Attended & Passing over the Stage:
Octa: And our New Blazeing Starre,
Pray heaven it bode no ill to Naples.
Lodo: Courts never want these Prodigyes;
shee's young, and tis no breach of Duty
To wish things well, but leave her to her Fancy.
Lett's Talke of something else.
Enter Asinello: Assinello
What's the matter Signior?
What Sunneshyne makes you looke so pleasant?
Flo: If you have a mind to Laugh Gentlemen
Here's a spectacle hard by——
Lodo: what ist
Flo: A Thing calls himselfe a Country gentleman
A strange medly made up of foole & knave.
That has it seemes money in his purse,
And is come to Court in hopes to buy an office:
And he talkes with as much confidence as if
he had one already.
Octa: Prethee where is he?
Flo: Nay he knowes not, tis a Labarinth
to him and he is lost int. he moves up & downe,
Like a firework upon a Line:
most of his Discourse is three Questions
where is the Queene; how to get an office,
And which is the way out o' the Court, for hee's lost int.
But see the Pageant Appeares himselfe.
Enter Asinello:
Asi: The strangest place that ere I came in: Yee heare
you looke lyke Civill gentlemen, Pray which is the way
out of the Court? I have been int theise two Houres
And I can find neither Beginning nor Ending.
Lodo: The way out o' the Court. cannot you find that, Sir?
Asi: No, but would you would Instruct me, Sir.
Lodo: Nay faces about. tis the very same way you Came in Sir;
there's no way lyke it.
Asi: But I cannot tell that, here are so many windings
and turnings that I have lost my selfe.
Octa: you are not the first man has been lost at Court.
Asi: I should be sorry sir, if I now add to the Number.
But to tell you truly I come for preferment
on Honorable Tearmes.
Flo: As how Sir?
Asi: why I have sould some estate in the Country
to facilitate my way. I hope you'l grant
I am a faire wooer.
Lodo: It cannot be Denyde,
Octa: And may Qualify you here, if well Employd.
Asi: But to tell I must Confesse, that ere I went farre
In this Elizium I should meet with a Cerberus,
or so that would looke grimme upon my passage,
But I have here my Sopps of gold to winne
him to that Complexion.
Lodo: The Queene has no Courtiers
of such Craveing Appetites, I Assure you.
Asi: I honour the Queene, Sir, and all her Relations,
But they say the King of Hungary has
some subjects in all Courts.
Flo: you are Cunning in Metaphor I perceave.
Asi: I should be loath to Disoblige any
As farre as my Abillityes Extend.
Octa: A most Ingenuos Expression.

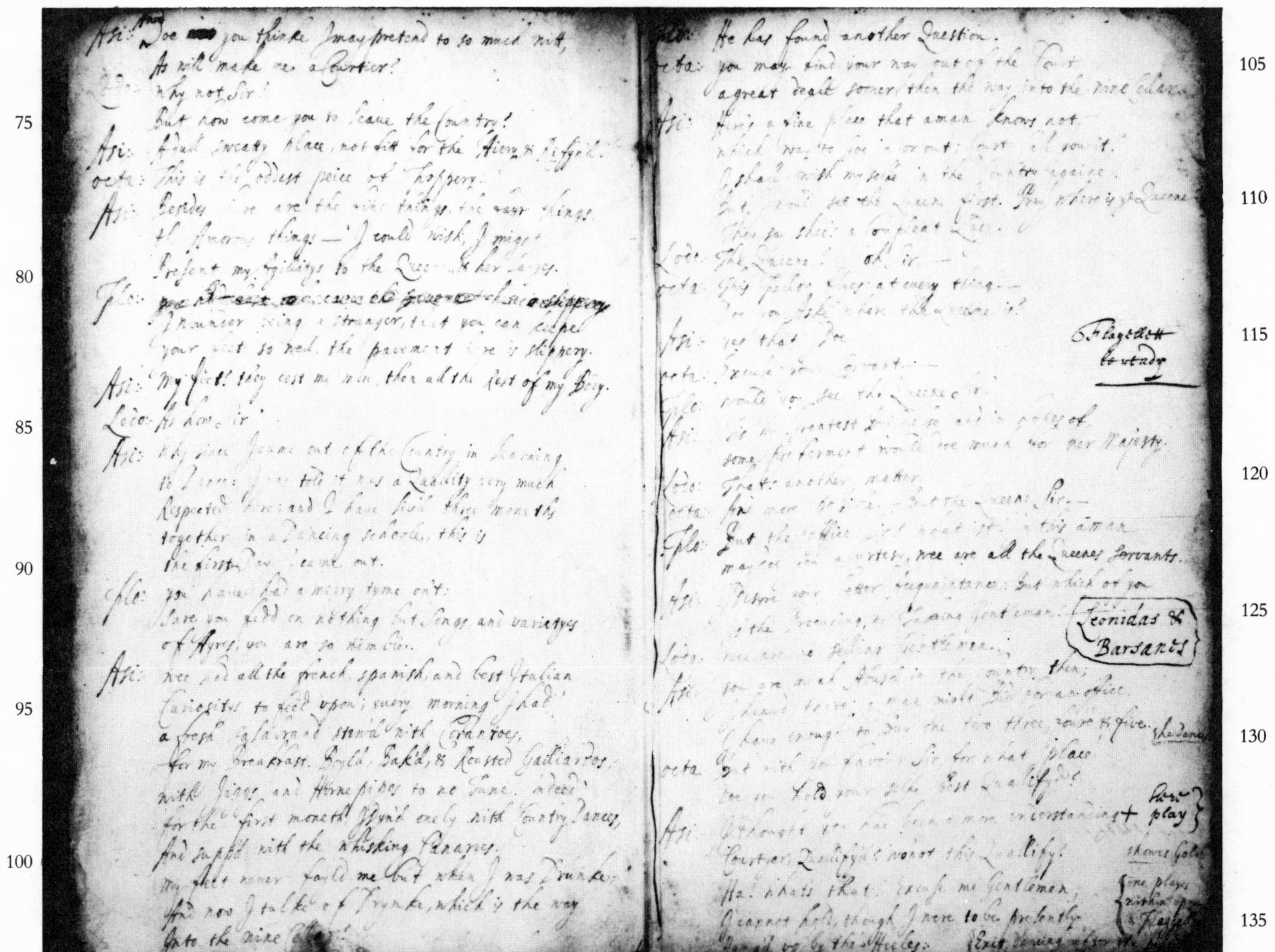

one playes / within vpon / a Flagellett

Exit, Dancing after the pipe.

II, i, 115–16, 132. These two sound effect notes are related: the musician needed to be warned of his cue (he may have played from his position in the music room), and the cue needed to be set more precisely than the author, at lines 134–36, indicated.

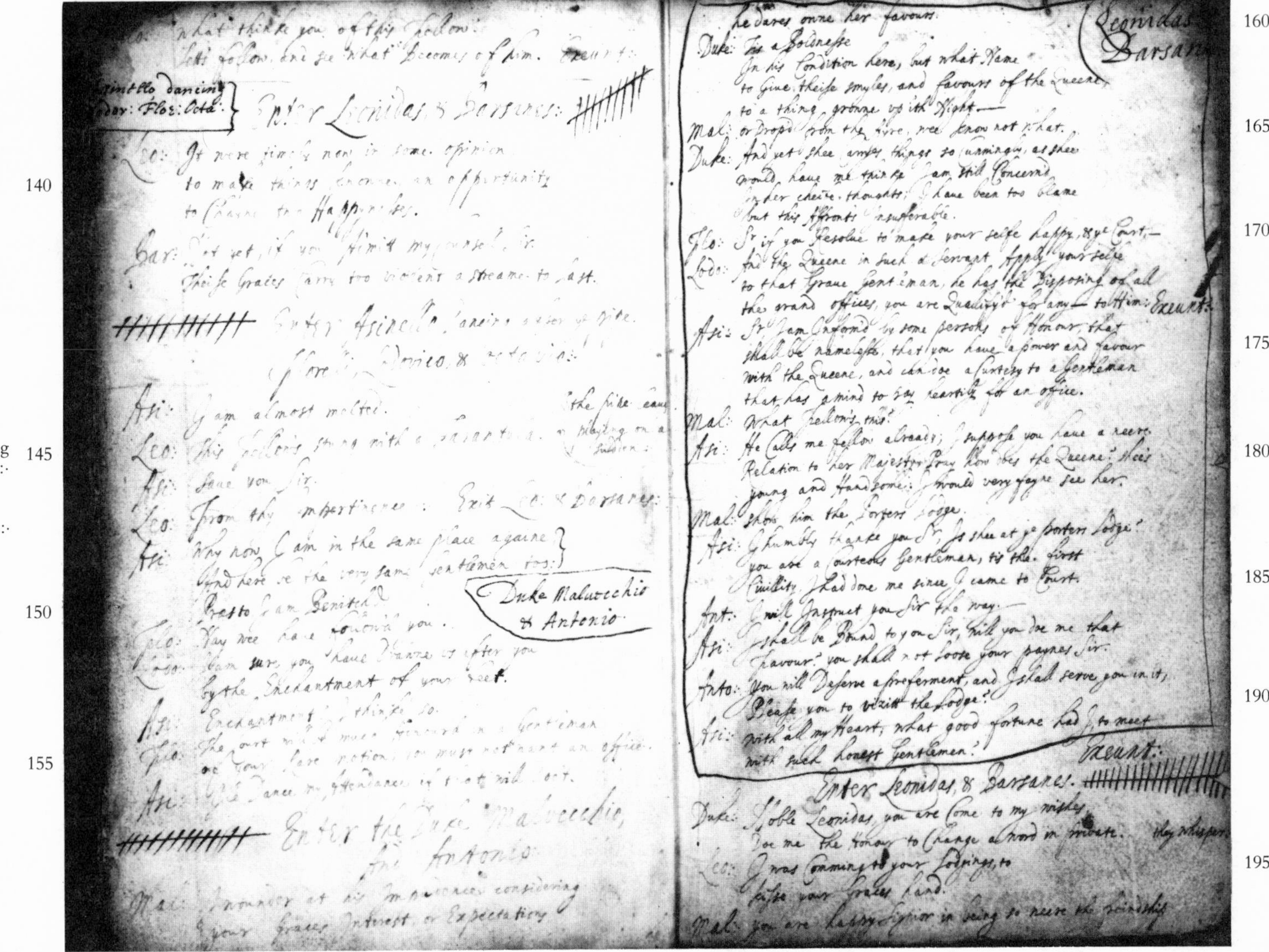

the pipe leaues / playing on a / sudden:·

Exit Leo: & Barsanes:·

2[d] whistle

[II, ii]

Not to be angry

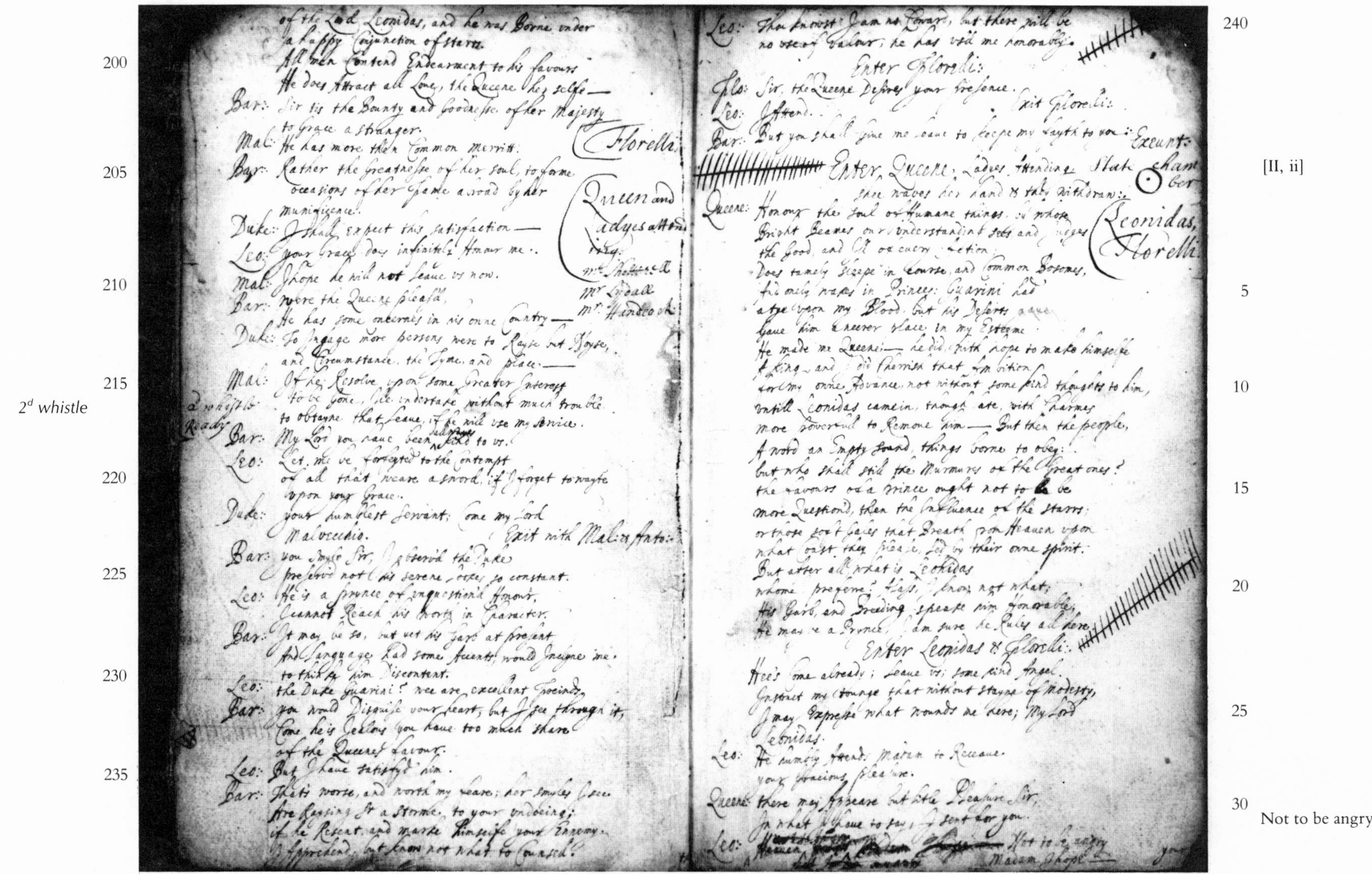

of the Lord Leonidas, and he was borne under
a happy Conjunction of starrs.
All men Contend Endearment to his favours
He does Attract all Love, the Queene her selfe—
Bar: Sir tis the Bounty and goodnesse of her Majesty
to grace a stranger.
Mal: He has more then Common merritt.
Bar: Rather the greatnesse of her soul, to forme
occasions of her fame abroad by her
munificence.
Duke: I shall expect this satisfaction—
Leo: Your Grace does infinitely Honour me.
Mal: I hope he will not leave us now.
Bar: were the Queene pleas'd,
He has some concernes in his owne Country—
Duke: To ingage more persons were to Rayse but Noyse,
and Circumstance, the Tyme, and place—
Mal: If he Resolve upon some Greater Interest
to be gone, Ile undertake without much trouble
to obtayne that leave, if he will use my Advice.
Bar: My Lord you have been [illegible] kind to us.
Leo: Let me be forgotten to the contempt
of all that weare a sword, if I forget to wayte
upon your Grace.
Duke: Your humblest servant; Come my Lord
Malvecchio. Exit with Mal: et Arato:
Bar: You smyle Sir, I observ'd the Duke
preserv'd not his serene lookes so constant.
Leo: He's a Prince of unquestion'd Honour,
I cannot Reach his worth in Character.
Bar: It may be so, but yet his Eyes at present
And language had some Accents would Incline me
to think him Discontent.
Leo: the Duke Guarini? wee are excellent friends,
Bar: you would Disguise your heart, but I see through it,
Come he's Jealous you have too much share
of the Queenes favour.
Leo: But I have satisfy'd him.
Bar: That's worse, and worth my feare; her smyles [illegible]
are Raysing it a storme, to your undoeing;
if he Resent, and marke himselfe your Enemy.
I apprehend, but know not what to Counsell.

Florelli.
Queen and Ladyes attending
Mrs Shottrell
Mrs Lydall
Mrs Hancock
2d whistle
Ready

Leo: Thou knowest I am no Coward, but there will be
no use of Valour; he has us'd me generously.
Enter Florelli:
Flo: Sir, the Queene Desires your presence.
Leo: I attend. Exit Florelli:
Bar: But you shall give me leave to keepe my fayth to you: Exeunt:
Enter Queene, Ladies Attending State Chamber
Shee waves her hand & they withdraw:
Queene: Honour the soul of Humane things, by whose
bright beames our understanding sees and judges
the Good, and Ill of every Action
Does tamely sleepe in Course, and Common persons,
And only wakes in Princes: Guarini has
a tye upon my Blood; but his Deserts have
gave him a neerer place in my Esteeme
He made me Queene— he did, with hope to make himselfe
a King; and I did Cherish that Ambition,
for my owne Advance, not without some kind thoughts to him,
untill Leonidas came in, though late, with Charmes
more Soverain to Remove him— But then the people,
A word an Empty sound, things borne to obey;
but who shall still the Murmurs of the Great ones?
The favours of a Prince ought not to be
more Question'd, then the Influence of the starrs;
or those soft gales that Breath from Heaven upon
what part they please, led by their owne spirit.
But after all, what is Leonidas
whome I preferre? Alas, I know not what,
His Garb, and Dressing speake him Honorable,
He may be a Prince, I am sure he Rules all here.
Enter Leonidas & Florelli:
Hee's come already; leave us; some kind Angel
Instruct my tounge that without stayne of modesty,
I may Expresse what wounds me here; My Lord
Leonidas.
Leo: He humbly attends, madam to Receave
your gracious pleasure.
Queene: there may appeare but little pleasure Sir,
In what I have to say, I sent for you.
Leo: Not to be angry
Madam, I hope—

Leonidas,
Florelli.

Challenge your Justice, and I Dare not Doubt

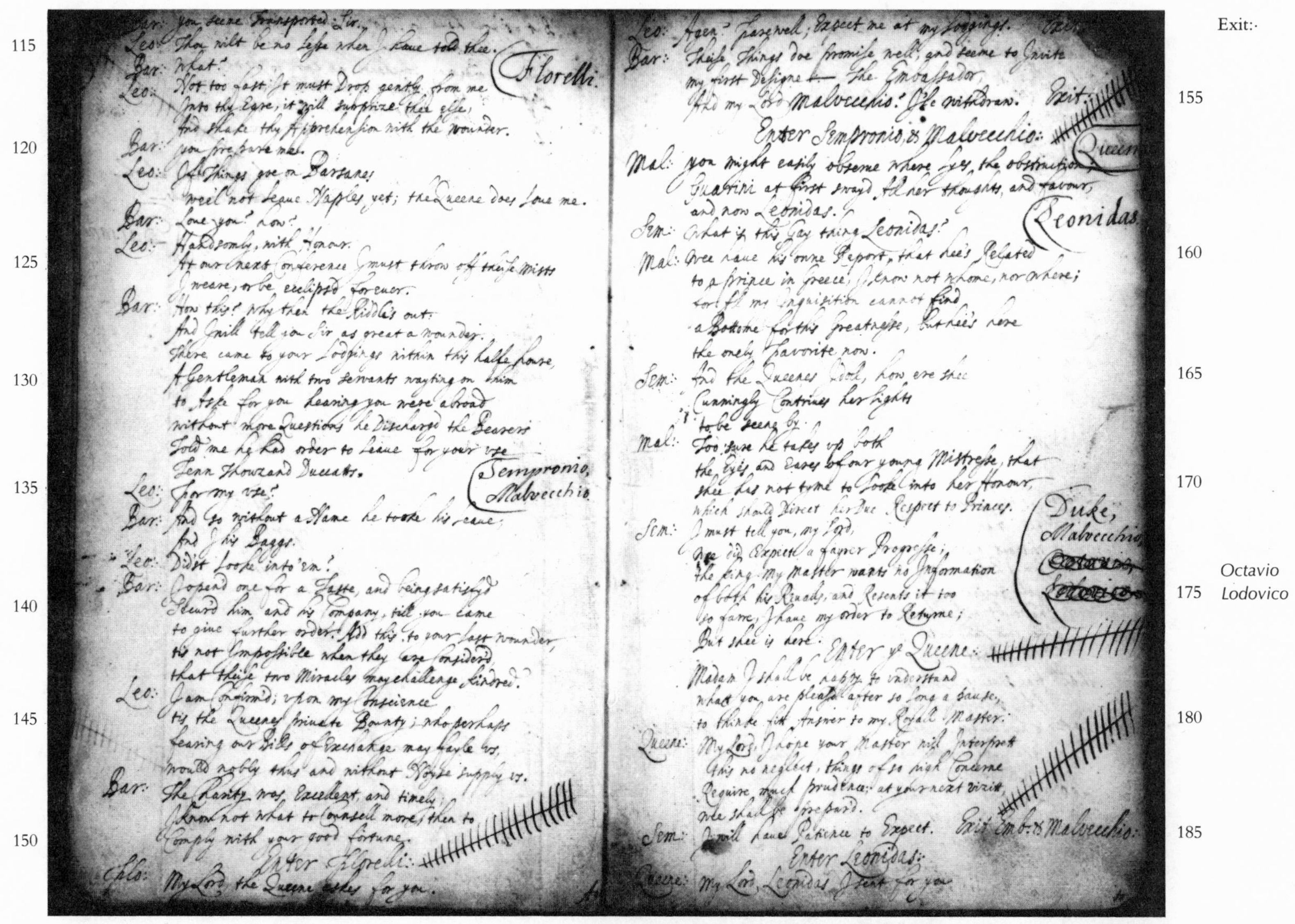

Bar: you seeme Transported Sir.
Leo: Thou wilt be no lesse when I haue told thee.
Bar: What?
Leo: Not too fast; It must Drop gently from me
Into thy Eare, it will surprize thee else,
And shake thy Apprehension with the wonder.
Bar: you free haue me.
Leo: All things goe on Barsanes;
I will not leaue Naples yet; the Queene does loue me.
Bar: Loue you? how?
Leo: Handsomly, with Honor.
At our next conference I must throw off theise Mists
I weare, or be ecclipsed forever.
Bar: How this? why then the Riddle's out.
And I will tell you Sir as great a wonder.
There came to your Lodgings within this halfe houre,
A Gentleman with two servants wayting on him
to aske for you hearing you were abroad
without more Questions he Discharged the Bearers
Told me he had order to leaue for your use
Tenn Thowsand Duccatts.
Leo: For my use?
Bar: And so without a Name he tooke his leaue;
And I his Baggs.
Leo: Didst Looke into 'em?
Bar: I opened one for a Taste, and being satisfyed
I secured him, and his Company, till you came
to giue further order. Add this to your last wonder,
tis not Impossible when they are considered
that theise two Miracles may challenge kindred.
Leo: I am confirmd; upon my conscience
tis the Queenes private Bounty; who perhaps
fearing our Bills of Exchange may faile us,
would nobly thus and without Noyse supply us.
Bar: The Charity was Excellent, and timely;
I know not what to counsell more, then to
comply with your good fortune.
Enter Florelli:
Flo: My Lord, the Queene askes for you.

Florelli.
Sempronio, Malvecchio

Leo: Agen? farewell; Expect me at my Lodgings. Exit
Bar: Theise Things doe promise well, and seeme to Invite
my first Designe — The Embassador,
And my Lord Malvecchio: I'le withdraw. Exit
Enter Sempronio & Malvecchio:
Mal: you might easily obserue where lyes the [illegible]
Guarini at first swayd all her thoughts, and favour,
and now Leonidas.
Sem: What is this Gay thing Leonidas?
Mal: Wee haue his owne Report, that hee's Related
to a Prince in Greece; I know not whome, nor where;
for all my Inquisition cannot find
a Bottome for this greatnesse, but hee's here
the onely Favorite now.
Sem: And the Queenes [illegible], how are shee
Cunningly Contriues her Lights
to be seene by.
Mal: Too sure he takes up both
the Eyes, and Eares of our young Mistresse, that
shee has not time to Looke into her Honour
which should Direct her Due Respect to Princes.
Sem: I must tell you, my Lord,
wee did Expect a fairer Progresse;
the King My Master wants no Information
of both his Remedy, and Resents it too
so farre, I haue my order to Returne;
But shee is here. Enter ye Queene.
Madam I shall be happy to understand
what you are pleasd after so long a pause,
to thinke fitt Answer to my Royall Master.
Queene: My Lord, I hope your Master will Interpret
this no neglect, things of so high Conserne
Require much prudence; at your next visit,
wee shall be prepard.
Sem: I will haue Patience to Expect. Exit Emb: & Malvecchio:
Enter Leonidas:
Queene: My Lord, Leonidas I sent for you

Queene
Leonidas
Duke, Malvecchio, ~~Octavio~~, ~~Lodovico~~

Exit:·

Octavio
Lodovico

II, ii, 173–74. Though Octavio and Lodovico are deleted from this warning (because the scene involving them, beginning at line 205, contains no lines for either character), their names in the author's stage direction after line 204 are not crossed out. I would guess that the warning is correct, and the prompter simply forgot to make the same deletion in the stage direction.

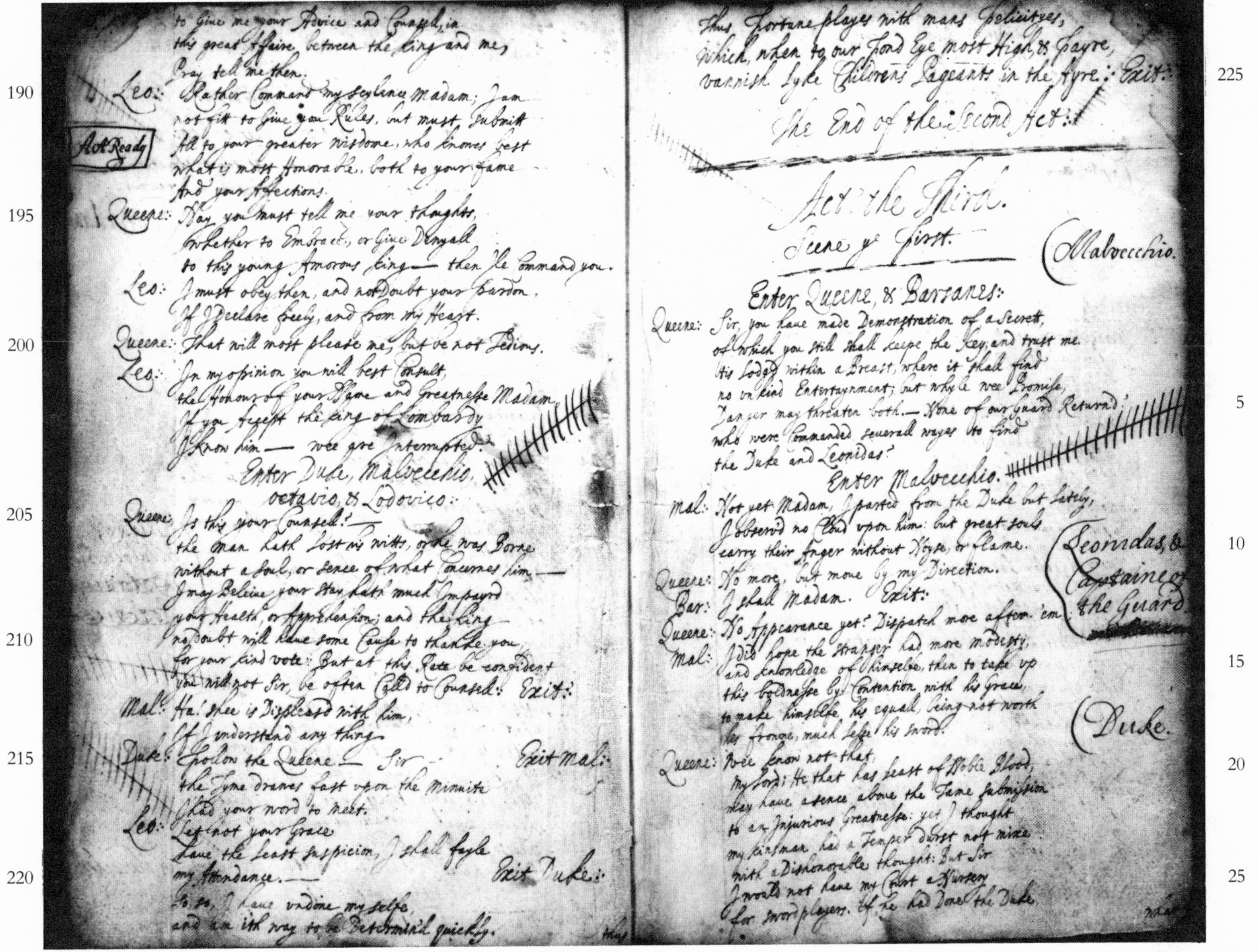

to Give me your Advice and Counsell, in
this great Affaire, between the King and me,
Pray tell me then.

Leo: Rather Command my Sylence Madam; I am
not fitt to Give you Rules, but must Submitt
All to your greater Wisdome, who knowes best
what is most Honorable, both to your Fame
And your Affections.

Act Ready

Queene: Nay, you must tell me your thoughts,
Whether to Embrace, or Give Denyall
to this young Amorous King— then Ile Command you.

Leo: I must obey then, and not Doubt your Pardon,
If I Declare freely, and from my Heart.

Queene: That will most please me, but be not Tedious.

Leo: In my opinion you will best Consult,
the Honour of your Name and Greatnesse Madam,
If you Accept the King of Lombardy
I know him— wee are Interrupted.

Enter Duke, Malvecchio, Octavio, & Lodovico:

Queene: Is this your Counsell?—
the man hath lost his witts, or he was Borne
without a Soul, or Sence of what Concernes him—
I may Beleive your Stay hath much Impayrd
your Health, or Apprehension; and the King
no doubt will have some Cause to thanke you
for your kind vote: But at this Rate be confident
you will not Sir, be often Called to Counsell: Exit:

Mal: Ha! shee is Displeasd with him,
If I understand any thing. Exit Mal:

Duke: Follow the Queene— Sir
the Tyme drawes fast upon the Minnite
I had your word to meet.

Leo: Let not your Grace
Have the least suspicion, I shall fayle
my Attendance.— Exit Duke:
So, so, I have vndone my selfe,
and am ith way to be Determin'd quickly.

thus

Thus Fortune playes with mans Felicityes,
which, when to our Fond Eye most High, & Fayre,
vannish Lyke Children's Pageants in the Ayre.: Exit:

The End of the Second Act:

Act the Third.

Scene ye First.

Malvecchio.

Enter Queene, & Barsanes:

Queene: Sir, you have made Demonstration of a Secrett,
of which you still shall keepe the Key, and trust me.
tis lodgd within a Breast, where it shall find
no vnkind Entertaynment; but whyle wee Promise,
Danger may threaten both.— None of our Guard Returnd:
who were Commanded severall wayes to find
the Duke and Leonidas?

Enter Malvecchio.

Mal: Not yet Madam, I parted from the Duke but lately,
I observ'd no Cloud upon him: but great souls
carry their Anger without Noyse, or flame.

Leonidas, & Captaine of the Guard

Queene: No more, but move by my Direction.

Bar: I shall Madam. Exit:

Queene: No Appearance yet? Dispatch more after 'em

Mal: I did hope the Stranger had more modesty,
and knowledge of himselfe, then to take up
this boldnesse by Contention with his Grace,
to make himselfe his equall, being not worth
his Frowne, much lesse his sword.

Duke.

Queene: Wee know not that,
my Lord: He that has least of Noble Blood,
May have a sence above the Tame submission
to an Injurious Greatnesse: yet I thought
my kinsman had a Temper durst not mixe
with a Dishonorable thought: But Sir
I would not have my Court a Nursery
for swordplayers. If he had Done the Duke

what

Queen:·

to yᵉ Duke:·

asyde:·

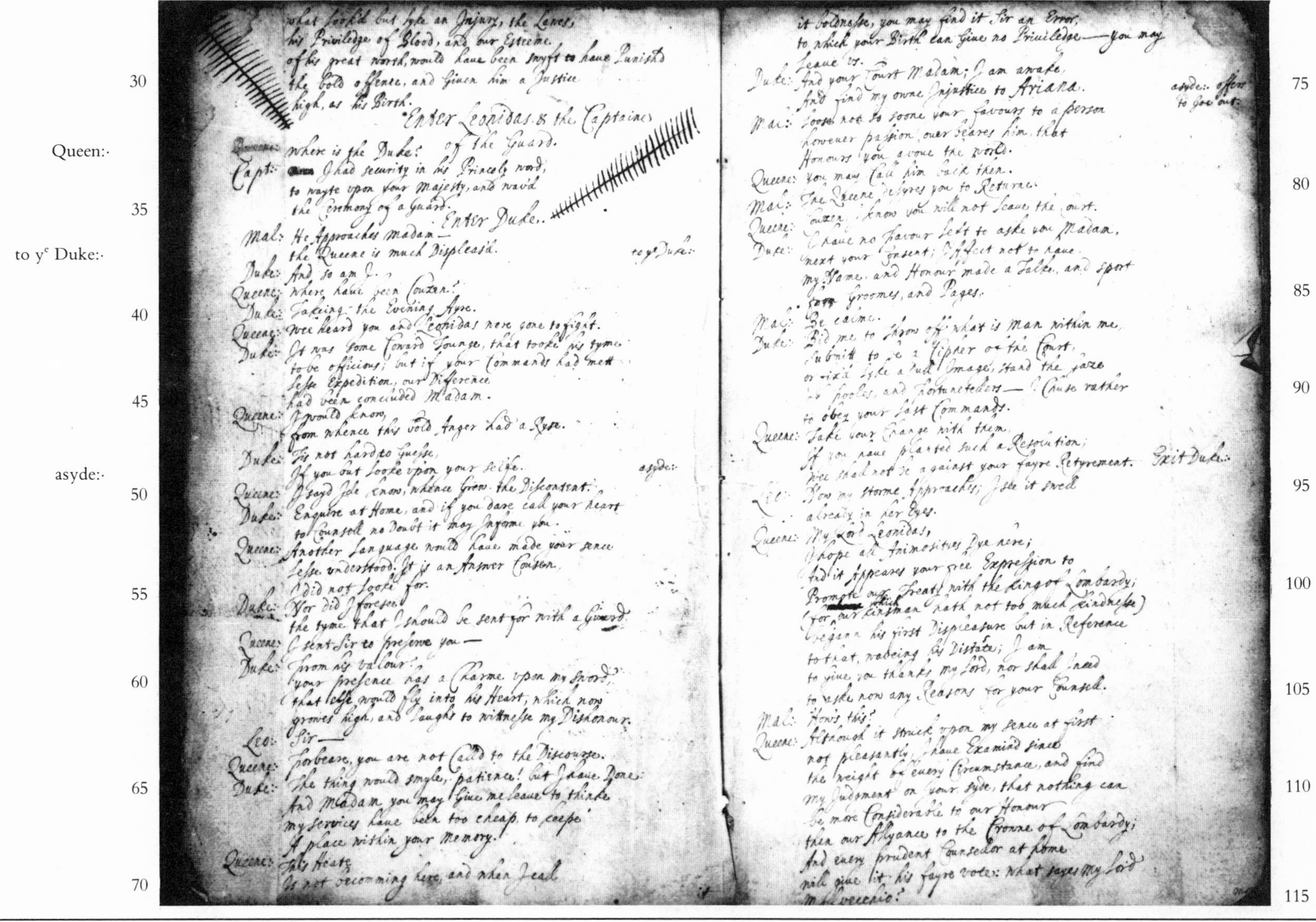

what looked but lyke an Injury, the Lawes, his Priviledge of Blood, and our Esteeme of his great worth, would haue been swyft to haue Punish'd the bold offence, and giuen him a Justice high, as his Birth.

Enter Leonidas & the Captaine of the Guard.

Queene: Where is the Duke?

Capt: I had security in his Princely word, to wayte upon your Majesty, and wav'd the Ceremony of a Guard.

Enter Duke.

Mal: He approaches Madam— the Queene is much Displeas'd. *to yᵉ Duke:·*

Duke: And so am I.

Queene: Where haue been Couzen?

Duke: Takeing the Evening Ayre.

Queene: Wee heard you and Leonidas were gone to fight.

Duke: It was some Coward Counsel, that tooke his tyme to be officious; but if your Commands had mett lesse Expedition, our Difference had been concluded Madam.

Queene: I would know, from whence this bold Anger had a Ryse.

Duke: Tis not hard to Guesse, If you but looke upon your selfe. *asyde:·*

Queene: I sayd I'de know, whence Grew the Discontent.

Duke: Enquire at Home, and if you dare call your heart to Counsell no doubt it may Informe you.

Queene: Another Language would haue made your sence lesse understood. It is an Answer Cousen I did not looke for.

Duke: Nor did I foresee the tyme that I should be sent for with a Guard.

Queene: I sent Sir to preserve you—

Duke: From his valour; your presence has a Charme upon my Sword, that else would fly into his Heart, which now growes high, and laughs to witnesse my Dishonour.

Leo: Sir—

Queene: Forbeare, you are not Call'd to the Discourse.

Duke: The thing would smyle, patience! but I haue Done. And Madam you may Giue me leave to thinke my services haue been too cheap, to keepe A place within your memory.

Queene: This Heate Is not becomming here, and when zeal it boldnesse, you may find it Sir an Error, to which your Birth can Giue no Priviledge— you may leave us.

Duke: And your Court Madam; I am awake, And find my owne Injustice to Ariana. *asyde:· offers to goe out:*

Mal: Loose not so soone your favours to a person however passion over beares him, that Honours you above the world.

Queene: You may Call him back then.

Mal: The Queene desyres you to Returne.

Queene: Couzen, I know you will not leave the Court.

Duke: I haue no favour left to aske you Madam, next your presence; I affect not to haue my Name and Honour made a Talke, and sport for Groomes and Pages.

Mal: Be calme.

Duke: Bid me to show off what is Man within me, Submit to be a Cipher of the Court, or fix'd lyke a dull Image, stand the gaze of fooles and fortunetellers— I Cause rather to obey your last Commands.

Queene: Take your Chance with them. If you haue planted such a Resolution; Wee shall not be against your fayre Retyrement. *Exit Duke:·*

Leo: Now my storme approaches; I see it swell already in her Eyes.

Queene: My Lord Leonidas, I hope all Animosities Dye here; And it appeares your free Expression to Prompt our Treaty with the King of Lombardy; (for our kinsman hath not too much kindnesse) Began his first Displeasure but in Reference to that, wanting his Distaste; I am to giue you thanks my Lord, nor shall I need to aske now any Reasons for your Counsell.

Mal: How's this?

Queene: Although it struck upon my sence at first not pleasantly, I haue Examin'd since the weight by every Circumstance, and find my Judgment on your syde, that nothing can be more Considerable to our Honour then our Alyance to the Crowne of Lombardy; And every prudent Counsellor at home will giue it his fayre voice: What sayes my Lord Malvecchio?

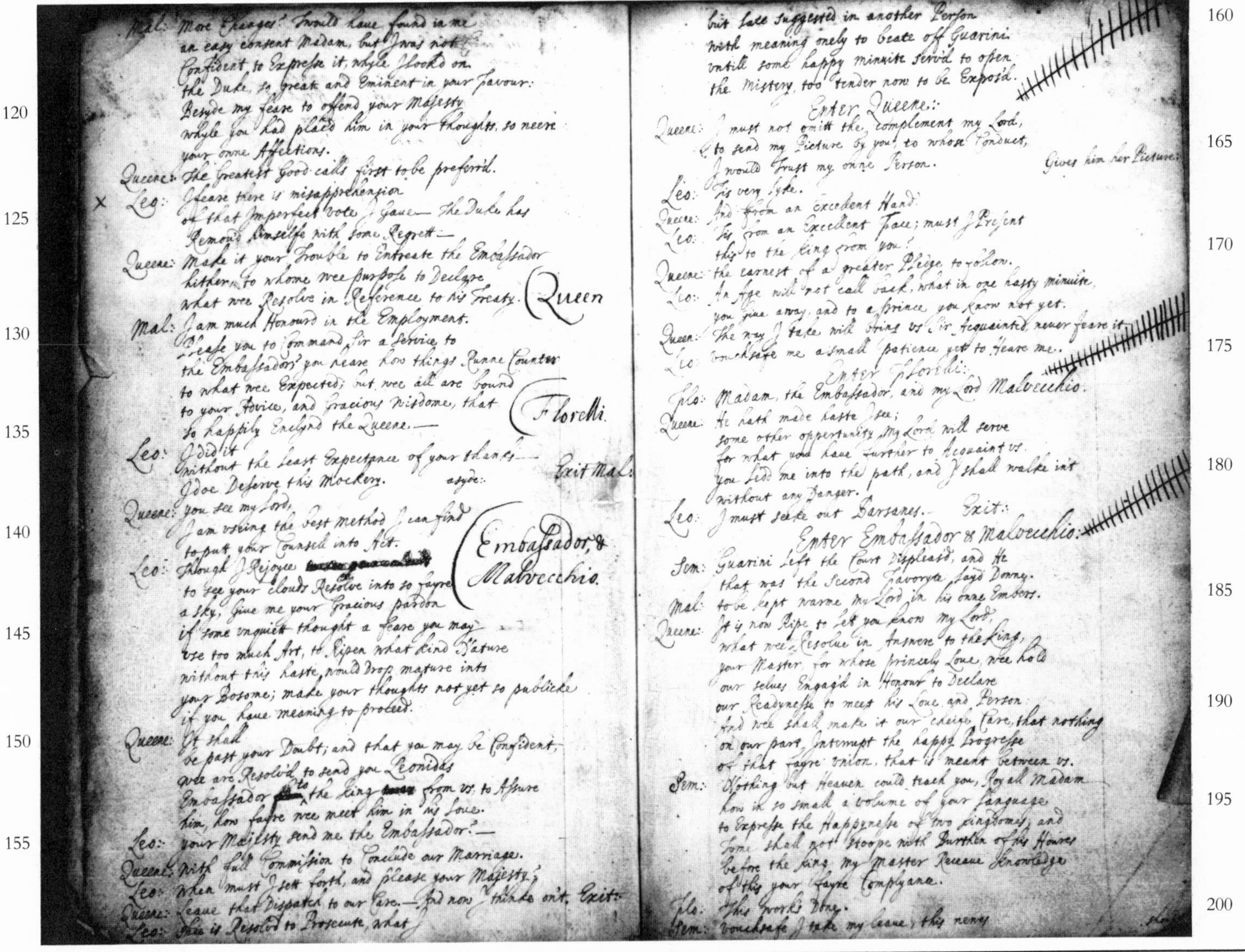

Mal: More Changes! I would have found in me
an easy consent Madam, but I was not
Confident to Expresse it, whyle I looked on
the Duke, so great and Eminent in your favour:
Beside my feare to offend your Majesty
whyle you had placed him in your thoughts, so neere
your owne Affections.
Queene: The Greatest Good calls first to be preferrd.
Leo: I feare there is misapprehension
of that Imperfect vote I gave— The Duke has
Removd himselfe with some Regrett—
Queene: Make it your Trouble to Entreate the Embassador
hither, to whome wee purpose to Declare
what wee Resolve in Reference to his Treaty. (Queen
Mal: I am much Honourd in the Employment.
Please you to Command, Sir a Service to
the Embassador; you heare how things Runne Counter
to what wee Expected; but wee all are bound
to your Advice, and Gracious Wisdome, that (Florelli.
so happily Enclynd the Queene.—
Leo: I did it
without the least Expectance of your thanks— Exit Mal:
I doe Deserve this Mockery. asyde:
Queene: you see my Lord,
I am useing the best method I can find
to put your Counsell into Act. (Embassador, &
Leo: Though I Rejoyce ~~[illegible]~~ Malvecchio.
to see your clouds Resolve into so fayre
a Sky, Give me your Gracious pardon
if some unquiett thought a feare you may
use too much Art, to Ripen what kind Nature
without this haste, would Drop mature into
your Bosome; make your thoughts not yet so publicke
if you have meaning to proceed.
Queene: It shall
be past your Doubt; and that you may be Confident,
wee are Resolvd to send you Leonidas
Embassador ~~[illegible]~~ to the King ~~[illegible]~~ from us, to Assure
him, how fayre wee meet him in his Love.
Leo: your Majesty send me the Embassador?—
Queene: With full Commission to Conclude our Marriage.
Leo: When must I sett forth, and please your Majesty?
Queene: Leave that Dispatch to our Care.— And now I thinke on't. Exit:
Leo: Shee is Resolvd to Prosecute, what

but late suggested in another Person
with meaning onely to beate off Guarini
untill some happy minuite servd to open
the Mistery, too tender now to be Exposd.
Enter Queene::
Queene: I must not omitt the complement my Lord,
to send my Picture by you, to whose Conduct,
I would Trust my owne Person. Gives him her Picture:
Leo: Tis very lyke.
Queene: And from an Excellent Hand.
Leo: Tis from an Excellent Face; must I Present
this to the King from you?
Queene: the earnest of a greater Pledge to follow.
Leo: An Age will not call back, what in one happy minuite
you give away, and to a Prince you know not yet.
Queen: The way I take will bring us Sir Acquainted, never feare it.
Leo: vouchsafe me a small patience yet to heare me.
Enter Florelli:
Flo: Madam, the Embassador, and my Lord Malvecchio.
Queene: He hath made haste I see;
some other opportunity My Lord will serve
for what you have further to Acquaint us.
you ledd me into the path, and I shall walke in't
without any Danger.
Leo: I must seeke out Barsanes.— Exit:
Enter Embassador & Malvecchio:
Sem: Guarini left the Court Displeasd, and He
that was the Second Favoryte, sayd Donny.
Mal: to be kept warme my Lord in his owne Embers.
Queene: It is now Ripe to let you know my Lord,
what wee Resolve in Answere to the King,
your Master, for whose princely Love, wee hold
our selves Engag'd in Honour to Declare
our Readynesse to meet his Love, and Person.
And wee shall make it our cheife Care, that nothing
on our part, Interrupt the happy Progresse
of that fayre Union, that is meant between us.
Sem: Nothing but Heaven could teach you, Royall Madam
how in so small a volume of your language
to Expresse the Happynesse of two Kingdomes, and
Time shall not stoope with Burthen of his Howres
before the King my Master Receave knowledge
of this your fayre Complyance.
Flo: This works Done.
Sem: vouchsafe I take my leave; this newes

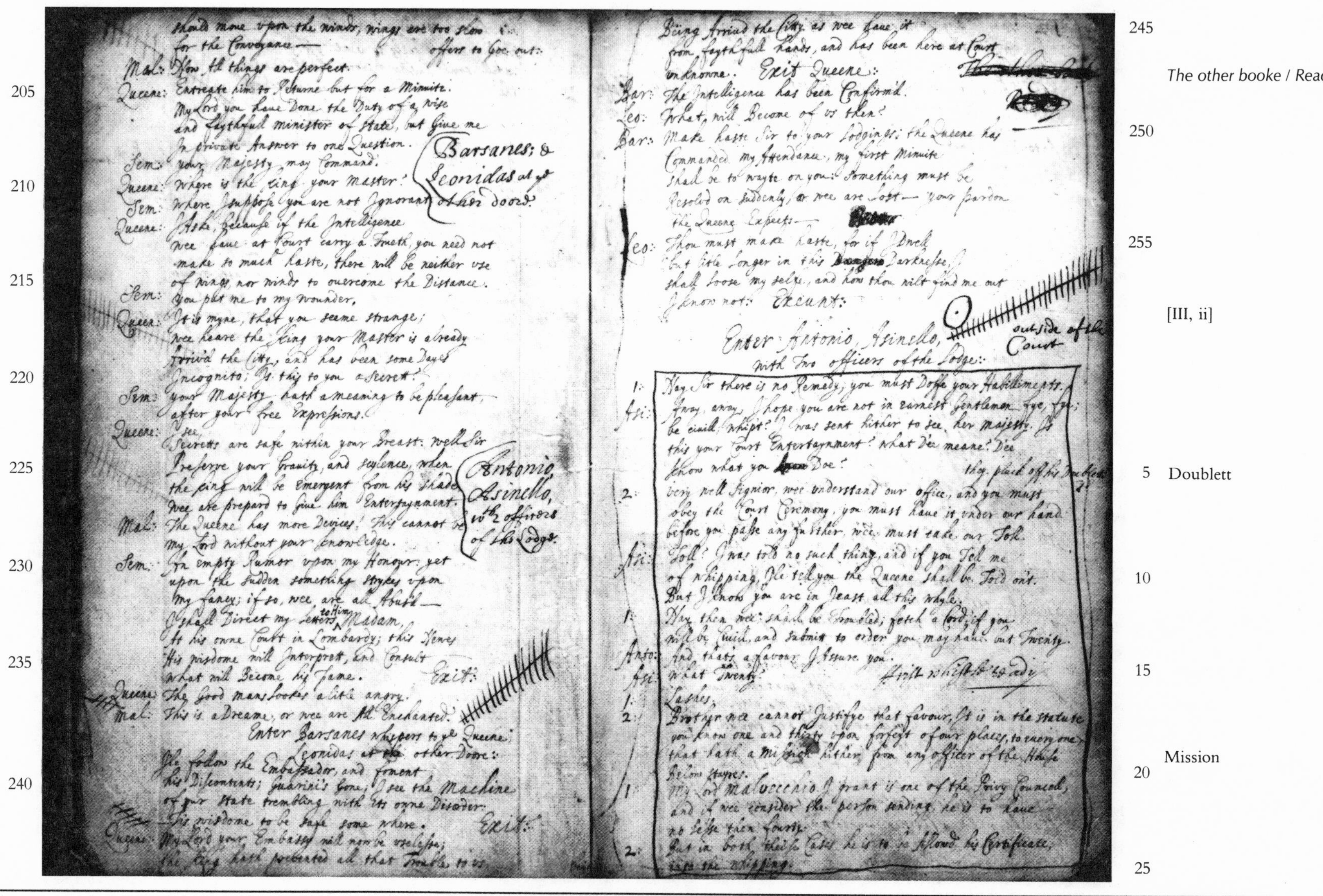

should move upon the winds, wings are too slow
for the Conveyance — offers to Goe out:
Mal: Now all things are perfect.
Queene: Entreate him to Returne but for a Minute.
My Lord you have Done the Duty of a wise
and faythfull minister of State, but give me
In private Answer to one Question.
Sem: your Majesty may Command.
Queene: where is the King your Master?
Sem: where I suppose you are not Ignorant
Queene: I aske, because if the Intelligence
wee have at Court carry a Truth, you need not
make so much haste, there will be neither use
of wings, nor winds to overcome the Distance.
Sem: you put me to my wonder.
Queen: It is myne, that you seeme strange;
wee heare the King your Master is already
Arriv'd the City, and has been some Days
Incognito; Is this to you a secret?
Sem: your Majesty hath a meaning to be pleasant
after your free Expressions.
Queene: I see,
secretts are safe within your Breast: well Sir
Preserve your Gravity, and Sylence, when
the King will be Emergent from his Shade
wee are prepard to give him Entertaynment.
Mal: The Queene has more Devices; This cannot be
my Lord without your knowledge.
Sem: An empty Rumor upon my Honour, yet
upon the sudden something strykes upon
my fancy; if so, wee are all Abus'd —
I shall Direct my letters to him Madam,
At his owne Court in Lombardy; this Newes
His wisdome will Interpret, and Consult
what will Become his Fame. Exit:
Queene: The good mans lookes a litle angry.
Mal: This is a Dreame, or wee are All Enchanted.
Enter Barsanes whispers to ye Queene:
Leonidas at the other Doore:
I'le follow the Embassador, and foment
his Discontents; Guarini's Gone; I see the Machine
of our State trembling with its owne Disorder.
Tis wisdome to be safe some where. Exit:
Queene: My Lord your Embassy will now be uselesse;
the King hath prevented all that Trouble to us

Barsanes: & Leonidas at ye other doore:

Antonio, Asinello, wth 2 officers of the Lodge:

Being Arriv'd the City as wee have it
from faythfull hands, and has been here at Court
unknowne. Exit Queene:
Bar: The Intelligence has been Confirm'd.
Leo: what will Become of us then?
Bar: Make haste Sir to your lodgings; the Queene has
Commanded my Attendance, my first Minute
shall be to wayte on you: something must be
Resolv'd on suddenly, or wee are lost — your pardon
the Queene Expects —
Leo: Thou must make haste, for if I dwell
but litle longer in this Darknesse,
I shall loose my selfe, and how thou wilt find me out
I know not: Exeunt:
Enter Antonio, Asinello,
with two officers of the Lodge:
1: Nay Sir there is no Remedy; you must Doffe your Habillements.
Asi: Away, away, I hope you are not in earnest Gentlemen, Fye, fye;
be civill, whipt? I was sent hither to see, her majesty. Is
this your Court Entertaynment? what Dee meane? Dee
know what you Doe? they pluck off his Doublet:
2: very well Signior, wee understand our office, and you must
obey the Court Ceremony, you must have it under our hand
before you passe any farther, wee must take our Toll.
Asi: Toll? I was told no such thing, and if you Tell me
of whipping, I'le tell you the Queene shall be Told on't.
But I know you are in Jeast all this while.
1: Nay then wee shall be Troubled; fetch a Cord; if you
will be Civil, and submit to order you may have but Twenty.
Anto: And, that's a favour I Assure you.
Asi: what Twenty?
1: Lashes,
2: Brother wee cannot Justifye that favour, It is in the statute
you know one and thirty upon forfeyt of our places, to every one
that hath a Mission hither from any officer of the House
Below stayres.
1: My Lord Malocchio I grant is one of the Privy Councell,
and if wee consider the person sending, he is to have
no lesse then fourty.
2: But in both these Cases he is to be allowd his Certificate,
to save the whipping.

outside of the Court

The other booke / Ready

[III, ii]

Doublett

Mission

III, i, 208–10. This reference to proscenium doors—a simple repeat of the author's stage direction—was to doors on opposite sides of the forestage. The prompt notes do not clarify for us just how many proscenium doors the Bridges Street Theatre had and how they were used in performance. Nor do other Restoration promptbooks, which suggests that either the use of the doors was so conventional that the promptbook did not have to contain such notes or that entrance-door information was kept elsewhere.

III, i, 237. Two cross-hatch marks are used for simultaneous entrances on opposite sides of the stage.

III, i, 242. The use of the cross-hatch symbol here is very curious; it normally serves to mark entrances, not exits.

III, i, 247–48. Here and at IV, i, 119–20 are references to another promptbook, which probably contained rewritten Asinello scenes prepared after the play was banned. The cuts in the text as we have it here, if they were observed, would have left the role of Asinello (played by John Lacy) little more than a bit part.

Anto:·

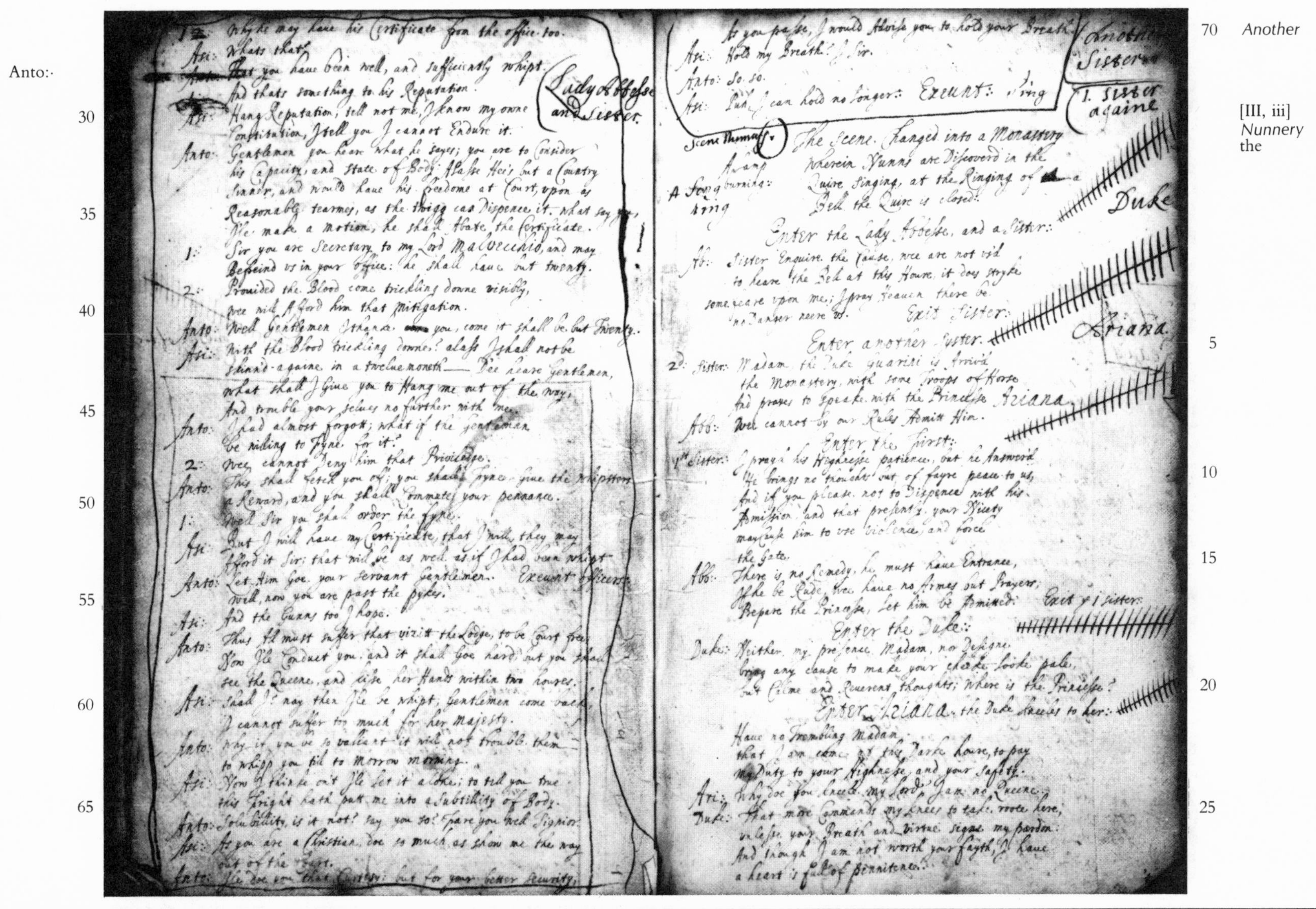

Another

[III, iii]
Nunnery
the

III, ii, 29–30. This warning is 44 lines before the entrance of the characters; since this is their first appearance in the play the prompter probably provided extra time to rouse the actresses from the scene or tiring room.

III, iii, opening. The lamp, choir of singers, and bell ring were not warned.

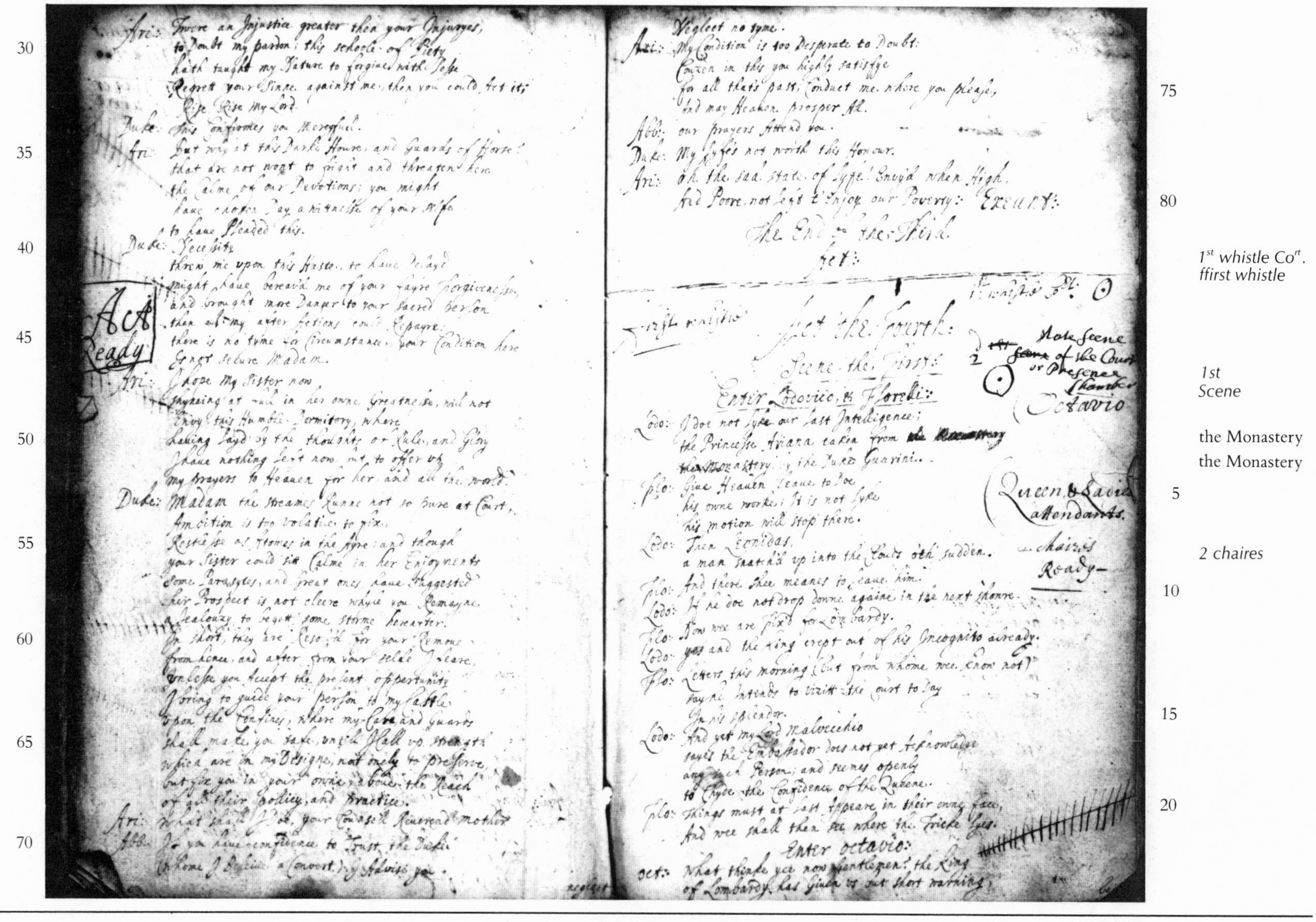

Ari: Twere an Injustice greater then your Injuryes,
to Doubt my pardon; this schoole of Piety
hath taught my Nature to forgive with lesse
Regrett your Sinne against me, then you could Act it;
Rise Rise my Lord.
Duke: This confirmes you Mercyfull.
Ari: But why at this Darke Houre, and Guards of Horse
that are not wont to visit and threaten here
the Calme of our Devotions; you might
have chosen, by a Miracle of your Wife
to have Pleaded this.
Duke: Necessity
threw me upon this Haste, to have Delay'd
might have bereav'd me of your fayre forgivenesse,
and brought more Danger to your sacred Person
then all my after Actions could Repayre.
there is no tyme for Circumstance: your Condition here
Grows Insecure Madam.
Ari: I hope my Sister now,
Rejoyceing at all in her owne Greatnesse, will not
Envy this Humble Dormitory, where
having layd by the thoughts or Rule, and Glory
I have nothing left now, but to offer up
my prayers to Heaven for her and all the world.
Duke: Madam the streames Runne not so sure at Court,
Ambition is too volatile to fixe.
Restlesse as flames in the fyre: and though
your Sister could sitt Calme in her Enjoyments
Some Parasytes, and great ones have suggested
their Prospect is not cleere while you Remayne.
a Jealousy to begett some storme hereafter.
In short, they are Resolv'd for your Remove
from hence, and after from your selfe I feare,
Unlesse you Accept the present opportunity
I bring to guide your person to my Castle
upon the Confines, where my Care and Guards
shall make you safe, untill I shall [illegible]
which are in my Designe, not only to Preserve,
but fixe you in your owne, above the Reach
of all their policy and Practice.
Ari: What shall I doe, your Counsell Reverend mother
Abb: If you have confidence to Trust the Duke
(whome I beleive a Convert) my Advise you
neglect

Act Ready

Neglect no tyme.
Ari: My Condition is too Desperate to Doubt:
Cozen in this you highly satisfye
for all that's past, Conduct me where you please,
And may Heaven prosper All.
Abb: our prayers attend you.
Duke: My Lyfe's not worth this Honour.
Ari: Oh the sad state of Lyfe! Envy'd when High,
And Poore, not left t'Enjoy our Poverty: Exeunt.
The End of the Third Act.

First whistle 1st whistle C°.

Act the Fourth.
Scene the First.

2 ~~1st Scene~~ State Scene of the Court or Presence Chamber
Octavio

Enter Lodovico, & Florelli.
Lodo: I doe not lyke our last Intelligence:
the Princesse Ariana taken from ~~the Monastery~~
the Monastery, by the Duke Guarini.
Flo: Give Heaven leave to doe
his owne workes; It is not lyke
his motion will stop there.
Lodo: Then Leonidas,
a man snatch'd up into the Clouds o'th' sudden.
Flo: And there shee meanes to leave him.
Lodo: If he doe not drop downe againe in the next showre.
Flo: Now wee are fix'd for Lombardy.
Lodo: yes and the King crept out of his Incognito already.
Flo: Letters this morning (but from whome wee know not)
sayes he Intends to visitt the Court to day
In his splendor.
Lodo: And yet my Lord Malvecchio
sayes the Embassador does not yet Acknowledge
any such Person; and seemes openly
to Chyde the Confidence of the Queene.
Flo: Things must at last appeare in their owne face,
And wee shall then see where the Tricke lyes.
Enter Octavio.
Oct: What thinke yee now Gentlemen? the King
of Lombardy has Given us but short warning.

Queen & Ladies attendants.
Chaires Ready

1st whistle Co[n].
ffirst whistle

1st Scene

the Monastery
the Monastery

2 chaires

Wm Harris

W. Harris

W. Harris

Abus'd, some witch-
crafts hangs

In his Revenge.

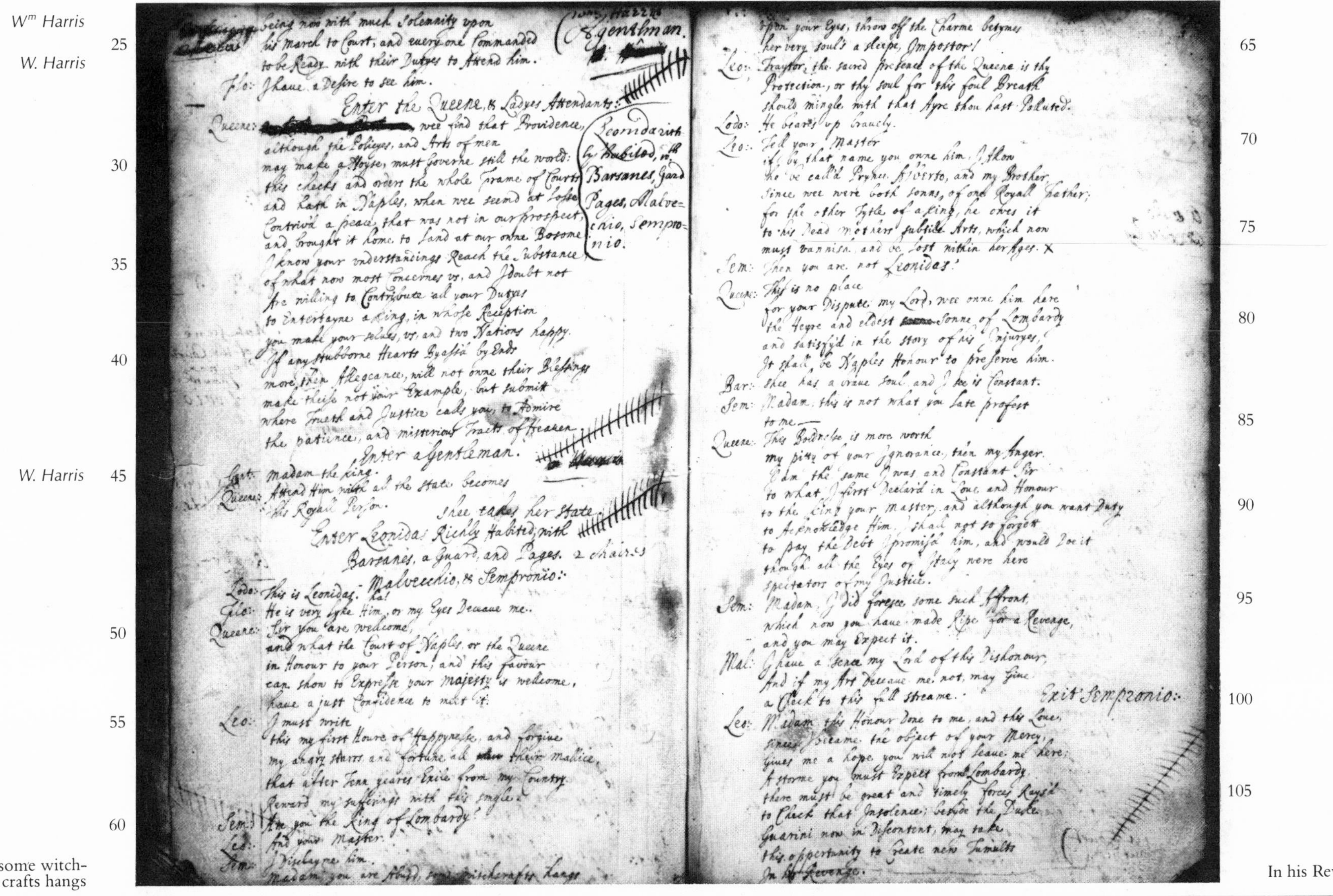

being now with much Solemnity upon
his march to Court, and every one Commanded
to be Ready with their Duties to Attend him.
Flo: I have a Desire to see him.
Enter the Queene, & Ladyes Attendants.
Queene: wee find that Providence,
although the Policyes, and Arts of men
may make a Noyse, must Governe still the world:
this checks and orders the whole Frame of Courts
and hath in Naples, when wee seem'd at Losse,
Contriv'd a Peace, that was not in our prospect,
and brought it home, to Land at our owne Bosome.
I know your understandings Reach the Substance
of what now most Concernes us, and I doubt not
are willing to Contribute all your Dutyes
to Entertayne a King, in whose Reception
you make your selves, us, and two Nations happy.
If any stubborne Hearts Byass'd by Ends
more, then Allegeance, will not owne their Blessings
make these not your Example, but submit
where Truth and Justice calls you, to Admire
the patience, and misterious Tracts of Heaven.
Enter a Gentleman.
Gent: madam the King.
Queene: Attend him with all the State becomes
this Royal Person. She takes her State.
Enter Leonidas Richly Habited, with
Barsanes, a Guard, and Pages. 2 chaires
Malvecchio, & Sempronio:
Lodo: This is Leonidas. ha!
Flo: He is very lyke Him, or my Eyes Deceave me.
Queene: Sir you are welcome,
and what the Court of Naples, or the Queene
in Honour to your Person, and this favour
can show to Expresse your majesty is welcome,
have a just Confidence to meet it.
Leo: I must write
this my first Houre of Happynesse, and forgive
my angry starrs and fortune all their mallice,
that after Tenn yeares Exile from my Country
Reward my sufferings with this smyle.
Sem: Are you the King of Lombardy?
Leo: And your Master.
Sem: I Disclayme him.
Madam you are Abus'd, some witchcrafts hangs

upon your Eyes, throw off the Charme betymes
her very soul's a sleepe, Impostor!
Leo: Traytor, the sacred presence of the Queene is thy
Protection, or thy soul for this foul Breath
should mingle with that Ayre thou hast Polluted.
Lodo: He beare's up bravely.
Leo: Tell your Master
if by that name you owne him, I them
He 'be call'd Prince Alberto, and my Brother
since wee were both sonnes of one Royall Father;
for the other Style of a King, he owes it
to his Dead mothers subtill Arts, which now
must vannish, and be lost within her Ashes. X
Sem: Then you are not Leonidas?
Queene: This is no place
for your Dispute: my Lord, wee owne him here
the Heyre and eldest Sonne of Lombardy
and satisfy'd in the story of his Injuryes,
It shall be Naples Honour to preserve him.
Bar: Shee has a brave soul, and I hee is Constant.
Sem: Madam, this is not what you late profest
to me.
Queene: This Boldnesse is more worth
my pitty of your Ignorance, then my Anger.
I am the same I was and Constant Sir
to what I first Declar'd in Love and Honour
to the King your master, and although you want Duty
to Acknowledge Him, I shall not so forget
to pay the Debt I promis'd him, and would Doe it
though all the Eyes of Italy were here
spectators of my Justice.
Sem: Madam, I did foresee some such Affront,
which now you have made Ripe for a Revenge,
and you may Expect it.
Mal: I have a Sence my Lord of this Dishonour,
And if my Art deceave me not, may Give
a Check to this full streame. Exit Sempronio:
Leo: Madam this Honour done to me, and this Love,
since I became the object of your Mercy,
gives me a hope you will not leave me here:
A storme you must Expect from Lombardy,
there must be great and timely forces Rays'd
to Check that Insolence; beside the Duke
Guarini now in Discontent, may take
this opportunity to Create new Tumults
In his Revenge.

IV, i, 24–26. The naming of actors, here, at IV, i, 45, and in other promptbooks, was usually restricted to those with minor roles, which were often nameless. The note here is muddled: it seems to indicate two characters, one to be played by Harris, but the stage direction for the entrance indicates only "a Gentleman." Harris's name was twice entered and canceled; perhaps there was confusion for a while as to who would play the role.

IV, i, 47. The prompter added a reference to the two chairs that were warned at line 8; they were probably carried on by the pages listed in the entrance stage direction. Not many properties are mentioned in Restoration promptbooks, and they were probably kept to a minimum. As with scenic notes, there may have been a property plot kept by the machinist, a list more complete than the prompter would need.

3^d whistle

Other booke ready

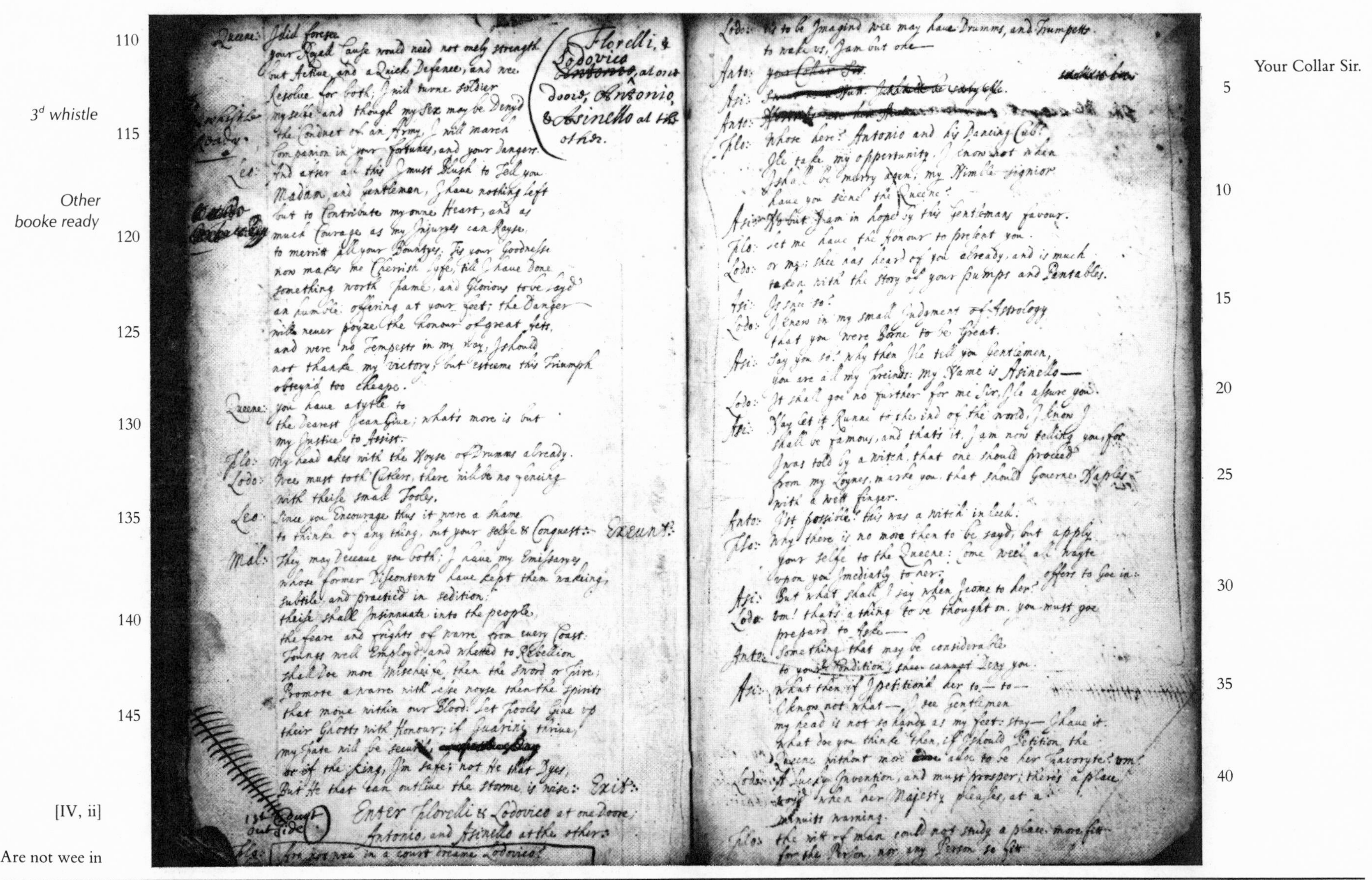

Your Collar Sir.

[IV, ii]

Flo:· Are not wee in

IV, ii, opening. This double entrance from opposite sides does not have the special cuing given the entrance at III, i, 237.

IV, ii, 1–77. The entire scene is clearly meant to be cut, but the prompter—or whoever decided on the cutting—forgot to continue the boxing on F22.

Exchequer —

Binion

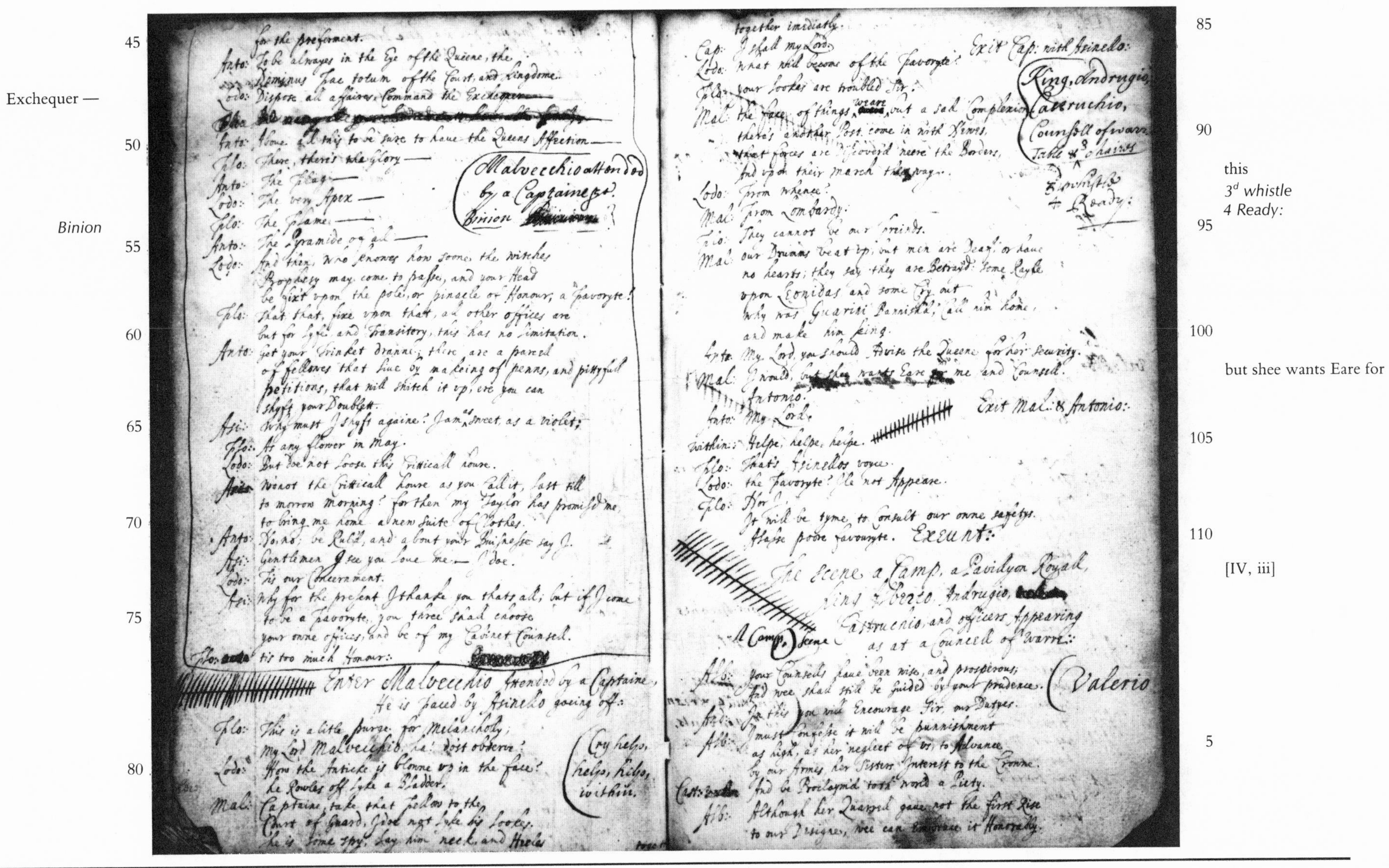
for the preferment.
Anto: To be always in the Eye of the Queene, the
Dominus Fac totum of the Court and kingdome.
Lodo: Dispose all affaires, Command the Exchequer
[struck out]
Anto: Above all this to be sure to have the Queens Affection —
Flo: There, there's the glory —
Anto: The Flag —
Lodo: The very Apex —
Flo: The Flame —
Anto: The Pyramide of all —
Lodo: And then, who knows how soone the witches
Prophesy may come to passe, and your Head
be fixt upon the pole, or pinacle of Honour, a favoryte!
Flo: That that, fixe upon that, all other offices are
but for lyfe and transitory, this has no limitation.
Anto: Get your Trinket drawne; there are a parcel
of fellowes that live by makeing of peans, and pittyfull
petitions, that will stitch it up, ere you can
shyft your Doublet.
Asi: Why must I shyft againe? I am as sweet as a violet;
Flo: As any flower in May.
Lodo: But doe not loose this criticall houre.
Asi: Why not the criticall houre as you call it, last till
to morrow morning? for then my Taylor has promised me
to bring me home a new suite of Clothes.
Anto: No, no; be Ruld, and about your buisnesse say I.
Asi: Gentlemen I see you love me — I doe.
Lodo: Tis our Concernment.
Asi: Why for the present I thanke you thats all; but if I come
to be a favoryte, you three shall choose
your owne offices, and be of my Cabinet Counsell.
Lo: tis too much Honour:
Enter Malvecchio attended by a Captaine,
He is faced by Asinello going off:
Flo: This is a litle purse for Melancholy;
My Lord Malvecchio, ha! dost observe?
Lodo: How the Anticke is blowne up in the face?
he Rowles off lyke a Bladder.
Mal: Captaine, take that fellow to the
Court of Guard, I doe not lyke his lookes.
he is some spy. lay him neck and Heeles

Malvecchio attended by a Captaine. Binion

Cry helpe, helpe, helpe, within.

together imediatly.
Cap: I shall my Lord. Exit Cap: with Asinello:
Lodo: What will become of the favoryte?
Flo: Your lookes are troubled Sir.
Mal: the face of things weares but a sad Complexion
there's another Post come in with Newes
that forces are discoverd neere the Borders,
and upon their march this way.
Lodo: From whence?
Mal: From Lombardy.
Flo: They cannot be our friends.
Mal: our Drums beat up, but men are deaf, or have
no hearts; they say they are Betrayd: some Rayle
upon Leonidas and some Cry out
why was Guariti Banishd? Call him home,
and make him king.
Anto: My Lord you should Advise the Queene for her security.
Mal: I would, but shee wants Eare for me and Counsell.
Antonio.
Anto: My Lord. Exit Mal: & Antonio:
within: Helpe, helpe, helpe.
Flo: That's Asinellos voyce
Lodo: the favoryte? ile not Appeare.
Flo: Nor I.
It will be tyme to consult our owne safetys.
Alasse poore favoryte. Exeunt:
The Scene a Camp, a Pavilyon Royall,
Alberto, Andrugio, Castruccio, and officers Appearing
as at a Councell of warre:
A Camp. Scene
Alb: Your Counsells have been wise, and prosperous;
And wee shall still be guided by your prudence.
In this you will Encourage Sir, our Dutyes.
I must confesse it will be punnishment
as high, as her neglect of us, to Advance
by our Armes, her Sisters Interest to the Crowne.
And be Proclaymd to the world a Piety.
Alb: Although her Quarrell gave not the first Rise
to our Designes, wee can embrace it Heartily.

King, Andrugio, Castruchio, Counsell of warr. Table & 3 chaires

whistle 4 Ready:

Valerio

this

3^d^ whistle

4 Ready:

but shee wants Eare for

[IV, iii]

IV, ii, 105. The cross-hatch symbol is here used, not for an entrance, but for offstage shouts; in some promptbooks it is used for sound effects, such as flourishes, involving musicians.

Alberto & Sem: whisper:·

Hughes
W[m] *Hughes*

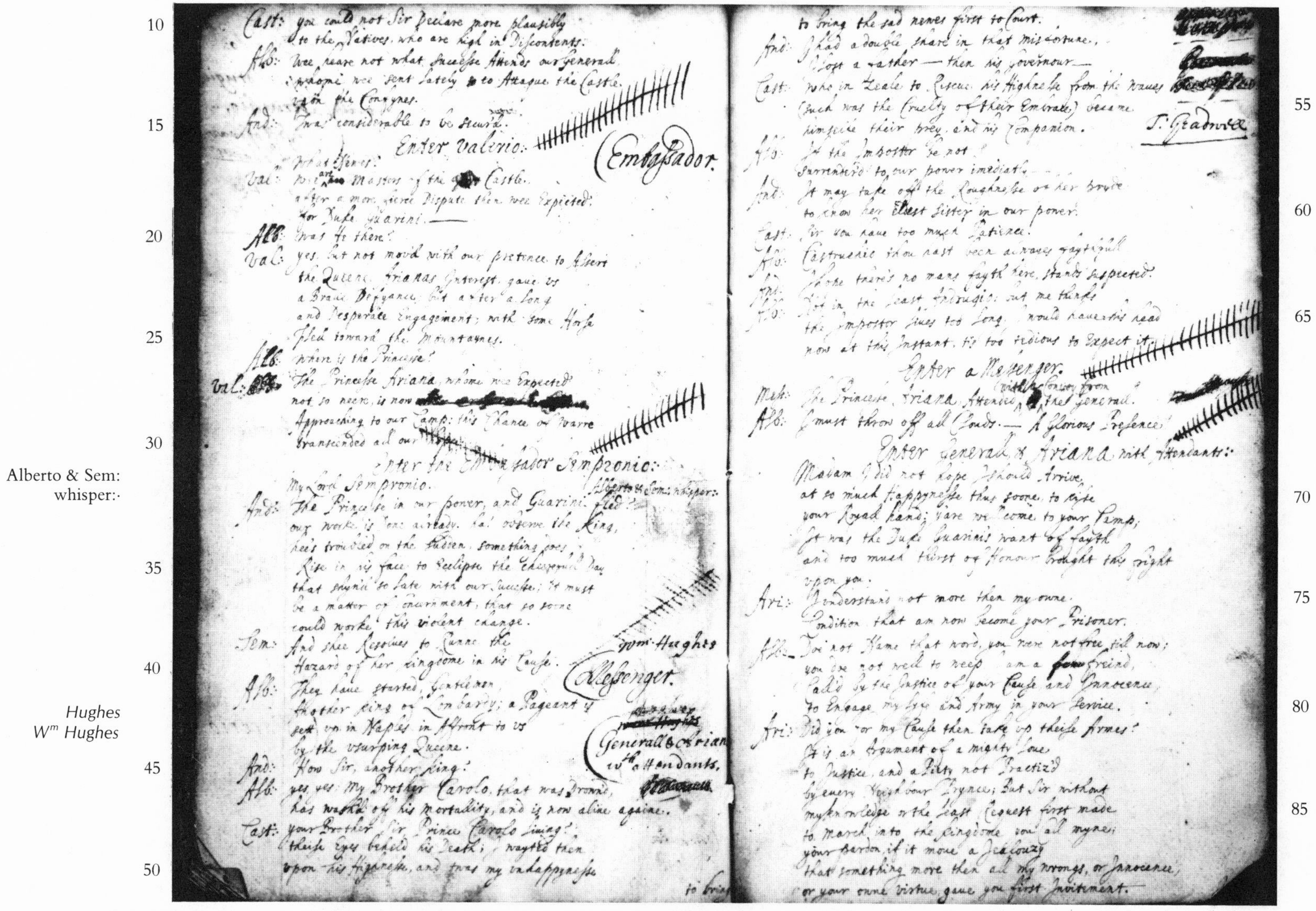
Cast: you could not Sir declare more plausibly
to the Natives, who are high in Discontents.
Alb: wee heare not what successe Attends our Generall
whome wee sent lately to Attaque the Castle
upon the Convoyes.
And: Twas considerable to be secur'd.
Enter Valerio.
What Newes?
Val: Wee are Masters of the Castle.
After a more fierce Dispute then wee Expected
For Duke Guarini. —
Alb: was he there?
Val: yes, but not mov'd with our pretence to Assert
the Queene Ariana's Interest, gave us
a Brave Defyance, but after a long
and desperate Engagement; with some Horse
fled toward the Mountaynes.
Alb: where is the Princesse?
Val: The Princesse Ariana, whome we Expected
not so neere, is now [deleted]
Approaching to our Camp: this Chance of Warre
transcends all our [deleted]
Enter the Ambassador Sempronio:
My Lord Sempronio.
And: The Princesse in our power, and Guarini fled
our worke is done already. ha! observe the King,
hee's troubled on the sudden. something does
Rise in his face to Ecclipse the cheerefull Day
that should be Late with our successe: It must
be a matter of concernment, that so soone
could worke this violent change.
Sem: And shee Resolves to runne the
Hazard of her Kingdome in his Cause.
Alb: They have started, Gentlemen,
Another King of Lombardy; a Pageant
sett up in Naples in Affront to us
by the usurping Queene.
And: How Sir, another King?
Alb: yes, yes: my Brother Carolo, that was drown'd,
has wash'd off his Mortality, and is now alive againe.
Cast: your Brother Sir, Prince Carolo living?
these Eyes beheld his Death; wayted then
upon his Highnesse, and was my unhappynesse
to bring

Embassador
Alberto & Sem: whisper:
Wm: Hughes
Messenger
[deleted]
Generall & Ariana with Attendants.

to bring the sad newes first to Court.
And: I had a double share in that misfortune,
I lost a Father — then his Governour —
Cast: who in Zeale to Rescue his Highnesse from the waves
(such was the Cruelty of their Embrace) became
himselfe their prey, and his Companion.
Alb: Is the Impostor he not
Surrendred to our power imediatly
And: It may take off the Roughness or her brave[?]
to know her Eldest Sister in our power.
Cast: Sir you have too much Patience.
Alb: Castruccio thou hast been always faythfull
I hope there's no want of fayth here, stands suspected.
And: Not in the least, I doubt: but me thinks
Alb: the Impostor lives too long. would have his head
now at this Instant. tis too tedious to Expect it.
Enter a Messenger.
Mes: The Princesse Ariana Attended with Honour from the Generall.
Alb: I must throw off all Clouds. — A glorious Presence!
Enter Generall & Ariana with Attendants:
Madam I did not hope I should Arrive
at so much Happynesse thus soone, to kisse
your Royal hand; Y'are welcome to your Camp;
It was the Duke Guarini's want of fayth
and too much thirst of Honour brought this fight
upon you.
Ari: I understand not more then my owne
Condition that am now become your Prisoner.
Alb: Doe not Name that word, you were not free till now;
you were not well to keepe I am a friend,
Call'd by the Justice of your Cause and Innocence
To Engage my Life and Army in your Service.
Ari: Did you for my Cause then take up these Armes?
It is an Argument of a mighty Love
to Justice, and a Piety not Practiz'd
by every Neighbour Prince; But Sir, without
my knowledge or the least Request first made
to march into the Kingdome you call myne;
your Pardon, if it move a Jealousy
that something more then all my wrongs, or Innocence
or your owne Virtue, gave you first Incitement.

[deleted]
T: Gradwell

IV, iii, 16. The warning for the Ambassador is only 15 lines before his entrance, but this and some of the other short warnings in the promptbook may have been placed where they were because of other matters requiring the prompter's attention. Note that here the prompter warned the Ambassador just as soon as he could after the entrance of Valerio, which he had to cue; Valerio's warning was short for the same reason. Entrances were obviously more critical than warnings, and this is evidence of how heavily the King's Company actors may have depended on the prompter for their cues.

IV, iii, 42–46. Here and at IV, iii, 51–56 are other examples of the frequent recasting of small roles. The deleted words just before Gradwell's name appear to be actors' names.

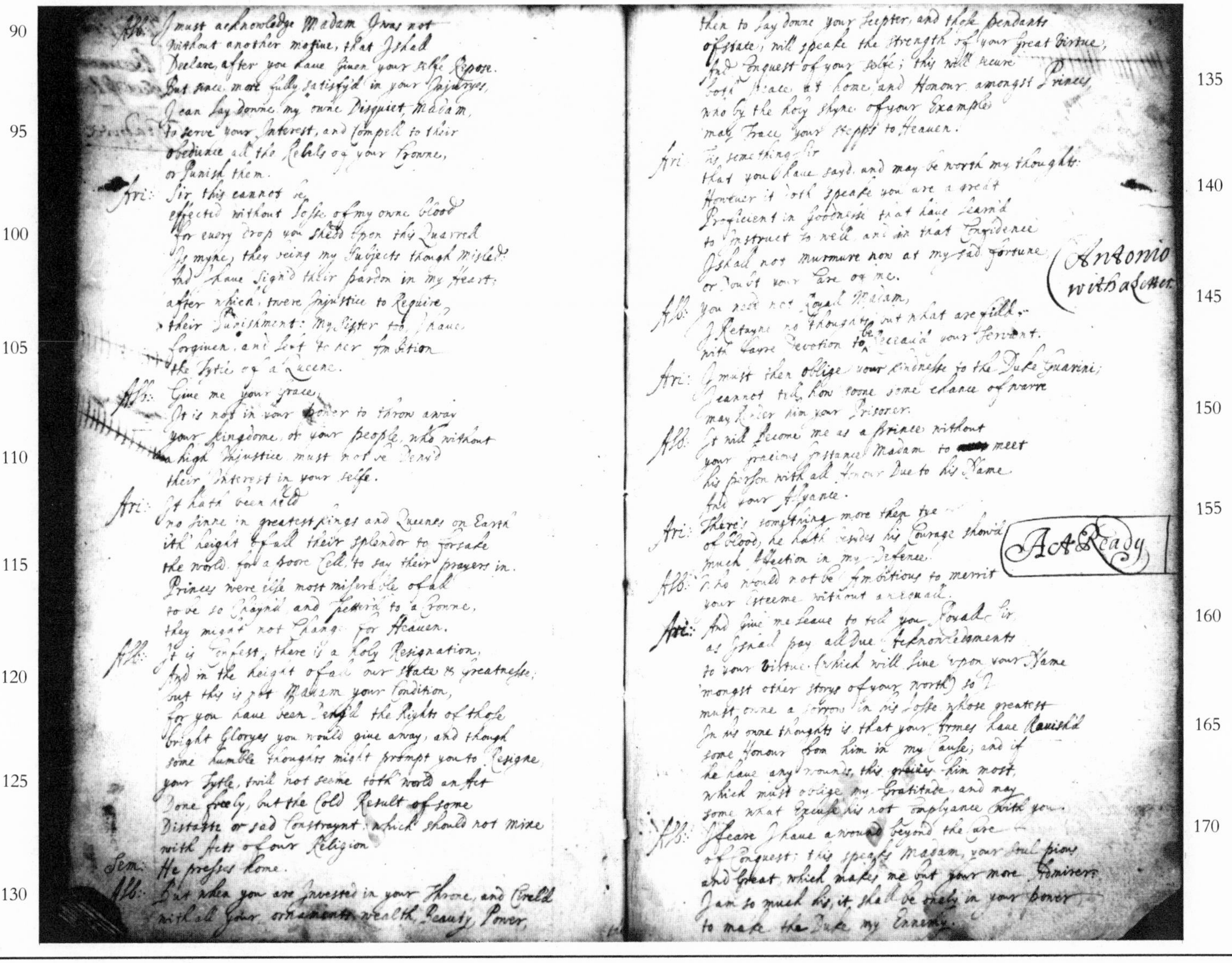

Alb: I must acknowledge Madam I was not
without another motive, that I shal
Declare, after you have given your selfe Repose.
But since more fully satisfy'd in your Injuryes,
I can lay downe my owne Disquiet, Madam,
to serve your Interest, and Compell to their
obedience all the Rebels of your Crowne,
or Punish them.

Ari: Sir this cannot be
effected without losse of my owne blood
for every drop you shed upon this Quarrell
Is myne, they being my Subjects though misled.
And I have sign'd their pardon in my heart;
after which, twere Injustice to Require
their Punishment: My sister too, I have
forgiven, and left to her Ambition
the Style of a Queene.

Alb: Give me your grace,
It is not in your Power to throw away
your kingdome or your people, who without
a high Injustice must not be Deny'd
their Interest in your selfe.

Ari: It hath been held
no sinne in greatest Kings and Queenes on Earth
ith' height of all their splendor to forsake
the world for a poore Cell, to say their prayers in.
Princes were else most miserable of all
to be so Chayn'd and fetter'd to a Crowne,
they might not Change for Heaven.

Alb: It is Confest, there is a holy Resignation,
And in the height of all our State & greatnesse;
but this is not Madam your Condition,
for you have been Denyd the Rights of those
bright Gloryes you would give away, and though
some humble thoughts might prompt you to Resigne
your Style, twill not seeme to th' world an Act
Done freely, but the Cold Result of some
Distaste or sad Constraynt, which should not mixe
with Acts of our Religion

Sem: He presses home.

Alb: But when you are Invested in your Throne, and Circled
with all your ornaments, wealth, Beauty, Power,
then to lay downe your Scepter, and those Pendants
of state, will speake the strength of your great Virtue,
And Conquest of your selfe; this will secure
both Peace at home and Honour amongst Princes,
who by the holy shyne of your Example
may trace your stepps to Heaven.

Ari: Tis something Sir
that you have sayd, and may be worth my thoughts:
However it doth speake you are a great
Proficient in goodnesse that have learn'd
to Instruct so well, and in that Confidence
I shall not murmure now at my sad fortune
or doubt your Care of me.

(Antonio with a Letter.

Alb: You need not Royall Madam,
I Retayne no thoughts but what are full
with fayre Devotion to be esteem'd your Servant.

Ari: I must then oblige your kindnesse to the Duke Guarini;
I cannot tell how soone some chance of warre
may render him your Prisoner.

Alb: It will become me as a Prince without
your gracious Instance Madam to meet
his person with all Honour Due to his Name
and your Alyance.

Ari: There's something more then tye
of blood, he hath besides his Courage show'd
much Affection in my Defence.

Act Ready

Alb: Who would not be Ambitious to merrit
your esteeme without a Reward.

Ari: And give me leave to tell you Royall Sir
as I shall pay all Due Acknowledgements
to your Virtue (which will live upon your Name
'mongst other storys of your worth) so I
must owne a sorrow in his losse whose greatest
In his owne thoughts is that your Armes have Ravish'd
some Honour from him in my Cause; and if
he have any wounds, this greives him most,
which must oblige my Gratitude, and may
some what Excuse his not Complyance with you.

Alb: I feare I have a wound beyond the care
of Conquest: this speaks Madam, your soul pious
and Great which makes me but your more Admirer.
I am so much his, it shall be onely in your power
to make the Duke my Ennemy.

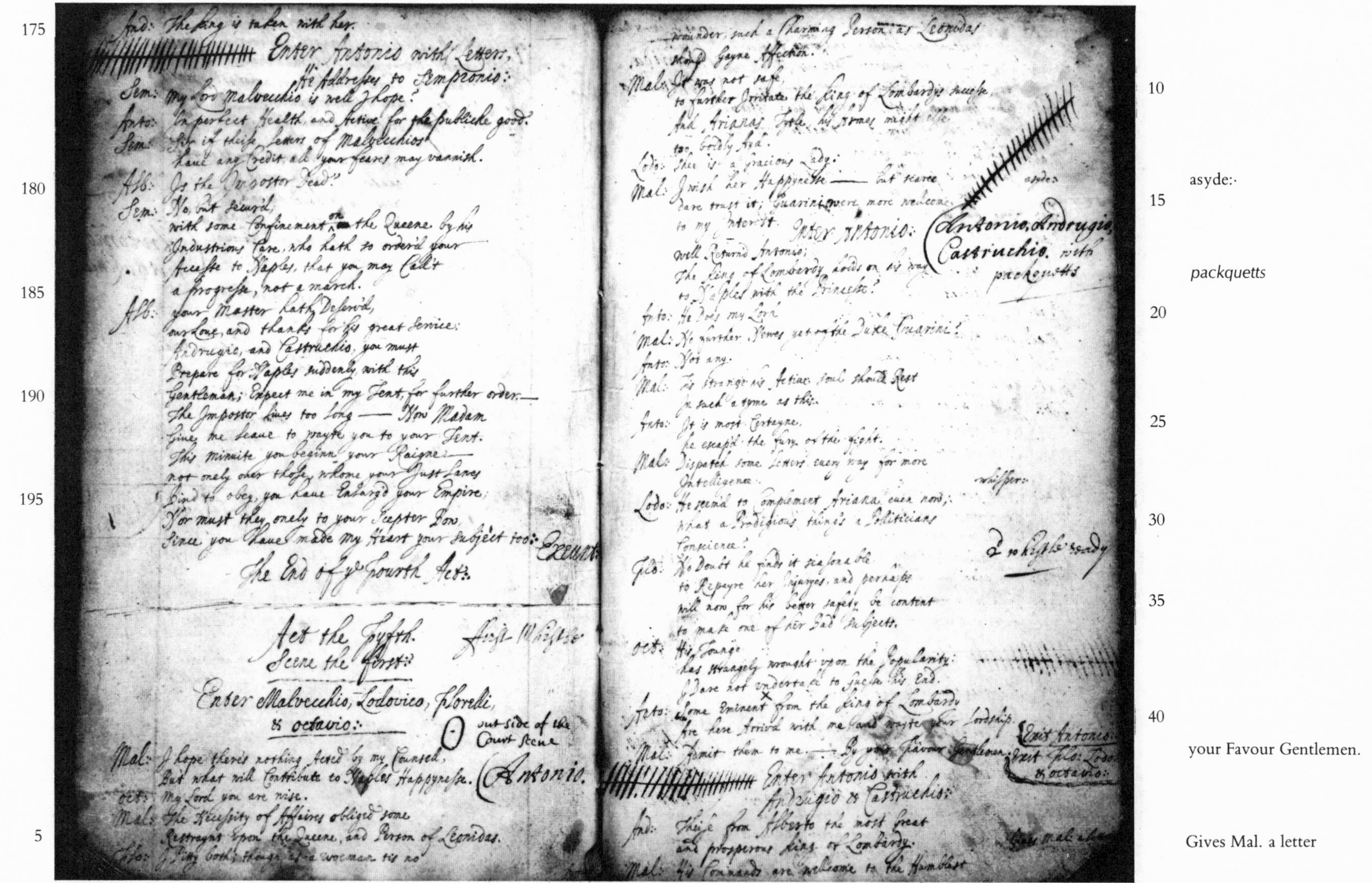

And: The King is taken with her.
Enter Antonio with Letters.
He Addresses to Sempronio:
Sem: My Lord Malvecchio is well I hope?
Anto: In perfect Health and Active for the publicke good.
Sem: If these Letters of Malvecchios have any Credit all your feares may vanish.
Alb: Is the Impostor dead?
Sem: No, but secured with some Confinement on the Queene by his Industrious Care, who hath so order'd your Accesse to Naples, that you may Call't a progresse, not a march.
Alb: your Master hath Deserv'd our Love, and thanks for his great Service: Andrugio, and Castruchio, you must Prepare for Naples suddenly with this Gentleman; Expect me in my Tent, for further order.— The Impostor lives too long — How Madam Give me leave to wayte you to your Tent. This minuite you beginn your Raigne: not onely over those, whome your Just Lawes Bind to obey, you have Enlarg'd your Empire; Nor must they onely to your Scepter Bow Since you have made my Heart your Subject too: Exeunt
The End of ye Fourth Act:
Act the Fyfth. Scene the first:
Act 5 Whistle
Enter Malvecchio, Lodovico, Floredi, & octavio:
outside of the Court Scene
Antonio.
Mal: I hope there's nothing Acted by my Counsell, But what will Contribute to Naples Happynesse.
Oct: My Lord you are wise.
Mal: The Necessity of Affaires oblig'd some Restraynt upon the Queene, and Person of Leonidas.
Flo: I pitty both; though as a woman tis no wounder such a Charming Person as Leonidas should Gayne Affection.
Mal: It was not safe to further Irritate the King of Lombardy's Neece And Arianas Title, his Armes might else too Easily Aid.
Lodo: Shee is a gracious Lady:
Mal: I wish her Happynesse — but scarce dare trust it; Guarini were more welcome to my Interest. asydes
Enter Antonio:
Antonio, Andrugio, Castruchio, with packquetts
Well Return'd Antonio; The King of Lombardy holds on his way to Naples with the Princesse?
Anto: He do's my Lord.
Mal: No further Newes yet of the Duke Guarini?
Anto: Not any.
Mal: Tis strange his Active soule should Rest In such a tyme as this.
Anto: It is most Certayne. he escap'd the fury of the fight.
Mal: Dispatch some Letters every way for more Intelligence.
Lodo: He seem'd to Complement Ariana even now; What a Prodigious thing's a Politicians Conscience? whisper
2 whistle ready
Flo: No Doubt he finds it seasonable to Repayre her Injuryes, and perhaps will now, for his better safety, be content to make one of her sad Subjects.
Oct: His Courage has strangely wrought upon the Popularity: I dare not undertake to guess his End.
Anto: Some Eminent from the King of Lombardy Are here Arriv'd with me and wayte your Lordship. Exit Antonio
Mal: Admit them to me. — By your Favour Gentlemen. Exit Flo. Lodo. & octavio:
Enter Antonio with Andrugio & Castruchio:
And: These from Alberto the most great and prosperous King of Lombardy. Gives Mal. a letter
Mal: His Commands are welcome to the Humblest

asyde:·

packquetts

your Favour Gentlemen.

Gives Mal. a letter

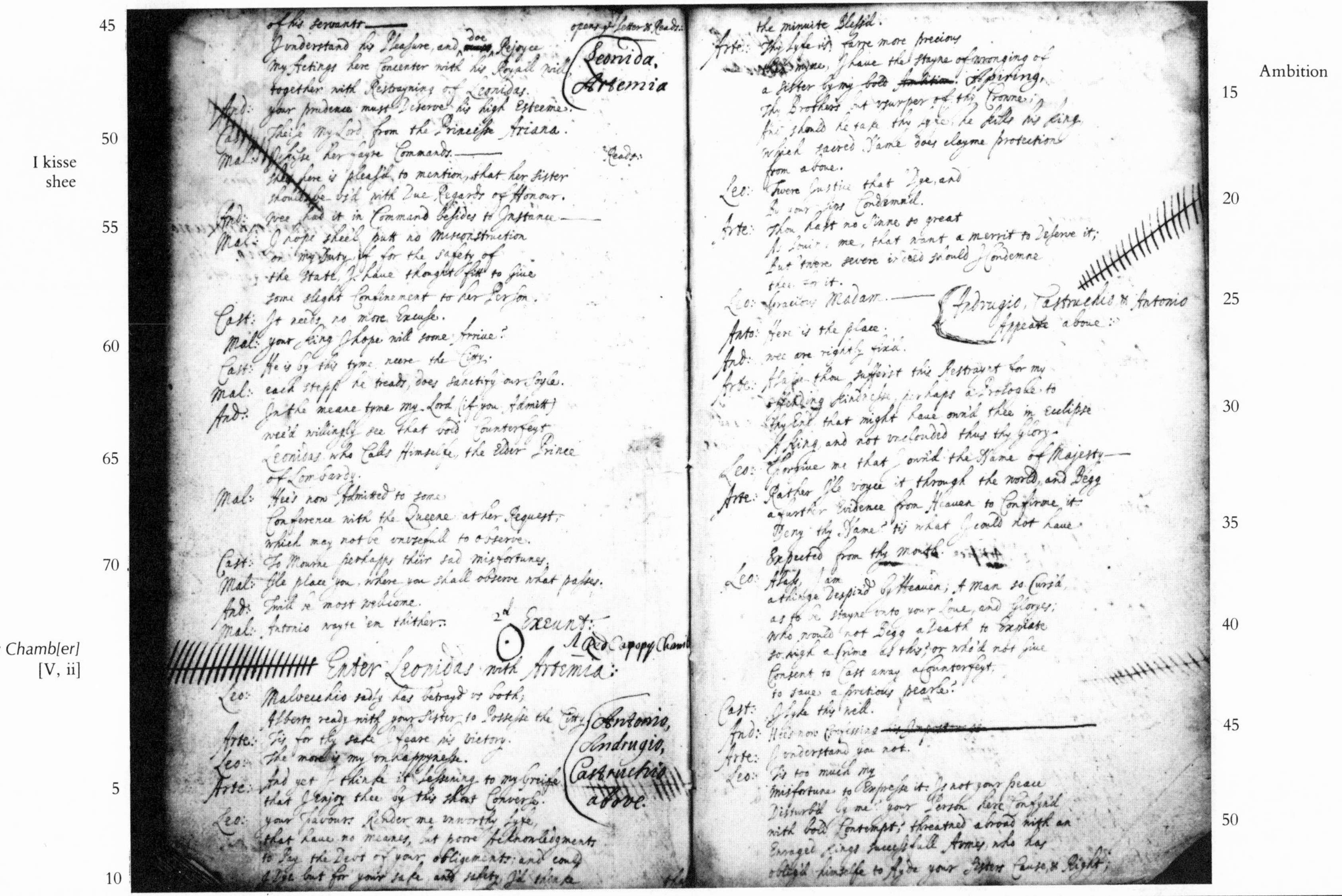

of his servants ——
I understand his Pleasure, and doe Rejoyce
My feelings here concenter with his Royall will
together with Restrayning of Leonidas. (opens ye Letter & Reads)
And: your prudence must deserve his high Esteeme.
Cast: These my Lord from the Princesse Ariana.
Mal: I kisse her fayre Commands. —— (Reads)
shee here is pleas'd to mention, that her sister
should be us'd with due Regards of Honour.
And: wee had it in Command besides to Instance ——
Mal: I hope shee'l putt no misconstruction
on my duty, if for the safety of
the State, I have thought fitt to give
some slight Confinement to her Person.
Cast: It needs no more Excuse.
Mal: your King I hope will soone arrive?
Cast: He is by this tyme neere the City.
Mal: each stepp he treads, does sanctify our Soyle.
And: In the meane tyme my Lord (if you admitt)
wee'd willingly see that void Counterfeyt
Leonidas who Calls Himselfe the Elder Prince
of Lombardy.
Mal: Hee's now admitted to some
Conference with the Queene at her Request,
which may not be unusefull to observe.
Cast: To Mourne perhapps their sad misfortunes.
Mal: Ile place you where you shall observe what passes.
And: Twill be most welcome.
Mal: Antonio wayte 'em thither.
Exeunt
(A Red Canopy Chamb)
(Leonida, Artemia)

Enter Leonidas with Artemia:
(Antonio, Andrugio, Castruchio above.)
Leo: Malvecchio sadly has betrayd us both;
Alberto ready with your Sister to Possesse the City.
Arte: Tis, for thy sake I feare his Victory.
Leo: The more is my unhappynesse.
Arte: And yet I thinke it lessening to my Greife
that I enjoy thee by this short Converse.
Leo: your favours Render me unworthy Lyfe,
that have no meanes, but poore Acknowledgements
to Pay the Debt of your obligements: and could
I lyve but for your sake and safety, I'd thinke
the minute blessed.
Arte: Thy Lyfe is farre more precious
then mine, I have the stayne of wronging of
a Sister by my bold Aspiring.
The Brothers but usurper of thy Crowne:
And should he take thy Lyfe, he kills his King
which sacred Name does clayme protection
from above.
Leo: Twere Justice that I dye, and
by your lipps Condemn'd.
Arte: thou hast no Crime so great
As mine, that want a merrit to deserve it;
but more severe is fate should I Condemne
thee to it.
Leo: Gracious Madam ——
(Andrugio, Castruchio & Antonio Appeare above)
Anto: Here is the place.
And: wee are rightly fixd.
Arte: Alasse thou sufferest this Restraint for my
offending kindnesse, perhaps a Prologue to
thy End that might have owned thee in Ecclipse
a King, and not unclouded thus thy glory.
Leo: Forbeare me that owned the Name of Majesty ——
Arte: Rather I'le voyce it through the world, and begg
a further Evidence from Heaven to Confirme it.
Deny thy Name? tis what I could not have
Expected from thy mouth.
Leo: Alas, I am
a thinge Despis'd by Heaven; A man so Curs'd
as to be stayned unto your Love and favours;
who would not begg a death to expiate
so high a Crime as this? or who'd not give
Consent to Cast away a Counterfeyt,
to save a pretious pearle?
Cast: I like thy will.
And: Hee's now Confessing ——
Arte: I understand you not.
Leo: Tis too much my
misfortune to Expresse it. Is not your peace
Disturb'd by me? your Person here Confin'd
with bold Contempt; threatned abroad with an
Enraged Kings successfull Armes, who has
oblig'd himselfe to ayde your Sisters Cause, & Right;

I kisse
shee

A Red Canopy Chamb[er]
[V, ii]

Ambition

Artifice me
Taske my Loue

perhaps

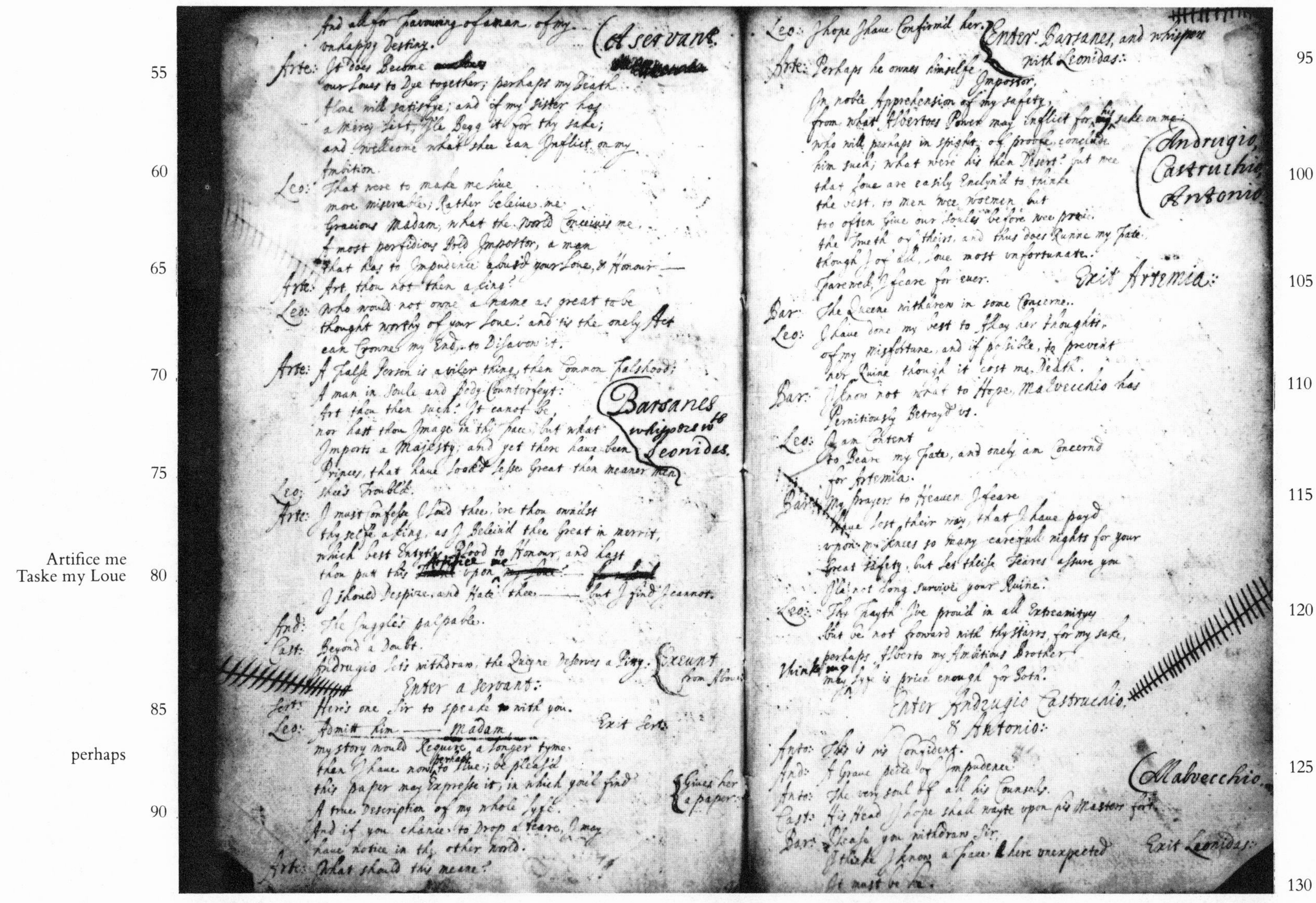

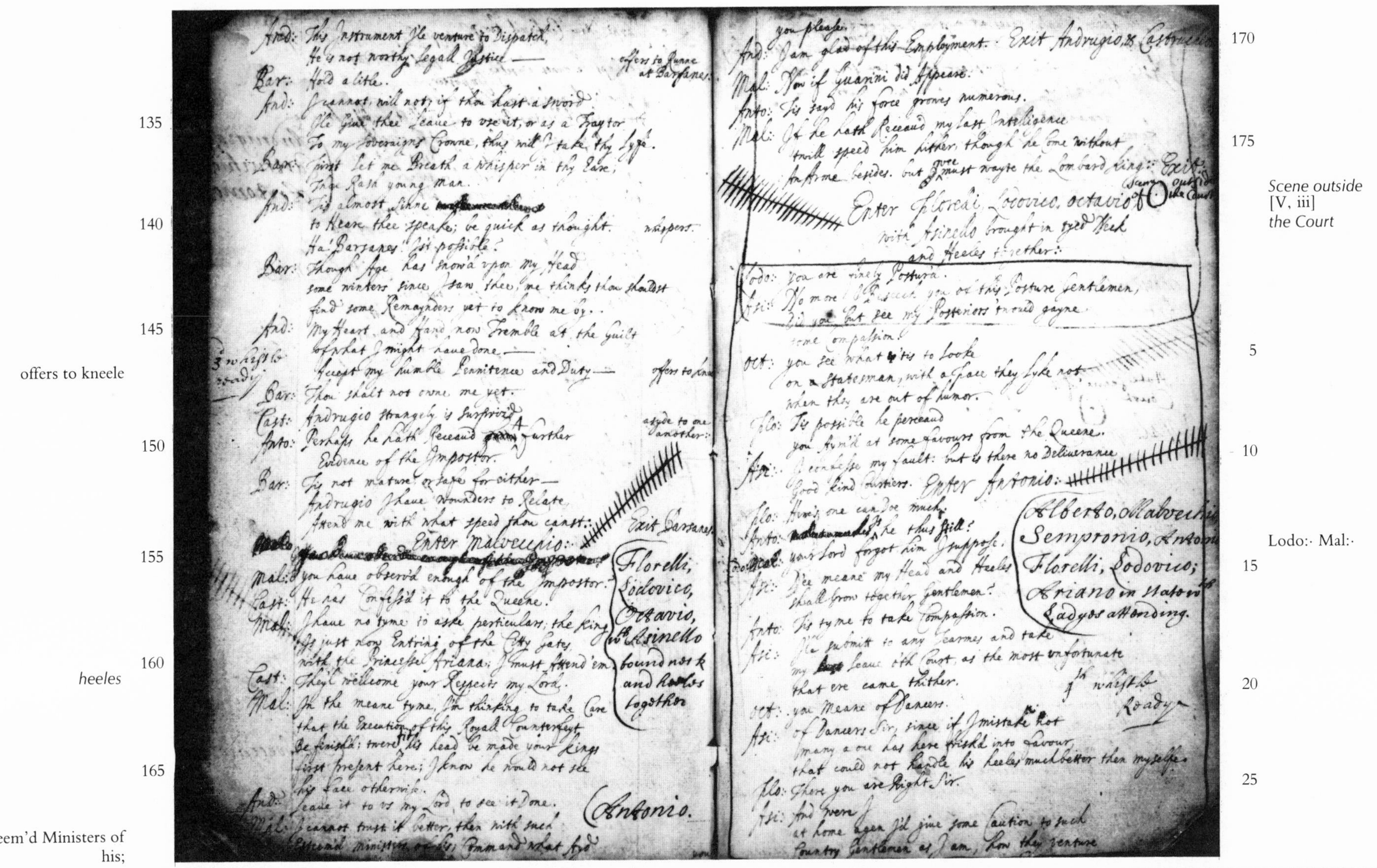

offers to kneele

heeles

Esteem'd Ministers of his;

Scene outside [V, iii] *the Court*

Lodo:· Mal:·

for Freedome
Deliuerance. they vnbind hi[m]

[V, iv]

wth a head

asyde:·

Flo:· And the Princesse Ariana

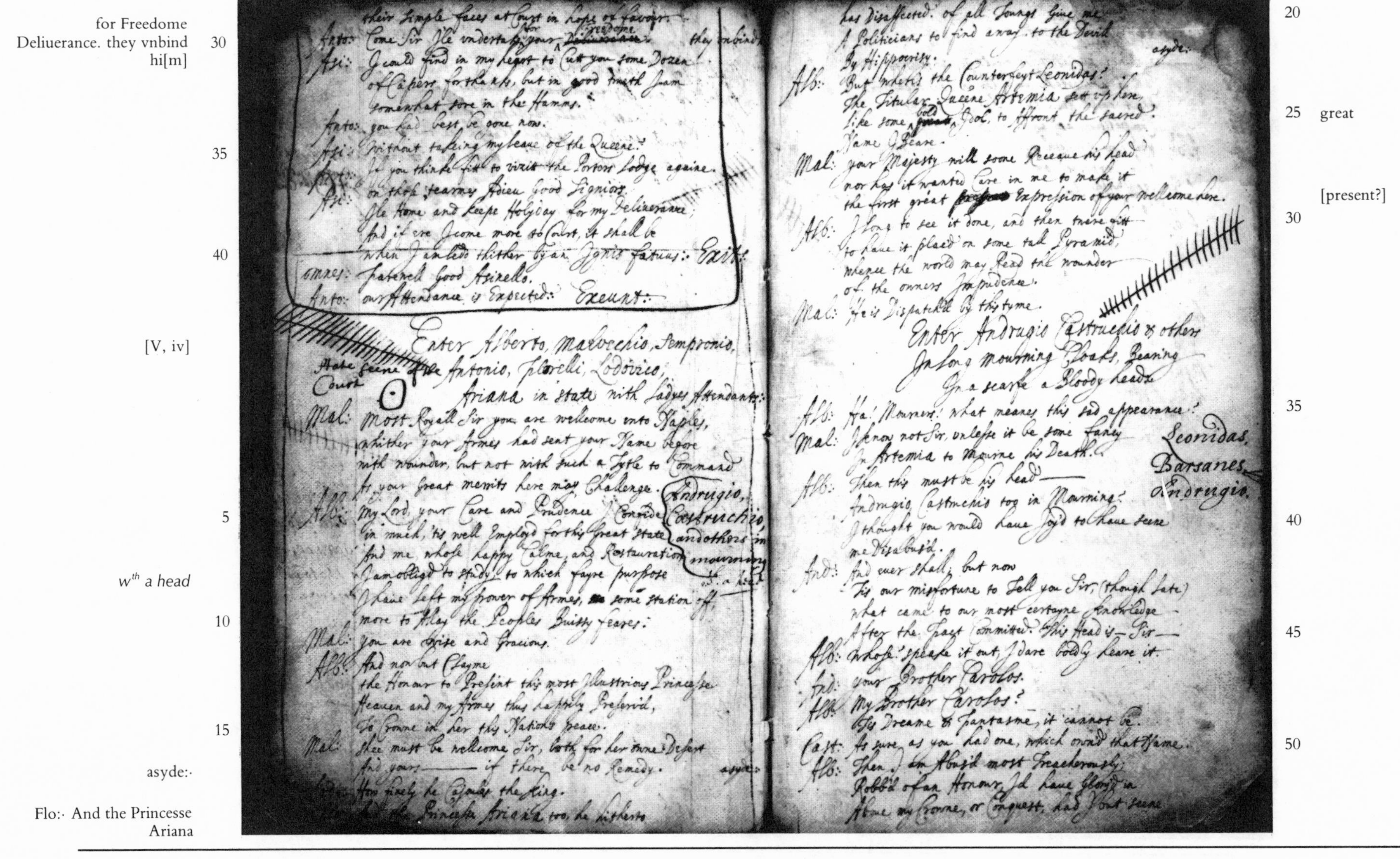

great

[present?]

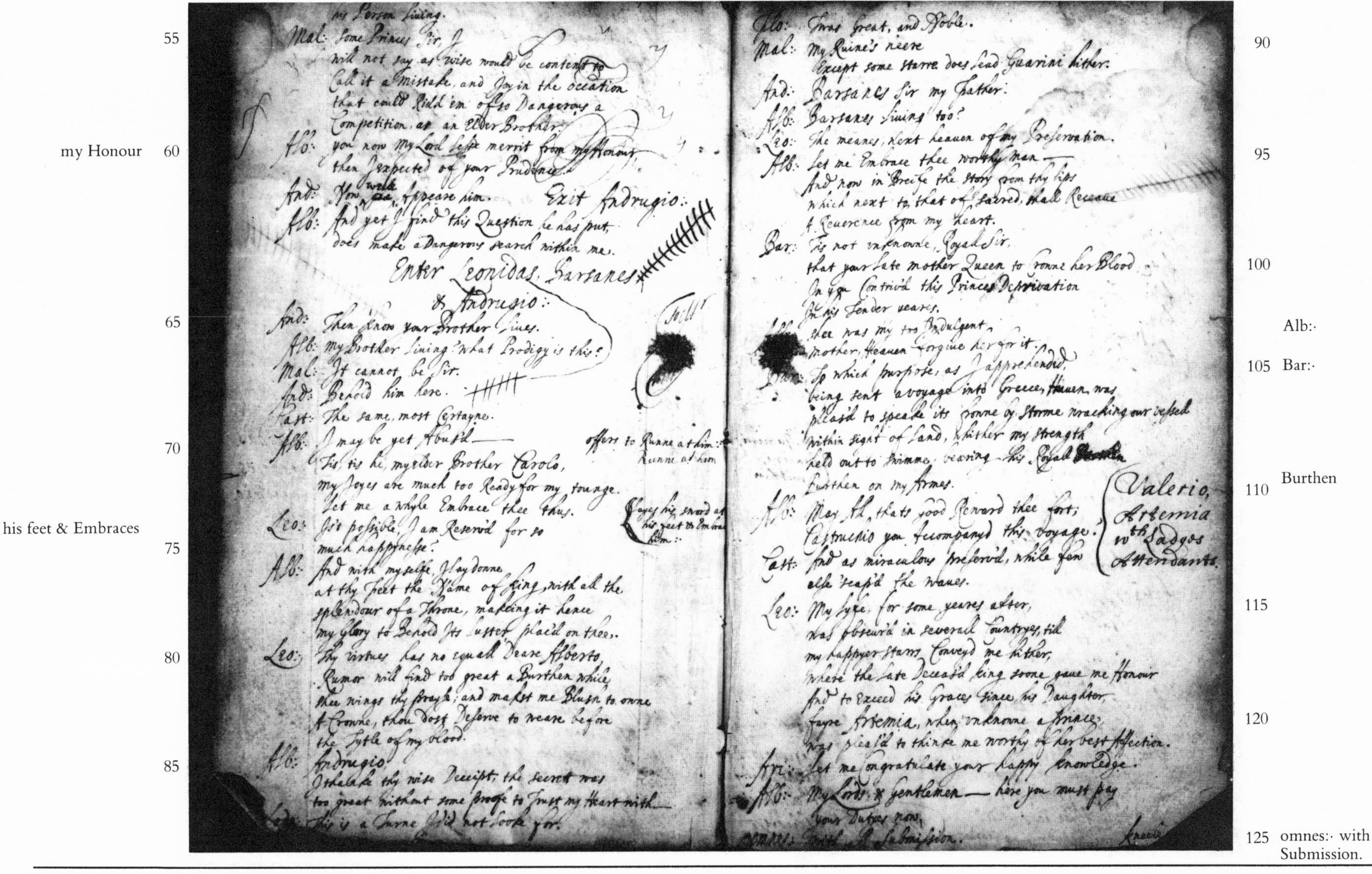

my Honour

his feet & Embraces

Alb:·

Bar:·

Burthen

omnes:· with all Submission.

V, iv, 68. This entrance cue seems to be for Leonidas, Barsanes, and Andrugio; the stage direction for their entrance is before line 65 and properly cued, but references to them in the lines do not come until line 68, at which point, apparently, they actually entered.

The

His thy

kneeles:·

Ari:· I hope Heauen has Decreed

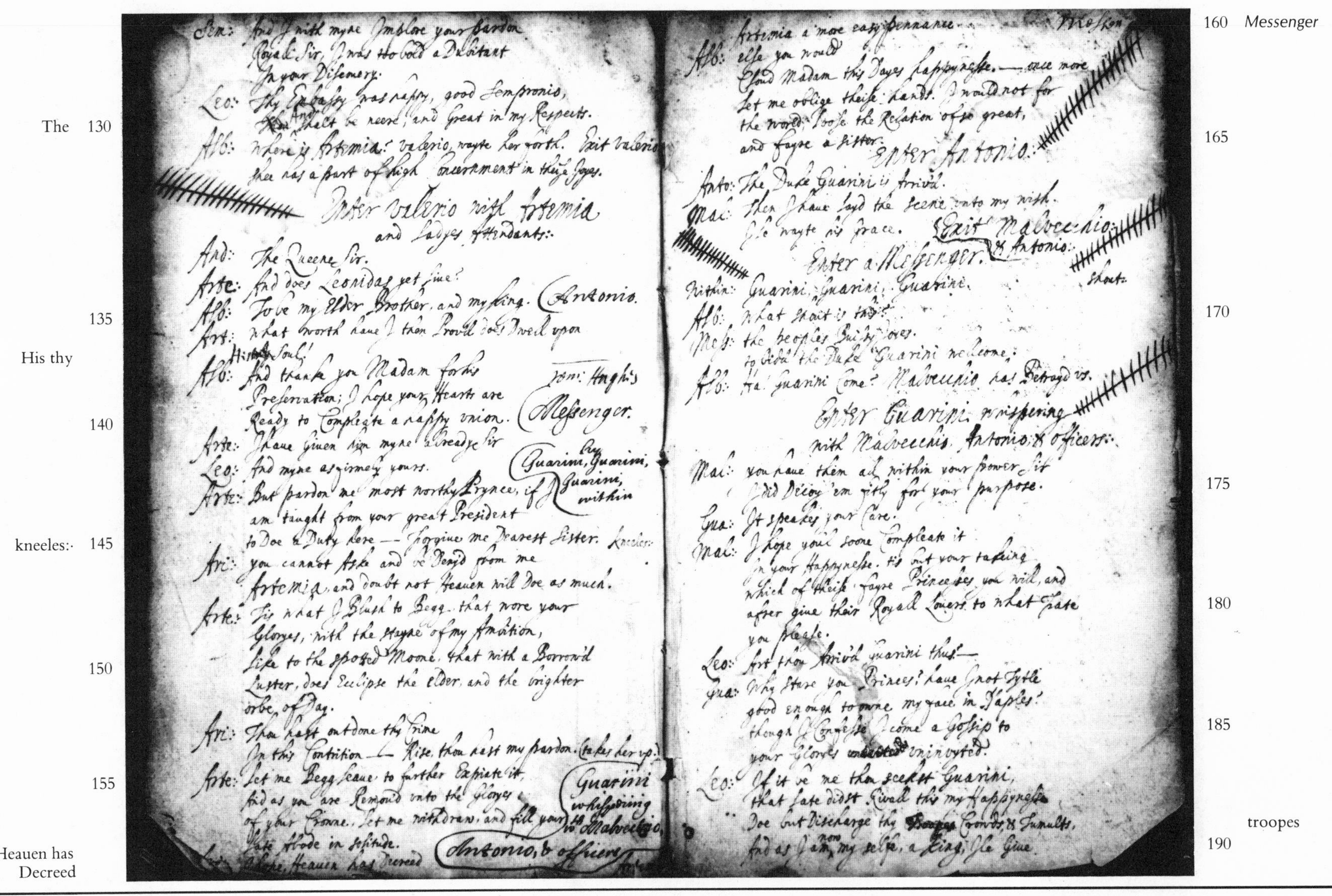

Messenger

troopes

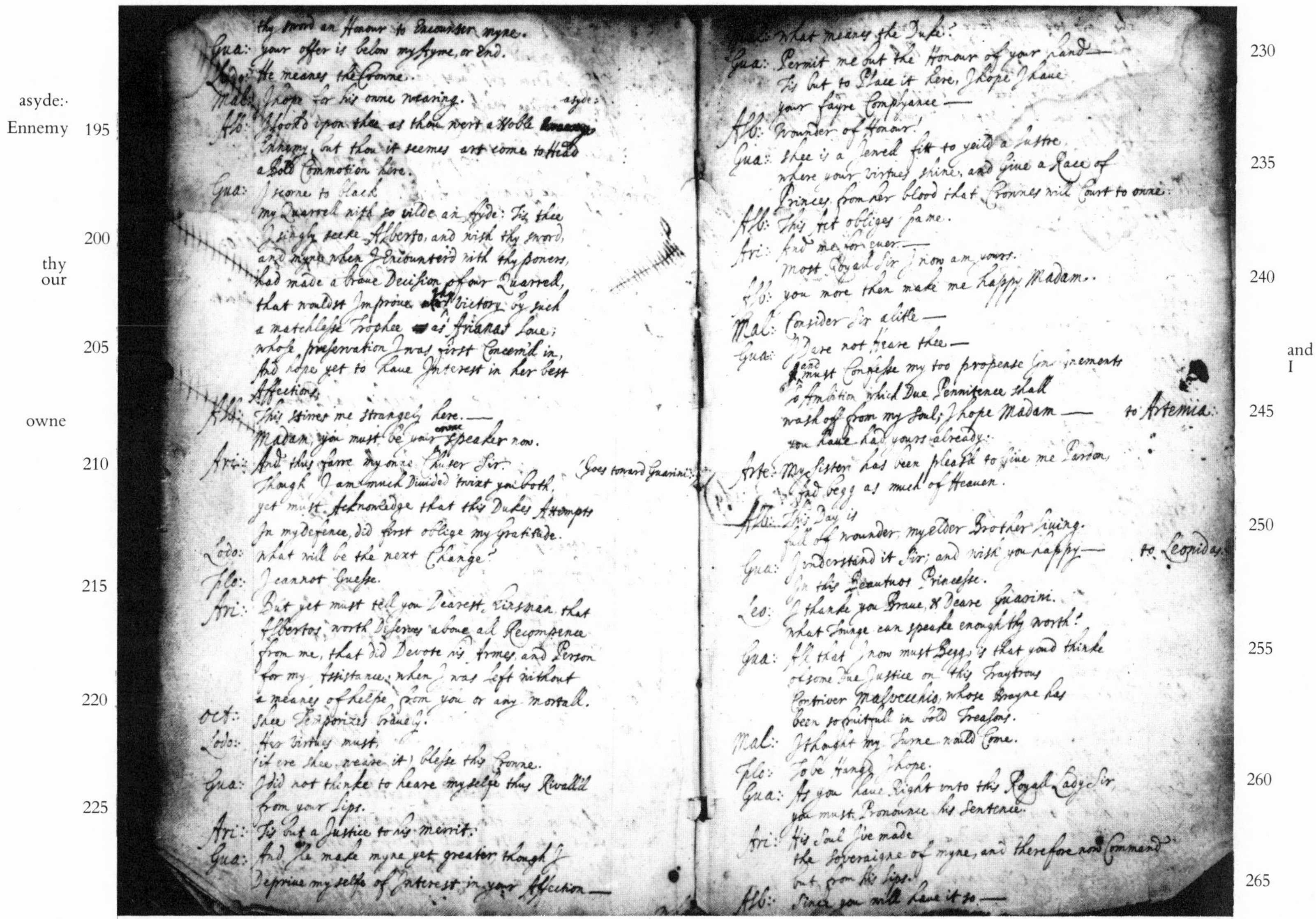
thy sword an Honour to Encounter myne.
Gua: your offer is below my ayme, or End.
Lodo: He meanes the Crowne.
Mal: I hope for his owne meaning. asyde:
Alb: I look'd upon thee as thou wert a Noble Enemy,
but thou it seemes art come to Head
a bold Commotion here.
Gua: I scorne to black
my Quarrell with so vilde an ayde: Tis thee
I singly seeke Alberto, and with thy sword,
and myne when I encounterd with thy powers,
had made a brave Decision of our Quarrell,
that would I improve thy victory by such
a matchlesse Trophee as Frianas Love;
whose preservation I was first Concern'd in,
And hope yet to have Interest in her best
Affections.
Alb: This stirres me strangely here.—
Madam, you must be your owne speaker now.
Ari: And this farre my owne Suiter Sir. (Goes toward Guarini:)
Though I am much divided twixt you both,
yet must acknowledge that this Dukes Attempts
In my defence, did first oblige my gratitude.
Lodo: what will be the next Change?
Flo: I cannot Guesse.
Ari: But yet must tell you Dearest Kinsman that
Albertos worth Deserves above all Recompence
from me, that did Devote his Armes, and Person
for my Assistance: when I was left without
a meanes of helpe from you or any mortall.
Oct: shee Temporizes bravely.
Lodo: Her virtues must,
(if ere shee weare it) blesse this Crowne.
Gua: I did not thinke to heare my selfe thus Rivall'd
from your Lips.
Ari: Tis but a Justice to his merrit.
Gua: And Ile make myne yet greater though I
Deprive my selfe of Interest in your Affection—

Ari: what meanes the Duke?
Gua: Permit me but the Honour of your hand—
Tis but to Place it here. I hope I have
your fayre Compliance—
Alb: Wonder of Honour!
Gua: shee is a Jewell fitt to yeild a Lustre
where your virtues shine, and give a Race of
Princes from her blood that Crownes will Court to owne.
Alb: This yet obliges fame.
Ari: And me for ever.
Most Royall Sir I now am yours.
Alb: you more then make me happy Madam.
Mal: Consider Sir a litle—
Gua: I dare not heare thee—
and I must Confesse my too propense Inclinements
to Ambition which Due Pennitence shall
wash off from my Soul; I hope Madam— to Artemia:
you have had yours already.
Arte: My Sister has been pleas'd to give me Pardon,
and I shall begg as much of Heaven.
Alb: This Day is
full of wonder, my elder Brother Living.
Gua: I understand it Sir; and wish you happy— to Leonidas.
In this Beautious Princesse.
Leo: I thanke you Brave, & Deare Guarini.
what Image can speake enough thy worth!
Gua: All that I now must Begg is that you'd thinke
of some due Justice on this Traytrous
Contriver Malvecchio, whose Brayne has
been so fruitfull in bold Treasons.
Mal: I thought my Tyme would Come.
Flo: To be Hang'd I hope.
Gua: As you have Right unto this Royall Lady Sir,
you must Pronounce his Sentence.
Ari: His Soul I've made
the Soveraigne of myne, and therefore now Commend
but from his Lips.
Alb: Since you will have it so—

asyde:-
Ennemy
thy
our
owne
and
I

Alb:· which to Enjoy may your

Leo:· you now will but

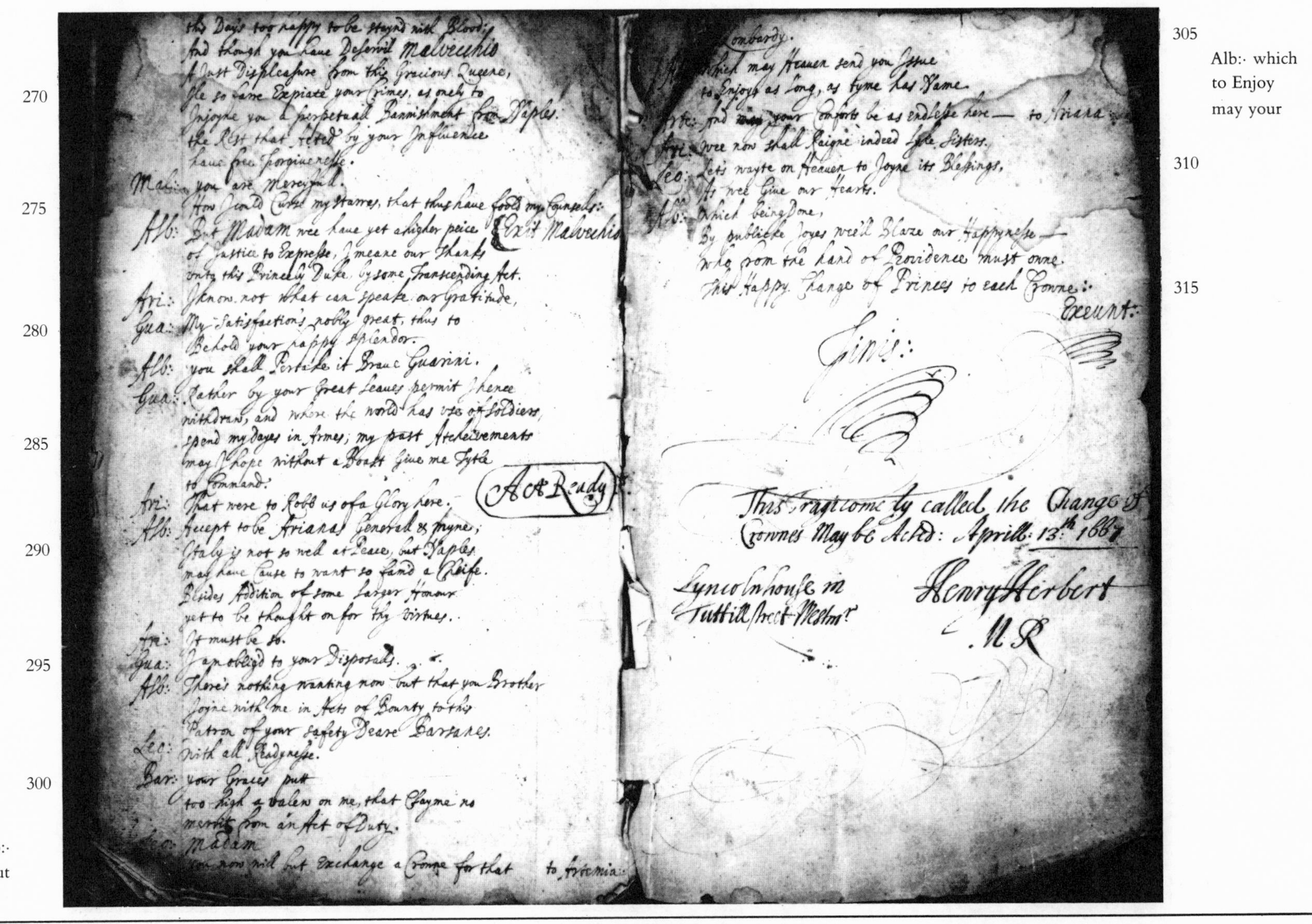
the Day's too happy to be stayn'd with Blood;
And though you have Deserv'd Malvecchio
A Just Displeasure from this Gracious Queene,
Ile so farre Expiate your Crimes, as onely to
Injoyne you a perpetuall Bannishment from Naples.
the Rest that acted by your Influence
have free forgivenesse.
Mal: you are Mercyfull.
How I could Curse my Starres, that thus have fool'd my Counsells: Exit Malvecchio
Alb: But Madam wee have yet a higher peice
of Justice to Expresse, I meane our Thanks
unto this Princely Duke, by some Transcending Act.
Ari: I know not what can speake our gratitude,
Gua: My Satisfaction's nobly great, thus to
Behold your happy Splendor.
Alb: you shall Partake it Brave Guarini.
Gua: Rather by your great leaves permit I hence
withdraw, and where the world has use of Soldiers,
spend my dayes in Armes; my past Atcheivements
may I hope without a Boast Give me Tytle
to Command.
Ari: That were to Robb us of a Glory here. Act Ready
Alb: Accept to be Ariana's Generall & myne;
Italy is not so well at Peace, but Naples
may have Cause to want so fam'd a Chiefe.
Besides Addition of some larger Honour
yet to be thought on for thy Virtues.
Ari: It must be so.
Gua: I am oblig'd to your Disposalls.
Alb: There's nothing wanting now but that you Brother
Joyne with me in Acts of Bounty to this
Patron of your safety Deare Barsanes.
Leo: With all Readynesse.
Bar: your Graces put
too high a valew on me, that Clayme no
meritt from an Act of Duty.
Leo: Madam
you now will but Exchange a Crowne for that to Ariana:
Lombardy.
Alb: Which may Heaven send you Issue
to Enjoy as long, as tyme has Name.
Ari: And may your Comforts be as endlesse here— to Ariana
Ari: wee now shall Raigne indeed lyke Sisters.
Leo: Lets wayte on Heaven to Joyne its Blessings,
It well Give our Hearts.
Alb: Which being Done,
By publicke Joyes wee'll Blaze our Happynesse—
Who from the hand of Providence must owne
This Happy Change of Princes to each Crowne:
Exeunt:
Finis:
This Tragicomedy called the Change of Crownes May be Acted: Aprill: 13th 1667
Henry Herbert
M R
Lyncolnhouse in Tuttill street Westmr

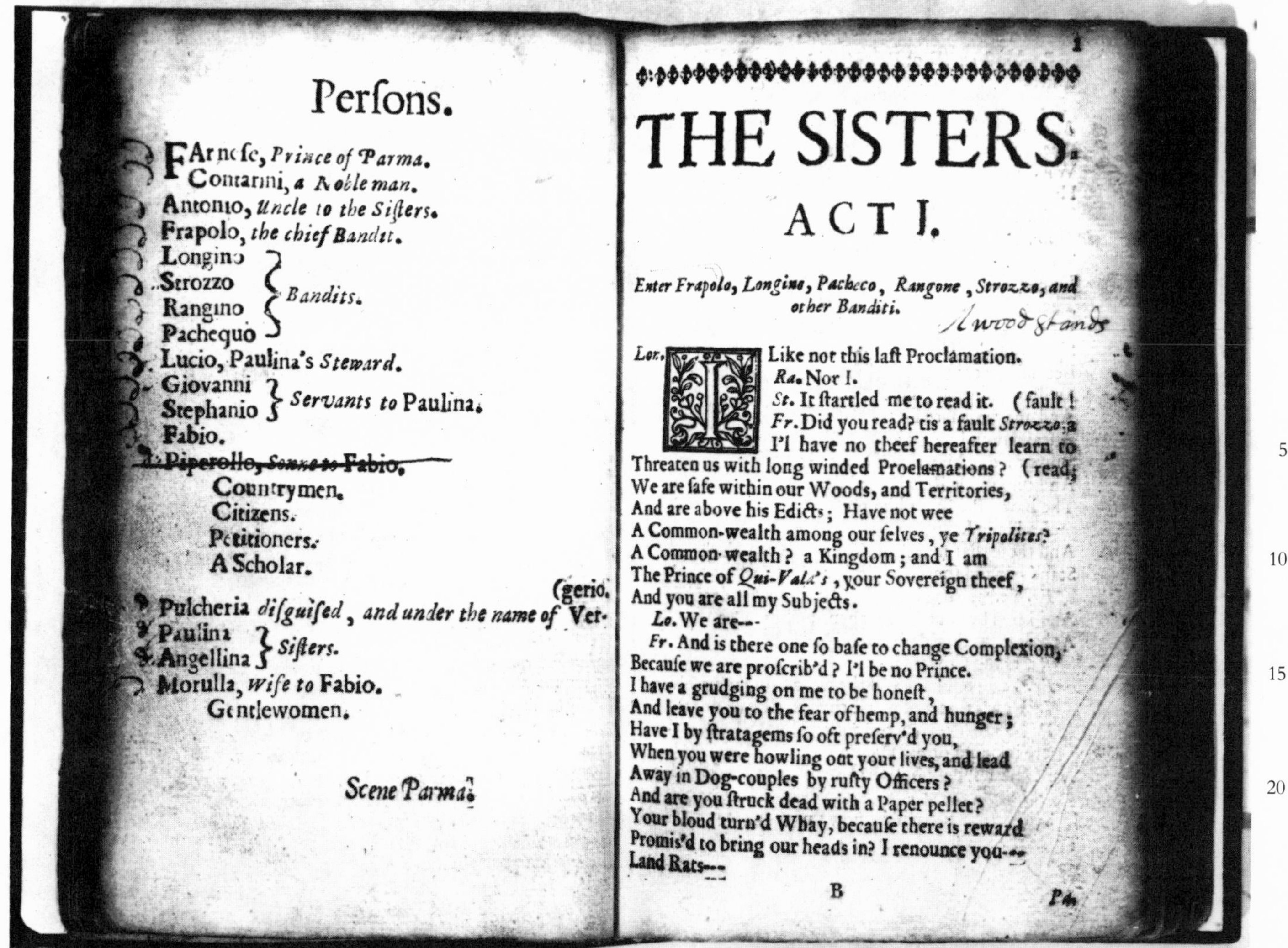

Perſons.

Farneſe, *Prince of Parma.*
Contarini, *a Noble man.*
Antonio, *Uncle to the Siſters.*
Frapolo, *the chief Bandit.*
Longino
Strozzo
Rangino
Pachequo } *Bandits.*
Lucio, Paulina's *Steward.*
Giovanni
Stephanio } *Servants to* Paulina.
Fabio.
~~Piperollo, *Sonne to* Fabio.~~
Countrymen.
Citizens.
Petitioners.
A Scholar.
Pulcheria *diſguiſed, and under the name of* Vergerio.
Paulina
Angellina } *Siſters.*
Morulla, *wife to* Fabio.
Gentlewomen.

Scene Parma.

1

THE SISTERS.

ACT I.

Enter Frapolo, Longino, Pacheco, Rangone, Strozzo, and other Banditi.

Lon. I Like not this laſt Proclamation.
Ra. Nor I.
St. It ſtartled me to read it.
Fr. Did you read? tis a fault *Strozzo*; a fault!
I'l have no theef hereafter learn to read;
Threaten us with long winded Proclamations?
We are ſafe within our Woods, and Territories,
And are above his Edicts; Have not wee
A Common-wealth among our ſelves, ye *Tripolites?*
A Common-wealth? a Kingdom; and I am
The Prince of *Qui-Vala's*, your Sovereign theef,
And you are all my Subjects.
Lo. We are---
Fr. And is there one ſo baſe to change Complexion,
Becauſe we are proſcrib'd? I'l be no Prince.
I have a grudging on me to be honeſt,
And leave you to the fear of hemp, and hunger;
Have I by ſtratagems ſo oft preſerv'd you,
When you were howling out your lives, and lead
Away in Dog-couples by ruſty Officers?
And are you ſtruck dead with a Paper pellet?
Your bloud turn'd Whay, becauſe there is reward
Promis'd to bring our heads in? I renounce you---
Land Rats---

B Pa-

The copy lacks the title page.

The Sisters by James Shirley. Reproduced by permission of the Folger Shakespeare Library, Washington, D.C.

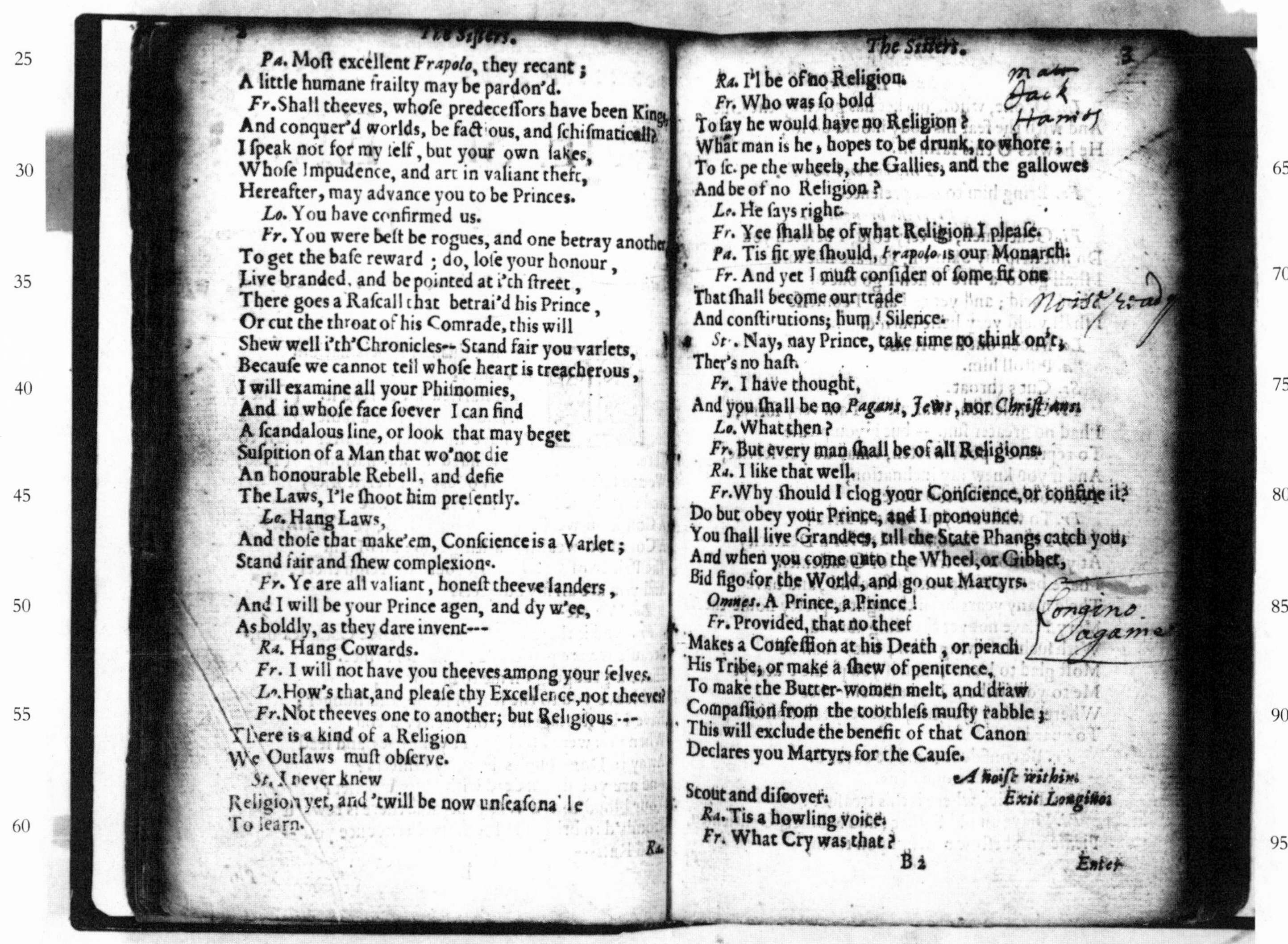

The Siſters.

Pa. Moſt excellent *Frapolo*, they recant;
A little humane frailty may be pardon'd.
Fr. Shall theeves, whoſe predeceſſors have been Kings,
And conquer'd worlds, be fact ious, and ſchiſmaticall?
I ſpeak not for my ſelf, but your own ſakes,
Whoſe Impudence, and art in valiant theft,
Hereafter, may advance you to be Princes.
Lo. You have confirmed us.
Fr. You were beſt be rogues, and one betray another
To get the baſe reward; do, loſe your honour,
Live branded, and be pointed at i'th ſtreet,
There goes a Raſcall that betrai'd his Prince,
Or cut the throat of his Comrade, this will
Shew well i'th'Chronicles-- Stand fair you varlets,
Becauſe we cannot tell whoſe heart is treacherous,
I will examine all your Phiſnomies,
And in whoſe face ſoever I can find
A ſcandalous line, or look that may beget
Suſpition of a Man that wo'not die
An honourable Rebell, and defie
The Laws, I'le ſhoot him preſently.
Lo. Hang Laws,
And thoſe that make'em, Conſcience is a Varlet;
Stand fair and ſhew complexion.
Fr. Ye are all valiant, honeſt theeve ſlanders,
And I will be your Prince agen, and dy w'ee,
As boldly, as they dare invent---
Ra. Hang Cowards.
Fr. I will not have you theeves among your ſelves.
Lo. How's that, and pleaſe thy Excellence, not theeves?
Fr. Not theeves one to another; but Religious --
There is a kind of a Religion
We Outlaws muſt obſerve.
St. I never knew
Religion yet, and 'twill be now unſeaſonable
To learn.
Ra.

The Siſters. 3

Ra. I'l be of no Religion.
Fr. Who was ſo bold
To ſay he would have no Religion?
What man is he, hopes to be drunk, to whore;
To ſcape the wheels, the Gallies, and the gallowes
And be of no Religion?
Lo. He ſays right.
Fr. Yee ſhall be of what Religion I pleaſe.
Pa. Tis fit we ſhould, *Frapolo* is our Monarch.
Fr. And yet I muſt conſider of ſome fit one
That ſhall become our trade
And conſtitutions; hum! Silence.
St. Nay, nay Prince, take time to think on't,
Ther's no haſt.
Fr. I have thought,
And you ſhall be no *Pagans*, *Jews*, nor *Chriſtians*
Lo. What then?
Fr. But every man ſhall be of all Religions.
Ra. I like that well.
Fr. Why ſhould I clog your Conſcience, or confine it?
Do but obey your Prince, and I pronounce
You ſhall live Grandees, till the State Phangs catch you;
And when you come unto the Wheel, or Gibbet,
Bid figo for the World, and go out Martyrs.
Omnes. A Prince, a Prince!
Fr. Provided, that no theef
Makes a Confeſſion at his Death, or peach
His Tribe, or make a ſhew of penitence,
To make the Butter-women melt, and draw
Compaſſion from the toothleſs muſty rabble;
This will exclude the benefit of that Canon
Declares you Martyrs for the Cauſe.
A noiſe within.
Scout and diſcover. *Exit Longino.*
Ra. Tis a howling voice.
Fr. What Cry was that?
B 2 *Enter*

I, i, 61. The incomplete word, *Mast*, is probably "Master."

I, i, 85–86. The warning for Longino is pointless; he is onstage at this point and will presently exit, only to reenter within two short lines. The prompter evidently went about his job mechanically, giving every entrance a warning.

I, i, 93. The *noise*, though warned, is not cued.

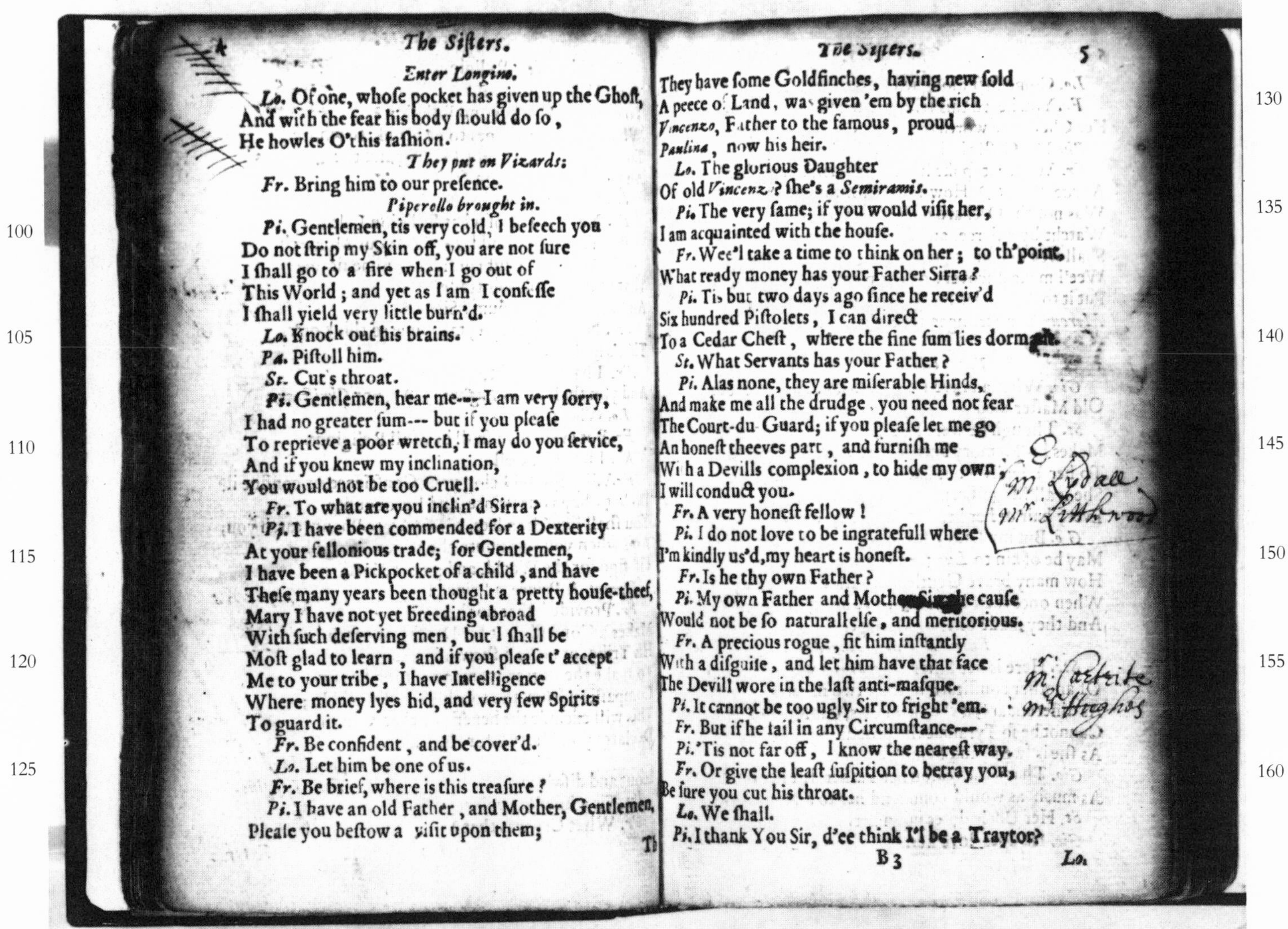

The Sisters.

Enter Longino.

Lo. Of one, whose pocket has given up the Ghost,
And with the fear his body should do so,
He howles O'this fashion.

They put on Vizards:

Fr. Bring him to our presence.

Piperello brought in.

Pi. Gentlemen, tis very cold, I beseech you
Do not strip my Skin off, you are not sure
I shall go to a fire when I go out of
This World; and yet as I am I confesse
I shall yield very little burn'd.
Lo. Knock out his brains.
Pa. Pistoll him.
St. Cut's throat.
Pi. Gentlemen, hear me--- I am very sorry,
I had no greater sum--- but if you please
To reprieve a poor wretch, I may do you service,
And if you knew my inclination,
You would not be too Cruell.
Fr. To what are you inclin'd Sirra?
Pi. I have been commended for a Dexterity
At your fellonious trade; for Gentlemen,
I have been a Pickpocket of a child, and have
These many years been thought a pretty house-theef,
Mary I have not yet breeding abroad
With such deserving men, but I shall be
Most glad to learn, and if you please t' accept
Me to your tribe, I have Intelligence
Where money lyes hid, and very few Spirits
To guard it.
Fr. Be confident, and be cover'd.
Lo. Let him be one of us.
Fr. Be brief, where is this treasure?
Pi. I have an old Father, and Mother, Gentlemen,
Please you bestow a visit upon them;
Th

The Sisters. 5

They have some Goldfinches, having new sold
A peece of Land, was given 'em by the rich
Vincenzo, Father to the famous, proud
Paulina, now his heir.
Lo. The glorious Daughter
Of old *Vincenzo*? she's a *Semiramis.*
Pi. The very same; if you would visit her,
I am acquainted with the house.
Fr. Wee'l take a time to think on her; to th'point,
What ready money has your Father Sirra?
Pi. Tis but two days ago since he receiv'd
Six hundred Pistolets, I can direct
To a Cedar Chest, where the fine sum lies dormant.
St. What Servants has your Father?
Pi. Alas none, they are miserable Hinds,
And make me all the drudge, you need not fear
The Court-du Guard; if you please let me go
An honest theeves part, and furnish me
With a Devills complexion, to hide my own;
I will conduct you.
Fr. A very honest fellow!
Pi. I do not love to be ingratefull where
I'm kindly us'd, my heart is honest.
Fr. Is he thy own Father?
Pi. My own Father and Mother, Sir, the cause
Would not be so naturall else, and meritorious.
Fr. A precious rogue, fit him instantly
With a disguise, and let him have that face
The Devill wore in the last anti-masque.
Pi. It cannot be too ugly Sir to fright 'em.
Fr. But if he fail in any Circumstance---
Pi. 'Tis not far off, I know the nearest way.
Fr. Or give the least suspition to betray you,
Be sure you cut his throat.
Lo. We shall.
Pi. I thank You Sir, d'ee think I'l be a Traytor?

B3 Lo.

I, i, 99. The cross-hatch cue mark for Piperello's entrance is placed a line before rather than right at his entrance. This is the case with many, but not all, of the entrance cues in the promptbook. Perhaps a cue that was advanced one line was for an entrance opposite prompt side if the signal had to be relayed by an assistant.

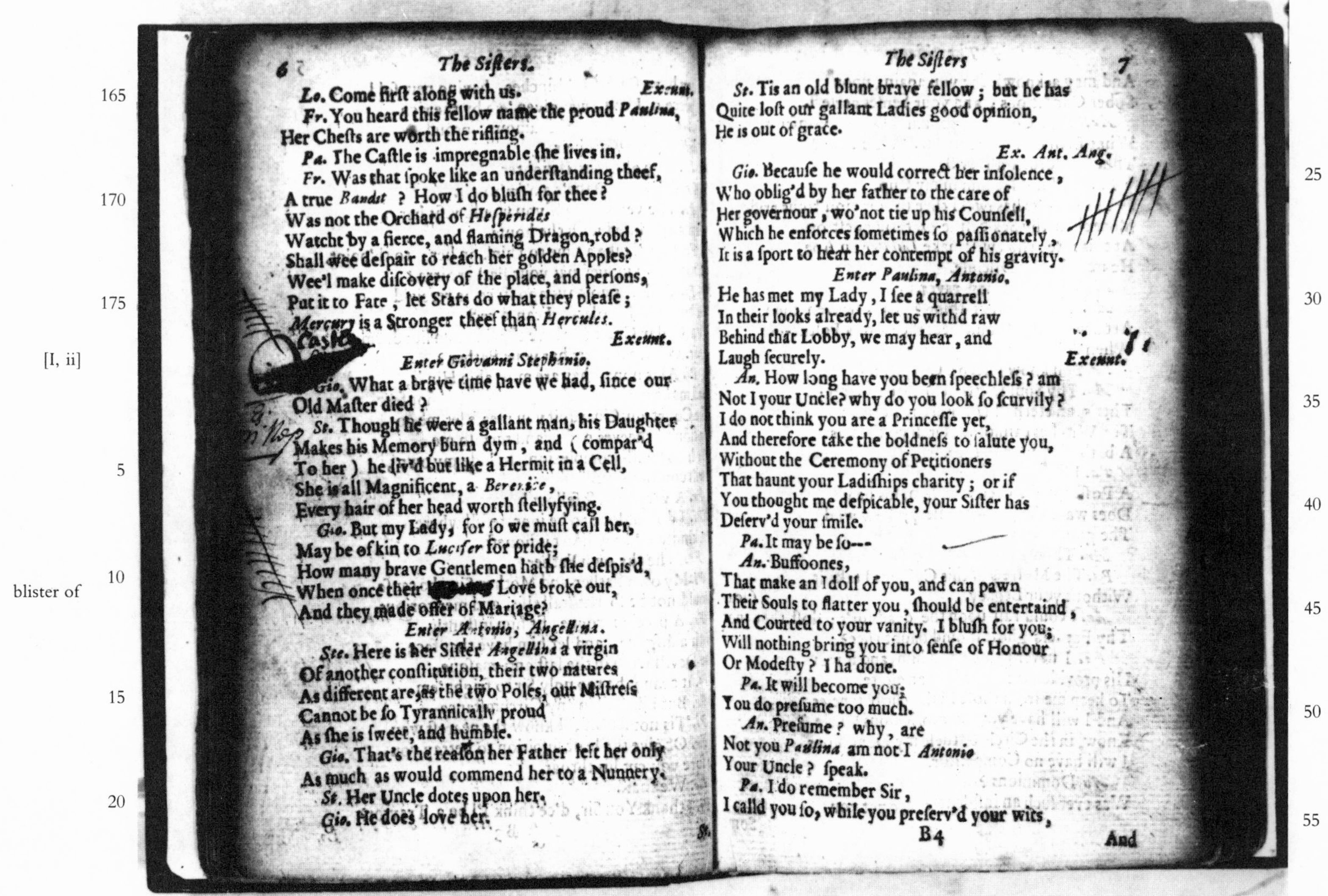

6 *The Siſters.*

Lo. Come firſt along with us. *Exeunt.*

Fr. You heard this fellow name the proud *Paulina*,
Her Cheſts are worth the rifling.

Pa. The Caſtle is impregnable ſhe lives in.

Fr. Was that ſpoke like an underſtanding theef,
A true *Bandit* ? How I do bluſh for thee?
Was not the Orchard of *Heſperides*
Watcht by a fierce, and flaming Dragon,robd ?
Shall wee deſpair to reach her golden Apples?
Wee'l make diſcovery of the place, and perſons,
Put it to Fate, let Stars do what they pleaſe;
Mercury is a Stronger theef than *Hercules*.

Exeunt.

Castle

[I, ii]

Enter Giovanni Stephanio.

Gio. What a brave time have we had, ſince our
Old Maſter died?

St. Though he were a gallant man, his Daughter
Makes his Memory burn dym, and (compar'd
To her) he liv'd but like a Hermit in a Cell,
She is all Magnificent, a *Berenice*,
Every hair of her head worth ſtellyfying.

Gio. But my Lady, for ſo we muſt call her,
May be of kin to *Lucifer* for pride;
How many brave Gentlemen hath ſhe deſpis'd,
blister of
When once their [illegible] Love broke out,
And they made offer of Mariage?

Enter Antonio, Angellina.

Ste. Here is her Siſter *Angellina* a virgin
Of another conſtitution, their two natures
As different are, as the two Poles, our Miſtreſs
Cannot be ſo Tyrannically proud
As ſhe is ſweet, and humble.

Gio. That's the reaſon her Father left her only
As much as would commend her to a Nunnery.

St. Her Uncle dotes upon her.

Gio. He does love her.

St.

The Siſters 7

St. Tis an old blunt brave fellow; but he has
Quite loſt our gallant Ladies good opinion,
He is out of grace.

Ex. Ant. Ang.

Gio. Becauſe he would correct her inſolence,
Who oblig'd by her father to the care of
Her governour, wo'not tie up his Counſell,
Which he enforces ſometimes ſo paſſionately,
It is a ſport to hear her contempt of his gravity.

Enter Paulina, Antonio.

He has met my Lady, I ſee a quarrell
In their looks already, let us withd raw
Behind that Lobby, we may hear, and
Laugh ſecurely. *Exeunt.*

An. How long have you been ſpeechleſs? am
Not I your Uncle? why do you look ſo ſcurvily?
I do not think you are a Princeſſe yet,
And therefore take the boldneſs to ſalute you,
Without the Ceremony of Petitioners
That haunt your Ladiſhips charity; or if
You thought me deſpicable, your Siſter has
Deſerv'd your ſmile.

Pa. It may be ſo---

An. Buffoones,
That make an Idoll of you, and can pawn
Their Souls to flatter you, ſhould be entertaind,
And Courted to your vanity. I bluſh for you;
Will nothing bring you into ſenſe of Honour
Or Modeſty? I ha done.

Pa. It will become you;
You do preſume too much.

An. Preſume? why, are
Not you *Paulina* am not I *Antonio*
Your Uncle? ſpeak.

Pa. I do remember Sir,
I calld you ſo, while you preſerv'd your wits,

B4 And

I, ii, opening. There is an ink blot over a portion of this note. One can almost make out the word under the blot, so the *Castle* description may have been modified in some way, such as *Castle chamber*.

I, ii, 3. The & probably refers to Antonio, who enters with Angellina, but why was the name not spelled out?

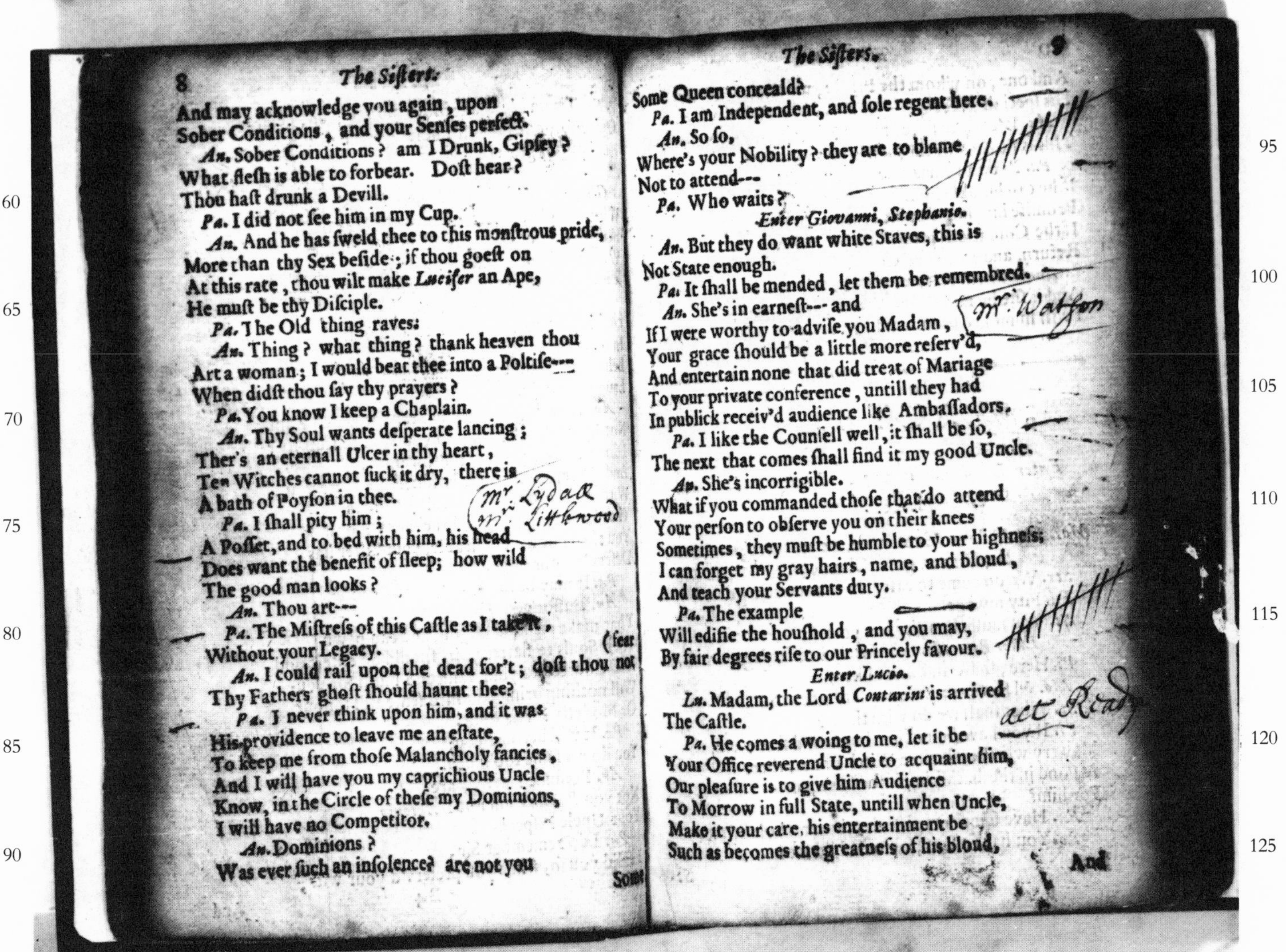

8 *The Siſters.*

And may acknowledge you again, upon
Sober Conditions, and your Senſes perfect.
An. Sober Conditions? am I Drunk, Gipſey?
What fleſh is able to forbear. Doſt hear?
Thou haſt drunk a Devill.
Pa. I did not ſee him in my Cup.
An. And he has ſweld thee to this monſtrous pride,
More than thy Sex beſide; if thou goeſt on
At this rate, thou wilt make *Lucifer* an Ape,
He muſt be thy Diſciple.
Pa. The Old thing raves.
An. Thing? what thing? thank heaven thou
Art a woman; I would beat thee into a Poltiſe---
When didſt thou ſay thy prayers?
Pa. You know I keep a Chaplain.
An. Thy Soul wants deſperate lancing;
Ther's an eternall Ulcer in thy heart,
Ten Witches cannot ſuck it dry, there is
A bath of Poyſon in thee.
Pa. I ſhall pity him;
A Poſſet, and to bed with him, his head
Does want the benefit of ſleep; how wild
The good man looks?
An. Thou art---
Pa. The Miſtreſs of this Caſtle as I take it,
Without your Legacy.
An. I could rail upon the dead for't; doſt thou not (fear
Thy Fathers ghoſt ſhould haunt thee?
Pa. I never think upon him, and it was
His providence to leave me an eſtate,
To keep me from thoſe Malancholy fancies,
And I will have you my caprichious Uncle
Know, in the Circle of theſe my Dominions,
I will have no Competitor.
An. Dominions?
Was ever ſuch an inſolence? are not you

Some

The Siſters. 9

Some Queen conceald?
Pa. I am Independent, and ſole regent here.
An. So ſo,
Where's your Nobility? they are to blame
Not to attend---
Pa. Who waits?
Enter Giovanni, Stephanio.
An. But they do want white Staves, this is
Not State enough.
Pa. It ſhall be mended, let them be remembred.
An. She's in earneſt--- and
If I were worthy to adviſe you Madam,
Your grace ſhould be a little more reſerv'd,
And entertain none that did treat of Mariage
To your private conference, untill they had
In publick receiv'd audience like Ambaſſadors.
Pa. I like the Counſell well, it ſhall be ſo,
The next that comes ſhall find it my good Uncle.
An. She's incorrigible.
What if you commanded thoſe that do attend
Your perſon to obſerve you on their knees
Sometimes, they muſt be humble to your highneſs;
I can forget my gray hairs, name, and bloud,
And teach your Servants duty.
Pa. The example
Will edifie the houſhold, and you may,
By fair degrees riſe to our Princely favour.
Enter Lucio.
Lu. Madam, the Lord *Contarini* is arrived
The Caſtle.
Pa. He comes a woing to me, let it be
Your Office reverend Uncle to acquaint him,
Our pleaſure is to give him Audience
To Morrow in full State, untill when Uncle,
Make it your care, his entertainment be
Such as becomes the greatneſs of his bloud,

And

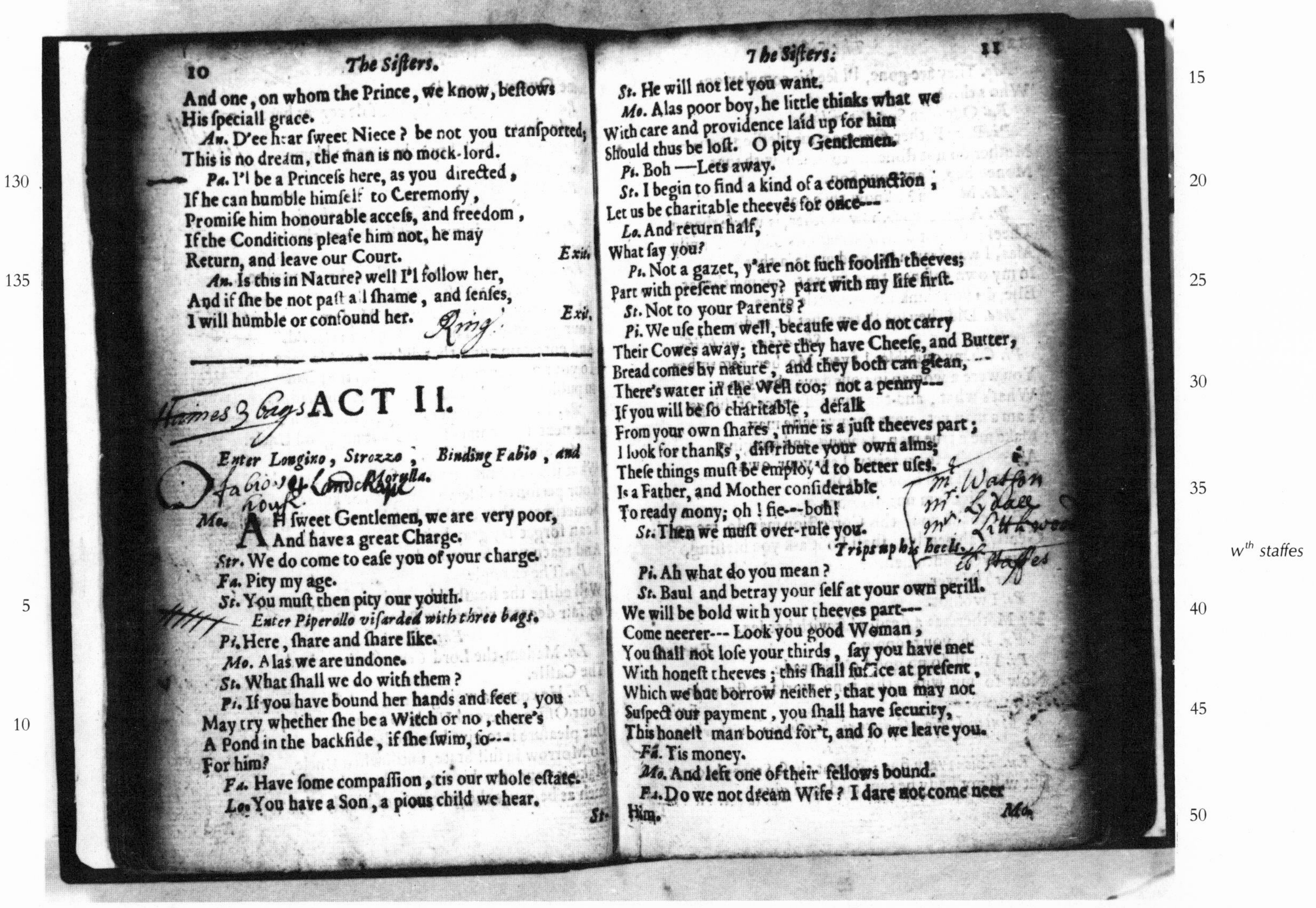

10 *The Sisters.*

And one, on whom the Prince, we know, bestows
His speciall grace.
An. D'ee hear sweet Niece? be not you transported;
This is no dream, the man is no mock-lord.
Pa. I'l be a Princess here, as you directed,
If he can humble himself to Ceremony,
Promise him honourable access, and freedom,
If the Conditions please him not, he may
Return, and leave our Court. *Exit.*
An. Is this in Nature? well I'l follow her,
And if she be not past all shame, and senses,
I will humble or confound her. *Exit.*

ACT II.

Enter Longino, Strozzo, Binding Fabio, and Morulla.

Mo. AH sweet Gentlemen, we are very poor,
And have a great Charge.
Str. We do come to ease you of your charge.
Fa. Pity my age.
St. You must then pity our youth.
Enter Piperollo visarded with three bags.
Pi. Here, share and share like.
Mo. Alas we are undone.
St. What shall we do with them?
Pi. If you have bound her hands and feet, you
May try whether she be a Witch or no, there's
A Pond in the backside, if she swim, so---
For him?
Fa. Have some compassion, tis our whole estate.
Lo. You have a Son, a pious child we hear.
St.

The Sisters. 11

St. He will not let you want.
Mo. Alas poor boy, he little thinks what we
With care and providence laid up for him
Should thus be lost. O pity Gentlemen.
Pi. Boh —Lets away.
St. I begin to find a kind of a compunction;
Let us be charitable theeves for once---
Lo. And return half,
What say you?
Pi. Not a gazet, y'are not such foolish theeves;
Part with present money? part with my life first.
St. Not to your Parents?
Pi. We use them well, because we do not carry
Their Cowes away; there they have Cheese, and Butter,
Bread comes by nature, and they both can glean, --
There's water in the Well too; not a penny---
If you will be so charitable, defalk
From your own shares, mine is a just theeves part;
I look for thanks, distribute your own alms;
These things must be employ'd to better uses.
Is a Father, and Mother considerable
To ready mony; oh! fie---boh!
St. Then we must over-rule you.
Trips up his heels.
Pi. Ah what do you mean?
St. Baul and betray your self at your own perill.
We will be bold with your theeves part---
Come neerer--- Look you good Woman,
You shall not lose your thirds, say you have met
With honest theeves; this shall suffice at present,
Which we but borrow neither, that you may not
Suspect our payment, you shall have security,
This honest man bound for't, and so we leave you.
Fa. Tis money.
Mo. And left one of their fellows bound.
Fa. Do we not dream Wife? I dare not come neer
Him. *Mo.*

wth staffes

II, i, 46. The text is missing an exit stage direction for Longino and Strozzo; the prompter probably should have supplied it, but this is more evidence that he did not concern himself with exits.

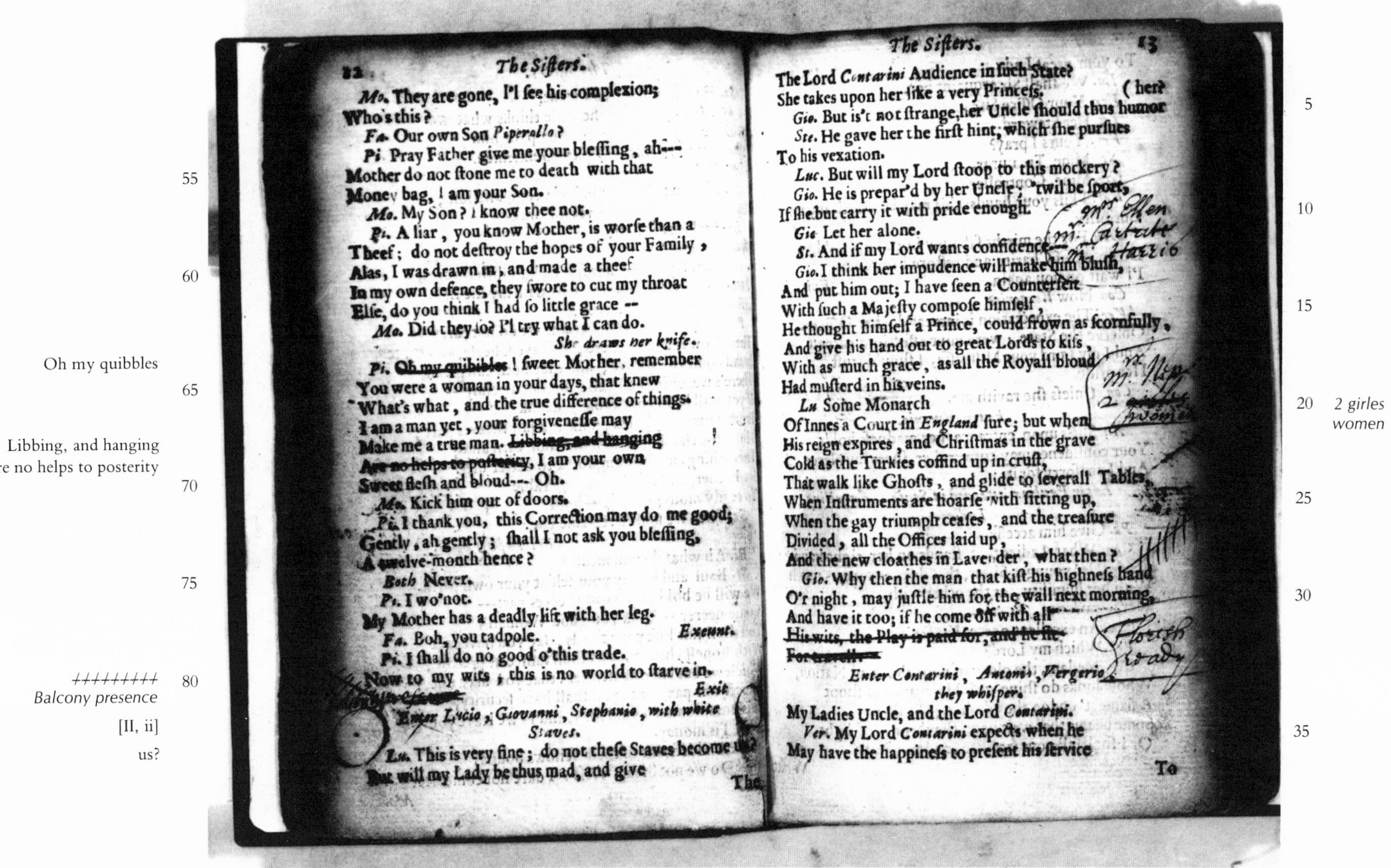

22. The Sisters.

Mo. They are gone, I'l see his complexion;
Who's this?
Fa. Our own Son *Piperallo*?
Pi. Pray Father give me your blessing, ah---
Mother do not stone me to death with that
Money bag, I am your Son.
Mo. My Son? I know thee not.
Pi. A liar, you know Mother, is worse than a
Theef; do not destroy the hopes of your Family,
Alas, I was drawn in, and made a theef
In my own defence, they swore to cut my throat
Else, do you think I had so little grace --
Mo. Did they so? I'l try what I can do.
She draws her knife.
Pi. Oh my quibibles! sweet Mother, remember
You were a woman in your days, that knew
What's what, and the true difference of things.
I am a man yet, your forgivenesse may
Make me a true man. Libbing, and hanging
Are no helps to posterity, I am your own
Sweet flesh and bloud--- Oh.
Mo. Kick him out of doors.
Pi. I thank you, this Correction may do me good;
Gently, ah gently; shall I not ask you blessing,
A twelve-month hence?
Both Never.
Pi. I wo'not.
My Mother has a deadly lift with her leg.
Fa. Boh, you tadpole. *Exeunt.*
Pi. I shall do no good o'this trade.
Now to my wits, this is no world to starve in.
Exit
Enter Lucio, Giovanni, Stephanio, with white Staves.
Lu. This is very fine; do not these Staves become us?
But will my Lady be thus mad, and give
The

The Sisters. 23

The Lord *Contarini* Audience in such State?
She takes upon her like a very Princess. (her?
Gio. But is't not strange, her Uncle should thus humor
Ste. He gave her the first hint, which she pursues
To his vexation.
Luc. But will my Lord stoop to this mockery?
Gio. He is prepar'd by her Uncle; 'twil be sport,
If she but carry it with pride enough.
Gio Let her alone.
St. And if my Lord wants confidence---
Gio. I think her impudence will make him blush,
And put him out; I have seen a Counterfeit
With such a Majesty compose himself,
He thought himself a Prince, could frown as scornfully,
And give his hand out to great Lords to kiss,
With as much grace, as all the Royall bloud
Had musterd in his veins.
Lu Some Monarch
Of Innes a Court in *England* sure; but when
His reign expires, and Christmas in the grave
Cold as the Turkies coffind up in crust,
That walk like Ghosts, and glide to severall Tables,
When Instruments are hoarse with fitting up,
When the gay triumph ceases, and the treasure
Divided, all the Offices laid up,
And the new cloathes in Lavender, what then?
Gio. Why then the man that kist his highness hand
O'r night, may justle him for the wall next morning,
And have it too; if he come off with all---
His wits, the Play is paid for, and he fit
For travell.
Enter Contarini, Antonio, Vergerio,
they whisper.
My Ladies Uncle, and the Lord *Contarini*.
Ver. My Lord *Contarini* expects when he
May have the happiness to present his service
To

Oh my quibbles

Libbing, and hanging
Are no helps to posterity

+++++++++
Balcony presence

[II, ii]

us?

2 girles
women

II, ii, opening. The presence of two circle symbols is probably not significant; the annotator apparently began to put his symbol and note on the right-hand side of the page, near the gutter, found he had insufficient room, and used the left margin instead.

II, ii, 32–33. The canceled lines are: "His wits, the Play is paid for, and he fit / For travell."

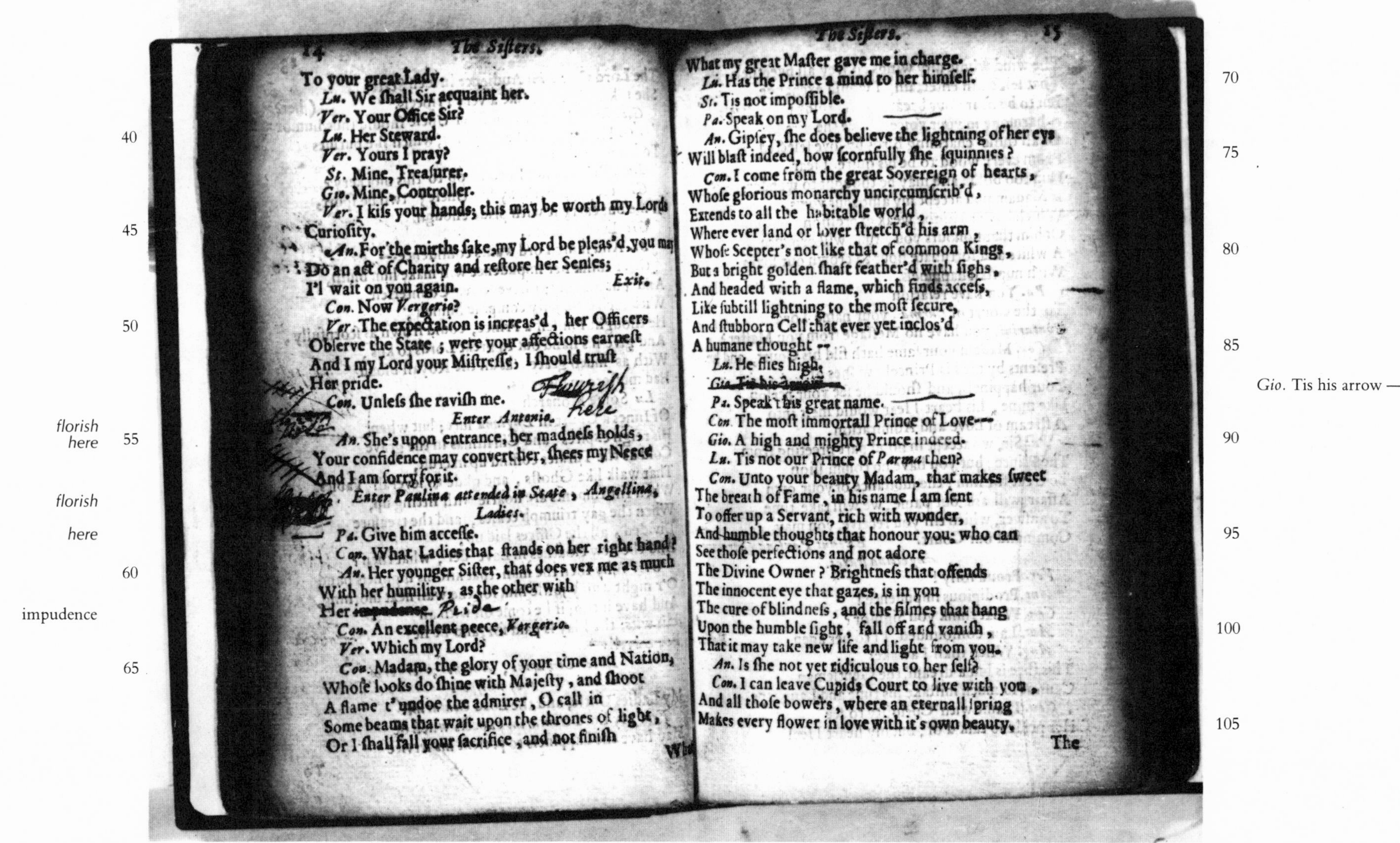

14 The Sisters.

To your great Lady.
Lu. We shall Sir acquaint her.
Ver. Your Office Sir?
Lu. Her Steward.
Ver. Yours I pray?
St. Mine, Treasurer.
Gio. Mine, Controller.
Ver. I kiss your hands; this may be worth my Lords
Curiosity.
An. For the mirths sake, my Lord be pleas'd, you may
Do an act of Charity and restore her Senses;
I'l wait on you again. *Exit.*
Con. Now *Vergerio*?
Ver. The expectation is increas'd, her Officers
Observe the State; were your affections earnest
And I my Lord your Mistresse, I should trust
Her pride.
Con. Unless she ravish me.
Enter Antonio.
An. She's upon entrance, her madness holds,
Your confidence may convert her, shee's my Neece
And I am sorry for it.
Enter Paulina attended in State, Angellina, Ladies.
Pa. Give him accesse.
Con. What Ladies that stands on her right hand?
An. Her younger Sister, that does vex me as much
With her humility, as the other with
Her impudence.
Con. An excellent peece, *Vergerio.*
Ver. Which my Lord?
Con. Madam, the glory of your time and Nation,
Whose looks do shine with Majesty, and shoot
A flame t'undoe the admirer, O call in
Some beams that wait upon the thrones of light,
Or I shall fall your sacrifice, and not finish
What

The Sisters. 15

What my great Master gave me in charge.
Lu. Has the Prince a mind to her himself.
St. Tis not impossible.
Pa. Speak on my Lord.
An. Gipsey, she does believe the lightning of her eys
Will blast indeed, how scornfully she squinnies?
Con. I come from the great Sovereign of hearts,
Whose glorious monarchy uncircumscrib'd,
Extends to all the habitable world,
Where ever land or lover stretch'd his arm,
Whose Scepter's not like that of common Kings,
But a bright golden shaft feather'd with sighs,
And headed with a flame, which finds access,
Like subtill lightning to the most secure,
And stubborn Cell that ever yet inclos'd
A humane thought --
Lu. He flies high.
Pa. Speak this great name.
Con. The most immortall Prince of Love--
Gio. A high and mighty Prince indeed.
Lu. Tis not our Prince of *Parma* then?
Con. Unto your beauty Madam, that makes sweet
The breath of Fame, in his name I am sent
To offer up a Servant, rich with wonder,
And humble thoughts that honour you; who can
See those perfections and not adore
The Divine Owner? Brightness that offends
The innocent eye that gazes, is in you
The cure of blindness, and the filmes that hang
Upon the humble sight, fall off and vanish,
That it may take new life and light from you.
An. Is she not yet ridiculous to her self?
Con. I can leave Cupids Court to live with you,
And all those bowers, where an eternall spring
Makes every flower in love with it's own beauty.
The

florish here

florish

here

impudence

Gio. Tis his arrow —

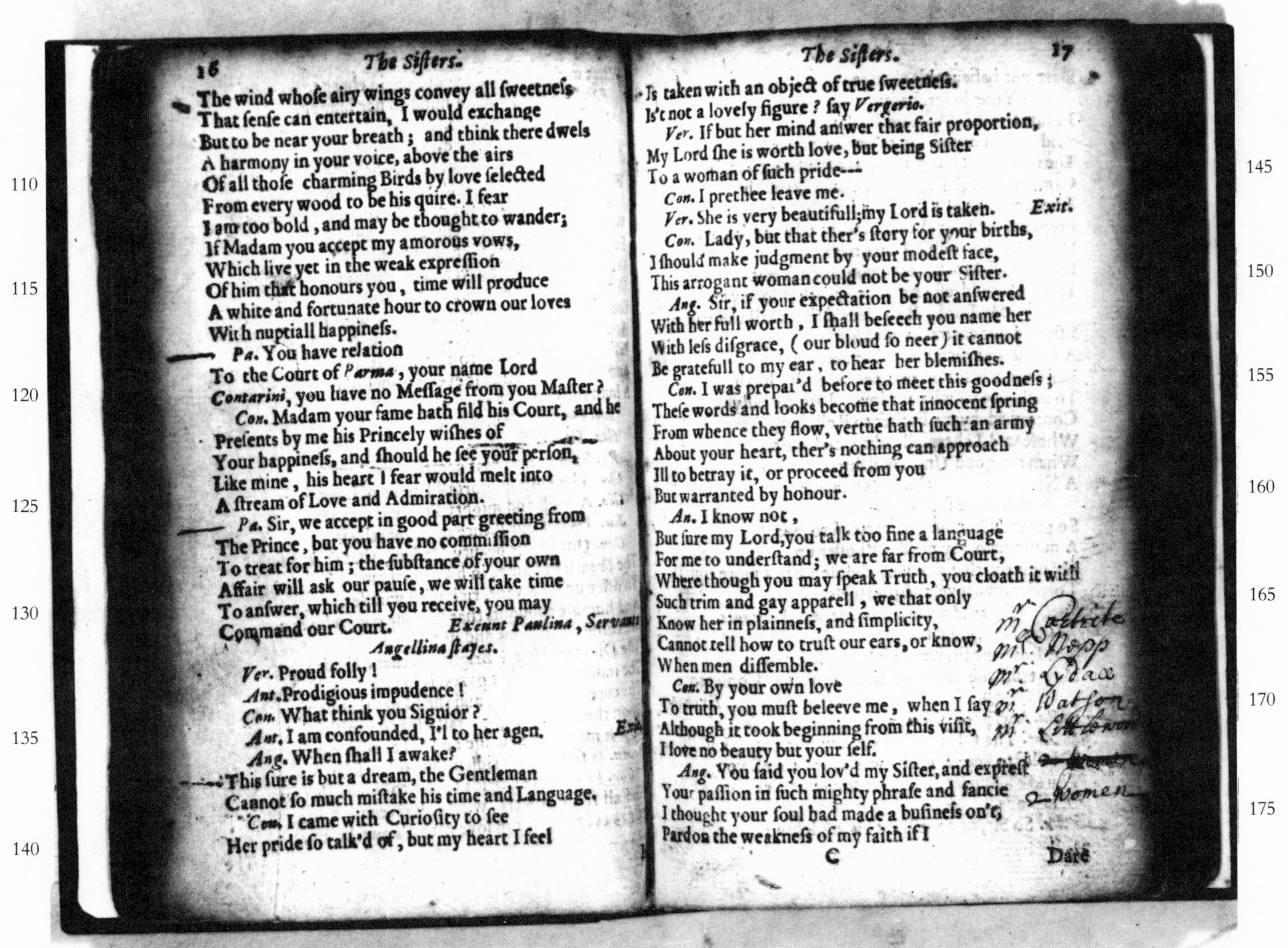

16 *The Siſters.*

The wind whoſe airy wings convey all ſweetneſs
That ſenſe can entertain, I would exchange
But to be near your breath; and think there dwels
A harmony in your voice, above the airs
Of all thoſe charming Birds by love ſelected
From every wood to be his quire. I fear
I am too bold, and may be thought to wander;
If Madam you accept my amorous vows,
Which live yet in the weak expreſſion
Of him that honours you, time will produce
A white and fortunate hour to crown our loves
With nuptiall happineſs.
Pa. You have relation
To the Court of *Parma*, your name Lord
Contarini, you have no Meſſage from you Maſter?
Con. Madam your fame hath fild his Court, and he
Preſents by me his Princely wiſhes of
Your happineſs, and ſhould he ſee your perſon,
Like mine, his heart I fear would melt into
A ſtream of Love and Admiration.
Pa. Sir, we accept in good part greeting from
The Prince, but you have no commiſſion
To treat for him; the ſubſtance of your own
Affair will ask our pauſe, we will take time
To anſwer, which till you receive, you may
Command our Court. *Exeunt Paulina, Servants*
Angellina ſtayes.
Ver. Proud folly!
Ant. Prodigious impudence!
Con. What think you Signior?
Ant. I am confounded, I'l to her agen. *Exit*
Ang. When ſhall I awake?
This ſure is but a dream, the Gentleman
Cannot ſo much miſtake his time and Language.
Con. I came with Curioſity to ſee
Her pride ſo talk'd of, but my heart I feel

The Siſters. 17

Is taken with an object of true ſweetneſs.
Is't not a lovely figure? ſay *Vergerio.*
Ver. If but her mind anſwer that fair proportion,
My Lord ſhe is worth love, but being Siſter
To a woman of ſuch pride---
Con. I prethee leave me.
Ver. She is very beautifull; my Lord is taken. *Exit.*
Con. Lady, but that ther's ſtory for your births,
I ſhould make judgment by your modeſt face,
This arrogant woman could not be your Siſter.
Ang. Sir, if your expectation be not anſwered
With her full worth, I ſhall beſeech you name her
With leſs diſgrace, (our bloud ſo neer) it cannot
Be gratefull to my ear, to hear her blemiſhes.
Con. I was prepar'd before to meet this goodneſs;
Theſe words and looks become that innocent ſpring
From whence they flow, vertue hath ſuch an army
About your heart, ther's nothing can approach
Ill to betray it, or proceed from you
But warranted by honour.
An. I know not,
But ſure my Lord, you talk too fine a language
For me to underſtand; we are far from Court,
Where though you may ſpeak Truth, you cloath it with
Such trim and gay apparell, we that only
Know her in plainneſs, and ſimplicity,
Cannot tell how to truſt our ears, or know,
When men diſſemble.
Con. By your own love
To truth, you muſt beleeve me, when I ſay mr Watson
Although it took beginning from this viſit,
I love no beauty but your ſelf.
Ang. You ſaid you lov'd my Siſter, and expreſt
Your paſſion in ſuch mighty phraſe and fancie 2 Women
I thought your ſoul had made a buſineſs on't,
Pardon the weakneſs of my faith if I
C Dare

II, ii, 173. The prompter apparently began to write *2 girles* but changed to *2 women* part way through, ending up with a confusing note that had to be deleted and rewritten.

(pardon sweet Virgin)

18 *The Siſters.*

Dare not believe this change.
Con. Your Siſter, Lady,
I came to viſit, not affect, I heard,
And had a purpoſe but to try how neer
The wonder of her pride (pardon ſweet Virgin)
Came to a truth, nor did I Court her with
The language of a meaning lover; but
Prepared by your Vncle, meant to make her ſee
Her miſerable folly; I dare not
Preſent ſuch Mockeries to you; ſuſpect not
This haſty addreſs; by your fair ſelf, I love you.
Ang. My Lord, If I beleev'd this, reall Courtſhip,
I ſhould not entertain your honour with a
A fruitleſs Expectation, but declare,
Beſides my want of fortune, beauty, birth,
To make me worth your love, I am already
Contracted by my Father to Religion,
Whoſe will I cheerfully obey, and wait
When my good Uncle will diſpoſe me to
A Nunnery. *Con.* A Nunnery?
Ang. Where for
So great an honour you pretend to me
A moſt unworthy maid, I'l offer up
My prayers, that you may chooſe a heart more equall
To your own love, and greatneſs.
Enter Antonio, Paulina, and Servants.
Con. Nay you muſt
Not leave me ſo, we are interrupted, you
May truſt me fair one with a neerer Conference.
Exeunt.
Pa. Alas poor old man.
Ant. The Old man before your borrowed Ladiſhip
Is bold to keep his head warm, and to tell you
You are a Puppet, take that to your titles
Of honour.
Pa. So Sir, none reſtrain his inſolence?
Ant.

The Siſters. 19

Ant. I'l make him ſwallow down his ſtaff of Office
That ſtirs. I ha'not done. Canſt be ſo impudent
To think his Lordſhip does not laugh at thee?
Your eys the thrones of light? a brace of Lanthorns,
In which two ſnuffs of Candle cloſe to th'ſocket,
Appear like fire-drakes, and will ſerve to light
A traveller into a Ditch. You Madam Majeſty,
And the glory of a Nation?
Tho'art a diſeaſe to Honour, Modeſty,
A Feaver in thy Fathers bloud, a Gangreen
Upon his name, a Pox upon thee for't;
Ther's one diſeaſe more, yet I have not done.
Pa. My Charity may invite, if theſe fits hold,
Some cloſe proviſion for you 'mong mad men;
I do command you leave my houſe.
Ant. I wo'not,
I'l fire the houſe; doſt hear? thou wo't burn well,
Th'aſt Oil enough about thy face, and all
Thy body Pitch, very combuſtible.
But I'l not be damn'd for thee, now I think on't,
And ſince no Counſell will prevail, I'l ſave
My ſelf. Before I go, give but a reaſon
Why thou doſt ſlight this gallant Lord, and ſquint
As if he were Groom or Foot man.
Pa. I'l tell you,
You would have the truth.
Ant. If thou canſt ſpeak any.
Pa. I do eſteem my ſelf
More equall for his Maſter.
Ant. Who, the Prince?
Pa. No, the blind Prince of Love, you are wiſe Uncle,
But I am out of Poetry.
Ant. I think I were beſt cut off thy head, and ſave
The Laws a labour--- Ther's no talking to her.
Pa. I am of your mind Uncle, you may edifie
Your charge, my younger Siſter, ſhe's not proud,
C2 Pray

Your eys the thrones of light? a brace of

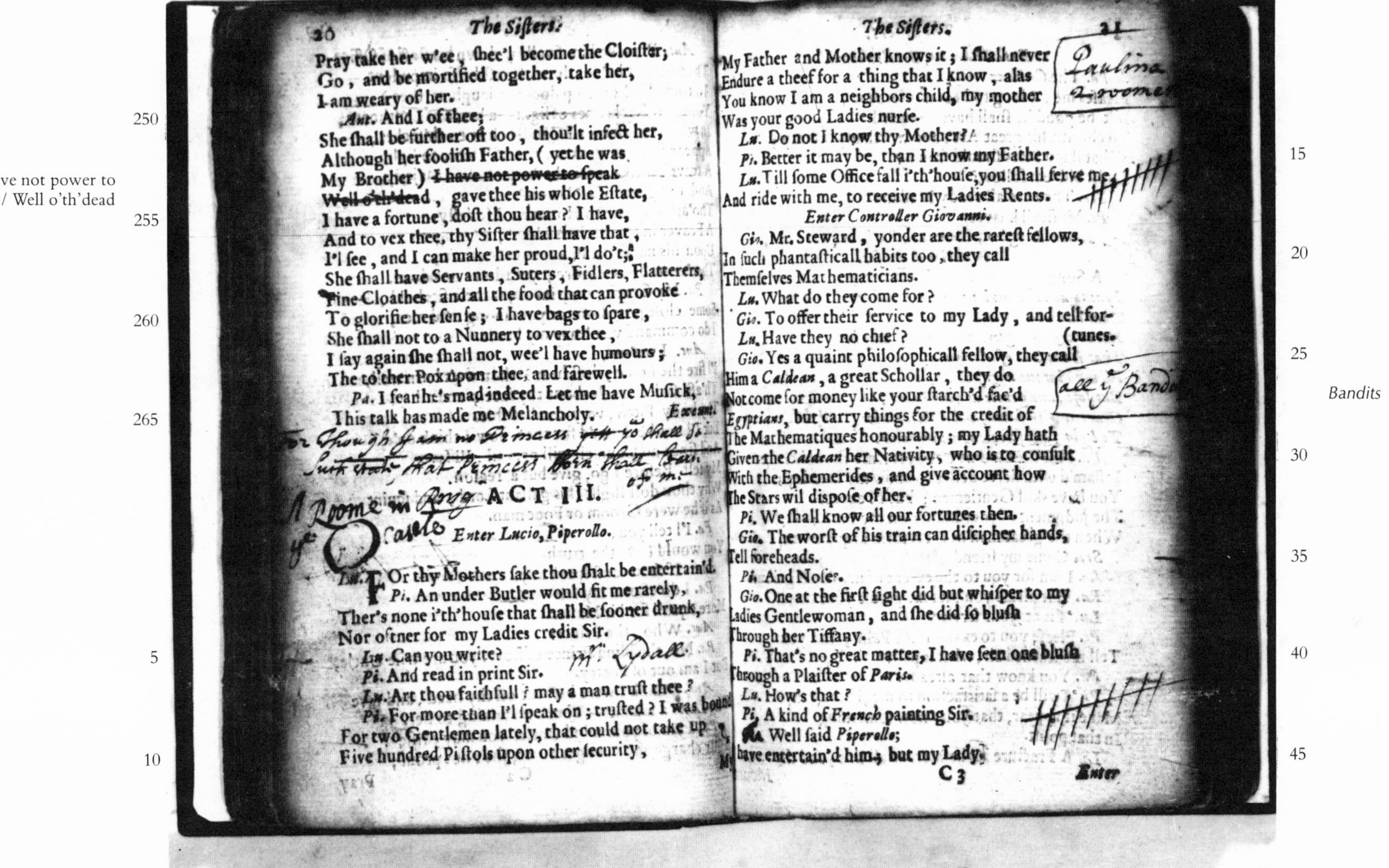

20 *The Sisters.*

Pray take her w'ee, shee'l become the Cloister;
Go, and be mortified together, take her,
I am weary of her.
Ant. And I of thee;
She shall be further off too, thou'lt infect her,
Although her foolish Father, (yet he was
My Brother) ~~I have not power to speak~~
~~Well o'th'dead~~, gave thee his whole Estate,
I have a fortune, dost thou hear? I have,
And to vex thee, thy Sister shall have that,
I'l see, and I can make her proud, I'l do't;
She shall have Servants, Suters, Fidlers, Flatterers,
Fine Cloathes, and all the food that can provoke
To glorifie her sense; I have bags to spare,
She shall not to a Nunnery to vex thee,
I say again she shall not, wee'l have humours;
The to'ther Pox upon thee, and farewell.
Pa. I fear he's mad indeed. Let me have Musick,
This talk has made me Melancholy. *Exeunt.*

For Though I am no Princess ~~yett~~ yo^u^ shall se
Such state that Princess born shall learn of me.

A Roome in ye Castle ACT III.

Enter Lucio, Piperollo.

Lu. For thy Mothers sake thou shalt be entertain'd.
Pi. An under Butler would fit me rarely,
Ther's none i'th'house that shall be sooner drunk,
Nor oftner for my Ladies credit Sir.
Lu. Can you write? m^r^ Lydall
Pi. And read in print Sir.
Lu. Art thou faithfull? may a man trust thee?
Pi. For more than I'l speak on; trusted? I was bound
For two Gentlemen lately, that could not take up
Five hundred Pistols upon other security,

The Sisters. 21

Paulina
2 women

My Father and Mother knows it; I shall never
Endure a theef for a thing that I know, alas
You know I am a neighbors child, my mother
Was your good Ladies nurse.
Lu. Do not I know thy Mother?
Pi. Better it may be, than I know my Father.
Lu. Till some Office fall i'th'house, you shall serve me,
And ride with me, to receive my Ladies Rents.

Enter Controller Giovanni.

Gio. Mr. Steward, yonder are the rarest fellows,
In such phantasticall habits too, they call
Themselves Mathematicians.
Lu. What do they come for?
Gio. To offer their service to my Lady, and tell for-
Lu. Have they no chief? (tunes.
Gio. Yes a quaint philosophicall fellow, they call
Him a *Caldean*, a great Schollar, they do
Not come for money like your starch'd fac'd
Egyptians, but carry things for the credit of
The Mathematiques honourably; my Lady hath
Given the *Caldean* her Nativity, who is to consult
With the Ephemerides, and give account how
The Stars wil dispose of her.
Pi. We shall know all our fortunes then.
Gio. The worst of his train can discipher hands,
Tell foreheads.
Pi. And Noses.
Gio. One at the first sight did but whisper to my
Ladies Gentlewoman, and she did so blush
Through her Tiffany.
Pi. That's no great matter, I have seen one blush
Through a Plaister of *Paris.*
Lu. How's that?
Pi. A kind of *French* painting Sir.
Lu. Well said *Piperollo*;
have entertain'd him, but my Lady.

all ye Bandits

C3 *Enter*

I have not power to speak / Well o'th'dead

Bandits

II, ii, 266–67. Paulina's added lines are: *For Though I am no Princess ~~yett~~ yo^w^ shall se / Such state that Princess born shall learn of me.*

III, i, 44. The prompter's *Lu* is written directly over the incorrect printed "*Gio.*"

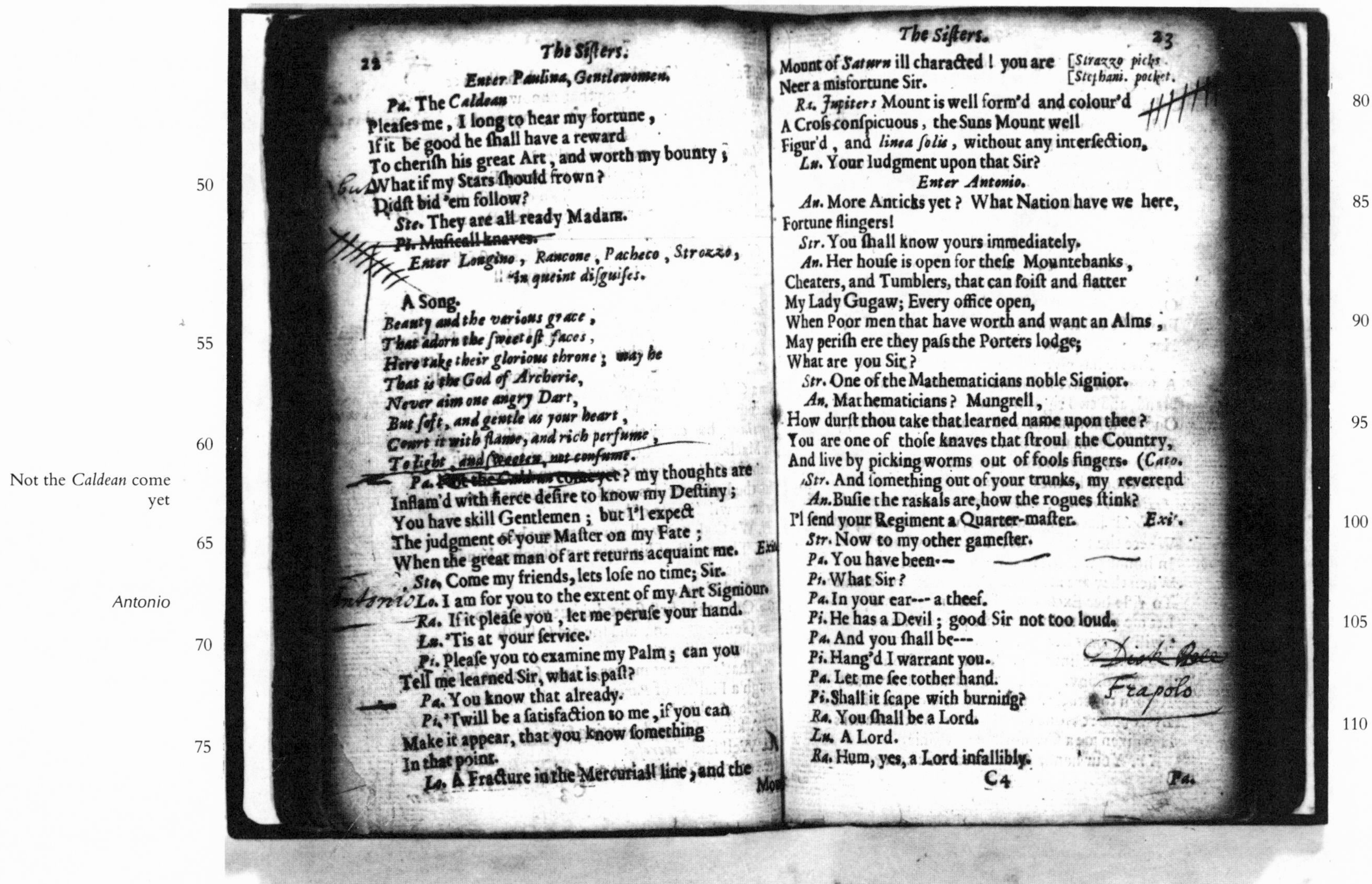

The Sisters. 22

Enter Paulina, Gentlewomen.

Pa. The Caldean
Pleases me, I long to hear my fortune,
If it be good he shall have a reward
To cherish his great Art, and worth my bounty;
What if my Stars should frown?
Didst bid 'em follow?
Ste. They are all ready Madam.
Pi. Musicall knaves.

Enter Longino, Rancone, Pacheco, Strozzo, in queint disguises.

A Song.
Beauty and the various grace,
That adorn the sweetest faces,
Here take their glorious throne; may be
That is the God of Archerie,
Never aim one angry Dart,
But soft, and gentle as your heart,
Court it with flame, and rich perfume,
To light, and sweeten, not consume.

Pa. Is not the Caldean come yet? my thoughts are
Inflam'd with fierce desire to know my Destiny;
You have skill Gentlemen; but I'l expect
The judgment of your Master on my Fate;
When the great man of art returns acquaint me. Exit.
Ste. Come my friends, lets lose no time; Sir.
Lo. I am for you to the extent of my Art Signiour.
Ra. If it please you, let me peruse your hand.
Lu. 'Tis at your service.
Pi. Please you to examine my Palm; can you
Tell me learned Sir, what is past?
Pa. You know that already.
Pi. 'Twill be a satisfaction to me, if you can
Make it appear, that you know something
In that point.
Lo. A Fracture in the Mercuriall line, and the
Mount

Not the *Caldean* come yet

Antonio

The Sisters. 23

Mount of Saturn ill characted! you are [Strozzo picks
Neer a misfortune Sir. [Stephani. pocket.
Ra. Jupiters Mount is well form'd and colour'd
A Cross conspicuous, the Suns Mount well
Figur'd, and linea solis, without any interfection.
Lu. Your Judgment upon that Sir?

Enter Antonio.

An. More Anticks yet? What Nation have we here,
Fortune flingers!
Str. You shall know yours immediately.
An. Her house is open for these Mountebanks,
Cheaters, and Tumblers, that can foist and flatter
My Lady Gugaw; Every office open,
When Poor men that have worth and want an Alms,
May perish ere they pass the Porters lodge;
What are you Sir?
Str. One of the Mathematicians noble Signior.
An. Mathematicians? Mungrell,
How durst thou take that learned name upon thee?
You are one of those knaves that stroul the Country,
And live by picking worms out of fools fingers. (Cato.
Str. And something out of your trunks, my reverend
An. Busie the raskals are, how the rogues stink?
I'l send your Regiment a Quarter-master. Exit.
Str. Now to my other gamester.
Pa. You have been---
Pi. What Sir?
Pa. In your ear--- a theef.
Pi. He has a Devil; good Sir not too loud.
Pa. And you shall be---
Pi. Hang'd I warrant you.
Pa. Let me see tother hand.
Pi. Shall it scape with burning?
Ra. You shall be a Lord.
Lu. A Lord.
Ra. Hum, yes, a Lord infallibly.
C4 Pa.

Frapolo

III, i, 53–61. The whole song was obviously cut; perhaps the young people in the company did not have a singer among their number. The entrance of the bandits, though seemingly cut along with the song, is cued and would certainly have come at this point. Stephanio has some lines just before and after the cut song, but no stage direction indicates when he entered; he probably came in with Paulina. The prompter should have inserted a note.

III, i, 107. As later notes make clear, Bell did indeed play Frapolo; to find his name deleted here is strange, but perhaps the prompter did not want to confuse himself with a note that might appear to be a warning for two characters instead of one.

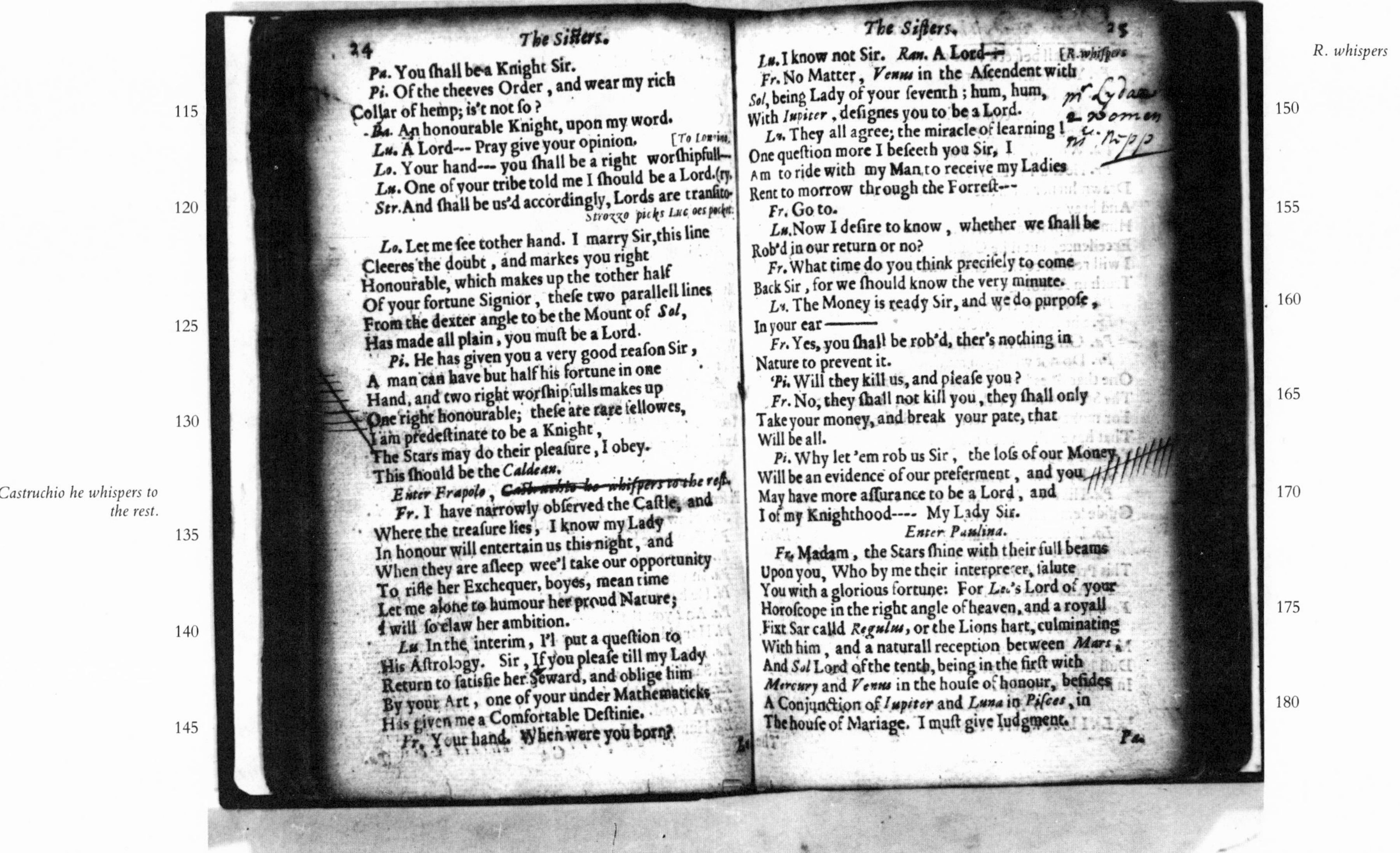

R. whispers

Castruchio he whispers to the rest.

24 *The Siſters.*

Pa. You ſhall be a Knight Sir.
Pi. Of the theeves Order, and wear my rich
Collar of hemp; is't not ſo?
Ba. An honourable Knight, upon my word.
Lu. A Lord--- Pray give your opinion. [*To Lonvino.*
Lo. Your hand--- you ſhall be a right worſhipfull—
Lu. One of your tribe told me I ſhould be a Lord.(ry.
Str. And ſhall be us'd accordingly, Lords are tranſito-
Strozzo picks Lucoes pocket.
Lo. Let me ſee tother hand. I marry Sir, this line
Cleeres the doubt, and markes you right
Honourable, which makes up the tother half
Of your fortune Signior, theſe two parallell lines
From the dexter angle to be the Mount of *Sol*,
Has made all plain, you muſt be a Lord.
Pi. He has given you a very good reaſon Sir,
A man can have but half his fortune in one
Hand, and two right worſhipfulls makes up
One right honourable; theſe are rare fellowes,
I am predeſtinate to be a Knight,
The Stars may do their pleaſure, I obey.
This ſhould be the *Caldean.*
Enter Frapolo, ~~*Castruchio he whiſpers to the reſt.*~~
Fr. I have narrowly obſerved the Caſtle, and
Where the treaſure lies, I know my Lady
In honour will entertain us this night, and
When they are aſleep wee'l take our opportunity
To rifle her Exchequer, boyes, mean time
Let me alone to humour her proud Nature;
I will ſo claw her ambition.
Lu. In the interim, I'l put a queſtion to
His Aſtrology. Sir, If you pleaſe till my Lady
Return to ſatisfie her Seward, and oblige him
By your Art, one of your under Mathematicks
Has given me a Comfortable Deſtinie.
Fr. Your hand. When were you born?

The Siſters. 25

Lu. I know not Sir. *Ran.* A Lord— [*R. whiſpers*
Fr. No Matter, *Venus* in the Aſcendent with
Sol, being Lady of your ſeventh; hum, hum,
With *Iupiter*, deſignes you to be a Lord.
Lu. They all agree; the miracle of learning!
One queſtion more I beſeech you Sir, I
Am to ride with my Man to receive my Ladies
Rent to morrow through the Forreſt---
Fr. Go to.
Lu. Now I deſire to know, whether we ſhall be
Rob'd in our return or no?
Fr. What time do you think preciſely to come
Back Sir, for we ſhould know the very minute.
Lu. The Money is ready Sir, and we do purpoſe,
In your ear———
Fr. Yes, you ſhall be rob'd, ther's nothing in
Nature to prevent it.
Pi. Will they kill us, and pleaſe you?
Fr. No, they ſhall not kill you, they ſhall only
Take your money, and break your pate, that
Will be all.
Pi. Why let 'em rob us Sir, the loſs of our Money,
Will be an evidence of our preferment, and you
May have more aſſurance to be a Lord, and
I of my Knighthood---- My Lady Sir.
Enter Paulina.
Fr. Madam, the Stars ſhine with their full beams
Upon you, Who by me their interpreter, ſalute
You with a glorious fortune: For *Leo's* Lord of your
Horoſcope in the right angle of heaven, and a royall
Fixt Sar calld *Regulus*, or the Lions hart, culminating
With him, and a naturall reception between *Mars*,
And *Sol* Lord of the tenth, being in the firſt with
Mercury and *Venus* in the houſe of honour, beſides
A Conjunction of *Iupiter* and *Luna* in *Piſces*, in
The houſe of Mariage. I muſt give Iudgment.
Pa.

III, i, following 133. With a stroke of the pen the mute character of Castruchio was dropped from the cast of characters, but even the author forgot him, for his name is not among the dramatis personae.

III, i, 171. The prompter should have added Giovanni and the two women to the entrance stage direction, since they were warned to enter with Paulina.

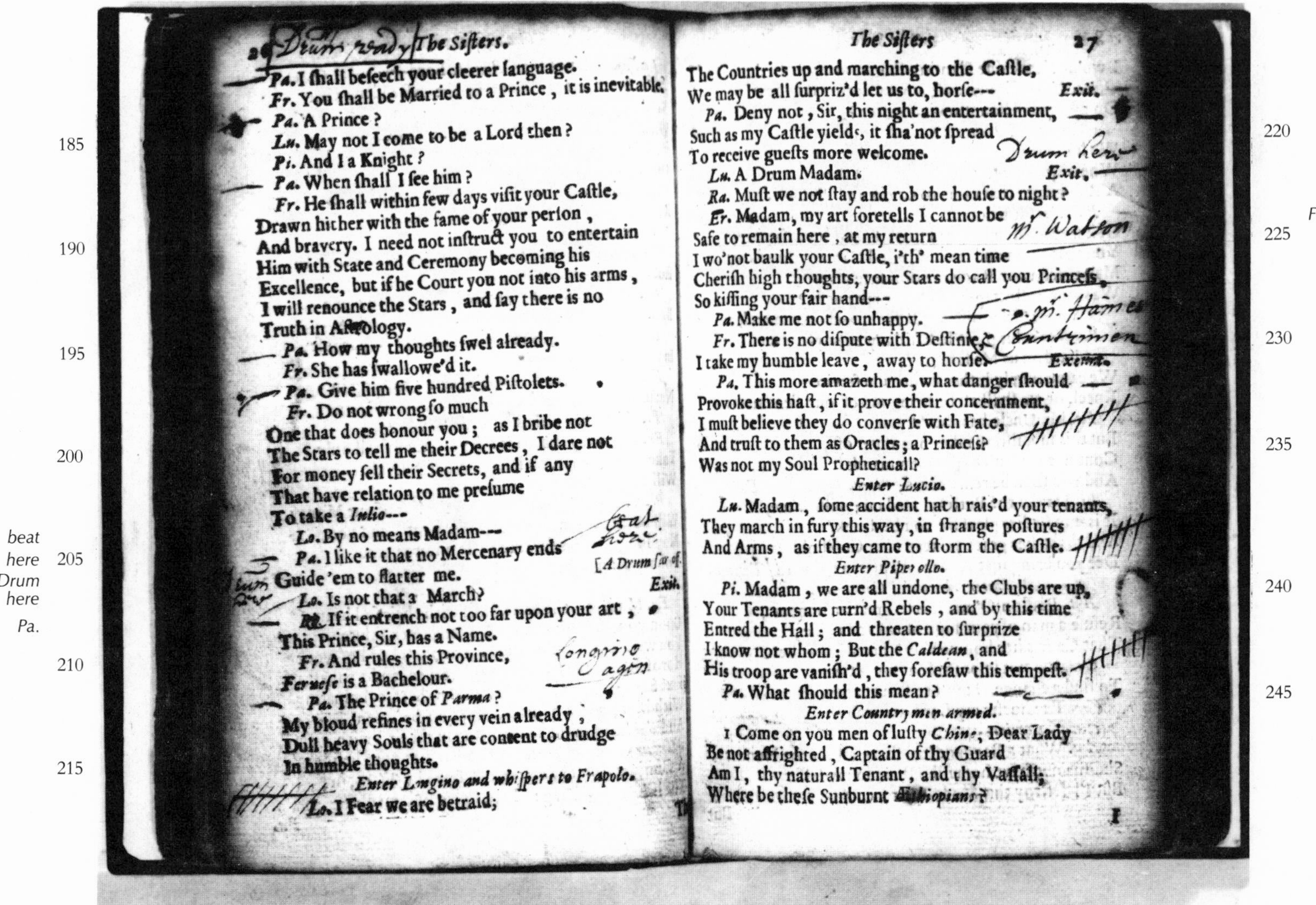

26 Drum ready The Sisters.

Pa. I shall beseech your cleerer language.
Fr. You shall be Married to a Prince, it is inevitable.
Pa. A Prince?
Lu. May not I come to be a Lord then?
Pi. And I a Knight?
Pa. When shall I see him?
Fr. He shall within few days visit your Castle,
Drawn hither with the fame of your person,
And bravery. I need not instruct you to entertain
Him with State and Ceremony becoming his
Excellence, but if he Court you not into his arms,
I will renounce the Stars, and say there is no
Truth in Astrology.
Pa. How my thoughts swel already.
Fr. She has swallowe'd it.
Pa. Give him five hundred Pistolets.
Fr. Do not wrong so much
One that does honour you; as I bribe not
The Stars to tell me their Decrees, I dare not
For money sell their Secrets, and if any
That have relation to me presume
To take a *Iulio*---
Lo. By no means Madam--- beat here
Pa. I like it that no Mercenary ends [*A Drum far of.*
Guide 'em to flatter me. *Exit.*
Lo. Is not that a March?
Pa. If it entrench not too far upon your art,
This Prince, Sir, has a Name.
Fr. And rules this Province, Longino agin
Ferneze is a Bachelour.
Pa. The Prince of *Parma*?
My bloud refines in every vein already;
Dull heavy Souls that are content to drudge
In humble thoughts.
Enter Longino and whispers to Frapolo.
Lo. I Fear we are betraid;

The Sisters 27

The Countries up and marching to the Castle,
We may be all surpriz'd let us to, horse--- *Exit.*
Pa. Deny not, Sir, this night an entertainment,
Such as my Castle yields, it sha'not spread
To receive guests more welcome. Drum here
Lu. A Drum Madam. *Exit.*
Ra. Must we not stay and rob the house to night?
Fr. Madam, my art foretells I cannot be
Safe to remain here, at my return Mr. Watson
I wo'not baulk your Castle, i'th' mean time
Cherish high thoughts, your Stars do call you Princess,
So kissing your fair hand---
Pa. Make me not so unhappy. Mr. Hames
Fr. There is no dispute with Destinie, & Countrimen
I take my humble leave, away to horse. *Exeunt.*
Pa. This more amazeth me, what danger should
Provoke this hast, if it prove their concernment,
I must believe they do converse with Fate,
And trust to them as Oracles; a Princess?
Was not my Soul Propheticall?
Enter Lucio.
Lu. Madam, some accident hath rais'd your tenants,
They march in fury this way, in strange postures
And Arms, as if they came to storm the Castle.
Enter Piperollo.
Pi. Madam, we are all undone, the Clubs are up,
Your Tenants are turn'd Rebels, and by this time
Entred the Hall; and threaten to surprize
I know not whom; But the *Caldean*, and
His troop are vanish'd, they foresaw this tempest.
Pa. What should this mean?
Enter Country men armed.
1 Come on you men of lusty *Chine*; Dear Lady
Be not affrighted, Captain of thy Guard
Am I, thy naturall Tenant, and thy Vassall;
Where be these Sunburnt *Æthiopians*?

I

beat here
Drum here
Pa.
Fr.

III, i, preceding 182. The small cross-hatch mark above the *Drum ready* warning must be a doodle, not a cue symbol. This single warning serves for a sequence of drum cues.

III, i, 206–44. The rapid sequence of cues and warnings would have kept the prompter very busy; he could not have managed without an assistant.

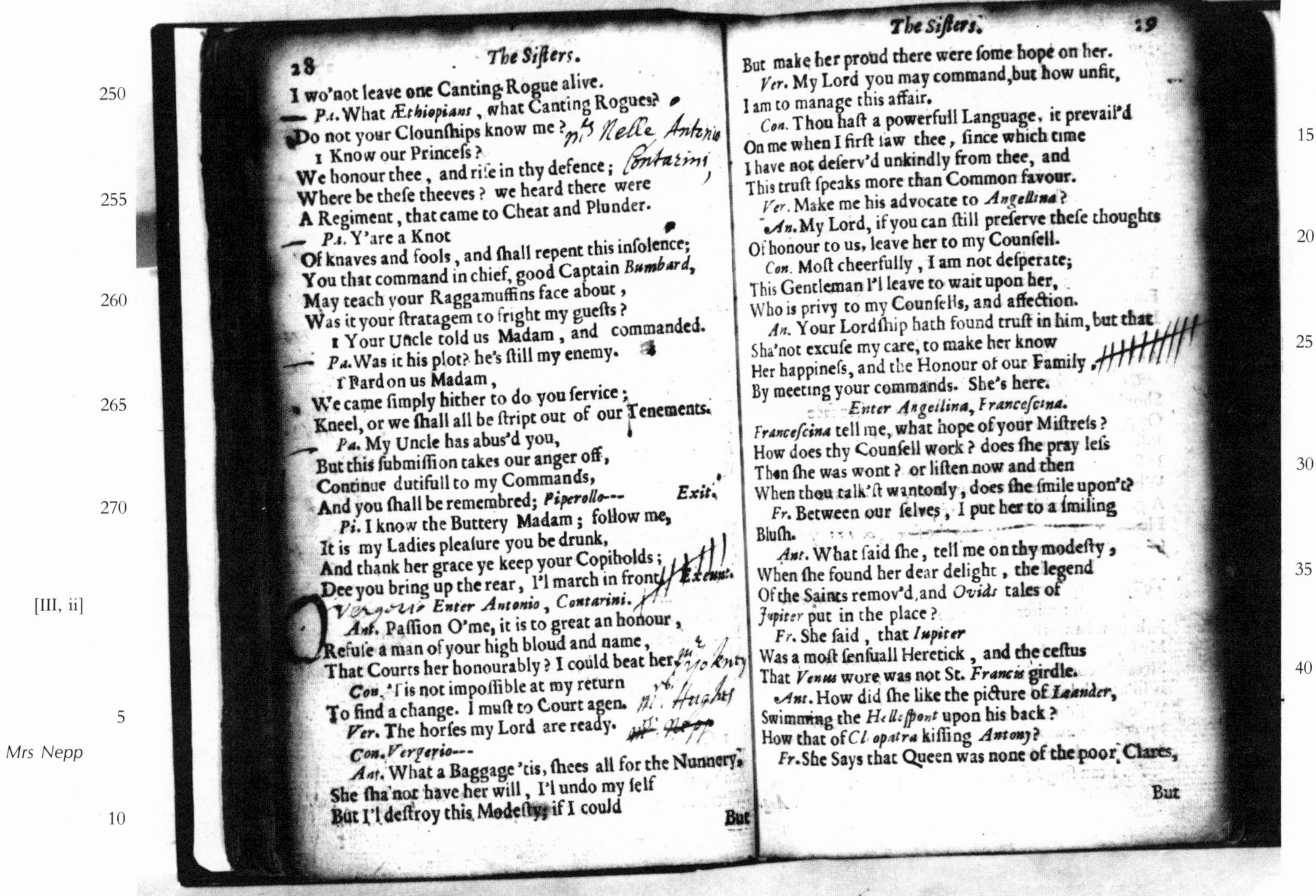

28 *The Siſters.*

I wo'not leave one Canting Rogue alive.
Pi. What *Æthiopians*, what Canting Rogues?
Do not your Clounſhips know me?
1 Know our Princeſs?
We honour thee, and riſe in thy defence;
Where be theſe theeves? we heard there were
A Regiment, that came to Cheat and Plunder.
Pi. Y'are a Knot
Of knaves and fools, and ſhall repent this inſolence;
You that command in chief, good Captain *Bumbard*,
May teach your Raggamuffins face about,
Was it your ſtratagem to fright my gueſts?
1 Your Uncle told us Madam, and commanded.
Pa. Was it his plot? he's ſtill my enemy.
1 Pardon us Madam,
We came ſimply hither to do you ſervice;
Kneel, or we ſhall all be ſtript out of our Tenements.
Pa. My Uncle has abus'd you,
But this ſubmiſſion takes our anger off,
Continue dutifull to my Commands,
And you ſhall be remembred; *Piperollo*--- *Exit.*
Pi. I know the Buttery Madam; follow me,
It is my Ladies pleaſure you be drunk,
And thank her grace ye keep your Copiholds;
Dee you bring up the rear, I'l march in front. *Exeunt.*
[III, ii] *Enter Antonio, Contarini.*
Ant. Paſſion O'me, it is to great an honour,
Refuſe a man of your high bloud and name,
That Courts her honourably? I could beat her.
Con. 'Tis not impoſſible at my return
To find a change. I muſt to Court agen.
Ver. The horſes my Lord are ready.
Mrs Nepp *Con. Vergerio*---
Ant. What a Baggage 'tis, ſhees all for the Nunnery.
She ſha'not have her will, I'l undo my ſelf
But I'l deſtroy this Modeſty, if I could
But

The Siſters. 29

But make her proud there were ſome hope on her.
Ver. My Lord you may command, but how unfit,
I am to manage this affair.
Con. Thou haſt a powerfull Language, it prevail'd
On me when I firſt ſaw thee, ſince which time
I have not deſerv'd unkindly from thee, and
This truſt ſpeaks more than Common favour.
Ver. Make me his advocate to *Angellina*?
An. My Lord, if you can ſtill preſerve theſe thoughts
Of honour to us, leave her to my Counſell.
Con. Moſt cheerfully, I am not deſperate;
This Gentleman I'l leave to wait upon her,
Who is privy to my Counſells, and affection.
An. Your Lordſhip hath found truſt in him, but that
Sha'not excuſe my care, to make her know
Her happineſs, and the Honour of our Family
By meeting your commands. She's here.
Enter Angellina, Franceſcina.
Franceſcina tell me, what hope of your Miſtreſs?
How does thy Counſell work? does ſhe pray leſs
Then ſhe was wont? or liſten now and then
When thou talk'ſt wantonly, does ſhe ſmile upon't?
Fr. Between our ſelves, I put her to a ſmiling
Bluſh.
Ant. What ſaid ſhe, tell me on thy modeſty,
When ſhe found her dear delight, the legend
Of the Saints remov'd, and *Ovids* tales of
Jupiter put in the place?
Fr. She ſaid, that *Jupiter*
Was a moſt ſenſuall Heretick, and the ceſtus
That *Venus* wore was not St. *Francis* girdle.
Ant. How did ſhe like the picture of *Leander*,
Swimming the *Hellespont* upon his back?
How that of *Cleopatra* kiſſing *Antony*?
Fr. She Says that Queen was none of the poor Clares,
But

III, ii, opening. The stage direction omits Vergerio, and the prompter dutifully added the name, but the machinist forgot to indicate what setting was to be used.

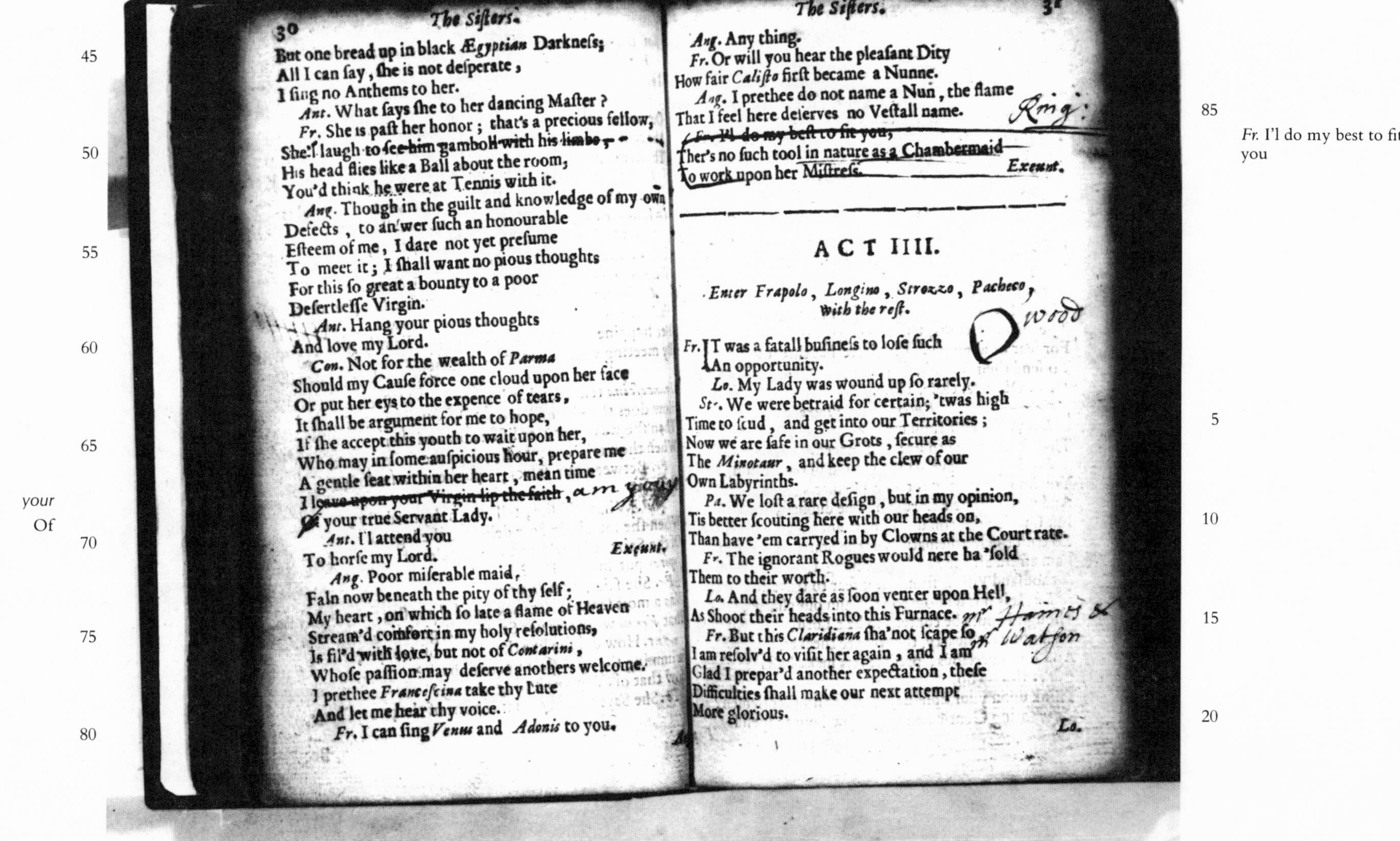

30 The Siſters.

But one bread up in black *Ægyptian* Darkneſs;
All I can ſay, ſhe is not deſperate,
I ſing no Anthems to her.
Ant. What ſays ſhe to her dancing Maſter?
Fr. She is paſt her honor; that's a precious fellow,
She'l laugh to ſee him gamboll with his limbs,
His head flies like a Ball about the room,
You'd think he were at Tennis with it.
Ang. Though in the guilt and knowledge of my own
Defects, to anſwer ſuch an honourable
Eſteem of me, I dare not yet preſume
To meet it; I ſhall want no pious thoughts
For this ſo great a bounty to a poor
Deſertleſſe Virgin.
Ant. Hang your pious thoughts
And love my Lord.
Con. Not for the wealth of *Parma*
Should my Cauſe force one cloud upon her face
Or put her eys to the expence of tears,
It ſhall be argument for me to hope,
If ſhe accept this youth to wait upon her,
Who may in ſome auſpicious hour, prepare me
A gentle ſeat within her heart, mean time
I leave upon your Virgin-lip the faith, am your
Of your true Servant Lady.
Ant. I'l attend you
To horſe my Lord. *Exeunt.*
Ang. Poor miſerable maid,
Faln now beneath the pity of thy ſelf;
My heart, on which ſo late a flame of Heaven
Stream'd comfort in my holy reſolutions,
Is fil'd with love, but not of *Contarini*,
Whoſe paſſion may deſerve anothers welcome.
I prethee *Franceſcina* take thy Lute
And let me hear thy voice.
Fr. I can ſing *Venus* and *Adonis* to you.

The Siſters. 31

Ang. Any thing.
Fr. Or will you hear the pleaſant Dity
How fair *Caliſto* firſt became a Nunne.
Ang. I prethee do not name a Nun, the flame
That I feel here deſerves no Veſtall name. Ring:
Fr. I'l do my beſt to fit you,
Ther's no ſuch tool in nature as a Chambermaid
To work upon her Miſtreſs. *Exeunt.*

ACT IIII.

Enter Frapolo, Longino, Strozzo, Pacheco, with the reſt. wood

Fr. It was a fatall buſineſs to loſe ſuch
An opportunity.
Lo. My Lady was wound up ſo rarely.
St. We were betraid for certain; 'twas high
Time to ſcud, and get into our Territories;
Now we are ſafe in our Grots, ſecure as
The *Minotaur*, and keep the clew of our
Own Labyrinths.
Pa. We loſt a rare deſign, but in my opinion,
Tis better ſcouting here with our heads on,
Than have 'em carryed in by Clowns at the Court rate.
Fr. The ignorant Rogues would nere ha 'ſold
Them to their worth.
Lo. And they dare as ſoon venter upon Hell,
As Shoot their heads into this Furnace. Mr Hamnes & Mr Watson
Fr. But this *Claridiana* ſha'not ſcape ſo,
I am reſolv'd to viſit her again, and I am
Glad I prepar'd another expectation, theſe
Difficulties ſhall make our next attempt
More glorious.
Lo.

your
Of

Fr. I'l do my best to fit you

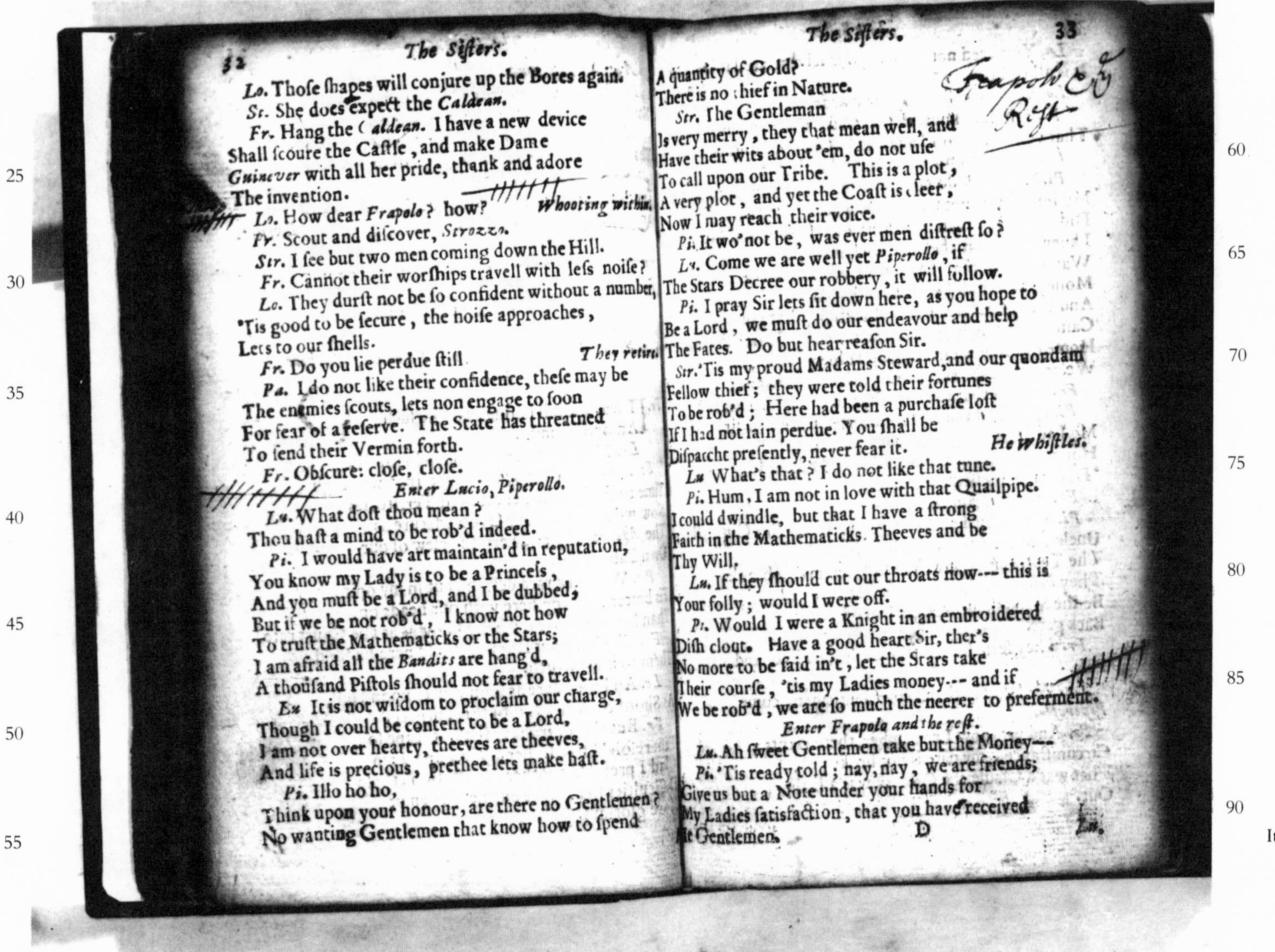

32 *The Siſters.*

Lo. Thoſe ſhapes will conjure up the Bores again.
St. She does expect the *Caldean.*
Fr. Hang the *Caldean.* I have a new device
Shall ſcoure the Caſtle, and make Dame
Guinever with all her pride, thank and adore
The invention.
Lo. How dear *Frapolo?* how? *Whooting within.*
Fr. Scout and diſcover, *Strozzo.*
Str. I ſee but two men coming down the Hill.
Fr. Cannot their worſhips travell with leſs noiſe?
Lo. They durſt not be ſo confident without a number,
'Tis good to be ſecure, the noiſe approaches,
Lets to our ſhells.
Fr. Do you lie perdue ſtill. *They retire.*
Pa. I do not like their confidence, theſe may be
The enemies ſcouts, lets non engage to ſoon
For fear of a reſerve. The State has threatned
To ſend their Vermin forth.
Fr. Obſcure: cloſe, cloſe.
Enter Lucio, Piperollo.
Lu. What doſt thou mean?
Thou haſt a mind to be rob'd indeed.
Pi. I would have art maintain'd in reputation,
You know my Lady is to be a Princeſs,
And you muſt be a Lord, and I be dubbed,
But if we be not rob'd, I know not how
To truſt the Mathematicks or the Stars;
I am afraid all the *Bandits* are hang'd,
A thouſand Piſtols ſhould not fear to travell.
Lu. It is not wiſdom to proclaim our charge,
Though I could be content to be a Lord,
I am not over hearty, theeves are theeves,
And life is precious, prethee lets make haſt.
Pi. Illo ho ho,
Think upon your honour, are there no Gentlemen?
No wanting Gentlemen that know how to ſpend

The Siſters. 33

A quantity of Gold?
There is no thief in Nature.
Str. The Gentleman
Is very merry, they that mean well, and
Have their wits about 'em, do not uſe
To call upon our Tribe. This is a plot,
A very plot, and yet the Coaſt is cleer,
Now I may reach their voice.
Pi. It wo'not be, was ever men diſtreſt ſo?
Lu. Come we are well yet *Piperollo*, if
The Stars Decree our robbery, it will follow.
Pi. I pray Sir lets ſit down here, as you hope to
Be a Lord, we muſt do our endeavour and help
The Fates. Do but hear reaſon Sir.
Str. 'Tis my proud Madams Steward, and our quondam
Fellow thief; they were told their fortunes
To be rob'd; Here had been a purchaſe loſt
If I had not lain perdue. You ſhall be
Diſpatcht preſently, never fear it. *He whiſtles.*
Lu What's that? I do not like that tune.
Pi. Hum, I am not in love with that Quailpipe.
I could dwindle, but that I have a ſtrong
Faith in the Mathematicks. Theeves and be
Thy Will.
Lu. If they ſhould cut our throats now--- this is
Your folly; would I were off.
Pi. Would I were a Knight in an embroidered
Diſh clout. Have a good heart Sir, ther's
No more to be ſaid in't, let the Stars take
Their courſe, 'tis my Ladies money--- and if
We be rob'd, we are ſo much the neerer to preferment.
Enter Frapolo and the reſt.
Lu. Ah ſweet Gentlemen take but the Money---
Pi. 'Tis ready told; nay, nay, we are friends;
Give us but a Note under your hands for
My Ladies ſatisfaction, that you have received
it Gentlemen. D *Lu.*

It

IV, i, 27. An ink blot obscures the word above the small cross-hatch symbol; it appears to be *shout* and may have been blotted in error.

IV, i, 57–58. y^e / *Rest* is a rather vague warning, but the prompter, presumably well in advance of rehearsals, was simply copying the information in the coming stage direction. "The rest" would have been the other bandits.

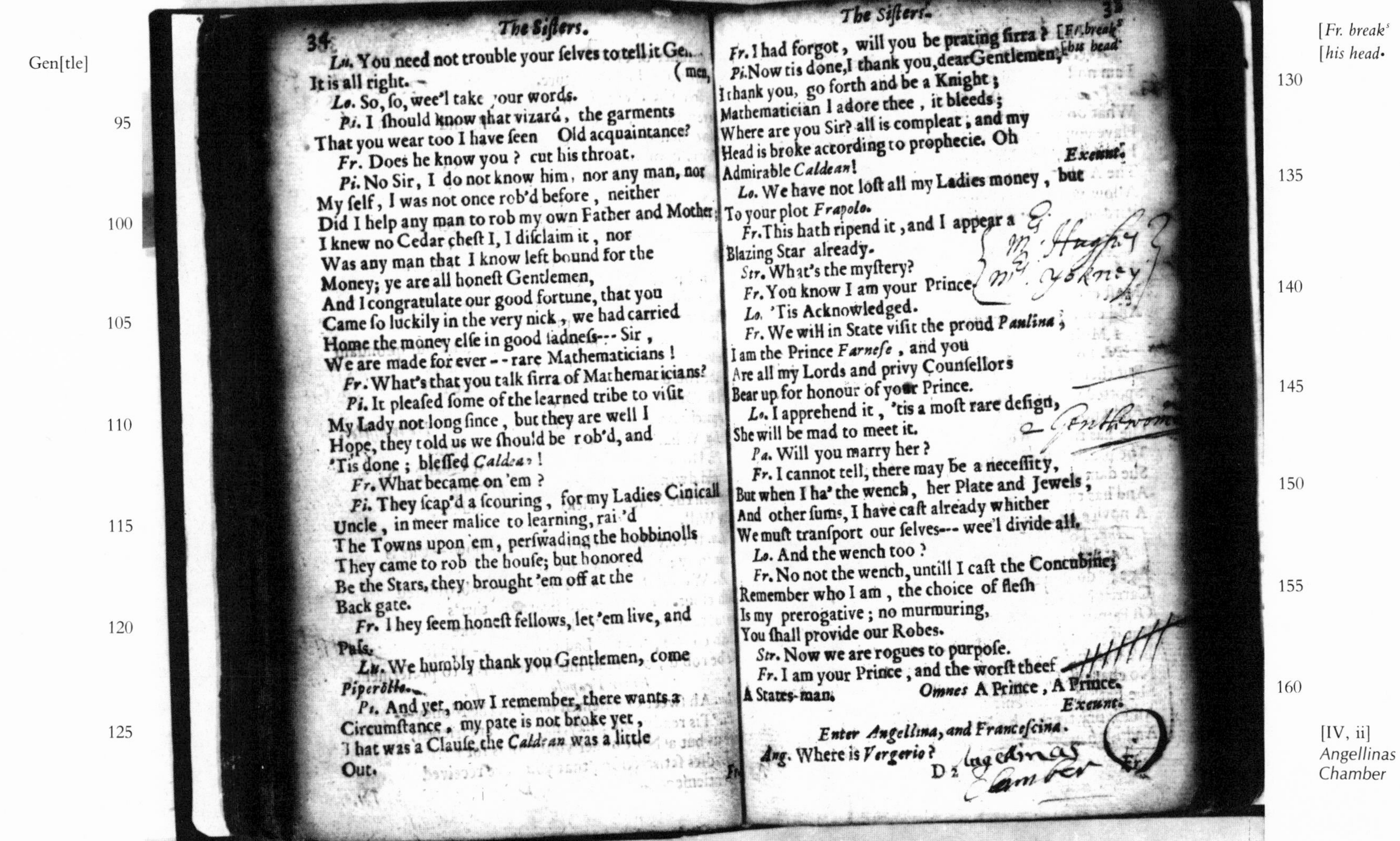

34 *The Sisters.*

Lu. You need not trouble your selves to tell it Gen- (men,
It is all right. -
Lo. So, so, wee'l take your words.
Pi. I should know that vizard, the garments
That you wear too I have seen Old acquaintance?
Fr. Does he know you? cut his throat.
Pi. No Sir, I do not know him, nor any man, nor
My self, I was not once rob'd before, neither
Did I help any man to rob my own Father and Mother;
I knew no Cedar chest I, I disclaim it, nor
Was any man that I know left bound for the
Money; ye are all honest Gentlemen,
And I congratulate our good fortune, that you
Came so luckily in the very nick, we had carried
Home the money else in good sadness--- Sir,
We are made for ever -- rare Mathematicians!
Fr. What's that you talk sirra of Mathematicians?
Pi. It pleased some of the learned tribe to visit
My Lady not long since, but they are well I
Hope, they told us we should be rob'd, and
'Tis done; blessed *Caldean*!
Fr. What became on 'em?
Pi. They scap'd a scouring, for my Ladies Cinicall
Uncle, in meer malice to learning, rais'd
The Towns upon 'em, perswading the hobbinolls
They came to rob the house; but honored
Be the Stars, they brought 'em off at the
Back gate.
Fr. They seem honest fellows, let 'em live, and
Pass.
Lu. We humbly thank you Gentlemen, come
Piperollo.
Pi. And yet, now I remember, there wants a
Circumstance, my pate is not broke yet,
That was a Clause the *Caldean* was a little
Out.

The Sisters. 35

Fr. I had forgot, will you be prating sirra? [Fr. breaks his head
Pi. Now tis done, I thank you, dear Gentlemen,
I thank you, go forth and be a Knight;
Mathematician I adore thee, it bleeds;
Where are you Sir? all is compleat, and my
Head is broke according to prophecie. Oh
Admirable *Caldean*! *Exeunt.*
Lo. We have not lost all my Ladies money, but
To your plot *Frapolo.*
Fr. This hath ripend it, and I appear a
Blazing Star already.
Str. What's the mystery?
Fr. You know I am your Prince.
Lo. 'Tis Acknowledged.
Fr. We will in State visit the proud *Paulina*;
I am the Prince *Farnese*, and you
Are all my Lords and privy Counsellors
Bear up for honour of your Prince.
Lo. I apprehend it, 'tis a most rare design,
She will be mad to meet it.
Pa. Will you marry her?
Fr. I cannot tell, there may be a necessity,
But when I ha' the wench, her Plate and Jewels,
And other sums, I have cast already whither
We must transport our selves--- wee'l divide all.
Lo. And the wench too?
Fr. No not the wench, untill I cast the Concubine;
Remember who I am, the choice of flesh
Is my prerogative; no murmuring,
You shall provide our Robes.
Str. Now we are rogues to purpose.
Fr. I am your Prince, and the worst theef
A States-man. *Omnes* A Prince, A Prince.
Exeunt.

Enter Angellina, and Francescina.

Ang. Where is *Vergerio*?
D2

Gen[tle]

[*Fr. break*[s]
[*his head*.

[IV, ii]
Angellinas Chamber

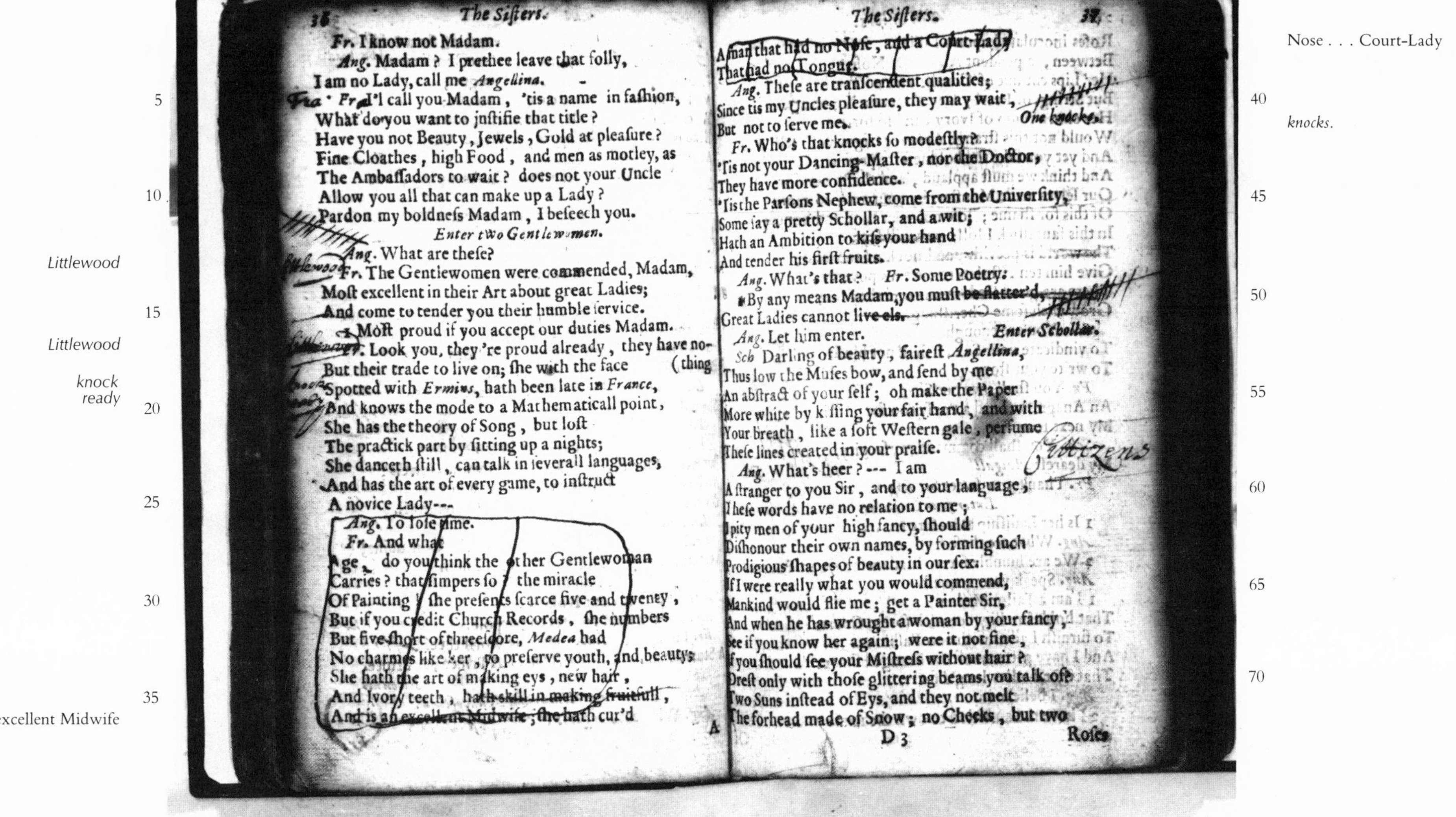

Fr. I know not Madam.
Ang. Madam? I prethee leave that folly,
I am no Lady, call me *Angellina*.
Fr. I'l call you Madam, 'tis a name in fashion,
What do you want to justifie that title?
Have you not Beauty, Jewels, Gold at pleasure?
Fine Cloathes, high Food, and men as motley, as
The Ambassadors to wait? does not your Uncle
Allow you all that can make up a Lady?
Pardon my boldness Madam, I beseech you.
Enter two Gentlewomen.
Ang. What are these?
Fr. The Gentlewomen were commended, Madam,
Most excellent in their Art about great Ladies;
And come to tender you their humble service.
1 Most proud if you accept our duties Madam.
Fr. Look you, they're proud already, they have nothing
But their trade to live on; she with the face
Spotted with *Ermins*, hath been late in *France*,
And knows the mode to a Mathematicall point,
She has the theory of Song, but lost
The practick part by sitting up a nights;
She danceth still, can talk in severall languages,
And has the art of every game, to instruct
A novice Lady---
Ang. To lose time.
Fr. And what
Age, do you think the other Gentlewoman
Carries? that simpers so? the miracle
Of Painting! she presents scarce five and twenty,
But if you credit Church Records, she numbers
But five short of threescore, *Medea* had
No charms like her, to preserve youth, and beauty;
She hath the art of making eys, new hair,
And Ivory teeth, hath skill in making fruitfull,
And is an excellent Midwife; she hath cur'd

A

A man that had no Nose, and a Court-Lady
That had no Tongue.
Ang. These are transcendent qualities;
Since tis my Uncles pleasure, they may wait,
But not to serve me. *One knocks.*
Fr. Who's that knocks so modestly?
'Tis not your Dancing-Master, nor the Doctor,
They have more confidence.
'Tis the Parsons Nephew, come from the University,
Some say a pretty Schollar, and a wit;
Hath an Ambition to kiss your hand
And tender his first fruits.
Ang. What's that? *Fr.* Some Poetry:
By any means Madam, you must be flatter'd,
Great Ladies cannot live else.
Ang. Let him enter. *Enter Schollar.*
Sch Darling of beauty, fairest *Angellina*,
Thus low the Muses bow, and send by me
An abstract of your self; oh make the Paper
More white by kissing your fair hand, and with
Your breath, like a soft Western gale, perfume
These lines created in your praise.
Ang. What's heer? --- I am
A stranger to you Sir, and to your language;
These words have no relation to me;
I pity men of your high fancy, should
Dishonour their own names, by forming such
Prodigious shapes of beauty in our sex:
If I were really what you would commend,
Mankind would flie me; get a Painter Sir,
And when he has wrought a woman by your fancy,
See if you know her again; were it not fine,
If you should see your Mistress without hair?
Drest only with those glittering beams you talk of?
Two Suns instead of Eys, and they not melt
The forhead made of Snow; no Checks, but two

Littlewood
Littlewood
knock
ready
excellent Midwife

Nose . . . Court-Lady
knocks.

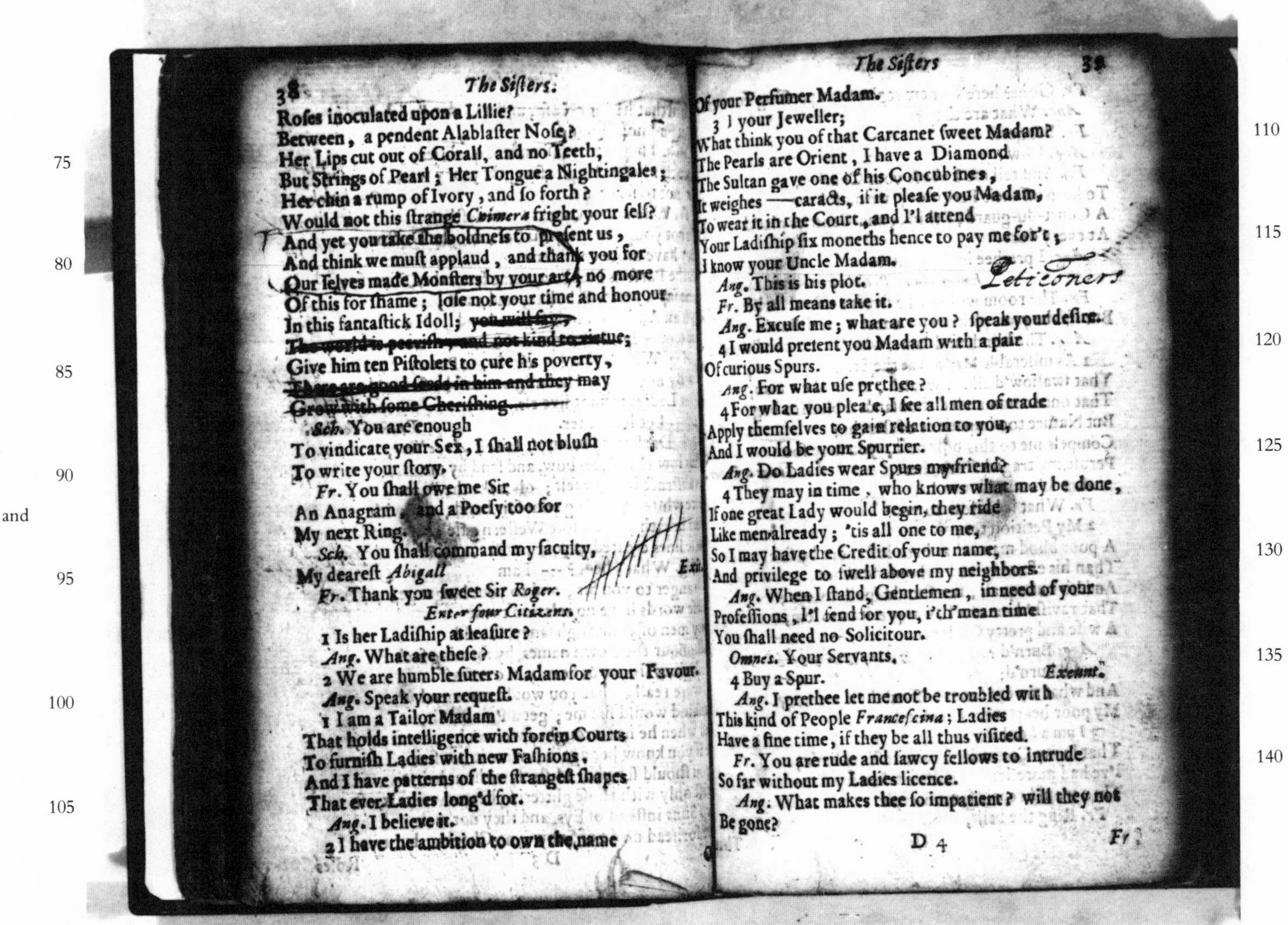

38 *The Sisters.*

Roses inoculated upon a Lillie?
Between, a pendent Alablaster Nose?
Her Lips cut out of Corall, and no Teeth,
But Strings of Pearl; Her Tongue a Nightingales;
Her chin a rump of Ivory, and so forth?
Would not this strange *Cimera* fright your self?
And yet you take the boldness to present us,
And think we must applaud, and thank you for
Our selves made Monsters by your art; no more
Of this for shame; lose not your time and honour
In this fantastick Idoll; ~~you will say,~~
~~The world is peevish, and not kind to virtue;~~
Give him ten Pistolets to cure his poverty,
~~There are good seeds in him and they may~~
~~Grow with some Cherishing.~~
Sch. You are enough
To vindicate your Sex, I shall not blush
To write your story.
Fr. You shall owe me Sir
An Anagram, and a Poesy too for
My next Ring.
Sch. You shall command my faculty,
My dearest *Abigall*. *Exit.*
Fr. Thank you sweet Sir *Roger.*
Enter four Citizens.
1 Is her Ladiship at leasure?
Ang. What are these?
2 We are humble suters Madam for your Favour.
Ang. Speak your request.
1 I am a Tailor Madam
That holds intelligence with forein Courts
To furnish Ladies with new Fashions,
And I have patterns of the strangest shapes
That ever Ladies long'd for.
Ang. I believe it.
2 I have the ambition to own the name

The Sisters 39

Of your Perfumer Madam.
3 I your Jeweller;
What think you of that Carcanet sweet Madam?
The Pearls are Orient, I have a Diamond
The Sultan gave one of his Concubines,
It weighes —caracts, if it please you Madam,
To wear it in the Court, and I'l attend
Your Ladiship six moneths hence to pay me for't;
I know your Uncle Madam.
Ang. This is his plot.
Fr. By all means take it.
Ang. Excuse me; what are you? speak your desire.
4 I would present you Madam with a paire
Of curious Spurs.
Ang. For what use prethee?
4 For what you please, I see all men of trade
Apply themselves to gain relation to you,
And I would be your Spurrier.
Ang. Do Ladies wear Spurs my friend?
4 They may in time, who knows what may be done,
If one great Lady would begin, they ride
Like men already; 'tis all one to me,
So I may have the Credit of your name,
And privilege to swell above my neighbors.
Ang. When I stand, Gentlemen, in need of your
Professions, I'l send for you, i'th' mean time
You shall need no Solicitour.
Omnes. Your Servants.
4 Buy a Spur. *Exeunt.*
Ang. I prethee let me not be troubled with
This kind of People *Francescina*; Ladies
Have a fine time, if they be all thus visited.
Fr. You are rude and sawcy fellows to intrude
So far without my Ladies licence.
Ang. What makes thee so impatient? will they not
Be gone?

D 4 *Fr.*

IV, ii, 83–84. The canceled lines are: "you will say, / The world is peevish, and not kind to virtue."

IV, ii, 86–87. The canceled lines are: "There are good seeds in him and they may Grow with some Cherishing."

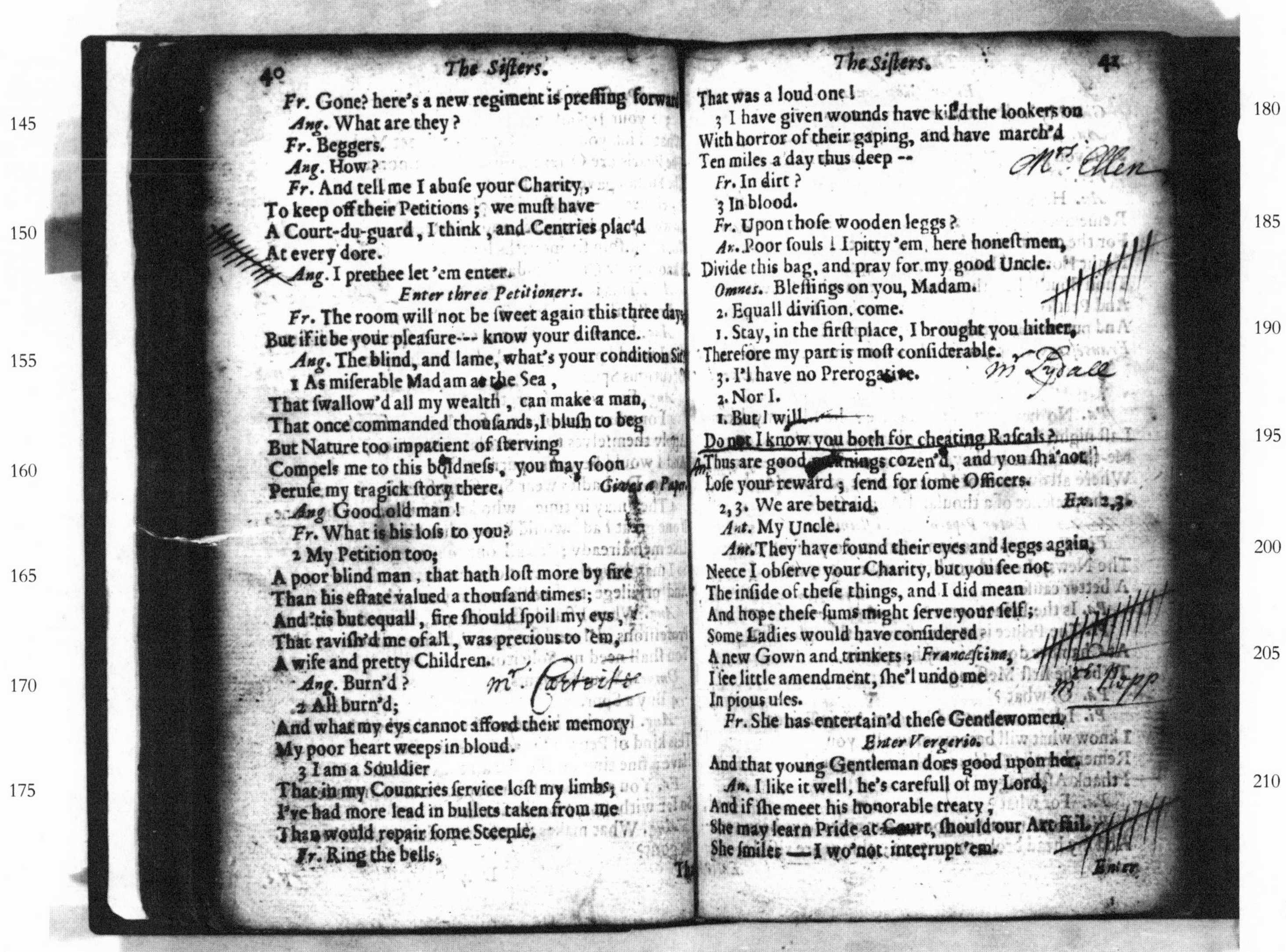

40 *The Sisters.*

Fr. Gone? here's a new regiment is pressing forward
Ang. What are they?
Fr. Beggers.
Ang. How?
Fr. And tell me I abuse your Charity,
To keep off their Petitions; we must have
A Court-du-guard, I think, and Centries plac'd
At every dore.
Ang. I prethee let 'em enter.
Enter three Petitioners.
Fr. The room will not be sweet again this three days
But if it be your pleasure--- know your distance.
Ang. The blind, and lame, what's your condition Sir?
1 As miserable Madam as the Sea,
That swallow'd all my wealth, can make a man,
That once commanded thousands, I blush to beg
But Nature too impatient of sterving
Compels me to this boldness, you may soon
Peruse my tragick story there. *Gives a Paper.*
Ang Good old man!
Fr. What is his loss to you?
2 My Petition too;
A poor blind man, that hath lost more by fire
Than his estate valued a thousand times;
And 'tis but equall, fire should spoil my eys,
That ravish'd me of all, was precious to 'em,
A wife and pretty Children.
Ang. Burn'd?
2 All burn'd;
And what my eys cannot afford their memory
My poor heart weeps in bloud.
3 I am a Souldier
That in my Countries service lost my limbs;
I've had more lead in bullets taken from me
Than would repair some Steeple.
Fr. Ring the bells,

41 *The Sisters.*

That was a loud one!
3 I have given wounds have kill'd the lookers on
With horror of their gaping, and have march'd
Ten miles a day thus deep --
Fr. In dirt?
3 In blood.
Fr. Upon those wooden leggs?
An. Poor souls! I pitty 'em, here honest men,
Divide this bag, and pray for my good Uncle.
Omnes. Blessings on you, Madam.
2. Equall division, come.
1. Stay, in the first place, I brought you hither,
Therefore my part is most considerable.
3. I'l have no Prerogative.
2. Nor I.
1. But I will.
Do not I know you both for cheating Rascals?
Thus are good meanings cozen'd, and you sha'not
Lose your reward; send for some Officers.
2, 3. We are betraid. *Ex. 2, 3.*
Ant. My Uncle.
Ant. They have found their eyes and leggs again,
Neece I observe your Charity, but you see not
The inside of these things, and I did mean
And hope these sums might serve your self;
Some Ladies would have considered
A new Gown and trinkets; *Francescina,*
I see little amendment, she'l undo me
In pious uses.
Fr. She has entertain'd these Gentlewomen,
Enter Vergerio.
And that young Gentleman does good upon her.
An. I like it well, he's carefull of my Lord,
And if she meet his honorable treaty,
She may learn Pride at Court, should our Art fail.
She smiles — I wo'not interrupt 'em.
Enter

IV, ii, 188. Though no stage direction provides an entrance for Antonio, the prompter caught the error and wrote in both a warning and a cue sign but not Antonio's name.

IV, ii, 196–97. The prompter again caught a printer's or author's error and marked these two lines for Antonio rather than the First Petitioner.

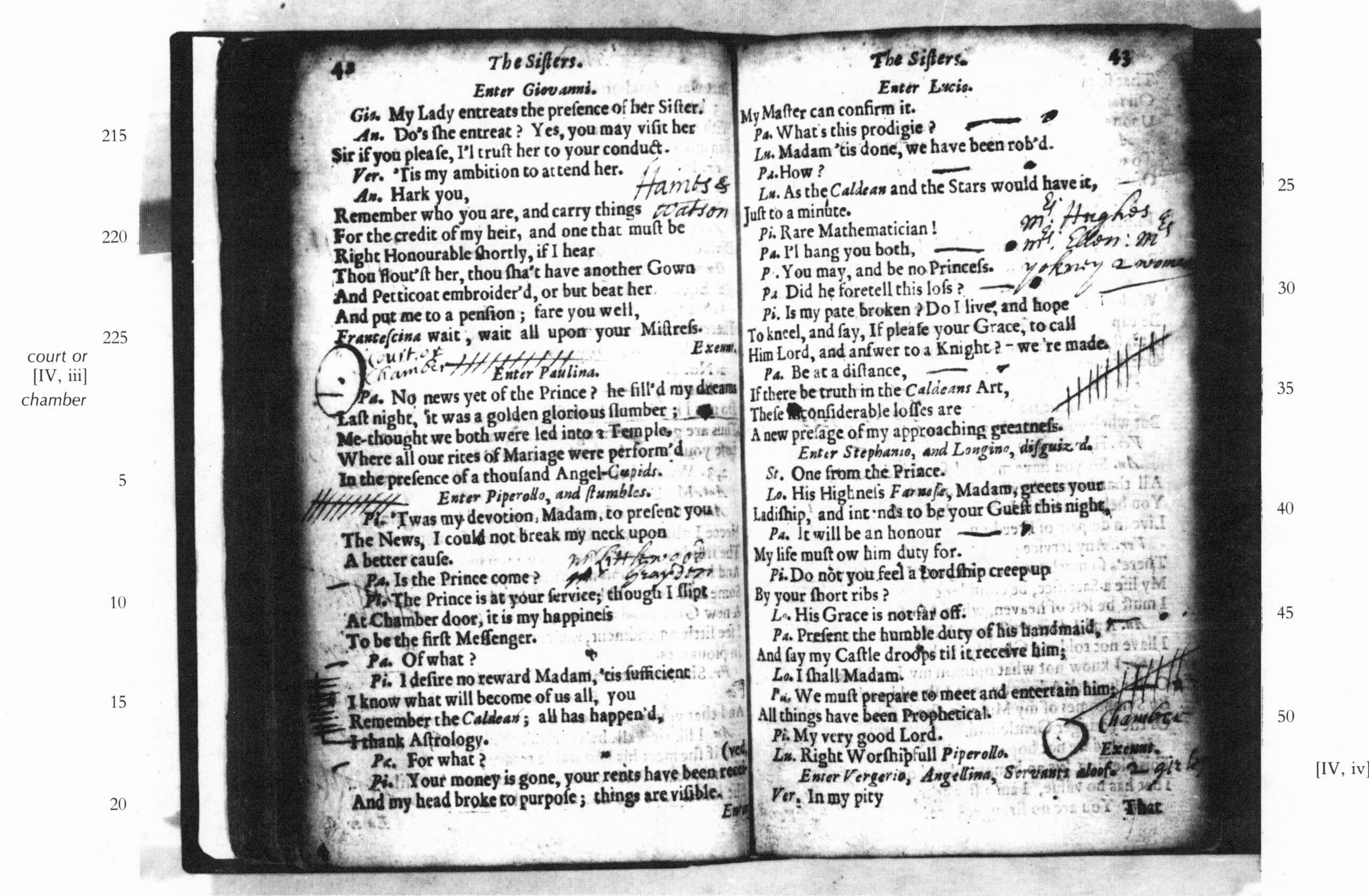

42 *The Sisters.*

Enter Giovanni.

Gio. My Lady entreats the presence of her Sister.
An. Do's she entreat? Yes, you may visit her
Sir if you please, I'l trust her to your conduct.
Ver. 'Tis my ambition to attend her.
An. Hark you,
Remember who you are, and carry things
For the credit of my heir, and one that must be
Right Honourable shortly, if I hear
Thou flout'st her, thou sha't have another Gown
And Petticoat embroider'd, or but beat her
And put me to a pension; fare you well,
Francescina wait, wait all upon your Mistress.

Exeunt.

court or [IV, iii] chamber

Enter Paulina.

Pa. No news yet of the Prince? he fill'd my dreams
Last night, 'it was a golden glorious slumber;
Me-thought we both were led into a Temple,
Where all our rites of Mariage were perform'd
In the presence of a thousand Angel-*Cupids*.

Enter Piperollo, and stumbles.

Pi. 'Twas my devotion, Madam, to present you
The News, I could not break my neck upon
A better cause.
Pa. Is the Prince come?
Pi. The Prince is at your service; though I slipt
At Chamber door, it is my happiness
To be the first Messenger.
Pa. Of what?
Pi. I desire no reward Madam, 'tis sufficient
I know what will become of us all, you
Remember the *Caldean*; all has happen'd,
I thank Astrology.
Pa. For what?
Pi. Your money is gone, your rents have been rece(ved)
And my head broke to purpose; things are visible.

The Sisters. 43

Enter Lucio.

My Master can confirm it.
Pa. What's this prodigie?
Lu. Madam 'tis done, we have been rob'd.
Pa. How?
Lu. As the *Caldean* and the Stars would have it,
Just to a minute.
Pi. Rare Mathematician!
Pa. I'l hang you both,
P. You may, and be no Princess.
Pa. Did he foretell this loss?
Pi. Is my pate broken? Do I live, and hope
To kneel, and say, If please your Grace, to call
Him Lord, and answer to a Knight? — we're made.
Pa. Be at a distance,
If there be truth in the *Caldeans* Art,
These inconsiderable losses are
A new presage of my approaching greatness.

Enter Stephano, and Longino, disguiz'd.

St. One from the Prince.
Lo. His Highness *Farnese*, Madam, greets your
Ladiship, and intends to be your Guest this night.
Pa. It will be an honour
My life must ow him duty for.
Pi. Do not you feel a Lordship creep up
By your short ribs?
Lo. His Grace is not far off.
Pa. Present the humble duty of his handmaid,
And say my Castle droops til it receive him;
Lo. I shall Madam.
Pa. We must prepare to meet and entertain him;
All things have been Prophetical.
Pi. My very good Lord.
Lu. Right Worshipfull *Piperollo*.

Exeunt.

[IV, iv]

Enter Vergerio, Angellina, Servants aloof.

Ver. In my pity

That

IV, iv, opening. Though the prompter noted that Francescina should be warned for this scene, he did not add her name to the entrance stage direction. He did, however, add the two girls—presumably the same as the two women who were warned.

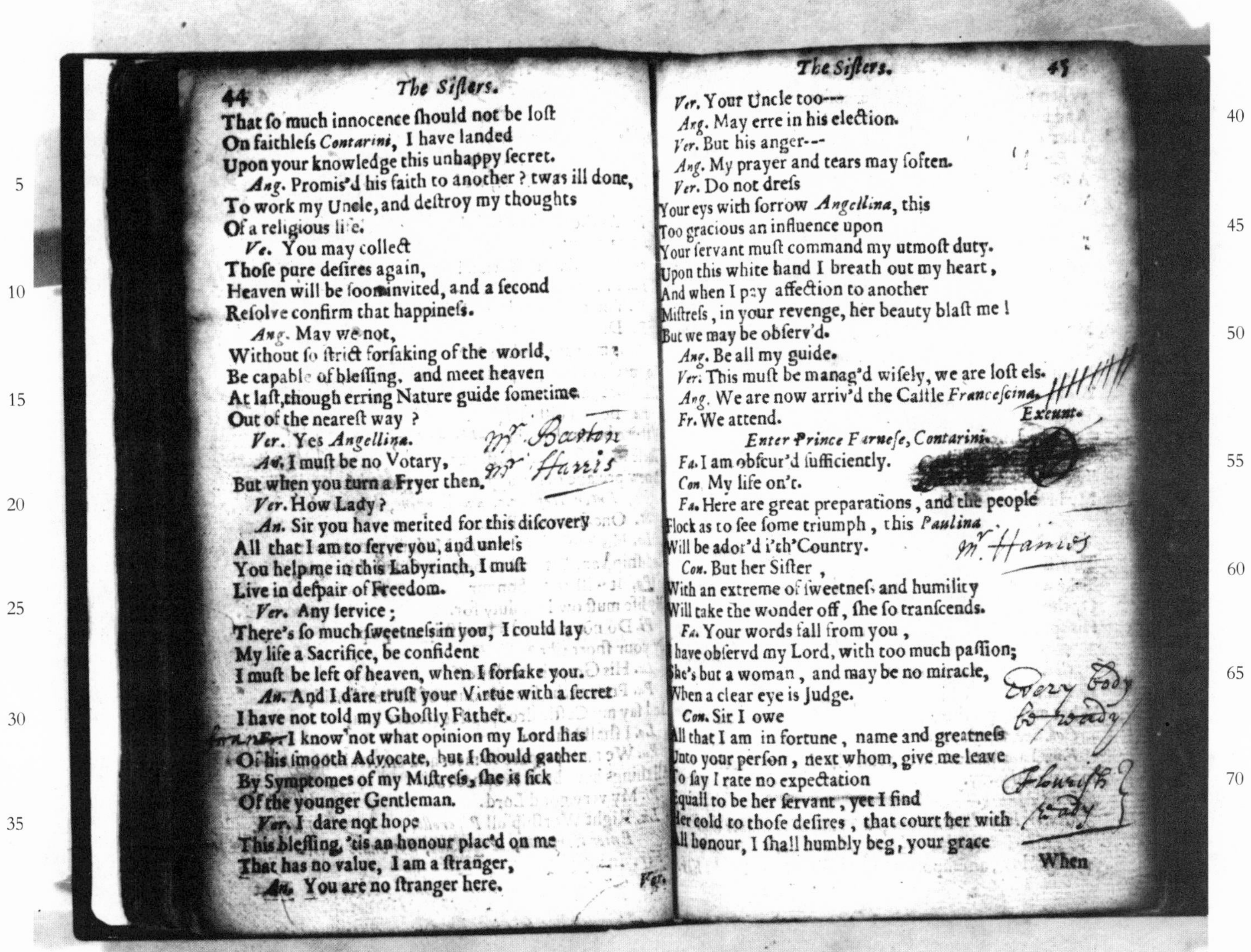

44 *The Siſters.*

That ſo much innocence ſhould not be loſt
On faithleſs *Contarini*, I have landed
Upon your knowledge this unhappy ſecret.
Ang. Promis'd his faith to another? twas ill done,
To work my Uncle, and deſtroy my thoughts
Of a religious life.
Ve. You may collect
Thoſe pure deſires again,
Heaven will be ſoon invited, and a ſecond
Reſolve confirm that happineſs.
Ang. May we not,
Without ſo ſtrict forſaking of the world,
Be capable of bleſſing, and meet heaven
At laſt, though erring Nature guide ſometime
Out of the neareſt way?
Ver. Yes *Angellina.*
An. I muſt be no Votary,
But when you turn a Fryer then.
Ver. How Lady?
An. Sir you have merited for this diſcovery
All that I am to ſerve you, and unleſs
You help me in this Labyrinth, I muſt
Live in deſpair of Freedom.
Ver. Any ſervice;
There's ſo much ſweetneſs in you, I could lay
My life a Sacrifice, be confident
I muſt be left of heaven, when I forſake you.
An. And I dare truſt your Virtue with a ſecret
I have not told my Ghoſtly Father.
Fr. I know not what opinion my Lord has
Of his ſmooth Advocate, but I ſhould gather
By Symptomes of my Miſtreſs, ſhe is ſick
Of the younger Gentleman.
Ver. I dare not hope
This bleſſing, 'tis an honour plac'd on me
That has no value, I am a ſtranger,
An. You are no ſtranger here.
Ver.

The Siſters. 45

Ver. Your Uncle too---
Ang. May erre in his election.
Ver. But his anger---
Ang. My prayer and tears may ſoften.
Ver. Do not dreſs
Your eys with ſorrow *Angellina*, this
Too gracious an influence upon
Your ſervant muſt command my utmoſt duty.
Upon this white hand I breath out my heart,
And when I pay affection to another
Miſtreſs, in your revenge, her beauty blaſt me!
But we may be obſerv'd.
Ang. Be all my guide.
Ver. This muſt be manag'd wiſely, we are loſt els.
Ang. We are now arriv'd the Caſtle *Franceſcina.*
Fr. We attend. *Exeunt.*
Enter Prince Farneſe, Contarini.
Fa. I am obſcur'd ſufficiently.
Con. My life on't.
Fa. Here are great preparations, and the people
Flock as to ſee ſome triumph, this *Paulina*
Will be ador'd i'th'Country.
Con. But her Siſter,
With an extreme of ſweetneſs and humility
Will take the wonder off, ſhe ſo tranſcends.
Fa. Your words fall from you,
I have obſervd my Lord, with too much paſſion;
She's but a woman, and may be no miracle,
When a clear eye is Judge.
Con. Sir I owe
All that I am in fortune, name and greatneſs
Unto your perſon, next whom, give me leave
To ſay I rate no expectation
Equall to be her ſervant, yet I find
Her cold to thoſe deſires, that court her with
All honour, I ſhall humbly beg, your grace
When

IV, iv, 31. The note *fran* in the margin, giving this speech to Francescina, is pointless, for the speech ascription is correct. Perhaps with Francescina, Frapolo, and, presently, Farnese, the prompter was momentarily confused about the abbreviations, just as was the printer at times.

IV, iv, 55–56. Apparently a scene shift was planned for this point and later omitted; the setting description is both crossed out and smudged over. Writing in 1920 Montague Summers quoted the note as reading ⊙ *Court or Castle*, yet he gave no indication that the note was crossed out and smudged. The University of Chicago copy does not indicate a canceled note either.

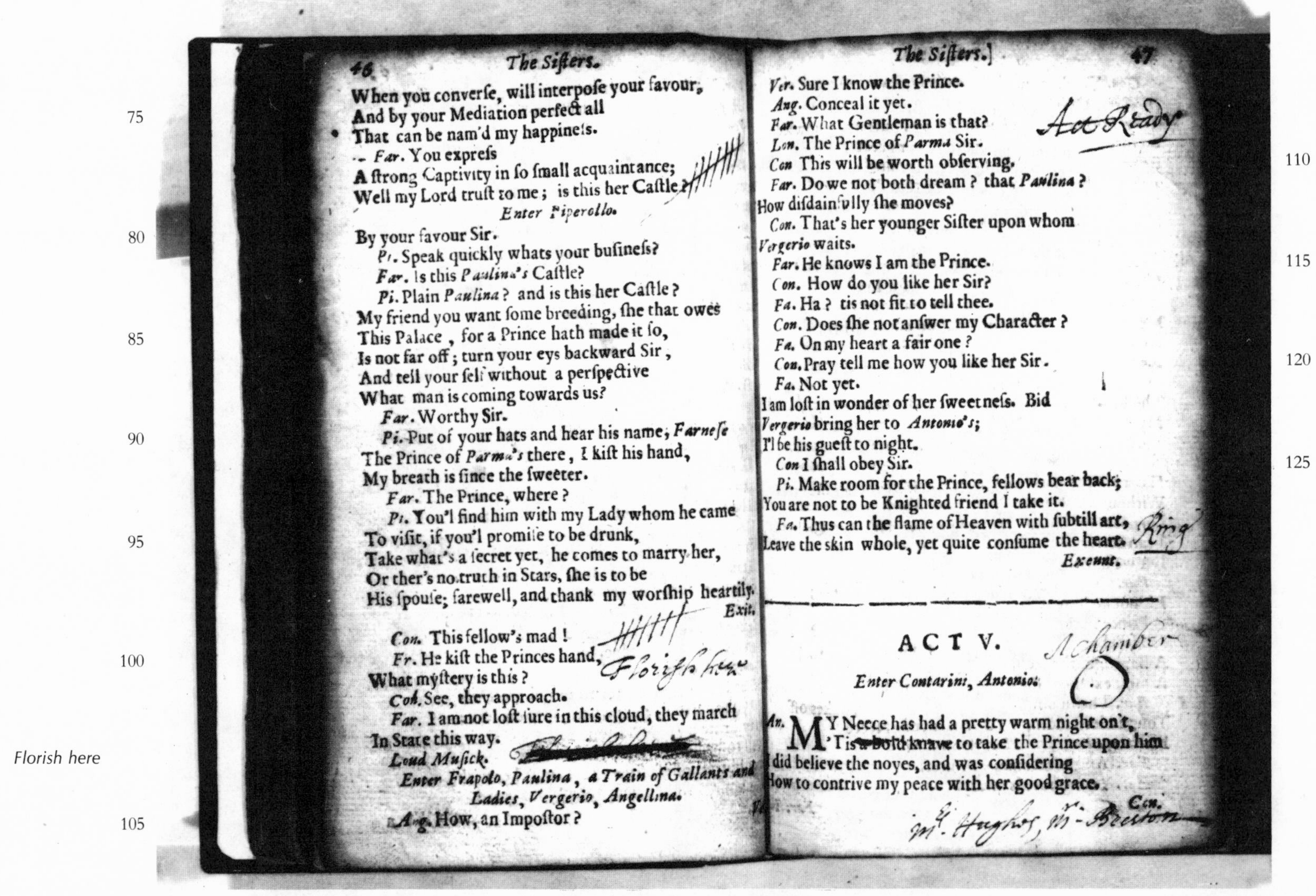

46 The Siſters.

When you converſe, will interpoſe your favour,
And by your Mediation perfect all
That can be nam'd my happineſs.
Far. You expreſs
A ſtrong Captivity in ſo ſmall acquaintance;
Well my Lord truſt to me; is this her Caſtle?

Enter Piperollo.

By your favour Sir.
Pi. Speak quickly whats your buſineſs?
Far. Is this *Paulina's* Caſtle?
Pi. Plain *Paulina*? and is this her Caſtle?
My friend you want ſome breeding, ſhe that owes
This Palace, for a Prince hath made it ſo,
Is not far off; turn your eys backward Sir,
And tell your ſelf without a perſpective
What man is coming towards us?
Far. Worthy Sir.
Pi. Put of your hats and hear his name; *Farneſe*
The Prince of *Parma's* there, I kiſt his hand,
My breath is ſince the ſweeter.
Far. The Prince, where?
Pi. You'l find him with my Lady whom he came
To viſit, if you'l promiſe to be drunk,
Take what's a ſecret yet, he comes to marry her,
Or ther's no truth in Stars, ſhe is to be
His ſpouſe; farewell, and thank my worſhip heartily. *Exit.*
Con. This fellow's mad!
Fr. He kiſt the Princes hand,
What myſtery is this?
Con. See, they approach.
Far. I am not loſt ſure in this cloud, they march
In State this way.
Loud Muſick.
Enter Frapolo, Paulina, a Train of Gallants and Ladies, Vergerio, Angellina.
Ang. How, an Impoſtor?

Florish here

The Siſters. 47

Ver. Sure I know the Prince.
Ang. Conceal it yet.
Far. What Gentleman is that?
Lon. The Prince of *Parma* Sir.
Con This will be worth obſerving.
Far. Do we not both dream? that *Paulina*?
How diſdainfully ſhe moves?
Con. That's her younger Siſter upon whom
Vergerio waits.
Far. He knows I am the Prince.
Con. How do you like her Sir?
Fa. Ha? tis not fit to tell thee.
Con. Does ſhe not anſwer my Character?
Fa. On my heart a fair one?
Con. Pray tell me how you like her Sir.
Fa. Not yet.
I am loſt in wonder of her ſweetneſs. Bid
Vergerio bring her to *Antonio's*;
I'l be his gueſt to night.
Con I ſhall obey Sir.
Pi. Make room for the Prince, fellows bear back;
You are not to be Knighted friend I take it.
Fa. Thus can the flame of Heaven with ſubtill art,
Leave the ſkin whole, yet quite conſume the heart.
Exeunt.

ACT V.

Enter Contarini, Antonio.

An. MY Neece has had a pretty warm night on't,
'Tis a bold knave to take the Prince upon him
I did believe the noyes, and was conſidering
How to contrive my peace with her good grace.
Con.

IV, iv, 99–104. The cross-hatch symbol here apparently cued both the flourish and the group entrance.

Con. You have no fear to suffer now?
Ant. I thank
Your Lordship, that has made my house and knowledg
So fortunate, by the presence of our great
Farnese, 'tis an honour makes me young;
And yet this Rascal troubles me, that durst
Come in the Princes name, and charge my Neece
So home too; Is't not Treason Sir?
Con. Of highest nature.
Ant. Let him then tast the Law; yet I commend
His Spirit, that would scorn to die for Felonie,
And when his head goes off the shame and grief
May help to break her heart: I do not love her,
And then my Girl, my *Angellina's* heir,
And you her Lord and mine.
Con. My hopes are fair,
The Prince himself having vouchsaf'd to be
My Advocate.
Ant. He must command all here.
Enter Farnese, and Angellina.
'Tis a good Prince, and loves you well, and let me
Without boast, tell you my Lord, she brings
No common Blood, though we live dark i'th' Country
I can derive her from the great *Ursini*,
But we have been eclips'd.
Far. Contarini leave us. You may stay *Antonio*;
Is't not an honour to your Family
A Prince should court your Neece into his arms?
Ant. I must confess, 'tis good enough for such
A Baggage, they will make together Sir,
A most excellent shew upon the Scaffold.
Far. The Impostor, and *Paulina's* pride, takes off
Your understanding; I do court your Neece
Fair *Angellina*. *Ant.* How Sir?
Far. And as becomes a Princess.
Ant. Your Grace is merry.
Far.

Far. I know not, but there's Magick in her eyes.
An. Magick? and she be a Witch, I ha' done with her.
Does he love *Angelina*? Please your Highness --
Do you affect this Girl?
Far. Religiously.
An. And have you all your Princely wits about ye?
Far. This Language is but coarse. I tell you Sir
The Virgin must be mine.
An. Your Whore?
Far. My Princess.
An. That's another matter.
Far. Shew your obedience,
You have commands upon her as a Father.
An. I know not what to say, but I'l perswade;
Hark you Neece, you hear what the Prince says,
'Tis now no time to think of Nunneries.
Be rul'd then, and love somebody; if you have
Promis'd my Lord, I say make good that promise,
If not, the Prince is worth considering.
The Gentleman will make you a round Jointure.
If thou beest free, love him, to vex thy Sister,
Who may upon submission be receiv'd
To Grace, and rise in time a Madam Nurse
To your heir apparent; I have done my duty.
But this is no great honesty, to cheat
My Lord. I see the greatest men are flesh
And blood, our souls are much upon a making;
All men that are in love deal with the Devil,
Only with this difference, he that dotes
Upon a Woman is absolutely possest;
And he that loves the least is haunted
With a Familiar.
Enter a Servant
Ser. Old *Fabio* Sir your Tenant, with much business
In's face, desires to speak with you, I could hardly
Keep him from pressing in, his Wife he sayes
Is Lunatick.
E *Ant.*

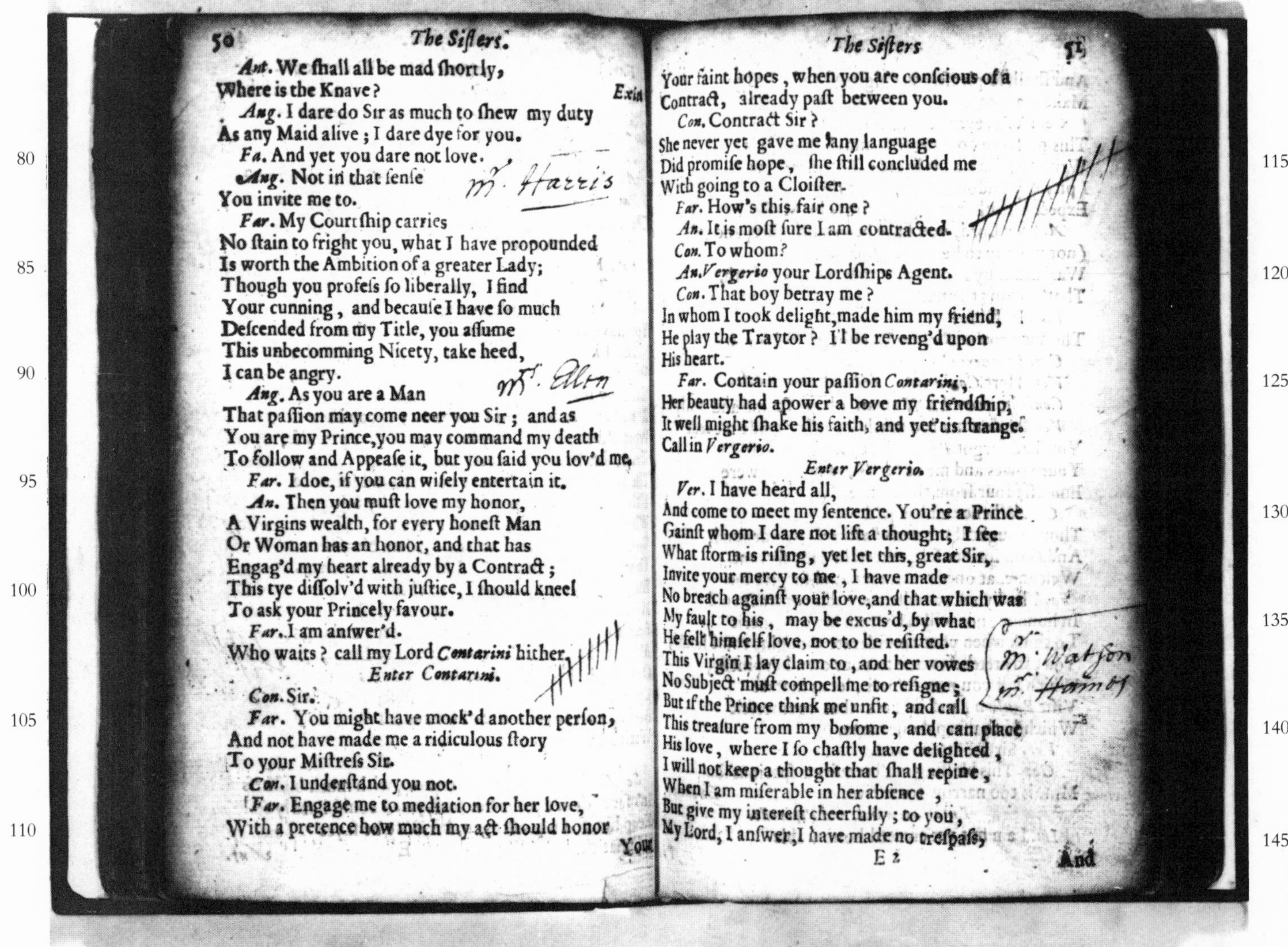

50 The Sisters.

Ant. We shall all be mad shortly,
Where is the Knave? *Exit*
Ang. I dare do Sir as much to shew my duty
As any Maid alive; I dare dye for you.
Fa. And yet you dare not love.
Ang. Not in that sense
You invite me to.
Far. My Courtship carries
No stain to fright you, what I have propounded
Is worth the Ambition of a greater Lady;
Though you profess so liberally, I find
Your cunning, and because I have so much
Descended from my Title, you assume
This unbecomming Nicety, take heed,
I can be angry.
Ang. As you are a Man
That passion may come neer you Sir; and as
You are my Prince, you may command my death
To follow and Appease it, but you said you lov'd me,
Far. I doe, if you can wisely entertain it.
An. Then you must love my honor,
A Virgins wealth, for every honest Man
Or Woman has an honor, and that has
Engag'd my heart already by a Contract;
This tye dissolv'd with justice, I should kneel
To ask your Princely favour.
Far. I am answer'd.
Who waits? call my Lord *Contarini* hither.
Enter Contarini.
Con. Sir.
Far. You might have mock'd another person,
And not have made me a ridiculous story
To your Mistress Sir.
Con. I understand you not.
Far. Engage me to mediation for her love,
With a pretence how much my act should honor
You

The Sisters 51

Your faint hopes, when you are conscious of a
Contract, already past between you.
Con. Contract Sir?
She never yet gave me any language
Did promise hope, she still concluded me
With going to a Cloister.
Far. How's this fair one?
An. It is most sure I am contracted.
Con. To whom?
An. *Vergerio* your Lordships Agent.
Con. That boy betray me?
In whom I took delight, made him my friend,
He play the Traytor? I'l be reveng'd upon
His heart.
Far. Contain your passion *Contarini*,
Her beauty had a power a bove my friendship,
It well might shake his faith, and yet 'tis strange.
Call in *Vergerio*.
Enter Vergerio.
Ver. I have heard all,
And come to meet my sentence. You're a Prince
'Gainst whom I dare not lift a thought; I see
What storm is rising, yet let this, great Sir,
Invite your mercy to me, I have made
No breach against your love, and that which was
My fault to his, may be excus'd, by what
He felt himself love, not to be resisted.
This Virgin I lay claim to, and her vowes
No Subject must compell me to resigne;
But if the Prince think me unfit, and call
This treasure from my bosome, and can place
His love, where I so chastly have delighted,
I will not keep a thought that shall repine,
When I am miserable in her absence,
But give my interest cheerfully; to you,
My Lord, I answer, I have made no trespass,
E 2 And

V, i, 118. The cue here is for Vergerio's entrance, and the prompter caught the error; Vergerio enters earlier than the stage direction indicates, in order to overhear the conversation.

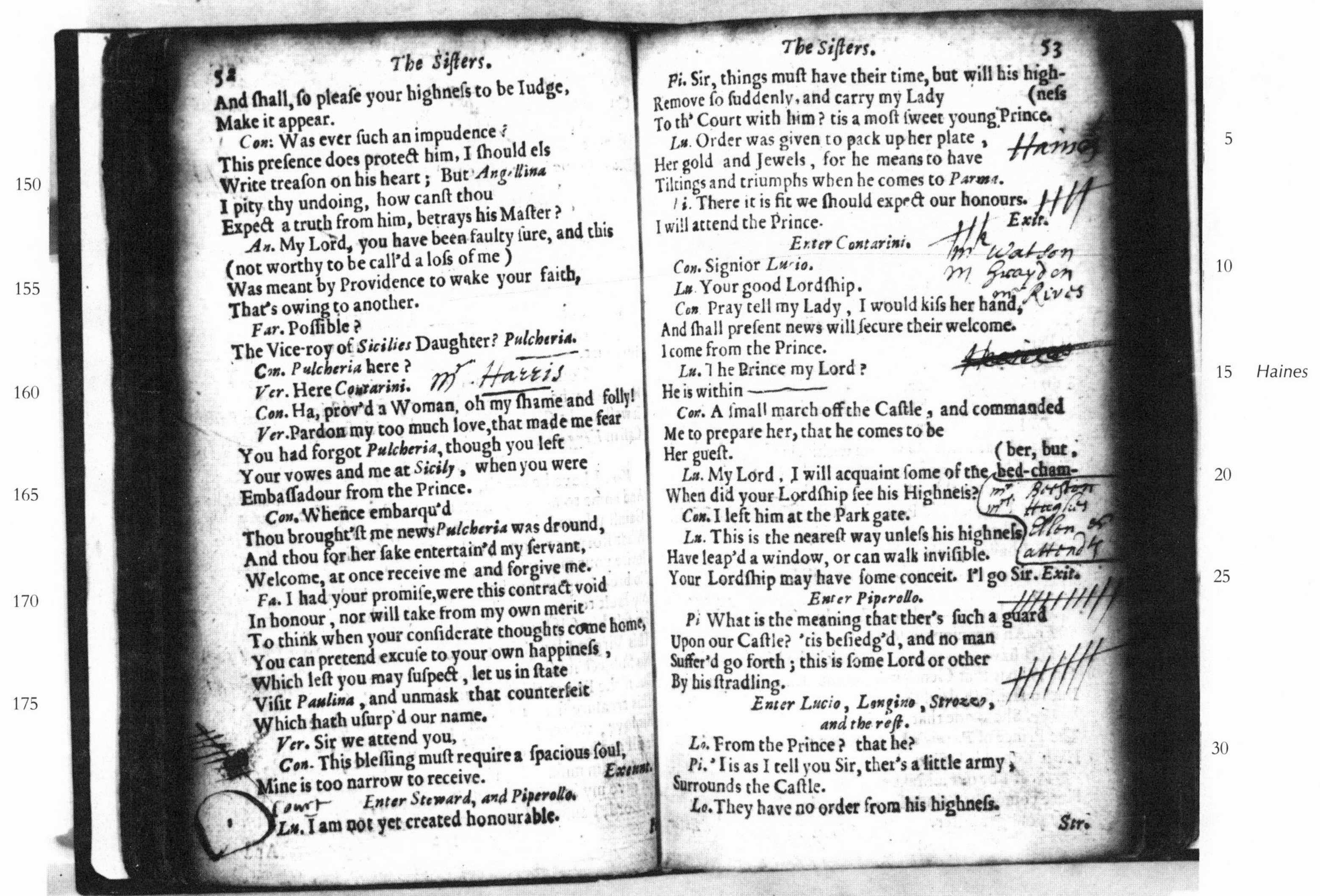

52 *The Siſters.*

And ſhall, ſo pleaſe your highneſs to be Iudge,
Make it appear.
Con: Was ever ſuch an impudence?
This preſence does protect him, I ſhould els
Write treaſon on his heart; But *Angellina*
I pity thy undoing, how canſt thou
Expect a truth from him, betrays his Maſter?
An. My Lord, you have been faulty ſure, and this
(not worthy to be call'd a loſs of me)
Was meant by Providence to wake your faith,
That's owing to another.
Far. Poſſible?
The Vice-roy of *Sicilies* Daughter? *Pulcheria*.
Con. *Pulcheria* here?
Ver. Here *Contarini*.
Con. Ha, prov'd a Woman, oh my ſhame and folly!
Ver. Pardon my too much love, that made me fear
You had forgot *Pulcheria*, though you left
Your vowes and me at *Sicily*, when you were
Embaſſadour from the Prince.
Con. Whence embarqu'd
Thou brought'ſt me news *Pulcheria* was dround,
And thou for her ſake entertain'd my ſervant,
Welcome, at once receive me and forgive me.
Fa. I had your promiſe, were this contract void
In honour, nor will take from my own merit
To think when your conſiderate thoughts come home,
You can pretend excuſe to your own happineſs,
Which leſt you may ſuſpect, let us in ſtate
Viſit *Paulina*, and unmask that counterfeit
Which hath uſurp'd our name.
Ver. Sir we attend you,
Con. This bleſſing muſt require a ſpacious ſoul,
Mine is too narrow to receive. *Exeunt*.
[V, ii] *Enter Steward, and Piperollo.*
Lu. I am not yet created honourable.

The Siſters. 53

Pi. Sir, things muſt have their time, but will his high-
Remove ſo ſuddenly, and carry my Lady (neſs
To th' Court with him? tis a moſt ſweet young Prince.
Lu. Order was given to pack up her plate,
Her gold and Jewels, for he means to have
Tiltings and triumphs when he comes to *Parma*.
Pi. There it is fit we ſhould expect our honours.
I will attend the Prince. *Exit*.
Enter Contarini.
Con. Signior *Lucio*.
Lu. Your good Lordſhip.
Con. Pray tell my Lady, I would kiſs her hand,
And ſhall preſent news will ſecure their welcome.
I come from the Prince.
Lu. The Brince my Lord? Haines
He is within ——
Con. A ſmall march off the Caſtle, and commanded
Me to prepare her, that he comes to be
Her gueſt.
Lu. My Lord, I will acquaint ſome of the bed-cham-
When did your Lordſhip ſee his Highneſs? (ber, but.
Con. I left him at the Park gate.
Lu. This is the neareſt way unleſs his highneſs
Have leap'd a window, or can walk inviſible.
Your Lordſhip may have ſome conceit. I'l go Sir. *Exit*.
Enter Piperollo.
Pi What is the meaning that ther's ſuch a guard
Upon our Caſtle? 'tis beſiedg'd, and no man
Suffer'd go forth; this is ſome Lord or other
By his ſtradling.
Enter Lucio, Longino, Strozzo, and the reſt.
Lo. From the Prince? that he?
Pi. 'Tis as I tell you Sir, ther's a little army,
Surrounds the Caſtle.
Lo. They have no order from his highneſs.
Str.

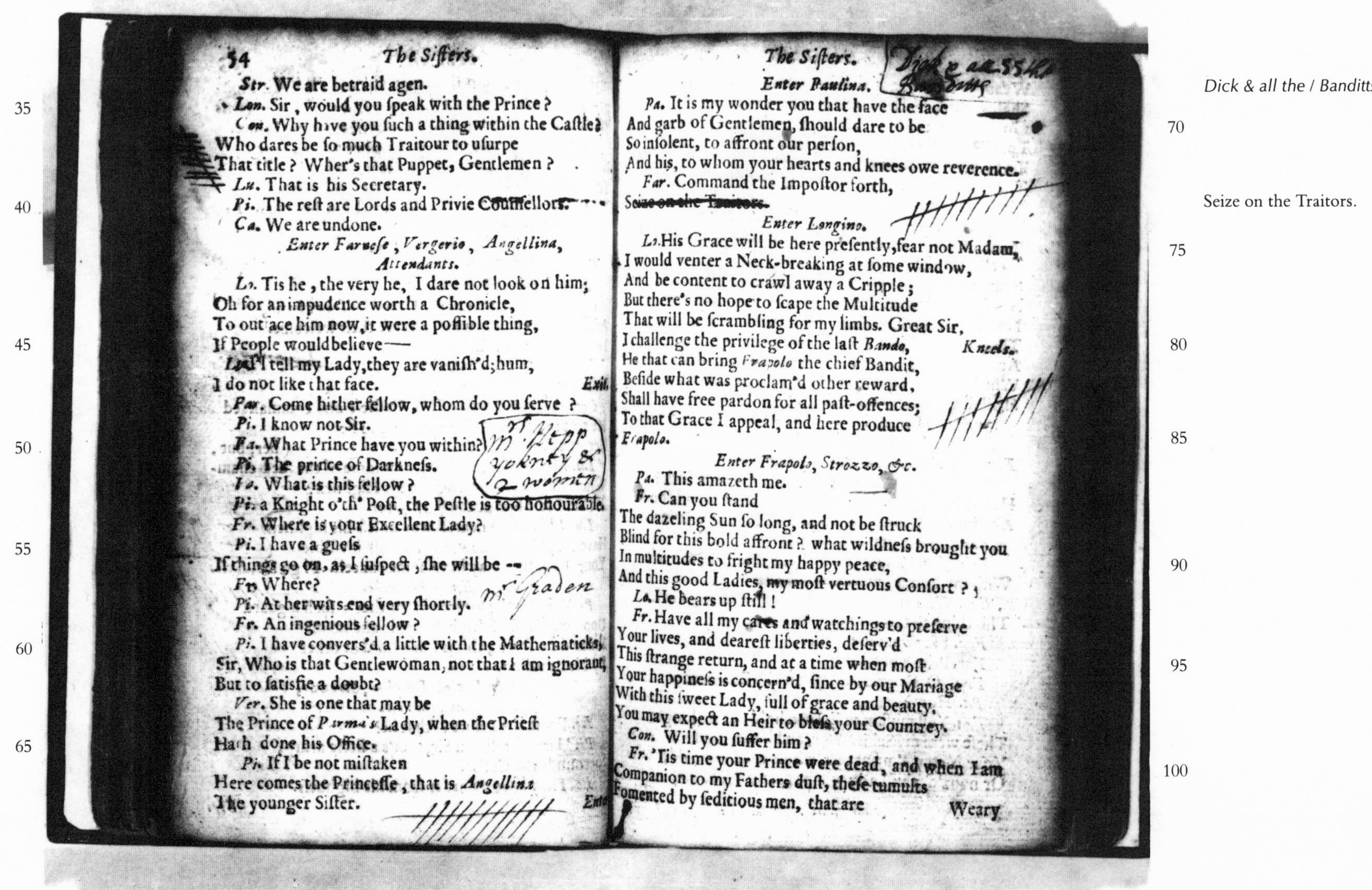

54 The Sisters.

Str. We are betraid agen.
Lon. Sir, would you speak with the Prince?
Con. Why have you such a thing within the Castle?
Who dares be so much Traitour to usurpe
That title? Wher's that Puppet, Gentlemen?
Lu. That is his Secretary.
Pi. The rest are Lords and Privie Counsellors.
Ca. We are undone.
Enter Farnese, Vergerio, Angellina, Attendants.
Lo. Tis he, the very he, I dare not look on him;
Oh for an impudence worth a Chronicle,
To out face him now, it were a possible thing,
If People would believe——
Lo. I'l tell my Lady, they are vanish'd; hum,
I do not like that face. Exit.
Far. Come hither fellow, whom do you serve?
Pi. I know not Sir.
Fa. What Prince have you within?
Pi. The prince of Darkness.
Fa. What is this fellow?
Pi. a Knight o'th' Post, the Pestle is too honourable.
Fr. Where is your Excellent Lady?
Pi. I have a guess
If things go on, as I suspect, she will be --
Fr. Where?
Pi. At her wits end very shortly.
Fr. An ingenious fellow?
Pi. I have convers'd a little with the Mathematicks,
Sir, Who is that Gentlewoman, not that I am ignorant,
But to satisfie a doubt?
Ver. She is one that may be
The Prince of Parma's Lady, when the Priest
Hath done his Office.
Pi. If I be not mistaken
Here comes the Princesse, that is Angellina
The younger Sister. Ente[r]

The Sisters.
Enter Paulina.
Pa. It is my wonder you that have the face
And garb of Gentlemen, should dare to be
So insolent, to affront our person,
And his, to whom your hearts and knees owe reverence.
Far. Command the Impostor forth,
Seize on the Traitors.
Enter Longino.
Lo. His Grace will be here presently, fear not Madam,
I would venter a Neck-breaking at some window,
And be content to crawl away a Cripple;
But there's no hope to scape the Multitude
That will be scrambling for my limbs. Great Sir,
I challenge the privilege of the last Bando, Kneels.
He that can bring Frapolo the chief Bandit,
Beside what was proclam'd other reward,
Shall have free pardon for all past-offences;
To that Grace I appeal, and here produce
Frapolo.
Enter Frapolo, Strozzo, &c.
Pa. This amazeth me.
Fr. Can you stand
The dazeling Sun so long, and not be struck
Blind for this bold affront? what wildness brought you
In multitudes to fright my happy peace,
And this good Ladies, my most vertuous Consort?
La. He bears up still!
Fr. Have all my cares and watchings to preserve
Your lives, and dearest liberties, deserv'd
This strange return, and at a time when most
Your happiness is concern'd, since by our Mariage
With this sweet Lady, full of grace and beauty,
You may expect an Heir to bless your Countrey.
Con. Will you suffer him?
Fr. 'Tis time your Prince were dead, and when I am
Companion to my Fathers dust, these tumults
Fomented by seditious men, that are
Weary

Dick & all the / Banditts

Seize on the Traitors.

V, ii, 54, 57, 59. The prompter did not correct the speech ascriptions here from "*Fr.*" to "*Far.*"

V, ii, 68. Francescina and the two women were warned for this entrance with Paulina, and their names should have been added to the stage direction.

Plenty

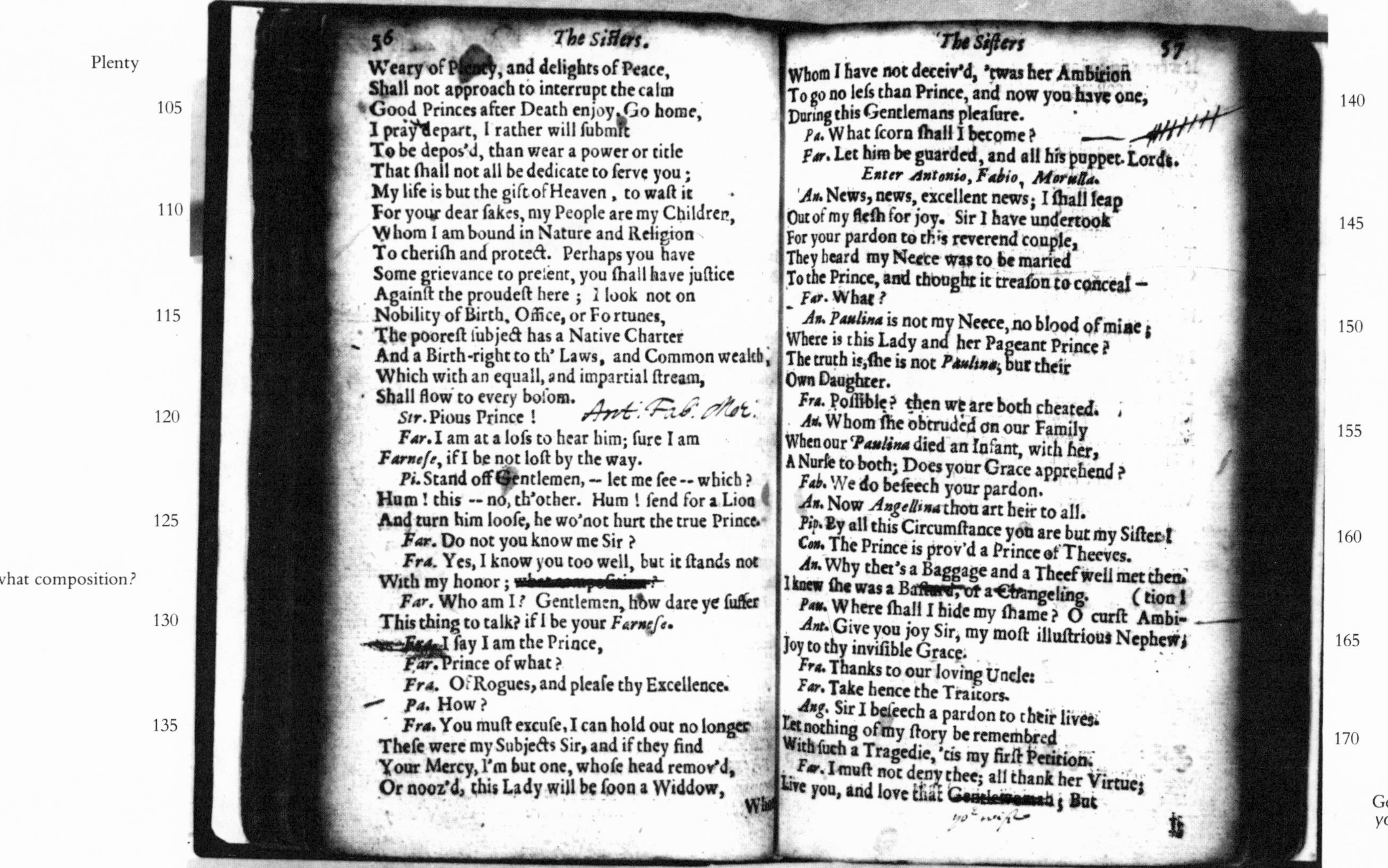

56 The Siſters.

Weary of Plenty, and delights of Peace,
Shall not approach to interrupt the calm
Good Princes after Death enjoy. Go home,
I pray depart, I rather will ſubmit
To be depos'd, than wear a power or title
That ſhall not all be dedicate to ſerve you;
My life is but the gift of Heaven, to waſt it
For your dear ſakes, my People are my Children,
Whom I am bound in Nature and Religion
To cheriſh and protect. Perhaps you have
Some grievance to preſent, you ſhall have juſtice
Againſt the proudeſt here; I look not on
Nobility of Birth, Office, or Fortunes,
The pooreſt ſubject has a Native Charter
And a Birth-right to th' Laws, and Common wealth,
Which with an equall, and impartial ſtream,
Shall flow to every boſom. Ant: Fab: Mor:
Str. Pious Prince!
Far. I am at a loſs to hear him; ſure I am
Farneſe, if I be not loſt by the way.
Pi. Stand off Gentlemen, -- let me ſee -- which?
Hum! this -- no, th'other. Hum! ſend for a Lion
And turn him looſe, he wo'not hurt the true Prince.
Far. Do not you know me Sir?
Fra. Yes, I know you too well, but it ſtands not
With my honor; ~~what compoſition?~~
Far. Who am I? Gentlemen, how dare ye ſuffer
This thing to talk? if I be your *Farneſe*.
~~*Fra.*~~ I ſay I am the Prince,
Far. Prince of what?
Fra. Of Rogues, and pleaſe thy Excellence.
Pa. How?
Fra. You muſt excuſe, I can hold out no longer
Theſe were my Subjects Sir, and if they find
Your Mercy, I'm but one, whoſe head remov'd,
Or nooz'd, this Lady will be ſoon a Widdow,
Wha

The Siſters 57

Whom I have not deceiv'd, 'twas her Ambition
To go no leſs than Prince, and now you have one,
During this Gentlemans pleaſure.
Pa. What ſcorn ſhall I become?
Far. Let him be guarded, and all his puppet-Lords.
Enter Antonio, Fabio, Morulla.
An. News, news, excellent news; I ſhall leap
Out of my fleſh for joy. Sir I have undertook
For your pardon to this reverend couple,
They heard my Neece was to be maried
To the Prince, and thought it treaſon to conceal —
Far. What?
An. *Paulina* is not my Neece, no blood of mine;
Where is this Lady and her Pageant Prince?
The truth is, ſhe is not *Paulina*, but their
Own Daughter.
Fra. Poſſible? then we are both cheated.
An. Whom ſhe obtruded on our Family
When our *Paulina* died an Infant, with her,
A Nurſe to both; Does your Grace apprehend?
Fab. We do beſeech your pardon.
An. Now *Angellina* thou art heir to all.
Pip. By all this Circumſtance you are but my Siſter!
Con. The Prince is prov'd a Prince of Theeves.
An. Why ther's a Baggage and a Theef well met then.
I knew ſhe was a ~~Baſtard, or a Changeling.~~ (tion!
Pau. Where ſhall I hide my ſhame? O curſt Ambi-
Ant. Give you joy Sir, my moſt illuſtrious Nephew;
Joy to thy inviſible Grace.
Fra. Thanks to our loving Uncle:
Far. Take hence the Traitors.
Ang. Sir I beſeech a pardon to their lives.
Let nothing of my ſtory be remembred
With ſuch a Tragedie, 'tis my firſt Petition.
Far. I muſt not deny thee; all thank her Virtue;
Live you, and love that ~~Gentlewoman~~; But
yor wife
It

what composition?

Gentlewoman
yo' wife

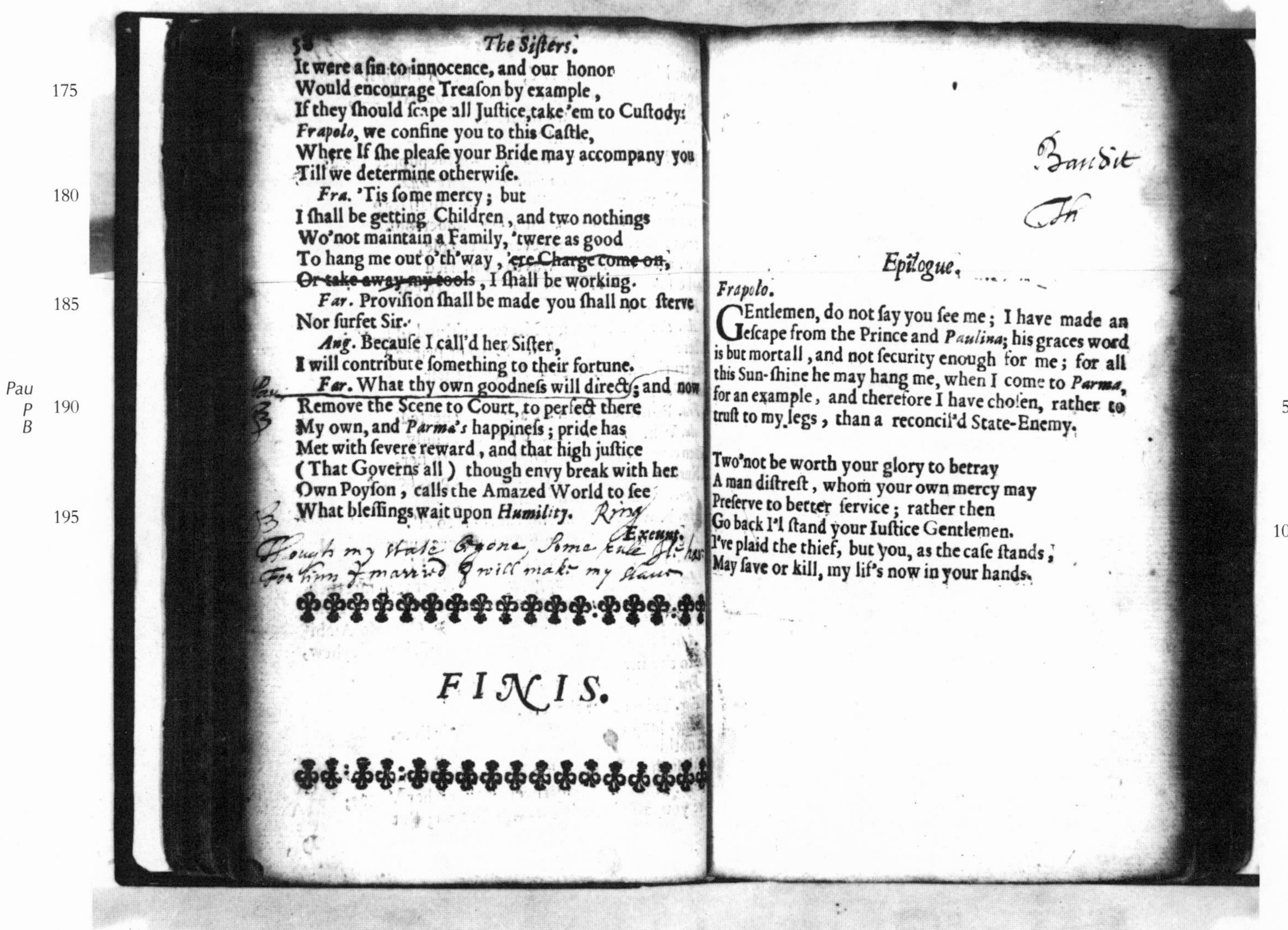

58 *The Sisters.*

It were a ſin to innocence, and our honor
Would encourage Treaſon by example,
If they ſhould ſcape all Juſtice, take 'em to Cuſtody:
Frapolo, we confine you to this Caſtle,
Where if ſhe pleaſe your Bride may accompany you
Till we determine otherwiſe.
Fra. 'Tis ſome mercy; but
I ſhall be getting Children, and two nothings
Wo'not maintain a Family, 'twere as good
To hang me out o'th'way, ~~ere Charge come on,~~
~~Or take away my tools~~, I ſhall be working.
Far. Proviſion ſhall be made you ſhall not ſterve
Nor ſurfet Sir.
Ang. Becauſe I call'd her Siſter,
I will contribute ſomething to their fortune.
Pau *Far.* What thy own goodneſs will direct; and now
P Remove the Scene to Court, to perfect there
B My own, and *Parma's* happineſs; pride has
Met with ſevere reward, and that high juſtice
(That Governs all) though envy break with her
Own Poyſon, calls the Amazed World to ſee
What bleſſings wait upon *Humility.* Ring
Exeunt.
Though my state begone, some rule Ile have
For him I married I will make my slaue

FINIS.

Epilogue.

Frapolo.

Gentlemen, do not ſay you ſee me; I have made an eſcape from the Prince and *Paulina*; his graces word is but mortall, and not ſecurity enough for me; for all this Sun-ſhine he may hang me, when I come to *Parma*, for an example, and therefore I have choſen, rather to truſt to my legs, than a reconcil'd State-Enemy.

Two'not be worth your glory to betray
A man diſtreſt, whom your own mercy may
Preſerve to better ſervice; rather then
Go back I'l ſtand your Iuſtice Gentlemen.
I've plaid the thief, but you, as the caſe ſtands,
May ſave or kill, my lif's now in your hands.

V, ii, 189–97. The markings indicate that Farnese spoke only the first phrase in the final speech, with the remainder, plus the two added lines, spoken by Paulina. Summers misquoted the additional lines and gave them to Frapolo. The two lines were apparently added after the prompt notes were entered, since the *Ring* cue comes before rather than after them. The cue should have been canceled and rewritten, otherwise the musicians might have been signaled too soon; or was music supposed to accompany the added lines? The curious doodles in the left margin I cannot interpret.

V, ii, 196–97. Paulina's added lines are: *Though my state begone, some rule Ile have / For him I married I will make my slaue.*

AGLAURA.

Presented at the Private-House
IN
Black Fryers,
By His Majesties Servants.

Written by
Sir JOHN SUCKLING.

LONDON,
Printed for *Humphery Moseley* at the Prince's Arms
in St. *Paul's* Churchyard. 1658.

Aglaura by Sir John Suckling. Reproduced by permission of the Bodleian Library, Oxford.

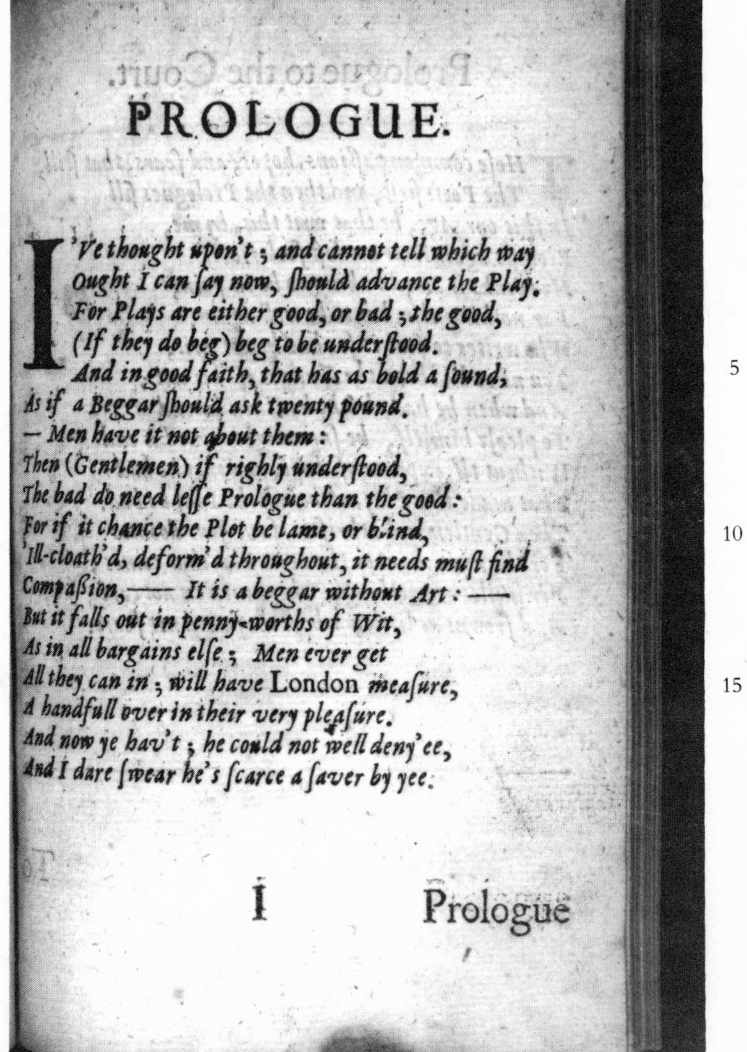

PROLOGUE.

I'Ve thought upon't; and cannot tell which way
Ought I can ſay now, ſhould advance the Play;
For Plays are either good, or bad; the good,
(If they do beg) beg to be underſtood.
And in good faith, that has as bold a ſound,
As if a Beggar ſhould ask twenty pound.
— Men have it not about them:
Then (Gentlemen) if righly underſtood,
The bad do need leſſe Prologue than the good:
For if it chance the Plot be lame, or blind,
Ill-cloath'd, deform'd throughout, it needs muſt find
Compaſſion,—— It is a beggar without Art: ——
But it falls out in penny-worths of Wit,
As in all bargains elſe; Men ever get
All they can in; will have London meaſure,
A handfull over in their very pleaſure.
And now ye hav't; he could not well deny'ee,
And I dare ſwear he's ſcarce a ſaver by yee.

I Prologue

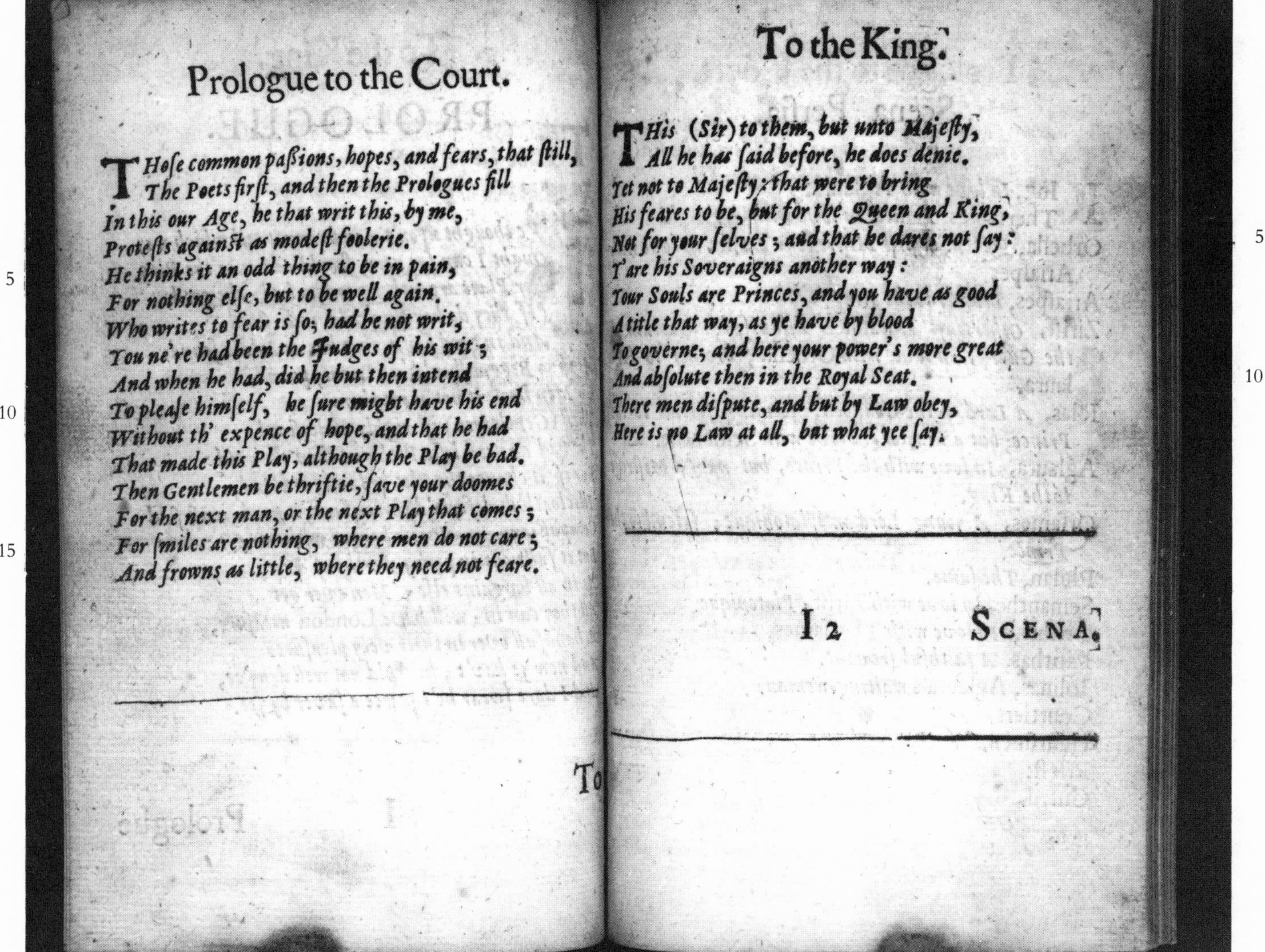

Prologue to the Court.

THoſe common paſsions, hopes, and fears, that ſtill,
The Poets firſt, and then the Prologues fill
In this our Age, he that writ this, by me,
Proteſts againſt as modeſt foolerie.
He thinks it an odd thing to be in pain,
For nothing elſe, but to be well again.
Who writes to fear is ſo; had he not writ,
You ne're had been the Judges of his wit;
And when he had, did he but then intend
To pleaſe himſelf, he ſure might have his end
Without th' expence of hope, and that he had
That made this Play, although the Play be bad.
Then Gentlemen be thriftie, ſave your doomes
For the next man, or the next Play that comes;
For ſmiles are nothing, where men do not care;
And frowns as little, where they need not feare.

To

To the King.

THis (Sir) to them, but unto Majeſty,
All he has ſaid before, he does denie.
Yet not to Majeſty; that were to bring
His feares to be, but for the Queen and King,
Not for your ſelves; and that he dares not ſay:
Y'are his Soveraigns another way:
Your Souls are Princes, and you have as good
A title that way, as ye have by blood
To governe; and here your power's more great
And abſolute then in the Royal Seat.
There men diſpute, and but by Law obey,
Here is no Law at all, but what yee ſay.

I2 SCENA.

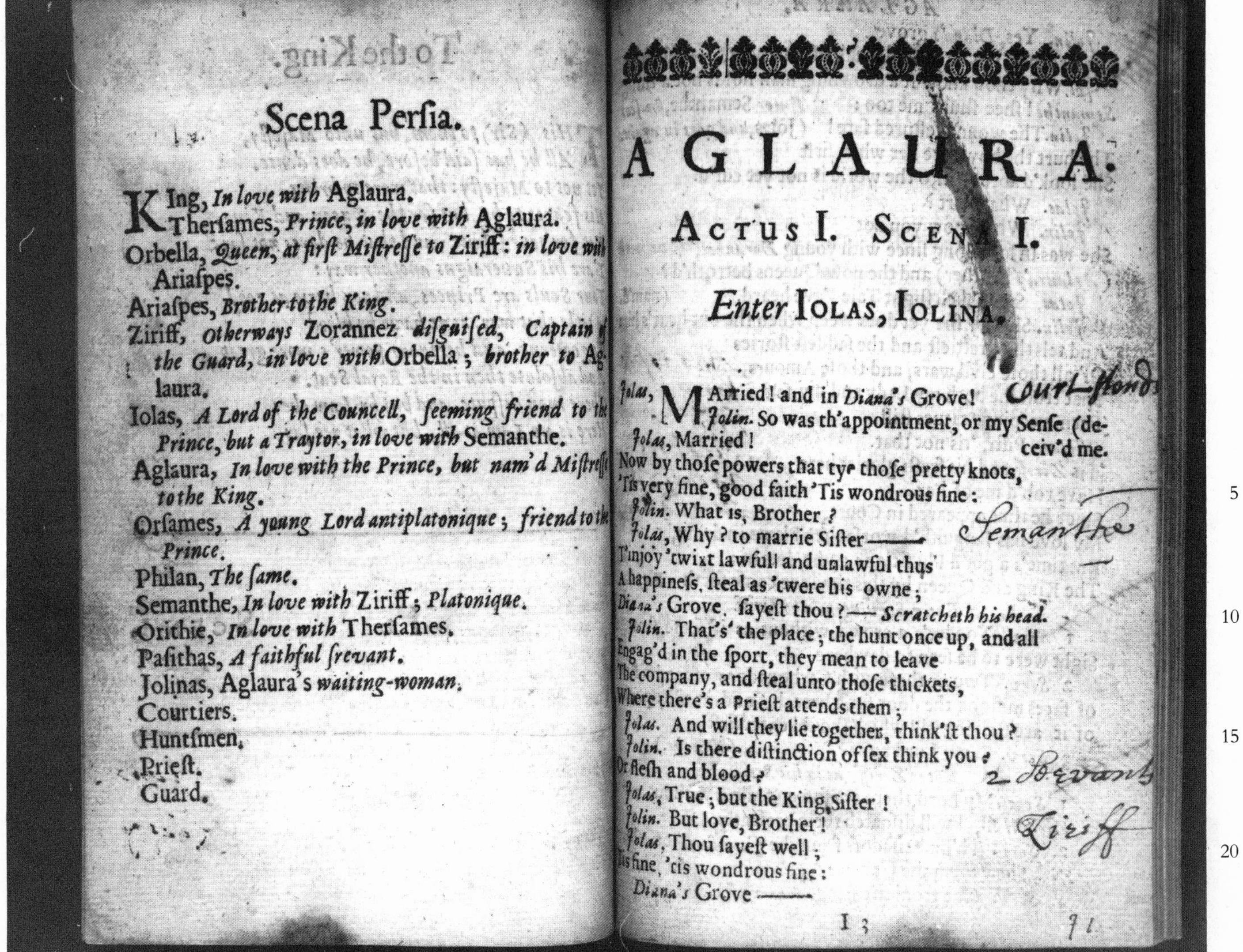

Scena Persia.

King, *In love with* Aglaura.
Thersames, *Prince, in love with* Aglaura.
Orbella, *Queen, at first Mistresse to* Ziriff: *in love with* Ariaspes.
Ariaspes, *Brother to the King*.
Ziriff, *otherways* Zorannez *disguised, Captain of the Guard, in love with* Orbella; *brother to* Aglaura.
Iolas, *A Lord of the Councell, seeming friend to the Prince, but a Traytor, in love with* Semanthe.
Aglaura, *In love with the Prince, but nam'd Mistresse to the King*.
Orsames, *A young Lord antiplatonique; friend to the Prince*.
Philan, *The same*.
Semanthe, *In love with* Ziriff; *Platonique*.
Orithie, *In love with* Thersames.
Pasithas, *A faithful srevant*.
Jolinas, Aglaura's *waiting-woman*.
Courtiers.
Huntsmen.
Priest.
Guard.

AGLAURA.

Actus I. Scena I.

Enter Iolas, Iolina.

Iolas, Married! and in *Diana's* Grove!
Iolin. So was th'appointment, or my Sense (deceiv'd me.
Iolas, Married!
Now by those powers that tye those pretty knots,
'Tis very fine, good faith 'Tis wondrous fine:
Iolin. What is, Brother?
Iolas, Why? to marrie Sister—— Semanthe
T'injoy 'twixt lawfull and unlawful thus
A happiness, steal as 'twere his owne;
Diana's Grove, sayest thou?—— *Scratcheth his head*.
Iolin. That's' the place; the hunt once up, and all
Engag'd in the sport, they mean to leave
The company, and steal unto those thickets,
Where there's a Priest attends them;
Iolas. And will they lie together, think'st thou?
Iolin. Is there distinction of sex think you?
Or flesh and blood? 2 Servants
Iolas, True; but the King, Sister!
Iolin. But love, Brother! Ziriff
Iolas, Thou sayest well;
'Tis fine, 'tis wondrous fine:
Diana's Grove ——

I 3 91

Jolin. Yes, *Diana's* grove,
But Brother, if you should speak of this now, —(so fast:
Jol. Why thou know'st a drowning man holds not a thing
Semanthe! shee shuns me too: *Enter* Semanthe, *she sees*
Jolin. The wound festured sure! (Jolas, *and goes in again.*
The hurt the boy gave her when first
She look'd abroad into the world is not yet cur'd.
Jolas. What hurt?
Jolin. Why, know you not
She was in love long since with young *Zorannes,*
(*Aglaura's* brother) and the now Queens betroth'd?
Jolas, Some such slight Tale I'ave heard. (nam'd,
Jolin. Slight? she yet does weep when she but hear's him
And tels the prettiest and the saddest stories
Of all those civil wars, and those Amours,
That trust me both my Lady and my self
Turn weeping Statues still.
Jolas. Pish, 'tis not that.
'Tis *Ziriff* and his fresh glories here
Have rob'd me of her.
Since he thus appeared in Court,
My love has languish'd worse then Plants in drought.
But time's a good Physician: come, lets in:
The King and Queen by this time are come forth. *Exeunt.*

Enter Serving-men to Ziriff.

1 *Serv.* Yonder's a crowd without as if some strange
Sight were to be seen to day here.
2 *Serv.* Two or three with Carbonadoes afore in stead
of faces mistook the door for a breach, and at the opening
of it, are striving still which should enter first.
3 *Serv.* Is my Lord busie? (*Knocks.*)

Enter Ziriff, as in his Studie.

1 *Serv.* My Lord, there are some Soldiers without —
Zir. Well, I will dispatch them presently.
2. *Serv.* Th'Embassadors from the *Cadusians* too —
Zir. Shew them the Gallerie.
3. *Serv.* One from the King ———

Zir

Zir. Again? I come, I come. *Exeunt Serving-men.*

Ziriff *solus.*

Greatness, thou vainer shadow of the Princes beams,
Begot by meere reflection, nourish'd in extreames;
First taught to creep, and live upon the glance,
Poorely to fare, till thine own proper strength
Bring thee to surfet of thy self at last:
How dull a Pageant, would this States-play seeme
To me now, were not my love and my revenge
Mixt with it?
Three tedious Winters have I waited here,
Like patient Chymists blowing still the coales,
And still expecting when the blessed hour
Would come, should make me master of
The Court *Elixar,* Power, for that turns all:
'Tis in projection now; down, sorrow, down,
And swell my heart no more, and thou wrong'd ghost
Of my dead father, to thy bed agen,
And sleep securely;
It cannot be long, for sure *Fate* must,
As't has been cruel, so a while be just. *Exit.*

Enter King and Lords, the Lords intreating for Prisoners.

King. I say they shall not live; our mercy
Would turn sin, should we but use it e're:
Pittie, and Love, the bosses only be
Of government meerly for show and Ornament.
Feare is the bit that mans proud will restraines,
And makes its vice its vertue — See it done.

Enter to them Queen, Aglaura, *Ladies, the King addresses himself to* Aglaura.

So early and so curious in your dresse, (fair Mistress?)
These prettie ambushes and traps for hearts
Set with such care to day, look like design:
Speak Lady, is't a massacre resolv'd?
Is conquering one by one grown tedious sport?
Or is the number of the taken such,

I 4 That

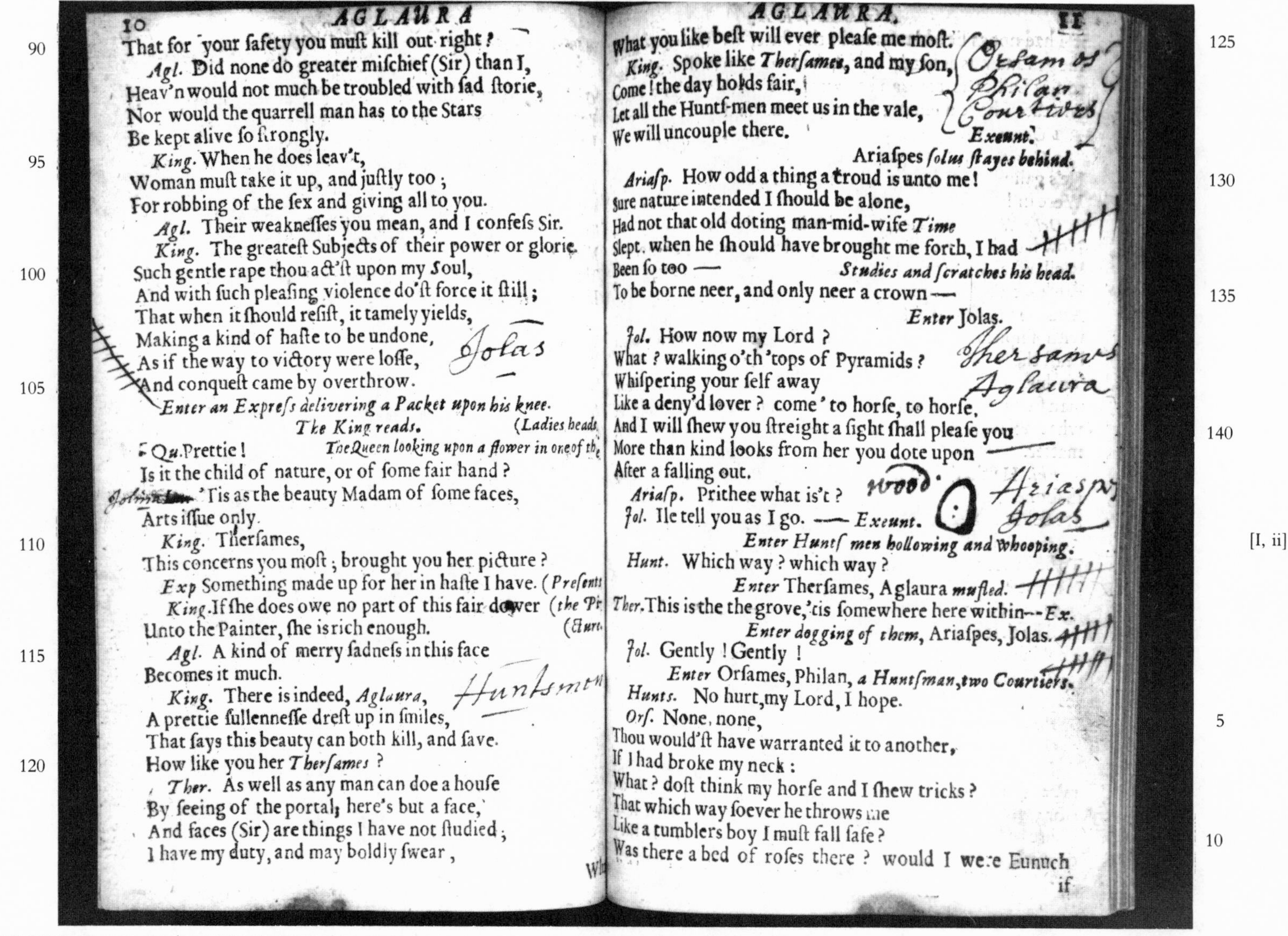

10 AGLAURA

That for your ſafety you muſt kill out-right?
Agl. Did none do greater miſchief (Sir) than I,
Heav'n would not much be troubled with ſad ſtorie,
Nor would the quarrell man has to the Stars
Be kept alive ſo ſtrongly.
King. When he does leav't,
Woman muſt take it up, and juſtly too;
For robbing of the ſex and giving all to you.
Agl. Their weakneſſes you mean, and I confeſs Sir.
King. The greateſt Subjects of their power or glorie.
Such gentle rape thou act'ſt upon my Soul,
And with ſuch pleaſing violence do'ſt force it ſtill;
That when it ſhould reſiſt, it tamely yields,
Making a kind of haſte to be undone,
As if the way to victory were loſſe,
And conqueſt came by overthrow.
Enter an Expreſs delivering a Packet upon his knee.
The King reads. (*Ladies heads*
Qu. Prettie! *The Queen looking upon a flower in one of the*
Is it the child of nature, or of ſome fair hand?
'Tis as the beauty Madam of ſome faces,
Arts iſſue only.
King. Therſames,
This concerns you moſt; brought you her picture?
Exp. Something made up for her in haſte I have. (*Preſents*
King. If ſhe does owe no part of this fair dower (*the Pi*
Unto the Painter, ſhe is rich enough. (*Aure.*
Agl. A kind of merry ſadneſs in this face
Becomes it much.
King. There is indeed, *Aglaura*,
A prettie ſullenneſſe dreſt up in ſmiles,
That ſays this beauty can both kill, and ſave.
How like you her *Therſames*?
Ther. As well as any man can doe a houſe
By ſeeing of the portal; here's but a face,
And faces (Sir) are things I have not ſtudied;
I have my duty, and may boldly ſwear,
Wh

AGLAURA. 11

What you like beſt will ever pleaſe me moſt.
King. Spoke like *Therſames*, and my ſon,
Come! the day holds fair,
Let all the Huntſ-men meet us in the vale,
We will uncouple there. *Exeunt.*
Ariaſpes *ſolus ſtayes behind.*
Ariaſp. How odd a thing a croud is unto me!
Sure nature intended I ſhould be alone,
Had not that old doting man-mid-wife *Time*
Slept, when he ſhould have brought me forth, I had
Been ſo too — *Studies and ſcratches his head.*
To be borne neer, and only neer a crown—
Enter Jolas.
Jol. How now my Lord?
What? walking o'th' tops of Pyramids?
Whiſpering your ſelf away
Like a deny'd lover? come to horſe, to horſe,
And I will ſhew you ſtreight a ſight ſhall pleaſe you
More than kind looks from her you dote upon
After a falling out.
Ariaſp. Prithee what is't?
Jol. Ile tell you as I go. —— *Exeunt.*
Enter Huntſmen hollowing and whooping. [I, ii]
Hunt. Which way? which way?
Enter Therſames, Aglaura *mufled.*
Ther. This is the grove, 'tis ſomewhere here within-- *Ex.*
Enter dogging of them, Ariaſpes, Jolas.
Jol. Gently! Gently!
Enter Orſames, Philan, *a Huntſman, two Courtiers.*
Hunts. No hurt, my Lord, I hope.
Orſ. None, none,
Thou would'ſt have warranted it to another,
If I had broke my neck:
What? doſt think my horſe and I ſhew tricks?
That which way ſoever he throws me
Like a tumblers boy I muſt fall ſafe?
Was there a bed of roſes there? would I were Eunuch
if

I, i, 125. Orsames and his group are warned before the Thersames group even though they enter later. The earlier warning may have been given because the entrance was opposite prompt side or because the group was larger or both.

I, ii, opening. The cross-hatch entrance cue for the Huntsmen is missing.

12 AGLAURA.

if I had not as lief h'a falne in the ftate, as where I did; the ground was as hard, as if it had been pav'd with Platonick Ladies hearts, and this unconfcionable fellow askes whether I have no hurt; where's my horfe?

1 Court. Making love to the next mare I think.

2 Court. Not the next I affure you,
He's gallop't away, as if all the fpurs i'th' field
Were in his fides.

Orf. Why there's it; the jades in the fafhion too.
Now ha's done me an injurie, he will not come nere me.
Well, when I hunt next, may it be upon a ftarv'd cow,
Without a faddle too.
And may I fall into a faw-pit, and not be taken up, but with fufpition of having been private with mine own beaft there. Now I better confider on't too, Gentlemen, 'tis but the fame thing we do at Court; here's every man ftriving who fhall be formoft, and hotly purfuing of what he feldome overtakes, or if he does, it's no great matter.

Phi. He that's beft hors'd (that is beft friended) gets in fooneft; and then all he has to do is to laugh at thofe that are behind. Shall we help you my Lord?

Orf. Prithee do —— ftay!
To be in view, is to be in favour,
Is it not?

Phi. Right,
And he that has a ftrong faction againft him, hunts, upon a cold fent, and may in time come to a loffe.

Orf. Here's one rides two miles about, while another leaps a ditch and is in before him.

Phi. Where note the indirect way's the neareft.

Orf. Good again ——

Phi. And here's another puts on, and fals into a Quagmire, (that is) follows the Court till he has fpent all (for your Court-quagmire is want of mony) there a man is fure to ftick, and then not one helps him out, if they do not laugh at him.

1 Court.

AGLAURA. 13

1 Court. What think you of him that hunts after my rate, And never fees the Deer?

2 Court. Why he is like fome young fellow that follows The Court, and never fees the King.

Orf. To fpur a horfe till he is tir'd, is

Phi. To importune a friend till he weary of you.

Orf. For then upon the firft occafion y'are thrown off,
As I was now. (mes.

Phi. This is nothing to the catching of your horfe, Orfa-

Orf. Thou fay'ft true, I think he is no tranfmigrated
Philofopher, & therefore not likely to be taken with morals,
Gentlemen - your help, the next I hope will be yours,
And then tw'ill be my turne —— *Exeunt.*

Enter again married, Therfames, Aglaura, *Prieft.*

Therf. Feare not my Dear; if when Loves diet
Was bare looks, and thofe ftoln too,
He yet did thrive! what then
Will he do now? when every night will be
A feaft, and every day frefh revelrie.

Agl. Will he not furfeit when he once fhall come
To groffer fare (my Lord) and fo grow fick?
And Love once fick, how quickly it will dye?

Ther. Ours cannot; 'tis as immortal as the things
That elemented it, which were our fouls:
Nor can they e're impair in health, for what
Thefe holy rites do warrant us to do,
More than our bodyes would for quenching thirft.
Come let's to horfe, we fhall be mift,
For we are envies mark, and Court eyes carry far.
Your prayers and filence Sir: —*to the Prieft.* *Exeunt.*

Enter Ariafpes, Jolas. [I, iii]

Ari. If it fucceed, I wear thee here my *Jolas*—

Jol. If it fucceed? will night fucceed the day?
Or hours one to another? is not his luft
The Idol of his foul? and was not fhe
The Idol of his luft? as fafely he might
Have ftoln the Diadem from off his head,

And

And he would leſs have miſt it.
You now, my Lord, muſt raiſe his jealouſie,
Teach it to look through the falſe optick, fear,
And make it ſee all double: Tell him the Prince
Would not have thus preſum'd but that he does
Intend worſe yet; and that his crown and life
Will be the next attempt
Ari. Right, and I will urge
How dangerous 'tis unto the preſent ſtate,
To have the creatures, and the followers
Of the next Prince (whom all now ſtrive to pleaſe)
Too near about him:
Jol. What if the male-contents that uſe
To come unto him were diſcovered?
Ari. By no means; for 'twere in vain to give
Him diſcontent (which too muſt needs be done)
If they within him gav't not nouriſhment.
Jol. Well, Ile away firſt, for the print's too big
If we be ſeen together.— *Exit.*
Ari. I have ſo fraught this Barke with hope, that it
Dares venture now in any ſtorm, or weather;
And if he ſink or ſplits, all's one to me.
" Ambition ſeems all things, and yet is none,
" But in diſguiſe ſtalkes to opinion
" And fooles it into faith, for every thing:
'Tis not with th'aſcending to a Throne,
As 'tis with ſtairs and ſteps that are the ſame;
For to a Crown, each humors a degree;
And as men change and differ, ſo muſt we.
The name of vertue doth the people pleaſe,
Not for their love to vertue, but their eaſe,
And Parrat Rumor I that tale have taught,
By making love I hold the womans grace;
'Tis the Courts double key, and entrance gets
To all the little plots; the fierie ſpirits
My love to Armes hath drawn into my faction;
All, but the minion of the Time, is mine,
And

And he ſhall be, or ſhall not be at all.
He that beholds a wing in pieces torn,
And knows not that to heav'n it once did bear
The high-flown and ſelfe-leſsning bird, will think
And call them idle Subjects of the wind:
When he that has the skill to imp and binde
Theſe in right places, will thus truth diſcover,
That borrowed inſtruments doe oft convey
The Soul to her propos'd Intents, and where
Our Stars deny, Art may ſupply— *Exit.*
Enter Semanthe, Orithia, Orſames, Philan.
Sem. Think you it is not then
The little jealouſies (my Lord) and fears,
Joy mixt with doubt, and doubt reviv'd with hope,
That crowns all love with pleaſure? theſe are loſt
When once we come to full fruition;
Like waking in the morning, when all night
Our fancy has been fed with ſome new ſtrange delight.
Orſ. I grant you, Madam, that the fears, and joys,
Hopes, and deſires, mixt with deſpairs, and doubts,
Do make the ſport in love; that they are
The very dogs by which we hunt the Hare;
But as the dogs would ſtop, and ſtreight give o're,
Were it not for the little thing before;
So would our paſſions; both alike muſt be
Fleſh't in the chaſe.
Ori. Will you then place the happineſs, but there,
Where the dull pow-man, and the plow-mans horſe
Can find it out? Shall Souls refin'd, not know
How to preſerve alive a noble flame,
But let it dy, burn out to appetite?
Sem. Love's a Chamelion, and would live on aire,
Phyſick for Agues, ſtarving is his food.
Orſ. Why? there's it now! a greater Epicure
Lives not on earth? my Lord and I have been
In's Privie kitchin, ſeen his bills of Fare.
Sem. And how, and how my Lord?
Orſ.

16 AGLAURA.

Orſ. A mighty Prince,
And full of curioſity —— Harts newly ſlain
Serv'd up intire, and ſtuck with little Arrows
In ſtead of Cloaves ——
Phi. Sometimes a cheek plumpt up
With broth, with cream and claret mingled
For ſauce, and round about the diſh
Pomegranate kernels ſtrew'd on leaves of Lillies.
Orſ. Then will he have black eyes, for thoſe of late
He feeds on much, and for variety
The gray——
Phi. You forget his cover'd diſhes
Of Jene-ſtrayes, and Marmalade of Lips,
Perfum'd by breath ſweet as the beanes firſt bloſſoms.
Sem. Rare!
And what's the drink to all this meat, my Lord?
Orſ. Nothing but pearl diſſolv'd, tears ſtill freſh fetch'd
From Lovers eyes, which if they cannot come to be
Warm in the carriage, are ſtreight cool'd with ſighs.
Sem: And all this rich proportion, perchance
We would allow him:
Orſ, True! but therefore this is but his common diet;
Onely ſerves
When his chief Cooks, *Liking* and *Opportunitie*,
Are out o'th'way; for when he feaſts indeed,
'Tis there where the wiſe people of the world
Did place the vertues, i'th' middle —— Madam.
Ori. My Lord there is ſo little hope we ſhould convert you;
And if we ſhould, ſo little got by it,
That wee'l not loſe ſo much upon't as ſleep.
Your Lordſhip ſervants ——
Orſ. Nay Ladies wee'l wait upon you to your chambers.
Phi. Prithee lets ſpare the complement, we ſhall do no (good.
Orſ. By this hand I'le trie.
They keep me faſting, and I muſt be praying. *Exeunt.*
[I, iv] Aglaura *undreſſing of her ſelf.* Jolina.
Agl. Undreſs me: ——

AGLAURA. 17

Is it not late *Jolina*?
It was the longeſt day, this ——
Enter Therſames.
Ther. Softly, as death it ſelf comes on,
When it does ſteal away the ſick mans breath,
And ſtanders by perceive it not,
Have I trod, the way unto theſe lodgings.
How wiſely do thoſe Powers
That give us happineſs, order it?
Sending us ſtill feares to bound our joys,
Which elſe would overflow and loſe themſelves:
See where ſhe ſits,
Like day retir'd into another world.
Deare mine! where all the beauty man admires
In ſcattered pieces, does united lie.
Where ſenſe does feaſt, and yet where ſweet deſire
Lives in its longing, like a Miſers eye,
That never knew, nor ſaw ſacietie:
Tell me, by what Approaches muſt I come
To take in what remains of my felicitie?
Agl. Needs there any new ones, where the breach
Is made already? you are entred here ——
Long ſince (Sir) here, and I have giv'n up all.
Ther. All but the Fort; and in ſuch wars, as theſe,
Till that be yielded up, there is no peace,
Nor triumph to be made; come! undo, undo,
And from theſe envious clouds ſlide quick
Into Loves proper Sphere, thy bed:
The wearie Traveller, whom the buſie Sun
Hath vex't all day, and ſcortch'd almoſt to tinder,
Nere long'd for night, as I have long'd for this.
What rude hand is that? *One knocks haſtily.*
Go *Jolina*, ſee but let none enter —— *Jolina goes to the door.*
Jol. 'Tis *Zeriff*, Sir.
Ther. — Oh ——
Something of weight hath fallen out it ſeems,
Which in his zeal he could not keep till morning.

But

18 *AGLAVRA.*

But one ſhort minute, Deare, into that chamber.
Enter Ziriff.
How now?
Thou ſtart'ſt, as if thy ſinnes had met thee,
Or thy Fathers ghoſt; what newes man?
Zir. Such as will ſend the blood of haſtie meſſages
Unto the heart, and make it call
All that is man about you into councell:
Where's the Princeſſe, Sir?
Ther. Why what of her?
Zir. The King muſt have her ——
Ther. How?
Zir. The King muſt have her (Sir)
Ther. Though feare of worſe makes ill ſtill reliſh better,
And this looke handſome in our Friendſhip, *Ziriff*,
Yet ſo ſevere a preparation —
There needed not: come, come! what iſt?
Ziriff *leads him to the doore, and ſhewes him a Guard.*
A Guard! *Ther ſames*,
Thou art loſt; betray'd
By faithleſſe and ungratefull man, *(and drawes*
Out of a happineſſe: — *He ſteps between the doore and him.*
The very thought of that,
Will lend my anger ſo much noble juſtice,
That wert thou maſter of as much freſh life,
As th'aſt been of villany, it ſhould not ſerve,
Nor ſtocke thee out, to glorie, or repent
The leaſt of it.
Zir. Put up: put up! ſuch unbecomming anger
I have not ſeene you weare before.
What? draw upon your Friend! *Diſcovers himſelfe.*
Doe you beleeve me right now? ——
Ther. I ſcarce beleeve mine eyes: — *Zorannes.*
Zir. The ſame, but how preſerv'd, or why
Thus long diſguis'd, to you a freer houre muſt ſpeake:
That y'are betrai'd is certaine, but by whom,
Unleſſe the Prieſt himſelfe, I cannot gheſſe.
Mo

AGLAURA. 19

More than the marriage, though he knowes not of;
If you now ſend her on theſe early ſummons
Before the ſparks are growne into a flame,
You do redeeme th' offence, or make it leſſe;
And (on my life) yet his intents are fair,
And he will but beſiege, not force affection.
So you gaine time; if you refuſe, there's but
One way; you know his power and paſſion.
Ther. Into how ſtrange a Labyrinth am I
Now falne! what ſhall I do *Zirannes*?
Zir. Doe (Sir) as Sea-men, that have loſt their light
And way: ſtrike ſaile, and lye quiet a while,
Your forces in the Province are not yet
In readineſſe, nor is our friend *Zephines*
Arriv'd at Delphos; nothing is ripe, beſides ——
Ther. Good heavens, did I but dream that ſhe was mine?
Upon imagination did I climbe up to
This height? let me then wake and dye:
Some courteous hand ſnatch me from what's to come,
And ere my wrongs have being give them end:
Zir. How poore and how unlike the Prince is this?
This trifle woman does unman us all:
Robs us ſo much it makes us things of Pittie.
Is this a time to loſe our anger in,
And vainly breathe it out? when all we have
Will hardly fill the ſaile of Reſolution,
And make us beare up high enough for action.
Ther. I have done (Sir) pray chide no more;
The ſlave whom tedious cuſtome has enur'd
And taught to think of miſerie as of food,
Counting it but a neceſſarie of life,
And ſo diſgeſting it, ſhall not ſo much as once
Be nam'd to patience, when I am ſpoken of:
Marke mee; for I will now undoe my ſelfe
As willingly, as virgins give up all firſt nights
To them they love: ——*Offers to go out.*
Zir. Stay, Sir, 'twere fit *Aglaura* yet were kept
K Tri

I, iv, 38. Aglaura and Jolina presumably exit at this point, but there is no stage direction to that effect, nor did the prompter correct the error.

I, iv, 54. The Guard was warned at line 15, but he is given no entrance cue.

In ignorance: I will dismiss the Guard,
And be my selfe againe. *Exit.*
Ther. In how much worse estate am I in now,
Than if I neare had known her! Privation
Is a miserie as much above bare wretchedness,
As that is short of happiness:
So when the Sun does not appear,
'Tis darker, cause it once was here.

Enter Ziriff, *speaks to* Orsames *and others half entred.*

Zir. Nay, Gentlemen,
There needs no force, where there is no resistance:
Ile satisfie the King my selfe.
Ther. —— Oh 'tis well y'are come,
There was within me fresh Rebellion,
And reason was almost unking'd agen.
But you shall have her Sir— *Goes out to fetch* Aglaura.
Zir. What doubtfull combats in this noble youth
Passion and Reason have!

Enter Thersames *leading* Aglaura.

Ther. Here Sir —— *Gives her, goes out.*
Agl. What means the Prince, my Lord?
Zir. Madam, his wiser fear has taught him to disguise
His Love, and make it looke a little rude at parting.
Affairs that do concerne all that you hope from
Happiness, this night force him away:
And left you should have tempted him to stay,
(Which he did doubt you would, and would prevaile)
He left you thus: he does desire by mee
You would this night lodg in the little Tower,
Which is in my command; the reasons why
Himself will shortly tell you.
Agl. 'Tis strange, but I am all obedience.— *Exeunt.*

Actus

ACTUS II. SCENA I.

Enter Thersames, Jolas *a Lord of the Counsel.*

Jol. I Told him so, Sir, urg'd 'twas no common knot,
That to the tying of it two powerfull Princes,
Vertue and Love were joyn'd, and that
A greater than these two was now
Engaged in it; Religion; but 'twould not do,
The corke of passion boy'd up all reason so
That what was said, swam but o'th' top of th' ear,
Near reach't the heart:
Ther. Is there no way for Kings to shew their power,
But in their Subjects wrongs? no subject neither
But his owne sonne?
Iol. Right Sir:
No quarrie for his lust to gorge on, but on what
You fairly had flown at and taken?
Well —— wert not the King, or wert indeed
Not you, that have such hopes, and such a crown
To venture, and yet ——
'Tis but a woman.
Ther. How? that But again, and thou art more injurious
Than he, and wouldst provoke me sooner.
Iol. Why Sir?
There are no Altars yet addrest unto her,
Nor sacrifice; if I have made her less
Than what she is, it was my love to you;
For in my thoughts, and here within, I hold her
The Noblest peece Nature ere lent our eyes,
And of the which, all Women else, are but
Weak counterfeits, made up by her journey-men:
But was this fit to tell you?
I know you value but too high all that,

K 2 And

I, iv, following 117. The entrance is not cued.
I, iv, following 126. The entrance is not cued.

II, i, opening. The opening entrance, warned by the *act ready* note at I, iv, 116, is not cued with a cross-hatch mark; this is characteristic of all act openings in the promptbook.

And in a losse we should not make things more;
'Tis miseries happinesse, that wee can make it lesse
By art, through a forgetfullnesse upon our ils;
Yet who can doe it here?
When every voice must needs, and every face,
By shewing what she was not, shew what she was.
Ther. Ile instantly unto him —*drawes.*
Iol. Stay Sir:
Though't be the utmost of my Fortunes hope
To have an equall share of ill with you:
Yet I could wish we sold this trifle life
At a far dearer rate, then we are like to doe,
Since 'tis a King's the Merchant.
Ther. Ha!
King! I! tis indeed!
And ther's no Art can canncell that high bond:
Iol. —He cooles againe. — (*to himselfe.*)
True Sir, and yet mee thinkes to know a reason —
For passive nature ne'r had glorious end;
And he that States preventions ever learn'd,
Knowes, 'tis one motion to strike and to defend.

Enter Serving-man.

Serv. Some of the Lords without, and from the King,
They say, wait you.
Ther. What subtle State trick now?
But one turne here, and I am back my Lord. — *Exit*
Iol. This will not doe; his resoutiou's like.
A skilfull horse-man and reason is the stirrop,
Which though a sudden shock may make — Thersames
It loose, yet does it meet it handsomly agen.
Stay, 'tmust be some sudden feare of wrong
To her, that may draw on sudden act
From him, and ruine from the King; for such
A spirit will not like common ones, be
Rais'd by every spell, 'tis in loves circle
Onely 'twill appeare.

Orsames Philan Courtiers Enter

Enter Thersames.

Ther. I cannot beare the burthen of my wrongs
One minute longer.
Iol. Why! what's the matter Sir?
Ther. They doe pretend the safety of the State:
Now, nothing but my marriage with *Gadusa*
Can secure th' adjoyning countrey to it;
Confinement during life for me if I refuse
Diana's Nunnerie for her — And at that Nunn'rie, *Iolas,*
Allegiance in me like the string of a Watch
Wound up too high, and forc'd above the nicke,
Ran back, and in a moment was unravell'd all.
Iol. Now by the love I beare to Justice,
That Nun'ry was too severe; when vertuous love's a crime,
What man can hope to scape a punishment,
Or who's indeed so wretched to desire it?
Ther. Right!
Iol. What answer made you, Sir!
Ther. None, they gave till to morrow,
And e're that be, or they or I
Must know our destiny.
Come friend let's in; there is no sleeping now;
For time is short, and we have much to doe. — *Exeunt,*

Enter Orsames, Philan, *Courtiers.*

Ors. Judge you, Gentlemen, if I be not as unfortunate
As a gamester thinks himselfe upon the losse
Of the last stake; this is the first she
I ever swore too heartily, and (by those eyes)
I think I had continued unperjur'd a whole moneth,
(And that's fair you'l say.)
1 *Court.* Very fair —
Ors. Had she not run mad betwixt. —
2 *Court.* How? mad?
Who? *Semanthe?*
Ors. Yea, yea, mad, ask *Philan* else.
People that want cleer intervalls talke not
So wildly: Ile tell you Gallants, 'tis now, since first I

Found my felf a little hot, and quivering 'bout the heart,
Some ten daies fince, (a tedious Ague) Sirs
(But what of that?)
The gracious glance, and little whifper paft,
Approaches made from th' hand unto the lip,
I came to vifit her, and (as you know we ufe)
Breathing a figh or two by the way of Prologue,
Told her that in Loves Phyfick 'twas a rule,
Where the difeafe had birth to feek a cure;
I had no fooner nam'd love to her, but fhe
Began to talke of Flames, and Flames
Neither devouring, nor devour'd of Aire,
And of Camelions —

1 *Court.* Oh the *Platoniques*!

2 *Court.* Thofe of the new religion in love! your Lord-
(fhip's merrie,
Troth, how do you like the humor on't?

Orf. As thou wouldft like red haire, or leannefs
In thy Miftrefs; fcurvily, 't does worfe with handfomnefs,
Than ftrong defire could do with impotence;
A meere trick to inhance the price of kiffes —

Phi. Sure thefe filly women, when they feed
Our expectation fo high, do but like
Ignorant Conjurers, that raife a Spirit
Which handfomly they cannot lay againe:

Orf. True, 'tis like fome that nourifh up
Young Lions till they grow fo great they are affraid of
Themfelves; they dare not grant at laft,
For feare they fhould not fatisfie.

Phi. Who's for the Town? I muft take up again.

Orf. This Villanous Love's as changeable as the Philofo-
phers Stone, and thy Miftrefs as hard to compafs too!

Ph. The Platonique is ever fo; they are as tedious
Before they come to the point; as an old man
Faln into the ftories of his youth.

2 *Court.* Or a widow into the praifes of her firft husband.

Orf. Well, if fhe hold out but one moneth longer,
If I doe not quite forget I ere beleagured there,
And remove the fiege to another place, may all

The

The curfes beguil'd virgins lofe upon their prejur'd lovers
Fall upon me.

Phi. And thou wouldft deferve 'em all.

Orf. For what?

Phi. For being in the company of thofe
That tooke away the Prince's Miftrefs from him.

Orf. Peace, that wil be redeem'd —
I put but on this wildneffe to difguife my felf;
There are brave things in hand, hark i'thy eare: --(*whifper*)

1. *Court.* Some fevere plot upon a maiden-head.
Thefe two young Lords make Love,
As Embroyderers work againft a Mask, night and day;
They think importunity a neerer way then merit,
And take women as School-boyes catch Squirrels;
Hunt 'em up and downe till they are wearie,
And fall down before 'em.

Orf. Who loves the Prince failes not —

Phi. And I am one: my injuries are great as thine,
And doe perfwade as ftrongly.

Orf. I had command to bring thee,
Fail not, and in thine one difguife.

Phi. Why in difguife?

Orf. It is the Princes Policie and love;
For if we fhould mifcarrie,
Some one taken might betray the reft
Unknowne to one another;
Each man is fafe, in his own valour;

2 *Court.* And what Mercers wife are you to cheapen now
In ftead of his filks?

Orf. Troth; 'tis not fo well; 'tis but a Cozen of thine —
Come *Philan* let's along: — *Exeunt.*

Enter Queen alone. [II, ii]

Orb. What is it thus within whifpering remorfe,
And calls Love Tyrant? all powers, but his,
Their rigour, and our fear, have made divine!
But every Creature holds of him by fenfe,
The fweeteft Tenure; yea! but my husbands brother:

K 4 And

And what of that? doe harmeleſſe birds or beaſts
Ask leave of curious Heraldrie at all?
Does not the wombe of one fair ſpring,
Bring unto the earth many ſweet rivers,
That wantonly doe one another chace,
And in one bed, kiſſe, mingle, and embrace?
Man (Natures heire) is not by her will ti'd,
To ſhun all creatures are alli'd unto him,
For then he ſhould ſhun all; ſince death and life
Doubly allies all them that live by breath:
The Aire that doth impart to all lifes brood
Refreſhing, is ſo neer to it ſelfe, and to us all,
That all in all is individuall:
But, how am I ſure one and the ſame deſire
Warmes *Ariaſpes*? for Art can keep alive
A beddrid love;

Enter Ariaſpes.

Ar. Alone, (Madam) and overcaſt with thought!
Uncloud--uncloud- for if we may believe
The ſmiles of Fortune, love ſhall no longer pine
In priſon thus, nor undelivered travell
With throws of fear, and of deſire about it.
The Prince, (like to a valiant beaſt in nets)
Striving to force a freedome ſuddenly,
Has made himſelfe at length, the ſurer prey:
The King ſtands only now betwixt, and is
Juſt like a ſingle tree that hinders all the proſpect:
'Tis but the cutting down of him, and we ——

Orb. Why would't thou thus inbarque int[o ſ]trange ſeas,
And trouble Fate for what we have already?
Thou art to me what thou now ſeek'ſt, a Kingdom.
And were thy love as great, as thy ambition,
I ſhould be ſo to thee.

Ari. Think you, you are not Madam?
As well and juſtly may you doubt the truths,
Tortur'd or dying men doe leave behind them:
But then my Fortune turns my miſerie,

When

When my addition ſhall but make you leſſe;
Shall I indure that head that wore a crowne,
For my ſake ſhould weare none? Firſt let me loſe
Th' Exchequer of my wealth, your love; nay, may
All that rich treaſurie you have about you,
Be rifled by the man I hated, and I looke on; Ziriff
Though youth be full of ſin, and heav'n be juſt,
So ſad a doome I hope they keep not from me
Remember what a quick Apoſtacie he made
When all his vowes were up to heav'n and you.
How, e're the Bridall torches were burnt out,
His flames grew weake, and ſicklier: think on that.
Think how unſafe you are, if ſhe ſhould now.
Not ſell her honour at a lower rate,
Than your place in his bed.

Orb. And would not you prove falſe too then?

Ari. By this--and this--loves break-faſt; (*Kiſſes her.*)
By his feaſts too yet to come, by all the
Beauty in this face, divinitie too great
To be Prophan'd ——

Orb. O doe not ſwear by that;
Cankers may eat that flow'r upon the ſtalke
(For ſickneſſe and miſchance are great devourers)
And when there is not in theſe cheeks and lips,
Left red enough to bluſh at perjurie,
When you ſhall make it, what ſhall I doe then?

Ari. Our ſoules by that time (Madam)
Will by long cuſtome ſo acquainted be,
They will not need that duller truch-man Fleſh,
But freely, and without thoſe poorer helps,
Converſe and mingle; mean time wee'll teach
Our loves to ſpeake, not thus to live by ſignes,
And action is his native language, Madam.

Enter Ziriff *unſeen.*

This box but open'd to the Senſe will doe't.

Orb. I undertake I know not what.

Ari. Thine own ſafety (Deareſt)

Let

Let it be this night, if thou do'ſt; *Whiſper and kiſſe.*
Love thy ſelf or me.
Orb. That's very ſudden.
Ari. Not if we be ſo, and we muſt now be wiſe,
For when their Sun ſets, ours begins to riſe. — *Exeunt,*

Ziriff *ſolus*

Zir. Then all my feares are true, and ſhe is falſe;
Falſe as a falling Star, or Glow-wormes fire:
This Devill Beauty is compounded ſtrangely,
It is a ſubtill point, and hard to know,
Whether't has in't more active tempting,
Or more paſſive tempted; ſo ſoon it forces,
And ſo ſoon it yeelds —
Good Gods! ſhee ſeiz'd my heart, as if from you
Sh'ad had Commiſſion to have uſ'd me ſo;
And all mankinde beſides — and ſhe, if the juſt Ocean
Makes more haſte to pay
To needy rivers, what it borrow'd firſt,
Then ſhe to give, where ſhe ne'er took;
Mee thinks I feele anger, Revenges Harbinger
Chalking up all within, and thruſting out
Of doores, the tame and ſofter paſſions; —
It muſt be ſo:
To love is noble frailtie, but poore ſin
When wee fall once to Love, unlov'd agen. *Exit.*

[II, iii] *Enter King* Ariaſpes, Jolas.

Ari. 'Twere fit your Juſtice did conſider, (Sir)
What way it tooke; if you ſhould apprehend
The Prince for Treaſon (which he never did)
And which, unacted, is unborn; (at leaſt will be believ'd ſo)
Lookers on, and the loud talking croud,
Will think it all but water colours
Laid on for a time;
And which wip'd off, each common eye would ſee,
Strange ends through ſtranger wayes:
King. Think'ſt thou I will compound with Treaſon then?
And make one feare anothers Advocate?

Iol. Vertue forbid Sir, but if you would permit,
Them to approach the roome (yet who would adviſe
Treaſon ſhould come ſo neer?) there would be then
No place left for excuſe.
King. How ſtrong are they?
Iol. Weake, conſidering
The Enterpriſe; they are but few in number,
And thoſe few too having nothing but
Their reſolutions conſiderable about them;
A Troop indeed deſign'd to ſuffer what
They come to execute.
King. Who are they are thus wearie of their lives?
Jol. Their names I canot give you.
For thoſe he ſent for, he did ſtill receive
At a back doore, and ſo diſmiſt them too.
But I doe think *Ziriff* is one.
King. Take heed! I ſhall ſuſpect thy hate to others,
Not thy love to me, begot this ſervice;
This Treaſon thou thy ſelf do'ſt ſay
Has but an houres age, and I can give accompt
Of him, beyond that time — Brother, in the little Tower
Where now *Aglaura's* priſoner,
You ſhall find him; bring him along;
He yet doth ſtand untainted in my thoughts,
And to preſerve him ſo,
He ſhall not ſtirr out of my eyes command
Till this great cloud be over.
Jol. Sir, 'twas the Prince who firſt —
King. I know all that! urge it no more!
I love the man;
And 'tis with paine we doe ſuſpect,
Where we do not diſlike.
Th'art ſure he will have ſome,
And that they will come to night?
Iol. As ſure as night will come it ſelf.
King. Get all your Guards in readineſs, we will our ſelf
Diſperſe them afterwards; and both be ſure

To wear your thoughts within: Ile act the reſt: *Exeunt.*
Enter Philan, Orſames, *Courtiers.*
2. *Court.* Well.—If there be not ſome great ſtorme towards,
Ne're truſt me; Whiſper (Court thunder) is in
Every corner, and there has been to day
About the Town a murmuring
And buzzing, ſuch as men uſe to make,
When they do feare to vent their feares; (heads,
1. *Court.* True, and all the Stateſ-men hang down their
Like full ear'd corne; two of them
Where I ſup't, askt what time of night it was,
And when twas told them, ſtarted, as if
They had been to run a race. (mirth
2. *Court.* The King too (if you mark him,) doth faign
And jollitie, but through them both,
Flaſhes of diſcontent and anger make eſcapes:
Orſ. Gentlemen! 'tis pitty heav'n
Deſign'd you not to make the Almanacks.
You gheſſe ſo ſhrewdly by the ill aſpects,
Or neere conjunctions of the great ones,
At what's to come ſtill; that without all doubt
The Countrey had been govern'd wholy by you,
And plow'd and reap'd accordingly; for mee,
I underſtand this myſterie as little
As the new love; and as I take it too,
'Tis much about the time that every thing
But Owles, and Lovers take their reſt;
Good night, *Philan* —— away—*Exit.*
1. *Court.* 'Tis early yet; let's go on the Queens ſide
And foole a little; I love to warme my ſelfe
Before I goe to bed, it does beget
Handſome and ſprightly thoughts, and makes
Our dreams half ſolid pleaſures.
2. *Court.* Agreed: *Exeunt.*

ACTUS

ACTUS III. SCENA I.

Enter Prince, Conſpirators.

Ther. COuldſt thou not find out *Ziriff*?
1. *Court.* Not ſpeak with him my Lord,
Yet I ſent in by ſeverall men.
Orſ. I wonder *Jolas* meets us not here too.
Ther. 'Tis ſtrange, but let's on now how ere,
When Fortunes, honour, life, and all's in doubt,
Bravely to dare, is bravely to get out. [ors]
Excurſions: The Guard upon them.
Ther. Betrai'd! betraid!
Orſ. Shift for your ſelfe Sir, and let us alone,
We will ſecure you way, and make our own. *Exeunt.*
Enter the King, and Lords.
King. Follow Lords and ſee quick execution done,
Leave not a man alive.
Who treads on fire, and does not put it out, [spes]
Diſperſes feare in many ſparks of doubt. *Exeunt.* [s]
Enter Conſpirators, and the Guard upon them. Three of the Conſpirators fall, and three of the Kings ſide: Orſames & Philan kill the reſt, they throw off their diſguiſes.
Orſ. Stand friends, an equal party——(Fight.) [rtiers]
Ph. Brave *Orſames* 'tis pleaſure to die neer thee.
Orſ. Talk not of dying *Philan*, we will live,
And ſerve the noble Prince agen: we are alone,
Off then with thy diſguiſe, & throw it in the buſhes;
Quick, quick; before the torrent comes upon us:
We ſhall be ſtreight good ſubjects, and I deſpair not
Of reward for this nights ſervice: So.——
We two now kill'd our friends! 'tis hard,
But 't muſt be ſo.
Enter Ariaſpes, Jolas, *two Courtiers, part of the Guard.*
Ari. Follow! Follow!
Oſr. Yes; ſo you may now, y'are not likely to overtake.
Jol.

32 AGLAURA.

Jol. *Orsames*, and *Philan*, how came you hither?
Ors. The neerest way it seems, you follow'd (thank you)
As if't had been through quicksets:
Jol. 'Sdeath have they all escap'd?
Ors. Not all, two of them we made sure;
But they cost deare, look here else.
Ari. Is the Prince there?
Phi. They are both Princes I thinke, (*views*
They fought like Princes I am sure. Jolas *pulls off the*
Jol. *Stephines*, and *Odiris* — we trifle.
Which way tooke the rest?
Ors. Two of them are certainly hereabouts.
Ari. Upon my life they swam the river;
Some streight to horse, and follow o're the bridge;
You and I my Lord, will search this place a little better.
Ors. Your Highness will I hope remember, who were
The men were in—
Ari Oh! fear not, your Mistress shall know y'are valiant.
Ors. *Philan!* if thou lov'st me, let's kill them upon the (place.
Phi. Fie: thou now art wilde indeed?
Thou taught'st me to be wise first,
And I will now keep thee so. Follow, follow. *Exeunt.*

[III, ii]

Enter Aglaura *with a Lute.*
The Prince comes and knocks within.

Ther. Madam!
Agl. What wretch is this that thus usurps
Upon the Priviledg of Ghosts, and walks
At mid-night?
Ther. Aglaura.
Agl Betray me not
My willing sence too soone, yet if that voyce
Be false.—
Ther. Open faire Saint, and let me in.
Agl. It is the Prince—
As willingly as those
That cannot sleep do light; welcome (Sir,) (*Opens.*)
Welcome above.— *Spies his sword drawn.*

AGLAURA. 33

Bless me, what means this unsheath'd minister of death?
If Sir, on me quick Justice be to pass,
Why this? absence alas, or such strange lookes
As you now bring with you, would kill as soone:
Ther. Softly! for I, like a hard hunted Deer,
Have only herded here; and though the crie
Reach not our eares, yet am I followd close:
O my heart! since I saw thee,
Time has been strangely Active, and begot
A Monstrous issue of unheard of Storie:
Sit; thou shalt have it all! nay, sigh not.
Such blasts will hinder all the passage;
Do'st thou remember how we parted last?
Agl. Can I forget it Sir?
Ther. That word of parting was ill plac'd, I sweare,
It may be ominous; but do'st thou know
Into whose hands I gave thee?
Agl. Yes, into *Ziriffs* Sir.
Ther That *Ziriff* was thy brother, brave *Zorannes*
Preserv'd by miracle in that sad day
Thy father fell, and since thus in disguise,
Waiting his just revenge.
Agl. You do amaze me, Sir.
Ther. And must doe more, when I tell all the storie.
The King the jealous King, knew of the marriage,
And when thou thought'st thy self by my direction,
Thou wert his prisoner;
Unlesse I would renounce all right,
And cease to love thee, (O strange, and fond request!)
Immur'd thou must have been in some sad place,
And lockt for ever from *Thersames* sight.
For ever— and that unable to indure
This night, I did attempt his life.
Agl. Was it well done Sir?
Ther. O no! extreamly ill!
For to attempt and not to act was poore:
Here the dead-doing Law, (like ill-paid Souldiers)
Leaves

III, ii, opening. Though the stage direction clearly states that Aglaura carries a lute, there is no prompt note to that effect. The lute may have been omitted. There are only two manuscript notes on properties in the promptbook (a letter in I, i and a warrant in IV, ii). Perhaps this also argues for a simplified production at Lincoln's Inn Fields Theatre.

34 AGLAURA.

Leaves the ſide 'twas on; to joyne with power,
Royall villany now will look ſo like to Juſtice;
That the times to come, and curious poſteritie
Will find no difference: weep'ſt thou *Aglaura*?
Come, to bed my Love!
And wee will there mock Tyrannie, and Fate,
Thoſe ſofter hours of pleaſure and delight,
That like ſo many ſingle Pearles, ſhould have
Adorn'd our thread of life, we will at once
By Loves Myſterious power and this nights help
Contract to one and make but one rich draught
Of all.
Agl. What mean you Sir?
Ther. To make my ſelf incapable of miſerie,
By taking ſtrong preſervatives of happineſs:
I would this night injoy thee:
Agl. Do, Sir, doe what you will with me,
For I am too much yours, to deny the right
How ever claim'd—but—
Ther. But what *Aglaura*?
Agl. Gather not Roſes in a wet and frowning hour,
They'll loſe their ſweets then, truſt me they will Sir.
What pleaſure can Love take to play his game out,
When death muſt keep the ſtakes?— *A noiſe without.*
Hark Sir — grave-bringers, and laſt minutes are at hand,
Hide, hide your ſelfe, for Loves ſake hide your ſelf.
Ther. As ſoon the ſun may hide himſelfe, as I.
The Prince of *Perſia* hide himſelf?
Agl. O talk not Sir; the Sunn does hide himſelf
When night and blackneſs comes— (then
Ther. Never ſweet Ignorance, he ſhines in th' other world
And ſo ſhall I, If I ſet here in glorie:
Enter *Opens the door. Enter Ziriff*
Ye haſtie ſeekers of life.
Sorannez.—
Agl. My brother!
If all the joy within me come not out,

AGLAURA. 35

To give a welcome to ſo deare an object?
Excuſe it Sir; ſorrow locks up all doores.
Zir. If there be ſuch a Toy about you, Siſter,
Keep't for your ſelf, or lend it to the Prince;
There is a dearth of that Commoditie,
And you have made it Sir. Now,
What is the next mad thing you mean to do?
Will you ſtay here? when all the Court's beſet
Like to a wood at a great hunt, and buſie miſcheife haſtes
To be in view, and have you in her power—
Ther. To mee all this —
For Great greife's deafe as well as it is dumbe,
And drives no trade at all with Counſell: (Sir)
Why doe you not Tutor one that has the Plague,
And ſee if he will feare an after ague fit.
Such is all miſcheif now to mee; there is none left
Is worth a thought; death is the worſt I know,
And that compar'd to ſhame, does look more lovely now
Than a chaſte Miſtreſs, ſet by common woman—
And I muſt court it Sir? (our ſelves:
Zir. No wonder if that heav'n forſake us when we leave
What is there done ſhould feed ſuch high deſpaire?
Were you but ſafe —
Agl. Deare (Sir) be rul'd,
If love be love, and magick too,
(As ſure it is where it is true;)
We then ſhall meet in abſence, and in ſpight
Of all divorce, freely enjoy together
What niggard Fate thus peeviſhly denies.
Ther. Yea: but if pleaſures be themſelves but dreames,
What then are the dreames of theſe to men?
That monſter, Expectation, will devoure
All that is within our hope or power,
And e're we once can come to ſhew how rich
We are, we ſhall be poore,
Shall we not *Sorannez*?
Zir. I underſtand not this,

L

III, ii, 74. The noise was not warned, but Ziriff, who was warned at line 34, probably made the noise and needed no further warning.

In times of envious penurie (such as these are)
To keepe but love alive is faire, we should not think
Of feasting him ; come (Sir)
Here in these lodgings is a little doore,
That leads unto another ; that again
Unto a vault that has his passage under
The little river, opening into the wood ;
From thence 'tis but some few minutes easie businesse
Unto a Servants house of mine (who for his faith
And honestie, hereafter must
Looke big in storie) there you are safe however ;
And when this Storme has met a little calme,
What wilde desire dares whisper to it selfe,
You may enjoy, and at the worst may steale :
Ther. what shall become of thee *Aglaura* then ?
Shall I leave thee their rages sacrifice?
And like dull Seamen threatned with a storme,
Throw all away I have, to save my self ?
Agl. Can I be safe when you are not, my Lord ?
Knowes Love in us divided happinesse?
Am I the safer for your being here ?
Can you give that you have not for your self?
My innocence is my best guard, and that your stay
Betraying it unto suspition, takes away.
If you did love mee ? — (*Kisse[s]*
(*Kisses him*
Ther. Grows that in question? then 'tis time to part-
When we shall meet again Heav'n only knowes;
And when we shall, I know we shall be old .
Love does not calculate the common way;
Minutes are houres there, and the houres are dayes,
Each day 's an yeare; and every yeare an age;
What will this come to think you?
Zir. Would this were all the ill,
For these are petty little harmeless nothings ;
Times horse runs full as fast hard borne and curb'd,
As in his full carreere, loose-rein'd and spurr'd:
Come: come, le's away.

Ther. Happinesse, such as men lost in miserie,
Would wrong in naming, 'tis so much above them.
All that I want of it, all you deserve,
Heav'n send you in my absence.
Agl. And miserie, such as wittie malice would
Lay out in curses, on the thing it hates,
Heav'n send me in the stead, if when you are gone
I welcome it but for your sake alone. — *Exeunt.*
Leads him out, & enters up out of the vault.
[III, iii]
Zir. Stir not from hence, Sir, til you hear from me,
So goodnight deare Prince
Ther. Goodnight deare friend.
Zir. When we meet next all this will but advance —
Joy never feasts so high,
As when the first course is of miserie. *Exeunt.*

L2 ACTUS.

38 AGLAURA.

ACTUS IV. SCENA I.

Enter three or four Courtiers.

1 *Court.* BY this light — a brave Prince,
He made no more of the Guard, than they
Would of a Taylor on a Mask night, that has refused
Trusting before.
2 *Court.* He's as Active as he is valiant too?
Did'st mark him how he stood like all the points
O'th' Compass, and as good Pictures,
Had his eyes, towards every man?
3 *Court.* And his sword too;
All th'otherside walk up and down the Court now,
As if they had lost their way, and stare
Like Grey-hounds, when the Hare has taken the furze.
1 *Court.* Right.
And have more troubles about them
Than a Serving man that has forgot his message
When he's come upon the place —
2 *Court.* Yonder's the King within chafing & swearing
Like an old Falconer upon the first flight
Of a young Hawke, when some Clowne
Has taken away the quarrie from her;
And all the Lords stand round about him,
As if he were to be baited, with much more feare,
And at much more distance,
Than a Countrey Gentlewoman sees the Lions the first
Look: he's broke loose.
Enter King and Lords.
Traitours
King. Find him; or by *Osiris* self, you all are Traitours
And equally shall pay to Justice; a single man,
And guiltie too, breake through you all!
Enter Ziriff.
Zir. Confidence!
(Thou paint of women and the States-mans wisdome,

AGLAURA. 39

Valour for Cowards, and of the guilties Innocence,)
Assist me now,
Sir, send these Starers off:
I have some business will deserve your privacie.
King. Leave us.
Jol. How the vil'ain swels upon us? — *Exeunt.*
Zir. Not to punish thought,
Or keep it long upon the wrack of doubt,
Know Sir,
That by corruption of the waiting woman,
The common key of secrets, I have found
The truth at last, and have discover'd all:
The Prince your Sonne was by *Aglaura's* meanes,
Convey'd last night unto the Cypress Grove,
Through a close vault that opens in the lodgings.
Hee does intend to joyn with *Carimania*,
But e're he goes, resolves to finish all
The rites of Love, and this night meanes,
To steale what is behind.
King. How good is Heav'n unto me!
That when it gave me Traitours for my Subjects,
Would lend me such a Servant!
Zi. How just (Sir) rather, —
That would bestow this Fortune on the poore;
And where your bountie had made debt so infinite
That it grew desperate, their hope to pay it —
King. Enough of that, thou do'st but gently chide
Me for a fault that I wil mend; for I
Have been too poore, and low in my rewards
Unto thy vertue: but to our business;
The question is, whether we shall rely
Upon our Guards again;
Zir. By no meanes Sir.
Hope on his future fortunes, or their Love
Unto his person, has so sicklied o're
Their resolutions, that we must not trust them.
Besides, it were but needless here;
L 3 He

IV, i, 53. *Fitz* was probably the violinist Theophilus Fitz, who evidently accompanied the song in the next scene. When he was supposed to enter is not clear; perhaps he played from offstage.

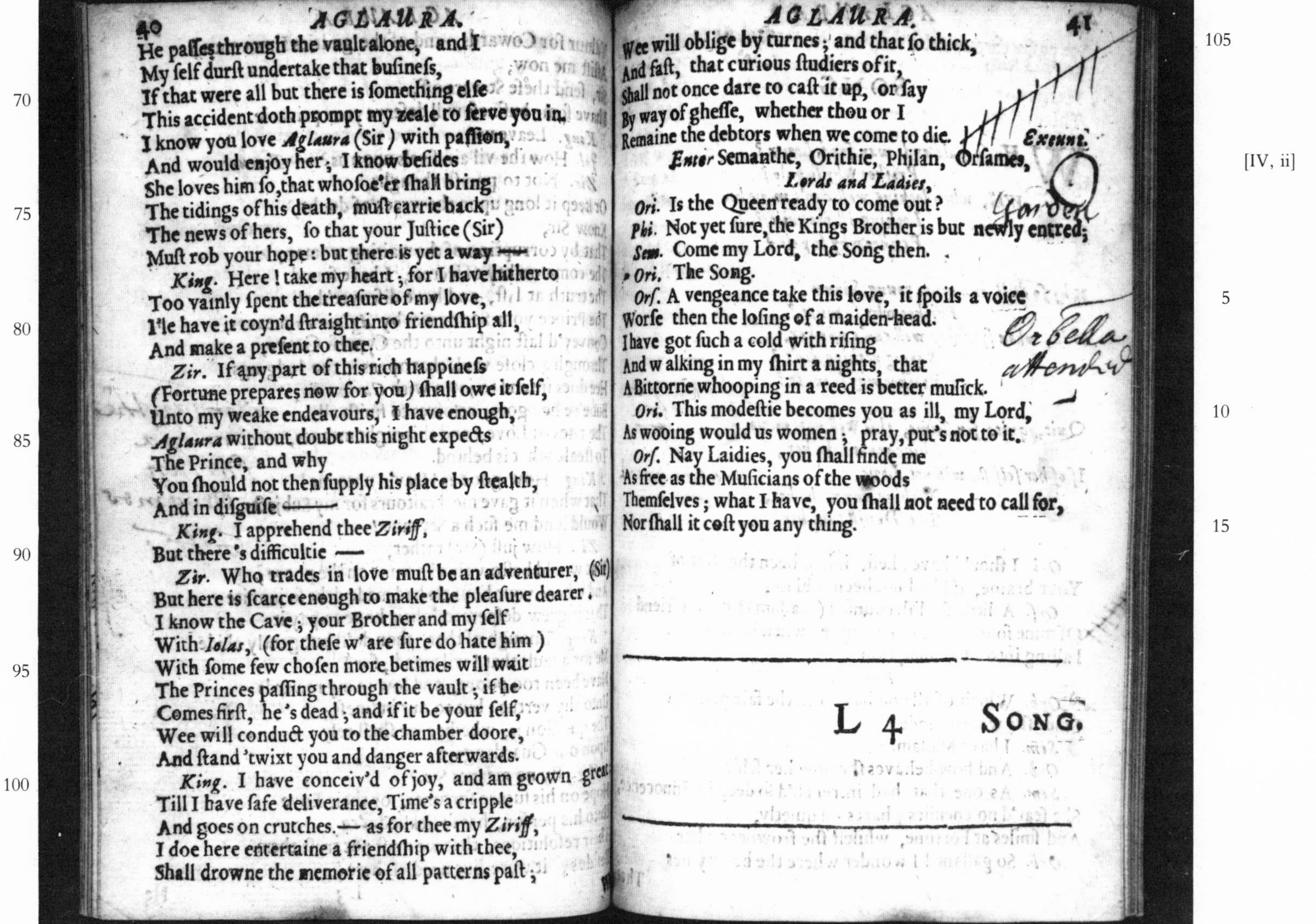

He paſſes through the vault alone, and I
My ſelf durſt undertake that buſineſs,
If that were all but there is ſomething elſe
This accident doth prompt my zeale to ſerve you in,
I know you love *Aglaura* (Sir) with paſſion,
And would enjoy her; I know beſides
She loves him ſo, that whoſoe'er ſhall bring
The tidings of his death, muſt carrie back
The news of hers, ſo that your Juſtice (Sir)
Muſt rob your hope: but there is yet a way ——

King. Here! take my heart; for I have hitherto
Too vainly ſpent the treaſure of my love,
I'le have it coyn'd ſtraight into friendſhip all,
And make a preſent to thee.

Zir. If any part of this rich happineſs
(Fortune prepares now for you) ſhall owe it ſelf,
Unto my weake endeavours, I have enough,
Aglaura without doubt this night expects
The Prince, and why
You ſhould not then ſupply his place by ſtealth,
And in diſguiſe ——

King. I apprehend thee *Ziriff*,
But there's difficultie ——

Zir. Who trades in love muſt be an adventurer, (Sir)
But here is ſcarce enough to make the pleaſure dearer.
I know the Cave; your Brother and my ſelf
With *Iolas*, (for theſe w'are ſure do hate him)
With ſome few choſen more betimes will wait
The Princes paſſing through the vault; if he
Comes firſt, he's dead; and if it be your ſelf,
Wee will conduct you to the chamber doore,
And ſtand 'twixt you and danger afterwards.

King. I have conceiv'd of joy, and am grown great
Till I have ſafe deliverance, Time's a cripple
And goes on crutches.— as for thee my *Ziriff*,
I doe here entertaine a friendſhip with thee,
Shall drowne the memorie of all patterns paſt;

Wee will oblige by turnes; and that ſo thick,
And faſt, that curious ſtudiers of it,
Shall not once dare to caſt it up, or ſay
By way of gheſſe, whether thou or I
Remaine the debtors when we come to die. *Exeunt.*

Enter Semanthe, Orithie, Philan, Orſames, [IV, ii]
Lords and Ladies,

Ori. Is the Queen ready to come out?

Phi. Not yet ſure, the Kings Brother is but newly entred;

Sem. Come my Lord, the Song then.

Ori. The Song.

Orſ. A vengeance take this love, it ſpoils a voice
Worſe then the loſing of a maiden-head.
I have got ſuch a cold with riſing
And walking in my ſhirt a nights, that
A Bittorne whooping in a reed is better muſick.

Ori. This modeſtie becomes you as ill, my Lord,
As wooing would us women; pray, put's not to it.

Orſ. Nay Laidies, you ſhall finde me
As free as the Muſicians of the woods
Themſelves; what I have, you ſhall not need to call for,
Nor ſhall it coſt you any thing.

L 4 SONG.

SONG,

Why so pale and wan fond Lover?
Prithee why so pale?
Will, when looking well can't move her,
Looking ill prevaile?
Prithee why so pale?

Why so dull and mute young Sinner?
Prithee why so mute?
Will, when speaking well can't win her,
Saying nothing doo't?
Prithee why so mute? Ariaspy

Quit, quit, for shame, this will not move Ziriffa
This cannot take her;
If of her self she will not Love, warrant
Nothing can make her,
The Devill take her.

Ori. I should have ghest, it had been the issue of
Your braine, if I had not been told so;
Ors. A little foolish counsell (Madam) I gave a friend
Of mine four or five yeares agoe, when he was
Falling into a Consumption.

Enter Queen.

Orb. Which of all you have seen the fair prisoner
Since she was confinde?
Sem. I have Madam.
Orb. And how behaves she now her self?
Sem. As one that had intrench'd so deep in Innocence,
She fear'd no enemies; bares all quietly,
And smiles at Fortune, whilest she frownes on her
Orb. So gallant! I wonder where the beauty lies

That

That thus inflames the royal blood? (them
Ori. Faces, Madam, are like books; those that do study
Know best; and to say truth, 'tis still
Much as it pleases the Courteous Reader.
Orb. These Lovers sure are like Astronomers,
That when the vulgar eye discovers but
A Skie above, studded with some few stars,
Finde out besides strange fishes, birds, and beasts.
Sem. As men in sicknes scorch'd into a raving
Do see the Devill, in all shapes and formes,
When standers-by wondring, ask where, and when;
So they in Love; for all's but feaver there,
And madness too.
Orb. That's too severe *Semanthe*;
But we will have your reasons in the park;
Are the doores open through the Gardens?
Lo. The King has newly led the way. *Exeunt.*

Enter Ariaspes: *Ziriff, with a Warrant sealed.*

Ari. Thou art a Tyrant, *Ziriff*: I shall die with joy.
Zir. I must confesse my Lord; had but the Princes ills
Prov'd sleight, and not thus dangerous,
He should have ow'd to me, at least I would Iolas
Have laid a claime unto his safetie; and
Like Physicians, that do challenge right
In Natures cures, look'd for reward and thanks;
But since 'twas otherwise, I thought it best
To save my self, and then to save the State.
Ari. 'Twas wisely done.
Zir. Safely I'me sure, my Lord! you know 'tis not
Our custome, where the Kings dislike once swells to hate,
There to engage our selves; Court friendship
Is a Cable, that in stormes is ever cut,
And I made bold with it; here is the warrant seal'd;
And for the execution of it, if you think
We are not stroug enough, we may have
Iolas, for him the King did name.

Ari

44 AGLAURA.

Ari. And him I would have named.
Zir. But is he not too much the Princes (Sir?)
Ari. He is as lights in Sceanes at Masques,
What glorius shew so e're he makes without,
I that set him there, know why, and how; *Enter* Jolas.
But here he is. ——
Come *Jolas*; and since the Heav'ns decreed,
The man whom thou should'st envie, should be such,
That all men else must do't; be not asham'd
Thou once wert guiltie of it;
But bless them, that they give thee now a meanes
To make a friendship with him, and vouchsafe
To find thee out a way to love, where well
Thou couldst not hate.
Jol. What meanes my Lord?
Ari. Here here he stands that has preserv'd us all!
That sacrific'd unto a publique good,
(The dearest privat good we mortals have)
Friendship: gave into our armes the Prince,
When nothing but the sword (perchance a ruine)
Was left to do it.
Iol. How could I chide my love, and my ambition now,
That thrust me upon such a quarell? here I do vow——
Zir. Hold, do not vow my Lord, let it deserve it first
And yet (if Heav'n bless honest mens intents)
'Tis not impossible.
My Lord, you will be pleas'd to inform him in particulars;
I must be gone. ——
The King I feare already has been left
Too long alone.
Ari. Stay —— the houre and place.
Zir. Eleven, under the Tarras walk;
I will nor faile you there. *Goes out, returns back agaian.*
I had forgot: ——
'Tmay be, the small remainder of those lost men
That were of the conspiracie, will come along with him
'Twere best to have some chosen of the Guard
With-

AGLAURA. 45

Within our call —— *Exit* Ziriff.
Ari. Honest, and carefull *Ziriff*! Jolas *stands musing.*
How now Planet-strook?
Iol. This *Ziriff* will grow great with all the world.
Ari. Shallow man, short-sighteder than Travelers in mists,
Or women that outlive themselves; do'st thou not see,
That whilest he does prepare a Tombe with one hand
For his friend, he digs a Grave with th' other for himself?
Iol. How so?
Ari. Do'st think he shall not feele the weight of this,
As well as poore *Thersames*?
Iol. Shall we then kill him too at the same instant?
Ari. And say, the Prince made an unluckie thrust.
Iol. Right.
Ari. Dul, dul, he must not dye so uselesly.
As when we wipe of filth from any place,
We throw away the thing that made it cleane,
So this once done, he's gone.
Thou know'st the People love the Prince; to their rage
Something the State must offer up; who fitter
Than thy rivall and my enemy?
Iol. Rare! our witness will be taken.
Ari. Pish! let me alone.
The Giants that made mountaines ladders,
And thought to take great *Jove* by force, were fooles;
Not hill on hill, but plot on plot, does make
Us sit above, and laugh at all below us. —— *Exeunt.*

[IV, iii]

Enter Aglaura *and a Singing Boy.*
Boy. Madam 'twill make you melancholy,
I'le sing the *Princes* Song, that's sad enough.
Agl. What you will Sir.

SONG.

NO, no, faire Heretique, it needs muſt be
But an ill Love in me,
And worſe for thee.

For were it in my Power,
To love thee now this hower
More than I did the laſt;

I would then ſo fall,
I might not Love at all;

Love that can flow, and can admit increaſe,
Admitts as well an Ebb, and may grow leſs.

2

True Love is ſtill the ſame; the torrid Zones,
And thoſe more frigid ones,
It muſt not know:

For Love grown cold or hot,
Is Luſt, or Friendſhip, not
The thing we have;

For that's a flame would die,
Held down, or up too high:

Then think I love more then I can expreſs,
And would love more, could I but love thee leſs.

Agl. Leave me! for to a Soule ſo out of Tune,
As mine is now, nothing is harmony:
When once the main-ſpring, *Hope*, is faln into
Diſorder; no wonder, if the leſſer wheeles,
Deſire, and *Joy*, ſtand ſtill; my thoughts like *Bees*

Whe

When they have loſt their King, wander
Confuſedly up and down, and ſettle no where.

Enter Orithie.

Orithie. flie! flie the roome,
As thou would'ſt ſhun the habitations
Which Spirits haunt, or where thy nearer friends
Walk after death; here is not only Love,
But Loves plague too — misfortune; and ſo high,
That it is ſure infectious!

Ori. Madam, ſo much more miſerable am I this way (than you,
That ſhould I pittie you, I ſhould forget my ſelf;
My ſufferings are ſuch, that with leſs patience
You may endure your own, than give mine Audience.
There is that difference, that you may make
Yours none at all but by conſidering mine!

Agl. O ſpeak them quickly then! the marriage day
To paſſionate Lovers never was more welcome,
Than any kinde of eaſe would be to me now.

Ori. Could they be ſpoke, they were not then ſo great.
I love, and dare not ſay I love, dare not hope,
What I deſire, yet ſtill too muſt deſire —
And like a ſtarving man brought to a feaſt,
And made ſay grace, to what he nere ſhall taſte,
Be thankfull after all, and kiſs the hand
That made the wound thus deep.

Agl. 'Tis hard indeed, but with what unjuſt ſcales
Thou took'ſt the wait of our miſ-fortunes,
Be thine own Judg now.
Thou mourn'ſt for loſs of that thou never had'ſt;
Or if thou hadſt a loſs, it never was
Of a *Therſames*.
Would'ſt thou not think a Merchant mad, *Orithie*,
If thou ſhould'ſt ſee him weep, and teare his haire,
Becauſe he brought not both the Indies home?
And would'ſt not think his ſorrows very juſt,
If having fraught his ſhip with ſome rich Treaſure,
He ſunk i' th' very Port? This is our caſe.

48 AGLAURA.

Ori. And do you think there is such odds in it ?
Would Heaven we women could as easily change
Our Fortunes as ('tis said) we can our minds.
I cannot (Madam) think them miserable,
That have the Princes Love.
Agl. He is the man then —
Blush not *Orithie*, 'tis a sin to blush
For loving him, though none at all to love him.
I can admit of rivalship without
A jealousie — nay shall be glad of it :
Wee two will sit, and think and sigh,
And sigh, and talk of love — and of *Thersames*.
Thou shalt be praising of his wit, while I
Admire he governs it so well :
Like this thing said thus, th' other thing thus done,
And in good language him for these adore,
While I want words to doo't yet do it more.
Thus will we doe, till death it self shall us
Divide, and then whose fate 'shall be to die
First of the two, by legacie shall all
Her love bequeath, and give her stock to her
That shall survive; for no one stock can serve
To love *Thersames* so as he'll deserve.

Enter King Ziriff.

King. What have we here impossibility?
A constant night, and yet within the room,
That, that can make the day before the Sunn?
Silent *Aglaura* too ?
Agl. I know not what you say :
Is't to your pittie, or your scorne I owe
The favor of this visit (Sir ?) for such
My fortune is, it doth deserve them both :
King. And such thy beauty is that it makes good
All Fortunes, sorrow lookes lovely here;
And there's no man that would not entertaine
His greifs as friends, were he but sure they'd shew
No worse upon him —— but I forget my self,

AGLAURA 49

I came to chide.
Agl. If I have sinn'd so high, that yet my punishment
Equalls not my crime,
Doe Sir; I should be loth to die in debt
To Justice how ill soe're I paid
The scores of Love. —
King. And those indeed thou hast but paid indifferently
To me, I did deserve at least faire death,
Not to be murthered thus in private :
That was too cruell, Mistress.
And I do know thou do'st repent, and wilt
Yet make me satisfaction :
Agl. What satisfaction Sir ?
I am no monster, never had two hearts;
One is by holy vowes anothers now,
And could I give it you, you would not take it,
For 'tis alike impossible for me
To love again, as you love Perjurie.
O Sir ! consider, what a flame love is.
If by rude meanes you think to force a light,
That of it self it would not freely give
You blow it out, and leave your self i' th' dark.
The Prince once gone, you may as well perswade
The light to stay behind, when the Sun posts
To th' other world, as me; alas ! we two
Have mingled soules more than two meeting brooks;
And whosoever is design'd to be
The murtherer of my Lord, (as sure there is,
Has anger'd heav'n so farr, that 'tas decreed
Him to encrease his punishment that way)
Would he but search the heart, when he has done,
He there would find *Aglaura* murthered too.
King. Thou hast o'rcome me, mov'd so handsomly
For pittie, that I will dis-inherit
The elder brother, and from this houre be
Thy Convert, not thy Lover. —
Ziriff. Dispatch away ——

And

51 AGLAURA.

And he that brings news of the Prince's welfare,
Look that he have the same reward we had decreed
To him brought tidings of his death.
'Tmust be a busie and bold hand, that would
Unlink a chain the Gods themselves have made:
Peace to thy thoughts: *Aglaura* — *Exit.*
Ziriff steps back and speakes.
Zir. What e're he sayes, beleeve him not *Aglaura*;
For lust and rage ride high within him now:
He knowes *Thersames* made th' escape from hence,
And does conceale it only for his ends:
For by the favour of mistake and night,
Hee hopes t'enjoy thee in the Princes roome;
I shall be mist — else I would tell thee more;
But thou mayest ghesse; for our condition
Admits no middle waies; either we must
Send them to Graves, or lie our selves in dust — *Exit.*
Aglaura *stands still and studies.*
Agl. Ha! 'tis a strange Act thought puts me now upon;
Yet sure my brother meant the self-same thing,
And my *Thersames* would have don't for me:
To take his life, that seeks to take away
The life of Life, (honour from me;) and from
The world, the life of honour, *Thersames*;
Must needs be something sure of kin to Justice.
If I do faile, th' attempt how'ere was brave,
And I shall have at worst a handsome grave — *Exit.*

[IV, iv] *Court*

Enter Jolas, Semanthe.
Semanthe *steps back*, Jolas *stayes her.*
Jol. What? are we grown, *Semanthe*, night, and day
Must one still vanish when the other comes?
Of all that ever Love did yet bring forth
(And 't has been fruitfull too) this is
The strangest issue. —
Sem. What my Lord?
Jol. Hate *Semanthe.*
Sem. You do mistake; if I do shun you, 'tis,

AGLAURA. 52

As bashfull debtors shun their Creditors,
I cannot pay you in the self-same coyn,
And am asham'd to offer any other.
Jol. It is ill done *Semanthe*, to plead bankrupt,
When with such ease you may be out of debt;
In loves dominions, native commoditie
Is currant payment; change is all the Trade,
And heart for heart the richest merchandize.
Sem. 'T would here bemean my Lord, since mine would (prove
In your hands but a Counterfeit, and yours in mine
Worth nothing; Sympathy, not greatness,
Makes those Jewells rise in value.
Jol. Sympathy! O teach but yours to love then,
And two so rich no mortall ever knew.
Sem. That heart would Love but ill that must be taught,
Such fires as these still kindle of themselves.
Jol. In such a cold, and frozen place as is
Thy breast, how should they kindle of themselves
Semanthe?
Sem Ask how the Flint can carry fire within:
'Tis the least miracle that love can do:
Jol. Thou art thy self the greatest miracle,
For thou art faire to all perfection,
And yet do'st want the greatest part of beautie,
Kindness; thy crueltie (next to thy self)
Above all things on earth takes up my wonder.
Sem. Call not that crueltie, which is our fate,
Beleeve me [illegible] the honest Swaine *Iolas*
That from the brow of some steep cliff far off,
Beholds a ship labouring in vain against
The boysterous and unrulie Elements, ne're had
Less power, or more desire to help than I; Less
At every sigh I die, and every look At
Does move; and any passion you will have
At Love, I have in store: I will be angrie, But
Quarrel with destiny and with my self
That 'tis no better; be melancholy, That

act ready

M And

52 *AGLAURA.*

And (though mine own diſaſters well might plead
To be in chief,) yours onely ſhall have place;
I'le pittie, and (if that's too low) I'le greive,
As for my ſinns, I cannot give you eaſe:
All this I do, and this I hope will prove
'Tis greater Torment not to love, than Love.—— *Exit.*
Iol. So periſhing Sailours pray to ſtormes,
And ſo they hear agen: So men
With death about them, look on Phyſitians that
Have given them o're, and ſo they turn away:
Two fixed Stars that keep a conſtant diſtance,
And by lawes made with themſelves muſt know
No motion excentrick, may meet as ſoon as we:
The anger that the fooliſh Sea does ſhew,
When it does brave it out, and roare againſt
A ſtuborn rock that ſtill denies it paſſage,
Is not ſo vaine and fruitleſs, as my prayers.
Ye mighty Powers of Love and Fate, where is
Your Juſtice here? It is thy part (fond Boy)
When thou do'ſt find one wounded heart, to make
The other ſo; but if thy Tyranny
Be ſuch, that thou wilt leave one breaſt to hate,
If we muſt live, and this ſurvive,
How much more cruel's Fate? —— *Exit.*

ACTUS

AGLAURA. 53

ACTUS V. SCENA I.

Enter Ziriff, Ariaſpes, Jolas.

Iol. A Glorious night!
Ari. Pray Heav'n it prove ſo.
Are we not there yet?
Zir. 'Tis about this hollow. *Enter the Cave.*
Ari. How now! what region are we got into?
Th' inheritance of night!
Are we not miſtaken a turning *Ziriff*,
And ſtept into ſome melancholy Devils Territorie?
Sure 'tis a part of the firſt *Chaos*,
That would endure no change.
Zir. No matter Sir, 'tis as proper for our purpoſe,
As the Lobbie for the waiting womans.
Stay you here. I'le move a little backward,
And ſo we ſhall be ſure to put him paſt
Retreat: you know the word if't be the prince. (*Goes to the mouth of the Cave.*
Enter King.
Here Sir, follow me, all's quiet yet.——
King. He's not come then?
Zir. No.
King. Where,s *Ariaſpes*?
Zir. Waiting within. *He leads him on, ſteps behind him, gives the falſe word, they kill the King.*
Iol. I do not like this waiting,
Nor this fellows leaving us.
Ari. This place does put odd thoughts into thee,
Then thou art in thine own nature too as jealous
As either Love or Honor: Come weare thy ſword in readi-
And think how near we are a Crown, (neſs,
Zir. Revenge!
So let's drag him to the light, and ſearch
His pockets, there may be papers there that will

M 2 Diſcover

54 *AGLAURA.*

Discover the rest of the Conspiratours.
Iolas, your hand — *Draw him out.*
Iol. Whom have we here? the King!
Zir. Yes and *Zorannes* too. Illo! hoe! *Enter* Pasithas *and others.*
Unarme them.
D'ee stare?
This for my Fathers injuries and mine: *Points to the Kings dead body.*
Half Love, half Duties Sacrifice;
This for the Noble Prince, an offering to friendship: (*runs at* Jolas
Iol. Basely and tamely! — *dies.*
Ari. What hast thou done?
Zir. Nothing — kill'd a Traitour,
So — away with them, and leave us,
Pasithas, be onely you in call.
Ari. What do'st thou pawse?
Hast thou remorse already murtherer?
Zir. No foole: 'tis but a difference I put
Betwixt the crimes: *Orbella* is our quarrel;
And I do hold it fit, that love should have
A nobler way of Justice than Revenge
Or Treason; follow me out of the wood,
And thou shalt be Master of this again: (*agen*
And then, best arme and title take it. *They go out and enter*
There — *Gives him his Sword.*
Ari. Extreamly good! Nature took paines I sware,
The villain and the brave are mingled handsomly.
Zir. 'Twas Fate that took it, when it decreed
We two should meet, nor shall they mingle now
We are brought together strait to part. — *Fight*
Ari. Some devil sure has borrowed this shape. *Pawse*,
My sword ne're stay'd thus long to find an entrance.
Zir. To guiltie men, all that appeares is Devil.
falls Come trifler, come, — *Fight again*, Ariaspes *falls*
Ari. Whither, whither, thou fleeting Coward life?
Bubble of time. Natures shame, stay; a little, stay!
Till I have look'd my self into revenge,
And star'd this Traytour to a carkasse first.

AGLAURA. 55

— It will not be: — *Falls.*
The Crowne, the Crowne, too
Now is lost, for ever lost — oh! —
Ambition's, but an *Ignis fatuus*, I see, Thersames
Misleading fond mortalitie,
That hurries us about, and sets us down
Just — where - we - first - begun — *Dies.*
Zir. What a great spreading mightie thing this was,
And what a nothing now? how soon poore man
Vanishes into his noone-tide shadow?
But hopes o're-fed have seldom better done: — (*Hollows.*)
Take up this lump of vanity, and honour, *Enter* Pasithas.
And carry it the back-way to my lodging,
There may be use of Statesmen, when th' are dead;
So. — for the Cittadell now, for in such times
As these, when the unruly multitude
Is up in swarmes, and no man knows which way
They'll take, 'tis good to have retreat. *Exeunt.*
Enter Thersames.
Ther. The Dog-star's got up high, it should be late:
And sure by this time every waking eare,
And watchfull eye is charm'd; and yet me thought
A noyse of weapons struck my eare just now.
'Twas but my fancie sure, and were it more, Aglaura
I would not tread one step that did not lead
To my *Aglaura*, stood all his Guard betwixt,
With lightning in their hands;
Danger! thou Dwarf drest up in Giants clothes,
That shew'st farr off still greater than thou art
Goe, terrifie the simple, and the Guiltie, such
As with false Opticks still do look upon thee;
But fright not Lovers, we dare look on thee
In thy worst shape, and meet thee in them too.
Stay — These trees I made my mark, 'tis hereabouts,
— Love guide me but right this night,
And Lovers shall restore thee back again
Those eyes the Poets took so boldly from thee. *Exit.*
M 3 *Aglaura*

V, i, 43. Apparently Pasithas makes an exit at this point, but there is no stage direction or prompt note to that effect. Pasithas enters at line 78, but that entrance is neither warned nor cued; that might suggest that he never left the stage but simply withdrew to the side.

[V, ii]

56 AGLAURA.

Aglaura *with a torch in one hand, and a dagger in the other.*

Agl. How ill this does become this hand, how much the (worse
This suits with this! one of the two should goe.
The shee within me sayes, it must be this —
Honor sayes this — and honor is *Thersames* friend.
What is that she then? it is not a thing
That sets a Price, not upon me, but on
Life in my name, leading me into doubt,
Which when't has done, it cannot light me out.
For feare does drive to Fate, or Fate if we
Do flie, oretakes, and holds us, til or death,
Or infamie, or both doth seize us — *Puts out the light.*
Ha! — would 'twere in agen!
Antiques and strange mishapes,
Such as the Porter to my soul, mine Eye,
Was ne'er acquainted with, Fancy let's in,
Like a distracted multitude, by some strange accident
Piec'd together, feare now afresh comes on,
And charges Love too home.
— He comes — he comes —
Woman, if thou would'st be the Subject of mans wonder,
Not his scorne hereafter, now shew thy self.

Enter Prince rising from the vault, she stabs him two or three times, he falls, she goes back to her chamber.

Sudden and fortunate!
My better Angel sure did both infuse
A strength, and did direct it. *Enter* Ziriff.

Zir. *Aglaura*!
Agl. Brother. ———
Zir. The same.
So slow to let in such a long'd for Guest?
Must joy stand knocking Sister? come, prepare,
Prepare. —
The King of *Persia's* comming to you strait!
The King — mark that.
Agl. I thought how Poore the joyes you brought with (you,
Were

AGLAURA. 57

Were in respect of those that were with me:
Joyes, are our hopes stript of their feares,
And such are mine; for know, deare Brother,
The King is come already and is gone — mark that.
Zir. Is this instinct, or riddle? what King? how gone?
Agl. The Cave will tell you more —
Zir. Some sad mistake — thou hast undone us all. *Goes out, enters hastily again.*
The Prince! the Prince! cold as the bed of earth
He lies upon, as senseless too! death hangs
Upon his lips
Like an untimely frost, upon an early Cherrie
The noble Guest, his Soule, took it so ill
That you should use his old Acquaintance so,
That neither prayers, nor teares, can e're perswade
Him back again. — Aglaura *swounes; rubs her.*
Hold hold! we cannot sure part thus!
Sister! *Aglaura*! *Thersames* is not dead,
It is the Prince that calls —
Agl. The Prince, where? —
Tell me, or I will strait go back again,
Into those Groves of Gessemine, thou took'st me from,
And find him out, or lose my self for ever.
Zir. For ever — I: there's it!
For in those Groves thou talk'st of,
There are so many by-wayes and odde turnings,
Leading unto such wide and dismall places,
That should we goe without a guide, or stir
Before Heav'n calls, 'tis strongly to be feared
We there should wander up and down for ever,
And be benighted to eternitie —
Agl. Benighted to eternitie? — What's that?
Zir. Why 'tis to be benighted to eternitie,
To sit i'th' darke, and do I know not what;
Unriddle at our own sad cost and charge,
The doubts the learned here do onely move —
Agl. What place have murtherers brother there? for sure
The murtherer of the Prince must have

M 4 A

are our

V, ii, following 21. The Prince's (Thersames') entrance is neither warned nor cued.

58 AGLAURA.

A punishment that Heav'n is yet to make.——
Zir. How is religion fool'd betwixt our loves,
And feares? poore Girle, for ought that thou hast done,
Thy Chaplets may be faire and flourishing,
As his in the *Elysium*:
Agl. Do you think so?
Zir. Yes I do think so.
The juster Judges of our Actions,
Would they have been severe upon
Our weaknesses,
Would (sure) have made us stronger.——
Fie! those teares
A Bride upon the marriage day as properly
Might shed as thou, here widdowes doo't
And marrie next day after:
To such a funeral as this, there should be
nothing common——
Wee'l mourn him so, that those that are alive
Shall think themselves more buried farr then he;
And wish to have his grave, to find his Obsequies:
But stay—the Body. *Brings up the body, she swoons and*
Agen! Sister — *Aglaura*—
O speak once more, once more look out fair Soule. ——
Shee's gone. ——
Irrevocably gone. —— And winging now the Aire,
Like a glad bird broken from some cage:
Poore Bankrupt heart, when't had not wherewithall
To pay to sad disaster all that was its due,
It broke——would mine would do so too.
My soule is now within me
Like a well metled Hauk, on a blind Faulkners fist,
Me thinks I feele it baiting to be gone:
And yet I have a little foolish businesse here
On earth; I will dispatch.—— *Exit.*

[V, iii]

Enter Pasithas, *with the body of* Ariaspes.
Pas. Let me be like my burthen, if I had not as
lieve kill two of the Blood-royal for him, as carrie one

59 AGLAURA.

of them; These Gentlemen of high actions are three times as heavie after death, as your private retir'd ones; look if he be not reduc'd to the state of a Courtier of the second forme now? and cannot stand upon his owne legs, nor do any thing without help, Hum.—— And what's become of the great Prince, in prison as they call it now, the toy within us, that makes us talke, and laugh, and fight, I! why there's it, well, let him be what he will, and where he will, I'le make bold with the old Tenement here. Come Sir—come along:—— *Exit.*

[V, iv]

Enter Ziriff.

Zir. All's fast too, here——
They sleep to night
I'their winding sheets I think, there's such
A general quiet.
Oh! here's light I warrant:
For lust does take as little rest, as care, or age.——
Courting her glasse, I sweare, fie! that's a flatterer Madam,
In me you shall see trulier what you are. (*Knocks. Ent. the Queen*
Orb. What make you up at this strange houre my Lord?
Zir. My businesse is my boldnesse warrant,
(Madam)
And I could well afford t'have been without it now,
Had Heav'n so pleas'd.
Orb. Tis a sad Prologue,
What followes in the name of vertue?
Zir. The King.
Orb. I, what of him? is well, is he not?
Zir. Yes.——
If to be free from the great load
Wee sweat and labour under, here on earth,
Be to be well, he is.
Orb. Why he's not dead, is he?
Zir. Yes Madam, slain — and the Prince too!
Orb. How? where?
Zir. I know not, but dead they are.
Orb. Dead?

Zir.

V, ii, 85 f. The phrasing *Queene & / Ladies behind* suggests an entrance upstage, from the shutter area.

V, iv, 8. The entrance of the Queen was warned but is not cued.

Zir. Yes Madam.
Orb. Did'ſt ſee them dead?
Zir. As I ſee you alive.
Orb. Dead!
Zir. Yes dead!
Orb. Well, we muſt all die;
The Siſters ſpin no cables for us mortals;
Th' are thred; and Time and chance —
Truſt me I could weep now;
But watrie diſtillations do but ill on graves,
They make the lodging colder. *She knocks.*
Zir. What would you Madam?
Orb. Why my friends, my Lord!
I would conſult and know, what's to be done.
Zir. Madam 'tis not ſo ſafe to raiſe the Court;
Things thus unſetled, if you pleaſe to have —
Orb. Where's *Ariaſpes*?
Zir. In's dead ſleep by this time I'm ſure.
Orb. I know he is not! find him inſtantly.
Zir. I'm gone, —— *Turns back again.*
But Madam, why make you choice of him, from whom
If the ſucceſſion meet diſturbance,
All muſt come of danger?
Orb. My Lord, I are not yet ſo wiſe, as to be jealous;
Pray diſpute no further.
Zir. Pardon me Madam, if before I goe
I muſt unlock a ſecret unto you! ſuch a one
As while the King did breathe durſt know no aire,
Zerannes lives.
Orb. Ha!
Zir. And in the hope of ſuch a day as this
Has lingred out a life, ſnatching, to feed
His almoſt famiſhed eyes,
Sights now and then of you, in a diſguiſe.
Orb. Strange! this night is big with miracle!
Zir. If you did love him, as they ſay you did,
And do ſo ſtill; 'tis now within your power!
Or

Orb. I would it were my Lord, but I am now
No private woman, If I did love him once
(And 'tis ſo long agoe, I have forgot)
My youth and Ignorance may well excus't.
Zir. Excuſe it?
Orb. Yes, excuſe it Sir.
Zir. Though I confeſs I lov'd his father much,
And pitie him, yet having offer'd it
Unto your thoughts, I have diſcharg'd a truſt;
And zeale ſhall ſtray no further.
Your pardon Madam: *Exit.* *Queen ſtudies.*
Orb. May be 'tis a plot to keep off *Ariaſpes*
Greatneſs, which he muſt feare, becauſe he knowes
He hates him: for theſe are Stateſ-men,
That when time has made bold with the King and Subject,
Throwing down all fence that ſtood betwixt their power
And others right, are on a change,
Like wanton Salmons coming in with floods,
That leap o're wyres and nets, and make their way
To be at the return to every one a prey.
Enter Ziriff, *and* Paſithas *throwing down the dead body of* Ariaſpes.
Orb. Ha! murthered too!
Treaſon — treaſon —
Zir. But ſuch another word, and half ſo loud,
And th'art, —
Orb. Why? thou wilt not murther me too?
Wilt thou villain?
Zir I do not know my temper — *Diſcovers himſelf.*
Look here vain thing, and ſee thy ſins full blown:
There's ſcarce a part in all this face, thou haſt
Not been forſworn by, and Heav'n forgive thee for't!
For thee I loſt a Father, Countrey, friends,
My ſelf almoſt, for I lay buried long;
And when there was no uſe thy love could pay
Too great, thou mad'ſt the principal a way.
Had I but ſtaid, and not began revenge
Till

V, iv, following 83. The entrance of Ziriff was not warned, but he just made an exit and probably needed no warning for his reentrance.

62 *AGLAURA.*

Till thou had'ſt made an end of changing,
I had had the Kingdome to have kill'd:
As wantons entring a Garden, take
The firſt faire flower they meet, and
Treaſure't in their laps;
Then ſeeing more, do make freſh choyce agen,
Throwing in one and one, till at the length
The firſt poor flower o're-charg'd, with too much weight
Withers, and dies:
So haſt thou delt with mee,
And having kill'd me firſt, I will kill— The last
Orb. Hold — hold —
Not for my ſake, but *Orbella's* (Sir) a bare scene
And ſingle death is ſuch a wrong to Juſtice,
I muſt needs except againſt it.
Find out a way to make me long a dying;
For death's no puniſhment; it is the ſenſe,
The paines and feares afore that makes a death:
To think what I had had, had I had you,
What I have loſt in loſing of my ſelf,
Are deaths farr worſe then any you can give:
Yet kill me quickly; for if I have time,
I ſhall ſo waſh this ſoule of mine with teares,
Make it ſo fine, that you would be afreſh
In love with it, and ſo perchance I ſhould (her head
Again come to deceive you. *She riſes up weeping, & hanging down*
Zir. So riſes day, bluſhing at nights deformitie:
And ſo the prettie flowers blubber'd with dew,
And ever waſht with raine, hang down their heads.
I muſt not look upon her: (*Goes towards him*)
Orb. Were but the Lillies in this face as freſh
As are the Roſes; had I but innocence
Joyn'd to their bluſhes, I ſhould then be bold,
For when they went on begging they were ne're deni'd;
'Tis but a parting kiſſe Sir—
Zir. I dare not grant it.—
Orb. Your hand Sir then, for that's a part I ſhall
Love

AGLAURA. 63

Love after death (if after death we love)
Cauſe it did right the wrong'd *Zorannes* here—
Steps to him and opens the box of poyſon, Zorannes *falls.*
Sleep, ſleep for ever, and forgotten too,
All but thy ills, which may ſucceeding time
Remember, as the Sea-man does his marks,
To know what to avoid: may at thy name
All good men ſtart, and bad too; may it prove
Infection to the Aire, that people dying of it
Nay help to curſe thee for me. *Turnes to the body of A-* (riaſpes.
Could I but call thee back as eaſily now;
But that's a Subject for our teares, not hopes!
There is no peicing Tulips to their ſtalks,
When they are once divorc'd by a rude hand;
All we can do is to preſerve in water
A little life, and give by curteous Art
What ſcanted Nature wants Commiſſion for; Pasithas
That thou ſhalt have: for to thy memorie
Such Tribute of moyſt ſorrow I will pay,
And that ſo purifi'd by love, that on thy grave
Nothing ſhall grow but Violets and Primroſes,
Of which too, ſome ſhall be
Of the myſterious number, ſo that Lovers ſhall
Come hither not as to a tomb but to an Oracle. *She knocks, and raiſes the Court.*
Enter Ladies and Courtiers, as out of their beds.
Orb. Come! come! help me to weep my ſelf away,
And melt into a grave, for life is but
Repentance nurſe, and will conſpire with memorie,
To make my houres my tortures.
Ori. What Scene of ſorrow's this? both dead?
Orb. Dead? I! and 'tis but half death's triumphs this,
The King and Prince lye ſomewhere, juſt
Such empty truncks as theſe.
Ori. The Prince?
Then in greifs burthen I muſt bare a part.
Sem. The noble *Ariaſpes*—valiant *Ziriff* too—*Weeps.*
Orb. Weep'ſt thou for him, fond Prodigall? do'ſt know
O

V, iv, 109 f. *The last / scene* seems to serve as a warning for all subsequent entrances, none of which is individually warned and most of which are not cued. The *Brennoralt* promptbook contains a similar warning.

On whom thou spend'st thy teares? this is the man
To whom we owe our ills; the false *Zorannes*
Disguis'd, not lost; but kept alive, by some
incensed power to punish *Persia* thus:
He would have kill'd me too; but Heav'n was just,
And furnisht me with meanes, to make him pay
This score of villanie, e're he could do more.

Enter Pasithas, *surveys the bodies, finds his Master.*

Pas. Were you his murth'rer then? —

Pasithas *runs to her, kills her, and flies.*

Ori. Ah me! the Queene. —

Rub her till she come to her selfe.

Sem. How do you Madam?
Orb. Well, — but I was better and shall — *Dies.*
Sem. Oh! she is gone for ever!

Enter Lords in their night gownes, Orsames, Philan.

Ors. What have we here?
A Church-yard? nothing but silence, and grave?
Ori. Oh! here has been (my Lords)
The blakest night the *Persian* world e're knew,
The King and Prince are not themselves exempt
From this arrest; but pale and cold, as these,
Have measured out their lengths.
Lo. Impossible! which way?
Sem. Of that we are as ignorant as you.
For while the Queene was telling of a Storie,
An unknown villain here has hurt her so,
That like a sickly Taper, she but made
One flash, and so expir'd:

Enter bearing in Pasithas.

Phi. Here he is, but no confession.
Or. Torture must force him then:
Though 'twill indeed but weakly satisfie
To know now they are dead, how they did die.
Phi. Come take the bodies up, and let us all
Goe drowne our selves in teares, this massacre
Has left so torne a State, that 'twill be Policie
As well as debt, to weep till we are blinde;
For who would see the miseries behinde?

Epilogue.

Epilogue.

Our play is done, and yours doth now begin:
What different Fancies, people now are in?
How strange, and odd a mingle it would make,
If e're they rise, 'twere possible to take
All votes. —
But as when an authentique watch is shown,
Each man windes up, and rectifies his own,
So in our very Judgments; first their sits
A grave Grand Jurie on it of Town-wits,
And they give up their verdict; then agin
The other Jurie of the Court comes in
(And that's of life and death) for each man sees
That oft condemns, what th'other Jurie frees:
Some three daies hence, the Ladies of the Town
Will come to have a Judgment of their own:
And after them, their servants; then the Citie,
For that is modest, and is still last wittie.
'Twill be a week at least yet e're they have
Resolv'd to let it live, or give't a grave:
Such difficultie there is to unite
Opinion, or bring it to be right.

Epiolgue

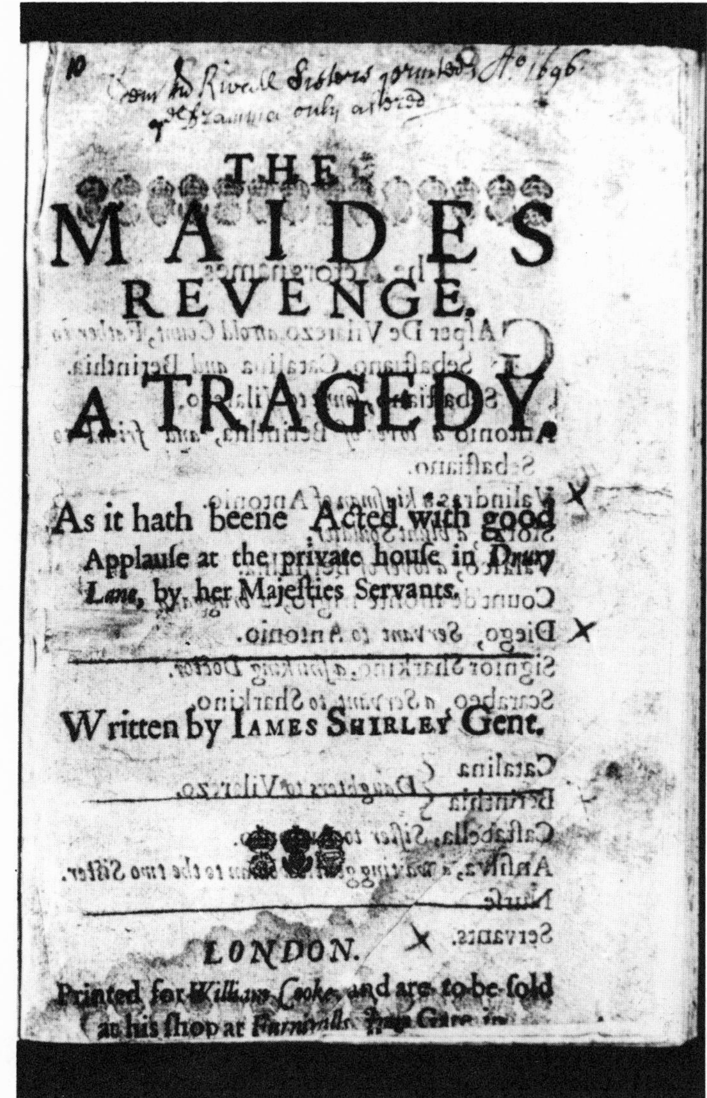

THE
MAIDES
REVENGE.
A TRAGEDY.

As it hath beene Acted with good Applause at the private house in *Drury Lane*, by her Majesties Servants.

Written by IAMES SHIRLEY Gent.

LONDON.
Printed for *William Cooke*, and are to be sold at his shop at *Furnivalls Inne Gate* in

The Maides Revenge by James Shirley. Purchased with funds from the Lillian Gish foundation and the Duplicates fund, 1975. Harvard Theatre Collection.

Title page. Cropped from the bottom is: "Holbourne. 1639."

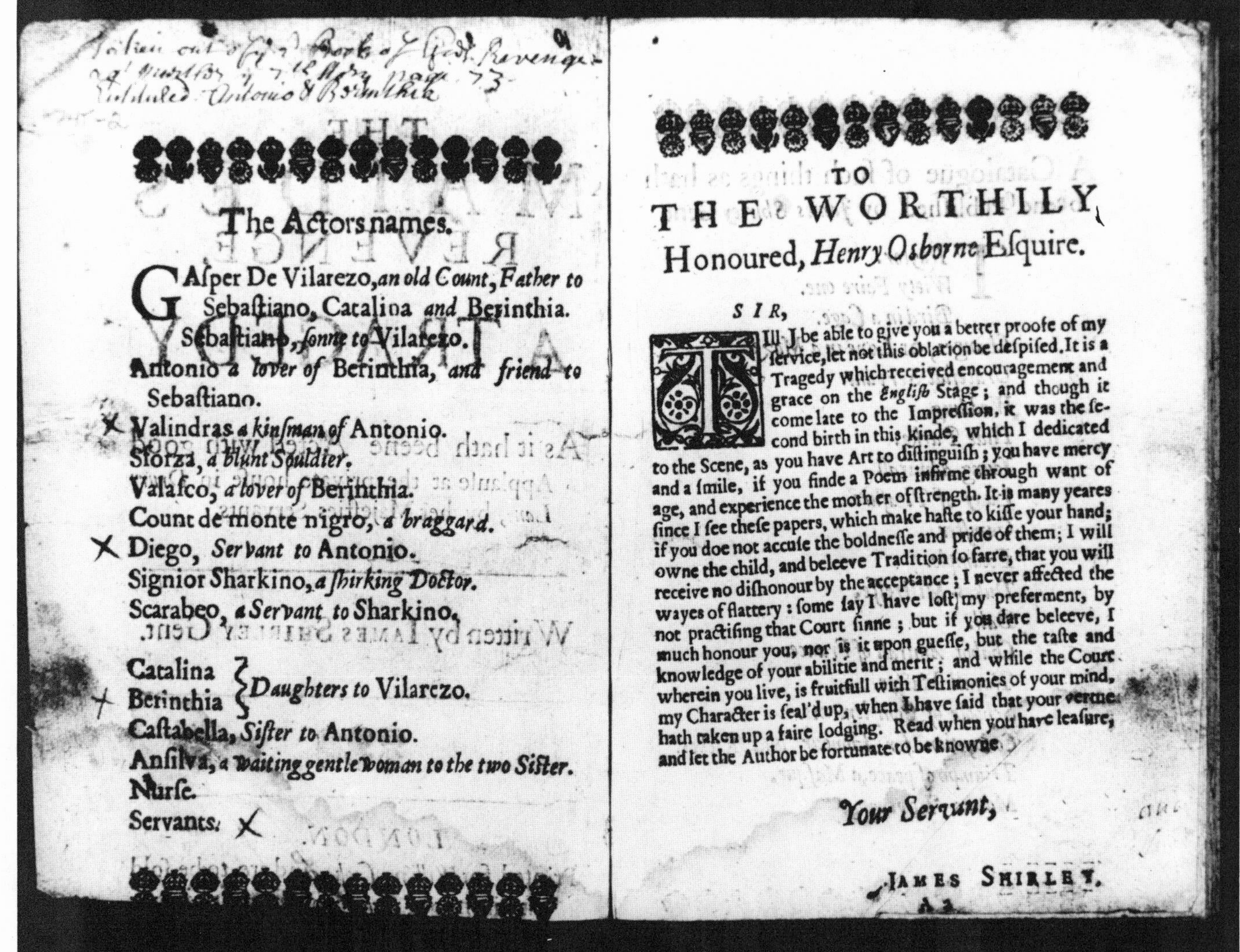

The Actors names.

GAsper De Vilarezo, *an old Count, Father to* Sebastiano, Catalina *and* Berinthia.

Sebastiano, *sonne to* Vilarezo.

Antonio *a lover of* Berinthia, *and friend to* Sebastiano.

Valindras *a kinsman of* Antonio.

Sforza, *a blunt Souldier.*

Valasco, *a lover of* Berinthia.

Count de monte nigro, *a braggard.*

Diego, *Servant to* Antonio.

Signior Sharkino, *a shirking Doctor.*

Scarabeo, *a Servant to* Sharkino.

Catalina }
Berinthia } *Daughters to* Vilarezo.

Castabella, *Sister to* Antonio.

Ansilva, *a waiting gentlewoman to the two Sister.*

Nurse.

Servants.

TO THE WORTHILY Honoured, *Henry Osborne* Esquire.

SIR,

TIll I be able to give you a better proofe of my service, let not this oblation be despised. It is a Tragedy which received encouragement and grace on the *English* Stage; and though it come late to the Impression, it was the second birth in this kinde, which I dedicated to the Scene, as you have Art to distinguish; you have mercy and a smile, if you finde a Poem infirme through want of age, and experience the mother of strength. It is many yeares since I see these papers, which make haste to kisse your hand; if you doe not accuse the boldnesse and pride of them; I will owne the child, and beleeve Tradition so farre, that you will receive no dishonour by the acceptance; I never affected the wayes of flattery: some say I have lost my preferment, by not practising that Court sinne; but if you dare beleeve, I much honour you, nor is it upon guesse, but the taste and knowledge of your abilitie and merit; and while the Court wherein you live, is fruitfull with Testimonies of your mind, my Character is seal'd up, when I have said that your vertue hath taken up a faire lodging. Read when you have leasure, and let the Author be fortunate to be knowne.

Your Servant,

JAMES SHIRLEY.

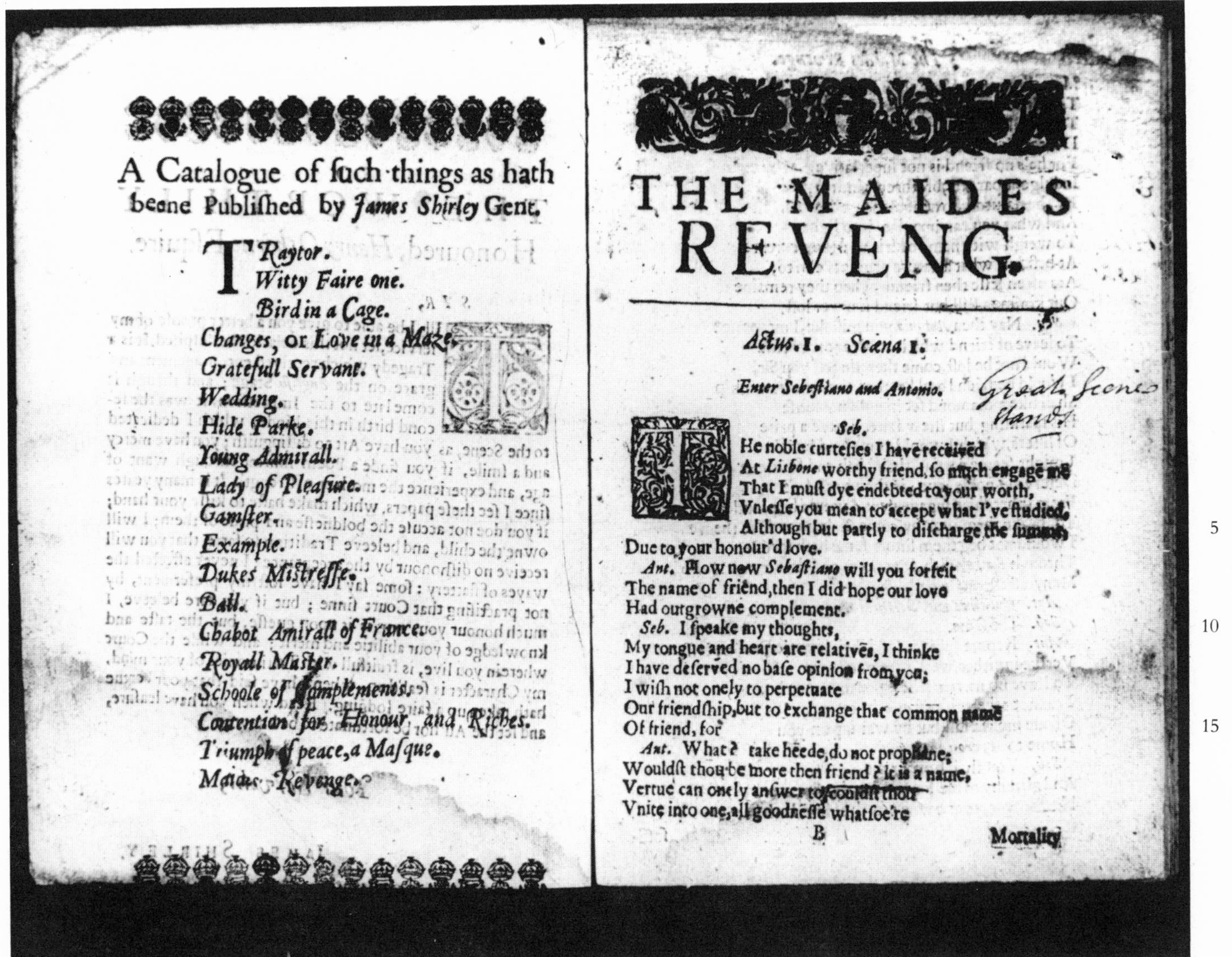

A Catalogue of such things as hath beene Published by *James Shirley* Gent.

Traytor.
Witty Faire one.
Bird in a Cage.
Changes, or *Love in a Maze.*
Gratefull Servant.
Wedding.
Hide Parke.
Young Admirall.
Lady of Pleasure.
Gamster.
Example.
Dukes Mistresse.
Ball.
Chabot Admirall of France.
Royall Master.
Schoole of Complements.
Contention for Honour, and Riches.
Triumph of peace, a Masque.
Maides Revenge.

THE MAIDES REVENG.

Actus. 1. *Scæna* 1.

Enter Sebastiano and Antonio.

Seb.
The noble curtesies I have received
At *Lisbone* worthy friend, so much engage me
That I must dye endebted to your worth,
Vnlesse you mean to accept what I've studied,
Although but partly to discharge the summe
Due to your honour'd love.
Ant. How now *Sebastiano* will you forfeit
The name of friend, then I did hope our love
Had outgrowne complement.
Seb. I speake my thoughts,
My tongue and heart are relatives, I thinke
I have deserved no base opinion from you;
I wish not onely to perpetuate
Our friendship, but to exchange that common name
Of friend, for
Ant. What? take heede, do not prophane;
Wouldst thou be more then friend? it is a name,
Vertue can onely answer to, couldst thou
Vnite into one, all goodnesse whatsoe're

B Mortality

I, i, 18–31. Exactly what was cut in Antonio's speech is not clear; apparently the manuscript markings in the middle of the speech were tentative. Probably everything after "answer to" in line 18 was omitted. Like many cuts in the text, this one seems to have been made to shorten the play by leaving out some of the flowery speeches.

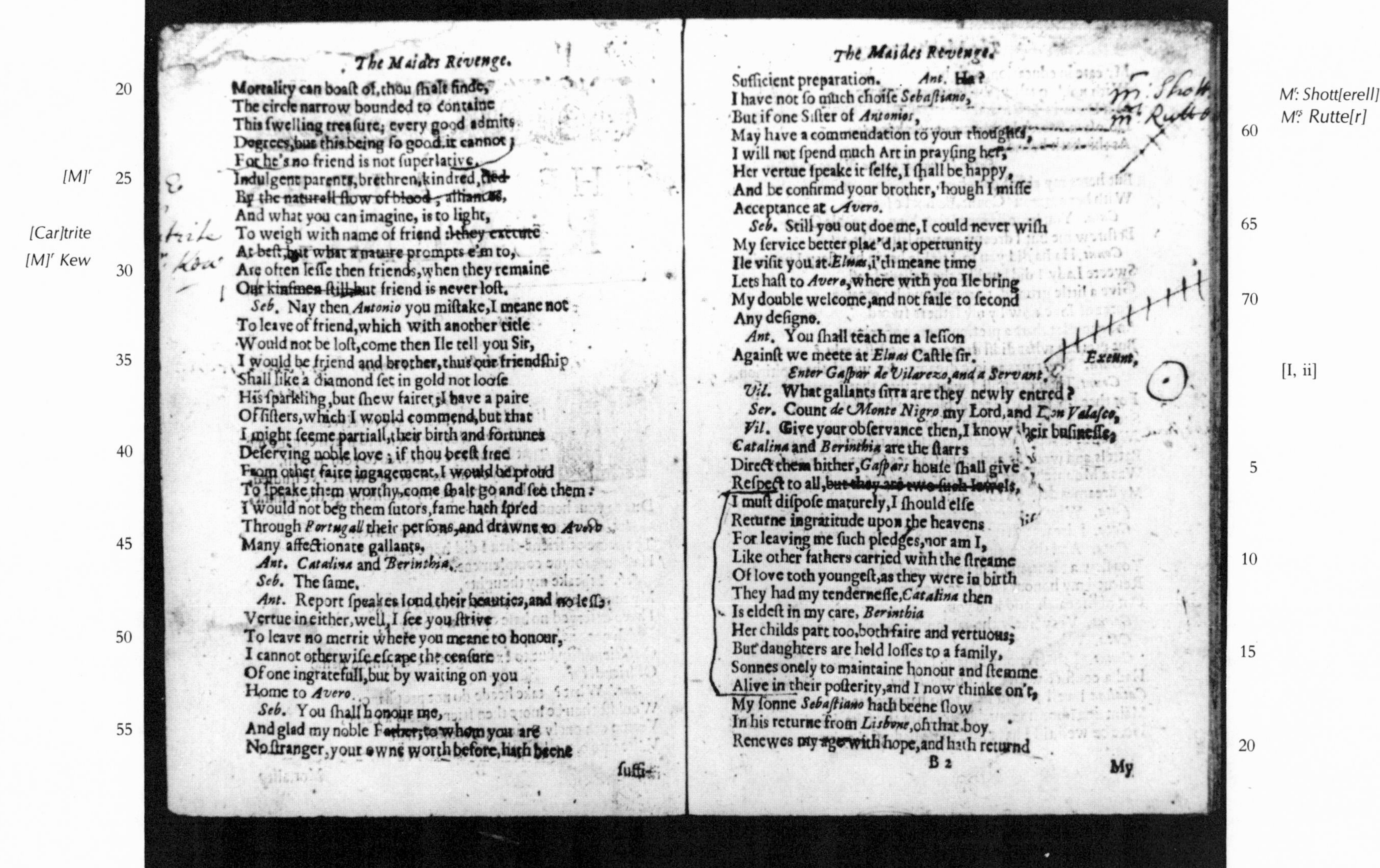

The Maides Revenge.

Mortality can boaſt of, thou ſhalt finde,
The circle narrow bounded to containe
This ſwelling treaſure; every good admits
Degrees, but this being ſo good it cannot;
For he's no friend is not ſuperlative.
[M]r Indulgent parents, brethren, kindred, tied
By the naturall flow of blood, alliances,
And what you can imagine, is to light,
[Car]trite To weigh with name of friend: they execute
[M]r Kew At beſt, but what a nature prompts e'm to,
Are often leſſe then friends, when they remaine
Our kinſmen ſtill, but friend is never loſt.
Seb. Nay then *Antonio* you miſtake, I meane not
To leave of friend, which with another title
Would not be loſt, come then Ile tell you Sir,
I would be friend and brother, thus our friendſhip
Shall like a diamond ſet in gold not looſe
His ſparkling, but ſhew fairer; I have a paire
Of ſiſters, which I would commend, but that
I might ſeeme partiall, their birth and fortunes
Deſerving noble love; if thou beeſt free
From other faire ingagement, I would be proud
To ſpeake them worthy, come ſhalt go and ſee them:
I would not beg them ſutors, fame hath ſpred
Through *Portugall* their perſons, and drawne to *Avero*
Many affectionate gallants.
Ant. *Catalina* and *Berinthia*.
Seb. The ſame.
Ant. Report ſpeakes loud their beauties, and no leſſe
Vertue in either, well, I ſee you ſtrive
To leave no merrit where you meane to honour,
I cannot otherwiſe eſcape the cenſure
Of one ingratefull, but by waiting on you
Home to *Avero*.
Seb. You ſhall honour me,
And glad my noble Father, to whom you are
No ſtranger, your owne worth before, hath beene

ſuffi-

The Maides Revenge.

Sufficient preparation. *Ant.* Ha?
I have not ſo much choiſe *Sebaſtiano*,
But if one Siſter of *Antonios*, Mr Shott[erell]
May have a commendation to your thoughts, Mrs Rutte[r]
I will not ſpend much Art in prayſing her,
Her vertue ſpeake it ſelfe, I ſhall be happy,
And be confirmd your brother, though I miſſe
Acceptance at *Avero*.
Seb. Still you out doe me, I could never wiſh
My ſervice better plac'd, at opertunity
Ile viſit you at *Elnas*, i'th meane time
Lets haſt to *Avero*, where with you Ile bring
My double welcome, and not faile to ſecond
Any deſigne.
Ant. You ſhall teach me a leſſon
Againſt we meete at *Elnas* Caſtle ſir. *Exeunt.*

Enter Gaſpar de Vilarezo, and a Servant. [I, ii]

Vil. What gallants ſirra are they newly entred?
Ser. Count *de Monte Nigro* my Lord, and *Don Velaſco*.
Vil. Give your obſervance then, I know their buſineſſe,
Catalina and *Berinthia* are the ſtarrs
Direct them hither, *Gaſpars* houſe ſhall give
Reſpect to all, but they are two ſuch Iewels,
I muſt diſpoſe maturely, I ſhould elſe
Returne ingratitude upon the heavens
For leaving me ſuch pledges, nor am I,
Like other fathers carried with the ſtreame
Of love toth youngeſt, as they were in birth
They had my tenderneſſe, *Catalina* then
Is eldeſt in my care, *Berinthia*
Her childs part too, both faire and vertuous;
But daughters are held loſſes to a family,
Sonnes onely to maintaine honour and ſtemme
Alive in their poſterity, and I now thinke on't,
My ſonne *Sebaſtiano* hath beene ſlow
In his returne from *Lisbone*, oft that boy
Renewes my age with hope, and hath returnd

B 2 My

The Maides Revenge.

My care in education, weight for weight
With noble quality, well belov'd byth beſt
Of Dons in *Spaine* and *Portugall*, whoſe loves
Do often ſtretch his abſence to ſuch length
As this hath beene.

Enter Count de monte Nigro, and Catalina.

But heres my eldeſt daughter
With her amorous Count, Ile not be ſeene, *Exit.*

Cata. You have beene abſent long my noble Count,
Beſhrew me but I dreamt on you laſt night.

Count. Ha ha, did you ſo, I tickle her in her ſleep I perceive;
Sweete Lady I did but like the valiant beaſt,
Give a little ground, to returne with a greater
Force of love, now by my fathers ſword
And gauntlet that's a pretious peece of vertue,
But prethee what didſt dreame of me laſt night?

Cata. Nay twas an idle dreame, not worth the repitition.

Count. Thou dreamſt I warrant thee, that I was fighting
[Mr] Burt
For thee up to the knees in blood, why I dare doo't,
[Mrs M]arshall
Such dreames are common with Count *de monte*
Nigro, my ſleepes are nothing elſe but rehearſals of
Battels, and wounds, and ambuſcadoes, *Donzell Delphebo*
Was a Mountebanke of vallour, *Roſicbeere* a puffe;
de[ser]ve
My dreames deſerve to be ith Chronicles.
[no]w

Cata. Why, now my dreame is out. *Count.* What?

Cata. I dreamt that you were fighting. *Count.* So.

Cata. And that in ſingle combate, for my ſake
You ſlew a giant, and you no ſooner had
Reſcued my honour, but there crept a pigmee
Out of the earth, and kild you.

Count. Very likely, the vallianſt man muſt dye.

Cata. What by a pigmee?

Count. I, thats another giant, I remember *Hercules*
Had a conflict with'em, oh my *Dona*
Catalina I well would I were ſo happy once to
Maintaine ſome honourable duell for thy ſake, I ſhall
fight, tis true
Nere be well, till I have kild ſome body; fight tis true.

I.

The Maides Revenge.

I have never yet fleſht my ſelfe in blood, no body
Would quarell with me, but I finde my ſpirit prompt
If occaſion would but winke at me, why not? wherefore has
Nature given me theſe brawny armes, this manly bulke,
And theſe Colloſſian ſupporters, nothing but to fling
The ſledge, or pitch the bare, and play with
Axletrees
Axletrees; if thou loveſt me, do but command me
Some worthy ſervice; pox a dangers I weigh 'em no
More than fleabitings, would ſome body did hate that
Face, now I wiſh it with all my heart.

Cata. Would you have any body hate me?

Count. Yes, Ide hate 'em, Ide but thruſt my hand into their
Mouth downe to the bottome of their bellies, plucke
Out their lungs and ſhake their inſides outward.

Enter Berinthia and Valaſco.

Ber. Noble Sir, you neede not heape more proteſtations,
I do beleeve you love me.

Val. Doe you beleeve I love, and not accept it?

Ber. Yes I accept it too, but apprehend me
As men doe guifts, whoſe acceptation does not
Binde to performe what every giver craves;
Without a ſtaine to virgin modeſty
I can accept your love, but pardon me,
It is beyond my power to grant your ſuite.

Val. Oh you too much ſubject a naturall guift,
And make your ſelfe beholding for your owne:
The Sunne hath not more right to his owne beames,
With which he gildes the day, nor the Sea lord
Of his owne waves.

Ber. Alaſſe, what is't to owne a paſſion
Without power to direct it, for I move,
Not by a motion I can call my owne,
But by a higher rapture, in obedience
To a father, and I have yet no freedome
To place affection, ſo you but endeere me
Without a merit.

Cata. Heres my ſiſter.

B 3 *Count.*

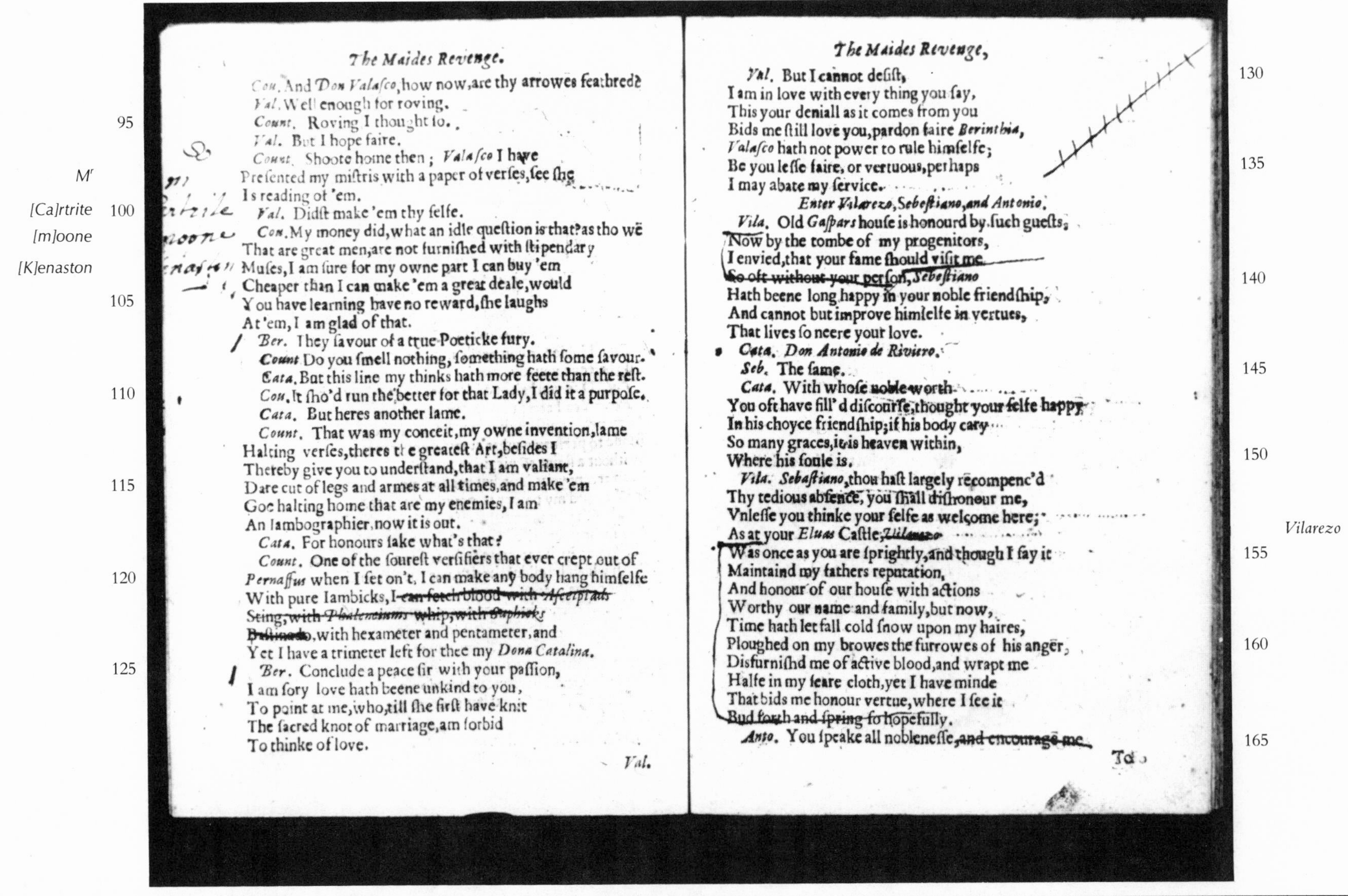

The Maides Revenge.

Cou. And *Don Valaſco*, how now, are thy arrowes feathred?
Val. Well enough for roving.
Count. Roving I thought ſo.
Val. But I hope faire.
Count. Shoote home then; *Valaſco* I have
Preſented my miſtris with a paper of verſes, ſee ſhe
Is reading of 'em.
Val. Didſt make 'em thy ſelfe.
Con. My money did, what an idle queſtion is that? as tho we
That are great men, are not furniſhed with ſtipendary
Muſes, I am ſure for my owne part I can buy 'em
Cheaper than I can make 'em a great deale, would
You have learning have no reward, ſhe laughs
At 'em, I am glad of that.
Ber. They ſavour of a true Poeticke fury.
Count Do you ſmell nothing, ſomething hath ſome ſavour.
Cata. But this line my thinks hath more feete than the reſt.
Cou. It ſho'd run the better for that Lady, I did it a purpoſe.
Cata. But heres another lame.
Count. That was my conceit, my owne invention, lame
Halting verſes, theres the greateſt Art, beſides I
Thereby give you to underſtand, that I am valiant,
Dare cut of legs and armes at all times, and make 'em
Goe halting home that are my enemies, I am
An Iambographier, now it is out.
Cata. For honours ſake what's that?
Count. One of the ſoureſt verſifiers that ever crept out of
Pernaſſus when I ſet on't, I can make any body hang himſelfe
With pure Iambicks, I ~~can fetch blood with *Aſceipiads*~~
~~Sting, with *Phaleneiums* whip, with *Suphicks*~~
~~Baſtinado~~, with hexameter and pentameter, and
Yet I have a trimeter left for thee my *Dona Catalina.*
Ber. Conclude a peace ſir with your paſſion,
I am ſory love hath beene unkind to you,
To point at me, who, till ſhe firſt have knit
The ſacred knot of marriage, am forbid
To thinke of love.
Val.

The Maides Revenge,

Val. But I cannot deſiſt,
I am in love with every thing you ſay,
This your deniall as it comes from you
Bids me ſtill love you, pardon faire *Berinthia*,
Valaſco hath not power to rule himſelfe;
Be you leſſe faire, or vertuous, perhaps
I may abate my ſervice.
Enter Vilarezo, Sebaſtiano, and Antonio.
Vila. Old *Gaſpars* houſe is honourd by ſuch gueſts,
Now by the tombe of my progenitors,
I envied, that your fame ſhould viſit me
~~So oft without your perſon~~, *Sebaſtiano*
Hath beene long happy in your noble friendſhip,
And cannot but improve himſelfe in vertues,
That lives ſo neere your love.
Cata. *Don Antonio de Riviero.*
Seb. The ſame.
Cata. With whoſe ~~noble worth~~
You oft have fill'd diſcourſe, thought your ſelfe happy
In his choyce friendſhip; if his body cary
So many graces, it is heaven within,
Where his ſoule is.
Vila. *Sebaſtiano*, thou haſt largely recompenc'd
Thy tedious abſence, you ſhall diſhonour me,
Vnleſſe you thinke your ſelfe as welcome here;
As at your *Eluas* Caſtle; ~~*Villarezo*~~
Was once as you are ſprightly, and though I ſay it
Maintaind my fathers reputation,
And honour of our houſe with actions
Worthy our name and family, but now,
Time hath let fall cold ſnow upon my haires,
Ploughed on my browes the furrowes of his anger,
Diſfurniſhd me of active blood, and wrapt me
Halfe in my ſeare cloth, yet I have minde
That bids me honour vertue, where I ſee it
~~Bud forth and ſpring ſo~~ hopefully.
Anto. You ſpeake all nobleneſſe, ~~and encourage me.~~
To

M^r
[Ca]rtrite
[m]oone
[K]enaston

Vilarezo

I, ii, 121–23. Canceled lines read: "I can fetch blood with *Asceipiads* / Sting, with *Phaleneiums* whip, with *Suphicks* / Bastinado."

The Maides Revenge.

To ſpend the greeneneſſe of my riſing yeares
So to th'advantage, that at laſt I may
Be old like you.
Vila. Daughters ſpeake his welcome, *Catalina.*
Cata. Sir you are moſt welcome.
Count. Howes that? ſhe ſayes he is moſt welcome, he were
Not beſt love her, ſhe never made me ſuch a reverence
For all the kiſſes I have beſtowed upon her ſince
First opened my affection, I do not like this
Fellow, I muſt be faine to uſe doctor *Sharkins* cunning.
Val. It were not truely noble to affront him;
My blood boyles in me, it ſhall coole againe,
The place is venerable by her preſence,
And I may be deceiv'd, *Valaſco* then
Keepe diſtance with thy feares.
Anto. How now *Antonio*, where haſt thou loſt thy ſelfe?
Strucke dead with Ladies eyes? I could ſtar-gaze
For ever thus, oh pardon love, gainſt whom
I often have prophan'd, and mockd thy fires,
punish me Thy flames now puniſh me, let me collect:
They are both excellent creatures, there is
A Majeſtie in *Catalinaes* eye, and every part carries ambition
Of Queene upon it, yet *Berinthia*
Hath ſomething more than all this praiſe, though ſhe
Command the world, this hath more power ore me;
Here I have loſt my freedome, not the Queene
Of Love could thus have wounded poore *Antonio*;
Ile ſpeake to her; Lady I'm an Novice, yet in love.
Ber. It may be ſo.
Anto. She jeſts at me, yet I ſhould be proud to be
Your ſervant.
Ber. I entertaine no ſervants that are proud.
Val. Divine *Berinthia*!
Anto. She checks my rudeneſſe, that ſo openly
I ſeeme to court her, and in preſence too
Of ſome that have engaged themſelves perhaps
To her already.

Vila.

The Maides Revenge.

Vila. Come let us in, my houſe ſpreads to receive you,
Which you may call your owne; Ile leade the way.
Cata. Pleaſe you walke Sir.
Ant. I will become me thus to waite on you. *Exeunt, manet Count, and Valaſco.* It
Count. Does not the foole ride us both?
Val. What foole? both, whom?
Count. That foole, both us, we are but horſes and may
Walke one another for ought I ſee before the doore, when he
Is alight and entred. I do not reliſh that ſame
Novice, he were not beſt gull me; harke you Don
Valaſco, what ſhals doe?
Val. Doe, why?
Count. This *Antonio* is a ſutor to one of 'em.
Val. I feare him not.
Coun. I do not feare him neither, I dare fight with him, and
He were ten *Antonios*, but the Ladies *Don*, the Ladies.
Val. *Berinthia*, to whom
I pay my love devotions, in my eare
Seemd not to welcome him, your Lady did.
Count. I but for all that he had moſt mind to your miſtris,
And I do not ſee but if he purſue it,
There is a poſſibility to ſcale the fort, Ladies
Mindes may alter, by your favour, I have leſſe
Cauſe to feare o'th two; if he love not *Catalina*
My game is free, and I may have a courſe in
Her Parke the more eaſily.
Val. Tis true, he preferred ſervice to *Berinthia*,
And what is ſhe then to reſiſt the vowes
Antonio if he love, dare heape upon her?
He's gracious with her father, and a friend
Deere as his boſome to *Sebaſtiano*,
And may be is directed by that brother
To aime at her, or if he make free choyce,
Berinthias beauty will draw up his ſoule.
Count. And yet now I thinke on't, he was very ſawcy
With my love to ſupport her arme, which ſhe

C Ac-

The Maides Revenge.

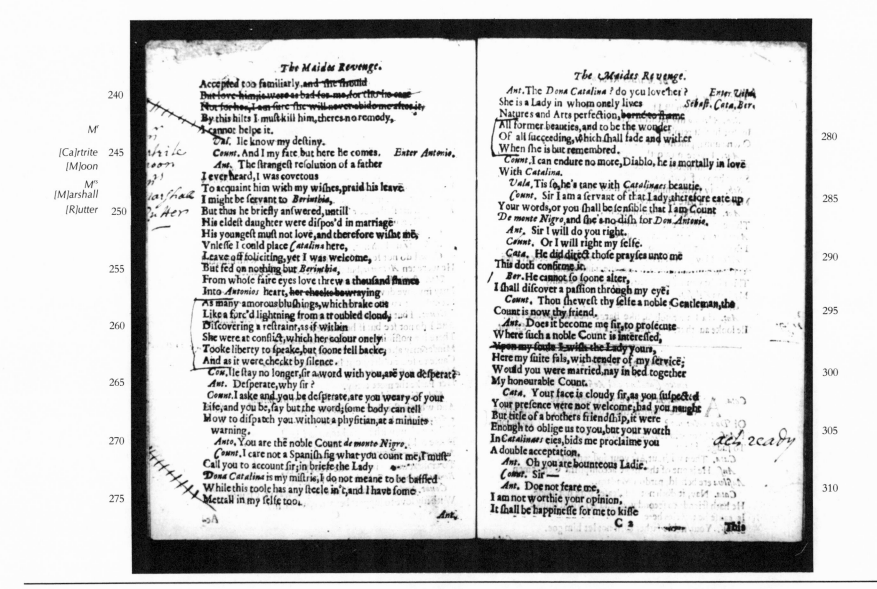

Accepted too familiarly, ~~and ſhe ſhould~~
~~But love him, it were as bad for me, for tho he cane~~
~~Not for her, I am ſure ſhe will never abide me after it,~~
By this hilts I muſt kill him, theres no remedy,
M^r I cannot helpe it.
Val. Ile know my deſtiny.
[Ca]rtrite *Count.* And I my fate but here he comes. *Enter Antonio.*
[M]oon *Ant.* The ſtrangeſt reſolution of a father
I ever heard, I was covetous
M^rs To acquaint him with my wiſhes, praid his leave
[M]arshall I might be ſervant to *Berinthia*,
[R]utter But thus he briefly anſwered, untill
His eldeſt daughter were diſpos'd in marriage
His youngeſt muſt not love, and therefore wiſht me,
Vnleſſe I could place *Catalina* here,
Leave off ſoliciting, yet I was welcome,
But fed on nothing but *Berinthia*,
From whoſe faire eyes love threw a thouſand flames
Into *Antonios* heart, ~~her cheeks bewraying~~
As many amorous bluſhings, which brake out
Like a forc'd lightning from a troubled cloud,
Diſcovering a reſtraint, as if within
She were at conflict, which her colour onely
Tooke liberty to ſpeake, but ſoone fell backe,
And as it were checkt by ſilence.
Cou. Ile ſtay no longer, ſir a word with you, are you deſperate?
Ant. Deſperate, why ſir?
Count. I aske and you be deſperate, are you weary of your
Life, and you be, ſay but the word; ſome body can tell
How to diſpatch you without a phyſitian, at a minuits
warning.
Anto. You are thē noble Count *de monte Nigro*.
Count. I care not a Spaniſh fig what you count me, I muſt
Call you to account ſir; in briefe the Lady
Dona Catalina is my miſtris, I do not meane to be baffled
While this toole has any ſteele in't, and I have ſome
Mettall in my ſelfe too.

Ant.

The Maides Revenge.

Ant. The *Dona Catalina*? do you love her? *Enter Vita. Sebaſt. Cata. Ber.*
She is a Lady in whom onely lives
Natures and Arts perfection, ~~borne to frame~~
All former beauties, and to be the wonder
Of all ſucceeding, which ſhall fade and wither
When ſhe is but remembred.
Count. I can endure no more, Diablo, he is mortally in love
With *Catalina*.
Vala. Tis ſo, he's tane with *Catalinaes* beautie.
Count. Sir I am a ſervant of that Lady, therefore eate up
Your words, or you ſhall be ſenſible that I am Count
De monte Nigro, and ſhe's no diſh for *Don Antonio*.
Ant. Sir I will do you right.
Count. Or I will right my ſelfe.
Cata. He did direct thoſe prayſes unto me
This doth confirme it.
Ber. He cannot ſo ſoone alter,
I ſhall diſcover a paſſion through my eye:
Count. Thou ſheweſt thy ſelfe a noble Gentleman, the
Count is now thy friend.
Ant. Does it become me ſir, to proſecute
Where ſuch a noble Count is intereſſed,
~~Upon my ſoule I wiſh the Lady~~ yours,
Here my ſuite fals, with tender of my ſervice;
Would you were married, nay in bed together
My honourable Count.
Cata. Your face is cloudy ſir, as you ſuſpected
Your preſence were not welcome; had you naught
But title of a brothers friendſhip, it were
Enough to oblige us to you, but your worth
In *Catalinaes* eies, bids me proclaime you
A double acceptation. act ready
Ant. Oh you are bounteous Ladie.
Count. Sir —
Ant. Doe not feare me,
I am not worthie your opinion,
It ſhall be happineſſe for me to kiſſe

C 2 This

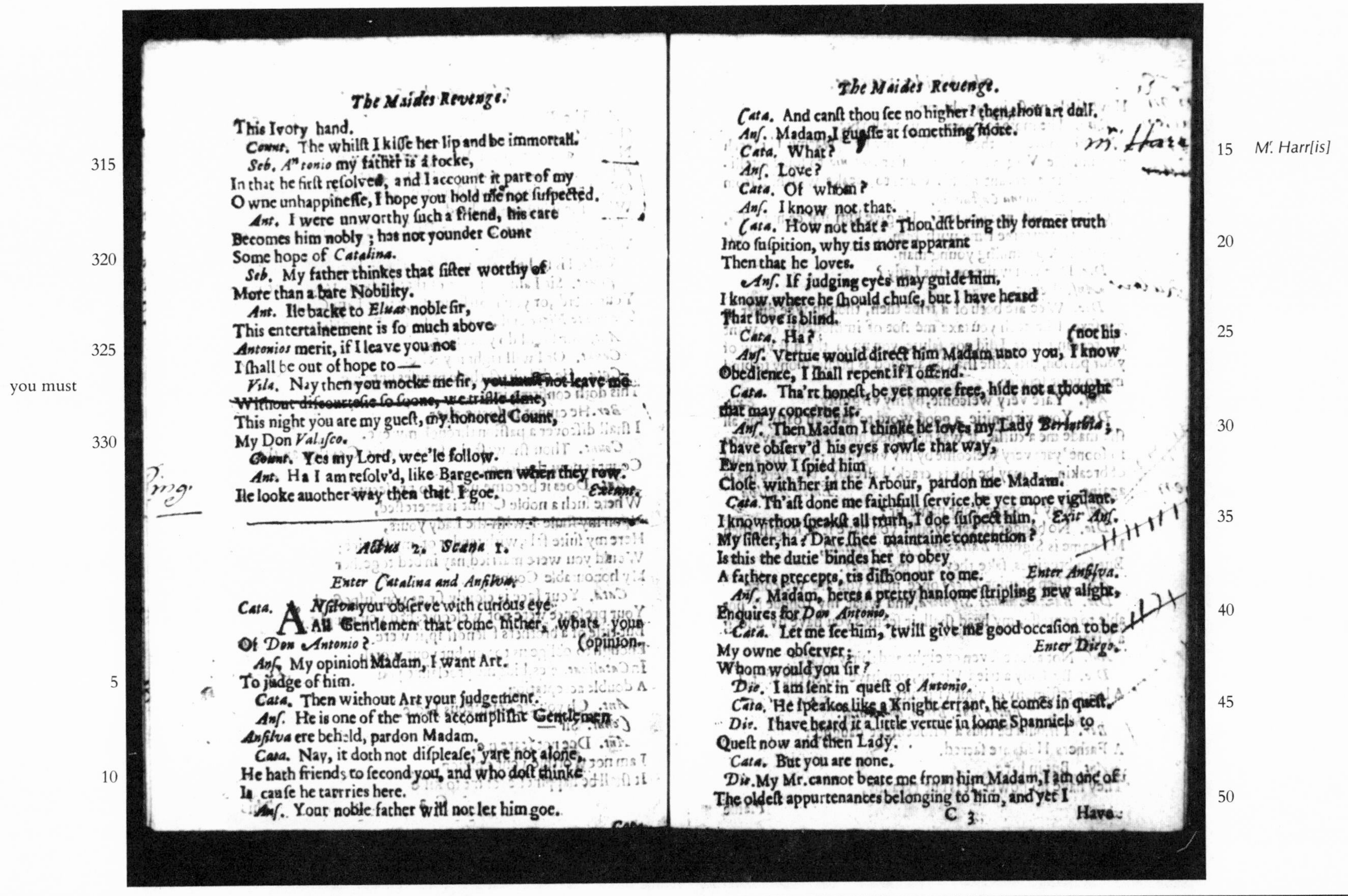

The Maides Revenge.

This Ivory hand.
Count. The whilſt I kiſſe her lip and be immortall.
Seb. *Antonio* my father is a rocke,
In that he firſt reſolved, and I account it part of my
Owne unhappineſſe, I hope you hold me not ſuſpected.
Ant. I were unworthy ſuch a friend, his care
Becomes him nobly; has not younder Count
Some hope of *Catalina*.
Seb. My father thinkes that ſiſter worthy of
More than a bare Nobility.
Ant. Ile backe to *Eluas* noble ſir,
This entertainement is ſo much above
Antonios merit, if I leave you not
I ſhall be out of hope to—

you must

Vila. Nay then you mocke me ſir, you muſt not leave me
Without diſcourteſie ſo ſoone, we trifle time,
This night you are my gueſt, my honored Count,
My Don *Valaſco*.
Count. Yes my Lord, wee'le follow.
Ant. Ha I am reſolv'd, like Barge-men when they row.
Ile looke another way then that I goe. *Exeunt.*

Actus 2. Scæna 1.

Enter Catalina and Anſilva.

Cata. Anſilva you obſerve with curious eye
All Gentlemen that come hither, whats your (opinion
Of *Don Antonio*?
Anſ. My opinion Madam, I want Art.
To judge of him.
Cata. Then without Art your judgement.
Anſ. He is one of the moſt accompliſht Gentlemen
Anſilva ere beheld, pardon Madam.
Cata. Nay, it doth not diſpleaſe, yare not alone,
He hath friends to ſecond you, and who doſt thinke
Is cauſe he tarries here.
Anſ. Your noble father will not let him goe.

The Maides Revenge.

Cata. And canſt thou ſee no higher? then thou art dull.
Anſ. Madam, I gueſſe at ſomething more.
Cata. What?

M'. Harr[is]

Anſ. Love?
Cata. Of whom?
Anſ. I know not that.
Cata. How not that? Thou'dſt bring thy former truth
Into ſuſpition, why tis more apparant
Then that he loves.
Anſ. If judging eyes may guide him,
I know where he ſhould chuſe, but I have heard
That love is blind.
Cata. Ha?
Anſ. Vertue would direct him Madam unto you, I know (not his
Obedience, I ſhall repent if I offend.
Cata. Tha'rt honeſt, be yet more free, hide not a thought
that may concerne it.
Anſ. Then Madam I thinke he loves my Lady *Berinthia*;
I have obſerv'd his eyes rowle that way,
Even now I ſpied him
Cloſe with her in the Arbour, pardon me Madam.
Cata. Th'aſt done me faithfull ſervice, be yet more vigilant,
I know thou ſpeakſt all truth, I doe ſuſpect him, *Exit Anſ.*
My ſiſter, ha? Dare ſhee maintaine contention?
Is this the dutie bindes her to obey
A fathers precepts, tis diſhonour to me. *Enter Anſilva.*
Anſ. Madam, heres a pretty hanſome ſtripling new alight,
Enquires for *Don Antonio*.
Cata. Let me ſee him, 'twill give me good occaſion to be
My owne obſerver; *Enter Diego.*
Whom would you ſir?
Die. I am ſent in queſt of *Antonio*.
Cata. He ſpeakes like a Knight errant, he comes in queſt.
Die. I have heard it a little vertue in ſome Spanniels to
Queſt now and then Lady.
Cata. But you are none.
Die. My Mr. cannot beare me from him Madam, I am one of
The oldeſt appurtenances belonging to him, and yet I
C 3 Have

II, i, 38. Ansilva's entrance was not warned, since she just left the stage.

M^r M^rs
[Kyn]aston
[Ma]rshall
[R]utter
[Mrs] Rutter

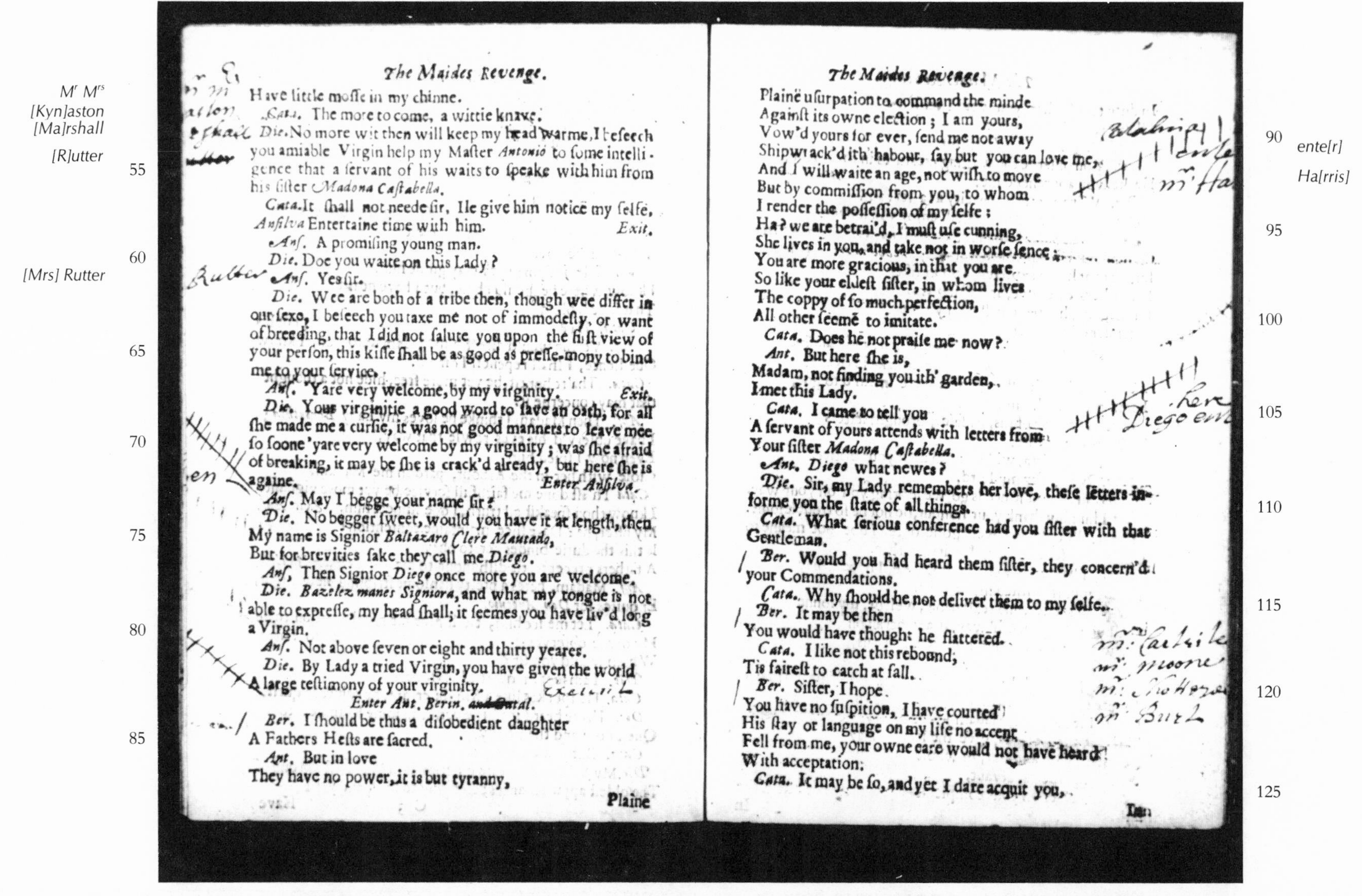

The Maides Revenge.

Have little mosse in my chinne.

Cata. The more to come, a wittie knave.

Die. No more wit then will keep my head warme, I beseech you amiable Virgin help my Master *Antonio* to some intelligence that a servant of his waits to speake with him from his sister *Madona Castabella.*

Cata. It shall not neede sir, Ile give him notice my selfe, *Ansilva* Entertaine time with him. *Exit.*

Ans. A promising young man.

Die. Doe you waite on this Lady?

Ans. Yes sir.

Die. Wee are both of a tribe then, though wee differ in our sexe, I beseech you take me not of immodesty, or want of breeding, that I did not salute you upon the first view of your person, this kisse shall be as good as presse-mony to bind me to your service.

Ans. Yare very welcome, by my virginity. *Exit.*

Die. Your virginitie a good word to save an oath, for all she made me a curtsie, it was not good manners to leave mee so soone 'yare very welcome by my virginity; was she afraid of breaking, it may be she is crack'd already, but here she is againe. *Enter Ansilva.*

Ans. May I begge your name sir?

Die. No begger sweet, would you have it at length, then My name is Signior *Baltazaro Clere Mautado,* But for brevities sake they call me *Diego.*

Ans, Then Signior *Diego* once more you are welcome.

Die. *Bazelez manes Signiora,* and what my tongue is not able to expresse, my head shall; it seemes you have liv'd long a Virgin.

Ans. Not above seven or eight and thirty yeares.

Die. By Lady a tried Virgin, you have given the world
A large testimony of your virginity.

Enter Ant. Berin. and Catal.

Ber. I should be thus a disobedient daughter
A Fathers Hests are sacred.
Ant. But in love
They have no power, it is but tyranny,

Plaine

The Maides Revenge.

Plaine usurpation to command the minde
Against its owne election; I am yours,
Vow'd yours for ever, send me not away
Shipwrack'd ith' habour, say but you can love me,
And I will waite an age, not wish to move
But by commission from you, to whom
I render the possession of my selfe;
Ha? we are betrai'd, I must use cunning,
She lives in you, and take not in worse sence
You are more gracious, in that you are
So like your eldest sister, in whom lives
The coppy of so much perfection,
All other seeme to imitate.
Cata. Does he not praise me now?
Ant. But here she is,
Madam, not finding you ith' garden,
I met this Lady.
Cata. I came to tell you
A servant of yours attends with letters from
Your sister *Madona Castabella.*
Ant. *Diego* what newes?

Die. Sir, my Lady remembers her love, these letters informe you the state of all things.

Cata. What serious conference had you sister with that Gentleman.

Ber. Would you had heard them sister, they concern'd your Commendations.

Cata. Why should he not deliver them to my selfe.

Ber. It may be then
You would have thought he flattered.
Cata. I like not this rebound;
Tis fairest to catch at fall.
Ber. Sister, I hope
You have no suspition, I have courted
His stay or language on my life no accent
Fell from me, your owne eare would not have heard
With acceptation:
Cata. It may be so, and yet I dare acquit you,

Iam

ente[r]
Ha[rris]

II, i, 72. Cropped note: *[ag]en*—that is, Ansilva reenters.

II, i, following 83. The prompter sensibly changed Catalina's entrance to line 89, where the author should have placed it.

II, i, 104 f. Cropped note: *here / Diego ent[ers].* Again the prompter corrected an author's error by providing an entrance for Diego.

The Maides Revenge.

In duty to a Father, you would wiſh me
All due reſpect, I know it.
Ant. *Diego.* *Die.* Sir.
Ant. You obſerve the waiting creatures in the blacke,
Harke, you apprehend me. *Whiſper.*
Die. With as much tenacity as a ſervant.
Cat. I hope ſir, now we ſhall enjoy you longer.
Ant. ~~The gods would ſooner be ſicke with Nectar,~~ than
~~Grow weary of ſuch faire ſocietie~~; madam *(Antonio*
But I am at home expected, a poore ſiſter,
My fathers care alive, and dying was
His Legacy, having out-ſtaid my time
Is tender of my abſence.
Enter Vilarezo, Sebaſtiano, Count, and Valaſco.
Cata. My Lord *Antonio* meanes to take his leave.
Vila. Although laſt night you were inclin'd to goe,
Let us prevaile this morning.
Cat. A ſervant of his, he ſaies, brought letters
To haſten departure.
Vila. Why ſirra, will you rob us of your maſter.
Die. Not guilty my Lord.
Count. Sir, if you'le needs go, we'le bring you on your way.
Ant. I humbly thank your honour, Ile not be ſo troubleſome.
Count. Would you were gone once, I doe not meane to
trouble my ſelfe ſo much I warrant thee.
Ant. I have now a charge upon me, I hope it may
Excuſe me, if I haſten my returne.
Vila. Tis faire, and reaſonable, well ſir, my ſonne
Shall waite on you oth' way, if any occaſion
Draw you to *Avero*, lets hope you'le ſee us,
You know your welcome.
Ant. My Lord the favours done me, would proclaime
I were too much unworthy not to viſit you,
Oft as I ſee *Averro*; Madam ~~I part with ſome unhappineſſe~~
~~To loſe your preſence~~, give me leave I may
Be abſent your admirer, to whoſe memory
I write my ſelfe a ſervant,
Count. Poxe on your complement, you were not beſt write
In

The Maides Revenge.

In her table-bookes.
Cata. You doe not know
What power you have o're me, that but to pleaſe you,
Can frame my ſelfe to take a leave ſo ſoone.
Vala. What thinke you of that my Lord?
Count. Why, ſhe ſayes ſhe has power to take her leave
So ſoone, no hurt ath' world in't, I hope ſhe is an
Innocent Lady. *To Berinth.*
Ant. The ſhallow rivers glide away with noiſe,
The deepe are ſilent, fare you well Lady.
Count. I told you he is a ſhallow fellow.
Vala. I know not what to thinke on't *Berinthia.*
Ant. Gentlemen happineſſe and ſucceſſe in your deſires.
Seb. Ile ſee you a league or two.
Vila. By any meanes, nay ſir.
Ant. *Diego.*
Die. My Lord I have a ſuite to you before I goe.
Vila. To me *Diego*, prethee ſpeake it.
Die. That while other Gentlemen are happy to devide their affections among the Ladies, I may have your honours leave to beare ſome good-will to this Virgin: *Cupid* hath throwne a dart at me, like a blinde buzzard as he was, and theres no recovery without a cooler; if I be ſent into theſe parts, I deſire humbly I may be bould to rub acquaintance with Miſtreſſe *Anſilva.*
Vila. With all my heart *Diego.*
Die. Madam, I hope you will not be an enemy to a poore Flye that is taken in the flame of the blind god.
Cata. You ſhall have my conſent ſir.
Vila. But what ſayes *Anſilva*, haſt thou a mind to a husband?
Anſ. I feare I am too young ſeven yeares hence were time enough for me.
Seb. Shees not full fortie yet ſir.
Die. I honour the Antiquitie of her maidenhead, thou Miſtreſſe of my heart.
Ant. Come lets away *Diego* our horſes-----
Vila. We'le bring you to the gate.
Count. Yes, wee'le bring him out of doores, would wee
D were

The Maides Revenge,

were ſhut of him. *Exeunt.* manet Anſilva.

Anſ. Hay ho, who would have thought I ſhould have benne in love with a ſtripling, have I ſeene ſo many maiden-heades ſuffer before me, and muſt mine come to the blocke at fortie yeares old, if this *Diego* have the grace to come on, I ſhall have no power to keepe my ſelfe chaſt any longer; how many maides have beene overrunne with this love? but heres my Lady. *Exit.*

Enter Catalina and Valaſco.

Cat. Sir, you love my ſiſter.
Val. With an obedient heart.
Cat. Where do you think *Don Antonio* hath made choice
To place his love?
Val. There where I wiſh it may grow older in deſire,
And be crown'd with fruitfull happineſſe.
Cat. Hath your affection had no deeper roote,
That tis rent up already, J had thought
It would have ſtood a Winter, but J ſee
A Summer ſtorme hath kil'd it, fare you well ſir.
Val. How's this, a Summers ſtorme!
Lady by the honour of your birth,
Put off theſe cloudes, you maze me, take off
The wonder you have put upon *Valaſco*,
And ſolve theſe riddles.
Cat. You love *Berinthia.*
Val. With a devoted heart, elſe may I die
Contempt of all mankinde, not my owne ſoule
Is deerer to me.
Cat. And yet you wiſh *Antonio* may be crown'd
With happineſſe in his love, he loves *Birinthia.*
Val. How?
Cat. Beyond expreſſion, to ſee how a good nature
Free' from diſhonour in it ſelfe, is backward
To thinke another guilty, ſuffers it ſelfe
Be poiſoned with opinion, did your eyes
Emptie their beames ſo much in admiration
Of your *Berinthias* beauty, you left none
To obſerve your owne abuſes.

Val.

The Maides Revenge.

Vala. Doth not *Antonio* dedicate his thoughts
To your acceptance, 'tis impoſſible,
I heard him praiſe you to the heavens, above 'em;
Made himſelfe hoarſe but to repeate your vertues
As he had beene in extaſie; love *Birinthia?*
Hell is not blacker than his ſoule, if he
Love any goodneſſe but your ſelfe.
Cat. That leſſon he with impudence hath reade
To my owne eares, but ſhall I tell you ſir?
We are both made but properties to raiſe
Him to his partiall ends, flattery is
The ſtalkeing horſe of pollicy, ſaw you not,
How many flames he ſhot into her eyes
When they were parting, for which ſhe pay'd backe
Her ſubtill teares, he wrung her by the hand,
Seem'd with the greatneſſe of his paſſion
To have beene o're borne, Oh cunning treachery!
Worthy our juſtice, true he commended me;
But could you ſee the Fountaine that ſent forth
So many cozening ſtreames, you would ſay *Styx*
Were Chriſtall to it, and waſt not to the Count,
Whom he ſuppos'd was in purſuite of me;
Nay, whom he knew did love me, that he might
Fire him the more to conſummate my marriage
That I diſpoſed he might have of acceſſe
To his belov'd *Berinthia*, the end
Of his deſires I can confirme it, he praid
To be ſo happy with my fathers leave
To be her amorous ſervant, which he nobly
Denied, partly expreſſing your engagements;
If you have leaſt ſuſpition of this truth:
But dee' thinke ſhe love you?
Val. I cannot challenge her, but ſhe has let fall
Something to make me hope, how thinke you ſhee's
Affected to *Antonio?*
Cat. May be
Luke warme as yet, but ſoone as as ſhees caught,
Inevitably his, without prevention,

D 2 For

The Maides Revenge.

For my owne part I hate him in whom lives
A will to wrong a Gentleman, for hee was
Acquainted with your love, 'twas my reſpect
To tender ſo your injury, I could not
[Ly]dall — Be ſilent in it, what you meane to doe
I leave to your owne thoughts.
[Mrs] Bowtell — *Val.* Oh ſtay ſweete Lady, leave me not to ſtruggle
Alone with this ~~univerſall~~ affliction;
You ſpeake even now *Berinthia* would be his
Without prevention, oh that Antidote,
That Balſome to my wound.
Cat. Alas I pitty you, and the more, becauſe
I ſee your troubles ſo amaze your judgement,
Ile tell you my opinion ſir oth' ſudden;
For him, he is not worth *Valaſco's* anger;
Onely thus, you ſhall diſcover to my Father,
She promis'd you her love, be confident
To ſay you did exchange faith to her; this alone
May chance aſſure her, and if not I hav't:
Steale her away, your love I ſee is honourable,
So much I ſuffer when deſert is wounded,
You ſhall have my aſſiſtance, you apprehend me.
[Ky]naston — *Val.* I am devoted yours, command me ever.
[H]arris — *Cat.* Keepe ſmooth your face and ſtill maintaine your wor-(ſhip
With *Berinthia*, things muſt be manag'd
And ſtrucke in the maturity, noble ſir; I wiſh
You onely fortunate in *Berinthias* love.
Val. Words are too poore to thanke you, I looke on you
As my ſafe guiding ſtarre. *Exit.*
Cat. But I ſhall prove a wandering ſtarre, I have
A courſe which I muſt finiſh for my ſelfe.
Glide on thou ſubtill mover, thou haſt brought
This inſtrument already for thy aymes,
Siſter, Ile breake a Serpents egge betimes,
And teare *Antonio* from thy very boſome;
Love is above all law of nature, blood,
Not what men call, but what that bides is good. *Exit.*
[II, ii] — *Enter Caſtabella and Villandras.*
Vil.

The Maides Revenge.

Vil. Be not ſo carefull Cooze, your brothers well.
Be confident if he were otherwiſe
You ſhould have notice, whom hath he to ſhare
Fortunes without you? all his ills are made
Leſſe by your bearing part, his good is doubled
By your communichaing.
Caſt. By this reaſon
All is not well, in that my ignorance
What fate hath hapned, barres me off the portion
Belongs to me ſiſter, but my care
Is ſo much greater, in that *Diego* whom
I charg'd to put on wings, if all were well,
Is dull in his returne. *Enter Antonio and Diego.*
Vil. His Maſter happily hath commanded him
To attend him homewards, this is recompenc'd
Already, looke they are come;
Y'are welcome ſir.
Ant. Oh ſiſter, ere you let fall words of welcome,
Let me unlade a treaſure in your eare
Able to weigh downe man.
Caſt. What treaſure brother, you amaze me.
Ant. Never was man ſo bleſt,
As heavens had ſtudied to enrich me here,
So am I fortunate.
Vil. You make me covetous.
Ant. I have a friend.
Vil. You have a thouſand ſir, is this your treaſure?
Ant. But I have one more worth then millions,
~~And he doth onely keepe alive that name~~
~~Of friendſhip in his breaſt~~, pardon *Villandros*,
Tis not to ſtraine your love, whom I have tried, — Cartr[ite]
My worthieſt cozen. — Bur[t]
Caſt. But where is this ſame friend, why came he not
To *Elnas* with you, ſure he cannot be — Rutt[er]
Deare to you Brother, to whom I am not indebted
At leaſt for you.
Dio. I have many deare friends too, my Taylor is one
To whom I am indebted

D 3 *Ant.*

II, ii, opening. The significance of the double circle is not clear. Since the machinist seems not to have been responsible for the few descriptions of settings in the copy, perhaps someone else—one unfamiliar with the shift cue symbol—drew the circles and dots. But see Appendix D, item 2.

The Maides Revenge.

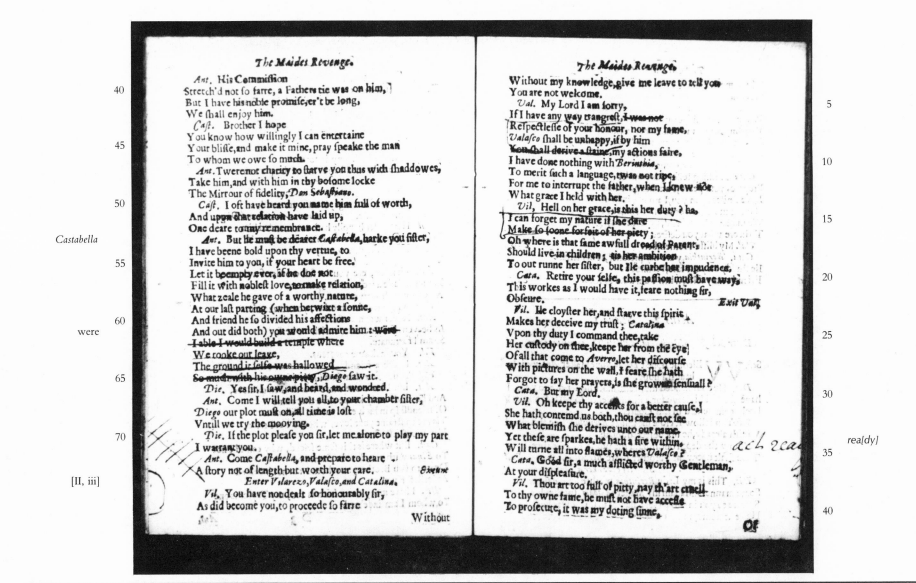

Ant. His Commiſſion
Stretch'd not ſo farre, a Fathers tie was on him,
But I have his noble promiſe,er't be long,
We ſhall enjoy him.
Caſt. Brother I hope
You know how willingly I can entertaine
Your bliſſe,and make it mine, pray ſpeake the man
To whom we owe ſo much.
Ant. Twere not charity to ſtarve you thus with ſhaddowes,
Take him,and with him in thy boſome locke
The Mirrour of fidelity,*Don Sebaſtiano.*
Caſt. I oft have heard you name him full of worth,
And upon that relation have laid up,
One deare to my remembrance.
Castabella *Ant.* But he muſt be dearer *Caſtabella*,harke you ſiſter,
I have beene bold upon thy vertue, to
Invite him to you, if your heart be free.
Let it be empty ever, if he doe not
Fill it with nobleſt love,to make relation,
What zeale he gave of a worthy nature,
At our laſt parting (when betwixt a ſonne,
And friend he ſo divided his affections
were And out did both) you would admire him: were
I able I would build a temple where
We tooke our leave,
The ground it ſelfe was hallowed
So much with his owne piety, *Diego* ſaw it.
Die. Yes ſir, I ſaw, and heard, and wondred.
Ant. Come I will tell you all, to your chamber ſiſter,
Diego our plot muſt on, all time is loſt
Vntill we try the mooving.
Die. If the plot pleaſe you ſir, let me alone to play my part
I warrant you.
Ant. Come *Caſtabella*, and prepare to heare
A ſtory not of length but worth your eare. *Exeunt*
[II, iii] *Enter Vilarezo, Valaſco, and Catalina.*
Vil. You have not dealt ſo honourably ſir,
As did become you, to proceede ſo farre
Without

The Maides Revenge.

Without my knowledge,give me leave to tell you
You are not welcome.
Val. My Lord I am ſorry,
If I have any way trangreſt, I was not
Reſpectleſſe of your honour, nor my fame,
Valaſco ſhall be unhappy,if by him
You ſhall derive a ſtaine,my actions faire,
I have done nothing with *Berinthia*,
To merit ſuch a language, twas not ripe,
For me to interrupt the father,when I knew not
What grace I held with her.
Vil. Hell on her grace,is this her duty? ha,
I can forget my nature if ſhe dare
Make ſo ſoone forfeit of her piety;
Oh where is that ſame awfull dread of Parents,
Should live in children; tis her ambition
To out runne her ſiſter, but Ile curbe her impudence.
Cata. Retire your ſelfe, this paſſion muſt have way,
This workes as I would have it,feare nothing ſir,
Obſcure. *Exit Val.*
Vil. Ile cloyſter her,and ſtarve this ſpirit,
Makes her deceive my truſt; *Catalina*
Vpon thy duty I command thee,take
Her cuſtody on thee,keepe her from the eye
Of all that come to *Averro*,let her diſcourſe
With pictures on the wall, I feare ſhe hath
Forgot to ſay her prayers,is ſhe growne ſenſuall?
Cata. But my Lord.
Vil. Oh keepe thy accents for a better cauſe,
She hath contemd us both,thou canſt not ſee
What blemiſh ſhe derives unto our name.
Yet theſe are ſparkes,he hath a fire within,
Will turne all into flames,wheres *Valaſco*? rea[dy]
Cata. Good ſir,a much afflicted worthy Gentleman,
At your diſpleaſure.
Vil. Thou art too full of pitty,nay th'art cruell
To thy owne fame,he muſt not have acceſſe
To proſecute, it was my doting ſinne,
Of

The Maides Revenge.

Of too much confidence in *Berinthia*,
Gave her ſuch libertie, on my bleſſing puniſh it,
Twill be a vertuous act, the ſnow I thought
Was not more innocent, more cold, more chaſte,
Why my command bound her in ribs of ice,
But ſhees diſſolv'd, to thee Ile leave her now,
Be the maintainer of thy Fathers vow. *Exit*
Val. Why I am undone now.
Cata. Nothing leſſe, this conflict
Prepares your peace, I am her guardian,
Love ſmiles upon you, I am not inconſtant,
Having more power to aſſiſt you, but away,
We muſt not be diſcri'd, expect ere long
To heere what you deſire.
Val. My bliſſe I remember. *Exit*
Cata. *Berinthia*, y'are my priſoner, at my leiſure
Ile ſtuddy on your fate, I cannot be
[rin]g
Friend to my ſelfe, when I am kind to thee. *Exit*

Actus. 3. Scæna 1.

Enter Sebaſtiano, Berinthia, Anſilva, Diego meetes them.

Seb. WElcome honeſt *Diego*, your Maſter *Antonio* is in health I hope.

Die. He commanded me, remember his ſervice to you, I have obtaind his leave for a ſmall abſence to perfect a ſuite I lately commenc'd in this Court.

Seb. You follow it cloſe me thinks *Berinthia*, I ſee this cloud
Vaniſh already, be not dejected, ſoone
Ile know the depth ont, ſhould the world forſake thee,
Thou ſhalt not want a brother deere *Berinthia*. *Exit*

Secretly gives her a Letter.

Die. This is my Lady *Berinthia*, prethee let me ſhew
Some manners; Madam my Maſter *Antonio* ſpeakes his
Service to you in this paper: alas Madam, I was but
Halfe at home, and I am returnd to ſee if I can recover

The

The Maides Revenge.

The tother peece of my ſelfe, ſo, was it not a reaſonable Complement.

Ber. *Antonio*, he's conſtant I perceive. *Exit*

Die. So, we are alone, ſweet Miſtreſſe *Anſilva*, I am bold
To renue my ſuite, which leaſt it ſhould either
Ma[rshall]
Fall or depend too long, having paſt my declaration,
agen
I ſhall deſire to come to a judgement.
My cauſe craves nothing but juſtice,
That is, that you would be mine; and now ſince
Your ſelfe is judge alſo, I beſeech you be not partiall
In your owne cauſe, but give ſentence for the plaintiffe, and I
I will diſcharge the fees of the Court on this faſhion.

Enter Berinthia.

Ber. Here is a haven yet to reſt my ſoule on,
In midſt of all unhappineſſe, which I looke on,
Ru[tter]
With the ſame comfort a diſtreſſed Sea man
A farre off, viewes the coaſt he would enjoy,
When yet the Seas doe toſſe his reeling barke,
Twixt hope and danger, thou ſhalt be conceald.

She miſtaking as ſhe moved, puts up the Letter, it fals downe.

Anſ. Heres my Lady *Berinthia*.

Die. Whatever I ſee my Lady *Berinthia*, and ſhe thinkes
Much, would ſhe had one to ſtoppe her mouth.

Anſ. But I muſt obſerve her, upon her fathers diſpleaſure,
She is committed to my Ladies cuſtody, who hath made
Me her keeper, ſhe muſt be lockt up.

Die. Ha, lockt up.

Anſ. Madam, it is now time you would retire to your owne Chamber.

Ber. Yes, prethee doe *Anſilva* in this gallery,
I breathe but too much aire, oh *Diego* youle have
An anſwer I perceive, ere you returne.

Exit

Die. My journey were to no purpoſe elſe Madam, I apprehend her, ile waite an opportunity, alas poore Lady, is my ſweete heart become a jaylor, there's hope of an office without money.
age[n]
Enter Anſilva haſtily.

Anſ. *Diego* I ſpy my Lady *Catalina* comming this way, pray ſhrowd your ſelfe behinde this cloth, I would be loath ſhee

E ſhould

II, iii, 48. Valasco was not given an entrance.

III, i, 43. The ——— ——— ——— *Exit* note appears to be in a hand different from that responsible for the actor warnings, cues, and other prompt notes. Berinthia and Ansilva leave the stage.

Burt

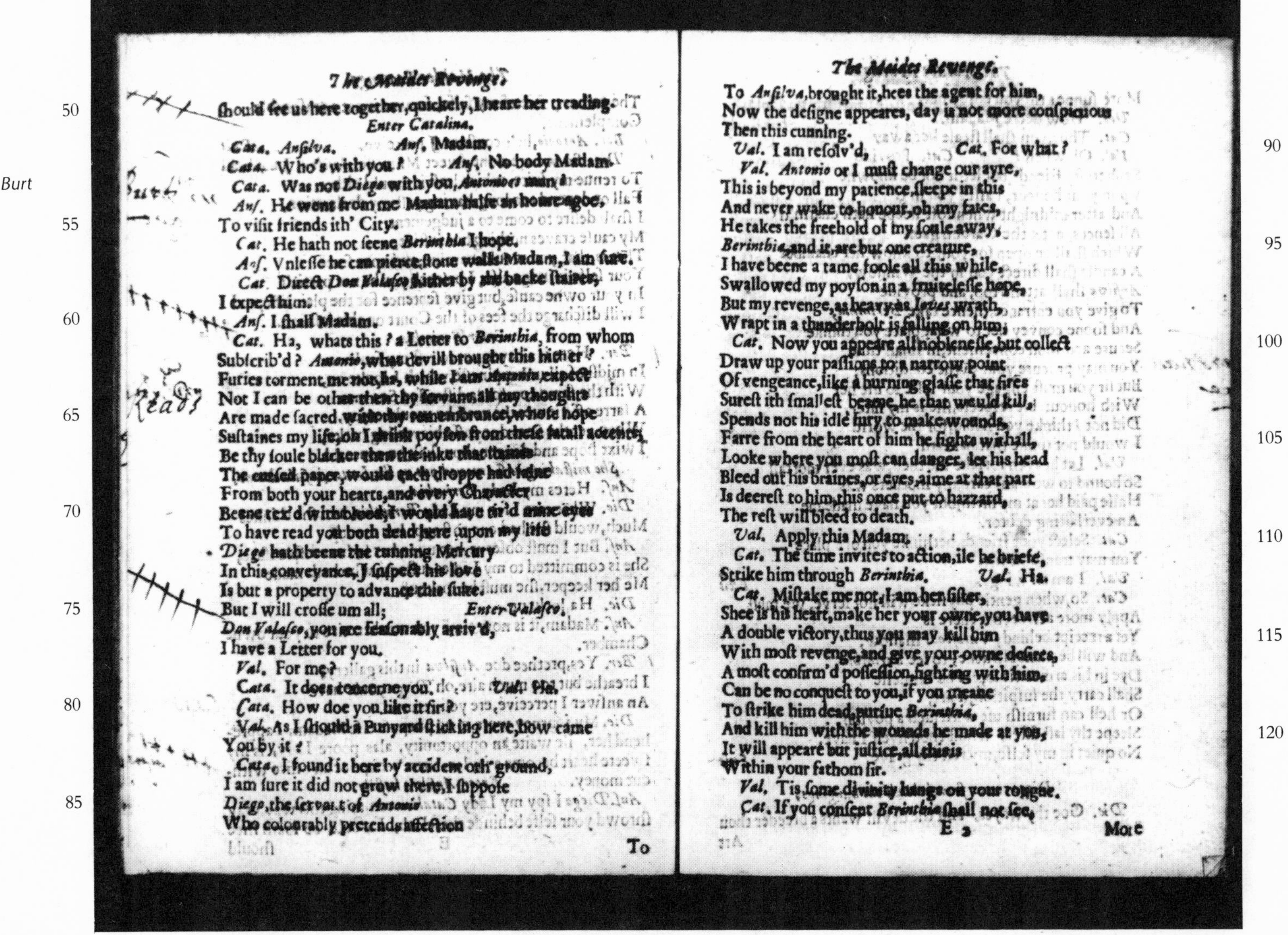

The Maides Revenge.

should see us here together, quickely, I heare her treading.

Enter Catalina.

Cata. Ansilva. Ans. Madam.
Cata. Who's with you? Ans. No body Madam.
Cata. Was not Diego with you, Antonioes man?
Ans. He went from me Madam halfe an houre agoe,
To visit friends ith' City.
Cat. He hath not seene Berinthia I hope.
Ans. Vnlesse he can pierce stone walls Madam, I am sure.
Cat. Direct Don Valasco hither by the backe staires,
I expect him.
Ans. I shall Madam.
Cat. Ha, whats this? a Letter to Berinthia, from whom
Subscrib'd? Antonio, what devill brought this hither?
Furies torment me not, ha, while I am thus expect
Not I can be other then thy servant, all my thoughts
Are made sacred with thy remembrance, whose hope
Sustaines my life; oh I drinke poyson from these fatall accents,
Be thy soule blacker then the inke that paints
The cursed paper, would each droppe had beene
From both your hearts, and every Character
Beene text'd with blood, I would have tir'd mine eyes
To have read you both dead here upon my life
Diego hath beene the cunning Mercury
In this conveyance, I suspect his love
Is but a property to advance this suite;
But I will crosse um all; Enter Valasco.
Don Valasco, you are seasonably arriv'd,
I have a Letter for you.
Val. For me?
Cata. It does concerne you. Val. Ha.
Cata. How doe you like it sir?
Val. As I should a Punyard sticking here, how came
You by it?
Cata. I found it here by accident o'th ground,
I am sure it did not grow there, I suppose
Diego, the servant of Antonio
Who colourably pretends affection

To

The Maides Revenge.

To Ansilva, brought it, hee's the agent for him,
Now the designe appeares, day is not more conspicuous
Then this cunning.
Val. I am resolv'd, Cat. For what?
Val. Antonio or I must change our ayre,
This is beyond my patience, sleepe in this
And never wake to honour, oh my fates,
He takes the freehold of my soule away,
Berinthia, and it, are but one creature,
I have beene a tame foole all this while,
Swallowed my poyson in a fruitelesse hope,
But my revenge, as heavy as Ioves wrath,
Wrapt in a thunderbolt is falling on him;
Cat. Now you appeare all noblenesse, but collect
Draw up your passions to a narrow point
Of vengeance, like a burning glasse that fires
Surest ith smallest beame, he that would kill,
Spends not his idle fury to make wounds,
Farre from the heart of him he fights withall,
Looke where you most can danger, let his head
Bleed out his braines, or eyes, aime at that part
Is deerest to him, this once put to hazzard,
The rest will bleed to death.
Val. Apply this Madam.
Cat. The time invites to action, ile be briefe,
Strike him through Berinthia. Val. Ha.
Cat. Mistake me not, I am her sister,
Shee is his heart, make her your owne, you have
A double victory, thus you may kill him
With most revenge, and give your owne desires,
A most confirm'd possession, fighting with him,
Can be no conquest to you, if you meane
To strike him dead, pursue Berinthia,
And kill him with the wounds he made at you,
It will appeare but justice, all this is
Within your fathom sir.
Val. Tis some divinity hangs on your tongue.
Cat. If you consent Berinthia shall not see,

E 3 More

III, i, 50. Diego steps behind hangings at this point; a curtain may have been hung at the shutter position at mid-stage.

The Maides Revenge.

More ſunnes till you enjoy her.
Val. How deere Madam.
Cat. Thus, you ſhall ſteale her away.
Val. Oh when? *Cat.* Provide
Such truſty friends, but let it not be knowne
Vpon your honour, I aſſiſt you in't.
And after midnight when ſoft ſleepe hath charm'd
All ſences, enter the Garden gate.
Which ſhall be open for you, to know her chamber
A candle ſhall direct you in the Window.
Anſilva ſhall attend too, and provide
To give you entrance, thence take *Berinthia*,
And ſoone convey her to what place you thinke
Secure and moſt convenient, in ſmall time
You may procure your owne conditions;
But ſir you muſt engage your ſelfe to uſe her
With honourable reſpects, ſhe is my ſiſter,
Did not I thinke you noble, for the world
I would not runne that hazzard.
Val. Let heaven forſake me then, was ever mortall
So bound to womans care, my mothers was
Halfe paid her at my birth, but you have made me
An everlaſting debtor.
Cat. Select your friends, bethinke you of a place
You may tranſpoſe her.
Val. I am all wings. *Exit.*
Cat. So, when gentle phyſicke will not ſerve, we muſt
Apply more active, but there is
Yet a receipt behind; *Valaſcoes* ſhallow,
And will be planet ſtrucke, to ſee *Berinthia*
Dye in his armes, tis ſo, yet he himſelfe
Shall carry the ſuſpition, if art,
Or hell can furniſh me with ſuch a poyſon,
Sleepe thy laſt ſiſter, whilſt thou liveſt I have,
No quiet in my ſelfe, my reſt thy grave. *Exit.*

Diego comes from behinde the hangings.

Die. Goe thy wayes, and the devill wants a breeder thou

E 2 Art

The Maides Revenge.

Art for him, one ſpirit and her ſelfe are able to furniſh
Hell and it were unprovided, but I am glad I heard all,
I ſhall love hangings the better while I live:
I pereceive ſome good may be done behind em,
But ile acquaint my Lady *Berinthia*,
Heres her chamber I obſerv'd: Madam, Madam
Berinthia. *Berinthia above.*
Ber. Whoſe there? Shark[ino]
Die. Tis I *Diego*, I am *Diego.* Scara[beo]
Ber. Honeſt *Diego*, what good newes.
Die. Y'are undone, undone loſt, undone for ever; it is time now to be ſerious.
Ber. Ha,
Die. Wheres my Maſter *Antonioes* Letter.
Ber. Here, where, ha, alas, I feare I have loſt it.
Die. Alas you have undone your ſelfe, and your ſiſter, my Lady *Catalina* hath found it, and is mad with rage, and envy againſt you; I overheard your deſtruction, ſhe hath ſhewed it to *Don Valaſco*, and hath plotted that he ſhall ſteale you away this night, the doores ſhall be left open the houre after twelve.
Ber. You amaze me, tis impoſſible.
Die. Doe not caſt away your ſelfe, by incredulity, upon my life your fate is caſt, nay more, worſe then that.
Ber. Worſe?
Die. You muſt be poyſoned too, oh ſhees a cunning devill, and ſhe will carry it ſo, that *Valaſco* ſhall bee ſuſpected for your death, what will you doe?
Ber. I am overcome with amazement?
Die. Madam remember with what noble love my Maſter *Antonio* does honour you, and now both ſave your ſelfe, and make him happy, how
Ber. I am loſt man.
Die. Feare not, I will engage my life for your ſafety,
Seeme not to have knowledge or ſuſpicion, be carefull
What you receive, leaſt you be poyſon'd, leave the
Reſt to me, I have a crotchet in my pate ſhall ſpoyle
Their muſicke, and prevent all danger I warrant you,

E 3 By

III, i, 138 f. Cropped note: *[Mrs M]arshall / [abo]ve.* She must have appeared in one of the balconies over the proscenium doors.

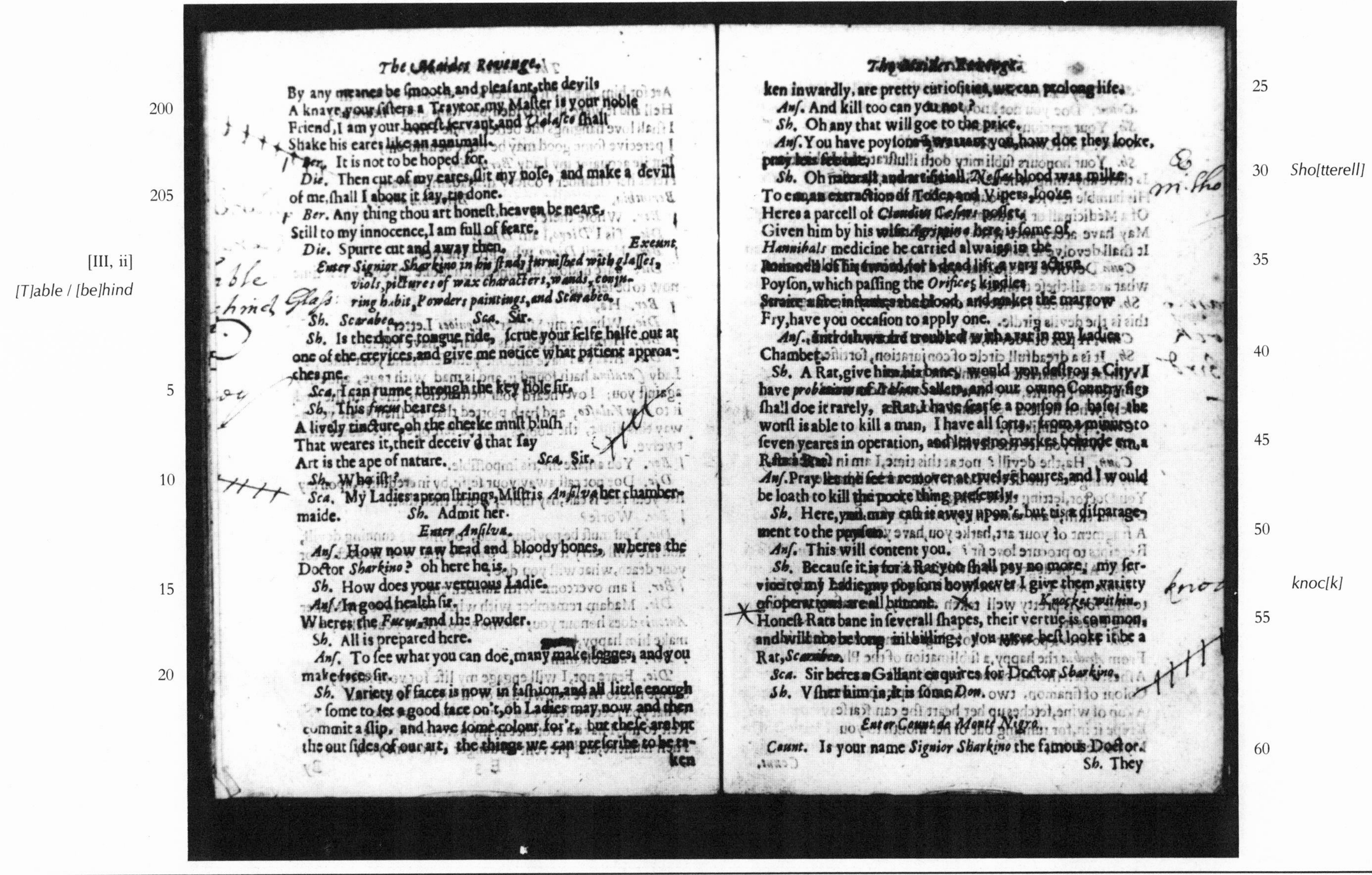

The Maides Revenge.

By any meanes be ſmooth, and pleaſant, the devils
A knave, your ſiſters a Traytor, my Maſter is your noble
Friend, I am your honeſt ſervant, and *Diaſco* ſhall
Shake his eares like an annimall.

Ber. It is not to be hoped for.

Dio. Then cut of my eares, ſlit my noſe, and make a devill of me, ſhall I about it ſay, tis done.

Ber. Any thing thou art honeſt, heaven be neare,
Still to my innocence, I am full of feare.

Dio. Spurre cut and away then. *Exeunt.*

[III, ii]

Enter Signior Sharkino in his ſtudy furniſhed with glaſſes, viols, pictures of wax characters, wands, conjuring habit, Powders paintings, and Scarabeo.

[T]able / [be]hind

Sh. Scarabeo. *Sca.* Sir.

Sh. Is the doore tongue tide, ſcrue your ſelfe halfe out at one of the crevices, and give me notice what patient approaches me.

Sca. I can runne through the key hole ſir.

Sh. This *fucus* beares
A lively tincture, oh the cheeke muſt bluſh
That weares it, their deceiv'd that ſay
Art is the ape of nature. *Sca.* Sir.

Sh. Who iſt?

Sca. My Ladies apron ſtrings, Miſtris *Anſilva* her chamber-maide. *Sh.* Admit her.

Enter Anſilva.

Anſ. How now raw head and bloody bones, wheres the Doctor *Sharkino*? oh here he is.

Sh. How does your vertuous Ladie.

Anſ. In good health ſir.
Wheres the *Fucus*, and the Powder.

Sh. All is prepared here.

Anſ. To ſee what you can doe, many make legges, and you make faces ſir.

Sh. Variety of faces is now in faſhion, and all little enough ſome to ſet a good face on't, oh Ladies may now and then commit a ſlip, and have ſome colour for't, but theſe are but the out ſides of our art, the things we can preſcribe to be taken inwardly, are pretty curioſities, we can prolong life.

The Maides Revenge.

Anſ. And kill too can you not?

Sh. Oh any that will goe to the price.

Anſ. You have poyſons I warrant you, how doe they looke, pray lets ſee one.

Sh. Oh naturall and artificiall, *Neſſus* blood was milke, To [illegible] an extraction of Todes and Vipers, looke
Heres a parcell of *Claudius Caeſars* poſſet,
Given him by his wife *Agrippina* here is ſome of
Hannibals medicine he carried alwaies in the
[illegible] of his ſword, for a dead lift, a very active
Poyſon, which paſſing the *Orifice*, kindles
[illegible] infames the blood, and makes the marrow
Fry, have you occaſion to apply one.

Sho[tterell]

Anſ. [illegible] troubled with a rat in my Ladies Chamber.

Sh. A Rat, give him his bane, would you deſtroy a City, I have *[illegible]* Sallets, and our owne Country figs ſhall doe it rarely, a Rat, I have ſcarſe a poyſon ſo baſe, the worſt is able to kill a man, I have all ſorts, from a minute to ſeven yeares in operation, and leave no markes behinde em, a [illegible]

Anſ. Pray let me ſee a remover at twelve houres, and I would be loath to kill the poore thing preſently.

Sh. Here, you may caſt it away upon't, but tis a diſparagement to the poyſon.

Anſ. This will content you.

Sh. Becauſe it is for a Rat you ſhall pay no more, my ſervice to my Ladie, my poyſons howſoever I give them, variety of operations are all honeſt. *Knockes within.*

knoc[k]

Honeſt Rats bane in ſeverall ſhapes, their vertue is common, and will not be long in killing; you were beſt looke it be a Rat, *Scarabeo.*

Sca. Sir heres a Gallant enquires for Doctor *Sharkino.*

Sh. Vſher him in, it is ſome *Don.*

Enter Count de Monte Nigro.

Count. Is your name *Signior Sharkino* the famous Doctor.

Sh. They

III, ii, 5. Cropped note: *[Mrs Cor]ey*. Her warning is unnecessarily short.

III, ii, 54. Scarabeo evidently makes an exit at this point.

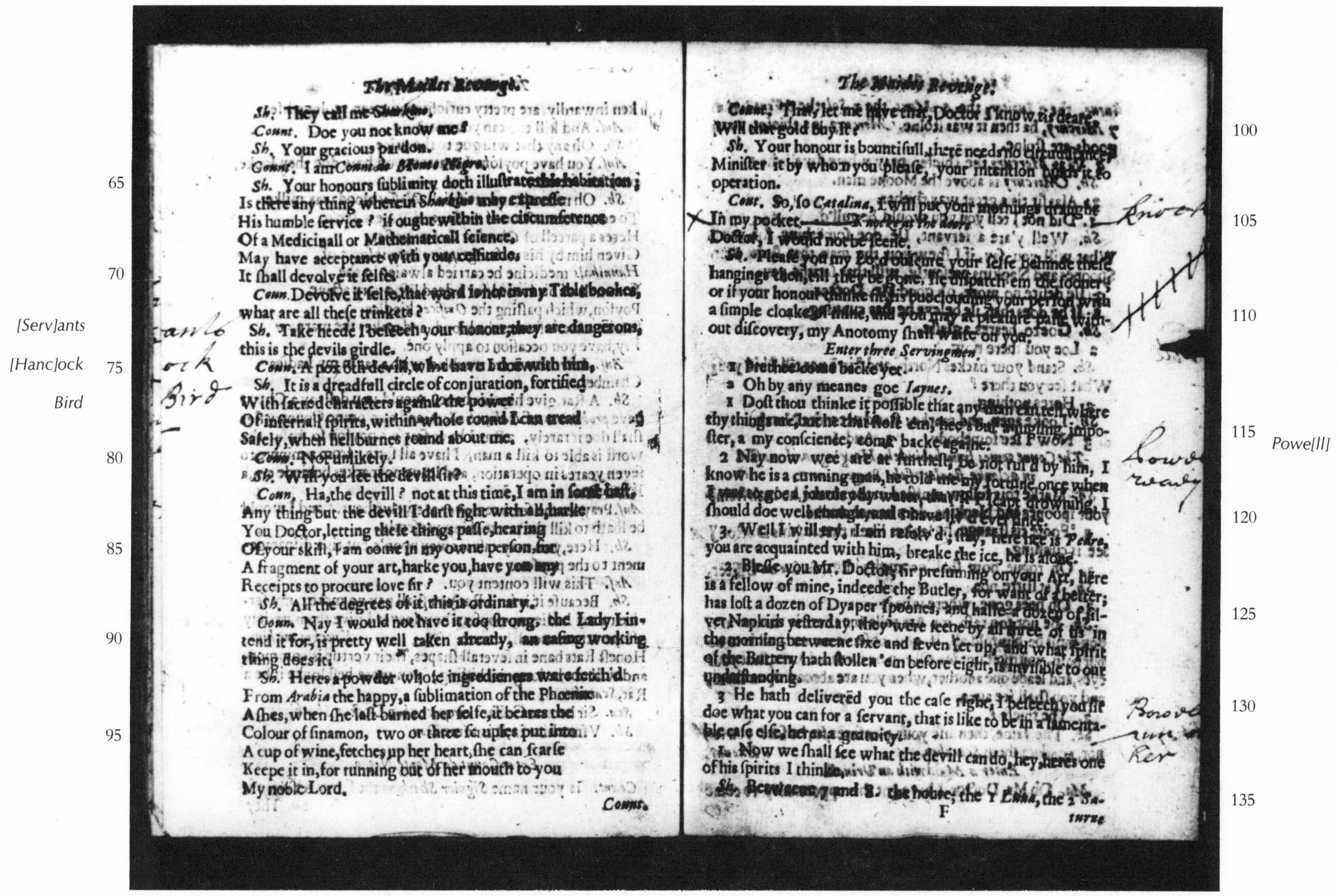

The Maides Revenge.

Sh. They call me *Sharkino*.
Count. Doe you not know me?
Sh. Your gracious pardon.
Count. I am *Conte de Monte Negro*.
Sh. Your honours sublimity doth illustrate this habitation;
Is there any thing wherein *Sharkino* may expresse
His humble service? if ought within the circumference
Of a Medicinall or Mathematicall science,
May have acceptance with your celsitude,
It shall devolve it selfe.
Coun. Devolve it selfe, that word is not in my Tablebookes,
what are all these trinkets?
Sh. Take heede I beseech your honour, they are dangerous,
this is the devils girdle.
Coun. A pox oth devill, what have I doe with him,
Sh. It is a dreadfull circle of conjuration, fortified
With sacred characters against the power
Of infernall spirits, within whose round I can tread
Safely, when hell burnes round about me.
Coun. Not unlikely.
Sh. Will you see the devill sir?
Coun. Ha, the devill? not at this time, I am in some hast,
Any thing but the devill I durst fight with all, harke
You Doctor, letting these things passe, hearing
Of your skill, I am come in my owne person, for
A fragment of your art, harke you, have you any
Receipts to procure love sir?
Sh. All the degrees of it, this is ordinary.
Coun. Nay I would not have it too strong, the Lady I intend it for, is pretty well taken already, an easing working thing does it.
Sh. Heres a powder whose ingredients ware fetch'd
From *Arabia* the happy, a sublimation of the Phoenix
Ashes, when she last burned her selfe, it beares the
Colour of sinamon, two or three scruples put into
A cup of wine, fetches up her heart, she can scarse
Keepe it in, for running out of her mouth to you
My noble Lord.

Count.

The Maides Revenge.

Count. That, let me have that, Doctor I know tis deare, Will this gold buy it?
Sh. Your honour is bountifull, there needs no circumstance, Minister it by whom you please, your intention brings it to operation.
Count. So, so *Catalina*, I will put your mothings draught In my pocket.——*Knocke at the doore.* Doctor, I would not be seene.
Sh. Please you my Lo. obscure your selfe behinde these hangings then, till they be gone, Ile dispatch 'em the sooner, or if your honour thinke fit, its but clouding your person with a simple cloake of mine, and you may at pleasure passe without discovery, my Anotomy shall waite on you.

Enter three Servingmen.

1 Prethee come backe yet.
2 Oh by any meanes goe *Iaynes*.
1 Dost thou thinke it possible that any man can tell where thy things are, but he that stole 'em, hee's but a juggling imposter, a my conscience, come backe againe.
2 Nay now wee are at furthest, be not fear'd by him, I know he is a cunning man, he told me my fortune once when I was to goe a journey by water, that [illegible] I should doe well [illegible] and I have liv'd ever since.
3 Well I will try, I am resolv'd, stay, here hee is *Pedro*, you are acquainted with him, breake the ice, he is alone.
2 Blesse you Mr. Doctor, sir presuming on your Art, here is a fellow of mine, indeede the Butler, for want of a better; has lost a dozen of Dyaper spoones, and halfe a dozen of silver Napkins yesterday, they were seene by all three of us in the morning betweene sixe and seven set up, and what spirit of the Buttery hath stollen 'em before eight, is invisible to our understanding.
3 He hath delivered you the case right, I beseech you sir doe what you can for a servant, that is like to be in a lamentable case else, heres a gratuity.
1 Now we shall see what the devill can do, hey, heres one of his spirits I thinke.
Sh. Betweene 7 and 8. the house, the 1 *Luna*, the 2 Saturne

F

[Serv]ants

[Hanc]ock

Bird

Powe[ll]

III, ii, 130 ff. Cropped note: *Powel[l] / run o[n] / her[e]*. Perhaps Martin Powell played Scarabeo.

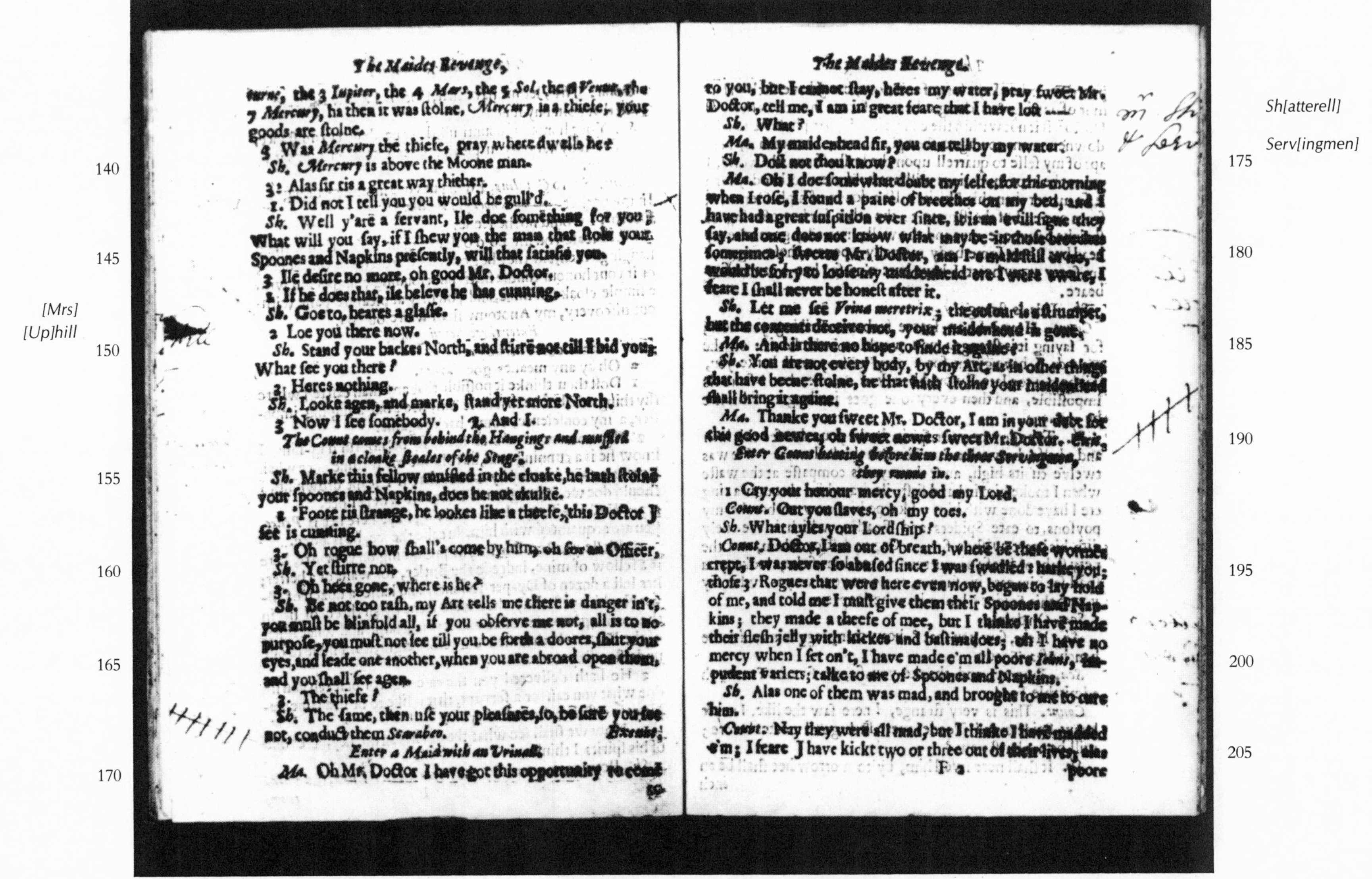

The Maides Revenge,

turne, the 3 Iupiter, the 4 Mars, the 5 Sol, the 6 Venus, the 7 Mercury, ha then it was ſtolne, Mercury is a thiefe, your goods are ſtolne.

3 Was Mercury the thiefe, pray where dwells he?

Sh. Mercury is above the Moone man.

3 Alas ſir tis a great way thither.

1. Did not I tell you you would be gull'd.

Sh. Well y'are a ſervant, Ile doe ſomething for you; What will you ſay, if I ſhew you the man that ſtole your Spoones and Napkins preſently, will that ſatisfie you.

3 Ile deſire no more, oh good Mr. Doctor.

1 If he does that, ile beleve he has cunning.

Sh. Goe to, heares a glaſſe.

2 Loe you there now.

Sh. Stand your backes North, and ſtirre not till I bid you: What ſee you there?

2 Heres nothing.

Sh. Looke agen, and marke, ſtand yet more North.

3 Now I ſee ſomebody. 2. And I.

The Count comes from behind the Hangings and muffled in a cloake ſteales of the Stage.

Sh. Marke this fellow muffled in the cloake, he hath ſtolne your ſpoones and Napkins, does he not ſkulke.

1 'Foote tis ſtrange, he lookes like a theefe, this Doctor I ſee is cunning.

3. Oh rogue how ſhall's come by him, oh for an Officer,

Sh. Yet ſtirre not.

3. Oh hee's gone, where is he?

Sh. Be not too raſh, my Art tells me there is danger in't, you muſt be blinfold all, if you obſerve me not, all is to no purpoſe, you muſt not ſee till you be forth a doores, ſhut your eyes, and leade one another, when you are abroad open them, and you ſhall ſee agen.

3. The thiefe?

Sh. The ſame, then uſe your pleaſures, ſo, be ſure you ſee not, conduct them Scarabeo. *Exeunt.*

Enter a Maid with an Urinall.

Ma. Oh Mr. Doctor I have got this opportunity to come

to you, but I cannot ſtay, heres my water, pray ſweet Mr. Doctor, tell me, I am in great feare that I have loſt ——

Sh[atterell]

Serv[ingmen]

Sh. What?

Ma. My maidenhead ſir, you can tell by my water.

Sh. Doſt not thou know?

Ma. Oh I doe ſomewhat doubt my ſelfe, for this morning when I roſe, I found a paire of breeches on my bed, and I have had a great ſuſpition ever ſince, it is an evill ſigne they ſay, and one does not know what may be in thoſe breeches ſometimes, ſweete Mr. Doctor, am I a maid ſtill or no, I would be ſorry to looſe my maidenhead ere I were aware, I feare I ſhall never be honeſt after it.

Sh. Let me ſee *Vrina meretrix*, the colour is ſtrumpet, but the contents deceive not, your maidenhead is gone.

Ma. And is there no hope to finde it againe?

Sh. You are not every body, by my Art, as in other things that have beene ſtolne, he that hath ſtolne your maidenhead ſhall bring it againe.

Ma. Thanke you ſweet Mr. Doctor, I am in your [illegible] for this good newes, oh ſweet newes ſweet Mr. Doctor. *Exit.*

Enter Count beating before him the three Servingmen, they runne in.

1 Cry your honour mercy, good my Lord.

Count. Out you ſlaves, oh my toes.

Sh. What ayles your Lordſhip?

Count. Doctor, I am out of breath, where be theſe wormes crept, I was never ſo abaſed ſince I was ſwadled: harke you; thoſe 3 Rogues that were here even now, began to lay hold of me, and told me I muſt give them their Spoones and Napkins; they made a theefe of mee, but I thinke I have made their fleſh jelly with kickes and baſtinadoes; oh I have no mercy when I ſet on't, I have made e'm all poore Iohns, impudent [illegible]; talke to me of Spoones and Napkins.

Sh. Alas one of them was mad, and brought to me to cure him.

Count. Nay they were all mad, but I thinke I have madded e'm; I feare I have kickt two or three out of their lives, alas

F 2 poore

[Mrs]
[Up]hill

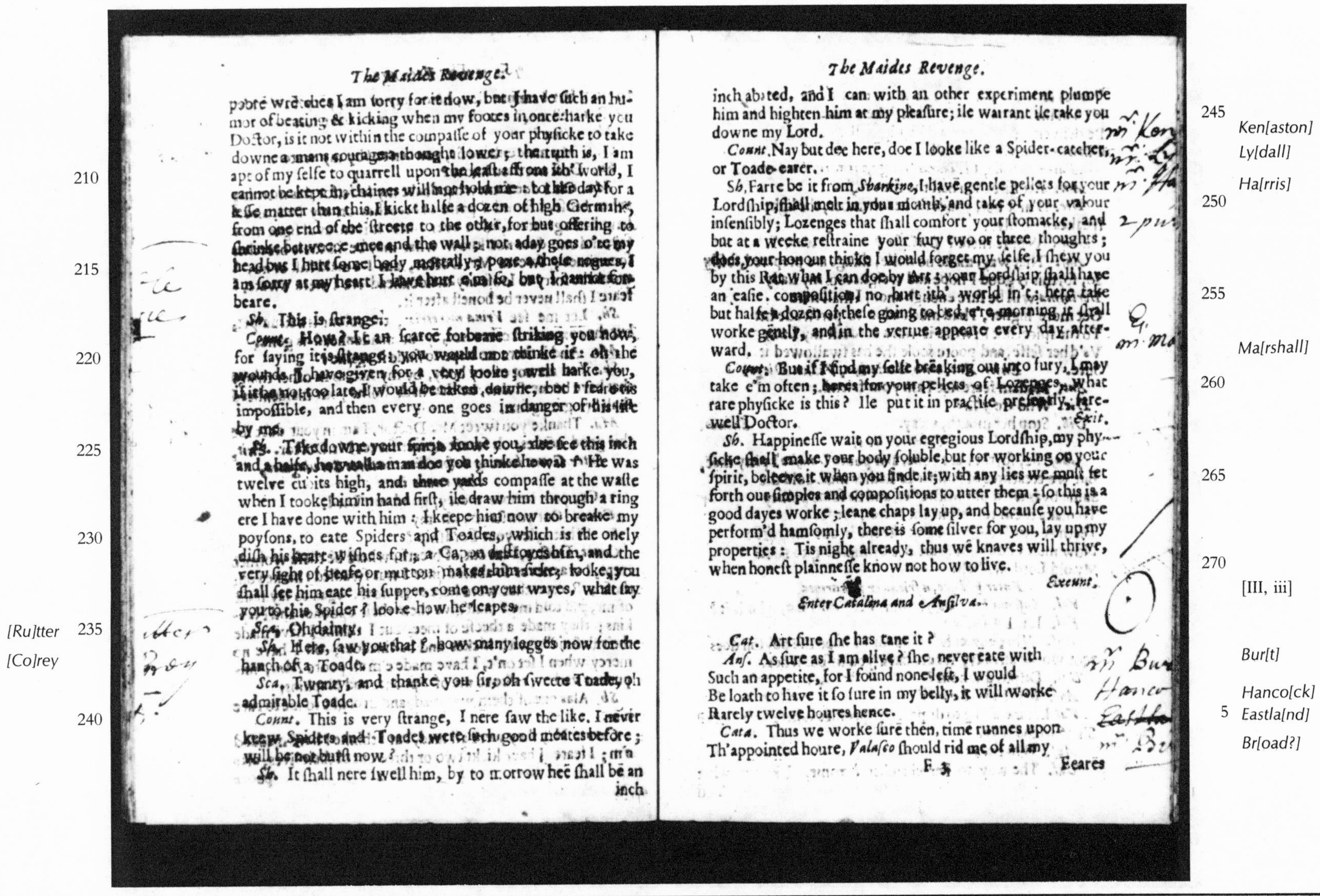

The Maides Revenge.

poore wretches I am sorry for it now, but I have such an humor of beating & kicking when my footes in once: harke you Doctor, is it not within the compasse of your physicke to take downe a mans courage a thought lower; the truth is, I am apt of my selfe to quarrell upon the least affront ith' world, I cannot be kept in, chaines will not hold me a tother day for a lesse matter than this, I kickt halfe a dozen of high Germanes, from one end of the streete to the other, for but offering to shrinke betweene mee and the wall; not a day goes o're my head but I hurt some body mortally, a pox a these rogues, I am sorry at my heart I have hurt em so, but I cannot forbeare.

[Ru]tter

Sh. This is strange.

[Co]rey

Count. How? I can scarce forbeare striking you now, for saying it is strange, you would not thinke it: oh the wounds I have given for a very looke; well harke you, if it be not too late, I would be taken downe, but I feare tis impossible, and then every one goes in danger of his life by me.

Sh. Take downe your spirit, looke you, doe see this inch and a halfe, how tall a man doe you thinke he was? He was twelve cubits high, and three yards compasse at the waste when I tooke him in hand first, ile draw him through a ring ere I have done with him: I keepe him now to breake my poysons, to eate Spiders and Toades, which is the onely dish his heart wishes for; a Capon destroyes him, and the very sight of beefe or mutton makes him sicke; looke you shall see him eate his supper, come on your wayes, what say you to this Spider? looke how he leapes.

Sca. Oh dainty.

Sh. Here, saw you that? how many legges now for the hanch of a Toade.

Sca. Twenty, and thanke you sir, oh sweete Toade, oh admirable Toade.

Count. This is very strange, I nere saw the like. I never knew Spiders and Toades were such good meates before; will he not burst now?

Sh. It shall nere swell him, by to morrow hee shall be an inch abated, and I can with an other experiment plumpe him and highten him at my pleasure; ile warrant ile take you downe my Lord.

Ken[aston]

Ly[dall]

Count. Nay but dee here, doe I looke like a Spider-catcher, or Toade-eater.

Ha[rris]

Sh. Farre be it from *Sharkino*, I have gentle pellets for your Lordship, shall melt in your mouth, and take of your valour insensibly; Lozenges that shall comfort your stomacke, and but at a weeke restraine your fury two or three thoughts; does your honour thinke I would forget my selfe, I shew you by this Rat what I can doe by art; your Lordship shall have an easie composition, no hurt ith' world in't; here take but halfe a dozen of these going to bed, e're morning it shall worke gently, and in the vertue appeare every day afterward.

Ma[rshall]

Count. But if I find my selfe breaking out into fury, I may take e'm often; heres for your pellets of Lozenges, what rare physicke is this? Ile put it in practise presently; farewell Doctor. *Exit.*

Sh. Happinesse wait on your egregious Lordship, my physicke shall make your body soluble, but for working on your spirit, beleeve it when you finde it; with any lies we must set forth our simples and compositions to utter them: so this is a good dayes worke; leane chaps lay up, and because you have perform'd hansomly, there is some silver for you, lay up my properties: Tis night already, thus we knaves will thrive, when honest plainnesse know not how to live. *Exeunt.*

[III, iii]

Enter Catalina and Ansilva.

Cat. Art sure she has tane it?

Bur[t]

Ans. As sure as I am alive? she never eate with
Such an appetite, for I found none left, I would
Be loath to have it so sure in my belly, it will worke
Rarely twelve houres hence.

Hanco[ck]

Eastla[nd]

Cata. Thus we worke sure then, time runnes upon
Th'appointed houre, *Valasco* should rid me of all my

Br[oad?]

F 3 Feares

III, ii, 215 f. There is not enough left of this cropped note to allow a reconstruction, nor is there anything in the text to suggest why a note was needed here. Perhaps it had to do with Sharkino's tricks.

III, ii, 251. The cropped note *2 pur* appears to be a reference to purses, but the text would not support that interpretation. The three actors just warned make their entrance disguised and perhaps with torches or lanterns; the note may have had something to do with their entrance.

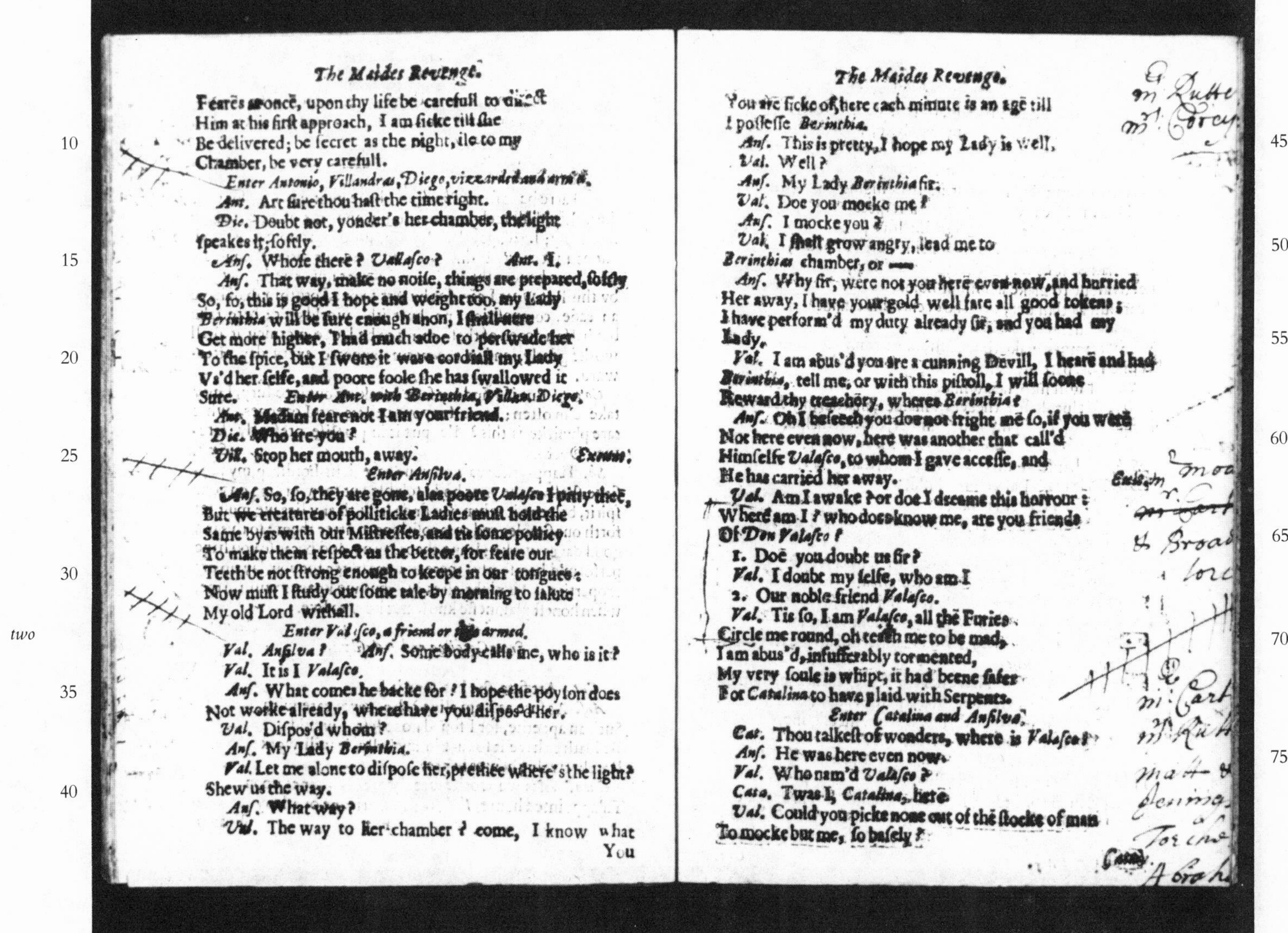

The Maides Revenge.

Feares at once, upon thy life be carefull to direct
Him at his firſt approach, I am ſicke till ſhe
Be delivered; be ſecret as the night, ile to my
Chamber, be very carefull.
Enter Antonio, Villandras, Diego, vizzarded and arm'd.
Ant. Art ſure thou haſt the time right.
Die. Doubt not, yonder's her chamber, the light
ſpeakes it; ſoftly.
Anſ. Whoſe there? *Vallaſco?* *Ant.* I.
Anſ. That way, make no noiſe, things are prepared, ſoftly
So, ſo, this is good I hope and weight too, my Lady
Berinthia will be ſure enough anon, I ſhall were
Get more higher, I had much adoe to perſwade her
To the ſpice, but I ſwore it ware cordiall my Lady
Vs'd her ſelfe, and poore foole ſhe has ſwallowed it
Sure. *Enter Ant. with Berinthia, Villan. Diego.*
Ant. Madam feare not I am your friend.
Die. Who are you?
Vill. Stop her mouth, away. *Exeunt.*
Enter Anſilva.
Anſ. So, ſo, they are gone, alas poore *Valaſco* I pitty thee,
But we creatures of politicke Ladies muſt hold the
Same byas with our Miſtreſſes, and tis ſome pollicy
To make them reſpect us the better, for feare our
Teeth be not ſtrong enough to keepe in our tongues:
Now muſt I ſtudy out ſome tale by morning to ſalute
My old Lord withall.
Enter Valaſco, a friend or two armed. *two*
Val. *Anſilva?* *Anſ.* Some body calls me, who is it?
Val. It is I *Valaſco.*
Anſ. What comes he backe for? I hope the poyſon does
Not worke already, where have you diſpos'd her.
Val. Diſpos'd whom?
Anſ. My Lady *Berinthia.*
Val. Let me alone to diſpoſe her, prethee where's the light?
Shew us the way.
Anſ. What way?
Val. The way to her chamber? come, I know what
You

The Maides Revenge.

You are ſicke of, here each minute is an age till
I poſſeſſe *Berinthia.*
Anſ. This is pretty, I hope my Lady is well.
Val. Well?
Anſ. My Lady *Berinthia* ſir.
Val. Doe you mocke me?
Anſ. I mocke you?
Val. I ſhall grow angry, lead me to
Berinthias chamber, or ——
Anſ. Why ſir, were not you here even now, and hurried
Her away, I have your gold well fare all good tokens;
I have perform'd my duty already ſir, and you had my
Lady.
Val. I am abus'd you are a cunning Devill, I heare and had
Berinthia, tell me, or with this piſtoll, I will ſoone
Reward thy treachery, wheres *Berinthia*?
Anſ. Oh I beſeech you doe not fright me ſo, if you were
Not here even now, here was another that call'd
Himſelfe *Valaſco*, to whom I gave acceſſe, and
He has carried her away.
Val. Am I awake? or doe I dreame this horrour:
Where am I? who doe know me, are you friends
Of *Don Valaſco*?
1. Doe you doubt us ſir?
Val. I doubt my ſelfe, who am I
2. Our noble friend *Valaſco.*
Val. Tis ſo, I am *Valaſco*, all the Furies
Circle me round, oh teach me to be mad,
I am abus'd, inſufferably tormented,
My very ſoule is whipt, it had beene ſafer
For *Catalina* to have plaid with Serpents.
Enter Catalina and Anſilva.
Cat. Thou talkeſt of wonders, where is *Valaſco*?
Anſ. He was here even now.
Val. Who nam'd *Valaſco*?
Cata. Twas I, *Catalina*, here.
Val. Could you picke none out of the ſtocke of man
To mocke but me, ſo baſely?

III, iii, 62. Cropped note: *Mr Moo[n]*—that is, Michael Mohun.

III, iii, 64 ff. Cropped note: *Mr Cart[wright] / & Broad / torc[h]*. Broad is an actor otherwise unknown. The note is cropped, and what can be seen may be the first part of a longer name, such as Broadhurst.

III, iii, 73 ff. Cropped note: *Mr Cart[wright] / Mrs Rut[ter] / Matt & / Jening[s?] / Torche[s] / Abrah[am Ivory?]*. *Matt* was probably the scene keeper and sometime actor Matthew Kempton; *Jening[s?]* is an actor otherwise unknown.

[Sha]ttrell

[torc]h

[Bu]rt

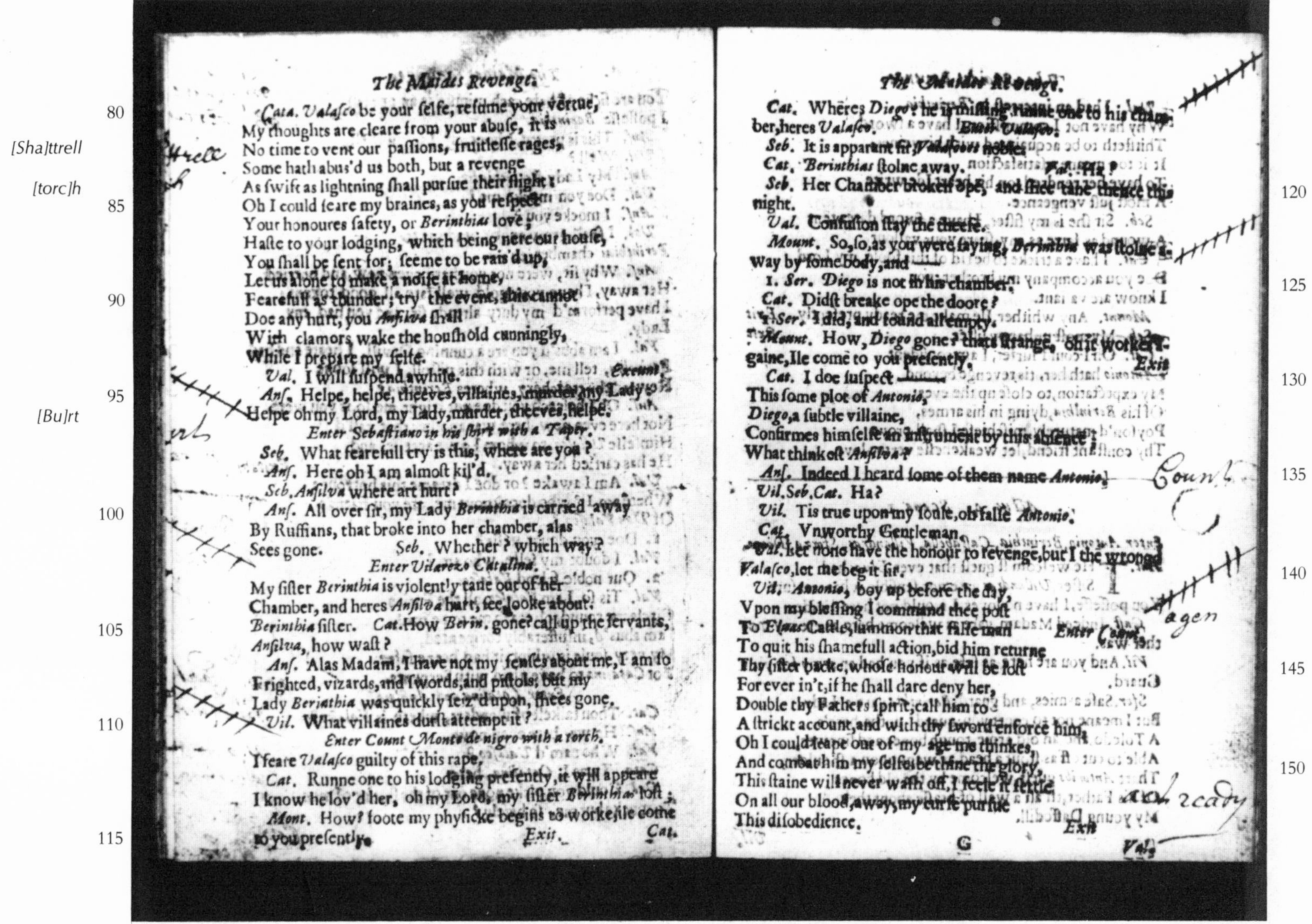

The Maides Revenge.

Cata. *Valaſco* be your ſelfe, reſume your vertue,
My thoughts are cleare from your abuſe, it is
No time to vent our paſſions, fruitleſſe rages,
Some hath abus'd us both, but a revenge
As ſwift as lightning ſhall purſue their flight:
Oh I could teare my braines, as you reſpect
Your honoures ſafety, or *Berinthias* love;
Haſte to your lodging, which being nere our houſe,
You ſhall be ſent for; ſeeme to be rais'd up,
Let us alone to make a noiſe at home,
Fearefull as thunder; try the event, this cannot
Doe any hurt, you *Anſilva* ſhall
With clamors wake the houſhold cunningly,
While I prepare my ſelfe.
Val. I will ſuſpend awhile. *Exeunt.*
Anſ. Helpe, helpe, theeves, villaines, murder my Lady:
Helpe oh my Lord, my Lady, murder, theeves, helpe.
Enter Sebaſtiano in his ſhirt with a Taper.
Seb. What fearefull cry is this, where are you?
Anſ. Here oh I am almoſt kil'd.
Seb. *Anſilva* where art hurt?
Anſ. All over ſir, my Lady *Berinthia* is carried away
By Ruffians, that broke into her chamber, alas
Sees gone. *Seb.* Whether? which way?
Enter Vilarezo Catalina.
My ſiſter *Berinthia* is violently tane out of her
Chamber, and heres *Anſilva* hurt, see looke about.
Berinthia ſiſter. *Cat.* How *Berin.* gone? call up the ſervants,
Anſilva, how waſt?
Anſ. Alas Madam, I have not my ſenſes about me, I am ſo
Frighted, vizards, and ſwords, and piſtols; but my
Lady *Berinthia* was quickly ſeiz'd upon, ſhees gone.
Vil. What villaines durſt attempt it?
Enter Count Monte de nigro with a torch.
I feare *Valaſco* guilty of this rape,
Cat. Runne one to his lodging preſently, it will appeare
I know he lov'd her, oh my Lord, my ſiſter *Berinthia* loſt;
Mont. How? ſoote my phyſicke begins to worke, Ile come
to you preſently. *Exit.*
Cat.

The Maides Revenge.

Cat. Wheres *Diego*? he is miſſing, runne one to his chamber, heres *Valaſco*. *Enter Valaſco.*
Seb. It is apparant ſir, *Valaſcoes* noble.
Cat. *Berinthias* ſtolne away. *Val.* Ha?
Seb. Her Chamber broken ope, and ſhee tane thence this night.
Val. Confuſion ſtay the theefe.
Mount. So, ſo, as you were ſaying, *Berinthia* was ſtolne away by ſome body, and ——
1. *Ser.* *Diego* is not in his chamber.
Cat. Didſt breake ope the doore?
1. *Ser.* I did, and found all empty.
Mount. How, *Diego* gone? thats ſtrange, oh it workes againe, Ile come to you preſently. *Exit*
Cat. I doe ſuſpect ——
This ſome plot of *Antonio*,
Diego, a ſubtle villaine,
Confirmes himſelfe an inſtrument by this abſence;
What think'ſt *Anſilva*?
Anſ. Indeed I heard ſome of them name *Antonio*.
Vil. Seb. Cat. Ha?
Vil. Tis true upon my ſoule, oh falſe *Antonio*.
Cat. Unworthy Gentleman.
Val. Let none have the honour to revenge, but I the wronged
Valaſco, let me beg it ſir.
Vil. *Antonio*, boy up before the day,
Upon my bleſſing I command thee poſt
To *Elvas* Caſtle, ſummon that falſe man *Enter Count.*
To quit his ſhamefull action, bid him returne
Thy ſiſter backe, whoſe honour will be loſt
For ever in't, if he ſhall dare deny her,
Double thy Fathers ſpirit, call him to
A ſtrickt account, and with thy ſword enforce him,
Oh I could leape out of my age me thinkes,
And combat him my ſelfe, be thine the glory,
This ſtaine will never waſh off, I feele it ſettle
On all our blood, away, my curſe purſue
This diſobedience. *Exit*
G Val.

III, iii, 123. The entrance cue is for the Servant who just went off; the author forgot to give him an exit and an entrance.

Val. I had an interest in *Berinthia*,
Why have not I commission, I have a sword,
Thirsteth to be acquainted with his veines;
It is too meane a satisfaction
To have her rendred, on his heart Ide write
A most just vengeance.
Seb. Sir she is my sister, I have a sword dares tent
A wound as farre as any; spare your vallour.
Cat. I have a tricke to be rid of this foole, my Lord
Doe you accompany my brother, you
I know are valiant.
Mount. Any whither, Ile make me ready presently. *Exit*
~~*Seb.* My most unhappy sister.~~ *Exit*
Cat. Oh I could surfet, I am confident
Antonio hath her, tis revenge beyond
My expectation, to close up the eyes
Of his *Berinthia*, dying in his armes,
Poyson'd maturely mischiefe, I shall prove
Thy constant friend, let weakenesse vertue love.

Caller

Actus. 4. Scena 1.

Enter Antonio, Berinthia, Castabella, Villandras, Sforza, Diego.

Ant. The welcom'st guest that ever *Eluas* had
Sister, *Villandras* yare not sensible what treasure
You possesse, I have no loves, I would not here divide.
Cast. Indeed Madam, yare as welcome here, as ere my mother was.
Vil. And you are here as safe, as if you had an army for your Guard.
Sfor. Safe armies, and guard; *Berinthia* yare a Lady,
But I meane not to court you: guard quotha, here's
A Toledo, and an old arme, tough bones and sinewes,
Able to cut off as stout a head as wags upon a shoulder;
That art *Antonios* guest, welcome by the old bones
Of his Father, th'ast a wall of brasse about thee
My young Daffodill.

Vil.

Vil. Nor thinke my noble cozen meaneth you any dishonour here.
Ant. Dishonour, it is a language I never understood; yet
Throw off your feares *Berinthia*, yare ith' power
Of him that dares not thinke
The least dishonour to you.
Sfor. True by this buffe jerkin, that hath look'd ith face of an Army, and he lies like a termagant, denies it, *Antonio* is Lord of the Castle, but ile command fire to the gunnes, upon any Renegado that confronts us, set thy heart at rest my gilloflower, we are all friends I warrant thee, and hees a Turke that does not honour thee from the haire of thy head, to thy pettitoes.
Ant. Come be not sad.
Cast. Put on fresh blood, yare not cheerefull, how doe you?
Ber. I know not how, not what to answer you,
Your loves I cannot be ungratefull to,
Yare my best friends I thinke, but yet I know not
With what consent you brought my body hither.
Ant. Can you be ignorant what plot was laid
To take your faire life from you.
Ber. If all be not a dreame, I doe remember
Your servant *Diego* told me wonders; and
I owe you for my preservation, but ~~[illegible]~~
Sfor. Shoote not at Buts, *Cupids* an archer, heres a faire marke, a fooles bolts soone shot, my names *Sforza* still, my double Daisie.
Cast. It is your happinesse you have escaped the malice of your sister.
Vil. And it is worth
A noble gratitude to have beene quit,
By such an honourer as *Antonio* is
Of faire *Berinthia*.
Ber. Oh but my Father, under whose displeasure I ever thinke.
Ant. You are secure.
Ber. As the poore Deere, that being pursuid, for safety
Gets up a rocke that over hangs the Sea,
Where all that she can see, is her destruction,

G 2 Before

The Maides Revenge.

Before the waves, behinde her enemies
Promiſe her certaine ruine.
Ant. Faine not your ſelfe ſo hapleſſe my *Berinthia*,
Raiſe your dejected thoughts, be merry, come,
Thinke I am your *Antonio.*
Caſt. It is not wiſdome
To let our paſſed fortunes trouble us,
Since were they bad, the memorie is ſweete,
That we have paſt them, looke before you Lady,
The future moſt concernes.
Ber. You have awak'd me, *Antonio* pardon,
Upon whoſe honour I dare truſt my ſelfe,
I am reſolv'd, if you dare keepe me here,
T'expect ſome happier iſſue.
Ant. Dare keepe thee here? with thy conſent, I dare
Deny thy Father, by this ſword I dare,
And all the world.
Sfor. Dare, what giant of vallour dares hinder us, from daring to ſlit the weaſands of them that dare ſay, wee dare not doe any thing, that is to be dared under the poles, I am old *Sforza*, that in my dayes have ſcoured rogues faces with hot bals, made em cut croſſe capers, and ſent them away with a powder, I have a company of roring bils upon the walls, ſhall ſpit fire in the faces of any ragamuffian that dares ſay, we dare not fight pell mell, and ſtill my name is *Sforza.*
Enter Diego haſtily.
Die. Sir your noble friend *don Sebaſtiano* is at the caſtle gate,
Ant. Your brother Lady, and my honoured friend,
[M]r Why doe the gates not ſpread themſelves, to open
At his arrivall *Sforza*, tis *Berinthiaes* brother,
[M]oone *Sebaſtiano* the example of all worth
And friendſhip, is come after his ſweete ſiſter,
[M]r *Ber.* Alas I feare.
Ant. Be not ſuch a coward Lady, he cannot come
[S]hottrell Without all goodneſſe waiting on him, *Sforza*,
Sforza I ſay, what precious time we loſe,
Sebaſtiano, I almoſt loſe my ſelfe
In joy to meete him, breake the iron barres
And

The Maides Revenge.

And give him entrance.
Sfor. Ile breake the wals downe, if the gates be too little.
Caſt. I much deſire to ſee him.
Ant. Siſter, now hees come, he did promiſe me
But a ſhort abſence, he of all the world
I would call brother, *Caſtabella* more
Then for his ſiſters love, oh hees a man
Made up of merit, my *Berinthia*
Throw off all cloudes, *Sebaſtianoes* come.
Ber. Sent by my Father to——
Ant. What, to ſee thee? he ſhall ſee thee here:
Reſpected like thy ſelfe, *Berinthia*,
Attended with *Antonio*, begirt with armies of thy ſervants.
Enter Sebaſtiano Mounte Nigro, Sforza.
Oh my friend.
Seb. Tis yet in queſtion ſir, and will not be
So eaſily proved.
Moun. No ſir, weele make you prove your ſelfe our friend.
Ant. What face have you put on? am I awake?
Or doe I dreame *Sebaſtiano* frownes.
Seb. *Antonio* I come not now to Complement,
While you were noble, I was not leaſt of them
You cald your friends, but you are guilty of
An action that deſtroyes that name.
Sfor. Bones a your Father, does he come to ſwagger,
My name is *Sforza* then.
Ant. No more,
I guiltie of an action ſo diſhonourable
Has made me unworthy of your friendſhip;
Come y'are not in earneſt, tis enough I know
My ſelfe *Antonio.*
Seb. Adde to him ungracefull.
Ant. Twas a foule breath delivered it, and were any
But *Sebaſtiano*, he ſhould feele the weight
Of ſuch a falſhood.
Seb. Siſter you muſt along with me.
Ant. Now by my Fathers ſoule, he that takes her hence
Unleſſe ſhe give conſent, treads on his grave,
G 3 Sebaſti-

Sebaſtiano,y'are unnoble then,
Tis I that ſaid it.
Mount. So it ſeemes.
Seb. *Antonio*,for here I throw of all
The ties of love,I come to fetch a ſiſter,
Diſhonourably taken from her father;
Or with my ſword to force thee render her;
Now if thou beeſt a Souldier redeliver,
Or keepe her with the danger of thy perſon,
Thou canſt not be my brother,till we firſt
Be allied in blood.
Ant. Promiſe me the hearing,
And ſhat have any ſatisfaction,
Becomes my fame.
Mount. So,ſo,he will ſubmit himſelfe,it will be our honor,
Ant. Wert in your power,would you not account it
A pretious victory, in your ſiſters cauſe,
To dye your ſword with any blood of him,
Sav'd both her life and honour?
Seb. I were ungratefull.
Ant. You have told your ſelfe,and I have argument to
prove this.
Seb. Why would you have me thinke,my ſiſter owes to
you ſuch preſervation?
Ant. Oh *Sebaſtiano*,
Thou doſt not thinke what devill lies at home
Within a ſiſters boſome,*Catalina*,
(I know not with what worſt of envy) laid
Force to this goodly building,and through poyſon
Had rob'd the earth of more then all the world,
Her vertue.
Seb. You muſt not beate my reſolution off
With theſe inventions ſir.
Ant. Be not cozend,
With your credulity,for my blood,I value it
Beneath my honour,and I dare by goodneſſe,
In ſuch a quarrell ſhed it but heare all,
And then you ſhall have fighting your heart full.
Valaſco

Valaſco was the man,appointed by
That goodly ſiſter to ſteale *Berinthia*,
And Lord himſelfe of this poſſeſſion,
Juſt at that time;but heare and tremble at it,
Shee by a cunning poyſon ſhould have breath'd
Her ſoule into his armes,within two houres,
And ſo *Valaſco* ſhould have borne the ſhame
Of theft and murther; how doe you like this ſir.
Seb. You amaze me ſir.
Ant. Tis true by honours ſelfe,heare it confirm'd,
And when you will,I am ready.
Vil. Pitty ſuch valour ſhould be imployd,
Vpon no better cauſe,they will enforme him.
Mount. Harke you ſir,dee thinke this is true?
Vil. I dare maintaine it.
Mount. Thats another matter,why then the caſe is
Altered,what ſhould we doe fighting,and loſe
Our lives to no purpoſe.
Sf. It ſeemes you are his ſecond.
Mount. I am *Count de Monte Nigro*.
Sfor. And my names *Sforza* ſir, you were not beſt to come
here to brave us, unleſſe you have more legges and armes at
home,I have a ſaza ſhall picke holes in your doublet,and firke
your ſhankes,my gallimaufry.
Seb. I cannot but beleeve it,oh *Berinthia*,
I am wounded ere I fight.
Ant. Holds your reſolve yet conſtant? if you have
Better opinion of your ſword,then truth,
I am bound to anſwer, but I would I had
Such an advantage gainſt another man,
As the juſtice of my cauſe,all vallour fights
But with a ſayle againſt it.
Vil. Take a time to informe your father ſir,my noble
Cozen is to be found here conſtant.
Seb. But will you backe with me then?
Ber. Excuſe me brother,I ſhall fall too ſoone
Vpon my ſiſters malice, whoſe foule guilt
Will make me expect more certaine ruine,
Ant.

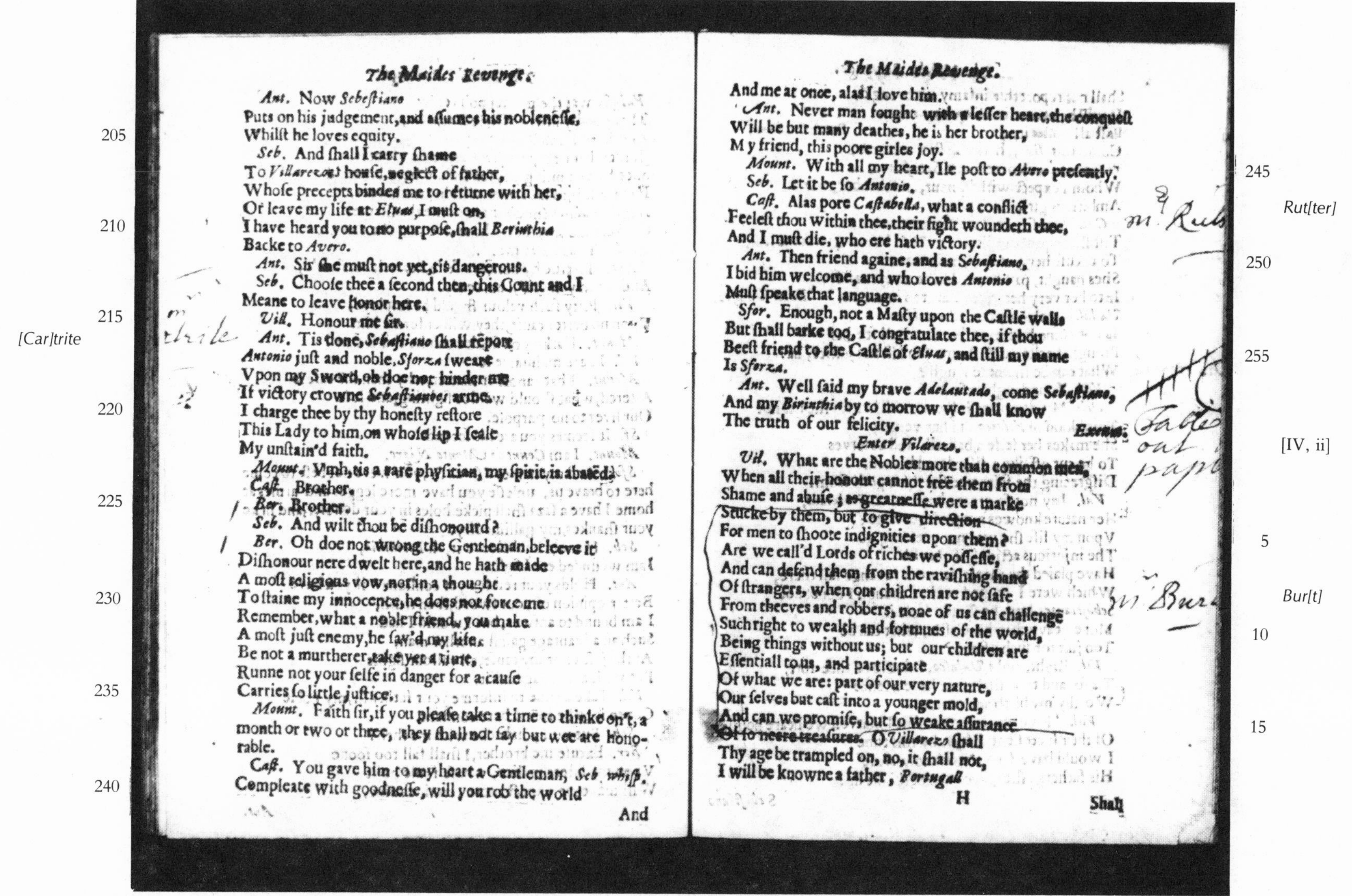

The Maides Revenge.

Ant. Now *Sebestiano*
Puts on his judgement, and assumes his noblenesse,
Whilst he loves equity.
Seb. And shall I carry shame
To *Villarezo's* house, neglect of father,
Whose precepts bindes me to returne with her,
Or leave my life at *Elvas*, I must on,
I have heard you to no purpose, shall *Berinthia*
Backe to *Avero*.
Ant. Sir she must not yet, tis dangerous.
Seb. Choose thee a second then, this Count and I
Meane to leave honor here.
Vill. Honour me sir.
Ant. Tis done, *Sebastiano* shall repor
[Car]trite
Antonio just and noble, *Sforza* sweare
Vpon my Sword, oh doe not hinder me
If victory crowne *Sebastianoes* arme.
I charge thee by thy honesty restore
This Lady to him, on whose lip I seale
My unstain'd faith.
Mount. Vmh, tis a rare physitian, my spirit is abated.
Cast. Brother.
Ber. Brother.
Seb. And wilt thou be dishonourd?
Ber. Oh doe not wrong the Gentleman, beleeve it
Dishonour nere dwelt here, and he hath made
A most religious vow, not in a thought
To staine my innocence, he does not force me
Remember, what a noble friend, you make
A most just enemy, he sav'd my life.
Be not a murtherer, take yet a time,
Runne not your selfe in danger for a cause
Carries so little justice.
Mount. Faith sir, if you please take a time to thinke on't, a month or two or three, they shall not say but wee are honorable.
Cast. You gave him to my heart a Gentleman, *Seb. whisp.*
Compleate with goodnesse, will you rob the world
And

The Maides Revenge.

And me at once, alas I love him.
Ant. Never man fought with a lesser heart, the conquest
Will be but many deathes, he is her brother,
My friend, this poore girles joy.
Mount. With all my heart, Ile post to *Avero* presently.
Seb. Let it be so *Antonio*.
Cast. Alas pore *Castabella*, what a conflict
Rut[ter]
Feelest thou within thee, their fight woundeth thee,
And I must die, who ere hath victory.
Ant. Then friend againe, and as *Sebastiano*,
I bid him welcome, and who loves *Antonio*
Must speake that language.
Sfor. Enough, not a Masty upon the Castle walls
But shall barke too, I congratulate thee, if thou
Beest friend to the Castle of *Elvas*, and still my name
Is *Sforza*.
Ant. Well said my brave *Adelantado*, come *Sebastiano*,
And my *Birinthia* by to morrow we shall know
The truth of our felicity. *Exeunt.*
[IV, ii]
Enter Vilarezo.
Vil. What are the Nobles more than common men,
When all their honour cannot free them from
Shame and abuse; as greatnesse were a marke
Stucke by them, but to give direction
For men to shoote indignities upon them?
Are we call'd Lords of riches we possesse,
And can defend them from the ravishing hand
Of strangers, when our children are not safe
Bur[t]
From theeves and robbers, none of us can challenge
Such right to wealth and fortunes of the world,
Being things without us; but our children are
Essentiall to us, and participate
Of what we are: part of our very nature,
Our selves but cast into a younger mold,
And can we promise, but so weake assurance
Of so neere treasures. O *Villarezo* shall
Thy age be trampled on, no, it shall not,
I will be knowne a father, *Portugall*
H Shall

IV, ii, 1. Cropped note: circle-and-dot symbol and *pape[r]*.

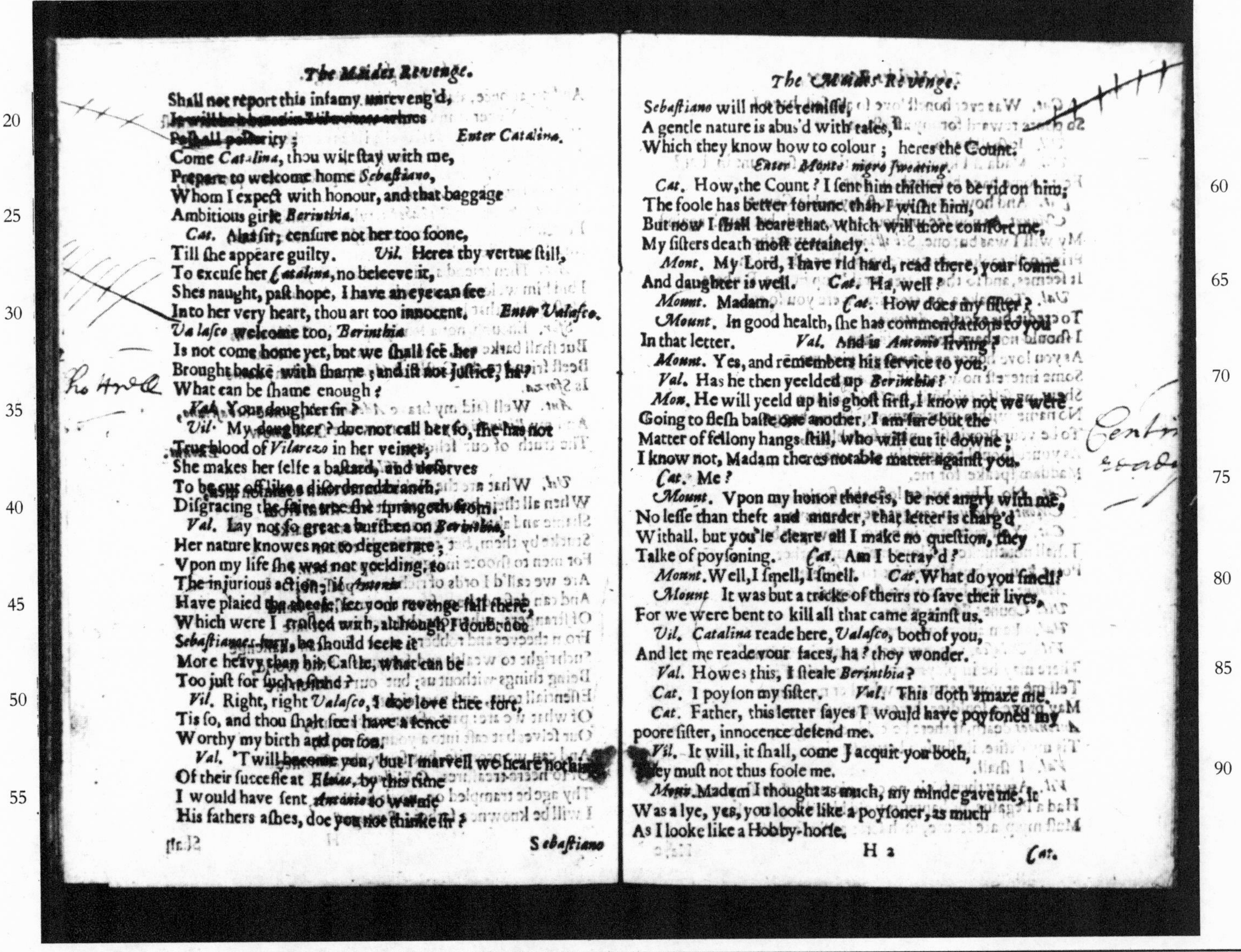

The Maides Revenge.

Shall not report this infamy unreveng'd,
Past all posterity; *Enter Catalina.*
Come *Catalina*, thou wilt stay with me,
Prepare to welcome home *Sebastiano*,
Whom I expect with honour, and that baggage
Ambitious girle *Berinthia*.
Cat. Alas sir, censure not her too soone,
Till she appeare guilty. *Vil.* Heres thy vertue still,
To excuse her *Catalina*, no beleeve it,
Shes naught, past hope, I have an eye can see
Into her very heart, thou art too innocent. *Enter Valasco.*
Valasco welcome too, *Berinthia*
Is not come home yet, but we shall see her
Brought backe with shame, and its not justice, ha?
What can be shame enough?
Val. Your daughter sir?
Vil. My daughter? doe not call her so, she has not
True blood of *Vilarezo* in her veines,
She makes her selfe a bastard, and deserves
To be cut off like a disordered branch,
Disgracing the faire tree she springeth from;
Val. Lay not so great a burthen on *Berinthia*,
Her nature knowes not to degenerate;
Vpon my life she was not yeelding, to
The injurious action, 'tis *Antonio*
Have plaied the theefe, let your revenge fall there,
Which were I trusted with, although I doubt not
Sebastianoes fury, he should feele it
More heavy than his Castle, what can be
Too just for such a fiend?
Vil. Right, right *Valasco*, I doe love thee fort,
Tis so, and thou shalt see I have a fence
Worthy my birth and person.
Val. 'Twill become you, but I marvell we heare nothing
Of their successe at *Elvas*, by this time
I would have sent *Antonio* to wait his
His fathers ashes, doe you not thinke sir?
Sebastiano

The Maides Revenge.

Sebastiano will not be remisse,
A gentle nature is abus'd with tales,
Which they know how to colour; heres the Count.
Enter Montenigro sweating.
Cat. How, the Count? I sent him thither to be rid on him,
The foole has better fortune than I wisht him,
But now I shall heare that which will more comfort me,
My sisters death most certainely.
Mont. My Lord, I have rid hard, read there, your sonne
And daughter is well. *Cat.* Ha, well?
Mount. Madam. *Cat.* How does my sister?
Mount. In good health, she has commendations to you
In that letter. *Val.* And is *Antonio* living?
Mount. Yes, and remembers his service to you,
Val. Has he then yeelded up *Berinthia*?
Mon. He will yeeld up his ghost first, I know not we were
Going to flesh baste one another, I am sure but the
Matter of fellony hangs still, who will cut it downe;
I know not, Madam theres notable matter against you.
Cat. Me?
Mount. Vpon my honor there is, be not angry with me,
No lesse than theft and murder, that letter is charg'd
Withall, but you'le cleare all I make no question, they
Talke of poysoning. *Cat.* Am I betray'd?
Mount. Well, I smell, I smell. *Cat.* What do you smell?
Mount It was but a tricke of theirs to save their lives,
For we were bent to kill all that came against us.
Vil. *Catalina* reade here, *Valasco*, both of you,
And let me reade your faces, ha? they wonder.
Val. Howes this, I steale *Berinthia*?
Cat. I poyson my sister. *Val.* This doth amaze me.
Cat. Father, this letter sayes I would have poysoned my
poore sister, innocence defend me.
Vil. It will, it shall, come I acquit you both,
They must not thus foole me.
Mont. Madam I thought as much, my minde gave me, it
Was a lye, yes, you looke like a poysoner, as much
As I looke like a Hobby-horse.
H 2 *Cat.*

IV, ii, 20–21. The canceled lines are: "It will be a barre in *Vilarezoes* armes / Past all posterity."

IV, ii, 72 f. The note is cropped, though apparently not severely; I read it *Centr / ready*. I cannot figure out what was to be ready. Perhaps it had something to do with the canceled masque in the next scene.

[M]oone
[B]outell
[Ky]naston
[M]arshall

[IV, iii]
Cast[le]

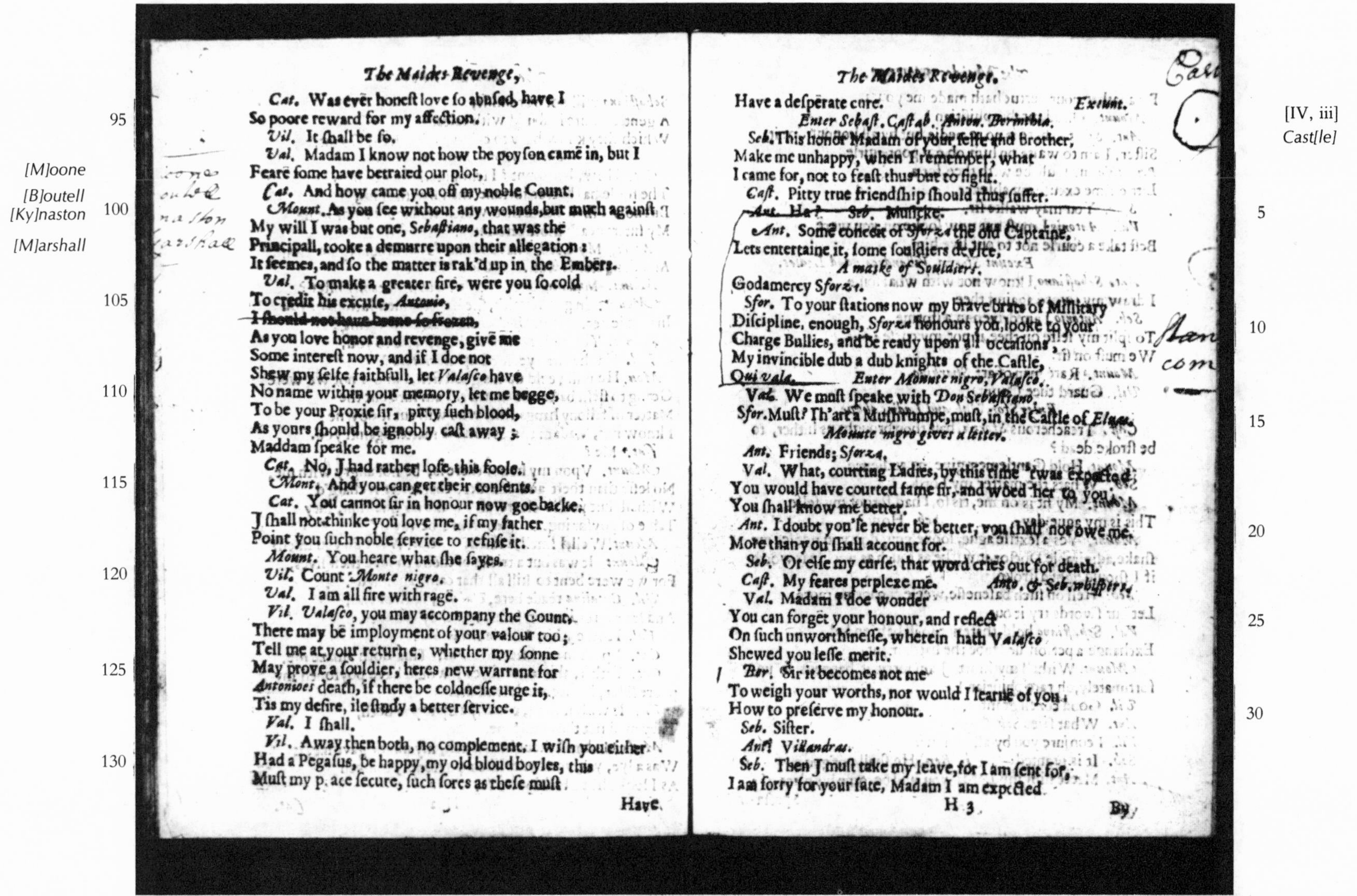

The Maides Revenge,

Cat. Was ever honest love so abused, have I
So poore reward for my affection.
Vil. It shall be so.
Val. Madam I know not how the poyson came in, but I
Feare some have betraied our plot,
Cat. And how came you off my noble Count.
Mount. As you see without any wounds, but much against
My will I was but one, *Sebastiano*, that was the
Principall, tooke a demurre upon their allegation:
It seemes, and so the matter is rak'd up in the Embers.
Val. To make a greater fire, were you so cold
To credit his excuse, *Antonio*,
~~I should not have beene so frozen,~~
As you love honor and revenge, give me
Some interest now, and if I doe not
Shew my selfe faithfull, let *Valasco* have
No name within your memory, let me begge,
To be your Proxie sir, pitty such blood,
As yours should be ignobly cast away;
Maddam speake for me.
Cat. No, I had rather lose this foole.
Mont. And you can get their consents.
Cat. You cannot sir in honour now goe backe.
I shall not thinke you love me, if my father
Point you such noble service to refuse it.
Mount. You heare what she sayes.
Vil. Count *Monte nigro*.
Val. I am all fire with rage.
Vil. *Valasco*, you may accompany the Count.
There may be imployment of your valour too;
Tell me at your returne, whether my sonne
May prove a souldier, heres new warrant for
Antonioes death, if there be coldnesse urge it,
Tis my desire, ile study a better service.
Val. I shall.
Vil. Away then both, no complement, I wish you either
Had a Pegasus, be happy, my old bloud boyles, this
Must my p ace secure, such sores as these must
Have.

The Maides Revenge.

Have a desperate cure. *Exeunt.*
Enter Sebast. Castab. Anton. Bermibla.
Seb. This honor Madam of your selfe and brother,
Make me unhappy, when I remember, what
I came for, not to feast thus but to fight.
Cast. Pitty true friendship should thus suffer.
~~*Ant.* Ha? *Seb.* Musicke.~~
Ant. Some conceit of *Sforza* the old Captaine,
Lets entertaine it, some souldiers device,
A maske of Souldiers.
Godamercy *Sforza*.
Sfor. To your stations now my brave brats of Millitary
Discipline, enough, *Sforza* honours you, looke to your
Charge Bullies, and be ready upon all occasions,
My invincible dub a dub knights of the Castle,
Qui vala. *Enter Monte nigro, Valasco.*
Val. We must speake with *Don Sebastiano*.
Sfor. Must? Th'art a Mushrumpe, must, in the Castle of *Elvas*.
Monte nigro gives a letter.
Ant. Friends; *Sforza*.
Val. What, courting Ladies, by this time 'twas expected,
You would have courted fame sir, and woed her to you.
You shall know me better.
Ant. I doubt you'se never be better, you shall not owe me.
More than you shall account for.
Seb. Or else my curse, that word cries out for death.
Cast. My feares perplexe me. *Anto. & Seb. whispers.*
Val. Madam I doe wonder
You can forget your honour, and reflect
On such unworthinesse, wherein hath *Valasco*
Shewed you lesse merit.
Ber. Sir it becomes not me
To weigh your worths, nor would I learne of you.
How to preserve my honour.
Seb. Sister.
Ant. *Villandras*.
Seb. Then I must take my leave, for I am sent for,
I am sorry for your fate, Madam I am expected
H 3 By

IV, iii, 11 f. Cropped note: *Stan / com.* I cannot decipher this note; it may have concerned the canceled masque.
IV, iii, 13. The entrance of Monte Nigro and Valasco was neither warned nor cued.

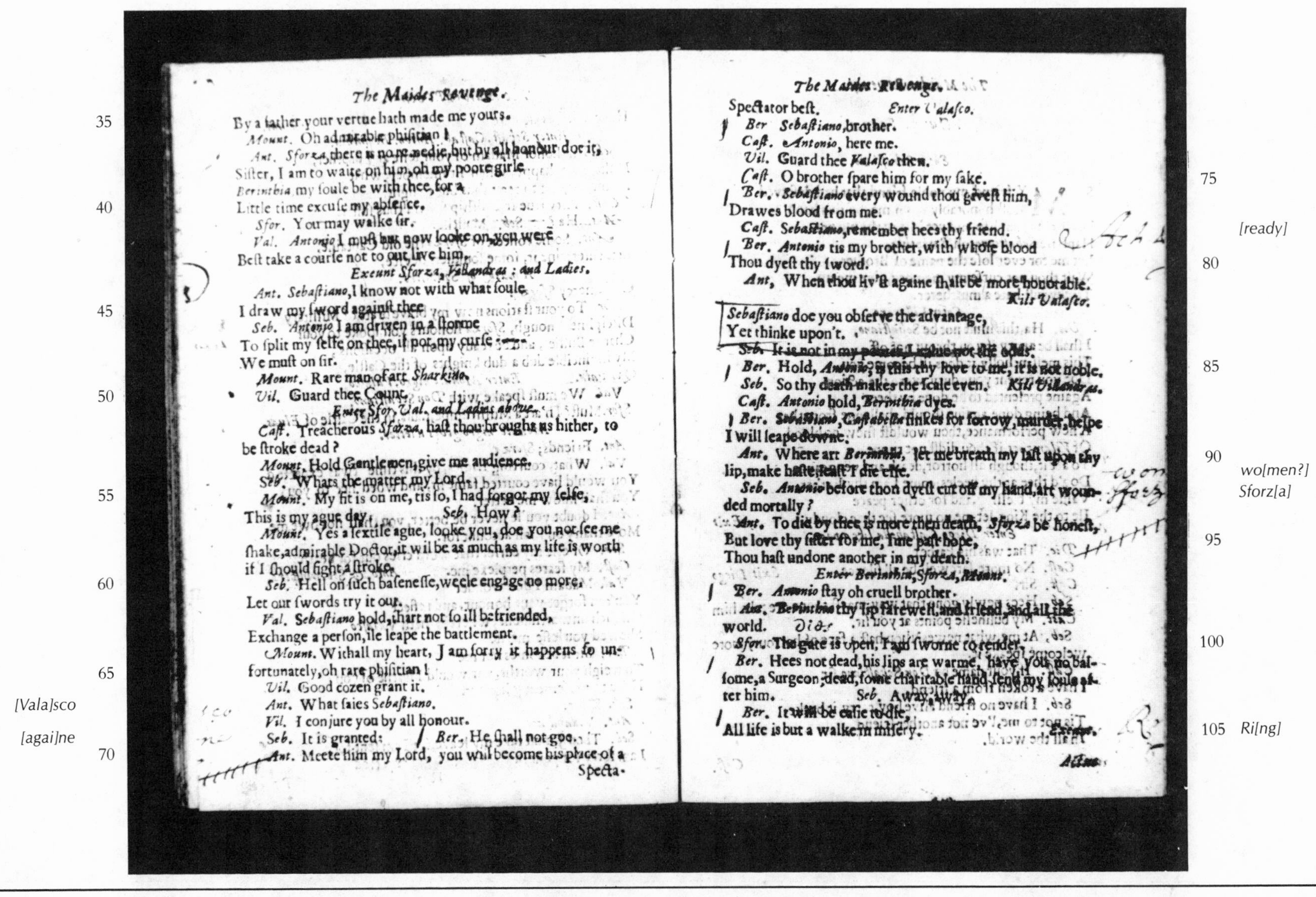

The Maides Revenge.

By a father your vertue hath made me yours.
Mount. Oh admirable phisitian !
Ant. Sforza, there is no remedie, but by all honour doe it;
Sister, I am to waite on him, oh my poore girle.
Berinthia my soule be with thee, for a
Little time excuse my absence.
Sfor. You may walke sir.
Val. Antonio I must but now looke on, you were
Best take a course not to out live him.
Exeunt Sforza, Villandras: and Ladies.
Ant. Sebastiano, I know not with what soule
I draw my sword against thee.
Seb. Antonio I am driven to a storme
To split my selfe on thee, if not, my curse ---
We must on sir.
Mount. Rare man of art Sharkino.
Vil. Guard thee Count.
Enter Sfor, Val. and Ladies above.
Cast. Treacherous Sforza, hast thou brought us hither, to
be stroke dead ?
Mount. Hold Gentlemen, give me audience.
Seb. Whats the matter my Lord.
Mount. My fit is on me, tis so, I had forgot my selfe,
This is my ague day. Seb. How ?
Mount. Yes a textile ague, looke you, doe you not see me
shake, admirable Doctor, it will be as much as my life is worth
if I should fight a stroke.
Seb. Hell on such basenesse, weele engage no more,
Let our swords try it out.
Val. Sebastiano hold, thart not so ill befriended,
Exchange a person, ile leape the battlement.
Mount. Withall my heart, I am sorry it happens so un-
fortunately, oh rare phisitian !
Vil. Good cozen grant it.
Ant. What saies Sebastiano.
Vil. I conjure you by all honour.
Seb. It is granted: Ber. He shall not goe.
Ant. Meete him my Lord, you will become his place of a
Specta-

The Maides Revenge.

Spectator best. Enter Valasco.
Ber. Sebastiano, brother.
Cast. Antonio, here me.
Vil. Guard thee Valasco then.
Cast. O brother spare him for my sake.
Ber. Sebastiano every wound thou gavest him,
Drawes blood from me.
Cast. Sebastiano, remember hees thy friend.
Ber. Antonio tis my brother, with whose blood
Thou dyest thy sword.
Ant. When thou liv'st againe shalt be more honorable.
Kils Valasco.
Sebastiano doe you observe the advantage,
Yet thinke upon't.
Seb. It is not in my power, I value not the odds.
Ber. Hold, Antonio, is this thy love to me, it is not noble.
Seb. So thy death makes the scale even. Kils Villandras.
Cast. Antonio hold, Berinthia dyes.
Ber. Sebastiano, Castabella sinkes for sorrow, murder, helpe
I will leape downe.
Ant. Where art Berinthia, let me breath my last upon thy
lip, make haste least I die else.
Seb. Antonio before thou dyest cut off my hand, art woun-
ded mortally ?
Ant. To die by thee is more then death, Sforza be honest,
But love thy sister for me, sure past hope,
Thou hast undone another in my death.
Enter Berinthia, Sforza, Mount.
Ber. Antonio stay oh cruell brother.
Ant. Berinthia thy lip farewell, and friend, and all the
world. Dies.
Sfor. The gate is open, I am sworne to render.
Ber. Hees not dead, his lips are warme, have you no bal-
some, a Surgeon, dead, some charitable hand send my soule af-
ter him. Seb. Away, away.
Ber. It will be easie to die.
All life is but a walke in misery. Exeunt.
Actus

IV, iii, following 43. There appears to be a cropped circle-and-dot shift symbol here, but the locale does not seem to change.

IV, iii, following 50. The entrance of Sforza and the ladies was not cued, but they made an exit a few lines earlier and probably needed no signal for their balcony entrance.

IV, iii, 63. Valasco apparently left the stage after his speech, but the author gave him no exit, nor did the prompter.

IV, iii, 89. Berinthia evidently leaves the balcony, but there is no indication of when she went there.

IV, iii, following 96. Berinthia, Sforza, and Monte Nigro enter, apparently below; there is no indication of when they left the stage.

The Maides Revenge.

Actus 5. Scan. 1.

Enter Sebastiano.

Seb. MY friend, my noble friend, that had deserved
Most honorably from me, by this hand
Divorc'd from life, and yet I have the use ont,
[H]arris Haplesse Sebastiano; oh Berinthia,
[Bow]tell Let me for ever lose the name of Brother,
Wilt thou not curse my memory, give me up
To thy just hate a murtherer.

Enter Villareza.

Vil. Ha, this must not be Sebastiano,
I shall be angry if you throw not off
This mellancholly, it does ill become you,
Doe you repent your duty, were the action
Againe presented to be done by thee
And being done, againe should challenge from thee
A new performance, thou wouldst shew no blood
Of Villarezoes, if thou didst not runne
To act it, though all horror, death and vengeance
Dog'd thee at thy heeles; come I am thy Father,
Value my blessing, and for other peace
Ile to the King, let me no more see thee cloudy. Exit

Enter Diego, Castabella like a page.

Die. That was his Father.
Cast. No more, farewell, be all silence. Exit Diego
Cast. Sir.
Seb. Hees newly gone that way, mayst soone ore take him
Cast. My businesse points at you sir.
Seb. At me, what newes? thou hast a face of horrour, more welcome speake it.
Cast. If your name be Don Sebastiano, sir
I have a token from a friend.
Seb. I have no friend alive boy, carry it backe,
Tis not to me, I've not another friend
In all the world.

Cast.

The Maides Revenge.

Cast. He that hath sent you sir this gift, did love you,
Youle say your selfe he did.
Seb. Ha, name him prethee.
Cast. The friend I came from was Antonio.
Seb. Thou lyest, and thart a villane, who hath sent thee
To tempt Sebastianoes soule to act on thee
Another death, for thus afrighting me.
Cast. Indeede I doe not mocke, nor come to afright you
Heaven knowes my heart, I know Antonioes dead,
But twas a gift he in his life design'd
To you, and I have brought it.
Seb. Thou dost not promise cozenage, what gift is it?
Cast. It is my selfe sir, while Antonio liv'd, I was his boy,
But never did boy loose so kinde a Master, in his life he
Promised he would bestow me, so much was his love
To my poore merit, on his dearest friend,
And nam'd you sir, if heaven should point out
To overlive him, for he knew you would
Love me the better for his sake, indeed
I will be very honest to you, and
Refuse no service to procure your love
And good opinion to me.
Seb. Can it be
Thou wert his boy, oh thou shouldst hate me then,
Th'art false, I dare not trust thee, unto him
Thou shewest thee now unfaithfull to accept
Of me, I kild him thy Master, twas a friend
He could commit thee to, I onely was,
Of all the stocke of men his enemy,
His cruellest enemy.
Cast. Indeede I am sure it was, he spoke all truth,
And had he liv'd to have made his Will, I know
He had bequeathed me as a legacy
To be your boy; alas I am willing sir
To obey him in it, had he laid on me
Command, to have mingled with his sacred dust,
My unprofitable blood, it should have beene
A most glad sacrifice, and 't had beene honour

I To

V, i, opening. The act apparently opened with a scene change; the edge of a circle-and-dot symbol is just visible in the left margin. Here and throughout the promptbook there are no cross-hatch marks for entrances at the beginnings of acts or scenes. The cropped note seems to read *[L]ong act*, but the act is short.

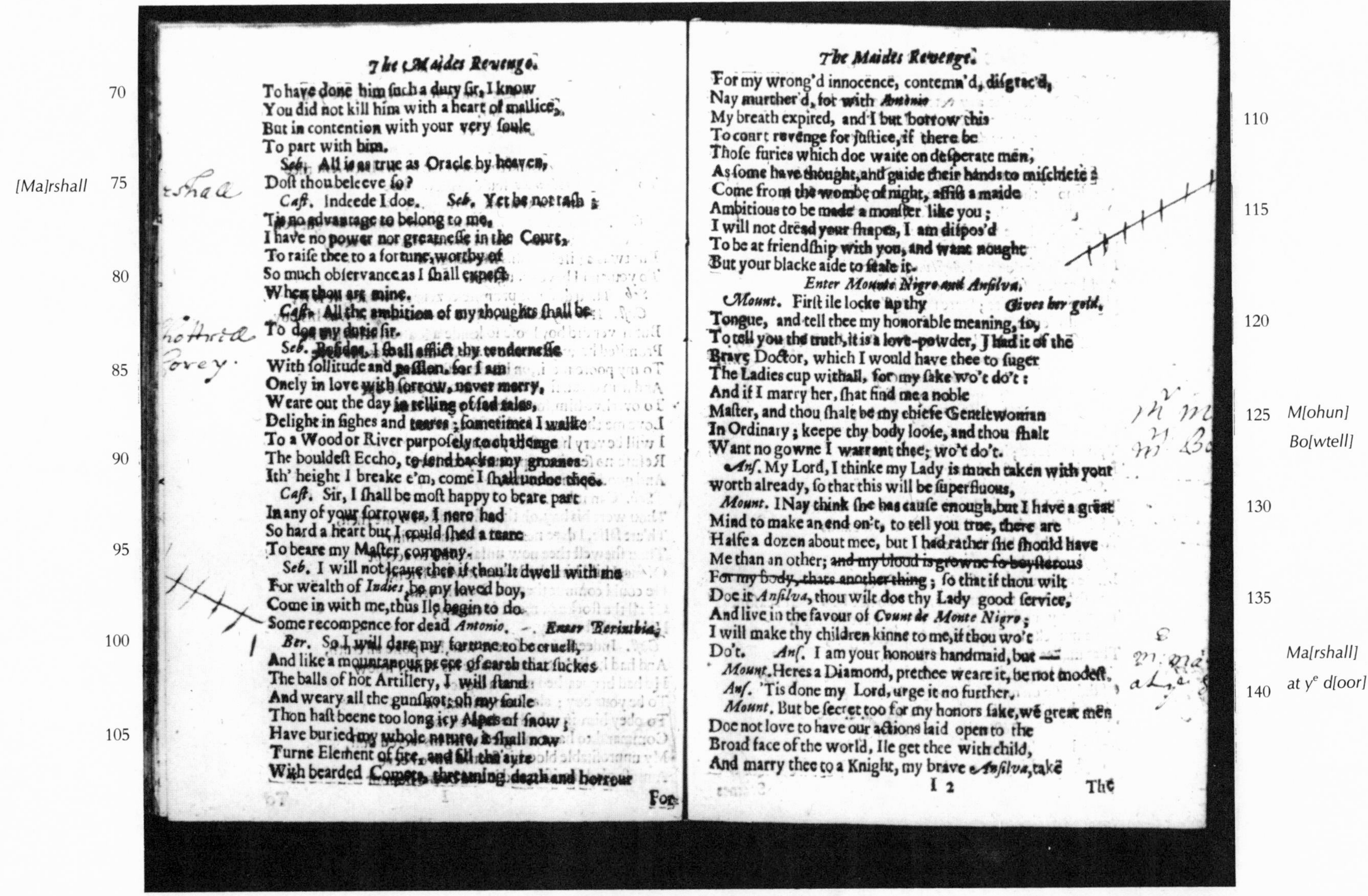

The Maides Revenge.

To have done him such a duty sir, I know
You did not kill him with a heart of mallice,
But in contention with your very soule
To part with him.
Seb. All is as true as Oracle by heaven,
Dost thou beleeve so? [Ma]rshall
Cast. Indeede I doe. *Seb.* Yet be not rash;
Tis no advantage to belong to me,
I have no power nor greatnesse in the Court,
To raise thee to a fortune, worthy of
So much observance as I shall expect
When thou art mine.
Cast. All the ambition of my thoughts shall be
To doe my dutie sir.
Seb. Besides, I shall afflict thy tendernesse
With sollitude and passion, for I am
Onely in love with sorrow, never merry,
Weare out the day in telling of sad tales,
Delight in sighes and teares; sometimes I walke
To a Wood or River purposely to challenge
The bouldest Eccho, to send backe my groanes
Ith' height I breake e'm, come I shall undoe thee.
Cast. Sir, I shall be most happy to beare part
In any of your sorrowes, I nere had
So hard a heart but I could shed a teare
To beare my Master company.
Seb. I will not leave thee if thou't dwell with me
For wealth of *Indies*, be my loved boy,
Come in with me, thus Ile begin to do.
Some recompence for dead *Antonio*. *Enter Berinthia.*
Ber. So I will dare my fortune to be cruell,
And like a mountanous peece of earth that suckes
The balls of hot Artillery, I will stand
And weary all the gunshot; oh my soule
Thou hast beene too long icy Alpes of snow;
Have buried my whole nature, it shall now
Turne Element of fire, and fill the ayre
With bearded Comets, threatning death and horrour
For

The Maides Revenge.

For my wrong'd innocence, contemn'd, disgrac'd,
Nay murther'd, for with *Antonio*
My breath expired, and I but borrow this
To court revenge for justice, if there be
Those furies which doe waite on desperate men,
As some have thought, and guide their hands to mischiefe;
Come from the wombe of night, assist a maide
Ambitious to be made a monster like you;
I will not dread your shapes, I am dispos'd
To be at friendship with you, and want nought
But your blacke aide to seale it.
Enter Monte Nigro and Ansilva.
Mount. First ile locke up thy *Gives her gold.*
Tongue, and tell thee my honorable meaning, to,
To tell you the truth, it is a love-powder, I had it of the
Brave Doctor, which I would have thee to suger
The Ladies cup withall, for my sake wo't do't:
And if I marry her, that find me a noble
Master, and thou shalt be my chiefe Gentlewoman M[ohun]
In Ordinary; keepe thy body loose, and thou shalt Bo[wtell]
Want no gowne I warrant thee; wo't do't.
Ans. My Lord, I thinke my Lady is much taken with your
worth already, so that this will be superfluous,
Mount. Nay think she has cause enough, but I have a great
Mind to make an end on't, to tell you true, there are
Halfe a dozen about mee, but I had rather she should have
Me than an other; and my blood is growne so boysterous
For my body, thats another thing; so that if thou wilt
Doe it *Ansilva*, thou wilt doe thy Lady good service,
And live in the favour of *Count de Monte Nigro*;
I will make thy children kinne to me, if thou wo't
Do't. *Ans.* I am your honours handmaid, but — Ma[rshall]
Mount. Heres a Diamond, prethee weare it, be not modest,
Ans. 'Tis done my Lord, urge it no further, at ye d[oor]
Mount. But be secret too for my honors sake, we great men
Doe not love to have our actions laid open to the
Broad face of the world, Ile get thee with child,
And marry thee to a Knight, my brave *Ansilva*, take
I 2 The

V, i, 99. The author forgot to give Sebastiano and Castabella an exit, and the prompter did not correct the mistake.

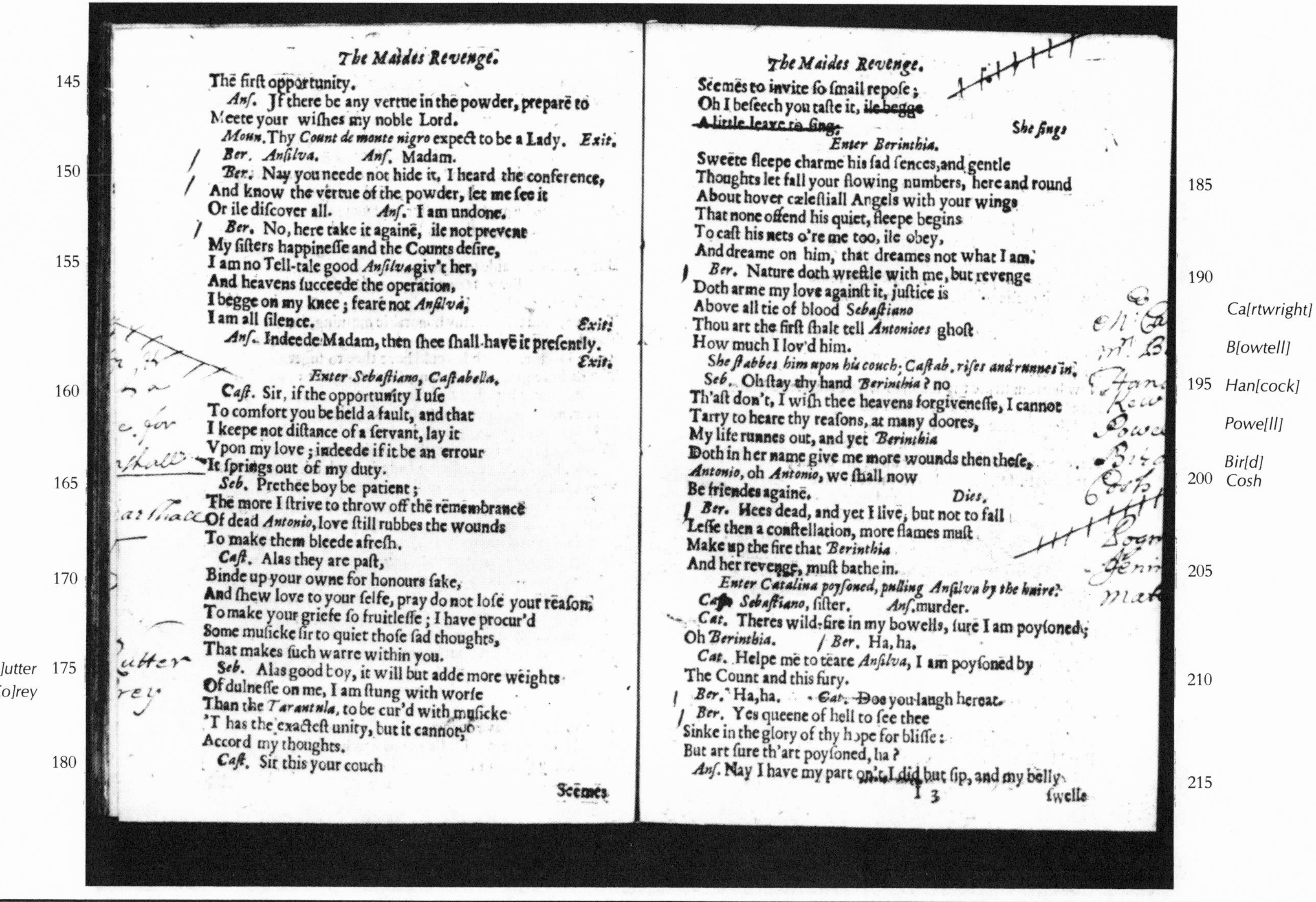

The Maides Revenge.

The first opportunity.

Ans. If there be any vertue in the powder, prepare to Meete your wishes my noble Lord.

Moun. Thy *Count de monte nigro* expect to be a Lady. *Exit.*

Ber. *Ansilva.* *Ans.* Madam.

Ber. Nay you neede not hide it, I heard the conference, And know the vertue of the powder, let me see it Or ile discover all. *Ans.* I am undone.

Ber. No, here take it againe, ile not prevent My sisters happinesse and the Counts desire, I am no Tell-tale good *Ansilva* giv't her, And heavens succeede the operation, I begge on my knee; feare not *Ansilva*, I am all silence. *Exit.*

Ans. Indeede Madam, then shee shall have it presently. *Exit.*

Enter Sebastiano, Castabella.

Cast. Sir, if the opportunity I use To comfort you be held a fault, and that I keepe not distance of a servant, lay it Vpon my love; indeede if it be an errour It springs out of my duty.

Seb. Prethee boy be patient; The more I strive to throw off the remembrance Of dead *Antonio*, love still rubbes the wounds To make them bleede afresh.

Cast. Alas they are past, Binde up your owne for honours sake, And shew love to your selfe, pray do not lose your reason; To make your griefe so fruitlesse; I have procur'd Some musicke sir to quiet those sad thoughts, That makes such warre within you.

Seb. Alas good boy, it will but adde more weights Of dulnesse on me, I am stung with worse Than the *Tarantula*, to be cur'd with musicke 'T has the exactest unity, but it cannot Accord my thoughts.

Cast. Sit this your couch

Scemes

The Maides Revenge.

Seemes to invite so small repose; Oh I beseech you taste it, ile begge A little leave to sing. *She sings*

Enter Berinthia.

Sweete sleepe charme his sad sences, and gentle Thoughts let fall your flowing numbers, here and round About hover cælestiall Angels with your wings That none offend his quiet, sleepe begins To cast his nets o're me too, ile obey, And dreame on him, that dreames not what I am.

Ber. Nature doth wrestle with me, but revenge Doth arme my love against it, justice is Above all tie of blood *Sebastiano* Thou art the first shalt tell *Antonioes* ghost How much I lov'd him.

She stabbes him upon his couch: Castab. rises and runnes in.

Seb. Oh stay thy hand *Berinthia*? no Th'ast don't, I wish thee heavens forgivenesse, I cannot Tarry to heare thy reasons, at many doores, My life runnes out, and yet *Berinthia* Doth in her name give me more wounds then these, *Antonio*, oh *Antonio*, we shall now Be friendes againe. *Dies.*

Ber. Hees dead, and yet I live, but not to fall Lesse then a constellation, more flames must Make up the fire that *Berinthia* And her revenge, must bathe in.

Enter Catalina poysoned, pulling Ansilva by the haire.

Cast. *Sebastiano*, sister. *Ans.* murder.

Cat. Theres wild-fire in my bowells, sure I am poysoned; Oh *Berinthia*. *Ber.* Ha, ha.

Cat. Helpe me to teare *Ansilva*, I am poysoned by The Count and this fury.

Ber. Ha, ha. *Cat.* Doe you laugh hereat.

Ber. Yes queene of hell to see thee Sinke in the glory of thy hope for blisse: But art sure th'art poysoned, ha?

Ans. Nay I have my part on't, I did but sip, and my belly

I 3 swells

[R]utter
[Co]rey

Ca[rtwright]
B[owtell]
Han[cock]
Powe[ll]
Bir[d]
Cosh

V, i, 160 ff. This badly cropped note may have concerned the couch needed in the scene.

V, i, 189. Castabella evidently leaves the stage after this speech.

V, i, 204 ff. Cropped note: *Bogr / Jenn[ings?] / Mat[thew?]*. *Bogr* is probably the beginning of a longer name; no known Restoration actor's name even remotely resembles it. *Mat* is probably Matthew Kempton.

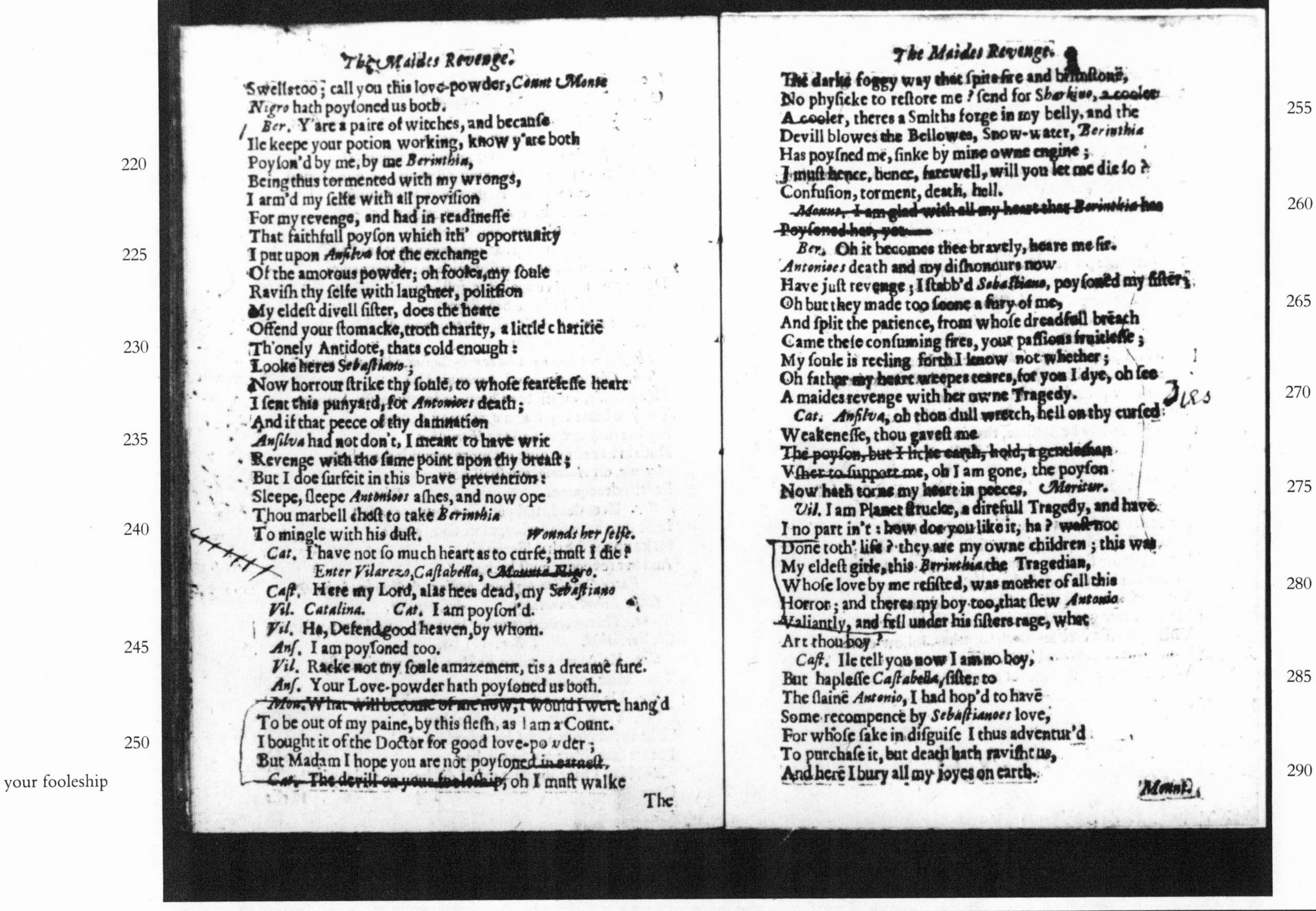

The Maides Revenge.

Swells too; call you this love-powder, Count Monte
Nigro hath poysoned us both.
Ber. Y'are a paire of witches, and because
Ile keepe your potion working, know y'are both
Poyson'd by me, by me Berinthia,
Being thus tormented with my wrongs,
I arm'd my selfe with all provision
For my revenge, and had in readinesse
That faithfull poyson which ith' opportunity
I put upon Ansilva for the exchange
Of the amorous powder; oh fooles, my soule
Ravish thy selfe with laughter, politition
My eldest divell sister, does the heate
Offend your stomacke, troth charity, a little charitie
Th'onely Antidote, thats cold enough:
Looke heres Sebastiano;
Now horrour strike thy soule, to whose fearelesse heart
I sent this punyard, for Antonioes death;
And if that peece of thy damnation
Ansilva had not don't, I meant to have writ
Revenge with the same point upon thy breast;
But I doe surfeit in this brave prevention:
Sleepe, sleepe Antonioes ashes, and now ope
Thou marbell chest to take Berinthia
To mingle with his dust. *Wounds her selfe.*
Cat. I have not so much heart as to curse, must I die?
Enter Vilarezo, Castabella, Mounte Nigro.
Cast. Here my Lord, alas hees dead, my Sebastiano
Vil. Catalina. Cat. I am poyson'd.
Vil. Ha, Defend good heaven, by whom.
Ans. I am poysoned too.
Vil. Racke not my soule amazement, tis a dreame sure.
Ans. Your Love-powder hath poysoned us both.
Mon. What will become of me now, I would I were hang'd
To be out of my paine, by this flesh, as I am a Count.
I bought it of the Doctor for good love-powder;
But Madam I hope you are not poysoned in earnest.
Cat. The devill on your fooleship, oh I must walke
The

your fooleship

The Maides Revenge.

The darke foggy way that spits fire and brimstone,
No physicke to restore me? send for Sharkino, a cooler
A cooler, theres a Smiths forge in my belly, and the
Devill blowes the Bellowes, Snow-water, Berinthia
Has poysned me, sinke by mine owne engine;
I must hence, hence, farewell, will you let me die so?
Confusion, torment, death, hell.
Mount. I am glad with all my heart that Berinthia has
Poysoned her, yet.
Ber. Oh it becomes thee bravely, heare me sir.
Antonioes death and my dishonours now
Have just revenge; I stabb'd Sebastiano, poysoned my sister;
Oh but they made too soone a fury of me,
And split the patience, from whose dreadfull breach
Came these consuming fires, your passions fruitlesse;
My soule is reeling forth I know not whether;
Oh father my heart weepes teares, for you I dye, oh see
A maides revenge with her owne Tragedy. Dies
Cat. Ansilva, oh thou dull wretch, hell on thy cursed
Weakenesse, thou gavest me
The poyson, but I licke earth, hold, a gentleman
Usher to support me, oh I am gone, the poyson
Now hath torne my heart in peeces. *Moritur.*
Vil. I am Planet strucke, a direfull Tragedy, and have
I no part in't: how doe you like it, ha? wast not
Done toth' life? they are my owne children; this was
My eldest girle, this Berinthia the Tragedian,
Whose love by me resisted, was mother of all this
Horror; and theres my boy too, that slew Antonio
Valiantly, and fell under his sisters rage, what
Art thou boy?
Cast. Ile tell you now I am no boy,
But haplesse Castabella, sister to
The slaine Antonio, I had hop'd to have
Some recompence by Sebastianoes love,
For whose sake in disguise I thus adventur'd
To purchase it, but death hath ravisht us,
And here I bury all my joyes on earth.
Mount.

V, i, 270. *Dies* was not written by the person who wrote the bulk of the prompt notes.

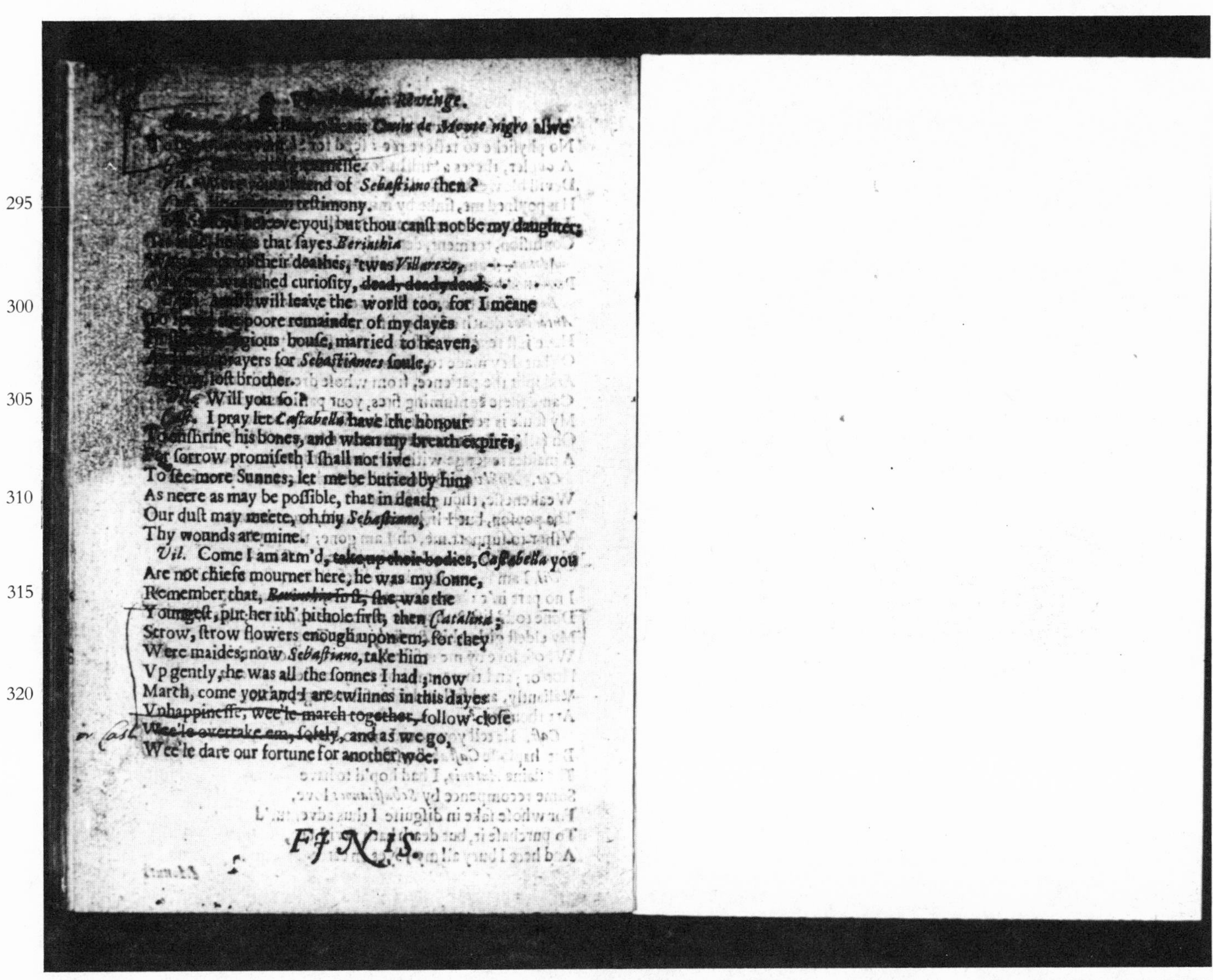
[illegible] *Revenge.*
[illegible] *Conte de Monte nigro* alive
[illegible]
[illegible]nesse.
Vil. [illegible] friend of *Sebastiano* then?
Cas. [illegible] testimony.
[illegible] beleeve you, but thou canst not be my daughter;
[illegible] that sayes *Berinthia*
[illegible] their deathes, 'twas *Villarezo*,
[illegible] wretched curiosity, dead, dead, dead,
Cas. [illegible] will leave the world too, for I meane
[illegible] the poore remainder of my dayes
[illegible] religious house, married to heaven,
[illegible] prayers for *Sebastianoes* soule,
[illegible] lost brother.
Vil. Will you so?
Cas. I pray let *Castabella* have the honour
To enshrine his bones, and when my breath expires,
For sorrow promiseth I shall not live
To see more Sunnes, let me be buried by him
As neere as may be possible, that in death
Our dust may meete, oh my *Sebastiano*,
Thy wounds are mine.
Vil. Come I am arm'd, take up their bodies, *Castabella* you
Are not chiefe mourner here, he was my sonne,
Remember that, *Berinthia* first, she was the
Youngest, put her ith' pithole first, then *Catalina*;
Strow, strow flowers enough upon em, for they
Were maides; now *Sebastiano*, take him
Vp gently, he was all the sonnes I had; now
March, come you and I are twinnes in this dayes
Vnhappinesse, wee'le march together, follow close
Cast. Wee'le overtake em, safely, and as we go,
Wee'le dare our fortune for another woe.

FINIS.

V, i, 322. Castabella evidently speaks the closing lines.

14

BRENNORALT.

A
TRAGEDY.

Presented at the Private-House
IN
Black-Fryers.

By his Majesties Servants.

Written by
Sir *JOHN SUCKLING.*

LONDON,
Printed for *Humphrey Moseley* at the Prince's Arms,
in St. *Pauls* Churchyard. 1658.

Brennoralt by Sir John Suckling. Reproduced by permission of the Bodleian Library, Oxford.

The Scæne Poland.

The Actors.

Sigismond— King of Poland.
Miesla.
Melidor. } Counsellors to the King.
A Lord.
Brennoralt —— a Discontent.
Doran — His Friend.
Villanor.
Grainevert. } Cavaliers and Officers under Brennoralt.
Marinel.
Stratheman.
Fresolin, Brother to Francelia.
Iphigene—— young Palatine of Florence.
Palatine of Mensecke, Governor, one of the chief (Rebels.
Palatine of York a Rebell.
Almerin, a gallant Rebell.
Morat, his Lieutenant Colonel.
Francelia, the Governors Daughter.
Orilla, a waiting woman to Francelia.
Raguelin, A servant in the Governors house, but Spie to Brennoralt.
Jaylor.
Guard.
Soldiers.

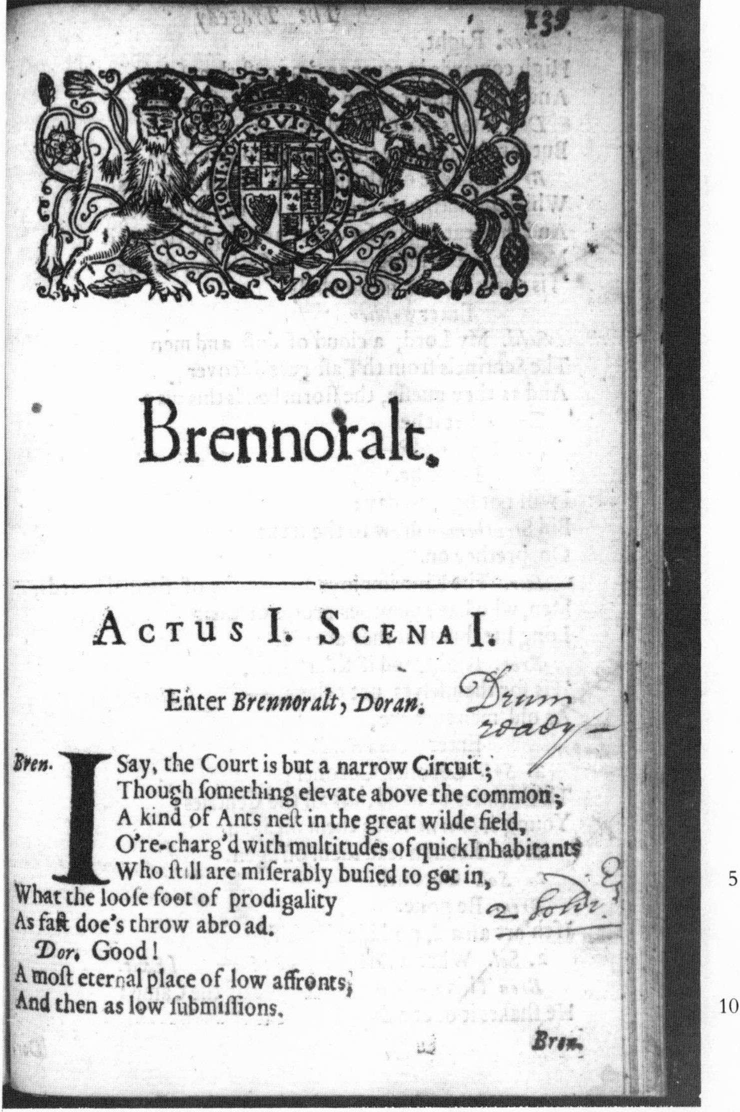

139

Brennoralt.

ACTUS I. SCENA I.

Enter *Brennoralt*, *Doran*. Drum ready

Bren. I Say, the Court is but a narrow Circuit;
Though ſomething elevate above the common;
A kind of Ants neſt in the great wilde field,
O're-charg'd with multitudes of quick Inhabitants
Who ſtill are miſerably buſied to get in,
What the looſe foot of prodigality
As faſt doe's throw abroad. 2 Soldr.
Dor. Good!
A moſt eternal place of low affronts;
And then as low ſubmiſſions.

Bren.

I, i, opening. *Drum ready* — warns alarms at three different places in the scene: at lines 19, 34, and 56.

I, i, 7. The simultaneous warning of two characters who do not enter together is unusual; most promptbooks separate such warnings, even when entrances are close together, so there will be no danger of cuing two actors to enter together when they should not.

140 *The Tragedy*

Bren. Right.
High cowards in revenges 'mongst themselves,
And only valiant when they mischief others.
Dor. Stars, that would have no names,
But for the ills they threaten in conjunction.
Bren. A race of shallow and unskilful Pilots,
Which do misguide the Ship even in the calme,
And in great storms serve but as weight to sink it
More, prethee more.—— (*Alarum within.*
'Tis musick to my melancholy.
Enter *Soldier.*
Sold. My Lord, a cloud of dust and men
The Sentinels from th'East gate discover;
And as they guesse, the storm bends this way.
Bren. Let it be.
Sol. My Lord?—
Bren. Let it be.
I will not fight to day:
Bid *Stratheman* draw to the trenches.
On, prethee on.
Dor. The King imploys a company of formal beards,
Men, who have no other proofs of their
Long life, but that they are old.
Bren. Right, and if th'art wise,
'Tis for themselves, not others,— (*Alarms*
As old men ever are, [a]llarm
Enter *second Soldier.*
2. *Sol.* Coronel, Coronel;
Th'Enemies at hand, kils all the Centries:
Young *Almerin* leads them on agen.
Bren. Let him lead them off agen.
2. *Sol.* Coronel.———
Bren. Be gone.
If th'art afraid, go hide thy self.
2. *Sol.* What a Divel ayles he?— (*Exit.*
Bren. This *Almerin's* the ague of the Camp:
He shakes it once a day.
Dor;

of Brennoralt. 141

Dor. Hee's the ill conscience rather:
He never lets it rest; would I were at home agen.
Sfoot we lie here i'th'trenches, as if it were
For a wind to carry us into th'other
World: every hour we expect ——
I'le no more on't.
Bre. Prethee——
Dor. Not I, by heaven.
Bre. What man! the worst is but fair death.
Dor. And what will that amount to? A fair Epitaph.
A fine account. ——— I'le home I swear.
Enter *Stratheman.*
Stra. Arme, arme my Lord,
And shew your self; all's lost else.
Dor. Why so?
Stra. The Rebels like an unruly flood,
Rowle o're the Trenches and throw down
All before them.
Bre. Ha?
Stra. We cannot make a stand.
Bre. He would out-rival me in honor too,
As well as love; but that he must not do.
Help me *Stratheman.* — (*Puts on Armor.*
The danger now grows worthy of our swords;
And, oh *Doran,* I would to heaven there were
No other stormes then the worst tempest here. (*Exeunt.*
Enter *Marinel,* throwing down one he carries.
Mari. There;
The Sun's the nearest Surgeon I know,
And the honestest; if thou recoverest, why so:
If not, the cure's paid, they have mauld us.
Enter *Grainevert,* with another upon his back.
Grain. A curse light on this powder;
It stays valor, ere it's half way on it's journey:
What a disadvantage fight we upon in this age?
He

I, i, 19. Here the prompter cued both an alarm and the entrance of the First Soldier with one cross-hatch mark. As in a few other promptbooks, some actor entrances are cued a line or two in advance of the actual entrance; perhaps these were entrances opposite prompt side, where an assistant cued the actor after receiving a cross-stage signal from the prompter.

He that did well heretofore,
Had the broad fair day to ſhew it in:
Witneſſes enough; we muſt beleeve one another——
'Tis night when we begin:
Eternal ſmoake and ſulphur.
Smalk; by this hand I can bear with thee
No longer; how now? dead as I live;
Stolne away juſt as he us'd to wench.
Well go thy ways, for a quiet drinker, and dier,
I ſhall never know thy fellow. (*ſearches his pockets.*
Theſe trifles too about thee;
Then never was an boneſter poor wretch
Borne I think——look i'th'other pocket too——hum,
[s]hout *Mar.* Who's that?
[r]eady *Grani.* 'Tis I; how go the matters?
Mar. Scurvily enough;
Yet ſince our Colonel came th've got no ground
Of us; A weak Sculler againſt Wind and Tide,
Would have done as much; hark!
This way the torrent bears. *Exeunt.*
alarm Enter *Freſolin, Almerin,* Rebels.
Freſ. The Villaines all have left us.
Alm. Would they had left their fears
[a]larm Behind them. But come, ſince we muſt——
Enter *Brennoralt, Soldiers.*
Stratheman *Bren.* Hoe! *Strathemen*;
Skirt on the left hand with the horſe,
And get betwixt theſe and that Body;
They'r new railled up for reſcue. *Dor.* Th'are ours.
Brennoralt charges through.
I do not ſee my game yet.—— *Exeunt.*
A ſhout within.
Enter *Brenoralt, Doran, Stratheman, Marinell.*
Bren. What ſhout is that?
Stra. They have taken *Almerin,* my Lord.
Bren.

Bren. *Almerin?* the Devil thank 'em for't:
When I had hunted hard all day,
And now at length unherded the proud Dear,
The Curs have ſnatch'd him up, ſound a Retreat;
There's nothing now behind. Who ſaw *Doran?*
Str. Shall we bring *Almerin* in?
Bre. No; gazing is low Triumph:
Convey him fairly to the King,
He fought it fairly——
Dor. What youth was that whom you beſtrid my Lord,
And ſav'd from all our ſwords to day?
Was he not of the Enemy?
Bre. It may be ſo——
Str. The Governors Son, *Freſolin,* his Miſtris brother. (*In*
Br. No matter who. 'Tis pitty the rough hand (*Dorans ear.*
Of war ſhould early courages deſtroy
Before they bud, and ſhew themſelves i'th'heat
Of Action——
Mar. I threw (my Lord) a youth upon a bank,
Which ſeeking after the retreat I found
Dead, and a woman, the pretty daughter
Of the Foreſter, *Lucilia.*
Bre. See, ſee *Doran*; A ſad experiment:
Woman's the Cowardly'ſt and coldeſt thing
The World brings forth: Yet Love, as fire works water,
Make it boyl o're, and do things contrary
To'ts proper nature——I ſhould ſhed a tear,
Could I tell how—— Ah poor *Lucilia!*
Thou did'ſt for me what did as ill become thee.
Pray ſee her gently buried——
Boy, ſend the Surgeon to the Tent; I bleed:
What lowſie Cottages th'ave given our ſouls?
Each petty ſtorm ſhakes them into diſorder;
And't coſts more paines to patch them up agen,
Then they are worth by much. I'm weary of
The Tenement.—— *Exeunt.*
Enter

I, i, 89. The cross-hatch sign evidently cues the reentrance of Marinell, though no printed or manuscript note brings him on. He was warned, however, at line 83.

I, i, following 106. The reentrance of Brennoralt, Doran, Stratheman, and Marinell was not warned, though all of the characters except Marinell just left the stage and probably needed no warning. Marinell left the stage 9 lines before this group entrance.

Enter *Villanor*, *Grainevert*, *Marinell*, ~~and *Strathe*[illegible]~~

Gra. *Villanor*! welcome, welcome, whence cameſt thou?

Vil. Look, I wear the Kings high-way ſtill on my boots.

Gra. A pretty riding phraſe, and how? and how?
Ladies cheap?

Vil. Faith, reaſonable:
Thoſe toys were never dear thou know'ſt;
A little time and induſtry they'l coſt;
But in good faith not much: ſome few there are
That ſet themſelves at mighty rates ——

Gra. Which we o'th' wiſe paſſe by,
As things o're-valued in the market.
I'ſt not ſo?

Vil. Y'have ſaid ſaid Sir. Harke you, your friend the Rivals (married.
Has obtain'd the long lov'd Lady, and is ſuch an aſſe after't.

Gra. Hum.
'Tis ever ſo.
The motions of married people, are as of
Other naturals; violent Gentlemen to the place,
And calm in it.

Mar. We know this too; and yet we muſt be fooling.

Gra. Faith, women are the baggage of life:
They are troubleſome, and hinder us
In the great march, and yet we cannot
Be without 'em.

Mar. You ſpeak very well,
And Soldier like.

Grain. What? thou art a wit too I warrant,
In our abſence?

Vil. Hum —no, no, a poor pretender,
A Candidate or ſo, 'gainſt the next Seſſions:
Wit enough to laugh at you here.

Gra. Like enough; valour's a crime
The wiſe have ſtill reproached unto the valiant,
And the fools too.

Vil. *Rallere a part, Gr. invert*;

What

What accommodations ſhall we find here?

Gra. Clean ſtraw (ſweet heart) and meat
When thou canſt get it.

Vil. Hum? ſtraw?

Gra. Yes.
That's all will be betwixt Inceſt;
You and your mother earth muſt lye together.

V. Prethee let's be ſerious; will this laſt?
How goes affaires?

G. Well.

V. But well?

G. Faith, 'tis now upon the turning of the ballance:
A moſt equall buſineſſe, betwixt Rebellion
And Loyaltie.

V. What doſt mean?

G. Why; which ſhall be the vertue, and which the vice.

V. How the Divell can that be?

G. Oh: ſucceſſe is a rare paint; hides all the uglineſſe.

V. Prethee, what's the quarrell?

G. Nay, for that excuſe us;
Aske the children of peace,
They have the leiſure to ſtudy it,
We know nothing of it; Liberty they ſay.

V. 'Sfoot, let the King make an Act
That any man may be unmarried agen;
There's liberty for them. A race
Of half-witted fellowes quarrell about freedome,
And all that while allow the bonds of Matrimony?

G. You ſpeak very well Sir.

Enter *King*, *Lords*, *Brennoralt*.

M. Soft; the King and Councell.

G. Look, they follow after like tyred ſpaniels:
Queſt ſometimes for company; that is, concurre:
And that's their buſineſs.

M. They are as weary of this ſport
As a young unthrift of's land:
Any bargain to be rid on't.

Can you blame them ?
Who's that ?
M. Brennoralt, our brave Coronel :
A diſcontent, but, what of that ? who is not ?
V. His face ſpeakes him one.
G. Thou art i'th' right.
He looks ſtill as if he were ſaying to
Fortune ; Huſwife, go about your buſines.
Come, let's retire to *Barathens* Tent.
Taſte a bottle, and ſpeak bold truths ;
That's our way now. *Ex. Manet. King and Lords.*
Mieſ. —— Think not of pardon, Sir,
Rigor and mercy us'd in States uncertainly,
And in ill times, look not like th' effects
Of vertue, but neceſſity : Nor will
They thank your goodneſs, but your fears.——
Melid. My Lords ;
Revenge in Princes ſhould be ſtill imperfect :
It is then handſom'ſt, when the King comes to
Reduce, not Ruine ——
Bre. Who puts but on the face of puniſhing,
And only gently cuts, but prunes rebellion :
He makes that flouriſh which he would deſtroy.
Who would not be a Rebel when the hopes
Are vaſte, the fears but ſmall ? [*Mel.*] Why, I would not.
Nor you my Lord, nor you, nor any here.
Fear keeps low ſpirits only in, the brave
Do get above it, when they do reſolve.
Such puniſhments in infancy of war,
Make men more deſperate, not the more yeelding.
The common people are a kind of flyes ;
They're caught with hony, not with wormwood, Sir.
Severity exaſp'rates the ſtirr'd humor ;
And State-diſtempers turns into diſeaſes.
Bre. The gods forbid, great *Polands* State ſhould be
Such as it dares not take right Phyſick. Quarter
To Rebels ? Sir ! when you give that to them,
Give

Give that to me, which they deſerve. I would
Not live to ſee it ——
3 *Lord.* Turn o're your own, and others Chronicles,
And you ſhall find (great Sir)
" That nothing makes a Civil war long liv'd,
" But ranſome and returning back the brands
Which unextinct, kindled ſtill fiercer fires.
Mieſ. Mercy beſtow'd on thoſe that do diſpute
With ſwords, do's looſe the Angels face it has,
And is not mercy Sir, but policy ;
With a weak vizard on ——
King. — Y' have met my thoughts
My Lords ; nor will it need larger debate.
To morrow, in the ſight of the beſiedg'd,
The Rebell dyes : *Mieſla*, 'tis your care.
The mercy of Heav'n may be offended ſo,
That it cannot forgive : Mortals much more,
Which is not infinite, my Lords. (*Exeunt.*
Enter *Iphigene*, *Almerin* (as in priſon.) [I, ii]
Iph. O *Almarin* ; would we had never known
The ruffle of the world ! but were again
By Stolden banks, in happy ſolitude ;
When thou and I, Shepherd and Shepherdeſs ;
So oft by turns, as often ſtill have wiſht,
That we as eas'ly could have chang'd our ſex,
As cloths ; but (alas!) all thoſe innocent joys,
Like glorious Mornings, are retir'd into
Dark ſullen clouds, before we knew to value
What we had. [*Alme.*] Fame & victory are light (*to himſelf*
Huſwifes, that throw themſelves into the arms,
Not of the valiant, but the fortunate.
To be tane, thus ! [*Iph.*] *Almerin* [*Alm.*] Nipt ith' bud
Of honour ! [*Iph.*] My Lord [*Alm.*] Foil'd ! & by the man
That do's pretend unto *Francelia* !
Iph. What is't you do, my *Almerin* ? ſit ſtill ?
And quarrel with the Winds, becauſe there is
A ſhipwrack tow'rds, and never think of ſaving
T 2 Th

I, ii, opening. The circle-and-dot symbol indicates a scene shift, but no description of the setting is given.

148 *The Tragedy*

The barke? [*Almer:*] The Barke? What should we do with
When the rich freight is lost: my name in armes? (that
Iph. ——— Who knowes
What prizes are behind, if you attend
And wait a second Voyage? [*Almer:*] Never, never:
There are no second Voyages in this,
The wounds of honour do admit no cure.
Iph. Those slight ones which misfortune gives, must needs.
Else, why should Mortals value it at all?
+++++– For who would toyle to treasure up a wealth;
Which weak inconstancy did keep, or might
Dispose of? —— Enter *Melidor.*
Oh my Lord, what news?
Mel. As ill as your own fears could give you;
The Councell has decreed him sudden death,
And all the wayes to mercy are blockt up. (*She weeps*
Almer. My *Iphigene* ——— (*and sighs.*
This was a misbecoming peice of love:
Women would manage a disaster better — (*Iphig. weeps &*
Again? thou art unkind ——— (*sighs agen.*
Thy goodness is so great it makes thee faulty:
For while thou think'st to take the trouble from me,
Thou givest me more, by giving me thine too.
Iph. Alas! I am indeed a uselesse trifle;
A dull, dull thing: For could I now do any thing
But grieve and pitty, I might help: my thoughts
Labour to find a way; but like to birds
In cages, though they never rest, they are
+++++– But where they did set out at first ———
Enter *Jaylor.*
Jay. My Lords, your pardon;
The prisoner must retire;
I have receiv'd an order from the King,
Denies accesse to any.
Iph. ——— He cannot be
So great a Tyrant. [*Almer.*] I thanke him; nor can
He use me ill enough: I only grieve
That

of Brennoralt. 149

That I must die in debt; a Bankrupt: Such
Thy love hath made me: My dear *Iphigene*
Farewell: It is no time for Ceremony.
Shew me the way I must ——— (*Exit.*
Iph. Griefe strove with such disorder to get out,
It stopt the passage, and sent backe my words
That were already on the place ——. [*Melid.*] stay, there
Is yet a way. [*Iph.*] O speak it! [*Mel.*] But there is
Danger in't *Iphigene*, to thee high danger.
Iph. Fright children in the dark with that, and let
Me know it: There is no such thing in nature
If *Almerin* be lost. [*Melid.*] Thus then; You must
Be taken pris'ner too, and by exchange
Save *Almerin.*
Iph. How can that be?
Mel. Why ——— (*studies.*
Step in, and pray him set his hand, about (*To the Jaylor.*
This distance; his seale too ———
Jay. My Lord, I know not what this is.
Mel. Setling of money-businesse, fool, betwixt us.
Jay. If't be no more ——— (*Exit.*
Mel. Tell him that *Iphigene* and I desire it:
I'le send by *Strathocles* his servant,
A Letter to *Morat* thus sign'd and seal'd,
That shall inform the sudden execution;
Command him as the only means
To save his life, to sallie out this night
Upon the quarters, and endevour prisoners.
Name you as most secure and slightest guarded,
Best pledge of safety; but charge him,
That he kill not any, if it be avoydable;
Lest't should inrage the King yet more,
And make his death more certain. (*Enter Jaylor with*
Jay. He understands you not (*the writing.*
He sayes; but he has sent it.
Melid. So ———
T 3 *Iph.* But

I, ii, 29. There is no explanation for two entrance cue signs for the entry of a single person, unless the prompter discovered in rehearsal that a more emphatic cue was needed or unless the cropping has lost us an explanatory note.

I, ii, 68. As in other promptbooks, *act ready* pairs off with the *Ring* cue at the end of the act. They sometimes, as here, concern a scene shift as well as entr'acte music and actor entrances.

150 The Tragedy

Iph. But should *Morat* mistrust now?
Or this miscarry?
Melid. ——— ——— ——— Come;
Leave it to me; I'le take the Pilots part;
And reach the Port, or perish in the Art. Ring *Exeunt.*

ACT II. SCENE I.

Table paper
Standish

Enter *Almerin* (in prison.)

Almer. Sleep is as nice as woman;
The more I court it, the more it flys me;
Thy elder brother will be kinde: yet,
Unsent for death will come. ——— To morrow ———
Well ——— What can to morrow do?
'Twill cure the sense of honour lost ———
I, and my discontents shall rest together,
What hurt is there in this?
But death against the will, Souldiers
Is but a slovenly kind of potion; Posth. Morris
And though prescrib'd by Heaven, Cue. Abram.
It goes against mens stomachs:
So does it at fourscore too; when the soul's
Mew'd up in narrow darkness;
Neither sees nor hears,—pish, 'tis meer fondness in our na-
A certain clownish cowardise, that still (ture;
Would stay at home, and dares not venture musick
Into forreign Countrys, though better then
It's own, ——— ha, what Countries? for we receive
Descriptions of th'other world from our Divines,
As blind men take relation of this from us: mr. Lacy
My thoughts lead me into the dark, mr. Shottrell
And there they'l leave me, I'le no more on't, mr. Harris
Within. (*Knocks*) ——— ——— ——— ——— Enter.
Some paper and a light, I'le write to th' King:
Desie

of BRENNORALT. 151

Desie him, and provoke a quick dispatch.
I would not hold this ling'ring doubtful State
So long again, for all that hope can give.
Enter 3 of the Guard (with paper and inck)
That sword does tempt me strangely ——— (*writing.*
Wer't in my hands, 'twere worth th' other two.
But then the Guard, ——— it sleeps or drinks; may be
To contrive it so that if I should not pass, ———
Why if I fall in't,
'Tis better yet then Pageantry;
A scaffold and spectators; { *One of the Guard peeps over his*
more souldier-like ——— { *shoulder.*
Uncivill villain, read my Letter? ——— (*Seizes his sword.*
1 Guar. Not I, not I my Lord.
Alm. Deny it too?
Guar. Murder, murder.
Guar. Arme, arme ——— (*The Guard runs out.*
Alm. I'le follow,
Give the alarum with them,
'Tis least suspitious ——— (*Arme, arme, arme.*
All ——— the enemy, the enemy ——— (*Enter Souldiers running over the Stage, one throwing away his armes.*
Soul. Let them come.
Let them come.
Let them come ——— ——— (Enter *Almerin.*
Alm. I hear fresh noise,
The camp's in great disorder: where am I now?
'Tis strangely dark ——— Goddess without eys
Be thou my guide, for ——— blindness and sight
Are equall sense, of equall use, this night.
Enter *Grainevert, Strathaman, Villanor, Marinell.* Stratheman
Gra. Trouble not thy self, childe of discontent:
'Twill take no hurt I warrant thee;
The State is but a little drunk,
And when 'tas spued up that that made it so,
'Twill be well agen, there's my opinion in short.
Mar. Th' art i'th' right,
The State's a pretty forehanded State,
And will do reason hereafter.

II, i, 11. *Cue* is the actor Nathaniel Kew (sometimes even spelled Q). This warning covers two separate entrances, one at line 28 for the guards and one at line 45 for the soldiers.

II, i, 17. The warning for music is odd, unless the poems beginning at line 71 were turned into songs; the first clear need for music is at line 171.

The Tragedy

Let's drink and talk no more on't.

All. ——A good motion, a good motion,

Let's drink;

Villa. I, I let's drink agen.

Stra. Come, to a Mistris.

Gra. Agreed.

Name, name.

Villa. Any body.——*Vermelia.*

Gra. Away with it.

She's pretty to walk with,
And witty to talk with,
And pleasant too to think on:
But the best use of all,
Is, her health is a stale,
And helps us to make us drink on.

Doran.

Stra. Excellent.

Gentlemen, if you say the word,
We'l vant credit, and affect high pleasure;
Shall we?

Villa. I, I, let's do that.

Stra. What think ye of the sacrifice now?

Mar. Come we'l ha't, — for trickling tears are vain.

Villa. The sacrifice? what's that?

Stra. Child of ignorance, 'tis a Camp health,
An *A—la—mode* one. *Grainevert* begin it.

Grain. Come give it me.

Let me see ——— (*Pins up a Rose.*
Which of them this Rose will serve.
Hum, hum, hum.

Bright Star o'th'lower Orbe, twinkling Inviter,
Which draw'st (as well as eyes) but set'st men righter:
For who at thee begins, comes to the place,
Sooner then he that sets out at the face:
Eyes are seducing lights, that the good women know,
And hang out these a nearer way to show.

Mar. Fine and patheticall: Come *Villanor.*

Vila. What's the matter?

Mar.

of BRENNORALT. 113

Mar. Come, your liquor, and your stanza's.
Lines, Lines.

Villa. Of what?

Mar. Why, of any thing your Mistris has given you.

Vil. Gentlemen, she never gave me any thing but a box
Oth'ear for offering to kisse her once.

Stra. Of that box then.

Mar. I, I, that box, of that box.

Villa. Since it must be,
Give me the poyson then. ——(*Drinks and spits.*

That box, fair Mistris, which thou gav'st to me,
In humane guesse, is like to cost me three
Three cups of Wine, and verses six,
The Wine will down, but verse for rime still sticks:
By which you all may easily Gentiles know,
I am a better drinker than a Poet. ——Enter Doran.

Mar. Doran,

Doran.

Gra. A Hall, a hall
To welcome our friend;
For some liquor call,
A new or fresh face,
Must not alter our pace,
But make us still drink the quicker:
Wine, Wine, oh'tis divine
Come fill it unto our brother:
What's at the tongues end,
It forth does send,
And will not a syllable smother
Then,
It unlocks the brest
And throwes out the rest,
And learnes us to know each other.
Wine ——*Wine.*——

Mr Hall
Mr Lydall
Mr Beeston
Mr Vener
Mr Marshall
Mr Rutter

Dor. Madlads, have you been here ever since?

Stra. Yes faith, thou seest the worst of us.
We——debauch——in discipline:
Four and twenty houres is the time:

II, i, 117. This warning is well in advance of the entrance at line 182, but it is for a group, and perhaps an elaborate procession was set up.

254 *The Tragedy*

Barruthen had the watch to night,
To morrow 'twill be at my Tent.
Dor. Good,
And d' you know what has faln out to night?
Stra. Yes:
Grainevert, and my Leiutenant Coronel;
But they are friends again.
Dor. Piſh, piſh —— the yong Palatine of Plocence,
And his grave Guardian ſurpris'd too night?
Carri'd by the enemy out of his quarters.
G. As a Chicken by a Kite out of a back ſide,
Was't not ſo?
D. Is that all?
G. Yes.
My Coronel did not love him:
He eats ſweet-meats upon a march too.
D. Well, hark ye;
Worſe yet; *Almerin*'s gone:
Forc'd the Court of Guard where he was priſoner,
And has made an eſcape.
G. So pale and ſpiritleſs a wretch,
Drew *Priams* curtain in the dead of night,
And told him half his *Troy* was burnt ——
He was of my mind. I would have done ſo my ſelf.
D. Well.
There's high ſuſpicions abroad:
Ye ſhall ſee ſtrange diſcoveries
I'th Councel of War.
G. What Councel?
D. One cal'd this morning.
Y' are all ſent to.
G. I will put on clean linnen, and ſpeak wiſely.
V. 'Sfoot we'l have a Round firſt.
G. By all means Sir.
Sings:
Come let the State ſtay,
And drink away,
There is no buſineſs above it:

of BRENNORALT. 255

It warms the cold brain,
Makes us ſpeak in high ſtrain,
He's a fool that do's not approve it.
The Macedon *youth*
Left behind him this truth,
That nothing is done with much thinking;
He drunk, and he fought,
Till he had what he ſought,
The world was his own by good drinking.
(*Exeunt*

Enter *Generall of the Rebels, Palatine of Trocke, Palatine of Menſecke, Francelia, Almerin, Morat, Iphigene.*

G. As your friend, my Lord, he has the priviledge of ours,
And may enjoy a liberty we would deny
To enemies.
A. I thank your Excellence; O *Iphigene*,
He does not know,
That thou the nobler part of friendſhip hold'ſt,
And do'ſt oblige, whilſt I can but acknowledge.
Men. Opportunity to Stateſ-men is as the juſt degree
Of heat to Chymiſts —— it perfects all the work,
And in this priſ'ner 'tis offer'd.
We now are there, where men ſhould ſtill begin;
To treat upon advantage,
The Palatine of *Trocke*, and *Menſecke*,
With *Almerin*, ſhall to the King;
Trumpet ready
Petitions ſhall be drawn,
Humble in form, but ſuch for matter,
As the bold *Macedonian* youth would ſend
To men he did deſpiſe for luxury.
The firſt begets opinion of the world,
Which looks not far, but on the outſide dwels:
Th'other inforces courage in our own,
For bold demands muſt boldly be maintain'd.
Pal. Let all go on ſtill in the publique name,
But keep an ear open to particular offers;
Liberty and publique good are like great *Oleos*

II, i, 196. This warning for a trumpet is far in advance of the cue at line 269, but there was doubtless a practical reason behind it. A musician had to come to stage level from the music room (possibly an upper side box). Within a few lines of the trumpeter's music cue he makes an entrance.

Muſt have the upper end ſtill of our tables,
Though they are but for ſhew.
Fra. Would I had ne're ſeen this ſhape, 't has poyſon in't,
Yet where dwells good, if ill inhabits there?
Min. —Preſſe much religion,
For though we dreſſe the ſcruples for the multitude,
And for our ſelves reſerve th' advantages,
(It being much pretext) yet it is neceſſary;
For things of faith are ſo abſtruſe and nice,
They will admit diſpute eternally:
So how ſoe're other demands appear, mr Moon
Theſe never can be prov'd unreaſonable; mr Kenaston
The ſubject being of ſo fine a nature, mr Bird
It not ſubmits it ſelf to ſenſe, but ſcapes
The trials which conclude all common doubts.
Fra. My Lord, you uſe me as ill Painters paint,
Who while they labour to make faces fair,
Neglect to make them like.
Iphi. Madam, there is no ſhipwrack of your
Vertues near, that you ſhould throw away
Any of all your excellencies
To ſave the deareſt, modeſty.
Gener. If they proceed with us, we can retreat unto
Our expoſitions, and the peoples votes.
If they refuſe us wholly, then we plead,
The King's beſieged, blockt up ſo ſtraitly
By ſome few, reliefe can find no way
To enter to the King, or to get out to us;
Exclaim againſt it loud,
Till the *Polonians* think it high injuſtice,
And wiſh us better yet.
Then eaſily do we riſe unto our ends;
And will become their envy through their pitty.
At worſt you may confirm our party there,
Increaſe it too: there is one *Brennoralt*,
Men call him Gallant, but a diſcontent;
My Coſen the King hath us'd him ill:
Him a handſome whiſper will draw.

The afternoon ſhall perfect
What we have looſely now reſolv'd.
Iphi. If in diſcourſe of beauty,
(So large an Empire) I do wander,
It will become your goodneſſe Madam,
To ſet me right.
And in a country where you your ſelf is Queen,
Not ſuffer ſtrangers loſe themſelves.
Gener. What making revenges *Palatine*?
And taking priſoners fair Ladies hearts?
Iphi. Yes my Lord.
And have no better fortune in this War,
Then in the other; for while I think to take,
I'am ſuprized my ſelf.
Fra. Diſſembler, would thou wert.
M. You are a Courtier my Lord;
The *Palatine* of *Plocence*, (*Almerin*)
Will grace the *Hymeneals*;
And that they may be while his ſtay here,
I'le court my Lord in abſence;
Take off for you the little ſtrangeneſſes
Virgins wear at firſt, ———— *Iphi. ſounds.*
Look to the *Palatine*.
Mer. How is't my deareſt *Iphigene*? Sound a parley here
Iph. Not well, I would retire.
G. A qualme.
M. His colour ſtole away; ſank down,
As water in a weather-glaſſe
Preſt by a warm hand.
Menſ. A cordiall of kind looks, —— (*Enter a Trum-*
From the King. (*pet blinded.*
M. Let's withdraw,
And hear him. ———— *Exit.*
Enter *Brennoralt, Doran, Raynelin.*
Dor. Yes to be married;
What are you mute now?
Bren. Thou cam'ſt too haſtily upon me, putſt
So cloſe the colours to mine eye, I could

Not

Not see. It is impossible. [*Dor.*] Impossible?
If't were impossible, it should be otherwise,
What can you imagine there of Constancy?
Where 'tis so much their nature to love change,
That when they say but what they are,
They excuse themselves for what they do?
Bren. She hardly knows him yet, in such an instant.
Dor. Oh you know not how fire flies,
When it does catch light matter, woman,
B. No more of that; She is
Yet the most precious thing in all my thoughts.
If it be so———— ————(*Stud'es.*)
I am a lost thing in the world *Doran.*
D. How?
Bren. Thou wilt in vain perswade me to be other
Life which to others is a Good that they
Enjoy, to me will be an evill, I
Shall suffer in————
Dor. Look on another face that's present remedy.
Bren. How ill thou doest conclude?
'Cause there are pestilent ayres, which kill men suddenly
In health, must there be soveraigne as suddenly,
To cure in sickness? 't never was in nature.
Exit, and
Enters again hastily.
Bren. I was a fool to think, Death only kept
The doors of ill-payed love, when or disdain,
Or spite could let me out as well————
Dor. Right; were I as you,
It should no more trouble me
To free my self of love,
Then to spit out that which made me sick.
Bren. Ile tell her so; that she may laugh at me,
As at a prisoner threatning his Guard,
He will break loose, and so is made the faster.
She hath charmes————(*Studies.*)
Doran can fetch in a rebellious heart,
Ev'n while it is conspiring liberty.
Oh

———— ———— ————Oh she hath all
The vertues of her sex, and not the vices,
Chaste and unsullied, as first op'ning Lillies,
Or untouch'd buds————
Dor. Chaste? why! do you honour me,
Because I throw my self not off a precipice?
'Tis her ruine to be otherwise!
Though we blame those that kill themselves (my Lord)
We praise not him that keeps himself alive,
And deserves nothing.
Bren. And 'tis the least,
She doe's triumph, when she does but appear:
I have as many Rivals as beholders.
Dor. All that encreases but our jealousies;
If you have now such qualmes for that you have not,
What will you have for that you shall possesse?
Bren. ————Dull heritique;
Know I have these, because I have not her
When I have her, I shall have these no more.
Her fancy now, her vertue then will govern:
And as I use to watch with doubtfull eye,
The wavering needle in the best Sun-dyall,
Till it has setled, then the troubles o're,
Because I know when it is Fixt, it's true:
So here my doubts are all afore me. Sure,
Doran, crown'd Conquerours are but the types
Of Lovers, which enjoy, and really
Possess what the other have in dreams. Ile send
A challenge to him.———— ———— ————
Dor. Do, and be thought a mad-man.
To what purpose?
If she love him she will but hate you more.
Lovers in favour (*Brennoralt*) are Gamesters
In good fortune; the more you set them;
The more they get,
Bren. I'le see her then this night, by Heaven I will.
Dor. Where, in the Citadell?
Bren. Know what, and why.————
Dor.

II, i, following 305. Brennoralt's entrance was not warned, since he just made an exit.

Dor. He raves, *Brennoralt* ?
Bren. Let me alone,
I conjure thee, by the discretion
Left betwixt us, (that's thine,
For mine's devour'd by injuries of fortune,)
Leave me to my self.
Dor. I have done.
Bren. Is there such a passage,
As thou hast told me of, into the Castle ?
Rag. There is my Lord.
Bren. And dar'st thou let me in ?
Rag. If you my Lord will venture.
Bren. There are no Century's near it.
Rag. None.
Bren. How to the Chamber afterward ?
Rag. Her woman.
Bren. What's she ?
Rag. A wicket to my Ladies secrets,
One that stands up to marriage with me.
Bren. There—upon thy life be secret.—(*flings a purse*.
Rag. Else,—All punishment to ingratitude.
Bren. Enough.
I am a storm within till I am there,
Oh *Doran* !
That that which is so pleasant to behold,
Should be such pain within !
Dor. Poor *Brennoralt* !
Thou art the Martyr of a thousand tyrants :
Love, Honour, and Ambition reign by turns ;
And shew their power upon thee.
Bren. Why, let them ; I'm still *Brennoralt* : " Ev'n Kings
" Themselves are by their servants rul'd sometimes ;
" Let their own slaves govern them at odde hours :
" Yet not subject their Persons or their Powers.
Exeunt.

ACT.

ACT III. SCENE I.

Enter *Iphigene* (*as in a Garden*)

Iphi. WHat have I got by changing place ?
But as a wretch which ventures to the Wars,
Seeking the misery with pain abroad,
He found, but wisely thought h' had left at home.
Fortune thou hast no tyranny beyond
This usage.— — (*Weepes*
Would I had never hop't
Or had betimes dispair'd, let never in
The gentle theif, or kept him but a guest,
Not made him Lord of all.
Tempests of wind thus (as my stormes of greife
Carry my teares, which should releive my heart)
Have hurried to the thankless Ocean clouds
And showers, that needed not at all the curtesie ;
When the poore plaines have languish't for the want ;
And almost burnt asunder.——
I'le have this Statues place, and undertake
At my own charge to keep the water full. —— (*Lies down*

Enter *Francelia*.

Fran. These fond Impressions grow too strong upon me
They were at first without design or end ;
Like the first Elements, that know not what
And why they Act and yet produce strange things ;
Poore innocent desires, journeying they know
Not whether : but now they promise to themselves
Strange things, grow insolent, threaten no rest
Till they be satisfi'd.
What difference was between these Lords ?
The one made love, as if he by assault
Would take my heart, so force't it to defence ;
While t' other blew it up with secret mines,
And left no place for it, here he is.

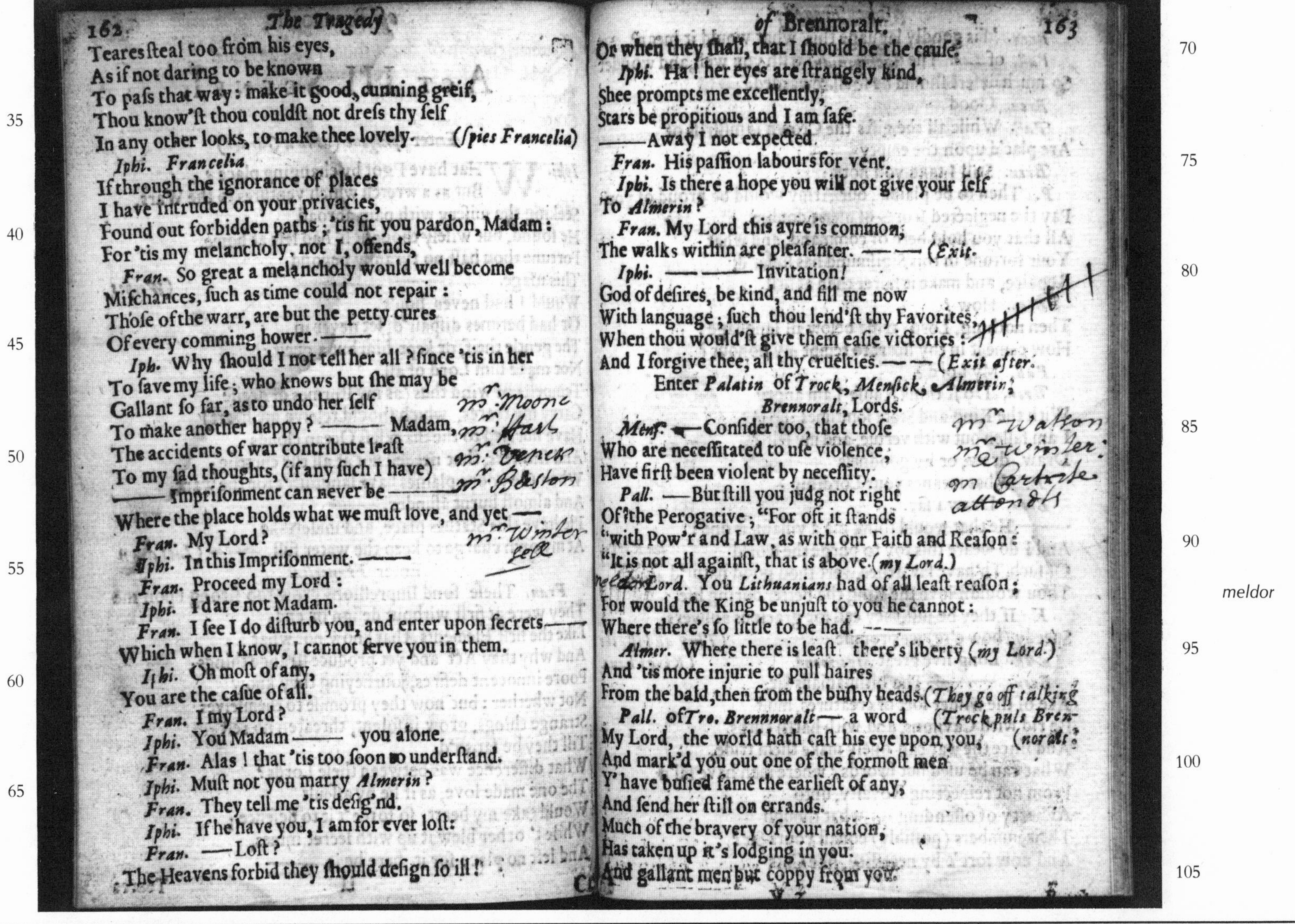

162 The Tragedy

Teares ſteal too from his eyes,
As if not daring to be known
To paſs that way: make it good, cunning greif,
Thou know'ſt thou couldſt not dreſs thy ſelf
In any other looks, to make thee lovely. (ſpies Francelia)
Iphi. Francelia
If through the ignorance of places
I have intruded on your privacies,
Found out forbidden paths; 'tis fit you pardon, Madam:
For 'tis my melancholy, not I, offends,
Fran. So great a melancholy would well become
Miſchances, ſuch as time could not repair:
Thoſe of the warr, are but the petty cures
Of every comming hower.——
Iph. Why ſhould I not tell her all? ſince 'tis in her
To ſave my life; who knows but ſhe may be
Gallant ſo far, as to undo her ſelf
To make another happy? —— Madam,
The accidents of war contribute leaſt
To my ſad thoughts, (if any ſuch I have)
—— Impriſonment can never be ——
Where the place holds what we muſt love, and yet ——.
Fran. My Lord?
Iphi. In this Impriſonment. ——
Fran. Proceed my Lord:
Iphi. I dare not Madam.
Fran. I ſee I do diſturb you, and enter upon ſecrets——
Which when I know, I cannot ſerve you in them.
Iphi. Oh moſt of any,
You are the caſue of all.
Fran. I my Lord?
Iphi. You Madam —— you alone.
Fran. Alas! that 'tis too ſoon to underſtand.
Iphi. Muſt not you marry *Almerin*?
Fran. They tell me 'tis deſig'nd.
Iphi. If he have you, I am for ever loſt:
Fran. ——Loſt?
The Heavens forbid they ſhould deſign ſo ill!

mr Moone
mr Hart
mr Beeston
mr Winter

of Brennoralt. 163

Or when they ſhall, that I ſhould be the cauſe.
Iphi. Ha! her eyes are ſtrangely kind,
Shee prompts me excellently,
Stars be propitious and I am ſafe.
——Away I not expected.
Fran. His paſſion labours for vent.
Iphi. Is there a hope you will not give your ſelf
To *Almerin*?
Fran. My Lord this ayre is common;
The walks within are pleaſanter. —— (*Exit.*
Iphi. —— —— Invitation!
God of deſires, be kind, and fill me now
With language; ſuch thou lend'ſt thy Favorites,
When thou would'ſt give them eaſie victories:
And I forgive thee; all thy cruelties.—— (*Exit after.*
Enter *Palatin* of *Trock*; *Menſick*, *Almerin*; *Brennoralt*, Lords.
Menſ. Conſider too, that thoſe
Who are neceſſitated to uſe violence,
Have firſt been violent by neceſſity.
Pall. —But ſtill you judg not right
Of the Perogative; "For oft it ſtands
"with Pow'r and Law, as with our Faith and Reaſon:
"It is not all againſt, that is above. (*my Lord.*)
Lord. You *Lithuanians* had of all leaſt reaſon; meldor
For would the King be unjuſt to you he cannot:
Where there's ſo little to be had. ——
Almer. Where there is leaſt, there's liberty (*my Lord.*)
And 'tis more injurie to pull haires
From the bald, then from the buſhy heads. (*They go off talking*
Pall. of *Tro. Brennoralt* —— a word (*Trock puls Brennoralt;*
My Lord, the world hath caſt his eye upon you,
And mark'd you out one of the formoſt men
Y' have buſied fame the earlieſt of any,
And ſend her ſtill on errands.
Much of the bravery of your nation,
Has taken up it's lodging in you.
And gallant men but coppy from you.

mr Watson
mr Winter
mr Cartwright
attend

III, i, 92. Since Melidor enters with the King, why he is warned here rather than with the rest of the group at line 85 is not clear. This warning is in another hand and may have been added by the prompter's assistant in rehearsal.

Bren. 'Tis goodly laguage this, what would it mean?
Pall. of *Tro.* The *Lithuanians* wish you well, and wonder
So much desert should be so ill rewarded.
Bren. Good
Pall. While all the gifts the Crown is mistriss of
Are plac'd upon the empty ———
Bren. Still I take you not.
P. Then to be plaine; our Army would be proud of you:
Pay the neglected scores of merit double.
All that you hold here of command, and what
Your fortune in this Sigismund has suffer'd,
Repaire, and make it fairer then at first.
Bren. How?
Then nothing, Lord; trifle below ill language:
How came it in thy heart to tempt my honour?
Pall. My Lord?
Bren. Do'st think 'cause I am angry
With the King and State somtimes
I am fallen out with vertue, and my self?
Draw, draw, or by goodness ———
P. What meanes your Lordship?
Bren. Draw I say.
——— He that would think me a villain, is one:
And I do weare this toy to purge the world
Of such. Th'have sav'd thee, wert thou good natur'd *Ent. K of Pol. Lords, Melid. Miesla.*
Thou wouldst love the King the better during life.
K. If they be just, they call for gracious answers;
Speedy, (how e're) we promise *(They all kisse the*
All. Long live great *Sigismond* *(Kings hand.*
Bren. ——— The Lithuanians Sir,
Are of the wilder sort of creatures, must
Be rid with Cavilons, and with harsh curbs.
And since the war can onely make them tride,
What can be used but swords? where men have fal'n
From not respecting Royalty, unto
A liberty of offending it: what though
Their numbers (possibly) equall yours Sir?
And now forc't by necessity, like Cats
In

In narrow roomes, they fly up in your face?
Think you Rebellion and Loyalty
Are empty names? and that in Subjects hearts
They don't both give, and take away the courage?
Shall we beleeve there is no difference
In good and bad? that there's no punishment,
Or no protection? forbid it Heaven!
If when great *Polands* honour, safety too,
Hangs in dispute, we should not draw our Swords,
Why were we ever taught to wear 'em Sir,
Mi. This late commotion in your Kingdom Sir,
Is like a growing Wen upon the face,
Which as we cannot look on but with trouble,
So take't away we cannot but with danger.
War there hath foulest face, and I most feare it
Where the pretence is fair'st. Religion
And Liberty, most specious names, they urge;
Which like the Bils of subtle Mountebanks,
Fill'd with great promises of curing all,
——— ——— Though by the wise,
Pass'd by unread as common consenage,
Yet, by th'unknowing multitude they're still
Admir'd and flock'd unto. ———
K. Is there no way
To disabuse them? *(Melid)* All is now too late.
'The Vulgar in Religion are like
'Unknown Lands; those that first possess them, have them.
Then, Sir, consider, justness of cause is nothing.
When things are risen to the point they are;
'Tis either not examin'd or beleev'd
Among the Warlike. ———
The better cause the *Grecians* had of *Trore*,
Yet were the Gods themselves divided in't;
And the foule ravisher found as good protection
As the much injur'd husband ———
Nor are you Sir, assur'd of all behinde you:
For though your person in your Subjects hearts
Stands highly honour'd, and belov'd, yet are
They

"[Sti]r'd

There certain acts of State, which men call grievances
Abroad; and though they bare them in the times
Of peace, yet will they now perchance, seek to
"Be free, and throw them off. "For know Dread Sir,
"The Common People are much like the Sea,
"That suffers things to fall and sink unto
"The bottom in a Calme, which in a storme
"[Sti]r'd and enrag'd, it lifts, and does keep up.
Then: Time distempers cures more safely Sir, Coth
Then Physick does, or instant letting-blood; morris
Religion now is a young Mistress there,
For which each man will fight, and dye at least Mr. Roscos
Let it alone a while, and t'will become Mrs. Rutter
A kind of marri'd wife: people will be Mrs. Marshall
Content to live with it in quietness.
(If that at least may be) my voyce is therefore Sir,
For Peace.——
Mins. Were Sir the question simply War or Peace,
It were nomore then shortly to be askt,
Whether we would be well or ill:
Since War the sickness of the Kingdome is,
And Peace the health: But here I do conceive
'Twill rather lye, whether we had not better,
Endure sharp sickness for a time, to enjoy
A perfect strength, then have it languish on us:
For peace and warr in an incestuous line
Have still begot each other——
Those men that highly now have broke all Lawes,
(The great one only 'tis 'twixt man and man)
What safety can they promise, though you give it?
Will they not still suspect, (and justly too)
That all those civill bonds (new made) should be
Broken again them? so being still
In feares and jealousies themselves, they must
Infect the People. "For in such a case
"The privat safety is the publick trouble,
Nor will they ever want prætext; "Since he
"That will maintain it with his sword hee's injur'd,
"May

May say't at any time ——
Then Sir, as terrible as war appeares,
My vote is for't, nor shall I ever care
How ugly my Physitians face shall be,
So he can do the cure.
Lord. In entring Physick,
I think Sir, none so much considers
The Doctors face, as his own body.
To keep on foot the war with all yours wants,
Is to let blood, and take strong potions
In dangerous sickness.
K. I see, and wonder not to find, my Lord,
This difference in opinion; the Subject's large:
Nor can we there too much dispute, where when
We erre, 'tis at a Kingdoms charges; Peace
And War are in themselves indifferent,
And time doth stamp them either good or bad;
But here the place is much considerable;
"War in our own is like to too much heat
"Within, it makes the body sick; when in
"Another Contrey 'tis but exercise;
"Conveighs that heat abroad, and gives it health.
To that I bend my thoughts; but leave it to
Our greater Councel, which we now assemble:
Meane time exchange of pris'ners only we
Assent unto ——— ———
Lord. Nothing of Truce Sir? [*K.*] No: wee'l not take up
Quiet at int'rest: perfect peace, or nothing.
"Cessations for short times in war, are like
"Small fits of health, in desp'rate maladies:
"Which while the instant pain seems to abate,
"Flatters into debauch and worse estate—— *Exeunt.*
Enter Iphigene *as leading to her chamber* Francelia;
Servants with lights; Morat, *and another Soldier.*
Iph. I have not left my self a fair retreate,
And must be now the blest object
Of your love, or subject of your scorne.

168 *The Tragedy*

Fran. I feare ſome treacherie ;
And that mine eyes have given intelligence.
Unleſs you knew there would be weak defence,
You durſt not think of taking in a heart,
As ſoon as you ſet down before it.
Iph. Condemn my Love not of ſuch fond Ambition,
It aimes not at a conqueſt,
But exchange, *Francelia*— (*whiſper.*
Mor. They're very great in this ſhort time.
Sol. 'Tis ever ſo :
Young and handſome
Have made acquaintances in nature ;
So when they meet, they have the leſs to do.
It is for age or uglineſs to make approaches,
And keep a diſtance.
Iph. When I ſhall ſee other perfection,
Which at the beſt will be but other vanity,
Not more I ſhall not love it——
Fran. 'Tis ſtill one ſtep not to deſpair, my Lord
Exeunt Iphig. Fran: ſervants.
Morat. Doeſt think he will fight ?
Sold. Troth it may be not :
Nature, in thoſe fine peeces, does as painters,
Hangs out a pleaſant Excellence
That takes the eye, which is indeed,
But a courſe canvas in the naked truth,
Or ſome ſlight ſtuffe.
Morat. I have a great mind to taſte him.
Sold. Fy ! a priſoner ?
Morat. By this hand if I thought——
He courted my Colonels Mrs in earneſt.
Wom. My Lord, my Lord,
My Lady thinks the Geſſemine walks
Will be the finer, the freſhneſs
Of th' morning takes off the ſtrength
O' th' heat ſhe ſayes.
Iph. 'Tis well.
Mor. Mewe——doe it ſo ? I ſuſpect vidly,
Wee'l follow him, and ſee if he be

of Brennoralt. 169

So farr quallified towards a ſouldier,
As to drink a craſh in's chamber— (*Raguelin puls the wai-*
R. Where are thoſe keyes ? (*ting woman back.*
Wom. Harke you, I dare not do it.
R. How ?
Wom. My Lady will finde
R. Scruples?
Are my hopes become your fears ?
There was no otherway I ſhould be any thing
In this lewd world,—and now——
'Sfoot, I know ſhe longs to ſee him too.
Wom. Does ſhe ?
R. Doe you think he would deſire it elſe ?
Wom. I, but————
R. Why, let me ſecure it all.
I'le ſay I found the Keys, or ſtole them : Come-
Wom. Well, if you ruine all now——
Here, theſe enter the garden from the works,
That the Privy walks, and that the back ſtaires,
Then you know my chamber.
R. Yes I know your chamber.—— *Exeunt.*
Enter Brennoralt.
Bren. He comes not.
One wiſe thought more, and I return :
I cannot in this act ſeperate the fooliſh
From the bold ſo farre, but ſtill it taſtes o'th raſh,
Why let it taſte, it taſts of love too ;
And to all actions't gives a pretty reliſh, that.
Enter Raguelin,
Rag. My Lord ?
Bren. Oh—here.
Rag. 'Sfoot y'are upon our Centries.
Move on this hand,—— *Exeunt.*
Enter (agen) Bren. and Raguel.
Bren. Where are we now ?
Ra. Entring part of the Fort,
Your Lordſhip muſt be wet a little. —— *Exeunt.*
Bren.

III, i, following 323. The reentrances of Brennoralt and Raguelin here and again at line 326 are not warned or cued, since they come in such quick succession. They were apparently considered a part of the stage movement that the actors took care of without the help of the prompter.

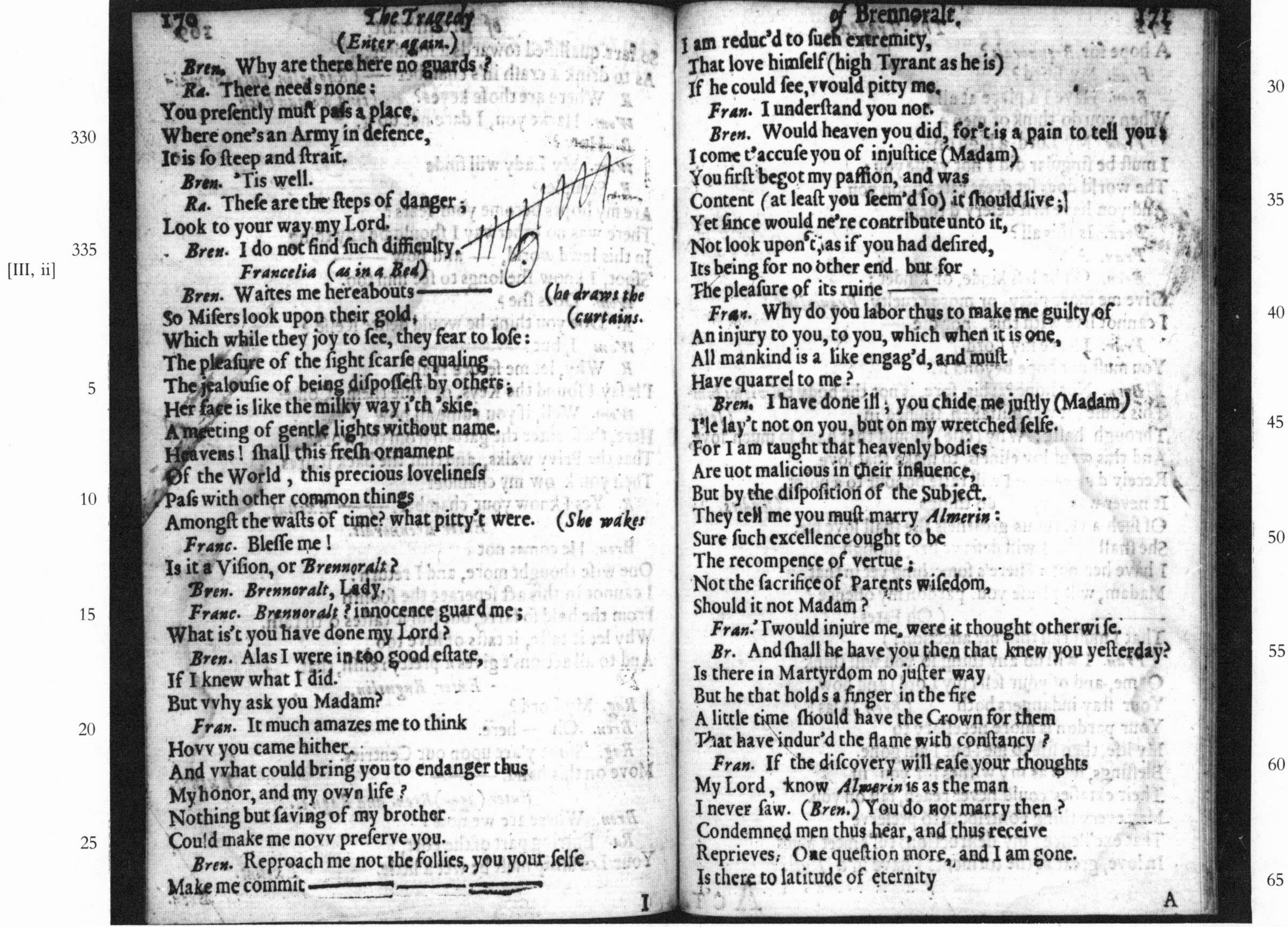

170 *The Tragedy*

(Enter again.)

Bren. Why are there here no guards ?
Ra. There needs none:
You presently must pass a place,
Where one's an Army in defence,
It is so steep and strait.
Bren. 'Tis well.
Ra. These are the steps of danger;
Look to your way my Lord.
Bren. I do not find such difficulty.

[III, ii]

Francelia (as in a Bed)
Bren. Waites me hereabouts——— *(he draws the curtains.*
So Misers look upon their gold,
Which while they joy to see, they fear to lose:
The pleasure of the sight scarse equaling
The jealousie of being dispossest by others;
Her face is like the milky way i'th 'skie,
A meeting of gentle lights without name.
Heavens! shall this fresh ornament
Of the World, this precious lovelines
Pass with other common things
Amongst the wasts of time? what pitty't were. *(She wakes*
Franc. Blesse me!
Is it a Vision, or *Brennoralt*?
Bren. *Brennoralt*, Lady.
Franc. *Brennoralt*? innocence guard me;
What is't you have done my Lord?
Bren. Alas I were in too good estate,
If I knew what I did.
But why ask you Madam?
Fran. It much amazes me to think
How you came hither,
And what could bring you to endanger thus
My honor, and my own life?
Nothing but saving of my brother
Could make me now preserve you.
Bren. Reproach me not the follies, you your selfe
Make me commit————

I

of Brennoralt. 171

I am reduc'd to such extremity,
That love himself (high Tyrant as he is)
If he could see, would pitty me.
Fran. I understand you not.
Bren. Would heaven you did, for't is a pain to tell you;
I come t'accuse you of injustice (Madam)
You first begot my passion, and was
Content (at least you seem'd so) it should live;
Yet since would ne're contribute unto it,
Not look upon't, as if you had desired,
Its being for no other end but for
The pleasure of its ruine———
Fran. Why do you labor thus to make me guilty of
An injury to you, to you, which when it is one,
All mankind is a like engag'd, and must
Have quarrel to me?
Bren. I have done ill; you chide me justly (Madam)
I'le lay't not on you, but on my wretched selfe,
For I am taught that heavenly bodies
Are uot malicious in their influence,
But by the disposition of the Subject.
They tell me you must marry *Almerin*:
Sure such excellence ought to be
The recompence of vertue;
Not the sacrifice of Parents wisedom,
Should it not Madam?
Fran. 'Twould injure me, were it thought otherwise.
Br. And shall he have you then that knew you yesterday?
Is there in Martyrdom no juster way
But he that holds a finger in the fire
A little time should have the Crown for them
That have indur'd the flame with constancy?
Fran. If the discovery will ease your thoughts
My Lord, know *Almerin* is as the man
I never saw. *(Bren.)* You do not marry then?
Condemned men thus hear, and thus receive
Reprieves; One question more, and I am gone.
Is there to latitude of eternity

A

III, ii, opening. A scene shift is called for, though no description of the setting is provided. The shift takes place while Brennoralt is onstage, a practice indicated in authors' stage directions in some plays and here confirmed in prompt notes. Raguelin was not given an exit, but he apparently went off at III, i, 334.

172 *The Tragedy.*

A hope for *Brennoralt*?
Fran. My Lord?
Bren. Have I a place at all;
When you do think of men?
Fran My Lord, a high one,
I must be singular did I not value you:
The world does set great rates upon you,
And you have first deserv'd them.
Bren. Is this all?
Fran. All.
Bren. Oh be less kinde, or kinder:
Give me more pitty, or more cruelty, *Francelia.*
I cannot live with this, nor die —
Fran. I feare my Lord,
You must not hope beyond it.
Bren. Not hope? This, sure, is not the body to (*views him-*
This soule; it was mistaken, shufled in (*selfe.*
Through haste: Why (else) should that have so much love,
And this want lov.eliness, to make that love
Receiv'd? ——— I will raise honour to a point,
It never was do things (*studies.*
Of such a vertuous greatness she shall love me.
She shall —— I will deserve her, though
I have her not: There's something yet in that.
Madam, wilt please you, pardon my offence?
——————— (Oh Fates!
That I must call thus my affection!)
Fran. I will do any thing so you will think
Of me, and of your self (my Lord) and how
Your stay indangers both — (*Bren.*) Alas!
Your pardon is more necessary to
My life, then life to me: but I am gone.
Blessings, such as my wishes for you, in
Their extasies, could never reach, fall on you.
May every thing contribute to preserve
That exc'llence (my destruction) till't meet joyes
In love, great as the torments I have in't. *Exit.*

ACT.

of Brennoralt 173

ACT IV. SCENE I.

Enter *Brennoralt.*

Bren. WHy so, 'tis well, Fortune I thank thee still;
I dare not call thee villaine neither.
'Twas plotted from the first,
That's certain, — it looks that way?
Hum ——— caught in a trap?
Here's something yet to trust to — (*To his sword.*
This was the entry, these the staires:
But whether afterwards;
He that is sure to perish on the land,
May quit the nicetie of Card and Compass:
And safe, to his discretion, put to Sea:
He shall have my hand to't. *Exit.*

Enter Raguelin, Orilla, (*the waiting-woman*)

Ra. Look:
By this light 'tis day.
Oril. Not by this, by t'other 'tis indeed.
Ra. Thou art such another piece of temptation.
My Lord raves by this time,
A hundred to one the Centinels
Will discover us too,
Then I do pray for night-watch.
Oril. Fie upon thee,
Thou art as fearful as a yong colt;
Boglest at every thing, fool.
As if Lovers had considered hours: I'le peep in (*she peeps.*
Ra. I am as weary of this wench,
As if I were married to her:
She hangs upon me like an Ape upon a horse
She's as common too as a Barbers glasse
Conscienc't too like a Dy-dapper.
Orilla. — there's no body within:
My

III, ii, 102. The end of the act was warned, but there is no ring cue. Perhaps there was no scene change, though Francelia and her bed must have been taken off; or possibly the lack of a ring cue meant that there was no entr'acte music. An interval may have been taken.

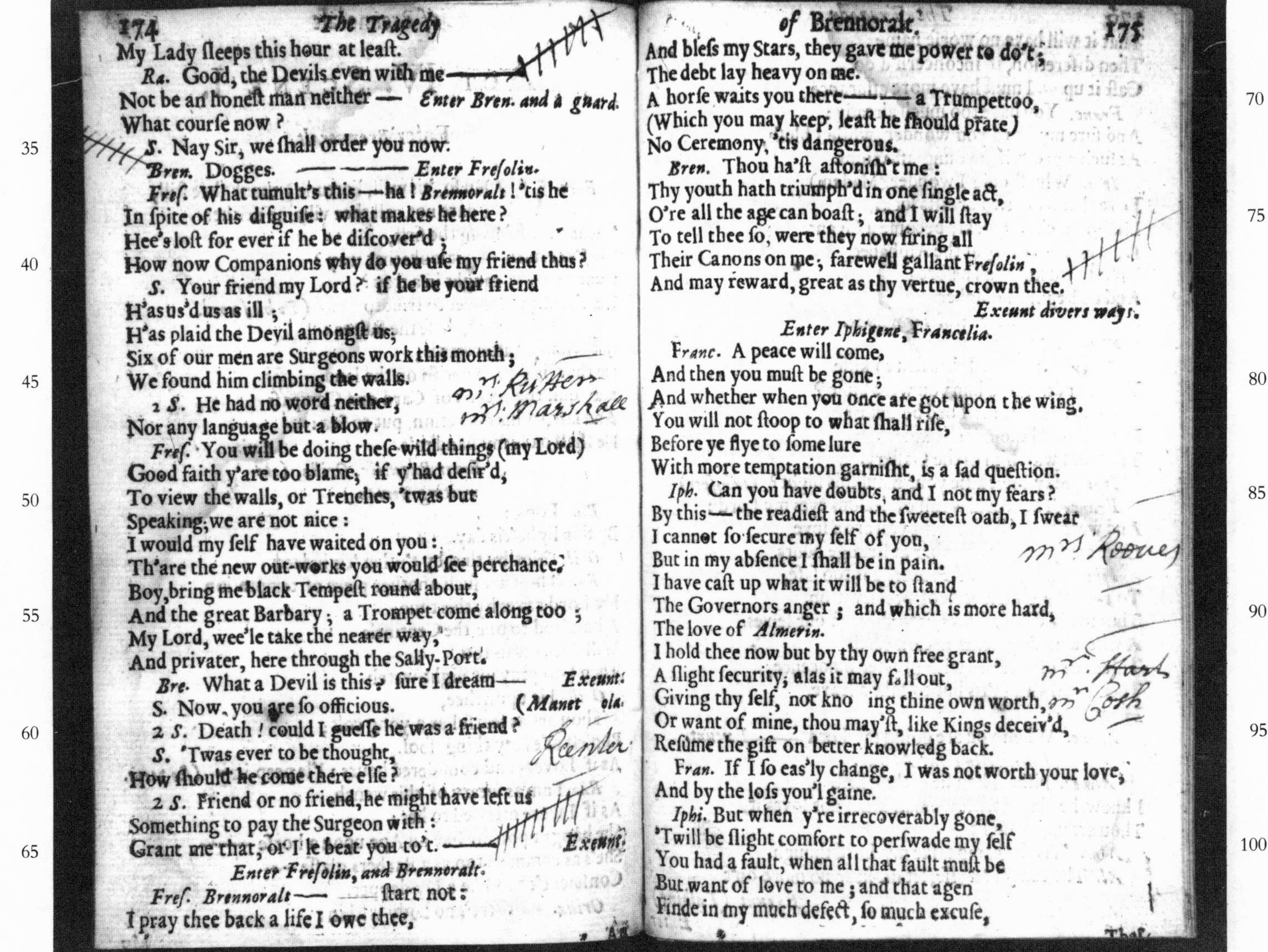

174 *The Tragedy*

My Lady ſleeps this hour at leaſt.
Ra. Good, the Devils even with me——
Not be an honeſt man neither —— *Enter Bren. and a guard.*
What courſe now ?
S. Nay Sir, we ſhall order you now.
Bren. Dogges. ———— *Enter Freſolin.*
Freſ. What tumult's this—ha ! *Brennoralt* ! 'tis he
In ſpite of his diſguiſe : what makes he here ?
Hee's loſt for ever if he be diſcover'd ;
How now Companions why do you uſe my friend thus ?
S. Your friend my Lord ? if he be your friend
H'as us'd us as ill ;
H'as plaid the Devil amongſt us;
Six of our men are Surgeons work this month ;
We found him climbing the walls.
2 *S.* He had no word neither,
Nor any language but a blow.
Freſ. You will be doing theſe wild things (my Lord)
Good faith y'are too blame, if y'had deſir'd,
To view the walls, or Trenches, 'twas but
Speaking; we are not nice :
I would my ſelf have waited on you :
Th'are the new out-works you would ſee perchance.
Boy, bring me black Tempeſt round about,
And the great Barbary ; a Trompet come along too ;
My Lord, wee'le take the nearer way,
And privater, here through the Sally-Port.
Bre. What a Devil is this ? ſure I dream—— *Exeunt.*
S. Now, you are ſo officious. (*Manet ola.*
2 *S.* Death ! could I gueſſe he was a friend ?
S. 'Twas ever to be thought,
How ſhould he come there elſe ?
2 *S.* Friend or no friend, he might have left us
Something to pay the Surgeon with :
Grant me that, or I'le beat you to't. —— *Exeunt.*
Enter Freſolin, and Brennoralt.
Freſ. Brennoralt—— ſtart not :
I pray thee back a life I owe thee,

of Brennoralt. 175

And bleſs my Stars, they gave me power to do't ;
The debt lay heavy on me.
A horſe waits you there—— a Trumpettoo,
(Which you may keep, leaſt he ſhould prate)
No Ceremony, 'tis dangerous.
Bren. Thou ha'ſt aſtoniſh't me :
Thy youth hath triumph'd in one ſingle act,
O're all the age can boaſt ; and I will ſtay
To tell thee ſo, were they now firing all
Their Canons on me ; farewell gallant *Freſolin*,
And may reward, great as thy vertue, crown thee.
Exeunt divers ways.
Enter Iphigene, Francelia.
Franc. A peace will come,
And then you muſt be gone ;
And whether when you once are got upon the wing,
You will not ſtoop to what ſhall riſe,
Before ye flye to ſome lure
With more temptation garniſht, is a ſad queſtion.
Iph. Can you have doubts, and I not my fears ?
By this—the readieſt and the ſweeteſt oath, I ſwear
I cannot ſo ſecure my ſelf of you,
But in my abſence I ſhall be in pain.
I have caſt up what it will be to ſtand
The Governors anger ; and which is more hard,
The love of *Almerin.*
I hold thee now but by thy own free grant,
A ſlight ſecurity, alas it may fall out,
Giving thy ſelf, not kno ing thine own worth,
Or want of mine, thou may'ſt, like Kings deceiv'd,
Reſume the gift on better knowledg back.
Fran. If I ſo eas'ly change, I was not worth your love,
And by the loſs you'l gaine.
Iphi. But when y're irrecoverably gone,
'Twill be ſlight comfort to perſwade my ſelf
You had a fault, when all that fault muſt be
But want of love to me ; and that agen
Finde in my much defect, ſo much excuſe,

IV, i, 61. *Reenter* is an unusual warning, here used instead of character or actor names, perhaps because the people involved in the entrance at line 65 just left the stage.

That it will have no worſe name
Then diſcretion, if inconcern'd do
Caſt it up— I muſt have more aſſurance.
Franc. You have too much already:
And ſure my Lord you wonder, while I bluſh;
At ſuch a growth in young affections.
Iphi. Why ſhould I wonder (Madam)
Love that from two breaſts ſucks,
Muſt or a child quickly become a Gyant.
Dunces in love ſtay at the Alphabet,
Th'inſpir'd know all before;
And do begin ſtill higher.

Enter waiting woman.

Woman. Madam;
Almerin, returned, has ſent to kiſſe
Your hands. I told him you were buſie?
Franc. Muſt I my Lord be buſie?
I may be civil though not kind.
Tell him I wait him in the Gallery.
Iphi May I not kiſſe your hand this night? (*Whiſper*)
Franc. The world is full of jealous eyes my Lord:
And were they all lockt up; you are a ſpye
Once entred in my chamber at ſtrange hours.
Iphi. The vertue of *Francelia* is too ſafe,
To need thoſe little Arts of preſervation.
Thus to divide our ſelves, is to diſtruſt our ſelves.
A Cherubin diſpatches not on earth
Th'affairs of heaven with greater innocence,
Then I will viſit; 'tis but to take a leave,
I begg.
Franc. When you are going my Lord ——*Exeunt.*

Enter Almerin, Morat.

Almer. Piſh. Thou lieſt, thou lieſt.
I know he playes with woman kind, not loves it.
Thou art impertinent ——
Mor. 'Tis the camp talke my Lord though.
Al. The camp's an aſſe, let me hear no more on't
Exeunt (*Talking*)
Enter

Enter Granivert, Villanor, Marinel.

Grani. And ſhall we have peace?
I am no ſooner ſober, but the State is ſo too:
If 't be thy will, a truce for a month only.
I long to refreſh my eyes, by this hand
They have been ſo tir'd with looking upon faces
Of this country.
Villa. And ſhall the *Donazella*
To whom we wiſh ſo well-a,
Look Babies agen in our eyes-a?
Grani. Ah —a ſprightly girle above fifteen,
That melts when a man but takes her by the hand
Eyes full, and quick; with breath
Sweet as double Violets,
And wholſome as dying leaves of Strawberries.
Thick ſilken eye browes, high upon the fore head;
And cheeks mingled with pale ſtreaks of red,
Such as the bluſhing morning never wore.
Villa. Oh my chops, my chops;
Grani. With narrow mouth, ſmall teeth,
And lips ſwelling as if ſhe pouted ———
Villa. Hold, hold, hold;
Grani. Haire curling, and cover'd like buds of *Marioram,*
Part tyed in negligence,
Part looſely flowing ——
Marin. Tyrant, tyrant, tyrant!
Grani. In a pink coulor taffata petticoat,
Lace't ſmock-ſleeves dangling;
This viſion ſtoln from her own bed,
And ruſling in ones chamber ———
Villa. Oh good *Granivert*, good *Granivert.*
Grani. With a wax candle in her hand,
Looking as if ſhe had loſt her way
At twelve at night.
Marin. Oh any hower, any hower.
Grani. Now I think on't, by this hand
I'le marry and be long-liv'd.
Villa. Long liv'd? how?
X Gran.

Grain. Oh he that has a Wife, eats with an appetite,
'Has a very good ſtomack to't firſt:
This living at large is very deſtructive,
Variety is like rare ſawces; provokes too far,
And draws on ſurfeits more then th'other.
Enter Doran.
Dor. So; is this a time to foole in?
G. What's the matter?
Dor. Draw out your choiſe men, and away to
Your Coronell immediately. There's work
Towards my boyes, there's work.
Grain. Art in earneſt?
Dor. By this light.
Grain. There's ſomething in that yet.
This moiety Warr
Twilight,
Neither night nor day,
Pox upon it:
A ſtorme is worth a thouſand
Of your calme;
There's more variety in it. *Exeunt.*
Enter Almerin, Fracelia, as talking earneſtly.
Alm. Madam, that ſhewes the greatneſs of my paſſion.
Fran. The imperfection rather: Jealouſie's
No better ſigne of love (my Lord) then feavers are
Of Life; they ſhew there is a Being, though
Impair'd, and periſhing: and that, affection
But ſick and in diſorder. I like't not.
Your ſervant—— *Exit.*
Al. So ſhort and ſowre? the change is viſible
Enter Iphigene.
Iph. Deare *Almerin* welcome, y' have been abſent long,
Alm. Not very long.
Iph. To me it hath appear'd ſo;
What ſayes our Camp? am I not blamed there?
Alm. They wonder——
Iph. While we ſmile——
How have you found the King inclining?
Alm. Well

Alm. Well.
The Treaty is not broken, nor holds it.
Things are where they were;
'Thas a kind of face of peace,
You my Lord may when you pleaſe return.
Iph. I *Almerin?*
Alm Yes my Lord, I'le give you an eſcape,
Iph. 'Tis leaſt in my deſires.
Alm. Hum!
Iph. Such priſons are beyond all liberty.
Alm. Is't poſſible?
Iph. Seems it ſtrange to you?
Alm. No, not at all.
What? you find the Ladies kind?
Iph. Civill ——— (*ſmiles.*
A. You make love well too they ſay (my Lord)
Iph. Paſs my time.
Alm Addreſs unto *Francelia?*
Iph. Viſit her.
Al D' you know ſhe is my Miſtreſs Palatine?
Iph. Ha?
Alm. D' you know ſhe is my Miſtreſs?
Iph. I have been told ſo.
Alm. And do you court her then?
Iph. Why?——— ——— (*ſmiles.*
If I ſaw the enemy firſt,
Would you not charge?
Alm. He do's allow it too by Heaven:
Laughs at me too; thou filcher of a heart,
Falſe as thy title to *Francelia,*
Or as thy friendſhip: which with this I do —(*dreames.*
Throw by—— draw.
Iph. What do you meane?
Alm. I ſee the cunning now of all thy love,
And why thou cameſt ſo tamely kind,
Suffering ſurpriſe. Draw.
Iph. I will not draw, kill me;
And I ſhall have no trouble in my death,

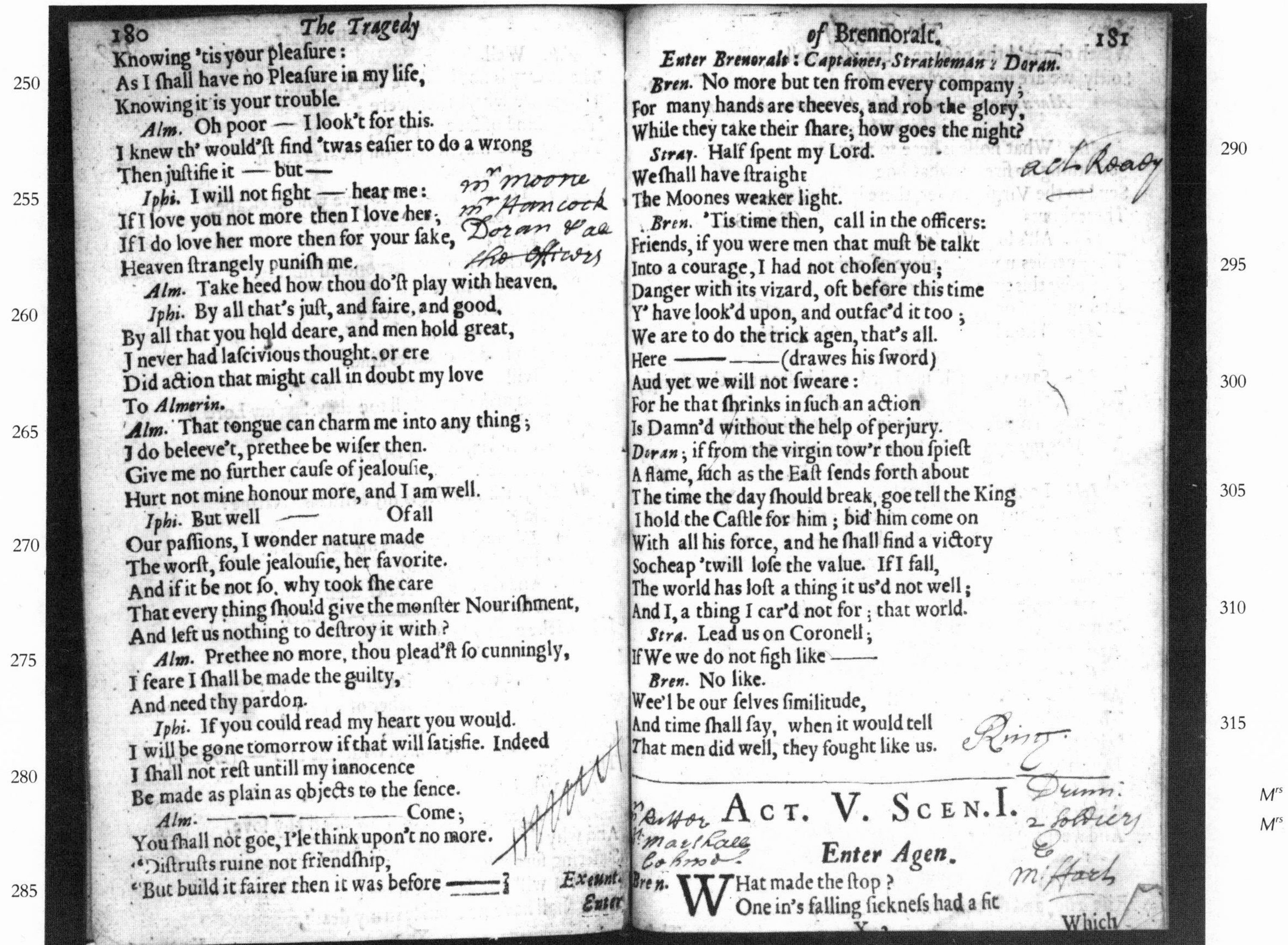

180 *The Tragedy*

Knowing 'tis your pleaſure:
As I ſhall have no Pleaſure in my life,
Knowing it is your trouble.
Alm. Oh poor — I look't for this.
I knew th' would'ſt find 'twas eaſier to do a wrong
Then juſtifie it — but —
Iphi. I will not fight — hear me:
If I love you not more then I love her,
If I do love her more then for your ſake,
Heaven ſtrangely puniſh me.
Alm. Take heed how thou do'ſt play with heaven.
Iphi. By all that's juſt, and faire, and good,
By all that you hold deare, and men hold great,
I never had laſcivious thought, or ere
Did action that might call in doubt my love
To *Almerin*.
Alm. That tongue can charm me into any thing;
I do beleeve't, prethee be wiſer then.
Give me no further cauſe of jealouſie,
Hurt not mine honour more, and I am well.
Iphi. But well —— Of all
Our paſſions, I wonder nature made
The worſt, foule jealouſie, her favorite.
And if it be not ſo, why took ſhe care
That every thing ſhould give the monſter Nouriſhment,
And left us nothing to deſtroy it with?
Alm. Prethee no more, thou plead'ſt ſo cunningly,
I feare I ſhall be made the guilty,
And need thy pardon.
Iphi. If you could read my heart you would.
I will be gone tomorrow if that will ſatisfie. Indeed
I ſhall not reſt untill my innocence
Be made as plain as objects to the ſence.
Alm. —————— Come;
You ſhall not goe, I'le think upon't no more.
"Diſtruſts ruine not friendſhip,
"But build it fairer then it was before —— *Exeunt.*
Enter

of Brennoralt. 181

Enter Brenoralt: Captaines, Stratheman: Doran.
Bren. No more but ten from every company;
For many hands are theeves, and rob the glory,
While they take their ſhare; how goes the night?
Stray. Half ſpent my Lord.
We ſhall have ſtraight
The Moones weaker light.
Bren. 'Tis time then, call in the officers:
Friends, if you were men that muſt be talkt
Into a courage, I had not choſen you;
Danger with its vizard, oft before this time
Y' have look'd upon, and outfac'd it too;
We are to do the trick agen, that's all.
Here ——— (drawes his ſword)
Aud yet we will not ſweare:
For he that ſhrinks in ſuch an action
Is Damn'd without the help of perjury.
Doran; if from the virgin tow'r thou ſpieſt
A flame, ſuch as the Eaſt ſends forth about
The time the day ſhould break, goe tell the King
I hold the Caſtle for him; bid him come on
With all his force, and he ſhall find a victory
So cheap 'twill loſe the value. If I fall,
The world has loſt a thing it us'd not well;
And I, a thing I car'd not for; that world.
Stra. Lead us on Coronell;
If We we do not figh like ——
Bren. No like.
Wee'l be our ſelves ſimilitude,
And time ſhall ſay, when it would tell
That men did well, they fought like us.

ACT. V. SCEN. I.

Enter Agen.

Bren. WHat made the ſtop?
One in's falling ſickneſs had a fit
Which

M^rs
M^rs

V, i, opening. There should be a warning for the actor Coysh, who played, among other characters in *Brennoralt*, Morat, who enters at line 13.

182 *The Tragedy*

Which choak'd the paſſage; but all is well:
Softly, we are neer the place. *Exeunt.*

Alarum within, and fight, then enter Almerin in his night-gown.

Alm. What noiſe is here to night?
Something on fire— what hoe,
Send to the Virgin-tower, there is diſorder—
Thereabouts *(Enter Sold.*

Sold. All's loſt, all's loſt!
The Enemies upon the place of armes:
And is by this time Maſter of that,
And of the Tower.

Alm. Thou lieſt.—— *(ſtrikes him.*

Enter *Morat.*

Mor. Save your ſelf my Lord, and haſte unto the Camp;
Ruine gets in on every ſide.

Alm. There's ſomething in it when this fellow flies.
Villaines, my armes, I'le ſee what Divel raignes.

[V, ii]

Enter *Iphigene, Francelia.*

Iphi. Look, the day breaks.

Fran. You think I'le be ſo kind, as ſwear
It does not now. Indeed I will not—

Iph. Will you not ſend me neither
Your picture when y'are gone?
That when my Eye is famiſh'd for a look,
It may have where to feed,
And to the painted Feaſt invite my heart.

Fran. Here, take this Virgin bracelet of my hair,
And if like other men thou ſhalt hereafter
Throw it with negligence,
'Mongſt the Records of thy weak female conqueſts,
Laugh at the kinde words, and myſtical contrivement,
If ſuch a time ſhall come,
Know I am ſighing then thy abſence *Iphigene*,
And weeping o're the falſe but pleaſing Image.

Enter *Almerin.*

Alm. Francelia, Francelia,
Riſe, riſe, and ſave thy ſelf, the Enemy

of Brennoralt. 183

That does not know thy worth, may elſe deſtroy it.
(throws open the door.

Ha! mine eyes grow ſick.
A plague has, through them, ſtolne into my heart;
And I grow dizzie, feet, lead me off agen,
Without the knowledg of my body.
I ſhall act I know not what elſe —*Exit.*

Franc. How came he in?
Dear *Iphigene* we are betrayd;
Lets raiſe the Caſtle, leſt he ſhould return.

Iph. That were to make all publique.
Fear not, Ile ſatisfie his anger:
I can do it

Franc. Yes, with ſome quarrel;
And bring my honor, and my love in danger— *Enter Almerin.*
Look he returnes, and wrecks of fury,
Like hurried clouds over the face of heaven,
Before a tempeſt, in his looks appears.

Alm. If they would queſtion what our rage doth act,
And make it ſin, they would not thus provoke men.
———I am too tame.
For if they live I ſhall be pointed at,
Here I denounce a war to all the World,
And thus begin it— *(runs at Iphigene)*

Iphi. What haſt thou done —*(falls)*

Franc. Ah me, help, help ——*(wounds Francelia)*

Iphi. Hold

Alm. 'Tis too late.

Iphi, Rather then ſhe ſhall ſuffer,
My fond deceits involve the innocent;
I will diſcover all.

Alm. Ha! what will he diſcover? —

Iphi. That which ſha'll make thee curſe
The blindneſs of thy rage.— *I am a woman.*

Alm. Ha, ha, ha, brave and bold!
Becauſe thy perjury deceived me once,
And ſaved thy life, thou thinkeſt to eſcape agen.
Impoſtor, thus thou ſhalt,——— *(runs at him.*

V, i, 17. There is no exeunt at the end of the scene.

Iphi. Oh hold—I have enough.
Had I hope of life, thou ſhould'ſt not have this ſecret.
Franc. What will it be now?
Iphi.— My Father having long deſir'd
A ſon to heir his great poſſeſſions,
And in ſix births ſucceſſively deceiv'd,
Made a raſh vow; oh how raſh vows are puniſhed!
That if the burthen then my mother went with
Prov'd not a male, he ne're would know her more.
Then was unhappy *Iphigene* brought forth,
And by the womens kindneſs nam'd a Boy;
And ſince ſo bred: (a cruel pitty as
It hath fallen out.) If now thou find'ſt that, which
Thou though'ſt a friendſhip in me, Love; forget it.
It was my joy,— and—death. ——(*faints.*
Alm. ——— For curioſity
'Ile ſave thee, if I can, and know the end
If't be but loſs of Blood;——— Breaſts!
By all that's good a woman'—*Iphigene.*
Iphi. I thank thee, for I was faine aſleep, before
I had diſpatcht. Sweeteſt of all thy ſexe,
Francelia, forgive me now; my love
Unto this man, and fear to loſe him, taught me
A fatal cunning, made me court you,— and
My own deſtruction. [*Franc.*] I am amaz'd.
Alm. And can it be? Oh mockery of heaven!
To let me ſee what my ſoul often wiſht,
And mak't my puniſhment, a puniſhment,
That were I old in ſins, were yet too great.
Iphi. Would you have lov'd me then? Pray ſay you woul'd;
For I, like teſtie ſickmen at their death,
Would know no news but health from the Phyſitian.
Alm. Can'ſt thou doubt that,
That haſt ſo often ſeen me extaſi'd,
When thou wert dreſt like woman,
Unwilling ever to beleeve thee man?
Iph. I have enough.
Alm. Heavens!

What thing ſhall I appear unto the world!
Here might my ignorance find ſome excuſe.
—————————— But, there,
I was diſtracted. None but one enrag'd
With anger to a ſavageneſs, would ere
Have drawn a ſword upon ſuch gentle ſweetneſs.
Be kind, and kill me; kill me one of you:
Kill me if't be but to preſerve my wits.
Deare *Iphigene*, take thy revenge, it will
Not miſbecome thy ſexe at all; for 'tis
An act of pity, not of cruelty,
Thus to diſpatch a miſerable man.
Franc. And thou wouldſt be more miſerable yet,
While like a bird made priſoner by it ſelf,
Thou beat'ſt and beat'ſt thy ſelf againſt every thing,
And do'ſt paſs by that which ſhould let thee out.
Alm. ———— Is it my fault?
Or heaven's? Fortune when ſhe would play upon me,
Like ill Muſitians, wound me up ſo high,
That I muſt crack ſooner then move in tune.
Franc. Still you rave,
While we for want of preſent help may periſh.
Alm. Right.
A Surgeon, I'le goe find one inſtantly.
The enemy too — I had forgot ——
Oh what fatality govern'd this night.
Exit.
Franc. How like an unthrifts caſe will mine be now?
For all the wealth he loſes ſhifts but 's place;
And ſtill the world enjoyes it: and ſo wil't you
Sweet *Iphigene*, though I poſſeſs you not.
Iphi. What excellence of Nature's this! have you
So perfectly forgiven already, as to
Conſider me a loſs? I doubt which Sexe
I ſhall be happier in. Climates of Friendſhip
Are not leſſe pleaſant, 'cauſe they are leſs ſcortching
Then thoſe of Love; and under them wee'l live:
Such poetrious links of that wee'l tye our ſouls
Together with, that the chains of the other

186 *The Tragedy*

Shall be grosse fetters to it. [*Franc.*] But I fear
I cannot stay the making. Oh would you
Had never un-deceiv'd me, for I'had dy'd with
Pleasure, beleeving I had been your Martyr.
Now ———
Iphi. She looks pale *Francelia* —
Franc. ——— ——— I cannot stay;
A hasty summons hurries me away:
And — gives — no — (*dies*)
Iphi. — ——— ——— Shee's gone,
She's gone. Life like a Dials hand hath stolne
From the fair figure e're it was perceiv'd.
What will become of me?— Too late, too late
Y'are come: you may perswade wild birds, that wing
The air, into a Cage, as soon as call
Her wandring spirits back.— ha!
Those are strange faces; there's a horror in them:
And if I stay, I shall be taken for
The murtherer. O in what streights they move
That wander 'twixt death, feares and hopes of love.
Exit.

A noise within, Enter Soldiers. She thinks them Almer.

Enter *Brennoral*, *Granivlet*, *Soldiers*.

Bren. Forbear, upon your lives, the place:
There dwells divinity within it. All else.
The Castle holds, is lawful prize,
Your valors wages. This I claim as mine,
Guard you the door ———
Grani. Coronel, shall you use all the women your self?
Bren. Away— 'tis unseasonable— (*draws the curtain*)
Awake fair Saint and blesse thy poor Idolator.
Ha! — pale? — and cold? — dead
The sweetest guest fled, murdered by heaven;
The purple streames not dry yet.
Some villaine has broke in before me,
Rob'd all my hopes: but I will find him out,
And kick his soul to hell— Ile doe't — { *dragging out Iphigene.*
Speak.
Iphi. What should I say?

Almerin
Soldier

of Brennoralt. 187

Iph. Alas, I do confess my self the unfortunate cause.
Bren. Oh d'you so.
Hadst thou been cause of all the plagues
That vex mankind, th'adst been an Innocent
To what thou art; thou shalt not think repentance. (*kils her*
Iph. Oh, thou wert too suddain.
And ——— (*dies.*
Bren. Was I so?
The lustful youth would sure have spoil'd her honor:
Which finding highly guarded, rage, and fear
To be reveal'd, counsell'd this villany. *Exeunt.*
Is there no more of them?
Enter *Almerin*.
Alm. Not enter?
Yes dogge, through thee — ha! a Coarse laid out
Instead of *Iphigene*: *Francelia* dead too? — *Enter Bren.*
Where shall I begin to curse
Bren. Here ——— If he were thy friend.
Alm. *Brennoralt.*
A gallant sword could ne're have come
In better time.
Bren. I have a good one for thee,
If that will serve the turn.
Alm. I long to trie it,
That sight doth make me desperate;
Sick of my self and the World.
Bren. Didst value him?
A greater villain did I never kill.
Alm Kill?
Bren. Yes.
Alm. Art sure of it?
Bren. May be I do not wake.
Alm. Th'ast taken then a guilt off from me,
Would have weigh'd down my sword,
Weakned me to low resistance.
I should have made no sports, hadst thou conceal'd it.
Know *Brennoralt* thy sword is stain'd in excellence,
Great as the World could coast. ———

V, ii, 142. The noises off were not warned.
V, ii, 147. The entrance of Brennoralt and the others was correctly advanced. They obviously enter before Iphigene's speech is completed.

V, ii, 182. Brennoralt's reentrance was not warned or cued, but he had left the stage for only a few lines.

188 *The Tragedy*

Bren. Ha—ha—how thou art abus'd?
Look there, there lies the excellence
Thou ſpeak'ſt of murdred; by him too;
He did confeſs he was the cauſe.
Alm. Oh Innocence ill underſtood, and much worſe us'd!
She was alas by accident, but I,
I was the cauſe indeed.
Bre. I will beleeve thee too, and kill thee—
Deſtroy all cauſes till I make a ſtop
In nature; for to what purpoſe ſhould ſhe
Work agen?
The last Scene
Alm. Bravely then;
The Title of a Kingdome is a trifle
To our quarrel Sir; know by ſad miſtake
I kil'd thy Miſtreſs *Brennoralt*,
And thou kild'ſt mine.
Bren. Thine?
Alm. Yes, that *Iphigene*,
Though ſhown as man unto the world,
Was woman, excellent woman—
Bren. I underſtand no riddles, guard thee.— (*Fight and*
Alm. O could they now look down, (*pauſe.*
And ſee how we two ſtrive,
Which firſt ſhould give revenge,
They would forgive us ſomething of the crime.
Hold prethee give me leave
To ſatisfie a curioſity—
I never kiſſed my *Iphigene* as woman.
Bren. Thou motion'ſt well, nor have I taken leave (*Riſing.*
It keeps a ſweetneſs yet——
As ſtills from Roſes, when the flowrs are gone.
Alm. Even ſo have two faint Pilgrims ſcorch't with heat,
Unto ſome neighbor fountain ſtept aſide,
Kneel'd firſt, then laid their warm lips to the Nymph,
And from her coldneſs took freſh life again,
As we do now——
Bren. Lets on our journey if thou art refreſht.
Alm. Come, and if there be a place reſerved
For

of Brennoralt. 189

For heighned ſpirits better then other,
May that which wearies firſt of ours have it. (*Fight a*
Bren. If I grow weary laugh at me, that's all. (*good while.*
Alm. —— Brave ſouls above which will (*Alm.* fals.
Be (ſure) inquiſitive for news from earth,
Shall get no other but that thou art Brave.
Enter *King*, *Stratheman*, *Lords*, *Minſe*
Stra. To preſerve ſome Ladies as we gueſt.
King. Still gallant *Brennoralt*, thy ſword not ſheath'd yet?
Buſie ſtill?——
Bren. Revenging Sir
The fowleſt murder ever blaſted ears,
Committed here by *Almerin* and *Iphigene*.
Alm. Falſe falſe; the firſt created purity
Was not more innocent then *Iphigene*.
Bren. Lives he agen?
Alm. Stay thou much wearied gueſt,
Till I have thrown a truth amongſt them——
We ſhall look back elſe to poſterity.
King. What ſays he?
Lord. Something concerning this he labors to
Diſcover.
Alm. Know it was I that kild *Francelia*.
I alone——
Minſ. O barberous return of my civilities!
Was it thy hand?
Alm. Hear and forgive me *Minſe*.
Entring this morning haſtily
With reſolution to preſerve
The fair *Francelia*, I found a thief
Stealing the treaſure (as I thought)
Belong'd to me. Wild in my mind
As ruin'd in my honor, in much miſtaken rage
I wounded both: then (oh) too late I found
My error: Found *Iphigene* a woman,
Acting ſtolne love, to make here own love ſafe,
And all my jealouſies impoſſible,
Whilſt I ran out to bring them cure;

V, ii, 215. *The last scene*, as in the promptbook for *Aglaura*, is similar to an act-end warning, but here it is placed closer to the end of the play, and it serves as a warning for only one entrance, not several.

Francelia dies ; and *Iphigene* found here ;
I can no more —— (*dies*)
King. Moſt ſtrange and intricate!
Iphigene a woman ?
Mel. With this ſtory I am guiltily acquainted,
The firſt concealments, ſince her love,
And all the ways to it I have been truſted with :
But Sir my grief joyned with the inſtant buſineſs
Beggs a deferment.
King. I am amaz'd till I do hear it out.
—— But ith' mean time,
Leaſt in theſe miſts merit ſhould loſe it ſelf,
——Thoſe forfeitures
Of *Trock* and *Menſeck* and *Brennoralt* are thine.
Bren. A Princely guilt ! But Sir it comes too late.
Like Sun-beams on the blaſted bloſſoms, do
Your favors fall : you ſhould have given me this
When't might have rais'd me in mens thoughts, and made
Me equal to *Francelia's* love : I have
No end, ſince ſhe is not ——
Back, to my private life I will return.
"Cattel, though weary, can trudg homewards, after.
King. This melancholy, time muſt cure : Come take
The bodies up, and lead the priſoners on ;
Triumph and Funerals muſt walk together,
Cypreſſe and Laurel twin'd make up one chaplet.
—— For we have got
The day ; but bought it at ſo dear a rate,
The victory it ſelfe's unfortunate. Ring— *Exeunt*

FINIS.

THE

WITTIE

FAIRE ONE.

A Comedie.

As it was preſented at the Private Houſe in DRVRY Lane.

By her Maieſties Servants.

By IAMES SHIRLEY.

HOR. SERM. lib. I.

Men' moveat cimex Pantilvis? aut crucier, quod
Vellicet abſentem Demetrius?
——————— *Demetri, teque Tigelli*
Diſcipulorum inter iubeo plorare Cathedras.

LONDON
Printed by *B. A.* and *T. F.* for WIL. COOKE, and are to be ſold at his ſhop, neere *Furnivals-Inne* Gate, in *Holborne*. 1633.

The Wittie Faire One by James Shirley. Reproduced by permission of the Bodleian Library, Oxford.

1633

TO THE TRVELY NOBLE KNIGHT

Sir EDWARD BVSHELL.

Ir, your candide censure of some vnworthy Poems which I haue presented to the world, long since made me your Seruant in my thoughts, and being vnwilling to rest long in the silent contemplation of your Noblenesse, I presumed at last to send this Comedy, *to kisse your hand, as the first degree to my greater happinesse in your more particular knowledge of me; It wanted no grace on the Stage, if it appeare acceptable to you in this new trimme of the Presse, it will improoue abroad, and you oblige the Author to acknowledge a fauour beyond the first applause. Pardon the rudenesse of my publike addresse to you, in the number of many whom which more excuse, I might haue interrupted. I am bold, but your mercy will incline you not to despise these (at the worst) but errors of my devotion, and the weak expression of his seruice, whose desires are to be knowne,*

Your true Honourer,

IAMES SHIRLEY.

A 2

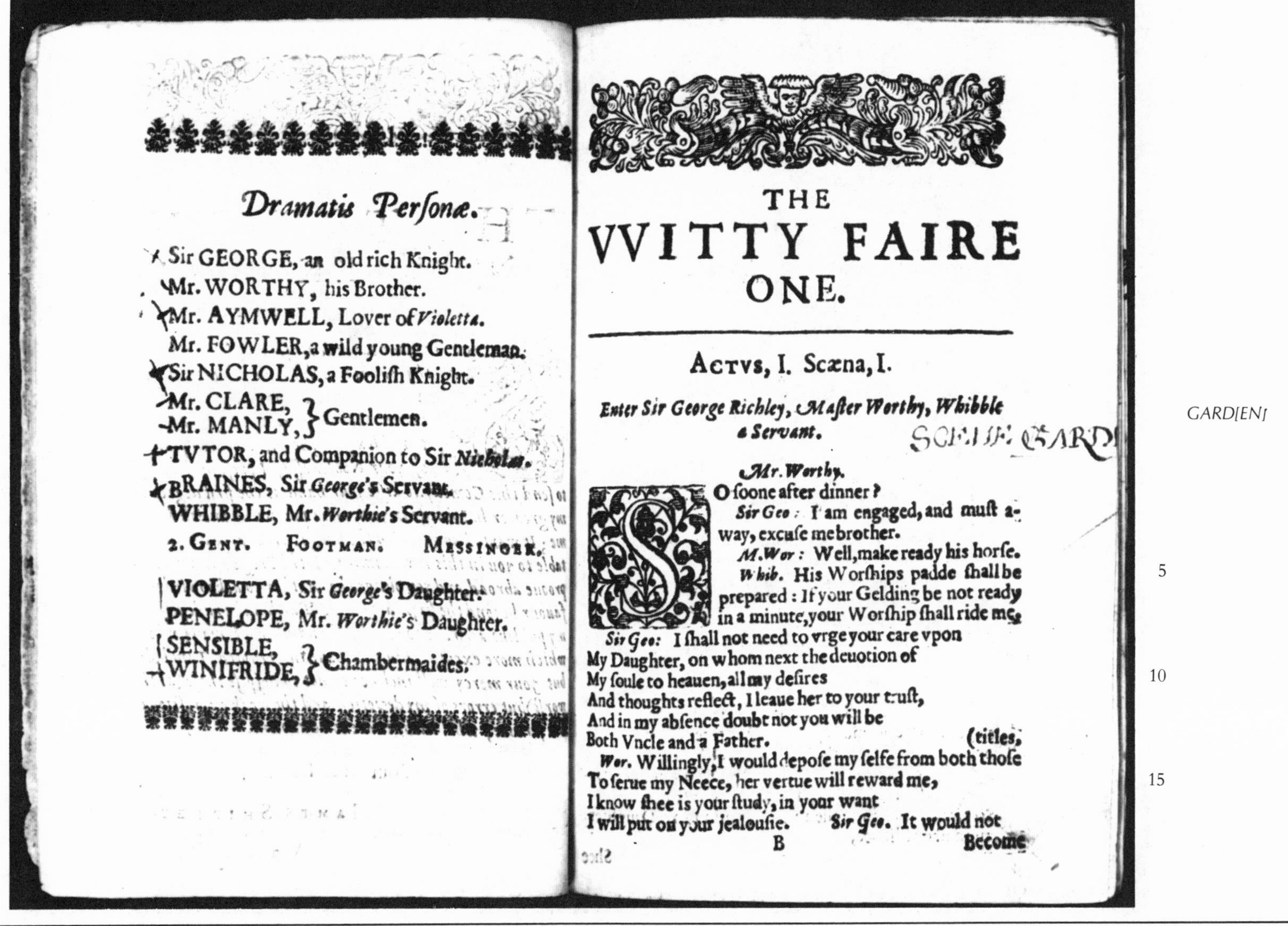

Dramatis Personæ.

Sir GEORGE, an old rich Knight.
Mr. WORTHY, his Brother.
Mr. AYMWELL, Lover of *Violetta*.
Mr. FOWLER, a wild young Gentleman.
Sir NICHOLAS, a Foolish Knight.
Mr. CLARE, } Gentlemen.
Mr. MANLY, }
TVTOR, and Companion to Sir *Nicholas*.
BRAINES, Sir *George's* Servant.
WHIBBLE, Mr. *Worthie's* Servant.
2. GENT. FOOTMAN. MESSINGER.

VIOLETTA, Sir *George's* Daughter.
PENELOPE, Mr. *Worthie's* Daughter.
SENSIBLE, } Chambermaides.
WINIFRIDE, }

THE
VVITTY FAIRE
ONE.

ACTVS, I. Scæna, I.

Enter Sir George Richley, Master Worthy, Whibble a Servant.

SCENE GARD[EN]

Mr. Worthy.
SO soone after dinner?
Sir Geo: I am engaged, and must away, excuse me brother.
M. Wor: Well, make ready his horse.
Whib. His Worships padde shall be prepared: If your Gelding be not ready in a minute, your Worship shall ride me.
Sir Geo: I shall not need to vrge your care vpon
My Daughter, on whom next the deuotion of
My soule to heauen, all my desires
And thoughts reflect, I leaue her to your trust,
And in my absence doubt not you will be
Both Vncle and a Father. (titles,
Wor. Willingly, I would depose my selfe from both those
To serue my Neece, her vertue will reward me,
I know shee is your study, in your want
I will put on your jealousie. *Sir Geo.* It would not

B Become

GARD[EN]

I, i, 14 ff. Faint pencil note: probably *Aymwell / Fowler / Clare*, as in the forthcoming stage direction. In the 1660s the pencil notes were doubtless quite readable. Because of their unusual nature, transcriptions of the pencil marginalia have been put here in the footnotes.

The witty Faire one

Become me to confine your entertainments,
Of friends and viſitants,but remember Brother,
Shee's now my ſole heyre, and by the late death
Of her twinne Siſter,ſhee deriues the right
Of all my wealth to her, Gallants I feare
I'th Towne hold too fruitfull intelligence
In theſe affaires, and if they be not watched
They'l with their wit charme all the Dragons guard,their
golden apples. *Worth.* There are ſuch indeed.
Sir Geo. Oh ſir, there are too many, not a Virgin
Left by her friends heyre to a noble fortune,
But ſhee's in danger of a Marriage
To ſome puft Title, what are theſe enter the Garden?

Enter Aymwell, Fowler, and Clare.

Wor. The Gentlemen that din'd with vs —
Aymw *Fow.* Why how now *Franck*,grown muſty on a ſud-dain?
Head hung, and playing the thiefe thus with your friends,
to ſteale your perſon from vs, what's the matter.
Aym. Nothing, nothing Gentlemen.
Clare. Very like, and yet you leaue our company for this
nothing.
Fow. Let's in againe to the Ladies. *Sir Geo.* What's he?
Wor. One Maſter *Fowler* a reputed wit
I'th Towne, affected by young Gentlemen
For his Converſe, yet liues vpon no penſion
But his owne Fortune,and a Faire one.
Th'other Mr. *Clare*, a friend to Mr. *Aymwell*, whom they
both ſeeme to ſollicite.
Sir Geo. Mr. *Aymwell*. *Wor.* A hopefull Gentleman.
Sir Geo. Brother, did you not obſerue at dinner
His eyes ſhoote beames vpon my Daughter (more
Then I was pleas'd with) Mr. *Aymwell* call you him,
I may ſuſpect vniuſtly, but ſuch lookes are often looſe con-
veyers. *Wor.* Make no part of him your feare.
Sir Geo. I doe not, when I call to mind my Daughters
vertue and obedience,
Shee

The witty Faire one.

Shee knowes my purpoſe to diſpoſe her to
Sir *Nicolas Treedle*.
Wor. And how doe you find her inclination?
Sir Geo. As I would direct it.
Wor. She will maintaine it to your comfort Sir,
How euer with what vigilance becomes me,
I will preſerue it,while ſhee remaines within my cuſtody.
Sir Geo. Ile leaue a Seruant to waite vpon her.
Wor. Braines. *Sir Geo.* The ſame.
Wor. He is a cunning fellow. *Sir Geo.* He has a ſconce,
Carryes ſome ſubtilty which he employes
Still honeſtly in diſcharge of any truſt committed to him.
Wor. Good. *Sir Geo.* And 'tis his pride.
He was nere o're-reached in any action.
Wor. He knowes his charge.
Sir Geo. Perfectly,but I looſe time, Sir *Nicolas*
Treedle expects me, this night i'the Countrey.
Wor. When dee returne?
Sir Geo. Within theſe three dayes at moſt,
Trouble your ſelfe no further.
Wor. Ile waite on you to your horſe Sir. *Exeunt.*

Enter Mr. Aymwell.

Aym. Sh'as ſhot a fire into my boſome, from
Her eye, or I haue drawne in,at mine owne,
Loue poyſon. Oh my ſtarres were too vngentle
To poynt her out the Miſtris of my thoughts,
Who is ſo much like them, aboue the hope
Of euer clyming too, I ſee a fatall
Impoſſibility deuide vs, yet
The more I would diſcharge this new gueſt, it
Strengthens it ſelfe within mee,and renewes
Vigour to keepe poſſeſſion, ſhe's aboue mee
And her great fortune makes my expectation
So dull and painfull, a great heyre her vncle?

Enter Mr. Worthy.

Wor. Mr. *Aymwell* what alone, come lets
To cards,where be the Gentlemen. *Aym.* Within Sir,
B 2 Has

I, i, 53. Faint pencil note: *Aymwe[ll]*.
I, i, 74. Faint pencil note: *Worth[y]*.
I, i, 76. Faint pencil note: *Vyolet[ta]*.

The witty Faire one.

H'as Sir *George Richley* left vs?
Wor. Some affaires importun'd his departure.
Aym. When shall wee expect him?
Wor. Three dayes hence: this your enquirie
Doth promise you haue busi nesse with him. *Aym.* Little,
But you did motion cards, Ile chuse my partner
And for a set or two I'me at your seruice.
Wor. Make your owne election.
Aym. Why dee mocke mee. *Wor.* How mocke you.
Aym. Yes? *Wor.* You doe not meane in earnest.
Aym. I shall be ray my passion *Wor.* I find him.
Aym. You may for I am lost. *Enter Mrs. Violette.*
Vio. Hee's here —good Vncle, is my father gone?
Wor. Yes, gentle Neece.
Vio. Delight in both your walkes
Ile take this Arbor.
Aym. So breakes the day and hides it selfe agen
Among the Westerne shades, were shee to dwell
Within your garden it should need no sunne,
Her smiles were powerfull to infuse a warmth
Into the flowers, her breath perfume your arbours
The trees grow rich in blossome and beare fruit
At the same instant, as 'twere euer Spring
And euer Summer when shee seates her selfe
Within some bower, the feathered Quiristers
Shall play theyr musicke to her and take pride
To warble aery notes till shee be weary,
Which when shee shall but with one Accent of
Her owne expresse, an hundred Nightingales
Shall fall downe dead from the soft boughes before her
For griefe to be orechaunted. *Wor.* Here's pretty madnes
Aym. 'Tis so, you haue done my passion iustice Sir
For loue is but a stragling from our reason.
Wor. If you doe loue my Neece, let you and I
Talke out of Metaphor. *Aym.* You know my Father.
Wor. Hee was my noble friend.
Aym. For his sake, giue me your free answere to
One question. *Wor.* What is't, promise your selfe
Wh

The witty Faire one.

What I can doe or say is at your seruice.
Aym. Is there a possibility, admit
I loved your Neece, shee might be wonne at last
To be my wife. *Wor.* Ile not dispute the extent
Of what is possible, yet my answere may be
Satisfactory. *Aym.* You were ever generous.
Wor. I were vnciuill not to reply to
A question, you shall finde my loue more fruitfull.
You shall haue both my answere and my counsell.
Aym. Let me imbrace a perfect friend.
Wor. D'ee know what
Fortune my young Neece may bring her husband.
Aym. I guesse a great one, but I set more value
Vpon her person, my affection springs
Not from her wealth. *Wor.* But yet her portion
Is worth your taking notice Master *Aymwell*,
Her Father is a man who though he write
Himselfe but Knight, keepes a warme house i'th Countrey
'Mongst his Tenants, takes no Lordly pride
To trauell with a Footman and a Page
To *London*, humbly rides 'th old fashion
With halfe a douzen wholesome Liueries,
To whom he gives Christian wages and not countenance
Alone to liue on, can spend by th' yeare
Eight hundred pounds, and put vp fine sleepes quietly
Without dreaming on Morgages or Statutes I
Or such like curses on his Land, can number
May be ten thousand pound in ready coyne
Of's owne, yet neuer bought an office for't,
Ha's plate no question, and Iewels too
In's old Ladies cabinet, beside
Other things worth an Inuentory, and all this
His daughter is an heyre too, now pray tell mee
What's your reuenue? *Aym.* Some 3. hundred pounds.
Wor. *Per annum?* Grant it, what expectation
Haue you abroad? *Aym.* None.
Wor. That's quickly summon'd.
You haue not made your loue knowne to my Neece yet.
B 3 *Aym.* No,

I, i, 150. I cannot imagine what *2 fro* means.

The witty Faire one.

Aym. No, my intention was to preacquaint you.
Wor. Y'haue done wiſely, doe not thinke on her
When y'are at prayers, ſhe will but puzzell
Your deuotion, theres no hope of her. *Aym.* Ha!
Wor. I meane for you to arriue at her, your owne diſpa-
rity in fortune. *Aym.* I doe finde it.
Wor. Excuſe my plainneſſe ſir, her Father lookes
A great deale higher, and to take away
Your leaſt incouragement, to proſecute
Within my knowledge ſhe's deſign'd already
To a wealthy Gentleman, and within few dayes
'Twill be a marriage, you ſhall but procure
Your owne affliction to employ your hope
Where things remaine ſo deſperate. *Aym.* I thanke you.
Wor. you doe your ſelfe more right. *Aym.* If ſuch affaires
Haue paſt, it were not noble to continue
This path, y'aue done me gentle office Sir
I muſt beleeue y'are generous, this new flame
My reaſon ſhall ſuppreſſe, before it growe
Too mighty for mee. *Wor.* It becomes you well,
Loue like to ſinne, inueterate is ſtrong
He preuents danger, that deſtroyes it yong.
Wor. Come to your freinds. *Exeunt.*

Enter Fowler, Penelope, Clare.

Fow. Your ſoft Starres will not let you be ſo cruell
Lady, to giue repulſe to a louer.
Cla. Doe not belieue him, he does but complement,
I ha' knowne him court a hundred, with as much
Formalitie, wooed 'em ith nuptiall cut, made verſes
O' their haire, ſet Lillies and Roſies, a whole
Garden i'their cheekes, cherries i'their lippes, ſtellifie their eyes, and yet in a twinckling. —
Penel. Sure you doe him wrong ſir. *Clare.* Wrong?
Fow. He meaſures my affection by the length of his own,
Prethee Satyre chuſe another walke, and leaue vs to inioy this, thou knowſt not my intent.
Cla. Thou mayſt be honeſt with one, and that's a miracle
and

The witty Faire one.

and will aske a ſtrong faith to beleeue it, I hope ſhee has more wit then to truſt your voluble courtſhip, Ile ſeeke out my friend *Aymwell.* *Vio. comes from the Arbor.*

Viol. Sir, if your engagement require no haſt.

Penel. I doe wonder a Gentleman of your knowledge ſhould ſo deceiue himſelfe.

Fow. Expreſſe your ſelfe Faireſt.

Penel. Faire ſir, I am not taken with your flatteries, I can ſee through you.

Fow. If you haue ſo actiue an eye Lady, you may ſee a throng of Paſſions flaming at my hart, ſet a fire by your beauty I proteſt t'ee; come, ſhame not your wiſdome to beleeue report or opinion ath'world, 'tis a malicious age we liue in, if your eares haue beene abuſed with any ill noiſe, a me you ſhall tell your ſelfe if you loue me, the world is a ſhameleſſe and miſerable detractor, you doe not deſpiſe me Lady. —

Penel. No, I pitty ſo handſome a Gentleman, and of So faire a fortune, ſhould want his eyes.

Fow. How blind? *Penel.* To your owne follies ſir.

Fow. Shall I ſweare I loue you, as I am a Gentleman.

Pen. As you are a Gentleman, I know you can ſweare any thing t'is a faſhion y'are moſt conſtant in, to bee religiouſly wicked, an oath in your mouth and a reſeruation in your heart is a common Courtſhip, doe not ſweare as you are a Gentleman. *Fow.* As I am an honeſt man.

Penel. Out vpon't, that's a worſe, my Taylor couzened me t'oher day with the ſame oath, ſaue your credit and let ſwearing alone, I dare take your word.

Fow. Well ſayd.

Penel. For a greater matter, but not for this, you and I ha not eaten a buſhell of ſalt yet, in time I may be conuerted, and thinke your tongue and heart keepe houſe together, for at this time I preſume they are very farre aſunder.

Fow. Would you haue my tongue in my heart Lady?

Penel. No by my troth, I would rather finde your heart in your tongue, but you are valiant, and 'tis onely feare they ſay, brings a mans heart vp to his mouth.

Fow. Why.

I, i, 164 ff. Faint pencil note: *[Pe]nelope / [Fo]wler / [Cl]are.*

I, i, 200. There are three indecipherable lines in the right margin.

The Witty Faire one.

Fow. Why, your wit is a tyrant now, pray tell me doe not you loue me mightily now aboue Potatoes, come I ſee the little blind Boy in your eyes already.

Pen. Loue you Sir?

Fow. Yes, I know by your bitterneſſe you wiſh me well and thinke there is ſome hope I may be wonne too, you take paines to whip me ſo handſomely, come Ile be a good child and kiſſe the rod.

Cla. You oblige my ſeruice to you, I am one
Aymwell called friend, and ſhall be happy to
Convay him any knowledge may concerne him.

Vio. Then briefly thus I vnderſtand he loues mee
Pray you doe him the true office of a friend
And councell him deſiſt, I am diſpos'd of
Already in my fathers thoughts, and muſt
Shew my obedience, he ſhall beget
But his owne trouble, if he moue it to
My Vnckle or my Father, and perhaps
Draw their ſuſpition and diſpleaſure
On me too, by ſo indiſcreet proceeding,
I would not haue a Gentleman of his worth
Doe himſelfe ſo great iniury to runne
A courſe of ſo much hazard, if you pleaſe
To beare the burden of my thankes for his
On my part vndeſeru'd opinion,
And make him ſenſible, in time hee may
Place his affection where he may expect
Better returne, you ſhall diſcharge a friendſhip
To him, and with it make my thoughts your debtor.

Cla. You haue expreſt a nobleneſſe in this
Were all of your mind Lady,
There would be leſſe Willow worne.

Fow. You would ha' me praiſe you now, I could ramble in your commendation. *Pen.* I thinke ſo.

Fow. Dee but thinke ſo, why you ſhall heare mee, Your hayres are *Cupids* Nets, a Forehead like the fayreſt coaſt of heauen without a cloud, your eybrow is loues bow

whiles

The witty Faire one.

whiles eyther Eye are arrowes drawne to wound, your lips the Temple or ſacred phane of kiſſes often as they meete exchanging Roſes, your tongue Loues lightning, necke the Milky path or throne where ſit the Graces, doe not I know that I haue abuſed you all this while, or doe you thinke I loue you a thought the better, or withall my Poeticall daubings can alter the complection of a hayre now.

Pen. I would not haue you ſir.

Fow. No diſpraiſe te'e
I haue ſeene as handſome a woman
Ride vpon a ſacke to Market, that neuer knew the impulſion of a Coate or the price of a Stammell petticoate, and I ha ſeene a worſe face in a Counteſſe; what's that? Muſt ye be proud becauſe men doe call you handſome, and yet though wee are ſo fooliſh to tell you ſo, you might haue more wit then to beeleeue it, your eyes may be matcht I hope, for your noſe there be richer in our ſexe, t'is true that you haue colour for your hayre wee graunt it, and for your cheekes, but what doe your teeth ſtand you in Lady, your lips are pretty but you lay 'em too open and men breath too much vpon 'em, for your tongue wee all leaue you ther's no conteſting, your hand is fine but your gloues whiter, and for your leg, if the commendation or goodneſſe of it bee in the ſmall, there be bad enow in Gentlemens ſtockings to compare with it; come remember y'are imperfect creatures without a man, be not you a Goddeſſe I know y'are mortall, and had rather make you my companion then my Idoll, this is no flattery now.

Enter Worthy, Aymwell, Braines.

Wor. Where be theſe Gentlemen.

Fow. How now *Franck*.

Wor. You looke well to your charge *Braines*.

Bra. A queſtion Sir, pray you, are you married Sir?

Cla. Why doſt thou aske?

Bra. Becauſe you ſhould anſwere me
I cannot ſee't in your forehead Sir.

Cla. How now my officious Trencher ſquire.

C *Wor.* Ex-

I, i, following 273. Faint pencil note: *Worthy / Aymwe[ll] / Brain[es].*

Wor. Excuse him Master *Clare*, t'is his blunt zeale
To doe his Master seruice, who enioy'd
His best care and vigilance vpon this
Gentlewoman. ***Cla.*** I am married Sir.

Bra. Then I hope y'aue met with your match already I ha nothing to say tee. ***Cla.*** This fellow's mad.

Bra. Nor my Master neither, though he left his braines behind him, I hope a man may aske a question Sir.

Wor. Come hither *Braines*.

Fow. A me life thou art in loue. ***Cla.*** You are not.

Fow. Doe not mistake your selfe for I am.

Cla. Caught, I am glad on't.

Fow. No indeed not caught neyther, therefore be not ouerioy'd good morality, why dost thou thinke it possible a womans face or any thing without her can inchaunt me.

Bra. Let me alone. (*Exit Uncle.*

Cla. Why dost thou court 'em then.

Fow. Why, to try their wits with which I sharpen my owne, dost thinke I am so mad to marry, sacrifice my liberty to a Woman, sell my patromony to buy them Feathers and new fashions, and maintaine a Gentleman Vsher to ride in my saddle when I am Knighted, and pointed at with *Pythagoras* for my tame sufferance, ha my Wardrop laid forth and my holiday breeches when my Lady pleases I shall take the ayre in a Coach with her, together with her Dog that is costiue, bee appointed my table what I shall eate, according as her Ladiship findes her owne body inclin'd, fed vpon this or that Melancholy dish by prescription, guarded with officious Sallets like a Prisoner in a throng, praise her beautifull allowance of course Mutton that haue the world of dainty flesh before me, 'twere a sinne to discretion and my owne freedome.

Bra. Young Mistris, I obserue you.

Cla. You doe not meane to dye in this faith.

Fow. Prethee doe not talke of Dying, a pox o'the Belman and his *Omniabenes*, but that I thinke I know thy Father, I should hardly belieue thou wert a Gentleman, how-

euer thy *Aristotles Ethicks* will make thee vncapable of their company shortly, if you Catechise thus you shall haue few Gentlemen your Disciples that haue any bloud or spirit about 'em, there's no discourse so becomming your Gallants now, as a Horse race or *Hide*-Parke? what Ladies lips are softest? what Fashion is most terse and Courtly? what newes abroad? which is the best Vaulting house? where shall we taste Canary and be drunke too night, talke a morality — heere be Ladies still, you shall heare me court one on 'em, I hope you wee' not report abroad among my friends that I loue her, 'tis the loue of mounting into her maydenhead I vow *Jacke*, and nothing else.

Cla. Y'are a mad Louer. *As Aymwell comes towards*

Bra. That was cunningly cast about. *Violetta she turnes*

Fow. Whither is't Lady? *and Exit.*

Pen. I'me walking in Sir.

Fow. I'le wayt on you, and after that abroad, 'tis an inuiting day, are you for the Coach. ***Penel.*** No.

Fow. Or for the Couch? Take mee a Companion for either. ***Penel.*** Neither.

Fow. How neither, blame your selfe if you be idle,
Howsoeuer you shall not be alone, make vse of
My arme Fairest, you will to your Lute, I heard you
Could touch it cunningly, pray blesse my eares a little.

Penel. My Lute's broke sir.

Fow. A string you meane, but 'tis no matter, your voyce is not, rauish a little with that, if you please I can helpe you to an heyre by this blacke eye which Nature hath giuen you, Ile not leaue you I'le follow yee. *Exeunt Fowler, and Penelope.*

Aym. All this from her?

Cla. You may belieue me Sir.

Aym. Why this to him, could shee not giue me
Repulse, but shee must thus proclaime it, I neuer
Mou'd it to her, her Vncle hath had no opportunity
To acquaint her what's the Mystery,
Prethee repeat agen the substance of what shee said.

Cla. With my best memory her words, shee wisht you

The witty Faire one.

not proceed for ſhee was already diſpos'd of in her Fathers thoughts.

Aym. In her fathers thoughts? Happily not in her owne.

Cla. It would be fruitleſſe to moue her Vncle or her Father in't.

Aym. H,not moue her Vncle or her Father?
This may beget encouragement hope I may to her
Propound my affection and be happy in't proceed.

Cla. She would be ſory a Gentleman of your worth
Should runne a Courſe of ſo much hazard.

Aym. Hazard, that word does yet imply there is a poſ-
(ſibilitie.

Cla. So with complement
Of her thankes for your fayre opinion of her,
Shee wiſht me make you ſenſible in time
To place your Loue where you might expect
Better returne.

Aym. Ah that's wormwood, let me ſee,better returne
This laſt returne hath ſpoyl'd the whole Terme
And vndone my ſuite, vm? No it doth admit
A faire Conſtruction:
Shee would ha me ſenſible in time to plant
My loue where I may expect better returne,
Why? That I may from her for ought I know.

Cla. *Amantes ſibi ſomnia fingunt*, how apt are Louers to conſter all to their deſires.

Aym. I wonnot let my Action fall.

Cla. Doe not build Caſtles.

Aym. I'le ſmooth it with her Vncle, if it hit
Oh I my bleſt Starres.

Cla. Hee's a bed already.

Aym. *Venus* aſſiſt one to thy Altar flies,
And I'le proclaime,thy ſonne hath found his eyes. *Exeunt.*

Explicit Actus primus.

ACTVS, II.

The witty Faire one.

ACTVS, II. Scena, I.

Enter Sir Nicholas Treedle, and a Servant.

Nic. VVHere's Marre-text my Chaplaine.

Ser. He's newly walked out of his Meditation in the Kitchin, into the Garden.

Nic. Bid him reade Prayers in the Dining-roome.

Serv. Before your Worſhip come?

Nic. I wo'not pray too day, doſt heere? Bid my Tutor come downe to mee. *Serv.* Which on them.

Nic. Why hee that reades Trauaile to me, the wit that I tooke vp in *Paules* in a tiffany Cloake without a hatband, now I haue put him into a doublet of Sattaine — ſtay hee's heere. *Enter Tutor.*

Nic. Morrow Tutor, what houre take you it?

Tu. It is no houre at all Sir. *Nic.* How? (Sir.

Tu. Not directly any houre, for it is betweene 8.and 9.

Nic. Very learnedly then I was ready betweene
Six and ſeauens too day.

Tu. Are you diſpos'd for Lecture.

Nic. Yes, yes Sir.

Tu. You remember my laſt prelection of the Diuiſion
Of the Earth into parts Reall and Imaginary:
The parts reall into Continent and Iland,
The ſubdiuiſion of the Continent, into *Peninſula*,
Iſtmus, and *Promontory*.

Nic. In troth Sir, I remember ſome ſuch things but I haue forgotten 'em. *Tu* What is an *Iſtmus*?

Nic. Why an *Iſtmus*, is an Elbow of land.

Tu. A Necke, a necke.

Nic. A necke? Why I was neere it, if you had let me alone, I ſhould haue come vp too't.

Tu. 'Twas well gueſt, what's an Iland?

Nic. An Iland is an high Mountaine, which ſhooteth it ſelfe into the Sea. *Tu.* That's a *Promontory*.

C 3 *Nic.*

I, i, 393. The word *ACT* served as a warning for actors, scene shifters, and musicians (if there was any entr'acte music). In King's Company promptbooks the word *Ring* is usually found at the end of an act, serving as a cue. Not so in this book, where all five act endings are warned but not cued. This is like the pattern set by the actor warnings, which are not matched by cue signs at the entrances.

II, i, opening. Cropped note: *Cham[ber].* The Duke's Company promptbooks often contain descriptions of the setting to be used, but none contains the circle-and-dot symbol indicating a whistle cue. The troupe may have used some other system for cueing scene changes.

II, i, 2. Faint pencil note: *Tutor.*

The witty Faire one.

Nic. Is't so? An Iland then is, no matter let it goe, 'tis not the first Iland wee ha lo't.

Tu. How are you perfect in your Circles? Great & lesse, Mutable and immutable, Tropicall and Polar.

Nic. As perfect in them as I am in these, faith I shall neuer come these things and omely, may not a man study Trauaile without these Circles, Degrees and altitudes you speake of? *Tu.* Yes, you may.

Nic. I doe not care for the neerest way, I ha time enough to goe about.

Tu. Very well, you shall lay aside your Globe then.

Nic. I, and if please you I will haue it stand in my hall to make my Tenants wonder in stead of the book of *Martyrs*.

Tu. It will doe well, now name what Kingdome or Prouince you haue most minde to.

Nic. What say you to *England*.

Tut. By no meanes, it is not in fashion with Gentlemen to study their owne Nation, you will discouer a dull easinesse if you admire not and with admiration prefer e not the weedes of other regiments before the most pleasant flowers of your owne garden, let your Iudgment reflect vpon a serious consideration who teaches you the minick posture of your body, the punctuality of your beard, the formality of your pace, the elbowes of your cloake, the heele of your boote, doe not other nations? Are not *Italian* heads, *Spanish* shoulders, *Dutch* bellies, and *French* legs, the onely Notions of your reformed *English* Gentlemen.

Nic. I am resolu'd to be ignorant of my owne country, say no more on't, what think you if I went ouer to *France* the first thing I did. *Tu.* By Sea?

Nic. Doe thinke I ha no more wit then to venture my selfe i'th salt water, I had rather be pickled and powdred at home by halfe that I had.

Tu. I apprehend you are cautious, it is safe trauelling in your study, but I will not read *France* to you. *Nic.* Not?

Tu. *Pardonne moy* it is vnnecessary, all the *French* fashions are here already or rather your *French* cuts.

Nic. Cuts?

Tu. Va-

The witty Faire one.

Scene

Tu. Vnderstand me, there are diuers *French* cuts.

Nic. We haue had too many *French* cuts already.

Tu. First, there is your cut of the head.

Ni. That's dangerous.

Tu. Pshew a haire a hayre, a perriwigge is your *French* cutte and in fashion with your most courtly Gallants, your owne hayre will naturally forsake you. Brai[nes] Whib[ble]

Nic. A bald reason.

Tu. Right obseru'd their prudent and weighty pollicy who haue brought up this artificiall head-peice, because no man should appeare light headed.

Nic. He had no sound head that inuented it.

Tu. Then there is the new cut of your doublet or slash the Fashion of your apparrell a queint cut.

Nic. Vpon Taffety.

Tu. Or what you please, the slash is the embleme of your valour, and besides declareth that you are open brested.

Nic. Open as much as you will but no valour.

Tu. Then Sir, there is the cut of your leg.

Nic. That's when a man is drunke, is it not?

Tu. Doe not stagger in your iudgement, for this cut is the grace of your body, I meane dancing o'th *French* cut i'th leg is most fashionable, beleeue it pupill a gentile carriage.

Nic. But it is faine to be supported sometime with a bottome. *Enter Seruant.*

Ser. Here is Sir *George Richley* Sir newly alighted.

Nic. Oh my Father in law that shalbe.

Tu. Then wee are cut off.

Nic. There is a match concluded between his daughter and me and now he comes for my answere conduct him to the gallery. *Tu.* Rather Sir meete him.

Nic. Let him goe before and tell him we are comming, weele be there as soone as hee. *Exeunt.*

Enter Braines, Whible.

Gard. — Gard[en] [II, ii]

Whi. *Braynes.* *Bra.* What's the matter.

Whi. Lets rifle the other bottle of wine.

Bra. Doe not indanger thy sconce. *Whi.* How?

Bra. I'le

II, i, 67. Faint pencil note: *[Se]rvant.*

II, i, 71. *Scene* is used here and elsewhere in this promptbook as a warning for a scene shift within an act; it is like the whistle warnings in the King's Company *Change of Crownes* promptbook.

Bra. I'le drink no more. *Whib.* Why?

Br. Becauſe I will not be drunke for any mans pleaſure.

Wh. Drunke?

Br. Tis good *Engliſh* now, t'was *Dutch*, may bee you ha ſome conſpiracy vpon mee.

Wh. I? Who has betrayed me? his Miſtris procured the Key of the Wine-ſeller, and bad me try if I could wind vp his braines handſomely, he knowes on't not one health more.

Br. Not, not, good *Whible* if you vrge agen I ſhall ſuſ- (pect.

Wh. Suſpect me?

Br. And beate you *Whible* if you be not ſatisfied.

Wh. I am, but in friendſhip.

Br. Doſt tempt me?

Wh. I will drinke your health and be drunke alone.

Br. This whelpe has ſome plot vpon men, I ſmell powder my young Miſtris would haue blowne vp my braines this Peter-gunner ſhould haue given fire, 'tis not the firſt time ſhee hath conſpired ſo but two not doe, I was neuer yet couzned in my life, and if I pawne my braines for a bottle of Sacke, or Claret, may my noſe as a brand for my negligence carry euerlaſting *Malmeſey* in it and be ſtudded with Rubies and Carbuncles, Miſtris you muſt pardon my officiouſneſſe, be as angry as a Tyger I muſt play the Dragon and watch your golden fleece, my Maſter has put me in truſt and I am not ſo eaſily corrupted. I ha but two eyes *Argus* had a hundred, but hee muſt be a cunning *Mercury* muſt pipe them both a ſleepe I can tell you And now I talke of ſleepe, my lodging is next to her chambers, it is a confidence in my Maſter to let his Liuery lye ſo neere her, Seruingmen haue e're now proved themſelues no Eunuches, with their Maſters Daughters, if I were ſo luſty as ſome of my owne tribe, it were no great labour to commit Burglary vpon a Maydenhead, but all my nouriſhment runs vpward into braines and I am glad on't, a temperate blood is ſigne of a good Liuer, I am paſt tilting, here ſhee is with the ſecond part of her to the ſame tune, an other maide that has a grudging

grudging of the greene ſicknes, and wants a man to recouer her.

Enter Violeta and Penelope.

Pen. Be this enough betweene vs, to bind each to helpe others deſignes.

Vio. Heere's *Breynes*, hee has not yet beene drencht.

Pe. Hee is too ſubtile. *Vio.* How now *Breynes*?

Br. As you ſee forſooth. *Pen.* Thou art very ſad.

Br. But I am in ſober ſadnes I thanke my ſtarres.

Vi. Witty.

Br. As much wit as will keepe *Breynes* from melting this hot weather.

Pen. A dry whooreſon not thus to be wrought vpon,

Br. Very good Sacke and Claret ith houſe.

Pen. Thou haſt not taſted.

Bre. O yes, o yes, my braines ſwimme in Canary exceeding, excellent Sacke, I thanke yee Ladies, I know t'is your pleaſure I ſhould not want o'th beſt blood o'th grape in hope there might be a ſtone in my cup to marre my drinking afterwards. *Enter Senſible.*

Miſtris *Senſible* what jigge ithe wind ſhe moues ſo nimbly.

Pen. From whom? *Sen.* Maſter *Fowler.*

Bre. A Letter? whence flew that paper kite.

Pen. What's this?

Br. An other incloſed without direction, happily obſerued.

Pen, If you can loue I will ſtudy to deſerue and be happy to giue you proofe of my ſervice, in the meane time it ſhalbe a teſtimony of your favour to deliuer this incloſed paper to your couzen from her ſervant *Aymwell*, farewell and remember F[illegible], looke you couzen what Mr. *Fowler* writes, I dare truſt you with the ſecret at your opportunity peruſe this paper.

Bre. Conveyances, I read iugling in that paper already, and though you put it vp I wo[illegible] not, oh, for ſo much Magick to coniure that paper out of her boſome into my pocket, now I doe long to know what pittifull louer, for it

---

II, ii, following 15. Faint pencil note: *[Vi]oletta / Pe]nelope.*

II, ii, following 42. Faint pencil note: *Sensibl[e] / letter.*

II, ii, 72. Faint pencil note: *Winifred.*

can be no other, is doing penance in that white sheete already, Mistris *Sensible* harke yee; whence came that letter?

Sen. From Master *Fowler* to my Mistris.

Br. It is a shee Letter it seemes.

Sen. A shee Letter why so?

Bre. Because it had a young one it'h belly on't, or I am much mistaken.

Pen. Does he not write like a bold gamester?

Br. And a bowling gamester too, for his byas was towards my Mistres, but I may chance to cast a rub in his way to keepe him from kissing.

Vio. Hee hath very good partes in him questionlesse, but doe you loue him.

Br. O the cunning of these Gipses, how when they list they can talke in a distinguishable dialect, they call men foxes but they make tame geese a some on vs, and yet like one a those in *Rome* I may prove so happy to preserue your distressed Capitoll, what newes brings this Kickshaw.

Enter Winifred.

Win. Master *Fowler* desires to speake with you.

Bre. Already he might ha deliuered his owne Letter.

Vio. Ile to my Chamber

Bre. It will doe very well.

Vio. I hope you wilbe carefull that I am not troubled with any visit of Gentlemen, it will become your officiousnesse good *Dametas* to haue a care of your charge *Pamela*.

Br. So, I can suffer this jeare. *Exit.*

Vio. Ha? is he gone? I'me glad on't, Ile take this opportunity to reade the Paper, Master *Aymwell* sent me no superscription?

Enter Breines.

Bre. Shee's at it already, thus farre of I can read her countenance if shee spare her voyce.

Vio. *I doe not court your fortune but your loue,*
If my wild apprehension of it, proue
My error, punish gently, since the fire
Came from your selfe that kindled my desire,

So

So my poore heart full of expectance lyes
To be your seruant or your sacrifice.

Vio. It shall bee answered. *Exit.*

Bre. It shall, the games a foote, were I best to discouer thus much, or reserue it to welcome home the old Knight withall, Ile be more familiar with this iugling, first, the Scriuener has a Name and if he be worth his owne eares he shall be worth my discouery.

Enter Fowler, and Penelope.

Here comes the Gallant and the tother toy now.

Pen. I receiued your Letter Sir?

Fow. In good time.

Pen. You might haue spared your hand a labour, if you had resolved to put your feete vpon this expedition.

Bre. Good.

Fow. I confesse I wrote something in my owne cause, but the chiefe cause was to conuay my friends affection to his Mistris.

Bre. And I will convey your affection to somebody else.

Pen Then you made me a property. (*Exit.*

Fow. 'Tis for your honour if you helpe any way to aduance an honest businesse, and yet mistake me not though the Racke should enforce from me without a second reason I had not wrote to you, yet for so much as concern'd my selfe by this kisse, my pen hath but set downe the resolution of my heart to serue you.

Pen. To serue me, how?

Fow. How? why any way, giue me your Liuery I'le weare it, or a Coate with a Cognizance by this light, I feare you are an Hereticke still and doe not beleeue as you should doe, come let me rectifie your Faith, serue you.

Pen. Since the Complement of Seruice came up, Gentlemen have had excuse for their loue: I would not have you serve me Sir.

Fow. Not serve you? Why dee thinke a man cannot loue and serve too.

Pen. Not one serve two, well.

D 2 *Fow.*

II, ii, following 95. Faint pencil note: *fowler / Penelope.*

II, ii, 105. Faint and badly cropped pencil note: *[re?]ent[er].*

The witty Faire one.

Fow. You are too literall, and yet i'th strict sence I have knowne a woman has served halfe a doozen Gentlemen handsomely, so, so, and yet the last had enough of her too, why should not one man serve two Gentlewomen, it argues against your Sexe, that you are more insatiable ath' two, but I have a simple affection I protest an Individuall, Ile never serve but one.

Penel. But one at once.

Fow. but one at once, and but one alwayes, by this Dymond.

Penel. Nay keepe your oath Sir.

Fow. I am forsworne if I doe not, for I vowed before I came to bestow it, come weare it in your bosome, it shall be an earnest of more precious jewels, though not of so bright a lustre that will follow.

Penel. I pray Sir resolve me one thing, and be plaine, Doe you love me?

Fow. Love you?

Pen. 'Tis my question.

Fow. 'Tis a very foolish one, to what purpose have I beene talking all this while, that you make it a question, has not it beene the Theame of all my discourse hitherto, that I doe love you. *Pen.* In what fence?

Fow. In what fence? Why in any fence at your owne choyce, or in all the fences together and you doubt me: I doe love to see your face, heare your voyce, smell your breath, touch your tree, and taste your golden Apples.

Pen. But this does not satisfie me.

Fow. You doe not doubt my sufficiency dee?

Pen. Now you're immodest, I onely askt if you love me.

Fow. And have not I told you? Pray teach me a better way to expresse it. Does a Wiseman love Fooles fortune, and Nobleman another beside my Lady? Does the Divell love an Usurer, a Great man his Flatterer, the Lawyer a Fat Terme, or the Physitian a dead time to thrive in.

Pen. Spare your selfe, this is but course love.

Fow. Ile spin it finer and finer every day Sweet, to plaine with thee, what dost thou think of me for a husband, I love thee that way. *Pen.* Would you did else.

Fow. Is there any thing in me would commend it selfe, that I may spare my other commendations, for I am resolved to be yours at any rate of my own praise, or what I can purchase from my friends.

Pen. Sir, if your meaning be no stranger to your language, although I cannot promise my selfe, you bind me to bee thankfull for it. *Fow.* She nibbles already.

Pen. But pardon me if I suspect you still, you are too wild and aery to be constant to that affection.

Enter Braines, and Worthy.

Bra. There be the Pigeons.

Wor. An't be no worse I care not, Mr. *Fowler* A most welcome Friend.

Fow. I would be to your daughter.

Bra. Let her use to entertaine him so, and hee'l bid himselfe welcome, harke you sir, you doe like his company? *Wor.* Yes.

Bra. So I say, but if I were worthy to give your daughter counsell, she should have a speciall care how she treads, for if this Gentleman be not a Whooremaster, he is very like one; and if she chance any way to cracke her *Venice-*Glasse, 'twill not be so easily sowdred.

Wor. Meddle with your charge Sir, and let her alone.

Bra. I have done, here is a fresh Gamester. *Enter Mr. Manley.*

Man. By your noble leave.

Wor. You'r welcome Sir.

Man. I was directed hither to find a Gentleman.

Fow. *Manly* how ist?

Manl. I was to inquire for you at your lodging.

Fow. Pray know this gentleman Lady, Master *Worthy* hee'le deserve your acquaintance.

Man. You oblige my services — but what make you heere my woman ferritor.

Wor. Come hither *Penelope.*

Fow. Solliciting a cause of *Venus.*

D 3 *Man.*

II, ii, following 175. Faint pencil note: *Braines / Worthy.*

II, ii, 191. Faint pencil note: *Man[ly].*

II, ii, following 200. Faint pencil note: *Aym[well] / Cla[re] / Br[aines].*

The Witty Faire one.

Man. I ſuſpect as much, but with her? is ſhee a whoore?
Fow. No but I'le doe the beſt to make her one,
She loues me already, that's ſome engagement
I dare truſt thee with my ſinnes, who's heere
Enter Mr. Aymwell, Mr. Clare, Braines, Aymwell and *Clare.*
Wor. Withdraw your ſelfe.
Fow. Franck. *Aym.* Maſter *Worthy.*
Wor. A knot of friends.
Aym. What of my letter?
Fow. 'Tis deliuered you muſt expect.
Wor. What newes gentlemen?
Aym. We heare none, you viſit the Exchange Sir, pray furniſh vs.
Br. What doe all theſe Butterflies here, I doe not like it.
Aym. I hope your daughter is in health.
Wor. Perfect, I thanke Heauen.
Aym. And your Neece at whoſe naming I'me bolde to tender my thankes for your laſt friendſhip, I might haue plung'd by this time into paſſion had not you nobly, iuſt as I was falling preuented my vnhappineſſe.
Wor. Your opinion of what I did, giues value to the action, howeuer 'twas a duty I was bound to.
Bra. This is the youth, I'le pawne my braines, harke you Sir, what doe you call this Gentleman.
Cla. Maſter *Aymwell.*
Bra. He may ſhoote ſhort for all his ayming,
He weares Batchellers buttons does he not.
Cl. Yes, old tupeny and loopes too, thou art iealous now.
Bra. One word more.
Fow. I haue a plot and thou muſt helpe me.
Man. Let it be a ſafe one. *Aym.* May we not ſee her?
Wor. Braines where's thy Miſtris?
Bra. She's a little buſie.
Fow. Who's that. *Wor.* my Neece.
Fow. And ſhee be but a little buſy ſhee's more then halfe at leaſure.
Bra. Doe not you know that a Woman is more troubled

The witty Faire one.

led with a little buſineſſe, then ſome man with mannaging the troubles of a whole common wealth, it has beene a prouerbe, as buſy as a Hen with one Chickin, marry and ſhee had twenty, twenty to one ſhe would not be ſo fond on'em.
Wor. He ſayes right, Gentlemen, wee are friends, it is my brothers pleaſure who is her father, to deny frequent acceſſe to her, till hee hath finiſht a deſigne, for my part, I am not of his minde, nor ſhall my daughter be a priſoner to his fancy, you ſee Sir I doe not ſeclude her, if ſhee chuſe within any limits of reaſon, I moue in her.
Aym. You ſpeake nobly.

Enter Whible.

Whi. Sir *George Richley* Sir, and Sir *Nickolas* are newly arriu'd.
Wor. My brother, acquaint my Neece.
Bra. T'is my office I'le doe it — *Exit.*
Man. Shall's ſtay?
Aym. By all meanes let's ſee the doughty Knight that muſt free the Lady from her Inchaunted Caſtle.
Cla. Didſt euer ſee him?
Aym. No, but I haue heard his character.
Man. Prethee let's ha't.
Aym. They ſay hee's one, was wiſe before hee was a man for then his folly was excuſeable, but ſince hee came to be of age, which had beene a queſtion till his death, had not the Law giuen him his Fathers Lands, he is growen wicked enough to be a Landlord, he does pray but once a yeare and that's for faire weather in harueſt, his inward ſences are ſound, for none comes from him hee ſpeakes wordes but no matter, and therefore is in Election to be of the Peace and Quorum, which his Tenants thinke him fit for, and his Tutors iudgement allowes, whom he maintaines to make him legs and ſpeeches, he feedes well himſelfe, but in obedience to government, he allowes his Servants faſting dayes; he loves Law, becauſe it kild his Father, whom the Parſon

---

II, ii, 245. Faint pencil note: *[Wh]ible*.

II, ii, 276 ff. Faint pencil note: *Tuto[r] / Rich[ly] / Tred[le]*.
II, ii, 285 ff. Faint pencil note: *Brai[nes] / Pene[lope] / Viol[etta]*.
II, ii, 290 f. Faint pencil note: *Winif[red] / Sensi[ble]*.

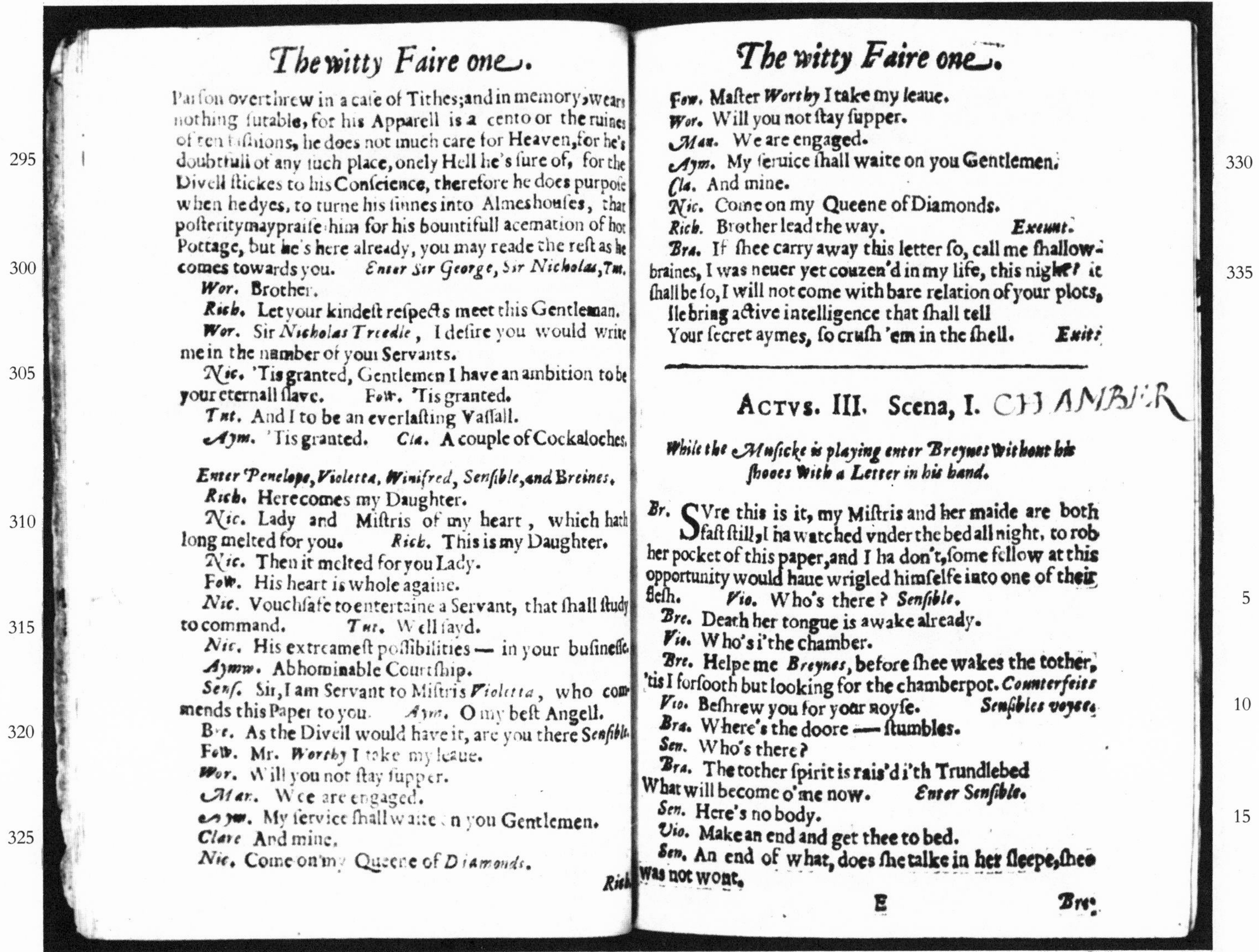

The witty Faire one.

Parson overthrew in a case of Tithes;and in memory,weares nothing sutable, for his Apparell is a cento or the ruines of ten fashions, he does not much care for Heaven,for he's doubtfull of any such place, onely Hell he's sure of, for the Divell stickes to his Conscience, therefore he does purpose when he dyes, to turne his sinnes into Almeshouses, that posterity may praise him for his bountifull acemation of hot Pottage, but he's here already, you may reade the rest as he comes towards you. *Enter Sir George, Sir Nicholas, Tut.*

Wor. Brother.

Rich. Let your kindest respects meet this Gentleman.

Wor. Sir *Nicholas Treedle*, I desire you would write me in the number of your Servants.

Nic. 'Tis granted, Gentlemen I have an ambition to be your eternall slave. *Fow.* 'Tis granted.

Tut. And I to be an everlasting Vassall.

Aym. 'Tis granted. *Cla.* A couple of Cockaloches.

Enter Penelope, Violetta, Winifred, Sensible, and Breines.

Rich. Here comes my Daughter.

Nic. Lady and Mistris of my heart, which hath long melted for you. *Rich.* This is my Daughter.

Nic. Then it melted for you Lady.

Fow. His heart is whole againe.

Nic. Vouchsafe to entertaine a Servant, that shall study to command. *Tut.* Well sayd.

Nic. His extreamest possibilities — in your businesse.

Aym. Abhominable Courtship.

Sens. Sir, I am Servant to Mistris *Violetta*, who commends this Paper to you. *Aym.* O my best Angell.

Bre. As the Divell would have it, are you there *Sensible*.

Fow. Mr. *Worthy* I take my leaue.

Wor. Will you not stay supper.

Man. Wee are engaged.

Aym. My service shall waite on you Gentlemen.

Clare And mine.

Nic. Come on my Queene of *Diamonds*.

Rich.

The witty Faire one.

Fow. Master *Worthy* I take my leaue.

Wor. Will you not stay supper.

Man. We are engaged.

Aym. My seruice shall waite on you Gentlemen.

Cla. And mine.

Nic. Come on my Queene of Diamonds.

Rich. Brother lead the way. *Exeunt.*

Bra. If shee carry away this letter so, call me shallow-braines, I was neuer yet couzen'd in my life, this night it shall be so, I will not come with bare relation of your plots,

Ile bring active intelligence that shall tell
Your secret aymes, so crush 'em in the shell. *Exit.*

ACTVS. III. Scena, I. CHAMBER

While the Musicke is playing enter Breynes without his shooes with a Letter in his hand.

Br. SVre this is it, my Mistris and her maide are both fast still, I ha watched vnder the bed all night, to rob her pocket of this paper, and I ha don't, some fellow at this opportunity would haue wrigled himselfe into one of their flesh. *Vio.* Who's there? *Sensible.*

Bre. Death her tongue is awake already.

Vio. Who's i'the chamber.

Bre. Helpe me *Breynes*, before shee wakes the tother, 'tis I forsooth but looking for the chamberpot. *Counterfeits*

Vio. Beshrew you for your noyse. *Sensibles voyce.*

Bra. Where's the doore — stumbles.

Sen. Who's there?

Bra. The tother spirit is rais'd i'th Trundlebed
What will become o'me now. *Enter Sensible.*

Sen. Here's no body.

Vio. Make an end and get thee to bed.

Sen. An end of what, does she talke in her sleepe, shee was not wont.

E Bre.

II, ii, 313. Faint pencil note: *ACT*.

II, ii, 327. The printer repeated six lines in error; the prompter did not bother to correct the mistake.

III, i, opening. Faint pencil note: *Sensi[ble]*.

III, i, 5. Faint pencil note: *Tuto[r]*.

The witty Faire one.

Bre. So, ſo, ha the ſpring is open
I might forget to make it faſt laſt night,
'Tis ſo, and happily ſome Curre or Cat
Has beene i'the chamber, for I heare a noyſe
About the doore, I'le make it faſt
And ſo, to bed againe, I thinke it is day already. *Exit.*
Enter Tutor in his gowne as from his ſtudy.
Tu. So this fancy wrote, for Sir *Nicholas* like a forked
Arrow points two wayes, wenches are caught with
Such conceipts, they will imagin't none of his
Inuention, then whoſe but mine my perſon does inuite
More acceptation, but the Father aymes
At the eſtate, no matter if I can
Inſinuate my ſelfe into her opinion
'Tis no impoſſibility, her portion
Will be enough for both, ſhall I liue ſtill
Dependant and not ſeeke wayes to aduance my
Selfe, buſy my braines in ballads to the giddy
Chambermaides, begger my ſelfe with purſe and pincaſin
When ſhee that is the Miſtris may be mine
T'will be a Maſter piece if I can gull him,
But he's here already. *Enter Sir Nicholas.*
Nic. Noble Tutor, Morrow to you, hay finiſhed
The whimzey for my Miſtris already?
Tu. I ha don't, this paper carries the Loue powder.
Nic. For feare you had forgotten me, I ha made a quib-
ling in praiſe of her my ſelfe, ſuch a one as will fetch vp her
heart Tutor.
Tu. That were a dangerous vomit Sir, take heed of that.
Nic. I but I will not hurt her I warrant thee, and ſhee
dy within a Twelue month and a day Ile be hangd for her.
Tu. Will you Sir. *Nic.* Marry will I, looke you Sir.
But firſt let me ſee yours, can you not write it in my owne
hand, I ſhall hardly read it.
Tut. I'le reade it to you. *Nic.* Sir *George* G'es mee't.
Enter Sir George, and Mr. Worthy.
Rich. See they are at it. *Nic.* And how doe you like it.
Wor. Mor-

The witty Faire one.

Wor. Morrow noble Sir *Nicholas.*
Ric. Morrow Gentlemen.
Nic. Morrow to you both, Sir *George* I ha been making
Poetry this morning. *Tut.* He has a ſubtile fancy.
Rich. What's the ſubiect?
Tu. No ſubiect, but the Queene of his affections.
Nic. I ſcorne ſubiects, 'tis my Empreſſe your Daughters
Muſe hath ſet my muſe on fire.
Tu. Reade Sir. *Nic.* No, you ſhall read 'em for me.
Tu. 'Tis a hue and cry Sir. *Ric.* A hue & cry, for what?
Nic. For what, why for ſomewhat I'le warrant you.
Tut. You may call it Loues hue and cry.
Nic. Call it what you will, I know what 'tis.
Wor. Are you ſo Poeticall.
Nic. I ha beene dabling in *Helicon*, next to trauaile 'tis
all my ſtudy marke the inuention.
Tutor reades.
In Loves name you are charg'd hereby
To make a ſpeedy hue and cry,
After a face who tother day
Came and ſtole my heart away;
For your directions in briefe
These are beſt markes to know the thiefe:
Her hayre a net of beames would prove,
Strong enough to Captive love:
Playing the Eagle, her cleere brow
Is a comely field of ſnow,
A ſparkling Eye, ſo pure a gray
As when it ſhines it needs no day:
Ivory dwelleth on her noſe
Lilly married to the roſe,
Have made her Cheeke the nuptiall bed
Lippes betray their Virgin weed
As they onely bluſht for this
That they one another kiſſe,
But obſerve beſide the reſt
You ſhall know this fellon beſt

E 2 By

III, i, 21. Faint pencil note: *[T]reedle.*
III, i, 29 f. Faint pencil note: *[R]ichly / [W]orthy.*

The witty Faire one.

By her Tongue, for if your Eare
Shall once a heavenly Musicke heare
Such as neither Gods nor men
But from that voyce shall heare, agen
That that is shee, Oh take her t'ee
None can rocke heaven asleepe but shee.

Nic. How doe you like my pipin of *Pernassus* Gentl men.

Ric. Wor. Very handsome.

Nic. Na, I'le warrant you, my Tutor has good furnim in him.

Wor. I doe not thinke hee made 'em.

Nic. Now you shall heare some verses of my ow making.

Rich. Your owne, did you not make these?

Tu. He betrayes himselfe.

Nic. Hum? yes I made 'em too my Tutor knowes.

Tu. I'le take my oath who made e'm.

Nic. But I wrote 'em for an other gentleman that h a Mistris.

Ric. My daughter you said.

Nic. I may say so, but that their faces are nothing ali you would hardly know one from tother, for your b ter vnderstanding I will read 'em my selfe — Her foote

Wor. Dee begin there?

Nic. Oh, I will rise by degrees.

Her foote is feat with Dyamond toes
But shee with legs of Ruby goes:
Thighes Loadstones, and doe draw vnto her
The Iron pinne of any wooer.

Wor. Pretious conceit.

Nic. *Her head.*

Ric. H r head?

Wor. You were betweene her thighes but now.

Nic. T is my conceit, I doe now meane to goe do wards agen, and meete where I left in the middle.

The witty Faire one.

Her head is Opall, *necke of* Saphyre,
Brea Carbuncles, *shine like a fire.*
And the naked truth to tell you,
The very mother of Pearle her belly:
How can shee chose but heare my groanes,
That is composed of precious stones.

Wo. I marry Sir. *Nic.* Now if you lik't you may.

Wo. A word with you Sir, pray what dee thinke of your (pupill,

Tu. I thinke nothing Sir.

Wo. But deale ingeniously, your opinion.

Tu. Shall I tell you?

Wo. Pray Sir.

Tu. Nothing.

Wo. I thinke so too, what doth my Brother meane to make this fond Election.

Tu. For my owne part you heare me say nothing, but the good parts and qualities of men are to be valued.

Wo. This fellow's a Knaue, I smell him.

Tu Some thing has some sauour.

Ni. When you please, name your owne time I'me ready to be married at midnight.

Ric. About a seavennight hence.

Nic. Let it be 3. or 4. I care not how soone, is breake-fast ready.

Ric. It waites vpon you.

Nic. I doe loue to eate and drinke in a morning, though I fast all day after.

Ric. Ile follow brother.

Wo. Wee'le both attend. *Exeunt.*

Enter Mr. Aymwell with a Letter. Tow[n] [III, ii]

Aym. This opportunity, let my couetous eye,
Take to enrich it selfe, but first prepare
With reuerence, as to an Alter bring
No carelesse but Religious beames along
With you to this new obiect, this small paper
Carries the volume of my humane fate
I hold my destiny, betwixt two fingers

E 3 And

III, i, preceding 126. *Sene* (that is, Scene) is a scene-shift warning.
III, i, 129 f. Faint pencil note: *Aym[well] / lette[r].*
III, i, 148 f. Faint pencil note: *Bo[y] / Cll[are].*
III, ii, 4–11. Faint pencil lines indicate that these lines, or some of them, were cut.

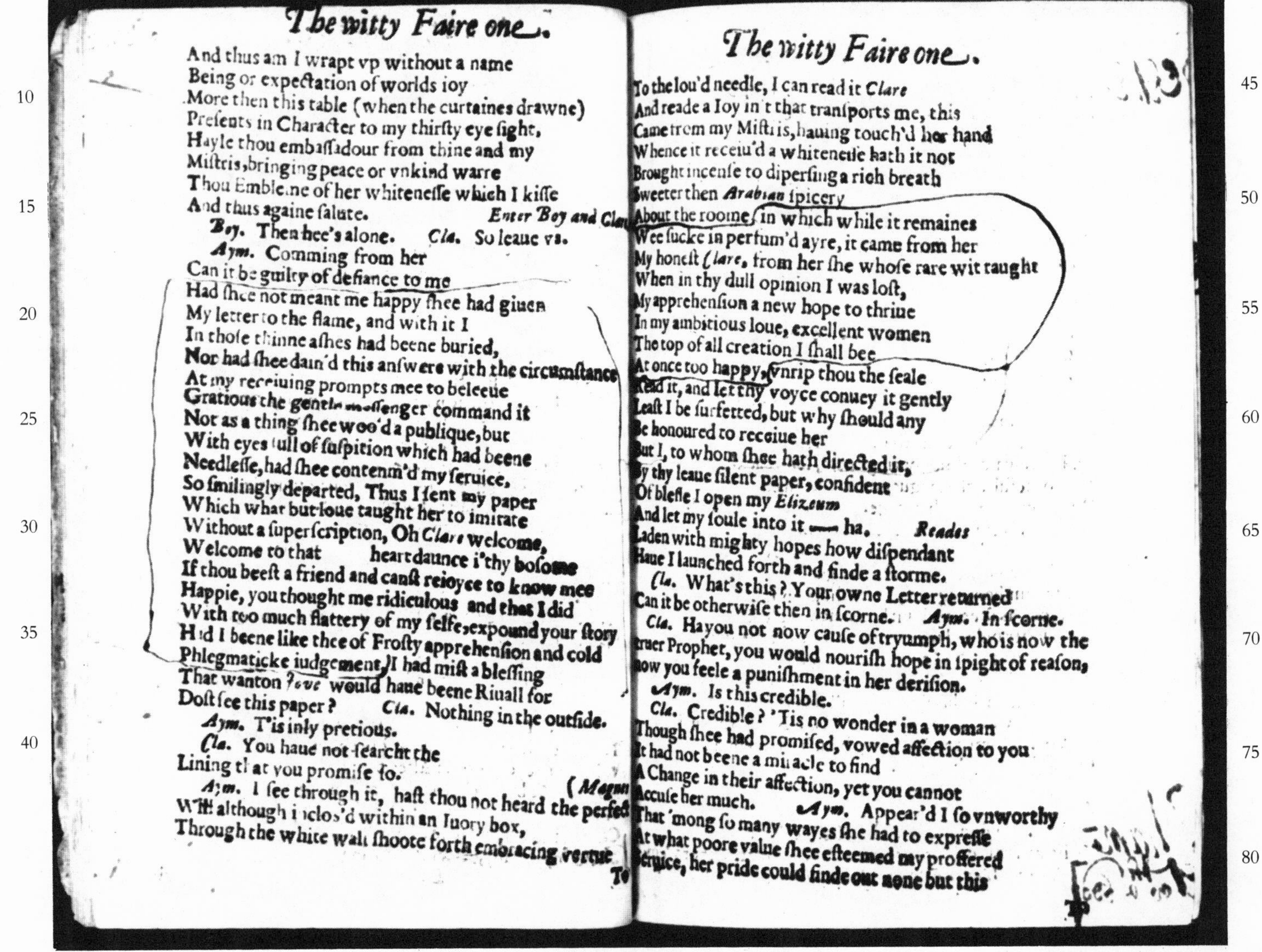

The witty Faire one.

And thus am I wrapt vp without a name
Being or expectation of worlds ioy
More then this table (when the curtaines drawne)
Presents in Character to my thirsty eye sight,
Hayle thou embassadour from thine and my
Mistris, bringing peace or vnkind warre
Thou Embleme of her whitenesse which I kisse
And thus againe salute. *Enter Boy and Cla.*
Boy. Then hee's alone. *Cla.* So leaue vs.
Aym. Comming from her
Can it be guilty of defiance to me
Had shee not meant me happy shee had giuen
My letter to the flame, and with it I
In those thinne ashes had beene buried,
Nor had shee dain'd this answere with the circumstance
At my receiuing prompts mee to beleeue
Gratious the gentle messenger command it
Not as a thing shee woo'd a publique, but
With eyes full of suspition which had beene
Needlesse, had shee contemn'd my seruice,
So smilingly departed, Thus I sent my paper
Which what but loue taught her to imitate
Without a superscription, Oh *Clare* welcome,
Welcome to that heart daunce i'thy bosome
If thou beest a friend and canst reioyce to know mee
Happie, you thought me ridiculous and that I did
With too much flattery of my selfe, expound your story
Had I beene like thee of Frosty apprehension and cold
Phlegmaticke iudgement, I had mist a blessing
That wanton *Loue* would haue beene Riuall for
Dost see this paper? *Cla.* Nothing in the outside.
Aym. T'is inly pretious.
Cla. You haue not searcht the
Lining that you promise so.
Aym. I see through it, hast thou not heard the perfect (*Magnet*
Will although inclos'd within an Iuory box,
Through the white wall shoote forth embracing vertue
To

The witty Faire one.

To the lou'd needle, I can read it *Clare*
And reade a Ioy in't that transports me, this
Came from my Mistris, hauing touch'd her hand
Whence it receiu'd a whitenesse hath it not
Brought incense to dipersing a rich breath
Sweeter then *Arabian* spicery
About the roome, in which while it remaines
Wee sucke in perfum'd ayre, it came from her
My honest *Clare*, from her she whose rare wit taught
When in thy dull opinion I was lost,
My apprehension a new hope to thriue
In my ambitious loue, excellent women
The top of all creation I shall bee
At once too happy, vnrip thou the seale
Read it, and let thy voyce conuey it gently
Least I be surfetted, but why should any
Be honoured to receiue her
But I, to whom shee hath directed it,
By thy leaue silent paper, confident
Of blesse I open my *Elizeum*
And let my soule into it —— ha. *Reades*
Laden with mighty hopes how dispendant
Haue I launched forth and finde a storme.
Cla. What's this? Your owne Letter returned
Can it be otherwise then in scorne. *Aym.* In scorne.
Cla. Ha you not now cause of tryumph, who is now the
truer Prophet, you would nourish hope in spight of reason,
now you feele a punishment in her derision.
Aym. Is this credible.
Cla. Credible? 'Tis no wonder in a woman
Though shee had promised, vowed affection to you
It had not beene a miracle to find
A Change in their affection, yet you cannot
Accuse her much. *Aym.* Appear'd I so vnworthy
That 'mong so many wayes she had to expresse
At what poore value shee esteemed my proffered
Seruice, her pride could finde out none but this

III, ii, 58–62. Faint pencil lines continue the cut through line 62.

The Witty Faire one.

To ſend me mine owne agen. *Cla.* Doe but imagine
You ſent a ſeruant with a meſſage to her,
Shee not within, he is return'd agen
Without an anſwere. *Aym.* Inciuility,
Shee might haue thank'd me, and ſubſcrib'd her name,
I was not bound to her obſeruance.
Cla. Come be free againe. *Aym.* I will be ſo, with this
That I could cancell my affection.
Cla. What doe you meane, it hauing touch'd her hand
Is full of incence and *Arabian* ſpicery
You are too prodigall of your perfume.
Aym. Doe not thou mocke me too.
Cla. Well, I ha done.
Aym. Would I had ſo I cannot empty all
My torment, wherefore ſhould a man loue woman
Such aery mockeries, nothing but meere *Eccboes*
That owe theyr being to our opinion
And in reward of honouring them, ſend backe
As ſcornefully the language we beſtowed.
Out of our too much dotage. *Cla.* If they ſend,
All they receiue from vs, accuſe them not
We haue our hearts againe. *Aym.* And Ile haue mine
I will, I ha not yet, here wants a gueſt
Inuite him home againe, Why ſhould not I
Be as coy as ſhee, and with as much neglect
Throw her behind my thoughts, inſtruct me with
Witty reuenge, and thou that ſee me toſſe
This ſhuttlecocke with as much pride, and when
I'me ſated with this ſport, let fall this vanity
Into as low diſdaine, pſhew. *Cla.* Nobly reſolu'd.
Aym. Come to a Tauerne, drench the memory
Of theſe poore thoughts.
Cla. Let's ſeeke out Maſter
Fowler and *Manly.*
Aym. And warm'd with ſacke, wee'l try
Who can make *Satyres* beſt. *Cla.* A match, lets to't
Enter Maſter Fowler, Manly like his Phiſitian.

[III, iii] *[C]ham / [b]er / wth a bed*

The witty Faire one.

Fow. And thou doſt not play the Doctor handſomely; Il'e ſet the Colledge of Phiſitians vpon thee for practiſing without a licence.

Man. Can you bee ſicke? *Fow.* I would but counterfeit. *Man.* So muſt I the Phiſitian.

Fow. I haue knowne a ſpruſe Empericke hath given his patient 2 or 3. ſtooles with the bare repetition of crude wordes, and knotty ſentences, which haue come from him like a Phlegme, which beſides the operation in the hearers, who admire him for't, while he beates like a drumme, at their barrell head, and turnes their braines like beere, does him the benefit to ſcowre his owne durty maw, whoſe dregs elſe would putrifie; and infeſt his cheekes worſe then a gangreene.

Man. Are you ſure ſhee will viſit you?

Fow. As ſure as I am well, for and I were ſicke and would ſleepe, I would rather, take a nap o'th ridge of *Etna*, and thee fall of deafning *Nilus*, then indure the viſitation, of any of their tribe— one knockes, my pillow and lay my head in the aking poſture. *One knocks*

Enter Aymwell and Clare.

Man. Tis *Aymwell* and *Clare.*

Aym. Where's my witty Bacchanalian, how now? what meanes this Apothecaries ſhop about thee, art Phyſicall?

Fow. Sicke, ſicke.

Aym. Didſt not looke in a glaſſe to day? how ſcuruily this nightcap ſhewes vpon thee.

Cla. What's the diſeaſe? *Man.* A feauer Sir.

Aym. Hang feauers, let's to the Tauerne, and inflame our ſelues, with luſty wine, ſucke in the ſpirit of Sacke, till wee bee Delphicke and propheſie my bully rooke.

Fow. Alas. *Aym.* Alaſſe, is that the diſeaſe, Drench her, drench her in ſack, ſicke for a laſſe, doe not foole thy ſelfe beyond the cure of Bedlam, be wiſe and well agen.

Fow. You are merry, it ſeemes you haue won the Lady.

Aym. What Lady? the Lady ith' Lobſter, I was halfe

F ſicke

III, ii, 86 ff. Faint pencil note: *[F]owler / [M]anly / [& a?] / [do]ctor.*

III, iii, 1 f. Faint pencil note: *Aym[well] / Cla[re].*
III, iii, 19. Faint pencil note: *Knoc[k].*
III, iii, 25 f. Faint pencil note: *Whib[ble] / Pene[lope].*

The witty Faire one.

ſicke for fooliſh thing called a woman, a toy tooke mee i'th
head, and had like to haue taken away my heart too but I
ha recouered, doe not truſt thy body with a Phiſitian, heele
make thy fooliſh bones goe without fleſh in a fortnight,
and thy ſoule walke without a body a ſeauennight after.

Man. Theſe are no Doctors?

Aym. Doctor? art a Pariſian, a Paduan, or a Leaden Do-
How many and be true to vs haſt thou kild the laſt (ctor?
Spring, will it puzzel thy arithmeticke, my pretious
Rectifier of nature, the wrong way, — faith
Thou muſt excuſe me *Iacke* that I cannot condole
With thee, by this whay beard of *Eſculapius*, I dare
Not endanger my ſelfe with ſo much mellancholly
Leaſt I fall into a relapſe — whom haue wee heere?

Enter Whibble and Penelope.

Wo. T'is reported that Maſter *Fowler* is ſick and keepes
his chamber, I hope hee's within.

Pen. Noble Sir. *Aym.* Fayre Lady.

Pen. How fare you Sir? *Fow.* The better to ſee you
heere. *Man.* Vpon the entrance of this Gentlewoman, I finde your griefe much altered.

Pen. Vpon mine?

Man. Yes, and by that I dare preſume to ſay you are the
cauſe of his diſtemper. *Pen.* I Sir?

Fow. A cunning Doctor

Man. For I obſerud ſo ſoone as his ſearching eye had
faſtned on her, his labouring pulſe that through his Feauor
did, before ſticke hard, and frequent now exceeds in both
theſe differences and this *Gallen* himſelfe found true vpon
a woman, that had doted vppon a Fencer. *Cla.* I?

Whi. Shee did long for tother bout then,

Fow. Giue vs leaue pray.

Aym. A very pretty fellow,

Cla. Well skild i'th pulſe.

Aym. You know my diſeaſe too dee not? will
not my complexion giue you the hint on't

Man. You are not very well. *Aym.* How Sir?

Man

The witty Faire one.

Does not thy very ſoule bluſh to deceiue me.

Bra: What's the matter Miſtris.

Vio: Here me I beſeech you.

Geo: I'th height and puzze of my care to make
Thee, happie? to conſpire thy ouerthrow
I wo'not heare.

Bra: Good Sir.

Vio. This was your worke you can read.

Bra: And write too the ſuperſcription of a Letter or
ſo. *Geo.* Where's *Senſible* *Enter Senſible.*
For your good ſeruice to your Miſtris houſewife
Packe vp your trinckets, I here diſcharge you.

Bra: I hope you are *Senſible.*

Vio: Oh wench my father hath my letter.

Sen: Yours?

Vio: And I miſtaking ſeal'd and return'd *Aymwell* that
which he ſent.

Sen: How came he by't.

Vio: Talke not of that, Oh for ſome art to helpe vs.

Bra: Let me councell you not to expreſſe any violence
in your paſſions, leaſt you marre the poſſibility of reclay-
ming her, it ſeemes *Aymwell* ha's miſt the intelligence,
where ſhame is inforc'd too much vpon the delinquent, it
begets rather an audacious defence of the ſin, then repentance, ſoft raine ſlides to the root, and nouriſhes, where
great ſtormes make a noyſe, wet but the skin a'th earth, and
runne away in a channell.

Sen: A moſt rare proiect.

Vio. It will appeare the ſame, both made together
Which ſince my ſiſters death I haue worne.

Geo: Which of my cares reward'ſt thou with this folly.

Vio. Sir can you pardon?

Geo. I loue you but too well, goe to your chamber.

Vio: But muſt wee part.

Geo: Diſpute it not.

Bra: Bu'y ſweet Miſtris *Senſible*, I hope wee ſhall
meete againe as merry as we part.

Sen:

III, iii, 72. Signatures F2 and F3 are lacking in the copy. On the missing F3, at the entrance of Braines, a new scene seems to begin.

III, iv, 86. Faint pencil note: *ACT*.

The witty Faire one.

Sen. 'Tis very violent,but wee obey your pleaſure, I haue onely apparrell and ſome few trifles.

Geo: Take 'em all we'e and be gone.

Vio. Beſide my owne misfortune, I haue cauſe to pitty thine, my father is diſpleas'd, and not iniuſtly, happy genius.— *Exeunt*

Geo: So, things muſt be mannag'd wiſely, I will haſten the marriage.

Bra: By all meanes let it be ſuddaine.

Geo: Within two dayes — to morrow.

Bra: I wo'not ſleepe, till ſhee be married, but carry things ſmooth, let not the Knight ſuſpect y'are troubled, your daughter will be fetc'ht about with a byas againe.

Geo: How thou deſeru'ſt me,let vs in.

Bra: Hereafter for my ſake, and ſubtle paines
Who ere is wiſe,let the world call him *Braines.*

ACTVS. IV. SCENA. I.

Enter Aymwell and Senſible.

Aym. CAn this be true?

Sen: As I haue faith to heauen.

Aym: Take this and this for thy ſweete ſtory, thou
Haſt entranc'd me with thy language; laden
With my diſpaires,like a diſtreſſed barke
I gaue my ſelfe vp loſt in the imagin'd
Tempeſt,but at point of ſtriking
Vpon a rocke, what a cæleſtiall gale
Makes my ſayles ſwell with comfort, and enforcing
My ſhip into the channell, I doe feele it
Bound on the waues,diſcretion at the helme
Which paſſion made forſaken, I now bleſſe
The Minute I weighed Anchor ; oh my deſtiny
Dwell longer on this thread and make it firme,

Vpon

The witty Faire one.

Vpon it hangs the weight of ſuch a fortune
That if it cracke, will ſwifter then *Ioues* flaming
Arrow, digge my graue i'th earths center,
Forgiue me ſacred ſexe of women that
In thought or ſillable I ha declaym'd
Againſt your goodneſſe, I will redeeme it
With ſuch religious honouring your names
That when I dye ſome neere thought ſtained Virgin
Shall make a relicke of my duſt, and throw
My aſhes like a charme vpon thoſe men,
Whoſe faithes they hold ſuſpected, to what pitch
Of bleſſedneſſe are my thoughts mounted.

Sen. Sir,
This is an opportunity for action
Time will runne faſt vpon the minute.

Aym. Pardon
The treſpaſſe of my ioy it makes me vilde
I am too well rewarded for thy ſuffering
Promiſe thy ſelfe a noble recompence.

Enter Manly, and Clare.

Man: Come ha you finiſht your diſcourſe yet.

Aym: Y'are my friends,
I was deceiued in my *Violetta*
Shee loues,ſh'as ſent me proofe, but a miſtake
Sent backe my letter,and detain'd her anſwere
Which was betray'd to her father,but keepe your wonder
To honour her rare wit, which if the ſtarres
Shew themſelues not malicious, will aſſure
All my deſires in her, a diuine proiect
She is the maſter engine, you muſt worke too,
Will you not friends?

Both: You know you may commaund vs.

Aym. Then ſpread your boſomes, you ſhall ſtraight procure
A caroach be ready a'th backſide a'my lodging,
Doe not looſe time in queſtioning, my fate
Depends vpon your haſt.

Man. Promiſe it done.

Aym: You ſhall diſguiſe your ſelfe I muſt employ you in rougher action.

Clar: I refuſe no office
To aduance your hopes.

Aym. My certaintie's, in thee,

G

The

IV, i, 3 f. Faint pencil note: *[M]anly / [C]lare*.

IV, i, 3–14. A pencil line in the left margin seems to indicate that these lines were to be cut. The cut appears to be continued to line 24 by another pencil line in the right margin, though the ink lines boxing lines 18–25 suggest a shorter cut.

IV, i, 17. *Sen[e]* (Scene) is a scene-shift warning.

IV, i, 34 f. Faint pencil note: *Violet[ta] / Tutor*.

The witty Faire one.

The frame of our whole building leanes,come on
Moue ſlowly time vntill our worke be done. *Exeun[t]*

[IV, ii] Chamber

Enter Violetta, Tutor.

Vio. I was not blind to your deſerts,
Nor can be ſo vngratefull now, as not
To giue encouragement to your affection
My father may command my perſon, neuer
My loue to marry *Treedle.*

Tu. Hee's an aſſe I made his beſt verſes for 'em.

Vio. I thought his fancy would not reach 'em.

Tu. His ſconce is drier then a Pumice.

Vio. There be wayes to preuent marriage for I'me already charged. *Tu.* Y'are wiſe,lets run away together.

Vio. But how ſhall I be ſure your loue is firme.

Tu. Try me and truſt me after.

Vio. And I will, for ſhall it be a hard taske Ile impoſe
on you, dare you fight?

Tu. If I like my enemy. *Vio.* 'Tis a poore old fellow,

Tu. Then I'le kill him, his name?

Vio. My fathers ſeruant *Braynes.* *Tu.* Hee's dead
By this time. *Vio.* Stay, there is a circumſtance
To be obſerued,by ſome meanes I'le procure
He waites on me to the *Strand* this afternoone.

Enter Sir Nicholas, and Whible.

Sir Nicholas? your eare for the reſt.

Tu. He will ſuſpect nothing by our priuacy,
He bad me take occaſion to vrge
His good parts to you, ſhould hee aske I'de ſweare
I did but preſſe his commendations.

Nic. Is thy name *Whible.*

Whi. Yes, an't pleaſe your worſhip.

Nic. I like thee the better for that my name's
Treedle.

Whi. I thanke your worſhip.

Nic. Haſt done looking a me.

Whi. Euery eye hath his obiect already.

Nic. A witty knaue,what place doſt thou occupie vnder thy Maſter.

Whi.

The witty Faire one.

Whi. I am commonly his journey-man Sir.

Nic. How? *Whi.* I looke to his Horſes ſir.

Nic. Wo't ſerue mee when I'me married.

Whi. Alas, I haue no good parts to commend me.

Nic. No good parts, and thou haſt but skill in Horſes
and Dogs, th'art fit for any Gentleman in *England.*

Vio. Iuſt at that place aſſault him.

Tu. By your faire hand I will. *Vio.* My Delight, how
fare you. *Nic.* I'me ſtudying ſome witty Poeſie for
thy wedding Ring,let me ſee —

Vio. Trouble not your head,*Whible* intreat my Father hi-
(ther.

Nic. No matter,I will ſend to the Vniuerſity.

Vio. Were you euer of any Colledge?

Nic. Colledge, I haue had a head in moſt ath' Butteries
of *Cambridge,* and 't has beene ſconc'd to purpoſe. I know
what belongs to Sizing and haue anſwered to my Que in
my dayes, I me free of the whole Vniuerſity, I commencd
with no worſe then his Maieſties footmen.

Vio. And euer ſince you haue had a running wit, you
were better conſult our wits at home, wee haue excellent
Poets i'th Towne they ſay.

Nic. I'th Towne? What makes ſo many Schollers then
come from *Oxford* and *Cambridge*, like Market women
with Dorſers full of lamentable Tragedies, and ridiculous
Comedies which they might here vent to the Players, but
they will take no money for 'em. *Vio.* Oh my deareſt!
How happie ſhall I bee when I'me married. *Kiſſe.*

Enter Sir George, Worthy.

Wor. Looke,they are ingendering at the lip.

Geo. I like it well. *Vio.* Why are our ioyes defer'd?

Nic. But till to morrow.

Vio. 'Tis an age me thinkes. *Nic.* Kind worme.

Wor. This cannot be deceit.

Vio. I want ſome trifles the *Exchange* will furniſh me,
Let it be your motion to my Father.

Nic. Father and Vncle you will excuſe our familiar
conuerſation, I vow Ile bee honeſt till I be married, not a

G 3 touch

IV, ii, 2 f. Faint pencil note: *Tredle / Whible.*

IV, ii, 37 f. Faint pencil note: *Richle[y] / Worth[y].*

Braines

The Witty Faire one.

touch of my flesh within the walls, onely the suburbs of her lips or hands, or so, and when, and when is to morrow the day, the day of coupling and so forth, haue you got a licence.

Geo. It shall be my next worke.

Nic. Pray doe, weel'e bee marryed here, but keepe our wedding at my owne house at *Croidon*, wee'le ha the City Waites downe with vs, and a noise of Trumpets, we can haue Drummes i'th Country, and the Traine-Band, and then let the Spaniards come and they dare, dost heare, heere's twenty peeces you shall fribble e'm away at the Exchange presently.

Geo: How Sir?

Nic: By this gold she shall Father, lay it out in Tooth-picks, I'le weare 'em out in my hat; come I'le with you for the lycence.

Geo. Who shall with her?

Wor. I must attend a proiect of my daughters. *Exit.*

Enter Braines.

Geo: Braines.

Bra: Sir.

Geo: Waite on my daughter to the Exchange, obserue her carefully.

Bra: point me a minute to returne with her, if I faile put my braines into 'th pot, and let 'em be seru'd vp with a Calues head, to morrow dinner.

Vio: It succeeds to my wish.

Nic. Violetta, look you lay out my gold at the Exchange in Bartholomew Fairings, farewell *Violetta.*

Bra: Come Mistris will you walke, I would faine see any mortall wit couzen me a my charge now, I will liue to be the shame of Pollititians, and when I am dead, be clapt vp into the Chronicles.

[IV, iii]

Enter Fowler.

Fow: Ah the desire of vnlawfull flesh, what a coniuring dost thou keepe within vs to lay this little spirit of conscience, the world and the divell, are tame and sprightlesse temp-

The witty Faire one.

temptations, poore traffique to this staple commoditie of Whooring: this is the place where I must take shipping for the Summer Islands, if she keepe touch, I will call them fortunate, and once a Weeke make a Love voyage to them. Ha! are we entertayn'd with Musicke?

Song.

Backe, backe againe, fond man forbeare,
Buy not a Minutes play too deare:
Come with Holy flame and bee
Welcome to Vertue and to mee.

Come with Holy flame and bee, welcome to Vertue and to me? Flame? I bring none wo' me, and I should be sorry to meete any fire workes here, for those hereafter I looke on 'em a farre off, and apprehend them with lesse feare, againe?

Song.

Love a thousand sweets distilling,
And with Nectar bosomes filling,
Charme all eyes that none may find vs,
Be above, before, behind vs;
And while wee thy pleasures tast
Enforce Time it selfe to stay,
And by fore-locke hold him fast
Least occasion slip away.

I marry, this is another manner of invitement, I'le to her but — *Enter Winifrid.*

Heere comes the squire of her Mistresses body, how does my little taper of Virgin waxe, thou hast beene in some dampe thou burnst blew me thinkes.

Win. Noble Sir.

Fow. What, a cold.

Win. A great cold, I ha lost my voyce.

Fow. And thou hast not lost thy Maydenhead 'tis ter, have a little care of thy Francke Tenement, tongue will come time enough to it selfe Ile war what place has she chosen for the Encounter?

G 3 *Pen.*

IV, ii, 78. Faint pencil note: *[F]owler.*
IV, ii, 88. Faint pencil note: *Musick.*

IV, iii, 8. Faint pencil note: *Winif[red].*
IV, iii, 20 f. Faint pencil note: *pene[lope] / Wort[hy].*
IV, iii, 25. Faint pencil note: *Wine[fred].*
IV, iii, 34–36. The Bodleian copy is torn; the missing words are "no mat- / and thy / rant thee."

The witty Faire one.

Win. Her chamber. *Fow.* Her chamber?

Win. 'Tis all darke.

Fow. Is't all darke, I commend her pollicy the better then the roome, and the deed that muſt bee done in't will be of one complexion, ſo ſhee be light I care not, prethee convey me to her. *Win.* Follow me.

Fow. As thy ſhadow woe bee to ſome a'the deere ſexe when a Chambermaid is Vſher to a Gentleman. *Exit.*

[IV, iv] *[Ch]amber*

Enter Miſtris Penelope and Worthy.

Pen. It ſhall be a harmeleſſe tryall Sir.

Wor. Goe too, I know thou art vertuous, put in execution thy purpoſe, I'le be within the reach of thy voyce.

Pen. It ſhall be my ſecurity,
What ill ſtarre, rul'd at my Natiuity,
That I ſhould be ſo miſerable to loue
A man, whoſe glory is his vice, whoſe ſtudy
Is but to ruine vertue. *Enter Winifrid.*

Win. Miſtreſſe? *Pen.* Heere *Winifrid.*

Win. The Gameſter waytes his entrance iocund as a Bridegroome, hee has forgot his Feauer.

Pen. Away you know your charge, be ready where are you Sir, Mr. *Fowler* *She Speakes hoarſe.* *Enter Fowler.*

Fow. Hell, if darkneſſe will carry it, yet hell cannot be ſo blacke.
There are too many flames in't, thy hand, what Monkes hole haſt thou brought me to, where's thy Miſtris.

Pen. This is the way.

Fow. Is this the way? it is a very blind one, the Diuell can hardly know me if hee meet me heere that's my comfort, yet if hee did, he loues the ſinne too well to interrupt ſo precious a meeting, prethee Child of darkneſſe conduct me to the handſome Fairie I muſt dance withall.

Pen. It ſeemes your Feauer hath left you. *Fow.* My I forget my ſelfe, I ſhould haue counterfeited ſicke while, but no matter and thy Miſtris know it not, ilfull in ſecrets, and I will deſerue it: two or 3 am in her preſence, will make her keepe her pro-

The witty Faire one.

promiſe, wo'me about the cure, for that ſhe thinkes I was ſo, prethee doe thy office and bring me to her, I hope ſhe is not within hearing.

Pen. Feare not. *Fow.* So about it then.

Pen. There's a fee belongs to my place firſt:

Fow. A fee belonging to your place, as I hope for a limbe of thy Miſtreſſe I had forgot it, there's gold I can feele it by this darkeneſſe: for thou ſeeſt I haue no light to ſweare by 'tis weight, quicke periwincle to thy miſtris now.

Pen. This is not enough.

Fow. There's more, take ſiluer and all.

Pen. This is nothing.

Fow. Is it nothing? by this hand wo'd I could ſee't, tis all I haue, wo't ſearch me?

Pen. There is another Fee belongs to vs.

Fow. Another Fee belongs to us? what's that? I muſt kiſſe her, th'haſt a downe lip, and doſt twang it handſomely, now to the buſineſſe.

Pen. This is not all I looke for:

Fow. Shee wo'not tempt me to come aloft will ſhe?

Pen. If you could ſee me I doe bluſh;

Wor. What does my daughter meane?

Fow. If I could ſee her ſhee does bluſh ſhee; ſayes tis ſo: oh the inſatiable deſires of Chamber-maydes! they were wont to looke no higher then the Groome or Seruingman and be thankefull, or if the Maſter would be pleaſed to let 'em ſhew him this lobby to'ther withdrawing chamber, or the turret in ſummer, and take occaſion to cōmend the ſcituation and ſo forth, 'twas after the Lady had beene ſeru'd, out of his owne meere motion and fauour, and 'twas taken as an endearement for euer of their ſeruice and ſecrecie, now they muſt be taſters to'em i'tho ſweete ſtane, Fees o'the Court muſt be payed, or no ſuit commenc'd with iniquity, O *Venus,* what will this world come to?

Pen. Heare me. *Fow.* Yes, I cannot ſee thee.

Pen.

IV, iii, 38. Faint pencil note: *[Fo]wler.*

IV, iv, 25–28. The torn page in the Bodleian copy caused the following to be lost: "Feauer / all this / thou art sk / fits when I."

The witty Faire one.

Pen. This chamber by my policy was made darke:

Fow. This chamber by your policy was made darke, so.

Pen. My Miſtris expected you without this ceremony.

Fow. Your Miſtris expects me, &c. cunning Gipſey.

Pen: But if you condiſcend not firſt:

Fow. But if I condiſcend not firſt, will ſhe threaten me?

Pen. To impart to me the ſweet pleaſure of your body.

Fow: To impart to you the ſweet pleaſure of my body,

Pen: Indeed you ſhall not imbrace my Miſtris and ſo forth.—

Fow. Indeed I ſhall not imbrace your Miſtris and ſo forth, you will iuſtifie this to her face, tis not that I ſtand vpon a cariere, but I wo'not be compeld to lye with any Whore in Chriſtendome, was euer ſuch a Goate in nature, why harke yee virgin aboue ground, for a darke roome or a ſellar are all one for you, you that are a degree aboue the Kitchin, and make your Maſters man run mad to heare you play ath' Virginals, whoſe breath though ſtrengthned with garlicke, you wo'd ſucke like a domeſticke Catte at midnight, will no dyet downe with you; but what is reſerued for your Miſtreſſes pallate, you are in hope to filch a point from my breeches, which executed at both ends, you will weare about your ſmutchy wriſt for a bracelet, I will ſeeke out thy Miſtris, rifle her Lady-ware in ſpight of thee, and giue my footmen charge not to kiſſe thee, and it would keep thee frō ſtarving, would I could ſee the way out agen:

Pen. I can betray and will.

Fow. Shee'le betray vs, ſhe has voyce enough for ſuch a miſchiefe, doſt heare, doe but conſider ſhe is thy Miſtris, there's ſome reaſon ſhe ſhould be prefer'd.

Pen. Il'e heare none.

Fow. Shee'le heare no reaſon, if the divell hath fed her blood with the hope of me, would he would furniſh her with an *Incubus* in my ſhape to ſerue her, or let a Satyre leape her, oh vnmercifull Chambermaides, the graue is ſooner ſatisfied then their wantonneſſe, doſt heare, wo't ha the truth on't, 'twas a condition betweene vs, and I ſwore no woman ſhould enioy me before her, there's conſcience I ſhould be honeſt to her, prethee be kind to a young ſinner, I will deſerue thee hereafter i'the height of dalliance.

Pen: I am i'the ſame humor ſtill:

Fow: She is i'the ſame humour ſtill, I muſt go through her to her Miſtris, art thou a Chriſtian?— Well tho'rt a braue girle, and I doe loue thy reſolution, and ſo ſoone as I haue preſented my firſt fruits to thy Miſtris onely for my oathes ſake I'le returne and ply thee with embraces, as I am a Gentleman prethee ſhew me the way.

Pen. I wo'not truſt you Sir,

Fow. Wo'not you truſt me? why come on then and there be no remedy.

Pen. Will you ſatisfie my deſire?

Fow. I'le doe my endeauour, I am vntruſſing as faſt as I can, nay and I be provock't, I am a Tyrant, haue at you Beauchamp.

Pen. *Winfryd.*

Enter Winfryd with light.

Fow: Ha you found your voyce, what
Meane you by this light?

Pen. That you ſhould ſee your ſhame

Fow. Cheated, ha?
Is this your loue to me, your noble loue
I did ſuſpect before how I ſhould find you,

Pen. Degenerated man, what mad diſeaſe
Dwels in thy veynes that does corrupt the flowings
Of generous bloud within thee,

Fow. Shall I not vault Gentlewoman?

Pen. What behaviour of mine
Gave thee ſuſpicion I could be
So loſt to vertue, to giue vp mine honour,
Poore man how thou didſt foole thy ſelfe
Goe home and pray thy ſinne may
Be forgiven, and with teares

H Waſh

IV, iv, 98 f. Faint pencil note: *[Wi]nfred / [ca]ndle.*

The witty Faire one.

Waſh thy polluted ſoule.
Wor. I like this well
And find her noble ayme.
Pen. Be man againe;
For yet thou art a Monſter, and this act
Publiſhed will make thee appeare ſo blacke and
Horrid, that euen beaſts will be aſhamed
Of thy ſociety, my goodneſſe in hope of
Your conuerſion makes me chides you ſo, [?]
Ha *Winifryd* doſt thou obſerue him, oh my heart
Is full of feare, I tremble to looke on him :
See of a ſuddaine what a paleneſſe has
Poſſeſt his face, doe not his eyes retyre
Into their hollow chambers, Sir how doe you?
Fow: Well. *Wor.* What new proiect's this?
Win. A ſuddaine change.
Sure heauen is iuſt vnto thy late impoſture,
And thou art puniſht now indeed with ſicknes
For mocking heauen I feare, oh doſt thou ſee. *Fow.* What
Pen. Death ſits vpon his forehead, I ne're ſaw
The horrour of a dying countenance,
But in this Gentleman, *Winifryd* to my cloſſet,
Fetch me the Cordial,
Fow. What de'e meane Gentlewomen,
I doe not feele any ſuch dangerous ſicknes.
Pen. What a hollow voyce he has, oh my misfortune
If he ſhould die here, fetch me ſome ſtrong waters.
Fow. No no, I can walke for 'em my ſelfe if need be.
Pen. He talks wildly:
I may ſuſpect him, if y'aue ſo much ſtrength
To walke, goe home, call your Phyſician,
And friends, diſpoſe of your eſtate, and ſettle
Your peace for heauen I doe beſeech you Sir.
My prayers ſhall begge a mercy on your ſoule:
For I haue no encouragement to hope
Your glaſſe hath many ſands, farewell Sir, cheriſh
Rare holy thoughts, that if your life ſoone end,
Your

The witty Faire one.

Your better part may to you Court aſcend, come to my Father. *Exeunt.*

Fow. What's the meaning a this ſicke and dying, I feele no paine, I haue heard of ſome dyed with conceite, if it ſhould kill me, I were a precious cockſcombe, was euer poore Gentleman brought into ſuch a fooliſh paradiſe prepared for a race, and mounting into th' ſaddle, I muſt goe home and dye, well, if I liue I'le quit your cunning, and for the more certainty, my reuenge may proſper, I wo'not ſay my prayers till it take effect. *Enter Tutor.* Tow[n] [IV, v]

Tut. This is the place where I muſt exerciſe my valour vpon *Braines*, I was ne're giuen to fight, but I'me engaged for ſuch a prize as I would challenge all the Noble ſciences in my owne defence.

Enter Aymowell, Clare, Manly.

Aym. I cannot ſpye 'em, yet, pray heauen no
Diſaſter croſſe our proiect,
Cla. What thing's that walkes about the doore?
Aym. One practiſing I
Thinke, the poſtures of a Fencer.
Tut. Things occurre worthy conſideration:

Were I beſt to ſpeake before I ſtrike him, or giue him blowes, and tell him reaſon afterwards. I doe not like expoſtulations, they proclaime our anger, and giue the enemy warning to defend himſelfe, I'le ſtrike him valiantly and in ſilence. *Cla.* What does he mutter?

Aym. What buſines ſtayes him here, ſome treachery.
Tut. Being reſolu'd to ſtrike before I ſpeake.
'Tis worth my iudgement, whether Fiſt or Sword
Shall firſt ſalute him, I'le be generous,
And giue him firſt two or three wholeſome buffets,
Which well laid on, may happily ſo maze him,
My weapon may be vſeleſſe, for I feare
Should I begin with ſteele, her very face
Would force me make too deepe inciſion,
And ſo there may be worke for Seſſions,
I like not that as valiant as I am,
Killing is common. H 2 Clare

IV, iv, following 158. Faint pencil note: *Aymwell / Clare / Manly.*

IV, v, 5. Faint pencil note: *Clare.*
IV, v, 7 f. Faint pencil note: *Brain[es] / Viole[tta].*
IV, v, 25 f. Faint pencil note: *[Braines] / [Violetta].*
IV, v, 27. Faint pencil note: *Ent* (that is, Enter Clare). The prompter should have deleted the incorrect stage direction for Clare's entrance at line 33.

The Witty Faire one.

Aym. *Clare*, they are in ſight, downe, downe, oh myra-
uiſht ſoule, what bliſſe is in this obiect ?
Tut. Ha they are comming, 'tis ſhe and the old Ruffia
he has but a ſcuruy countenance, I ha th'aduantage in th
firſt blow, and I ſhou'd be very ſorry, he ſhould beate m
in the concluſion.

Enter Clare.

Cla. Why does this fellow ſtay ?
Tut. I muſt on, ſhe has ſpyed me through her maske,
I ſee her ſmile already, and command
A preſent Battery.

Enter Braines before Violetta.

Cla. Will this fellow preuent my office, *he goes tow-
ard him with a quarrelling face*, ha, I'le not engage m
ſelfe, then 'tis ſo: *withdrawes*
Vio. Helpe, helpe. *She runs in & preſently ſlips o*
Bra. Miſtris ſtay. *Sencible dreſt like her Miſtri*
Feare nothing, alas good Gentlewoman, you blacke Mag
death, *I*'de treade him into the kennell amongſt his ki
dred.
Tut. Hold, helpe, murder,
Bra. We ſhall haue the whole ſtreete about's preſen
let's on our iourney, whoorſon Mole-catcher !
And ye had not beene wo'me, I would haue cut
Him into more pieces then a Taylors caſhin,
Sir *Nicholas* ſhall know on't too. *Exeunt.*
Tut. They are gone together, Poxe a this toughnes,
Has made an Aſſe of me, next him doe I hate the Law
Moſt abominably, for if I might kill and not be hang'd!
For him 'two'd neuer trouble me, ſhall *I* looſe my repu-
tion, So ? I'le venture an other pounding, but *I*'le be
veng'd on him. *Exeunt*

Enter Braines before Senſible.

Bra. My Miſtris is growne very thrifty of her vo
a'the ſudden, I haue ask'd her 2. or three queſtions, and
anſwers me with holding out her hand, as the poſte at
Albanes, that points the way to *London*, either ſhee
gro

The witty Faire one.

growne ſullen, or the fright ſhe was in late like a Wolfe
that ſees a man firſt, hath taken away her voyce,—*I*'le
make her ſpeake to me—He ſtayes, ſhe puts him forward
with her hand.—Said you forſooth— will it not doe,
what a bleſſed comfort ſhal he enioy if ſhe continue ſpeech-
leſſe, the *Perſians* did worſhip a God vnder the name of
Silence, and ſure Chriſtians may haue an excuſe for their
*I*dolatry, if they can find a woman whom nature hath po-
ſted into the world with a tongue, but no ability to make
vſe of that miſerable Organ, what doe you thinke 'tis a
clocke ? two not ſtrike, ha? how now Mrs. treading a to-
ſide, this is your way to the Exchange. *She ſlips away.*
Sen. My way you ſawcie Clowne, take that,
Bra. You are bountifull, 'tis more then I look't for.

She vnmaskes.

Sen. What ha you to ſay to me Sirra, cannot a Gentlewomã
Bra. Ha ah my *Braines* melt, *I* am undone, *I* am vndone,
you *Succubus* where is my Miſtris? *Proſerpine* ſpeake.

Enter Tutor with Sericants.

Tut. That's he, your office.
Serg. We arreſt you Sir.
Bra. Me you Toades ?
Sen. Howe's this ?
Tut. Away with him to Priſon, 'tis no ſlight action, at
your perils Sergeants—my fayreſt Miſtris.
Sen. Miſtris—*I*'le humour this plot for the mirth ſake.

Exeunt.

Bra. Sirra *Tadpoole* what dee' meane, *I* owe him not a
penny by this fleſh, he has a conſpiracy vpon me, *I* charge
ye in the Kings name vnbind me.
Serg. We charge you i'th Kings name obey vs,
Bra. May you liue to be arreſted ath' Pox, and dye in a
Dungeon, nay *I*nnes a Court Gentlemen, at ſnext trimming
ſhaue your eares and noſes off, and then ducke you in their
owne boggards.

H 3 ACTVS.

IV, v, following 37. Faint pencil note: *[B]raines / [S]ensible.*
IV, v, following 58. Faint pencil note: *[T]utor / [S]erge[ants].*
IV, v, 74. Faint pencil note: *AC[T].*
IV, v, 93. There is no exeunt at the end of the act.

ACTVS. V. SCENA. I.

Enter Sir George, Sir Nicholas, Mr. Worthy.

Nic. SO, now we have got a Lycense, I would see who dares marry your daughter besides my selfe, is she come from the *Exchange* yet?

Wor. Not yet Sir. *Enter a Messenger.*

Mes. Your servant *Braines* remembers his duty in this Paper. *Geo.* Letters!

Nic. Letters, let me read em.

Geo. Your patience Sir.

Wor. I doubt all is not well, what if some misfortune should now befall your Mistris, I hope you have Armour of Patience?

Nic. I and of Proofe too at home, as much as my Hall can hold, the Story of the Prodigall can hardly be seen for't; I have Pikes and Gunnes, enough for me and my Predecessors, a whole Wardrope of Swords and Bucklers, when you come home you shall see 'em.

Geo. A Conspiracy. *Nic.* Oh Treason.

Geo. My man *Braines* is arrested by your Tutor, a plot to take away my daughter, she is gone.

Wor. I did prophesie too soone.

Nic. My Tutor read travell to me, and run away. With my Wench — a very Peripatetike — what shall I doe then, and some had arrested and clapt her up too — we should have knowne where to find her — dee heare, I did not meane to marry with a Licence.

Wor. How Sir?

Nic. No Sir, I did meane to marry with your daughter Am I a Gull? *Wor.* Have Patience.

Nic. I will have no patience, I will have [illegible], why does not *Braines* appeare?

Wor. His heeles are not at liberty, he's in Prison.

Nic. In Prison, why and he had beene hanged, he might have brought us word.

Geo. I'me rent with vexation, Sirra goe you with me to the Prison. *Exit George and Messenger.*

Wor. What will you doe?

Nic. Ile geld my Tutor.

Wor. You were best finde him first.

Nic. Nay I will finde him, and find him agen and I can light on him, let me alone, Ile take halfe a doozen wo'mee and about it instantly. *Exit.*

Wor. I wish thee well Neece, but a better husband.

Enter Fowler.

Who's yonder, 'tis Master *Fowler*, at an excellent opportunity. *Exit.*

Fow. I doe walke still, by all circumstance I am alive, not sicke in any part but my head, which has only the pangs of invention, and is in travell of some pretious revenge, for my worse then Masculine affront, what if I report abroad shee's dishonest, I cannot doe 'em a worse turne then to say so: some of our Gallants take a pride to belye poore Gentlewomen a that fashion, and thinke the discourse an honour to 'em; confidently boast the fruition of this or that Lady, whose hand they never kist with the Glove off: and why may not I make it my revenge, to blurre their fames a little for abusing me.

Enter two Friends at severall Doores.

1. Well met friend, what? thou lookest sad.

2. You will excuse me, and beare a part, when I tell the cause.

1. What's the Newes?

2. Our Friend Master *Fowler's* dead.

Fow. *Fowler*! Ha? 2. Mr. *John Fowler*.

Fow. That's I, that's I, ha? 2. The same.

Fow. Dead, am I dead?

1. It cannot be; I saw him but this morning Lusty and pleasant, how dyed hee?

2. Suddenly. 1. Where?

2. At Master *Worthies* house.

1. Dead?

V, i, opening. Faint pencil note: *mess[enger]*.
V, i, following 18. Faint pencil note: *[Fo]wler*.

V, i, 38. Faint pencil note: *2 fren[ds]*.

1. Dead! 2. Too true Sir.
Fow. I wo'd not beleeve my ſelfe ſicke, belike I am
dead, 'tis more then I know yet.
1. He was a Sutor to Maſter *Worthies* daughter.
2. Miſtris *Penelope*, right.
Fow. By all circumſtance they meane me, theſe Gentlemen know me too, how long is it ſince I departed? Some
miſtake ——
1. How poore a thing is life, that we cannot
Promiſe a Minutes certainty, i'th height
And ſtrength of youth, falling to duſt agen. (man?
Fow. Ha, ha, Gentlemen, what d'ee thinke a'the dead
2. 'Tis the laſt Office I can doe him, now to waite on
him to the Earth. (ſee me?
Fow. Coxcombes d'ee not know me, I'me alive, dee not
1. He was a noble Fellow, and deſerves
A memory, if my braine have not loſt
All his Poeticke juyce, it ſhall goe hard
But Ile ſqueeze out an Elegie.
Fow. For whom my furious Poet, ha, not know me, doe
I walke inviſible, or am I my owne Ghoſt, and you wo'not
ſee me, you ſhall feele me, you have a nimble pate, I may
chance ſtrike out ſome flaſh of wit —— no ——
Enter Maſter Worthy.
Here comes another, ſave you Maſter *Worthy.*
1. Sir I heard ill newes, Maſter *Fowlers* dead.
Wor. He is indeed Sir. *Fow.* Indeed you lye Sir.
Wor. I ſaw his eyes ſeal'd up by death, and him
Rapt in his laſt ſheet.
1. Where's his body? *Wor.* At my ſad houſe Sir.
Fow. Is my body at your houſe?
Wor. I did hope Gentlemen, we ſhould ha found
My houſe his Bridall Chamber, not his Coffin.
But Heaven muſt be obey'd, my daughter lov'd him,
And much laments his loſſe.
Fow. Very good, then I am dead, am I not?
Wor. You both were in the number of his friends,

I hope you'll adde your preſence to the reſt, a'the Funerall.
Fow. Whoſe Funerall, you man of *Bedlam.*
2. Cry mercy Sir, pray keepe your way.
1. It is a duty which without invitement
We are both prompt to diſcharge.
Fow. Maſter *Worthy*, Gentlemen d'ee heare. *Ex. man.* *Fow.*
Is't poſſible, not know me, not ſee me, I am ſo thinne, and
aery, I ha ſlipt out a'the world it ſeemes, and did not know
on't — if I be dead, what place am I in, where am I?
This is not Hell, ſure I feele no torment, and there is too
little company, no 'tis not Hell —— and I ha not liv'd after the rate of going to Heaven; yet beſide, I met iuſt now
a Vſurer, that onely deales upon ounces, and carries his
Scales at his Girdle, with which he uſes to weigh, not
mens neceſſities, but the Plate he is to lend mony upon, can
this fellow come to Heaven? Here a poore fellow is put
i'th ſtockes for being drunke, and the Conſtable himſelfe
reeling home, charges others i'th Kings name to ayde him.
There's a ſpruce Captain, newly crept out of a Gentleman
Vſher, and ſhufled into a Buffe Iurkin with gold Lace, that
never ſaw ſervice beyond *Finsbury* or the *Artillery* Garden, marches waving a deſperate Feather in his Ladies beaver, while a poore Souldier, bred up in the Schoole of
Warre all his life, yet never commenc'd any degree of Cō-
mander, wants a peece of Braſſe, to diſcharge a wheaten
Bullet to his belly no — this is not Heaven I know by the
people that traffique in't, where am I then? Vmh Ile to
Worthies before they bury me, and informe my ſelfe better
what's become a me, if I finde not my ſelfe there in a Coffin, there's hope I may revive agen, if I be dead, I am in a
world very like the other, I will get me a female ſpirit to
converſe withall and kiſſe, and be merry, and imagine my
ſelfe alive againe. *Exit.*
Enter Sir Nicholas, Whibble, Footman. [V, ii]
Nic. Come follow me, and be valiant my Maſters.
Whib. Remember your ſelfe Sir, this is your Worſhips
Footeman, and for mine owne part, though I be not cut
I
accor-

V, i, following 67. Faint pencil note: *[Wo]rthy.*

V, i, following 108. Faint pencil note: *Treed[le] / Whib[ble] / footm[an]*. Just above this in the right margin is a pencilled squiggle with no apparent meaning.

according to your cloth, I am a true Servant of yonrs, whe d'ee thinke we shall finde 'em?

Nic. Where? where dost thou thinke?

Footm. I thinke where his worship thinkes.

Nic. No matter, whether we finde 'em or no, but whe we have taken 'em as if they be not 'tis their owne fau for we are ready, for *Violetta* upon submission, I will co mit marriage with her, but for the Rogue my Tutor —

Whib. What will you doe with him?

Nic. Ile doe nothing to him, thou shalt kill him for m

Whib. It will shew better in your Footman.

Nic. Thou sayest right, he can run him through quickl but 'tis no matter who, and the worst come to the wor 'tis but a hanging matter, and Ile get a pardon first or la I would kill him my selfe, but that I should bee tax to kill a poore worme, more then ever I did in my life, be sides 'tis not with my credit to be hang'd.

Whib. And please your Worship, Ile make a faire mo on, take your choyce Sir *Nicholas*, whether we shall ki him and you'll be hang'd for him, or you shall be hang'd fo him, and we'll kill him.

Footm. Vnder correction, I think it were better to ta him Prisoner.

Nic. I like my Footmans reason, we'll take him fi Prisoner, and whosoever hath a minde to be hang'd, m kill him afterwards, — oh that I had him heere now, could cut him in pieces on my Rapiers point.

Whib. Has not your Worship beene at Fence Schoole

Nic. At Fence Schoole? I thinke I have, Ile play so ma for so many, I name no weapons, with any High *Germa* English Fencer of them all — Canst not thou Fen *Whibble?*

Whib. I Sir alas —

Nic. 'Tis but thus and thus, and there's a man at yo Mercy, I would cleave a Button, and 'twere as broad the brim of your hat now, oh that I had but my Friend b to kill a litle, prithee try me *Whibble*.

Wh

The witty Faire one.

Whib. I am none of your friends.

Nic. Why then and thou lovest me, be my foe a litle, for about or so. (aside.

Whib. I care not much to exercise your Worship, stand

Nic. Stay let me see first — there's it — I cannot with my honour wound thee, I doe not stand upon the oddes of my weapon which is longer then thine, but thou seest thine is shorter then mine by a handfull too much is too much.

Enter Tutor and Sensible.

Footm. Your Tutor Sir, and Mistris *Violetta*.

Nic. How! Downe with him some body — hee's gone, follow him close — Oh run away cowardly rascall, will ye not fight against three? Mistris it is my fortune you see or my destiny, to recover your lost Virginity, I am sorry for nothing, but that I ha shed no bloud in your rescue: but where there is no valour to be expected, 'tis best to put up with valour and reputation, would the Rascall my Tutor have popt in before me? I'm glad I have prevented him, — dee heare — your father's mad, and I'm litle better my selfe, but let's be wise, loose no time, I know a Parson shall divide us into man and wife ere any body think on't, Ile make all sure now, Ile not be put into any more of these frights, ile marry you, if any man dare runaway with you afterward, let it light upon mine owne head, and that's the worse I am sure they can doe me. *Exeunt.*

Enter Worthy, and two friends.

Wor. Gentlemen I thanke you, you carried it
To my desire most cunningly.

1: D'ee thinke 'thas taken?

2. I am covetous to see the event.

Wor. Pray sit — *Penelope.* *Enter Penelope.*

1. In mourning.

Wor. All parties in the ingagement.

Pen. You oblige a womans service.

2. Gentle Lady
And if it prove fortunate, the designe

I 2 Will

V, ii, following 22. Faint pencil note: *Tutor / sensible*.
V, ii, 41 f. Faint pencil note: *[W]orthy / 2 frie[nds]*.
V, ii, 46. Faint pencil note: *Penel[ope]*.
V, ii, following 53. Faint pencil note: *Winnif[red] / Fowle[r]*.
V, ii, 58. Faint pencil note: *Hea[rse]*.

Will be your honour, and the deed it selfe
Reward us in his benefit, he was ever wilde

1. Assured your ends are noble, we are happy in'.

Enter Winifrid.

Win. Master *Fowler.* *Wor.* Is he come already?

Pen. Remove the hearse into this Chamber
In your noblenesse, I desire you will
Interpret fairely what I am to personate
And by the Story you will finde I haue
Some cause of passion.

[V, iii]

Enter Fowler. *The Hearse brought in, Taper*

[&?]

Fow. This is the roome I sickned in, and by report dye in, umh I have heard of spirits walking with aeriall bodie and ha beene wondered at by others, but I must only wo der at my selfe, for if they be not mad, I'me come to m owne buriall, certaine these clothes are substantiall, I ow my Taylor for 'em to this houre, if the Divell bee not m Taylor, and hath furnish'd me with another suit very lik it — This is no magicall noyse, essentiall gold and silve What doe I with it if I be dead? Here are no reckoning to be payd with it, no Taverne Bils, no midnight Reve with the costly Tribe of amorous she sinners, now I ca not spend it, would the poore had it, by their prayer might hope to get out of this new pittifull Purgatory, or a least know which way I came in to't —— Here they a in mourning, what a Divell doe they meane to doe wi me — not too many teares Lady, you will but spoyle yo eyes, and draw upon 'em the misery of Spectacles, doe n you know me neyther?

Pen. Oh Master *Fowler.*

Fow. Ha, out wa't, nay and the woman but acknowled me alive, there's some hope a me.

Pen. I loved thee living with a holy flame to purge t errours of thy wanton youth.

Fow. I'me dead againe.

Pen. This made thy soule sue out so hasty a Divorce.

A

And flee to aery dwellings, hath
Left vs thy cold pale figure, which wee haue
Commission but to chamber vp in
Melancholly dust, where thy owna wormes
Like the false servants of some great man shall
devoure thee first.

Fow. I am wormes meate,

Pen. We must all dye.

Fow: Woo'd some of you would do't quickly, that I might ha company,

Pen. But wert thou now to liue againe with vs
And that by miracle thy soule should with thy
Body haue second marriage, I beleeue
Thou woo'dst study to keepe it a chast Temple, holy
Thoughts like Fumes of sacred incense houering
About this heart, then thou wo'dst learne to be
Above thy frailties, and resist the flatteries of
Smooth-fac'd lust.

Fow. This is my Funerall sermon.

Pen. The burden of which sinne, my feares perswade me, both hastned and accompanied thy death.

Wor. This sorrow is vnfruitfull.

Pen. I ha done,
May this prayer profit him, woo'd his soule were
As sure to gaine heauen as his bodie's, here,

2. We must hope the best, he was an inconstant young man, frequenting of some companies, had corrupted his nature, and a little debauched him.

Fow. In all this sermon I haue heard little commendations of our deare brother departed, rich men doe not goe to th'pithole without Complement of Christian burial, it seemes if I had liu'd to ha made a will, and bequeathed so much legacy as would purchase some Preacher a neate Cassocke, I should ha dyed in as good estate and assurance for my soule as the best Gentleman i'th Parish, had my Monument in a conspicuous place of the Church, where I should ha beene cut in a forme of prayer, as if I had beene cal'd

I 3 away

The witty Faire one.

away at my devotion, and ſo for haſt to be in heauen, went thither with my booke and ſpectacles — do'e heare Lady and Gentlemen, is it your pleaſure to ſee me, though not know me? and to enforme a walking buſines when this ſo much lamented brother of yours departed out of this world, in his life I had ſome relation to him, what diſeaſe dyed he of pray? who is his heire yet at Cōmon Law, for he was warme in the poſſeſsiou of Lands, thanke his kind father, who hauing beene in a conſumption ſixteene yeares, one day aboue all the reſt hauing nothing els to doe, dyed, that the young man might be a Landlord, according to the cuſtome of his anceſtors:

1. I doubt the proiect,

Fow. You ſhould be his heyre or executor at leaſt by your dry eyes, Sir I commend thee, what a miſerable folly 'tis to weepe for one that's dead, and has no ſence of our lamentation, Wherefore were Blackes inuented? to ſaue our eyes their tedious diſtillations, 'tis enough to be ſad in our habits, they haue cauſe to weep that haue no mourning Cloth, 'tis a ſigne they get little by the dead, and that's the greateſt ſorrow now adayes, you lou'd him Lady, to ſay truth you had little cauſe, a wild young man, yet and hee were aliue againe, as that's in vaine to wiſh you know, he may perchance be more ſenſible, & reward you with better ſeruice, ſo you would not proclaime his weaknes, — faith ſpeake well a'th dead hereafter, and bury all his faults with him, will ye, what are theſe all the gueſts? ha? what papers? ſome Elegy or Epitaph? who ſubſcribes? oh this is your Poetry.

How he dyed ſome doe ſuppoſe
How he liued the Pariſh knowes,
Whether he's gone to heauen or hell,
Aske not me I cannot tell.

Very well would the Gentleman your friend were aliue to giue you thanks for 'em.

What haue we more?

Under-

The witty Faire one.

Underneath, the fayre not wiſe,
Too ſelfelou'd Narciſſus *eyes,*
Yet his ſad deſtruction came
From no Fountaine *but a flame,*
Then youth Quench your hot deſires,
Purge your thoughts with chaſter fyres,
Leaſt with him it be too late,
And death triumph in your fate
Hither all you Virgins come,
Strow your teares vpon this Tombe.
Perhaps a limely weeping may
So diſpoſe his ſcorched clay,
That a chaſt and ſnowy flower
May reward your gentle ſhower.

Very well done vpon ſo dead a ſubiect, by the Virgin that's in't, you ſhould owe this parcell of Poetry Lady.

Pen. A womans muſe ſir,

Fow. Oh now you can anſwere me, am I dead ſtill?

Pen. Yes:

Fow. Then you talke to a dead man.

Pen. I doe.

Fow. Where am I dead?

Pen. Here, euery where.
Y'are dead to vertue, to all noble thoughts,
And till the proofe of your conuerſion
To piety winne my faith, you are to me
Without all life, and charity to my ſelfe,
Bids me endeauour with this ceremouy
To giue you buriall if hereafter I
Let in my memory to my thoughts, or ſee you,
You ſhall but repreſent his ghoſt or ſhadow
Which neuer ſhall haue power to fright my innocence.
Or make my cheeke looke pale, my ends are compos'd,
And here in ſight of heauen.

Fow: Stay,
Thart a Noble girle, and doſt deſerue
To marry with an Emperour, remoue

This

V, iii, 117 f. Faint pencil note: *Richly / Bra[ines].*

The witty Faire one.

This sad thing from vs, you doe know me Gentlemen
Witnesse my death to vanity, quitting all
Vnchast desires, reuiue me in thy thoughts,
And I will loue as thou hast taught me nobly
And like a husband, by this kisse the seale
That I doe shake my wanton slumber off,
And wake to vertue.
Wor. Meete it daughter.
Pen. Now you begin to liue:
Fow. I will grow old i'th study of my honour, this last conflict hath quite ore'come me, make me happy in the stile of your sonne.
Wor. My blessings multiply.
Gent. We congratulate this euent.
Wor. See my brother. *Enter Sir George, Braines.*
Bra. Let not your rage be so high Sir, I ha more cause to be mad,
Geo. Thou? *Bra:* I.
Geo. I haue lost my daughter.
Bra. But I haue lost my credit, that had nothing else to liue. I was more proud of that then you could be of twenty daughters,
Wor. Haue you found 'em?
Geo. Not, not, and yet this old Ruffian will not let me vex for it, he sayes the greatest losse is his.
Bra. And I'le maintaine it, 'twas my boast that I was neuer couzned in my life, haue I betrayed so many plots, discouered letters, deciphered Characters, stript knavery to the skinne, and layd open the very soule of Conspiracie, deserv'd for my cunning to bee called *Braines* both Towne and Country over, and now to forfeit 'em, to see 'em drencht in a muddy stratagem, cheated by a woman, and a pedancieall lousie Woodmonger, 'tis abhominable; patience I abhorre thee, I desire him that bids me goe hang my selfe, which is the way to *Surgeans* Hall I'le beg to ha my skull cut, I have a suspition my Braines are filcht, and my head has beene late stuft with Woodcocks

The Witty Faire one.

cocks Feathers.
Fow. Be not mad.
Bra. I will in spight of any man here, who shall hinder me if I have a minde too't.
Geo. Your happinesse removes my affliction, ha!
Enter Whibble, Tutor.
Whib: Where is Sir *Nicholas*? we have brought the Gentleman.
Bra. Are you there —— this was the Champion that justled me, shall I fetch a Dog-whip, or let me cut him up he will make excellent meat for the Divels Trencher, Ile carve him Sirra.
Geo. Forbeare, where is my daughter? villaine confesse.
Tut. Alas Sir, I was waiting upon her home, Sir *Nicholas* met me, and tooke her from me.
Geo. Wor. Sir *Nicholas*!
Whib. Yes Sir *Nicholas*, hath Mistris *Violetta*, I am a witnesse.
Bra. Why did he iustle me, there began the treachery, aske him that?
Tut: I pray y' sir let it be forgotten, I ha bin kickt for't.
Enter at one Dore Mr, Aymwell, Violetta, Manly, Clare, *at the other,* Sir Nicholas *and* Sensible.
Whib. Here she is, no there she is.
Geo. Sir *Nicholas:*
Wor: I am amaz'd:
Nic. Stay which is my wife?
Geo. Here's my daughter.
Bra. Mistris!
Fow. Fine iugling. *Francke* whence commest?
Aym: From the Priest, if you have any ioy for me, We are married.
Nic. Are there not two Sir *Nicholasses*, pray what d'ee call this Gentlewoman?
Aymw. Her name's *Violetta.*
Viol. Father your pardon.
Nic. This is fine yfaith, well may a woman mistake her hus-

K

V, iii, following 154. Faint pencil note: *[W]hible / [Tu]tor.*

V, iii, following 172. Faint pencil note: *Aymw[ell] / Violet[ta] / Manly / Clare / Tred[le] / Sensib[le].*

The witty Faire one.

husband, when a man that is the wiser Vessell cannot know his owne wife. *Geo.* Marryed to *Aymwell*!

Man. Cla. We are Witnesses.

Nic. A good iest yfaith, hearke you, were you ever Catechiz'd? What is your name forsooth?

Sens. Faith Sir guesse.

Aymw. All passion will be fruitlesse but of ioy.

Nic. Sensible? Came I from *Croydon* for a Chambermaid? D'ee heare every body I ha married *Sensible*!

Man. Cla. We are witnesses of that too.

Nic. No no, this is my wife.

Aymw. Touch her not with a rude hand.

Nic. Why, I know she meant to be my wife, and onely I ha married her, as folkes goe to Law, by Attourney, she is but her Deputy, for the more state I married her proxie.

Bra. Doe not deceive your selfe Sir, though Princes depute men to marry their wives, women doe not use to be Cyphers, she is your wife in law, let me counsell you sir to prevent laughter, some body hath been cozened, I name no body, sure it was your fortune to marry this wench, which cannot now be undone, seeme not to be sorry for't, they doe purpose to ieere you out of your skinne else.

Nic. Say'st thou so?

Bra. Be confident and laugh at them first, that they are so simple to think that you are guld, commend your choice, and say 'twas a trick of yours to deceive their expectation.

Nic. Come hither Madam *Treedle*, Gentlemen, you thinke now, I have but an ill match on't, and that as they say I am cheated, doe not beleeve it —— a Lady is a Lady, a bargaine is a bargaine, and a Knight is no Gentleman, so much for that —— I grant I married her, in her Mistresses name, and though (as great men, that use to choose wives for their favourites or Servants, when they have done with 'em) I could put her off to my Footman or my Tutor here, I wo'not, I will maintain her my wife and publish her, d'ee see, publish her to any man that shall laugh at it, my owne Ladybird.

Fow.

The witty Faire one.

Fow. You are happy Sir, in being deceiv'd, he is a noble Gentleman.

Wor. Sir *Nicholas* has releast her,
Let your consent be free then.

Geo. You have wonne it
Be my lov'd children, and I with a ioy
Flow in all Bosomes. *Braines* we are reconcil'd.

Nic. Tutor we pardon.

Fow. You may Sir, he was my engine, now,
What sayes my factious servant, nay, wee're friends,
The greatest Politician may bee
Deceiv'd sometimes, wit without braines yee see.

Bra. And braines without wit too.

Fowl. Franck th[illegible] art married, and Sir *Nicholas* has made a Lady, I h[illegible]oose a great while, and doe purpose to be made fast to [illegible] Gentlewoman. *Exeunt.*

FINIS.

This Play, called THE WITTY FAIRE ONE, as it was Acted on the Stage, may be Printed, this 14. of *January*. 1632.

HENRY HERBERT.

V, iii, 231. Faint pencil note: *[A]CT.*

THE

ORDINARY,

A Comedy,

Written by
WILLIAM CARTVVRIGHT,
M. A. Ch. Ch. Oxon.

LONDON,
Printed for *Humphrey Moſeley*, and
are to be ſold at his ſhop at the Sign of
the Princes Armes in St *PAVLS*
Churchyard. 1651.

The Ordinary by William Cartwright. Reproduced by permission of the University of Illinois Library at Urbana-Champaign.

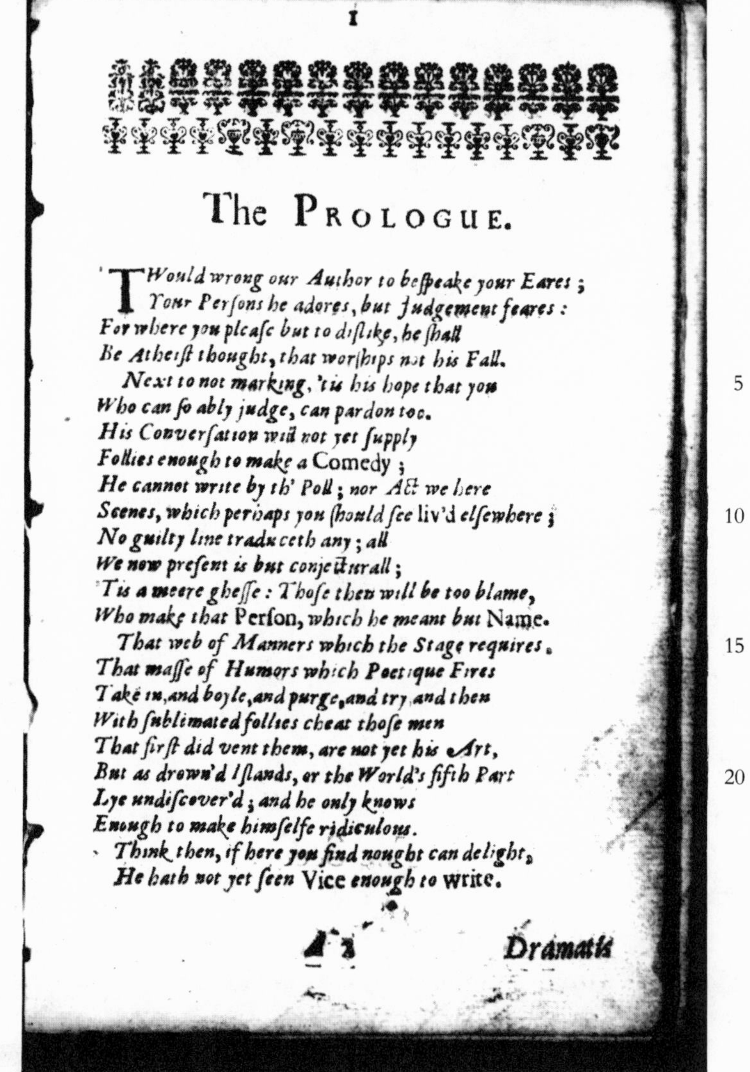

1

The Prologue.

'TWould wrong our *Author* to beſpeake your *Eares*;
Your Perſons he adores, but *Judgement* feares:
For where you pleaſe but to diſlike, he ſhall
Be Atheiſt thought, that worſhips not his *Fall*.
Next to not marking, 'tis his hope that you
Who can ſo ably judge, can pardon too.
His *Converſation* will not yet ſupply
Follies enough to make a Comedy;
He cannot write by th' *Poll*; nor *Act* we here
Scenes, which perhaps you ſhould ſee liv'd elſewhere;
No guilty line traduceth any; all
We now preſent is but conjecturall;
'Tis a meere gheſſe: Thoſe then will be too blame,
Who make that Perſon, which he meant but Name.
That web of *Manners* which the *Stage* requires.
That maſſe of *Humors* which *Poetique Fires*
Take in, and boyle, and purge, and try, and then
With ſublimated follies cheat thoſe men
That firſt did vent them, are not yet his *Art*,
But as drown'd *Iſlands*, or the *World's* fifth *Part*
Lye undiſcover'd; and he only knows
Enough to make himſelfe ridiculous.
Think then, if here you find nought can delight,
He hath not yet ſeen Vice enough to write.

A 2 Dramatis

Dramatis Personæ.

Heare-say——An Intelligencer.
Slicer——A Lieutenant.
Meanewell, Littleworth disguiz'd, a decay'd Knights Son.
} Complices in the Ordinary.
Shape——A Cheater.
Sir *Tho. Bitefigg*——A covetous Knight
Simon Credulous——A Citizen.
Andrew——his Son, suter to Mrs *Jane*.
Robert Moth——An Antiquary.
Caster. *Have-at-all.* } ——Gamesters.
Rimewell——A Poet.
Bag-shot.——A decay'd Clerke.
Sir *Christopher*——A Curate.
Vicar *Catchmey.*——A Cathedrall singing-man.
} Clubbers at the Ordinary.
Mrs *Jane*——Daughter to Sir *Thomas*.
Priscilla——Her Maid.
Joane Pot-lucke——A Vintners Widow.
Shopkeeper. Chirurgeon. } Officers. Servants.

The Scene,

LONDON.

ACT. I. SCEN. I.

{ *Hearesay, Slicer,* *Shape, Meanewell.* }

Hear. WE're made my Boys, we're made; me thinks I am
Growing into a thing that will be worship'd.
Slic. I shall sleep one day in my Chaine, and Skarlet
At *Spittle*-Sermon.
[*Shap.*] Were not my wit such
I'd put out monies of being Maior.
But O this braine of mine! that's it that will
Barre me the City Honour.
Hear. We're cry'd up
O'th' sudden for the sole Tutors of the Age.
Shap. Esteem'd discreet, sage, trainers up of youth.
Hear. Our house becomes a place of Visit now.
Slic. In my poore judgement 'tis as good my Lady
Should venture to commit her eldest sonne
To us, as to the Inns of Court: hee'l be
Undone here only with lesse Ceremony.

A 3 *Hear.* Speak

Shap.

2 The ORDINARY.

Hear. Speak for our credit my brave man of War.
What, *Meane-well*, why ſo lumpiſh?
Mean. Pray y' be quiet.
Hear. Thou look'ſt as if thou plott'ſt the calling in
O'th' *Declaration*, or th' *Aboliſhing*
O'th' *Common-Prayers*; cheare up; ſay ſomething for us.
Mean. Pray vexe me not.
Slic. Theſe fooliſh puling ſighs
Are good for nothing, but to endanger Buttons.
Take heart of grace man.
Mean. Fie y'are troubleſome.
Hear. Nay fare you well then Sir. [*Ex. Hea. Sli. Sha.*
Mean. My Father ſtill
Runs in my mind, ~~meets all my thoughts, and~~ doth
~~Mingle himſelfe in all~~ my Cogitations,
Thus to ſee eager villaines drag along
Him, ~~unto whom they crouch'd; to ſee him hal'd~~,
That ne'r knew what compulſion was, but when
His vertues did incite him to good deeds,
~~And keep my ſword dry~~ ——— O unequall Nature!
Why was I made ſo patient as to view,
And not ſo ſtrong as to redeeme? why ſhould I
Dare to behold, and yet not dare to reſcue?
Had I been deſtitute of weapons, yet
Arm'd with the only name of Son, I might
Have outdone wonder. Naked Piety
Dares more than Fury well-appointed; Bloud
Being never better ſacrific'd, than when
It flowes to him that gave it. But alas,
The envy of my Fortune did allow
That only, which ſhe could not take away,
Compaſſion; that which was not in thoſe ſavage,
And knowing Beaſts; thoſe Engines of the Law,
That even kill as uncontroul'd, as that.
How doe I grieve, when I conſider from
What

The ORDINARY. 3

What hands he ſuffer'd! hands that doe excuſe
Th' indulgent Priſon; ſhackles being here
A kind of Reſcue. Young man tis not well
To ſee thy aged Father thus confin'd.
Good, good old man; alas thou'rt dead to me,
Dead to the world, and only living to
That which is more than death, thy miſery:
The Grave could be a comfort: And ſhall I ———
O would this Soule of mine ——— But Death's the wiſh
Of him that feares; hee's lazie that would dye.
I'le live and ſee that thing of wealth, that worme
Bred out of ſplendid mucke; that Citizen
Like his owne ſully'd Wares throwne by into
Some unregarded corner, and my Piety
Shall be as famous as his Avarice;
His Son whom we have in our Tuition
Shall be the Subject of my good Revenge;
I'le count my ſelfe no child, till I have done
Something thats worth that name: my Braine ſhall be
Buſie in his undoing; and I will
Plot ruine with Religion; his diſgrace
Shall be my Zeales contrivement; and when this
Shall ſtile me Son againe, I hope 'twill be
Counted not wrong, but Duty. When that time
Shall give my Actions growth, I will caſt off
This brood of Vipers: and will ſhew that I
Doe hate the Poyſon, which I meane t' apply. *Exit.*

ACT. I. SCEN. II.

Mrs Potlucke

Pot. Now help good Heaven! 'tis ſuch an uncouth
To be a widow out of Term-time --- I (thing
Doe feele ſuch aguiſh Qualmes, and dumps and fits,
A 4 And

A purse

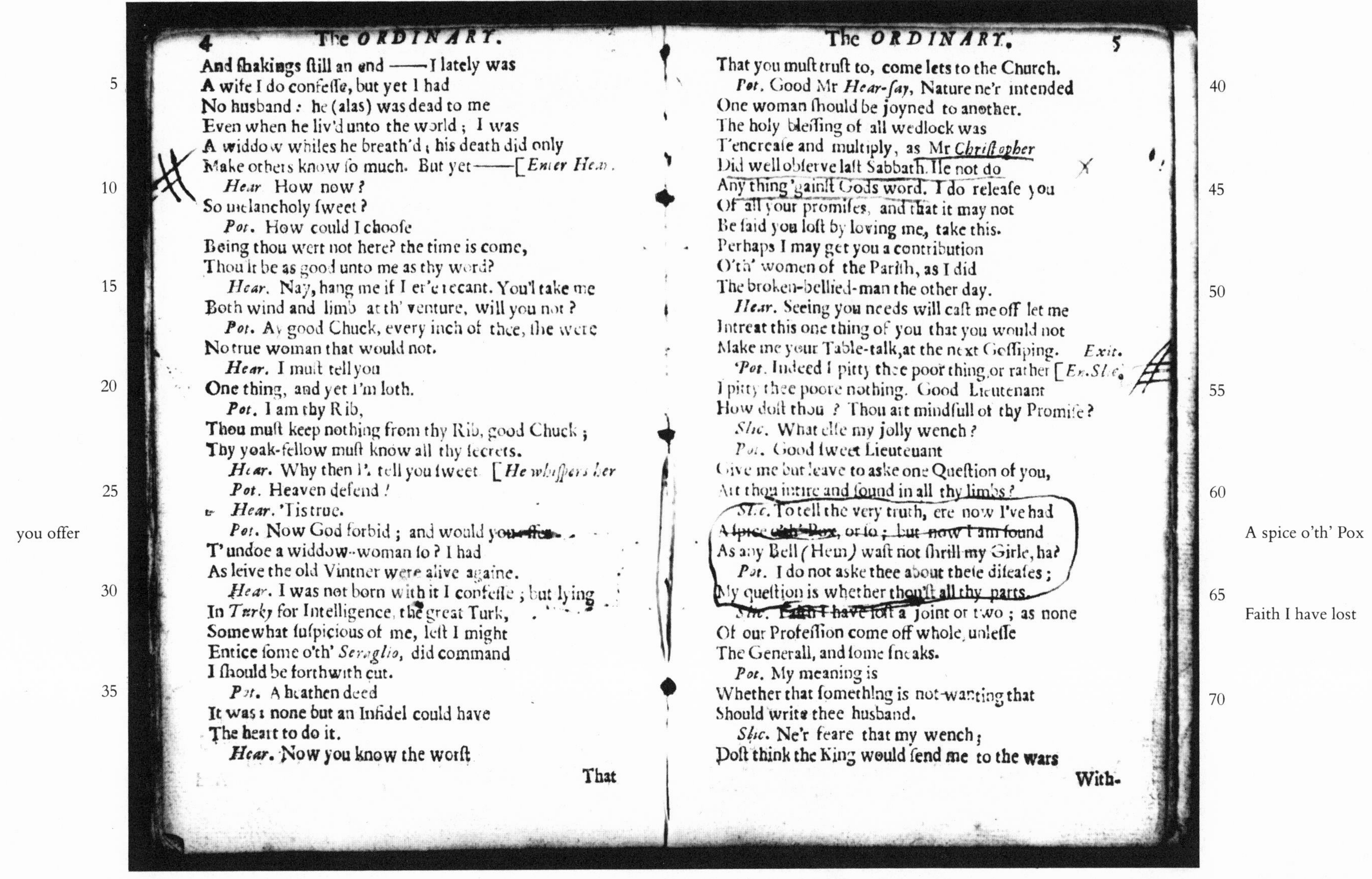

4 The ORDINARY.

And ſhakings ſtill an end ——I lately was
A wife I do confeſſe, but yet I had
No husband: he (alas) was dead to me
Even when he liv'd unto the world; I was
A widdow whiles he breath'd; his death did only
Make others know ſo much. But yet——[*Enter Hear.*
Hear How now?
So melancholy ſweet?
Pot. How could I chooſe
Being thou wert not here? the time is come,
Thou lt be as good unto me as thy word?
Hear. Nay, hang me if I er'e recant. You'l take me
Both wind and limb at th' venture, will you not?
Pot. Ay good Chuck, every inch of thee, ſhe were
No true woman that would not.
Hear. I muſt tell you
One thing, and yet I'm loth.
Pot. I am thy Rib,
Thou muſt keep nothing from thy Rib, good Chuck;
Thy yoak-fellow muſt know all thy ſecrets.
Hear. Why then I'l tell you ſweet [*He whiſpers her*
Pot. Heaven defend!
Hear. 'Tis true.
Pot. Now God forbid; and would you offer
T' undoe a widdow-woman ſo? I had
As leive the old Vintner were alive againe.
Hear. I was not born with it I confeſſe; but lying
In *Turky* for Intelligence, the great Turk,
Somewhat ſuſpicious of me, leſt I might
Entice ſome o'th' *Seraglio*, did command
I ſhould be forthwith cut.
Pot. A heathen deed
It was: none but an Infidel could have
The heart to do it.
Hear. Now you know the worſt
That

The ORDINARY. 5

That you muſt truſt to, come lets to the Church.
Pot. Good Mr *Hear-ſay*, Nature ne'r intended
One woman ſhould be joyned to another.
The holy bleſſing of all wedlock was
T'encreaſe and multiply, as Mr *Chriſtopher*
Did well obſerve laſt Sabbath. Ile not do
Any thing 'gainſt Gods word. I do releaſe you
Of all your promiſes, and that it may not
Be ſaid you loſt by loving me, take this.
Perhaps I may get you a contribution
O'th' women of the Pariſh, as I did
The broken-bellied-man the other day.
Hear. Seeing you needs will caſt me off let me
Intreat this one thing of you that you would not
Make me your Table-talk, at the next Goſſiping. *Exit*.
Pot. Indeed I pitty thee poor thing, or rather [*En. Slic*.
I pitty thee poore nothing. Good Lieutenant
How doſt thou? Thou art mindfull of thy Promiſe?
Slic. What elſe my jolly wench?
Pot. Good ſweet Lieutenant
Give me but leave to aske one Queſtion of you,
Art thou intire and ſound in all thy limbs?
Slic. To tell the very truth, ere now I've had
A ſpice o'th' Pox, or ſo; but now I am ſound
As any Bell (Hem) waſt not ſhrill my Girle, ha?
Pot. I do not aske thee about theſe diſeaſes;
My queſtion is whether thou'ſt all thy parts.
Slic. Faith I have loſt a joint or two; as none
Of our Profeſſion come off whole, unleſſe
The Generall, and ſome ſneaks.
Pot. My meaning is
Whether that ſomething is not-wanting that
Should write thee husband.
Slic. Ne'r feare that my wench;
Doſt think the King would ſend me to the wars
With-

you offer

A spice o'th' Pox

Faith I have lost

I, ii, 9. This is one of the few entrance cues in the copy, and it seems designed to call attention to an entrance within a scene and an entrance stage direction that is not centered and hence not easily noticed. But there are several such stage directions that are not marked like this.

I, ii, 43–45. Did Herbert underline these words to commend them? Evans thinks this was Herbert's way of marking a deletion, but this is hardly a line he would cut. Elsewhere in the copy he appears to have been the one responsible for scratching out oaths, sometimes vigorously. He often let bawdiness stand, but he had a sharp eye for blasphemy.

Without I had my weapons? Eunuchs are not
Men of imploiment in theſe dayes; his Majeſty
Hath newly put me on a peece of ſervice;
And if I e're come off (which I doe feare
I ſhan't, the danger is ſo great) brave Widow
Wee'l to't and get Commanders.
Potl. If you can
Leave me, I can leave you: there are other men
That won't refuſe a Fortune when 'tis proffer'd.
Slic. Well, I muſt to his Majeſty, think on't;
So fare thee well. Thine to his very Death,
That is a Month or two perhaps, *D. Slicer.* [*Ex. En. Sha.*
Potl. Kind Maſter *Shape*, you are exceeding welcome.
Here hath bin Mr *Hearſay*, and Lieutenant
Slicer: You may gheſſe at their buſineſſe, but
I hope you thinke me faithfull.
Sh. I beleeve it &
~~The memory of your Husbands aſhes, which~~
~~Scarce yet are cold, extinguiſheth all flames~~
~~That tend to kindling any Love-fire:~~ 'Tis
A vertue in you, which I muſt admire
That only you amongſt ſo many ſhould
Be the ſole Turtle of the Age.
Potl. I doe
Beare him in memory I confeſſe; but when
I doe remember what your promiſe was
When he lay ſicke, it doth take ſomething from
The bitterneſſe of Sorrow. Woman was
Not made to be alone ſtill.
Sh. Tender things
At ſeventeen may uſe that plea; but you
Are now arriv'd at Matron: theſe young ſparkes
Are rak'd up, I preſume, in ſager Embers.
Potl. Nay don't abuſe her that muſt be your Wife;
You might have pitty, & not come with your nicknames,
And

And call me Turtle: have I deſerv'd this?
Sh. If that you once hold merits, I have done;
I'm glad I know what's your Religion.
Potl. What's my Religion? 'tis well known there hath
Been no Religion in my houſe e'r ſince
My Husband dy'd. *Ent. Slic. Hearſay.*
Hear. How now ſweet *Shape*? ſo cloſe
Alone w' your Widow.
Sh. Sirs dare you beleeve it?
This thing, whoſe prayer it hath been theſe ten
Yeares, that ſhe may obtaine the ſecond tooth,
And the third haire, now dotes on me, on me
That doe refuſe all that are paſt ſixteen.
Slic. Why ~~faith~~ this was her ſute to me juſt now. faith
Hear. I had the firſt on't then. A Coachman, or
A Groome were fitter far for her.
Slic. You doe
Honour her too much to thinke ſhe deſerves
A thing that can luſt moderately, give her
The ſorrell Stallion in my Lords long ſtable.
~~*Sha.* Or the ſame colour'd Brother, which is worſe.~~
Potl. Why Gentlemen ——
~~*Hear.* Foh, foh I ſhe hath let fly.~~ *Hear.* Foh, foh!
~~*Potl.* Doe y' think I have no more manners than~~ ſo?
~~*Sha.* Nay faith I can excuſe her for that: But~~ Nay faith
~~I muſt confeſſe ſhe ſpoke, which is all one.~~
Slic. Her breath would rout an Army, ſooner than
That of a Cannon.
Hear. It would lay a Devill
Sooner than all *Trithemius* charmes.
Sha. Heark how
It bluſters in her noſthrils like a wind
In a foule Chimney.
Potl. Out you baſe companions,
You ſtinking Swabbers.
Hear. For

8 The ORDINARY.

Hear. For her gate, that's ſuch,
As if her noſe did ſtrive t'outrun her heels.
Sha. She's juſt ſix yards behind, when that appears;
It ſaves an Uſher Madam.
Pot. You are all
Moſt foul-mouth'd knaves to uſe a woman thus. (ther.
Sli. Your playſter'd face doth drop againſt moiſt wea-
Sha. Fie, how you writh it; now it looks juſt like
A ruffled boot.
Slic. Or an oyld paper Lanthorn.
Hear. Her noſe the candle in the midſt of it.
Sha. How bright it flames? Put out your noſe good Lady
You burn day-light.
Pot. Come up you lowſie Raskals.
Hear. Not upon you for a Kingdom good *Joane*,
The great Turk, *Joane* —— the great Turk.
Slic. Kiſſe him Chuck,
Kiſſe him Chuck open'd mouth'd and be reveng'd.
Pot. Hang you baſe cheating Varlet.
Slic. Don't you ſee
December in her face?
Sha. Sure the Surveyer
Of the high-waies will have to do with her
For not keeping her countenance paſſable.
Hear. There lies a hoare froſt on her head, and yet
A conſtant thaw in her noſe.
Sha. She's like a peece
Of fire-wood, dropping at one end, and yet
Burning i'th' midſt.
Slic. O that endeavouring face!
When will your coſtiveneſſe have done good Madam?
Hear. Do you not heare her Guts already ſqueake
Like Kitſtrings?
Slic. They muſt come to that within
This two or three yeares; by that time ſhee'l be
True

This two or

The ORDINARY. 9

True perfect Cat: They practiſe before hand.
Pot. I can endure no longer, though I ſhould
Throw off my womanhood.
Hear. No need, that's done
Already: nothing left thee, that may ſtile thee
Woman but Luſt, and Tongue; no fleſh but what
The vices of the ſex exact, to keep them
In heart.
Sli: Thou art ſo leane and out of caſe
That 'twere abſurd to call thee Devill incarnate.
Slic. Th'art a dry Devill troubled with the luſt
Of that thou haſt not, fleſh.
Pot. Rogue, Raskall, Villaine,
Ile ſhew your cheating tricks Faith: all ſhall
Be now laid open. Have I ſuffer'd you
Thus long i' my houſe, and ne'r demanded yet
One penny rent, for this? Ile have it all,
By this good bleſſed light I will.
Hear. You may
If that you pleaſe undo your ſelf, you may.
I will not ſtrive to hinder you. There is
Something contriving for you, which may be
Perhaps yet brought about. a Match or ſo;
A proper fellow; 'tis a trifle, that;
A thing you care not for I know. Have I
Plotted to take you off from theſe to match you
In better ſort, and am us'd thus? As for
The Rent you aske, here take it, take your money;
Fill, choake your gaping throat. But if as yet
You are not deaf to counſell, let me tell you
It had been better that you ne'r had took
It may ſtop ſome proceedings.
Pot. Mr *Hearſay*,
You know you may have even my heart out of
My belly (as they ſay) if you'l but take
The

vices of the sex exact

Sli: Sha.

this good blessed light . . . *stet*

The paines to reach it out ; I am sometimes
Peevish I doe confesse ; here take your money.
Hear. No.
Potl. Good Sir.
Hear. No, keep it and hoord it up.
My purse is no safe place for it.
Potl. Let me
Request you that you would be pleas'd to take it.
Hear. Alas 'twould only trouble me : I can
As willingly goe light, as be your Treasurer.
Potl. Good Mr *Slicer* speake to him to take it,
Sweet Mr *Shape*, joyne with him.
Slic. Nay, be once
O're-rul'd by a woman.
Sha. Come, come, you shall take it.
Potl. Nay ~~Faith~~ you shall ; here put it up good Sir.
Hear. Upon intreaty I'm content for once ;
But make no Custome of't; you doe presume
Upon my easie foolishnesse ; 'tis that
Makes you so bold : were it another man
He ne'r would have to doe with you. But marke me,
If e'r I find you in this mood againe
I'le dash your hopes of Marriage for ever.
Ex. all but Hear.

Faith

ACT. I. SCEN. 3.

To him,
Meanewell, Andrew.

And. GOd save you Tutors both.
Mean. Fie *Andrew*, fie ;
What kisse your hand ? you smell, not complement.
Hear. Besides, you come too near when you salute.
Your breath may be discover'd ; and you give

Ad-

[I, iv, 62]

Distinguish each of them by severall sents ——
Hear. A grove of Pikes are rushes to him, hail
More frights you, than a shower of Bullets him ——
Slic. The Dutch come up like broken beer ; the Irish
Savour of Usquebaugh ; the Spanish they
Smell like unto perfume at first, but then
After a while end in a fatall steame ——
Hear. One Drum's his Table, the other is his Musick.
His Sword's his Knife, his Colours are his Napkins,
~~Carves nourishing Horse, as he is us'd to do~~
~~The hostile Paguim, or we venison~~ : Eates
Gunpowder with his meat instead of Pepper,
Then drinks o'r all his Bandeleers, and fights ——
Slic. Secrets are rank'd and order'd in his belly,
Just like Tobacco leaves laid in a sweat.
Here lies a row of Indian secrets, then
Something of's own on them ; on that another
Of China Counsels, cover'd with a lidd
Of New-found-land discoveries ; next, a bed
Of Russia Policies, on them a lay
Of Pretter-Johnson whispers ——
Hear. Slights a tempest ;
Counts lightning but a giving fire , and thunder
The loud report when heaven hath discharg'd.
H' hath with his breath supplyd a breach.
When he's once fixt no Engine can remove him.
Slic. 'Twould be a Policy worth hatching, to
Have him disflected, if 'twere not too cruell.
All states would lye as open as his bowels.
Turkey in's bloudy Liver ; *Italy*
Be found in's reines ; *Spaine* busie in his Stomack ;
Venice would float in's Bladder ; *Holland* saile
Up and down all his veines ; *Bavaria* lie
Close in some little gut, and *Ragioni*
Di Stato generally reek in all :

B 4 Crid

Horse
hostile Paguim

I, iii, following 5. Pages 11 through 14 are missing in the copy.

Cred. I ſee my Son's too happy; he is born
To be ſome man of Action, ſome Engine
For th'overthrow of Kingdomes.
Troth
Hear. ~~Troth~~ he may
Divert the Torrent of the Turkiſh rule
Into ſome other Tract; damme up the ſtreame
Of that vaſt headlong Monarchy, if that
He want not meanes to compaſſe his intents.
Cred. The Turkiſh Monarchy's a thing too big
For him to mannage; he may make perhaps
The Governour of ſome new little Iſland,
And there plant Faith and Zeale: But for the preſent
M'ambition 's only to contrive a Match
Between Sir *Thomas Bite-figg's* only Daughter,
And (if I may ſo call him now) my Son;
'Twill raiſe his Fortunes ſomewhat.
We have got *There is one*
Slic. ~~We have got~~ [struck out]
There is
One that will doe more good with's tongue that way
Than that uxorious ſhowre that came from Heaven,
But you muſt oyle it firſt.
Cred. I underſtand you.
Greaze him i'th' fiſt you meane: there's juſt ten Peeces,
'Tis but an earneſt: If he bring't about,
then
I'le make thoſe then a hundred.
Hear. Think it done. *Ex.Cred.& Ent.Sh.Mean.*

ACT. I. SCEN. V.

Shape

Hearesay, Slicer, Meanewell, ~~*Shape.*~~

OUr life methinks is but the ſame with others
To couzen, and be couzen'd, makes the Age.
~~The Prey and Feeder are that Civill thing~~
That Sager heads call
~~That Sager heads call Body Politick.~~
Body Politick
Here is the only difference; others cheat
By

By ſtatute, but we do't upon no grounds.
The fraud's the ſame in both, there only wants
Allowance to our way: the Common-wealth
Hath not declar'd her ſelf as yet for us;
Wherefore our Policy muſt be our Charter.
Mea. Well mannag'd Knav'ry is but one degree
Below plaine Honeſty.
Slic. Give me villany
That's circumſpect, and well advis'd, that doth
Colour at leaſt for goodneſſe. If the Cloake
And Mantle were pull'd off from things, 'twould be
As hard to meet an honeſt Action as
A liberall Alderman, or a Court Nun.
Hear. Knowing then how we muſt direct our ſteps,
Let us chalk out our paths; you, *Shape*, know yours.
Shap. Where e'r I light on Fortune, my Commiſſion
Will hold to take her up: I'l eaſe my ſilken
Friends of that idle luggage, we call Money.
Hear. For my good toothleſſe Counteſſe, let us try
To win that old Emerit thing, that like
An Image in a German clock, doth move,
Not walke, I meane that rotten Antiquary.
Mean. Hee'l ſurely love her, 'cauſe ſhe looks like ſome
Old ruin'd peece, that was five Ages backward.
Hear. To the great Veſtry wit, the Livery braine,
My Common-Councell Pate, that doth determine
A City buſineſſe with his gloves on's head,
We muſt apply good hope of wealth and meanes.
Slic. That griping Knight Sir *Thomas* muſt be call'd
With the ſame lure: he knows t' a crum how much
Loſſe is in twenty dozen of Bread, between
That which is broke by th' hand, and that is cut,
Which way beſt keeps his Candles, bran or ſtraw,
What tallow's loſt in putting of 'm out
By ſpittle, what by foot, what by the puffe,
B 3 What

What by the holding downwards, and what by
The extinguisher; which week will longest be
In lighting, which spend fastest; he must heare
Nothing but Moyties, and Lives, and Farmes,
Coppies, and Tenures; he is deaf to th'rest.
Mean. I'l speak the language of the wealthy to him.
My mouth shall swill with Bags, Revenues, Fees,
Estates, Reversions, Incomes, and assurance.
He's in the Gin already, for his Daughter
Shee'l be an easie purchase.
Hear. I do hope
We shall grow famous; have all sorts repaire
As duly to us, as the barren Wives
Of aged Citizens do to St *Antholins.*
Come let us take our Quarters: we may come
To be some great Officers in time,
And with a reverend Magisterial frown,
Passe sentence on those faults that are our own. *ExOm.*

3 Baily fighting

ACT. II. SCENE I.

Have-at *Have-at-all, Slicer, Hearsay,* having rescued him
Covin Garden. in a Quarrell.

Have. 'Tis destin'd, I'l be valiant, I am sure
I shall be beaten with more credit then,
Than now I do escape. *Lieutenant* hast
Bethought thy self as yet? hast any way
To make my Sword fetch bloud?
Slic. You never yet
Did kill your man then?
Have. No.
Hear. Nor get your Wench
With child I warrant?
Have.

Have. O Sir.
Slic. You're not quite
Free of the Gentry till y'have marrd one man
And made another: when one fury hath
Cryd quit with t'other, and your Lust repair'd
What Anger hath destroyd, the Titles yours,
Till then you do but stand for't.
Have. Pox! who'd be Pox
That vile scorn'd Name, that stuffs all Court-gate Bils?
Lieutenant thou mayst teach me valour yet.
Slic. Teach thee? I will inspire thee man. I'l make
Thy name become a terrour, and to say
That *Have-at-all* is comming, shall make roome
As when the Bears are in Procession.
Heark hither *Franke*—— *They consult.*
Hear. That's good, but——
Slic. How think'st now?
Hear. Nay he will pay you large—lie. [*aloud*
Have. Pay, what else?
Hear. Make him beleeve the Citizen's his Guest,
The Citizen that he is his.
Slic. Concluded;
Would you fight fair or conquer by a spell?
Have. I do not care for Witchcraft; I would have would
My strength relie meerlie upon it self.
Slic. There is a way that I ne'r shew'd it yet,
But to one Spaniard, and 'twas wondrous happy.
Have. Think me a second Spaniard worthy Sir.
Slic. Then listen. The design is by a dinner;
An easie way you'l say, I'l say a true;
Hunger may break stone walls, it ne'r hurts men.
Your cleanly feeder is your man of valour.
What makes the Peasant grovel in his muck,
Humbling his crooked soule, but that he eates
Bread just in colour like it? Courage ne'r
B 4 Vouch-

II, i, opening. Rarely did prompters make notes on stage action. The bailiffs fighting was not called for by the author, but it is the kind of stage business players might add.

26 The ORDINARY.

Vouchſaf'd to dwell a minute, where a ſullen
Pair of brown loaves darken'd the durty Table;
Shadows of bread, not bread. You never knew
A ſolemn Son of Bagpudding and Pottage
Make a Commander; or a Tripe-eater
Become a Tyrant: he's the Kingdoms arm
That can feed large, and choicely.
Have. If that be
The way, I'l eat my ſelf into courage,
And will devour valour enough quickly.
Slic. 'Tis not the caſual eating of thoſe meats,
That doth procure thoſe Spirits, but the order,
And manner of the meal; the ranking of
The diſhes, that does all; elſe he that hath
The greateſt range would be the hardeſt man.
Thoſe goodly Juments of the Guard would fight
(As they eat Beef) after ſix ſtone a day;
The Spit would nouriſh great Attempts; my Lord
Would lead a Troop, as well as now a Maſque;
And force the Enemies ſword with as much eaſe
As his Miſtriſſes Bodkin. Gallants would
Owe valour to their Ordinaries, and fight
After a crown a meal.
Have. I do conceive
The Art is all in all. If that you'l give
A bill of your directions, I'l account
My ſelf oblig'd unto you for my ſafety.
Slic Take it then thus. All muſt be Souldier-like;
No diſh but muſt preſent Artilery.
Some military inſtrument in each.
Imprimis ſixe or ſeven yards of Tripe
Diſplay'd inſtead o'th' Enſign.
Have. Why, you ſaid,
Tripe-eaters ne'r made Tyrants.
Slic. Peace Sir, Learners
Muſt

The ORDINARY. 27

Muſt be attentive and beleeve. Do y' think
Wee'l eat this? 'tis but for formalitie;
Item a Coller of good large fat Brawn
Serv'd for a Drum, waited upon by two
Fair long black Puddings lying by for drumſticks;
Item a well grown Lamprey for a Fife;
Next ſome good curious Marchpanes made into
The form of Trumpets: Then in order ſhall
Follow the Officers. The Captain firſt
Shall be preſented in a warlike Cock,
Swiming in whitebroth, as he's wont in bloud;
The Sergeant Major he may buſtle in
The ſhape of ſome large Turkey; For my ſelf,
Who am Leiutenant, I'm content there be
A Buſtard only; let the Corporall
Come ſweating in a Breaſt of Mutton, ſtuff'd
With Pudding, or ſtrut in ſome aged Carpe,
Either doth ſerve I think. As for Perdues
Some choice Sous'd-fiſh brought couchant in a diſh
Among ſome fennell, or ſome other graſſe,
Shews how they lie i'th' field. The Souldier then
May be thus rank'd. The common one Chicken,
Duck, Rabbet, Pidgeon. For the more Gentile,
Snipe, Woodcock, Partridge, Pheaſant, Quail will ſerve.
Hear. Bravelie contriv'd.
Slic. That weapons be not wanting
Wee'l have a dozen of bones well charg'd with marrow
For Ordnance, Muskets, Petronels, Petarrs;
Twelve yards of Sauſage by inſteed of Match;
And Caveari then prepar'd for wild-fire.
Hea. Rare Rogue! how I do love him now me thinks.
Slic. Next wee'l have true fat, eatable old Pikes;
Then a freſh Turbut brought in for a Buckler,
With a long Spitchcock for the ſword adjoyn'd;
Wee'l bring the ancient weapons into play.
Have-

II, i, 82. Here and at line 86 are *X* marks, the significance of which is not clear. They come at points where Slicer is presenting an "Item" in his description, so perhaps the marks are cues for some bits of accompanying stage business or offstage sound effects.

22 The ORDINARY.

Have. Moſt rare by ~~heaven~~.
Slic. Peaches, Apricocks,
And Malecotoons, with other choiſer Plums
Will ſerve for large ſiz'd Bullets; then a diſh
Or two of Peaſe for ſmall ones. I could now
Tell you of Pepper in the ſtead of Powder,
But that 'tis not in faſhion 'mongſt us Gallants;
If this might all ſtand upon Drum heads, 'twould
Work ſomewhat better.
Have. Wil't ſo? then we'l have 'em
From every ward i'th' City.
Slic. No I'm loath
To put you to ſuch charge: for once, a long
Table ſhall ſerve the turn; 'tis no great matter.
The main thing's ſtill behind: we muſt have there
Some Fort to ſcale; a veniſon paſtie doth it:
You may have other Pies inſtead of outworks;
Some Sconces would not be amiſſe, I think.
When this is all prepar'd, and when we ſee
The Table look like a pitch'd Battel, then
Wee'l give the word, Fall too, ſlaſh, kill, and ſpoile;
Deſtruction, rapine, violence, ſpare none.
Hear. Thou haſt forgotten Wine, Lieutenant, wine.
Slic. Then to avoid the groſſe abſurdity
Of a dry Battel, cauſe there muſt ſome bloud
Be ſpilt (on th' enemies ſide I mean) you may
Have there a Rundlet of briſk Claret, and
As much of Aligant, the ſame quantitie
Of Tent would not be wanting, 'tis a wine
Moſt like to bloud. Some ſhal bleed fainter colours,
As Sack, and Whitewine. ~~Some that have the itch~~
~~[illegible]~~
~~Shall [illegible] in't.~~
When this is done fight boldly; write your ſelf
The tenth or 'leventh Worthy, which you pleaſe,
Your

The ORDINARY. 23

Your choice is free.
Have. I'l be the gaming Worthy;
My word ſhall be Twice twelve; I think the dice
Ne'r mounted any upon horſeback yet.
Sl. Wee'l bring your friends & ours to this large dinner:
It works the better eaten before witneſſe.
Beware you ſay 'tis yours: Confeſſion is
One ſtep to weakneſſe, private Conſcience is
A Theater to valour. Let's be cloſe.
Old *Credulous*, and his Son, and Mr *Caſter*
Shall all be there.
Have. But then they will grow valiant
All at my charge.
Slic. Ne'r fear't; th' unknowing man
Eates only Fleſh, the underſtanding Valour;
His ignorance i'th' myſtery keeps him coward:
To him 'tis but a Meale; to you 'tis vertue.
It ſhall be kept here.
Hav. No fitter place; there is
An old rich Clutchfiſt Knight, Sir *Thomas Bitefig*,
Invite him too; perhaps I may have luck,
And break his Purſe yet open for one hundred.
A Uſurer is ſomewhat exorable
When he is full; He ne'r lends money empty.
Slic. Diſcreet, and wiſely done; I was about
T' have prompted it.
Hear. Stout Mr *Haveatall*
Lets be ſworn Brothers.
Have. ~~[illegible]~~ thou fear'ſt Ile beat thee Pox
After I've eaten. Doſt thou think I'l offer't?
By my ~~next~~ meale ~~I wont~~: nay I do love meale I
My friends, how ~~e'n. I~~ do but think how I e'r: I
Shall baſtinado o'r the Ordinaries.
Arm'd with my ſword, Battoone and foot Ile walk
To give each rank its due. No one ſhall ſcape,
But

II, i, 146–48. The canceled lines are: "Some that have the itch / (As there are Taylors still in every Army) / Shall run with Renish, that hath Brimstone in't."

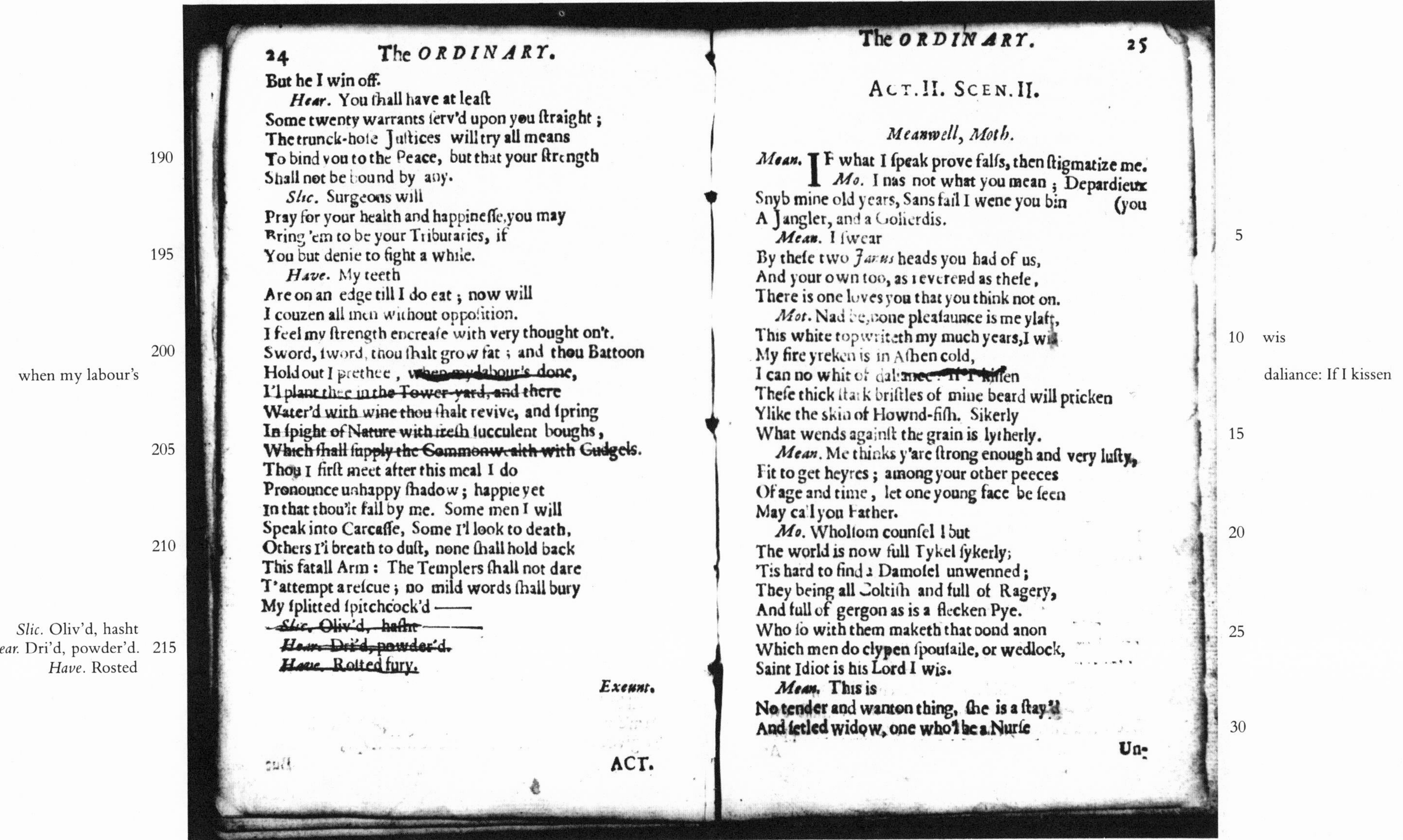

24 The ORDINARY.

But he I win off.
Hear. You ſhall have at leaſt
Some twenty warrants ſerv'd upon you ſtraight;
The trunck-hoſe Juſtices will try all means
To bind you to the Peace, but that your ſtrength
Shall not be bound by any.
Slic. Surgeons will
Pray for your health and happineſſe,you may
Bring 'em to be your Tributaries, if
You but denie to fight a while.
Have. My teeth
Are on an edge till I do eat; now will
I couzen all men without oppoſition.
I feel my ſtrength encreaſe with very thought on't.
Sword, ſword, thou ſhalt grow fat; and thou Battoon
Hold out I prethee, ~~when my labour's done,~~ when my labour's
I'l ~~plant thee in the Tower-yard, and there~~
~~Water'd with wine thou ſhalt revive, and ſpring~~
~~In ſpight of Nature with freſh~~ ſucculent boughs,
~~Which ſhall ſupply the Commonwealth with~~ Cudgels.
Thou I firſt meet after this meal I do
Pronounce unhappy ſhadow; happie yet
In that thou'lt fall by me. Some men I will
Speak into Carcaſſe, Some I'l look to death,
Others I'l breath to duſt, none ſhall hold back
This fatall Arm: The Templers ſhall not dare
T'attempt a reſcue; no mild words ſhall bury
My ſplitted ſpitchcock'd ——
~~*Slic.* Oliv'd, haſht~~ —— *Slic.* Oliv'd, hasht
~~*Hear.* Dri'd, powder'd.~~ *Hear.* Dri'd, powder'd.
~~*Have.* Roſted~~ fury. *Have.* Rosted

Exeunt.

ACT.

The ORDINARY. 25

ACT. II. SCEN. II.

Meanwell, Moth.

Mean. If what I ſpeak prove falſe, then ſtigmatize me.
Mo. I nas not what you mean; Depardieux
Snyb mine old years, Sans fail I wene you bin (you
A Jangler, and a Golierdis.
Mean. I ſwear
By theſe two *Janus* heads you had of us,
And your own too, as reverend as theſe,
There is one loves you that you think not on.
Mot. Nad be, none pleaſaunce is me ylaft,
This white topwriteth my much years, I wis wis
My fire yreken is in Aſhen cold,
I can no whit of dal~~iance: If I kiſſen~~ daliance: If I kissen
Theſe thick ſtark briſtles of mine beard will pricken
Ylike the skin of Hownd-fiſh. Sikerly
What wends againſt the grain is lytherly.
Mean. Me thinks y'are ſtrong enough and very luſty,
Fit to get heyres; among your other peeces
Of age and time, let one young face be ſeen
May call you Father.
Mo. Wholſom counſel I but
The world is now full Tykel ſykerly;
'Tis hard to find a Damoſel unwenned;
They being all Coltiſh and full of Ragery,
And full of gergon as is a flecken Pye.
Who ſo with them maketh that bond anon
Which men do clypen ſpouſaile, or wedlock,
Saint Idiot is his Lord I wis.
Mean. This is
No tender and wanton thing, ſhe is a ſtay'd
And ſetled widow, one who'l be a Nurſe

Un-

II, i, 204. Though "succulent boughs" does not appear to have been marked for deletion, it was probably cut with the rest of the line. Deletion marks are frequently sketchy in promptbooks, and in some cases what is left to be spoken by the actors makes no sense. A prompter would be chiefly concerned with the beginning and end of a deletion, so an illogical marking such as this one might not have mattered.

Unto you in your latter daies.
Mo. A Norice
Some dele yſtept in age I ſo mote I gone
This goeth aright, how highteth ſhe ſay you?
Mean. Mrs *Joane Potluck*, Vintner *Potluck's* widow.
Mo. *Joane Potluck* Spinſter. Lore me o thing mere
Alouten, what time gan ſhe brendle thus?
Mean. On Thurſday morning laſt.
Mo. Y' bleſſed Thurſday,
Ycliped ·liped ſo from *Thor* the Saxons God.
Ah benedicite I might ſoothly ſayne,
Mine mouth hath itched all this livelong day
All night me met eke, that I was at Kirke;
My heart gan quapp full oft. *Dan Cupido*
Sure ſent thylke ſweven to mine head.
Mean. You ſhall
Know more if you'l walk in. *Exit Meanwel,*
Mo. Wend you beforne;
Cembeth thy ſelf, and pyketh now thy ſelf;
Sleeketh thy ſelf; make cheere much Digne good *Robert*:
I do arret thou ſhalt acquainted bin
With Nymphs and Fawny, and Hamadryades;
And yeke the ſiſterne nine Pierides
That were tranſmued into Birds, nemp'd Pyes,
Metamorphoſeos wat well what I mean.
I is as Jollie now as fiſh in Seine. *Exeunt.*

ACT. II. SCEN. III.

new ordinary

Hearſay, Caſter, Shape.

Hear. CAn I lie hid no where ſecurely from
The throng, and preſſe of men? muſt every
Become a Theater, where I ſeek ſhelter? (place
And

[II, iii, 144]

I will aſcend to the Groom Porters next.
Flie higher Games, and make my mincing Knights
Walk muſing in their knotty Freeze abroad;
For they ſhall have no home. There ſhall not be
That pleaſure that I'l baulk: I'l run o'r Nature;
And when I've ranſack'd her, I'l weary Art;
My means I'm ſure will reach it. Let me ſee
'Twill yearly be——By Heav'n I know not what——
Heav'n
Hear. Ne'r think to ſum it, 'tis impoſſible;
You ſhall ne'r know what Angels, Peeces, Pounds,
Theſe names of want and beggary mean; your tongue
Shall utter nought but millions: you ſhall meaſure,
Not count your moneys; your revenews ſhall
Be proud and inſolent, and unruly;
They ſhall encreaſe above your conquer'd ſpendings
In ſpight of their exceſſe; your care ſhall be
Only to tame your riches, and to make them
Grow ſober, and obedient to your uſe.
Caſt. I'l ſend ſome forty thouſand unto *Pauls*;
Build a Cathedral next in *Banbury*;
Give Organs to each Pariſh in the Kingdom;
And ſo root out the unmuſicall Elect.
I'l pay all Souldiers whom their Captaines won't;
Raiſe a new Hoſpitall for thoſe maim'd People
That have been hurt in gaming; Then build up
All Colleges, that Ruine hath demoliſh'd,
Or, interruption left unperfect.
Hear. 'Twil
Never be done I think, unleſs you do it.
Provide the wealthieſt Gameſters, there's but one
Thing that can do us wrong, Diſcovery.
You have no enemie, but frailty.
Caſt. Night
And ſilence are loud names, compar'd with me.
Hear. I ſee the tide of Fortune rowling in.
C 2 With

II, iii, following 3. Pages 27 through 30 are missing in the copy.

Without reſiſtance. Go, be cloſe, and happy. *Exeunt.*

ordin: Continues

ACT. II. SCEN. IV.

Coven Garden

Andrew, Meanwell.

And. VPon my Conſcience now he cheated me;
I could have never loſt it elſe ſo ſtrangely.
Mean. What is a paltry cloak to a man of worth?
It barr'd men only o'th' ſight of your body:
Your handſomneſſe will now appear the better.
And. He was as like our Mr *Shape*, as could be;
But that he had a patch upon his Cheek,
And a black beard, I ſhould have ſworn 'twere he:
It was ſome body in his cloaths I'm ſure.
Mean. Some cunning Cheater upon my life won
His cloak and ſuit too.
And. There it is for certain.
Pies take him, doth he play for cloaks ſtill? Surely
He hath a Fly only to win good cloaths. [*Enter Sha.*
Sha. The Pox and Plague take all ill fortune! this
The ſecond time that he hath cheated me:
My very beſt ſuit that I had!
And. How now?
What loſt your cloak, and ſuit? A jeſt I vow;
I vow a pretty jeſt: 'odsnigs I gueſs'd ſo;
I ſaw him have it on; it made him look as like you,
As like you —— 'Tis a Rogue, a meer Decoy.
Sha. A Rogue, a meer Decoy? and yet like me?
And. Nay hold, I mean he is a Rogue, when that
He hath his own cloaths on. D'y' think that I
Would call him ſo, when he is in your ſuit?
Sha. No more of that good *Andrew*, as you love me
Keep in your wit.
And. Speak Tutor, do I uſe

To

To quarrell? ſpeak good Tutor.
Mean. That wit *Andrew*
Of yours will be th'undoing of you, if [illegible]
You uſe't no better.
And. ~~Faith~~ I thought I might *Faith*
Have broke a witty jeſt upon him, being
I've loſt my cloak.
Mean. True, but he has loſt his too:
And then you know that is not lawfull wit. [*Enter Hear.*
Hear. Here's Mr *Credulous*, and old Sir *Thomas*,
They have ſome buſineſſe with you.
Mean. Bring 'em in.
Sha My buſineſſe lies not here Sirs, fare you well. [*Ex.*
A. For Gods ſake don't you tell old Sim on't now. [*Sh.*

ACT II. SCEN. V.

To them, Sir *Thomas Biteſig*, *Credulous.*

Mea. GOd ſave you good Sir *Thomas.*
Sr Tho. Save you Sir.
Mean. You'r welcome Mr *Credulous.*
Cred. Come hither;
Whither do you ſteal now? what? where's your cloak?
And. Going to ſoiles ev'n now, I put it off.
Mea. To tell you truth he hath loſt it at Doublets.
Cred. With what a lie you'd flap me in the mouth?
Thou haſt the readieſt invention
To put off any thing —— thou hadſt it from
Thy mother I'l be ſworn; 'tnere came from me.
Mean. Peace as you love your ſelf; if that the Knight
Should once perceive that he were given to gaming,
'Twould make him break the match off preſently.
Cred. Sr *Thomas* here's my Son; he may be yours,
If you pleaſe to accept him.

C 3 *And*

34 The ORDINARY.

And. Father don't
Give me away for this: try me once more.
Sr *Tho.* I like his perſon well enough, if that
You'l make him an Eſtate convenient.
Mean. He hath more in him Sir than he can ſhew;
He hath one fault, he's ſomething covetous.
Sr *Tho.* Mary a very commendable fault.
Cred. He is deſcended of no great high bloud:
He hath a Houſe, although he came of none.
His Grandfather was a good Livery man,
Paid ſcot and lot, old *Timothy Credulous*
My Father, though I ſay it that ſhould not.
Sr *Tho.* I don't regard this thing, that you call bloud:
'Tis a meer name, a ſound.
Mean. Your Worſhip ſpeaks only
Juſt like your ſelf; me thinks he's noble,
That's truely rich: men may talk much of Lines,
Of Arms, of Bloud, of Race, of Pedigree,
Houſes, Deſcents, and Families; they are
But empty noiſe God knows, the idle breath
Of that puff nothing Honour; Formall words,
Fit for the tongues of men that ne'r knew yet
nay, what vertue — What Stem, what Gentry, nay, what vertue lies
In great Revenues — In great Revenues.
Sr *Tho.* Well and pithy ſaid.
You may work on my Daughter, and prevaile,
For that yong ſtripling: Tis a fooliſh wench,
An unexperienc'd Girle, ſhe'd like to have been
Caught by Sir *Robert Littleworths* Son, if that
I had not baniſh'd him my houſe: a youth
Honeſt enough I think, but that he's poor;
Born to more Name than Fortune.
Cred. He is ſafe
For ever wooing. I have laid his Father
Out of harm's way; there's picking meat for him:
And

The ORDINARY. 35

And God knows where he's gon; he hath not been
Seen this long while; he's ſure turn'd vagabond;
No ſight of him ſince th' Arreſt of his Father.
Andrew addreſſe your ſelf too good Sir *Thomas.*
And. 'Slid Father you're the ſtrangeſt man— I won't.
Cre. As God ſhall mend me thou'rt the proudeſt thing-- — As God shall mend
Thou canſt not complement, but in Capariſons.
And. What's that to you? I'd fain ſay ſomething yet;
But that I can't my loſſes do ſo vex me.
Cred. Come think not on't my Boy, I'l furniſh thee.
And. Sir, though ———
Cred. Nay, to't I ſay; help him Sir, help him.
And. Sir, though without my cloak at this time ——
To morrow I ſhall have one ——— give me leave
Barely to ſay —— I am your ſervant Sir ———
In hoſe and doublet.
Cred. I'l do what you told me.
Hear. Take heed: it that you do't hee'l gueſſe you'r giv'n
To idle ſpendings, and ſo croſſe the match.
I will invite him as to my ſelf.
Cred. Do ſo.
Hear. Sir *Thomas*, if you'l pleaſe ſo far to grace us,
As be a gueſt to morrow here, we ſhall
Study hereafter to deſerve the favour.
Sr *Tho.* Although I do not uſe to eat at Ord'naries,
Yet to accept your courteſie, good friends,
I'l break my wonted cuſtome.
Hear. You ſhall have it
With a free heart.
Sr *Tho.* If I thought otherwiſe,
I do aſſure you, I'd not venture hither.
Exeunt.

ACT.

ACT.III. SCENE I.

Moth.

Moth. HArrow alas! I ſwelt here as I go;
Brenning in fire of little *Cupido.*
I no where hoart yfeele, but on mine head.
Huh, huh, huh, ſo; ycapred very wele.
I am thine Leeke, thou *Chaucer* eloquent;
Mine head is white, but o mine taile is green.
This is the Palyes where mine Lady wendeth

Saint Francis, *and Saint* Benedight,
Bleſſe this houſe from wicked wight,
From the Night-mare and the Goblin,
That is hight good fellow Robin.
Keep it from all evill Spirits,
Fayries, Weezels, Rats and Ferrets,
From Curfew time
To the next prime.

Come forth mine Duck, mine Bryd, mine honycomb.
Come forth mine Cinamon. *Enter Mrs Potluck.*
Pot. Who is't that cals?
Mo. A Knight moſt Gent.
Pot. What is your pleaſure Sir?
Mo. Thou art mine pleaſure, by dame *Venus* brent;
So freſh thou art, and therewith ſo lycand.
Pot. Alas! I am not any flickering thing:
I cannot boaſt of that ſlight-fading gift
You men call beauty; all my handſomneſſe
Is my good breeding, and my honeſty.

I could plant red, where you now yellow ſee;
But painting ſhews an harlot.
Moth. Harlot, ſo
Called from one *Harlotha* Concubine
To deignous *Wilhelme*, hight the Conqueror.
Pot. Were he ten *Williams*, and ten Conquerors
I'd have him know't, I ſcorn to be his Harlot.
I never yet did take preſſe-money to
Serve under any one.
Moth. Then take it now.
Werme kiſſe! Thine lips ytaſte like marrow milk;
Me thinketh that freſh butter runneth on them.
I grant well now, I do enduren woe,
As ſharp as doth the *Titius* in Hell,
Whoſe ſtomack fowles do tyren ever more,
That highten Vultures, as do tellen Clerkes.
Pot. You've ſpoke my meaning, though I do not know
What 'tis you ſaid. Now ſee the fortune on't;
We do know one anothers Souls already;
The other muſt needs follow. Where's your dwelling?
Mo. Ycloſe by *Alderſgate* there dwelleth one
Wights clypen *Robert Moth*; now *Alderſgate*
Is hotten ſo from one that *Aldrich* hight;
Or elſe of Elders, that is, ancient men;
Or elſe of Aldern trees which growden there;
Or elſe as Heralds ſay, from *Aluredus*:
But whence ſo e'r this Yate ycalled is
There dwelleth *Robert Moth* thine Paramour.
Pot. Can you be conſtant unto me as I
Can be to you?
Moth. By *Woden* God of Saxons,
From whence comes Wenſday, that is Wodenſday,
Truth is a thing that ever I will keep,
Unto thylke in which I creep into
My Sepulchre; I'l be as faithfull to thee,

As Chaunticleere to Madam Partelot.
Pot. Here then I give away my heart to you,
As true a heart as ever widow gave.
Moth. I *Robert Moth*, this tenth of our King
Give to thee *Joan Potluck* my biggeſt crumpe Ring;
And with it my Carcaſſe entire I bequeathen
Under my foot to Hell, above my head to heaven:
And to witneſſe that this is ſooth,
I bite thy red lip with my tooth.
Pot. Though for a while our bodies now muſt part,
I hope they will be joyn'd hereafter.
Moth. O!
And muſt we part? alas, and muſt we ſo?
Sin it may be no bet, now gang in peace. *Ex. Potluck*
Though ſoft into mine bed I gin to ſink
To ſleep long as I'm wont to done, yet all
Will be for naught; I may well lig and wink,
But ſleep ſhall there none in this heart yſink. *Exit*

Coven G
Red-Lyon feilds
New hall

ACT. III. SCEN. II.

Credulous, and *Shape* dogging him.

Cred. SO now the Morgage is mine own outright;
I ſwear by the faith of my Body now
It is a pretty thing, o' my corporal Oath
A very pretty thing. Beſides the houſe,
Orchards, and Gardens: ſome two hundred Acres
Of Land that beareth as good Country corn,
For Country corn, as may be.
Shap. As I'd have it.
Cr. How now good friend! where doſt thou live? doſt (thou
Know *Caſter's* Farme?
Shap. Yes Sir; I fear 'tis gon:
Sure *Caſter's* Farme is caſt away.
Cred.

Cred. A jeſt!
Good troth a good one of a Country one;
I ſee there's wit there too. Then thou doſt know it.
Shap. I am affraid I ſhall not know it long;
I ſhall loſe my acquaintance.
Cred. 'Snigs another!
A very perillous head, a dangerous brain.
Sha. God bleſſe my Maſter, and the Devil take
Some body elſe.
Cred. Um! that's not quite ſo good
As th' other two; that ſome body elſe is me:
(Now you ſhall ſee how hee'l abuſe me here
To mine own face) why ſome Body elſe good Brother?
Sha. The rich gout rot his bones; an hungry, old,
Hard griping Citizen, that only feeds
On Heyrs and Orphans goods, they ſay muſt have it:
One that ne'r had the wiſdom to be honeſt;
And's therefore Knave, 'cauſe 'tis the eaſier Art.
I know he hath not given half the worth on't.
'Tis a meer cheat.
Cred. 'Slid Brother thou haſt paid him 'Slid
To th'utmoſt, though he hath not paid thy Maſter.
Now is my wit up too: this Land I ſee
Will make men thrive i'th' brain.
Sha. Would he were here,
Who e'r he be, I'd give him ſomewhat more
Into the bargain: a baſe thin-jaw'd ſneaksbill
Thus to work Gallants out of all. It grieves me
That my poor Tenement too goes into th' ſale.
Cred. What have I done? now wit deliver me.
If he know I am he, hee'l cut my throat;
I never ſhall enjoy it: ſure it was
Your Maſters ſeeking friend; he would ne'r elſe
Have had to doe with it; he that bought it is
A very honeſt man; and if you pleaſe him
Will

Will deale with you. I may ſpeak a word
In your behalf: 'twont be the worſe for you.
Sha. I'm going Sir unto him; do you know
Where I may find him?
Cred. What if I am he?
Sha. I am afraid he is not half ſo honeſt
As you do ſeem.
Faith *Cred.* ~~Faith~~ I'm the ſame; I try'd
What metal thou waſt made of: I perceive
Thou wilt not flinch for th' wetting; thou mayſt be
My Bayliff there perhaps.
Sha. And't pleaſe your Worſhip.
Cred. So now the caſe is alter'd.
Sha. I do know
It was my Maſters ſeeking, you would ne'r
Have had to do with't elſe. He ſent me to you
For the laſt hundred pound, by the ſame token,
That you invited him to th' eating houſe.
Cred. (O this ſimplicity! he does not know
Yet what an Ordnary means.) I was now coming
To have paid it in.
Shap. I'l ſave your Worſhip that
Labour an't pleaſe you: let me now begin
My Bayliffeſhip.
Cred. 'Snigs wiſer yet than ſoe.
Where is thy Maſter?
Shap. Sir, my Maſter's here
I thank my ſtars; but Mr *Caſter* is
At an Horſe-race ſome ten miles off.
Cred. VVhy then
I'l ſtay till he returns; 'twill be by dinner.
Sha. Your beſt way's now to ſend it; if by chance
The race go on his ſide, your VVorſhip may
Faile of your purchaſe.
Cred. 'Snigs and that's conſiderable.

Here,

Here, here, make haſte with it; but e'r thou goeſt
Tell me, is't a pretty thing?
Sha. O' my corporall Oath,
A very pretty thing: beſides the houſe
Orchards, and Gardens, ſome two hundred Acres
Of Land that beareth as good Country Corne,
God give you luck on't.
Cred. Right as I did ſay,
Ev'n word by word. But prethee ſtay a little;
VVhat Meadow ground's there? Paſture in proportion?
Sha. As you would wiſh Sir; I'm in haſte.
Cred. Nay Bayliffe
But one word more, and I have done; what place
Is there to dry wet linnen in?
Sha. O twenty
To hang up cloaths, or any thing you pleaſe.
Your VVorſhip cannot want line-room. God be wi' you.
Cred. But this once and——
Sha. I muſt be gone —— The Race. [*Exit Shape.*
Cred. Little thinkſt thee how diligent thou art
To little purpoſe. 'Snigs I pitty him;
VVhat haſte he makes to cheat himſelf! poor foole!
Now I am ſafe the wretch muſt pardon me
For his poor Tenement; all's mine. I'l ſow
One ground or other every month with Peaſe:
And ſo I will have green ones all the year.
Theſe Yeomen have no Policie i'th' world. *Exit.*

ACT III. SCEN. III

Priſcilla, Meanwell.

Priſ. PRay y' entertain your ſelf a while, untill
I give my Miſtris notice of your preſence.
I'd leave a book with you, but that I ſee

You

42 The *ORDINARY.*

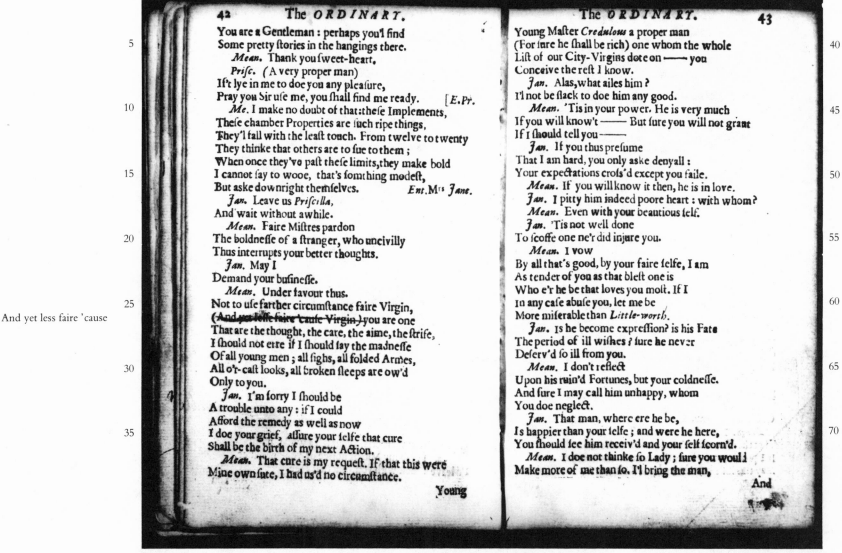

You are a Gentleman : perhaps you'l find
Some pretty ſtories in the hangings there.
Mean. Thank you ſweet-heart,
Priſc. (A very proper man)
Iſt lye in me to doe you any pleaſure,
Pray you Sir uſe me, you ſhall find me ready. [*E.Pr.*
Me. I make no doubt of that:theſe Implements,
Theſe chamber Properties are ſuch ripe things,
They'l fall with the leaſt touch. From twelve to twenty
They thinke that others are to ſue to them ;
When once they've paſt theſe limits,they make bold
I cannot ſay to wooe, that's ſomthing modeſt,
But aske downright themſelves. *Ent.*M[rs] *Jane.*
Jan. Leave us *Priſcilla,*
And wait without awhile.
Mean. Faire Miſtres pardon
The boldneſſe of a ſtranger, who uncivilly
Thus interrupts your better thoughts.
Jan. May I
Demand your buſineſſe.
Mean. Under favour thus.
Not to uſe farther circumſtance faire Virgin,
~~(And yet leſſe faire 'cauſe Virgin)~~ you are one
That are the thought, the care, the aime, the ſtriſe,
I ſhould not erre if I ſhould ſay the madneſſe
Of all young men ; all ſighs, all folded Armes,
All o'r-caſt looks, all broken ſleeps are ow'd
Only to you.
Jan. I'm ſorry I ſhould be
A trouble unto any : if I could
Afford the remedy as well as now
I doe your grief, aſſure your ſelfe that cure
Shall be the birth of my next Action.
Mean. That cure is my requeſt. If that this were
Mine own ſute, I had us'd no circumſtance.
Young

And yet less faire 'cause

The *ORDINARY.* 43

Young Maſter *Credulous* a proper man
(For ſure he ſhall be rich) one whom the whole
Liſt of our City-Virgins dote on —— you
Conceive the reſt I know.
Jan. Alas,what ailes him ?
I'l not be ſlack to doe him any good.
Mean. 'Tis in your power. He is very much
If you will know't —— But ſure you will not graut
If I ſhould tell you ——
Jan. If you thus preſume
That I am hard, you only aske denyall :
Your expectations croſs'd except you faile.
Mean. If you will know it then, he is in love.
Jan. I pitty him indeed poore heart : with whom?
Mean. Even with your beautious ſelf.
Jan. 'Tis not well done
To ſcoffe one ne'r did injure you.
Mean. I vow
By all that's good, by your faire ſelfe, I am
As tender of you as that bleſt one is
Who e'r he be that loves you moſt. If I
In any caſe abuſe you, let me be
More miſerable than *Little-worth.*
Jan. Is he become expreſſion? is his Fate
The period of ill wiſhes ? ſure he never
Deſerv'd ſo ill from you.
Mean. I don't reflect
Upon his ruin'd Fortunes, but your coldneſſe.
And ſure I may call him unhappy, whom
You doe neglect.
Jan. That man, where ere he be,
Is happier than your ſelfe ; and were he here,
You ſhould ſee him receiv'd and your ſelf ſcorn'd.
Mean. I doe not thinke ſo Lady ; ſure you would
Make more of me than ſo. I'l bring the man,
And

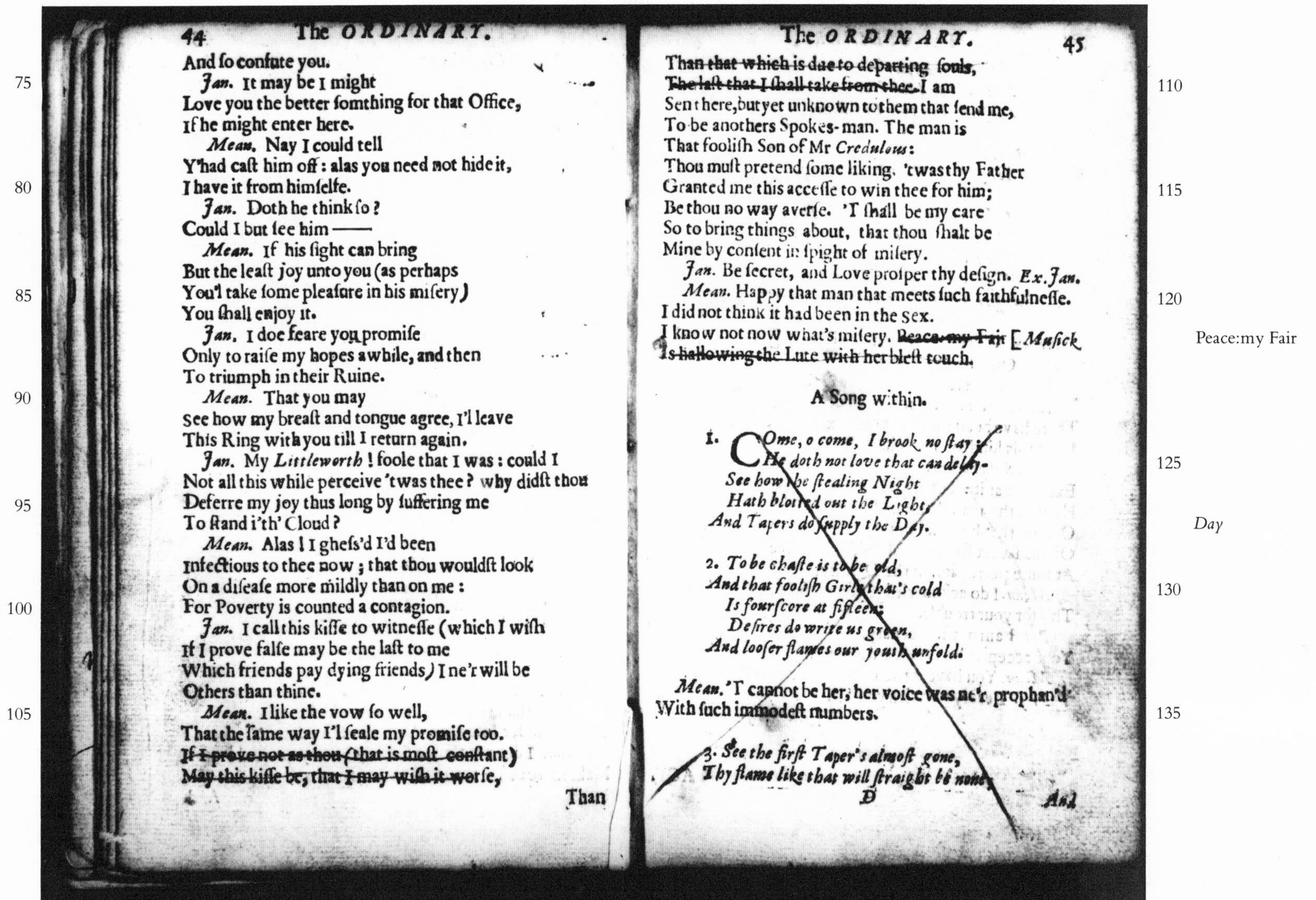

44 The ORDINARY.

And ſo confute you.
Jan. It may be I might
Love you the better ſomthing for that Office,
If he might enter here.
Mean. Nay I could tell
Y'had caſt him off: alas you need not hide it,
I have it from himſelfe.
Jan. Doth he think ſo?
Could I but ſee him ——
Mean. If his ſight can bring
But the leaſt joy unto you (as perhaps
You'l take ſome pleaſure in his miſery)
You ſhall enjoy it.
Jan. I doe feare you promiſe
Only to raiſe my hopes awhile, and then
To triumph in their Ruine.
Mean. That you may
See how my breaſt and tongue agree, I'l leave
This Ring with you till I return again.
Jan. My *Littleworth*! foole that I was: could I
Not all this while perceive 'twas thee? why didſt thou
Deferre my joy thus long by ſuffering me
To ſtand i'th' Cloud?
Mean. Alas! I gheſs'd I'd been
Infectious to thee now; that thou wouldſt look
On a diſeaſe more mildly than on me:
For Poverty is counted a contagion.
Jan. I call this kiſſe to witneſſe (which I wiſh
If I prove falſe may be the laſt to me
Which friends pay dying friends) I ne'r will be
Others than thine.
Mean. I like the vow ſo well,
That the ſame way I'l ſeale my promiſe too.
~~If I prove not as thou (that is moſt conſtant)~~
~~May this kiſſe be, that I may wiſh it worſe,~~
Than

The ORDINARY. 45

Than ~~that which is due to departing~~ ſouls,
~~The laſt that I ſhall take from thee.~~ I am
Sent here, but yet unknown to them that ſend me,
To be anothers Spokes-man. The man is
That fooliſh Son of Mr *Credulous*:
Thou muſt pretend ſome liking. 'twas thy Father
Granted me this acceſſe to win thee for him;
Be thou no way averſe. 'T ſhall be my care
So to bring things about, that thou ſhalt be
Mine by conſent in ſpight of miſery.
Jan. Be ſecret, and Love proſper thy deſign. *Ex. Jan.*
Mean. Happy that man that meets ſuch faithfulneſſe.
I did not think it had been in the Sex.
I know not now what's miſery. ~~Peace my Fair~~ [*Muſick*
~~Is hallowing the Lute with her bleſt touch.~~

A Song within.

1. *Come, o come, I brook no ſtay;*
He doth not love that can delay.
See how the ſtealing Night
Hath blotted out the Light,
And Tapers do ſupply the Day.

2. *To be chaſte is to be old,*
And that fooliſh Girl that's cold
Is fourſcore at fifteen;
Deſires do write us green,
And looſer flames our youth unfold.

Mean. 'T cannot be her, her voice was ne'r prophan'd
With ſuch immodeſt numbers.

3. *See the firſt Taper's almoſt gone,*
Thy flame like that will ſtraight be none,
D And

Peace:my Fair

Day

III, iii, 122. The printed direction calling for music should have been deleted, since the song was cut.

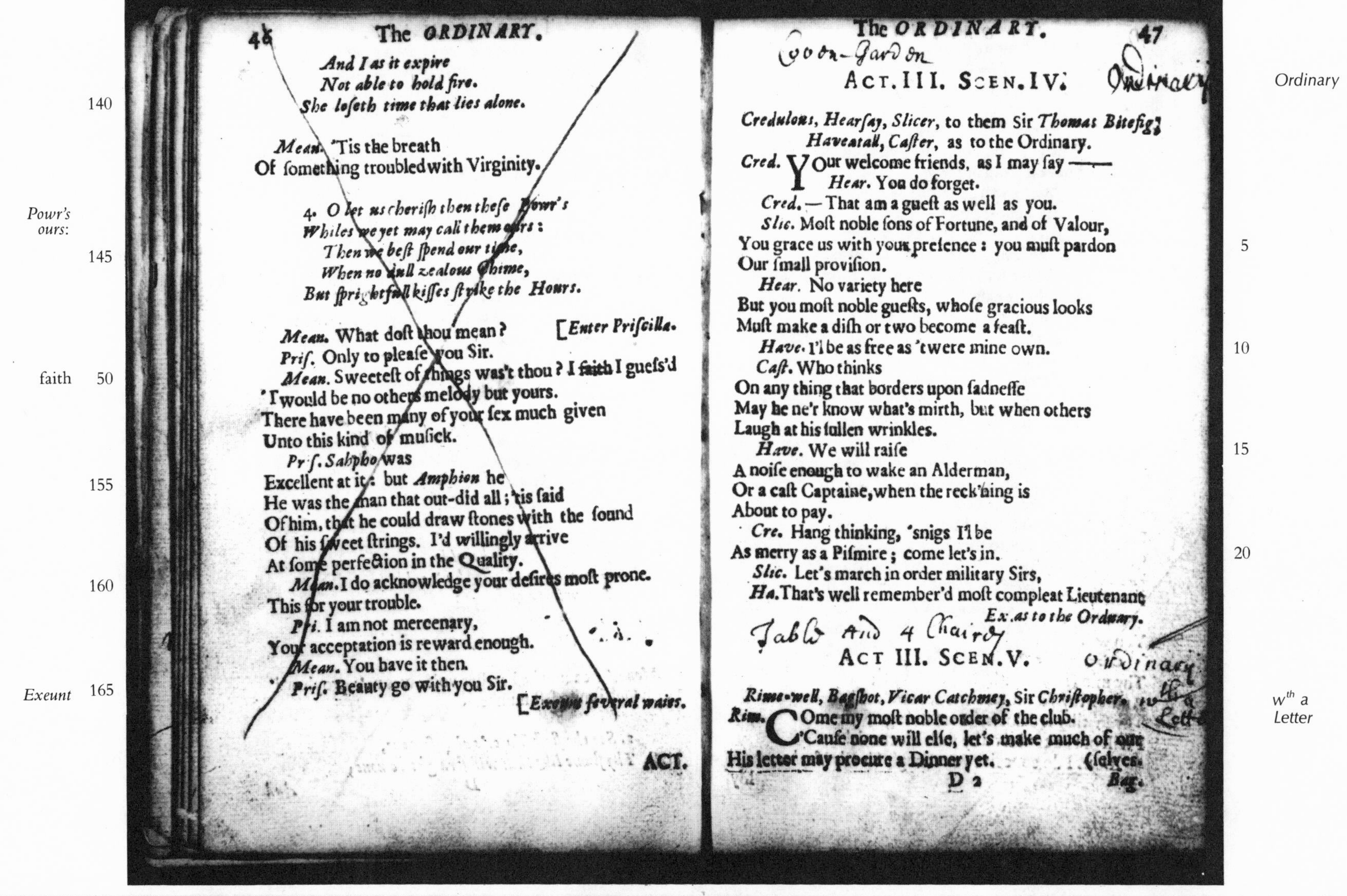

46 The ORDINARY.

And I as it expire
Not able to hold fire.
She loseth time that lies alone.

Mean. 'Tis the breath
Of something troubled with Virginity.

4. O let us cherish then these Powr's
Whiles we yet may call them ours:
Then we best spend our time,
When no dull zealous Chime,
But sprightfull kisses strike the Hours.

Mean. What dost thou mean? [*Enter Priscilla.*
Pris. Only to please you Sir.
Mean. Sweetest of things was't thou? I faith I guess'd
'Twould be no others melody but yours.
There have been many of your sex much given
Unto this kind of musick.
Pris. Sappho was
Excellent at it: but *Amphion* he
He was the man that out-did all; 'tis said
Of him, that he could draw stones with the sound
Of his sweet strings. I'd willingly arrive
At some perfection in the Quality.
Mean. I do acknowledge your desires most prone.
This for your trouble.
Pri. I am not mercenary,
Your acceptation is reward enough.
Mean. You have it then.
Pris. Beauty go with you Sir. [*Exeunt severall waies.*

ACT.

The ORDINARY. 47

Coven-Garden

ACT. III. SCEN. IV. Ordinary

Credulous, Hearsay, Slicer, to them Sir *Thomas Bitefig,* *Haveatall, Caster,* as to the Ordinary.

Cred. Your welcome friends, as I may say ——
Hear. You do forget.
Cred. — That am a guest as well as you.
Slic. Most noble sons of Fortune, and of Valour,
You grace us with your presence: you must pardon
Our small provision.
Hear. No variety here
But you most noble guests, whose gracious looks
Must make a dish or two become a feast.
Have. I'l be as free as 'twere mine own.
Cast. Who thinks
On any thing that borders upon sadnesse
May he ne'r know what's mirth, but when others
Laugh at his sullen wrinkles.
Have. We will raise
A noise enough to wake an Alderman,
Or a cast Captaine, when the reck'ning is
About to pay.
Cre. Hang thinking, 'snigs I'l be
As merry as a Pismire; come let's in.
Slic. Let's march in order military Sirs,
Ha. That's well remember'd most compleat Lieutenant.
Ex. as to the Ordinary.

Table And 4 Chairs

ACT III. SCEN. V. Ordinary

Rime-well, Bagshot, Vicar Catchmey, Sir *Christopher.* with a Letter

Rim. Come my most noble order of the club.
'Cause none will else, let's make much of our (selves.
His letter may procure a Dinner yet.

D 2 *Bag.*

Powr's ours:
faith
Exeunt
Ordinary
wth a Letter

48 The *ORDINARY.*

Bag. Cheer up Sir *Kit*, thou lookſt too ſpiritually:
ſee too much of the Tith-pig in thee.
Ch. I'm not ſo happy: *Kit's* as hungry now
As a beſieged City, and as dry
As a Dutch Commentator. This vile world
Ne'r thinks of Qualities: good truth I think
'T hath much to anſwer for. Thy Poetry
Rimewell and thy voice Vicar *Catchmey*, and
Thy Law too *Bagſhot* is contemn'd: 'tis pitty
Profeſſions ſhould be ſlighted thus. The day
Will come perhaps, when that the Commonwealth
May need ſuch men as we. There was a time
When Coblers were made Church-men, and thoſe black'd
Smutch'd Creatures thruſt into white Surpliſſes,
Look'd like ſo many Magpies, and did ſpeak
Juſt as they, by rote. But now the Land
Surfets forſooth. Poor Labourers in Divinity
Can't earn their groat a day, unleſſe it be
Reading of the Chriſtian buriall for the dead:
When they ev'n for that reaſon truly thank
God for thus taking this their Brother to him.
Catch. Something profane Sir *Chriſtopher*.
Chri. When I
Levell my larger thoughts unto the Baſis
Of thy deep ſhallowneſs, am I prophane?
Henceforth I'l ſpeak, or rather not ſpeak, for
I will ſpeak darkly.
Catch. There's one comfort then
You will be brief.
Chri. My briefneſs is prolix;
Thy mind is bodily, thy ſoul corporeal;
And all thy ſubtile faculties are not ſubtile,
Thy ſubtilty is dulneſs. I am ſtrong.
I will not be conceiv'd by ſuch Mechanicks.
Rime. I do conceive you though Sir *Chriſtopher*,
My

The *ORDINARY.* 49

My Muſe doth ſometimes take the ſelfſame flight.
Chri. *Pauci, pauci quos aequus amavit.*
But Quadrageſſimall wits, and fancies leane
As ember weeks (which therefore I call leane,
Becauſe they're fat) theſe I do doom unto
A knowing ignorance; he that's conceiv'd
By ſuch is not conceiv'd; ſenſe is non-ſenſe
If underſtood by them. I'm ſtrong again.
Rime. You err moſt Orthodoxly ſweet Sir *Kit*.
Chri. I love that though I hate it: and I have
A kind of diſagreeing conſent to't.
I'm ſtrong, I'm ſtrong again. Let's keep theſe two
In deſperate hope of underſtanding us.
Ridles, and Clouds are very lights of ſpeech:
I'l vaile my careleſſe anxious thoughts, as 'twere
In a perſpicuous cloud, that I may
Whiſper in a loud voice, and ev'n be ſilent
When I do utter words; words did I call them?
My words ſhall be no words, my voice no voice;
My noiſe no noiſe, my very language ſilence.
I'm ſtrong, I'm ſtrong: good Sir you underſtand not.
Bag. Nor do deſire; 'tis meerly froth, and barme,
The yeſt that makes your thin ſmall Sermons work.
Chri. Thou hold'ſt thy peace moſt vocally. Again.
Catch. I hate this Bilke.
Chri. Thou loveſt 'cauſe thou doſt hate.
Thy injuries are Courteſies. Strong again.
Cat. Good *Sampſon* uſe not this your Aſſes jaw-bone.
Chri. Thou'ſt got my love by loſing it; that earneſt
Jeſt hath regain'd my ſoul. *Sampſon* was ſtrong;
He kill'd a thouſand with an Aſſes-jawbone. { *Ent. a Serv.*
And ſo will I. 'ſt, 'ſt— good friend d'y'hear? { *as paſſing by* *wth a Lette[r]*
Here is a letter friend to Mr *Meanwell*.
Bag. Any Reverſions yet? nothing tranſmiſs'd?
Rime. No gleanings *James*? no Trencher Analects?
D 3 Ser-

Ser. Parly a little with your ſtomacks Sirs.
Catch. There's nothing ſo ridiculous as the hungry:
A faſting man is a good jeſt at any time.
Ser. There is a Gentleman without, that will'd me
To ask if you'l admit of him among you,
He can't endure to be in good company.
Catc. Your merry *James*; yes by all means good *James*;
Admit quoth he? what elſe? pray y' ſend him in. *Ex. Se.*
Let's be reſolv'd to fall out, now then he
Shall have the glory to compoſe the Quarrel,
By a good dozen of pacificall Beere.
Rime. Bag. Agreed, agreed.
Chri. My Coat allows no Quarrell.
Rime. The Colour bears't if you'l venture the ſtuffe,
The tenderneſſe of it I do confeſſe
Somewhat denies a grapling.
Chri. I will try,
Perhaps my Spirit will ſuggeſt ſome anger. [*Ent. And.*
An. Save you boon ſparks: wil't pleaſe you to admit me?
Chri. Your Worſhip graceth us in condeſcending
To levell thus your preſence humble Sir.
And. What may I call your name moſt reverend Sir?
Bag. His name's Sir *Kit*.
Chri. My name is not ſo ſhort,
'Tis a triſſyllable, an't pleaſe your Worſhip;
But vulgar tongues have made bold to profane it
With the ſhort ſound of that unhallowed Idoll
They call a Kit. Boy learn more reverence.
Bag. Yes, to my Betters.
And. Nay friends, do not quarrel.
Chri. It is the holy cauſe, and I muſt quarrell.
Thou Son of Parchment, got between the Standiſh
And the ſtiff Buckram bag: thou that maiſt call
The Pen thy Father, and the inke thy Mother,
The ſand thy Brother, and the wax thy Siſter,
And

And the good Pillory thy Couzen remov'd,
I ſay learn reverence to thy Betters.
Bag. Set up an hour-glaſſe; hee'l go on untill
The laſt ſand make his Period.
Chri. 'Tis my cuſtome,
I do approve the Calumny: the words
I do acknowledge, but not the diſgrace:
Thou vile ingroſſer of unchriſtian deeds.
Bag. Good *Iſrael Inſpiration* hold your tongue;
It makes far better Muſick, when you Noſe
Sternolds, or *Wiſdoms* Meeter.
Catch. By your leave
You fall on me now Brother.
Rim. 'Tis my cauſe,
You are too forward Brother *Catchm*.
Catch. I
Too forward?
Rim. Yes I ſay you are too forward
By the length of your *London* meaſure Beard.
Catch. Thou never couldſt entreat that reſpite yet
Of thy diſhoneſty as to get one hair
To teſtifie thy Age.
Bag. I'm beardleſſe too;
I hope you think not ſo of me?
Chri. Yes verily,
Not one hairs difference 'twixt you both.
Rim. Thou violent Cuſhion-thumper, hold thy tongue,
The Furies dwell in it.
Catch. Peace good Sir *Kit*.
Chri. Sir *Kit* again? Thou art a *Lopez*; when
One of thy legs rots off (which will be ſhortly)
Thou'lt beare about a Quire of wicked Paper,
Defil'd with ſanctified Rithmes,
And Idols in the frontiſpiece: that I
May ſpeak to thy capacity, thou'lt be
D 4 A

A Balladmonger.
Catch. I ſhall live to ſee thee
Stand in a Play-houſe doore with thy long box,
Thy half-crown Library, and cry ſmall Books.
By a good godly Sermon Gentlemen ——
A judgment ſhewn upon a Knot of Drunkards ——
A pill to purge out Popery— The life
And death of *Katherin Stubs* ——
Chri. Thou wilt viſit windows;
Me thinks I hear thee with thy begging tone
About the break of day waking the Brethren
Out of their morning Revelations.
And. Brave ſport Ifaith.
Rime. Pray y'good Sir reconcile them.
If that ſome Juſtice be i'th' Ordinary now
Hee'l bind them to the peace for troubling him.
Bag. Why ſhould he not good Sir, it is his office.
An. Now 'tis o' this ſide; o for a pair of Cudgels!
Rime. Peace Inkhorn, there's no muſick in thy tongue.
Catc. Thou and thy Rime lye both, the tongue of man
Is born to muſick naturally.
Rime. Thou thing,
Thy belly looks like to ſome ſtrutting hill,
O'r ſhadow'd with thy rough beard like a wood.
Chri. Or like a larger Jug, that ſome men call
[A] Bellarmine, but we a Conſcience; — A
[Wh]ereon the lewder hand of Pagan workman — Whereon
[Ov]er the proud ambitious head hath carv'd — Over
An [I]doll large with beard Epiſcopal, — An Idoll . . . beard Episcopal
Making the Veſſel look like Tyrant *Eglon.*
Catch. Prophane again Sir *Chriſtopher* I take it.
Chri. Muſt I be ſtrong again? thou humane beaſt,
Who'rt only eloquent when thou ſayſt nothing,
And appear'ſt handſome while thou hid'ſt thy ſelf,
I'm holy 'cauſe prophane.
And.

And. Couragious Raskals,
Brave Spirits, Souldiers in their daies I warrant.
Bag. Born in the field I do aſſure your Worſhip:
This Quarrelling is meat and drink to them.
Rime. Thou lyeſt. *Bag.* Nay then I do defie thee thus.
[*Ba. draws his Inkhorn and* Ri. *catcheth off* Sr Chr. *hat and ſpectacles.*]
Rime. And thus I am prepar'd to anſwer thee.
Ch. For the good Sts. ſake part them; I am blind,
If that my Spectacles ſhould once miſcarry.
Rime. Caytiff, this holy inſtrument ſhall quaile thee. — holy
Bag. And this ſhall ſend thee to thy couzen furies.
Chri. I feel a film come o'r mine eyes already,
I muſt look out an Animal conductive,
I mean a Dog.
And. Pray y'beat not out his eyes in
Anothers hands. *Chri.* Moſt ſtrongly urg'd.
Catch. Your words
Are meerly wind. *James* ho! what *James*! ſome beer.
They're maſtive Dogs, they won't be parted Sir,
Without good ſtore of Liquor. [*Ent. Serv. with beere.*
And. I will ſouce them.
Ser. Drink t' 'em Sir, if that you'l have 'em quiet.
An. Is that the way? here's to you my friends; a whol one.
Ba. Were't not for that good Gentleman thou'dſt ſmoak (for't.
Ri. Had I not vow'd ſome reverence to his preſence.
Thou hadſt been nothing.
Bag. 'Fore *Mars* I was dry;
This valour's thirſty: fill to my Antagoniſt.
Rime. No, mine own diſh will ſerve: I'm ſingular.
Few veſſels ſtill do well; I carry this
To drink my beer, while others drink their ſack.
I am abſtemious *Rimewel*: I hate wine
Since I ſpake treaſon laſt i'th' Celler. Here
Give me thy hand, thou child of fervency.
Didſt

Didst thou mistrust thy spectacles?
It was no anger, 'twas a Rapture meerly.
Chris. Drink, and excuse it after. *James* your help.
Come Man of voice keep time while that I drink.
This moisture shall dry up all injuries,
Which I'l remember only to forget;
And so hereafter, which I'm wont to call
The future now, I'l love thee stubbornly.
Your beer is like my words, strong, stinging geare.
Catch. Here little Lawyer, let's be friends hereafter;
I love this reconcilement with my heart.
And. 'Tis the best deed that e'r I did: O my conscience
I shall make a good Justice of the Peace,
There had been bloud-shed, if I had not stickled.
Ser. More bloud been spilt I warrant than beer now.
And. That Inkhorn is a deadly dangerous weapon:
It hath undone one quarter of the Kingdom.
Chris. Men should forgive; but thou art far, yea far
From it O *Bagshot*; thou'rt in love with hate;
Blesse me! I see the Fiend still in his looks;
He is not reconcilable with drink;
Hee'l never love truly, till he eat with me.
The nature of his Spirit asketh meat:
He hath a Woolf in's breast; food must appease him.
And. Cold meat will doe it, wil't not?
Rim. Any thing———
That may imploy the teeth.
And. Goe *James* provide;
You are not merry yet.
Catch. To satisfie you
In that point, we will sing a Song of his.
And. Let's ha't; I love these Ballads hugeously.

The

The Song.

1. Catch. *THen our Musick is in prime;*
When our teeth keep triple time;
Hungry Notes are fit for Knels:
May lankenes be
No Quest to me.
The Bagpipe sounds, when that it swels.
Chor. *May lankenes*, &c.

2. Bagsh. *A Mooting Night brings wholsome smiles,*
When John an Okes, and John a Stiles,
Doe greaze the Lawyers Satin.
A Reading-Day
Frights French away,
The Benchers dare speak Latin.
Chor. *A Reading*, &c.

3. Rim. *He that's full doth Verse compose;*
Hunger deales in sullen Prose:
Take notice and discard her.
The empty Spit
Ne'r cherish'd Wit,
Minerva *loves the Larder.*
Chor. *The empty Spit*, &c.

4. Chr. *First to break Fast, then to dine,*
Is to conquer Bellarmine:
Distinctions then are budding.
Old Sutcliffs *Wit*
Did never hit,
But after his Bag-pudding.
Chor. *Old* Sutcliffs *Wit*, &c.

And. Most

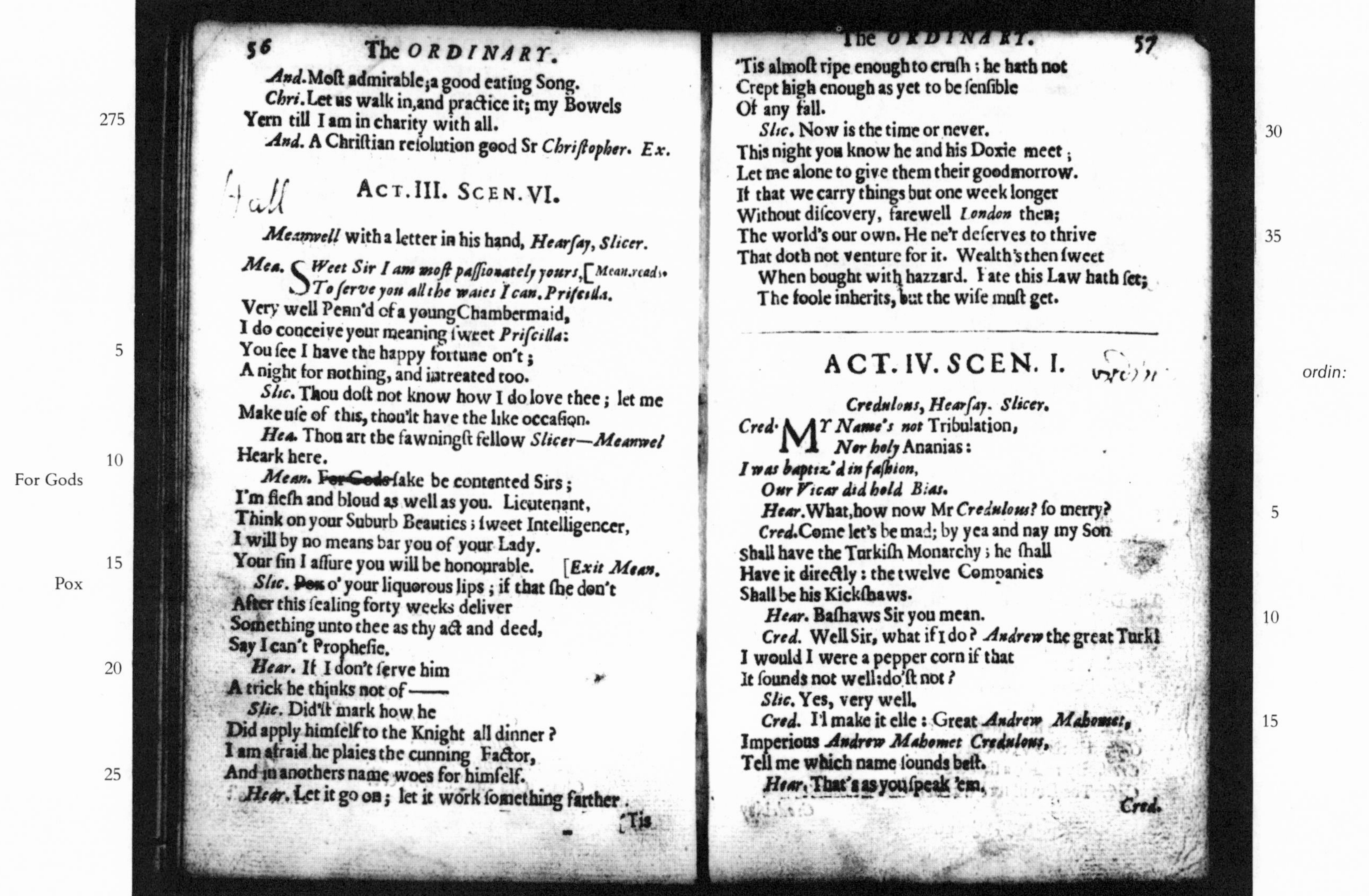

And. Moſt admirable; a good eating Song.
Chri. Let us walk in, and practice it; my Bowels
Yern till I am in charity with all.
And. A Chriſtian reſolution good Sr *Chriſtopher. Ex.*

Act. III. Scen. VI.

Meanwell with a letter in his hand, *Hearſay, Slicer.*

Mea. *Sweet Sir I am moſt paſſionately yours,* [*Mean. reads.*
To ſerve you all the waies I can. Priſcilla.
Very well Penn'd of a young Chambermaid,
I do conceive your meaning ſweet *Priſcilla*:
You ſee I have the happy fortune on't;
A night for nothing, and intreated too.
Slic. Thou doſt not know how I do love thee; let me
Make uſe of this, thou'lt have the like occaſion.
Hea. Thou art the fawningſt fellow *Slicer—Meanwel*
Heark here.
For Gods *Mean.* For Gods ſake be contented Sirs;
I'm fleſh and bloud as well as you. Lieutenant,
Think on your Suburb Beauties; ſweet Intelligencer,
I will by no means bar you of your Lady.
Your ſin I aſſure you will be honourable. [*Exit Mean.*
Pox *Slic.* Pox o' your liquorous lips; if that ſhe don't
After this ſealing forty weeks deliver
Something unto thee as thy act and deed,
Say I can't Propheſie.
Hear. If I don't ſerve him
A trick he thinks not of——
Slic. Did'ſt mark how he
Did apply himſelf to the Knight all dinner?
I am afraid he plaies the cunning Factor,
And in anothers name woes for himſelf.
Hear. Let it go on; let it work ſomething farther.
'Tis

'Tis almoſt ripe enough to cruſh; he hath not
Crept high enough as yet to be ſenſible
Of any fall.
Slic. Now is the time or never.
This night you know he and his Doxie meet;
Let me alone to give them their goodmorrow.
If that we carry things but one week longer
Without diſcovery, farewell *London* then;
The world's our own. He ne'r deſerves to thrive
That doth not venture for it. Wealth's then ſweet
When bought with hazzard. Fate this Law hath ſet;
The foole inherits, but the wiſe muſt get.

ACT. IV. SCEN. I. ordin:

Credulous, Hearſay. Slicer.

Cred. MY *Name's not* Tribulation,
Nor holy Ananias:
I was baptiz'd in faſhion,
Our Vicar did hold Bias.
Hear. What, how now Mr *Credulous?* ſo merry?
Cred. Come let's be mad; by yea and nay my Son
Shall have the Turkiſh Monarchy; he ſhall
Have it directly: the twelve Companies
Shall be his Kickſhaws.
Hear. Baſhaws Sir you mean.
Cred. Well Sir, what if I do? *Andrew* the great Turk!
I would I were a pepper corn if that
It ſounds not well: do'ſt not?
Slic. Yes, very well.
Cred. I'l make it elſe: Great *Andrew Mahomet,*
Imperious *Andrew Mahomet Credulous,*
Tell me which name ſounds beſt.
Hear. That's as you ſpeak 'em.
Cred.

III, vi, 38. There should have been an exeunt at the end of the scene.

58 The *ORDINARY.*

Cred. Oatemeleman *Andrew*, *Andrew* Oatmeleman.
Hear. *Ottoman* Sir you meane.
Cred. Yes *Ottoman.*
Then Mrs *Jane*, Sir *Thomas Bitefiggs* Daughter,
That may be the ſhe Great Turk, if ſhe pleaſe me.
Sli. The Sign o'th' half Moon that hangs at your door,
Is not for nought.
Cred. That's the Turks Armes they ſay;
The Empire's deſtin'd to our houſe directly.
Hang Shop-books, give's ſome Wine, hay for a noiſe
Of Fidlers now.
Hear. The Great Turk loves no Muſick.
Cred. Doe's he not ſo? nor I. I'l light Tobacco
With my Sum-totals; my Debt-books ſhall ſole
Pyes at young *Andrew's* Wedding: cry you mercy;
I would ſay Gentlemen the Great Turks Wedding.
My Deeds ſhall be ſlic'd out in Taylors Meaſures;
They all imploy'd in making Mrs *Mahomet*
New Gowns againſt the time; hang durty wealth.
Sl. What ſhould the Great Turks father do wth wealth?
Cred. 'Snigs I would fain now heare
Some fighting News. [*Ent. Caſt.*
Slic. There's one will furniſh you I warrant you.
Caſt. Pox! — Plague! — Hell! — Death!
Damn'd luck! — this 'tis! ———
The Devill take all Fortunes: never man
Came off ſo; quite and clean defunct by Heaven —
Heaven
Not a peece left.
Cred. What all your Ord'nance loſt?
Caſt. But one to bear, and loſe it! all the world
Was ſure againſt me.
Cred. 'Snigs how many fell?
Caſt. He threw twice twelve.
Cred. By'r Lady a ſhrewd many.
Caſt. The Devill ſure was in his hand I think.
Cred. Nay

The *ORDINARY.* 59

Cred. Nay, if the Devill was againſt you, then ——
Caſt. But one for to be hit in all the time ——
And that too ſafe enough to any ones thinking;
'T ſtood on eleven.
Cred. 'Slid a mighty ſlaughter;
But did he ſtand upon elev'n at once?
Caſt. The Plague take all impertinencies, peace.
Cred. Theſe Souldiers are ſo cholerick there is
No dealing with 'em; then they've loſt the day.
Caſt. 'Twas ten to one by Heaven all the while.
Heaven
Cred. And yet all kill'd at laſt? hard fortune faith.
faith
What news from *Bruxels*? or the *Hague*? d'y' heare
Ought of the Turks deſigns?
Caſt. I'l make thee news
For the Coranti Dotard.
Cred. Ay, the Coranti,
What doth that ſay?
Caſt. O hell! thou fooliſh thing
Keep in that tongue of thine, or—
Slic. Good now peace,
He's very furious when he's mov'd.
Hear. This 'twas.
You muſt be ventring without your Fancy-man.
Cred. What Officer's that Fancy-man, Lieutenant?
Some great Commander ſure.
Caſt. Pox! let it go;
Pox
I'l win't again: 'twas but the Reliques of
An idle hundred.
Cred. 'Snigs and well remember'd.
You did receive the hundred that I ſent you
To th' Race this morning by your man, my Bayliffe?
Caſt. Take him away, his wine ſpeaks in him now.
Cred. Godſnigs the Farme is mine, and muſt be ſo.
Slie. Debate theſe things another time, good friends.
Enter Haveatall.
Come

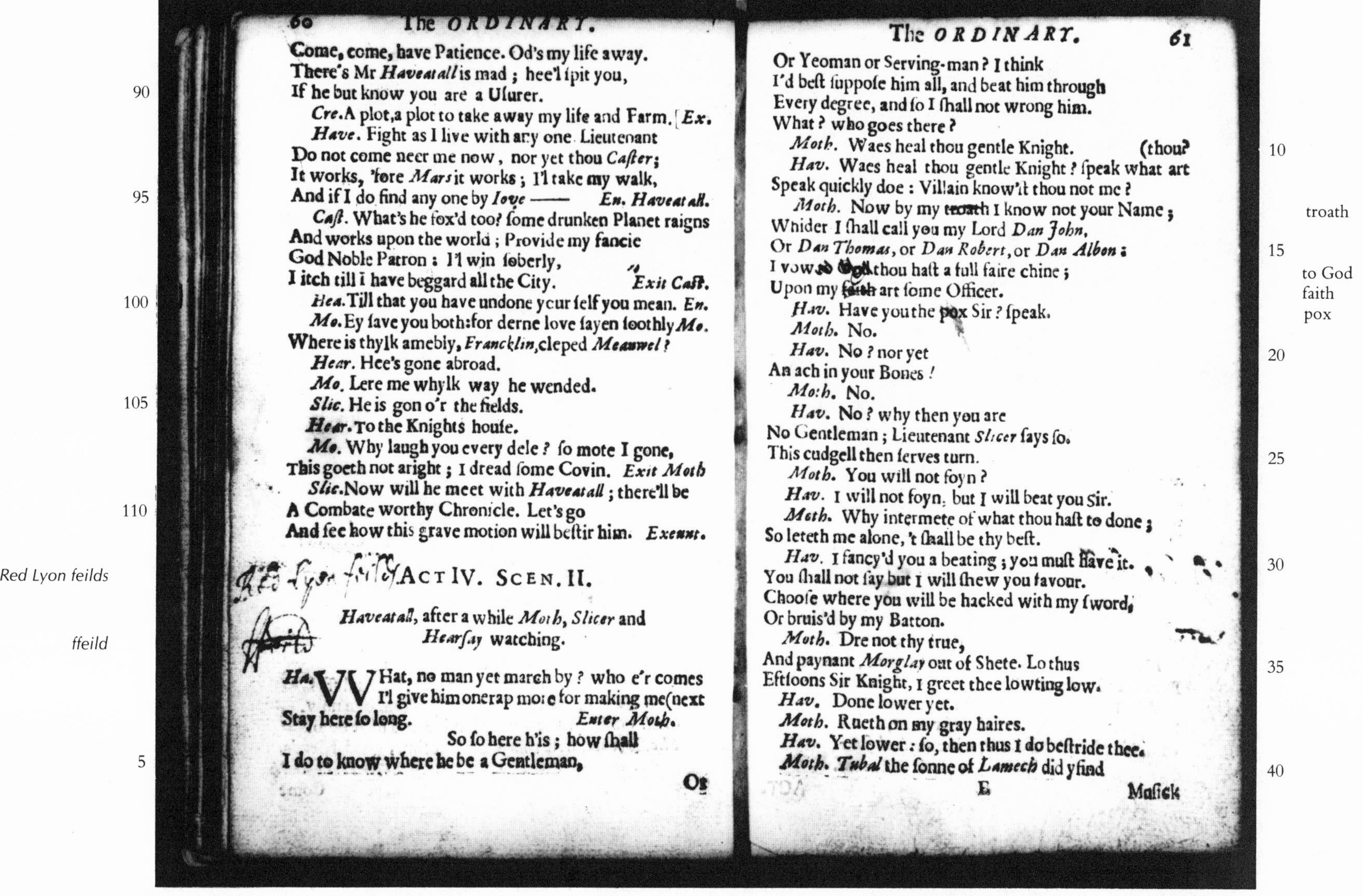

60 The ORDINARY.

Come, come, have Patience. Od's my life away.
There's Mr *Haveatall* is mad; hee'l ſpit you,
If he but know you are a Uſurer.
Cre. A plot, a plot to take away my life and Farm. [*Ex.*
Have. Fight as I live with any one Lieutenant
Do not come neer me now, nor yet thou *Caſter*;
It works, 'fore *Mars* it works; I'l take my walk,
And if I do find any one by *Jove* —— *En. Haveatall.*
Caſt. What's he fox'd too? ſome drunken Planet raigns
And works upon the world; Provide my fancie
God Noble Patron: I'l win ſoberly,
I itch till I have beggard all the City. *Exit Caſt.*
Hea. Till that you have undone your ſelf you mean. *En.*
Mo. Ey ſave you both: for derne love ſayen ſoothly *Mo.*
Where is thylk amebly, *Francklin*, cleped *Meanwel*?
Hear. Hee's gone abroad.
Mo. Lere me whylk way he wended.
Slic. He is gon o'r the fields.
Hear. To the Knights houſe.
Mo. Why laugh you every dele? ſo mote I gone,
This goeth not aright; I dread ſome Covin. *Exit Moth*
Slic. Now will he meet with *Haveatall*; there'll be
A Combate worthy Chronicle. Let's go
And ſee how this grave motion will beſtir him. *Exeunt.*

Red Lyon feilds

ACT IV. SCEN. II.

ffeild

Haveatall, after a while *Moth*, *Slicer* and *Hearſay* watching.

Ha. WHat, no man yet march by? who e'r comes
I'l give him one rap more for making me (next
Stay here ſo long. *Enter Moth.*
So ſo here h'is; how ſhall
I do to know where he be a Gentleman,
Or

The ORDINARY. 61

Or Yeoman or Serving-man? I think
I'd beſt ſuppoſe him all, and beat him through
Every degree, and ſo I ſhall not wrong him.
What? who goes there?
Moth. Waes heal thou gentle Knight. (thou?
Hav. Waes heal thou gentle Knight? ſpeak what art
Speak quickly doe: Villain know'ſt thou not me?
Moth. Now by my troath I know not your Name;
Whider I ſhall call you my Lord *Dan John*,
Or *Dan Thomas*, or *Dan Robert*, or *Dan Albon*:
I vow to God thou haſt a full faire chine;
Upon my faith art ſome Officer.
Hav. Have you the pox Sir? ſpeak.
Moth. No.
Hav. No? nor yet
An ach in your Bones!
Moth. No.
Hav. No? why then you are
No Gentleman; Lieutenant *Slicer* ſays ſo.
This cudgell then ſerves turn.
Moth. You will not foyn?
Hav. I will not foyn, but I will beat you Sir.
Moth. Why intermete of what thou haſt to done;
So leteth me alone, 't ſhall be thy beſt.
Hav. I fancy'd you a beating; you muſt have it.
You ſhall not ſay but I will ſhew you favour.
Chooſe where you will be hacked with my ſword,
Or bruis'd by my Batton.
Moth. Dre not thy true,
And paynant *Morglay* out of Shete. Lo thus
Eftſoons Sir Knight, I greet thee lowting low.
Hav. Done lower yet.
Moth. Rueth on my gray haires.
Hav. Yet lower: ſo, then thus I do beſtride thee.
Moth. *Tubal* the ſonne of *Lamech* did yfind
E Muſick

troath
to God
faith
pox

IV, i, 95. Haveatall should have been given an exit, not an entrance.

Muſick by knocking Hammers upon Anviles;
Let go thine blows, thylke Art is no compleat.
Hav. Doſt thou make me a Smith thou Rogue? a *Tubal?*
Moth. Harrow alas! flet *England*, flet *England*:
Dead is *Edmond*.
Hav. Take that for hiſtory.
O brave Lieutenant now thy dinner works.
Mo. I nis not *Edmond Ironſide* God wot.
Ha. More provocation yet? I'l ſeal thy lips.
Mo. A twenty Devil way! So did the Saxon
Upon thylke plain of *Sarum*, done to death
By treachery, the Lords of merry *England*
Nem etur Saxes.
Have. Villain doſt abuſe me
In unbaptized language? do not anſwer; [*Moth entreats by ſigns.*
If that thou doſt, by *Iove* I'l ſtrangle thee.
Do you make mouths you Raskall thus at me?
You're at dumb Service now: why, this is more
Unſufferable than your old patch'd gibberiſh;
This ſilence is abuſe. I'l ſend thee to
The Place of it, where thou ſhalt meet with *Oſwald*,
Vortigern, *Harold*, *Hengiſt*, *Horſey*, *Knute*,
Alured, *Edgar*, and *Cunobeline*. [*Slic. Hear ſtep in.*
Thus, thus I ſheath my Sword.
Slic. Redoubled Knight
Enough, 'tis thy foe doth vanquiſh'd lie
Now at thy mercy, mercy notwithſtand,
For he is one the trueſt Knight alive,
Though conquer'd now he lie on lowly ground.
Ha. Thou ow'ſt thy life to my Lieutenant, Caitife.
Breath and be thankfull.
Mo. I reche not thine yeſt;
Maugre thine head, algate I ſuffer none,
I am thine lefe, thine deere, mine *Potluck Jone*.
Exeunt.

ACT.

ACT. IV. SCEN. III. Hall.

Andrew, *Priſcilla*.

And. Faireſt of things — tralucent creature—Hang me
If I do know what's next.
Priſ. This meant to mee?
And. Faireſt of things— tralucent creature— rather
Obſcured Deity—— 'Tis gone again.
Lady will you eat a peece of Gingerbread?
Priſ. You might have better manners than to ſcoff
One of my breeding.
An. Heark; indad I love you.
Priſ. Alas!
An. I vow I burn in love, as doth
A penny Faggot.
Priſ. Hey ho!
An. And I ſhall
Blaze out Sir reverence if ye do not quench me.
Priſ. Indeed now?
An. Though I ſay't that ſhould not ſay't,
I am affected towards you ſtrangely.
Priſ. Now who'd have thought it?
An. There's a thing each night
Comes to my Bedshead and cries Matrimony,
Matrimony *Andrew*.
Priſ. [blotted] forbid. God
An. It is
Some Spirit that would joyn us.
Pri. Goodly, goodly.
An. Then do I ſhake all over.
Priſ. Doth it ſo?
An. Then ſhake again.
Priſ. I pray you now.

64 The ORDINARY.

And. Then cry
Faireſt of things —— tralucent creature —— rather
Obſcured Deity, ſweet Mrs *Jane*,
I come I come.
Priſc. Sweet Sir you are deceiv'd:
I'm but her woeman; here ſhe comes her ſelf. [*En.* Mrs *Ja.*
And. Now as my Father ſaith, I would I were
A Cucumber if I know what to doe.
Jan. Why how now *Priſ?* who's that that uſeth you
So lovingly?
And. Faireſt of things —— 'tis one
Tralucent Creature —— 'tis —— Ay that it is
One ——
Priſ. That would willingly run out of doores,
If that he had but Law enough.
And. I ſay ——
Jan. Nay ben't afraid: here's none ſhall doe you harm.
An. 'Tis one that brought his Pigs to the wrong market.
You keep your woman here ſo fine, that I
Had like t'have made a proper buſineſſe on't
Before I was aware. If any thing
Doe prove amiſſe, indeed-law you ſhall be
The Father on't. But know tralucent Creature
I am come off entire, and now am yours
Whole, *Andrew Creaulous*, your ſervants ſervant.
Jan. Methinks you contradict your ſelf: how can you
Be wholly mine, and yet my ſervants ſervant?
And. I doe but complement in that (I ſee
Downright's the beſt way here) if thou canſt love
I can love too. Law thee there now. I'm rich.
Jan. I uſe not to look after riches; 'tis
The perſon that I aime at.
And. That is me;
I'm proper, handſome, faire, clean-limb'd: I'm rich.
Jan. I muſt have one that can direct and guide me;

The ORDINARY. 65

A Guardian rather than a Husband; for
I'm fooliſh yet.
An. Now ſee the luck on't Lady
So am I too I faith. faith
Jan. And who e'r hath me
Will find me to be one of thoſe things which
His care muſt firſt reform.
An. Do not doubt that;
I have a head for Reformation:
This noddle here ſhall do it. I am rich.
Jane. Riches create no love; I fear you mean
To take me for formality only,
As ſome ſtaid peece of houſholdſtuff perhaps
Fit to be ſeen 'mong other ornaments:
Or at the beſt I ſhall be counted but
A name of dignity; not entertain'd
For love but State; one of your train, a thing
Took to wipe off ſuſpicion from ſome fairer
To whom you have vow'd Homage.
An. Do not think
I've any Plots or Projects in my Head,
I will do any thing for thee that thou
Canſt name or think on.
Priſ. Pray you try him Miſtris,
By my Virginity I think hee'l flinch.
And. By my Virginity (which is as good
As yours I'm ſure) by my Virginity
If that we men have any ſuch thing (as
We men haue ſuch a thing) I do beleeve
I will not flinch. Alas! you don't know *Andrew*.
Jan. Can you obtain but ſo much reſpite from
Your other Soverains ſervice, as to keep
Your Eye from gazing on her for a while?
An. If I do look on any woman, nay,
If I do caſt a ſheeps eye upon any
E 3 But

IV, iii, 36. This is another entrance cue, and the emphasis in both margins may have been because the actress playing Jane had been offstage since III, iii, 119 and needed a special warning.

66 The ORDINARY.

But your ſweet ſelf, may I loſe one of mine :
Marry I'l keep the other howſoe'r.
Jane. I know not how I may beleeve you ; you'l
Swear you ne'r caſt a glance on any, when
Your eye hath baited at each face you met.
An. Blind me good now : being you miſtruſt, I will
Be blinded with this handkercheife ; you ſhall
See that I love you now. So, let me have
But any reaſonable thing to lead me home,
I do not care though 't be a Dog, ſo that
He knows the way, or hath the wit t'enquire it.
Jane. That care Sir ſhall be mine. [*Ex. Iane, and Priſ.*
An. I doubt not, but
I ſhall be in the Chronicle for this,
Or in a Ballad elſe. This handkercheif
Shall be hung up i'th' Pariſh Church inſteed
Of a great ſilken flag to fan my grave :
With my Arms in't, pourtray'd in good blew thread
With this word underneath : *This, this was he*
That ſhut his eyes becauſe he would not ſee.
Hold who comes there ? [*Ent. Mean. Shape.*
Mean. One Sir to lead you home.
An. Who ? Tutor *Meanwell* ?
Sha. Yes I do commit you
Unto your truſty friend, If you perform
This vow we may—— { Shape counterfeits Mrs Janes voice.
An. I'l ſay your ſentence out,
Be man and wife.
Sha. If you'l do ſomething elſe
That I'l propoſe.
An. Pray make your own conditions.
Sha. You'l promiſe me you'l not be jealous of me ?
An. Do what you will I'l truſt you.
Sha. never hire
Any to tempt me ?
An.

The ORDINARY. 67

An. By this light (I would ſay
By this darkneſſe) I never will. call Rim · Baygh: W
Sha. Nor mark Kit. Catchm:
On whom I laugh ? ——
An. No.
Sha. Nor ſuſpect My ſmiles,
My nods, my winks ?——
An. No, no.
Sha. Nor yet keep count
From any Gallants viſit ?
An. I'l ne'r reckon ;
You ſhall do what you will.
Sha. You'l never ſet
Great Cheſts and Formes againſt my Chamber Door,
Nor pin my ſmock unto your ſhirt a nights,
For fear I ſhould ſlip from you ere you wake ?
An. As I do hope for Day I will not.
Sha. Give me
Some ſmall pledge from you to aſſure your love;
If that you yet prove falſe, I may have ſomething
To witneſſe your inconſtancy. I'l take
This little Ruby : this ſmall bluſhing ſtone
From your fair finger.
An. Take it Sweet : there is
A Diamond in my Bandſtring, if you have
A mind to that I pray make uſe of 't too.
Sha. In troth a ſtone of luſtre, I aſſure you
It darts a pretty light, a veget ſpark ;
It ſeems an Eye upon your Breaſt.
An. Nay take it,
For loves ſake take it then ; leave nothing that
Looks like an Eye about me.
Sha. My good *Andrew*,
'Cauſe of thy reſolution, I'l perform
This office for thee. Take my word for't, this
E 4 Shall

IV, iii, 136. This is the only actor warning in the copy. The players involved in the entrance may have needed a special warning because IV, iv was omitted, and their entrance was advanced by several pages.

Leave out this scene.

Shall ne'r betray thee. *Ex. Shape.*
An. Farewell honeſt *Jany*,
I cannot ſee to thank thee my ſweet *Jany*.
Tutor, your hand good Tutor, lead me wiſely.
Mea. Take comfort man; I have good news for thee:
Thine eyes ſhall be thine own before next morning.
Exeunt.

ACT IV. SCEN. IV.

Shape, Chirurgion, Mercer.

Sha. HEe's a good friend of mine, and I preſume
Upon your ſecreſie.
Chi. O Sir —— the Deed
By which it came was not more cloſe. D'y' think
I would undo me ſelf by twitting? 'twere
To bring the Gallants all about mine Ears,
And make me mine own Patient. I'm faithfull,
And ſecret, though a Barber.
Sha Nay, but hear me;
Hee's very modeſt: 'twas his firſt attempt
Procur'd him this infirmity; he will
Be baſhfull I am ſure, and won't be known
Of any ſuch thing at the firſt; you muſt
Be ſure to put him to't.
Chi. Let me alone,
He knows not yet the world I do perceive.
It is as common now with Gentlemen,
As 'tis to follow faſhion; only here
Lyeth the difference, that they keep in this
A little longer. I ſhall have ſo much
Upon your word Sir?
Sha. If you do perform
The cure by that time (twenty peeces Sir.)
You

You are content?
Mer. Yes Sir.
Chi. It ſhall be done *Ex. Shape.*
According to your own preſcription.
Sit down I pray you Sir, this Gentleman
Is a good friend of yours.
Mer. Indeed he is
A very honeſt man as any one
Can wiſh to deal with verily.
Chi. Beleeve't
He loves you very well.
Mer. I am moſt ready
To do him any ſervice truly; pray you
Good Brother don't delay me, I'm in haſte.
Chi. Indeed, and truly, verily good Brother;
How could theſe milk-ſop words e'r get him company
That could procure the Pox? where do you feel
You grief moſt trouble you?
Mer. I'm very well.
What mean you Brother?
Chi. Nay, be not ſo modeſt;
'Tis no ſuch hainous fault, as that you ſhould
Seek thus to hide it: meer ill fortune only ——
Mer. Surely you do forget your ſelf.
Chi. Come, come,
He told me you'ld be ſhamefac'd; you muſt be
Wary hereafter.
Mer. (I do perceive
He is a little mad indeed; the Gentleman
Told me ſo much juſt as I came along)
Yes, yes, I'l be wary, I'l take heed,
Come pray y' diſpatch me.
Chi. So, I like you now.
It is the cuſtome of moſt Gentlemen
Not to confeſſe untill they feel their bones
Begin

Begin t' admoniſh 'em.
Mer. You are i'th' right:
Good friend make haſte; I've very urgent buſineſſe.
Chi. Not raſhly neither; Is your Griſtle ſound?
Me thinks 'tis very firm as yet to th' touch.
You fear no danger there as yet Sir, do you?
Mer. No, I'l aſſure you. (He muſt have his humour;
I ſee he is not to be croſs'd.)
Chi. When did you
Feel the firſt grudging on't? 'tis not broke out
In any place?
Mer. No, no: I pray y' diſpatch me.
Chi. Theſe things deſire deliberation;
Care is requir'd.
Mer. Good Brother go t'your Cheſt.
Chi. How can I know what Med'cines to apply,
If that you tell me not where lies your grief?
Mer. Nay good now let me go.
Chi. I muſt not Sir,
Nor will not truly: truſt me you will wiſh
You had confeſs'd and ſuffer'd me in time,
When you ſhall come to dry burnt Racks of Mutton,
The Syren, and the Tub.
Mer. So now enough;
Pray fetch me what you promis'd.
Chi. Are you wild,
Or mad? I do proteſt I ne'r did meet
A Gentleman of ſuch perverſneſſe yet.
I find you juſt as I was told you ſhould.
Mer. I loſe the taking, by my ſwear, of taking
As much, whiles that I am receiving this.
Chi. I will not hinder you, if that you do
Prefer your gain before your health.
Mer. Well then
I pray you tell it out; we Tradeſmen are not

Ma-

Maſters of our own time.
Chi. What would you have?
Mer. What would I have? as if you did not know;
Come come leave jeſting now at laſt good Brother.
Chi. I am in earneſt Sir.
Mer. Why, I would have
My money Sir, the twenty peeces that
The Gentleman did give you order now
To pay me for the Velvet, that he bought
This morning of me.
Chi. O! the Gentleman ——
Mer. You ſhould not make a laughing ſtock good Bro- (ther
Of one that wrongs you not; I do profeſſe
I won't be fubb'd enſure your ſelf.
Chi. The Gentleman!
Oh! oh! the Gentleman! is this the cure
I ſhould perform? truly I dare not venture
Upon ſuch deſperate Maladies.
Mer. You are
But merrily diſpos'd?
Chi. Indeed they are
Too high for my ſmall Quality; verily
Perhaps good Brother you might periſh under
Mine hands truly; I do profeſs I am not
Any of your bold Mountebanks in this.
Mer. You're ſtill diſpos'd——
Chi. To laugh at you good Brother.
Gull'd by my ſwear, by my ſwear gull'd; he told me
You had a ſmall infirmity upon you,
A griefe of youth, or two; and that I ſhould
Have twenty peeces for the cure. He ask'd you
If that you were content, you anſwered yes.
I was in hope I'd gain'd a Patient more;
Your beſt way is to make haſte after him.
Mer. Now could I beat my ſelf for a wiſe fool

That

That I was,thus to trust him. *Exit.*

Chi. B'w'y' Brother.

'Fore [blotted] a good one. O! the Gentleman. *Ex laughing.*

God

ACT. IV. SCEN. V.

Rimewell, Bagshot, Catchmey, Sir *Christopher*; A Song at a window; congratulating (as they think) Mr *Meanwels* Marriage.

1. *Whiles early light springs from the skies,*
A fairer from your Bride doth rise;
A brighter Day doth thence appear,
And make a second morning there:
Her blush doth sled
All o'r the bed,
Clean shamefac'd beames
That spread in streames,
And purple round the modest aire.

2. *I will not tell what shreeks, and cries,*
What Angry Dishes, and what ties,
What pretty oaths then newly born
The listning Taper heard there sworn:
Whiles froward she
Most peevishly
Did yielding fight
To keep o'r night
What shee'd have profer'd you ere morn.

3. *Faire, we know, maids do refuse*
To grant what they do come to lose.
Intend a Conquest you that wed;
They would be chastly ravished.
Not any kisse

From

From Mrs Pris,
If that you do
Perswade and woe.
Know pleasure's by extorting fed.

4. *O may her arms wax black and blew*
Only by hard encircling you:
May she round about you twine
Like the easie twisting Vine;
And whiles you sip
From her full lip
Pleasures as new
As morning Dew,
Let those soft Tyes your hearts combine.

Sing. [blotted] give you joy Mr *Meanwell.* [blotted] give your Worship good morrow.

God . . . God

Rim. Come let's be going.

Chr. Hold,a blow I'l have,
One jerk at th' times, wrap'd in a benediction
O'th' Spouses teeming, and I'l go with you.

A Song.

Now thou our future Brother,
That shalt make this Spouse a Mother,
Spring up, and Dod's *blessing on't.*
Shew thy little sorrell Pate
And prove regenerate
Before thou be brought to the Font.
May the Parish Surplice be
Cut in peeces quite for thee,
To wrap thy soft body about;
So 'twill better service do
Reformed thus into

The

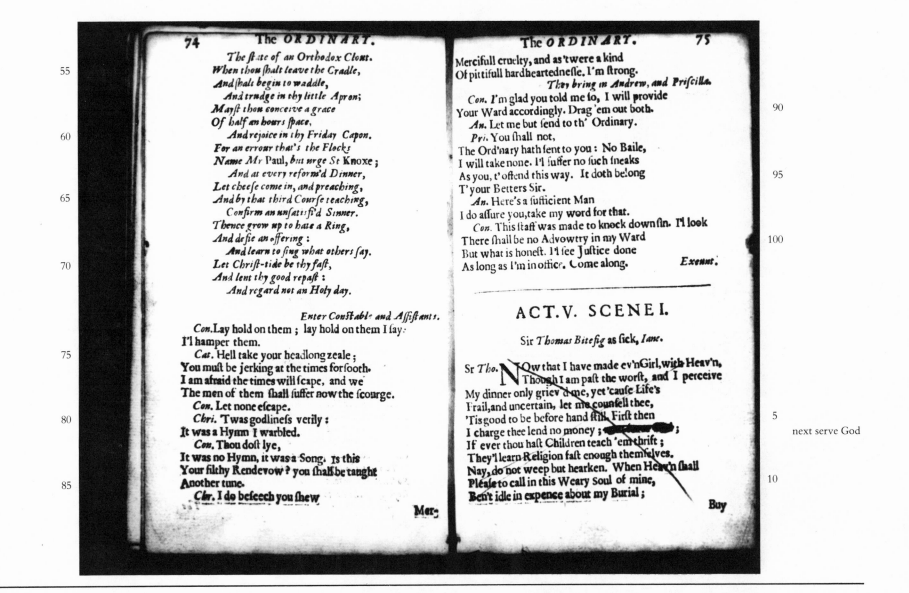

The ſtate of an Orthodox Clout.
When thou ſhalt leave the Cradle,
And ſhalt begin to waddle,
And trudge in thy little Apron;
Mayſt thou conceive a grace
Of half an hours ſpace,
And rejoice in thy Friday Capon.
For an errour that's the Flocks
Name Mr Paul, *but urge St* Knoxe;
And at every reform'd Dinner,
Let cheeſe come in, and preaching,
And by that third Courſe teaching,
Confirm an unſatisfi'd Sinner.
Thence grow up to hate a Ring,
And defie an offering:
And learn to ſing what others ſay.
Let Chriſt-tide be thy faſt,
And lent thy good repaſt:
And regard not an Holy day.

Enter Conſtable and Aſſiſtants.

Con. Lay hold on them; lay hold on them I ſay.
I'l hamper them.
Cat. Hell take your headlong zeale;
You muſt be jerking at the times forſooth.
I am afraid the times will ſcape, and we
The men of them ſhall ſuffer now the ſcourge.
Con. Let none eſcape.
Chri. 'Twas godlineſs verily:
It was a Hymn I warbled.
Con. Thou doſt lye,
It was no Hymn, it was a Song. Is this
Your filthy Rendevow? you ſhall be taught
Another tune.
Chr. I do beſeech you ſhew

Mer-

Mercifull cruelty, and as 'twere a kind
Of pittifull hardheartedneſſe. I'm ſtrong.
They bring in Andrew, and Priſcilla.
Con. I'm glad you told me ſo, I will provide
Your Ward accordingly. Drag 'em out both.
An. Let me but ſend to th' Ordinary.
Pri. You ſhall not,
The Ord'nary hath ſent to you: No Baile,
I will take none. I'l ſuffer no ſuch ſneaks
As you, t'offend this way. It doth belong
T'your Betters Sir.
An. Here's a ſufficient Man
I do aſſure you, take my word for that.
Con. This ſtaff was made to knock down ſin. I'l look
There ſhall be no Advowtry in my Ward
But what is honeſt. I'l ſee Juſtice done
As long as I'm in office. Come along. *Exeunt.*

ACT. V. SCENE I.

Sir *Thomas Biteſig* as ſick, *Jane.*

Sr *Tho.* Now that I have made ev'n Girl, with Heav'n,
Though I am paſt the worſt, and I perceive
My dinner only griev'd me, yet 'cauſe Life's
Frail, and uncertain, let me counſell thee,
'Tis good to be before hand ſtill. Firſt then
I charge thee lend no money; [blacked out]; next serve God
If ever thou haſt Children teach 'em thrift;
They'l learn Religion faſt enough themſelves.
Nay, do not weep but hearken. When Heav'n ſhall
Pleaſe to call in this Weary Soul of mine,
Be'n't idle in expence about my Burial;

Buy

Buy me a ſhroud, any old ſheet will ſerve
To cloath corruption; I can rot without
Fine linnen; 'tis but to enrich the Grave,
And adorn ſtench, no reverence to the dead,
To make 'em crumble more luxuriouſly.
One Torch will be ſufficient to direct
The footſteps of my Bearers. If there be
Any ſo kind as to accompanie
My body to the Earth, let them not want
For entertainment, prethee ſee they have
A ſprig of Roſemary dip'd in common water,
To ſmell to as they walk along the ſtreets.
Eatings and drinkings are no obſequies.
Raiſe no oppreſſing Pile to load my Aſhes;
But if thou'l needs b' at charges of a Tomb,
Five or ſix foot of common ſtone engrav'd
With a good hopefull word, or elſe a couple
Of capital letters filled up with pitch,
Such as I ſet upon my Sheep, will ſerve;
State is not meet for thoſe that dwell in duſt.
Mourn as thou pleaſeſt for me, plainneſs ſhews
True grief: I give thee leave to do it for
Two or three years, if that thou ſhalt think fit.
'Twill ſave expence in cloaths. And ſo now be
My bleſſing on thee, and my means hereafter.

Jan. I hope Heav'n will not deal ſo rigidly
With me, as to preſerve me to th' unwelcome
Performance of theſe ſad injunctions.

ACT

ACT V. SCEN. II.

To them *Meanwell*.

Hall

Mean. GOod health unto you Sir.
Sr *Tho.* I have the more
By reaſon of the care you took in ſending
A Confeſſor unto me.
Mean. I? a Confeſſor?
Sure there is ſome deſign, ſome trick or other
Put on you by thoſe men, who never ſleep
Unleſs they've cheated on that Day.
Sir *Tho.* I hope
You do'nt mean your Partners my good friends?
Mean. They ne'r deſerve the name of friends, they do
Covet, not love. If any came from them,
It was ſome Vulture in a holy habit,
Who did intend your Carkaſſe, nor your ſafety;
Indeed I know not of't, I've all this while
Appear'd another to you than I am. *Diſcloſeth himſelf.*
Perhaps you know me now. I'm he whom you
Pleas'd to forbid your houſe, whom Mr *Credulous*
Takes leave to ſtile loſt man, and Vagabond.
Sr *Tho.* That I forbad you Sir my houſe was only
In care to my Daughter, not in hate to you.
Mean. That I frequented it without your leave,
Was both in love to you, and to your Daughter;
That I have all this while liv'd thus diſguis'd,
Was only to avert the ſnare from you,
Not to intrap you; that you might not be
Blinded by thoſe, who like to venemous Beaſts,
Have only ſight to poyſon; that you might not
Ruine your Daughter in a complement.
Sir *Tho.* This may b' your plot, and this diſcoverie

E Feign'd

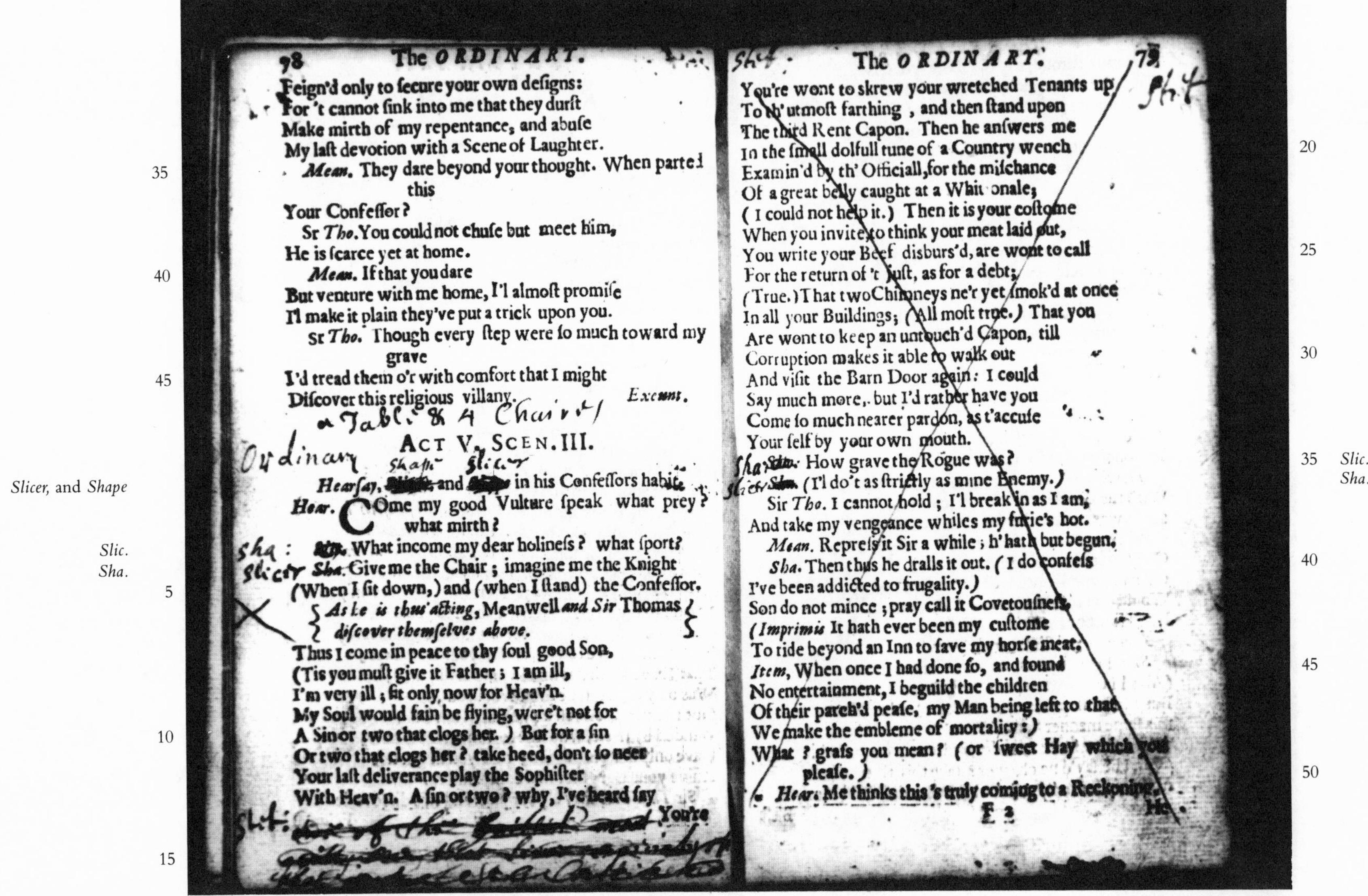

78 The ORDINARY.

Feign'd only to ſecure your own deſigns:
For 't cannot ſink into me that they durſt
Make mirth of my repentance, and abuſe
My laſt devotion with a Scene of Laughter.
Mean. They dare beyond your thought. When parted this
Your Confeſſor?
Sr *Tho.* You could not chuſe but meet him,
He is ſcarce yet at home.
Mean. If that you dare
But venture with me home, I'l almoſt promiſe
I'l make it plain they've put a trick upon you.
Sr *Tho.* Though every ſtep were ſo much toward my grave
I'd tread them o'r with comfort that I might
Diſcover this religious villany. *Exeunt.*

a Table & 4 Chairs

ACT V. SCEN. III.

Ordinary Shape Slicer

Slicer, and Shape

Hearſay, and in his Confeſſors habit.
Hear. Come my good Vulture ſpeak what prey? what mirth?

Slic.
Sha.

Sha: What income my dear holineſs? what ſport?
Slicer *Sha.* Give me the Chair; imagine me the Knight
(When I ſit down,) and (when I ſtand) the Confeſſor.
As he is thus acting, Meanwell *and Sir* Thomas *diſcover themſelves above.*
Thus I come in peace to thy ſoul good Son,
(Tis you muſt give it Father; I am ill,
I'm very ill; fit only now for Heav'n.
My Soul would fain be flying, were't not for
A Sin or two that clogs her.) But for a ſin
Or two that clogs her? take heed, don't ſo neer
Your laſt deliverance play the Sophiſter
With Heav'n. A ſin or two? why, I've heard ſay
Slic: You're

Sha The ORDINARY. 79 Sha

You're wont to ſkrew your wretched Tenants up
To th' utmoſt farthing, and then ſtand upon
The third Rent Capon. Then he anſwers me
In the ſmall dolfull tune of a Country wench
Examin'd by th' Officiall, for the miſchance
Of a great belly caught at a Whitſonale;
(I could not help it.) Then it is your coſtome
When you invite, to think your meat laid out,
You write your Beef disburs'd, are wont to call
For the return of 't juſt, as for a debt;
(True.) That two Chimneys ne'r yet ſmok'd at once
In all your Buildings; (All moſt true.) That you
Are wont to keep an untouch'd Capon, till
Corruption makes it able to walk out
And viſit the Barn Door again: I could
Say much more, but I'd rather have you
Come ſo much nearer pardon, as t'accuſe
Your ſelf by your own mouth.
Sha *Slic.* How grave the Rogue was?
Slicer *Sha.* (I do't as ſtrictly as mine Enemy.)

Slic.
Sha.

Sir *Tho.* I cannot hold; I'l break in as I am,
And take my vengeance whiles my furie's hot.
Mean. Repreſs it Sir a while; h' hath but begun.
Sha. Then thus he dralls it out. (I do confeſs
I've been addicted to frugality.)
Son do not mince; pray call it Covetouſneſs.
(*Imprimis* It hath ever been my cuſtome
To ride beyond an Inn to ſave my horſe meat;
Item, When once I had done ſo, and found
No entertainment, I beguild the children
Of their parch'd peaſe, my Man being left to that.
We make the embleme of mortality:)
What? graſs you mean? (or ſweet Hay which you pleaſe.)
Hear. Me thinks this 's truly coming to a Reckoning. He

F 2

V, iii, 6. The *X* instead of the # mark is used here to cue an entrance above.

V, iii, 14–16. Evans's reconstruction of the manuscript lines at the bottom of the page is: *one of the G[?]liest and / guilty one [?s] that lives especially of / that (?)worst (?)of Sins (?)Covetise.* Evans supposes that the lines were originally intended for insertion near the large *X* at line 5, but that mark is surely an entrance cue for Meanwell and Sir Thomas.

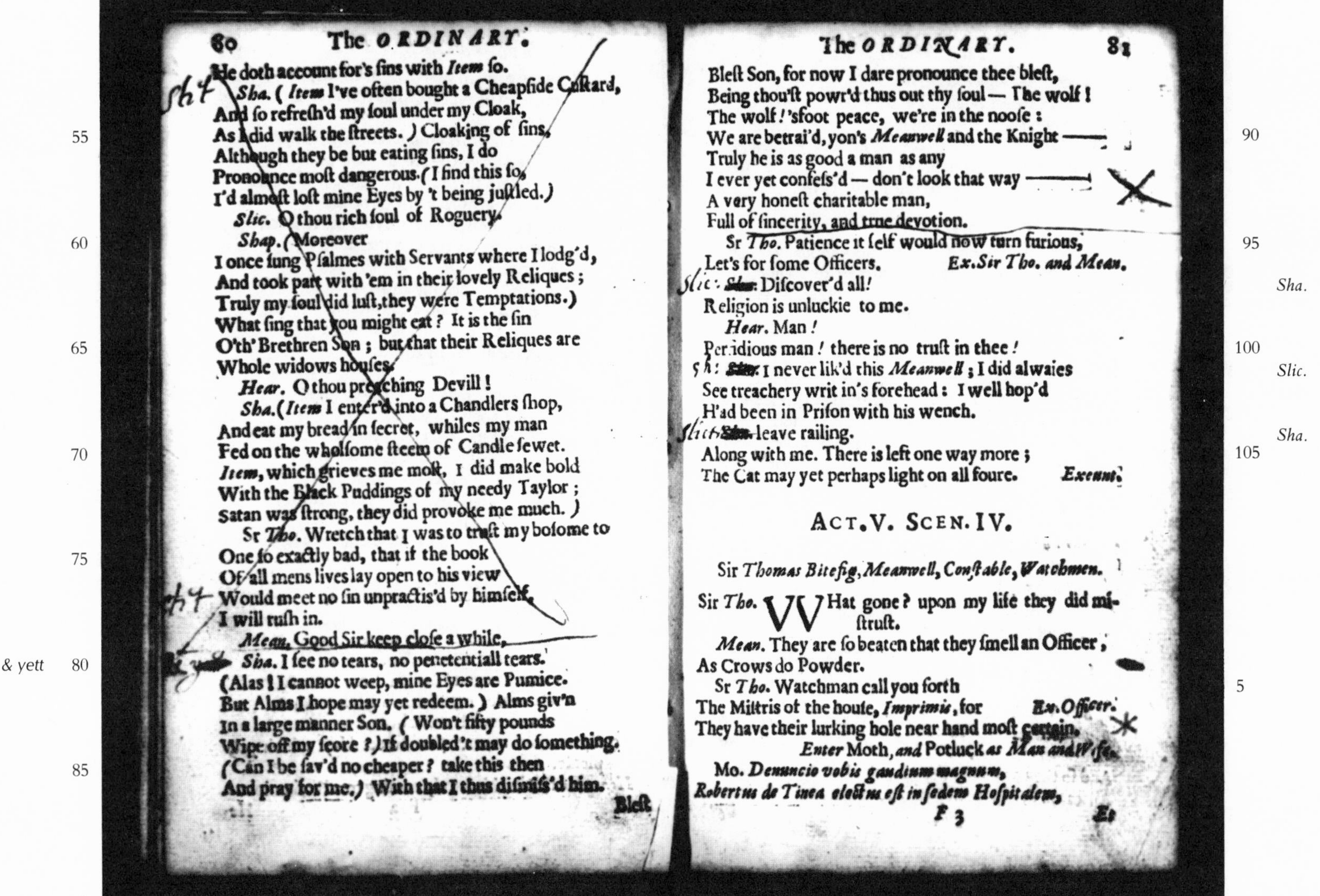

60 The ORDINARY.

He doth account for's ſins with *Item* ſo.
Sha. (*Item* I've often bought a Cheapſide Cuſtard,
And ſo refreſh'd my ſoul under my Cloak,
As I did walk the ſtreets.) Cloaking of ſins,
Although they be but eating ſins, I do
Pronounce moſt dangerous. (I find this ſo,
I'd almoſt loſt mine Eyes by 't being juſtled.)
Slic. O thou rich ſoul of Roguery.
Shap. (Moreover
I once ſung Pſalmes with Servants where I lodg'd,
And took part with 'em in their lovely Reliques;
Truly my ſoul did luſt, they were Temptations.)
What ſing that you might eat? It is the ſin
O'th' Brethren Son; but that their Reliques are
Whole widows houſes.
Hear. O thou preaching Devill!
Sha. (*Item* I enter'd into a Chandlers ſhop,
And eat my bread in ſecret, whiles my man
Fed on the wholſome ſteem of Candle ſewet.
Item, which grieves me moſt, I did make bold
With the Black Puddings of my needy Taylor;
Satan was ſtrong, they did provoke me much.)
Sr *Tho.* Wretch that I was to truſt my boſome to
One ſo exactly bad, that if the book
Of all mens lives lay open to his view
Would meet no ſin unpractis'd by himſelf.
I will ruſh in.
Mean. Good Sir keep cloſe a while.
Sha. I ſee no tears, no penetentiall tears.
(Alas! I cannot weep, mine Eyes are Pumice.
But Alms I hope may yet redeem.) Alms giv'n
In a large manner Son. (Won't fifty pounds
Wipe off my ſcore?) If doubled 't may do ſomething.
(Can I be ſav'd no cheaper? take this then
And pray for me.) With that I thus diſmiſs'd him.
Bleſt

The ORDINARY. 81

Bleſt Son, for now I dare pronounce thee bleſt,
Being thou'ſt powr'd thus out thy ſoul — The wolf!
The wolf! 'ſfoot peace, we're in the nooſe:
We are betrai'd, yon's *Meanwell* and the Knight —
Truly he is as good a man as any
I ever yet confeſs'd — don't look that way —
A very honeſt charitable man,
Full of ſincerity, and true devotion.
Sr *Tho.* Patience it ſelf would now turn furious;
Let's for ſome Officers. *Ex. Sir Tho. and Mean.*
Slic. Diſcover'd all!
Religion is unluckie to me.
Hear. Man!
Perfidious man! there is no truſt in thee!
Sha. I never lik'd this *Meanwell*; I did alwaies
See treachery writ in's forehead: I well hop'd
H'ad been in Priſon with his wench.
Sha. leave railing.
Along with me. There is left one way more;
The Cat may yet perhaps light on all foure. *Exeunt.*

ACT. V. SCEN. IV.

Sir *Thomas Bitefig, Meanwell, Conſtable, Watchmen.*

Sir *Tho.* WHat gone? upon my life they did miſtruſt.
Mean. They are ſo beaten that they ſmell an Officer,
As Crows do Powder.
Sr *Tho.* Watchman call you forth
The Miſtris of the houſe, *Imprimis*, for *Ex. Officer.*
They have their lurking hole near hand moſt certain.
Enter Moth, *and* Potluck *as Man and Wife.*
Mo. *Denuncio vobis gaudium magnum,*
Robertus de Tinea electus eſt in ſedem Hoſpitalem,
F 3 Et

& yett

Sha.

Slic.

Sha.

V, iii, 92. The meaning of the marginal *X* and of the horizontal line at line 94 is not clear, but they appear to be related.

V, iv, 7. The * is related to a similar mark at line 147, but just how the scene was to be rearranged is not clear. The intention was apparently to have lines 148–211 shifted forward and inserted after line 6.

Et aſſumit ſibi nomen Galfridi.
Joy comes to our houſe. I *Robert Moth* am
Cheſen into thylk Hoſpitall ſeat,
Thylk Baſon of *Jone Potluck*, Vintners Widow,
And do tranſmue my name to Giffery.
New foyſons byn ygraced with new Titles.
Come buſs.
Pot. Fie! Mr *Giffery* I ſwear
You make m' aſham'd 'fore all this Company.
Sir *Tho.* Sir, if you be the Maſter of this houſe,
You've harbor'd here a company of cheating Villains,
Which we are come to apprehend.
Pot. Pray y' look,
Search every Corner, here's no cheats. I'm ſure
The houſe was clear before your Worſhip entred.
Con. Make faſt the Doors for fear they do eſcape.
Let's in and ferret out theſe cheating Rakehels.
As the Watchmen go in and out about the Rooms Hearſay, Slicer, *and* Shape *mingle themſelves with 'em, being accounted Watchmen, and ſo paſs without diſcovery.*
Enter 1. *Watchman, and Hearſay.*
Heare: 1 Watch. ~~Hear.~~ 'Tis very certain they are not in the houſe.
Sr *Tho.* They had no time to get away.
Hear. Why then,
It may be being they are ſuch cunning Fellows,
They have the trick of going inviſible.
Enter 2 *Watchman, and Slicer.*
2 *Watch.* There's no place left unſearch'd but Pots and Mouſeholes.
Slic. They're either gone or in the Houſe that's certain.
Heare 2 Watchm. ~~Slic.~~ That cannot be; the Doors were ſhut I'm ſure,
And ſo they could not get out; the Rooms then are
All ſearch'd, and ſo they cannot be within.
Slic.

Slic. I'l lay my neck to a farthing, then they're vaniſh'd.
Hear. Sunk like the Queen, they'l riſe at Queenhive ſure.
Enter Conſtable, and other Watchmen, and Shape *among 'em, bringing in* Credulous, *and* Caſter.
Sha. Moſt certain theſe are two of them: for this
Old Knave, I'l take my Oath that he is one.
Con. Confeſs, confeſs, where are your other Comrads?
Cre. I am as honeſt as the skin that is
Between thy Brows?
Con. What skin between my Brows?
What skin thou knave? I am a Chriſtian;
And what is more, a Conſtable; what skin?
Sr *Tho.* You are miſtaken friends.
Con. I cry you mercy.
Sha. The Conſtable may call you any thing
In the Kings name upon ſuſpicion.
Sr *Tho.* We're cheated friends; theſe men o'th' Ordnary
Have gull'd us all this while, and now are gone.
Caſt. I am undon. Ne'r let me live if that
I did not think th' would gull me, I perceive
Fanſie doth much; ſee how 'tis come to paſs.
Cred. Where is my Son God bleſſe him? where is *Andrew?*
Pray God they have not taken him along;
He hath a perilous wit to be a cheat;
He'd quickly come to be his Majeſties Taker.
Con. I took one *Andrew Credulous* this morning
In diſhoneſt Adultery with a Trull.
And if he be your Son he is in Priſon.
Cred. Their villany o' my life. Now as I am
A Freeman and a Grocer, I had rather
Have found forty pounds; I pray go fetch him. *Ex. officer.* Slicer
Sr *Tho.* I'm ſorry that your Son takes theſe lewd courſes; etc
He is not fit to make a Husband of.
Cred.

Cre. Do not condemn before you hear. I'l warrant
Though he be guilty yet hee's innocent.

Enter Haveatall.

Mo. Hent him, for dern love Hent him; I done drad
His Viſage foul, yfrounct with glowing eyr.

Have. I come t' excuſe my ruder uſage of you.
I was in drink when that I did it; 'twas
The Plot of thoſe baſe Knaves, I hear are gone,
To teach me valour by the ſtrength of Wine;
Naming that courage which was only fury.
It was not wilfully.

Mo. I do not reche
One bean for all. This Buſs is a blive guerdon.
Hence Carliſhneſſe yferre. 'Tis a ſooth ſaw,
Had I but venged all mine herme,
Mine Cloak had not been furred half ſo werme.

Enter Officers with Andrew, Priſcilla, *and the four that were taken at the Window ſinging.*

Cre. Now Sir you ſhall hear all. Come *Andrew* tell me,
How camſt thou hither?

An. Truly Mr *Meanwel*
Told me that I ſhould meet with M[rs] *Jane*,
And there I found her Chamber-maid.

Cre. D'y'ſee?
Your Chamber-maid Sir *Thomas*; out you whore.

An. Take heed what you ſay Father, ſhee's my wife.

Cre. I would thou'rt in thy grave, then 'twere the better
Fortune o'th' two.

Priſ. Indeed this reverend Man
Joyn'd us i'th' Priſon.

Chr. Marriage is a Bond,
So no place fitter to perform it in. Come hither Daughter

Come hither daughter

Sr *Tho.* Send for my Daughter hither, wee'l know all.

Come . . . Send for my Daughter hither
hither

What are you Sir?

Chr. A workman in the Clergie.

Con.

Con. Yes, this is one I took at th' Window ſinging,
With theſe three other vagrant Fellows here.

Chri. I was in body there, but not in mind,
So that my ſin is but inchoately perfect,
And I though in a fault did not offend,
And that for three reaſons. Firſt, I did yield
Only a kind of unwilling conſent.
Secondly, I was drawn as 'twere by their
Impulſive gentleneſs. Mark Sir I'm ſtrong.
Thirdly, I deem'd it not a womans-ſhambles:
Fourthly and laſtly, that I ſung was only
An holy wiſh. Once more Beloved.

Sr *Tho.* Peace!
Y'have ſaid enough already. How came you
To ſing beneath the Window?

Rime. Mr *Hearſay*
Told us that Mr *Meanwell* was new married,
And thought it good that we ſhould gratifie him,
And ſhew our ſelves to him in a Feſtennine.

Cre. That Raskall *Meanwel* was the cauſe of all,
I would I had him here.

Sr *Tho.* Why? this is he, & now my son in law

& now my son in law

Sr *Robert Littleworth* his Son, he hath
Diſclos'd their vilanies; he is no cheat.

Mean. God ſave you Mr *Credulous*; you have
Forgotten me perhaps, I'm ſomewhat chang'd,
You ſee your loſt man's found; your Vagabond
Appears at laſt.

Cre. Go, you are a gibing ſcab:
Leave off your flouting; you're a beardleſs Boy;
I am a Father of Children.

Mean. And your Son
Will be ſo ſhortly, if he han't ill luck.
To vex you more, that hundred pounds you ſent
To Mr *Caſter*, *Shape* i'th' habit of

A

A Country fellow gull'd you of.
Cred. That Raskall;
Thou ſhewſt thy wit t' abuſe an old man thus.
As God ſhall mend me I will hamper thee.
Thou'ſt been diſguis'd here all this while, thou haſt;
Would I were braid in mine own morter, if
I do not call th' in Queſtion the next Terme
For counterfeiting of the Kings Subjects.
Come away from him Sirrah, come along.

This Scene comes in at this ✱ *Ex. Cred. And. Priſc.*

Mean. There's a Trunk they've left behind; I have
Seiz'd it for you; ſo that you'l be no loſer.
Sir *Tho.* If you can find a way whereby I may
Reward this courteſie of yours, I ſhall
Confeſs my ſelf engaged doubly to you,
Both for the benefit and its requitall. *Ent. Jane.*
Mean. The appearance of your Daughter here ſuggeſts
Something to ask, which yet my thoughts call boldneſs.
Sir *Tho.* Can ſhe ſuggeſt yet any good, that is
So expert grown in this fleſh Brokery?
Mean. O do not blot that Innocence with ſuſpicion,
Who never came ſo neere a blemiſh yet,
As to b'accus'd. To quit you of ſuch thoughts
I did receive a tempting letter from
That Strumpet that's gone out (as ſin is bold
To try even where no hope is) I made promiſe,
But to ſecure my ſelf, and withall ſound
Th' affections of young *Credulous* unto
Your vertuous Daughter, told him he ſhould meet her
Where I agreed to meet her Chambermaid.
The blame muſt all be mine.
Sr *Tho.* 'Tis her deliverance.
Shee hath eſcap'd two Plagues, a luſtfull fool.
Mean. I dare not challenge her I do confeſs,
As a reward due to my ſervice, and
If

If you deny her me, aſſure your ſelf
I'l never draw her from obedience:
I will not love her to procure her ruine,
And make m' affection prove her Enemy.
Sr *Tho.* You ſpeak moſt honeſtly, I never did
Think ill of your intents, but alwaies gave
A teſtimony to your life as large
As were your merits. But your fortunes are
Unequal, there's the want.
Mean. What's there defective
Love ſhall ſupply: True, Mr *Credulous*
Is a rich man, but yet wants that which makes
His riches uſefull, free diſcretion.
He may be ſomething in the Eye o'th' World;
But let a knowing man that can diſtinguiſh
Between Poſſeſſions, and good parts, but view him,
And prize impartially, he will be rated
Only as Cheſts, and Caskets, juſt according
To what he holds. I valew him, as I
Would an Exchequer, or a Magazine.
He is not vertuous, but well ſtor'd, a thing
Rather well victuall'd then well qualified.
And if you pleaſe to caſt your Eye on me,
Some moneys will call back my Fathers Lands
Out of his lime-twig fingers, and I ſhall
Come forth as gay as he.
Sr *Tho.* I'l ſtrive no longer
For fear I ſeem t' oppoſe felicity.
If ſhee'l give her conſent y'are one.
Jan. It is
The voice of Angels to me: I had thought
Nothing in all the ſtore of nature could
Have added to that love, wherewith I do
Reverence that name, my Father, till that you
Spoke this.
Sr *Tho.*

Sir *Tho*. I know your former Loves; grow up
Into an aged pair, yet ſtill ſeem young.
May you ſtand freſh, as in your Pictures ſtill, ent Moth Pot
And only have the reverence of the Aged. come along
I thank you for your pains Mr Conſtable,
You may diſmiſs your Watch now.
Hear: Sha. A pox on't!
That after all this ne'r a man to carry
To Priſon? muſt poor Tradeſmen be brought out
And no body clap'd up?
Mean. That you mayn't want
Employment, friends take this I pray and drink it.
Sli. Sir, when y'are cheated next we are your ſervants—
Ex. all but Shape, Hear. Slic.

ACT V. SCEN. V.

Shape, Slicer, Hearſay.

Sha. Lye thou there Watchman; how the knave that's look'd for
May often lurck under the Officer!
Invention I applaud thee.
Hear. London aire
Me thinks begins to be too hot for us.
Slic. There is no longer tarrying here, let's ſwear
Fidelity to one another, and
So reſolve for *New England*.
Hear. 'Tis but getting
A little Pigeon-hole reformed Ruff——
Slic. Forcing our Beards into th'Orthodox bent——
Sha. Noſing a little Treaſon 'gainſt the King;
Bark ſomething at the Biſhops, and we ſhall
Be eaſily receiv'd.
Hear. No fitter Place,

They

They are good ſilly People; Souls that will
Be cheated without trouble: One eye is
Put out with Zeal, th'other with Ignorance,
And yet they think they're Eagles.
Sha. We are made
Juſt fit for that Meridian: no good work's
Allow'd there; Faith, Faith is that they call for,
And we will bring it 'em.
Slic. What Language ſpeak they?
Hear. Engliſh, and now and then a Root or two
Of Hebrew, which wee'l learn of ſome Dutch Skipper
That goes along with us this Voyage; Now
We want but a good Wind, the Brethrens ſighs
Muſt fill our ſailes. For what old *England* won't
Afford, *New England* will. You ſhall hear of us
By the next Ship that comes for Proſelytes.
Each ſoyl is not the good mans Country only;
Nor is the lot his to be ſtill at home:
Wee'l claime a ſhare, and prove that Nature gave
This Boon, as to the good, ſo to the knave. *Exeunt.*

This Comedy, called the Ordinary ~~the Reformations obserued~~ obserued
may bee Acted, not otherwise not otherwise
January 15. 1671
Henry Herbert
MR

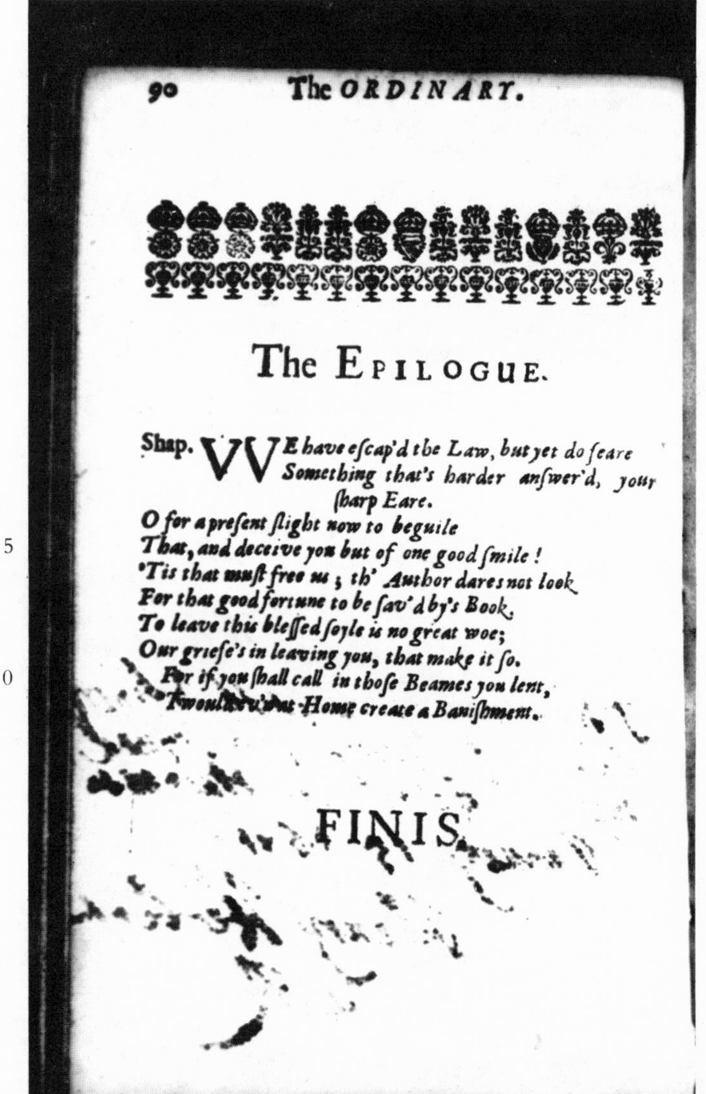

90 The ORDINARY.

The EPILOGUE.

Shap. WE have eſcap'd the Law, but yet do feare
Something that's harder anſwer'd, your ſharp Eare.
O for a preſent ſlight now to beguile
That, and deceive you but of one good ſmile!
'Tis that muſt free us; th' Author dares not look
For that good fortune to be ſav'd by's Book.
To leave this bleſſed ſoyle is no great woe;
Our griefe's in leaving you, that make it ſo.
For if you ſhall call in thoſe Beames you lent,
'Twould ev'n at Home create a Baniſhment.

FINIS.

'Twould ev'n at Home create

THE

LADY-ERRANT.

A

Tragi-Comedy.

Written by

Mr WILLIAM CARTVVRIGHT,
Late Student of *Christ-Church* in
OXFORD, and Proctor of
the *University*.

LONDON,
Printed for *Humphrey Moseley*, and
are to be sold at his shop at the Sign of
the Princes Armes in St PAVLS
Churchyard. 1651.

The Lady-Errant by William Cartwright. Reproduced by permission of the University of Illinois Library at Urbana-Champaign.

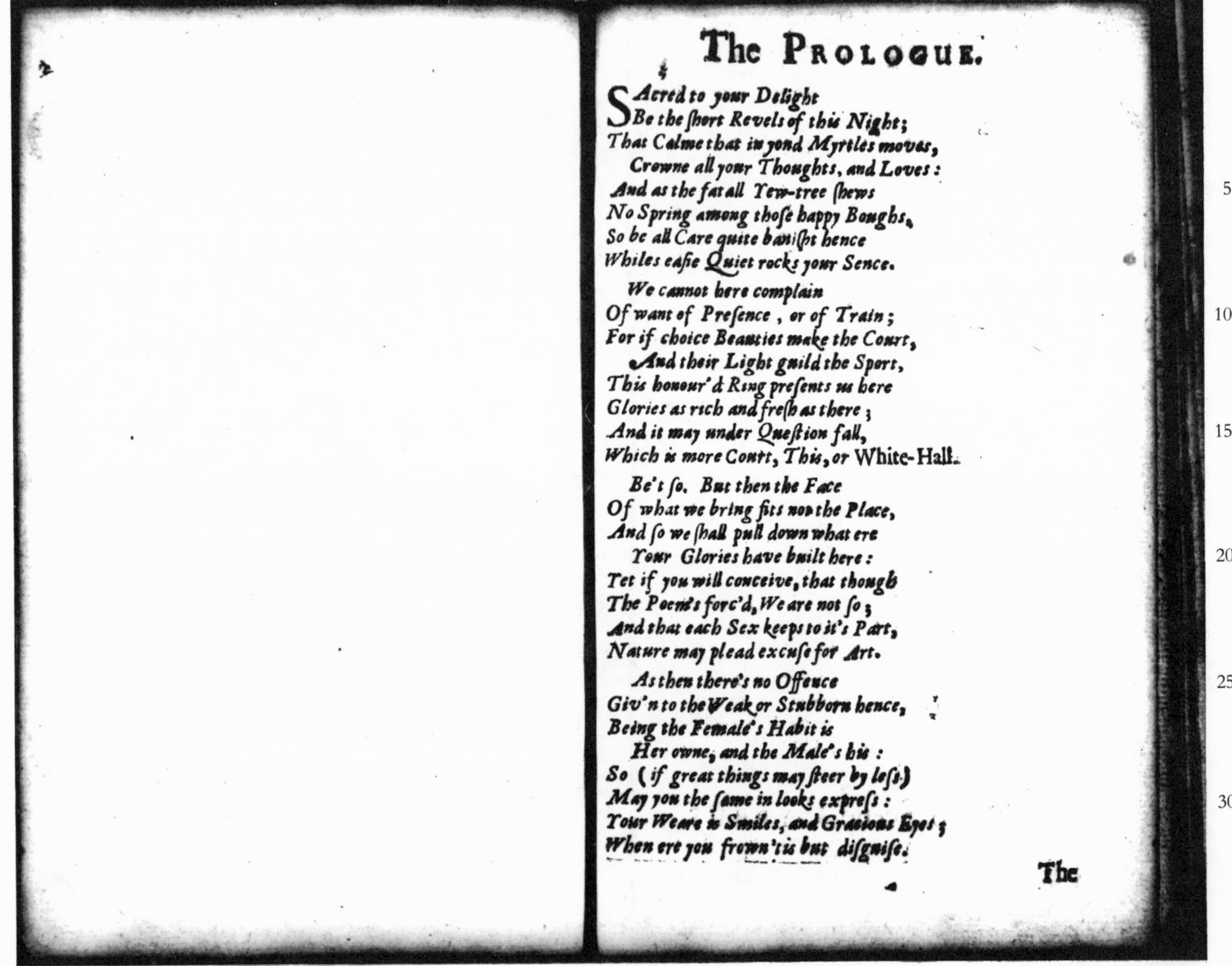

The Prologue.

SAcred to your Delight
Be the short Revels of this Night;
That Calme that in yond Myrtles moves,
Crowne all your Thoughts, and Loves:
And as the fatall Yew-tree shews
No Spring among those happy Boughs,
So be all Care quite banisht hence
Whiles easie Quiet rocks your Sence.

We cannot here complain
Of want of Presence, or of Train;
For if choice Beauties make the Court,
And their Light guild the Sport,
This honour'd Ring presents us here
Glories as rich and fresh as there;
And it may under Question fall,
Which is more Court, This, or White-Hall.

Be't so. But then the Face
Of what we bring fits not the Place,
And so we shall pull down what ere
Your Glories have built here:
Yet if you will conceive, that though
The Poet's forc'd, We are not so;
And that each Sex keeps to it's Part,
Nature may plead excuse for Art.

As then there's no Offence
Giv'n to the Weak or Stubborn hence,
Being the Female's Habit is
Her owne, and the Male's his:
So (if great things may steer by less)
May you the same in looks express:
Your Weare is Smiles, and Gracious Eyes;
When ere you frown 'tis but disguise.

The

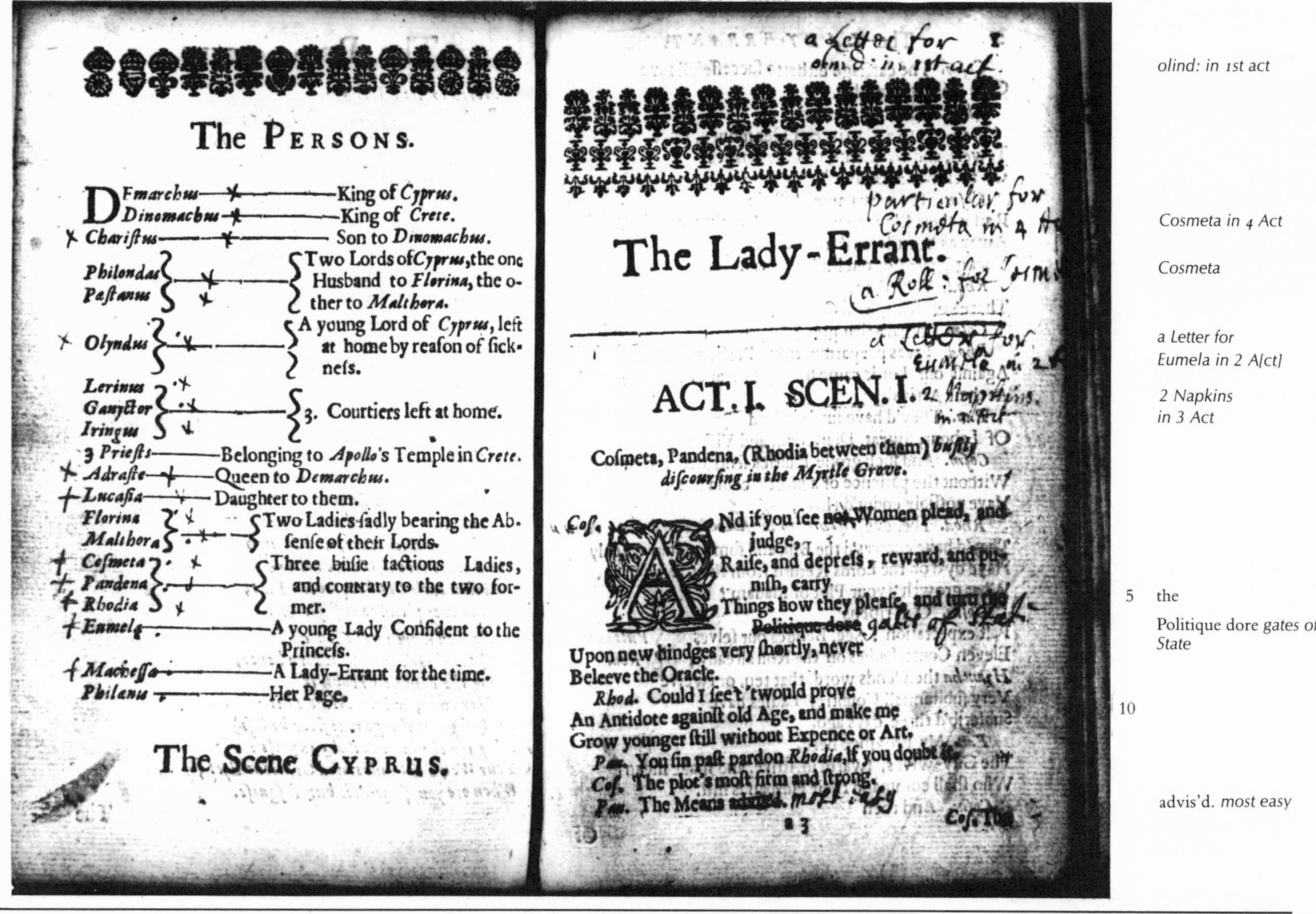

The Persons.

- Demarchus — King of *Cyprus*.
- *Dinomachus* — King of *Crete*.
- *Charistus* — Son to *Dinomachus*.
- *Philondas*, *Pastanus* — Two Lords of *Cyprus*, the one Husband to *Florina*, the other to *Malthora*.
- *Olyndus* — A young Lord of *Cyprus*, left at home by reason of sickness.
- *Lerinus*, *Ganyctor*, *Iringus* — 3. Courtiers left at home.
- *3 Priests* — Belonging to *Apollo*'s Temple in *Crete*.
- *Adraste* — Queen to *Demarchus*.
- *Lucasia* — Daughter to them.
- *Florina*, *Malthora* — Two Ladies sadly bearing the Absense of their Lords.
- *Cosmeta*, *Pandena*, *Rhodia* — Three busie factious Ladies, and contrary to the two former.
- *Eumela* — A young Lady Confident to the Princess.
- *Machessa* — A Lady-Errant for the time.
- *Philanus* — Her Page.

The Scene Cyprus.

The Lady-Errant.

ACT. I. SCEN. I.

Cosmeta, Pandena, (Rhodia between them) *busily discoursing in the Myrtle Grove.*

Cos. And if you see not Women plead, and judge,
Raise, and depress, reward, and punish, carry
Things how they please, and turn the Politique dore
Upon new hindges very shortly, never
Beleeve the Oracle.
Rhod. Could I see't 'twould prove
An Antidote against old Age, and make me
Grow younger still without Expence or Art.
Pan. You sin past pardon *Rhodia*, if you doubt it.
Cos. The plot's most firm and strong.
Pan. The Means advised.

B 3 *Cos.* The

olind: in 1st act

Cosmeta in 4 Act

Cosmeta

a Letter for Eumela in 2 A[ct]

2 Napkins in 3 Act

the

Politique dore *gates of State*

advis'd. *most easy*

Dramatis Personae. The significance of the *X* marks is not clear; perhaps someone considering the casting of the parts ticked off the character names as decisions were reached.

I, i, opening. For a discussion of the properties in *The Lady-Errant* see the commentary in the first part of this book.

2 The *LADY-ERRANT.*

Cosm. The carriage hitherto successefull; we
Gain daily to our side.
Rhod. Doe they come in?
Pan. As to a Marriage; Offer money, Plate,
Jewels, and Garments, nay the Images
Of their Male-Gods.
Cosm. The very name of Rule
Raises their Blouds, and makes 'em throw their Wealth
Away as heartily, as if they were
Young Heires, or old Philosophers.
Rhod. Why then,
There's one care sav'd *Cosmeta.*
Cosm. What's that pray?
Rhod. I was preparing strong Preservatives
Against our Lords came home, for fear of fainting
At their Arrivall.
Pan. They'd have smelt indeed
Of Labour, Sweat, Dust, Man, and Victory.
Cosm. And such grosse Rustick sents, that a Court nose
Without the patience of a Stoick, could not
Have possibly endur'd them.
Rhod. I believe [handwritten: they would have smelt so rank]
~~They'd~~ have encreas'd the Bill, and some would weekly — *I would* They'd
Have dy'd of the Lords Return from the *Cretan* War:
What growth 's your Plot of Madam?
Cosm. O it ripens
Past expectation! See, Besides our selves { *Puls out a Roll.*
Eleven Court-Ladies on the Roll already;
Hyantha then sends word, that ten, or twelve
Very substantiall Countrey-Ladies have
Subscrib'd three days ago.
Pan. My Province here,
The City-wives, swarm in, strive, and make means
Who shall command their Husbands first.
Cosm. And then
Of

The *LADY-ERRANT.* 3

Of Countrey Gentlewomen, and their eldest daughters,
More than can write their Names; 'Tis now past danger.
Rhod. But, Madam, how'l you gain the men at home?
Cos. For that brace & half of Courtiers there, *Ganyctor,*
Lerinus, and *Iringus,* they are mine,
Fast in the Net, if I but pitch it only. (ly.
Rhod. Look where they come, pray sweare 'em present-

ACT. I. SCEN. II.

Ganyctor, Lerinus, Iringus.

Cosm. I'Ll give 'em but my hand to kiss, and 'twill
Bind 'em as fast, as if it were the holiest
Of the best *Sibyls* Leaves.
Pan. Favour your tongues;
Let's lie in Ambush here a while, and listen
What they discourse of.
Rhod. Why of Women I warrant y'.
Cosm. Peace *Rhodia,* peace, close sweet *Pandena,* close!
Irin. Lerinus, this hath been the worst Spring that
I ever knew.
Lerin. Faith it has', for *Flora*
Still challeng'd it before, but now *Bellona*
Hath got the time: Roses and Violets were
The fruit o'th' Season formerly, but now
Laying, and raising Sieges: Building up
And pulling down of Castles; Manning, and
Demolishing of Forts have sign'd the Months.
Gan. Where beauteous Ladies number'd, & were guarded
By the enamor'd Lizards (~~as if *Cadmus*~~ [handwritten: but now] — *Cadmus*
~~In envy had reserv'd some Serpents teeth~~ — reserv'd some
~~And sown 'em there~~) hard watchings and rough Guards
Fill and make up the field.
(*Cosm.* Most smoothly said,
And like a Cowardly Poet.
Irin. There's a feare
a 4 The

4 The *LADY-ERRANT.*

The Women too will rise at home.
Ler. Their fingers
Itch to be tamp'ring with the wheels o'th' State.
Gan. 'Tis very well my Lord *Olyndus* then
Is left at home.
does
Ler. How does his Lordship now?
Still angry that his Majesty would not let
His Sickness go against the Enemy?
Irin. He finds the hardest Wars at home, he hath
Visits, and Onsets, that molest him more
Than all his griefs. He now complains of health;
The eager Ladyes do besiege him hourly,
Not out of love so much, as want of men;
Any thing now, that wears but Breeches only,
Is plotted, and projected for as much
or an
As a new Fashion, or an Office 'bove Stairs,
Ler. They do call this their time of Persecution,
Sweat they are living Martyrs.
Gan. Then the Punishment
Must make 'em so; I'm sure the cause will never.
Ler. A man is striven for as eagerly
As the last loaf in a great depth of Famine.
Irin. You won't believe what I shall tell you now;
Pandena and sweet *Rhodia* at this instant
Both love me, hate each other, eager Rivals;
The one enshrines her Mellons in pure Chrystall,
And as the fruit doth ripen, so her hopes
Of me doe ripen with it——
(*Pan.* Monstrous fellow!)
Irin. The other counts her Apricots, and thinks
So many kisses grow there; lays 'em naked
And open to the Sun, that it may freely
Smile on her vegetable Embraces.
(*Rho.* Good! do you hear this, Madam?)
Cos. Peace and let him on.
Irin.

The *LADY-ERRANT.* 5

Irin. The one presents me, and the other presents me
Gums, Spicknard-boxes, Fruits, and early Roses,
Figs, Mushrooms, Bulbi, and what not? I am
More reverenc'd than their Houshold-God, and taste
and taste
Their store before him still.
(*Cosm.* Close yet for my sake.)
Irin. And proud *Cosmeta*——
(*Pan.* Nay you must hear't out too.)
Irin. She, that, if there were Sexes 'bove the Moon,
VVould tempt a Male Idea, and seduce
A Separate Hee-Substance into Lewdness,
Hath smil'd, glanc'd, wink'd, and trod upon my toes,
Sent smooth Epistles to me, whom I let
Pass unregarded, as a suing Beauty,
And one that makes my triumph up——
[*As he speaks* Cosmeta *and the other two Ladies approach.*
Fair Ladies
You make my Triumph up in that I see you.
Cosm. VVhat? have you been at the VVars then Cap-(tain?
Irin. Madam
I've stood o'th' shore, and wisht well to our Fleet.
Cos. If that be all, pray how comes so much Crest
Crest,
And Scarfe, and Boot to be misplac'd on you?
and Boot
Gan. Is't not a time of VVar, dear Lady?
Pan You follow
The times then, though you won't the Camp.
Ler. 'Tis fit
VVe should be in the Field-fashion however.
Rho. 'Cause you intend the VVars at home perhaps.
Irin. Troth the beleagering of you, Lady, will
Hardly deserve the name of a Siedge; you'll yeeld
So easily on the first approach.
Cosm. You doe
Mistake her, Sir, she means, that you intend
To take great Towns at home——
Pan.

6 The *LADY-ERRANT.*

Pan. Demolish Castles,
And high-built Pyes at once———

at once

Rho. Gaine Sconces 'twixt
The first and second Course———
Cosm. And in the vertue
Of the large *Cretan* Jar kill men at Table.
Irin. No Lady, we do stay at home to make 'em;
Pan. The Wars indeed 'll exhaust the Kingdom much.
Cos. And fit tis that should some way be supply'd.
Irin. You won't corrupt me, Madam? pray forbear.
Cos. No, Sir, I will not do the State that harm;
For the Corruption of one Coward must
Needs be the Generation of another.
Ler. I'll warrant th'Issue will be truly valiant.
Rho. And how so Captain *Stay-by-it?*
Pan. Madam, he
Can neither fight nor speak: I'll tell you how.
That you're a Coward, Sir, is granted: Thus then;
Either your Father was valiant, or was not.
Irin. A very sure division, Lady, that.
Pan. If he were valiant, and you a Coward,
'Tis your Sons course next to be valiant;
But if he were not valiant, and that
You are a Coward of a Coward, then
Your Lineall Issue must be valiant needs,
Because two Negatives make an Affirmative.
Cosm. A most invincible Argument!
Irin. This shall not
Serve I assure you, say what e're you will
You shall not reason me to your Bed-side.
Rho. No, Sir.
Cos. Not though we send you Mellons?
Pan. Ripen'd Hopes?
Rho. Apricocks, Figges?
Pan. Vegetable Embraces.

Cosm.

The *LADY-ERRANT.* 7

Cos. And smooth Epistles? Go you vile abusers
Of what you cannot compass; 'cause you nourish
Desires, you will discharge the sin on us.
Irin. Ladies you're much deceiv'd: had you the Apho-
Of th'Art perfect, that each word should go (risms
With a designe, that not an Eye should be
Lift up, or cast down without mystery——— (looks,
Ler. Could you force sighs, faigne passions, manage
Season your jests, speak with a Manner still——— grace

grace
Manner . . . *grace*

Gan. Should you consult a Decade of Chambermaids,
And sadly advise with your Chrystall Oracles,
In which Attire your Beauties would appear
Most strong; in what contrivance your sweet Graces
Would be most fierce, and overcome Spectators,
You should not have one look to quench the fire.
Ler. You shall be Vestals by compulsion still———
Irin. You shall make Verses to me e're I've done; of
Call me your *Cælia*, your *Corinna*, and braue
Make me the Man o'th' Book in some Romance, heroe
And after all I will not yield.

to

braue
o'th' Book . . . *heroe*

Rho. You're got
Into a safe field of Discourse, where you
Are sure, that Modestie will not suffer us mi my
To answer you in a direct line.

that . . . us

Cosm. You were
Wont to go whining up and down, and make
Dismall Soliloquies in shady Woods———
Pan. Discourse with Trees———
Rho. And Dialogue with Eccho's and wood Nymphs
Cos. Send Messages by Birds, make discreet Thrushes
Your trusty Agents 'twixt your Loves and you———
Rho. Which Loves you call'd Nymphs———
Cos. When indeed they were
Milkmaids, or some such Drudges. This your rating
And prizing of your selves, and standing off,

Comes

8 The *LADY-ERRANT*.

Comes not from any bett'ring of your Judgements,
But from your Mouth's being out of taste.
Pan. Pray y' what
Employment are you fit for?
Ler. Ile assure you
None about you.
Cos. Their whole Employment is
To goe Embassadors 'twixt retir'd Ladies——
Pan. To ask how this great Ladies Physick wrought—
~~*Rho.* Give an account o'th' vertue of her Drugs.~~
Cos. Make perfect Audit of the Tale of sighs
Some little Dog did breath in his first sleep:
Goe you Reproach and Refuse of your Countrey.
Gan. You speak most valiantly Heroick Lady.
Ler. Pray *Venus* you permit the Lords to rule
The Common-wealth again, when they come home.
Pan. Know Sir, they shall not——
Cos. And you shall consent,
Ayd, and assist us in't ~~in spight of you~~,
Willing or unwilling, all's one.
Irin. Wee'll leave you.
Gan. Your Company grows dangerous.
Ler. 'Tis half Treason
To hear you talk.
Pan. Before you 'tis very safe. *Ex. Gan. Irin. Ler.*
You'l never dare t' engage your selves so much
I'th' Army, as to inform the King of't.
Rho. Come,
Let us away too.
Cos. We will vex 'em through
All sorts of Torment, meet 'em at each Corner,
Write Satyrs, and make Libels of 'em, put 'em
In Shows, & Mock-Shows, Masques, & Plaies, present 'em
In all Dramatique Poetry: they shall
Be sung i'th Markets, wee'll not let 'em rest
Till

The *LADY-ERRANT*. 9

Till themselves sue to be o'th' Female *Covenant*.

ACT. I. SCEN. III.

To them *Eumela*.

Pan. But hold, here comes *Eumela*.
Cos. Lady Secretary
Unto our future State. ~~God~~ give you joy. knigh[t]
Eum. You bestow Offices, ~~as City Mothers~~
After their Travail, do give Flowers between
Their House and *Juno*'s Temple, to the next to
They meet, or as you do your Ribbands, to Squire[s]
Entangle, not Reward.
Pan. Then you are Wise
And Politique still——
Rho. Of the Male-faction Lady?
Cos. And you will suffer by Prescription still?
But to be serious now; what do you do? (Rule:
Eum. That which you would, if you should come to
Wake, Sleep, Rise, Dress, Eat, Visit, and Converse,
And let the State alone.
Cos. Y'are very short.
Eum. Indeed I am somewhat now in haste; I'm going
To meet a pair of Ladies, that would willing
Keep their own Sex, and not turn Lords.
Pan. You mean
Florina, and *Malthora*, those that are
Sad now, that one day they may be ~~in History~~ in History
~~Under the name of Turtles.~~ Turtles
Cos. What Dialect may
Those Ladies grieve in? *Dorick* or *Ionick*?
Doe they make Verses yet?
Eum. Their Manners are
A kind of *Satyr* upon yours; though they
Intend

10 The *LADY-ERRANT.*

Intend it not, the people read 'em so.
Rho. 'Cause they have laid aside their Jewels, and so
Blinded their Garments——
Cos. 'Cause they eat their sweet-meats
In a black Closet, they are counted faithfull,
The sole *Penelope's* o'th' time, the Ladies
Of the chaste Web i'th' absence of their Lords.
Eum. Your sadnesse would be such perhaps, if you
Would take the pains to shew the Art of Mourning.
Rho. Is there another way of grieving then?
Eum. This is not grief, but stands to be thought grief:
They are not of such vaunting popular sorrow;
Their Tapers are not dy'd in dismall hue,
And set in Ebon Candlesticks; they wear
No sad black Sarcenet Smocks, nor do they smutch
Their women, to be serv'd by mourning Faces;
That This were to grieve to Ostentation,
Not to a reall friendship.
Pan. Is there friendship
Think you 'twixt man and wife?
Eum. You'll say, perhaps,
You, and your Husband, have not been friends yet.
Pan. Madam, you prophecy.
Eum. I might be thought t'have done so,
Had I foretold a truth to come, but this
Is History already.
Cos. If they do not this,
Nor wear the day out in a hoodwinkt room,
Where there's no living thing besides the Clock,
Nor yet take Physick to look pale, what doe they?
Eum. They grieve themselves, their Doctors grieves not
They do that in the Absence of their Lords [for them:
That you would in the Presence of your own.
your
fair as
Kitchin's
Cos. You see we look as fat, and faints ever——
Eum. Your Kitchin's warm, your Box, and Pencils
fail not.
Pan.

The *LADY-ERRANT.* 11

Pan. —VVe are as long in dressing as before——;
Eum. And have the same Romancys read, the same
Letters brought to you, whilst y'are doing it. out
Rho. —Sleep, and take rest, and then, and altogether
Speak as much wit as we did before the wars. as then
Eum. And to as little purpose.
Cos. Fie *Eumela!*
That you should be so obstinate, as to hear
VVealth, Honour, Pleasure, Rule, and every good
Knock at your door, and yet not let 'em in.
Eum. Madam, I know my Looking-glasse won't shew
The altering o'th' State, when it presents
The changes of my Face, and that I cannot
Order the Kingdome, as I do my Hair.
Enter *Florina* and *Malthora.*
Pan. Yonder's your business; Madam, there are three
Sad things arriv'd, two Ladies and a Lute.
Cos. But shall I write you down before you go
The thirteenth in the Rowl of the Asserters
Of Female Liberty?
Eum. If Liberty be the thing
You so much stand for, pray you give me mine;
I neither grant, nor yet deny; I will
Consider.
Cos. VVe dismiss you, Madam, then
Unto your serious Counsell.
Eum. Fare you well.
Exeunt Cosm. Pan. Rho.

ACT.

without
Desarts, Rocks
secret thoughts Eumela
are

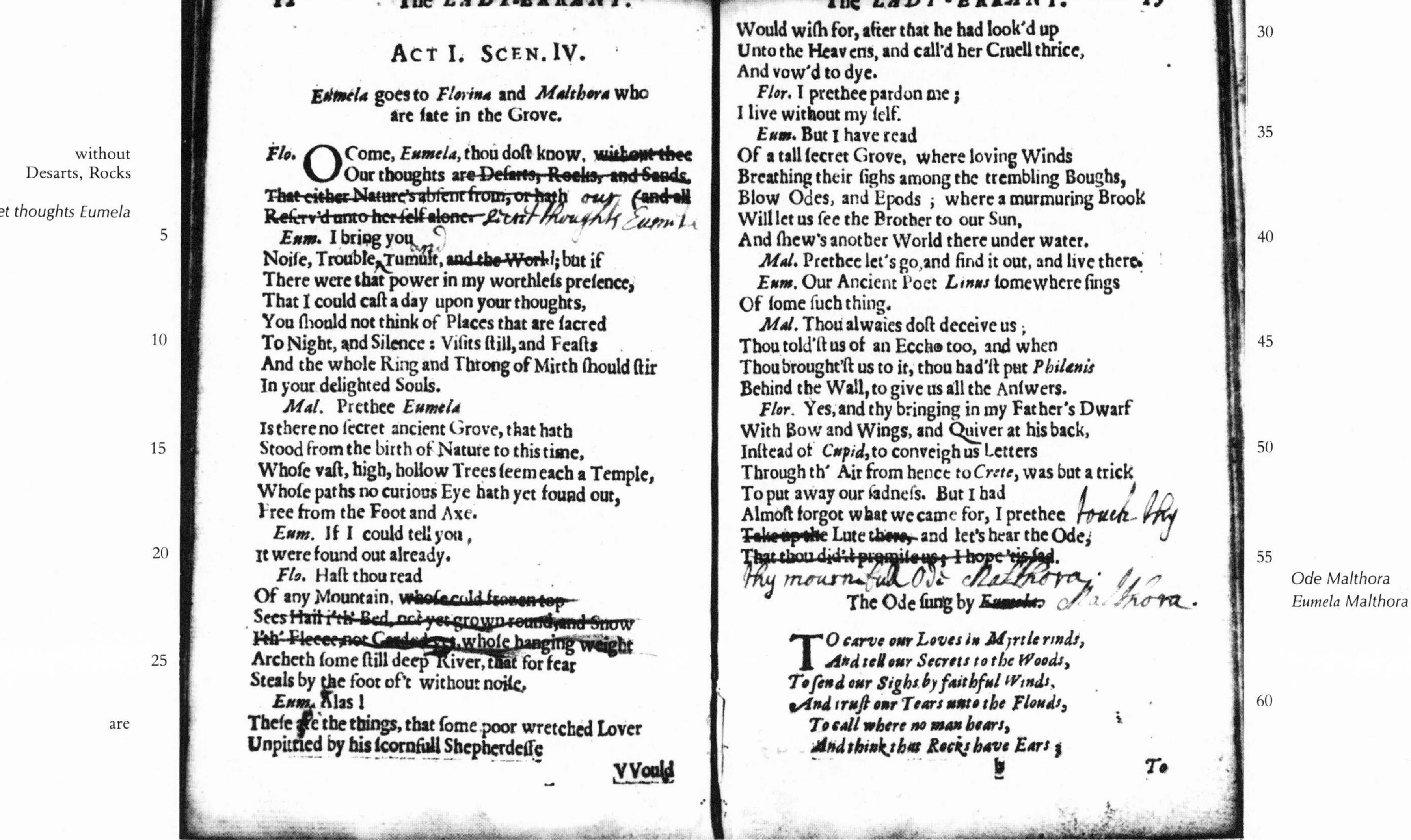

ACT I. SCEN. IV.

Eumela goes to *Florina* and *Malthora* who are sate in the Grove.

Flo. O Come, *Eumela*, thou dost know, ~~without thee~~
Our thoughts are ~~Desarts, Rocks, and Sands,~~
~~That either Nature's absent from, or hath~~ our ~~(and all~~
~~Reserv'd unto her self alone.~~ secret thoughts Eumela
Eum. I bring you
Noise, Trouble, Tumult, ~~and the World~~; but if
There were that power in my worthless presence,
That I could cast a day upon your thoughts,
You should not think of Places that are sacred
To Night, and Silence: Visits still, and Feasts
And the whole Ring and Throng of Mirth should stir
In your delighted Souls.
Mal. Prethee *Eumela*
Is there no secret ancient Grove, that hath
Stood from the birth of Nature to this time,
Whose vast, high, hollow Trees seem each a Temple,
Whose paths no curious Eye hath yet found out,
Free from the Foot and Axe.
Eum. If I could tell you,
It were found out already.
Flo. Hast thou read
Of any Mountain, ~~whose cold frozen top~~
Sees ~~Hail i'th' Bed, not yet grown round, and Snow~~
~~I'th' Fleece, not Carded yet, whose hanging weight~~
Archeth some still deep River, that for fear
Steals by the foot of't without noise,
Eum. Alas!
These are the things, that some poor wretched Lover
Unpitied by his scornfull Shepherdesse
VVould

Would wish for, after that he had look'd up
Unto the Heavens, and call'd her Cruell thrice,
And vow'd to dye.
Flor. I prethee pardon me;
I live without my self.
Eum. But I have read
Of a tall secret Grove, where loving Winds
Breathing their sighs among the trembling Boughs,
Blow Odes, and Epods; where a murmuring Brook
Will let us see the Brother to our Sun,
And shew's another World there under water.
Mal. Prethee let's go, and find it out, and live there.
Eum. Our Ancient Poet *Linus* somewhere sings
Of some such thing.
Mal. Thou alwaies dost deceive us;
Thou told'st us of an Eccho too, and when
Thou brought'st us to it, thou had'st put *Philanis*
Behind the Wall, to give us all the Answers.
Flor. Yes, and thy bringing in my Father's Dwarf
With Bow and Wings, and Quiver at his back,
Instead of *Cupid*, to conveigh us Letters
Through th' Air from hence to *Crete*, was but a trick
To put away our sadness. But I had
Almost forgot what we came for, I prethee touch thy
~~Take up the~~ Lute ~~there~~, and let's hear the Ode;
~~That thou did'st promise us; I hope 'tis sad.~~
thy mournfull Ode Malthora;
The Ode sung by ~~Eumela~~. Malthora.

TO carve our Loves in Myrtle rinds,
And tell our Secrets to the Woods,
To send our Sighs by faithful Winds,
And trust our Tears unto the Flouds,
To call where no man hears,
And think that Rocks have Ears;

b To

Ode Malthora
Eumela Malthora

I, iv, 22–24. The canceled lines are: "whose cold frozen top / Sees Hail i'th' Bed, not yet grown round, and Snow / I'th' Fleece, not Carded yet, whose hanging weight."

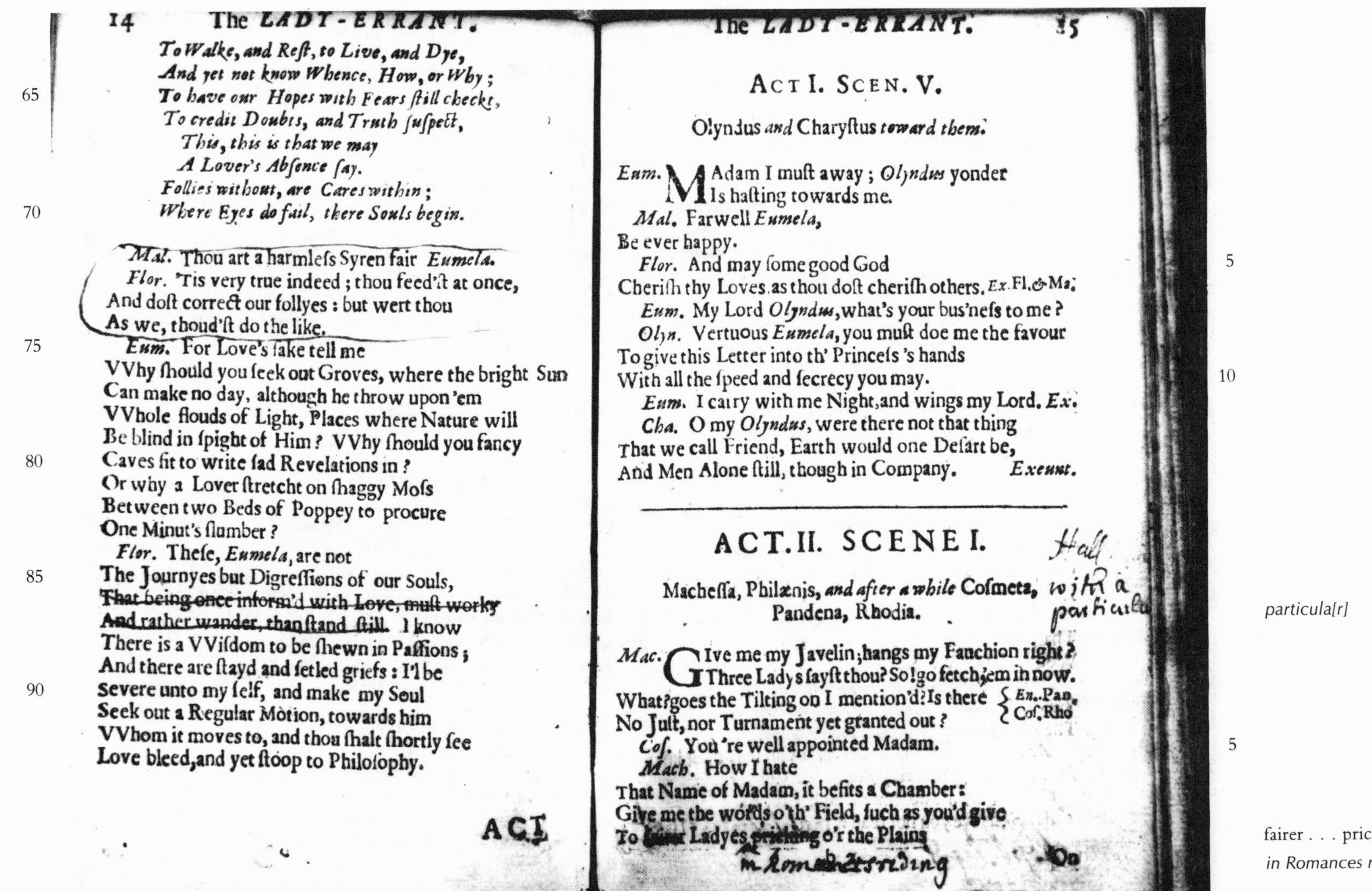

14 The LADY-ERRANT.

To Walke, and Reſt, to Live, and Dye,
And yet not know Whence, How, or Why;
To have our Hopes with Fears ſtill check't,
To credit Doubts, and Truth ſuſpect,
This, this is that we may
A Lover's Abſence ſay.
Follies without, are Cares within;
Where Eyes do fail, there Souls begin.

Mal. Thou art a harmleſs Syren fair *Eumela.*
Flor. 'Tis very true indeed; thou feed'ſt at once,
And doſt correct our follyes: but wert thou
As we, thoud'ſt do the like.
Eum. For Love's ſake tell me
VVhy ſhould you ſeek out Groves, where the bright Sun
Can make no day, although he throw upon 'em
VVhole flouds of Light, Places where Nature will
Be blind in ſpight of Him? VVhy ſhould you fancy
Caves fit to write ſad Revelations in?
Or why a Lover ſtretcht on ſhaggy Moſs
Between two Beds of Poppey to procure
One Minut's ſlumber?
Flor. Theſe, *Eumela*, are not
The Journyes but Digreſſions of our Souls,
~~That being once inform'd with Love, muſt worky~~
~~And rather wander, than ſtand ſtill.~~ I know
There is a VViſdom to be ſhewn in Paſſions;
And there are ſtayd and ſetled griefs: I'l be
Severe unto my ſelf, and make my Soul
Seek out a Regular Motion, towards him
VVhom it moves to, and thou ſhalt ſhortly ſee
Love bleed, and yet ſtoop to Philoſophy.

ACT

The LADY-ERRANT. 15

ACT I. SCEN. V.

Olyndus *and* Charyſtus *toward them.*

Eum. Madam I muſt away; *Olyndus* yonder
Is haſting towards me.
Mal. Farwell *Eumela*,
Be ever happy.
Flor. And may ſome good God
Cheriſh thy Loves as thou doſt cheriſh others. *Ex.* Fl. & Ma.
Eum. My Lord *Olyndus*, what's your bus'neſs to me?
Olyn. Vertuous *Eumela*, you muſt doe me the favour
To give this Letter into th' Princeſs's hands
With all the ſpeed and ſecrecy you may.
Eum. I carry with me Night, and wings my Lord. *Ex.*
Cha. O my *Olyndus*, were there not that thing
That we call Friend, Earth would one Deſart be,
And Men Alone ſtill, though in Company. *Exeunt.*

ACT. II. SCENE I. Hall with a particula

Macheſſa, Philænis, *and after a while* Coſmeta, Pandena, Rhodia.

Mac. Give me my Javelin; hangs my Fauchion right?
Three Ladys ſayſt thou? So! go fetch 'em in now.
What? goes the Tilting on I mention'd? Is there { En. Pan. Coſ. Rho
No Juſt, nor Turnament yet granted out?
Coſ. You're well appointed Madam.
Mach. How I hate
That Name of Madam, it befits a Chamber:
Give me the words o' th' Field, ſuch as you'd give
To ~~fairer~~ Ladyes ~~pricking~~ o'r the Plains
in Romances riding
On

particula[r]

fairer . . . pricking
in Romances riding

II, i, opening. Cosmeta apparently brings in a bill of particulars when she enters, but the property is not used, and the note must be an error. A "particular" *is* needed in Act IV, and this note should have appeared at the opening of IV, i.

On foaming Steeds. But I do pardon you.
Shews not this Scarf and Fauchion far more comely,
Than paultry pyebald Ribbands, ~~and young~~ Bodkins?
and young Bodkins
Pan. ~~You wear a rigid Beauty, fierce Delights.~~
Rho. Your Pleasures threaten, and your stubborn Graces
Tempt, and defend at once.
Mach. Why now y'are right.
And what say'st thou, my little Noon-tide shadow?
My trusty Pigmy?
Phil. Now indeed, and truly ——
Mach. Hell o' these simpring Protestations!
Thou sinfull Inch of short Mortality,
Give Ear to my instructions: here I swear
By th' Sacred Order of my Lady-Errantry,
If thou effeminat'st thy discourse once more
With these precise, minc'd, Little Sisters-Vows,
Thy breath is forfeit.
Phi. By that bloudy Fauchion ——
Mach. I there's a Wench, spit from the mouth of *Ma-*
Bellona was thy Nurse. (*vors!*
Phi. — And that fierce Javelin,
I'd rather see a Plume o'rshade your back
With a large, ~~generous~~ Carelesness; than a bunch
Of fidling Feathers hang before you, just
As modest fig-leaves do in naked Pictures.
Mach. Thou little 'Vantage ~~of Mankind, thou~~ Grain
That Nature put into the Scales to make
Weight to the VVorld, thou tak'st me very much.
Phi. The Sable Fan, which you wore last upon
Your white Lawn-Apron, made you shew just like
The Ace of Clubs, with a black spot i'th' middle.
Mac. VVhy how now little Mischief? is't not knavish
And waggish, like a very Page o'th' Court?
Cos. VVhat use do you mean her for?
Mach. Have you not read? that Ladies-Errant
kept Pages
kept Pages
To

To summon Knights from th' tops of Castle wals. Knock
knock
Pan. I fancy those brave Scythian Heroines; read
read[y]
Those Noble, valiant *Amazons* like you.
Mach. Nature did shew them only as my Types.
Cos. There's nothing wanting but adventures: We
shall quickly now requite the Errant Knights
That help distressed Ladies to their wishes.
Mach. I'l disobliege our Sex. If that you find
Any imprison'd, or inchanted
Tell him *Machessa*'s his deliver~~ance~~ er.
deliverance er
Said I *Machessa*? Hold! that word *Machessa*
Sailes through my Lips with too small breath. I'l have
A Name that Mouths shall travell with: let's see?
Wee'l put a Prologue to it: So! I have it;
It is concluded — *Monster-quelling-Woman-*
Obliging-Man-delivering-Machessa,
She, She is his deliverance: tell him so.
Ph. Do she that can; I would you'd change your Name;
'Tis longer than your Self, and if it were
Some three foot shorter, 'twere as high as I am. [*One knocks.* Knoc
Knoc[k]
Mach. See who 'tis knocks; you do not know your
Bellona, hear my Name, and send Adventures. (Office;

ACT. II. SCEN. II.

To them *Ganyctor*, *Lerinus*, *Iringus*.

Cos. THe Courtiers Madam; work for us! remember.
Pray stand aside as soon as we begin.
Gan. Save you *Machessa*.
Mach. I've a Name besides,
By which I mean Posterity shall know me;
The word is grown: 'tis *Monster-quelling-Woman-*
Obliging-Man-delivering-Machessa.
Irin. Sweet *Monster-quelling-Woman-ob-* and so forth:
b 3 Wee've

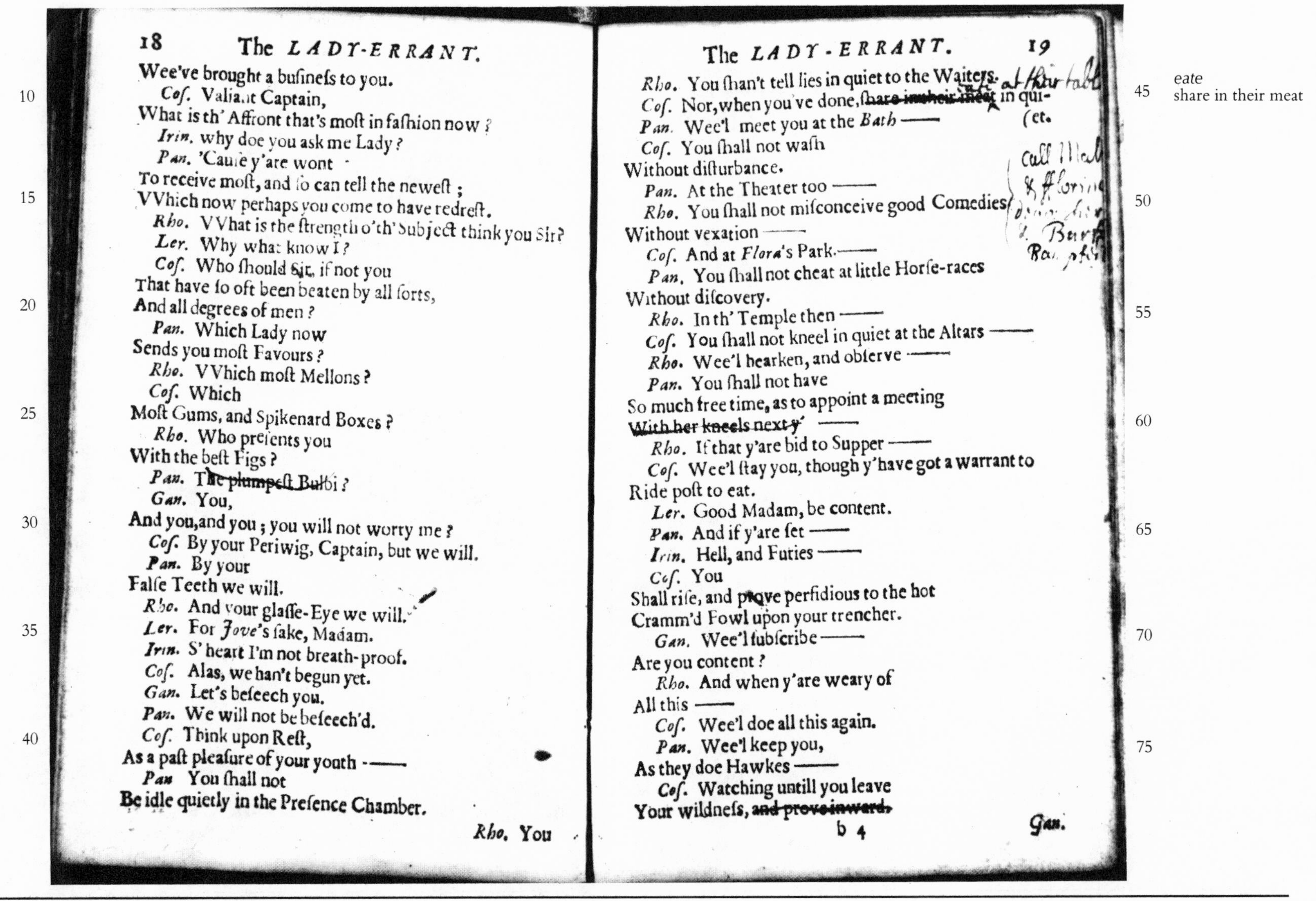

18 The LADY-ERRANT.

Wee've brought a buſineſs to you.
Coſ. Valiant Captain,
What is th' Affront that's moſt in faſhion now?
Irin. why doe you ask me Lady?
Pan. 'Cauſe y'are wont
To receive moſt, and ſo can tell the neweſt;
VVhich now perhaps you come to have redreſt.
Rho. VVhat is the ſtrength o'th' Subject think you Sir?
Ler. Why what know I?
Coſ. Who ſhould Sir, if not you
That have ſo oft been beaten by all ſorts,
And all degrees of men?
Pan. Which Lady now
Sends you moſt Favours?
Rho. VVhich moſt Mellons?
Coſ. Which
Moſt Gums, and Spikenard Boxes?
Rho. Who preſents you
With the beſt Figs?
Pan. T~~he plumpeſt Bul~~bi?
Gan. You,
And you, and you; you will not worry me?
Coſ. By your Periwig, Captain, but we will.
Pan. By your
Falſe Teeth we will.
Rho. And your glaſſe-Eye we will.
Ler. For *Jove*'s ſake, Madam.
Irin. S'heart I'm not breath-proof.
Coſ. Alas, we han't begun yet.
Gan. Let's beſeech you.
Pan. We will not be beſeech'd.
Coſ. Think upon Reſt,
As a paſt pleaſure of your youth ——
Pan You ſhall not
Be idle quietly in the Preſence Chamber.

Rho. You

The LADY-ERRANT. 19

Rho. You ſhan't tell lies in quiet to the Waiters.
Coſ. Nor, when you've done, ~~ſhare in their meat~~ in qui-
(et.
Pan. Wee'l meet you at the *Bath* ——
Coſ. You ſhall not waſh
Without diſturbance.
Pan. At the Theater too ——
Rho. You ſhall not miſconceive good Comedies
Without vexation ——
Coſ. And at *Flora*'s Park ——
Pan. You ſhall not cheat at little Horſe-races
Without diſcovery.
Rho. In th' Temple then ——
Coſ. You ſhall not kneel in quiet at the Altars ——
Rho. Wee'l hearken, and obſerve ——
Pan. You ſhall not have
So much free time, as to appoint a meeting
~~With her kneels next y'~~ ——
Rho. If that y'are bid to Supper ——
Coſ. Wee'l ſtay you, though y'have got a warrant to
Ride poſt to eat.
Ler. Good Madam, be content.
Pan. And if y'are ſet ——
Irin. Hell, and Furies ——
Coſ. You
Shall riſe, and prove perfidious to the hot
Cramm'd Fowl upon your trencher.
Gan. Wee'l ſubſcribe ——
Are you content?
Rho. And when y'are weary of
All this ——
Coſ. Wee'l doe all this again.
Pan. Wee'l keep you,
As they doe Hawkes ——
Coſ. Watching untill you leave
Your wildneſs, ~~and prove inward.~~

b 4 *Gan.*

eate
share in their meat

II, ii, 48. This is the only certain actor warning in the copy. I take the word *deoo:* to mean ditto—that is, a call for the three men (Sherwood, Burford, and Bampfield) who evidently participated in the dance at line 88.

Gan. Hear y'Madam——
Ler. We will ~~sub~~scribe. subscribe
Cos. Come quickly then, lest that
We take a toy, and will not let you. { *Mach. steps in and draws till they all pass out.*
Mach. Stay.
The Gods have destin'd this should be the first
Of my Adventures—go—y'are free.
Irin. Our thanks Ent: fflo: Maltho. [o]f
Will be too small a Recompence. [*Exeunt* Gan. Irin. Ler.
Mach. The Deed
Will pay it self; Vertue's not Mercenary:
Or, if it be, mine is not. So; I do
Begin to come in Action now. To do
And suffer, doth engross whole Nature, and
I will engross both them; I'l set all free,
But only Glory; her I'l Captive lead,
Making her Trumpet only sound my Name,
That is, the Sexe's. I am all their Fame.
How goes your Bus'ness on?
Pan. Vertue and Fortune
Joyn in it both.
Cos. Eumela is come over,
Hath undertook the Machin, and hath promis'd
To bring it to that pass, that neither Queen,
Nor Princess shall gainsay't. *Florina*, and
Malthora both have given in their Reasons,
Which I have answer'd, and convinc'd.
Mach. If that
It come to any danger, let me know it.
Exeunt Mach. Phi.

ACT.

Act. II. Scen. III.

To them *Eumela.*

Rho. Eumela welcome; does your bus'ness thrive?
Eum. Too fast.
Cos. What? have you sent to th' Ports?
Eum. All's safe.
Machessa's ours you say——
Pan. Yes, and *Philandra.*
Eum. Cleora and *Earina* busie Sticklers,
Oenone and *Hermione* sent as Emissaries
To try the farther Cities — ~~*Paxia* hath~~
~~A pretty stroke among the Privy Chamber~~
Cos You've lost no time.
Eum. Nor will, *Cosmeta*—
Psecas, and *Dorcas*, *Cloe*, and *Plecusa*,
Philis, and *Glauca*, swore this morning all
As I was dressing.
Rho. On what Book I pray?
Eum. On the Greek Epigrams, Madam, or *Anacreon*,
I know not which: they bind alike.
Cos. What hopes
Have we o'th' Women of *Lapythia*?
How stand the Dames of *Salamin* affected?
Eum. Why *Lycas* sent to give them a fair Largess strong Greek
Of ~~Leaves and~~ Wine, & then, whiles that well cheers 'em, Leaves and
Eugenia brings 'em a most promising Answer
From some corrupted Oracle, and so leads
The superstitious Souls to what she pleaseth.
This is a ground, a thing suppos'd. The Plot
Is wholly now upon *Florina*, there
It knits, and gathers, breaks, and joyns again;
She's Wise, and Noble — we must find a way

Not

II, ii, 88 ff. The new speech is: *Ler. And to show our Joy if they / please we'l join / with 'em in a / dance.*

Not thought on yet to gain her.
Pan. But the Queen
And Princeſs ——
Eum. They perceive the buſineſs ripens,
That it doth move the limbs, and can for need
Shift, and defend it ſelf, and therfore doe
By me make promiſe of a generall meeting
As ſoon as may be : i'th' mean time, we have
Full leave to gather any Contributions,
Gold, Silver, Jewels, Garments, any thing
Conducing to maintain the Publique Cauſe.
Omn. Goddeſs *Eumela!*
Eum. Goe, fall off, the Princeſs
I'l Is at hand —— ~~I~~goe mingle Counſels.
Exeunt Coſ.Rho.Pan.

Act. II. Scen. IV.

Lucaſia to *Eumela.* a Letter

Luc. Eumela you are come moſt opportunely.
Eu. This to your Highneſs from my L. *Olyndus.*
[*delivers the Letter.*]
Luc. You're happy that your Love is with you ſtill,
That you can ſee, and hear, and ſpeak to him.
Venus doth favour you more than the whole
Mars for her sake's Kingdome *Eumela* : ~~Mars for her ſake 's kind to you~~.
Eum. I muſt confeſs it happy : but *Olyndus*
Cannot be brought to think it ſo ; he fears
His ſickneſs will by ſome be conſtru'd Love ;
Which, if his Valour in his Country's danger
Durſt give the upper hand, ev'n at the Altar,
Though *Venus* did her ſelf look on, hee'd pull
Out of his Breaſt, and caſt aſide, as ſome
Unhallow'd part o'th' Sacrifice.

Luc. His

Luc. His King
Hath found him truly valiant. E'r I open
This Paper, you muſt ſtate one Point, *Eumela*,
Suppoſe me buſie in the holy Rites
Of our adored *Venus* : if by chance
I caſt mine Eye upon ſome Princely viſage,
And feel a Paſſion, is the Goddeſs wrong'd ?
Or the Religion leſſe ?
Eum. Our Loves what are they
But howerly Sacrifices, only wanting
The preaſe and tumult of Solemnity ?
If then i'th' heat ~~and Achme~~ of Devotion and Achme
We drink a new flame in, can it be ought
But to increaſe the Worſhip ? and what Goddeſs
Was ever angry that the holy Prieſt
Increas'd her Fires, and made 'em burn more clear ?
Luc. True, but ſuppoſe the Face then ſeen doth never
Appear more ~~after~~, is not that a ſign after
The Goddeſs is diſpleas'd ?
Eum. That it a while
Appears not, is to cheriſh, not extinguiſh
The Paſſion thence conceiv'd : as Perſecutions
Make Piety ſtronger ſtill, and bring th' Afflicted
Unto the glory of renowned Martyrs.
Luc. But is there then no hope but that ? Alas !
This man perhaps might periſh in ſome War
As now (But O ye Gods avert the Fate !) [*to her ſelf.*
And then th' unhappy ſighing Virgin fall
From ~~that~~ her feigned Heaven.
Eum. It cannot be ;
Venus deſtroyes her Deity, if She ſhew
And then delude : She will not loſe what once
She hath made her own ; She that knits hearts by th' Eyes,
Will keep the knot faſt by their Entercourſe ,
If you have once but ſeen, and lov'd, ~~permis~~ leave *leave*

The

24 The *LADY-ERRANT*.

The reſt unto the Deity. Will it pleaſe
Your Highneſs to peruſe the Letter? 'tis
Of moment I preſume: why bluſh you Madam?
And, while I aſk you, why look pale?
Luc. *Eumela*,
The ſuppoſition's truth; lately, thou knoweſt,
I did aſſiſt at *Venus* Sacrifice;
He, whom I ſaw, and lov'd, ſaw, and lov'd too,
And now hath writ — but let *Olyndus* tell him
I will not ſee him, though he were the Soul
Of all Mankind.
Eum. I will.
Luc. Hear me — yet if
He have a true undoubted Friend, he may
Send him, I'l meet him in the Myrtle Grove,
And tell him more.
Eum. I will obey.
Luc. But ſtay——
And yet that's all.
Eum. I go. [*Exit* Eumela.
Luc. The Soul doth give
Brightneſs to th' Eye, and ſome ſay, That the Sun,
If not enlight'ned by th' Intelligence
That doth inhabit it, would ſhine no more
Than a dull Clod of Earth: ſo Love, that is
Brighter than Eye, or Sun, if not enlight'ned
By Reaſon, would ſo much of Luſtre loſe
As to become but groſs, and foul Deſire;
I muſt refine his Paſſion; None can wooe
Nobly, but he that hath done Nobly too.

ACT.

for they are neare in ye Grove Mad.

The *LADY-ERRANT*. 25

ACT. III. SCEN. V.

To her *Florina* and *Malthora*.

Mal. YOur Highneſs here alone?
Luc. But ſo long only
As gives you leave to aſk. What? ſad *Florina*?
I'd thought your Soul had dwelt within it ſelf,
Been ſingle a full preſence, and that you
Had ſet your ſelf up your own Trophy now
Full of true Joy.
Flo. T'is hard to caſt off that
That we call Paſſion, we may veyl, and cloud it,
But 'twill break out at laſt. True Joy is that
Which now I cannot have.
Luc. How ſo *Florina*?
Flo. True Joy conſiſts in Looks, and Words, and Letters,
Which now an Abſence, equall to Divorce,
Hath wholly barr'd us of.
Luc. Looks, Words, and Letters!
Alas they are but only ſo much Air
Diverſly form'd, & ſo the food of that
Changeable Creature; not the Viands of
True conſtant Lovers.
Flo. But, if I ſee not,
Is not my Joy grown leſs, who could not love
'Till I firſt ſaw? and if I hear not, can
I have the perfect Harmony of pleaſure,
Who ſomething ow to words that I firſt yeelded?
Luc. Who ever yet was won by words? we come
Conquer'd, and when we grant, we do not yeeld,
But do confeſs that we did yeeld before.
But be thoſe Senſes ſome Contentments, Madam,
You muſt not yet make them the great, and true
Eſſential

II, iv, following 79. The new scene should have been numbered II, v.

Eſſentiall Joy that only can conſiſt
In the bright perfect Union of two Spirits.
Mal. But ſeeing thoſe Spirits cannot work, but by
The Organs of the Body, 'tis requir'd
That (to the full perfection of this Joy)
Bodies ſhould be near-Neighbours too.
Flo. I muſt
Confeſs that I ſubſcribe unto the Princeſs,
And ſomwhat too to you: the Preſence may
Conveigh, and fill, and poliſh Joy; but yet
To ſee, or hear, cannot be Joyes themſelves.
And where this Preſence is deny'd, the Soul
Makes uſe of higher, and more ſubtle means,
And by the ſtrength of thought creates a Preſence
Where there is none.
Mal. Alas! how we doe loſe
Our ſelves in ſpeculation of our Loves,
As if they were unbody'd Eſſences!
Luc. I would
Eumela now were here; Shee'd tell us, All
Is the ſame Joy, as Love from ſight, or thought,
Is the ſame Love; and that Love's turning to
Either of them, is only but a Needle
Turning to ſeverall points, no diverſe flame,
But only divers degrees of the ſelf-ſame.
Come Madam let's away and ſeek her out. [*Exeunt.*

ACT II. SCENE VI.

Chariſtus, Olyndus.

Cha. NOt ſee me, ſay you, though I were the Soul
Of all Mankind?
Olyn. They were the words ~~return'd~~———
But if he have a true ~~undoubted~~ friend,

very

Send

Send him, I'l tell him more.
Cha. Have I deſerved
My Country, now in danger, where I had
Took Honour Captive, and for ever fixt her
~~As an Intelligence~~ unto my Sword,
~~To move~~ and guide ~~it~~? have I ſcorn'd my Fortunes,
And laid aſide the Prince? have I contemn'd
That much priz'd thing call'd Life, and wreſtled with
Both Winds and Flouds, through which I have arriv'd
Hither at laſt? and all this not to ſee her?
Olyn. Doth ſhe betray, or undiſguiſe you to
The State? Doth ſhe forbid you, Sir, to love?
Affection is not wanting, where 'tis wiſe;
She only doth forbid you that you ſee her.
Cha: Only forbid me to be happy, only
Forbids me to enjoy my ſelf; What could
She more, were I her Enemy? *Olyndus*
Haſt thou at no time told her, that there was
A *Cretan* call'd thee Friend?
Olyn. Why do you ask?
Cha. Perhaps Sh' hath found this way to ſend for thee.
Oly. Though I have thought it worth the boaſting, that
Chariſtus is my friend, yet by that Word,
Sacred to Noble Souls, I never had
So much acceſs to tell her any thing,
Much leſs my Friendſhip.
Cha. Thou ſhalt go *Olyndus.*
Olyn. When my eyes ſee her, yours do; when I talk,
'Tis you that talk; we are true friends, and one,
Nay that one interchang'd; for I am you.
Cha. 'Tis true thou art my friend, ſo much my friend,
That my ſelf am not more my ſelf, than thou art:
If thou doſt go, I go— But ſtay — Didſt not
Thou ſay mine eyes were thine? thou didſt: if that
Be ſo, then thou muſt love her too, and then——

Olyn.

28 The LADY-ERRANT.

Olyndus thou must stay.
Olyn. She loves you so,
(As my *Eumela* doth inform me) that
No humane Image can deface the Print
That you have drawn i'th' Tablet of her Soul.
Cha. If ~~that~~ she loves me so, why then she must
Love thee so too; for thou and I are one.
Olyn. Why then, Sir, if you go your self, the issue
Will be the same however, so, when she
Loves you Shee'l love me too.
Cha. We are both one
In hearts and minds *Olyndus*: but those Minds
Are cloath'd with Bodies. Bodies that do oft ——
I know not what ——— yet thou hast an *Eumela*,
A fair *Eumela* trust me —— Thou must go ———
But use not any Language, Gesture, Looks,
That may be constru'd ought above Respect;
For thou art young and Beautifull, and Valiant,
And all that Ladies long for.
Olyn. When I prove
So treacherous to my Friend, my self, my fair
Eumela, mark me with that hatefull brand
That Ignominy hath not discover'd yet,
~~But doth reserve to~~ fear the ~~foulest Monster~~
~~That shall appear in Nature.~~
Cha. I beleeve thee:
Yet something bids me still not let thee go.
But I'l not hearken to it; though my Soul
Should tell me 'twere not fit, I'd not beleeve
My Soul could think so.
Olyn. How resolve you then?
Cha. Do what thou wilt. I do beleeve — and yet
I do — I know not what — O my *Lucasia*!
O my *Olyndus*! divers waies I bend,
Divided 'twixt the Lover, and the Friend. *Exeunt.*
ACT.

Monster / That shall appear in Nature

The LADY-ERRANT. 29

ACT. III. SCENE I.

Olyndus *to* Lucasia *in the Grove.*

Olyn. M~~A May't please your Highness,~~ Madam—
I have a friend so much my self, that I
Cann't say he's absent now, yet he hath sent me
To be here present for him: we enterchange
Bosoms, and Counsels, Thoughts and Souls so much,
That he entreats you to conceive you spake
To him in me; All that you shall deposite here, is safe.
~~Will be in safe, and faithfull Ears~~; the same
Trust you expect from him, shall keep your words,
And the same Night conceal 'em: 'tis *Charistus*
The noble *Cretan*.
Luc. When you said your Friend,
The rest was needless; I conceive him all
That makes up Vertue, all that we call Good
Whom you *Olyndus* give your Soul to; yet
I'd rather court his Valour, than his Love,
Did he shine bright in Armour, call for Dangers,
Eager to cut his way through stubborn Troops,
~~Ev'n this my softness, arm'd as he, could follow~~
~~And prompt his Arm, supply him with fresh Fury,~~
~~And dictate higher dangers~~. Then when Dust
And Bloud hath smear'd him (a disguise more worthy
Of Princes far, than that he wears) I could
Embrace him fresh from Conquest, and conceive him
As fair as ever any yet appear'd
To longing Virgins in their ~~Amorous~~ Dreams.
Olyn. Fury could never from the Den of danger
Awake that horror yet, that bold *Charistus*
Durst

And dictate higher dangers

Amorous

Durſt not attempt, ſtand equall with, and then
Conquer, and trample, and contemn.
Luc. Revenge
And Hate I do confeſs, may ſometimes carry
The Soul beyond it ſelf to do, and ſuffer :
But the things then are Furious, not Great, strong
And ſign the Actor Headlong, but not Vertuous.
Olyn. He that can do this, Madam, and Love too,
Muſt needs be vertuous ; that holy Flame
Clean and untainted, as the freſh deſires
Of Infant Saints, enters not Souls that are
Of any foul Complexion. He that Loves,
Even in that he Loves, is good : and as
He is no leſs an Atheiſt, that denies
The Gods to be moſt happy, than the Man
That dares Affirm there are no Gods at all ;
So he's no leſs an Heretick, that ſhall
Deny Love to be Vertuous, than he
That dares Affirm there is no Love at all.
Luc. But he hath left his Country now, when that
Her Wealth, her Name, her Temples, and her Altars,
Her Gods, and Liberty, ſtand yet upon
Th'uncertain Dye; when Danger cals his Arm ,
And Glory ſhould arreſt his Spirit there ;
And this to Court one , whom he knows not, whether
She may think Vertue a meer Airy word,
And Honour but a blaſt, invented to
Make catching Spirits dare, and do high things.
Olyn. That you are Vertuous, is aknowledge, that
All muſt confeſs ~~they have, but only thoſe~~
frame ~~That have not Eyes~~ : For if that Souls frame Bodies,
Architect And that the Excellence of the Architect
Appear in the perfection of the Structure,
Whether you have a Soul enrich'd with vertues,
Muſt be a blind Man's doubt : Nature dares not
Thruſt

Thruſt out ſo much deceit into the World ;
'Twould make us not beleeve her works were meant
For true firm Peeces, but Deluſions only.
Luc. Though I muſt not agree t' you, to paſs by
What you have ſaid , If I were Vertuous,
You muſt confeſs him ſo far ignorant yet,
As not to know whether I'd Love, or no.
Oly. This Knowledge is of more Extent than th' other.
For being that to be lov'd is the Effect
Of your own worths, you muſt love all mens Loves
As a Confeſſion of your Graces, that
Your ſelves have drawn from them. That which your (Beauty
Produceth, is a Birth as dear unto you,
As are your Children.
Luc. Should there more than one
Love us (if this hold) we muſt love them too,
And ſo that Sacred Tye that joyns the Soul
To one, and but to one, were but a Fable,
A thing in Poetry, not in the Creature.
Olyn. One is your Trophy : and he Lov'd as That
The Reſt but Witneſſes : thus Princes, when
They Conquer Princes, though they only count
Thoſe Names of Glory, and Renown, their Victory,
Take yet their meaner Subjects in, as fair
Acceſſes to their Triumphs, who, although
They are not the main Prize, are ſomewhat yet
That doth confirm that there was worth, ~~and~~ force,
To which the Main did juſtly yeeld.
Luc. Be't then like
That I do ~~love~~ his Love, I am not yet love
Bound to accept it in what ſhape ſoever
It doth appear ; the Manner, Time, and Place
May not be reliſh'd, though the thing be lik'd.
Olyn. For theſe he doth expect your Dictates, with
As much Religion, as he would the Anſwers
C 2 Of

Of Sacred Oracles, and with the ſame
Vow of Performance.

Luc. You muſt tell him then.
He muſt go back, and there do Honorably;
Succour his Country, cheer the Souldier, fight,
~~Spend~~, and ~~disburſe~~ the Prince, where e'r he goes,
Get him a Name, and Title upon *Cyprus.*
I will not ſee him 'till he hath Conquer'd, ~~till~~
~~He hath rid high in Triumph,~~ and when this
Is done, let him conſider then, it is
My Father, & my Subjects, and my Kingdom
That he hath Conquer'd.

Olyn. I am an Agent only,
And therefore muſt be faithful.

Luc. But withall
To ſhew that I reject him not, you may
Tell him, that being he hath ſuch a friend,
Whiles he is abſent I will love *Olyndus*
Inſtead of him. [*Exit* Lucaſia.

Olyn. But that my Friend is in me
I ſhould have deem'd it Sacrilege, to have had
A thought like that ſuggeſted. My *Chariſtus*,
Were he not ſomething carefull in his Love,
(I will not call him Jealous) were beyond
The ~~Lot~~ of Man: I muſt not tell him all,
Some may be hid; yet how ſhall I unriddle
The Myſtery of this Anſwer? But the knots
That Love doth tye, himſelf will only find
The way to looſe ——

Spend, and disburse

Lot

ACT. III. SCEN. II.

To him Chariſtus.

——And here *Chariſtus* comes.
Souls once poſſeſs'd, as his, are moſt impatient,
They meet what they ſhould ſtay for.

Cha.

Cha. Dear *Olyndus*,
Pardon that I expect not, but make haſt
To intercept my Doom. Others perhaps
May wait the punctuall Minute, and obſerve
The juſt and even Period: but *Chariſtus*
Doth love too ſlow, when time, and Sun can bind him
Unto a regular Motion.

Olyn. Would you had
Been there your ſelf! would you had drunk in all
The Looks, Words, Graces, and Divinities
That I have done! I'm like the Prieſt that's full
Of his inſpiring God, and am poſſeſs'd
With ~~ſo much~~ rapture, ~~that methinks I could~~
~~Bear up my ſelf without a Wing, or Chariot,~~
~~And hover o'r the Earth, ſtill dropping ſomething~~
~~That ſhould take root in Kingdoms, and come up~~
~~The Good of people.~~

Cha. Let me ask thee then
As we do thoſe that do come freſh from Viſions,
What ſaw'ſt thou there?

Olyn. That which I ſee ſtill, that
Which will not out; I ſaw a Face that did
Seem to participate of Flames, and ~~Flowers;~~ angells
~~Eyes in which Light combin'd with Jet to make~~
~~Whiteneſs be thought the Blot, and Black hereafter~~
~~Purchaſe the Name of Innocence, and Luſtre.~~
The whole was but one ſolid Light, and had I
Not ſeen our Goddeſs riſing from the Flouds
Pourtray'd leſs fair, leſs Goddeſs, I had thought
The thing I ſaw, and talk'd with, muſt have been
The Tutelar Deity of this our Iſland.

Cha. That I ſhould let thee go! that I ſhould be
So impious to my ſelf, as not to break
Her great Commands, and ſo become a Martyr
By daring to be happy 'gainſt her will ——

C 3 But

angells

But on *Olyndus.*
Olyn. You may think this
The Height, the Acme, and the All of her:
But when I tell you, that She hath a Mind
That hides all this, ~~and makes it not appear~~,
~~Diſparaging as 'twere, what ever may~~
~~Be ſeen without her~~, then you'l thus exclame;
Nature, thou wert o'rſeen to put ſo mean
A Frontiſpeece to ſuch a Building.
Cha. Give me,
O quickly give me the whole Miracle,
Or preſently I am not.
Olyn. Think, *Chariſtus,*
Think out the reſt, as 'tis, I cannot ſpeak it.
Cha. Alas! what ſhould I think?
Olyn Conceive a Fire
Simple and thin; to which that Light we ſee,
And ſee by, is ſo far impure, that 'tis
Only the ſtain, and blemiſh of the World;
And if it could be plac'd with it in one
And the ſame Tablet, would but only ſerve
As bound and ſhadow to it: Then conceive
A Subſtance that the Gods have ſet apart,
And when they would put generous Motions
Into a Mortall Breaſt, do take the Soul
And couch it there, ſo that what e'r we call
Vertue in us, is only but a Turning
And Inclination toward her from whom
This Pow'r was firſt deriv'd.
Cha. What preſent God
Lent thee his Eyes, and ſtood blind by, whiles thou
Did'ſt gaze, and ſurfet on theſe Glories?
Olyn. ~~Others~~
Do Love the ſhape, the Geſture, and the Man,
But She the Vertue. Mark *Chariſtus.* She
Saies

Saies *S*he could Court you ring'd about with Dangers,
Doat on you ſmear'd, ~~and ſtiff~~ with ~~hoſtile~~ Bloud, and stiff with hostile
Count and exact your wounds, as a due ſum
You are to pay to Valour; All which when
I told her was in Love, ſhe ſaid I did
Preſent a ſpark, when ſhe deſir'd a full
And glorious Conſtellation —— to be ſhort,
*S*he ſaies you muſt go back, do honourably,
Get you a Name upon the *Cyprian* Forces;
And bids when you have done all this, conſider
It is her Father, and his *S*ubjects, and
His Kingdome that you conquer ——
Cha. And her ſelf
That I ſhall loſe by doing ſo. ~~If I~~
~~Return, and Crete be Conquer'd, then She will~~
~~Count me Spoyl, and Luggage; and my Love~~
~~Only a Slave's Affection.~~ If I Conquer,
And *Cyprus* follow my Triumphant Chariot,
My Love wil then be Tyranny: and *S*he,
How can ſhe light an Hymeneal Torch
From her lov'd Countries Flame? I am rejected,
Chariſtus is a Name of ſcorn.
Olyn. VVhat Fates
Dare throw that Name upon my Friend? To ſhew
That ſhe rejects you not, becauſe there is
That Truſt, that Faith, and that Confuſion of
Chariſtus and *Olyndus* 'twixt us, in the mean
VVhiles he is abſent, tell him, ſaith ſhe, that
I'll love *Olyndus* in his ſtead.
Cha. How! Man
Th' haſt dealt diſhonourably. This the Light?
And this the Fire that makes that Light a ſtain?
Olyn. This I foretold my ſelfe: my good *Chariſtus*
Let not your Anger carry you beyond your
~~The bent of~~ Reaſon; can I give account The bent of
c 4 Of

Of others Passions? did I first conceive
The words my self; then speak 'em?
Cha. O ye Gods!
Where is the Faith? where the *Olyndus* now?
Th' hast been a Factor for thy self: I'd thought
I'd sent a Friend, but he's return'd a Merchant,
And will divide the Wealth.
Olyn. Far be that Brand
From your *Olyndus*! far from your *Lucasia*!
She hath a Face hath so much Heaven in it,
And this *Olyndus* so much Worship of it,
That he must first put on another Shape,
And become Monster, e'r he dare but look
Upon her with a thought that's ~~Masculine.~~ is not noble
Cha. Peace ~~Treachery~~! I am too cold; my Anger
Is dull and lazy yet. I'l search that Breast,
And dig out falshood from the secret'st Corner
In all thy Heart, here, in the very place
That thou hast wrong'd me.
Olyn. There is nothing here
That my *Charistus* knows not. Pray you open,
And search, and judge; and when you find all true,
Say you destroy'd a Friend.
Cha. It is your Art
I see to wooe, but I will make you speak
Something that is not Flattery.
Olyn. *Olyndus*
Ne'r lov'd the Man as friend yet, whom he did
Treat as an Enemy. 'Tis one part of Valour
That I durst now receive, conceal, and help you,
Here in the Bosome of that State, which ~~hath~~ is now
~~Cast out a spear into the *Cretan* Field,~~ fighting
~~And bid you War.~~ against yo: country
Cha. Thou hast already here
Betray'd my Love; thy falshood will proceed
Unto

[t]raytor

Unto my Person next. I'd thought I'd been in a friend's arms
~~Clasp'd in Embraces~~, but I find I am
Entangled in a Net.
Olyn. Y'are safe as in house
~~The Bosome of~~ your Father; take this Veyl
Of Passion from your Eyes; and you'l behold
The same *Olyndus* still.
Cha. The same Deceiver,
The same false perjur'd Man. Draw, or by Heaven,
That now should Thunder and revenge my wrongs,
Thou shalt dye sluggishly.
Olyn. Recall your self,
And do but hear ——
Cha. What words a Coward will
Fawn on me with, to keep an abject life,
Not worth the saving.
Olyn. Witness all ye Gods
That govern Friendship, how unwillingly
I do unty the Knot.
Cha. Draw quickly, lest
It may be known I am the *Cretan* Prince,
And so my juster Fury be not suffer'd
To scourge a timorous and perfidious Man.
Oly. Though thou stand'st here an Enemy, and we have
The Pledge of all the *Cretan* State, yet know
Though all our Island's People did look on,
And thou proclaim'st thy self to be the Man,
They should not dare to know the Prince, untill
I'd done this Sacrifice to Honour.
Cha. So!

They fight, and wound each other dangerously, and then retire, Charistus to Lucasia's Myrtle, and Olyndus to the next adjoyning, and leaning there speak.

Olyn.

arm[s]
Clasp'd in Embraces

The Bosome of

III, ii, 139–41. The revised lines read: "~~hath~~ *is now* / Cast out a spear into the *Cretan* Field, *fighting* / ~~And bid you War.~~ *against yo: country*."

38 The *LADY-ERRANT.*

Olyn. I have not long to ſtay 'mongſt Mortals now,
And then you may ſearch all thoſe Corners that
You talk'd of in my Heart. But if you find
Ought that is falſhood towards you, or more
Than reverence to *Lucaſia,* may I want
The Honour of a Grave —— Hear O ye Gods,
(Ye Gods whom (but a while) and I am with you
Lucaſia is as ſpotleſs, as the Seat
That you prepare for Virgin Lovers!
Cha. I
Have wrong'd thee, my *Olyndus,* wrong'd thee much,
But do not chide me; there's not life enough
Left in me to make uſe of Admonition.
Olyn. If you ſurvive, love your *Lucaſia;* 'twill
Make your *Olyndus* happy; for the good
Of the ſurviving Friend, ſome holy men
Say, doth pertain unto the Friend Departed.
Cha. Vertuous *Lucaſia!* and hadſt thou *Olyndus*
Not been ſo too, my Gods had fought for me;
But I muſt dye —— *Olyndus.* [Chariſtus *faints.*
Olyn. Heaven forbid
That my *Chariſtus* periſh! I have only
Strength left to wiſh: If I can creep yet to thee
I'l help thee all I can. [Olynd. *ſinks*
Cha. And I will meet thee;
[*They creep one to the other and ſo embrace.*]
Let us embrace each other yet. The Fates
Preſerve our Friendſhip, and would have us equall,
Equall ev'n in our Angers: we ſhall go
Down equall to the Shades both, two waies equall,
As Dead, as Friends. And when *Lucaſia* ſhall
Come down unto us (which the Heavens forbid
Should be as yet) I'l not be Jealous there.

ACT.

has
is

hear me
whom

The *LADY-ERRANT.* 39

ACT. III. SCEN. III.

To them as they lye groveling, and embracing thus, Macheſſa *and* Philænis.

Phi. O Me! Good Heavens! had you the Balſam, Lady,
Now that you told me of, 'twould do ſomegood.
Mach. This is *Olyndus,* that the honour'd Stranger;
Brave Spirits are a Balſam to themſelves:
There is a Nobleneſs of Mind, that heals
Wounds beyond Salves— look not, but help *Philænis,*
Gather the Weapons, and the reſt up quickly;
Where two are wrong'd, I ought to ſuccour both.
{ Macheſſa *carries 'em out.*

ACT. III. SCEN. IV.

Lucaſia, Florina, Malthora Eumela.

Lu. Madam, ne'r fear your Dream, for that is only
The reliques of your day-time thoughts, that are
Preſerv'd by'our Soul, to make a Scene i'th' Night.
Eum. Have you not dream'd the like before?
Mal. Yes thrice.
Eum. Why then *Paſtanus* now hath periſh'd thrice,
Or elſe y' have ſometimes dream'd in vain.
Flor. Eumela,
I told her this, and that her troubled Sleeps
Were one Love ſtill waking.
Luc. Wee'l divert Nicias
This anxious fear. Reach me the Lute *Eumela.*
Have you not heard how *Venus* did complain
For her belov'd *Adonis?* The young Poet,
That was deſir'd to give a Language to
Th' afflicted Goddeſs, thought her words were theſe.
The

Continu[es]

one
call her Nicias in to dance a Jigg
me *lets heare*

III, iv, 15–16. The canceled lines are: "That was desir'd to give a Language to / Th' afflicted Goddess, thought her words were these."

The Ode.

Cal. WAke my Adonis, *do not dye;*
One Life's enough for thee and I.
Where are thy words? thy wiles?
Thy Loves, thy Frowns, thy smiles?
Alas in vain I call;
One death hath snatch'd 'em all:
Yet Death's not deadly in that Face,
Death in those Looks it self hath Grace,

'Twas this, 'twas this I feard
When thy pale Ghost appear'd;
This I presag'd when thund'ring Jove
Tore the best Myrtle in my Grove;
When my sick Rose-buds lost their smell,
And from my Temples untouch'd fell;
And 'twas for some such thing
My Dove did hang her Wing.

Whither art thou my Deity gone?
Venus *in* Venus *there is none.*
In vain a Goddess now am I
Only to Grieve, and not to dye.
But I will love my Grief,
Make Tears my Tears relief;
And Sorrow shall to me
A new Adonis *be.*

Deity
none
dye

And this no Fates can rob me of, whiles I
A Goddess am to Grieve, and not to Dye.

Flor. Madam, they say 'twas in this very Grove
The Goddess thus complain'd.

ACT.

ACT. III. SCEN. V.

To them Philænis *with a couple of Napkins.*

Eum. HOw now *Philænis?*
Are you turn'd Sewer to the Lady-Errant?
Phi. Lady I'm sent to wipe away the Bloud
From these two Myrtles ground.
Eum. Bless me! what Bloud *Philænis?*
Luc. I hope the Song will not prove ominous.
Phi. 'Tis fit we have some Wars at home too, else
My Lady would have no employment left.
Luc. What Wars? whose Bloud?
Phi. A pair of froward Lovers,
Olyndus, and the Stranger, fought, it seems,
Here till they almost kill'd themselves: and when
Neither did fear, but both did faint, it seems
Olyndus lean'd there, and the Stranger there,
And with their Blouds besmear'd the Trees a little;
We did not think your Highness should have seen it.

these two Myrtles
ground

Trees a

They rise amaz'd, the Princess repairs to the Tree where Charistus *bled, and* Eumela *to the Tree where her* Olyndus *bled.*

Luc. Is this *Olyndus* way of mingling Souls?
Eum. Is this the Others Enterchange of Breasts?
Luc. O Heavens! durst your *Olyndus* thus?
Eum. O Heav'ns,
And O ye Gods too! durst that other this?
Luc. Did he then stay behind for this *Eumela?*
Eum. And did he leave his Country to destroy
One worth it all, here in our very Bosoms?
Luc. H' has ruin'd one, whose like if Nature will
Shew to the World again, she must lay up,

And

had love
He was a Princess's thoughts; 'twas I that
And signs you Dread, and Soveraign

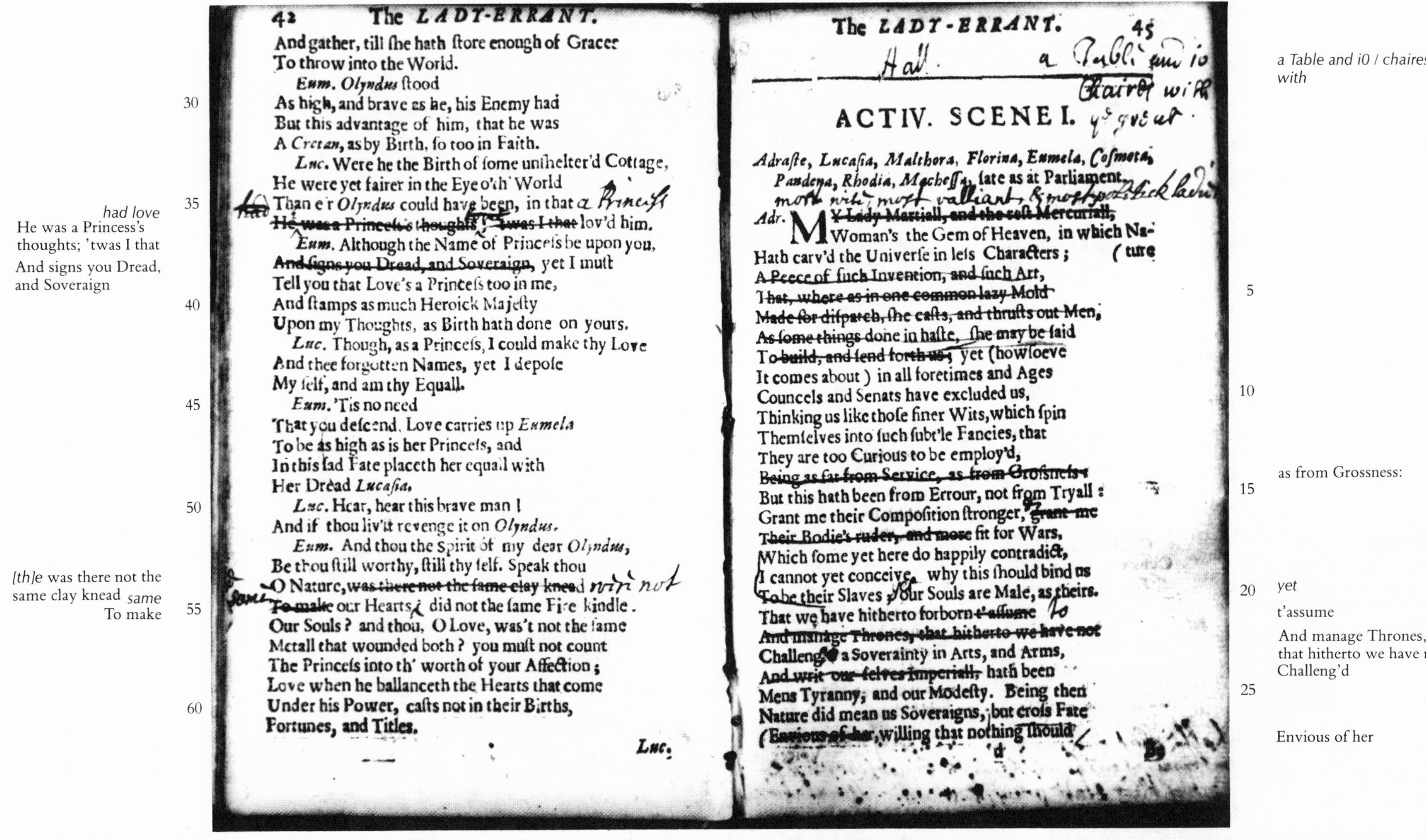

42 The LADY-ERRANT.

And gather, till ſhe hath ſtore enough of Grace:
To throw into the World.
Eum. Olyndus ſtood
As high, and brave as he, his Enemy had
But this advantage of him, that he was
A *Cretan*, as by Birth, ſo too in Faith.
Luc. Were he the Birth of ſome unſhelter'd Cottage,
He were yet fairer in the Eye o'th' World
Than e'r *Olyndus* could have been, in that
He was a Princeſs's thoughts; 'twas I that lov'd him.
Eum. Although the Name of Princeſs be upon you,
And ſigns you Dread, and Soveraign, yet I muſt
Tell you that Love's a Princeſs too in me,
And ſtamps as much Heroick Majeſty
Upon my Thoughts, as Birth hath done on yours.
Luc. Though, as a Princeſs, I could make thy Love
And thee forgotten Names, yet I depoſe
My ſelf, and am thy Equall.
Eum. 'Tis no need
That you deſcend. Love carries up *Eumela*
To be as high as is her Princeſs, and
In this ſad Fate placeth her equall with
Her Dread *Lucaſia.*
Luc. Hear, hear this brave man!
And if thou liv'ſt revenge it on *Olyndus.*
Eum. And thou the Spirit of my dear *Olyndus*,
Be thou ſtill worthy, ſtill thy ſelf. Speak thou
O Nature, was there not the ſame clay knead
To make our Hearts, did not the ſame Fire kindle
Our Souls? and thou, O Love, was't not the ſame
Metall that wounded both? you muſt not count
The Princeſs into th' worth of your Affection;
Love when he ballanceth the Hearts that come
Under his Power, caſts not in their Births,
Fortunes, and Titles.
Luc.

The LADY-ERRANT. 45

ACT IV. SCENE I.

Adraſte, Lucaſia, Malthora, Florina, Eumela, Coſmeta, Pandena, Rhodia, Macheſſa, ſate as at Parliament.

Adr. MY Lady Martiall, and the reſt Mercuriall,
Woman's the Gem of Heaven, in which Nature
Hath carv'd the Univerſe in leſs Characters;
A Peece of ſuch Invention, and ſuch Art,
That, where as in one common lazy Mold
Made for diſpatch, ſhe caſts, and thruſts out Men,
As ſome things done in haſte, ſhe may be ſaid
To build, and ſend forth us; yet (howſoever
It comes about) in all foretimes and Ages
Councels and Senats have excluded us,
Thinking us like thoſe finer Wits, which ſpin
Themſelves into ſuch ſubt'le Fancies, that
They are too Curious to be employ'd,
Being as far from Service, as from Groſsneſs:
But this hath been from Errour, not from Tryall:
Grant me their Compoſition ſtronger, grant me
Their Bodie's ruder, and more fit for Wars,
Which ſome yet here do happily contradict,
I cannot yet conceive, why this ſhould bind us
To be their Slaves; our Souls are Male, as theirs.
That we have hitherto forborn t'aſſume
And manage Thrones, that hitherto we have not
Challeng'd a Soveraignty in Arts, and Arms,
And writ our ſelves Imperiall, hath been
Mens Tyranny, and our Modeſty. Being then
Nature did mean us Soveraigns, but croſs Fate
(Envious of her, willing that nothing ſhould

[th]e was there not the same clay knead *same*
To make

a Table and i0 / chaires with

as from Grossness:

yet

t'assume

And manage Thrones, that hitherto we have not Challeng'd

Envious of her

III, v, following 61. Pages 43 and 44 are missing from the copy.

IV, i, opening. The property note about the table and chairs seems to break off just before the end: *y*^e^ *great*—what? A description of the setting may have been intended, such as a great hall. The canceled line, "Lady Martiall, and the rest Mercuriall," is replaced by: *most wise, most valliant, & most politick Ladies.*

46 The LADY-ERRANT;

Be perfect upon Earth) ſtill kept us under;
Let us, i'th'name of Honour, riſe unto
The pitch of our Creation. Now's the time;
The beſt and ableſt men are abſent, thoſe
That are left here behind are either Fooles,
Or Wiſe men overgrown, which is all one.
Aſſert your ~~ſelves into~~ your Liberty then,
Stand firm, and high, put theſe good Reſolutions
Forth into Action; then, in ſpight of Fate,
A Female Hand ſhall turn the Wheel of State.
Om. Inſpir'd *Adraſte*!
Om. Moſt divine *Adraſte*! Eumila
Adr. If that you reliſh this let ~~Miſtris Speaker~~
On to the reſt.
Om. On, on, on, on, on, on!
Eum. Moſt Willing, moſt Agreeing, moſt Potent,
And moſt free Ladies, *&c.*——
'Tis fit all things ſhould be reduc'd unto
Their Primeve Inſtitution, and firſt Head;
Woman was then as much as Man, thoſe Stones
Which *Pyrrha* caſt, made as fair Creatures as
Deucalion's did: that his ſhould be ſet up
Carv'd, and Ador'd, but hers kept down, and trampled,
Came from an ancient Injury; what Oracle, and
What voice from Heaven commanded that?
Coſ. Moſt true!
Obſerve that Ladies.
Sibyl's Leaf by *Juno* *Pan.* ~~Sibyl's Leaf by Juno~~!
Eum. He that ſaies Woman is not fit for Policy,
Doth give the Lie to Art; for what man ~~hath~~ such had
~~More ſorts of Looks? more Faces? who puts off~~
~~More ſeverall Colours? Men, compar'd in this,~~
~~Are only Dough-bak'd Women; not as once~~
~~Maliciouſly one call'd us Dough-bak'd Men.~~
Coſ. 'Tis no ſingle
halfe that cunning, in mannageing an
intrigue, as wee haue, haue they not learnt the
best of their state policy, their wise dissimulation
Voice;

The LADY-ERRANT. 47

Voice; the whole Sex ſpeaks in her.
Eum. Some few yet
Do ſpeak againſt our Paſſions, but with greater of their owne
Rail at our Lightneſs, but 'tis out of Humour;
Rather Diſeaſe than Reaſon; ~~they being ſuch~~
~~As wipe off what they ſpit.~~ For Heav'n forbid
That any ſhould vouchſafe to ſpeak againſt us
But rough Philoſophers, and rude Divines,
And ſuch like dull Profeſſions. But wee'l now
Shew them our Paſſions are our Reaſons Edge,
And that, which they call Lightneſs, only is
An Art to turn our ſelves to ſeverall Points.
Time, Place, Minds, People, all things now concur
To re-eſtate us there where Nature plac'd us:
Not a Male more muſt enter *Cyprus* now.
Coſ. No, nor an Eunuch, nothing that hath been
Male heretofore.
Pan. No, nor Hermophrodite;
Nothing that is half Male. A little Spark
Hath often kindled a whole Town; we muſt
Be cautelous in the leaſt.
Eum. That then they may not
Regain the Iſland, all the Havens muſt
Be ſtor'd, and guarded.
Coſ. Very fit they ſhould.
Eum. Next to the Havens, Caſtles out of hand
Muſt be repair'd, Bulwarks, and Forts, and Sconces
Be forthwith rear'd.
Coſ. 'Tis time we were about them.
Eum. Arms then muſt be bought up, and Forces rais'd;
Much, much is to be done—
Pan. Why let *Macheſſa*
About it ſtraight.
Eum. I ſee agreeing Minds,
Your Hearts and Courage very ready, but
d 2 Where

IV, i, following 62. The added lines are: *halfe that cunning, in mannageing an / intrigue, as wee haue, haue they not learnt the / best of their state policy, their wise dissimulation / [from us (?)].*

Where is the Nerve and Sinew of this Action?
Where ſhall we have the Mony to do this?
Coſ. Wee'l give our hair for Cordage, and our fineſt
Linnen for Sails, rather than this Deſign
Shall be once daſh'd for want.
Pan. There's much already
Come in———
Coſ. And more doth dayly.
Pan. Hearts and Purſes
Concur unto the Action.
Coſ. We have Notes
Of the particular Contributions.
Eum. Her Majeſty would have you read 'em, that
She may know what to truſt to.
Coſ. From the Temple [*She reads.*
We do expect ten dozen of Chalices,
But they are hid, or elſe already gone—
Eum. This is not what you have, but what y' have not.
Coſ. We tell you this, that you mayn't take it ill,
That we ha'n't borrow'd ſome o'th' Holy Plate.
Well then, to what we have— Firſt from the Court
Ten Veſſels of Corinthian Braſs, with divers
Peeces of *Polyclet*, and *Phydias*,
Parrhaſius, *Zeuxes*, and *Protogenes*,
Apelles, and ſuch like great Maſter-hands.
Eum. Statues, and Pictures do but little good
Againſt the Enemy.
Coſ. Pray y' hear it out:
Rich Cabinets then, which, though they do contain
Treaſure immenſe and large, have nothing yet
Within them richer than themſelves.
Eum. What hold they?
Coſ. Pearls, Rubies, Emralds, Amethyſts, and Saphirs,
Cryſolits, Jaſpers, Diamonds, two whereof
Do double the twelfth Caract: beſides Sparks

Enough

Enough to ſtick the Roof o'th' Banquetting Houſe,
And make it ſeem an Heav'n.
Eum. VVell, on *Coſmeta.*
Coſ. Twelve ſtanding Goblets, two ~~more~~ rich and (maſſy.
~~The one bears *Bacchus* ſitting on a Vine,~~
~~Squeezing out Purple liquor, Th' other hath~~
~~*Silenus* riding on his patient Beaſt,~~
~~And Satyrs dancing after him. More yet,~~
Twelve other ~~leſs~~ engraven with leſs Stories,
As Loves, and Months, and Quarters of the year,
Nymphs, Shepheards, and ſuch like—This from the Court.
Eum. VVhat from the City?
Pan. Purple Robes, and Furs [*Pan. reads.*
In great abundance— Baſons and large Ewers,
Flagons, and Diſhes, Plates, and Voyders, all
Rich and unwieldy. And beſides all this,
Gold Chains, and Caudle-Cups innumerable.
Eum. The Contribution's much—
Pan. But yet not ended———
Twelve City Ladies ſend us word, they have
Twelve Iron Cheſts, and rib'd with Iron too,
VVherein they do ſuſpect there lies a Mine,
That hath not ſeen the Sun for ſix *Olympiads.*
Eum. Let 'em be got in ſuddenly; we muſt
Be hot and eager in our undertakings.
The VVealth's enough; the Eaſt was overrun
By the bold *Macedonian* Boy with leſs.
VVas't not *Macheſſa*? But I pray you nothing
From the poor Country Villagers?
Pan. Very little;
Hoop-rings, and Childrens VVhiſtles, and ſome forty
Or fifty dozen of gilt-Spoons, ~~that's all.~~
Eum. Let it be haſtily deliver'd all
Into her Majeſties Treaſury.
Coſ. Under favour,

d 3 VVe

less

bodkins & a bushel of thimbles

this treasure

50 The LADY-ERRANT.

We think *Machessa* would be very fit,
Both to take in, and to disburse. this treasure.
Eum. It is not
For any private Interest that She asks it,
But for the Publike good.
Pan. ~~Perhaps,~~ But yet
The People will think better, if it be
Entrusted in a Subject's hand, and Hers
Especially who never had a Husband--
Cos. No, nor a Child ~~as yet.~~
Adr. Why be it so;
You shall dispose't *Machessa.*
Mach. I consider
The trust you give me; see the weight, and Nature,
The Price and Moment of the Cause; Know next
My Order binds me not to be endow'd
With any Wealth or Utensill, besides
My Steed, my Habit, Arms, and Page; To which
When I prove false, let him that weaves my Story
(Whether he be a Courtier, or perhaps
A Scholar that writes worse) bring me no higher
Than to scratch'd Faces, and such Suburb brangles.
Truth is the Essence of our Order, we
Who are Errants cannot deceive ~~and Be~~ his Antick.
Adr. Let us away: though the Male-Gods may frown,
The Female part of Heaven is sure our own [*She whis.* Eu.
Eum. Noble *Machessa* all your deeds I see { Ex. Adrast. Cal. &c. *Manent* Eu. Machessa.
Tend to the Scope of Honour.
Mach. Were she seated
Upon the top of some high craggy Rock,
Whose Head were in ~~the Country of the~~ Thunder,
Guarded with watchfull Dragons, I will climb,
And ravish her from thence, to have my Name
Turn'd o'r from Age to Age, as something that
Ought to outlive the Phœnix, and dye only
With

The LADY-ERRANT. 51

With Men and Time.
Eum. Though you Court Danger thus,
I hope you will not scorn bright Glory, if
She come an easier way.
Mach. I ~~look to her,~~ court her, and
Not ~~to~~ her Cloaths, and Habit.
Eum. Will you be
Famous in History then? fill swelling Volumes
With your sole Name? be read aloud, and high
I'th' *Cyprian* Annals? and live fresh upon
The Tongue of Fame for ever? ~~will you stand~~
~~High on your Steed in Brass,~~ and be at once
~~The stop of Strangers, and~~ the Natives Worship,
By one fair Peacefull Action?
Mach. Brave *Eumela,*
To say I'l do't is lazy; it is done.
Eum. 'Tis the Queen's sute besides,
And She shall thank you.
Mach. Honour is my Queen,
And my Deeds thank themselves. But say, *Eumela,*
Quickly, what is't?
Eum. Why only send this Wealth,
That's put into your hands, unto the Army,
And so defeat this folly that they here
So eagerly pursue.
Mach. By Heav'n I'll first
Scatter the Ashes of my Ancesters,
Burn and demolish Temples, or pull down
The Statue of our Goddess, whiles her self
Stood with the proudest thunder to defend it;
You ought to thank me, that you have popos'd it,
And yet still live.
Eum. But pray you reason it.
Mach. Follies of idle Creatures! who e'r heard
Of Ladies Errant yet that stood to Reason?
d 4 But

52 The *LADY-ERRANT.*

But you that brag of Books, and Reading, and
I know not what unneceſſary Learning,
Tell me, did brawny *Hercules*, who wand'red
I'th' Lion's skin, and Club, or well-ſet *Theſeus*
That trod his ſteps, e'r do the like?
Eum. No. VVomen
Ne'r came to ſuch a pitch of danger yet
~~As to be baniſh'd all~~: then who e'r truſted
Theſeus, or *Hercules* with ten Drachmas? who
Could know their Minds that way? This ſingle deed
VVill make *Macheſſa* go beyond his *Pillars*,
And th' other's Fame. They quell'd but ſingle Robbers,
You will defeat thouſands of Rebels. They
Help'd ſome poor Village, or ſome Town perhaps,
You will redeem a Nation.
Mach. Thou ſay'ſt ſomething;
But I ſhall break my faith.
Eum. To whom? to thoſe
That have before broke theirs unto their Prince?
Mach. They'l curſe me too.
Eum. As bold *Macheſſa* hunts not
The Praiſe of People, ſo ſhe can contemn
Their Curſe, when ſhe doth well. Conſider too
Nations will curſe you more if you aſſiſt 'em.
Mach. But 'tis againſt my Order to deceive.
Eum. 'Tis more againſt your Order to aſſiſt
Rebellious Perſons 'gainſt their King. Beſides,
Doth not your Oath enjoyn you to relieve
Diſtreſſed men? who more diſtreſſed now
Than is the King, and th'Army? fear not words;
You are not Treacherous unto them, but faithfull
Unto your ſelf. Why ſtands this Helmet here?
VVhy do you wear this Fauchion? to what uſe
Carry this Javelin?
Mach. Not to help women; no,

Men

The *LADY-ERRANT.* 53 all

Men are my Oath. All ſhall be ſent *Eumela*,
The King muſt have it: wee'l be famous ——
Eum. But
You muſt be ſecret 'till it all come in.
Mach. And you'l aſſiſt me in the ſending of 't?
Eum. Take you no care for that, 'tis done.
Mach. But will
The Queen not take it ill?
Eum. 'Tis her great fear,
You'l ſcarce be brought to yeeld it up. Away,
Go, and delude 'em on, y'are ſafe, and may
Deceive in Conſcience now.
Mach. Bellona bleſs thee! [*Exit* Macheſſa.
Eum. But how ſhall we now conveigh it to 'em?

ACT. IV. SCEN. II.

To her Philondas *and* Pæſtanus *as having ſtoln from the Army.*

—Heav'n's of the Plot! No fitter men. *Jove* bleſs me!
My Lord *Philondas*, and my Lord *Paſtanus*!
This your appearance to me's like the firſt
Appearance to a new admitted Prieſt,
And I am quite as doubtfull now as he,
Not knowing whether 't be my fancy, or
The God, that makes the Viſion.
Phil. Dear *Eumela*,
Thou know'ſt we do appear to Ladies ſtill
In ~~very~~ fleſh and bloud. Though we may talk
Of ſpirituall Love, my Lord, and I, you know,
Could ne'r creep in at Key-holes yet; I'm ſure
We pay for th' opening of the doors, *Eumela*.
Eum. My Lord you make *Paſtanus* bluſh.
Paſt. I hope

I

IV, i, above 277. In the upper right-hand corner of page 53, badly cropped, is a manuscript note that appears to be *all d*. This is probably a call for the players who acted Philondas and Paestanus, who enter 14 lines later. If so, we can judge how badly cropped the copy is, for a normal actor warning would list the names of the actors or the characters to be called; all that can be seen here is the beginning of the prompt note. Before the copy was cropped, actor warnings may have appeared throughout the promptbook.

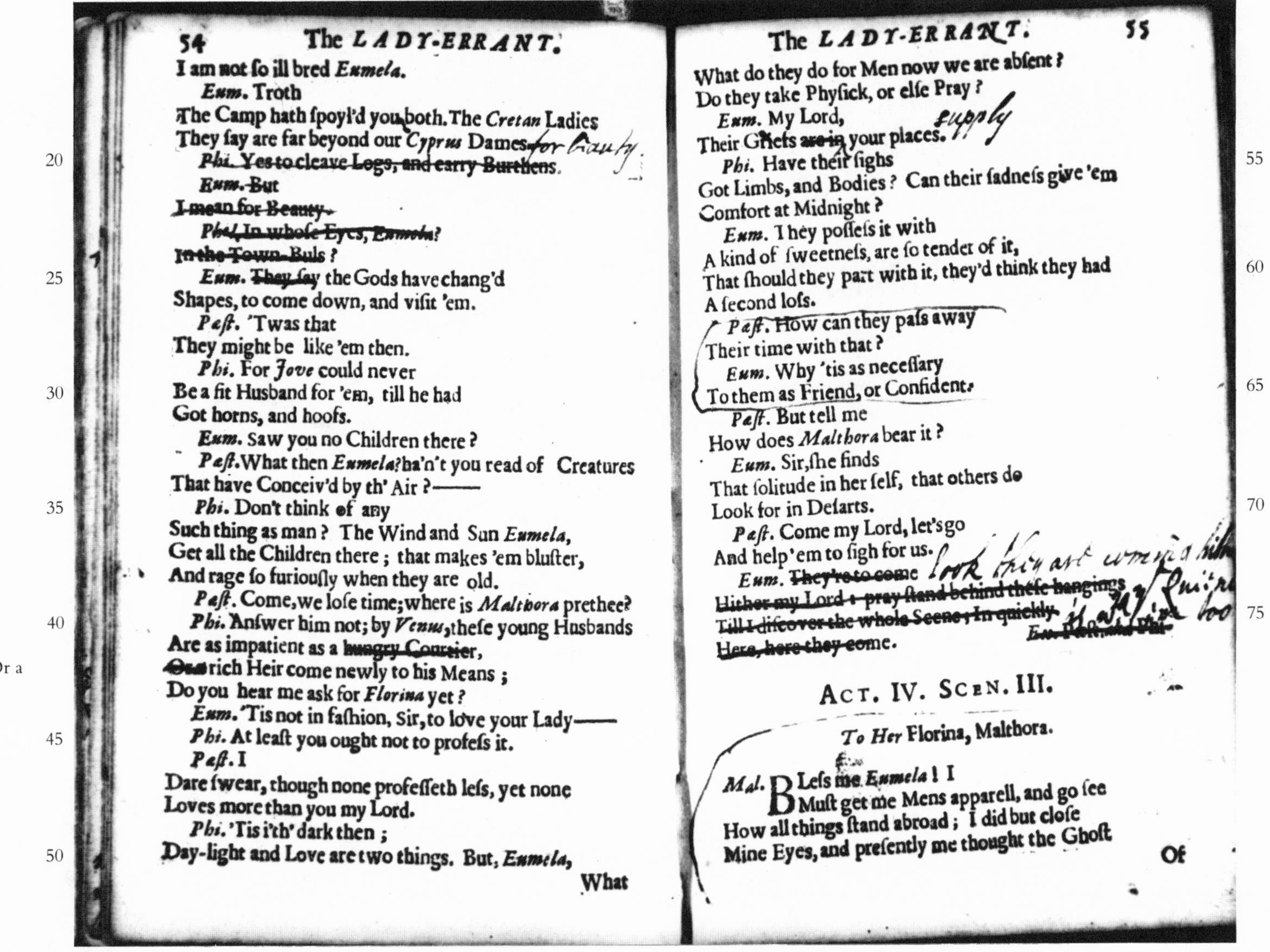

54 The *LADY-ERRANT.*

I am not ſo ill bred *Eumela.*
Eum. Troth
The Camp hath ſpoyl'd you both. The *Cretan* Ladies
They ſay are far beyond our *Cyprus* Dames~~.~~ for beauty
~~*Phi.* Yes to cleave Logs, and carry Burthens.~~
~~*Eum.* But~~
~~I mean for Beauty.~~
~~*Phi.* In whoſe Eyes, *Eumela*?~~
~~In the Town-Buls?~~
Eum. ~~They ſay~~ the Gods have chang'd
Shapes, to come down, and viſit 'em.
Paſt. 'Twas that
They might be like 'em then.
Phi. For *Jove* could never
Be a fit Husband for 'em, till he had
Got horns, and hoofs.
Eum. Saw you no Children there?
Paſt. What then *Eumela*? ha'n't you read of Creatures
That have Conceiv'd by th' Air?——
Phi. Don't think of any
Such thing as man? The Wind and Sun *Eumela*,
Get all the Children there; that makes 'em bluſter,
And rage ſo furiouſly when they are old.
Paſt. Come, we loſe time; where is *Malthora* prethee?
Phi. Anſwer him not; by *Venus*, theſe young Husbands
Are as impatient as a ~~hungry Courtier~~,
~~Or a~~ rich Heir come newly to his Means;
Do you hear me ask for *Florina* yet?
Eum. 'Tis not in faſhion, Sir, to love your Lady——
Phi. At leaſt you ought not to profeſs it.
Paſt. I
Dare ſwear, though none profeſſeth leſs, yet none
Loves more than you my Lord.
Phi. 'Tis i'th' dark then;
Day-light and Love are two things. But, *Eumela*,
What

The *LADY-ERRANT.* 55

What do they do for Men now we are abſent?
Do they take Phyſick, or elſe Pray?
Eum. My Lord,
Their Griefs ~~are in~~ supply your places.
Phi. Have their ſighs
Got Limbs, and Bodies? Can their ſadneſs give 'em
Comfort at Midnight?
Eum. They poſſeſs it with
A kind of ſweetneſs, are ſo tender of it,
That ſhould they part with it, they'd think they had
A ſecond loſs.
Paſt. How can they paſs away
Their time with that?
Eum. Why 'tis as neceſſary
To them as Friend, or Confident.
Paſt. But tell me
How does *Malthora* bear it?
Eum. Sir, ſhe finds
That ſolitude in her ſelf, that others do
Look for in Deſarts.
Paſt. Come my Lord, let's go
And help 'em to ſigh for us.
Eum. ~~They're to come~~ look they are coming hith
~~Hither my Lord; pray ſtand behind theſe hangings~~
~~Till I diſcover the whole Scene; In quickly.~~
~~Here, here they come.~~ ~~*Ex. Paſt. and Phi.*~~

ACT. IV. SCEN. III.

To Her Florina, Malthora.

Mal. Bleſs ~~me~~ *Eumela*! I
Muſt get me Mens apparell, and go ſee
How all things ſtand abroad; I did but cloſe
Mine Eyes, and preſently me thought the Ghoſt
Of

Or a

IV, ii, 73–76. The new lines are: *Look they are coming hith[er] / y^e Queene / is wth em too / Ex.* Paest. and *Phi.*

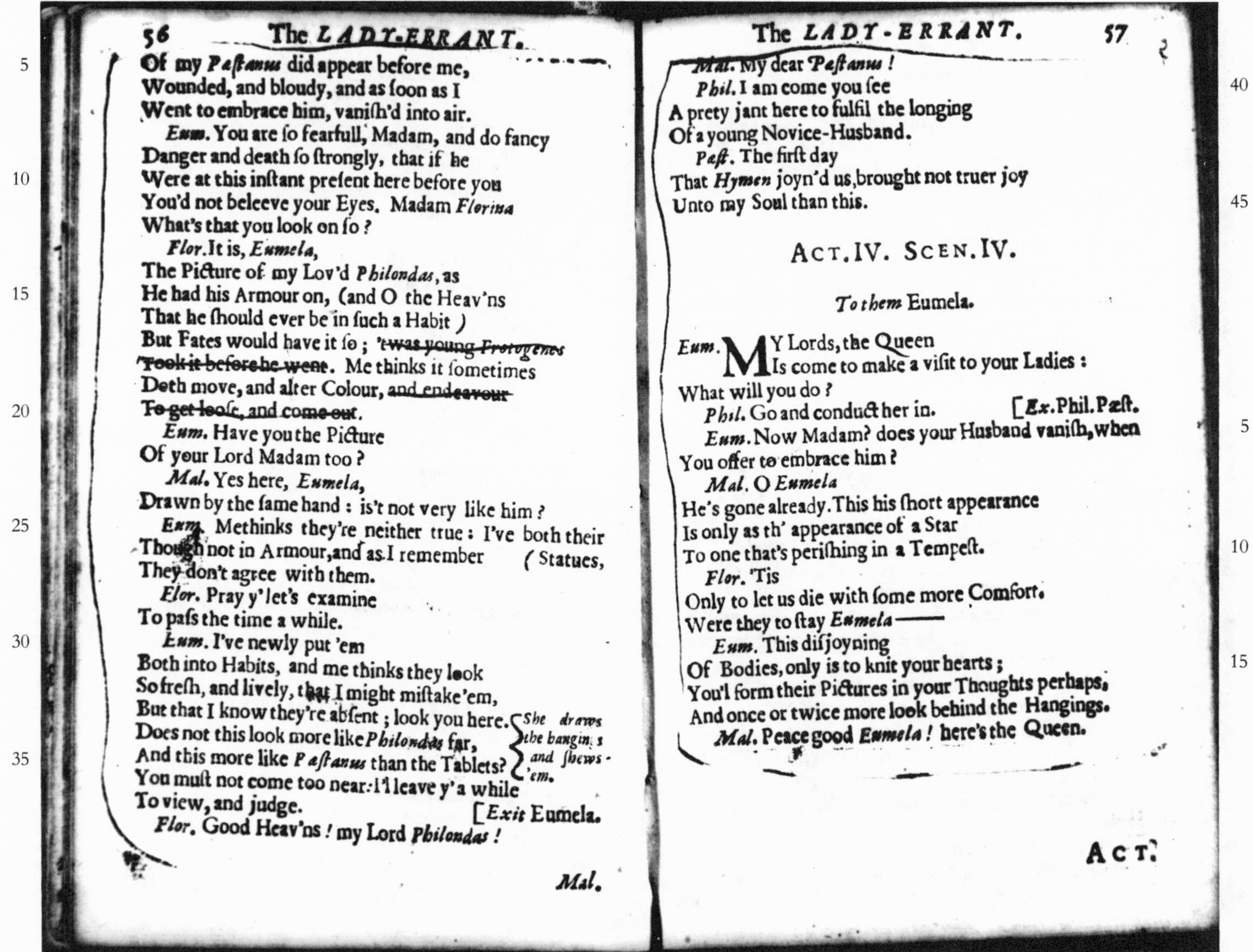

56 The LADY-ERRANT.

Of my *Pastanus* did appear before me,
Wounded, and bloudy, and as soon as I
Went to embrace him, vanish'd into air.
Eum. You are so fearfull, Madam, and do fancy
Danger and death so strongly, that if he
Were at this instant present here before you
You'd not beleeve your Eyes. Madam *Florina*
What's that you look on so?
Flor. It is, *Eumela*,
The Picture of my Lov'd *Philondas*, as
He had his Armour on, (and O the Heav'ns
That he should ever be in such a Habit)
But Fates would have it so; ~~'twas young Protogenes~~
~~Took it before he went~~. Me thinks it sometimes
Doth move, and alter Colour, ~~and endeavour~~
~~To get loose, and come out~~.
Eum. Have you the Picture
Of your Lord Madam too?
Mal. Yes here, *Eumela*,
Drawn by the same hand: is't not very like him?
Eum. Methinks they're neither true: I've both their
Though not in Armour, and as I remember (Statues,
They don't agree with them.
Flor. Pray y'let's examine
To pass the time a while.
Eum. I've newly put 'em
Both into Habits, and me thinks they look
So fresh, and lively, that I might mistake'em,
But that I know they're absent; look you here. { *She draws the hangings and shews 'em.*
Does not this look more like *Philondas* far,
And this more like *Pastanus* than the Tablets?
You must not come too near: I'l leave y'a while
To view, and judge. [*Exit* Eumela.
Flor. Good Heav'ns! my Lord *Philondas*!
Mal.

The LADY-ERRANT. 57

Mal. My dear *Pastanus*!
Phil. I am come you see
A prety jant here to fulfil the longing
Of a young Novice-Husband.
Past. The first day
That *Hymen* joyn'd us, brought not truer joy
Unto my Soul than this.

ACT. IV. SCEN. IV.

To them Eumela.

Eum. MY Lords, the Queen
Is come to make a visit to your Ladies:
What will you do?
Phil. Go and conduct her in. [*Ex.* Phil. Past.
Eum. Now Madam? does your Husband vanish, when
You offer to embrace him?
Mal. O *Eumela*
He's gone already. This his short appearance
Is only as th' appearance of a Star
To one that's perishing in a Tempest.
Flor. 'Tis
Only to let us die with some more Comfort.
Were they to stay *Eumela*——
Eum. This disjoyning
Of Bodies, only is to knit your hearts;
You'l form their Pictures in your Thoughts perhaps,
And once or twice more look behind the Hangings.
Mal. Peace good *Eumela*! here's the Queen.

ACT.

IV, iii, 33. Cartwright's stage direction about the drawing back of the hangings was written in pre-Restoration times, yet the prompter did not delete the business and substitute, say, a note for opening the shutters. We have very little evidence to go on, but apparently traverse curtains were sometimes used in lieu of shutters in the Restoration theatres. Stage directions in Settle's *Love and Revenge*, Behn's *The Feigned Courtesans*, and Lee's *Caesar Borgia*—all Dorset Garden plays—imply the use of hangings, apparently at one of the shutter positions. See also the prompt notes in *Tyrannick Love*.

ACT. IV. SCEN. V.

Florina, Malthora
Philondas, Paestanus

To them *Adraſte*, ~~*Philondas*, *Paſtanus*~~.

Adr. Chariſtus,
Heir to the *Cretan* Kingdom loſt, ~~ſay you?~~ — say you?

Phi. Yes, and ſuſpected to lye hid in *Cyprus*.

Adr. And this is that doth ſtop the War?

Paſt. This, and
Th' Equality of Forces.

Adr. Do our men
Awake, and rouze themſelves?

Phi. Rich noble Spirits,
And Minds that have kept Altars burning ſtill,
To Glory break out dayly, ſhewing how
Peace and Religion did not ſink, but calm 'em:
This blaſt will ſwell 'em big, and high, and make 'em
Ride Conquerours o'r the Flouds.

Adr. They do not ſleep then?

Phi. No, nor watch lazily; the World will ſee,
He, whoſe bleſt goodneſs hath kept War from us,
Hath not took Courage from us too; When his
Sad ſtudy'd Councels did remove the danger,
They did not then remove the Mind. The Arm
Of this days *Cyprus*, if provok'd, will ſtrike
As deep as *Cyprus* ſix Olympiads backwards,
And the unquiet *Cretan* ſhall appear
But as he did of old, our Exerciſe,
More than our Foe: a people that we ſuffer
To breath, and be, to keep our ſelves in breath.

Adr. What doth the King?

Paſt. More than the meaneſt ſouldier,
Yet ſtill comes freſh from Actions: his Commands
Are great, but his Examples greater ſtill.

Phil.

Phi. With his uncover'd head he dares the Thunder,
Slights hail and ſnow, and wearies out a Tempeſt,
Then after all he ſhakes himſelf, and gives
Rain, as the Heavens did before, but with
A more ſerene Aſpect. He doth exact
Labour, and hardneſs, hunger, heat, and cold,
~~And duſt~~, as his Prerogatives, and counts them — dust
Only his ſerious Pleaſures; Others Wars
Are not ſo manly as his Exerciſes,
And pitch'd Fields often are more eaſie ſervice
Than his meer Preparations.

Adr. 'Tis enough;
Y' have ſpoke a Compoſition, ſo made up
Of Prince and Souldier, that th' admiring World
May imitate, not equall. Come, my Lords,
I have a buſineſs to employ you back with. *Exeunt.*

ACT. IV. SCEN. VI.

Lucaſia, Eumela, Chariſtus, Olyndus.

Luc. I muſt confeſs, had not this Action been
Tainted with private Intereſt, but born
From zeal unto the Publique, then it might
Have been read Valour, as it is, it will
Be ſtil'd but Fury.

Eum. Madam it had then
Been only Valour, now 'tis Love and Valour.

Luc. VVhere thoſe Religious Names, King, Country, (Father,
Are trampled over, can you call it Valour?

Cha. If trampled o'r for you. To hazard all
Theſe holy Names, of Subject unto King,
Of Prince to Country, and of Son to Father,
And whil'ſt I ſpar'd to ſhed the ſmalleſt drop

Of

IV, v, opening. The deletion of the names of Philondas and Paestanus from the entrance direction appears to be an error, for both have lines in the scene. Florina and Malthora are added, since their entrance at the opening of IV, iii was cut.

Of Bloud, that might be once call'd yours, to have
That ignominious Name of Coward hurl'd on me,
And take up all their Places; what elſe is it
But to eſteem your ſelf a Prize, that doth
Abſolve me from all theſe, and make me ſtand
Above the rate of mortals.
Olyn. Father, Country,
State, Fortunes, Commonwealth, th'are Names that Love
Is not concern'd in, that looks higher ſtill,
And overſees all theſe.
Luc. It is not Love then;
For that, as it is Valiant, ſo it is
Juſt, Temperate, Prudent, ſummons all thoſe Noble
Heroick Habits into one rich Maſs,
And ſtamps them Honour.
Eum. But that Honour is
A Valour beyond that of Mortals, ſtriving
Who ſhall poſſeſs moſt of this Mole-hill Earth.
a *Olyn.* That Honour is a Juſtice, that doth ſee
Meaſures, and Weights, Axes, and Rods below it.
Eu. A Temperance not concern'd in Meats, and Wines.
that *Olyn.* A Prudence that doth write *Chariſtus* now
A better Patriot, than the ſober'ſt Stateſman
That plots the good of *Crete.*
Luc. If he that cares not
For things, be thence above them; if he ſees
More nobly, that doth draw the Veyl before
His Eyes to Lower Objects, then *Chariſtus*
Soares high, and nothing ſcapes him.
Cha. Fair *Lucaſia,*
I am not ſo immodeſt, as to challenge
The leaſt of theſe my ſelf: but yet in that
I love your Vertues, they are all mine own.
Luc. And yet you fear'd I was anothers, whom
I durſt not publiquely avow. Do y'think
My

My Love could ſtoop to ſuch Contrivances?
Or if I meant a ſubject of ſuch worth,
I needed to pretend a Prince?
Olyn. It is not
Lucaſia's Love, that dares not call the Eye
Of Day to try it: But where Love's engag'd
To ſuch a Treaſure as your ſelf, what can
Be thought ſecure? It ſtands and watches ſtill,
And fears it's very helps; could any love
Lucaſia and be careleſs, 'twere a fault
Would make him not deſerve her.
Luc. Could you then
Think I could be ſo impious unto Love
As to divide *Eumela* and *Olyndus?*
Or elſe ſo treacherous unto Friendſhip, as
To part *Eumela* and my ſelf? Being Hearts
Are Temples, and both ſorts of Love moſt Sacred,
To have wrong'd either had been Sacrilege
Worthy the horrid'ſt Thunder.
Eum. Love drinks in ye poyson of
All that may feed ſuſpicion, but is deaf
To what may clear it; 'tis engag'd ſo much
To th' Object, that it views the Object only,
And weighs not what attends it.
Luc. Where the Heart
Offends, you blame the Paſſion. Love it ſelf
Is never undiſcreet, but he that Loves.
Cha. Wiſdome and Love at once were never yet
Permitted to a God, I muſt not then
Preſume they meet in me. If Love admits
Diſcretion, if it Ponder, and Conſider,
Search, and Compare, and Judge, and then Reſolve; Resolve
'Tis Policy, not Affection: give it Eyes,
Counſell, and Order, and it ceaſeth. What
Though it firſt brake from out the Chaos? 'twas
e
To

~~To make another in the Creature. Distance,~~
~~Figure, and Lineament are things that come~~
~~From something more~~ Advis'd; Love never leads,
It still transports. The Motions which it feels
Are Fury, Rapture, Extasie, and such
As thrust it out full of ~~Instinct, and~~ Deity,
To meet what it desires.

ye Instinct, and

Luc. Alas I it self
Hath Eyes, but 'tis our Blindness that doth veyl them:
If Love could not consist with Wisdome, then
The World were govern'd by one generall Madness.
Olynd. 'Tis not deni'd but that we may have Wisdom
Before we Love, as men may have good Eyes
Before they fix them on the Sun: but dwell they
A while upon it, and they straight grow blind
From those admired Beauties.
Luc. But if Love
Do not consider, why then doth it fear?
Why doth it form *Chimeras* to it self,
And set up Thought 'gainst Thought? why is't alike
Tortur'd with Truth, and Falshood? why afflicted
As much from Doubts, as Certainties?
Cra. This is
Not from Distrust, but Care; Love is not perfect
Till it begins to fear. It doth not know
The worth of that it seeks, unless it be
Anxious, and troubled for it: And this is
Not any thought of Blemish in the thing
It loves, but only Study to preserve it.

Distrust,

Lu. Who puts a Snake 'mongst Flowers to preserve 'em?
~~Or who pours Poyson into Crystall that~~
~~It may be kept from cracking?~~ Jealousie
What art thou? thou could'st not come down from Hea-
For no such Monsters can inhabit there. (v'n;
Eum. Nor can it spring from Hell; for it is born
Of

Of Love, and there is nought but Hate.
Luc. Pray y' tell me
Who joyn'd it unto Love? who made them swear
So firm a Friendship?
Olyn. The same Deity
That joyn'd the Sun and Light, the same that knits
The Life and Spirit.
Luc. These preserve each other:
But that doth twine and wreath it self about
Our growing Loves, as Ivy 'bout the Oak;
We think it shelters, when (alas!) we find
It weakens, and destroys.
Eum. It is not Jealousie
That ruins Love, but we our selves, who will not
Suffer that fear to strengthen it; Give way
And let it work, 'twill fix the Love it springs from
In a staid Center.
Luc. ~~What it works I know not,~~
But it must needs suppose ~~Defect in one,~~
Either Defect of Merit in the Lover,
Or in the Lov'd, of Faith; you cannot think
That I give Others Favours, when your self
Boast such a store of Merits.
Cha. O *Lucasia,*
Rather than be so impious as to think
That you want Faith, I must confess a want
Of Merit in my self; (which would there were not.)
And being it is so, I was compell'd
To fear lest one more worthy than my self
Might throw me from my happiness. Consider
That you are born t' enrich the Earth, and then
If you will have one Love and not be Jealous,
You must convert your Eye upon your Eye,
Make your own Heart Court your own Heart, and be
Your self a servant to your self.

it . . . Defect in one

64 The *LADY-ERRANT.*

Luc. But doth not
This Paſſion ceaſe at laſt?
Olyn. It ceaſeth to
Diſturb, but ſtill remains to quicken Love ;
As Thunder ceaſeth when't hath purg'd the Air,
And yet the Fire which caus'd it ſtill remains
To make it move the livelier.
Luc. Were it quiet,
What Hand, *Chariſtus*, would More ſweetly move
The Orbs of this our Iſland? who fetch in
More frequent Conqueſts? and who more become
The Triumphs than your ſelf?
Cha. Beleeve *Chariſtus*
Errours
Dreams; ~~Errours~~, falſe Opinions, ſlippery Hopes,
And Jealous Fears are now his Spoyl, his Captives,
which *while*
And follow Love's Triumphant Chariot, ~~which~~ *while*
His Soul ſits high in, and o'looks the vain
Things of this lower World.
Luc. Lucaſia did
Only retire, not ſlie; Let's to the Grove,
And by the Conſummation of our Loves
Under thoſe Myrtles (which as yet perhaps
Preſerve the bluſhing Marks of thoſe your Angers)
Appeaſe th' offended Goddeſs.
Olyn. This your Union
Will make your Kingdoms joyn; *Cyprus* and *Crete*
Will meet in your Embraces.
Eum. Our Hearts are
Love's ord'nary Employment: 'tis a Dart
Of a more ſcattering Metall that ſtrikes you;
When he wounds Princes, he wounds Nations too.
Exeunt.

ACT

The *LADY-ERRANT.* 65

ACT V. SCENE I.

Pandena, Coſmeta, Rhodia, meeting *Macheſſa* and *Philanis.*

Coſ. Lady *Macheſſa*, opportunely met.
Pan. What ſtore of Arms prepar'd?
Mach. The Country's layd;
Spits, Andirons, Racks, and ſuch like Utenſils
Are in the very Act of Metamophoſis;
Art is now ſitting on them, and they will
Be hatch'd to Engins ſhortly.
Pan. Pray y' how doth
The Muſter-Roule encreaſe?
Mach. As faſt as *Chloe*
Can take their Names; we ſhall be all great Women.
Phil. Pray y' what Reward ſhall you and I have Lady?
Mach. Why I will be the Queen o'th' *Amazons*,
And thou o'th' *Pigmies*.
Phil. I, but who ſhall place us
In the *Amazonian*, and *Pigmean* Throne?
Mach. Who but our Swords *Philanis*? when we have
Setled the Government here at home, we will
Lead out an Army 'gainſt thoſe Warlike Dames,
And make 'em all our Vaſſals.
Phil. Theſe left handed
Ladies are notable Politicians.
The King of *Monomotapa* you may
Be ſure will be your Enemy, or elſe
The Book deceives me. But the *Agags* they
Will ſure be for you.
Caſ. Who may the *Agags* be?

E 3 *Phil.*

Phi. Why a black ugly People, that do turn
The inſide of their Eye-lids outward, that
They may look lovely; if they catch the *Amazons*,
They ſowce 'em ſtraight, as we do Pig, by quarters,
Or elſe do pickle 'em up for Winter Sallads.
Mac. How did you come by all this Knowledge *Phil?*
You are a learned Page.
Phil. Lady, do y' think
I never read to th' Women in the Nurs'ry?
But will you loſe one of your Breaſts? tis pitty
That your left Pap ſhould be burnt off.
Mach. Why Gyrl?
What uſe will there be of it?
Phi. To give ſuck.
You muſt go ſeek out ſome brave *Alexander*,
And beg ſome half a dozen of Children of him,
Or elſe you'l be no true bred *Amazon*.
Pan. Muſt they have *Macedonian* Fathers then?
Phil. I think the *Amazonian* Queen doth ſwear
To no ſuch Article when She is Crown'd;
But ord'narily they do ſo; yet howe'r
Your Grace may ſend for the three Courtiers,
That you deliver'd from theſe Ladies here,
They would be glad to be employ'd in any
Such State-affairs. But I'd almoſt forgot
The *Pigmies* Conqueſt.
Pho. Have you read of them too?
Phil. Though ſome ſay that their Souls are only ſtopt
Into their Bodies, juſt as ſo much Quick-ſilver
Is put into hot Loves, to make 'em dance
As long as th' heat continues; yet, beleeve it,
They are a ſubt'le Nation, a moſt ſhrew'd
Adviſing People.
Coſ. How'l you then ſubdue them?
Phil. By Policy, ſet Hays, and Traps, and Springs,
And

And Pitfals for 'em. And if any do
Dwell in the Rocks, make holes upon the top
As deep as Cups, and fill 'em up with Wine;
You ſhall have one come preſently, and ſip,
And when he finds the ſweetneſs, cry *Chin, Chin*:
Then all the reſt good Fellows ſtraight come out,
And tipple with him till they fall aſleep;
Then we may come and pack 'em up in Hampers,
Or elſe in Hand-baskets, and carry 'em whither
We pleaſe our ſelves.
Mach. A notable Stratagem!
You'l never leave your Policies *Phil.*
Phi. But yet
We muſt draw out ſome Souldiers howe'r.
Coſ. There's no great need of Souldiers; Their Camp's
No larger than a Ginger-bread Office.
Pan. And the Men little bigger.
Phil. What half Heretick
Book tels you that?
Rho. The greateſt ſort they ſay
Are like ſtone-pots with Beards that do reach down
Unto their knees.
Coſ. They're carri'd to the Wars then
As Chickens are to Market, all in Dorſers,
Some thirty Couple on a Horſe.
Phil. You read
Only Apocryphall Hiſtory. Beleeve me
They march moſt formally: I know't there will
Be work enough for Souldiers.
Mach Wee'l train up
All the young Wenches of the City here
On purpoſe for this Expedition,
And't ſhall be call'd the Female War.
Phil. I fear
They won't be ſtrong enough to go againſt 'em;
c 4 They

They have an Enemy doth vex 'em more
Than Horſe or Man can.
Mach. Who, the Cranes you mean?
I'l beg a Patent of Her Majeſty
To take up all that fly about the Country,
For the *Pigmean* Service
Phil. I, but who
Shall's have to Diſcipline 'em ſo, that we
May fly 'em at them off our fiſts?
Mach. They fly
In a moſt war-like Figure naturally:
However we may have a Net caſt o'r
Th' Artyllery Yard, and ſend for th' Gentleman
That bridles Stags, and makes 'em draw Coaches,
Hee'l exerciſe 'em in a Month or two,
And bring 'em to it eaſily.
Phil. We muſt carry
Six or ſev'n hundred of Bird-Cages
And Cony-Coopes along with us.
Mach. For what?
Phil. T' impriſon Rebels, and there feed 'em up
With Milk, and Dazy-roots. I will ſo yerk
The little Gentlemen.
play *Cos.* You muſt not pla[y]
The Tyrant o'r the Wretches.
Phil. You ſhall ſee [*Draws her Sword.*
How I'l behave my ſelf. This foreſide blow
Cuts off thrice three, this back-blow thrice three more,
This foreright thruſt ſpits half a dozen of 'em,
Bucklers and all, like ſo many Larkes with Sage
Between them; then this down-right cleaves a ſtubborn
Two-footed Rebell from the Crown o'th' head
Down to the twiſt, and makes him double forked
Like a Turn Stile, or ſome ſuch Engin. Others
I'l knock pall-mall, and make the wretched Caitiffs
Meaſure

Meaſure their length upon their Mother Earth,
And ſo beſtride 'em, and cry Victory.
Mach. And what'l you do, when you are ſeated in
The Throne, to win your Subjects Love *Philenis*?
Phil. I'l ſtand upon a Cricket, and there make
Fluent Orations to 'em; call 'em Truſty
And Well-beloved, Loyall, and True Subjects,
And my good People: Then I'l mount on Horſeback,
Shew 'em my little Majeſty, and ſcatter
Five or ſix hundred ſingle pence among 'em,
Teach 'em good Language by cleft ſticks, and Bay-leaves,
And Civilize 'em finally by Puppet-Plays.
Cos. Moſt ſtudi'd, and adviſ'd!
Pan. The heart of Wiſdome!
Rho. And Soul of Policy!
Mach. Come little Queen,
Wee'l go and make her Majeſty acquainted
With all the Plot; 'twill take her certainly. *Exeunt.*

ACT. V. SCEN. II.

Pallace For Church to be read[y] — [to?] be read[y]

Adraſte, Lucaſia, Chariſtus, Olyndus, Eumela, Florina, Malthora, in Myrtle wreathes.

Adr. WAs all the Treaſure ſhip'd?
Eum. All, but the Pictures,
And Statues, they'r reſerv'd. I ſaw the Luxury,
And wealth of *Cyprus* ſail. The Souldier doth
By this time gaze upon't.
Adr. The news, *Chariſtus*,
Of your Adventures here, I dare preſume
Hath joyn'd both Armies now. Me thinks I ſee
The *Cyprians* ſtanding here, the *Cretans* there,
And, in a ſpace between them, both Kings meeting
In

70 The *LADY-ERRANT.*

In a moſt ſtrong Embrace, and ſo provoking
Clamors and ſhouts from both ſides, and a joyfull
Clattring of Weapons.
Cha. Beautious Queen, your Vertues
~~Are greater far than Fame; and you your ſelf~~
~~Greater than them! Though Gold and Purple~~ do
~~Adorn your head, yet you have Wove your ſelf~~
~~Far~~ richer Diadems ~~from your Royall Acts~~,
And made ~~your ſelf Immortall by produci~~ng
~~Immortall things. But though your wreath of Vertue~~
Hath made what e'r the Sun beholds in all
His courſe enamor'd by you, yet if I
May pull one ſingle one from out the reſt,
There's none, for which you have more Altars rais'd
Unto your Name, than for that Noble Love,
Whoſe flames you keep ſtill burning in your ſelf,
And cheriſh in all others.
Adr. Sir, you have Conquer'd
A Princeſs, and in her a Queen: I am
Th'addition to your Triumph. We ow much
To you *Olyndus.*
Olyn. I can challenge nothing
But my *Chariſtus* Friendſhip. 'Tis to him
You ow theſe ſeeds of Peace. Although his Father
Appear'd ſo tender of him, that when he
Came hither ſecretly to view the Rites
Of *Venus*, which *Lucaſia* then perform'd,
The aged Man haſted to th' Oracle
To know what Fortune ſhould attend his Son,
And, for an unexpected anſwer, did
Baniſh thoſe Prieſts for which our King now fights:
Yet for all this, ev'n in this heat of danger,
H'hath made another Venture, and the Kingdom
Now grieves his ſecond loſs.
Adr. Do you know the anſwer

That

The *LADY-ERRANT.* 71

That the God gave to his enquiring Father,
For which the King did baniſh all the Prieſts?
Olyn. I may repeat it now, th'Event aſſures me
It meant you no Misfortune. It was this;
Chariſtus *ſhall his Country ſave,*
If he become his Enemies Slave.
Adr. I hope th'Event will not fulfill it.
Olyn. 'Tis
Fulfill'd enough to make an Oracle true.
Adr. I hope you have no Enemies, and for Slave
The Gods avert it!
Olyn. He's *Lucaſia*'s Servant,
There's that fulfill'd; *Cyprus* is now reputed
The *Enemy* to *Crete*; but as for true
And reall Enemies to you *Chariſtus,*
The World hath none ſo Barbarous; your Vertues
Have under this diſguiſe ſhew'd ſo much Prince,
That they betrai'd you ſtill to ~~any~~ Eye euerie any
~~That could diſcern.~~
Cha. Honour'd *Olyndus*, you
Outdo me ſtill. Friends ſhould be alwaies equall;
You muſt take off, ~~and pare~~ your Vertues, that *lessen*
You may go even with me. I ow much
To you, *Eumela*, too.
Adr. Her ſervice hath
Preſerv'd the Kingdom, and refounded *Cyprus.*
Cha. Two ~~Scepters~~ are her Debters. Scepters
Adr. But, *Eumela*,
You might have told me ſooner, that *Lucaſia*
Began to feel a Paſſion; you ne'r knew
That I deſtroy'd true vertuous Loves; it is
A pleaſure to me to perceive their Buddings,
To know their Minutes of Encreaſe, their Stealths,
And ſilent Growings; and I have not ſpar'd
To help, and bring them on.

Eum.

Eum. You have ſo favour'd
Agreeing Souls, that all the VVorld confeſſeth
Your own is perfect Harmony. But where
The God is Blind, ſhould not the Creature be
Silent, and Cloſe? That which is bred by whiſpers
VVould dye if once proclam'd.
Mal. *Cal.* ~~If it were any,~~
~~It was a fault of Trust~~; 'tis more Injuſtice Madam
To betray ſecret Love, than to make known
Counſels of State. *Cupid* hath his Cabinet, council too
To which, if any prove unfaithfull, he
Straight wounds him with the Leaden Shaft, and ſo
They live tormented, and dye ſcorn'd.
Adr. No more;
'Tis well: I meant not to Accuſe, but Praiſe.
Have you ſet ſome to watch, and ſignifie
The King's Return?
Eum. Three peacefull Courtiers,
Lerinus, and *Ganyctor*, and *Iringus*,
Deſir'd that they might bring the News, and ſo
Are gone unto the Port.
Adr. My Ladies, you
I hope will clear up now.
Flor. I have too much
Joy to expreſs it.
Mal. Could you ſee my heart,
You'd view a Triumph there.

ACT. V. SCEN. III.

To them *Philanis*.

Phil. AND't pleaſe your Highneſs
There are three Ladies wait without, who, if
You have a vacant Ear, are come t' inform you

Of

Of ſomething neer concerns the State.
Adr. The old
Vexation's buſie ſtill —— *Pandena* and
Coſmeta, and the other —— are they not?
Tell 'em they may come in — How ſhall we do,
Eumela, now to ſtop their Clamour? [Ex. Phi.
Eum. 'Tis eaſie;
There's nothing yet provided; the Return
O'th' King being now ſo ſudden, 'twill amaze 'em,
And make 'em kneel for mercy to you, if
You do but threaten to diſcloſe the Plot.

ACT. V. SCEN. IV.

To them *Coſmeta*, *Pandena*, *Rhodia*.

Adr. YOur buſineſs Ladies?
Coſ. Pleaſe you to diſmiſs
Thoſe Faces that have Beards?
Adr. Fear not, they ſhall not
Betray your Counſels.
Coſ. Pleaſe your Highneſs then,
There's fear that our Deſign will come to nought,
Our Truſt is falſi[illegible]'d.
Adr. How ſo?
Coſ. VVe came
To a[illegible] *Macheſſa* about VVeapons, and
She p[illegible]eſently demands, how many caſes
Of Knives, ~~what Forks~~ we have, ~~Teſting, or Carving?~~
Pan. Talk we of Swords, ſhe asks what Criſping ~~Pins~~ Iron
And Bodkins we could gueſs might eaſily be
Rais'd through the Common-wealth?
Rho. VVe ſpake of Armour,
She ſtraight replies, ſend in your ſteel Combs, with
The Steels you ſee your Faces in, wee'l quickly

Con-

what Forks . . . Testing or Carving? Pins

Convert 'em into Greaves, and Gorgets.
Coſ. If
This be not treaſon 'gainſt the Female State,
Beleeve not Policy, nor me.
Eum. Why ſhe
Was your own choice; you cri'd her up as one
That having neither Child, nor Husband, would
Take to her ſelf the Commonwealth as both.
Coſ. We do ſuſpect your ſadneſs ſweet *Florina.*
Rho. And your retir'dneſs too *Malthora,* (as
Demure as you ſtand here) is deep engag'd.
Pan. Nor is *Eumela* free.
Mal. VVhence do you gather it?
Coſ. Pray y' why thoſe Myrtle wreaths? why your
And your Doors Crown'd? (Gates dreſt?
Flo. In hope our Lords will ſhortly
Enter, and Crown 'em more.
Coſ. Moſt evident!
Can there be bolder Falſhood? Did we not
Agree to keep out Husbands from our City
And our Minds too? And yet behold there are
Garlands and Flowers prepar'd; and they to be
Receiv'd as Lovers. Husbands are at beſt
But a ſad kind of pleaſure; one good Look,
And a Salute's enough at any time
For the Good-man o'th' Family.
Flo. Pray y' allow
Affection more Expreſſions; Love doth ceaſe
To be, when that it breaks not out into
Thoſe ſigns of Joy; as Souls ceaſe to be Souls
VVhen they leave off to ſhew their Operations.
Pan. This is no time for vain Philoſophy,
VVe are to have a fine State of it ſhortly,
VVhen Ladies once begin to utter Axioms,
And raiſe a Faction 'gainſt the ſeven Sages.

Act

ACT. V. SCEN. V.

Macheſſa.

Mac. And't pleaſe your Highneſs, three Embaſſadors,
Sent from the *Cretan* State, do crave admittance.
Adr. Uſher 'em in. [*Ex.* Ma. [Eum. *whiſpers the Qu.*
Coſ. There's life you ſee i'th' bus'neſs;
Let's yet be true. The fame of our Exploit
Already makes us ſought to. There's an Honour
Not uſuall too i'th' Number of 'em; when
Arriv'd there three before from the ſame State?
And't pleaſe you, let *Pandena, Rhodia,* and I,
Manage their Entertainment?
Adr. Do ſo.
Pan. It ſhall
All be to th' honour of the Female State.
Coſ. Prepare your ſelf *Pandena,* here they come.

ACT V. SCENE VI.

To them Macheſſa *uſhering* Lerinus, Iringus, *and* Ganyctor, *as Embaſſadors.*

Ler. Moſt Gratious, moſt Renowned, and moſt (Beautious.
Coſ. Pray y' be not troubleſome; We're taken (up
VVholy with the Affairs o'th' Kingdom now.
Irin. VVhen will your Ladiſhip have a Vacancy?
Pan. You are Impertinent; True Politicians
Do never uſe to anſwer on the ſudden.
Rho. It is not now as heretofore; the times
Are grown more wiſe, and more reſerv'd; there are
Matters on foot far greater; you muſt wait ——
You are Embaſſadors.

Gan

Gan. We ſhould not think ſo,
But that you're pleas'd to tell us ſo ; your uſage
Hath a far different Dialect from your Tongue.
Coſ. Were there not VVomen in your Kingdom fit
For this Imployment ? I perceive your State
Is utterly unfurniſh'd, that it cannot
Send forth three Female Agents.
Irin. 'Tis not, Madam,
such brittle ware — The cuſtome of our Maſter to commit [MS: such brittle ware]
a peece of Chrystall — His Kingdom's ſecrets to ~~a peece of Chryſtall~~ ;
That were not to Negotiate, but Betray.
Pa. You ſhall meet VVomen here, that are not ~~Cryſtal~~, [MS: glass]
Thoſe that will find out you, and hide themſelves.
Rho. You ſhall not need the help of an Interpreter
VVhen we give Audience ; Speak what Tongue you will
You ſhall be underſtood, each one of us
H[illegible] more than one.
Ler. VVe eaſily beleeve it,
~~Though you ſhould ſpeak none elſe beſides your Native.~~
Coſ. Pray ſtand you by, and wait a while.
Ler. VVe obey.
Coſ. Now will they think the better of us ; 'tis
The way to bring our ſelves in Credit by
Neglecting of 'em thus. I'd have 'em know
VVe were to be ſaluted at their coming.
Pan. Their State is very unhappy, that it is
So unprovided : I beleeve theſe are
The very wiſeſt in the Kingdom ; for
They have no Manners.
Rho. You gueſs rightly, Madam ;
The greateſt Counſellors and Lawyers ſcarce
Know how to make a Leg.

ACT.

ACT. V. SCEN. VII.

To them *Philenis*.

Phil. ARm, arm, arm, arm,
The King, and Lords are within ſight. Here
Pray take my Sword, and Helmet. (Madam,
Coſ. Worthy Gentlemen,
Do y' ~~come~~ to proffer aid from th' *Cretan* King — come
To help us 'gainſt the Men ?
Irin. No Ladies : we
Come but to tell you that the King is Landed, [MS: They discover themselves.]
We are your fellow-Subjects.
Coſ. Fellow-Villaines
~~Among your ſelves~~. *Eumela*, we may thank
You for all this.
Pan. But Siſter of the Sword,
Great Lady Stickler —
Mach. Be patient pray y' a while— Take you this Hel-
And you this Fauchion Sir, and you this Lance; (met,
Embaſſadours ſtill muſt be diſmiſs'd with Preſents.
Rho. Where is our Plate ?
Pan. Our Wealth ?
Coſ. Our Jewels ?
Mach. Folly !
Did not my Order bind me to aſſiſt
Diſtreſſed men ?
Coſ Who would e'r truſt a VVoman ?
Mach. The Queen will give y' a fair account.
Adr. 'Tis no
Time to debate things now. The truth is, all
VVas ſhip'd, and ſent the King, as one great Preſent
From all the *Cyprian* VVomen. If you do
Deſire that he ſhould know how it was rais'd,

f For

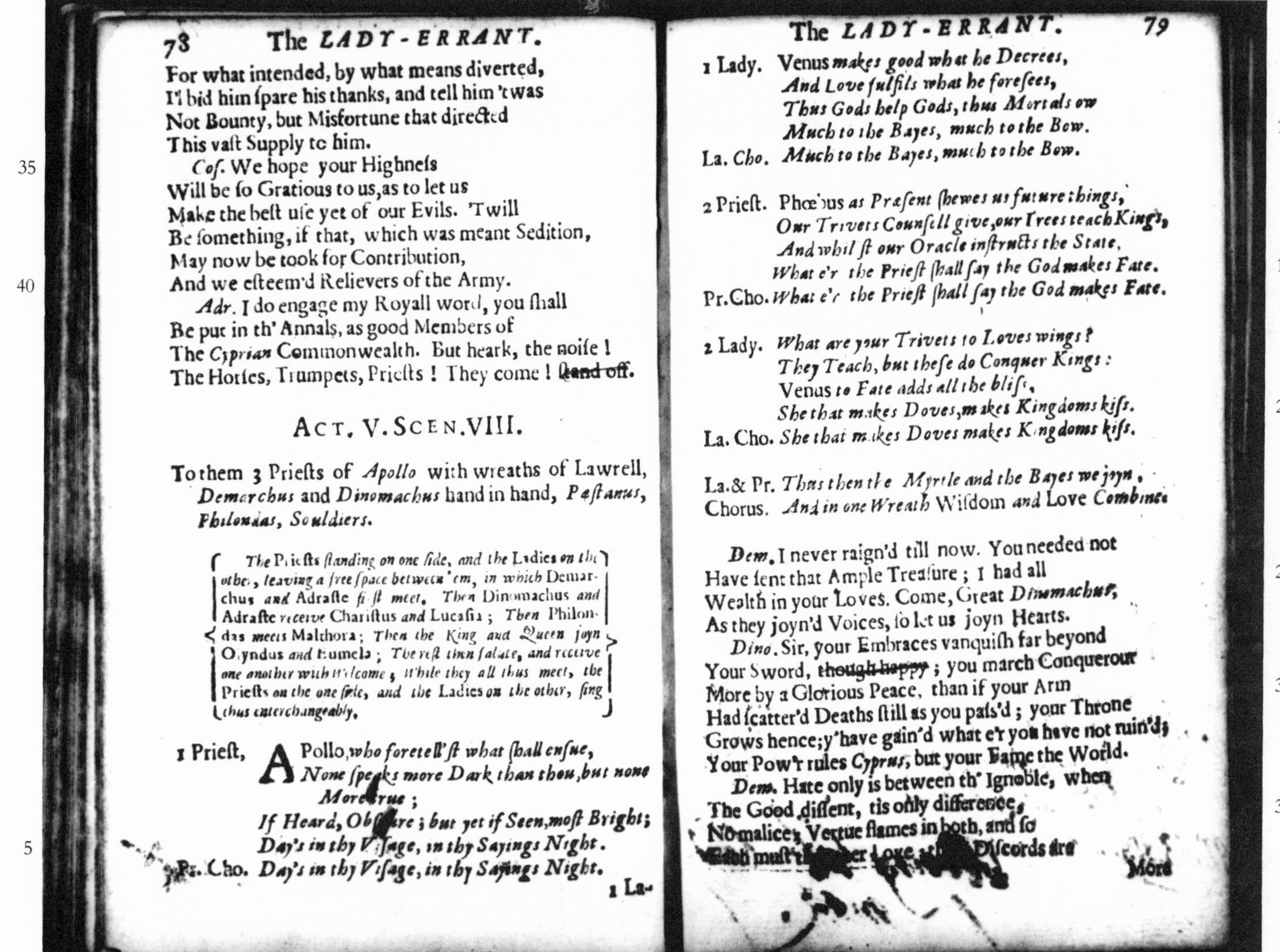

78 The LADY-ERRANT.

For what intended, by what means diverted,
I'l bid him ſpare his thanks, and tell him 'twas
Not Bounty, but Misfortune that directed
This vaſt Supply to him.
Coſ. We hope your Highneſs
Will be ſo Gratious to us, as to let us
Make the beſt uſe yet of our Evils. 'Twill
Be ſomething, if that, which was meant Sedition,
May now be took for Contribution,
And we eſteem'd Relievers of the Army.
Adr. I do engage my Royall word, you ſhall
Be put in th' Annals, as good Members of
The *Cyprian* Commonwealth. But heark, the noiſe!
The Horſes, Trumpets, Prieſts! They come! ~~ſtand off.~~

ACT. V. SCEN. VIII.

To them 3 Prieſts of *Apollo* with wreaths of Lawrell, *Demarchus* and *Dinomachus* hand in hand, *Peſtanus*, *Philondas*, *Souldiers*.

The Prieſts ſtanding on one ſide, and the Ladies on the other, leaving a free ſpace between 'em, in which Demarchus *and* Adraſte *firſt meet. Then* Dinomachus *and* Adraſte *receive* Chariſtus *and* Lucaſia; *Then* Philondas *meets* Malthora; *Then the King and Queen joyn* Olyndus *and* Eumela; *The reſt then ſalute, and receive one another with welcome; While they all thus meet, the* Prieſts *on the one ſide, and the* Ladies *on the other, ſing thus enterchangeably,*

1 Prieſt, APollo, *who foretell'ſt what ſhall enſue,*
None ſpeaks more Dark than thou, but none
More true;
If Heard, Obſcure; but yet if Seen, moſt Bright;
Day's in thy Viſage, in thy Sayings Night.
Pr. Cho. *Day's in thy Viſage, in thy Sayings Night.*

1 La-

The LADY-ERRANT. 79

1 Lady. Venus *makes good what he Decrees,*
And Love fulfils what he foreſees,
Thus Gods help Gods, thus Mortals ow
Much to the Bayes, much to the Bow.
La. Cho. *Much to the Bayes, much to the Bow.*

2 Prieſt. Phœbus *as Preſent ſhewes us future things,*
Our Trivets Counſell give, our Trees teach Kings,
And whilſt our Oracle inſtructs the State,
What e'r the Prieſt ſhall ſay the God makes Fate.
Pr. Cho. *What e'r the Prieſt ſhall ſay the God makes Fate.*

2 Lady. *What are your Trivets to Loves wings?*
They Teach, but theſe do Conquer Kings:
Venus *to Fate adds all the bliſs,*
She that makes Doves, makes Kingdoms kiſs.
La. Cho. *She that makes Doves makes Kingdoms kiſs.*

La. & Pr. *Thus then the Myrtle and the Bayes we joyn,*
Chorus. *And in one Wreath* Wiſdom *and* Love *Combine.*

Dem. I never raign'd till now. You needed not
Have ſent that Ample Treaſure; I had all
Wealth in your Loves. Come, Great *Dinomachus*,
As they joyn'd Voices, ſo let us joyn Hearts.
Dino. Sir, your Embraces vanquiſh far beyond
Your Sword, ~~though happy~~; you march Conquerour
More by a Glorious Peace, than if your Arm
Had ſcatter'd Deaths ſtill as you paſs'd; your Throne
Grows hence; y'have gain'd what e'r you have not ruin'd;
Your Pow'r rules *Cyprus*, but your Fame the World.
Dem. Hate only is between th' Ignoble, when
The Good diſſent, tis only difference,
No malice; Vertue flames in both, and ſo
Each muſt the other Love; their Diſcords are

More

true
Obscure

Each must the other Love; their Discords are

V, viii, opening. I presume that the palace setting (serving for a church) mentioned in the notes at the opening of V, ii, was used for this final scene. The warning for the use of the setting is very far in advance, perhaps because the final scene is an elaborate one. There are no other warnings for settings in the promptbook.

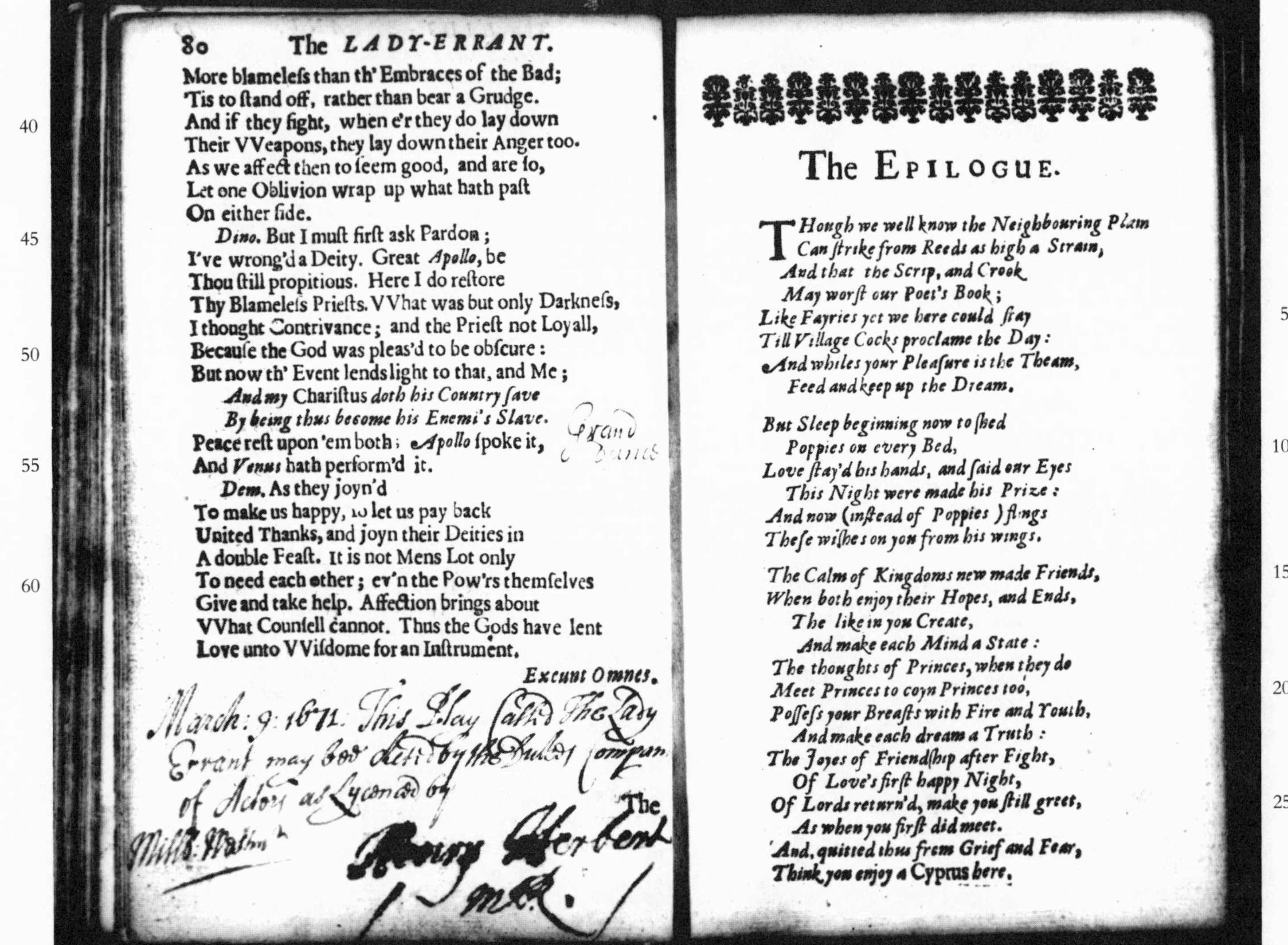

80 The *LADY-ERRANT.*

More blameleſs than th' Embraces of the Bad;
'Tis to ſtand off, rather than bear a Grudge.
And if they fight, when e'r they do lay down
Their VVeapons, they lay down their Anger too.
As we affect then to ſeem good, and are ſo,
Let one Oblivion wrap up what hath paſt
On either ſide.
Dino. But I muſt firſt ask Pardon;
I've wrong'd a Deity. Great *Apollo*, be
Thou ſtill propitious. Here I do reſtore
Thy Blameleſs Prieſts. VVhat was but only Darkneſs,
I thought Contrivance; and the Prieſt not Loyall,
Becauſe the God was pleas'd to be obſcure:
But now th' Event lends light to that, and Me;
And my Chariſtus *doth his Country ſave*
By being thus become his Enemi's Slave.
Peace reſt upon 'em both; *Apollo* ſpoke it,
And *Venus* hath perform'd it.
Dem. As they joyn'd
To make us happy, so let us pay back
United Thanks, and joyn their Deities in
A double Feaſt. It is not Mens Lot only
To need each other; ev'n the Pow'rs themſelves
Give and take help. Affection brings about
VVhat Counſell cannot. Thus the Gods have lent
Love unto VViſdome for an Inſtrument.

Exeunt Omnes.

Grand Dance

March: 9: 1671. This Play called The Lady Errant may bee acted by the Duke's Company of Actors as Lycenced by

Millb: Westm'

Henry Herbert
M. R.

Millb: Westm' Henry Herbert / M. R.

The EPILOGUE.

Though we well know the Neighbouring Plain
Can ſtrike from Reeds as high a Strain,
And that the Scrip, and Crook
May worſt our Poet's Book;
Like Fayries yet we here could ſtay
Till Village Cocks proclame the Day:
And whiles your Pleaſure is the Theam,
Feed and keep up the Dream.

But Sleep beginning now to ſhed
Poppies on every Bed,
Love ſtay'd his hands, and ſaid our Eyes
This Night were made his Prize:
And now (inſtead of Poppies) flings
Theſe wiſhes on you from his wings.

The Calm of Kingdoms new made Friends,
When both enjoy their Hopes, and Ends,
The like in you Create,
And make each Mind a State:
The thoughts of Princes, when they do
Meet Princes to coyn Princes too,
Poſſeſs your Breaſts with Fire and Youth,
And make each dream a Truth:
The Joyes of Friendſhip after Fight,
Of Love's firſt happy Night,
Of Lords return'd, make you ſtill greet,
As when you firſt did meet.
And, quitted thus from Grief and Fear,
Think you enjoy a Cyprus *here.*

V, viii, following 63. In the license note following the text only Herbert's signature is in his hand.

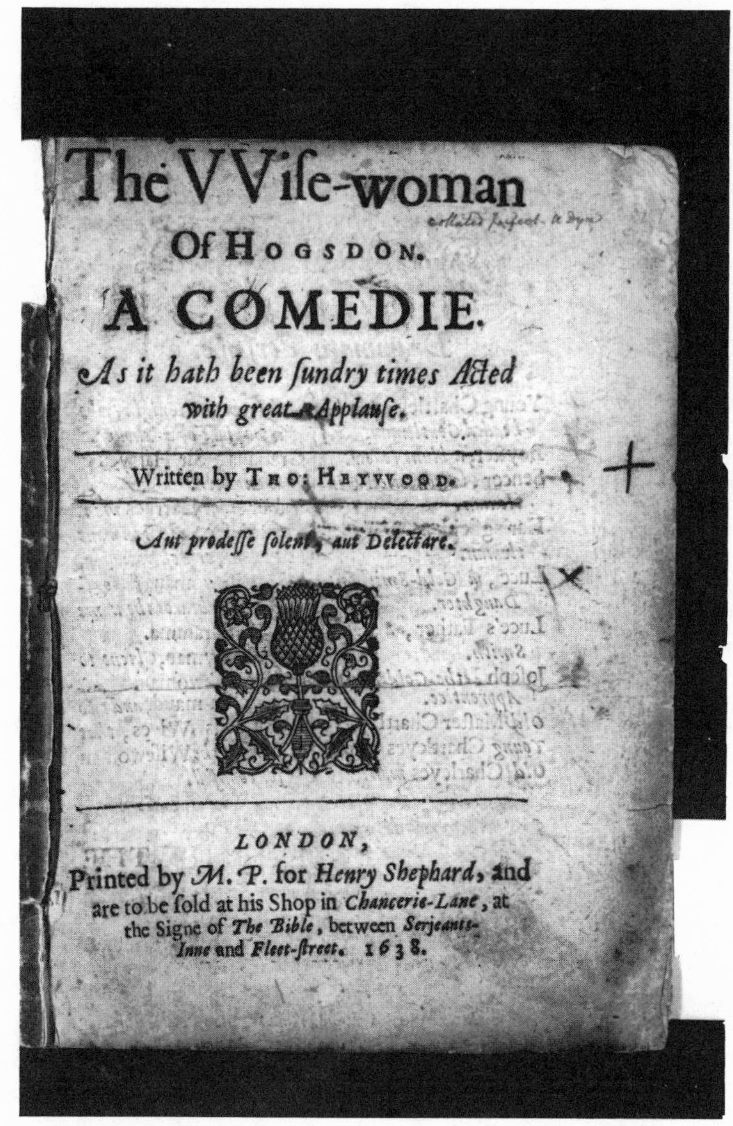

The VVise-woman
Of Hogsdon.
A COMEDIE.
As it hath been sundry times Acted with great Applause.
Written by Tho: Heywood.
Aut prodesse solent, aut Delectare.
LONDON,
Printed by *M. P.* for *Henry Shephard*, and are to be sold at his Shop in *Chancerie-Lane*, at the Signe of *The Bible*, between *Serjeants-Inne* and *Fleet-street*. 1638.

The Wise-Woman of Hogsdon by Thomas Heywood. Reproduced by permission of the Folger Shakespeare Library, Washington, D.C.

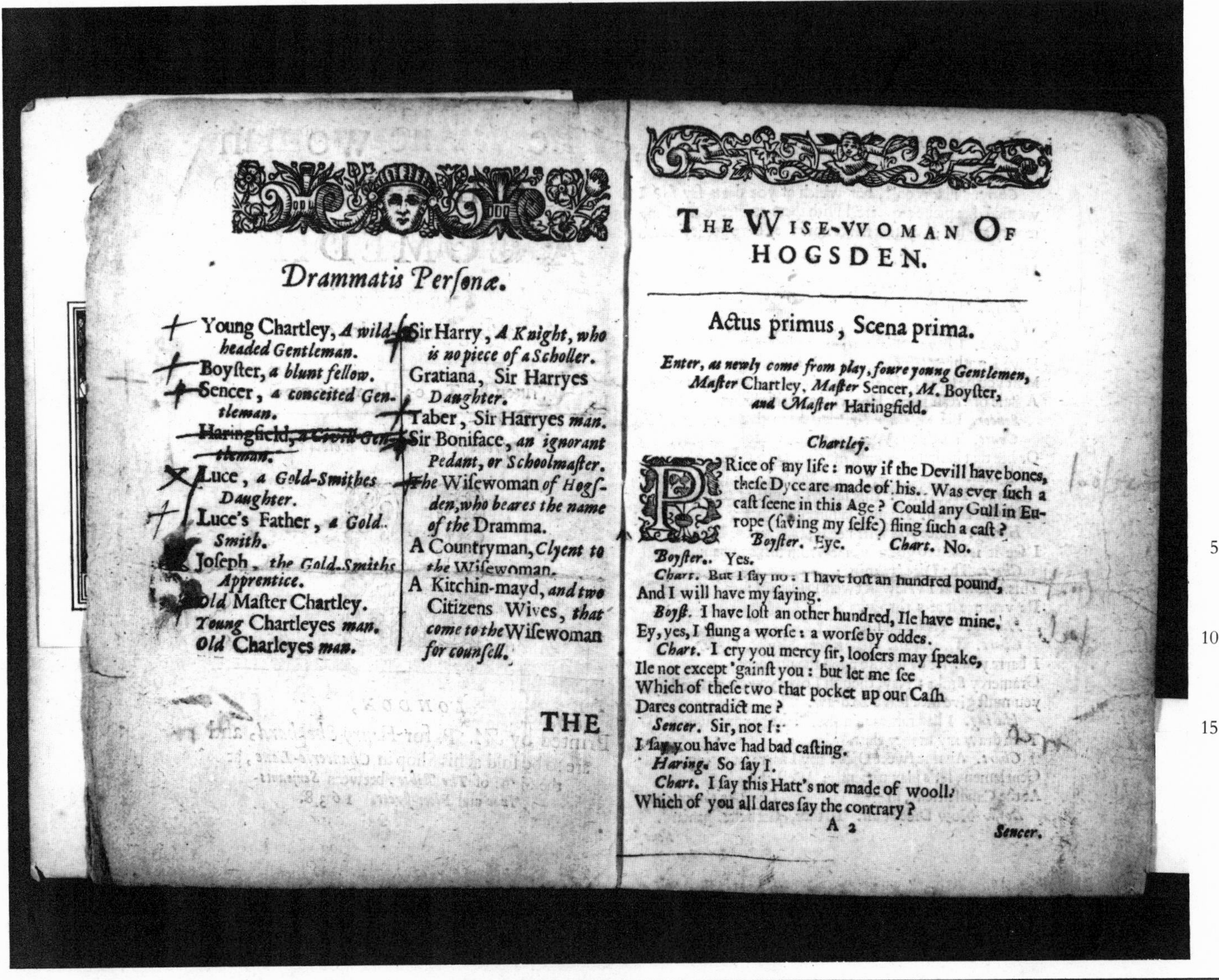

Drammatis Personæ.

Young Chartley, *A wild-headed Gentleman.*
Boyster, *a blunt fellow.*
Sencer, *a conceited Gentleman.*
~~Haringfield, a Civill Gentleman.~~
Luce, *a Gold-Smithes Daughter.*
Luce's Father, *a Gold-Smith.*
Joseph, *the Gold-Smiths Apprentice.*
Old Master Chartley.
Young Chartleyes *man.*
Old Charleyes *man.*
Sir Harry, *A Knight, who is no piece of a Scholler.*
Gratiana, Sir Harryes *Daughter.*
Taber, Sir Harryes *man.*
Sir Boniface, *an ignorant Pedant, or Schoolmaster.*
The Wisewoman *of Hogsden, who beares the name of the* Dramma.
A Countryman, *Clyent to the* Wisewoman.
A Kitchin-mayd, *and two* Citizens Wives, *that come to the* Wisewoman *for counsell.*

THE

THE WISE-WOMAN OF HOGSDEN.

Actus primus, Scena prima.

Enter, as newly come from play, foure young Gentlemen, Master Chartley, *Master* Sencer, *M.* Boyster, *and Master* Haringfield.

Chartley.

Price of my life: now if the Devill have bones,
these Dyce are made of his. Was ever such a
cast seene in this Age? Could any Gull in Europe
(saving my selfe) fling such a cast?
Boyster. Eye. *Chart.* No.
Boyster. Yes.
Chart. But I say no: I have lost an hundred pound,
And I will have my saying.
Boyst. I have lost an other hundred, Ile have mine,
Ey, yes, I flung a worse: a worse by oddes.
Chart. I cry you mercy sir, loosers may speake,
Ile not except 'gainst you: but let me see
Which of these two that pocket up our Cash
Dares contradict me?
Sencer. Sir, not I:
I say you have had bad casting.
Haring. So say I.
Chart. I say this Hatt's not made of wooll:
Which of you all dares say the contrary?

A 2 *Sencer.*

Dramatis Personae. The marks beside the names are clearly connected with the casting, for all the characters marked have actors' names attached to them in the prompt notes—except Gratiana, not marked here but played by Mrs. Coysh.

I, i, opening. There are some faint, indecipherable notes down the right margin of the page.

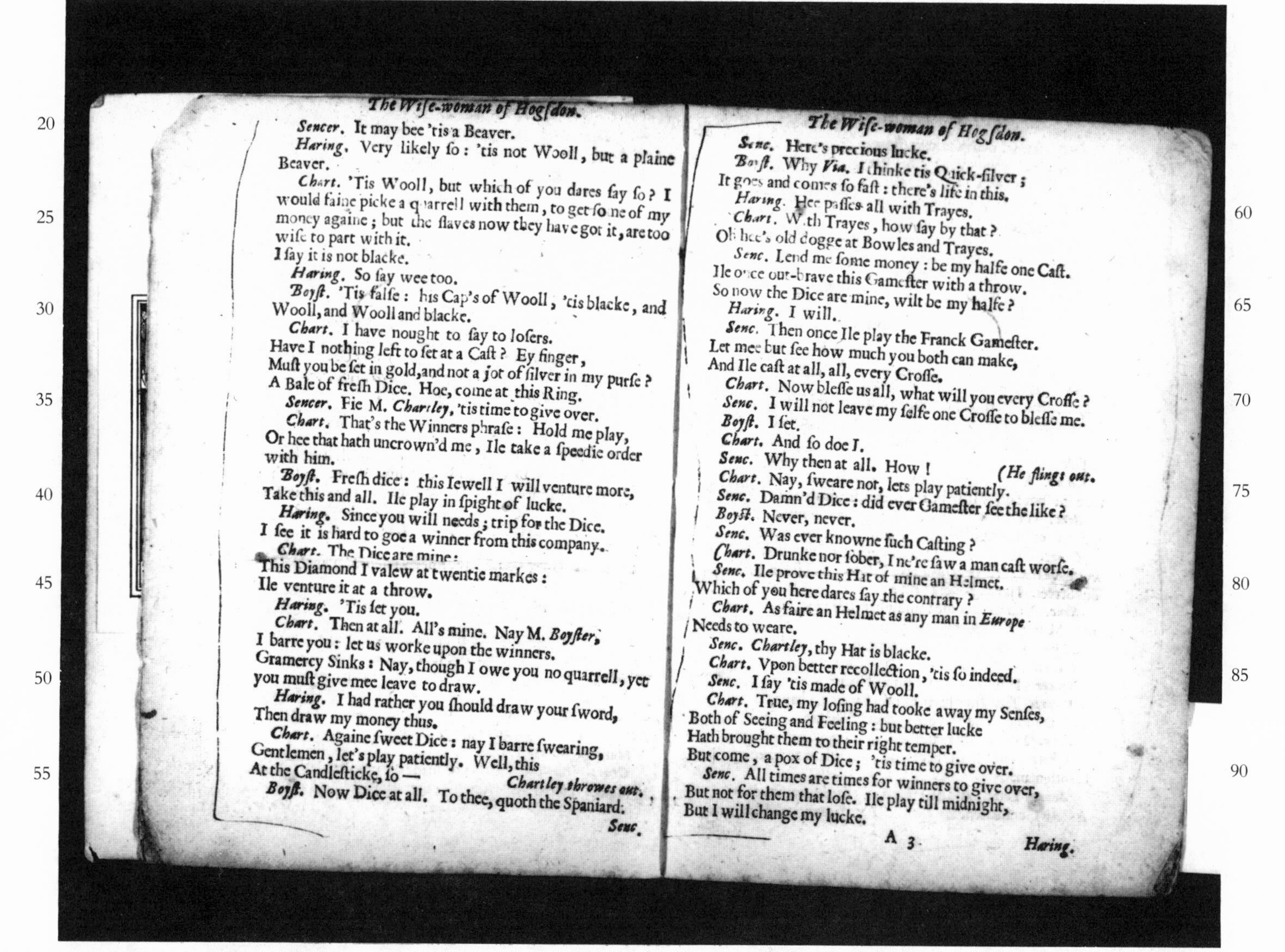

Sencer. It may bee 'tis a Beaver.
Haring. Very likely so: 'tis not Wooll, but a plaine Beaver.
Chart. 'Tis Wooll, but which of you dares say so? I would faine picke a quarrell with them, to get some of my money againe; but the slaves now they have got it, are too wise to part with it.
I say it is not blacke.
Haring. So say wee too.
Boyst. 'Tis false: his Cap's of Wooll, 'tis blacke, and Wooll, and Wooll and blacke.
Chart. I have nought to say to losers.
Have I nothing left to set at a Cast? Ey finger,
Must you be set in gold, and not a jot of silver in my purse?
A Bale of fresh Dice. Hoe, come at this Ring.
Sencer. Fie M. *Chartley*, 'tis time to give over.
Chart. That's the Winners phrase: Hold me play,
Or hee that hath uncrown'd me, Ile take a speedie order with him.
Boyst. Fresh dice: this Iewell I will venture more,
Take this and all. Ile play in spight of lucke.
Haring. Since you will needs; trip for the Dice.
I see it is hard to goe a winner from this company.
Chart. The Dice are mine:
This Diamond I valew at twentie markes:
Ile venture it at a throw.
Haring. 'Tis set you.
Chart. Then at all. All's mine. Nay M. *Boyster*,
I barre you: let us worke upon the winners.
Gramercy Sinks: Nay, though I owe you no quarrell, yet you must give mee leave to draw.
Haring. I had rather you should draw your sword,
Then draw my money thus.
Chart. Againe sweet Dice: nay I barre swearing,
Gentlemen, let's play patiently. Well, this
At the Candlesticke, so — *Chartley throwes out.*
Boyst. Now Dice at all. To thee, quoth the Spaniard.
Senc.

Senc. Here's precious lucke.
Boyst. Why *Via.* I thinke tis Quick-silver;
It goes and comes so fast: there's life in this.
Haring. Hee passes all with Trayes.
Chart. With Trayes, how say by that?
Oh hee's old dogge at Bowles and Trayes.
Senc. Lend me some money: be my halfe one Cast.
Ile once out-brave this Gamester with a throw.
So now the Dice are mine, wilt be my halfe?
Haring. I will.
Senc. Then once Ile play the Franck Gamester.
Let mee but see how much you both can make,
And Ile cast at all, all, every Crosse.
Chart. Now blesse us all, what will you every Crosse?
Senc. I will not leave my selfe one Crosse to blesse me.
Boyst. I set.
Chart. And so doe I.
Senc. Why then at all. How! *(He flings out.*
Chart. Nay, sweare not, lets play patiently.
Senc. Damn'd Dice: did ever Gamester see the like?
Boyst. Never, never.
Senc. Was ever knowne such Casting?
Chart. Drunke nor sober, I ne're saw a man cast worse.
Senc. Ile prove this Hat of mine an Helmet.
Which of you here dares say the contrary?
Chart. As faire an Helmet as any man in *Europe*
Needs to weare.
Senc. *Chartley*, thy Hat is blacke.
Chart. Vpon better recollection, 'tis so indeed.
Senc. I say 'tis made of Wooll.
Chart. True, my losing had tooke away my Senses,
Both of Seeing and Feeling: but better lucke
Hath brought them to their right temper.
But come, a pox of Dice; 'tis time to give over.
Senc. All times are times for winners to give over,
But not for them that lose. Ile play till midnight,
But I will change my lucke.
A 3 *Haring.*

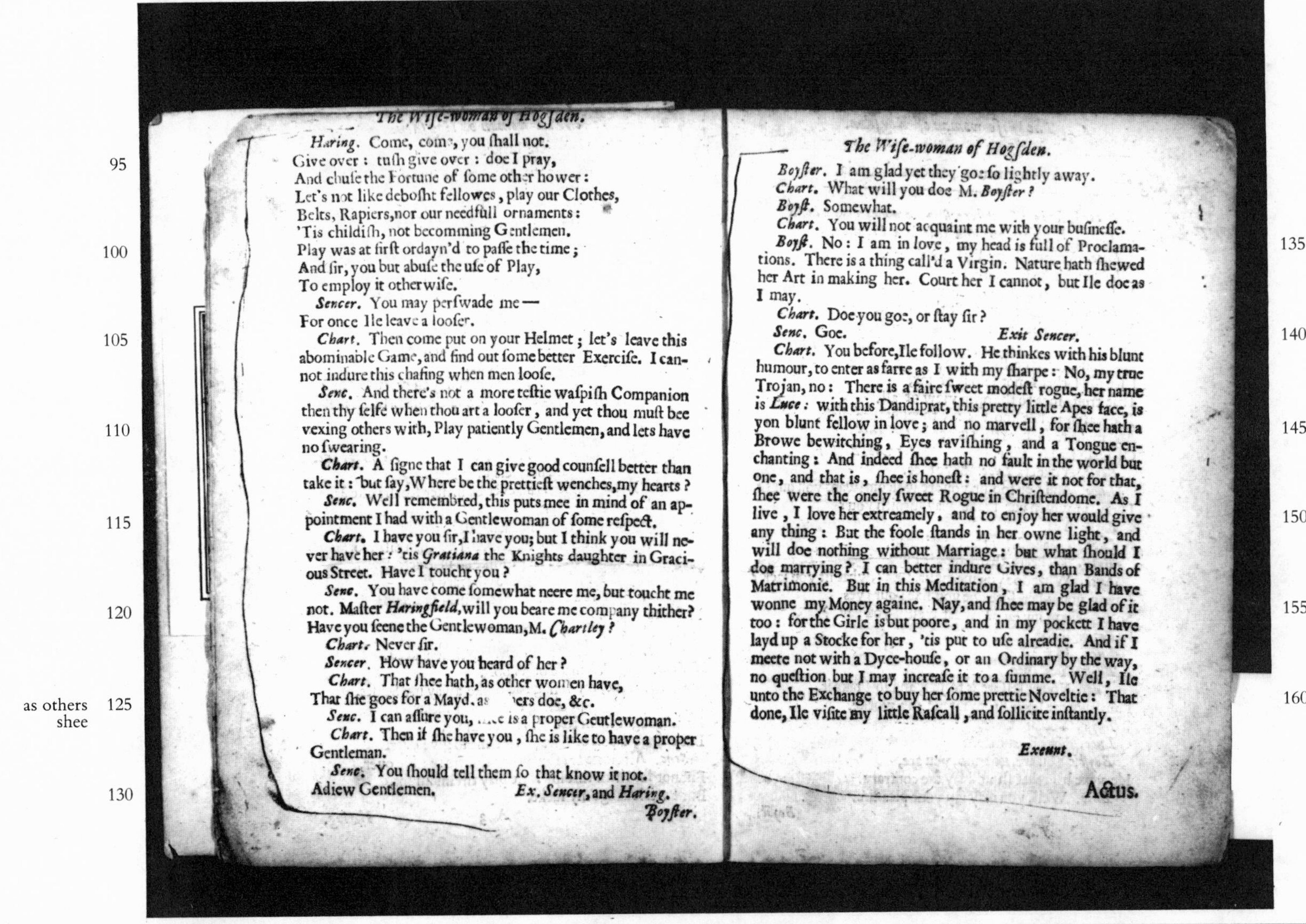

The Wife-woman of Hogſden.

Haring. Come, com:, you ſhall not.
Give over: tuſh give over: doe I pray,
And chuſe the Fortune of ſome other hower:
Let's not like deboſht fellowes, play our Clothes,
Belts, Rapiers, nor our needfull ornaments:
'Tis childiſh, not becomming Gentlemen.
Play was at firſt ordayn'd to paſſe the time;
And ſir, you but abuſe the uſe of Play,
To employ it otherwiſe.

Sencer. You may perſwade me—
For once Ile leave a looſer.

Chart. Then come put on your Helmet; let's leave this abominable Game, and find out ſome better Exerciſe. I cannot indure this chafing when men looſe.

Senc. And there's not a more teſtie waſpiſh Companion then thy ſelfe when thou art a looſer, and yet thou muſt bee vexing others with, Play patiently Gentlemen, and lets have no ſwearing.

Chart. A ſigne that I can give good counſell better than take it: but ſay, Where be the pretrieſt wenches, my hearts?

Senc. Well remembred, this puts mee in mind of an appointment I had with a Gentlewoman of ſome reſpect.

Chart. I have you ſir, I have you; but I think you will never have her: 'tis *Gratiana* the Knights daughter in Gracious Street. Have I toucht you?

Senc. You have come ſomewhat neere me, but toucht me not. Maſter *Haringfield*, will you beare me company thither? Have you ſeene the Gentlewoman, M. *Chartley*?

Chart. Never ſir.

Sencer. How have you heard of her?

Chart. That ſhee hath, as other women have,
That ſhe goes for a Mayd, as [others] doe, &c. [as others shee]

Senc. I can aſſure you, [shee] is a proper Gentlewoman.

Chart. Then if ſhe have you, ſhe is like to have a proper Gentleman.

Senc. You ſhould tell them ſo that know it not.
Adiew Gentlemen. *Ex. Sencer, and Haring.*

Boyſter.

The Wiſe-woman of Hogſden.

Boyſter. I am glad yet they goe ſo lightly away.

Chart. What will you doe M. *Boyſter*?

Boyſt. Somewhat.

Chart. You will not acquaint me with your buſineſſe.

Boyſt. No: I am in love, my head is full of Proclamations. There is a thing call'd a Virgin. Nature hath ſhewed her Art in making her. Court her I cannot, but Ile doe as I may.

Chart. Doe you goe, or ſtay ſir?

Senc. Goe. *Exit Sencer.*

Chart. You before, Ile follow. He thinkes with his blunt humour, to enter as farre as I with my ſharpe: No, my true Trojan, no: There is a faire ſweet modeſt rogue, her name is *Luce*: with this Dandiprat, this pretty little Apes face, is yon blunt fellow in love; and no marvell, for ſhee hath a Browe bewitching, Eyes raviſhing, and a Tongue enchanting: And indeed ſhee hath no fault in the world but one, and that is, ſhee is honeſt: and were it not for that, ſhee were the onely ſweet Rogue in Chriſtendome. As I live, I love her extreamely, and to enjoy her would give any thing: But the foole ſtands in her owne light, and will doe nothing without Marriage: but what ſhould I doe marrying? I can better indure Gives, than Bands of Matrimonie. But in this Meditation, I am glad I have wonne my Money againe. Nay, and ſhee may be glad of it too: for the Girle is but poore, and in my pockett I have layd up a Stocke for her, 'tis put to uſe alreadie. And if I meete not with a Dyce-houſe, or an Ordinary by the way, no queſtion but I may increaſe it to a ſumme. Well, Ile unto the Exchange to buy her ſome prettie Noveltie: That done, Ile viſite my little Raſcall, and ſollicite inſtantly.

Exeunt.

Actus.

The Wiſe-woman of Hogſdon.

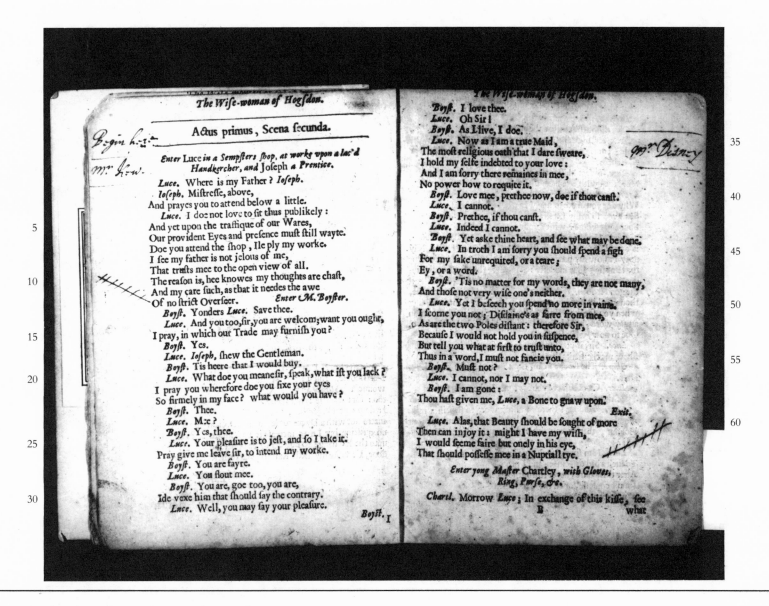

Actus primus, Scena ſecunda.

Enter Luce *in a Sempſters ſhop, at worke vpon a lac'd Handkercher, and* Ioſeph *a Prentice.*

Luce. Where is my Father? *Ioſeph.*
Ioſeph. Miſtreſſe, above,
And prayes you to attend below a little.
Luce. I doe not love to ſit thus publikely:
And yet upon the traffique of our Wares,
Our provident Eyes and preſence muſt ſtill wayte.
Doe you attend the ſhop, Ile ply my worke.
I ſee my father is not jelous of me,
That truſts mee to the open view of all.
The reaſon is, hee knowes my thoughts are chaſt,
And my care ſuch, as that it needes the awe
Of no ſtrict Overſeer. *Enter M. Boyſter.*
Boyſt. Yonders *Luce.* Save thee.
Luce. And you too, ſir, you are welcom; want you ought,
I pray, in which our Trade may furniſh you?
Boyſt. Yes.
Luce. *Ioſeph,* ſhew the Gentleman.
Boyſt. Tis heere that I would buy.
Luce. What doe you meane ſir, ſpeak, what iſt you lack?
I pray you wherefore doe you fixe your eyes
So firmely in my face? what would you have?
Boyſt. Thee.
Luce. Mee?
Boyſt. Yes, thee.
Luce. Your pleaſure is to jeſt, and ſo I take it.
Pray give me leave ſir, to intend my worke.
Boyſt. You are fayre.
Luce. You flout mee.
Boyſt. You are, goe too, you are,
Ide vexe him that ſhould ſay the contrary.
Luce. Well, you may ſay your pleaſure.

Boyſt. I

The Wiſe-woman of Hogſdon.

Boyſt. I love thee.
Luce. Oh Sir!
Boyſt. As I live, I doe.
Luce. Now as I am a true Maid,
The moſt religious oath that I dare ſweare,
I hold my ſelfe indebted to your love:
And I am ſorry there remaines in mee,
No power how to requite it.
Boyſt. Love mee, prethee now, doe if thou canſt.
Luce. I cannot.
Boyſt. Prethee, if thou canſt.
Luce. Indeed I cannot.
Boyſt. Yet aske thine heart, and ſee what may be done.
Luce. In troth I am ſorry you ſhould ſpend a ſigh
For my ſake unrequited, or a teare;
Ey, or a word.
Boyſt. 'Tis no matter for my words, they are not many,
And thoſe not very wiſe one's neither.
Luce. Yet I beſeech you ſpend no more in vaine.
I ſcorne you not; Diſdaine's as farre from mee,
As are the two Poles diſtant: therefore Sir,
Becauſe I would not hold you in ſuſpence,
But tell you what at firſt to truſt unto,
Thus in a word, I muſt not fancie you.
Boyſt. Muſt not?
Luce. I cannot, nor I may not.
Boyſt. I am gone:
Thou haſt given me, *Luce,* a Bone to gnaw upon.
Exit.
Luce. Alas, that Beauty ſhould be ſought of more
Then can injoy it: might I have my wiſh,
I would ſeeme faire but onely in his eye,
That ſhould poſſeſſe mee in a Nuptiall tye.

Enter yong Maſter Chartley, *with Gloves, Ring, Purſe, &c.*

Chartl. Morrow *Luce*; In exchange of this kiſſe, ſee what

B

I, ii, opening. The play is cut to begin at this point, the entire first scene with its expository information about the gambling young men being cut. Note that no setting is indicated in the notes—and so throughout.

I, ii, 12. The cross-hatch mark is used for entrance cues, as in King's Company promptbooks.

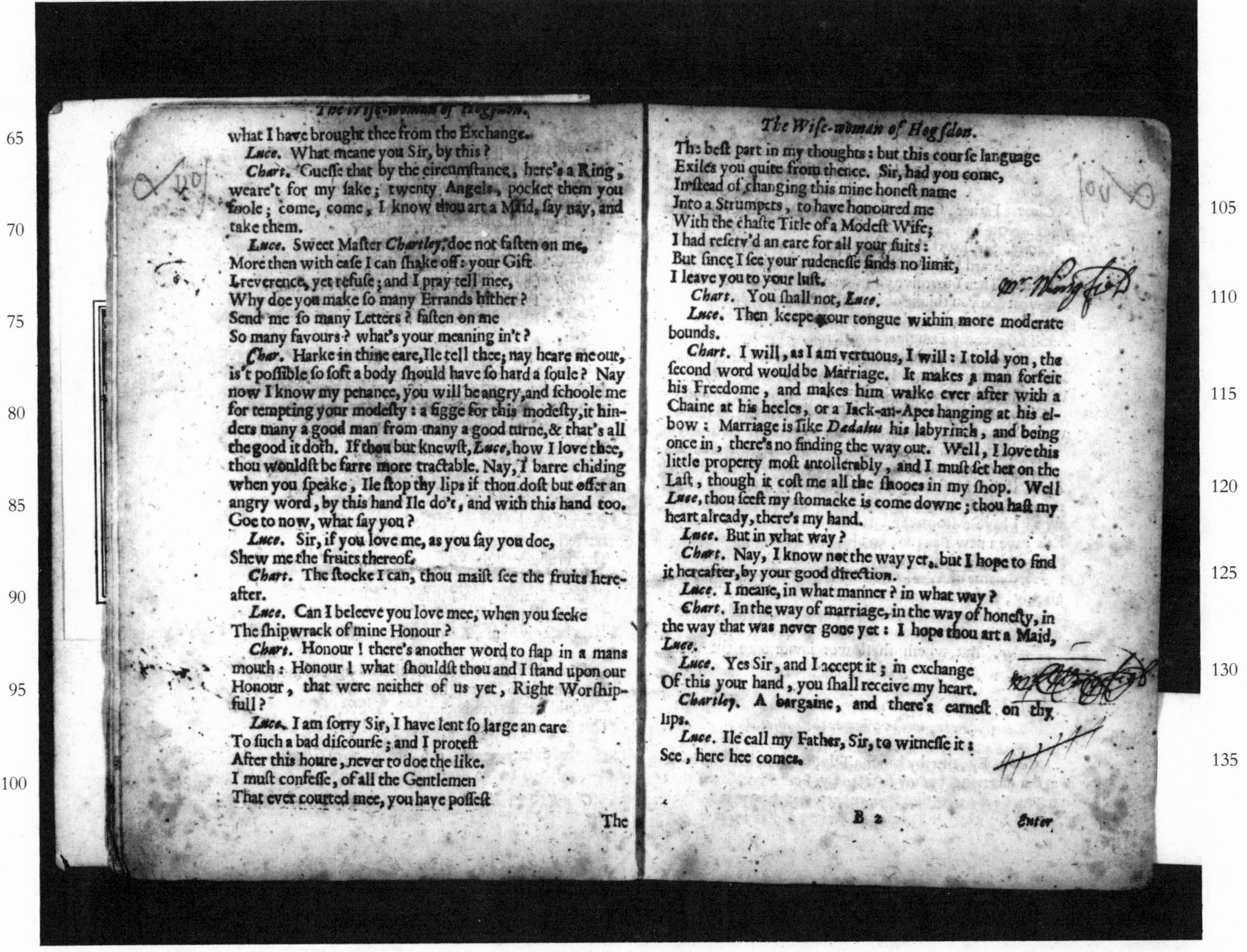

The Wise-woman of Hogsdon.

what I have brought thee from the Exchange.

Luce. What meane you Sir, by this?

Chart. Guesse that by the circumstance, here's a Ring, weare't for my sake; twenty Angels, pocket them you foole; come, come, I know thou art a Maid, say nay, and take them.

Luce. Sweet Master *Chartley*, doe not fasten on me,
More then with ease I can shake off: your Gift
I reverence, yet refuse; and I pray tell mee,
Why doe you make so many Errands hither?
Send me so many Letters? fasten on me
So many favours? what's your meaning in't?

Char. Harke in thine eare, Ile tell thee; nay heare me out, is't possible so soft a body should have so hard a soule? Nay now I know my penance, you will be angry, and schoole me for tempting your modesty: a figge for this modesty, it hinders many a good man from many a good turne, & that's all the good it doth. If thou but knewst, *Luce*, how I love thee, thou wouldst be farre more tractable. Nay, I barre chiding when you speake, Ile stop thy lips if thou dost but offer an angry word, by this hand Ile do't, and with this hand too. Goe to now, what say you?

Luce. Sir, if you love me, as you say you doe,
Shew me the fruits thereof.

Chart. The stocke I can, thou maist see the fruits hereafter.

Luce. Can I beleeve you love mee, when you seeke
The shipwrack of mine Honour?

Chart. Honour! there's another word to flap in a mans mouth: Honour! what shouldst thou and I stand upon our Honour, that were neither of us yet, Right Worshipfull?

Luce. I am sorry Sir, I have lent so large an eare
To such a bad discourse; and I protest
After this houre, never to doe the like.
I must confesse, of all the Gentlemen
That ever courted mee, you have possest

The

The Wise-woman of Hogsdon.

The best part in my thoughts: but this course language
Exiles you quite from thence. Sir, had you come,
Instead of changing this mine honest name
Into a Strumpets, to have honoured me
With the chaste Title of a Modest Wife;
I had reserv'd an eare for all your suits:
But since I see your rudenesse finds no limit,
I leave you to your lust.

Chart. You shall not, *Luce.*

Luce. Then keepe your tongue within more moderate bounds.

Chart. I will, as I am vertuous, I will: I told you, the second word would be Marriage. It makes a man forfeit his Freedome, and makes him walke ever after with a Chaine at his heeles, or a Iack-an-Apes hanging at his elbow: Marriage is like *Dedalus* his labyrinth, and being once in, there's no finding the way out. Well, I love this little property most intollerably, and I must set her on the Last, though it cost me all the shooes in my shop. Well *Luce*, thou seest my stomacke is come downe; thou hast my heart already, there's my hand.

Luce. But in what way?

Chart. Nay, I know not the way yet, but I hope to find it hereafter, by your good direction.

Luce. I meane, in what manner? in what way?

Chart. In the way of marriage, in the way of honesty, in the way that was never gone yet: I hope thou art a Maid, *Luce.*

Luce. Yes Sir, and I accept it; in exchange
Of this your hand, you shall receive my heart.

Charley. A bargaine, and there's earnest on thy lips.

Luce. Ile call my Father, Sir, to witnesse it:
See, here hee comes.

B 2 Enter

I, ii, 67. I cannot decipher the mark in the left margin.

I, ii, 130. The warning for Mr. Wingfield was obviously set too close to his entrance; the prompter crossed it out and moved it to line 109.

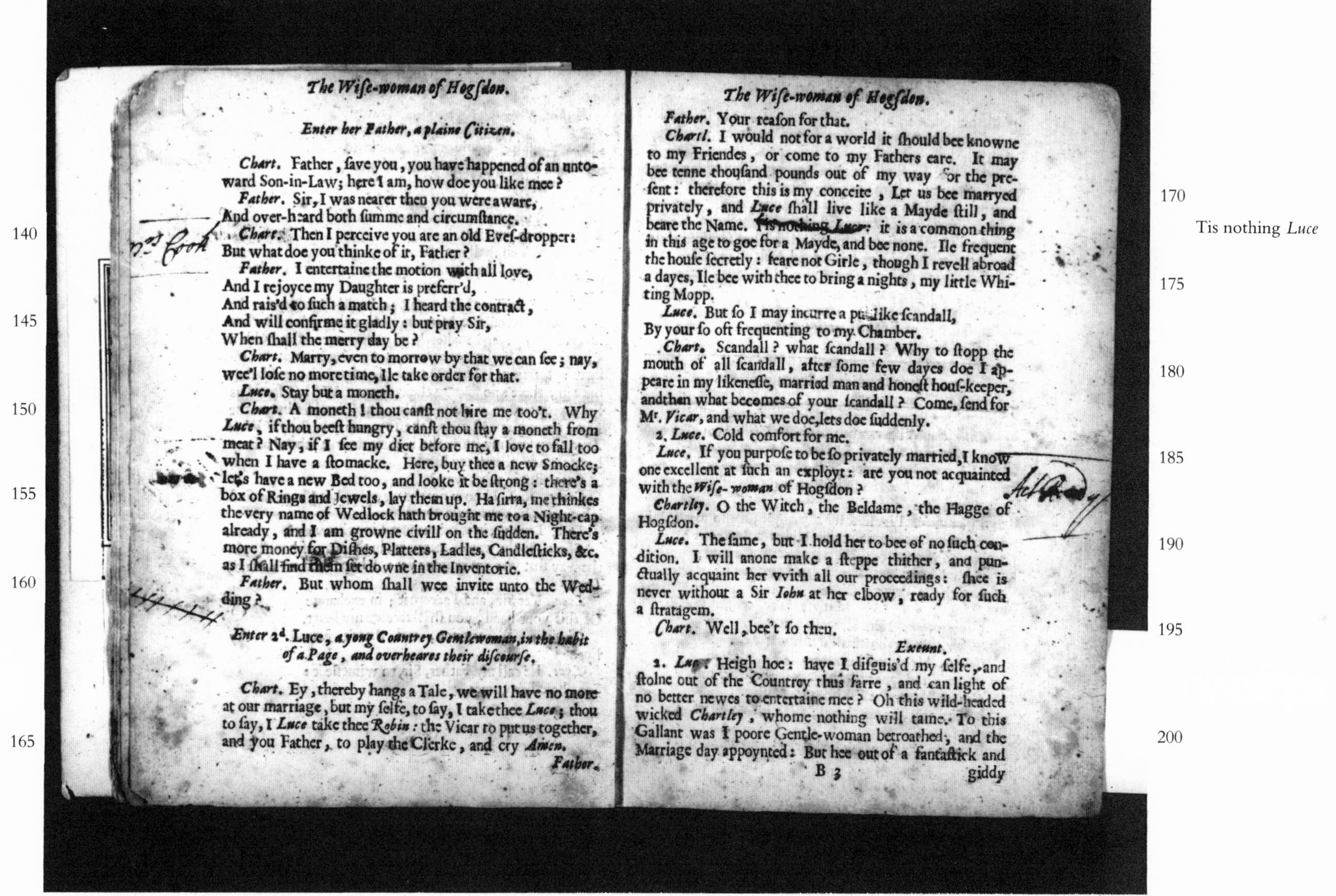

The Wiſe-woman of Hogſdon.

Enter her Father, a plaine Citizen.

Chart. Father, ſave you, you have happened of an untoward Son-in-Law; here I am, how doe you like mee?

Father. Sir, I was nearer then you were aware,
And over-heard both ſumme and circumſtance.

Chart. Then I perceive you are an old Eveſ-dropper:
But what doe you thinke of it, Father?

Father. I entertaine the motion with all love,
And I rejoyce my Daughter is preferr'd,
And rais'd to ſuch a match; I heard the contract,
And will confirme it gladly: but pray Sir,
When ſhall the merry day be?

Chart. Marry, even to morrow by that we can ſee; nay, wee'l loſe no more time, Ile take order for that.

Luce. Stay but a moneth.

Chart. A moneth! thou canſt not hire me too't. Why *Luce*, if thou beeſt hungry, canſt thou ſtay a moneth from meat? Nay, if I ſee my diet before me, I love to fall too when I have a ſtomacke. Here, buy thee a new Smocke; let's have a new Bed too, and looke it be ſtrong: there's a box of Rings and Jewels, lay them up. Ha ſirra, me thinkes the very name of Wedlock hath brought me to a Night-cap already, and I am growne civill on the ſudden. There's more money for Diſhes, Platters, Ladles, Candleſticks, &c. as I ſhall find them ſet downe in the Inventorie.

Father. But whom ſhall wee invite unto the Wedding?

Enter 2d. Luce, a yong Countrey Gentlewoman, in the habit of a Page, and overheares their diſcourſe.

Chart. Ey, thereby hangs a Tale, we will have no more at our marriage, but my ſelfe, to ſay, I take thee *Luce*; thou to ſay, I *Luce* take thee *Robin*: the Vicar to put us together, and you Father, to play the Clerke, and cry *Amen*.

Father.

The Wiſe-woman of Hogſdon.

Father. Your reaſon for that.

Chartl. I would not for a world it ſhould bee knowne to my Friendes, or come to my Fathers eare. It may bee tenne thouſand pounds out of my way for the preſent: therefore this is my conceite, Let us bee marryed privately, and *Luce* ſhall live like a Mayde ſtill, and beare the Name. Tis nothing *Luce*: it is a common thing in this age to goe for a Mayde, and bee none. Ile frequent the houſe ſecretly: feare not Girle, though I revell abroad a dayes, Ile bee with thee to bring a nights, my little Whiting Mopp.

Luce. But ſo I may incurre a publike ſcandall,
By your ſo oft frequenting to my Chamber.

Chart. Scandall? what ſcandall? Why to ſtopp the mouth of all ſcandall, after ſome few dayes doe I appeare in my likeneſſe, married man and honeſt houſ-keeper, and then what becomes of your ſcandall? Come, ſend for Mr. *Vicar*, and what we doe, lets doe ſuddenly.

2\. *Luce.* Cold comfort for me.

Luce. If you purpoſe to be ſo privately married, I know one excellent at ſuch an exployt: are you not acquainted with the *Wiſe-woman* of Hogſdon?

Chartley. O the Witch, the Beldame, the Hagge of Hogſdon.

Luce. The ſame, but I hold her to bee of no ſuch condition. I will anone make a ſteppe thither, and punctually acquaint her vvith all our proceedings: ſhee is never without a Sir *John* at her elbow, ready for ſuch a ſtratagem.

Chart. Well, bee't ſo then.

Exeunt.

2\. *Luce.* Heigh hoe: have I diſguis'd my ſelfe, and ſtolne out of the Countrey thus farre, and can light of no better newes to entertaine mee? Oh this wild-headed wicked *Chartley*, whome nothing will tame. To this Gallant was I poore Gentle-woman betroathed, and the Marriage day appoynted: But hee out of a fantaſtick and

B 3 giddy

Tis nothing *Luce*

Aymes shall bee

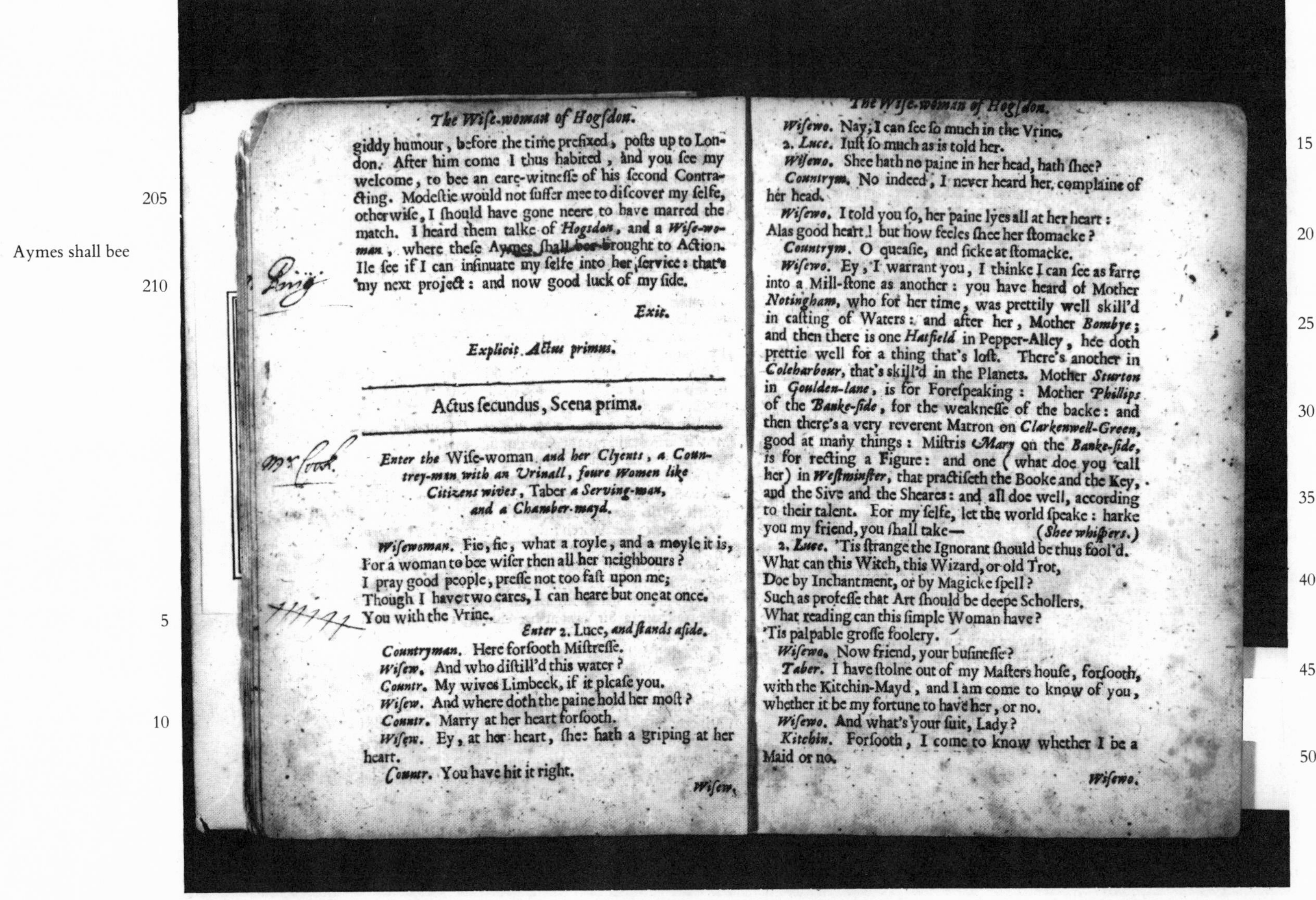

The Wiſe-woman of Hogſdon.

giddy humour, before the time prefixed, poſts up to London. After him come I thus habited, and you ſee my welcome, to bee an eare-witneſſe of his ſecond Contracting. Modeſtie would not ſuffer mee to diſcover my ſelfe, otherwiſe, I ſhould have gone neere to have marred the match. I heard them talke of *Hogsdon*, and a *Wiſe-woman*, where theſe Aymes ſhall bee brought to Action. Ile ſee if I can inſinuate my ſelfe into her ſervice: that's my next project: and now good luck of my ſide.

Exit.

Explicit Actus primus.

Actus ſecundus, Scena prima.

Enter the Wiſe-woman *and her Clyents, a Countrey-man with an Urinall, foure Women like Citizens wives,* Taber *a Serving-man, and a Chamber-mayd.*

Wiſewoman. Fie, fie, what a toyle, and a moyle it is,
For a woman to bee wiſer then all her neighbours?
I pray good people, preſſe not too faſt upon me;
Though I have two eares, I can heare but one at once.
You with the Vrine.

Enter 2. Luce, *and ſtands aſide.*

Countryman. Here forſooth Miſtreſſe.

Wiſew. And who diſtill'd this water?

Countr. My wives Limbeck, if it pleaſe you.

Wiſew. And where doth the paine hold her moſt?

Countr. Marry at her heart forſooth.

Wiſew. Ey, at her heart, ſhe hath a griping at her heart.

Countr. You have hit it right.

Wiſew.

The Wiſe-woman of Hogſdon.

Wiſewo. Nay, I can ſee ſo much in the Vrine.

2. Luce. Iuſt ſo much as is told her.

Wiſewo. Shee hath no paine in her head, hath ſhee?

Countrym. No indeed, I never heard her complaine of her head.

Wiſewo. I told you ſo, her paine lyes all at her heart: Alas good heart! but how feeles ſhee her ſtomacke?

Countrym. O queaſie, and ſicke at ſtomacke.

Wiſewo. Ey, I warrant you, I thinke I can ſee as farre into a Mill-ſtone as another: you have heard of Mother *Notingham*, who for her time, was prettily well skill'd in caſting of Waters: and after her, Mother *Bombye*; and then there is one *Hatfield* in Pepper-Alley, hee doth prettie well for a thing that's loſt. There's another in *Colebarbour*, that's skill'd in the Planets. Mother *Sturton* in *Goulden-lane*, is for Foreſpeaking: Mother *Phillips* of the *Banke-ſide*, for the weakneſſe of the backe: and then there's a very reverent Matron on *Clarkenwell-Green*, good at many things: Miſtris *Mary* on the *Banke-ſide*, is for recting a Figure: and one (what doe you call her) in *Weſtminſter*, that practiſeth the Booke and the Key, and the Sive and the Sheares: and all doe well, according to their talent. For my ſelfe, let the world ſpeake: harke you my friend, you ſhall take— *(Shee whiſpers.)*

2. Luce. 'Tis ſtrange the Ignorant ſhould be thus fool'd.
What can this Witch, this Wizard, or old Trot,
Doe by Inchantment, or by Magicke ſpell?
Such as profeſſe that Art ſhould be deepe Schollers.
What reading can this ſimple Woman have?
'Tis palpable groſſe foolery.

Wiſewo. Now friend, your buſineſſe?

Taber. I have ſtolne out of my Maſters houſe, forſooth, with the Kitchin-Mayd, and I am come to know of you, whether it be my fortune to have her, or no.

Wiſewo. And what's your ſuit, Lady?

Kitchin. Forſooth, I come to know whether I be a Maid or no.

Wiſewo.

II, i, opening. The wives cited here differ somewhat from the descriptions in the dramatis personae.

Wisewo. Why, art thou in doubt of that?

Kitchin. It may bee I have more reason then all the world knowes.

Taber. Nay, if thou com'st to know whether thou beest a Maid or no, I had best aske to know whether I be with child or no.

Wisew. Withdraw into the Parlour there, Ile but talke with this other Gentlewoman, and Ile resolve you presently.

Taber. Come *Sisly*, if shee cannot resolve thee, I can, and in the Case of a Mayden-head doe more then shee, I warrant thee.

Exeunt.

The Wom. Forsooth I am bold, as they say.

Wisew. You are welcome Gentlewoman.—

Wom. I would not have it knowne to my Neighbours, that I come to a Wise-woman for any thing, by my truly.

Wisewom. For should your Husband come and find you here.

Wom. My Husband woman, I am a Widdow.

Wisewom. Where are my braines? 'tis true, you are a Widdow; and you dwell, let me see, I can never remember that place.

Wom. In *Kentstreet.*

Wisewom. Kentstreet, Kentstreet! and I can tell you wherfore you come.

Wom. Why, and say true?

Wisewom. You are a Wagge, you are a Wagge: why, what doe you thinke now I would say?

Wom. Perhaps, to know how many Husbands I should have.

Wisewom. And if I should say so, should I say amisse?

Wom. I thinke you are a Witch.

Wisewom. In, in, Ile but reade a little of *Ptolomie*, and *Erra Pater*; and when I have cast a Figure, Ile come to you presently. *Exit Wom.*

Now

Mr. Disny

Now Wagge, what wouldst thou have?

2. *Luce.* If this were a Wisewoman, shee could tell that without asking. Now me thinkes I should come to know whether I were a Boy or a Girle; forsooth I lacke a service.

Wisewo. By my Fidelitie, and I want a good trusty Lad.

2. *Luce.* Now could I sigh, and say, Alas, this is some Bawd trade-falne, and out of her wicked experience, is come to bee reputed wise. Ile serve her, bee't but to pry into the mysterie of her Science.

Wisewo. A proper stripling, and a wise, I warrant him; here's a penie for thee, Ile hire thee for a yeare by the Statute of *Winchester*: prove true and honest, and thou shalt want nothing that a good Boy—

2. *Luce.* Here Wise-woman you are out againe, I shall want what a good Boy should have, whilst I live: well, here I shall live both unknowne, and my Sex unsuspected. But whom have wee here?

Enter Master ~~*Haringfield, and*~~ Chartley *halfe drunke.* Haringfield, *and*

~~*Chart.* Come *Haringfield*,~~ now wee have beene drinking of Mother Red-caps Ale, let us now goe make some sport with the Wise-woman.

Haring. Wee shall be thought very wise men, of all such as shall see us goe in to the Wise-womans.

Chartley. See, heere shee is; how now Witch? How now Hagge? How now Beldame? You are the Wise-woman, are you? and have wit to keepe your selfe warme enough, I warrant you.

Wisewo. Out thou knave.

2. *Luce.* And will these wild oates never be sowne?

Chart. You Inchantresse, Sorceresse, Shee-devill; you Madam *Hecate*, Lady *Proserpine*, you are too old, you Hagge, now, for conjuring up Spirits your selfe; but you keepe prettie yong Witches under your roofe, that can doe that.

C

Wisew.

Haring. I prethee let's be civill *Chart.*

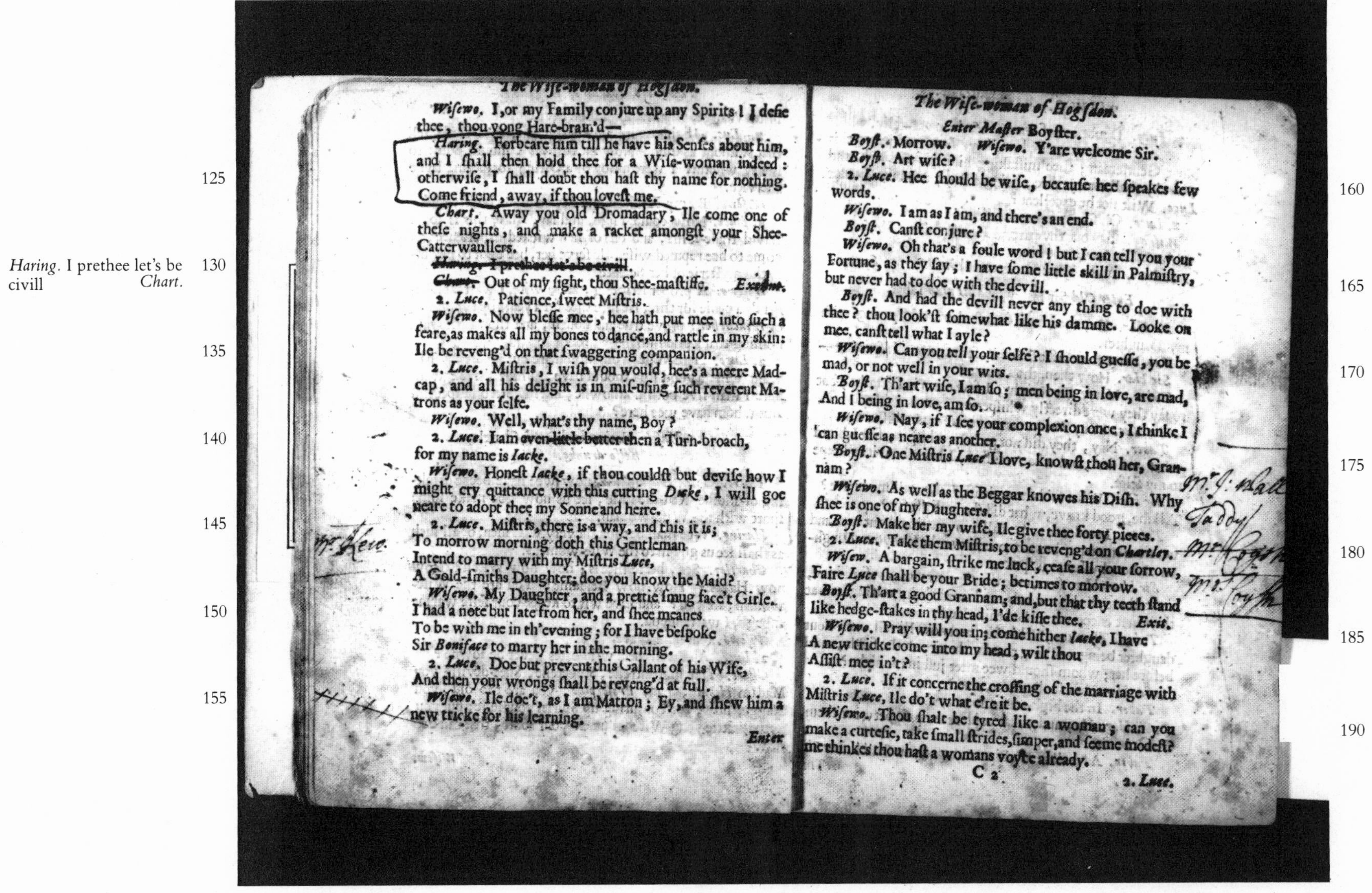

The Wiſe-woman of Hogſdon.

Wiſewo. I,or my Family conjure up any Spirits! I defie thee, thou yong Hare-brain'd—

Haring. Forbeare him till he have his Senſes about him, and I ſhall then hold thee for a Wiſe-woman indeed: otherwiſe, I ſhall doubt thou haſt thy name for nothing. Come friend, away, if thou loveſt me.

Chart. Away you old Dromadary, Ile come one of theſe nights, and make a racket amongſt your Shee-Catterwaullers.

~~*Haring.* I prethee let's be civill.~~

~~*Chart.*~~ Out of my ſight, thou Shee-maſtiffe. *Exeunt.*

2. Luce. Patience, ſweet Miſtris.

Wiſewo. Now bleſſe mee, hee hath put mee into ſuch a feare, as makes all my bones to dance, and rattle in my skin: Ile be reveng'd on that ſwaggering companion.

2. Luce. Miſtris, I wiſh you would, hee's a meere Madcap, and all his delight is in miſ-uſing ſuch reverent Matrons as your ſelfe.

Wiſewo. Well, what's thy name, Boy?

2. Luce. I am ~~even little better~~ then a Turn-broach, for my name is *Iacke.*

Wiſewo. Honeſt *Iacke*, if thou couldſt but deviſe how I might cry quittance with this cutting *Dicke*, I will goe neare to adopt thee my Sonne and heire.

2. Luce. Miſtris, there is a way, and this it is;
To morrow morning doth this Gentleman
Intend to marry with my Miſtris *Luce*,
A Gold-ſmiths Daughter; doe you know the Maid?

Wiſewo. My Daughter, and a prettie ſmug fac't Girle.
I had a note but late from her, and ſhee meanes
To be with me in th'evening; for I have beſpoke
Sir *Boniface* to marry her in the morning.

2. Luce. Doe but prevent this Gallant of his Wife,
And then your wrongs ſhall be reveng'd at full.

Wiſewo. Ile doe't, as I am Matron; Ey, and ſhew him a new tricke for his learning.

Enter

The Wiſe-woman of Hogſdon.

Enter Maſter Boyſter.

Boyſt. Morrow. *Wiſewo.* Y'are welcome Sir.

Boyſt. Art wiſe?

2. Luce. Hee ſhould be wiſe, becauſe hee ſpeakes few words.

Wiſewo. I am as I am, and there's an end.

Boyſt. Canſt conjure?

Wiſewo. Oh that's a foule word! but I can tell you your Fortune, as they ſay; I have ſome little skill in Palmiſtry, but never had to doe with the devill.

Boyſt. And had the devill never any thing to doe with thee? thou look'ſt ſomewhat like his damme. Looke on mee, canſt tell what I ayle?

Wiſewo. Can you tell your ſelfe? I ſhould gueſſe, you be mad, or not well in your wits.

Boyſt. Th'art wiſe, I am ſo; men being in love, are mad, And I being in love, am ſo.

Wiſewo. Nay, if I ſee your complexion once, I thinke I can gueſſe as neare as another.

Boyſt. One Miſtris *Luce* I love, knowſt thou her, Grannam?

Wiſewo. As well as the Beggar knowes his Diſh. Why ſhee is one of my Daughters.

Boyſt. Make her my wife, Ile give thee forty pieces.

2. Luce. Take them Miſtris, to be reveng'd on *Chartley*.

Wiſew. A bargain, ſtrike me luck, ceaſe all your ſorrow, Faire *Luce* ſhall be your Bride; betimes to morrow.

Boyſt. Th'art a good Grannam; and, but that thy teeth ſtand like hedge-ſtakes in thy head, I'de kiſſe thee. *Exit.*

Wiſewo. Pray will you in; come hither *Iacke*, I have
A new tricke come into my head, wilt thou
Aſſiſt mee in't?

2. Luce. If it concerne the croſſing of the marriage with Miſtris *Luce*, Ile do't what e're it be.

Wiſewo. Thou ſhalt be tyred like a woman; can you make a curteſie, take ſmall ſtrides, ſimper, and ſeeme modeſt? me thinkes thou haſt a womans voyce already.

C 2 *2. Luce.*

II, i, 175. Why the names of Mr. and Mrs. Coysh were canceled in this warning is not clear, since Sencer and Gratiana have an entrance following line 240.

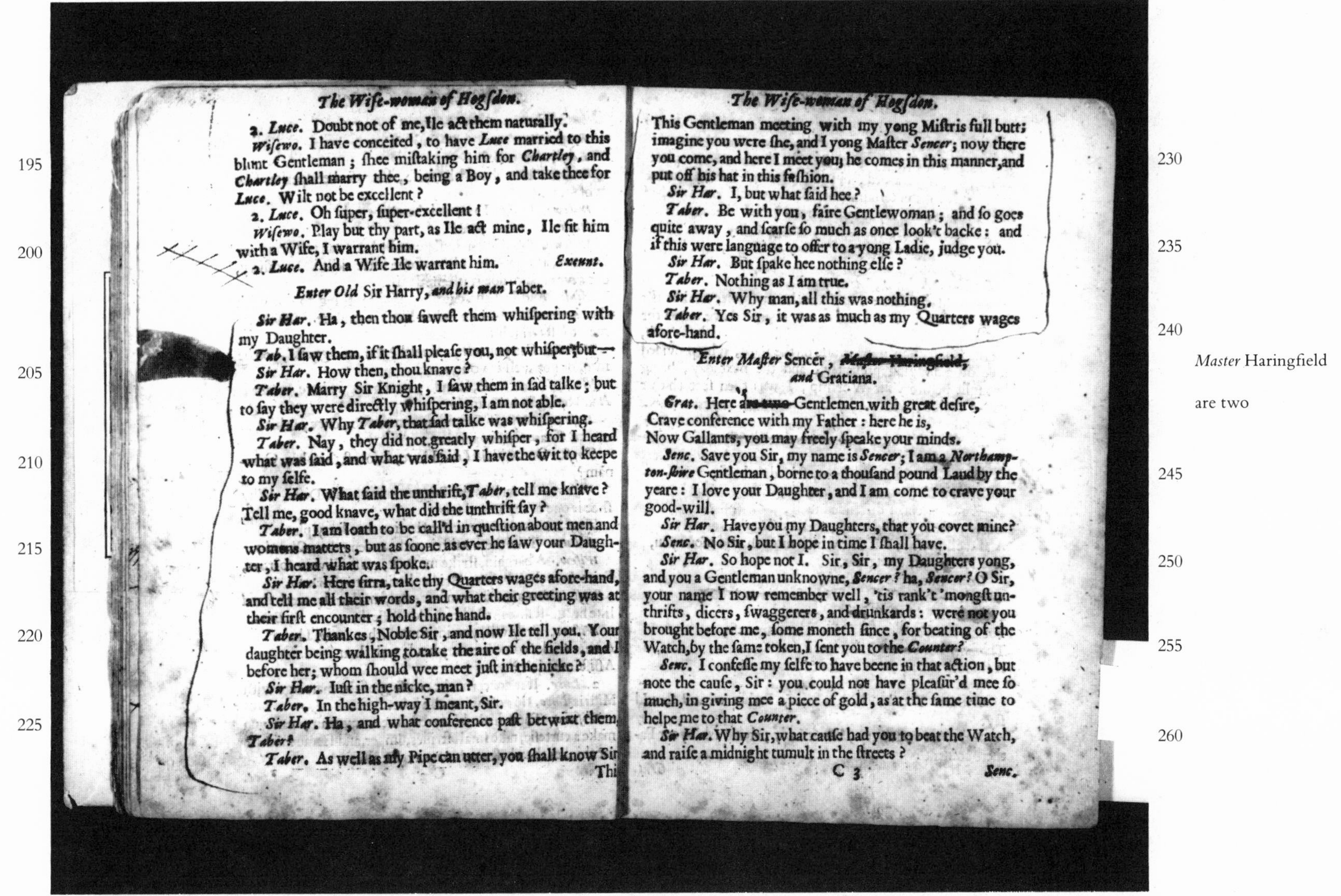

2. *Luce.* Doubt not of me, Ile act them naturally.

Wiſewo. I have conceited, to have *Luce* married to this blunt Gentleman; ſhee miſtaking him for *Chartley*, and *Chartley* ſhall marry thee, being a Boy, and take thee for *Luce*. Wilt not be excellent?

2. *Luce.* Oh ſuper, ſuper-excellent!

Wiſewo. Play but thy part, as Ile act mine, Ile fit him with a Wife, I warrant him.

2. *Luce.* And a Wife Ile warrant him. *Exeunt.*

Enter Old Sir Harry, *and his man* Taber.

Sir Har. Ha, then thou ſaweſt them whiſpering with my Daughter.

Tab. I ſaw them, if it ſhall pleaſe you, not whiſper; but—

Sir Har. How then, thou knave?

Taber. Marry Sir Knight, I ſaw them in ſad talke; but to ſay they were directly whiſpering, I am not able.

Sir Har. Why *Taber*, that ſad talke was whiſpering.

Taber. Nay, they did not greatly whiſper, for I heard what was ſaid, and what was ſaid, I have the wit to keepe to my ſelfe.

Sir Har. What ſaid the unthrift, *Taber*, tell me knave?
Tell me, good knave, what did the unthrift ſay?

Taber. I am loath to be call'd in queſtion about men and womens matters, but as ſoone as ever he ſaw your Daughter, I heard what was ſpoke.

Sir Har. Here ſirra, take thy Quarters wages afore-hand, and tell me all their words, and what their greeting was at their firſt encounter; hold thine hand.

Taber. Thankes, Noble Sir, and now Ile tell you. Your daughter being walking to take the aire of the fields, and I before her; whom ſhould wee meet juſt in the nicke?

Sir Har. Iuſt in the nicke, man?

Taber. In the high-way I meant, Sir.

Sir Har. Ha, and what conference paſt betwixt them, *Taber*?

Taber. As well as my Pipe can utter, you ſhall know Sir

Thi-

This Gentleman meeting with my yong Miſtris full butt; imagine you were ſhe, and I yong Maſter *Sencer*; now there you come, and here I meet you; he comes in this manner, and put off his hat in this faſhion.

Sir Har. I, but what ſaid hee?

Taber. Be with you, faire Gentlewoman; and ſo goes quite away, and ſcarſe ſo much as once look't backe: and if this were language to offer to a yong Ladie, judge you.

Sir Har. But ſpake hee nothing elſe?

Taber. Nothing as I am true.

Sir Har. Why man, all this was nothing.

Taber. Yes Sir, it was as much as my Quarters wages afore-hand.

Enter Maſter Sencer, *and* Gratiana.

Master Haringfield

Grat. Here's Gentlemen with great deſire,
Crave conference with my Father: here he is,
Now Gallants, you may freely ſpeake your minds.

are two

Senc. Save you Sir, my name is *Sencer*; I am a *Northampton-ſhire* Gentleman, borne to a thouſand pound Land by the yeare: I love your Daughter, and I am come to crave your good-will.

Sir Har. Have you my Daughters, that you covet mine?

Senc. No Sir, but I hope in time I ſhall have.

Sir Har. So hope not I. Sir, Sir, my Daughters yong, and you a Gentleman unknowne, *Sencer*? ha, *Sencer*? O Sir, your name I now remember well, 'tis rank't 'mongſt unthrifts, dicers, ſwaggerers, and drunkards: were not you brought before me, ſome moneth ſince, for beating of the Watch, by the ſame token, I ſent you to the *Counter*?

Senc. I confeſſe my ſelfe to have beene in that action, but note the cauſe, Sir: you could not have pleaſur'd mee ſo much, in giving mee a piece of gold, as at the ſame time to helpe me to that *Counter*.

Sir Har. Why Sir, what cauſe had you to beat the Watch, and raiſe a midnight tumult in the ſtreets?

Gallant! is that Gentleman too? *Haring.*

best, sooner . . . this

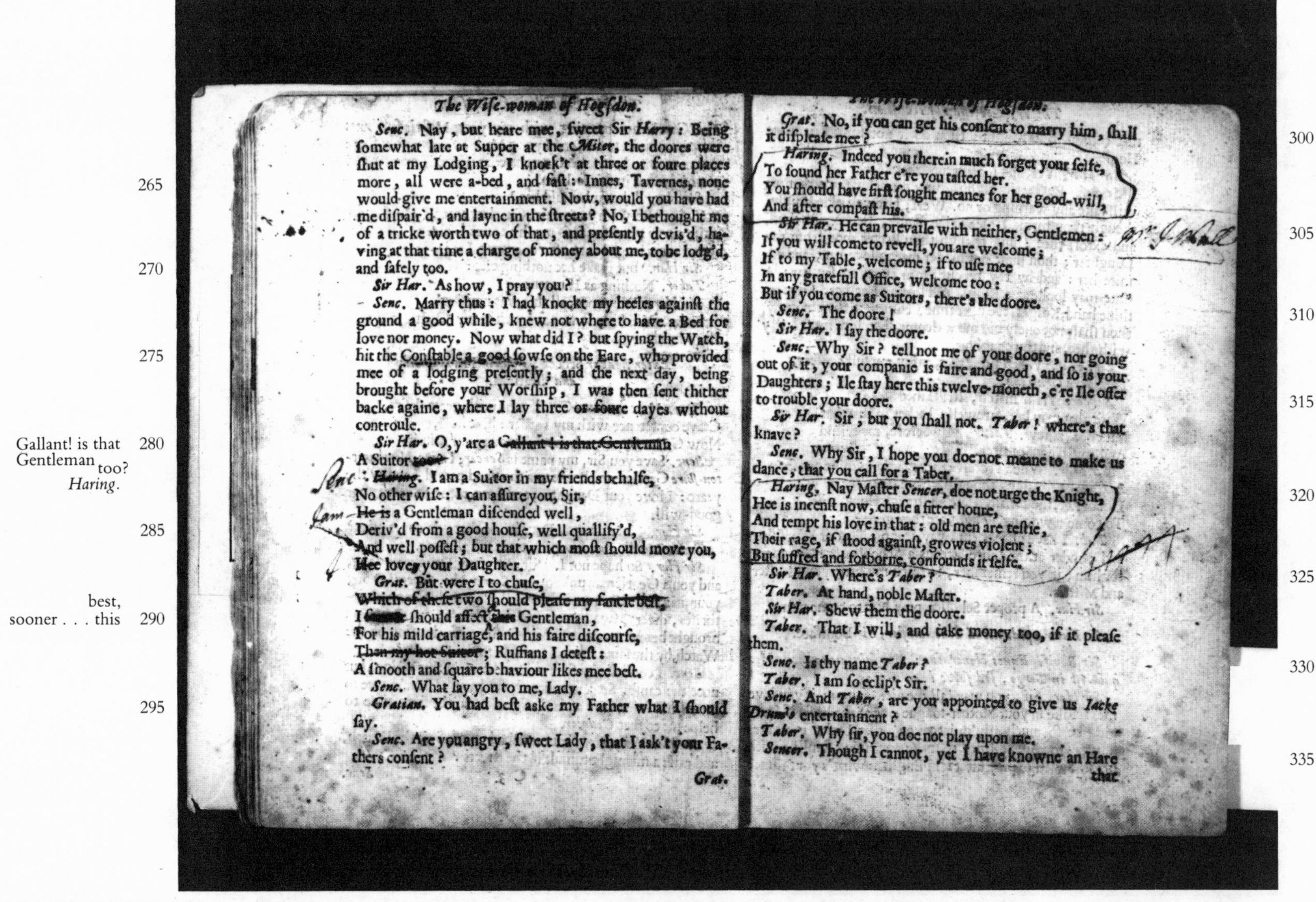

The Wiſe-woman of Hogſdon.

Senc. Nay, but heare mee, ſweet Sir *Harry*: Being ſomewhat late at Supper at the *Miter*, the doores were ſhut at my Lodging, I knock't at three or foure places more, all were a-bed, and faſt: Innes, Tavernes, none would give me entertainment. Now, would you have had me diſpair'd, and layne in the ſtreets? No, I bethought me of a tricke worth two of that, and preſently deviſ'd, having at that time a charge of money about me, to be lodg'd, and ſafely too.

Sir Har. As how, I pray you?

Senc. Marry thus: I had knockt my heeles againſt the ground a good while, knew not where to have a Bed for love nor money. Now what did I? but ſpying the Watch, hit the Conſtable a good ſowſe on the Eare, who provided mee of a lodging preſently; and the next day, being brought before your Worſhip, I was then ſent thither backe againe, where I lay three or foure dayes without controule.

Sir Har. O, y'are a Gallant! is that Gentleman
A Suitor too?

Haring. I am a Suitor in my friends behalfe,
No other wiſe: I can aſſure you, Sir,
He is a Gentleman diſcended well,
Deriv'd from a good houſe, well quallify'd,
And well poſſeſt; but that which moſt ſhould move you,
Hee loves your Daughter.

Grat. But were I to chuſe,
Which of theſe two ſhould pleaſe my fancie beſt,
I ſhould affect this Gentleman,
For his mild carriage, and his faire diſcourſe,
Than my hot Suitor; Ruffians I deteſt:
A ſmooth and ſquare behaviour likes mee beſt.

Senc. What ſay you to me, Lady.

Gratian. You had beſt aske my Father what I ſhould ſay.

Senc. Are you angry, ſweet Lady, that I ask't your Fathers conſent?

Grat.

The Wiſe-woman of Hogſdon.

Grat. No, if you can get his conſent to marry him, ſhall it diſpleaſe mee?

Haring. Indeed you therein much forget your ſelfe,
To ſound her Father e're you taſted her.
You ſhould have firſt ſought meanes for her good-will,
And after compaſt his.

Sir Har. He can prevaile with neither, Gentlemen:
If you will come to revell, you are welcome;
If to my Table, welcome; if to uſe mee
In any gratefull Office, welcome too:
But if you come as Suitors, there's the doore.

Senc. The doore!

Sir Har. I ſay the doore.

Senc. Why Sir? tell not me of your doore, nor going out of it, your companie is faire and good, and ſo is your Daughters; Ile ſtay here this twelve-moneth, e're Ile offer to trouble your doore.

Sir Har. Sir, but you ſhall not. *Taber!* where's that knave?

Senc. Why Sir, I hope you doe not meane to make us dance, that you call for a Taber.

Haring. Nay Maſter *Sencer*, doe not urge the Knight,
Hee is incenſt now, chuſe a fitter houre,
And tempt his love in that: old men are teſtie,
Their rage, if ſtood againſt, growes violent;
But ſuffred and forborne, confounds it ſelfe.

Sir Har. Where's *Taber*?

Taber. At hand, noble Maſter.

Sir Har. Shew them the doore.

Taber. That I will, and take money too, if it pleaſe them.

Senc. Is thy name *Taber*?

Taber. I am ſo eclip't Sir.

Senc. And *Taber*, are you appointed to give us *Iacke Drum's* entertainment?

Taber. Why ſir, you doe not play upon me.

Sencer. Though I cannot, yet I have knowne an Hare

that

II, i, 325. There should be a stage direction here to bring on Taber; the prompter caught the error and supplied an entrance cue.

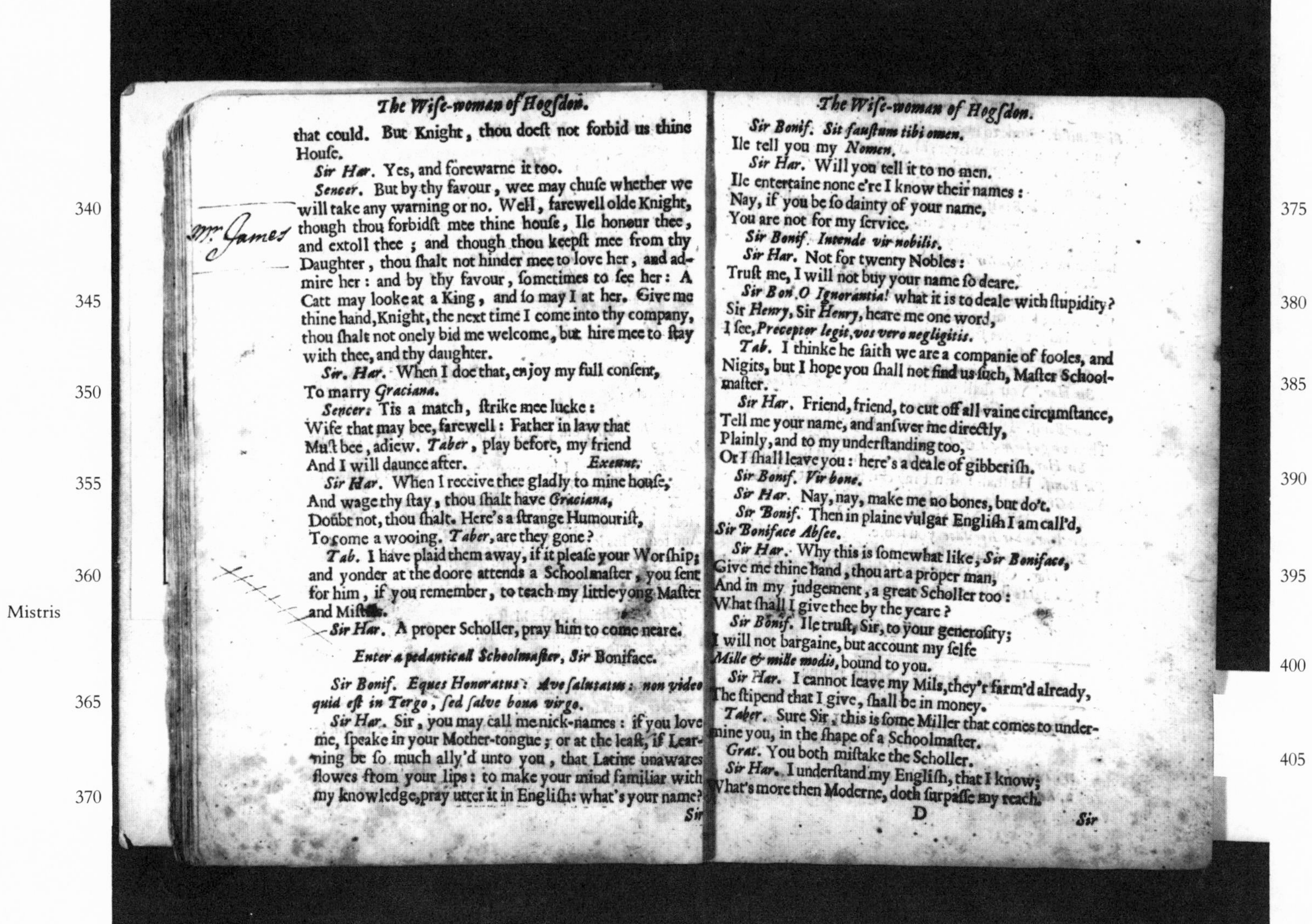

that could. But Knight, thou doest not forbid us thine Houſe.

Sir Har. Yes, and forewarne it too.

Sencer. But by thy favour, wee may chuſe whether we will take any warning or no. Well, farewell olde Knight, though thou forbidſt mee thine houſe, Ile honour thee, and extoll thee; and though thou keepſt mee from thy Daughter, thou ſhalt not hinder mee to love her, and admire her: and by thy favour, ſometimes to ſee her: A Catt may looke at a King, and ſo may I at her. Give me thine hand, Knight, the next time I come into thy company, thou ſhalt not onely bid me welcome, but hire mee to ſtay with thee, and thy daughter.

Sir. Har. When I doe that, enjoy my full conſent,
To marry *Graciana.*

Sencer: Tis a match, ſtrike mee lucke:
Wife that may bee, farewell: Father in law that
Muſt bee, adiew. *Taber*, play before, my friend
And I will daunce after. *Exeunt.*

Sir Har. When I receive thee gladly to mine houſe,
And wage thy ſtay, thou ſhalt have *Graciana,*
Doubt not, thou ſhalt. Here's a ſtrange Humouriſt,
To come a wooing. *Taber*, are they gone?

Tab. I have plaid them away, if it pleaſe your Worſhip; and yonder at the doore attends a Schoolmaſter, you ſent for him, if you remember, to teach my little yong Maſter and Miſt[...].

Mistris

Sir Har. A proper Scholler, pray him to come neare.

Enter a pedanticall Schoolmaſter, Sir Boniface.

Sir Bonif. Eques Honoratus: Ave ſalutatus: non video quid eſt in Tergo, ſed ſalve bona virgo.

Sir Har. Sir, you may call me nick-names: if you love me, ſpeake in your Mother-tongue; or at the leaſt, if Learning be ſo much ally'd unto you, that Latine unawares flowes from your lips: to make your mind familiar with my knowledge, pray utter it in Engliſh: what's your name?

Sir Bonif. Sit fauſtum tibi omen.
Ile tell you my *Nomen.*

Sir Har. Will you tell it to no men.
Ile entertaine none e're I know their names:
Nay, if you be ſo dainty of your name,
You are not for my ſervice.

Sir Bonif. Intende vir nobilis.

Sir Har. Not for twenty Nobles:
Truſt me, I will not buy your name ſo deare.

Sir Bon. O Ignorantia! what it is to deale with ſtupidity?
Sir *Henry*, Sir *Henry*, heare me one word,
I ſee, *Preceptor legit, vos vero negligitis.*

Tab. I thinke he ſaith we are a companie of fooles, and Nigits, but I hope you ſhall not find us ſuch, Maſter Schoolmaſter.

Sir Har. Friend, friend, to cut off all vaine circumſtance,
Tell me your name, and anſwer me directly,
Plainly, and to my underſtanding too,
Or I ſhall leave you: here's a deale of gibberiſh.

Sir Bonif. Vir bone.

Sir Har. Nay, nay, make me no bones, but do't.

Sir Bonif. Then in plaine vulgar Engliſh I am call'd,
Sir Boniface Abſee.

Sir Har. Why this is ſomewhat like, *Sir Boniface,*
Give me thine hand, thou art a proper man,
And in my judgement, a great Scholler too:
What ſhall I give thee by the yeare?

Sir Bonif. Ile truſt, Sir, to your generoſity;
I will not bargaine, but account my ſelfe
Mille & mille modis, bound to you.

Sir Har. I cannot leave my Mils, they'r farm'd already,
The ſtipend that I give, ſhall be in money.

Taber. Sure Sir, this is ſome Miller that comes to undermine you, in the ſhape of a Schoolmaſter.

Grat. You both miſtake the Scholler.

Sir Har. I underſtand my Engliſh, that I know;
What's more then Moderne, doth ſurpaſſe my reach.

D

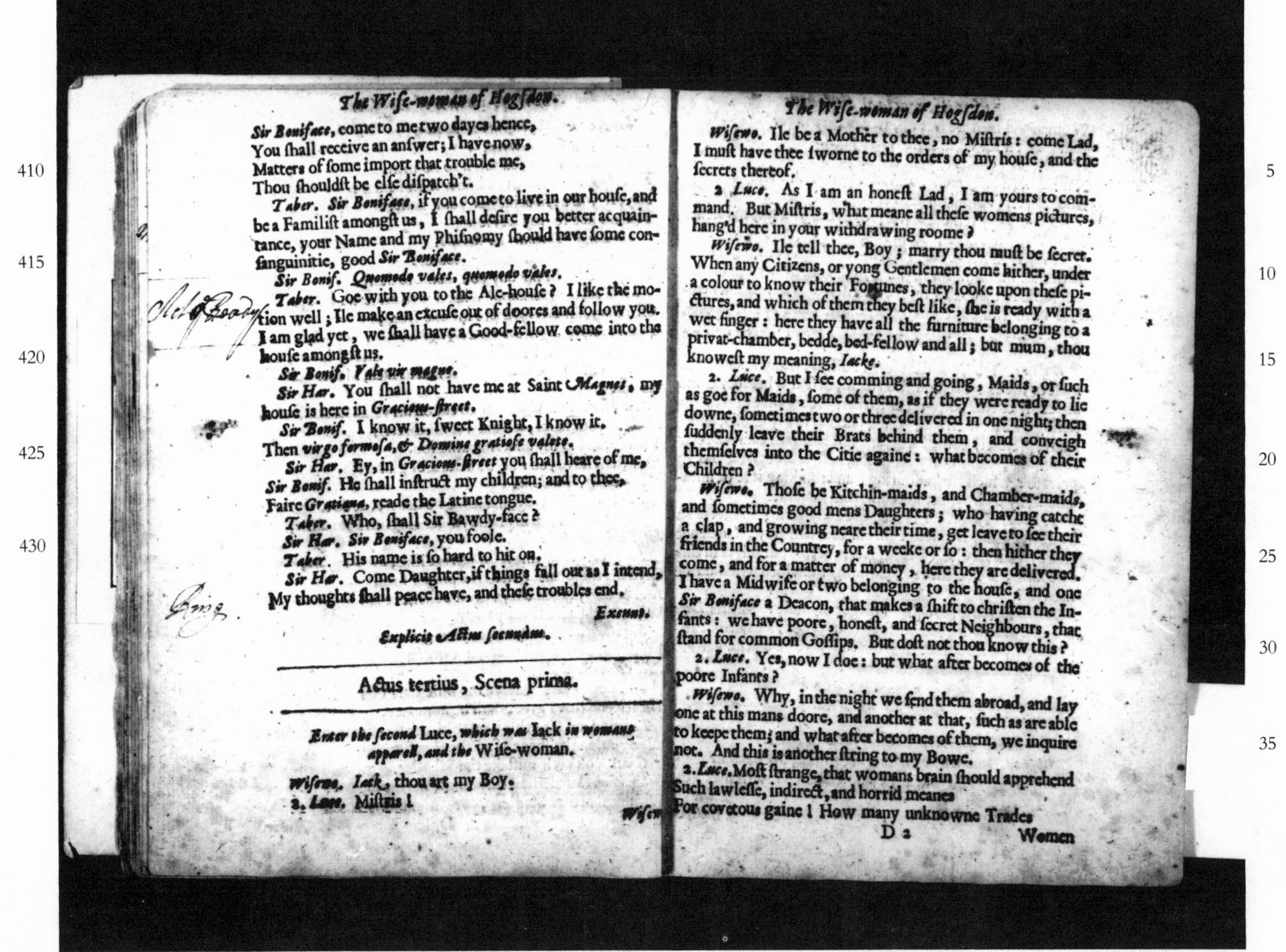

The Wise-woman of Hogsdon.

Sir Boniface, come to me two dayes hence,
You ſhall receive an anſwer; I have now,
Matters of ſome import that trouble me,
Thou ſhouldſt be elſe diſpatch't.

Taber. *Sir Boniface*, if you come to live in our houſe, and be a Familiſt amongſt us, I ſhall deſire you better acquaintance, your Name and my Phiſnomy ſhould have ſome conſanguinitie, good *Sir Boniface*.

Sir Bonif. *Quomodo vales, quomodo vales.*

Taber. Goe with you to the Ale-houſe? I like the motion well; Ile make an excuſe out of doores and follow you. I am glad yet, we ſhall have a Good-fellow come into the houſe amongſt us.

Sir Bonif. *Vale vir magne.*

Sir Har. You ſhall not have me at Saint *Magnes*, my houſe is here in *Gracious-ſtreet*.

Sir Bonif. I know it, ſweet Knight, I know it.
Then *virgo formoſa, & Domine gratioſe valete.*

Sir Har. Ey, in *Gracious-ſtreet* you ſhall heare of me,

Sir Bonif. He ſhall inſtruct my children; and to thee,
Faire *Gratiana*, reade the Latine tongue.

Taber. Who, ſhall Sir Bawdy-face?

Sir Har. *Sir Boniface*, you foole.

Taber. His name is ſo hard to hit on.

Sir Har. Come Daughter, if things fall out as I intend,
My thoughts ſhall peace have, and theſe troubles end.

Exeunt.

Explicit Actus ſecundus.

Actus tertius, Scena prima.

Enter the ſecond Luce, *which was* Iack *in womans apparell, and the* Wiſe-woman.

Wiſewo. *Iack*, thou art my Boy.

2. Luce. Miſtris!

Wiſew

The Wiſe-woman of Hogſdon.

Wiſewo. Ile be a Mother to thee, no Miſtris: come Lad, I muſt have thee ſworne to the orders of my houſe, and the ſecrets thereof.

2 Luce. As I am an honeſt Lad, I am yours to command. But Miſtris, what meane all theſe womens pictures, hang'd here in your withdrawing roome?

Wiſewo. Ile tell thee, Boy; marry thou muſt be ſecret. When any Citizens, or yong Gentlemen come hither, under a colour to know their Fortunes, they looke upon theſe pictures, and which of them they beſt like, ſhe is ready with a wet finger: here they have all the furniture belonging to a privat-chamber, bedde, bed-fellow and all; but mum, thou knoweſt my meaning, *Iacke*.

2. Luce. But I ſee comming and going, Maids, or ſuch as goe for Maids, ſome of them, as if they were ready to lie downe, ſometimes two or three delivered in one night; then ſuddenly leave their Brats behind them, and conveigh themſelves into the Citie againe: what becomes of their Children?

Wiſewo. Thoſe be Kitchin-maids, and Chamber-maids, and ſometimes good mens Daughters; who having catche a clap, and growing neare their time, get leave to ſee their friends in the Countrey, for a weeke or ſo: then hither they come, and for a matter of money, here they are delivered. I have a Midwife or two belonging to the houſe, and one *Sir Boniface* a Deacon, that makes a ſhift to chriſten the Infants: we have poore, honeſt, and ſecret Neighbours, that ſtand for common Goſſips. But doſt not thou know this?

2. Luce. Yes, now I doe: but what after becomes of the poore Infants?

Wiſewo. Why, in the night we ſend them abroad, and lay one at this mans doore, and another at that, ſuch as are able to keepe them; and what after becomes of them, we inquire not. And this is another ſtring to my Bowe.

2. Luce. Moſt ſtrange, that womans brain ſhould apprehend
Such lawleſſe, indirect, and horrid meanes
For covetous gaine! How many unknowne Trades

D 2 Women

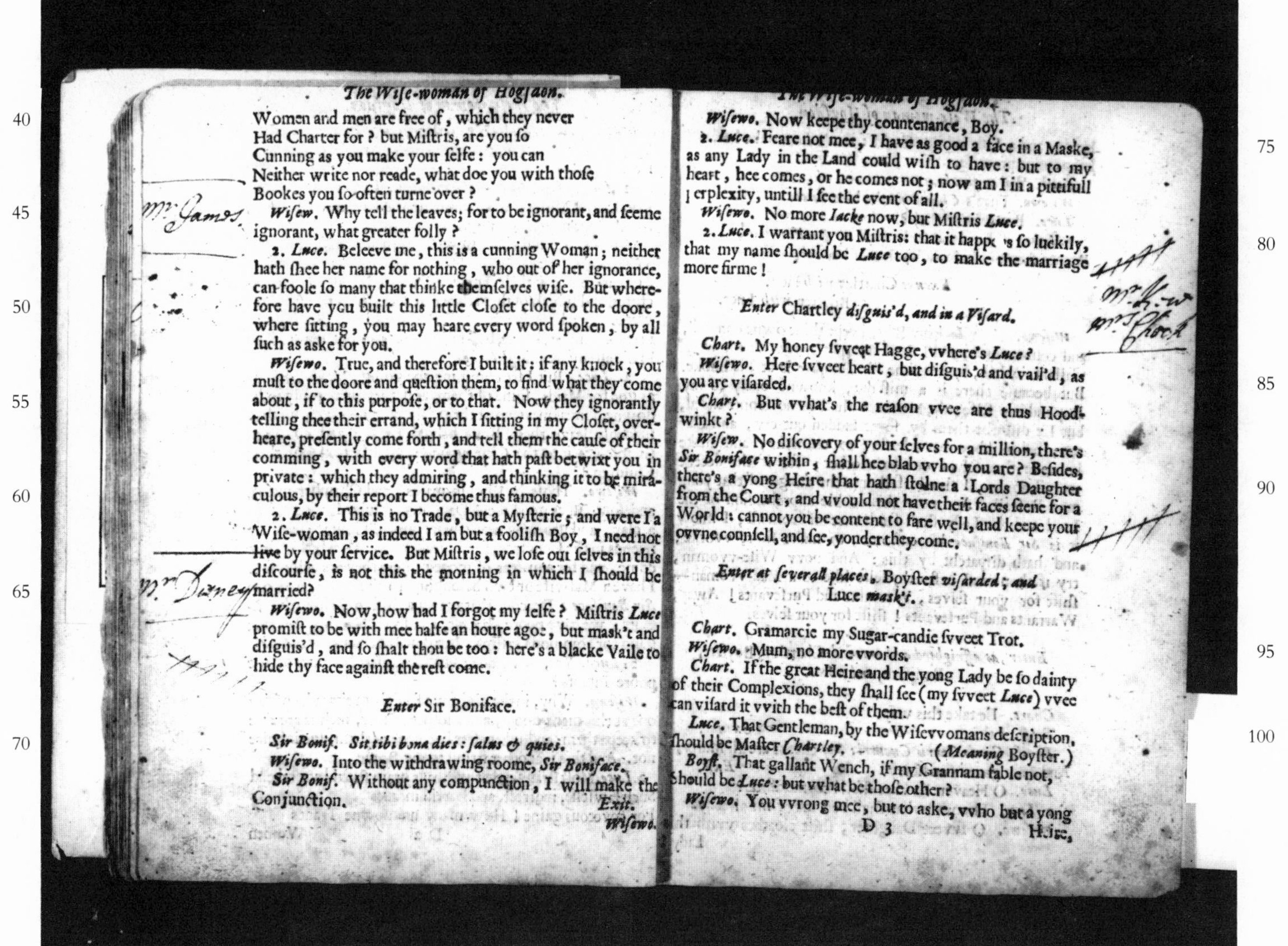

The Wise-woman of Hogsdon.

Women and men are free of, which they never
Had Charter for? but Mistris, are you so
Cunning as you make your selfe: you can
Neither write nor reade, what doe you with those
Bookes you so often turne over?

Wisew. Why tell the leaves; for to be ignorant, and seeme ignorant, what greater folly?

2. *Luce.* Beleeve me, this is a cunning Woman; neither hath shee her name for nothing, who out of her ignorance, can foole so many that thinke themselves wise. But wherefore have you built this little Closet close to the doore, where sitting, you may heare every word spoken, by all such as aske for you.

Wisewo. True, and therefore I built it; if any knock, you must to the doore and question them, to find what they come about, if to this purpose, or to that. Now they ignorantly telling thee their errand, which I sitting in my Closet, overheare, presently come forth, and tell them the cause of their comming, with every word that hath past betwixt you in private: which they admiring, and thinking it to be miraculous, by their report I become thus famous.

2. *Luce.* This is no Trade, but a Mysterie; and were I a Wise-woman, as indeed I am but a foolish Boy, I need not live by your service. But Mistris, we lose our selves in this discourse, is not this the morning in which I should be married?

Wisewo. Now, how had I forgot my selfe? Mistris *Luce* promist to be with mee halfe an houre agoe, but mask't and disguis'd, and so shalt thou be too: here's a blacke Vaile to hide thy face against the rest come.

Enter Sir Boniface.

Sir Bonif. *Sit tibi bona dies: salus & quies.*

Wisewo. Into the withdrawing roome, *Sir Boniface*.

Sir Bonif. Without any compunction, I will make the Conjunction. *Exit.*

Wisewo.

The Wise-woman of Hogsdon.

Wisewo. Now keepe thy countenance, Boy.

2. *Luce.* Feare not mee, I have as good a face in a Maske, as any Lady in the Land could wish to have: but to my heart, hee comes, or he comes not; now am I in a pittifull perplexity, untill I see the event of all.

Wisewo. No more *Iacke* now, but Mistris *Luce*.

2. *Luce.* I warrant you Mistris: that it happens so luckily, that my name should be *Luce* too, to make the marriage more firme!

Enter Chartley *disguis'd, and in a Visard.*

Chart. My honey swveet Hagge, vvhere's *Luce*?

Wisewo. Here svveet heart, but disguis'd and vail'd, as you are visarded.

Chart. But vvhat's the reason vvee are thus Hoodwinkt?

Wisew. No discovery of your selves for a million, there's *Sir Boniface* within, shall hee blab vvho you are? Besides, there's a yong Heire that hath stolne a Lords Daughter from the Court, and vvould not have their faces seene for a World: cannot you be content to fare well, and keepe your ovvne counsell, and see, yonder they come.

Enter at severall places, Boyster *visarded; and* Luce *mask't.*

Chart. Gramarcie my Sugar-candie svveet Trot.

Wisewo. Mum, no more vvords.

Chart. If the great Heire and the yong Lady be so dainty of their Complexions, they shall see (my svveet *Luce*) vvee can visard it vvith the best of them.

Luce. That Gentleman, by the Wisevvomans description, should be Master *Chartley*. (*Meaning* Boyster.)

Boyst. That gallant Wench, if my Grannam fable not, should be *Luce*: but vvhat be those other?

Wisewo. You vvrong mee, but to aske, vvho but a yong

D 3 Heire,

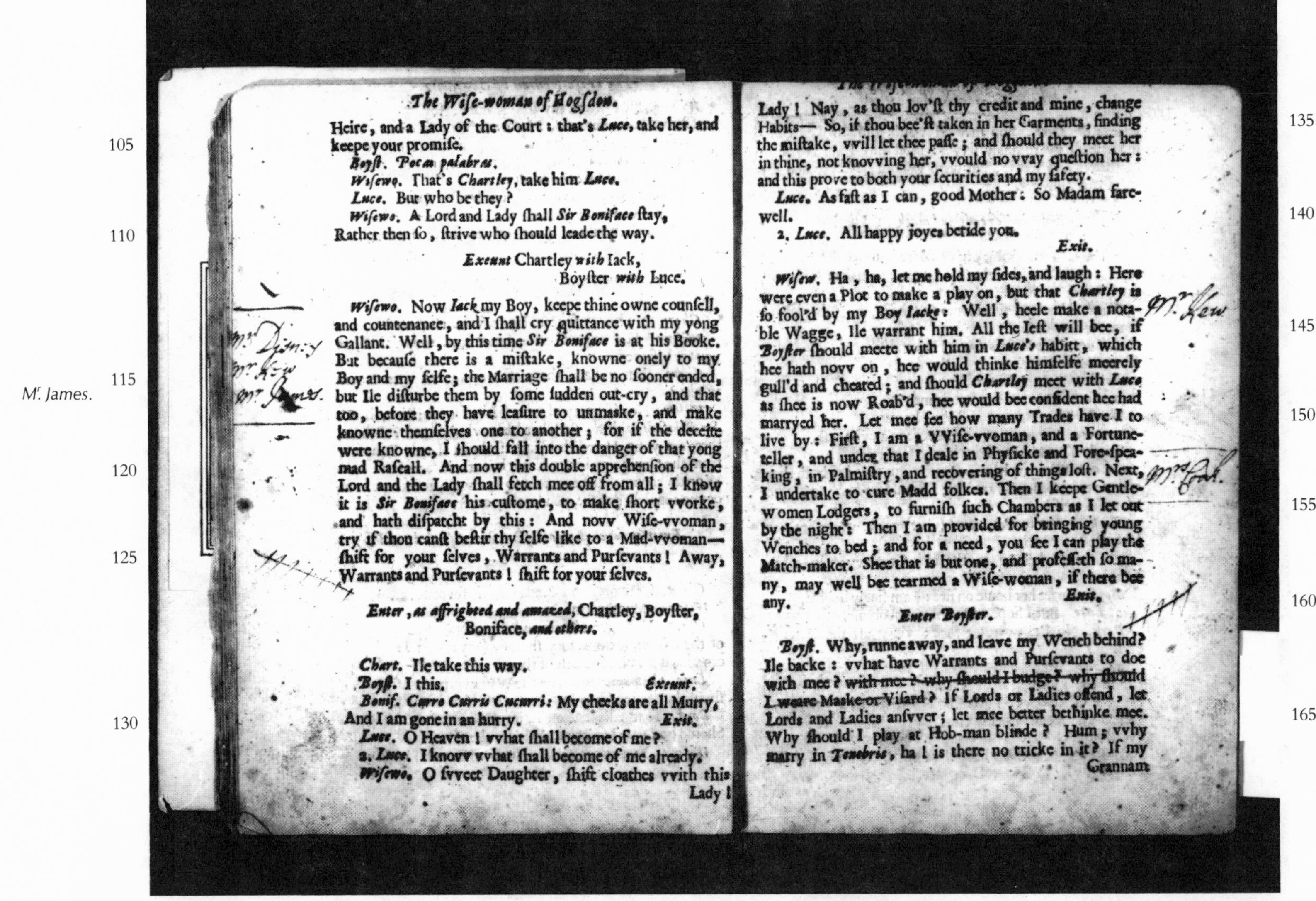

The Wiſe-woman of Hogſdon.

Heire, and a Lady of the Court: that's *Luce*, take her, and keepe your promiſe.

Boyſt. *Poca palabras.*

Wiſewo. That's *Chartley*, take him *Luce.*

Luce. But who be they?

Wiſewo. A Lord and Lady ſhall *Sir Boniface* ſtay,
Rather then ſo, ſtrive who ſhould leade the way.

Exeunt Chartley *with* Iack, Boyſter *with* Luce.

Mr. James.

Wiſewo. Now *Iack* my Boy, keepe thine owne counſell, and countenance, and I ſhall cry quittance with my yong Gallant. Well, by this time *Sir Boniface* is at his Booke. But becauſe there is a miſtake, knowne onely to my Boy and my ſelfe; the Marriage ſhall be no ſooner ended, but Ile diſturbe them by ſome ſudden out-cry, and that too, before they have leaſure to unmaske, and make knowne themſelves one to another; for if the deceite were knowne, I ſhould fall into the danger of that yong mad Raſcall. And now this double apprehenſion of the Lord and the Lady ſhall fetch mee off from all; I know it is *Sir Boniface* his cuſtome, to make ſhort worke, and hath diſpatcht by this: And now Wiſe-woman, try if thou canſt beſtir thy ſelfe like to a Mad-woman— ſhift for your ſelves, Warrants and Purſevants! Away, Warrants and Purſevants! ſhift for your ſelves.

Enter, as affrighted and amazed, Chartley, Boyſter, Boniface, *and others.*

Chart. Ile take this way.

Boyſt. I this. *Exeunt.*

Bonif. *Curro Curris Cucurri:* My cheeks are all Murry,
And I am gone in an hurry. *Exit.*

Luce. O Heaven! what ſhall become of me?

2. Luce. I know what ſhall become of me already.

Wiſewo. O ſweet Daughter, ſhift cloathes with this Lady! Nay, as thou lov'ſt thy credit and mine, change Habits— So, if thou bee'ſt taken in her Garments, finding the miſtake, will let thee paſſe; and ſhould they meet her in thine, not knowing her, would no way queſtion her: and this prove to both your ſecurities and my ſafety.

Luce. As faſt as I can, good Mother: So Madam farewell.

2. Luce. All happy joyes beride you. *Exit.*

Wiſew. Ha, ha, let me hold my ſides, and laugh: Here were even a Plot to make a play on, but that *Chartley* is ſo fool'd by my Boy *Iacke*: Well, heele make a notable Wagge, Ile warrant him. All the Ieſt will bee, if *Boyſter* ſhould meete with him in *Luce's* habitt, which hee hath now on, hee would thinke himſelfe meerely gull'd and cheated; and ſhould *Chartley* meet with *Luce* as ſhee is now Roab'd, hee would bee confident hee had marryed her. Let mee ſee how many Trades have I to live by: Firſt, I am a Wiſe-woman, and a Fortune-teller, and under that I deale in Phyſicke and Fore-ſpeaking, in Palmiſtry, and recovering of things loſt. Next, I undertake to cure Madd folkes. Then I keepe Gentle-women Lodgers, to furniſh ſuch Chambers as I let out by the night: Then I am provided for bringing young Wenches to bed; and for a need, you ſee I can play the Match-maker. Shee that is but one, and profeſſeth ſo many, may well bee tearmed a Wiſe-woman, if there bee any. *Exit.*

Enter Boyſter.

Boyſt. Why, runne away, and leave my Wench behind? Ile backe: what have Warrants and Purſevants to doe with mee? ~~with mee? why ſhould I budge? why ſhould I weare Maske or Viſard?~~ If Lords or Ladies offend, let Lords and Ladies anſwer; let mee better bethinke mee. Why ſhould I play at Hob-man blinde? Hum; why marry in *Tenebris*, ha! is there no tricke in it? If my Grannam

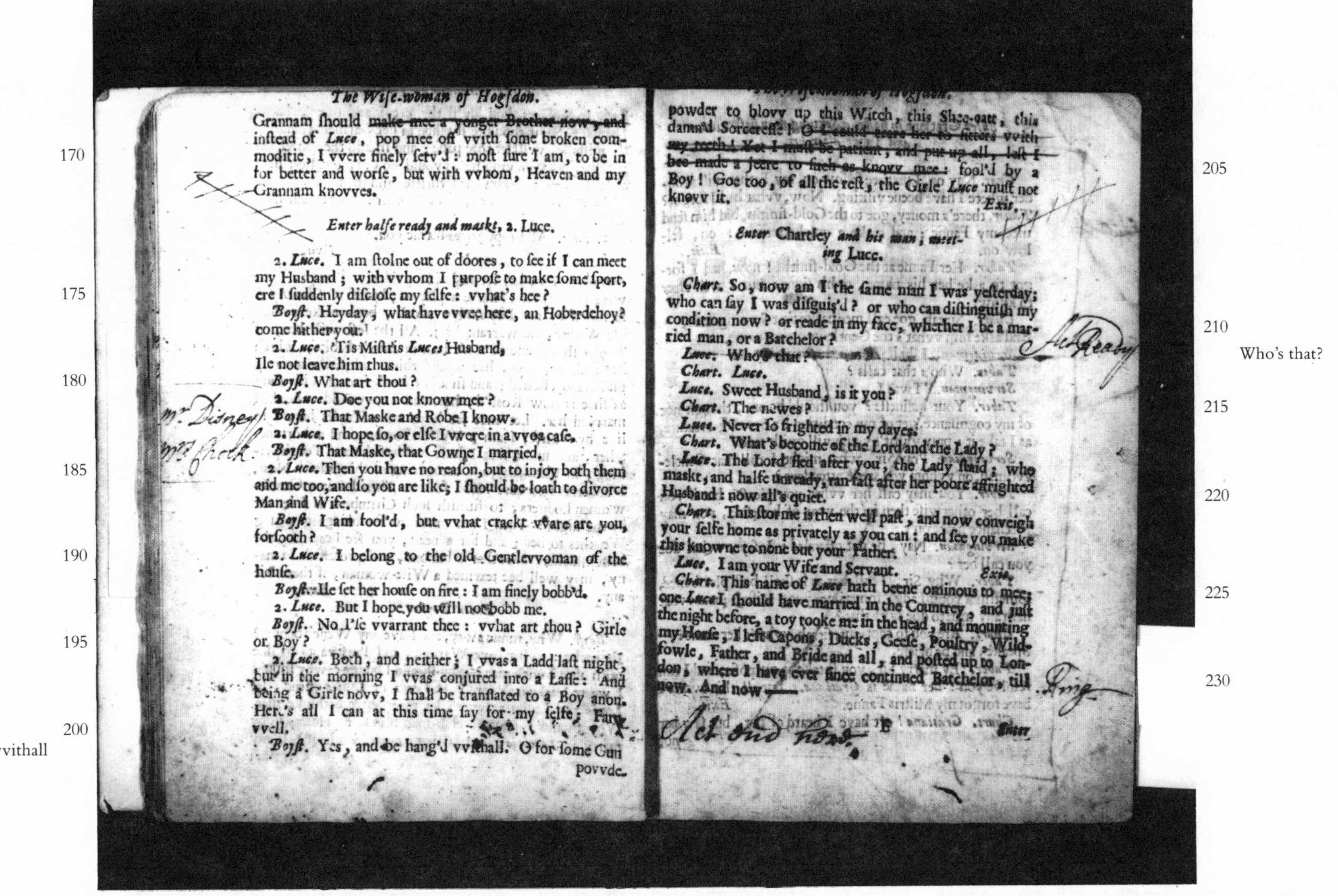

The Wise-woman of Hogsdon.

Grannam should make mee a yonger Brother now, and instead of *Luce*, pop mee off vvith some broken commoditie, I vvere finely serv'd: most sure I am, to be in for better and worse, but with vvhom, Heaven and my Grannam knovves.

Enter halfe ready and maskt, 2. Luce.

2. *Luce.* I am stolne out of doores, to see if I can meet my Husband; with vvhom I purpose to make some sport, ere I suddenly disclose my selfe: vvhat's hee?

Boyst. Heyday, what have vvee here, an Hoberdehoy? come hither you.

2. *Luce.* 'Tis Mistris *Luces* Husband, Ile not leave him thus.

Boyst. What art thou?

2. *Luce.* Doe you not know mee?

Boyst. That Maske and Robe I know.

2. *Luce.* I hope so, or else I vvere in a vvoe case.

Boyst. That Maske, that Gowne I married.

2. *Luce.* Then you have no reason, but to injoy both them and me too, and so you are like; I should be loath to divorce Man and Wife.

Boyst. I am fool'd, but vvhat crackt vvare are you, forsooth?

2. *Luce.* I belong to the old Gentlevvoman of the house.

Boyst. Ile set her house on fire: I am finely bobb'd.

2. *Luce.* But I hope you will not bobb me.

Boyst. No, I'le vvarrant thee: vvhat art thou? Girle or Boy?

2. *Luce.* Both, and neither; I vvas a Ladd last night, but in the morning I vvas conjured into a Lasse: And being a Girle novv, I shall be translated to a Boy anon. Her's all I can at this time say for my selfe; Farevvell.

Boyst. Yes, and be hang'd vvithall. O for some Gun powder to blovv up this Witch, this Shee-catt, this damn'd Sorceress! O I could teare her to fitters vvith my teeth! Yet I must be patient, and put up all, lest I bee made a jeere to such as knovv mee: fool'd by a Boy! Goe too, of all the rest, the Girle *Luce* must not knovv it. *Exit.*

Enter Chartley and his man; meeting Luce.

Chart. So, now am I the same man I was yesterday; who can say I was disguis'd? or who can distinguish my condition now? or reade in my face, whether I be a married man, or a Batchelor?

Luce. Who's that?

Chart. *Luce.*

Luce. Sweet Husband, is it you?

Chart. The newes?

Luce. Never so frighted in my dayes.

Chart. What's become of the Lord and the Lady?

Luce. The Lord fled after you, the Lady staid; who maskt, and halfe unready, ran fast after her poore affrighted Husband: now all's quiet.

Chart. This storme is then well past, and now conveigh your selfe home as privately as you can: and see you make this knowne to none but your Father.

Luce. I am your Wife and Servant. *Exit.*

Chart. This name of *Luce* hath beene ominous to mee; one *Luce* I should have married in the Countrey, and just the night before, a toy tooke me in the head, and mounting my Horse, I left Capons, Ducks, Geese, Poultry, Wildfowle, Father, and Bride and all, and posted up to London, where I have ever since continued Batchelor, till now. And now——

Enter

vvithall

Who's that?

III, i, 203–5. The canceled lines are: "O I could teare her to fitters vvith / my teeth! Yet I must be patient, and put up all, lest I / bee made a jeere to such as knovv mee:"

III, i, 231. The act is to end at this point, though on the pages that follow not all the dialogue is marked for omission.

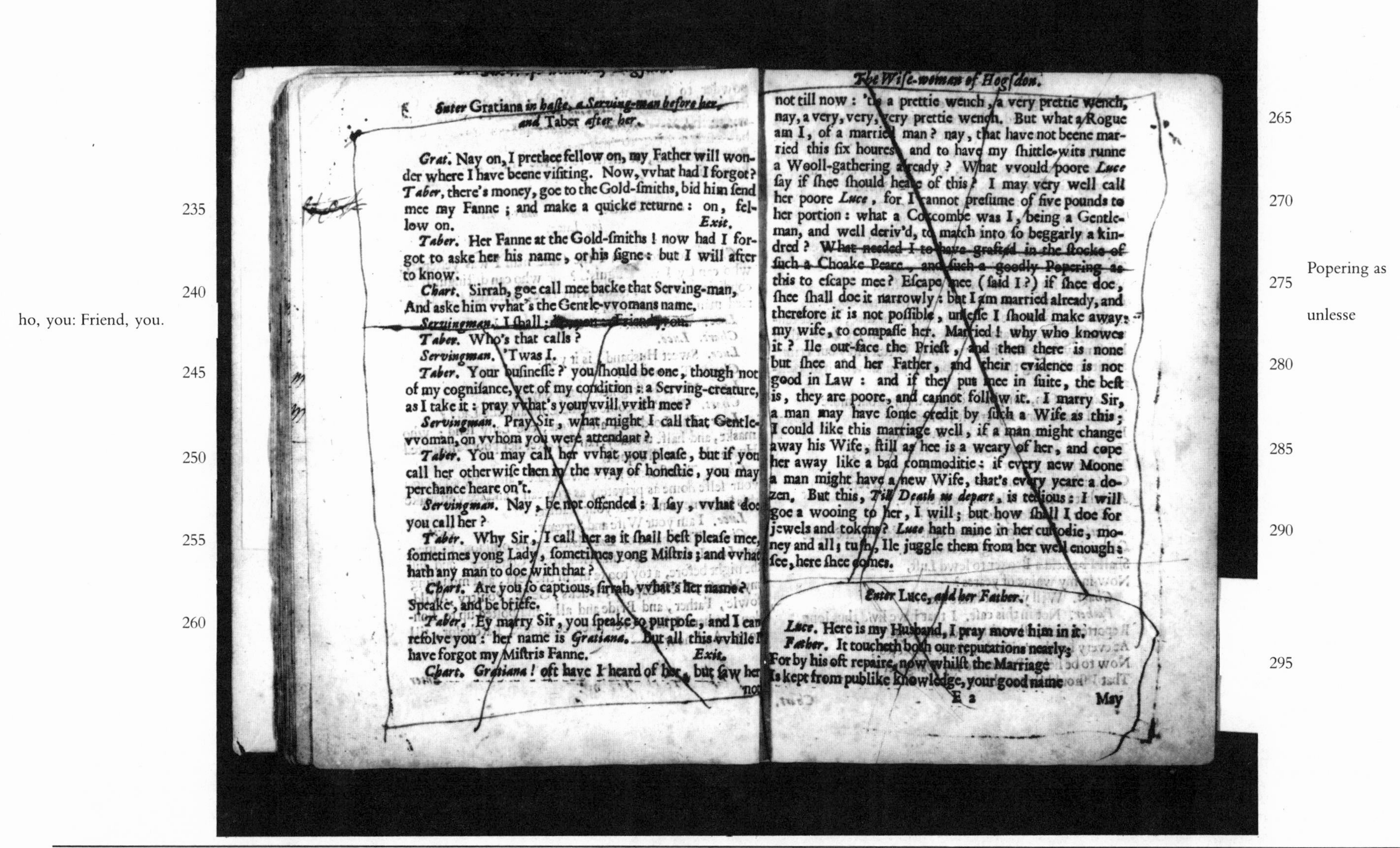

Enter Gratiana *in haste, a Serving-man before her, and* Taber *after her.*

Grat. Nay on, I prethee fellow on, my Father will wonder where I have beene viſiting. Now, vvhat had I forgot? *Taber*, there's money, goe to the Gold-ſmiths, bid him ſend mee my Fanne; and make a quicke returne: on, fellow on. *Exit.*

Taber. Her Fanne at the Gold-ſmiths! now had I forgot to aske her his name, or his ſigne: but I will after to know.

Chart. Sirrah, goe call mee backe that Serving-man, And aske him vvhat's the Gentle-vvomans name.

Servingman. I ſhall: ... Friend, you.

ho, you: Friend, you.

Taber. Who's that calls?

Servingman. 'Twas I.

Taber. Your buſineſſe? you ſhould be one, though not of my cogniſance, yet of my condition: a Serving-creature, as I take it: pray vvhat's your vvill vvith mee?

Servingman. Pray Sir, what might I call that Gentle-vvoman, on vvhom you were attendant?

Taber. You may call her vvhat you pleaſe, but if you call her otherwiſe then in the vvay of honeſtie, you may perchance heare on't.

Servingman. Nay, be not offended: I ſay, vvhat doe you call her?

Taber. Why Sir, I call her as it ſhall beſt pleaſe mee, ſometimes yong Lady, ſometimes yong Miſtris; and vvhat hath any man to doe with that?

Chart. Are you ſo captious, ſirrah, vvhat's her name? Speake, and be briefe.

Taber. Ey marry Sir, you ſpeake to purpoſe, and I can reſolve you: her name is *Gratiana.* But all this vvhile I have forgot my Miſtris Fanne. *Exit.*

Chart. Gratiana! oft have I heard of her, but ſaw her not

The Wiſe-woman of Hogſdon.

not till now: 'tis a prettie wench, a very prettie wench, nay, a very, very, very prettie wench. But what a Rogue am I, of a married man? nay, that have not beene married this ſix houres, and to have my ſhittle-wits runne a Wooll-gathering already? What vvould poore *Luce* ſay if ſhee ſhould heare of this? I may very well call her poore *Luce*, for I cannot preſume of five pounds to her portion: what a Coxcombe was I, being a Gentleman, and well deriv'd, to match into ſo beggarly a kindred? What needed I to have grafted in the ſtocks of ſuch a Choake Peare, and ſuch a goodly Popering as this to eſcape mee? Eſcape mee (ſaid I?) if ſhee doe, ſhee ſhall doe it narrowly: but I am married already, and therefore it is not poſſible, unleſſe I ſhould make away my wife, to compaſſe her. Married! why who knowes it? Ile out-face the Prieſt, and then there is none but ſhee and her Father, and their evidence is not good in Law: and if they put mee in ſuite, the beſt is, they are poore, and cannot follow it. I marry Sir, a man may have ſome credit by ſuch a Wife as this; I could like this marriage well, if a man might change away his Wife, ſtill as hee is a weary of her, and cope her away like a bad commoditie: if every new Moone a man might have a new Wife, that's every yeare a dozen. But this, *Till Death us depart*, is tedious: I will goe a wooing to her, I will; but how ſhall I doe for jewels and tokens? *Luce* hath mine in her cuſtodie, money and all; tuſh, Ile juggle them from her well enough: ſee, here ſhee comes.

Popering as

unlesse

Enter Luce, *and her Father.*

Luce. Here is my Husband, I pray move him in it.

Father. It toucheth both our reputations nearly.
For by his oft repaire, now whilſt the Marriage
Is kept from publike knowledge, your good name

E 2 May

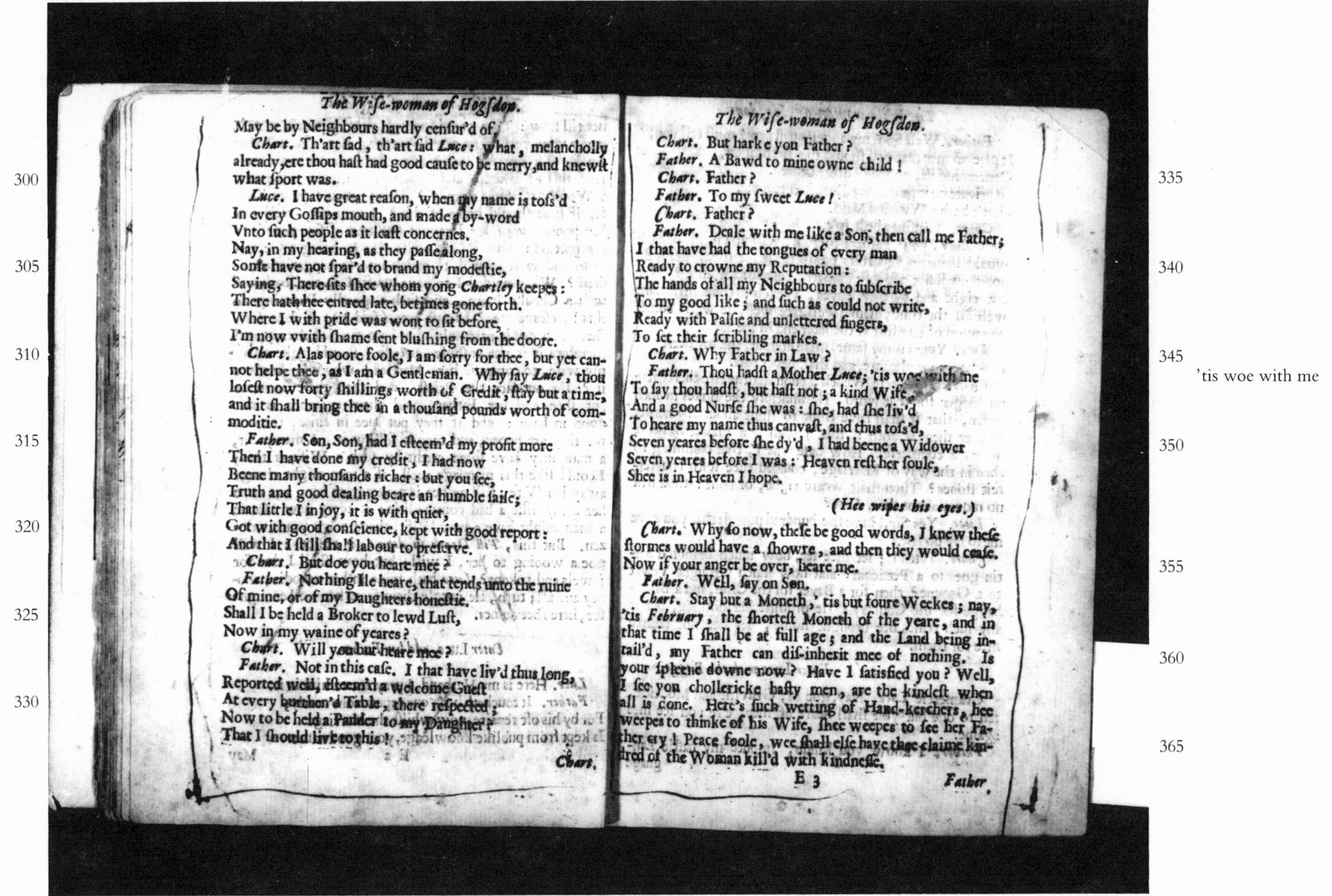

The Wise-woman of Hogsdon.

May be by Neighbours hardly censur'd of.

Chart. Th'art sad, th'art sad *Luce*: what, melancholly already, ere thou hast had good cause to be merry, and knewst what sport was.

Luce. I have great reason, when my name is toss'd
In every Gossips mouth, and made a by-word
Vnto such people as it least concernes.
Nay, in my hearing, as they passe along,
Some have not spar'd to brand my modestie,
Saying, There sits shee whom yong *Chartley* keepes:
There hath hee entred late, betimes gone forth.
Where I with pride was wont to sit before,
I'm now with shame sent blushing from the doore.

Chart. Alas poore foole, I am sorry for thee, but yet cannot helpe thee, as I am a Gentleman. Why say *Luce*, thou losest now forty shillings worth of Credit, stay but a time, and it shall bring thee in a thousand pounds worth of commoditie.

Father. Son, Son, had I esteem'd my profit more
Then I have done my credit, I had now
Beene many thousands richer: but you see,
Truth and good dealing beare an humble saile;
That little I injoy, it is with quiet,
Got with good conscience, kept with good report:
And that I still shall labour to preserve.

Chart. But doe you heare mee?

Father. Nothing Ile heare, that tends unto the ruine
Of mine, or of my Daughters honestie.
Shall I be held a Broker to lewd Lust,
Now in my waine of yeares?

Chart. Will you but heare mee?

Father. Not in this case. I that have liv'd thus long,
Reported well, esteem'd a welcome Guest
At every burthen'd Table, there respected;
Now to be held a Pandar to my Daughter?
That I should live to this!

Chart.

The Wise-woman of Hogsdon.

Chart. But harke you Father?

Father. A Bawd to mine owne child!

Chart. Father?

Father. To my sweet *Luce*!

Chart. Father?

Father. Deale with me like a Son, then call me Father;
I that have had the tongues of every man
Ready to crowne my Reputation:
The hands of all my Neighbours to subscribe
To my good like; and such as could not write,
Ready with Palsie and unlettered fingers,
To set their scribling markes.

Chart. Why Father in Law?

Father. Thou hadst a Mother *Luce*; 'tis woe with me
To say thou hadst, but hast not; a kind Wife,
And a good Nurse she was: she, had she liv'd
To heare my name thus canvast, and thus toss'd,
Seven yeares before she dy'd, I had beene a Widower
Seven yeares before I was: Heaven rest her soule,
Shee is in Heaven I hope.

(*Hee wipes his eyes.*)

Chart. Why so now, these be good words, I knew these stormes would have a showre, and then they would cease. Now if your anger be over, heare me.

Father. Well, say on Son.

Chart. Stay but a Moneth, 'tis but foure Weekes; nay, 'tis *February*, the shortest Moneth of the yeare, and in that time I shall be at full age; and the Land being intail'd, my Father can dis-inherit mee of nothing. Is your spleene downe now? Have I satisfied you? Well, I see you chollericke hasty men, are the kindest when all is done. Here's such wetting of Hand-kerchers, hee weepes to thinke of his Wife, shee weepes to see her Father cry! Peace foole, wee shall else have thee claime kindred of the Woman kill'd with kindnesse.

E 3 *Father*

'tis woe with me

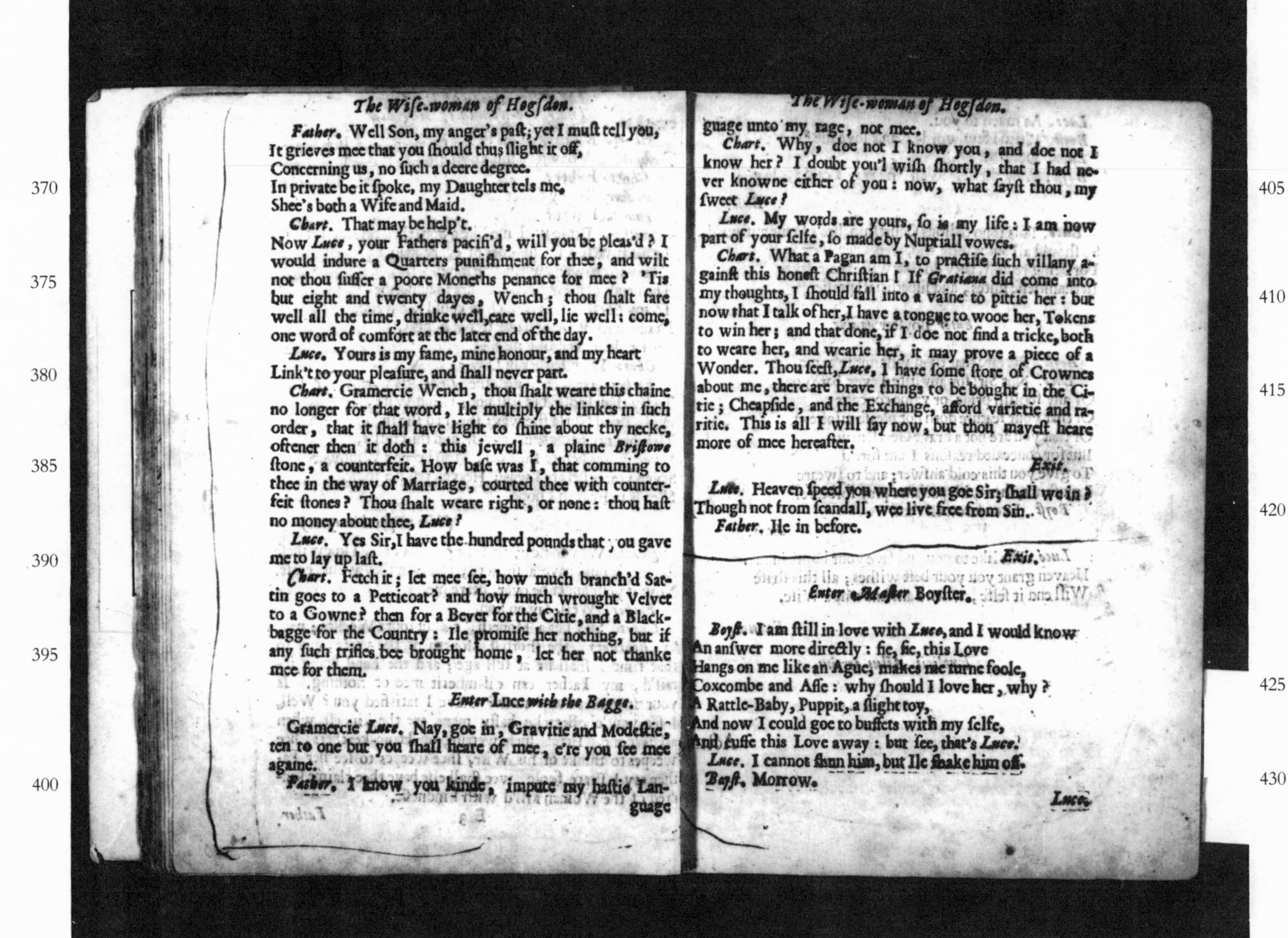

The Wife-woman of Hogsdon.

Father. Well Son, my anger's paſt; yet I muſt tell you,
It grieves mee that you ſhould thus ſlight it off,
Concerning us, no ſuch a deere degree.
In private be it ſpoke, my Daughter tels me,
Shee's both a Wife and Maid.

Chart. That may be help't.
Now *Luce*, your Fathers pacifi'd, will you be pleas'd? I would indure a Quarters puniſhment for thee, and wilt not thou ſuffer a poore Moneths penance for mee? 'Tis but eight and twenty dayes, Wench; thou ſhalt fare well all the time, drinke well, eate well, lie well: come, one word of comfort at the later end of the day.

Luce. Yours is my fame, mine honour, and my heart
Link't to your pleaſure, and ſhall never part.

Chart. Gramercie Wench, thou ſhalt weare this chaine no longer for that word, Ile multiply the linkes in ſuch order, that it ſhall have light to ſhine about thy necke, oftener then it doth: this jewell, a plaine *Briſtowe* ſtone, a counterfeit. How baſe was I, that comming to thee in the way of Marriage, courted thee with counterfeit ſtones? Thou ſhalt weare right, or none: thou haſt no money about thee, *Luce*?

Luce. Yes Sir, I have the hundred pounds that ; ou gave me to lay up laſt.

Chart. Fetch it; let mee ſee, how much branch'd Sattin goes to a Petticoat? and how much wrought Velvet to a Gowne? then for a Bever for the Citie, and a Black-bagge for the Country: Ile promiſe her nothing, but if any ſuch trifles bee brought home, let her not thanke mee for them.

Enter Luce *with the Bagge.*

Gramercie *Luce.* Nay, goe in, Gravitie and Modeſtie, ten to one but you ſhall heare of mee, e're you ſee mee againe.

Father. I know you kinde, impute my haſtie Language

The Wife-woman of Hogsdon.

guage unto my rage, not mee.

Chart. Why, doe not I know you, and doe not I know her? I doubt you'l wiſh ſhortly, that I had never knowne either of you: now, what ſayſt thou, my ſweet *Luce*?

Luce. My words are yours, ſo is my life: I am now part of your ſelfe, ſo made by Nuptiall vowes.

Chart. What a Pagan am I, to practiſe ſuch villany againſt this honeſt Chriſtian! If *Gratiana* did come into my thoughts, I ſhould fall into a vaine to pittie her: but now that I talk of her, I have a tongue to wooe her, Tokens to win her; and that done, if I doe not find a tricke, both to weare her, and wearie her, it may prove a piece of a Wonder. Thou ſeeſt, *Luce*, I have ſome ſtore of Crownes about me, there are brave things to be bought in the Citie; Cheapſide, and the Exchange, afford varietie and raritie. This is all I will ſay now, but thou mayeſt heare more of mee hereafter.

Exit.

Luce. Heaven ſpeed you where you goe Sir; ſhall we in?
Though not from ſcandall, wee live free from Sin.

Father. Ile in before.

Exit.

Enter Maſter Boyſter.

Boyſt. I am ſtill in love with *Luce*, and I would know
An anſwer more directly: fie, fie, this Love
Hangs on me like an Ague, makes me turne foole,
Coxcombe and Aſſe: why ſhould I love her, why?
A Rattle-Baby, Puppit, a ſlight toy,
And now I could goe to buffets with my ſelfe,
And cuffe this Love away: but ſee, that's *Luce*.

Luce. I cannot ſhun him, but Ile ſhake him off.

Boyſt. Morrow.

Luce.

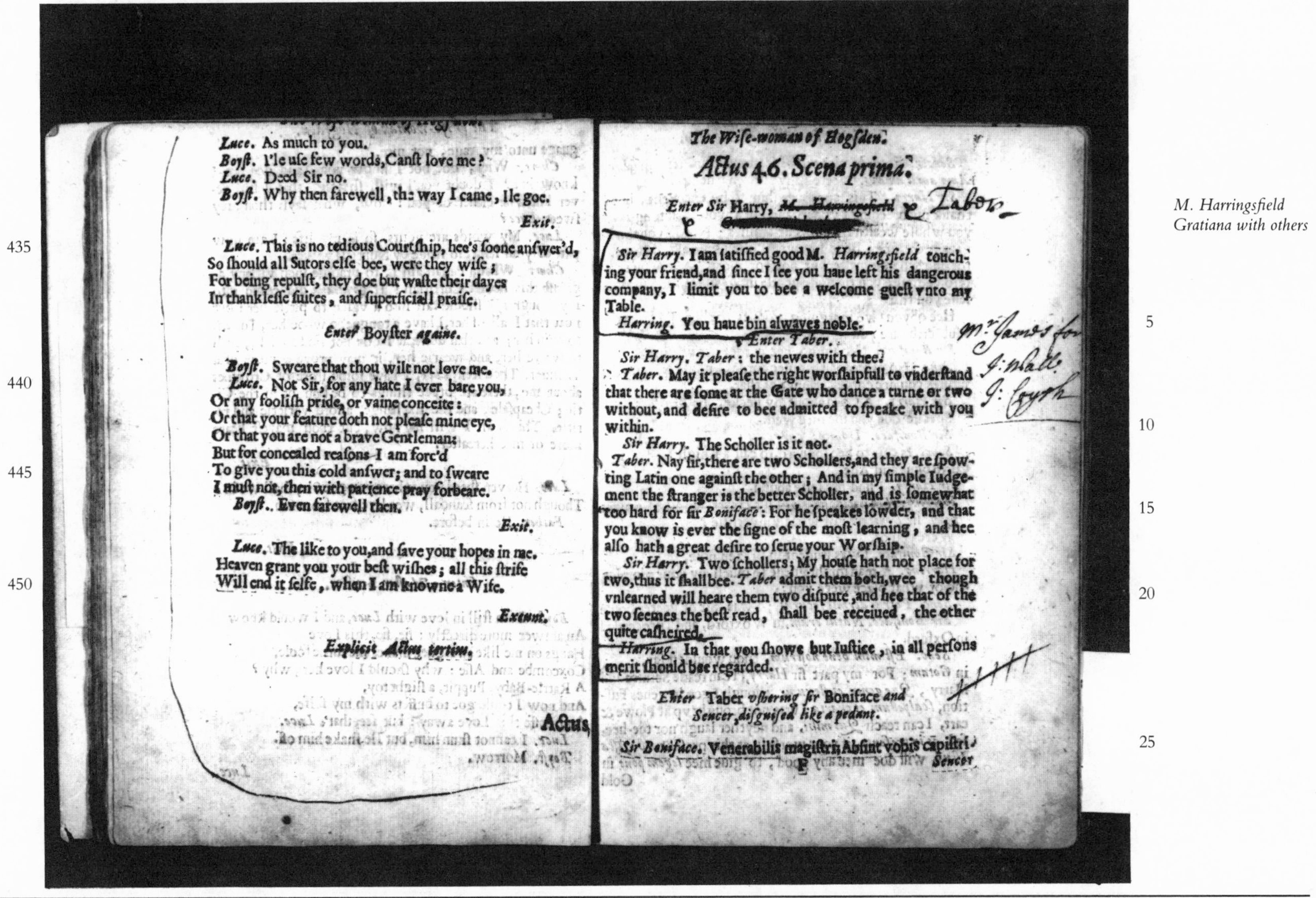

Luce. As much to you.
Boyſt. I'le uſe few words, Canſt love me?
Luce. Dead Sir no.
Boyſt. Why then farewell, the way I came, Ile goe.
Exit.

Luce. This is no tedious Courtſhip, hee's ſoone anſwer'd,
So ſhould all Sutors elſe bee, were they wiſe;
For being repulſt, they doe but waſte their dayes
In thankleſſe ſuites, and ſuperficiall praiſe.

Enter Boyſter *againe.*

Boyſt. Sweare that thou wilt not love me.
Luce. Not Sir, for any hate I ever bare you,
Or any fooliſh pride, or vaine conceite:
Or that your feature doth not pleaſe mine eye,
Or that you are not a brave Gentleman:
But for concealed reaſons I am forc'd
To give you this cold anſwer; and to ſweare
I muſt not, then with patience pray forbeare.
Boyſt. Even farewell then. *Exit.*

Luce. The like to you, and ſave your hopes in me.
Heaven grant you your beſt wiſhes; all this ſtrife
Will end it ſelfe, when I am knowne a Wife.
Exeunt.

Explicit Actus tertius.

Actus

The Wiſe-woman of Hogſden.

Actus 4 6. Scena prima.

Enter Sir Harry, M. Harringsfield & Taber

Sir Harry. I am ſatiſfied good M. *Harringsfield* touching your friend, and ſince I ſee you haue left his dangerous company, I limit you to bee a welcome gueſt vnto my Table.
Harring. You haue bin alwayes noble.
Enter Taber.
Sir Harry. Taber: the newes with thee?
Taber. May it pleaſe the right worſhipfull to vnderſtand that there are ſome at the Gate who dance a turne or two without, and deſire to bee admitted to ſpeake with you within.
Sir Harry. The Scholler is it not.
Taber. Nay ſir, there are two Schollers, and they are ſpowting Latin one againſt the other; And in my ſimple Iudgement the ſtranger is the better Scholler, and is ſomewhat too hard for ſir *Boniface*: For he ſpeakes lowder, and that you know is ever the ſigne of the moſt learning, and hee alſo hath a great deſire to ſerue your Worſhip.
Sir Harry. Two ſchollers; My houſe hath not place for two, thus it ſhall bee. *Taber* admit them both, wee though vnlearned will heare them two diſpute, and hee that of the two ſeemes the beſt read, ſhall bee receiued, the other quite caſheired.
Harring. In that you ſhowe but Iuſtice, in all perſons merit ſhould bee regarded.

Enter Taber *vſhering ſir* Boniface *and* Sencer, *diſguiſed like a pedant.*

Sir Boniface. Venerabilis magiſtri; Abſint vobis capiſtri.
Sencer

M. Harringsfield
Gratiana with others

IV, i, opening. The act should be numbered 4, not 46, of course. The meaning of the two e marks is not clear.

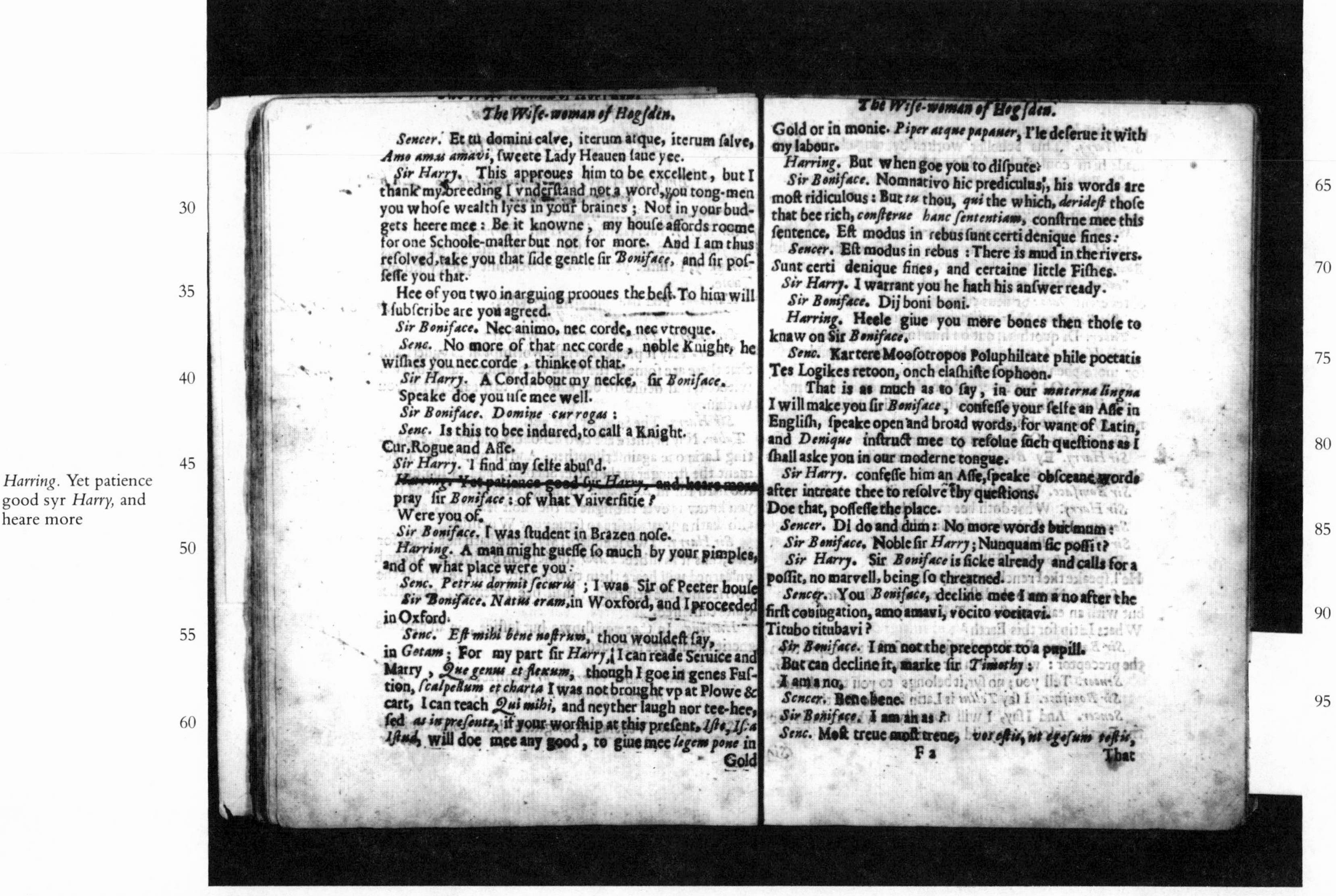

The Wife-woman of Hogsdin.

Sencer. Et tu domini calve, iterum atque, iterum salve, *Amo amas amavi*, sweete Lady Heauen saue yee.

Sir Harry. This approues him to be excellent, but I thank my breeding I vnderstand not a word, you tong-men you whose wealth lyes in your braines; Not in your budgets heere mee: Be it knowne, my house affords roome for one Schoole-master but not for more. And I am thus resolved, take you that side gentle sir *Boniface*, and sir possesse you that.

Hee of you two in arguing prooues the best. To him will I subscribe are you agreed.

Sir Boniface. Nec animo, nec corde, nec vtroque.

Senc. No more of that nec corde, noble Knight, he wishes you nec corde, thinke of that.

Sir Harry. A Cord about my necke, sir *Boniface.* Speake doe you use mee well.

Sir Boniface. *Domine cur rogas*:

Senc. Is this to bee indured, to call a Knight. Cur, Rogue and Asse.

Sir Harry. I find my selfe abus'd.

~~*Harring.* Yet patience good sir *Harry*, and heare more~~

Harring. Yet patience good syr *Harry*, and heare more

pray sir *Boniface*: of what Vniversitie? Were you of.

Sir Boniface. I was student in Brazen nose.

Harring. A man might guesse so much by your pimples, and of what place were you:

Senc. *Petrus dormit securus*; I was Sir of Peeter house.

Sir Boniface. *Natus eram*, in Woxford, and I proceeded in Oxford.

Senc. *Est mihi bene nostrum*, thou wouldest say, in *Gotam*; For my part sir *Harry*, I can reade Seruice and Marry, *Que genus et flexum*, though I goe in genes Fustion, *scalpellum et charta* I was not brought vp at Plowe & cart, I can teach *Qui mihi*, and neyther laugh nor tee-hee, sed *as in presente*, if your worship at this present, *Iste, Ista Istud*, will doe mee any good, to giue mee *legem pone* in Gold or in monie. *Piper atque papauer*, I'le deserue it with my labour.

Harring. But when goe you to dispute?

Sir Boniface. Nomnativo hic prediculus, his words are most ridiculous: But *tu* thou, *qui* the which, *iderides* those that bee rich, *consterue hanc sententiam*, constrne mee this sentence. Est modus in rebus sunt certi denique fines:

Sencer. Est modus in rebus: There is mud in the rivers. Sunt certi denique fines, and certaine little Fishes.

Sir Harry. I warrant you he hath his answer ready.

Sir Boniface. Dij boni boni.

Harring. Heele giue you more bones then those to knaw on Sir *Boniface.*

Senc. Kartere Moosotropos Poluphiltate phile poetatis Tes Logikes retoon, onch elashiste sophoon.

That is as much as to say, in our *materna lingua* I will make you sir *Boniface*, confesse your selfe an Asse in English, speake open and broad words, for want of Latin, and *Denique* instruct mee to resolue such questions as I shall aske you in our moderne tongue.

Sir Harry. confesse him an Asse, speake obsceane words after intreate thee to resolve thy questions. Doe that, possesse the place.

Sencer. Di do and dum: No more words but mum:

Sir Boniface. Noble sir *Harry*; Nunquam sic possit?

Sir Harry. Sir *Boniface* is sicke already and calls for a possit, no marvell, being so threatned.

Sencer. You *Boniface*, decline mee I am a no after the first coniugation, amo amavi, vocito vocitavi. Titubo titubavi?

Sir Boniface. I am not the preceptor to a pupill. But can decline it, marke sir *Timothy*: I am a no,

Sencer. Bene bene.

Sir Boniface. I am an as?

Senc. Most treue most treue, *vos estis, ut ego sum testis*,

F 2 That

IV, i, 50–51. Haringfield's speech should have been cut or reassigned. See also lines 64 and 73–74, where again the prompter failed to change the character's lines.

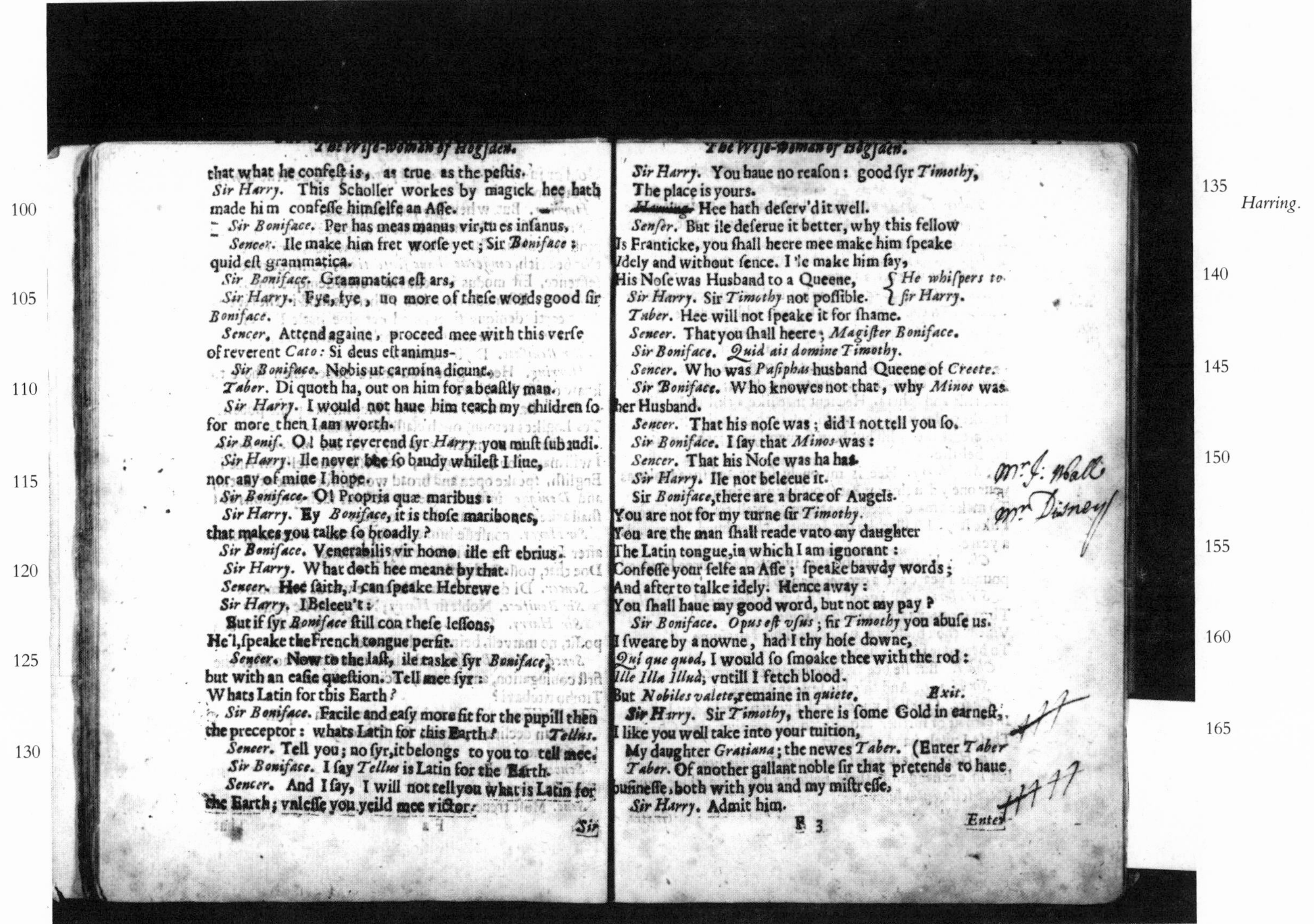

that what he confeſt is, as true as the peſtis.
Sir Harry. This Scholler workes by magick hee hath made him confeſſe himſelfe an Aſſe.
Sir Boniface. Per has meas manus vir, tu es inſanus,
Sencer. Ile make him fret worſe yet; Sir *Boniface*: quid eſt grammatica.
Sir Boniface. Grammatica eſt ars,
Sir Harry. Fye, fye, no more of theſe words good ſir *Boniface.*
Sencer. Attend againe, proceed mee with this verſe of reverent *Cato*: Si deus eſt animus-
Sir Boniface. Nobis ut carmina dicunt.
Taber. Di quoth ha, out on him for a beaſtly man.
Sir Harry. I would not haue him teach my children ſo for more then I am worth.
Sir Bonif. O! but reverend ſyr *Harry* you muſt ſubaudi.
Sir Harry. Ile never bee ſo baudy whileſt I liue,
nor any of mine I hope.
Sir Boniface. O! Propria quæ maribus:
Sir Harry. By *Boniface*, it is thoſe maribones,
that makes you talke ſo broadly?
Sir Boniface. Venerabilis vir homo ille eſt ebrius.
Sir Harry. What doth hee meane by that.
Sencer. Hee ſaith, I can ſpeake Hebrewe
Sir Harry. I Beleeu't:
But if ſyr *Boniface* ſtill con theſe leſſons,
He'l, ſpeake the French tongue perfit.
Sencer. Now to the laſt, ile taske ſyr *Boniface*, but with an eaſie queſtion. Tell mee ſyr:
Whats Latin for this Earth?
Sir Boniface. Facile and eaſy more fit for the pupill then the preceptor: whats Latin for this Earth? *Tellus.*
Sencer. Tell you; no ſyr, it belongs to you to tell mee.
Sir Boniface. I ſay *Tellus* is Latin for the Earth.
Sencer. And I ſay, I will not tell you what is Latin for the Earth; vnleſſe you yeild mee victor.

Sir Harry. You haue no reaſon: good ſyr *Timothy,*
The place is yours.
~~*Harring.*~~ Hee hath deſerv'd it well. *Harring.*
Senſer. But ile deſerue it better, why this fellow
Is Franticke, you ſhall heere mee make him ſpeake
Idely and without ſence. I'le make him ſay,
His Noſe was Husband to a Queene, { *He whiſpers to ſir Harry.*
Sir Harry. Sir *Timothy* not poſſible.
Taber. Hee will not ſpeake it for ſhame.
Sencer. That you ſhall heere; *Magiſter Boniface.*
Sir Boniface. *Quid ais domine Timothy.*
Sencer. Who was *Paſiphas* husband Queene of *Creete.*
Sir Boniface. Who knowes not that, why *Minos* was her Husband.
Sencer. That his noſe was; did I not tell you ſo.
Sir Boniface. I ſay that *Minos* was:
Sencer. That his Noſe was ha has.
Sir Harry. Ile not beleeue it.
Sir *Boniface*, there are a brace of Angels.
You are not for my turne ſir *Timothy.*
You are the man ſhall reade vnto my daughter
The Latin tongue, in which I am ignorant:
Confeſſe your ſelfe an Aſſe; ſpeake bawdy words;
And after to talke idely. Hence away:
You ſhall haue my good word, but not my pay?
Sir Boniface. *Opus eſt vſus*; ſir *Timothy* you abuſe us.
I ſweare by a nowne, had I thy hoſe downe,
Qui que quod, I would ſo ſmoake thee with the rod:
Ille Illa Illud; vntill I fetch blood.
But *Nobiles valete*, remaine in *quiete.* *Exit.*
Sir Harry. Sir *Timothy*, there is ſome Gold in earneſt,
I like you well take into your tuition,
My daughter *Gratiana*; the newes *Taber.* (Enter *Taber*
Taber. Of another gallant noble ſir that pretends to haue buſineſſe, both with you and my miſtreſſe.
Sir Harry. Admit him.

very gallant, in his hand / a Lady.

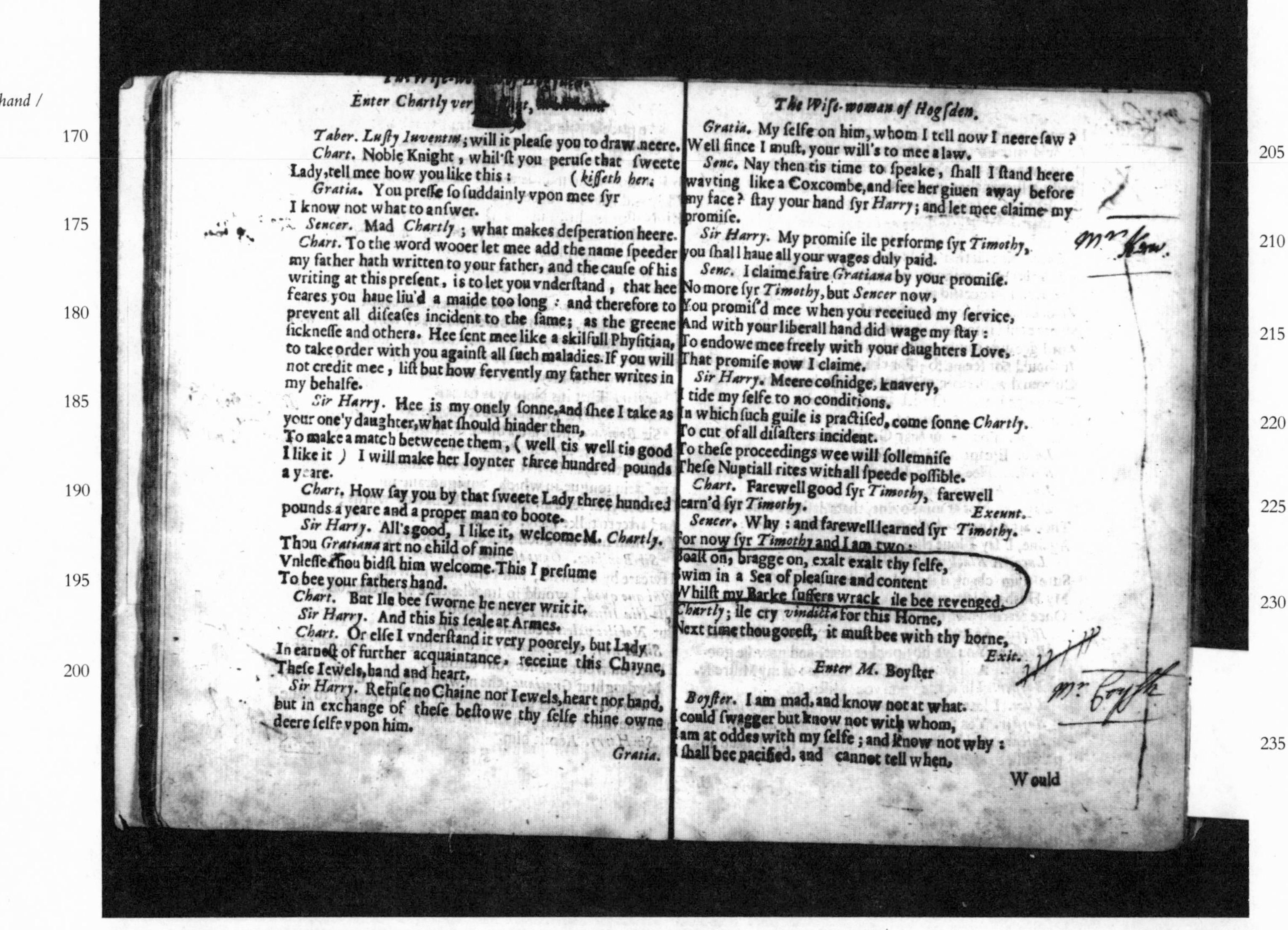

Enter Chartly ver[y gallant,]

Taber. Lusty Iuventus; will it please you to draw neere.

Chart. Noble Knight, whil'st you peruse that sweete Lady, tell mee how you like this: (*kisseth her.*

Gratia. You presse so suddainly vpon mee syr
I know not what to answer.

Sencer. Mad *Chartly*; what makes desperation heere.

Chart. To the word wooer let mee add the name speeder my father hath written to your father, and the cause of his writing at this present, is to let you vnderstand, that hee feares you haue liu'd a maide too long: and therefore to prevent all diseases incident to the same; as the greene sicknesse and others. Hee sent mee like a skilfull Physitian, to take order with you against all such maladies. If you will not credit mee, list but how fervently my father writes in my behalfe.

Sir Harry. Hee is my onely sonne, and shee I take as your onely daughter, what should hinder then,
To make a match betweene them, (well tis well tis good I like it) I will make her Ioynter three hundred pounds a yeare.

Chart. How say you by that sweete Lady three hundred pounds a yeare and a proper man to boote.

Sir Harry. All's good, I like it, welcome M. *Chartly.*
Thou *Gratiana* art no child of mine
Vnlesse thou bidst him welcome. This I presume
To bee your fathers hand.

Chart. But Ile bee sworne he never writ it.

Sir Harry. And this his seale at Armes.

Chart. Or else I vnderstand it very poorely, but Lady
In earnest of further acquaintance, receiue this Chayne,
These Iewels, hand and heart.

Sir Harry. Refuse no Chaine nor Iewels, heart nor hand, but in exchange of these bestowe thy selfe thine owne deere selfe vpon him.

Gratia.

The Wise-woman of Hogsden.

Gratia. My selfe on him, whom I tell now I neere saw?
Well since I must, your will's to mee a law.

Senc. Nay then tis time to speake, shall I stand heere wavting like a Coxcombe, and see her giuen away before my face? stay your hand syr *Harry*; and let mee claime my promise.

Sir Harry. My promise ile performe syr *Timothy*, you shall haue all your wages duly paid.

Senc. I claime faire *Gratiana* by your promise.
No more syr *Timothy*, but *Sencer* now,
You promis'd mee when you receiued my service,
And with your liberall hand did wage my stay:
To endowe mee freely with your daughters Love,
That promise now I claime.

Sir Harry. Meere cosnidge, knavery,
I tide my selfe to no conditions.
In which such guile is practised, come sonne *Chartly.*
To cut of all disasters incident.
To these proceedings wee will sollemnise
These Nuptiall rites withall speede possible.

Chart. Farewell good syr *Timothy*, farewell learn'd syr *Timothy*. *Exeunt.*

Sencer. Why: and farewell learned syr *Timothy.*
For now syr *Timothy* and I am two:
Boast on, bragge on, exalt exalt thy selfe,
Swim in a Sea of pleasure and content
Whilst my Barke suffers wrack ile bee revenged,
Chartly; ile cry *vindicta* for this Horne,
Next time thou gorest, it must bee with thy horne,
Exit.

Enter M. Boyster

Boyster. I am mad, and know not at what.
I could swagger but know not with whom,
I am at oddes with my selfe; and know not why:
I shall bee pacified, and cannot tell when,

Would

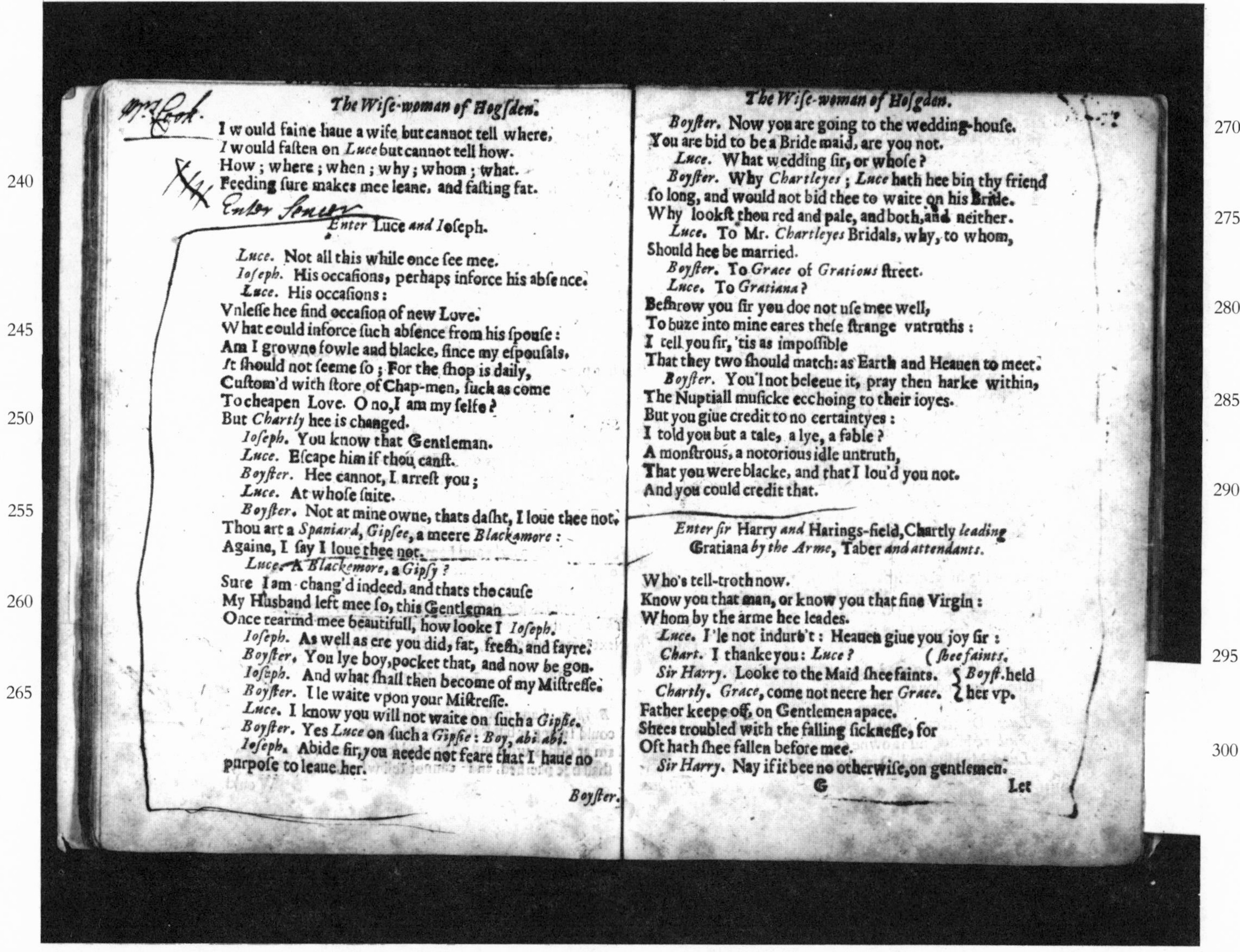

The Wife-woman of Hogfden.

I would faine haue a wife but cannot tell where,
I would fasten on *Luce* but cannot tell how.
How ; where ; when ; why ; whom ; what.
Feeding fure makes mee leane, and fafting fat.

Enter Luce *and* Iofeph.

Luce. Not all this while once fee mee.
Iofeph. His occafions, perhaps inforce his abfence.
Luce. His occafions :
Vnleffe hee find occafion of new Love.
What could inforce fuch abfence from his fpoufe :
Am I growne fowle and blacke, fince my efpoufals,
It fhould not feeme fo ; For the fhop is daily,
Cuftom'd with ftore of Chap-men, fuck as come
To cheapen Love. O no, I am my felfe?
But *Chartly* hee is changed.
Iofeph. You know that Gentleman.
Luce. Efcape him if thou canft.
Boyfter. Hee cannot, I arreft you ;
Luce. At whofe fuite.
Boyfter. Not at mine owne, thats dafht, I loue thee not.
Thou art a *Spaniard, Gipfee*, a meere *Blackamore* :
Againe, I fay I loue thee not.
Luce. A *Blackemore*, a *Gipfy* ?
Sure I am chang'd indeed, and thats the caufe
My Husband left mee fo, this Gentleman
Once tearmd mee beautifull, how looke I *Iofeph.*
Iofeph. As well as ere you did, fat, frefh, and fayre.
Boyfter. You lye boy, pocket that, and now be gon.
Iofeph. And what fhall then become of my Miftreffe.
Boyfter. Ile waite vpon your Miftreffe.
Luce. I know you will not waite on fuch a *Gipfie.*
Boyfter. Yes *Luce* on fuch a *Gipfie* : *Boy, abi abi.*
Iofeph. Abide fir, you neede not feare that I haue no
purpofe to leaue her.

Boyfter.

The Wife-woman of Hofgden.

Boyfter. Now you are going to the wedding-houfe.
You are bid to be a Bride maid, are you not.
Luce. What wedding fir, or whofe?
Boyfter. Why *Chartleyes* ; *Luce* hath hee bin thy friend
fo long, and would not bid thee to waite on his Bride.
Why lookft thou red and pale, and both, and neither.
Luce. To Mr. *Chartleyes* Bridals, why, to whom,
Should hee be married.
Boyfter. To *Grace* of *Gratious* ftreet.
Luce. To *Gratiana* ?
Befhrow you fir you doe not ufe mee well,
To buze into mine eares thefe ftrange vntruths :
I tell you fir, 'tis as impoffible
That they two fhould match: as Earth and Heauen to meet.
Boyfter. You'l not beleeue it, pray then harke within,
The Nuptiall muficke ecchoing to their ioyes.
But you giue credit to no certaintyes :
I told you but a tale, a lye, a fable ?
A monftrous, a notorious idle untruth,
That you were blacke, and that I lou'd you not.
And you could credit that.

Enter fir Harry *and* Harings-field, Chartly *leading*
Gratiana *by the Arme*, Taber *and attendants.*

Who's tell-troth now.
Know you that man, or know you that fine Virgin :
Whom by the arme hee leades.
Luce. I'le not indurb't : Heauen giue you joy fir :
Chart. I thanke you : *Luce* ? (*fhee faints.*
Sir Harry. Looke to the Maid fhee faints. { *Boyft.* held
Chartly. *Grace*, come not neere her *Grace.* { her vp.
Father keepe off, on Gentlemen apace.
Shees troubled with the falling fickneffe, for
Oft hath fhee fallen before mee.
Sir Harry. Nay if it bee no otherwife, on gentlemen.

G Let

IV, i, above 237. The warning for Mrs. Cook (who played the Second Luce) is for an entrance at line 386, after the extensive cut. Not all of the cutting is clearly marked, but the intention was evidently to omit everything after line 240 through line 380.

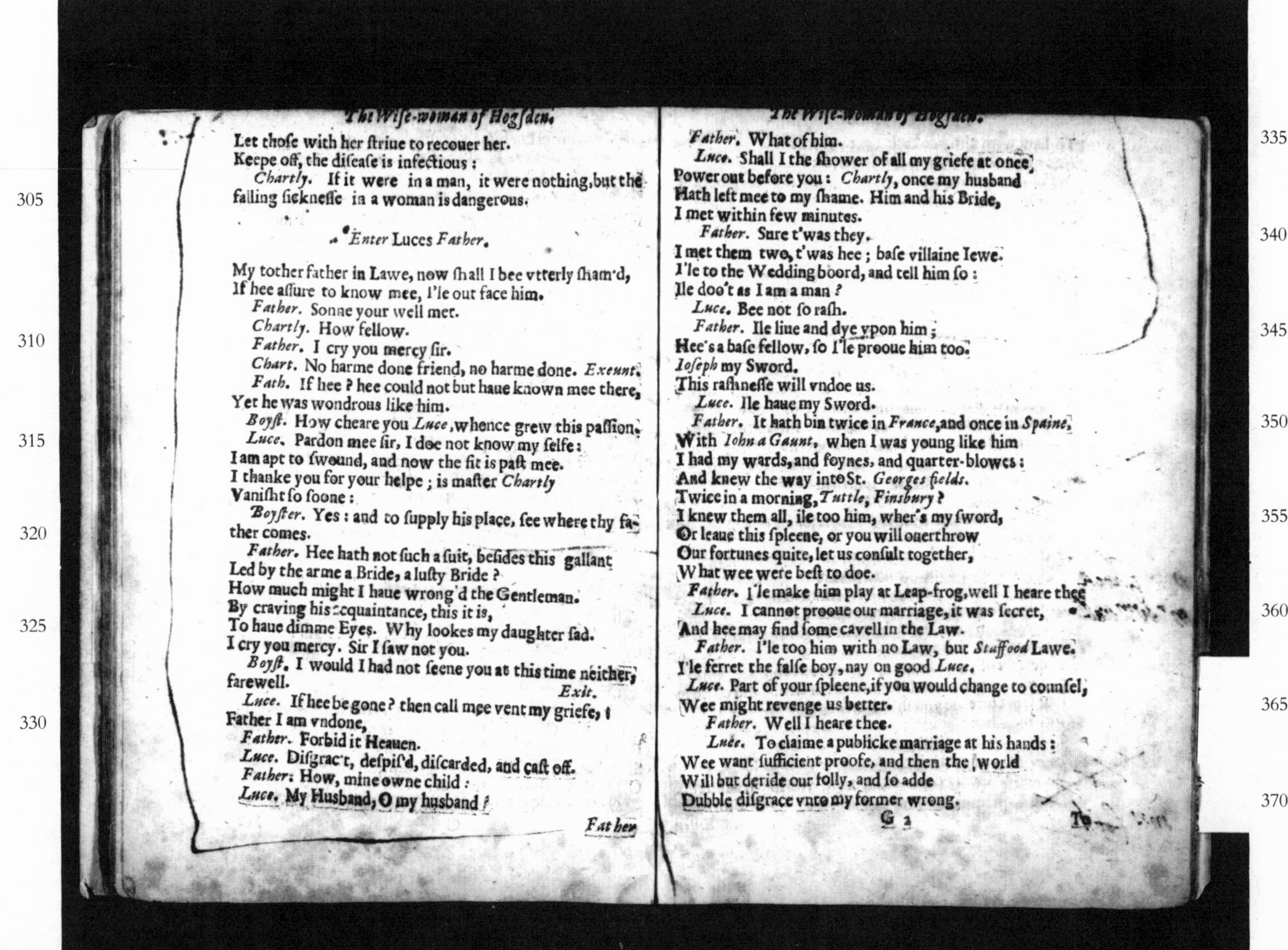

The Wise-woman of Hogsdon.

Let those with her striue to recouer her.
Keepe off, the disease is infectious:
Chartly. If it were in a man, it were nothing, but the falling sicknesse in a woman is dangerous.

Enter Luces *Father.*

My tother father in Lawe, now shall I bee vtterly sham'd,
If hee assure to know mee, I'le out face him.
Father. Sonne your well met.
Chartly. How fellow.
Father. I cry you mercy sir.
Chart. No harme done friend, no harme done. *Exeunt.*
Fath. If hee? hee could not but haue known mee there,
Yet he was wondrous like him.
Boyst. How cheare you *Luce*, whence grew this passion.
Luce. Pardon mee sir, I doe not know my selfe:
I am apt to swound, and now the fit is past mee.
I thanke you for your helpe; is master *Chartly*
Vanisht so soone:
Boyster. Yes: and to supply his place, see where thy father comes.
Father. Hee hath not such a suit, besides this gallant
Led by the arme a Bride, a lusty Bride?
How much might I haue wrong'd the Gentleman.
By craving his acquaintance, this it is,
To haue dimme Eyes. Why lookes my daughter sad.
I cry you mercy. Sir I saw not you.
Boyst. I would I had not seene you at this time neither, farewell. *Exit.*
Luce. If hee be gone? then call mee vent my griefe,
Father I am vndone,
Father. Forbid it Heauen.
Luce. Disgrac't, despis'd, discarded, and cast off.
Father. How, mine owne child:
Luce. My Husband, O my husband!

Father

The Wise-woman of Hogsdon.

Father. What of him.
Luce. Shall I the shower of all my griefe at once,
Power out before you: *Chartly*, once my husband
Hath left mee to my shame. Him and his Bride,
I met within few minutes.
Father. Sure t'was they.
I met them two, t'was hee; base villaine Iewe.
I'le to the Wedding boord, and tell him so:
Ile doo't as I am a man?
Luce. Bee not so rash.
Father. Ile liue and dye vpon him;
Hee's a base fellow, so I'le prooue him too.
Ioseph my Sword.
This rashnesse will vndoe us.
Luce. Ile haue my Sword.
Father. It hath bin twice in *France*, and once in *Spaine*,
With *Iohn a Gaunt*, when I was young like him
I had my wards, and foynes, and quarter-blowes:
And knew the way into St. *Georges fields.*
Twice in a morning, *Tuttle, Finsbury*?
I knew them all, ile too him, wher's my sword,
Or leaue this spleene, or you will ouerthrow
Our fortunes quite, let us consult together,
What wee were best to doe.
Father. I'le make him play at Leap-frog, well I heare thee
Luce. I cannot prooue our marriage, it was secret,
And hee may find some cavell in the Law.
Father. I'le too him with no Law, but *Stafford* Lawe.
I'le ferret the false boy, nay on good *Luce*,
Luce. Part of your spleene, if you would change to counsel,
Wee might revenge us better.
Father. Well I heare thee.
Luce. To claime a publicke marriage at his hands:
Wee want sufficient proofe, and then the world
Will but deride our folly, and so adde
Dubble disgrace vnto my former wrong.

G 2 To

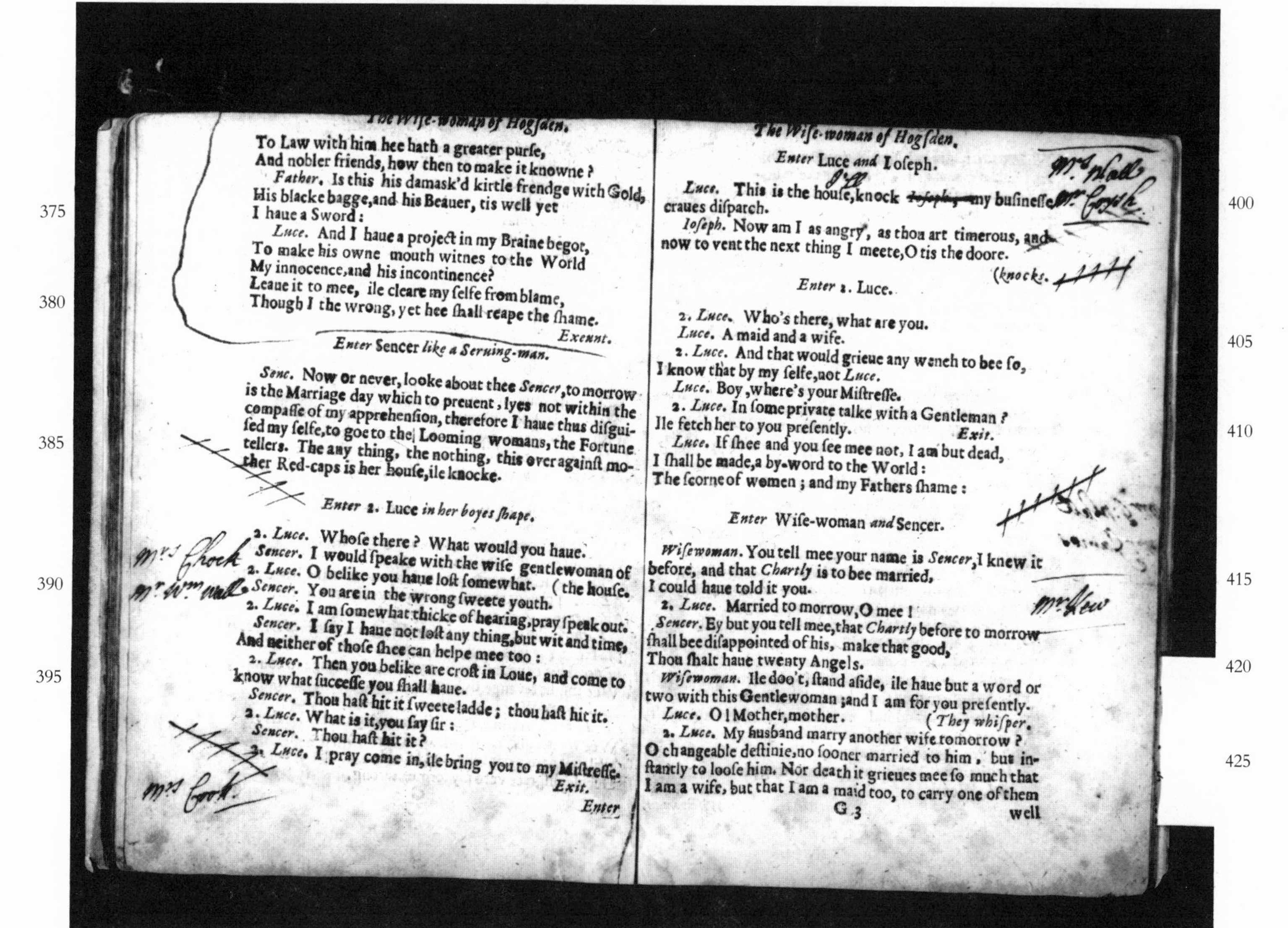

The Wise-woman of Hogsden.

To Law with him hee hath a greater purse,
And nobler friends, how then to make it knowne?

Father. Is this his damask'd kirtle frendge with Gold,
His blacke bagge, and his Beauer, tis well yet
I haue a Sword:

Luce. And I haue a project in my Braine begot,
To make his owne mouth witnes to the World
My innocence, and his incontinence?
Leaue it to mee, ile cleare my selfe from blame,
Though I the wrong, yet hee shall reape the shame.
Exeunt.

Enter Sencer *like a Seruing-man.*

Senc. Now or never, looke about thee *Sencer*, to morrow is the Marriage day which to preuent, lyes not within the compasse of my apprehension, therefore I haue thus disguised my selfe, to goe to the Looming womans, the Fortune tellers. The any thing, the nothing, this over against mother Red-caps is her house, ile knocke.

Enter 2. Luce *in her boyes shape.*

2. *Luce.* Whose there? What would you haue.

Sencer. I would speake with the wise gentlewoman of the house.

2. *Luce.* O belike you haue lost somewhat.

Sencer. You are in the wrong sweete youth.

2. *Luce.* I am somewhat thicke of hearing, pray speak out.

Sencer. I say I haue not lost any thing, but wit and time, And neither of those shee can helpe mee too:

2. *Luce.* Then you belike are crost in Loue, and come to know what successe you shall haue.

Sencer. Thou hast hit it sweete ladde; thou hast hit it.

2. *Luce.* What is it, you say sir:

Sencer. Thou hast hit it?

2. *Luce.* I pray come in, ile bring you to my Mistresse.
Exit.

Enter

The Wise-woman of Hogsden.

Enter Luce *and* Ioseph.

Luce. This is the house, knock Ioseph, my businesse craues dispatch.

Ioseph. Now am I as angry, as thou art timerous, and now to vent the next thing I meete, O tis the doore.
(*knocks.*

Enter 2. Luce.

2. *Luce.* Who's there, what are you.

Luce. A maid and a wife.

2. *Luce.* And that would grieue any wench to bee so, I know that by my selfe, not *Luce.*

Luce. Boy, where's your Mistresse.

2. *Luce.* In some private talke with a Gentleman? Ile fetch her to you presently. *Exit.*

Luce. If shee and you see mee not, I am but dead,
I shall be made, a by-word to the World:
The scorne of women; and my Fathers shame:

Enter Wise-woman *and* Sencer.

Wisewoman. You tell mee your name is *Sencer*, I knew it before, and that *Chartly* is to bee married, I could haue told it you.

2. *Luce.* Married to morrow, O mee!

Sencer. Ey but you tell mee, that *Chartly* before to morrow shall bee disappointed of his, make that good, Thou shalt haue twenty Angels.

Wisewoman. Ile doo't, stand aside, ile haue but a word or two with this Gentlewoman; and I am for you presently.

Luce. O Mother, mother. (*They whisper.*

2. *Luce.* My husband marry another wife tomorrow? O changeable destinie, no sooner married to him, but instantly to loose him. Nor death it grieues mee so much that I am a wife, but that I am a maid too, to carry one of them

G 3 well

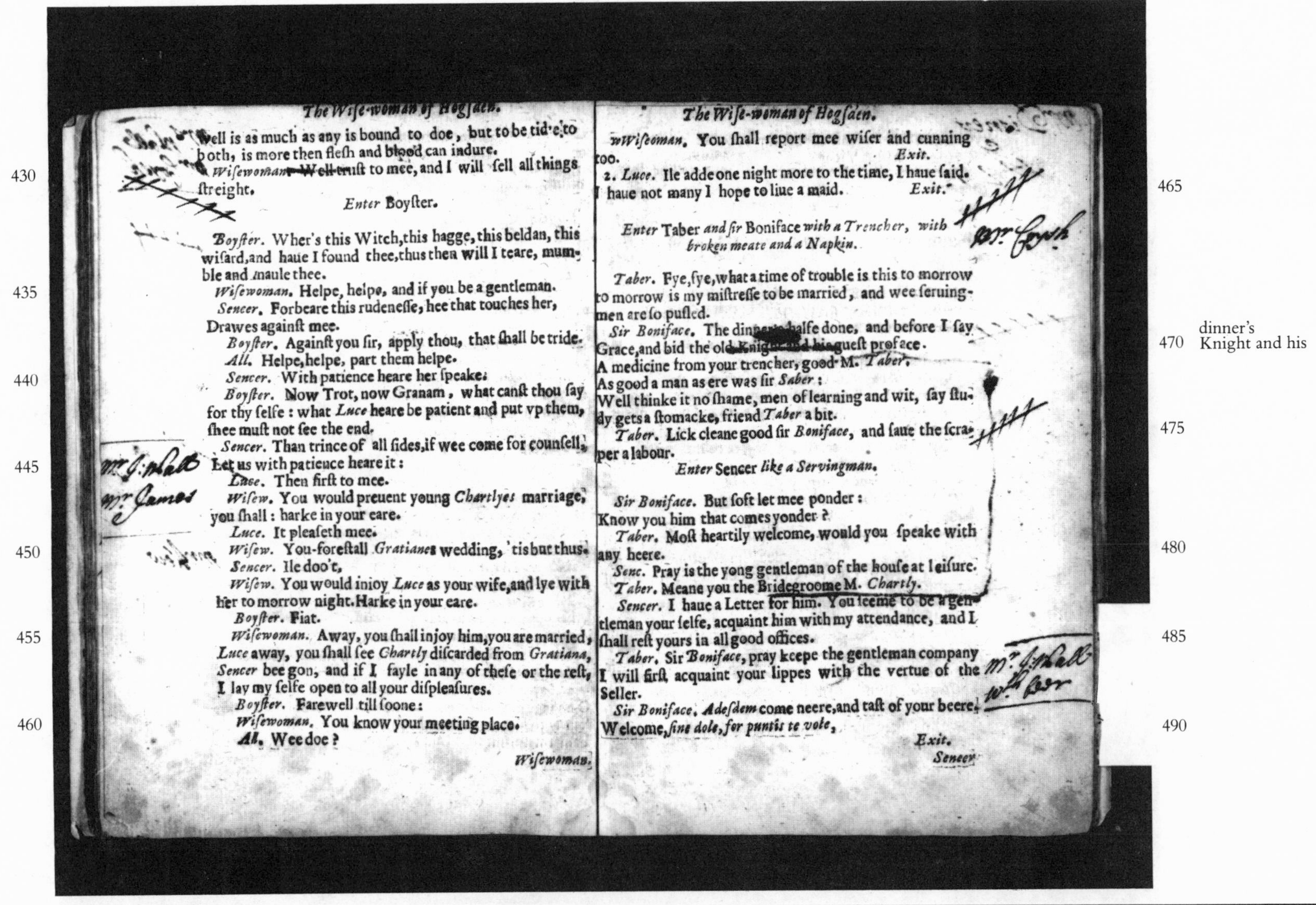

The Wife-woman of Hogsden.

Well is as much as any is bound to doe, but to be tid'e to both, is more then flesh and blood can indure.

Wisewoman. Well trust to mee, and I will sell all things streight.

Enter Boyster.

Boyster. Wher's this Witch, this hagge, this beldan, this wisard, and haue I found thee, thus then will I teare, mumble and maule thee.

Wisewoman. Helpe, helpe, and if you be a gentleman.

Sencer. Forbeare this rudenesse, hee that touches her, Drawes against mee.

Boyster. Against you sir, apply thou, that shall be tride.

All. Helpe, helpe, part them helpe.

Sencer. With patience heare her speake.

Boyster. Now Trot, now Granam, what canst thou say for thy selfe: what *Luce* heare be patient and put vp them, shee must not see the end.

Sencer. Than trince of all sides, if wee come for counsell, Let us with patience heare it:

Luce. Then first to mee.

Wisew. You would preuent young *Chartlyes* marriage, you shall: harke in your eare.

Luce. It pleaseth mee.

Wisew. You-forestall *Gratianes* wedding, 'tis but thus.

Sencer. Ile doo't,

Wisew. You would inioy *Luce* as your wife, and lye with her to morrow night. Harke in your eare.

Boyster. Fiat.

Wisewoman. Away, you shall injoy him, you are married, *Luce* away, you shall see *Chartly* discarded from *Gratiana*, *Sencer* bee gon, and if I fayle in any of these or the rest, I lay my selfe open to all your displeasures.

Boyster. Farewell till soone:

Wisewoman. You know your meeting place.

Al. Wee doe?

Wisewoman.

The Wise-woman of Hogsden.

wWiseoman. You shall report mee wiser and cunning too. *Exit.*

2. *Luce.* Ile adde one night more to the time, I haue said. I haue not many I hope to liue a maid. *Exit.*

Enter Taber *and sir* Boniface *with a Trencher, with broken meate and a Napkin.*

Taber. Fye, fye, what a time of trouble is this to morrow to morrow is my mistresse to be married, and wee seruingmen are so pusled.

Sir Boniface. The dinners halfe done, and before I say Grace, and bid the old Knight and his guest proface.
A medicine from your trencher, good M. *Taber.*
As good a man as ere was sir *Saber*:
Well thinke it no shame, men of learning and wit, say study gets a stomacke, friend *Taber* a bit.

Taber. Lick cleane good sir *Boniface*, and saue the scraper a labour.

Enter Sencer *like a Servingman.*

Sir Boniface. But soft let mee ponder:
Know you him that comes yonder?

Taber. Most heartily welcome, would you speake with any heere.

Senc. Pray is the yong gentleman of the house at leisure.

Taber. Meane you the Bridegroome M. *Chartly.*

Sencer. I haue a Letter for him. You seeme to be a gentleman your selfe, acquaint him with my attendance, and I shall rest yours in all good offices.

Taber. Sir *Boniface*, pray keepe the gentleman company I will first acquaint your lippes with the vertue of the Seller.

Sir Boniface. *Adesdem* come neere, and tast of your beere.
Welcome, *fine dole, for puntis te vole,*

Exit.

Sencer

dinner's
Knight and his

IV, i, 487. Taber exits at this point to get beer, though no stage direction takes him off; the prompter still warned him for his entrance at line 491.

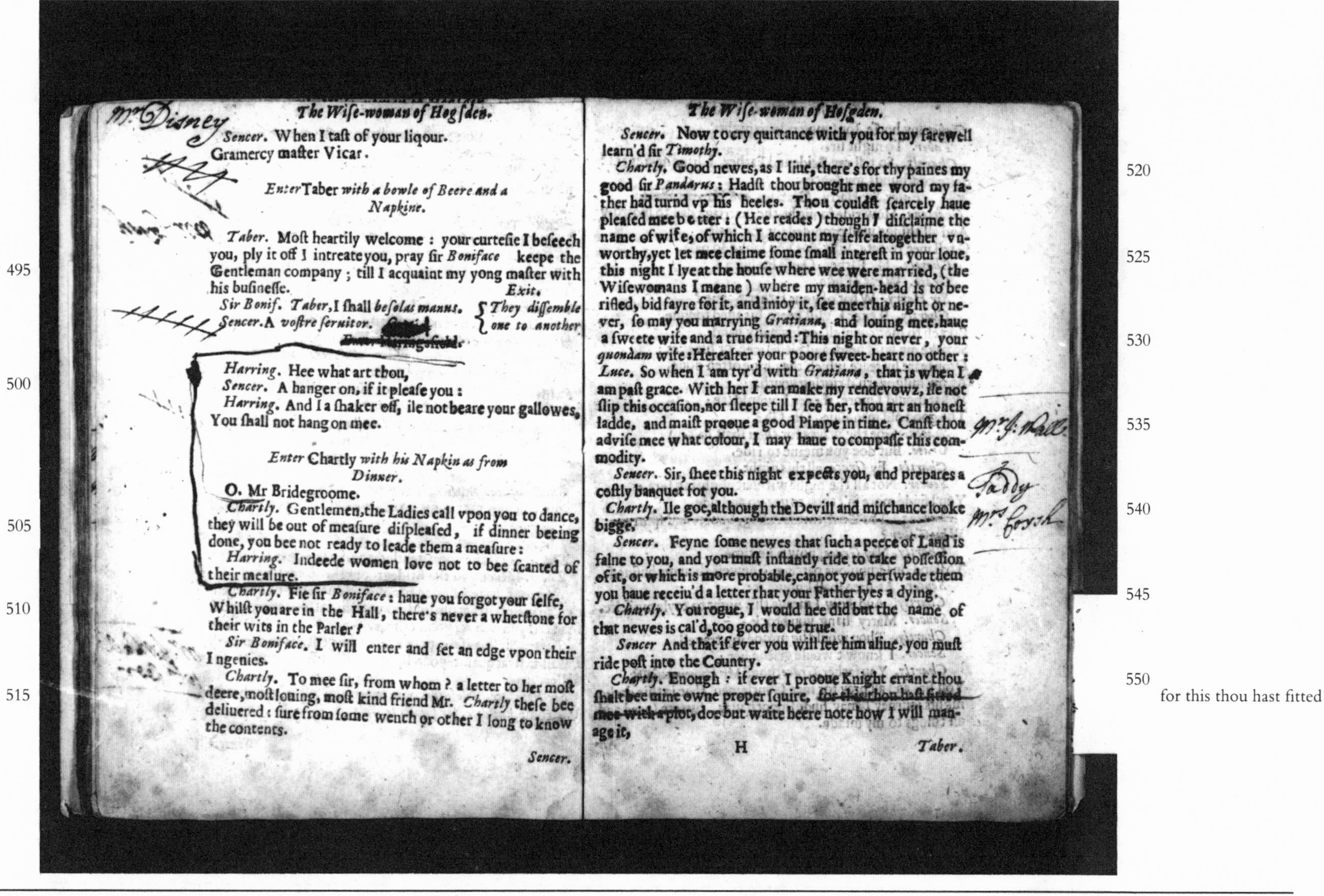

The Wiſe-woman of Hogſden.

Sencer. When I taſt of your liqour.
Gramercy maſter Vicar.

Enter Taber *with a bowle of Beere and a Napkine.*

Taber. Moſt heartily welcome: your curteſie I beſeech you, ply it off I intreate you, pray ſir *Boniface* keepe the Gentleman company; till I acquaint my yong maſter with his buſineſſe. *Exit.*

Sir Bonif. Taber, I ſhall *beſolas manus.*
Sencer. A *voſtre ſeruitor.* { *They diſſemble one to another*

~~Enter Haringsfield.~~

Harring. Hee what art thou,
Sencer. A hanger on, if it pleaſe you:
Harring. And I a ſhaker off, ile not beare your gallowes, You ſhall not hang on mee.

Enter Chartly *with his Napkin as from Dinner.*

O. Mr Bridegroome.
Chartly. Gentlemen, the Ladies call vpon you to dance, they will be out of meaſure diſpleaſed, if dinner beeing done, you bee not ready to leade them a meaſure:
Harring. Indeede women love not to bee ſcanted of their meaſure.
Chartly. Fie ſir *Boniface*: haue you forgot your ſelfe, Whilſt you are in the Hall, there's never a whetſtone for their wits in the Parler?
Sir Boniface. I will enter and ſet an edge vpon their Ingenies.
Chartly. To mee ſir, from whom? a letter to her moſt deere, moſt louing, moſt kind friend Mr. *Chartly* theſe bee deliuered: ſure from ſome wench or other I long to know the contents.

Sencer.

The Wiſe-woman of Hoſgden.

Sencer. Now to cry quittance with you for my farewell learn'd ſir *Timothy.*
Chartly. Good newes, as I liue, there's for thy paines my good ſir *Pandarus*: Hadſt thou brought mee word my father had turnd vp his heeles. Thou couldſt ſcarcely haue pleaſed mee better: (Hee reades) though I diſclaime the name of wife, of which I account my ſelfe altogether vnworthy, yet let mee claime ſome ſmall intereſt in your loue, this night I lye at the houſe where wee were married, (the Wiſewomans I meane) where my maiden-head is to bee rifled, bid fayre for it, and inioy it, ſee mee this night or never, ſo may you marrying *Gratiana*, and louing mee, haue a ſweete wife and a true friend: This night or never, your *quondam* wife: Hereafter your poore ſweet-heart no other: *Luce.* So when I am tyr'd with *Gratiana*, that is when I am paſt grace. With her I can make my rendevowz, ile not ſlip this occaſion, nor ſleepe till I ſee her, thou art an honeſt ladde, and maiſt proue a good Pimpe in time. Canſt thou adviſe mee what colour, I may haue to compaſſe this commodity.
Sencer. Sir, ſhee this night expects you, and prepares a coſtly banquet for you.
Chartly. Ile goe, although the Devill and miſchance looke bigge.
Sencer. Feyne ſome newes that ſuch a peece of Land is falne to you, and you muſt inſtantly ride to take poſſeſſion of it, or which is more probable, cannot you perſwade them you haue receiu'd a letter that your Father lyes a dying.
Chartly. You rogue, I would hee did but the name of that newes is cal'd, too good to be true.
Sencer And that if ever you will ſee him aliue, you muſt ride poſt into the Country.
Chartly. Enough: if ever I proue Knight errant thou ſhalt bee mine owne proper ſquire, ~~for this thou haſt fitted mee with a plot,~~ doe but waite heere note how I will manage it,

H *Taber.*

for this thou hast fitted

IV, i, following 498. The entrance cue sign is actually for Chartley, who has a speech after the indicated cut. I cannot decipher the blotted word.

IV, i, 553. There should be an entrance and an entrance cue sign for Taber here; he was warned at line 535.

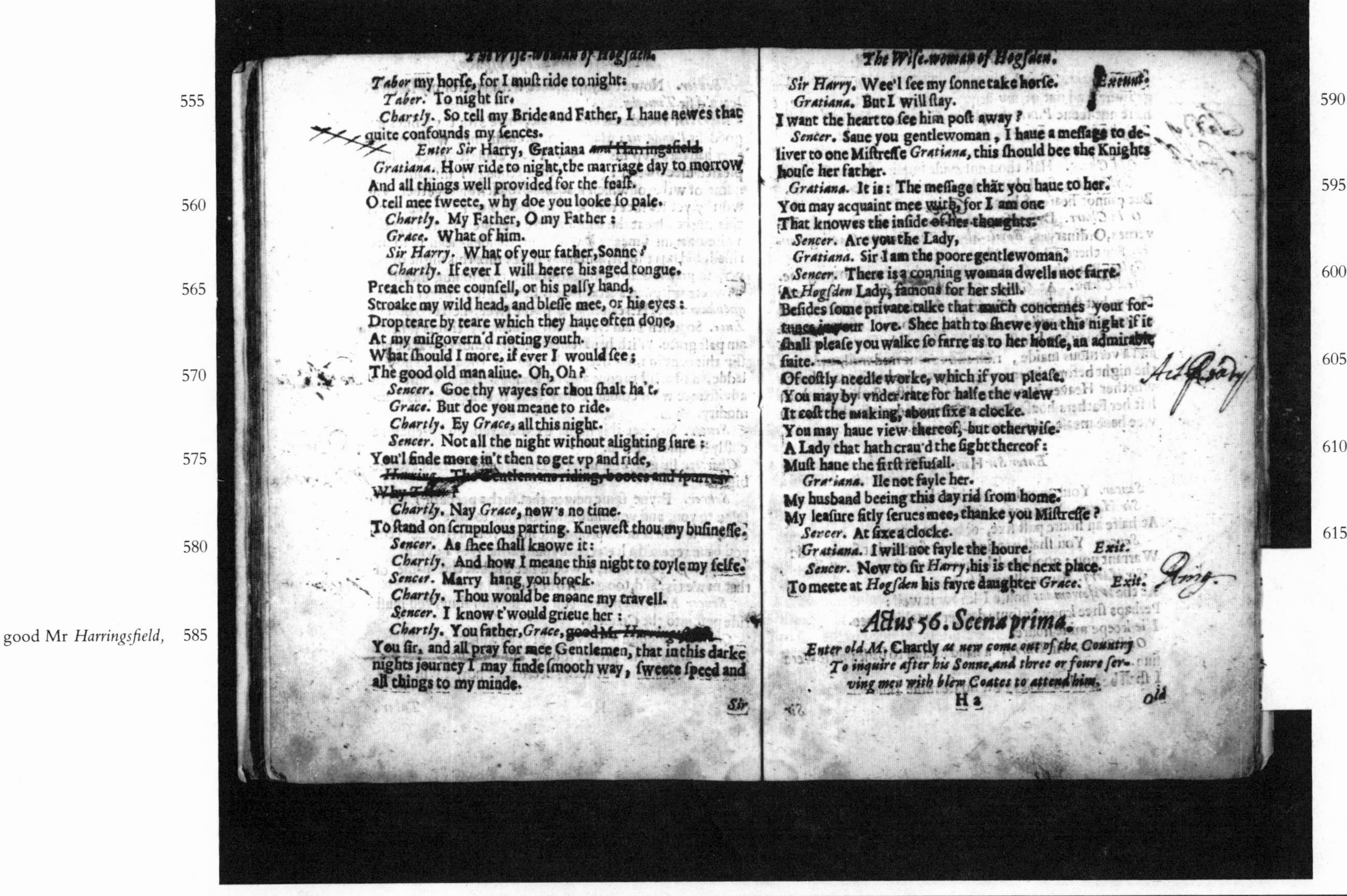

The Wise-woman of Hogsden.

Tabor my horse, for I must ride to night:

Taber. To night sir.

Chartly. So tell my Bride and Father, I haue newes that quite confounds my sences.

Enter Sir Harry, Gratiana ~~and Harringsfield.~~

Gratiana. How ride to night, the marriage day to morrow And all things well provided for the feast. O tell mee sweete, why doe you looke so pale.

Chartly. My Father, O my Father:

Grace. What of him.

Sir Harry. What of your father, Sonne?

Chartly. If ever I will heere his aged tongue.
Preach to mee counsell, or his palsy hand,
Stroake my wild head, and blesse mee, or his eyes:
Drop teare by teare which they haue often done,
At my misgovern'd rioting youth.
What should I more, if ever I would see;
The good old man aliue. Oh, Oh?

Sencer. Goe thy wayes for thou shalt ha't.

Grace. But doe you meane to ride.

Chartly. Ey *Grace,* all this night.

Sencer. Not all the night without alighting sure:
You'l finde more in't then to get vp and ride,

~~*Harring.* The Gentlemans riding, bootes and spurres~~
~~Why *Tabor?*~~

Chartly. Nay *Grace,* now's no time.
To stand on scrupulous parting. Knewest thou my businesse?

Sencer. As shee shall knowe it:

Chartly. And how I meane this night to toyle my selfe.

Sencer. Marry hang you brack.

Chartly. Thou wouldst be meane my travell.

Sencer. I know t'would grieue her:

good Mr *Harringsfield,*

Chartly. You father, *Grace,* ~~good Mr Harringsfield~~
You sir, and all pray for mee Gentlemen, that in this darke nights journey I may finde smooth way, sweete speed and all things to my minde.

Sir

The Wise-woman of Hogsden.

Sir Harry. Wee'l see my sonne take horse. *Exeunt.*

Gratiana. But I will stay.
I want the heart to see him post away?

Sencer. Saue you gentlewoman, I haue a message to deliver to one Mistresse *Gratiana,* this should bee the Knights house her father.

Gratiana. It is: The message that you haue to her.
You may acquaint mee with, for I am one
That knowes the inside of her thoughts.

Sencer. Are you the Lady,

Gratiana. Sir I am the poore gentlewoman.

Sencer. There is a cunning woman dwells not farre
At *Hogsden* Lady, famous for her skill.
Besides some private talke that much concernes your fortunes in your love. Shee hath to shewe you this night if it shall please you walke so farre as to her house, an admirable suite.
Of costly needle worke, which if you please,
You may by vnder-rate for halfe the valew
It cost the making, about sixe a clocke.
You may haue view thereof, but otherwise.
A Lady that hath crau'd the sight thereof:
Must haue the first refusall.

Gratiana. Ile not fayle her.
My husband beeing this day rid from home.
My leasure fitly serues mee, thanke you Mistresse?

Sencer. At sixe a clocke.

Gratiana. I will not fayle the houre. *Exit.*

Sencer. Now to sir *Harry,* his is the next place.
To meete at *Hogsden* his fayre daughter *Grace.* *Exit.*

Actus 56. Scena prima.

Enter old M. Chartly *as new come out of the Country To inquire after his Sonne, and three or foure serving men with blew Coates to attend him.*

H 2 old

IV, i, 576–77. The canceled speech is: "*Harring.* The Gentlemans riding, bootes and spurres / Why *Tabor?*"

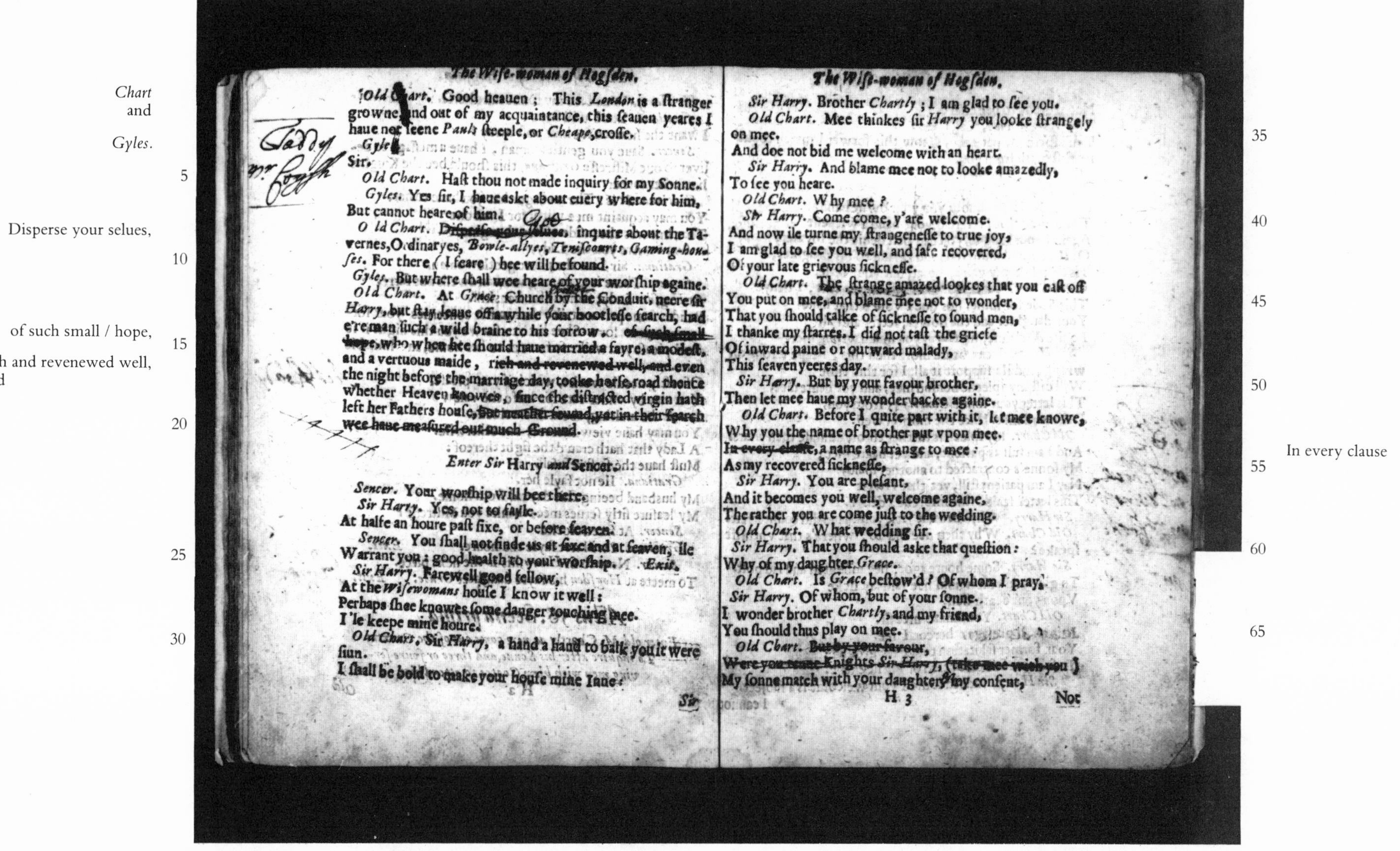

The Wise-woman of Hogsdon.

Old Chart. Good heauen; This *London* is a stranger
growne, and out of my acquaintance, this seauen yeares I
haue not seene *Pauls* steeple, or *Cheape-*crosse.
Gyles.
Sir.
Old Chart. Hast thou not made inquiry for my Sonne.
Gyles. Yes sir, I haue askt about euery where for him,
But cannot heare of him.
Old Chart. Disperse your selues, inquire about the Ta-
vernes, Ordinaryes, *Bowle-allyes, Tenis-courts, Gaming-hou-
ses.* For there (I feare) hee will be found.
Gyles. But where shall wee heare of your worship againe.
Old Chart. At *Grace-*Church by the Conduit, neere sir
Harry, but stay, leaue off a while your bootlesse search, had
e're man such a wild braine to his sorrow, of such small
hope, who when hee should haue married a fayre, a modest,
and a vertuous maide, rich and revenewed well, and euen
the night before the marriage day, tooke horse, road thence
whether Heauen knowes, since the distracted virgin hath
left her Fathers house, but neither found, yet in their search
wee haue measured out much Ground.
Enter Sir Harry *and* Sencer.
Sencer. Your worship will bee there.
Sir Harry. Yes, not to fayle.
At halfe an houre past sixe, or before seauen.
Sencer. You shall not finde us at sixe and at seauen, Ile
Warrant you: good health to your worship. *Exit.*
Sir Harry. Farewell good fellow,
At the *Wisewomans* house I know it well:
Perhaps shee knowes some danger touching mee.
I'le keepe mine houre.
Old Chart. Sir Harry, a hand a hand to balk you it were
sinn.
I shall be bold to make your house mine Inne.
Sir

The Wise-woman of Hogsdon.

Sir Harry. Brother *Chartly*; I am glad to see you.
Old Chart. Mee thinkes sir *Harry* you looke strangely
on mee.
And doe not bid me welcome with an heart.
Sir Harry. And blame mee not to looke amazedly,
To see you heare.
Old Chart. Why mee?
Sir Harry. Come come, y'are welcome.
And now ile turne my strangenesse to true joy,
I am glad to see you well, and safe recovered,
Of your late grievous sicknesse.
Old Chart. The strange amazed lookes that you cast off
You put on mee, and blame mee not to wonder,
That you should talke of sicknesse to sound men,
I thanke my starres, I did not tast the griefe
Of inward paine or outward malady,
This seaven yeeres day.
Sir Harry. But by your favour brother,
Then let mee haue my wonder backe againe.
Old Chart. Before I quite part with it, let mee knowe,
Why you the name of brother put vpon mee.
In every clause, a name as strange to mee:
As my recovered sicknesse,
Sir Harry. You are plesant,
And it becomes you well, welcome againe,
The rather you are come just to the wedding.
Old Chart. What wedding sir.
Sir Harry. That you should aske that question:
Why of my daughter *Grace.*
Old Chart. Is *Grace* bestow'd? Of whom I pray.
Sir Harry. Of whom, but of your sonne.
I wonder brother *Chartly*, and my friend,
You should thus play on mee.
Old Chart. But by your favour,
Were you tenne Knights *Sir Harry*, (take mee with you)
My sonne match with your daughter, my consent,
H 3 Not

Chart and *Gyles.*

Disperse your selues,

of such small / hope,

rich and revenewed well, and

In every clause

V, i, 19–20. The canceled lines are: "but neither found yet in their search / wee haue measured out much Ground."

V, i, 66–67. The canceled lines are: "But by your favour, / Were you tenne Knights *Sir Harry*, (take mee with you)."

Shall not make mee approue it

Mrs Cook.

It is an ill presage

see mee

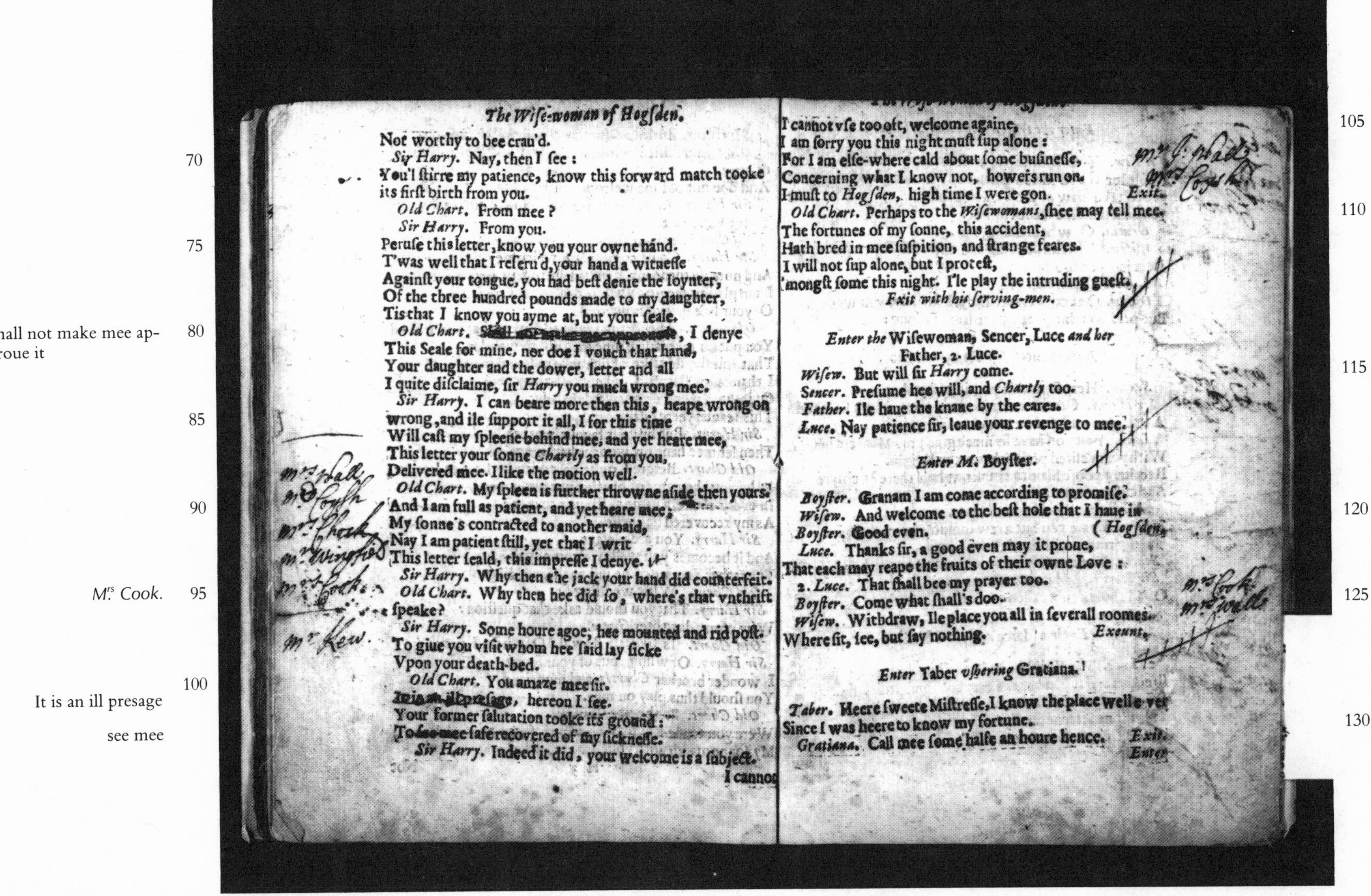

The Wise-woman of Hogsden.

Not worthy to bee crau'd.
Sir Harry. Nay, then I see:
You'l stirre my patience, know this forward match tooke its first birth from you.
Old Chart. From mee?
Sir Harry. From you.
Peruse this letter, know you your owne hand.
T'was well that I reseru'd, your hand a witnesse
Against your tongue, you had best denie the Ioynter,
Of the three hundred pounds made to my daughter,
Tis that I know you ayme at, but your seale.
Old Chart. Shall not make mee approue it, I denye
This Seale for mine, nor doe I vouch that hand,
Your daughter and the dower, letter and all
I quite disclaime, sir *Harry* you much wrong mee.
Sir Harry. I can beare more then this, heape wrong on wrong, and ile support it all, I for this time
Will cast my spleene behind mee, and yet heare mee,
This letter your sonne *Chartly* as from you,
Delivered mee. I like the motion well.
Old Chart. My spleen is further throwne aside then yours.
And I am full as patient, and yet heare mee;
My sonne's contracted to another maid,
Nay I am patient still, yet that I writ
This letter seald, this impresse I denye.
Sir Harry. Why then the jack your hand did counterfeit.
Old Chart. Why then hee did so, where's that vnthrift speake?
Sir Harry. Some houre agoe, hee mounted and rid post.
To giue you visit whom hee said lay sicke
Vpon your death-bed.
Old Chart. You amaze mee sir.
It is an ill presage, hereon I see.
Your former salutation tooke its ground:
To see mee safe recovered of my sicknesse.
Sir Harry. Indeed it did, your welcome is a subject
I cannot

I cannot vse too oft, welcome againe,
I am sorry you this night must sup alone:
For I am else-where cald about some businesse,
Concerning what I know not, howe'rs run on.
I must to *Hogsden*, high time I were gon. *Exit.*
Old Chart. Perhaps to the *Wisewomans*, shee may tell mee.
The fortunes of my sonne, this accident,
Hath bred in mee suspition, and strange feares.
I will not sup alone, but I protest,
'mongst some this night. I'le play the intruding guest.
Exit with his serving-men.

Enter the Wisewoman, Sencer, Luce *and her* Father, 2. Luce.

Wisew. But will sir *Harry* come.
Sencer. Presume hee will, and *Chartly* too.
Father. Ile haue the knaue by the eares.
Luce. Nay patience sir, leaue your revenge to mee.

Enter M. Boyster.

Boyster. Granam I am come according to promise.
Wisew. And welcome to the best hole that I haue in (*Hogsden.*
Boyster. Good even.
Luce. Thanks sir, a good even may it proue,
That each may reape the fruits of their owne Love:
2. Luce. That shall bee my prayer too.
Boyster. Come what shall's doo.
Wisew. Withdraw, Ile place you all in severall roomes.
Where sit, see, but say nothing. *Exeunt.*

Enter Taber *vshering* Gratiana.

Taber. Heere sweete Mistresse, I know the place well ever since I was heere to know my fortune.
Gratiana. Call mee some halfe an houre hence. *Exit.*
Enter

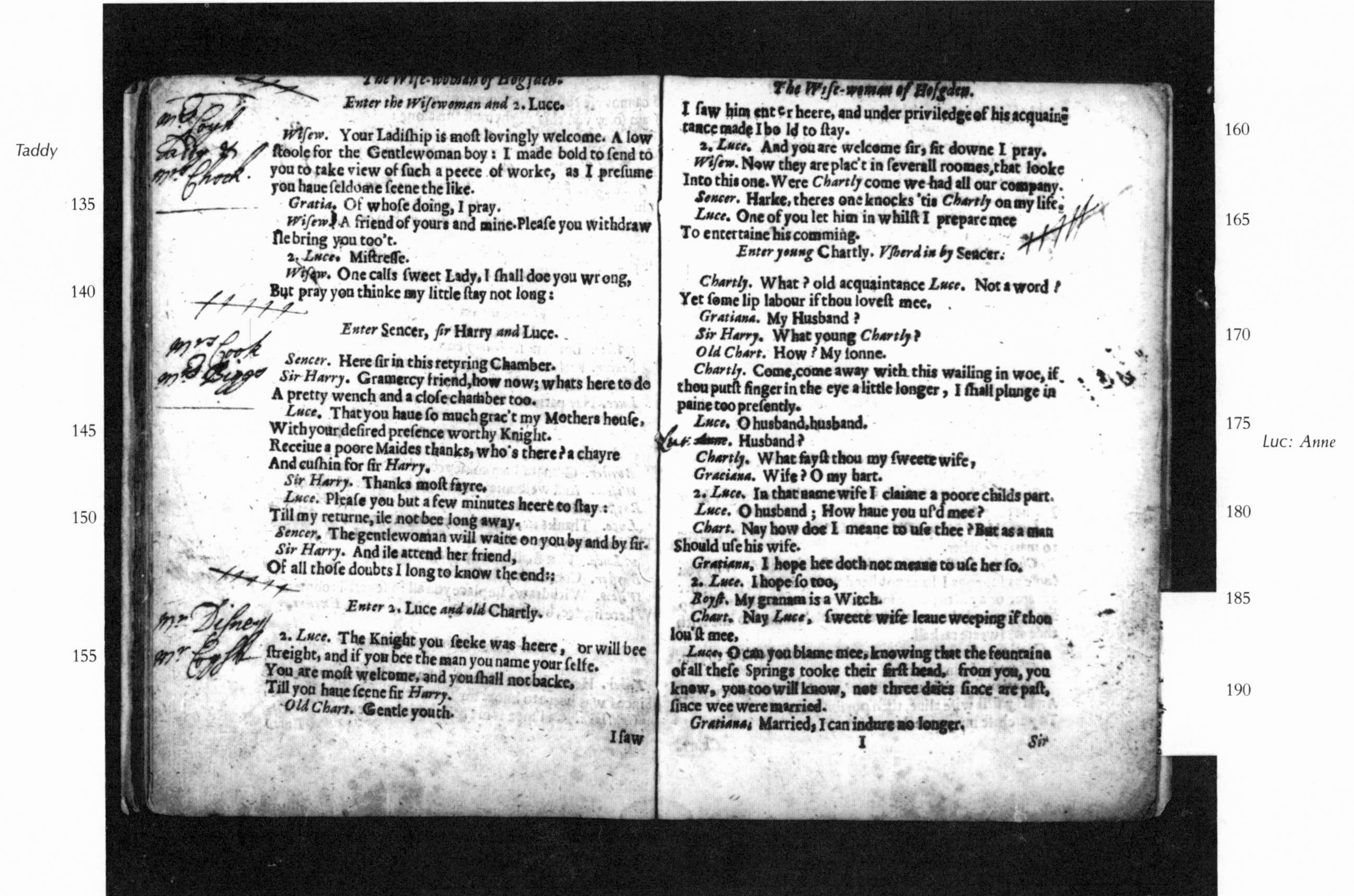

The Wise-woman of Hogsden.

Enter the Wisewoman and 2. Luce.

Taddy

Wisew. Your Ladiship is most lovingly welcome. A low stoole for the Gentlewoman boy: I made bold to send to you to take view of such a peece of worke, as I presume you haue seldome seene the like.

Gratia. Of whose doing, I pray.

Wisew. A friend of yours and mine. Please you withdraw Ile bring you too't.

2. *Luce.* Mistresse.

Wisew. One calls sweet Lady, I shall doe you wrong,
But pray you thinke my little stay not long:

Enter Sencer, *sir* Harry *and* Luce.

Sencer. Here sir in this retyring Chamber.

Sir Harry. Gramercy friend, how now; whats here to do
A pretty wench and a close chamber too.

Luce. That you haue so much grac't my Mothers house,
With your desired presence worthy Knight.
Receiue a poore Maides thanks, who's there? a chayre
And cushin for sir *Harry.*

Sir Harry. Thanks most fayre.

Luce. Please you but a few minutes heere to stay:
Till my returne, ile not bee long away.

Sencer. The gentlewoman will waite on you by and by sir.

Sir Harry. And ile attend her friend,
Of all those doubts I long to know the end:;

Enter 2. Luce *and old* Chartly.

2. *Luce.* The Knight you seeke was heere, or will bee streight, and if you bee the man you name your selfe.
You are most welcome, and you shall not backe,
Till you haue seene sir *Harry.*

Old Chart. Gentle youth.

I saw

The Wise-woman of Hosgden.

I saw him enter heere, and under priviledge of his acquaintance made I bold to stay.

2. *Luce.* And you are welcome sir, sit downe I pray.

Wisew. Now they are plac't in severall roomes, that looke
Into this one. Were *Chartly* come we had all our company.

Sencer. Harke, theres one knocks 'tis *Chartly* on my life.

Luce. One of you let him in whilst I prepare mee
To entertaine his comming.

Enter young Chartly. *Vsherd in by* Sencer.

Chartly. What? old acquaintance *Luce.* Not a word?
Yet some lip labour if thou lovest mee.

Gratiana. My Husband?

Sir Harry. What young *Chartly*?

Old Chart. How? My sonne.

Chartly. Come, come away with this wailing in woe, if thou putst finger in the eye a little longer, I shall plunge in paine too presently.

Luce. O husband, husband.

Anne. Husband?

Luc: Anne

Chartly. What sayst thou my sweete wife,

Graciana. Wife? O my hart.

2. *Luce.* In that name wife I claime a poore childs part.

Luce. O husband; How haue you us'd mee?

Chart. Nay how doe I meane to use thee? But as a man
Should use his wife.

Gratiana. I hope hee doth not meane to use her so.

2. *Luce.* I hope so too,

Boyst. My granam is a Witch.

Chart. Nay *Luce,* sweete wife leaue weeping if thou lou'st mee,

Luce. O can you blame mee, knowing that the fountaine of all these Springs tooke their first head, from you, you know, you too will know, not three daies since are past, since wee were married.

Gratiana. Married, I can indure no longer.

I Sir

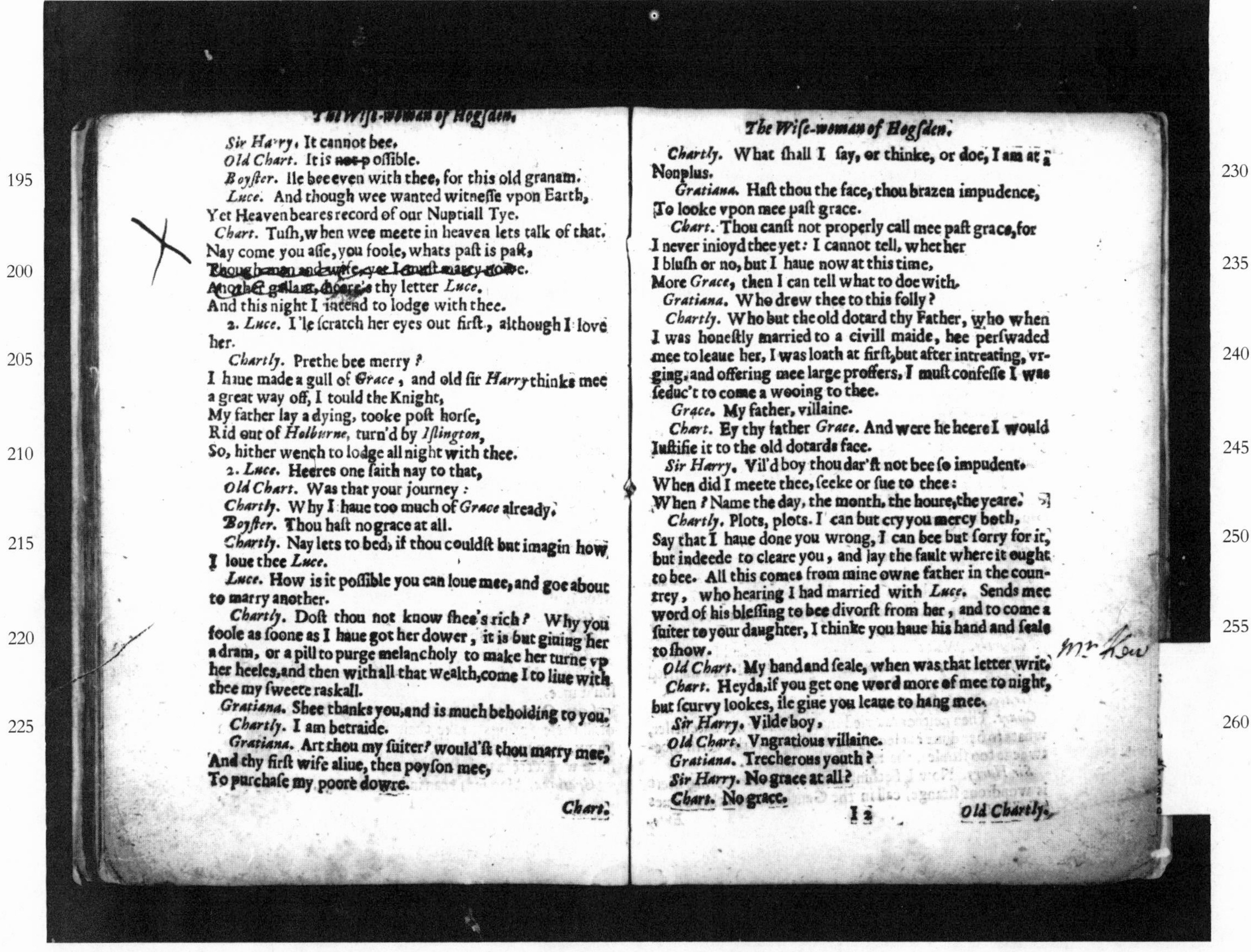

The Wise-woman of Hogsdon.

Sir Harry. It cannot bee.
Old Chart. It is not possible.
Boyster. Ile bee even with thee, for this old granam.
Luce. And though wee wanted witnesse vpon Earth,
Yet Heaven beares record of our Nuptiall Tye.
Chart. Tush, when wee meete in heaven lets talk of that.
Nay come you asse, you foole, whats past is past,
Though man and wife, yet I must marry nowe.
Another gallant, heere's thy letter *Luce*,
And this night I intend to lodge with thee.
2. Luce. I'le scratch her eyes out first, although I love her.
Chartly. Prethe bee merry?
I haue made a gull of *Grace*, and old sir *Harry* thinks mee a great way off, I tould the Knight,
My father lay a dying, tooke post horse,
Rid out of *Holburne*, turn'd by *Islington*,
So, hither wench to lodge all night with thee.
2. Luce. Heeres one saith nay to that,
Old Chart. Was that your journey:
Chartly. Why I haue too much of *Grace* already.
Boyster. Thou hast no grace at all.
Chartly. Nay lets to bed, if thou couldst but imagin how I loue thee *Luce*.
Luce. How is it possible you can loue mee, and goe about to marry another.
Chartly. Dost thou not know shee's rich? Why you foole as soone as I haue got her dower, it is but giuing her a dram, or a pill to purge melancholy to make her turne vp her heeles, and then with all that wealth, come I to liue with thee my sweete raskall.
Gratiana. Shee thanks you, and is much beholding to you.
Chartly. I am betraide.
Gratiana. Art thou my suiter? would'st thou marry mee,
And thy first wife aliue, then poyson mee,
To purchase my poore dowre.

Chart.

The Wise-woman of Hogsden.

Chartly. What shall I say, or thinke, or doe, I am at a Nonplus.
Gratiana. Hast thou the face, thou brazen impudence,
To looke vpon mee past grace.
Chart. Thou canst not properly call mee past grace, for I never inioyd thee yet: I cannot tell, whether
I blush or no, but I haue now at this time,
More *Grace*, then I can tell what to doe with.
Gratiana. Who drew thee to this folly?
Chartly. Who but the old dotard thy Father, who when I was honestly married to a civill maide, hee perswaded mee to leaue her, I was loath at first, but after intreating, vrging, and offering mee large proffers, I must confesse I was seduc't to come a wooing to thee.
Grace. My father, villaine.
Chart. By thy father *Grace*. And were he heere I would Iustifie it to the old dotards face.
Sir Harry. Vil'd boy thou dar'st not bee so impudent.
When did I meete thee, seeke or sue to thee:
When? Name the day, the month, the houre, the yeare.
Chartly. Plots, plots. I can but cry you mercy both,
Say that I haue done you wrong, I can bee but sorry for it, but indeede to cleare you, and lay the fault where it ought to bee. All this comes from mine owne father in the countrey, who hearing I had married with *Luce*. Sends mee word of his blessing to bee divorst from her, and to come a suiter to your daughter, I thinke you haue his hand and seale to show.
Old Chart. My hand and seale, when was that letter writ?
Chart. Heyda, if you get one word more of mee to night, but scurvy lookes, ile giue you leaue to hang mee.
Sir Harry. Vilde boy,
Old Chart. Vngratious villaine.
Gratiana. Trecherous youth?
Sir Harry. No grace at all?
Chart. No grace.

I 2 Old Chartly.

V, i, 200–201. The canceled lines are: "Though man and wife, yet I must marry nowe. / Another gallant, heere's."

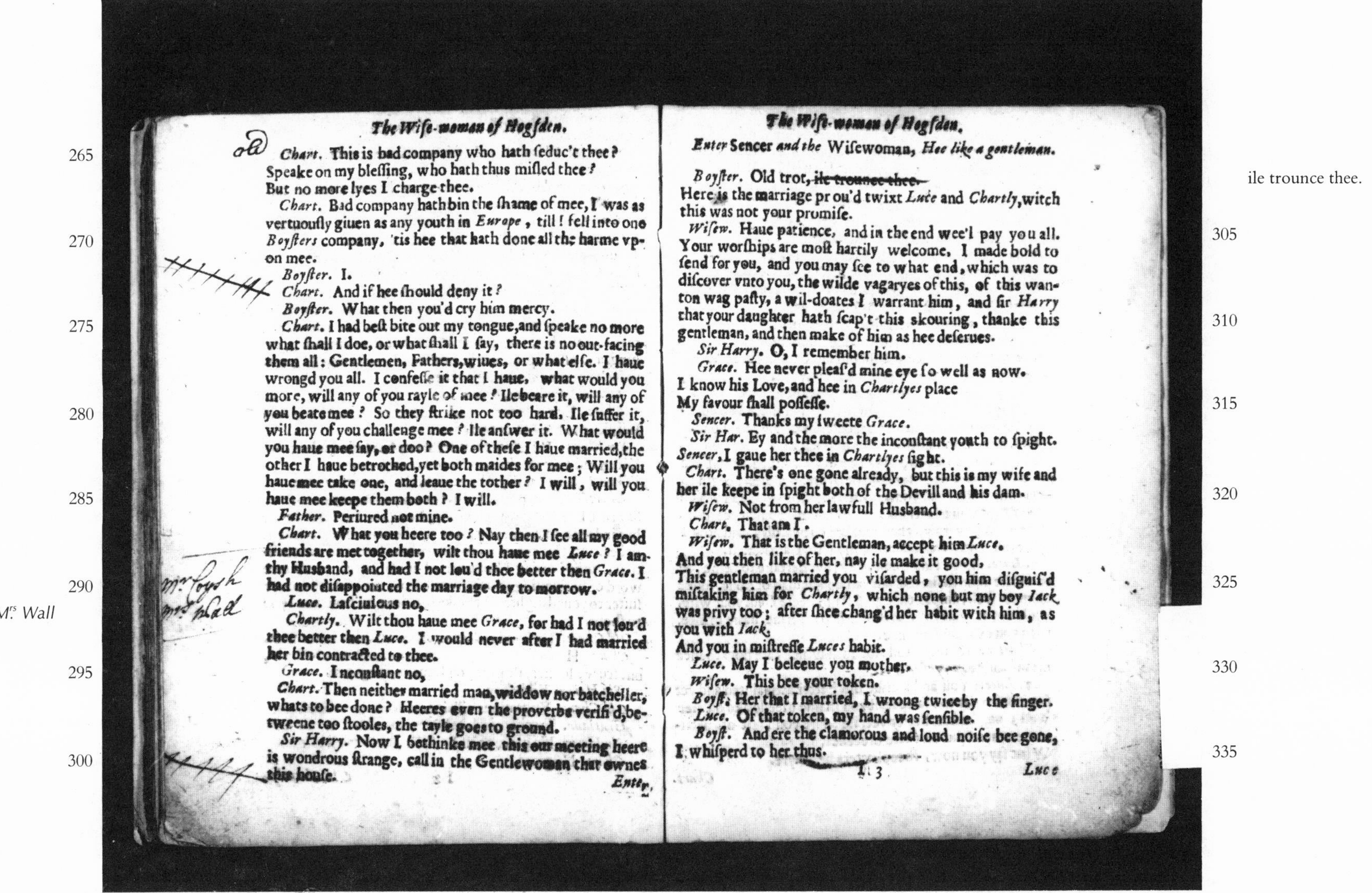

The Wiſe-woman of Hogſden.

Chart. This is bad company who hath ſeduc't thee?
Speake on my bleſſing, who hath thus miſled thee?
But no more lyes I charge thee.

Chart. Bad company hath bin the ſhame of mee, I was as vertuouſly giuen as any youth in *Europe*, till I fell into one *Boyſters* company, 'tis hee that hath done all the harme vpon mee.

Boyſter. I.

Chart. And if hee ſhould deny it?

Boyſter. What then you'd cry him mercy.

Chart. I had beſt bite out my tongue, and ſpeake no more what ſhall I doe, or what ſhall I ſay, there is no out-facing them all: Gentlemen, Fathers, wiues, or what elſe. I haue wrongd you all. I confeſſe it that I haue, what would you more, will any of you rayle of mee? Ile beare it, will any of you beate mee? So they ſtrike not too hard. Ile ſuffer it, will any of you challenge mee? Ile anſwer it. What would you haue mee ſay, or doo? One of theſe I haue married, the other I haue betrothed, yet both maides for mee; Will you haue mee take one, and leaue the tother? I will, will you haue mee keepe them both? I will.

Father. Periured not mine.

Chart. What you heere too? Nay then I ſee all my good friends are met together, wilt thou haue mee *Luce*? I am thy Husband, and had I not lou'd thee better then *Grace*, I had not diſappointed the marriage day to morrow.

Mrs Wall

Luce. Laſciuious no,

Chartly. Wilt thou haue mee *Grace*, for had I not lou'd thee better then *Luce*. I would neuer after I had married her bin contracted to thee.

Grace. Inconſtant no,

Chart. Then neither married man, widdow nor batcheller, whats to bee done? Heeres euen the prouerbe verifi'd, betweene two ſtooles, the tayle goes to ground.

Sir Harry. Now I bethinke mee this our meeting heere is wondrous ſtrange, call in the Gentlewoman that ownes this houſe.

Enter,

The Wiſe-woman of Hogſden.

Enter Sencer *and the* Wiſewoman, *Hee like a gentleman.*

Boyſter. Old trot, ~~ile trounce thee.~~

ile trounce thee.

Here is the marriage prou'd twixt *Luce* and *Chartly*, witch this was not your promiſe.

Wiſew. Haue patience, and in the end wee'l pay you all. Your worſhips are moſt hartily welcome, I made bold to ſend for you, and you may ſee to what end, which was to diſcouer vnto you, the wilde vagaryes of this, of this wanton wag paſty, a wil-doates I warrant him, and ſir *Harry* that your daughter hath ſcap't this skouring, thanke this gentleman, and then make of him as hee deſerues.

Sir Harry. O, I remember him.

Grace. Hee neuer pleaſ'd mine eye ſo well as now.
I know his Love, and hee in *Chartlyes* place
My fauour ſhall poſſeſſe.

Sencer. Thanks my ſweete *Grace.*

Sir Har. Ey and the more the inconſtant youth to ſpight.
Sencer, I gaue her thee in *Chartlyes* ſight.

Chart. There's one gone already, but this is my wife and her ile keepe in ſpight both of the Deuill and his dam.

Wiſew. Not from her lawfull Husband.

Chart. That am I.

Wiſew. That is the Gentleman, accept him *Luce*,
And you then like of her, nay ile make it good,
This gentleman married you viſarded, you him diſguiſ'd miſtaking him for *Chartly*, which none but my boy *Iack* was privy too; after ſhee chang'd her habit with him, as you with *Iack*,
And you in miſtreſſe *Luces* habit.

Luce. May I beleeue you mother.

Wiſew. This bee your token.

Boyſt. Her that I married, I wrong twice by the finger.

Luce. Of that token, my hand was ſenſible.

Boyſt. And ere the clamorous and loud noiſe bee gone, I whiſperd to her thus.

I 3 Luce

V, i, 272. The cue sign, in view of the warning for Boyster (the actor Kew) at line 256, is clearly for Boyster's speech, but he has been overhearing and making asides regularly during the scene. Perhaps the cue means that there was a piece of stage business that had to be signaled or that in rehearsal Kew had missed his cue.

forgot by me

shee skatters her hayre

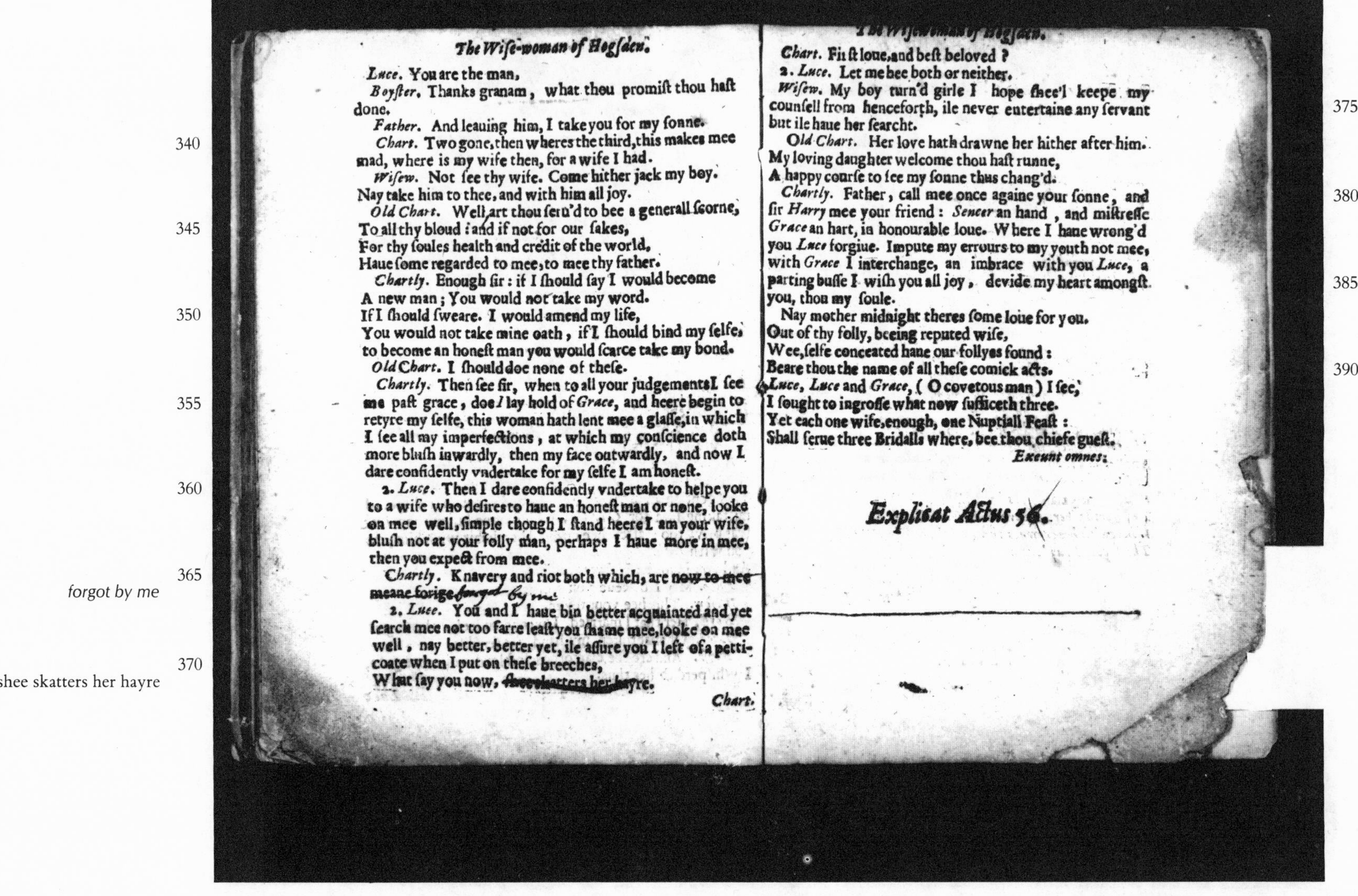

The Wise-woman of Hogsden.

Luce. You are the man,

Boyster. Thanks granam, what thou promist thou hast done.

Father. And leauing him, I take you for my sonne.

Chart. Two gone, then wheres the third, this makes mee mad, where is my wife then, for a wife I had.

Wisew. Not see thy wife. Come hither jack my boy.
Nay take him to thee, and with him all joy.

Old Chart. Well art thou seru'd to bee a generall scorne,
To all thy bloud: and if not for our sakes,
For thy soules health and credit of the world,
Haue some regarded to mee, to mee thy father.

Chartly. Enough sir: if I should say I would become
A new man; You would not take my word.
If I should sweare. I would amend my life,
You would not take mine oath, if I should bind my selfe,
to become an honest man you would scarce take my bond.

Old Chart. I should doe none of these.

Chartly. Then see sir, when to all your judgements I see me past grace, doe I lay hold of *Grace*, and heere begin to retyre my selfe, this woman hath lent mee a glasse, in which I see all my imperfections, at which my conscience doth more blush inwardly, then my face outwardly, and now I dare confidently vndertake for my selfe I am honest.

2. *Luce.* Then I dare confidently vndertake to helpe you to a wife who desires to haue an honest man or none, looke on mee well, simple though I stand heere I am your wife, blush not at your folly man, perhaps I haue more in mee, then you expect from mee.

Chartly. Knavery and riot both which, are ~~now to mee meane forige~~ forgot by me

2. *Luce.* You and I haue bin better acquainted and yet search mee not too farre least you shame mee, looke on mee well, nay better, better yet, ile assure you I left of a petticoate when I put on these breeches,
What say you now, ~~shee skatters her hayre.~~

Chart.

The Wise-woman of Hogsden.

Chart. First loue, and best beloved?

2. *Luce.* Let me bee both or neither.

Wisew. My boy turn'd girle I hope shee'l keepe my counsell from henceforth, ile never entertaine any servant but ile haue her searcht.

Old Chart. Her love hath drawne her hither after him.
My loving daughter welcome thou hast runne,
A happy course to see my sonne thus chang'd.

Chartly. Father, call mee once againe your sonne, and sir *Harry* mee your friend: *Sencer* an hand, and mistresse *Grace* an hart, in honourable loue. Where I haue wrong'd you *Luce* forgiue. Impute my errours to my youth not mee, with *Grace* I interchange, an imbrace with you *Luce*, a parting busse I wish you all joy, devide my heart amongst you, thou my soule.

Nay mother midnight theres some loue for you.
Out of thy folly, beeing reputed wise,
Wee, selfe conceated haue our follyes found:
Beare thou the name of all these comick acts.
Luce, Luce and *Grace*, (O covetous man) I see,
I sought to ingrosse what now sufficeth three.
Yet each one wise, enough, one Nuptiall Feast:
Shall serue three Bridalls where, bee thou chiefe guest.

Exeunt omnes.

Explicit Actus 5.

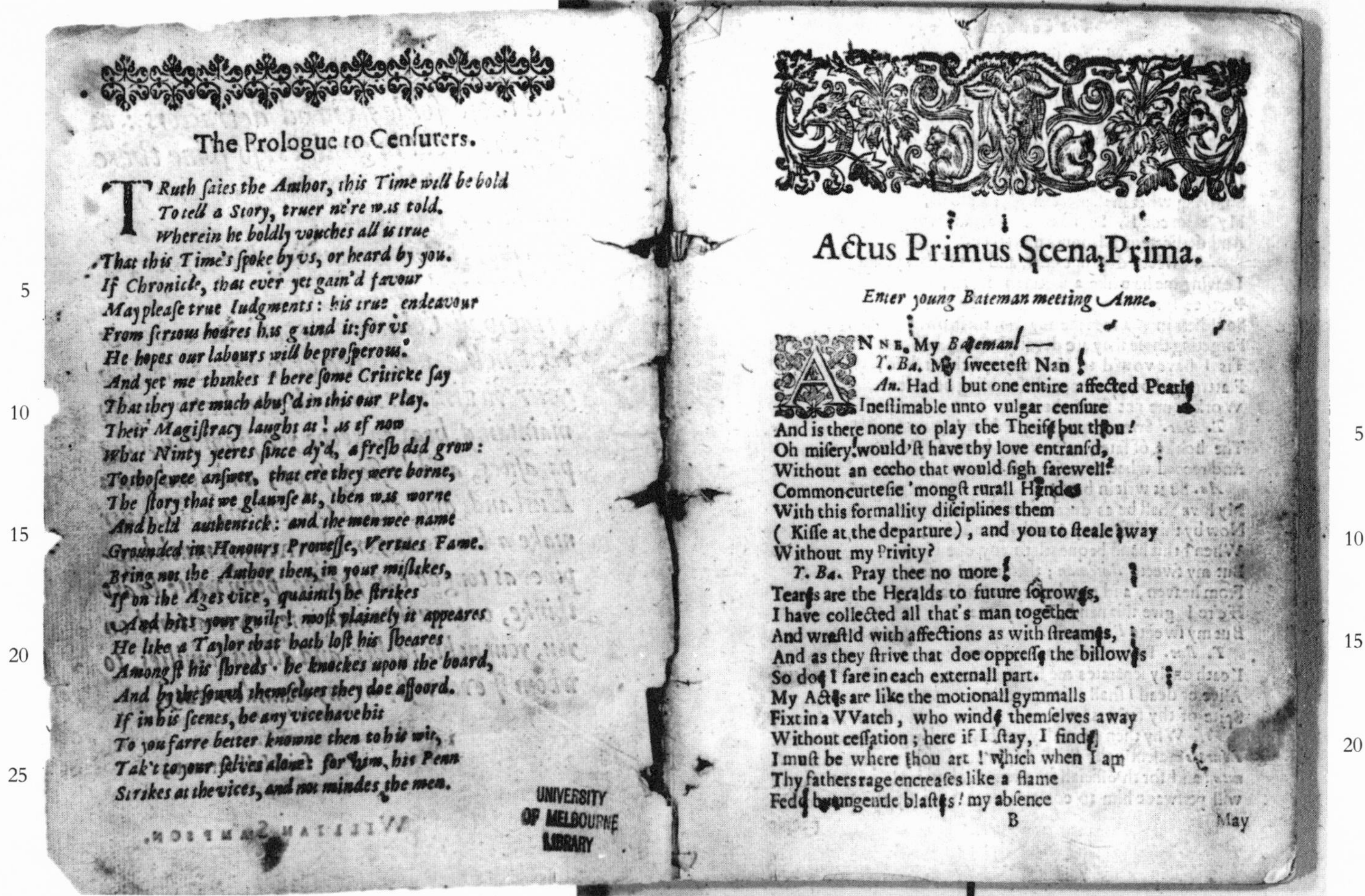

The Prologue to Censurers.

Truth saies the Author, this Time will be bold
To tell a Story, truer ne're was told.
Wherein he boldly vouches all is true
That this Time's spoke by us, or heard by you.
If Chronicle, that ever yet gain'd favour
May please true Iudgments: his true endeavour
From serious houres has gaind it: for us
He hopes our labours will be prosperous.
And yet me thinkes I here some Criticke say
That they are much abus'd in this our Play.
Their Magistracy laught at! as if now
What Ninty yeeres since dy'd, afresh did grow:
To those wee answer, that ere they were borne,
The story that we glaunse at, then was worne
And held authentick: and the men wee name
Grounded in Honours Prowesse, Vertues Fame.
Bring not the Author then, in your mislikes,
If on the Ages vice, quaintly he strikes
And hits your guilt! most plainely it appeares
He like a Taylor that hath lost his sheares
Amongst his shreds, he knockes upon the board,
And by the sound themselves they doe afoord.
If in his scenes, be any vice have hit
To you farre better knowne then to his wit,
Tak't to your selves alone: for him, his Penn
Strikes at the vices, and not mindes the men.

WILLIAM SAMPSON.

Actus Primus Scena Prima.

Enter young Bateman meeting Anne.

Anne. My Bateman!—
Y. Ba. My sweetest Nan!
An. Had I but one entire affected Pearle
Inestimable unto vulgar censure
And is there none to play the Theife but thou!
Oh misery! would'st have thy love entrans'd,
Without an eccho that would sigh farewell?
Common curtesie 'mongst rurall Hindes
With this formallity disciplines them
(Kisse at the departure), and you to steale away
Without my Privity?
Y. Ba. Pray thee no more!
Teares are the Heralds to future sorrowes,
I have collected all that's man together
And wrastld with affections as with streames,
And as they strive that doe oppresse the billowes
So doe I fare in each externall part.
My Acts are like the motionall gymmalls
Fixt in a VVatch, who winde themselves away
Without cessation; here if I stay, I finde
I must be where thou art! which when I am
Thy fathers rage encreases like a flame
Fedd by ungentle blasts! my absence
B May

The copy lacks a title page.

The Vow-Breaker by William Sampson. Reproduced by permission of the University of Melbourne Library.

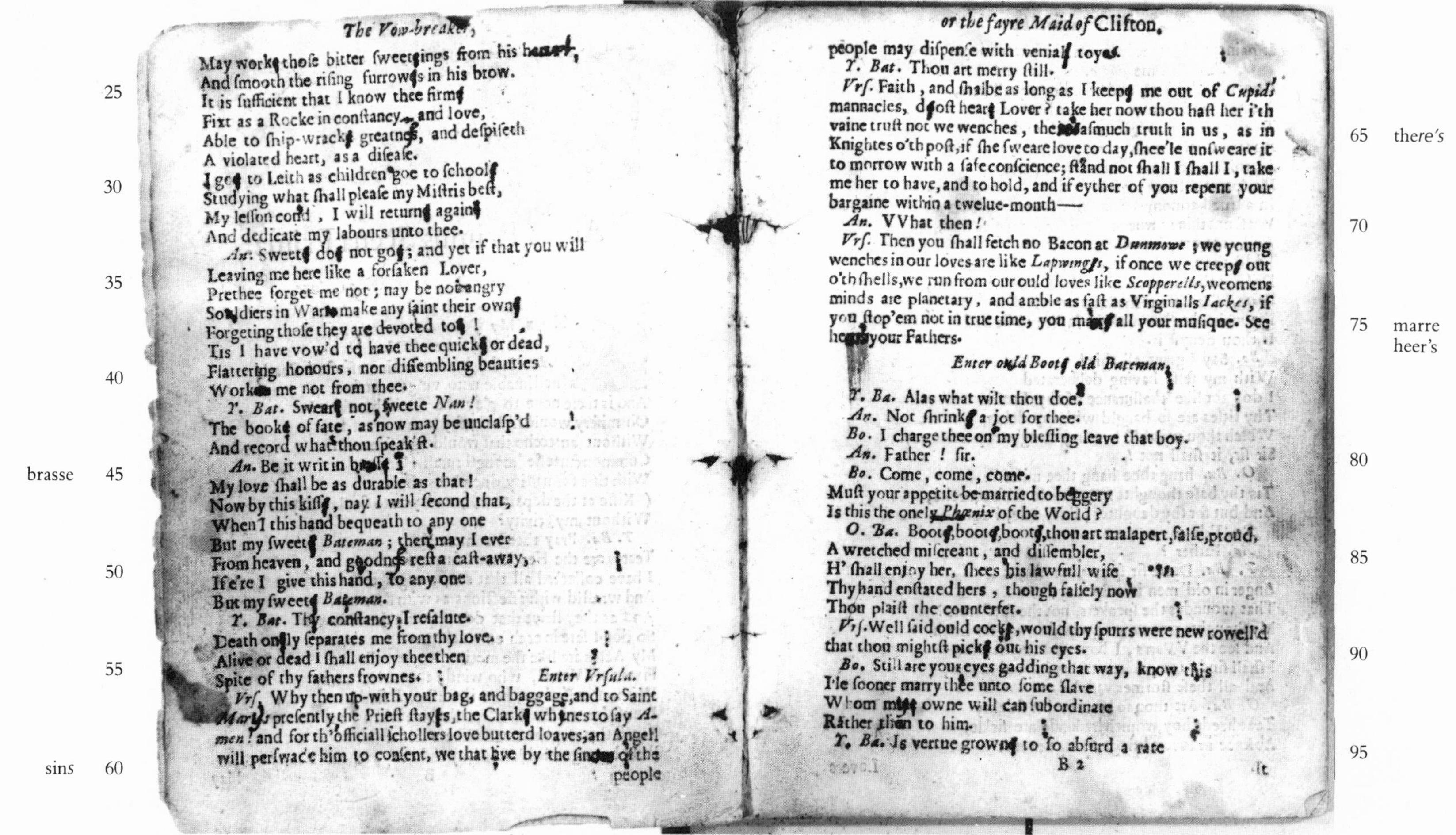

The Vow-breaker,

May worke those bitter ſweetnings from his heart,
And ſmooth the riſing furrowes in his brow.
It is ſufficient that I know thee firme
Fixt as a Rocke in conſtancy, and love,
Able to ſhip-wracke greatnes, and deſpiſeth
A violated heart, as a diſeaſe.
I goe to Leith as children goe to ſchoole
Studying what ſhall pleaſe my Miſtris beſt,
My leſſon cond , I will returne againe
And dedicate my labours unto thee.
An. Sweete doe not goe; and yet if that you will
Leaving me here like a forſaken Lover,
Prethee forget me not ; nay be not angry
Souldiers in Warre make any ſaint their owne
Forgeting thoſe they are devoted too !
Tis I have vow'd to have thee quicke or dead,
Flattering honours, nor diſſembling beauties
Worke me not from thee.
Y. Bat. Sweare not, ſweete *Nan!*
The booke of fate, as now may be unclaſp'd
And record what thou ſpeak'ſt.
An. Be it writ in braſſe ! brasse
My love ſhall be as durable as that!
Now by this kiſſe, nay I will ſecond that,
When I this hand bequeath to any one
But my ſweete *Bateman* ; then may I ever
From heaven, and goodnes reſt a caſt-away,
If e're I give this hand, to any one
But my ſweete *Bateman.*
Y. Bat. Thy conſtancy, I reſalute.
Death onely ſeparates me from thy love.
Alive or dead I ſhall enjoy thee then
Spite of thy fathers frownes. *Enter Vrſula.*
Vrſ. Why then up with your bag, and baggage, and to Saint *Marys* preſently the Prieſt ſtayes, the Clarke whines to ſay *Amen!* and for th'officiall ſchollers love butterd loaves, an Angell will perſwade him to conſent, we that live by the finders of the people sins

or the fayre Maid of Clifton.

people may diſpenſe with veniall toyes.
Y. Bat. Thou art merry ſtill.
Vrſ. Faith, and ſhalbe as long as I keepe me out of *Cupids* mannacles, doſt heare Lover ? take her now thou haſt her i'th vaine truſt not we wenches, there's asmuch truth in us, as in Knightes o'th poſt, if ſhe ſweare love to day, ſhee'le unſweare it to morrow with a ſafe conſcience; ſtand not ſhall I ſhall I, take me her to have, and to hold, and if eyther of you repent your bargaine within a twelue-month— there's
An. VVhat then!
Vrſ. Then you ſhall fetch no Bacon at *Dunmowe* ; we young wenches in our loves are like *Lapwings*, if once we creepe out o'th ſhells, we run from our ould loves like *Scopperells*, weomens minds are planetary, and amble as faſt as Virginalls *Iackes*, if you ſtop'em not in true time, you marre all your muſique. See heere's your Fathers. marre heer's

Enter ould Boote old Bateman.

Y. Ba. Alas what wilt thou doe.
An. Not ſhrinke a jot for thee.
Bo. I charge thee on my bleſſing leave that boy.
An. Father ! ſir.
Bo. Come, come, come.
Muſt your appetite be married to beggery
Is this the onely *Phœnix* of the World ?
O. Ba. Boote, boote, boote, thou art malapert, falſe, proud,
A wretched miſcreant, and diſſembler,
H' ſhall enjoy her, ſhees his lawfull wife I wake
Thy hand enſtated hers, though falſely now
Thou plaiſt the counterfet.
Vrſ. Well ſaid ould cocke, would thy ſpurrs were new rowell'd that thou mightſt picke out his eyes.
Bo. Still are your eyes gadding that way, know this
I'le ſooner marry thee unto ſome ſlave
Whom mine owne will can ſubordinate
Rather then to him.
Y. Ba. Is vertue growne to ſo abſurd a rate

B 2 It

The Vow-breaker,

It gaines   It gaines no better credit with base wordlings.
O. Ba. Tell me *Boote.*
Does not his birth, and breeding equall hers,
Are not my revenues correspondent
in   To equall thine; his purity in bloud
Runs in as sweete a streame, and naturall heate
As thine, or hers; his exteriour parts
May parralell hers, or any others
In a true harmony of lawfull love.
Wast not thine owne motion, didst not give way,
And entercourse to their privacies?
Didst thou not make me draw conveighances
Did not th'assurance of thy Lands seeme proball,
Boote, *Boote* thou shall not carry it thus
ther's   I'le make thee know ther's justice to be had
If thou denyst it.
Bo. Say I grant all this!
With my selfe having deliberated
I doe not like 'thassurance of thy Lands
Thy titles are so bangld with thy debts,
Which thou wouldst have my daughters portion pay.
Sir sir, it shall not!
O. Ba. hang thee hang thee miser!
Tis thy base thoughts forge these false conceits,
And but for thy daughter, I'de, i'de, i'de.
Bo. I'de come, come.
An. Father?
Dear   *Y. Ba.* Deare sir spare your fury!
Anger in old men is a Lunacy
That woundes the speakers, not the spectators?
My thoughts are now embarqu'd to goe for Leith
And see the VVarrs, I hope e're my returne
I shall finde temperate weather in your lookes,
And all these stormes vanishd.
O. Ba. Art thou so built on her fidelity
Take heede boy; women by kinde are fickle,
Absence in lovers brings strange events

Lovers

or the fayer Maid of Clifton.

Lovers that hourely kisse finde due regard
But those that absent are oft lose reward.
I doubt not of her firmenesse, but tis common
An absent lover thrives not with a woman.
Tis good counsell, boy, and worth observance.
But thou darst trust her?
Y. Ba. With my life sir.
O. Ba. Goe on then in thy entended purpose
Noble sir *Jarvis* whose man thou art,   *Jarvis* whose
I know will furnish thee.   furnish
Bo. This works to my designe, and gives free way
For wealthy Germans to my daughters love.
Come hither *Nan!*
Urs. I thought the wind was in that doore; by my virginity a
young wench were better be heire to a swine-heards chines, then
a rich mans bagges! we must be coupld in wed-locke like your
Barbary horse, and *Spanish* Gennet, for breede sake, house
to house, and land to land, the devill a jot of love? poore
simple virginity, that us'd to be our best Dowry is now growne   our
as bare as a serving-mans cloake that has not had a good nap   nap
this seven yeares.

Enter Clifton, and a Shoomaker. X

O. Ba. Well *Boote* time may make us friends.
Bo. Weele thinke on't *Bateman!* X
Clif. How many paire of shooes knave ha?   shooes
Sho. By Saint *Hugh* sir *Jarvis* foure thousand paire.
Clif. For every knave two paire good sauce against kyb'd heeles
by my hollidam; well shod, and clad will mak'em fight like
men! the North is could, subject to frostes, and snowes, and tis
bad fighting without vittle, and cloth! for which I have provided well for both; forty horse loades, and twently Carrs of
vittle, twill stop a good breach in a souldiours belly! my man
shall pay thee huffir by my Hollidam! my old Neighbour rich   my *Hollidam*
Boote, and *Bateman*, is this brabling matter ended yet! shall he   brabling matter ended
have her, by my *Hollidam* not yet, the knave shall serve his   have her,
Queene first, see the warres, where twill do him good to see

B 3   knocks

I, i, following 153. The *X* at the entrance of Clifton and the Shoemaker is the first of several in the copy. A second *X* follows within two lines. In some later instances the second mark precedes rather than follows the *X* that serves as a cue.

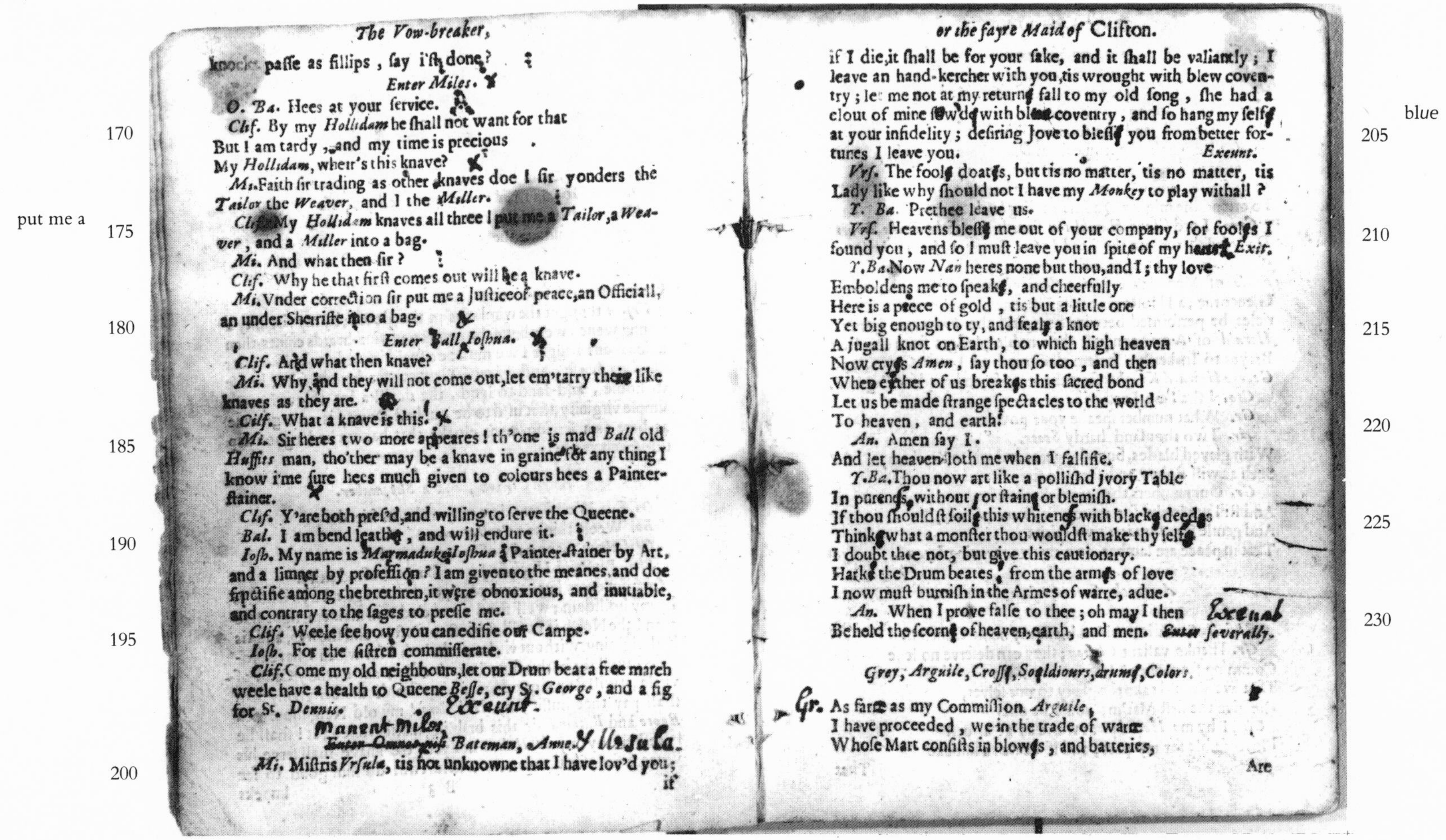

The Vow-breaker,

knocks paſſe as fillips, ſay i'ſt done?

Enter Miles.

O. Ba. Hees at your ſervice.

Clif. By my *Hollidam* he ſhall not want for that

But I am tardy, and my time is precious

My *Hollidam*, wheir's this knave?

Mi. Faith ſir trading as other knaves doe I ſir yonders the *Tailor* the *Weaver*, and I the *Miller*.

Clif. My *Hollidam* knaves all three I put me a *Tailor*, a *Weaver*, and a *Miller* into a bag. — put me a

Mi. And what then ſir?

Clif. Why he that firſt comes out will be a knave.

Mi. Vnder correction ſir put me a Juſticeof peace, an Officiall, an under Sheriffe into a bag.

Enter Ball, Ioſhua.

Clif. And what then knave?

Mi. Why, and they will not come out, let em'tarry their like knaves as they are.

Cilf. What a knave is this!

Mi. Sir heres two more appeares! th'one is mad *Ball* old *Huffits* man, tho'ther may be a knave in graine for any thing I know i'me ſure hees much given to colours hees a Painter-ſtainer.

Clif. Y'are both preſ'd, and willing to ſerve the Queene.

Bal. I am bend leather, and will endure it.

Ioſh. My name is *Marmaduke Ioſhua* & Painter-ſtainer by Art, and a limner by profeſſion? I am given to the meanes, and doe ſpectifie among the brethren, it were obnoxious, and inutiable, and contrary to the ſages to preſſe me.

Clif. Weele ſee how you can edifie our Campe.

Ioſh. For the ſiſtren commiſſerate.

Clif. Come my old neighbours, let our Drum beat a free march weele have a health to Queene *Beſſe*, cry St. *George*, and a fig for St. *Dennis.* Exeunt.

Manent Miles,

~~Enter Omnes~~ [illegible] *Bateman, Anne.* & Ursula.

Mi. Miſtris *Vrſula*, tis not unknowne that I have lov'd you; if

or the fayre Maid of Clifton.

if I die, it ſhall be for your ſake, and it ſhall be valiantly; I leave an hand-kercher with you, tis wrought with blew coventry; let me not at my returne fall to my old ſong, ſhe had a clout of mine ſow'de with blew coventry, and ſo hang my ſelfe at your infidelity; deſiring Jove to bleſſe you from better fortunes I leave you. *Exeunt.* — blue

Vrſ. The foole doates, but tis no matter, 'tis no matter, tis Lady like why ſhould not I have my *Monkey* to play withall?

Y. Ba. Prethee leave us.

Vrſ. Heavens bleſſe me out of your company, for fooles I found you, and ſo I muſt leave you in ſpite of my heart. *Exit.*

Y. Ba. Now *Nan* heres none but thou, and I; thy love
Emboldens me to ſpeake, and cheerfully
Here is a peece of gold, tis but a little one
Yet big enough to ty, and ſeale a knot
A jugall knot on Earth, to which high heaven
Now cryes *Amen*, ſay thou ſo too, and then
When either of us breakes this ſacred bond
Let us be made ſtrange ſpectacles to the world
To heaven, and earth!

An. Amen ſay I.
And let heaven loth me when I falſifie.

Y. Ba. Thou now art like a polliſhd jvory Table
In pureneſs, without or ſtaine or blemiſh.
If thou ſhouldſt ſoile this whiteneſs with blacke deedes
Thinke what a monſter thou wouldſt make thy ſelfe
I doubt thee not, but give this cautionary.
Harke the Drum beates, from the armes of love
I now muſt burniſh in the Armes of warre, adue.

An. When I prove falſe to thee; oh may I then
Beheld the ſcorne of heaven, earth, and men. Exeunt *Enter ſeverally.*

Grey, Arguile, Croſſe, Souldiours, drums, Colors.

Gr. As farre as my Commiſſion *Arguile*,
I have proceeded, we in the trade of warre
Whoſe Mart conſiſts in blowes, and batteries,

Are

I, i, following 199. The prompter's notes clarify the author's stage direction. An editor might have done the same thing. Many of the emendations in the copy are of an editorial nature but also theatrical—correcting entrances and exits, for instance.

Are like ſmall Rivers that muſt keepe their bounds,
Till the Queene Ocean command them riſe.
Dunbarr can witnes where we skirmiſhd laſt
I require the hoſtages be deliverd
Twixt *England*, and the federary Lords.

Arg. Peruſe this bedroule from *Duke Chattenreault*
Wherein their names are, their perſons attend
At *Inſkeith*, and with willingnes are bound
To attend the mighty Queene of *England*.

Grey. Lord *Claud-Hambleton* fourth ſon of the *Duke, Robert Dowglaſſe* brother to the Lord *James Stuart*! *Archibald Dowglaſſe* Lord of Loughennell *George Gram* ſecond ſon to the *Earle* of Menteich; *James Coningham* ſon to the *Earle* of Glencorne; all Hoſtages to the Queene of *England* till the Articles be performed betwixt her, and the *Federary* Lordes. *Herald* of Armes conduct theſe noble pledges from the Red Brayes to Inskeith, ſee'em delivered to *James Croft*, and *George Howard Knights* from thence to be embarqd for *England*.

Cro. I ſhall my Lord.

Gr. What number ſpeake your powers

Ar. Two thouſand hardy *Scots*,
With glaved blades, bum daggers, and white Kerchers,
Such as will fight, and face the fiery *French*.

Gr. Our numbers then are eight thouſand
And ſtill we looke for more, ſir *Francis Leake*,
And gentle Sir, *Jarvis*; two ſpirits
That in peace are lambes, in warr two ravening Lyons.

A march, Enter Clifton, Souldiers.

Clif. A Souldiers wiſhes bleſſe my noble Generall.

Gr. Thanks valiant *Clifton*; they can deſerve no leſſe
Comming from thee? I ſee you emulate
That we ſhould take the glory to our ſelves,
I'le give the firſt Alar'm, youle be one.

Clif. I by my *Hollidam* at warre as at a feaſt
I'le ſcramble for my part, and if I catch a knocke

That

That honour which a Souldiour wins in warrs
Is of low price unles he bring home ſcarrs

Gr. What number ſir *Jarvis*?

Clif. Five hundred, and fifty tall white coates,
Fellowes that will face a murdering Cannon,
When it blowes rancks into the Aire as Chaffe
Yet dreadles they ſhall ſtand it, and not ſhrinke,
Right *Nottingham* ſhire Lads.

Gr. Tis well don!
Our bands are well divided, yours my Lord
Keepe the greene Bul-warke, mine the weſt Gate,
You ſir *Jarvis* the water-ports to Inskeith,
Pelham from *Pelhamus* Mount plaies at the Towne
How now what Trumpets this?

A Trumpet, Enter Trumball.

Trum. From the Queene Regent of *Scotland* I come — come
To thee Lord Generall of the *Engliſh* Force.
She craves a treaty with the Lords of *England*
To know why thus they enter on her groundes,
Depopulate her Countries, Plough her Plaines:
If lawfull cauſe ſhe finds on enterview, — enterview,
She will ſubſcribe to *England*, ſue a peace,
Otherwiſe by Article ſheele confirm't;
This is under her highnes hand, and ſeale,
This is my meſſage.

Gr. Whats thy name?

Trum. *Trumball*, Serejant Trumpetter to her Grace. — *Trumball*, Serejant

Gr. Her Princely offer we accept *Rowge Croſſe*
Herrald at Armes, command ſir *George Howard*
Sir *James Crofts*, and my ſon *Arthur Grey*
To ſhew her Grace my Soveraignes grevances
I'th interim wee'le ſheath our burniſhd blades
Which had bene duld in ſcarlet long ere this. — *duld*
But for thy meſſage.

C

Enter

~~*Enter Trumbull.*~~

Trum. I ſhall report you honourable. Exit.

Clif. My *Hollidam* I like not theſe ſignes of peace
Theſe *French* Flyes worke on advantages
I'le not truſt 'em.

Gr. To prevent which each ſtand on his guard; your eares my Lord.

Ioſ. Reſolve me; doe they kill men ith warrs, and ne're give warning?

Mi. Not ſo much time, Jo! as a theife has at *Nottingham* Gallowes.

Ioſ. Tirany, tirany; may a not pray in ſincerity nor requeſt the breethren, and ſiſters to have care of a departing brother.

Mi. No *Io*! nothing but downe-right blowes, juſt as you fell Okes, or kill Oxen.

Ioſ. Moſt heatheniſh, and diabollicall; and do they ſhoote Bullets?

Mi. My Jo, as thicke as haile a man may hit his owne father.

Ioſ. Oh *Infidells*, and *Barbarians*; what will not the wicked doe, kill men with bullets! oh theſe Guns, they are dangerous things they ſprung from the whoore, a *Fryer* was the inventor, and they ſmell of the Dragon! oh my poore Puſſe-cat; ſinfull man thou art *Io*: to bring the poore Puſſe forth to dy by a Gun! a poore Puſſe, ſilly harmeleſſe Puſſe.

Mi. Ty her behind, then if thou runſt ſhee may ſave thee.

Ioſ. I run! thou prophane tranſlater I ſcorne to run, my Cat, and I will enter battell 'gainſt the wicked! I run. ✗

to Cross. *Gr.* Why returne ſo ſoone. — to Cross.

Enter Croſſe. ✗

Croſ. This my Lord
Making for Edenborough to the Queene,
Nine hundred ſhot, and five hundred Corſlets,
Came forth of Leith, under the conduct
Of *Mortigue*, and *Doyſells* their Colonells.
We wiſh'd them peaceably returne to Leith

Since

Since contrary to all Lawes of Armes
They now had iſſud? *Mortigue* replide
They on their maſters ground reſolved ſtood
And from their miſtris would not budge a foote
For any *Engliſh* breathing. *Exit Croſſe.*

Gr. Were not our promiſe given to the Queene
On which they build advantages, i'de make
Theſe *French* Rats run as Wolves from fire,
Bid'em retire, and tell them thus from us
Weele make them win their ground ere they ſtand on't.
Nothing but circumvention in the *French*.

Clif. By my *Hollidam* juglers, conſtant in nothing but Inconſtancy, thats the *French* Merchandize.

Ioſ. And doe they fight, as it is in the painted cloth, of the nine worthies, of *Ioſhua*, *Hector*, *Ceſar*, *Arthur*, *Charle-Magne*, *Iudas*, *Machabeus*, and *Godfrey Bollogine*.

Mil. Yes *Io*: they doe.

Ioſ. In the painted cloth *Joſhua* ſtands formoſt

Bal. With his Cat in ſtead of a Scutchion.

Ioſ. *Ball* thou art full of rebukes—

Enter Croſſe.

Croſ. Arme, arme, arme, regardles of true honour
Your meſſage is deſide, and facing the van
Diſchargd a thouſand ſhot, the Crag, and Chappell
They make a refuge 'gainſt our great Artillery

Gr. Let the bow-men ſhoote their ſlighteſt Arrowes,
As thicke as haile, the Musketteers ſhall follow
Alarum then; tis our firſt enterpriſe
When cowards fall the valiant ſpirits riſe. *Ex. Omnes.*

After ſkirmiſhes Enter Grey, Arguile, young Bateman with Colors, Clifton, Souldieers, priſoners.

Gray: The Crag, and Chappells ours, and the *French*
Like Hares are leapd out of fierce Greyhounds gripes.
Doyſells, and *Mortigue*, out-ran their Collours,

And

The Vow-breaker,

And with all expedition tooke the Towne.
Y. Ba. Whose Colors I display.
Gr. How many of the *French* this day are falne ?
Arg. Sevenscore my Lord, and prisoners of noble worth.
Poiteerz, Augois, Burbon, Shamoont, Shaloone,
Labrosse, and of the *English* meerely one man slaine.
Gr. Thanks unto heaven whose arme was our defence,
What's he that beares the *French* armes displaid ?
Clif. A servant of mine, his name *Bateman* ?
Gr. Theirs forty Angells for thy good daies service,
And if thy merit retaine an Ancients place.
Y. Ba. I thanke your honour.
Iof. My prisoner is an *Anabaptist*, all I desire is that I may
convert him,
Mi. It must be in's drinke then, else hees none o'th right
brethren;
Come *Gr.* Ca[illegible] noble *Arguile*, and worthy *Clifton*
After these, toiles of bloud, and massacre,
Let's quench our raging motions in the Grape,
And in the *French-mans* Vine drinke his confusion ?
Proud *France* shall know that our *Elizaes* Name,
Drives to confusion those that steale her Fame. *Ex. Omnes.*

Enter Anne, and Ursula.

An. Do'st thou not beleeve it ?
Vrs. Let me faile of my best wishes, and I doe, I cannot
amuse my thoughts to't, thou maist as soone perswade me that
a Spiders VVeb will catch a swarme of Bees as thou marry *Ger-*
man! his head's like a *Welch-mans* Crest on S. *Davies* day ? he
lookes like a hoary Frost in *December*, now *Venus* blesse me,
i'de rather ly by a Statue ?
An. Thou art pleasant still.
In nat'rall things we see that Herbes, and Plants
In autumne ever doe receive perfection,
As they, so man, never attaines his height
Till in the autumne of his growing age
Experience like a Mistris beautifies him,
With

or the fayre Maid of Clifton.

With silver haires, badges of experience.
Of wisdome, honours, counsell, knowledge, arts,
With all th'endowmens vertue hath in store.
Contrarily greene headed youth
Being in the spring or summer of his age,
Is prone to surfets, riots, intemperancies,
And all the stocke of ills that vice is queene of;
Vrs. Thou wrests a good text to an ill sense ? but none but
fooles would ly in beds of snow that might couch in Roses ?
but it may bee Cozen; but it may bee Cuz ? you follow the Cuz
fashion of our Country Knights that marry your old *London*
VVidowes; tis but keeping a handsome Chamber-maide, they
are necessary evills, and will serve with a small Dowery
afterwards to make parsons wives ? you know my meaning
Cuz.
An. He brings wealth, promotion, and tis the way.
Vrs. To your ruine; to your blacke father presently ? cocke
him with the herbe Moly that will put bloud in's cheekes ? let
him be dieted like your *Barbary* horse ? heele neere stand to
his tacklings else ? feede him with *Vipers* flesh that will make
his white head blacke ? doost thou refuse youthfull *Bateman*
to ly with wealthy *Germane*, reject a Mine of vertue, for a
Mountaine of muck ? *Cupid* blesse thee, for i le sweare, he has
blinded thee as blind as a *Bat*.
An. I lov'd young *Bateman* in my childish daies,
Have vow'd to have him, and he againe to me,
But what of that, foolish lovers vowes
Like breath on steele, as soone are of, as on,
German is wealthy and by him I gaine
Recourse amongst the modest sagest dames ?
VVealth has a priviledge that beauty cannot,
Bateman is young, embellish'd with a naturall,
Active, and generous, unspotted beauty,
German is old, indebted much to age,
Yet like ould *Æson*, gold can make him young,
Gold like a second nature can elixate,
Make the deformed faire, the faire seeme fowle,
C 3 And

I, i, 387. This is one of several places in the play where a change of locale is evident but the prompter gave no indication of a scene change.

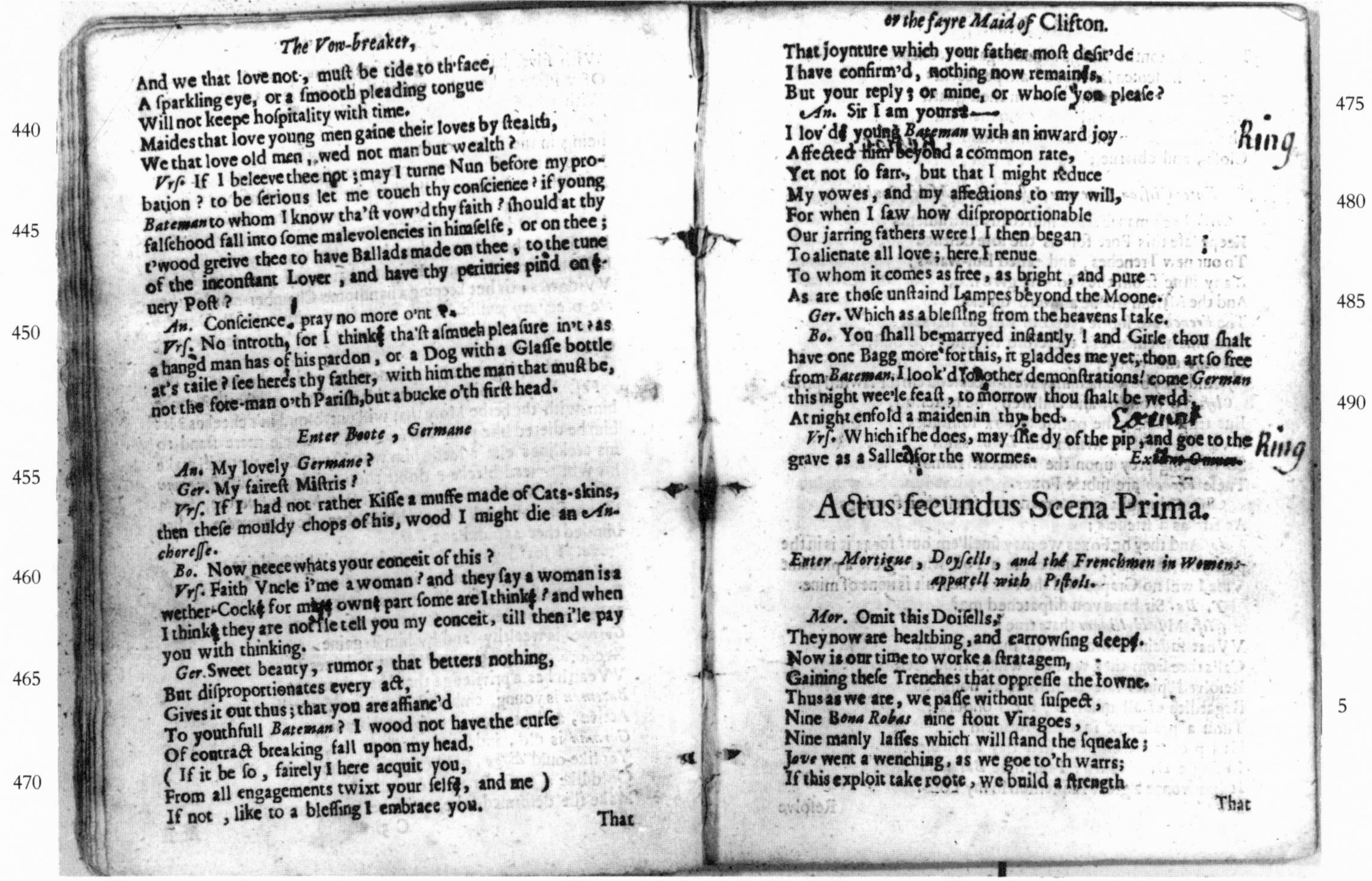

The Vow-breaker,

And we that love not, muſt be tide to th'face,
A ſparkling eye, or a ſmooth pleading tongue
Will not keepe hoſpitality with time.
Maides that love young men gaine their loves by ſtealth,
We that love old men, wed not man but wealth?

Vrſ. If I beleeve thee not; may I turne Nun before my probation? to be ſerious let me touch thy conſcience? if young *Bateman* to whom I know tha'ſt vow'd thy faith? ſhould at thy falſehood fall into ſome malevolencies in himſelfe, or on thee; t'wood greive thee to have Ballads made on thee, to the tune of the inconſtant Lover, and have thy periuries pin'd on every Poſt?

An. Conſcience, pray no more o'nt.

Vrſ. No introth, for I thinke tha'ſt aſmuch pleaſure in't as a hang'd man has of his pardon, or a Dog with a Glaſſe bottle at's taile? ſee here's thy father, with him the man that muſt be, not the fore-man o'th Pariſh, but a bucke o'th firſt head.

Enter Boote, Germane

An. My lovely *Germane*?

Ger. My faireſt Miſtris!

Vrſ. If I had not rather Kiſſe a muffe made of Cats-skins, then theſe mouldy chops of his, wood I might die an *Anchoreſſe*.

Bo. Now neece whats your conceit of this?

Vrſ. Faith Vncle i'me a woman? and they ſay a woman is a wether-Cocke for mine owne part ſome are I thinke? and when I thinke they are not i'le tell you my conceit, till then i'le pay you with thinking.

Ger. Sweet beauty, rumor, that betters nothing,
But diſproportionates every act,
Gives it out thus; that you are affianc'd
To youthfull *Bateman*? I wood not have the curſe
Of contract breaking fall upon my head,
(If it be ſo, fairely I here acquit you,
From all engagements twixt your ſelfe, and me)
If not, like to a bleſſing I embrace you.

That

or the fayre Maid of Clifton.

That joynture which your father moſt deſir'de
I have confirm'd, nothing now remaines,
But your reply; or mine, or whoſe you pleaſe?

An. Sir I am yours—
I lov'de young *Bateman* with an inward joy
Affected him beyond a common rate,
Yet not ſo farr, but that I might reduce
My vowes, and my affections to my will,
For when I ſaw how diſproportionable
Our jarring fathers were! I then began
To alienate all love; here I renue
To whom it comes as free, as bright, and pure
As are thoſe unſtaind Lampes beyond the Moone.

Ger. Which as a bleſſing from the heavens I take.

Bo. You ſhall be marryed inſtantly! and Girle thou ſhalt have one Bagg more for this, it gladdes me yet, thou art ſo free from *Bateman*, I look'd for other demonſtrations! come *German* this night wee'le feaſt, to morrow thou ſhalt be wedd,
At night enfold a maiden in thy bed.

Vrſ. Which if he does, may ſhe dy of the pip, and goe to the grave as a Sallet for the wormes. *Exeunt Omnes.*

Actus ſecundus Scena Prima.

Enter Mortigue, Doyſells, and the Frenchmen in Womens-apparell with Piſtols.

Mor. Omit this Doiſells,
They now are healthing, and carrowſing deepe.
Now is our time to worke a ſtratagem,
Gaining theſe Trenches that oppreſſe the towne.
Thus as we are, we paſſe without ſuſpect,
Nine *Bona Robas* nine ſtout Viragoes,
Nine manly laſſes which will ſtand the ſqueake;
Jove went a wenching, as we goe to'th warrs;
If this exploit take roote, we build a ſtrength

That

I, i, 477. *Ring* warnings and cues (here and at line 493) are for act endings. They occur regularly in this promptbook but differ somewhat in form from those found in other books; "Act Ready" is a safer warning than *Ring*, which looks like a cue.

I, i, 493. The original stage direction read: "Exeunt Omnes." The annotator altered it to Ex*it*.

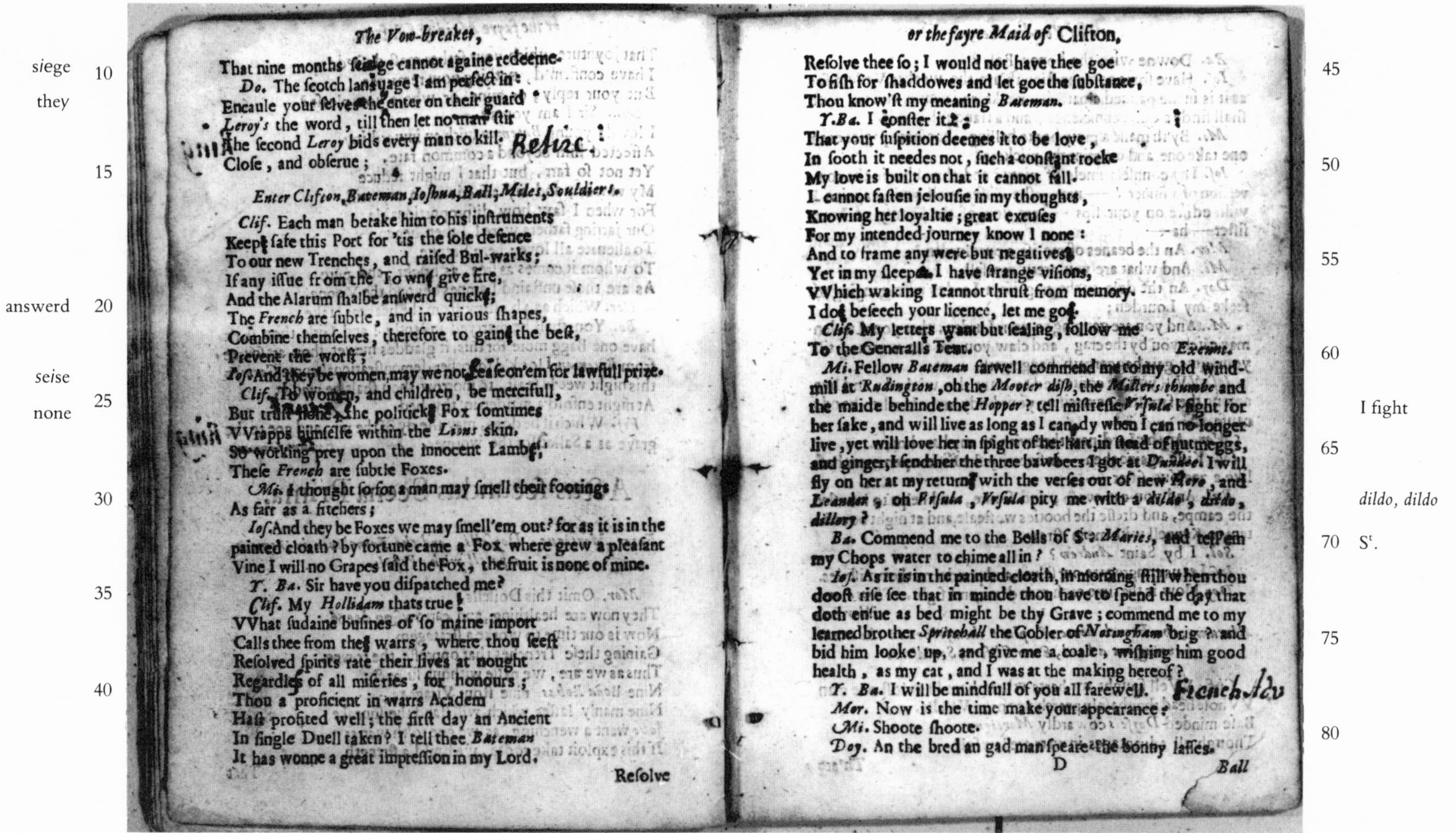

The Vow-breaker,

That nine months seidge cannot againe redeeme.
Do. The scotch language I am perfect in:
Encaule your selves, the enter on their guard
Leroy's the word, till then let no man stir
The second *Leroy* bids every man to kill. Retire.
Close, and obserue;

Enter Clifton, Bateman, Ioshua, Ball, Miles, Souldiers.

Clif. Each man betake him to his instruments
Keep safe this Port for 'tis the sole defence
To our new Trenches, and raised Bul-warks;
If any issue from the Towne give fire,
And the Alarum shalbe answerd quick;
The *French* are subtle, and in various shapes,
Combine themselves, therefore to gaine the best,
Prevent the worst;
Ios. And they be women, may we not sease on'em for lawfull prize.
Clif. To women, and children, be mercifull,
But trust none, the politick Fox somtimes
VVrapps himselfe within the *Lions* skin,
So working prey upon the innocent Lambe;
These *French* are subtle Foxes.
Mi. I thought so for a man may smell their footings
As farr as a fitchers;
Ios. And they be Foxes we may smell'em out? for as it is in the painted cloath? by fortune came a Fox where grew a pleasant Vine I will no Grapes said the Fox, the fruit is none of mine.
Y. Ba. Sir have you dispatched me?
Clif. My *Hollidam* thats true!
VVhat sudaine busines of so maine import
Calls thee from these warrs, where thou seest
Resolved spirits rate their lives at nought
Regardless of all miseries, for honours;
Thou a proficient in warrs Academ
Hast profited well; the first day an Ancient
In single Duell taken? I tell thee *Bateman*
It has wonne a great impression in my Lord.

Resolve

or the fayre Maid of Clifton,

Resolve thee so; I would not have thee goe
To fish for shaddowes and let goe the substance,
Thou know'st my meaning *Bateman.*
Y. Ba. I conster it;
That your suspition deemes it to be love,
In sooth it needes not, such a constant rocke
My love is built on that it cannot fall.
I cannot fasten jelousie in my thoughts,
Knowing her loyaltie; great excuses
For my intended journey know I none:
And to frame any were but negatives;
Yet in my sleepe I have strange visions,
VVhich waking I cannot thrust from memory.
I doe beseech your licence, let me goe.
Clif. My letters want but sealing, follow me
To the Generall's Tent. *Exeunt.*
Mi. Fellow *Bateman* farwell commend me to my old windmill at *Rudington*, oh the *Mooter dish*, the *Millers thumbe* and the maide behinde the *Hopper*? tell mistresse *Vrsula* I fight for her sake, and will live as long as I can dy when I can no longer live, yet will love her in spight of her hart, in stead of nutmeggs, and ginger, I sendher the three bawbees I got at *Dundee.* I will fly on her at my returne with the verses out of new *Hero*, and *Leander*, oh *Vrsula*, *Vrsula* pity me with a *dildo*, *dildo*, *dillory*?
Ba. Commend me to the Bells of S^t. *Maries*, and tell'em my Chops water to chime all in?
Ios. As it is in the painted cloath, in morning still when thou doost rise see that in minde thou have to spend the day that doth ensue as bed might be thy Grave; commend me to my learned brother *Spritchall* the Gobler of *Notingham* brig? and bid him looke up, and give me a coale, wishing him good health, as my cat, and I was at the making hereof?
Y. Ba. I will be mindfull of you all farewell. French Adv
Mor. Now is the time make your appearance?
Mi. Shoote shoote.
Doy. An the bred an gad man speare the bonny lasses.

D

Ball

siege
they
answerd
seise
none
I fight
dildo, dildo
S^t.

II, i, 14. *Retire*, and the note at line 78, *French Adv[ance]*, are typical additions in the copy which correct or augment the author's stage directions or clarify stage action implied in the dialogue. Most Restoration patent-house promptbooks prove that prompters did not try to record the movement of the actors. But if this was a promptbook for a production at one of the fairs, with a pickup cast, it would have been useful for the prompter to concern himself with such matters.

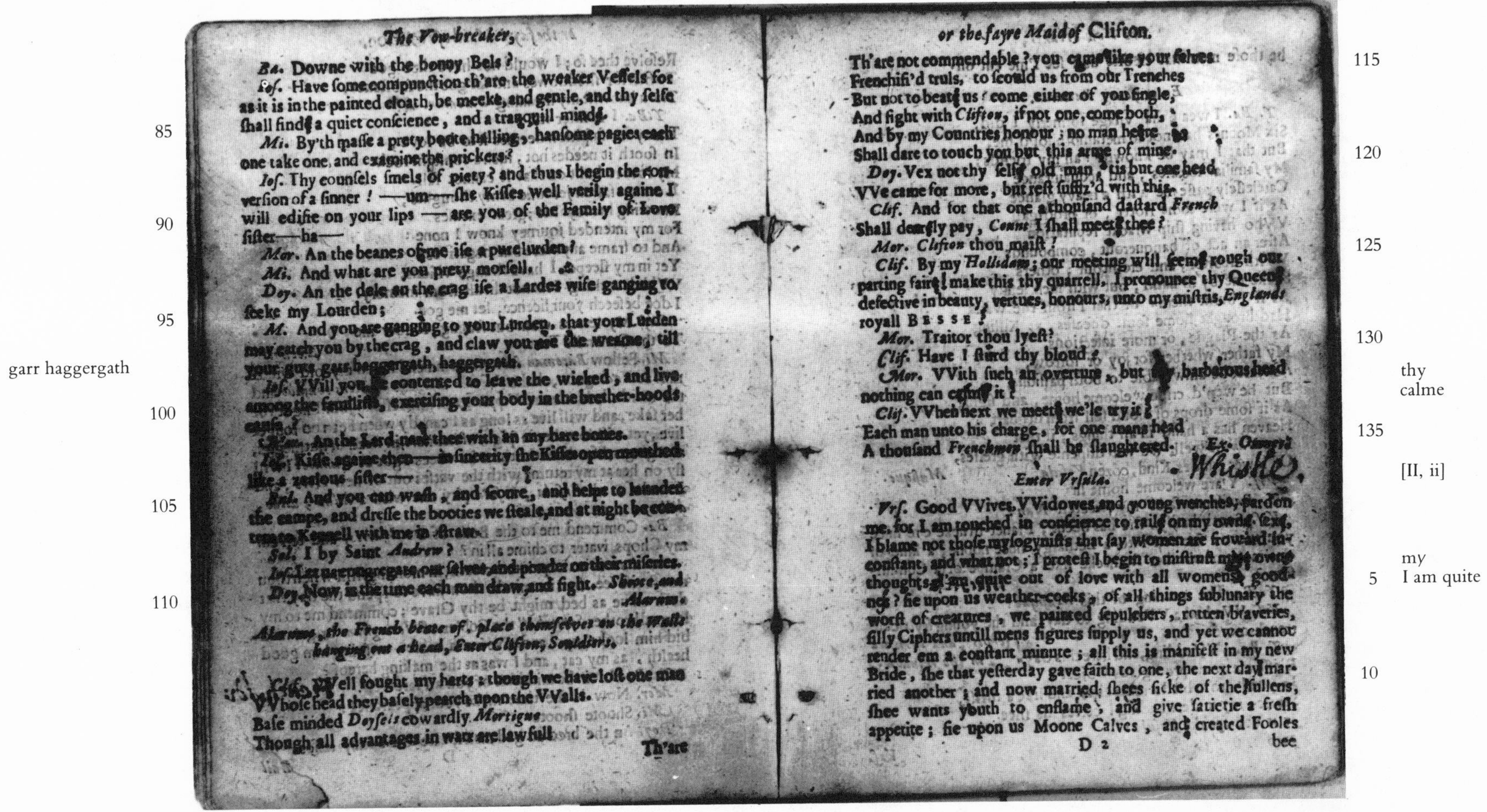

The Vow-breaker,

Ba. Downe with the bonny Bels?

Iof. Have ſome compunction th'are the weaker Veſſels for as it is in the painted cloath, be meeke, and gentle, and thy ſelfe ſhall finde a quiet conſcience, and a tranquill minde.

Mi. By'th maſſe a prety boote halling, hanſome pagies each one take one, and examine the prickers?

Iof. Thy counſels ſmels of piety? and thus I begin the converſion of a ſinner! ——um——ſhe Kiſſes well verily againe I will edifie on your lips —— are you of the Family of Love ſiſter——ha——

Mor. An the beanes of me iſe a pure lurden!

Mi. And what are you prety morſell.

Doy. An the dele on the crag iſe a Lardes wife ganging to ſeeke my Lourden;

M. And you are ganging to your Lurden, that your Lurden may catch you by the crag, and claw you ... till your guts gaas haggergath, haggergath.

garr haggergath

Iof. VVill you be contented to leave the wicked, and live among the familiſts, exerciſing your body in the brether-hoods cauſe?

Mor. An the Lord ... thee with an my bare bones.

Iof. Kiſſe againe then——in ſincerity ſhe Kiſſes open mouthed like a zealous ſiſter——

Bal. And you can waſh, and ſcoure, and helpe to launder the campe, and dreſſe the booties we ſteale, and at night be content to Kennell with me in ſtraw.

Sol. I by Saint *Andrew*?

Iof. Let us congregate our ſelves, and ponder on their miſeries.

Doy. Now is the time each man draw, and fight. *Shoote, and Alarum.*

Alarums, the French beate of. place themſelves on the Walls hanging out a head, Enter Clifton, Souldiers.

Clif. VVell fought my harts: though we have loſt one man
VVhoſe head they baſely pearch upon the VValls.
Baſe minded *Doyſels* cowardly *Mortigue*
Though all advantages in warr are lawfull

Th'are

or the fayre Maid of Clifton.

Th'are not commendable? you came like your ſelves
Frenchifi'd truls, to ſcould us from our Trenches
But not to beate us: come either of you ſingle,
And fight with *Clifton*, if not one, come both,
And by my Countries honour; no man heere
Shall dare to touch you but this arme of mine.

Doy. Vex not thy ſelfe old man, 'tis but one head
VVe came for more, but reſt ſuffiz'd with this.

Clif. And for that one a thouſand daſtard *French*
Shall dearely pay, *Come* I ſhall meete thee?

Mor. *Clifton* thou maiſt!

Clif. By my *Hollidam*; our meeting will ſeeme rough our parting faire! make this thy quarrell. I pronounce thy Queene defective in beauty, vertues, honours, unto my miſtris, *Englands* royall BESSE!

Mor. Traitor thou lyeſt?

Clif. Have I ſtird thy bloud?

Mor. VVith ſuch an overture, but thy barbarous head nothing can caſuiſt it?

thy calme

Clif. VVhen next we meete we'le try it!
Each man unto his charge, for one mans head
A thouſand *Frenchmen* ſhall be ſlaughtered. *Ex. Omnes.*

Whistle.

[II, ii]

Enter Vrſula.

Vrſ. Good VVives, VVidowes, and young wenches, pardon me, for I am touched in conſcience to raile on my owne ſexe, I blame not thoſe myſogyniſts that ſay women are froward inconſtant, and what not; I proteſt I begin to miſtruſt mine owne thoughts, I am quite out of love with all womens goodneſs? fie upon us weather-cocks, of all things ſublunary the worſt of creatures, we painted ſepulchers, rotten braveries, ſilly Ciphers untill mens figures ſupply us, and yet we cannot render em a conſtant minute; all this is manifeſt in my new Bride, ſhe that yeſterday gave faith to one, the next day married another; and now married ſhees ſicke of the ſullens, ſhee wants youth to enflame, and give ſatietie a freſh appetite; fie upon us Moone Calves, and created Fooles

D 2 bee

my
I am quite

II, ii, opening. *Whistle* is the first of several scene shift cues, unique to this promptbook and the one for *The Change of Crownes.* The cue *Ring* also served as a shift cue at act openings. None of the whistle cues in the text is warned.

The Vow-breaker,

be those men that credit us, I see i'me cut off.

Enter young Bateman.

Y. Ba. I weare that visage formerly I did,
have Six Moones has not so metamorphos'd me,
But that I may be knowne ? all my friends;
My familiar societes, and acquaintance
Carelessely passe me with a heavy glance
As if I were some rioter, or prodigall
VVho having ship-wrackt reputation
After an act of banquerout, compounds
VVith debitor, and creditour ; others
Shake me by th hand, but with such lenity
As if I burnt them ? or that I from the warrs
Had brought home some diseases, as Killing
As the Plague, or more infectious.
My father, whether for joy or sorrow,
[illegible] be answerable to both passions,
sigh'd But he wep'd, cries welcome home, and sighs,
As if some drops of bloud fell from his hart
Heaven has a hand in all things ; if that
My *Nan* be well; we will dispense with greifes,
[illegible] Kind, cozen *Vrsula*, *Musique.*
[illegible] Y'are welcome home sir.
[illegible] How fares my sweetest *Nan* ?
[illegible] badly, she has beene, Planet-strucke e're since
[illegible] she fell into a Lethargy since noone, a kind of
[illegible] over her stomacke like a Crampe or a Conuul-
[illegible] *Musicke.*
Y. Ba. The meaning of this *Musique* ?
Vrs. VVe had a VVedding to day, and the young fry tickle
much more. *Jervis, and Nan are*
Y. Ba. A VVedding, and here this day. *in the Window.*
Blesse me what prodigious Object
Is yond, that blasts mine eines, and like a theife,
Steales my understanding ! certes tis shee.
Is it not speake *Vrsula* ?

Vrs.

or the fayre Maid of Clifton.

Vrs. I know not, for had she as many bodies as harts, she might be here, and yonder too. .
Y. Ba. Now by my life——
Vrs. Nay sweare not ; if you have any ill language to spare I'le send my Cozen to you presently. *Exeunt.*
Y. Ba. Strange feares assaile my senses, and begins
Conflicts of despaires, doubts, and feares,
And but I have a resolution fixt
On her fidelity ; this frontispice
And other entertainments might confirme
Former presages.

Enter Anne, & Vrsula.

An. VVho ist would speake with me ?
Vrs. One that may be jealous though he weares no yellow.
Y. Ba. Her sight like to a cordiall has expell'd
All former grosse suggestions, me thinkes
I tast my happines e're I touch it.
An. Beshrew thy hart for this.
Vrs. Beshrew your owne false, if there be ill tis of your owne begetting i'le provide Cocke-brothes, and caudles for your old Cock-sparow. *Exeunt.* there
Y. Ba. Shees dumbe with joy, and I like to a man
Intranc'd with joyes un-utterable, cannot speake ?
But I have lost my selfe, I am awake,
And see a substance more then dreamers doe,
Thus in the armes of love I doe enfould thee.
An. I doe not know you——touch me not ?
Y. ba. I wonder then how I dare know my selfe,
When thou forget'st me ! I had thought
Had I ben sullide with the sooty *Moore*,
Or tan'd with heate like some *Egiptian* slave,
Or spoted like the *Persian Leopardes*,
Or in the worst forme can be term'd,
Or imagin'd, yet thou coulds have knowne me,
I am thy *Bateman Nan* !
An. If you be *Bateman* ;

D 3 T'were

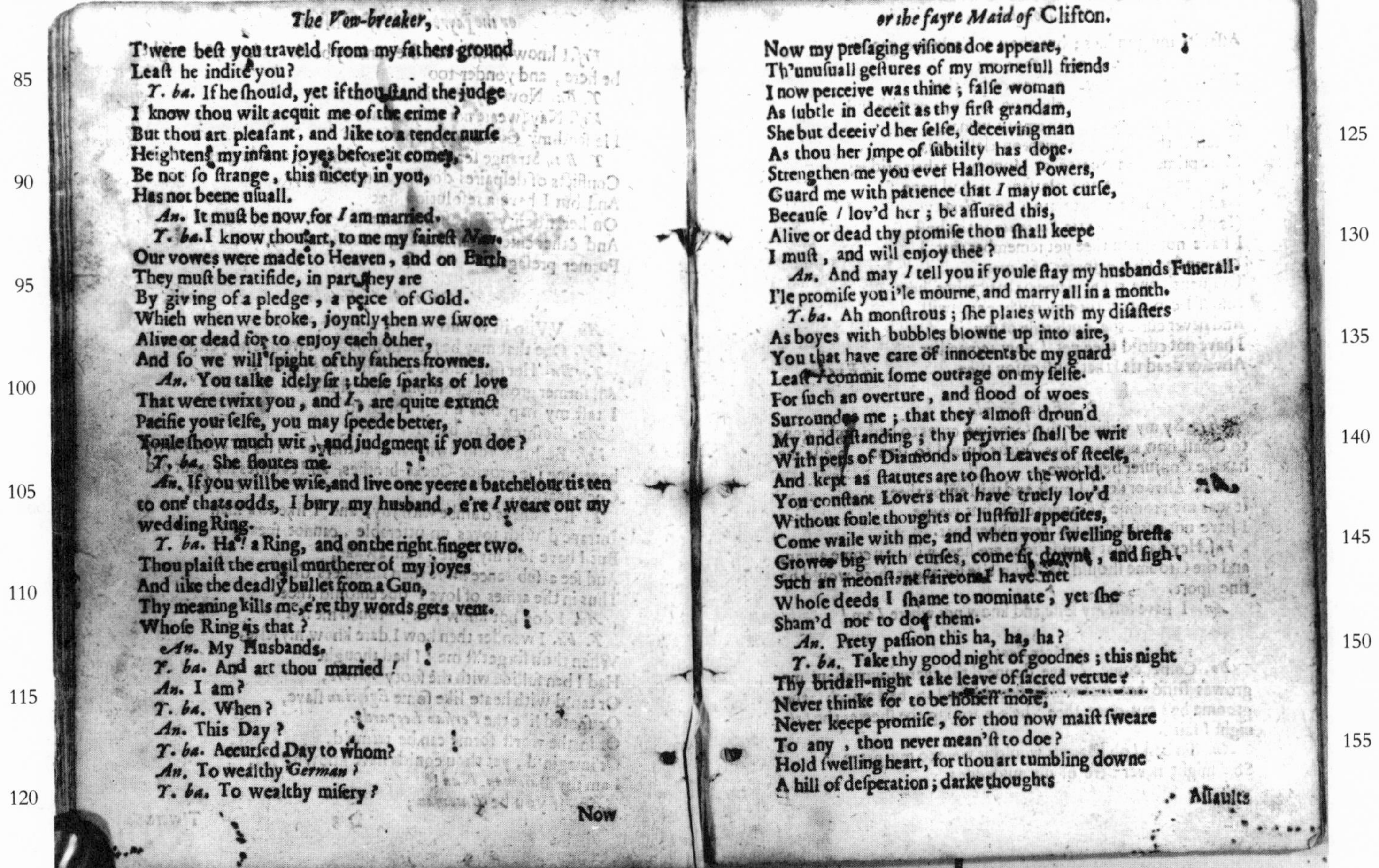

The Vow-breaker,

T'were beſt you traveld from my fathers ground
Leaſt he indite you?
T. ba. If he ſhould, yet if thou ſtand the judge
I know thou wilt acquit me of the crime?
But thou art pleaſant, and like to a tender nurſe
Heightens my infant joyes before it comes,
Be not ſo ſtrange, this nicety in you,
Has not beene uſuall.
An. It muſt be now, for *I* am married.
T. ba. I know thou'art, to me my faireſt *Nan.*
Our vowes were made to Heaven, and on Earth
They muſt be ratifide, in part they are
By giving of a pledge, a peice of Gold.
Which when we broke, joyntly then we ſwore
Alive or dead for to enjoy each other,
And ſo we will ſpight of thy fathers frownes.
An. You talke idely ſir; theſe ſparks of love
That were twixt you, and *I*, are quite extinct
Pacifie your ſelfe, you may ſpeede better,
Youle ſhow much wit, and judgment if you doe?
T. ba. She floutes me.
An. If you will be wiſe, and live one yeere a batchelour tis ten to one thats odds, I bury my husband, e're *I* weare out my wedding Ring.
T. ba. Ha! a Ring, and on the right finger two.
Thou plaiſt the cruell murtherer of my joyes
And like the deadly bullet from a Gun,
Thy meaning kills me, e're thy words gets vent.
Whoſe Ring is that?
An. My Husbands.
T. ba. And art thou married!
An. I am?
T. ba. When?
An. This Day?
T. ba. Accurſed Day to whom?
An. To wealthy *German*?
T. ba. To wealthy miſery?

Now

or the fayre Maid of Clifton.

Now my preſaging viſions doe appeare,
Th'unuſuall geſtures of my mornefull friends
I now perceive was thine; falſe woman
As ſubtle in deceit as thy firſt grandam,
She but deceiv'd her ſelfe, deceiving man
As thou her impe of ſubtilty has done.
Strengthen me you ever Hallowed Powers,
Guard me with patience that *I* may not curſe,
Becauſe *I* lov'd her; be aſſured this,
Alive or dead thy promiſe thou ſhall keepe
I muſt, and will enjoy thee?
An. And may *I* tell you if youle ſtay my husbands Funerall.
I'le promiſe you i'le mourne, and marry all in a month.
T. ba. Ah monſtrous; ſhe plaies with my diſaſters
As boyes with bubbles blowne up into aire,
You that have care of innocents be my guard
Leaſt I commit ſome outrage on my ſelfe.
For ſuch an overture, and flood of woes
Surroundes me; that they almoſt droun'd
My underſtanding; thy perjuries ſhall be writ
With pens of Diamonds upon Leaves of ſteele,
And kept as ſtatutes are to ſhow the world.
You conſtant Lovers that have truely lov'd
Without foule thoughts or luſtfull appetites,
Come waile with me, and when your ſwelling breſts
Growes big with curſes, come ſit downe, and ſigh,
Such an inconſtant faire one I have met
Whoſe deeds I ſhame to nominate, yet ſhe
Sham'd not to doe them.
An. Prety paſſion this ha, ha, ha?
T. ba. Take thy good night of goodnes; this night
Thy bridall-night take leave of ſacred vertue:
Never thinke for to be honeſt more,
Never keepe promiſe, for thou now maiſt ſweare
To any, thou never mean'ſt to doe?
Hold ſwelling heart, for thou art tumbling downe
A hill of deſperation; darke thoughts

Aſſaults

The Vow-breaker,

Aſſaults my goodnes; but thou ſhalt keepe promiſe
Alive or dead, I will enjoy thee yet.
I have not curſ'd thee yet, remember that;
And when th'aſt ſtaind thy innocent ſheetes with luſt,
And with ſaciety fild thy empty veines,
Weari'd the night with wanton dalliances,
More prime then Goates, or Monkeys in their prides;
Call then to minde how pleaſant this had bene
Had it not bene adulterate; for *German*
(Is not thy husband; tis *Bateman* is the beſt.
I have not curſ'd thee yet remember that.)
I'le muſter up the forces of a man,
To quench the riſing flames that harbor here
And if I can forget thee, by my hopes I will
And never curſe the Auth'reſſe of my ill.
I have not curſ'd thee yet! now remember
Exit nt. Alive or dead tis I that muſt enjoy thee. *Exeunt.*

Enter Vrſula.

Urſ. By my virginity the Groome cryes to bed, night goes
to Goaſt, how now another *Niobe* turn'd to ſtone, bleſſe me
has the Conjurer bene here.

An *An.* Alive or dead I muſt, and will enjoy thee,
It was my promiſe? *I* cannot chuſe but weepe.
I have not curſ'd thee yet, remember that.

Vrſ. Hey day what inundations are here, will you come away,
and the Groome ſhould geld himſelfe for anger there would be
fine ſport.

An. I have loſt my ſelfe, and know not where *I* am!

Enter Boote.

Bo. Come, come, *I* have daunc'd till every joynt about me
but that which should be growes ſtiffe ~~but that which ſhould be~~ to bed wench, the
groome he's out-gone thee, he's warming the ſheetes the firſt
night *I* faith.

An. To bed! oh heavens, would it were to my grave
So *I* might never here of my miſdeedes

I

or the fayre Maid of Clifton,

I have not curſ'd thee yet! remember that
Alive or dead I muſt, and will enjoy thee
How like the deadly towling of a Bell
A peale of ſadd preſages were his words. A peale of sadd presages

Bo. Ha, weeping; this is not cuſtomary on bridall-nights, this is not customary
Neece who was with your Cuz to night?

Vrſ. Vncle there was a certaine man.

Bo. Ay Ay, but where is that certaine man? *Ay Ay*

Vrſ. There is the woman, but the certaine man is gon

An. A certaine man indeede, for whom I now
Could weepe a Sea, to waſh out my pollutions?

Bo. But *nimble Chaps, tongue Trotter, Neatſ-Young* M[rs] *Magpy*
What was this certaine man called?

Vrſ. With reverence Vncle his name was *Bateman*.

Bo. An undermining Knave, I will indite him,
For daring to ſet foote upon my ground?
This day his father hath arreſted me
Vpon an action of a thouſand poundes
A precontract betwixt his ſon, and thee;
To bed my wench, *Bateman* ſhall ſurely finde
Me maſter of my words, when his proves winde. *Ex. Omnes.*

Enter Mortigue meeting Cliſton.

Clif. Thou keepſt thy promiſe *Mortigue.*

Mor. In all things as befits a man of worth
Thou haſt abuſ'd my princely miſtris name
Sully'd her royalties with infamies,
And from thy throat, as from a Serpents chaps.
Belch'd poyſons 'gainſt the Dowager of *France*;
To prove theſe falſe I made this ſally forth
Only to embate thee.

Clif. By my *Hollidam,*
I'me glad I've wak'd thy temper!
The end ſtill finds it ſelfe in every act,
And ſo ſhalt thou in thy preſumptuous braves?
The honour of my miſtris makes me young
Her name ſhootes majeſty into my lookes,

E Valour

II, ii, 182. I cannot make out the word substituted for "geld."

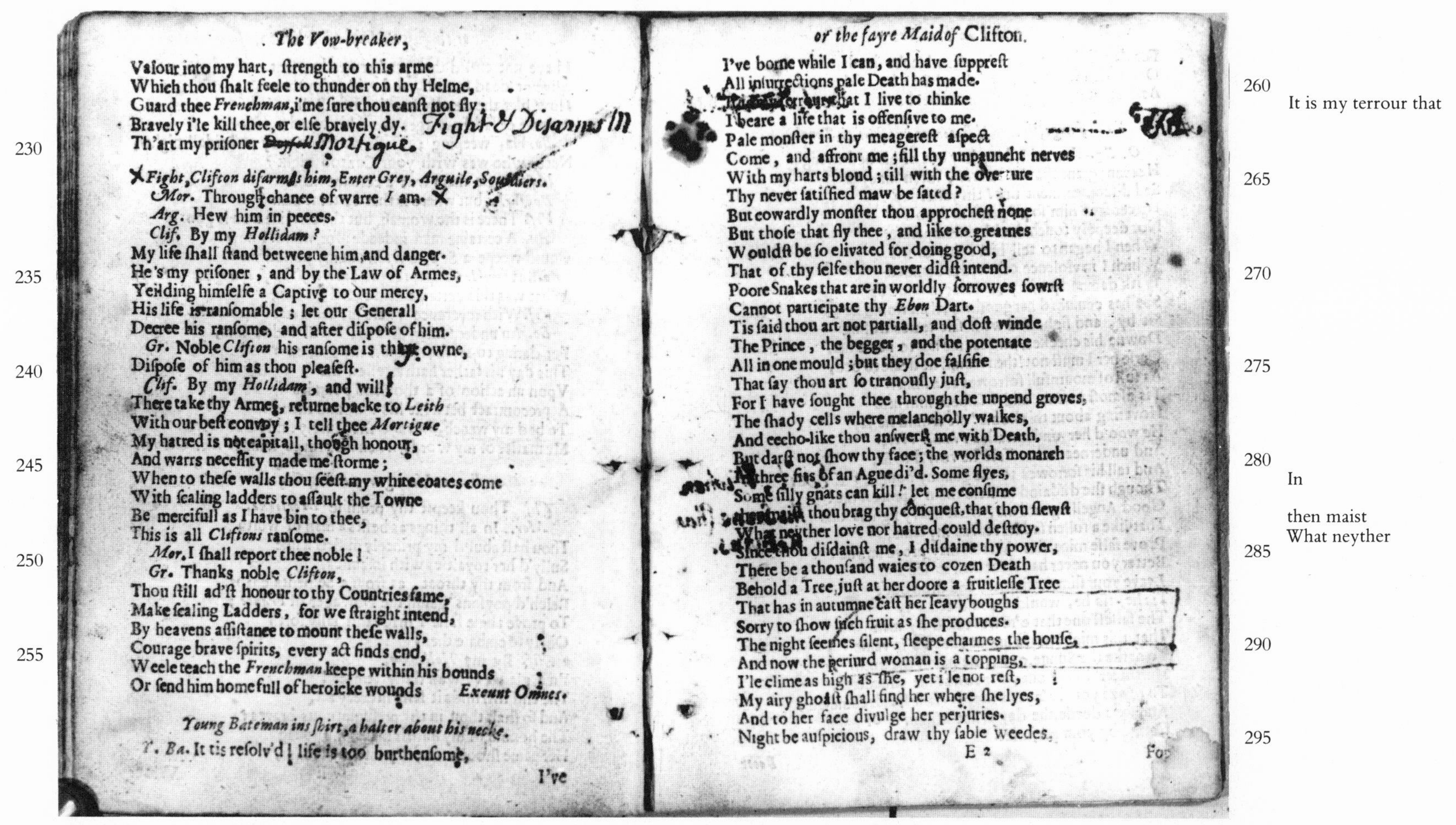

The Vow-breaker,

Valour into my hart, ſtrength to this arme
Which thou ſhalt feele to thunder on thy Helme,
Guard thee *Frenchman*, i'me ſure thou canſt not fly;
Bravely i'le kill thee, or elſe bravely dy. Fight & Disarms M
Th'art my priſoner Mortigue.

Fight, Clifton diſarmes him, Enter Grey, Arguile, Souldiers.

Mor. Through chance of warre *I* am.
Arg. Hew him in peeces.
Clif. By my *Hollidam*?
My life ſhall ſtand betweene him, and danger.
He's my priſoner, and by the Law of Armes,
Yeilding himſelfe a Captive to our mercy,
His life is ranſomable; let our Generall
Decree his ranſome, and after diſpoſe of him.
Gr. Noble *Clifton* his ranſome is thy owne,
Diſpoſe of him as thou pleaſeſt.
Clif. By my *Hollidam*, and will,
There take thy Armes, returne backe to *Leith*
With our beſt convoy; I tell thee *Mortigue*
My hatred is not capitall, though honour,
And warrs neceſſity made me ſtorme;
When to theſe walls thou ſeeſt my white coates come
With ſcaling ladders to aſſault the Towne
Be mercifull as I have bin to thee,
This is all *Cliftons* ranſome.
Mor. I ſhall report thee noble!
Gr. Thanks noble *Clifton*,
Thou ſtill ad'ſt honour to thy Countries fame,
Make ſcaling Ladders, for we ſtraight intend,
By heavens aſſiſtance to mount theſe walls,
Courage brave ſpirits, every act finds end,
Weele teach the *Frenchman* keepe within his bounds
Or ſend him home full of heroicke wounds *Exeunt Omnes.*

Young Bateman in's ſhirt, a halter about his necke.

Y. Ba. It tis reſolv'd; life is too burthenſome,
I've

or the fayre Maid of Clifton.

I've borne while I can, and have ſuppreſt
All inſurrections pale Death has made.
It is my terrour that I live to thinke
I beare a life that is offenſive to me.
Pale monſter in thy meagereſt aſpect
Come, and affront me; fill thy unpauncht nerves
With my harts bloud; till with the overture
Thy never ſatiſfied maw be ſated?
But cowardly monſter thou approcheſt none
But thoſe that fly thee, and like to greatnes
Wouldſt be ſo elivated for doing good,
That of thy ſelfe thou never didſt intend.
Poore Snakes that are in worldly ſorrowes ſowrſt
Cannot participate thy *Eben* Dart.
Tis ſaid thou art not partiall, and doſt winde
The Prince, the begger, and the potentate
All in one mould; but they doe falſifie
That ſay thou art ſo tiranouſly juſt,
For I have ſought thee through the unpend groves,
The ſhady cells where melancholly walkes,
And eecho-like thou anſwerſt me with Death,
But darſt not ſhow thy face; the worlds monarch
In three fits of an Ague di'd. Some flyes,
Some ſilly gnats can kill! let me conſume
then maiſt thou brag thy conqueſt, that thou ſlewſt
What neyther love nor hatred could deſtroy.
Since thou diſdainſt me, I diſdaine thy power,
There be a thouſand waies to cozen Death
Behold a Tree, juſt at her doore a fruitleſſe Tree
That has in autumne caſt her leavy boughs
Sorry to ſhow ſuch fruit as ſhe produces.
The night ſeemes ſilent, ſleepe charmes the houſe,
And now the periurd woman is a topping,
I'le clime as high as ſhe, yet i'le not reſt,
My airy ghoaſt ſhall find her where ſhe lyes,
And to her face divulge her perjuries.
Night be auſpicious, draw thy ſable weedes,
E 2 For

It is my terrour that

In

then maist
What neyther

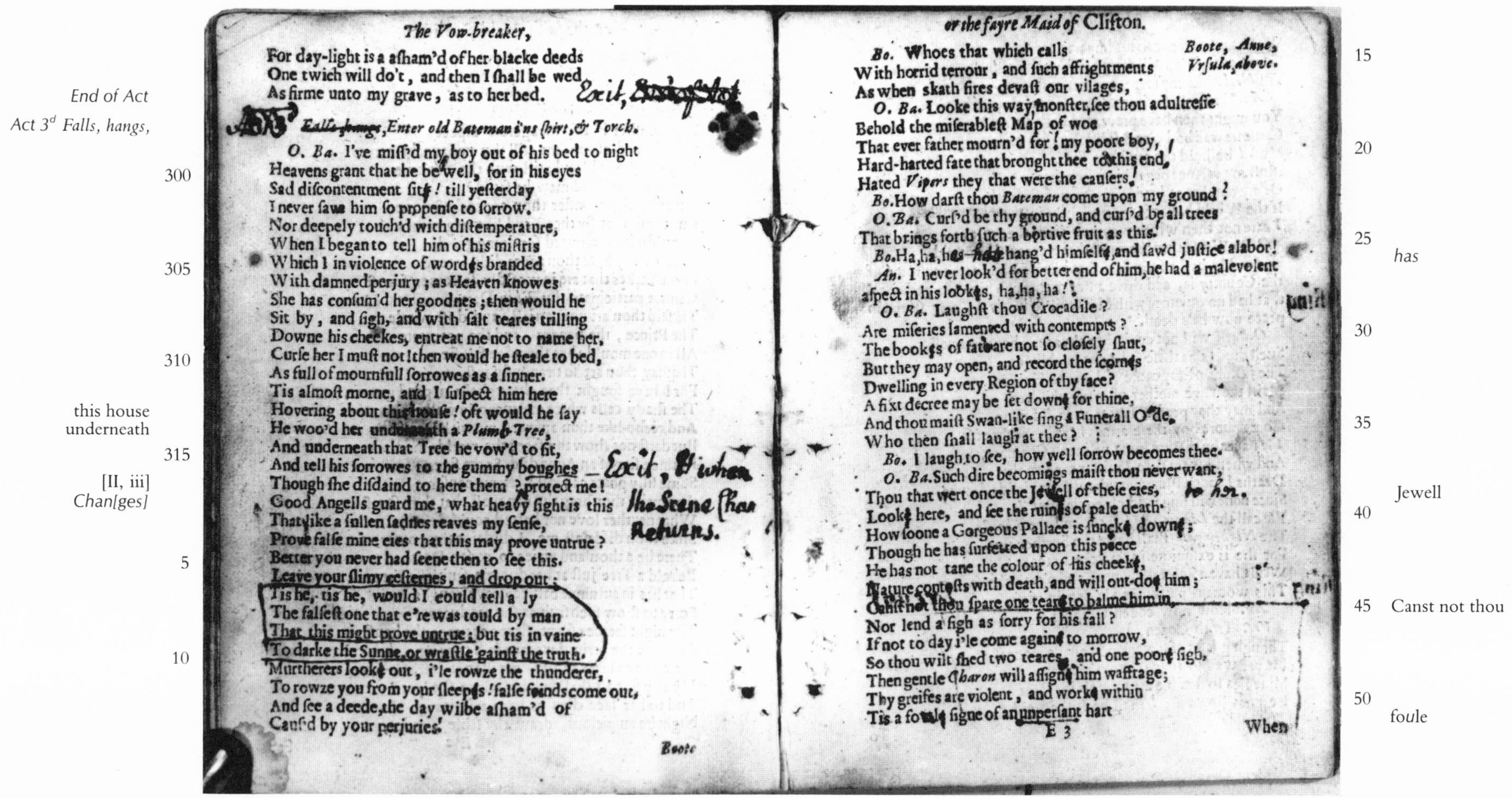

The Vow-breaker,

For day-light is a aſham'd of her blacke deeds
One twich will do't, and then I ſhall be wed
As firme unto my grave, as to her bed. Exit, — *End of Act*

Act 3^d^ Falls, hangs, *Falls hangs, Enter old Bateman in's ſhirt, & Torch.*

O. Ba. I've miſs'd my boy out of his bed to night
Heavens grant that he be well, for in his eyes
Sad diſcontentment ſits ! till yeſterday
I never ſaw him ſo propenſe to ſorrow.
Nor deepely touch'd with diſtemperature,
When I began to tell him of his miſtris
Which I in violence of words branded
With damned perjury ; as Heaven knowes
She has conſum'd her goodnes ; then would he
Sit by, and ſigh, and with ſalt teares trilling
Downe his cheekes, entreat me not to name her,
Curſe her I muſt not ! then would he ſteale to bed,
As full of mournfull ſorrowes as a ſinner.
Tis almoſt morne, and I ſuſpect him here
Hovering about this houſe ! oft would he ſay — *this house*
He woo'd her underneath a *Plumb Tree*, — *underneath*
And underneath that Tree he vow'd to ſit,
And tell his ſorrowes to the gummy boughes — Excit, & when
Though ſhe diſdaind to here them ? protect me ! — *[II, iii]* the Scene chan
Good Angells guard me, what heavy ſight is this — *Chan[ges]* Returns.
That like a ſullen ſadnes reaves my ſenſe,
Prove falſe mine eies that this may prove untrue ?
Better you never had ſeene then to ſee this.
Leave your ſlimy ceſternes, and drop out ;
Tis he, tis he, would I could tell a ly
The falſeſt one that e're was tould by man
That this might prove untrue ; but tis in vaine
To darke the Sunne, or wraſtle 'gainſt the truth.
Murtherers looke out, i'le rowze the thunderer,
To rowze you from your ſleeps ! falſe feinds come out,
And ſee a deede, the day wilbe aſham'd of
Cauſ'd by your perjuries.

Boote

or the fayre Maid of Clifton.

Bo. Whoes that which calls — *Boote, Anne, Vrſula, above.*
With horrid terrour, and ſuch affrightments
As when skath fires devaſt our vilages,
O. Ba. Looke this way, monſter, ſee thou adultreſſe
Behold the miſerableſt Map of woe
That ever father mourn'd for ! my poore boy,
Hard-harted fate that brought thee to this end,
Hated *Vipers* they that were the cauſers.
Bo. How darſt thou *Bateman* come upon my ground ?
O. Ba. Curſ'd be thy ground, and curſ'd be all trees
That brings forth ſuch a bortive fruit as this.
Bo. Ha, ha, hes hang'd himſelfe, and ſaw'd juſtice alabor! — *has*
An. I never look'd for better end of him, he had a malevolent
aſpect in his lookes, ha, ha, ha !
O. Ba. Laughſt thou Crocadile ?
Are miſeries lamented with contempts ?
The bookes of fate are not ſo cloſely ſhut,
But they may open, and record the ſcornes
Dwelling in every Region of thy face ?
A fixt decree may be ſet downe for thine,
And thou maiſt Swan-like ſing a Funerall Ode,
Who then ſhall laugh at thee ?
Bo. I laugh to ſee, how well ſorrow becomes thee.
O. Ba. Such dire becomings maiſt thou never want,
Thou that wert once the Jewell of theſe eies, to her. — *Jewell*
Looke here, and ſee the ruins of pale death.
How ſoone a Gorgeous Pallace is ſuncke downe ;
Though he has ſurfeited upon this peece
He has not tane the colour of his cheeke,
Nature contests with death, and will out-doe him ;
Canst not thou ſpare one teare to balme him in, — *Canst not thou*
Nor lend a ſigh as ſorry for his fall ?
If not to day i'le come againe to morrow,
So thou wilt ſhed two teares, and one poore ſigh,
Then gentle *Charon* will aſſigne him wafftage ;
Thy greifes are violent, and worke within
Tis a fowle ſigne of an unperſant hart — *foule*

E 3 When

II, ii, 298 ff. For a discussion of how the producers handled the hanging scene and the discovery by Old Bateman of his dead son, see the commentary in the first part of this book.

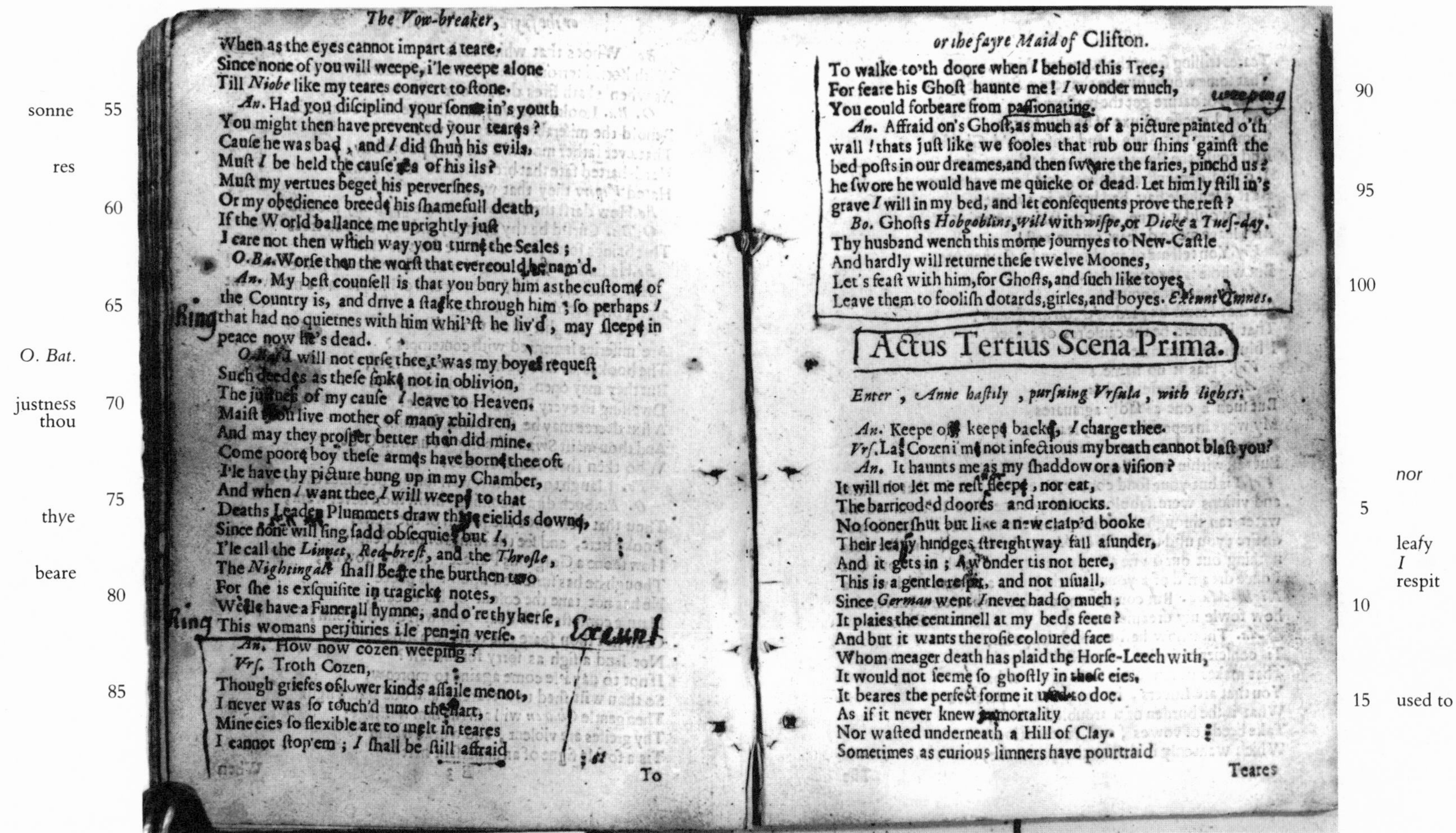

The Vow-breaker,

When as the eyes cannot impart a teare.
Since none of you will weepe, i'le weepe alone
Till *Niobe* like my teares convert to ſtone.
An. Had you diſciplind your ſonne in's youth
You might then have prevented your teares?
Cauſe he was bad, and *I* did ſhun his evils,
Muſt *I* be held the cauſe of his ils?
Muſt my vertues beget his perverſnes,
Or my obedience breede his ſhamefull death,
If the World ballance me uprightly juſt
I care not then which way you turne the Scales;
O. Ba. Worſe then the worſt that ever could be nam'd.
An. My beſt counſell is that you bury him as the cuſtome of the Country is, and drive a ſtake through him; ſo perhaps *I* that had no quietnes with him whil'ſt he liv'd, may ſleepe in peace now he's dead.
O. Bat. I will not curſe thee, t'was my boyes requeſt
Such deedes as theſe ſinke not in oblivion,
The juſtneſs of my cauſe *I* leave to Heaven.
Maiſt thou live mother of many children,
And may they proſper better then did mine.
Come poore boy theſe armes have borne thee oft
I'le have thy picture hung up in my Chamber,
And when *I* want thee, *I* will weepe to that
Deaths Leaden Plummets draw thine eielids downe,
Since none will ſing ſadd obſequies but *I*,
I'le call the *Linnet*, *Red-breſt*, and the *Throſtle*,
The *Nightingale* ſhall beare the burthen too
For ſhe is exſquiſite in tragicke notes,
Wee'le have a Funerall hymne, and o're thy herſe,
This womans perjuiries i'le pen in verſe. Exeunt
An. How now cozen weeping?
Vrſ. Troth Cozen,
Though griefes of lower kinds aſſaile me not,
I never was ſo touch'd unto the hart,
Mine eies ſo flexible are to melt in teares
I cannot ſtop'em; *I* ſhall be ſtill affraid
To

or the fayre Maid of Clifton.

To walke to'th doore when *I* behold this Tree;
For feare his Ghoſt haunte me! *I* wonder much,
You could forbeare from paſſionating. weeping
An. Affraid on's Ghoſt, as much as of a picture painted o'th wall! thats juſt like we fooles that rub our ſhins 'gainſt the bed poſts in our dreames, and then ſweare the faries, pinchd us? he ſwore he would have me quicke or dead. Let him ly ſtill in's grave *I* will in my bed, and let conſequents prove the reſt?
Bo. Ghoſts *Hobgoblins, Will* with *wiſpe*, or *Dicke* a *Tueſ-day*.
Thy husband wench this morne journyes to New-Caſtle
And hardly will returne theſe twelve Moones,
Let's feaſt with him, for Ghoſts, and ſuch like toyes
Leave them to fooliſh dotards, girles, and boyes. *Exeunt Omnes.*

Actus Tertius Scena Prima.

Enter, Anne haſtily, purſuing Vrſula, with lights.

An. Keepe off keepe backe, *I* charge thee.
Vrſ. Las Cozen i'me not infectious my breath cannot blaſt you?
An. It haunts me as my ſhaddow or a viſion?
It will not let me reſt, ſleepe, nor eat,
The barricoded doores and iron locks.
No ſooner ſhut but like a new claſp'd booke
Their leafy hindges ſtreightway fall aſunder,
And it gets in; *I* wonder tis not here,
This is a gentle reſpit, and not uſuall,
Since *German* went *I* never had ſo much;
It plaies the centinnell at my beds feete?
And but it wants the roſie coloured face
Whom meager death has plaid the Horſe-Leech with,
It would not ſeeme ſo ghoſtly in theſe eies,
It beares the perfect forme it uſed to doe.
As if it never knew immortality
Nor waſted underneath a Hill of Clay.
Sometimes as curious limners have pourtraid
Teares

sonne
res
O. Bat.
justness
thou
thye
beare

nor
leafy
I
respit
used to

The Vow-breaker,

Teares triiling from the weeping *Niobe,*
That ſome would ſweare the very picture wept,
Nor art of nature got the maſtery? — And art
So did I gueſſe affluxe of briniſh teares
Came from this Aiery, and unfadom'd Ghoſt?
And could the Painters of this age draw ſighes
I could demonſtrate ſighes, and heavy groanes
As if a ſenſible hart had broke in twaine?
Then would it turne, and cry falſe woman.
And leave me to deſcant on the reſt!
Vrſ. You tell me of an object, and a ſtrange one,
But whoſe is the reſemblance?
An. Ay there's the point, — *Ay ther's*
~~For that I muſt be pardon'd; oh my frame~~
That I ſhould be the cauſe'res of a deed,
I bluſh to nominate. — blush
Vrſ. Has it no name!
An. Yes ſweete *Vrſula,*
But ſuch a one as ſadly agrauates
My woes in repetition; pray leave me
I am addicted to contemplation
But reſt within my call.
Vrſ. Tis but your fond conceit; I've heard you ſay that dreames and viſions were fabulous; and yet one time I dream't fowle water ran through the floore, and the next day the houſe was on fire; you uſ'd to ſay *Hobgoblins, Fairies,* and the like were nothing but our owne affrightments, and yet oh my troth Cuz I once dream'd of a young batchelour, and was ridd with a *Night-Mare.* But come, ſo my conſcience be cleere I never care how fowle my dreames are. *Exit.*
An. Thou now haſt touch'd the point,
Tis conſcience is the Larum Bell indeede
That makes us ſenſible of our good or bad! — our
You that are Lovers, by me you may perceive — you
What is the burden of a troubled minde
Take heede of vowes, and proteſtations
Which wantonly in dalliancies you make,
The

or the fayre Maid of Cliſton.

The eie of Heaven is on you, and your oaths
Are regiſtred; which if you breake, ~~bleſſe me.~~ Bleſs me! — blesse me.

Enter Ghoſt.

Gho. Thou can'ſt not fly me, now, thou perjur'd Maid!
There is no Cavern in the Earth's vaſt entrailes — vast
But I can through as pearceant as the light,
And finde thee, though thou wer't entomb'd in ſtone,
Thou can'ſt not catch my unſubſtantiall part,
For I am aire, and am not to be touch'd.
From flaming fires of burning *Phlegeton,*
I have a time limited to walke,
Vntill the morning Cocke ſhall ſummon me — *now*
For to retire to miſty *Erebus.*
My pilgrimage has no ceſſation, long,
Vntill I bring thee with me to the place
Where *Rhadamant,* and ſable *Æacus* dwell.
Alive or dead, tis I that muſt enjoy thee,
To tell the ſtory where we ſpirits live
Would plucke *Vermilion* from thy Roſie cheekes,
And make them pale, as Snowy *Apennines,*
And from thoſe eies draw liquid ſtreames of teares
More full of iſſue than a ~~ſleepy~~ Fountaine, ſteep, — steepy
Alive or dead I muſt, and will enjoy thee,
Thinke on thy promiſes, thy broken Vows!
An. Diſtraction like an Ague ſeizes me,
I know not whether I ſee here, or ſpeake,
My intellectuall parts are frozen up
At ſight of thee, thou fiery *Effigies*
Of my wrong'd *Bateman.*

Enter Boote, Vrſula.

Bo. What weeping againe?
An. Doe you not ſee it?
Bo. See! what? I ſee nothing but a Bird fly o're the houſe.
Vrſ. Nor I, but a blinde Buzzard lookes as like her husband as may be.
F *An.*

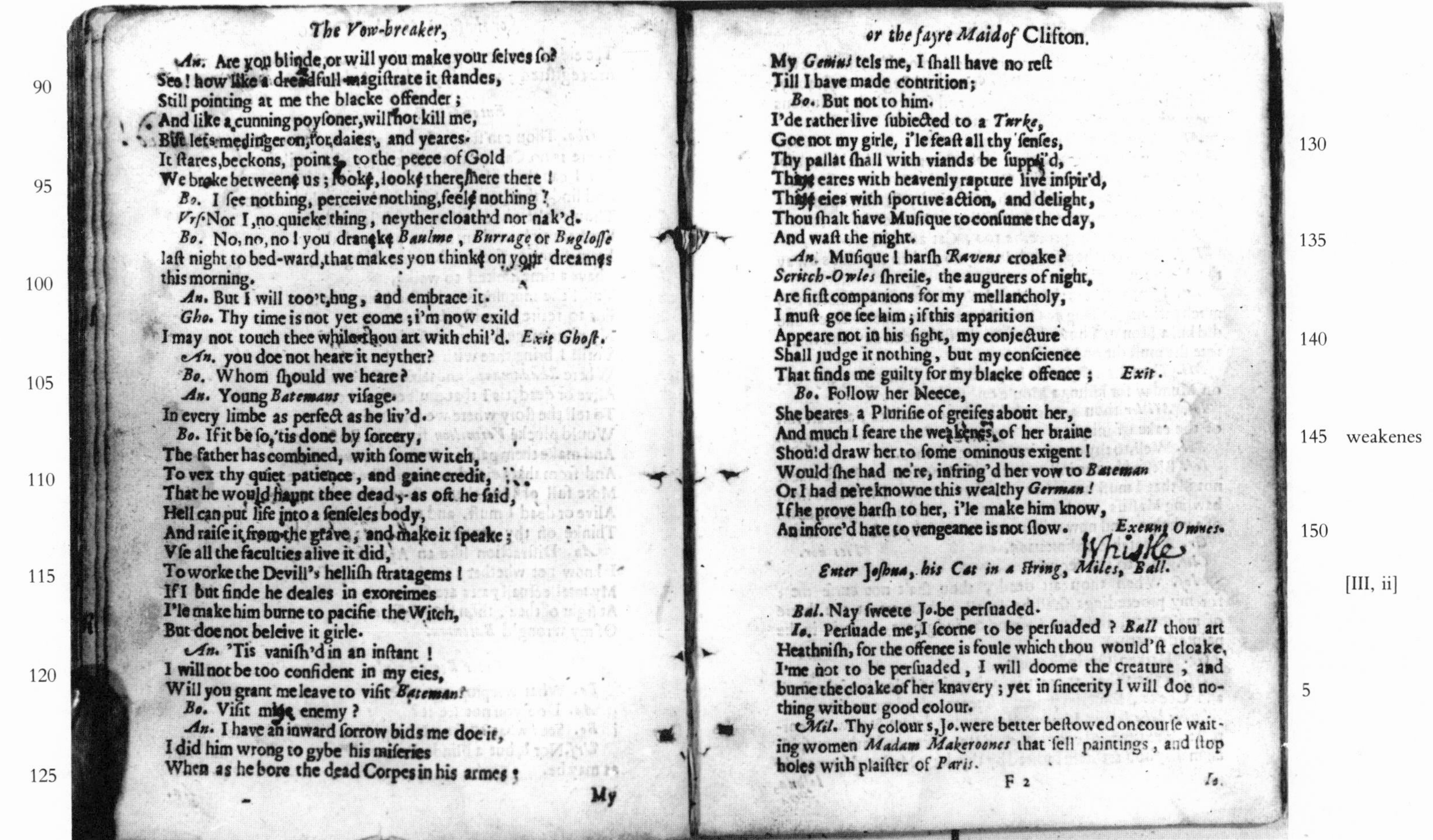

The Vow-breaker,

An. Are you blinde, or will you make your selves so?
See! how like a dreadfull magistrate it standes,
Still pointing at me the blacke offender;
And like a cunning poysoner, will not kill me,
But lets me linger on, for daies, and yeares.
It stares, beckons, points, to the peece of Gold
We broke betweene us; looke, looke there, there there!
Bo. I see nothing, perceive nothing, feele nothing?
Urs. Nor I, no quicke thing, neyther cloath'd nor nak'd.
Bo. No, no, no! you dranke *Baulme*, *Burrage* or *Buglosse*
last night to bed-ward, that makes you thinke on your dreames
this morning.
An. But I will too't, hug, and embrace it.
Gho. Thy time is not yet come; i'm now exild
I may not touch thee whilst thou art with chil'd. *Exit Ghost.*
An. you doe not heare it neyther?
Bo. Whom should we heare?
An. Young *Batemans* visage.
In every limbe as perfect as he liv'd.
Bo. If it be so, 'tis done by sorcery,
The father has combined, with some witch,
To vex thy quiet patience, and gaine credit,
That he would haunt thee dead, as oft he said,
Hell can put life into a senseles body,
And raise it from the grave, and make it speake;
Use all the faculties alive it did,
To worke the Devill's hellish stratagems!
If I but finde he deales in exorcimes
I'le make him burne to pacifie the Witch,
But doe not beleive it girle.
An. 'Tis vanish'd in an instant!
I will not be too confident in my eies,
Will you grant me leave to visit *Bateman*?
Bo. Visit mine enemy?
An. I have an inward sorrow bids me doe it,
I did him wrong to gybe his miseries
When as he bore the dead Corpes in his armes;

My

or the fayre Maid of Clifton.

My *Genius* tels me, I shall have no rest
Till I have made contrition;
Bo. But not to him.
I'de rather live subiected to a *Turke*,
Goe not my girle, i'le feast all thy senses,
Thy pallat shall with viands be supply'd,
Thine eares with heavenly rapture live inspir'd,
Thine eies with sportive action, and delight,
Thou shalt have Musique to consume the day,
And wast the night.
An. Musique! harsh *Ravens* croake?
Scritch-Owles shreile, the augurers of night,
Are first companions for my mellancholy,
I must goe see him; if this apparition
Appeare not in his sight, my conjecture
Shall judge it nothing, but my conscience
That finds me guilty for my blacke offence; *Exit.*
Bo. Follow her Neece,
She beares a Plurisie of greifes about her,
And much I feare the weaknes, of her braine weakenes
Should draw her to some ominous exigent!
Would she had ne're, infring'd her vow to *Bateman*
Or I had ne're knowne this wealthy *German*!
If he prove harsh to her, i'le make him know,
An inforc'd hate to vengeance is not slow. *Exeunt Omnes.*

Whiske

Enter Joshua, his Cat in a string, Miles, Ball. [III, ii]

Bal. Nay sweete *Jo.* be persuaded.

Io. Persuade me, I scorne to be persuaded? *Ball* thou art Heathnish, for the offence is foule which thou would'st cloake, I'me not to be persuaded, I will doome the creature, and burne the cloake of her knavery; yet in sincerity I will doe nothing without good colour.

Mil. Thy colours, *Jo.* were better bestowed on course waiting women *Madam Makeroones* that sell paintings, and stop holes with plaister of *Paris*.

F 2 *Io.*

Iof. Miller, Miller, thou art not mealy mouth'd ; thoſe be the Heathen bables, the May-poles of time, and Pageants of vanity, but I will convince them of error , and ſcoure their pollutions away with the waters of my exhortations.

Mi. Why ſhould'ſt thou hang thy Cat?

Iof. Thou art ſaucy, *Miller*, & ought'ſt not to Cathechiſe me ſo,

Bal. And it were but for Country ſake.

Mi. Sweete Jo. conſider thy Cat is thy Countriman,

Bal. Hang a poore Cat for killing a Mouſe?

Mi. Knowing the proverbe too , Cat after Kinde.

Bal. As it is in the painted cloath too ; when the Cat's away the Mouſe will play.

Iof. I, but as it is in the painted cloath, beware in time for too much patience, to Dog or Cat will breede too much offence. She did kill a Mouſe, I but when? on the forbidden day, and therefore ſhe muſt die on Munday.

Mi. Then ſhall thy zeale be proclaim'd, for hanging thy Cat on Munday for killing a Mouſe on Sunday.

Iof. Miller thou art drunke in thy enormities , and art full of the cake of iniquity. Enter *Gray, Arguile, Clifton.*

Bal. Well, to thy execution we commit thee.

Iof. Bleſſed be the inſtruments of ſilence ; poore Puſſe take it not ill that I muſt hang thee , by that meanes I free thee from bawling Maſtifs , and ſnarling Currs ; I have brought thee up of a whelpe , and now will have a care of thy end.

A notable *Gr.* A notable exhortation. *Ties her.*

Clif. Liſt to the ſequell ;

Iof. When thou art dead , thou ſhalt not curſe me ; for my proceedings ſhall be legall ; thou art at the barre of my mercy, and thus I aſcend to judgment, as it is in the painted cloath.

Gr. Harken the inditement.

Iof. Tybert the Cat ; as it is in the painted cloath, of the Bull, and Cocke , ſometimes houſe-keeper, drudger or ſcourer to *Marmaduke Ioſhua*, Limner alias painter-ſtainer, & now the corrector or extirper of vermine, as Rats, Mice, and other waſpiſh animalls; thou art here indited by thy deare Maſter *Marmaduke Ioſhua*,

Ioſhua for breaking of the high-day, what ſayſt thou for thy ſelfe? guilty or not guilty ? hah.

Gr. Would ſhe could mew *non* guilty.

Iof. Know'ſt thou not , thou ſilly Cat , that thy brethren will not Kill the Calfe nor roſt the Mutton nor boyle their fleſh Pots on the high-day ? was it not decree'd by our learned brother *Abolt Cabbidge* , Cobler of *Amſterdam* , that they ſhould be held uncleane, and not worthy of the meanes that did it , and did not expect Cratchet Coole his proud fleſh in the Leene for making insurrection on the high day ? making

Clif. A point well watred.

Iof Did not *Nadab* the Sowe-gelder make a gaunt of his gelt for being cumberſome on the high-day ? Ha thy ſilence argues guilt ; haſt thou not ſeene the whole conventicle of brothers, and ſiſters walke to St. *Anns*, and not ſo much as a fructifying Kiſſe on the high—

Gr. It ſeemes the elect Kiſſe weekely.

Iof. And muſt thou kill a Mouſe ? oh thou wicked Cat; could'ſt not turne up the white of the eie for the poore creature? thou gluttonous Cat, thou art now arraigned, I adjudge thee to be hanged this munday, for killing a Mouſe yeſterday being the high-day. *Offers to hang her.*

Gr. Stay, ſtay, a pardon, a pardon !

Iof. I am hot in my zeale , and fiery in expedition,

Clif. Wee'le talke with you hereafter.

Iof. I was executing a point of juſtice, equity, and conſcience.

Gr. A pleaſant Tragecomedy, the Cat being ſcap't, + Trumpet.
What Trumpets this?

Enter Croſſe.

Crof. Monlucke , Biſhop of *Valens*,
Newly anchor'd in the haven of *Inſkeith*,
Deſires ſafe convoy by your honours forces,
From the red Brayes to *Edenborough* Caſtle,
The reſt on entervew he will impart.
Such entertainment, as the warre affourds

The Vow-breaker,

The Drum the Fiffe, the thundering Cannon,
The ſhrill Trumpets, andall war-like Cymballs,
Such Muſique as in warrs Souldiers meaſure
Beſtow on him; come he in warr or peace
He ſhalbe welcome?
Io. Oh that prophane ſupleſſe, ho, ho, ho.

Enter Monluckk, attendants ſaluta,

Dauphins *Mon.* Mary, King Dauphins wiſe, *Dowager* of *France*,
And heire apparant to the *Scottiſh* Crowne,
Hearing of devaſtations in her Lands,
And the oppreſſions that her neighbour Princeſſe
With rough hoſtility grindes her people,
Me her Legat ſhe ſends to *Edenburgh*,
To parley with her Mother the Queene Regent,
And Article A peace twixt her deare ſiſter,
The Queene of *England*, and the Lords of *Scotland*.
If our conditions may be made with honour,
This is my meſſage.
Gr. Eyther for peace or warre.
The Queene my Miſtris now is arm'd for both,
For like a vertuons Princeſſe, and a Mother
O're us her loving ſubjects, and her ſons,
She knowing a Kings ſecurity reſts,
In the true love, and welfare of her people,
for Raiſ'd this hoſtility for to guard her ſelfe,
Not to offend, but to defend her owne,
Her Secretary *Sicill* now attends
On the like Embaſy for *Edenburgh*,
Whither your ſelfe ſhall ſafely be convoy'de.
Mon. You are an honourable foe.
Gr. Will the Queene,
Lay by her nicety, rough fil'd phraſe,
And not articulate too much with *England*?
For by the power of warr e're two ſuns riſe
Weele mount the walls of *Leith*, and ſacrifize,

He,

or the fayre Maid of Cliſton.

Her guilded Towres, and her *French* inſulters;
In flames of fire; we vow to hazard lives,
And honours in the enterprize. *Exeunt Omnes.*
Whistle

[III, iii]

Enter Anne, with a Torch, Vrſula, Bateman, wailing his Picture.

An. Softly, ſoftly; fie on your creaking ſhooes, what noiſe they make; ſhut the Dores cloſe, it does not here us a jot, looke well to the Darneicke Hangings, that it play not the Court Page with us.

Vrſ. Heer's not ſo much as a ſhaddow to affright us, for mine owne part neyther *Incubus* nor *Sucubus* can do't; I feare not what a quicke thing can doe, and I thinke y'ore dead things are too quiet to do any harme. do

An. Yet all is cleere, no frightfull viſion
Nor Ghoſtly apparition hauntes me yet;
Yonders thy father, good powres aſſiſt me,
That I may gaine his patience to heare me,
And I am hartily ſatiſfied. heartily
O. Ba. Pigmalion doated on the peece he made,
So doe not I upon thy pourtraiture.
I doe but hang thy faire reſemblance here
To tell me of thy immortality.
How ſenſible young Cedars are o'th winde,
When as the aged Oake affronts all ſtormes con
'Tis death, and natures fault, for the Diamond,
Of blooming youth, deſpiſe decaying age.
He might have tane thee el'ſe, and left thee boy. el'se
An. Whom talkes he too? my life, Coz, he has a ghoſt too!
Yet I ſee nothing.
Ba. How now *Hyena*; why camſt thou hither?
Com'ſt thou againe to gybe my miſeries?
Has thy maligneing harted father ſent thee malignant
To ſcoffe my ſorowes? keepe off I charge thee,
Thou did'ſt bewitch my poore boy with a Kiſſe,
Thy breath is ſure infectious, and I feare

Theirs

The Vow-breaker,

Their's something in thee smells of sorcery.
Stand at distance.
An. Good sir, use patience,
That in extremity is soveraigne Balme,
Teares be my witnes I come to comfort you,
Yet I see nothing.
Ba. Teares? 'tis impossible!
Marble will drop, and melt against the raine,
And from the cragy Rocks, Fountainous Flouds
Oft get inforced issues; but to gaine
Relenting teares from thy obdurate harte
'Tis impossible, as to force Fire from snow
Water from flint, say the Sun shall not shine,
As well upon the begger as the King,
That is alike indifferent to all.
Vrs. Good sir remember,
Forgivenes is an Atribute of Heaven.
She has a harty sorrow for her sinnes,
And comes to make attonement, if you please.
An. Still I nothing any where.
Ba. Pray listen;
Say, Would not that Physitian be well hang'd
That for his practise sake ~~kills~~ his patient, kills,
And after pleades a sorrow to his freinds?
She weepes, an evidence of a harty sorrow,
My boy would not have seene her weepe thus long,
But hee'd have minister'd comfort to my teares
Play'd the theife with my eies too.
An. Yet all is safe; sure it was but my dreams,
Sir you had a son, bless me 'tis here now. *Enter Ghost.*
In the same figure that it us'd to be.
Peace is more deare, and pretious unto me
Then a nights rest, to a man turmoil'd in Law.
My eies set he re un-mou'd, i'le gaze with thee,
Untill the windowes of my head drop out.
But then my minds wilbe afflicted too.
For what is unseen there, is visible here.
Lead

or the fayre Maid of Clifton.

Leade me, i'le follow though to a desart,
Or any uncouth place, worke thy vengeance,
And doe not torture me alive; ~~neyther~~ neyther.
Gho. All things keep their time!
An. Let all times daughters, which are daies, convert
To one ~~day~~ and bring me to my period, day,
Ba. Whom converses she withall?
Vrs. To her unseen fancies.
An. See with eies of wonder! see!
Ba. What should I see?
An. Aske you what? why 'tis your son,
Just as he di'd, looke, looke, there, there, there.
Ba. Is this thy sorow, com'st thou to mock me?
An. Just heavens not I! see how it smiles on you,
On me it hurles a dejected looke. *Takes the Picture.*
Ba. Because I hang his Picture ~~neare~~ my bed, near
Com'st thou to laugh me out out, fond-ling, no! mock
See thus I gaze on it; stroke his snowy hands,
And prune the curled tresses of his locks,
Which the Arts-man neatly has dishevell'd.
Vrs. Good sir; have patience, her's is true sorow,
And not derision.
Stands betweene the Picture, & Ghost.
An. Another *Ganimede*!
This eye, and yon'd are one? this front, that lip.
This cheeke a litle ruddier shows then that,
The very ashie palenes of his face,
~~The mossie downe still growing on his chin,~~
And so his Alablaster finger pointing
To the bracelet, whereon the peece of gold
We broke betweene us hangs.
Ba. Certes she's madd.
An. Pray come hither,
You shade this Picture from the pearsant Sun,
And curtaine it, to keepe it from the dust,
Why are you not as chary then of that?
It lookes as it were cold, alas poor Picture,
G *Ba.*

III, iii, 58. Beginning with this line the corrector sometimes rubbed out letters instead of canceling them with pen strokes.

III, iii, 94. The canceled line is: "The mossie downe still growing on his chin."

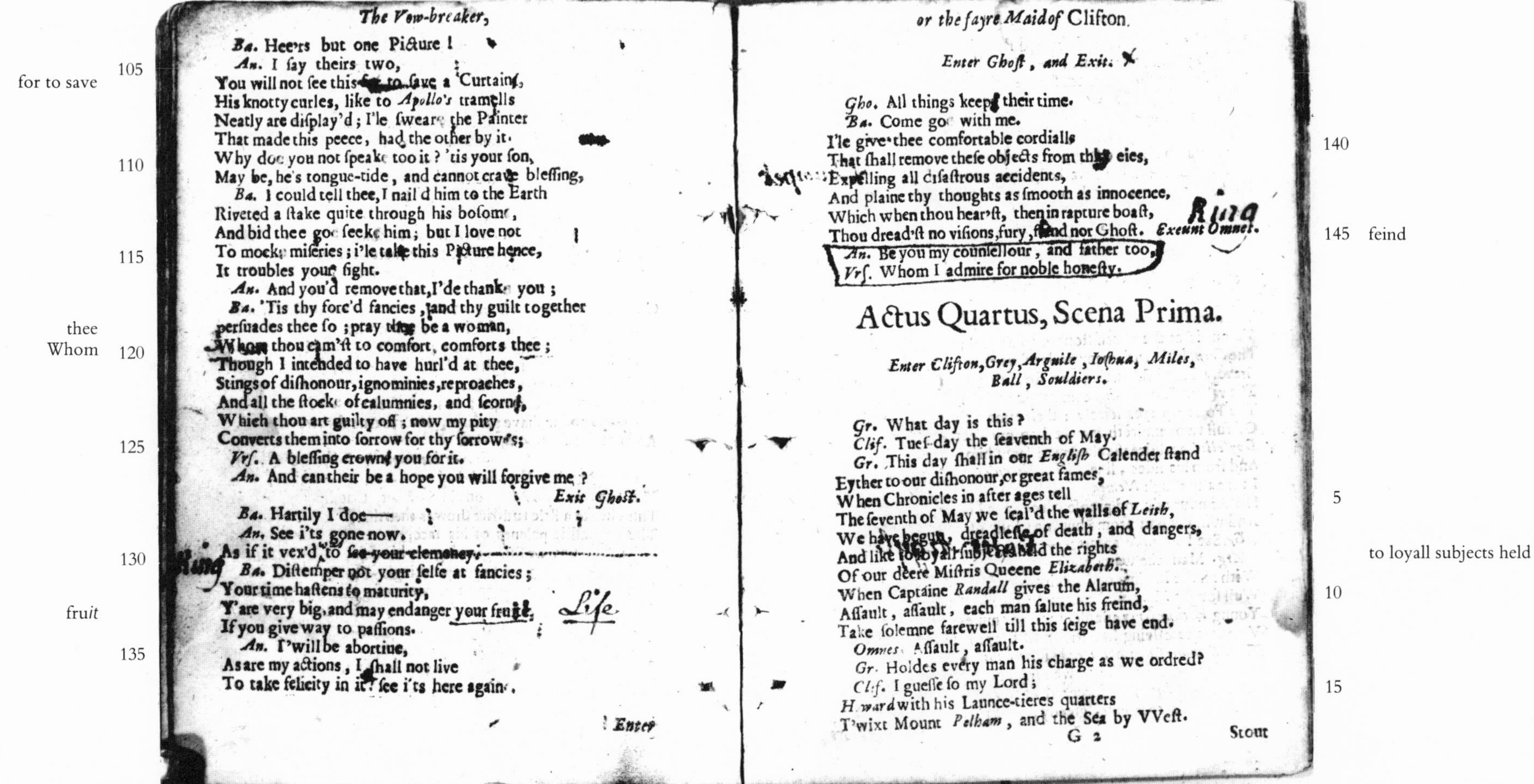

The Vow-breaker,

Ba. Hee'rs but one Picture !
An. I say theirs two,
You will not see this for to save a Curtain,
His knotty curles, like to *Apollo's* tramells
Neatly are display'd; I'le sweare the Painter
That made this peece, had the other by it.
Why doe you not speake too it? 'tis your son,
May be, he's tongue-tide, and cannot crave blessing,
Ba. I could tell thee, I nail'd him to the Earth
Riveted a stake quite through his bosome,
And bid thee goe seeke him; but I love not
To mocke miseries; i'le take this Picture hence,
It troubles your sight.
An. And you'd remove that, I'de thanke you;
Ba. 'Tis thy forc'd fancies, and thy guilt together
perswades thee so; pray thee be a woman,
Whom thou cam'st to comfort, comforts thee;
Though I intended to have hurl'd at thee,
Stings of dishonour, ignominies, reproaches,
And all the stocke of calumnies, and scorne,
Which thou art guilty off; now my pity
Converts them into sorrow for thy sorrowes;
Vrs. A blessing crowne you for it.
An. And can their be a hope you will forgive me?
Exit Ghost.
Ba. Hartily I doe——
An. See i'ts gone now.
As if it vex'd to see your clemency.
Ba. Distemper not your selfe at fancies;
Your time hastens to maturity,
Y'are very big, and may endanger your fruit.
If you give way to passions.
An. I'will be abortive,
As are my actions, I shall not live
To take felicity in it; see i'ts here againe.
Enter

or the fayre Maid of Clifton.

Enter Ghost, and Exit.

Gho. All things keepe their time.
Ba. Come goe with me.
I'le give thee comfortable cordialls
That shall remove these objects from thine eies,
Expelling all disastrous accidents,
And plaine thy thoughts as smooth as innocence,
Which when thou hear'st, then in rapture boast,
Thou dread'st no visions, fury, fiend nor Ghost. *Exeunt Omnes.*
An. Be you my counsellour, and father too,
Vrs. Whom I admire for noble honesty.

Actus Quartus, Scena Prima.

Enter Clifton, Grey, Arguile, Ioshua, Miles, Ball, Souldiers.

Gr. What day is this?
Clif. Tues-day the seaventh of May.
Gr. This day shall in our *English* Calender stand
Eyther to our dishonour, or great fames,
When Chronicles in after ages tell
The seventh of May we seal'd the walls of *Leith*,
We have begun, dreadlesse of death, and dangers,
And like loyall subjects held the rights
Of our deere Mistris Queene *Elizabeth*.
When Captaine *Randall* gives the Alarum,
Assault, assault, each man salute his freind,
Take solemne farewell till this seige have end.
Omnes. Assault, assault.
Gr. Holdes every man his charge as we ordred?
Clif. I guesse so my Lord;
Howard with his Launce-tieres quarters
T'wixt Mount *Pelham*, and the Sea by West.
G 2 Stout

for to save
thee
Whom
fru*it*
feind
to loyall subjects held

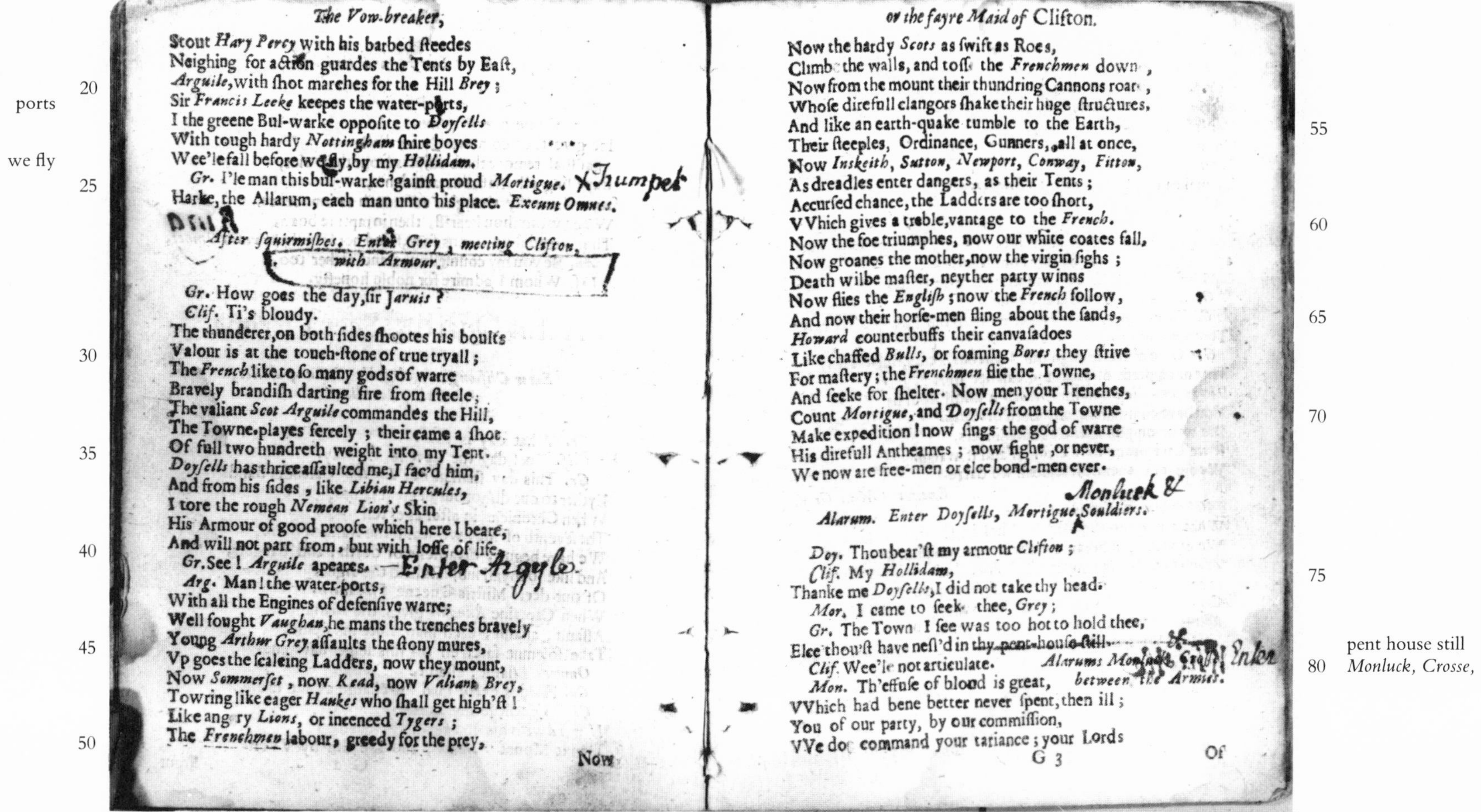

The Vow-breaker;

Stout *Hary Percy* with his barbed ſteedes
Neighing for action guardes the Tents by Eaſt,
Arguile, with ſhot marches for the Hill *Brey*;
Sir *Francis Leeke* keepes the water-perts, ports
I the greene Bul-warke oppoſite to *Doyſells*
With tough hardy *Nottingham* ſhire boyes
Wee'le fall before weſly, by my *Hollidam*. we fly
Gr. I'le man this bul-warke 'gainſt proud *Mortigue.* Trumpet
Harke, the Allarum, each man unto his place. *Exeunt Omnes.*

After ſquirmiſhes. Enter Grey, meeting Cliſton, with Armour.

Gr. How goes the day, ſir *Jaruis*?
Clif. Ti's bloudy.
The thunderer, on both ſides ſhootes his boults
Valour is at the touch-ſtone of true tryall;
The *French* like to ſo many gods of warre
Bravely brandiſh darting fire from ſteele;
The valiant *Scot Arguile* commandes the Hill,
The Towne playes fercely; their came a ſhot
Of full two hundreth weight into my Tent.
Doyſells has thrice aſſaulted me, I fac'd him,
And from his ſides, like *Libian Hercules*,
I tore the rough *Nemean Lion's* Skin
His Armour of good proofe which here I beare,
And will not part from, but with loſſe of life.
Gr. See! *Arguile* apeares. Enter Argyle
Arg. Man! the water-ports,
With all the Engines of defenſive warre;
Well fought *Vaughan*, he mans the trenches bravely
Young *Arthur Grey* aſſaults the ſtony mures,
Vp goes the ſcaleing Ladders, now they mount,
Now *Sommerſet*, now *Read*, now *Valiant Brey*,
Towring like eager *Haukes* who ſhall get high'ſt!
Like ang ry *Lions*, or incenced *Tygers*;
The *Frenchmen* labour, greedy for the prey,

Now

or the fayre Maid of Clifton.

Now the hardy *Scots* as ſwift as Roes,
Climb the walls, and toſſe the *Frenchmen* down,
Now from the mount their thundring Cannons roar,
Whoſe direfull clangors ſhake their huge ſtructures,
And like an earth-quake tumble to the Earth,
Their ſteeples, Ordinance, Gunners, all at once,
Now *Inskeith*, *Sutton*, *Newport*, *Conway*, *Fitton*,
As dreadles enter dangers, as their Tents;
Accurſed chance, the Ladders are too ſhort,
VVhich gives a treble, vantage to the *French*.
Now the foe triumphes, now our white coates fall,
Now groanes the mother, now the virgin ſighs;
Death wilbe maſter, neyther party winns
Now flies the *Engliſh*; now the *French* follow,
And now their horſe-men fling about the ſands,
Howard counterbuffs their canvaſadoes
Like chaffed *Bulls*, or foaming *Bores* they ſtrive
For maſtery; the *Frenchmen* flie the Towne,
And ſeeke for ſhelter. Now men your Trenches,
Count *Mortigue*, and *Doyſells* from the Towne
Make expedition! now ſings the god of warre
His direfull Antheames; now fight, or never,
We now are free-men or elce bond-men ever.

Alarum. Enter Doyſells, Mortigue, Monluck & *Souldiers.*

Doy. Thou bear'ſt my armour *Cliſton*;
Clif. My *Hollidam*,
Thanke me *Doyſells*, I did not take thy head.
Mor. I came to ſeeke thee, *Grey*;
Gr. The Town I ſee was too hot to hold thee,
Elce thou'ſt have neſl'd in thy pent-houſe ſtill. pent house still
Clif. Wee'le not articulate. *Alarums Monluck, Croſſe,* Enter Monluck, Crosse,
Mon. Th'effuſe of blood is great, *between the Armies.*
VVhich had bene better never ſpent, then ill;
You of our party, by our commiſſion,
VVe doe command your tariance; your Lords

G 3 Of

IV, i, following 73. The prompter did not need to bring on Monluck with the others here, for the author indicated at line 80 that Monluck was to enter; but since the prompter changed the character's entrance, he should have deleted Monluck from the direction at line 80.

The Vow-breaker,

Of *England*, and of *Scotland* we entreat
A litle patience till your *Heralds* ſpeak.
Croſ. William Cecill the *Queen*es Secretary,
Wotton Deane of *Canterbury*, and *York*,
With ſir *Ralph Sadler* joynt Commiſſioners,
Commands thee *Iohn* Lord *Grey* of *Wilton*,
Now Generall of her Majeſties forces,
To make immediate repaire to *Edenburgh*,
And preſent lay by all hoſtility,
From this houre untill ſeven a Clocke at night.
Mon. The like on your allegiance to *Mary Dowager* of *France*,
and Queene of *Scots*, we doe commend.
Mor. We obey, and inſtant will give order.
Gr. The like doe you ſir *Iarvis*,
Clif. Now we have beaten them out of the Towne, they come
To compoſition.
Gr. Give order through our Trenches, Tents, Bul-warks,
That not a peece of great nor ſmaller ſhot
Prove preiudiciall to the *French*; untill from us
You have commiſſion; my Lord of *Valens*
I'le waite on you to the commiſſioners,
If we have peace 'tis welcome, and if warre.
We are for eyther object, both we dare.
Exeunt Mon. Grey.
Clif. My *Hollidam.*
What a new monſter *England* has begot
We cannot fight becauſe we want commiſſion?
Mortigue, Doyſells, by my juſt *Hollidam*
It greives me that we muſt not fight it out.
Come le'ts ſhake hands, 'till ſeven at night all freinds
After ſuch greetings, as on warre depends.
Doy. VVe dread not chances. *Exeunt Omnes.*
Whistle

Doy. VVe dread not chances.

[IV, ii]

A bed covered with white. Enter Pratle, Magpy, Long-tongue, Barren with a Child, Anne in bed.

Pra. Lord, lord, what pretty impes you are in your majorities!
Marg.

or the fayre Maid of Clifton.

Mag. Is it a man-child Mother *Pratle*?
Pra. No in-ſooth goſſip *Mag-py* it is one of us, heavens bleſſe the babie, and a well appointed jmpe it is.
Lon. See how it ſmiles.
Barr. That's a ſigne of anger, t'will be a ſhrow I lay my life.
Pra. No, no, Miſtris *Barren*, an Infant ſmiling, and a Lambes bleating is a ſigne of fertility, it is ſo in *Artimedorus*; you frown'd when you were borne, and thats the reaſon you are ſo ſteril; *Artimedorus* ſaith ſo in his fourth booke.
Mag. VVhat pretty dimples it has!
Long. Fathers none nyes.
Pra. None noſe.
Barr. Smooth fore-head!
Mag. Cherry lip!
Pra. Had it bene a man-child, their had bene three evident ſignes of a whoremaſter; a Roman Noſe, Cherry Lip, and a bald Pate, for ſo *Artimedorus* in his Problems.
Mag. VVell, well, whoſoever got it, 'tis as like none father as an Apple to a Nut, inſooth Goſſip *Pratle* it is.
Long. It ſmiles ſtill! ſure it was begot in a merry houre.
Barr. Then I was got in a merry vaine; for praiſ'd be to memory my Mother ſaid I hung the lip at my nativity.
Mag. Lord Mother *Pratle* doe the Moderns report ſo?
Pra. I ſurely Goſſip *Mag-py*, and it is a great ſigne of frugality if the Starres, and Planets be concordant; for ſaith *Artimedorus*, if it be borne under *Venus*, it will be faire as you are, if under *Sol*, Rich as you are, and if under *Mercurie*.
Mag. Good Mother *Pratle* what is that god *Mercury*? is it he that makes the white *Mercury* waters, Ladies ſcoure their faces withall!
Pra. I ſurely Goſſip, and ſtop their wrinkles with too, and ſaith *Artimedorus*, in his third booke of his Moderns, if borne under *Caſtor*, and *Pollux*, ſtore of children.
Mag. Caſtor, and *Bollux*?
Pra. You ſpeake broad Goſſip, 'tis *Pollux*.
Mag.

Caster, and *Bollux*
speake broad Gossip, 'tis
Pollux

Bollux be it then

Mag. ~~Why *Bollux* be it then~~; surely *Barren* was not born under *Bollux*, for she has bene married this seven years, and never had child,

Bar. By your favour Gossip *Mag-py*, you were born under *Caster*, and *Pollux* then, for you had two children before you were married.

Enter Vrsula.

Pra. Insooth Gossip, she has given you a veny; Good lack mistris *Vrsula*, where have you negotiated Your selfe; you should have bene present, and have Negotiated your selfe about the Maxims, and principles Of child-bearing; what? you had a Mother?

Vrs. And a Father too, Mother mid-night.

Pra. No matter for the father; we talk of the surer side, you may be sure to know your mother, when your mother hardly knows your father; 'tis a very facetious point, as *Artimedorus* in his booke of dreams sets it downe.

Enter Boote.

Vrs. Here comes my Vncle.

Pra. Off with your hat sir, you come not here without reverence, see if the little infidell smile not on him, buss, buss, it.

Bo. Heavens blesse the babe! what wares bear my Little infidell?

Pra. Blesse the baby, it has sufficient if it live to be of the sages.

Bo. I mean carries it an *English* Pen, and Inke-horne Or a dutch watch tankerd?

Pra. Blesse the baby—it has—ey marry has it!

Bo. Is it a boy, has it a purse, and two pence in't?

Pra. Blesse the baby, it has a purse, and no money in't yet, but it may have, and it please the destinies.

Bo. A purse, and no money; by St *Antony* I thought the groome went drunke to bed, he stole to't so early——

Pra. Looke how it smiles.

Bo. Admit me to the mother;

Vrs. She's now awake, sir.

Bo. I give my thanks to heaven daughter *Nan*,
Whose providence hath made thee a mother,
Rejoyce thou in the first fruits of thy wombe,
If any sad distempers trouble thy mind,
Sing lullabies unto this pretty babe,
And they will vanish; this must be now thy comfort;

An. Just heaven; I might have taken comfort
In this pretty babe; now it is too late,
Leave me your blessing Sir; and depart hence,

Bo. You have some private occasions, i'me not to question. Neece bring the groaning cheese, and all requisites, I must supply the fathers place, and bid god-fathers. *Exit.*

An. Good women whose help I had but now.
'Tis almost now of that necessity
It was before: I pray be vigilant,
For if you slumber, or shut your eie-lids,
You never shall behold my living corps.

Pra. Blesse us daughter say not so! I hope you will not part in a trance, nor steale away in a qualme; come, come what should be your reason?

An. Nothing but a dreame.

Pra. An't be a dreame, let me come to it; was it a sorrowfull dream? *Artimedorus* saith their be divers kinds of meates engender dreams; as *Beanes*, long *Peason Lentills*, *Cole-worts*, *Garlicke*, *Onions*, and the like; *Leekes*, *Ches-Nuts*, and other opening Roots, as *Rad-dish*, *Carrets*, *Skirrets*, *Parsenips*; now there is some flesh is provocative too; as the *Hart*, the *Bore*, the old *Hare*, and *Beefe*; and then of fowles, as the *Crane*, *Ducke*, *Drake*, *Goose*, and *Bustard*; if you tasted any of these they will engender dreams.

An. Pray marke me, and let my words be written
Within your minds, as in a manuscript,
That when it proves so, you may say I told it.

Lon. Peace, and hear her dream.

An. Me thought I walk'd a long the verdant banks
Of fertill Trent, at an un-uſuall time,
The winter quarter; when *Herb s*, and *Flowers*
Natures choiſeſt braveries are dead.
When every ſapleſſe Tree fad's at the roote;
Yet then, though contrary to nature,
Vpon thoſe banks where foaming ſurges beate,
I gatherd *Flowers*, *Roſes* red, and *Damaske*,
Love *Pauncies*, *Pincks*, and gentle *Daffadils*,
That ſeldome budde before the Spring time comes,
Daiſies, *Cowſlopps*, *Harebells*, *Marigoulds*,
But not one bending *Violet* to be ſeene.
My apron full, I thought to paſſe away;
And make a Garland of theſe fragrancies;
Juſt as I turn'd, I ſpide a lovely perſon,
Whoſe countenance was full of ſplendancy
With ſuch embelliſhings, as I may imagine
Better then name them; it bad me follow it,
Then me thought, it went upon the water,
As firmely as on land; I covetous
To parley with ſo ſweet a frontiſ-peece
Leap'd into th'water, and ſo dround my ſelfe.
Pray watch me well this night; for if you ſleepe.
I ſhall goe gather *Flowers*, and then youle weepe

Vrſ. T'was a ſtrange dreame!

Pra. But a very true one; looke you *Artimedorus* in his third booke of his Moderns ſaith to dreame of *Flowers* is very good to a woman in child-bed; it argues ſhe ſhall ſoone enjoy her husband; to walke on the Seas ſpecifies to a man, delight, but to a woman a diſſolute life, for the Sea is like a harlot, a glicery face, and a broken heart. Come, come, doe you ſleepe? wee'le watch; by this good drink; Goſſip *Mag-py*, I was almoſt dry.

An. Lay the babe by me that I may Kiſſe it;

Pra. So, ſo, ſhe ſleepes, come ſit round, and lets have a Carrouſe to the litle infidell.

Vrſ. I marry ſir this is a ſilent hour, their teeth will not let

their tongues wag. VVell drunck Mother mid-night, now will ſhe ſweare by this VVine, till ſhe ſoke the Pot were it a fathome deepe.

Pra. By this good liquor, it is ſo.

Vrſ. Here's ſweete ſwearing, and deepe vowes, ſhe goes to'th bottome at every oath.

Mag. And I'faith Goſſip *Long-tongue* when peipes the *Onion* out o'th parſley-bed, when ſhall's come to your feaſt?

Lon. Truely Goſſip *Mag-py* when *Caſter*, and *Pollux* raignes.

Vrſ. Sweete Mother *Pratle* what be thoſe *Caſter*, and *Pollux*?

Pra. Twinns daughter that rule moſt the ſigne being in *Virgo*, looke you Goſſip *Barren*, could you once dreame of ſore eies you ſhould be ſure of children?

Barr. Good ſooth Mother *Pratle*, the firſt time I dream'd, I was with child I got a husband preſently.

Pra. By this dyet-bread, *Artimedorus* ſaith ſo; marke Miſtris *Vrſula*, to dreame to have Lyce, eyther in head or body, in ſome quantity ſignifies a proper man well appointed; and by this drinke I dream'd my husband when he came firſt a woing; came i'th liknes of a Kentiſh twindle Pippen; that is juſt, as if two ſtones grew together, no ſooner was I married, but I had two ſonnes preſently juſt as *Artimedorus* ſaith by this diet-bread.

Vrſ. They have ſworne all the VVine, and Banquet away.

Barr. I know not what your twindles are, but i'me ſure I tender *Caſtor*, and *Pollux* as dearely as any of you; I cannot dreame, heigho—

Pra. You begin to be ſleepy; I can preſcribe you a medicine of *Poppy*, *Mandragora*, and other drowſy Sirrops; heiday, all a ſleepe? if my charge ſleepes, let me reſt, for by this drinke i'me heavy too— *All ſleep.*

Vrſ. Their all aſleepe I have a heavy ſloth,
Come o're my eie-lids; *Somiſdore* hath ſtrucke me,
I cannot wake, and muſt give way to reſt,

The Vow-breaker,

Sleepe. Enter Ghoſt!

Gh. Deaths eldeſt daughter, ſleepe, with ſilencies
Has charm'd yond beldams, no jarring clock,
Nor murmuring wind, dares oppoſe juſt fate.
Awake fond mortall ne're to ſleepe againe,
Now is the time I come to claime my promiſe,
Alive or dead I muſt, and will enjoy thee.
An. Bleſſe me I was in my dreame againe; ha!
Mothers, Cozens, Mid-wiſe, all drown'd in ſleepe?
Then my decreed houre is here ſet downe
I must I muſt away?
Gh. With expedition;
The Ferry-man attends thee at the verge
Of *Cocitus*, and ſooty *Acheron*,
into And he ſhall waft thee into *Tartarus*,
Where, perjury, and falſe-hood finds reward
There ſhalt thou reade thy hiſtory of faults,
And mong'ſt the furies finde juſt recompence,
I'le bring thee over Turrets, Towres, and Steeples,
O're ſhady Groves, brineiſh Mears, and Brookes,
The flattring Sea to me is navigable,
O're ſteepy Mountaines, and the craggy Rocks,
Whoſe heights Kiſſe Starres, and ſtop the flying Clouds
does Weele through as ſwift as *Swallowes* in recourſe.
The Chaunteclere ſummons my retreat,
period Signing a period to my pilgrimage;
nipping frosts From nipping froſts, and penetrating blaſtes
Could Snowes, blacke thawes, and miſty killing deawes.
I'le lead thee to the ever-flaming Furnace,
That like a Feaver fed by oppoſite meates,
Engenders, and conſumes it ſelfe with heate.
I'le peirce the Aire as with a thunder bolt,
And make thy paſſage free; make ſpeede away,
Thy broken contract now thou goeſt to pay.

Enter

or the fayre Maid of Cliſton.

Enter Shee leaving her bed.

An. Oh helpe, ſuccour: help! wives, cozens, Mid-wives,
Good Angels guard me, I goe, but cannot tell,
Whether my journey be, to Heaven or hell. Sinks with Ghost Whether . . . *ghost*
Vrſ. I have ſlept this houre, how, d'yee cozen? ha? cozen, here;
me, where, alas no where, ah me ſhe's gon, ſhe's gon. Ah
Pra. Heigho; what's the matter Miſtris *Vrſula.*
Vrſ. Alas! my cozen, ſhe's gon, ſhe's gon!
Mar. Mary *Jove* forbid.
Long. I did not like her dreame.
Barr. Nor I, I promiſe you.
Pra. Diſpatch every one ſeverall waies ſome to th' feilds ſome to'th water-ſide; las 'tis but a fit, twill be over preſently—away, away ſeverally.

Exeunt, and Enter Boote. to Ursula.

Bo. What meanes this noiſe how comes my doores open at this time o'th night; I hope my daughters well,
Vrſ. Oh ſir ſhee is—
Bo. Not dead I hope.
Vrſ. I know not that neyther; but whilſt we
After long watching tooke a litle reſt
She's ſtolne out of her bed, and fled away,
The doores quite open, and the infant here.

Enter Women bringing Anne. *Enter Women bringing Anne.*

Bo. Heaven bleſſe her; I am ſtrucke dead with grief
She has been ſubject to diſtemper'd paſſions
Jove grant ſhe works no harme upon her ſelfe,
Me thinkes ſhe ſhould not for the infants ſake,
Poore babe it ſmiles, it lacks no mother yet.
Till it miſſe the breſt, ſhe cannot be farre
But they may find her out; their's a great Snow

H 3 Falne

IV, ii, 216. The prompter added a sensible and theatrical exit for Anne; the author forgot to provide any kind of exit for her.

The Vow-breaker,

Fal'n this night, and by her foot steps they may
Easily trace her, where she is.
Ves. Oh misery!
Behold the saddest spectacle of woe,
That ever mortall eies took notice of.
Pra. We trac'd her through the Snow, step, by step,
Untill we came unto the River side,
Where like a cunning *Hare* she had indented
To cozen her persuers, and cozen'd her selfe
For dround we found her on the River side
Nigh Collicke Ferry.
Bo. Oh my poore girle!

Women Return with Anne drownd

Enter Bateman with his Picture.

Ba. Oh my poore boy!
Bo. How happy had I beene if she had liv'd?
Ba. How happy had I beene if he had liv'd?
Bo. Whoes that which eechoes me, playing the wanton
With my miseries?
Ba. I come to see how sorrow does become thee
Doo'st thou remember that?
Bo. What mak'st thou here, is there no other wracke,
To work my miseries higher, but thy self,
And art thou come for that? oh my poore girle.
Ba. Monster, behold my poore boys Picture,
Thou would'st not shed a teare, nor lend a sigh,
Poore emblem of a penitential heart,
When in these arms I hug'd my dead boyes corps,
Now monster, who i'st will weep or sigh, for thine?
Bo. Monster thou troublest me.
Ba. Murderer I will.
See what the fruits of wealth have brought thee now,
An everlasting scandall to thy name.
A conscience full of horror, and black deeds;
Natures externall superfluities
Her white, and red Earth, rubbidg, drosse, and oare,
Which

or the fayre Maid of Clifton.

Which she but lent thee to keep: Marts withall,
Thou hast converted to most grosse abuses,
Thou would'st not else have scorn'd my poore boys love,
To match with wealthy *German*; see thy fruits,
Thy bases, and foundations now are sunke,
And look there lyes the ruines of thy workes.
Bo. Oh misery! my hart-strings cracke with grief,
Yet will not burst, oh say, hast thou yet done?
Ba. No, I will make thee sensible of thy ils,
First thou art causer of thy daughters death,
For thou enforc'd her to the breach of faith;
Next my sons ruin, whom parac'd like,
Thou laugd'st at in his fatall tragedy;
Whom but a villain that abjures all lawes,
That breaks all precepts, both of heave'ns, and man,
And natures too could have done this; should I
Like one that dares affront divinity
Laugh at thy daughters fall.
Bo. Hast thou done yet?
I do beseech thee for this infants sake,
Which sets a smiling brow on miseries,
And even by instinct, prayes thee to forgive,
Commiserate my woes; it greives me now
I did deri'd thy miseries; be but content
I'le weep till thou shalt say, it is enough,
So that we may be friends.
Ba. I cannot chuse.
But bear a burden in calamities;
Our angers have like tapers spent themselves,
And only lighted others, and not us.
Striving like great men for supremacy!
We have confounded one anothers goodnes,
Come we will be freinds, i'le dig a soleme cell,
Which shall be hung with sables round about,
Where we will sit, and write the tragedy
Of our poore children; i'le ha'it so set down
As not one eye that vewes it, but shall weep.
Ne

IV, ii, 243 ff. The entrance of the women with the body of Anne was correctly changed to here from the stage direction following line 234.

Nor any ear, but ſadly ſhall relent,
For never was a ſtory of more ruth,
Then this of him,and her,yet nought but truth. *Exeunt Omnes.*

Actus Quintus , Scena Prima.

Enter Arguile, Clifton, Monlucke, Jo. *Ball, Miles, Souldiers Mortigue, Doyſells, Souldiers on the Walls.*

Clif. After the hand of warre has raz'd your walls
Affrighting peace from your *Jvory* beds,
And like the reaper with his angry ſickle
Leaves the Earth full of ſoares, and wounds,
Yet after plaſters her with her owne crop;
So come we after warr, bloudy turmoiles
To bring you peace, which had you ſued before,
Thouſands that now ly boweld in the earth
Had liv'd to memory what we have done.
Set ope your gates,& with ſpred armes embrace her
For which as followes yee have articulated,

Mon. Which we, *Monluck,* Biſhop of *Valence*
Labroſſe , *Amyens* joynt commiſſioners
For the moſt chriſtian *King,* and *Queene,*
*Francis,*and *Mary* of *France,* and *Scotland,*
Have Confirm'd.

Mor. Doy. Which,we as duty binds,muſt obey.

Clif. The Articles thus followe, The moſt mighty Princeſſe *Elizabeth* by the grace of God , of *England, France,* and *Ireland Queene*, defendor of the faith, &c and the moſt Chriſtian *King* , *Francis*, and *Mary* , by the ſame grace *King* , and *Queene* of *France* , and *Scotland* have bore Record upon a reconcilation of peace , and amity to be inviolably kept betweene them, their ſubjects, Kingdomes, and confines; and therefore in their names it is ſtraitly commanded to all manner of perſons , borne under their obeyſances,

ſances , or being in their ſervices, to lay by all hoſtility eyther by Sea or Land , and to keepe good peace eyther with other from this time forwards , as they will anſwer therto , at their utmoſt perils ; long live *Elizabeth, Francis,*and *Mary* ;

Omn. Long live *Elizabeth* , &c.

Mor. We much deſire to heare the Articles,
On which this peace ſtands fully ratifi'd.

Clif. They are thirteene in number ;
The principall,and of moſt effect , are theſe,
That the *French* Souldiers , and all men of warre
Leave the Realme of *Scotland* in twenty daies,
Sixe ſcore Souldiers , onely are excepted,
Three ſcore of them to remaine at *Inskeith*,
And three ſcore, at the Caſtle of *Dun-barr,*
Their wages to be paid from the eſtates
of *Scotland* ;and to live lawfull ſubjects
To the Lawes, and ordinances of that Realme,
All fortifications in, or, about *Leith*,
Which by the *French* was built, ſhalbe defaced,
That *France* conveigh not any man of warre
Nor ammunition into this Land,
Without a free conſent in Parliament,
Of the three eſtates of theſe great Kingdomes.
That *Francis*,and *Mary King*, and *Queene* of *France*,
From henceforth beare not the Armes of *England*
Which ſolely appertaine to our dread Miſtris
The *Queene* of *England* , and to no other.
Theſe as you hope for peace, you muſt obſerve.

Mor. We ſubjects are the hands,Kings are the heads,
And what the head commands, the hands muſt act,
Our barrocadoed portalls ſhall flie ope,
And yeild entrance ; if war-like *Clifton* pleaſe,
As we have fought together , ſo wee'le feaſt,
Such viands,as a raized Towne can yeild
You ſhall receive ; noble ſir *Francis Leake*
Hath in this manner proclam'd this peace
On the North-ſide whom we will gratulate

The Vow-breaker,

With tearmes of honour, will it pleaſe you enter?
Clif. By my *Hollidam*, we accept your offer;
Lay by your armes; ſtill after frayes come feaſts,
To which we Souldiers, are most welcom'd gueſts; most
Unbrace our drums, inſtead of warr's Allarmes, *Exeunt Omnes.*
Wee'le meete, like conſtant lovers, arme in armes (*niſi Croſſe, Bal.*

Bal. See, *Joſhua*, is enter'd, one cup of briske Orleance Makes him i'th temper he was when he leap'd into *Leene.*

Croſ. Will he be drunk?

Bal. Moſt ſwine-like, and then by the vertue of his good liquor he's able to convert any Browniſticall ſiſter.

Croſ. An excellent quality!

Bal. Nay, in that mood, you ſhall have him, inſtead of preſenting *Pyramus*, and *Thiſbe*, perſonate *Cato Cenſorious*, and his three ſons, only in one thing he's out, one of *Cato's* ſons hang'd himſelfe, and that he refer's to a dumbe ſhow;

Croſ. Me thinks he ſhould hang himſelfe for the jeſt ſake.

Bal. As he did his Cat for killing a Mouſe on Sunday, ſee! he has top'd the cannikin already; now will he ſing treaſon familiarly, being ſober, aske him why he did it: in ſincerity, it was not he, it was his drinke.

Enter Joſhua, reeling with Jacks.

Ioſ. As it is in the painted cloath, in ſincerity; good liquor quickens the ſpirit.

When from the warrs I doe returne,
And at a cup of good Ale, mourne.
I'le tell how Townes without fire we did burne,
and is not that a wonder?

Bal. That's more then the painted cloath!
Ioſ. *I'le tell how that my Generall,*
Enter'd the breach, and ſcal'd the wall,
And made the formoſt battery of all,
and is not that a wonder?

Croſ.

or the fayre Maid of Clifton.

Croſ. Admirable!
Ioſ. *How that we went to take a Fort,*
And tooke it too in warr-like ſort
I'le ſweare that a ly is a true report,
and is not that a wonder?

Croſ. Ther's wonder in that, Jo!
How that we Souldiers, had true pay,
And cloath, and vit'les every day,
And never a Captaine ran away,
and is not that a wonder?

Bal. Nay, and but ſixe daies to'th weeke.

Ioſ. Is there any man here deſires to edyfie? I am in the humour of converting; I was converted in my drink, and ſo are moſt of my bretheren; I'le ſtand while I am able, and then will go ſleep on it. *Exit Ioſ.*

Bal. Hee's gone both waies; ſee the *French* Lords, & our's enter.

Muſique, Enter. Lord Grey, Clifton, Arguile, attendants Monlucke, Mortigue, Doyſells, all embrace.

Mon. On honorable tearmes we now embrace.
Gr. If what we articl'd be full perform'd
Clif. They are my Lord in each particular,
And the *French* ready to depart the Town,
By my *Hollidam*, they have feaſted us.
Not like to foes but friends, 'tis my wonder,
That a beſeiged Towne could yeild ſuch Cates,
In ſuch extremities, and exigents,
Full forty ſeverall meſſes, yet not one,
Eyther of fiſh or fleſh, onely one diſh,
Which was the daintieſt, (a powder'd horſe)
That, I took notice off.
Gr. Large ſtomacks, and empty ſallet diſhes
Are the *French-mans* viandes; his banquetings,
Cloyes not the ſtomack, but gives ſatiety,
A freſh appetite; that makes the body

I 2 Active

Active, and full of generous fires,
Full dishes are like potions unto them,
I know not whether nicety or want;
Clif. By my *Hollidam*; want, want,
Give me the *English* chine, and that feedes men,
And they that feed well, certainly will fight
Vnless some *Woolf*, or maw-*Worm* be internate;
Arg. I relish your opinion.
Gr. Lords of *France* you may depart at pleasure.
F. Lo. Prosperity, and peace ever t'wixt *France*, and *England*.
E. Lo. Amen saith *England*; when *France* forgets her pride
England will honour her,
Gr. Come my co-mates in warre,
Our Souldiers instantly shall march for *Barwick*,
The *Duke* of *Norfolk*, waites their arrivall.
Sir *Francis Leake* shall give them safe conduct,
You, *Arguile*, *Clifton*, and my selfe
With expedition are for *Nottingham*,
To meete our peerlesse princesse *Elizabeth*
Who in her progresse there will lay her Court.
Arguile shall there receive the hostages
Due to the federary Lords of *Scotland*,
Wee'le turne warr's clangors into musik's sweete,
And like new vested pares in wed-locke meet. *Exeunt Omnes.*

Enter. Miles, and Ball.

Bal. What if it were a Puppet-play?

Mi. Absurd! absurd! thei'le be out in turning up the white of the eies, besides, ther's none of us can speake i'th nose.

Bal. Yes, *Joshua*;

Mi. Most abhominable! wood'st thou have a Puritan speake to a Play; a Puppet Play! thou ought'st to be burn'd for thy hereticall conceit, why thou poison'd sowter, wood'st thou have a Puritan speake to a Play? still give me the hobby-Horse.

Bal. But who shall play the hobby-Horse, Master *Major*?

Mi. I hope, I looke, as like a hobby-Horse as Master *Major* I have not liv'd to these yeares, but a man woo'd thinke I should

be

V, i, following 162. The rest of the pages (signatures I3–K2) are missing.

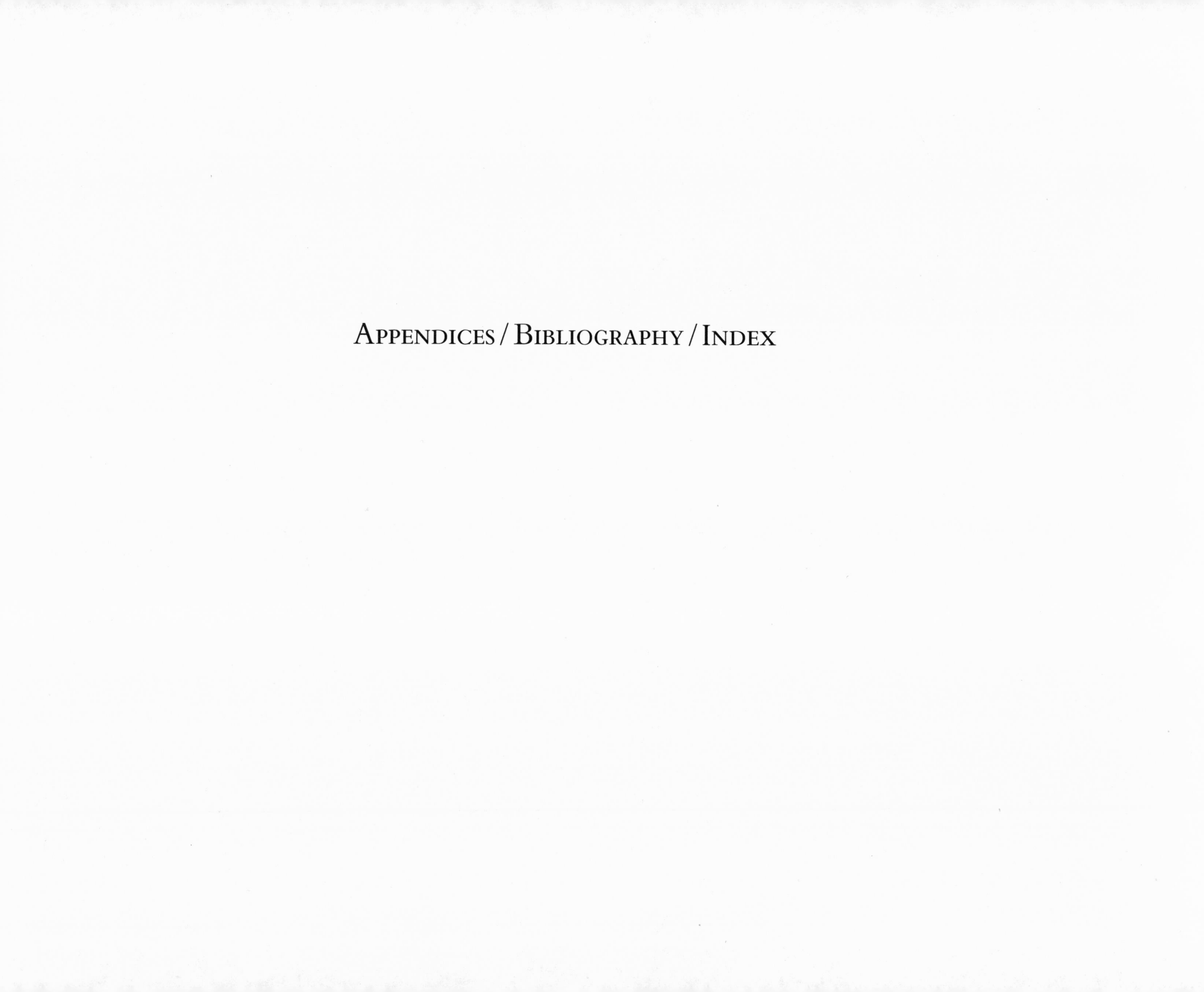

Appendices / Bibliography / Index

Appendix A

Dublin Promptbooks for Shakespeare's Plays

Though only two Shakespearean promptbooks have been found for the London theatres of the Restoration period, a remarkable number have been discovered for productions in the 1670s and 1680s at the Smock Alley Theatre in Dublin. In his *Shakespearean Prompt-Books of the Seventeenth Century* G. Blakemore Evans provides detailed examinations of the books for *Twelfth Night*, *Henry VIII*, *Macbeth*, *King Lear*, *Othello*, *1 Henry IV*, *A Midsummer Night's Dream*, and *Hamlet*, all of which contain prompt notes, and *The Merry Wives of Windsor*, *The Comedie of Errors*, and *The Winter's Tale*, which show playhouse cuts. Gunnar Sorelius in *Shakespeare Quarterly*, describes the contents of the Smock Alley *1* and *2 Henry IV*. Now lost is the promptbook for *Julius Caesar*, and lost copies of *Measure for Measure*, *The Tempest*, and *Troilus and Cressida* probably also had Smock Alley prompt notes.

Another (?) promptbook for *Measure for Measure*, thought by Professor Shattuck to have been prepared by John Downes for a production by Betterton's Company in London shortly after 1700, has notes in the same hand as that found in the Dublin *Belphegor* promptbook of the 1670s (or possibly 1680s). The *Measure for Measure* copy is at the Folger Shakespeare Library (Prompt. Meas. 2); it is the Gildon adaptation of Shakespeare's play, published in 1700, and may be the "lost" Smock Alley copy. Actors mentioned in the notes are Carlisle, Floyd, Wilshire (names, remarkably, of London players of the Restoration; these were perhaps relatives of a later generation), possibly Mlle Girardo, who performed in London in the first decade of the eighteenth century, and Smeton, who acted in *Belphegor* in Dublin, appeared in London in the 1690s, and evidently returned to Dublin. The copy contains actor warnings, a music cue, and some cuts but no technical notes.

The promptbooks show that Dublin prompters prepared their copies in much the same way as did their London counterparts. The circle-and-dot symbol for scene shifts appears in some of the Smock Alley Shakespeare books, as does the cross-hatch entrance cue sign. Actors, music, and properties are warned, but the Dubliners tended to use the term "ready" rather than "call." Prompt notes include descriptions of stage settings to be used, and the ends of acts are warned and cued as in some London copies. The *Macbeth* promptbook has notes concerning the use of the curtain, a feature of London theatres that was mentioned by authors in their stage directions but rarely by prompters in their marginalia. The Dublin books contain, like those for London theatres, many indications of passages to be omitted in performance and are interesting examples of how Shakespeare was butchered.

Appendix B

Belphegor *by John Wilson*

Manuscript play, c. 1677, with very complete manuscript prompt notes for a production at the Smock Alley Theatre, Dublin, in 1677–78 or possibly 1682–83; Folger MS Vb 109 (old number: MS 827.1). Dating discussed by Allen Stevenson in "The Case of the Decapitated Cast," *Shakespeare Quarterly*, 6 (Summer 1955), 275–96; by G. Blakemore Evans in a letter in 1974 to Laetitia Yeandle of the Folger Shakespeare Library; and by R. C. Bald in "Shakespeare on the Stage in Restoration Dublin," *PMLA*, 56 (1941), 369–78. Cast discussed by William Smith Clark II in *The Early Irish Stage* (Oxford: Clarendon Press, 1955), pp. 80–83. Reproduced here by permission of the Folger Shakespeare Library, Washington, D.C.

Though this study of Restoration promptbooks has been restricted to books prepared by professional London groups, the theatre in London was so closely related to that in Dublin that an example of Smock Alley procedures is needed for sake of comparison. The *Belphegor* promptbook is an unusually rich one and has never been published. Some of the actors named in it performed in London, and while some of the Dublin prompter's practices were different, many were similar to those found in London.

Kathleen Lesko, who has prepared a scholarly edition of *Belphegor* for her George Washington University dissertation, has been able to show that the prologue and epilogue, added in 1690 to the end of the manuscript, and emendations throughout the script, are in John Wilson's hand. The 1691 first quarto of the play incorporated some but not all of his corrections, and it contains some changes that do not appear in the promptbook. Perhaps Wilson made a clean copy of the manuscript we have here, omitting the prompt notes (no traces of which appear in the 1691 quarto) and making some further corrections before giving it to his London printer. The Smock Alley players would probably not have relinquished their promptbook and allowed it to be carried to London to serve as the basis for the first quarto, though that may have happened.

The promptbook reveals, in addition to the hand of the scribe who wrote out the text, three or perhaps four hands. Hand B is that of Wilson; hand C made a number of prompt notes in red pencil; and hand D, working in ink, also supplied many prompt notes. Marks indicating cuts may have been made by a fourth hand or by either C or D. Hand D also appears in the promptbook for Gildon's version of *Measure for Measure* (1700) at the Folger Shakespeare Library.

Cast

Actors' names appear occasionally throughout the promptbook and permit a partial reconstruction of the cast. But, as is typical of most Restoration promptbooks, whenever actors are called by name it is usually because they are playing minor characters, often roles with no names, as will be seen here. Thus we know hardly any of the casting for the major parts.

Head (of the infernal spirit)	Cudworth
Boy (singer)	Richard Barnes
Servants	William Peer, George Lee, William Pinkethman
Woman (servant)	Mrs. Wall
Woman	Margaret Osborn
Watch	Smeton
Officers	William Peer, Kit
Belzebub	John Freeman
Attendants	T. Brown, Porter (?)

The prompter had a terrible time with Pinkethman's name, spelling it variously "nikini," "Pnikim," and "pnikiman." "Kit" could be a first or last name. "Porter" is my guess at an almost indecipherable note. The marginalia suggest that Bright played Marone and T. Brown the important part of Grimaldi, but since the notes are otherwise consistent in naming only minor performers, I think Bright was a stagehand and Brown played an Attendant (who enters at the same time as Grimaldi at one point). Clark and the *Biographical Dictionary of Actors*, II, 338, mistakenly, I think, identify Bright as the London actor George Bright.

Staging

The most interesting notes in the promptbook have to do with staging: actor warnings, descriptions of settings, the handling of special effects, and the like. The author's stage directions were often specific enough about locales that the machinist did not need to provide any amplification. Between the two, the scene plot is complete.

Act & Scene	*Author's Description*	*Machinist's Description*
I, i	"A Stately Roome in Roderigo's house."	None
I, ii	"A Stately Roome in Grimaldis house."	None
I, iii	"The first Scene agen."	None
II, i	"The first Scene agen."	None
II, ii	"A noble Roome in Montalto's house."	None
II, iii	"The first Scene agen."	None
II, iv	"The scene of Montalto's house"	None
III, i	"Roderigo's house"	None; but: *2 chairs set / on.*
III, ii	"Montalto's house."	*ordinary* and *j^t. Sce.*

The playhouse notes on the setting here are confusing. There was no indication in II, ii, when the Montalto setting was first used, that what they labeled the "ordinary" setting should be employed, but that is repeated in V, iii, so it must be correct. But the machinist also designated this, surely by mistake, the *j^t. sce*—that is, the first scene (Roderigo's house); the note is partly blotted and probably should have been canceled completely.

III, iii	"Roderigo's house"	*1^t. Sce.*
III, iv	None	*Town.*
III, v	"A Vineyard."	None
IV, i	"The first Scene." (Wilson's added note)	None
IV, ii	"Roderigo's house"	*1^t S* and *Scene continues*

Act & Scene	*Author's Description*	*Machinist's Description*
IV, iii	"The Vineyard Scene." (Wilson's added note)	None
IV, iv	"Grimaldi's House."	None
V, i	"A Street Scene." (Wilson's added note)	None
V, ii	"A great Hall."	*flat pallace* and ~~*Hall*~~ and (at V, ii, 18): *[G?] Hall*
V, iii	"Montaltos house"	*Ordinary*

There are no circle-and-dot symbols or whistle warnings in the promptbook, but the Dublin promptbooks for *Othello* and *1 Henry IV* use the symbol. R. C. Bald in "Shakespeare on the Stage in Restoration Dublin" (p. 375), was not convinced that the circle-and-dot symbol signaled a scene shift, for he noted that the symbol did not appear every time a change of scene was indicated. But promptbooks of the period are full of such inconsistencies. Whether or not the Dubliners used a whistle to cue scene shifts we cannot tell.

Several London promptbooks contain symbols or words to cue entrances of actors; in place of those the *Belphegor* book reveals a system of abbreviations indicating which entrance door should be used; the abbreviation apparently served as both a door indication and a mark to call the prompter's attention to an entrance. As can be seen from the listing below, the prompter was casual about the actual form his door indications took. The notes begin at the opening of I, ii, and there is no apparent reason why earlier entrances were not signaled.

I, ii, opening	*W np*
I, ii, 115	*w. np*
I, iii, opening	*E. Lower*
I, iii, 25	*1 W ~~E~~ Lower*
I, iii, 53	*E L.*
II, i, opening	*E. Lower.*
II, i, 56	*E. L.*
II, i, 143	*E 1*
II, ii, opening	*W. L.*
II, ii, 10	*W. 1*
II, ii, 69	*W. L.*
II, iii, opening	*E. 1.*
II, iii, 81	*E L.*
II, iv, opening	*W. up.*
III, i, opening	*E. L.*
III, i, 37	*W L*
III, ii, opening	*w up*
III. ii, 4	*E. L.*
III, iii, opening	*E npp*
III, iii, 5	*E n p*
III, iii, 42	*E. L*
III, iv, opening	*w. &. E n[p]*
IV, i, opening	*E. L.*
IV, ii, opening	*E. l.*
IV, ii, 31	*W. up.*
IV, ii, 69	*E up 1*
IV, ii, 90	*E. L.*
IV, ii, 138	*E L*
IV, iii, opening	*E upp*
IV, iv, opening	~~*W.*~~ *E. up.*
V, i, opening	*W u*
V, i, 11	*up*
V, ii, opening	*E L*
V, iii, opening	*W : up*

Some of the notes were hastily written, and *np* is clearly just a poorly-written *up*. But the pattern is clear. At the Smock Alley Theatre there must have been two proscenium doors (or entranceways) on each side of the forestage, as in some London theatres of the time, and they are here identified as upper and lower. The use of *E* and *W* was certainly for East and West, though one would think that prompt and opposite prompt would have been easier for people inside a building. The fact that compass directions were used suggests that the prompter at Smock Alley, instead of being offstage on one side, was in a central position downstage, as in opera houses.

Some entrance cues do not supply all the information needed, and some entrances are not marked at all; in so complete a promptbook that is most strange.

The ringing of a bell, which in London usually cued the end of an act, did not have the same meaning in Dublin, at least for the production of *Belphegor*. Bell signals for *Belphegor* concerned the use of trapdoors, elevators, and accompanying sound effect cues. At I, i, 162 the ring of a bell signaled stagehands in the substage to raise the head of the infernal spirit (the actor Cudworth), and another ring at line 170 told them to lower it. Similarly, at III, v, 86 a ring was used to bring up four spirits; at IV, iii, 122 a bell signaled Belzebub's entrance; and at IV, iii, 190 a bell cued his sinking exit. The warnings for the bell cues served as warnings for the actors as well as for the substage workers. At V, i, 56 we read: *Bright ready / at great Trap*; at line 97 "Marone is throwne upon the stage" from below, and the prompt note (canceled) tells us: ~~*Ring for great*~~ */ Trap* ———. From these notes we learn that Smock Alley, as one might expect, had at least two trapdoors in the stage, a "great" one and at least one other, presumably smaller. The cancellation of the bell cue in this case may have been because the actor playing Marone (not Bright, who was evidently a stagehand) would have thrown himself up through the trap opening—with some help from Bright, but an elevator was clearly not used. The bell, then, must have been a signal to work the elevator to create a rising or sinking effect. The final use of the trapdoors in the play comes at V, iii, 148, when

Roderigo sinks, leaving a carcass behind. A bell cues the sinking; the warning for it at line 122 is for the thunder drum. That single warning seems to have sufficed for whatever trap business was coming up and for the various people involved—stagehands, a musician, and the actor.

Act-end warnings and cues are similar to those found in London promptbooks but with some variations. Acts I, II, and III are all warned with *act ready* notes; the act-end cue for Act I is a whistle, not a bell. Acts II, III, IV, and V have no act-end cues.

The *Belphegor* promptbook contains many more notes on properties than one finds in most London prompt copies of the period: a paper with writing on it for Roderigo, a necklace, a chain and medal, a white box, a bag of gold (apparently in place of the casket of jewels called for by the author), a purse, two chairs, a lantern, a light, pistols, letters, boxes, a key, an elbow chair, and a paring shovel; there are many properties cited in stage directions which are not listed in the prompt notes: a cane, a hatchet, dummy bodies, a spade, and the like. Some are essential to the stage action and must have been used, so why did the prompter not call attention to them?

Given the combination of stage directions and prompt notes in the copy one could come close to a reproduction of most of the elements of the original production—except, of course, the acting and costuming. Those two important elements find no place in any promptbooks of the period from either Dublin or London.

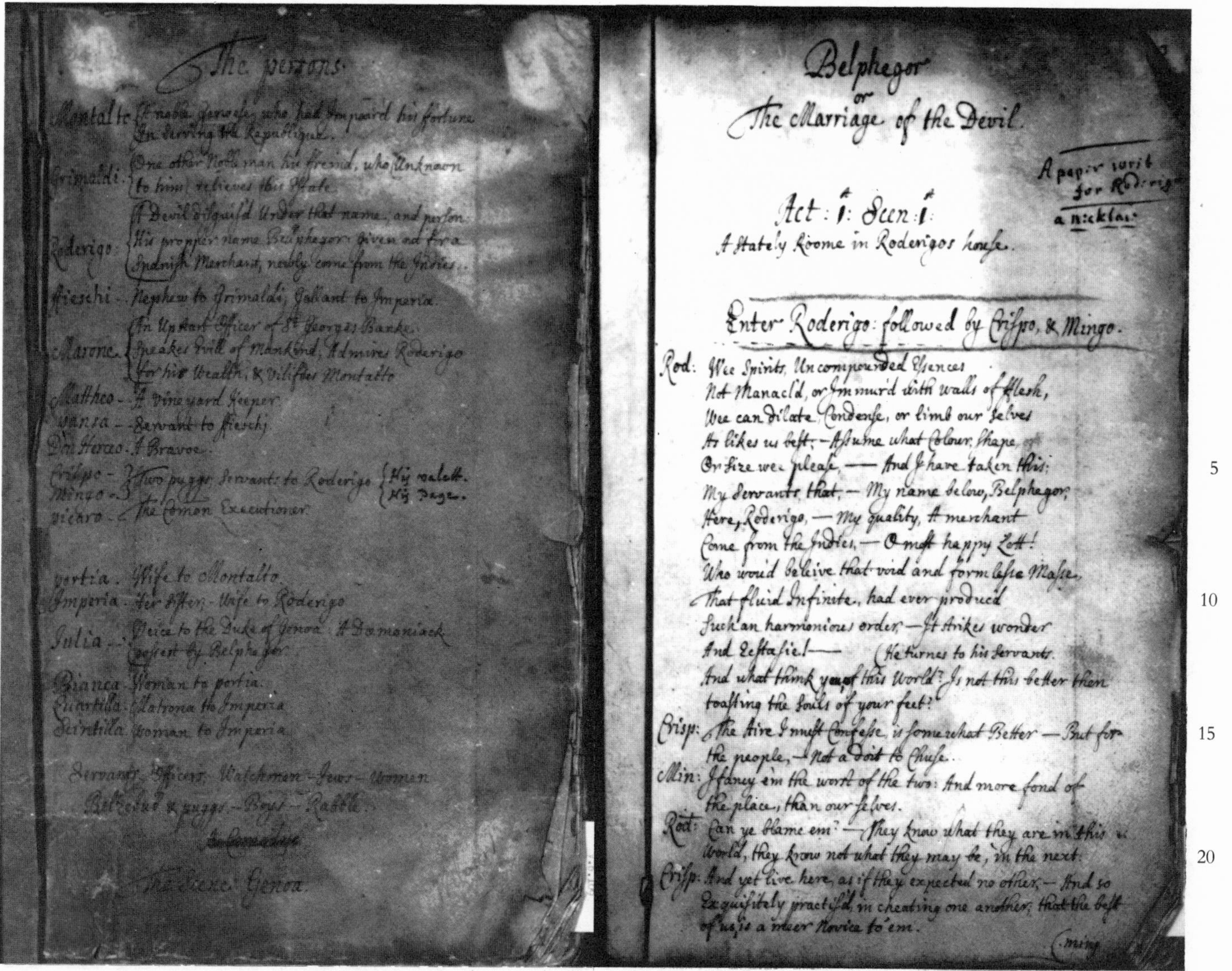

The persons.

Montalto — A noble Genoese, who had impair'd his fortune In serving the Republique.
Grimaldi — One other Noble man his friend, who (unknown to him) relieves this State.
Roderigo — A Devil disguis'd under that name, and person. His propper name Belphegor. Given out for a Spanish Merchant, newly come from the Indies.
Fieschi — Nephew to Grimaldi, Gallant to Imperia.
Marone — An Upstart Officer of St Georges Banke. Speakes ill of Mankind, Admires Roderigo for his Wealth, & Vilifies Montalto.
Mattheo — A Vineyard keeper.
Panza — Servant to Fieschi
Don Hercio — A Bravoe.
Crispo — } Two puggs, Servants to Roderigo { His valett.
Mingo — } { His Page.
Picaro — The Comon Executioner.

Portia — Wife to Montalto.
Imperia — Her Sister, Wife to Roderigo.
Julia — Neice to the Duke of Genoa. A Dæmoniack possest by Belphegor.
Bianca — Woman to Portia.
Quartilla — Matrona to Imperia.
Scintilla — Woman to Imperia.

Servants, Officers, Watchmen, Jews, Women, Belzebub & puggs, Boys, Rabble.

The Scene Genoa.

Belphegor or The Marriage of the Devil.

A paper writ for Roderigo
a necklace

Act: 1: Scen: 1:
A stately Roome in Roderigos house.

Enter Roderigo: followed by Crispo, & Mingo.

Rod: Wee Spirits, Uncompounded Essences
Not Manacl'd, or Immur'd with walls of flesh,
Wee can dilate, Condense, or limb our selves
As likes us best; — Assume what Colour, shape, or
Or size wee please, — And I have taken this:
My Servants, that, — My name below, Belphegor,
Here, Roderigo, — My quality, A merchant
Come from the Indies, — O most happy Lott!
Who would beleive that void and formlesse Masse,
That fluid Infinite, had ever produc'd
Such an harmonious order, — It strikes wonder
And Extasie! — (He turnes to his servants.
And what think you of this World? Is not this better then
toasting the soles of your feet?

Crisp: The Aire I must Confesse is somewhat Better — But for
the people, — Not a doit to Chuse.

Min: I fancy em the worst of the two: And more fond of
the place, than our selves.

Rod: Can ye blame em? — They know what they are in this
World, they know not what they may be, in the next.

Crisp: And yet live here, as if they expected no other, — And so
Exquisitely practis'd in cheating one another, that the best
of us, is a meer Novice to'em.
(Ming

Belphegor by John Wilson. Reproduced by permission of the Folger Shakespeare Library, Washington, D.C.

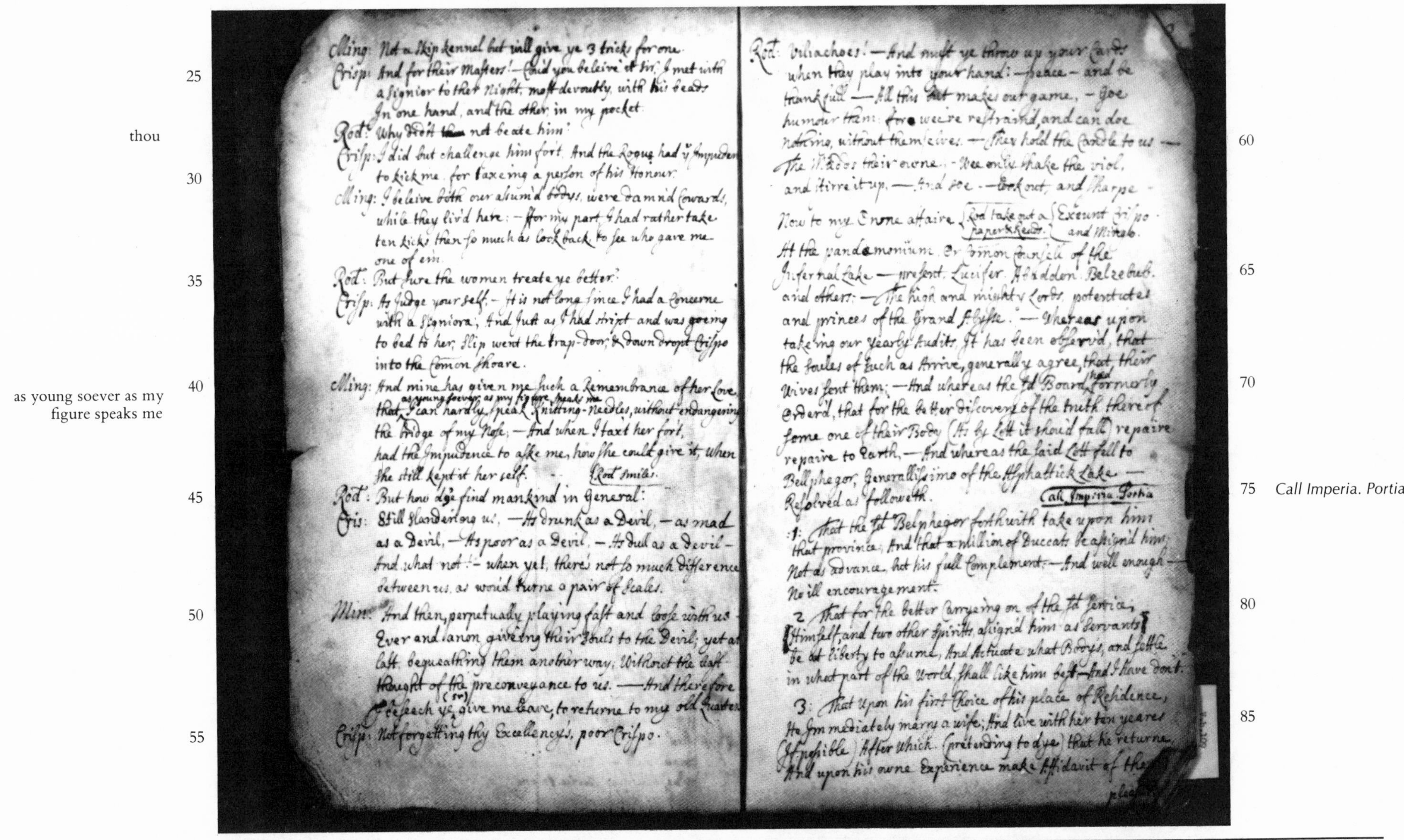

Ming: Not a Skip kennel but will give ye 3 tricks for one.
Crisp: And for their Masters! — Could you beleive it sir, I met with a Signior to that Night, most devoutly, with his beads In one hand, and the other in my pocket.
Rod: Why didst thou not beate him?
Crisp: I did but challenge him for't. And the Rogue had ye Impudence to kick me, for taxeing a person of his Honour.
Ming: I beleive both our assum'd bodys, were damn'd cowards, while they liv'd here: — for my part I had rather take ten kicks then so much as look back to see who gave me one of em.
Rod: But sure the women treate ye better?
Crisp: As Judge your self. — It is not long since I had a Concerne with a Signiora; And just as I had stript and was going to bed to her, slip went the trap-door, & down dropt Crispo into the Comon shoare.
Ming: And mine has given me such a Remembrance of her Love, that, as young soever as my figure speaks me, I can hardly speak. Knitting-Needles, without endangering the bridge of my Nose; — And when I taxt her for't, had the Impudence to aske me, how she could give it, when she still kept it her self. — [Rod smiles.]
Rod: But how d'ye find mankind in General:
Cris: Still slandering us, — As drunk as a Devil, — as mad as a Devil, — As poor as a Devil, — As dull as a devil — And what not! — when yet, there's not so much difference between us, as would turne a pair of Scales.
Min: And then, perpetually playing fast and loose with us — Ever and anon giveing their Souls to the Devil; yet at last, bequeathing them another way; Without the least thought of the preconveyance to us. — And therefore (sir) I beseech ye, give me leave, to returne to my old Quarters.
Crisp: Not forgetting thy Excellency's, poor Crispo.

Rod: Villachoes! — And must ye throw up your Cards when they play into your hand: — peace — and be thankfull — All this but makes our game. — Goe humour them: For we're restrain'd, and can doe nothing, without them selves. — They hold the Candle to us — The Widdows their owne. — We only shake the viol, and stirre it up. — And soe — Look out, and sharpe —
Now to my owne affaire. [Rod take out a paper & Reads.] [Exeunt Crispo and Mingo.]
At the pandemonium. Or Comon Councell of the Infernal Lake — present: Lucifer. Abaddon. Belzebub. and others: — The high and mighty Lords, potentates and princes of the Grand Abysse: — Whereas upon takeing our yearly Audits, It has been observ'd, that the Soules of such as Arrive, generally agree, that their Wives sent them; — And whereas the sd Board had formerly Order'd, that for the better discovery of the truth thereof some one of their Body (As by Lott it should fall) repaire to Earth. — And whereas the said Lott fell to Bellphegor, Generallissimo of the Alphaltick Lake — Resolved as followeth. [Call Imperia. Portia]
1: That the sd Belphegor forthwith take upon him that province; And that a million of Duccats be assign'd him; Not as advance, but his full Complement. — And well enough — Ne'ill encouragement.
2 That for the better Carryeing on of the sd service; [Himself, and two other Spirits, assign'd him as Servants] be at liberty to assume, And Actuate what Bodys, and settle in what part of the World, shall like him best. — And I have don't.
3: That upon his first Choice of his place of Residence, He Immediately marry a wife; And live with her ten yeares (If possible) After which (pretending to dye) that he returne And upon his owne Experience make Affidavit of the pleas

thou

as young soever as my figure speaks me

Call Imperia. Portia

I, i, 28. The text is full of canceled words or lines, and the manuscript is sometimes illegible. I have deciphered or clarified where I could but have had to leave some cancels unexplained.

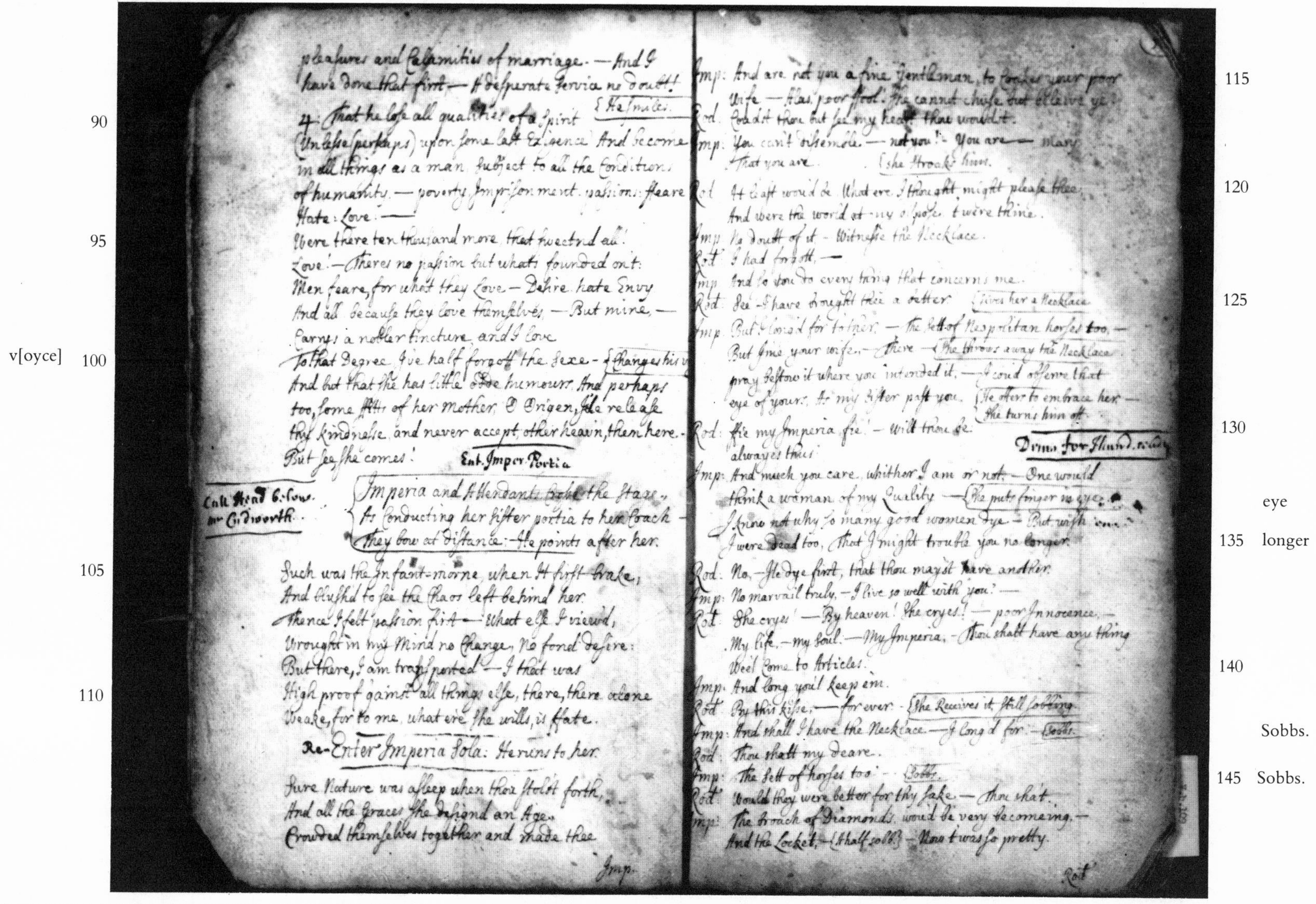

pleasures and Calamities of marriage. — And I
have done that first — A desperate service no doubt!
4 That he lose all qualities of a Spirit {He smiles.
(Unlesse perhaps) upon some last Existence And become
in all things as a man subject to all the Condition
of humanity — poverty. Imprisonment. passions: Feare
Hate: Love —
Were there ten thousand more that sweetned all!
Love! — Theres no passion but whats founded on't:
Men feare, for what they Love — Desire. hate Envy
And all because they love themselves — But mine, —
Carryes a nobler tincture and I love
To that Degree I've half forgot the sexe — {Changes his v
And but that she has little of the humour, And perhaps
too, some of her mother & Origen, she'l release
this kindnesse and never accept other heaven, then here.
But see she comes! Ent. Imper. Portia
Call Head below Mr Cudworth
{Imperia and Attendants Cross the Stage
As Conducting her sister portia to her Coach
They bow at distance: He points after her.
Such was the Infant-morne when it first brake,
And blush'd to see the Chaos left behind her.
Thence I felt passion first — What else I view'd,
Wrought in my mind no Change, No fond desire:
But there, I am transported — I that was
High proof gainst all things else, there, there alone
Weake, for to me, what ere she wills, is Fate.
Re-Enter Imperia Sola: He runs to her.
Sure Nature was asleep when thou stol'st forth,
And all the Graces she design'd an Age,
Crowded themselves together and made thee
Imp.

Imp: And are not you a fine Gentleman, to forsake your poor
Wife — Has poor Rod. She cannot chuse but believe ye.
Rod. Could'st thou but see my heart thou would'st.
Imp: You can't dissemble. — not you! — You are — Many
that you are. {She strokes him.
Rod. At least would be what ere I thought might please thee,
And were the world at my dispose, t'were thine.
Imp: No doubt of it — Witnesse the Necklace.
Rod. I had forgott. —
Imp: And so you do every thing that concerns me.
Rod. See I have brought thee a better {Gives her a Necklace
Imp: But I long'd for t'other, — the sett of Neapolitan horses too, —
But give your wife — there — {She throws away the Necklace
pray bestow it where you intended it, — I could observe that
eye of yours, to my sister past you. {He offers to embrace her — she turns him off
Rod: Fie my Imperia fie! — Will thou be
always thus!
Drums for Thund.
Imp: And much you care, whither I am or not, — One would
think a woman of my Quality — {She puts finger in eye.
I know not why so many good women dye — But with 'em
I were dead too, that I might trouble you no longer.
Rod. No, — I'le dye first, that thou mayst have another.
Imp: No marvail truly, — I live so well with you! —
Rod. She cryes! — By heaven! she cryes! — poor Innocence.
My life, — my soul. — My Imperia, — Thou shalt have any thing
Wee'l come to Articles.
Imp: And long you'l keep em.
Rod. By this kisse, — for ever. {She Receives it, still sobbing
Imp: And shall I have the Necklace — I long'd for. — Sobbs.
Rod. Thou shalt my deare.
Imp: The sett of horses too — Sobbs.
Rod. Would they were better for thy sake — Thou shalt.
Imp: The broach of Diamonds, would be very becoming, —
And the Locket, — {Thou shalt} — Now t'was so pretty.
Rod.

v[oyce]

eye

longer

Sobbs.

Sobbs.

I, i, 104. Unlike London promptbooks for the King's Company, where entrances were cued with a cross-hatch mark, the Dublin prompter simply named the characters—in this case, Imperia and Portia. The actor Cudworth played the Head; several other minor actors are mentioned in the prompt notes; a partial reconstruction of the cast is in the commentary.

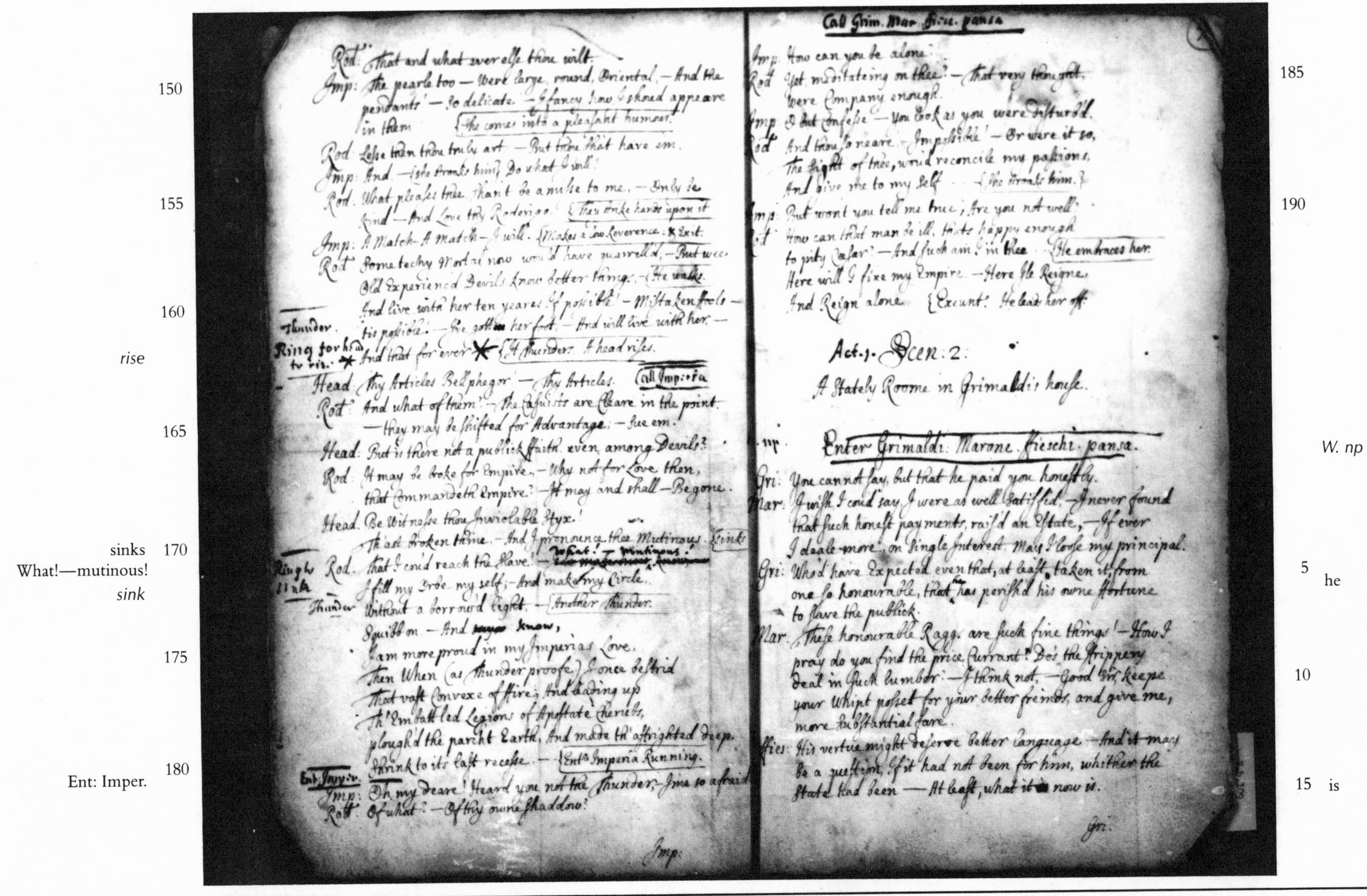

rise

sinks

What!—mutinous!

sink

Ent: Imper.

W. np

he

is

I, i, 162. For a discussion of the trapdoor warnings and cues see the commentary.

I, ii, opening. *W np* (which should read *W up*) stands for upper door, West side; the Dubliners identified entranceways as either East or West and upper or lower. A compilation of the entrance notes and a discussion of them is in the commentary.

And

Whence

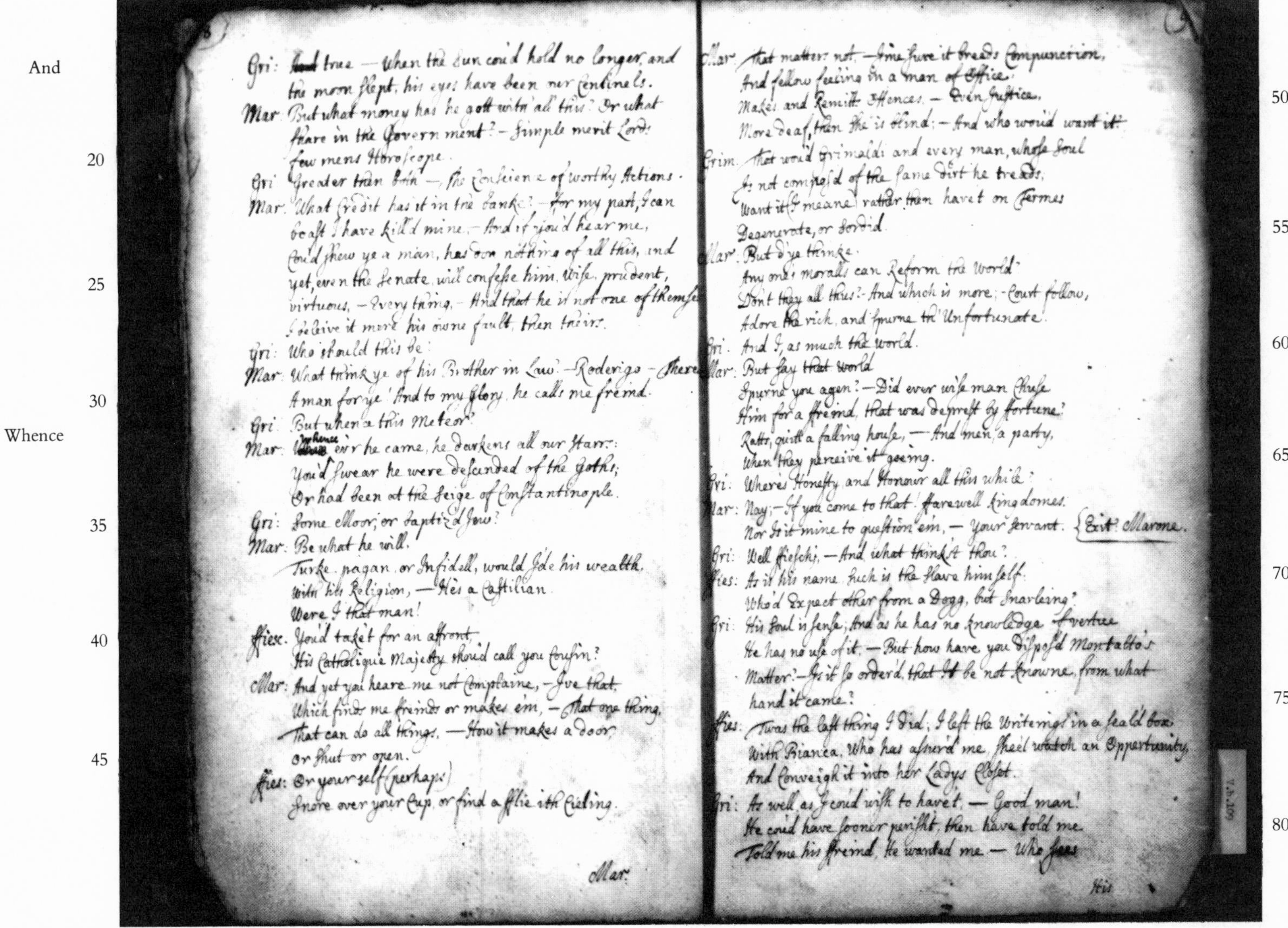

Gri: And true — when the sun cou'd hold no longer, and
the moon slept, his eyes have been our Centinels.
Mar: But what money has he gott with all this? Or what
share in the Govern ment? — Simple merit Lord:
few mens Horoscope.
Gri: Greater then both — The Conscience of worthy Actions.
Mar: What Credit has it in the banke? — For my part, I can
boast I have kill'd mine. — And if you'd hear me,
I cou'd shew ye a man, has don nothing of all this, and
yet, even the Senate will confesse him, Wise, prudent,
virtuous, — Every thing. — And that he is not one of themselves
I beleive it more his owne fault, then theirs.
Gri: Who should this be:
Mar: What think ye of his Brother in Law? — Roderigo — There's
A man for ye! And to my glory, he calls me freind.
Gri: But whence this Meteor?
Mar: Whence ever he came, he darkens all our Starrs:
You'd swear he were descended of the Goths;
Or had been at the Seige of Constantinople.
Gri: Some Moor, or baptiz'd Jew?
Mar: Be what he will.
Turke, pagan, or Infidell, would Ide his wealth,
with his Religion, — He's a Castilian
Were I that man!
Fiesc. You'd take't for an affront,
His Catholique Majesty should call you Cousin?
Mar: And yet you heare me not Complaine, — I've that,
Which finds me freinds or makes em, — That one thing,
That can do all things. — How it makes a door,
Or shut or open.
Fies: Or your self (perhaps)
Snore over your Cup, or find a flie ith Cieling.

Mar:

Mar: That matters not. — I'me sure it breeds Compunction,
And fellow feeling in a man of Office:
Makes and Remitts Offences. — Even Justice,
More deaf, then she is blind: — And who would want it.
Grim: That would Grimaldi and every man, whose Soul
Is not compos'd of the same dirt he treads,
Want it (I meane) rather then have't on Termes
Degenerate, or Sordid.
Mar: But d'ye thinke
Any one's moralls can Reform the World?
Don't they all thus? — And which is more; — Court follow,
Adore the rich, and spurne th' Unfortunate.
Gri: And I, as much the world.
Mar: But say that world
Spurne you agen? — Did ever wise man Chuse
Him for a freind, that was deprest by fortune?
Ratts, quitt a falling house, — And men, a party,
When they perceive it going.
Gri: Where's Honesty and Honour all this while?
Mar: Nay; — If you come to that! farewell kingdomes.
Nor Is it mine to question em, — Your servant. {Exit. Marone.
Gri: Well Fieschi, — And what think'st thou?
Fies: As is his name, such is the slave himself:
Who'd Expect other from a Dogg, but Snarleing?
Gri: His Soul is sense; And as he has no knowledge of vertue
He has no use of it. — But how have you dispos'd Montalto's
Matter? — Is it so order'd, that It be not knowne, from what
hand it came?
Fies: Twas the last thing I did; I left the Writeings in a seal'd box,
With Bianca, Who has assur'd me, shee'l watch an Oppertunity,
And Conveigh it into her Ladys Closet.
Gri: As well as I cou'd wish to have't, — Good man!
He cou'd have sooner perisht, then have told me
Told me his freind, He wanted me — Who sees

His

w. np:

His freinds Distresse, and stayes till he's entreated,
He comes too late. — Tis an Extorted Kindnesse
Left ere it comes, and shews he wanted will.

Call Montalto portia chain & Med.l

I have don't at all: — But this Marone sticks in my Stoma[ck]
Whence truly is he?

Fiesc: Wanza I think, Remembers the first plantation

Man: That do! Sir — from the time he first came to towne in Second Mourning, — that is in a Livery as Ragged and tatter'd as an Hee Goate. — His hatt right beggars block No crown to 't, — His doublet and breeches so suitable that in a darke morning, hed have mistaken one for to'ther, — His stockings without feete, or Anckles, like a Chandlers drawing-sleeves. And those too, he durst not trust off his leggs for feare of crawling away; — In a word A thing made up of so many several parishes, that you'd have taken him at first sight for a frontispeice of the Resurrection.

Fies: Thence he came in, as a Sub-Collector And thence, into St Georges Banke And now, being in his Nature Insolent, this Imaginary Reputation, has made him Intollerable.

Gri: And for his other Quality, I know somewhat my selfe —
He never forgave beyond the Opportunity of a Revenge;
Or spake well of any man, but to his greater disadvantag[e]
A pretty Gentleman. — But — tis pitty —

Fiesc: Nay worse, shall play both the Devils parts,
Of tempter, and Accuser: provoke his freind into a freedom
of talke, And then, Informe it.

Gri: Enough, — And for feare of any mistake, make another
step to Bianca. [Exit Fieschi: pansa: manet Grimaldi.
And this man thrive! — O Lucian thy Gods! — the groanes
Of Deprest virtue, And loud laughters of Exalted folly,
gave first Name to the fortunate Island, where men
slept themselves away, in the Melancholly Contemplations,
Between Vertue and Successe.

Enter

Enter Montalto and portia. a Chain & Medal

Gri: You have prevented me — I was just comeing,
To give you Joy. — The Senate have at last
Consider'd your Services.

Mon: And sent me a Gugaw
An Empty Nothing — ith — [Montalto takes out a Chaine and Medall and showes it.]

Gri: Twas never intended
Beyond a mark of Honour; and a pledge
Of future Kindnesse.

Mon: Tis a Beast that serves
A Common wealth, for when has spent his blood
And sunk his fortune to support the pride,
And Luxury of those few, that cheat the rest
He streight becomes the Object of their scorne
Or Jealousie.

Gri: How oddly my freind argues,
Against himselfe — Have you not serv'd the State
These twenty yeares? — And can you think it wisedome,
To quarrell now: Or now, when reasonably
You might Expect the fruite of all your hazards,
Arme them against you? — Virtue, Merit, worth,
Nev'r wanted Enemys; — Make not you more.

Mon: When they behold themselves thro' their false Opticks,
They swell a Gnatt into an Elephant.
When others, — How they turne the Glasse! and lessen
A Mountain to a Molehill.

Gri: Are you the only man has been so serv'd?
Who deserv'd better for a Law-giver
Than Solon? — Or Captaine then Thrasibulus?
Or Orator, then Demosthenes? Yet Athens,
Ungratefull Athens, banish'd the two first,
And slew the Latter; — Unto whom ow'd Rome
More, than to Manlius, who when her Capitol
was

12

was growne too hott for Jupiter preserv'd it:
Or what might not Camillus have pretence to
Who when she was reduc'd to her last stake,
push'd it, and won it. — What shou'd I mention
Rutilius, Scipio, Hannibal, Themistocles
Men famous in their Ages. — yet they fell
fell where they most deserv'd.

Mon: How my blood curdles at it! And methinks,
I feel a kind of Currishness shot through me;
And want no property of a Dog, but fawneing,
The necessary to a Riseing man.

Por: Is this that fortitude, my Montalto?
This, that Heroick Vertue, you taught me?
Sure, tis not the Montalto I have seene
When victory sate perching on his Helme:
Or that Montalto, when Opprest by Numbers,
He lost the day, And yet brought home more Glory,
Than if he had been Conqueror: Yet still,
Still the same even temper; Unconcern'd,
At Losse or Victory.

Mon: Wou'd't not heate a man,
To view his wounds, which like so many mouths,
Speak out his wrongs the Lowder: t'ave consum'd
Himself to warme Ingratitude.

Por: The fruite
Of Worthy Actions, is to have done em;
And every man that will; may give't himself.

Mon: How can I stand my breast, against a torrent
Of Adverse Fortune.

Por: Tis your greater glory
To stemm that flood. — How're you beholding to her
That she cou'd passe the Herd, and single you,
To Combate her.

Mon:

Call Quartilla 13
Scintilla

Mon: But she has Cut my Sinewes.

Por: The more your Honor, — I have heard you say
That Roman was more glorious in his Scortcht,
Than Armed hand. — Do not distrust yourself,
And you must Conquer her; — The Constant man,
Is master of himself, and Fortune too.

Mon: Blesse me. — Thou glorious woman, never made
Of Common Earth! — I am concern'd for thee.

Por: To the World's fondlings, be their World — With me,
My one Montalt' out weighs the Apparition.
The Airy dreame, which, when they think a substance,
Graspe at it they awake and find it Nothing:
Were had it any thing worthy our Love
It were a mind that can content it.

Mon: Brave woman!
And who mightst bring philosophy to manners.

Por: If you call this philosophy tis what
Its first Inventors meant it, ere our pedants;
Had made it, rather difficult, than great.
Come my Montalto, come, — And let th' Example
Of others virtue, now engage your owne;
Their Glory, your Imitation.

Mon: Thou hast ore come my portia, — And I'll trye
If that Content, the larger World denys;
May be found in our selves, — Even poverty,
If it can be content, has lost its Name.
He never has enough that gapes for more
Opinion was never Rich, Nor Content poore.

Por: Now how I love this Rugged Honesty,
Like the first matter, has all the seeds of good,
Only wants forme, and Order.

{ Exeunt.

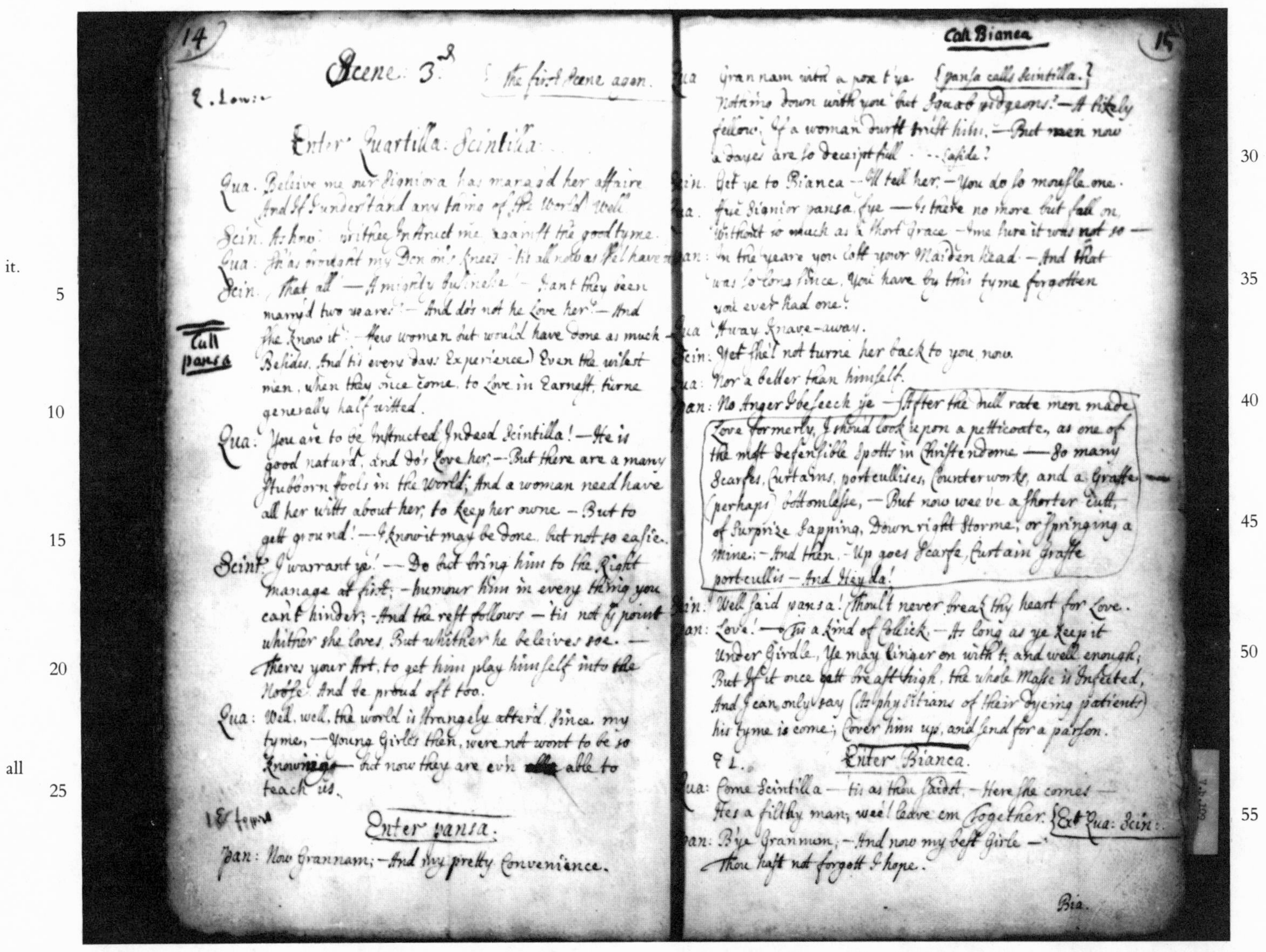

14

Scene. 3d. the first Scene agen.

E. Lowr.

Enter Quartilla. Scintilla.

Qua. Beleive me our Signiora has manag'd her affaire
And If I understand any thing of the World Well
Scin. As how. prithee Instruct me against the good tyme.
Qua. Sh'as brought my Don on's knees - tis all not as [illegible] have [illegible]
Scin. That all — A mighty businesse! - Hant they been
marry'd two yeares? — And do's not he Love her? — And
she know it? — Few women but would have done as much —

Call Pansa

Besides. And tis every days Experience) Even the wisest
men. when they once come. to Love in Earnest, turne
generally half witted.
Qua: You are to be Instructed Indeed Scintilla! — He is
good natur'd, and do's Love her; — But there are a many
stubborn fools in the World; And a woman need have
all her witts about her, to keep her owne — But to
gett ground! — I know it may be done. but not so easie.
Scint: I warrant ye! — Do but bring him to the Right
manage at first; - humour him in every thing you
can't hinder; - And the rest follows — tis not ye point
whither she loves. But whither he beleives soe. —
Theres your Art. to get him play himself into the
Noose. And be proud of't too.
Qua: Well. well. the world is strangely alter'd. since my
tyme, — Young Girles then, were not wont to be so
Knowing — but now they are ev'n able able to
teach us.

1 E: Lower

Enter Pansa.

Pan: How Grannam; — And thy pretty Convenience.

Call Bianca

15

Qua Grannam with a pox t'ye. {Pansa calls Scintilla.}
Nothing down with you but Squab pidgeons! — A likely
fellow; If a woman durst trust him. — But men now
a dayes are so deceipt full - - {aside.}
Scin. Get ye to Bianca - - I'll tell her; — You do so mouzle one.
Qua. Fye Signior Pansa. fye — Is there no more but fall on,
Without so much as a short Grace — I'me sure it was not so —
Pan: In the yeare you lost your Maiden head — And that
was so long since, You have by this tyme forgotten
you ever had one!
Qua Away Knave - away.
Scin: Yet she'l not turne her back to you now.
Qua: Nor a better than himself.
Pan: No Anger I beseech ye — After the dull rate men made
Love formerly, I shoud look upon a petticoate, as one of
the most defensible spotts in Christendome — So many
Scarfes. Curtains, portcullises, Counterworks, and a Grafte
(perhaps) bottomlesse, — But now wee've a shorter cutt,
of Surprize Sapping, Down right Storme; or springing a
mine; - And then, - Up goes Scarfe, Curtain Grafte
portcullis — And Hey da!
Scin: Well said Pansa! Thou'lt never break thy heart for Love.
Pan: Love! — Tis a kind of Collick. — As long as ye keep it
Under Girdle, Ye may Linger on with't, and well enough;
But If it once gett breast high, the whole Masse is Infected,
And I can only say (As physitians of their dyeing patients)
his tyme is come; Cover him up, and send for a parson.
E L.
Enter Bianca.
Qua: Come Scintilla — tis as thou saidst, — Here she comes —
Hes a filthy man; wee'l leave em together. {Ext Qua: Scin:
Pan: B'ye Grannum, — And now my best Girle —
Thou hast not forgott I hope.

Bia.

it.

all

I, iii, below 25. The prompter wrote *E Lower*, then wrote *W* over the *E* in red pencil.

I, iii, 40–47. The cut was not made by the prompter. The sequence of speeches doesn't make much sense without the deleted speech.

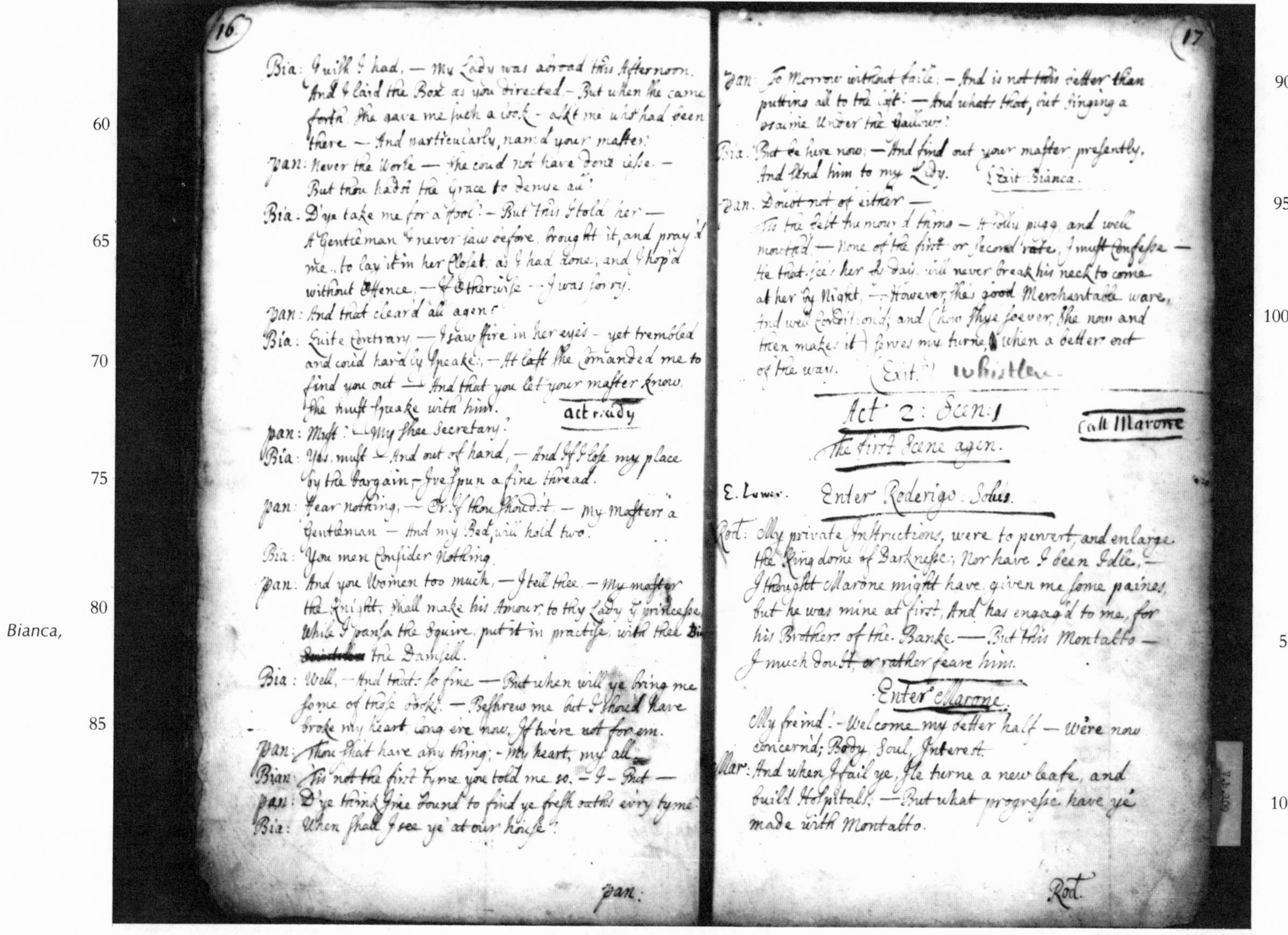

16

Bia: I wish I had. — My Lady was abroad this Afternoon.
And I laid the Box as you directed. — But when she came
forth she gave me such a look — askt me who had been
there — And particularly, nam'd your master.
Pan: Never the worse — she coud not have done lesse. —
But thou hadst the Grace to denye all?
Bia: D'ye take me for a fool? — But this I told her —
A Gentleman I never saw before, brought it, and pray'd
me, to lay it in her Closet, as I had done; and I hop'd
without Offence. — If Otherwise — I was sorry.
Pan: And that clear'd all agen.
Bia: Quite Contrary — I saw fire in her eyes — yet trembled
and could hardly speake; — At last she Comanded me to
find you out — And that you let your master know,
she must speake with him. act ready
Pan: Must? — My shee Secretary?
Bia: Yes, must — And out of hand, — And If I lose my place
by the bargain — I've spun a fine thread.
Pan: Fear nothing, — Or, if thou shoud'st — My Master's a
Gentleman — And my Bed, will hold two.
Bia: You men Consider Nothing.
Pan: And you Women too much, — I tell thee — My master
the Knight, shall make his Amour, to thy Lady ye princesse,
While I Pansa the Squire, put it in practise, with thee Bi-
~~[struck through]~~ the Damsell.

Bianca,

Bia: Well, — And that's so fine — But when will ye bring me
some of those Books? — Beshrew me but I shoud have
broke my heart long ere now, If twere not for em.
Pan: Thou shalt have any thing; — My heart, my all —
Bian: Tis not the first tyme you told me so. — I — But —
Pan: D'ye think I'me bound to find ye fresh oaths evry tyme?
Bia: When shall I see ye at our house?

Pan:

17

Pan: To Morrow without faile; — And is not this better than
putting all to the test — And whats that, but singing a
psalme Under the Gallows?
Bia: But be here now; — And find out your master presently,
And send him to my Lady. Exit Bianca.
Pan: Doubt not of either —
Tis the best humour'd thing — A Jolly pugg, and well
mouth'd — None of the first or second rate, I must Confesse —
He that sees her by day, will never break his neck to come
at her by Night, — However, she's good Merchantable ware,
And well Condition'd; and (how shye soever she now and
then makes it) serves my turne, when a better's out
of the way. Exit. whistle

Act 2: Scen: 1 Call Marone
The first Scene agen.

E. Lower. Enter Roderigo. Solus.

Rod: My private Instructions, were to pervert, and enlarge
the Kingdome of Darknesse; Nor have I been Idle. —
I thought Marone might have given me some paines,
but he was mine at first, And has engag'd to me, for
his Brothers of the Banke. — But this Montalto —
I much doubt, or rather feare him.
Enter Marone.
My freind! — Welcome my better half — We're now
concern'd; Body, Soul, Interest.
Mar: And when I fail ye, Ile turne a new leafe, and
build Hospitalls. — But what progresse have ye
made with Montalto.

Rod.

II, i, opening. The warning for Roderigo's entrance is the *act ready* at I, iii, 72. This is a pattern throughout the promptbook at the beginnings of acts.

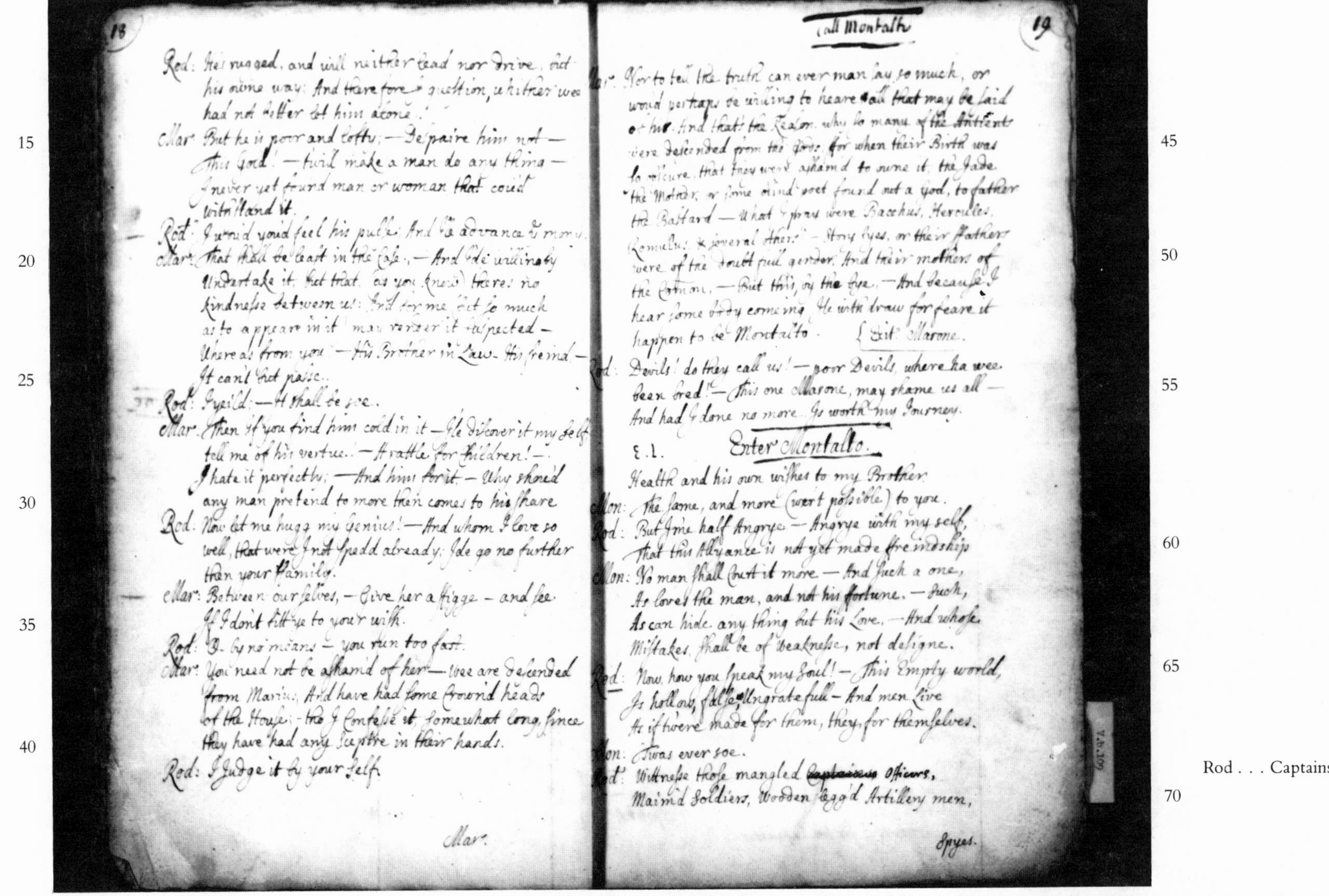

18

Rod: He's rugged, and will neither lead nor drive, but his owne way: And therefore 'tis a question, whither wee had not better let him alone.

Mar: But he is poor and lofty. — Despaire him not — This Gold! — twill make a man do any thing — I never yet found man or woman that could withstand it.

Rod: I would you'd feel his pulse: And I'le advance the money.

Mar: That shall be least in the case. — And I'de willingly undertake it, but that, as you know, there's no kindnesse between us: And for me but so much as to appeare in it may render it suspected — Whereas from you — His Brother in Law — His freind — It can't but passe.

Rod: I yeild: — It shall be soe.

Mar: Then if you find him cold in it — I'le discover it my self, tell me of his vertue. — A rattle for children! — I hate it perfectly; — And him for it. — Why shou'd any man pretend to more then comes to his share

Rod. Now let me hugg my Genius! — And whom I love so well, that were I not spedd already; I'de go no further than your Family.

Mar: Between our selves, — Give her a figge — and see If I don't fitt ye to your wish.

Rod: O. by no means — you run too fast.

Mar: You need not be asham'd of her — wee are descended from Marius; And have had some crown'd heads of the House; tho I confesse it somewhat long since they have had any Scepter in their hands.

Rod: I judge it by your self.

Mar.

call Montalto

19

Mar: Nor to tell the truth can ever man say so much, or would perhaps be willing to heare all that may be said of her. And that's the Reason why so many of the Antients were descended from the Gods: for when their Birth was so obscure, that they were asham'd to owne it, the Jade the Mother, or some kind poet found out a God, to father the Bastard — What were Bacchus, Hercules, Romulus, & severall others? — Stony Eyes, or their fathers were of the doubtfull gender: And their mothers of the Common. — But this, by the bye. — And because I hear some body coming, I'le with draw for feare it happen to be Montalto. [Exit Marone.

Rod: Devils! do they call us! — poor Devils, where ha wee been bred! — This one Marone, may shame us all — And had I done no more, 'tis worth my Journey.

S.1. Enter Montalto.

Health and his own wishes to my Brother.

Mon: The same, and more (wer't possible) to you.

Rod: But I'me half Angrye — Angrye with my self,
That this Allyance is not yet made friendship

Mon: No man shall court it more — And such a one,
As loves the man, and not his fortune. — Such,
As can hide any thing but his Love. — And whose
Mistakes, shall be of weaknesse, not designe.

Rod: Now, how you speak my Soul! — This Empty world,
Is hollow, false, Ungratefull — And men Live
As if 'twere made for them, they for themselves.

Mon: 'Twas ever soe.

Rod: Witnesse those mangled ~~Captaines~~ Officers,
Maim'd Soldiers, Wooden legg'd Artillery men,

Spyes.

Rod . . . Captains

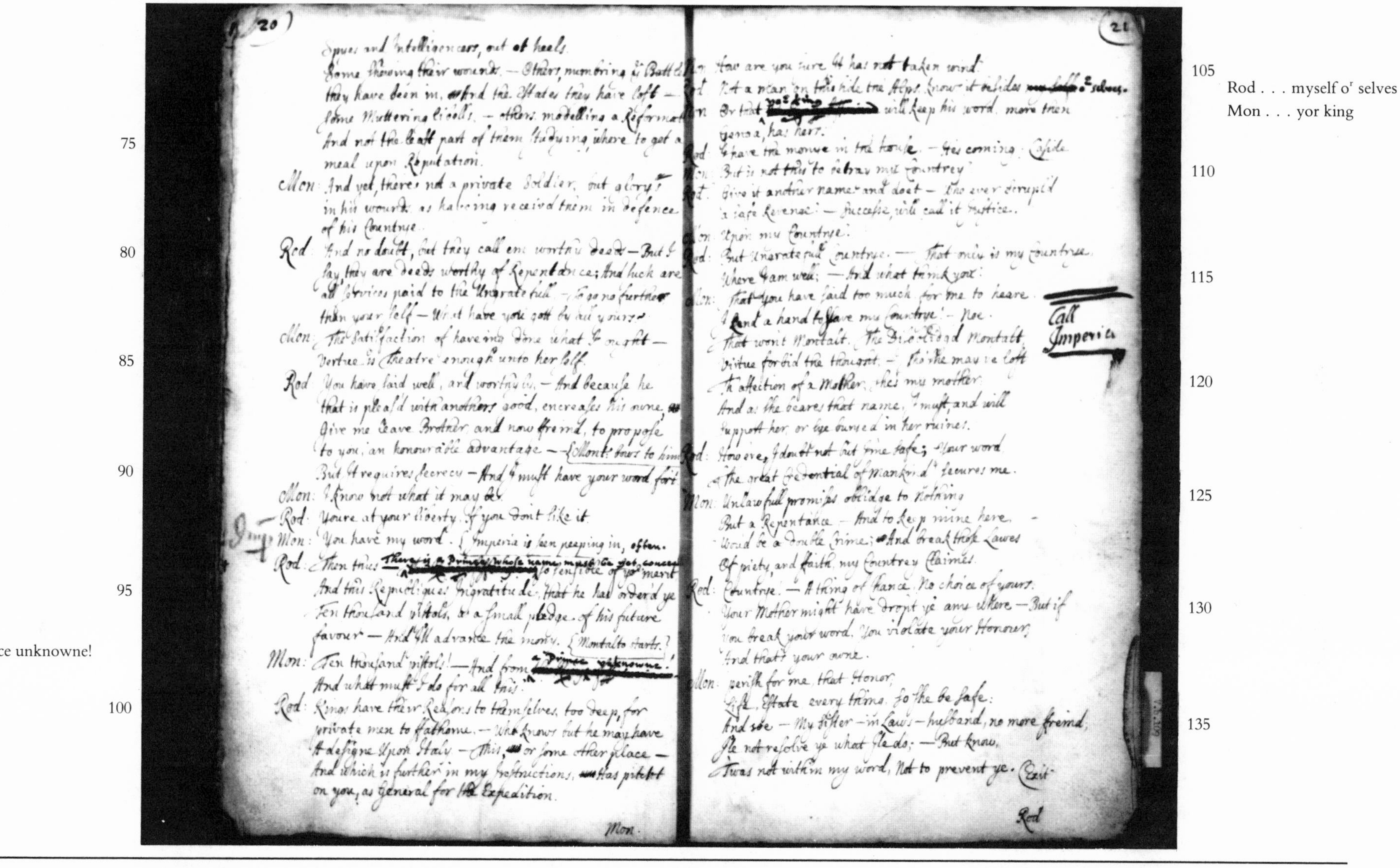

Rod . . . myself oʳ selves

Mon . . . yor king

a Prince unknowne!

II, i, 93. Imperia should have been warned for this "peeping" entrance.

II, i, above 94. Wilson's replacement line is: "There is a Prince whose name must be yet conceal'd." The original line is indecipherable.

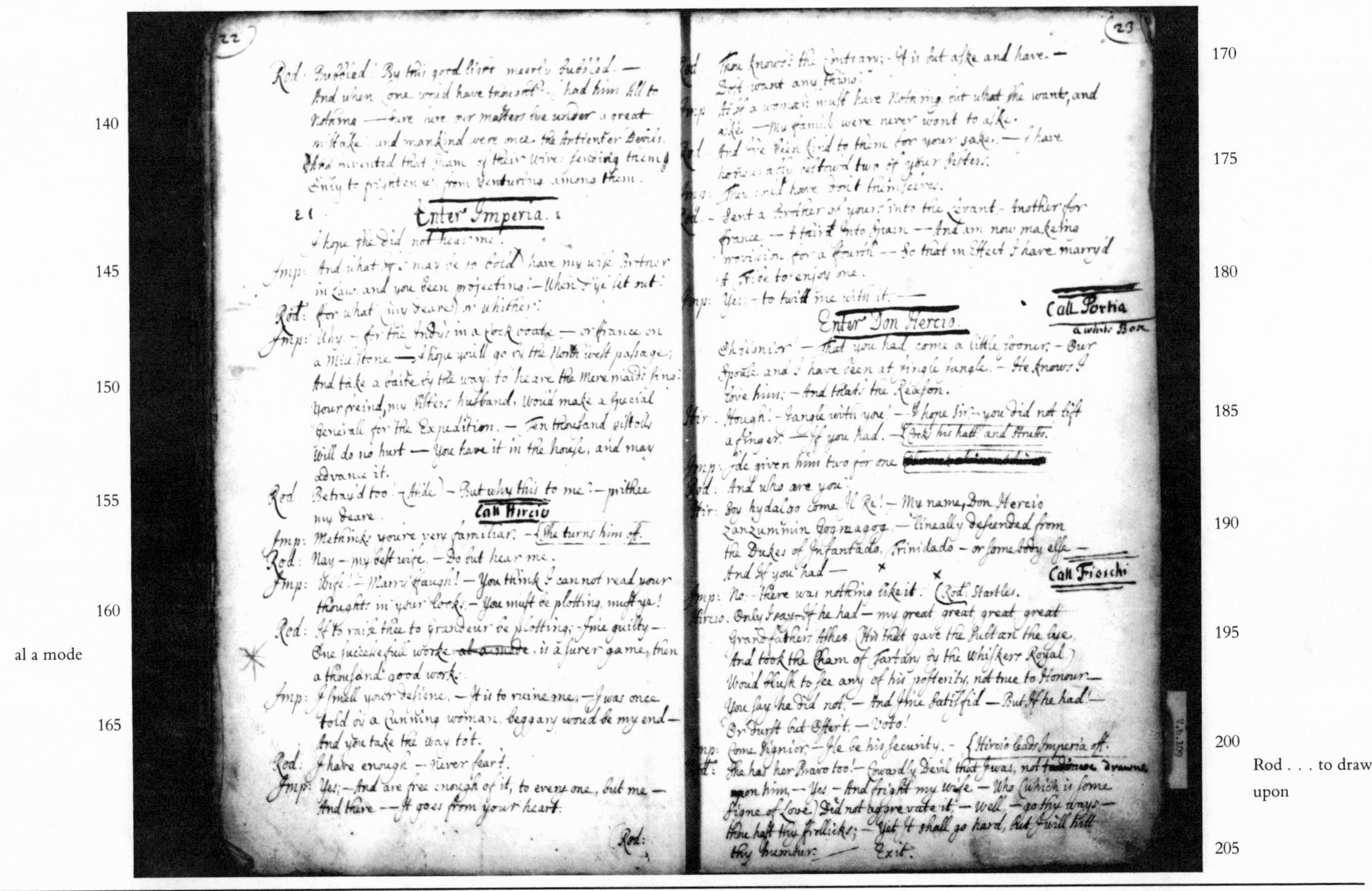

22

Rod: Bubbled! By this good Light meerly bubbled.—
And when one would have thought—I had him All to
nothing—sure sure our matters live under a great
mistake: and mankind were mee the Antienter Devils.
Who invented that shame of their Wives: fencing them,
Only to frighten us, from venturing among them.

Enter Imperia.

I hope she did not hear me.

Imp: And what (if I may be so bold) have my wise Brother
in Law and you been projecting?—When d'ye set out?

Rod: For what (my deare) or whither?

Imp: Why—for the Indies in a Cock boate—or France on
a Mill stone—I hope you'll go by the North west passage;
And take a baite by the way, to heare the Mere maids sing:
Your freind, my sisters husband, would make a special
Generall for the Expedition.—Ten thousand pistolls
Will do no hurt—You have it in the house, and may
advance it.

Rod: Betray'd too! (Aside)—But why this to me?—prithee
my deare.

Call Hircio

Imp: Methinks you're very familiar.—{She turns him of.

Rod: Nay—my best wife,—Do but hear me.

Imp: Wife!—Marry faugh!—You think I can not read your
thoughts in your looks.—You must be plotting, must ye!

Rod: If to raise thee to Grandeur be plotting;—I'me guilty—
One successefull worke [illegible], is a surer game, then
a thousand good work.

al a mode

Imp: I smell your designe,—It is to ruine me,—I was once
told by a Cunning woman, beggary would be my end—
And you take the way tot.

Rod: I have enough—never feart.

Imp: Yes;—And are free enough of it, to every one, but me—
And there—It goes from your heart.

Rod:

23

Rod: Thou knowst the contrary;—'Tis but aske and have.—
Dost want any thing?

Imp: Is't a woman must have Nothing but what she wants, and
askes.—My family were never wont to aske.

Rod: And I've been kind to them for your sake.—I have
honourably bestow'd two of your sisters.

Imp: They could have don't themselves.

Rod: Sent a Brother of yours into the Levant—Another for
France—A third into Spain—And am now makeing
provision for a fourth—So that in Effect I have marry'd
A Tribe to enjoy one.

Imp: Yes;—to twitt me with it.—

Enter Don Hercio.

Call Portia
a white Box

Oh Signior!—That you had come a little sooner.—Our
Spouse and I have been at single jangle.—He knows I
love him;—And that's the Reason.

Hir: Hough!—Jangle with you!—I hope Sir,—you did not lift
a finger.—If you had.—{Cocks his hatt and struts.

Imp: I'de given him two for one [illegible]

Rod: And who are you?

Hir: Soy hydalgo come il Re!—My name, Don Hercio
Zanzummin Gogmagog,—lineally descended from
the Dukes of Infantado, Trinidado—or some body else—
And if you had—

Call Fioschi

Imp: No—there was nothing like it. (Rod: Startles.

Hircio. Only I say—If he had—my great great great great
Grandfathers Ashes (His that gave the Sultan the lye,
And took the Cham of Tartary by the Whiskers Royal)
Would blush to see any of his posterity, not true to Honour—
You say he did not,—And I'me satisfid—But, If he had!—
Or durst but offert,—Voto!

Imp: Come Signior,—Ile be his security.—{Hircio leads Imperia off.

Rod: She has her Bravo too!—Cowardly Devil that I was, not [illegible] drawne
upon him,—Yes—And fright my wife.—Who (which is some
signe of Love) Did not aggravate it.—Well,—go thy ways—
thou hast thy frollicks;—Yet It shall go hard, but I will hitt
thy humour.— Exit.

Rod . . . to drawe upon

24

Act 2: Scen 2:

w. 1. Scen A noble Roome in Montalto's house

Enter Portia: Sola. a whit: Box

Por: My husband is convinced and so am I.
The Action in all its circumstances
Must be Grimaldi's, for't can be none but his:
And yet I'me rackt between the two Extreams,
Of freindship to him: And my just resentments:
To his false Nephew — All unknown to us.
The generous Grimaldi: has restor'd
My husbands fortune. — his degenerous Nephew,
Has taken this Occasion to renew
His long rejected Love.

w. 1. Enter Fieschi as at a stand.
And gazeing on her.

Fies: Her vertue sure.
Has wrought Impossibilities! and added,
New Graces to her person, — As if Infinity,
Coud be encreast!

Por: I sent for ye, Fieschi;
But it had been more honourable in you,
Not to have giv'n me cause, — Your worthy Unkle,
Has to his frequent Obligations,
Added a fresh — I need not tell ye what.

Fies: And tis his satisfaction, that he wanted
Neither the will, nor meanes of doing it.

Por: Debts, are discharg'd with payment — Benefitts,
pay what wee can, there will be still Arreare.
But, — for his Nephew to profane that freindship!
I coud be angrye. — verily, I coud
And woud, wer't not to make anothers ill
My owne affliction.

25

Fies: Blame your ~~owne~~ vertue then.
Montalto lov'd it, — And the self-same cause
That absolves him absolves Fieschi too.
He rested not in speculation only,
And shall I turne Philosopher?

Por: I'me his,
And only his: And there fore barr'd to you.

Fies: But Natures free; And walks not by Restraint.
But Choice —

Por: And I have mine —

Fies: Shee never found
Those fine dear words of Honour, Jealousie!
Shee never Impal'd free woman; — Or design'd
A thing so Excellent. for one's embrace.

Por: Enough, — ~~and~~ when that I ever heard ye, was as much
Against my will as the Concealing it,
Against my duty — Noe — A vertuous woman
Takes no more liberty, than what she ought.

Fies: At least blame Love not me; — I've often rais'd
Your great Idea in my Soul; — And (as
A Diamond only cuts a Diamond)
Set your owne vertue, gainst your self, ~~—~~ Yet still,
Love, gets the upper ground, and pours upon me:
So weake a fence is vertue, against Love.

Por: Wee still Excuse our selves, — The fault lyes not
In vertue. But our Resolutions:
Coud wee once make our Actions, worke up
To our Intentions, the worke were done!
There — Take your Idle what so'ere it be;
I know the hand too well, to open it.

Call Grimaldi
Montalto

She takes out a long white
Box & throws it towards him

Fies: And will you still torment me, with the sight,
of a forbidden good?

Por: Not good to you
Because forbidden; — If you're wise, begone.

Fiesc

He is goeing off as forgetting ye box She kicks it after him;—he takes it up

But

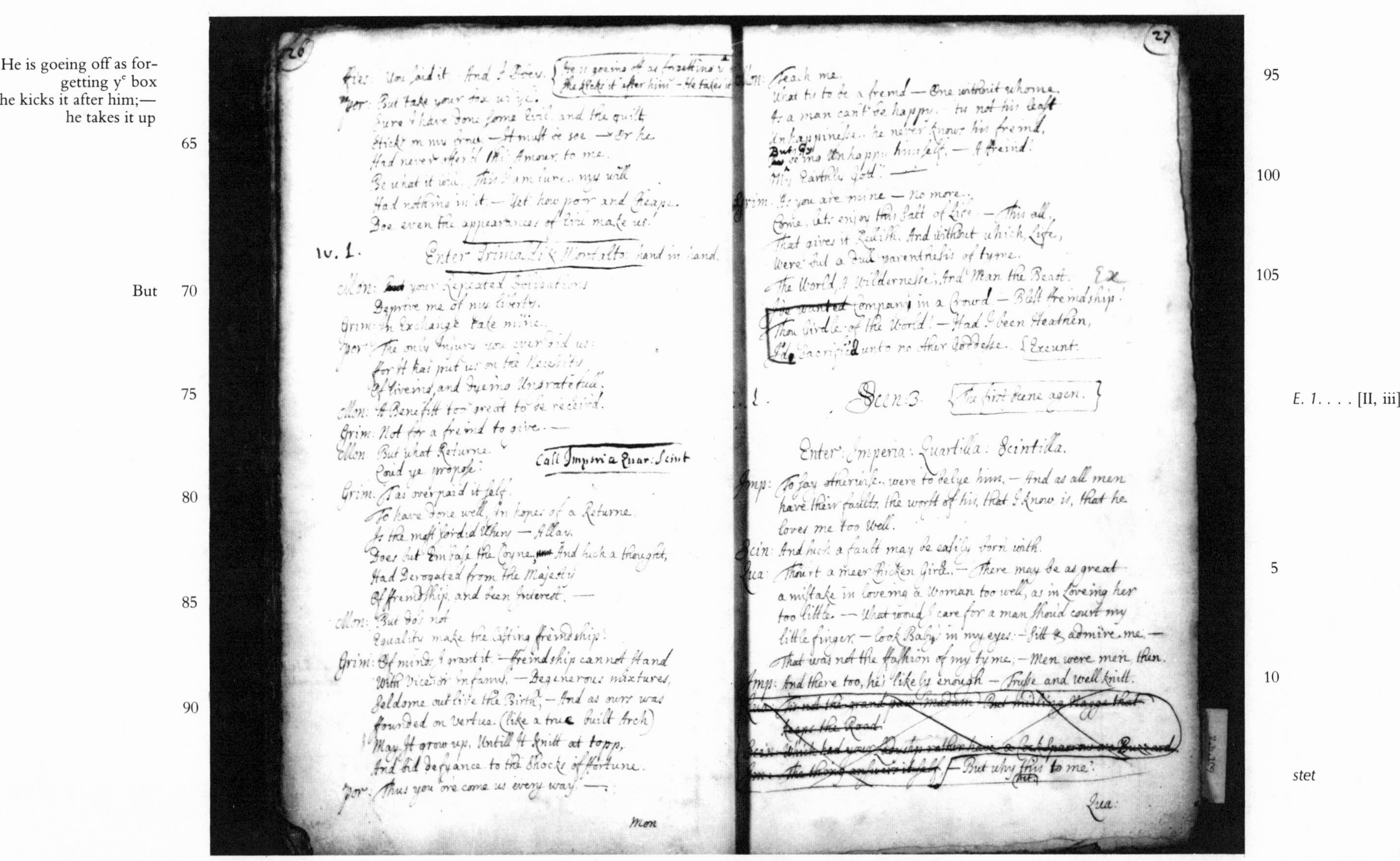

E. 1. . . . [II, iii]

stet

II, iii, 11–14. The canceled lines are: "Qua: Tis not the grand paw (Madam) But midling Nagge that / keeps the Road. / Scin: Which had your Ladyshp rather have a Cock Sparrow or a Buzzard. / Im: The thing answers itself."

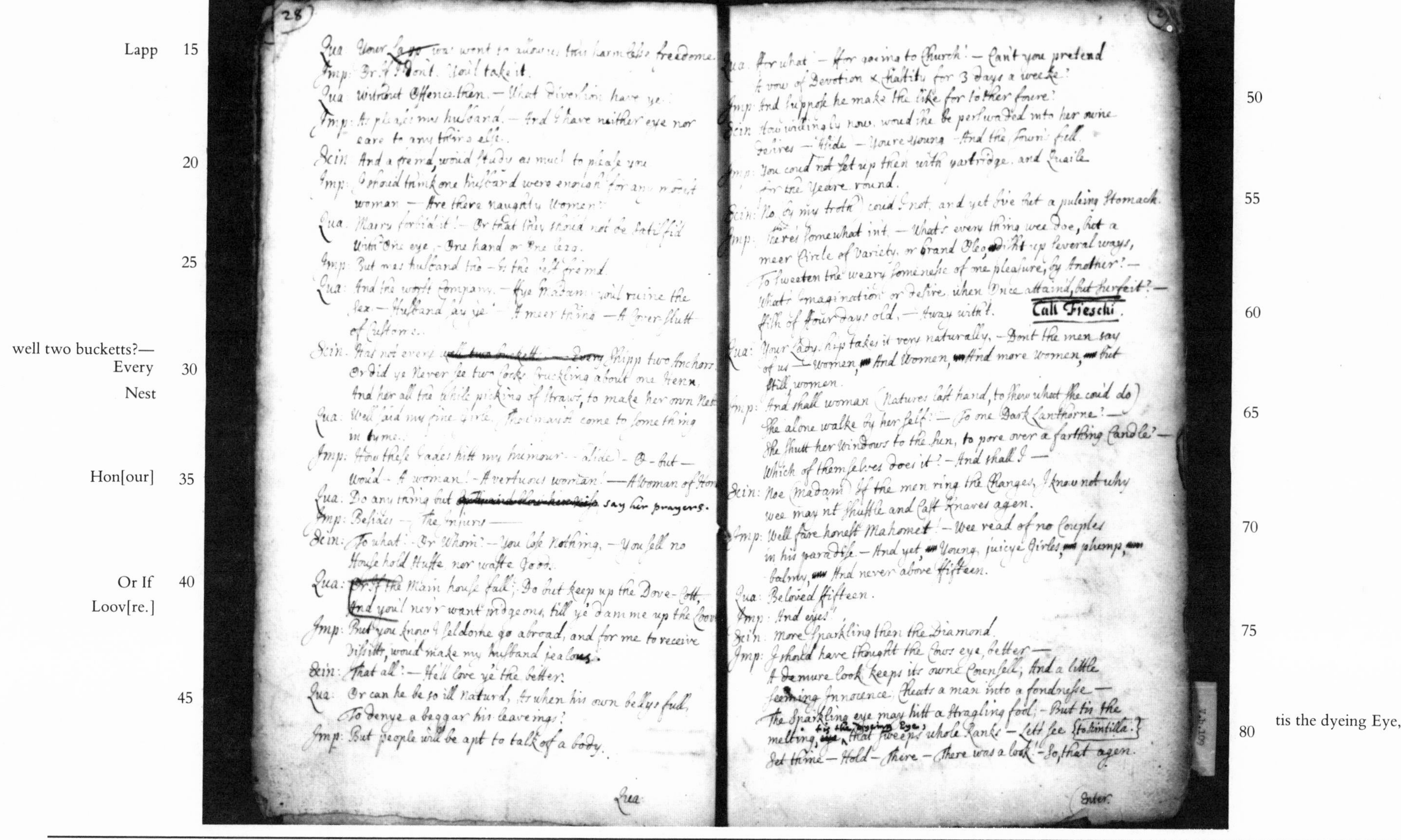

28

Qua: Your Lapp you want to allow this harmless freedome.
Imp: Or, if I dont, You'l take it.
Qua: Without Offence, then.— What Diversion have ye.
Imp: To please my husband.— And I have neither eye nor care to any thing else.
Dein: And a friend, would study as much to please you
Imp: I should think one husband were enough for any modest woman.— Are there naughty Women?
Qua: Marry forbid it!— Or that they should not be satisfid with One eye— One hand or One legg.
Imp: But my husband too— Is the best friend.
Qua: And the worst Company.— Fye Madam you'l ruine the Sex.— Husband, say ye? A meer thing— A Cover-slutt of Custome.
Dein: Was not every ~~well two buckett— Every~~ Shipp two Anchors Or did ye Never see two Cocks truckling about one Henn, And her all the while picking of strawe, to make her own Nest.
Qua: Well said my fine Girle, Shee must come to some thing in tyme.
Imp: How these Jades hitt my humour— (aside)— O— but— Would— A woman!— A vertuous woman!— A Woman of Hon
Qua: Do any thing but ~~[illegible]~~ say her prayers.
Imp: Besides— the Injury
Dein: To what? Or Whom?— You lose Nothing,— You sell no House hold stuffe nor waste Good.
Qua: ~~Or if~~ the Main house fall; Do but keep up the Dove-Cott, And you'l never want pidgeons, till ye dam me up the Loov
Imp: But you know I seldome go abroad, and for me to receive Visitts, would make my husband jealous.
Dein: That all:— He'll love ye the better.
Qua: Or can he be so ill Natur'd, as when his own bellys full, To denye a beggar his leavings?
Imp: But people will be apt to talk of a body.

Qua

Qua: For what— For going to Church?— Can't you pretend A vow of Devotion & Chastity for 3 days a weeke?
Imp: And suppose he make the like for tother three?
Dein: How willingly now, would she be perswaded into her owne desires— (Aside)— Youre young— And the Towne full.
Imp: You could not sett up then with partridge, and Quaile for the yeare round.
Dein: No, by my troth, could I not, and yet Ive but a puleing stomack.
Imp: Theres somewhat in't.— What's every thing wee doe, but a meer Circle of Variety, or Grand Olio dish't up severall ways, To sweeten the wearysomeness of one pleasure, by Another?— What's Imagination or Desire, when Once attain'd, but surfeit?— Filth of four days old,— Away with't. **Call Fieschi.**
Qua: Your Ladyship takes it very naturally,— Dont the men say of us— Women, And Women, And more Women, but still women.
Imp: And shall woman (Natures last hand, to shew what she could do) She alone walke by her self?— To one Dark Lanthorne?— She shutt her Windows to the sun, to pore over a farthing Candle?— Which of themselves does it?— And shall I—
Dein: Noe Madam, If the men ring the Changes, I know not why wee may nt shuffle and Cast Knaves agen.
Imp: Well fare honest Mahomet!— Wee read of no Couples in his paradise— And yet, Young, juicye Girles, plump, balmy, And never above Fifteen.
Qua: Beloved Fifteen.
Imp: And eyes!
Dein: More sparkling then the Diamond.
Imp: I should have thought the Eyes eye, better— A demure look keeps its owne Counsell; And a little seeming Innocence. Heats a man into a fondnesse— The sparkling eye may hitt a straggling fool;— But tis the melting, ~~eye~~, tis the dyeing Eye, that sweeps whole Ranks— Lett see Stabintilla.— Set thine— Hold— there— there was a look!— So, that agen.

Enter.

Lapp
well two bucketts?— Every
Nest
Hon[our]
Or If
Loov[re.]
tis the dyeing Eye,

beckons off
Scint: E[xeunt.]

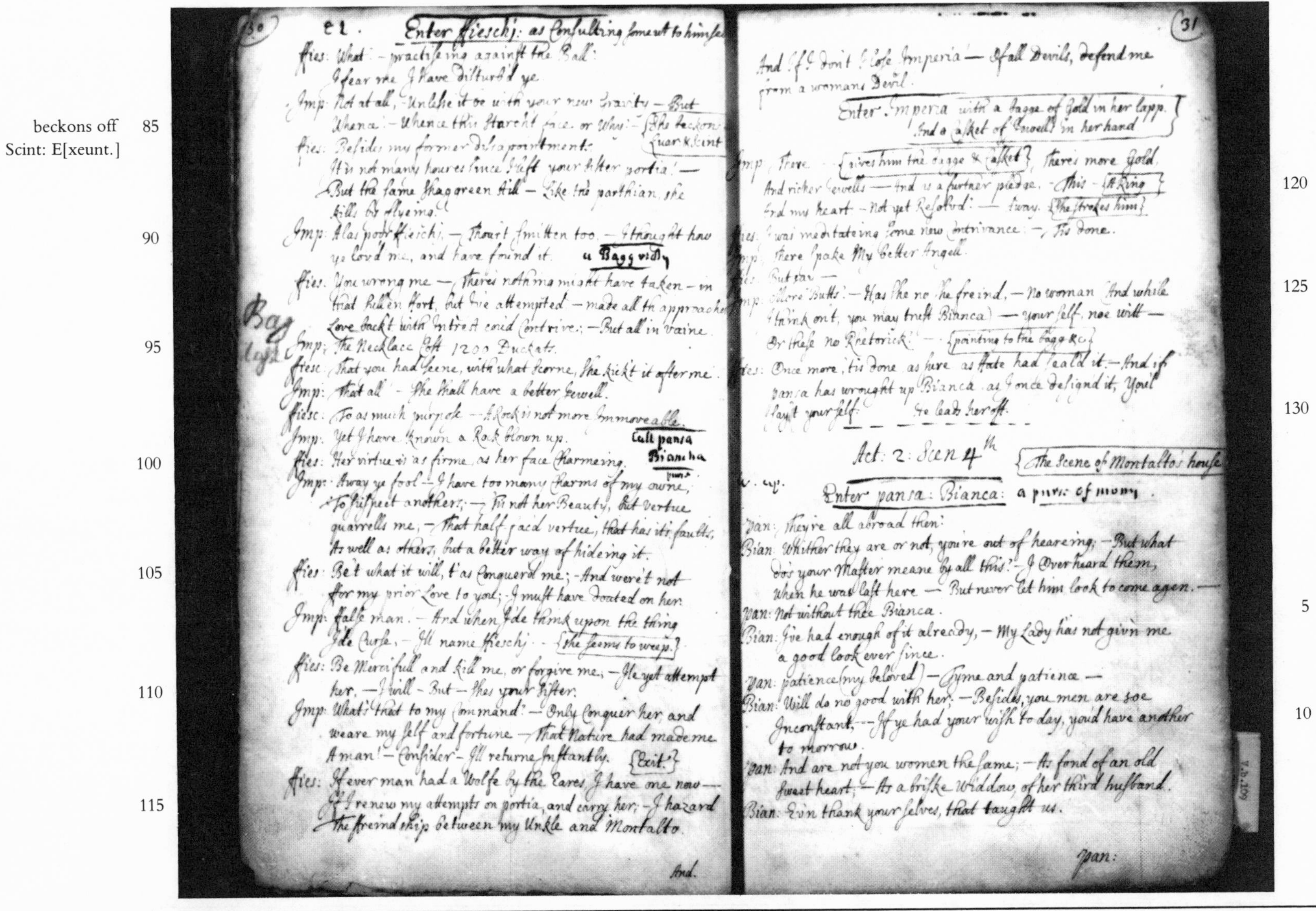

II, iii, 95. *left* presumably refers to stage left, where Imperia will enter, but why did the prompter not use East or West?

II, iii, following 118. Imperia's reentrance was not warned, but she had just left the stage.

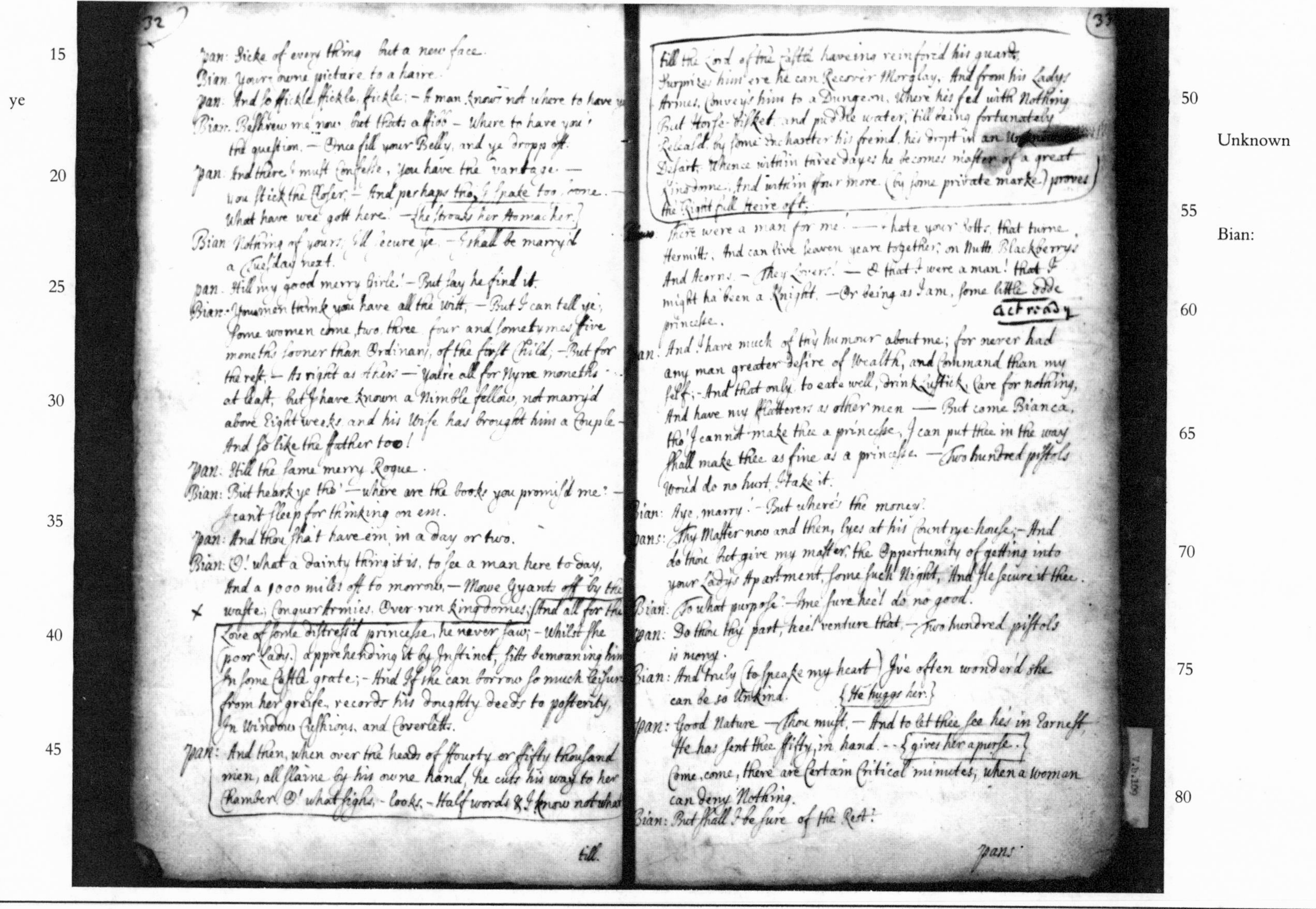

32

Pan: Sicke of every thing but a new face.
Bian: Your're meere picture to a haire.
Pan: And so fickle, fickle, fickle; — A man know's not where to have y
Bian: Beshrew me now but that's a kiss — Where to have you? the question. — Once fill your Belly, and ye dropp off.
Pan: And there I must Confesse, you have the vantage. — You stick the Closer, — And perhaps tho' I spake too, some. What have wee gott here. — {she strokes her stomacher.}
Bian: Nothing of yours; I'll secure ye. — I shall be marry'd a Tuesday next.
Pan: Still my good merry Girle! — But say he find it.
Bian: You men think you have all the Witt; — But I can tell ye; Some women come two three four and sometymes five moneths sooner than Ordinary of the first Child, — But for the rest, — As right as them. — You're all for Nyne moneths at least, but I have known a Nimble fellow, not marry'd above Eight weeks and his Wife has brought him a Couple — And so like the father too!
Pan: Still the same merry Rogue.
Bian: But heark ye tho' — where are the books you promis'd me? — I can't sleep for thinking on em.
Pan: And thou shalt have em in a day or two.
Bian: O! what a dainty thing it is, to see a man here to day, And a 1000 miles off to morrow, — Mowe Gyants off by the waste; Conquer Armies. Over run Kingdomes; And all for the Love of some distress'd princesse, he never saw; — Whilst she poor Lady, apprehending it by Instinct, sitts bemoaning him In some Castle grate; — And If she can borrow so much Leisure from her greife, records his doughty deeds to posterity, In Window Cushions, and Coverletts.
Pan: And then, when over the heads of fourty or fifty thousand men, all slaine by his owne hand, he cuts his way to her Chamber! O' what sighs, — Looks. — Half words & I know not what

till.

33

till the End of the fifth haveing reinforc'd his guards, Surprizes him ere he can Recover Morglay, And from his Ladys Armes, Convey's him to a Dungeon, where hee's fed with Nothing But Horse-Bisket, and puddle water; till being fortunately Releas'd by some Enchaunter his freind, hee's dropt in an [illegible] Desart. Whence within three dayes he becomes master of a great Kingdome; And within four more (by some private marke) proves the Right full Heire oft.
[illegible] There were a man for me. — I hate your Sotts, that turne Hermitts, And can live seaven yeare together, on Nutts Blackberrys And Acorns. — They Lovers! — O that I were a man! that I might ha' been a Knight. — Or being as I am, some little odde princesse. act ready
Pan: And I have much of thy humour about me; for never had any man greater desire of Wealth, and Command than my self; — And that only to eate well, drink Justick, Care for nothing, And have my flatterers as other men — But come Bianca, tho' I cannot make thee a princesse, I can put thee in the way shall make thee as fine as a princesse. — Two hundred pistols Would do no hurt, I take it.
Bian: Aye, marry. — But where's the money?
Pans: Thy Master now and then, lyes at his Countrye-house; — And do thou but give my master, the Opportunity of getting into your Lady's Apartment, some such Night, And I'le secure it thee.
Bian: To what purpose? — Ime sure hee'l do no good.
Pan: Do thou thy part, hee'l venture that. — Two hundred pistols is mony.
Bian: And truly (to speake my heart) I've often wonder'd she can be so Unkind. {He huggs her.}
Pan: Good Nature — thou must, — And to let thee see he's in Earnest He has sent thee fifty in hand. — {gives her a purse.} Come, come, there are Certain Critical minutes, when a woman can deny Nothing.
Bian: But shall I be sure of the Rest?

Pans

ye

Unknown

Bian:

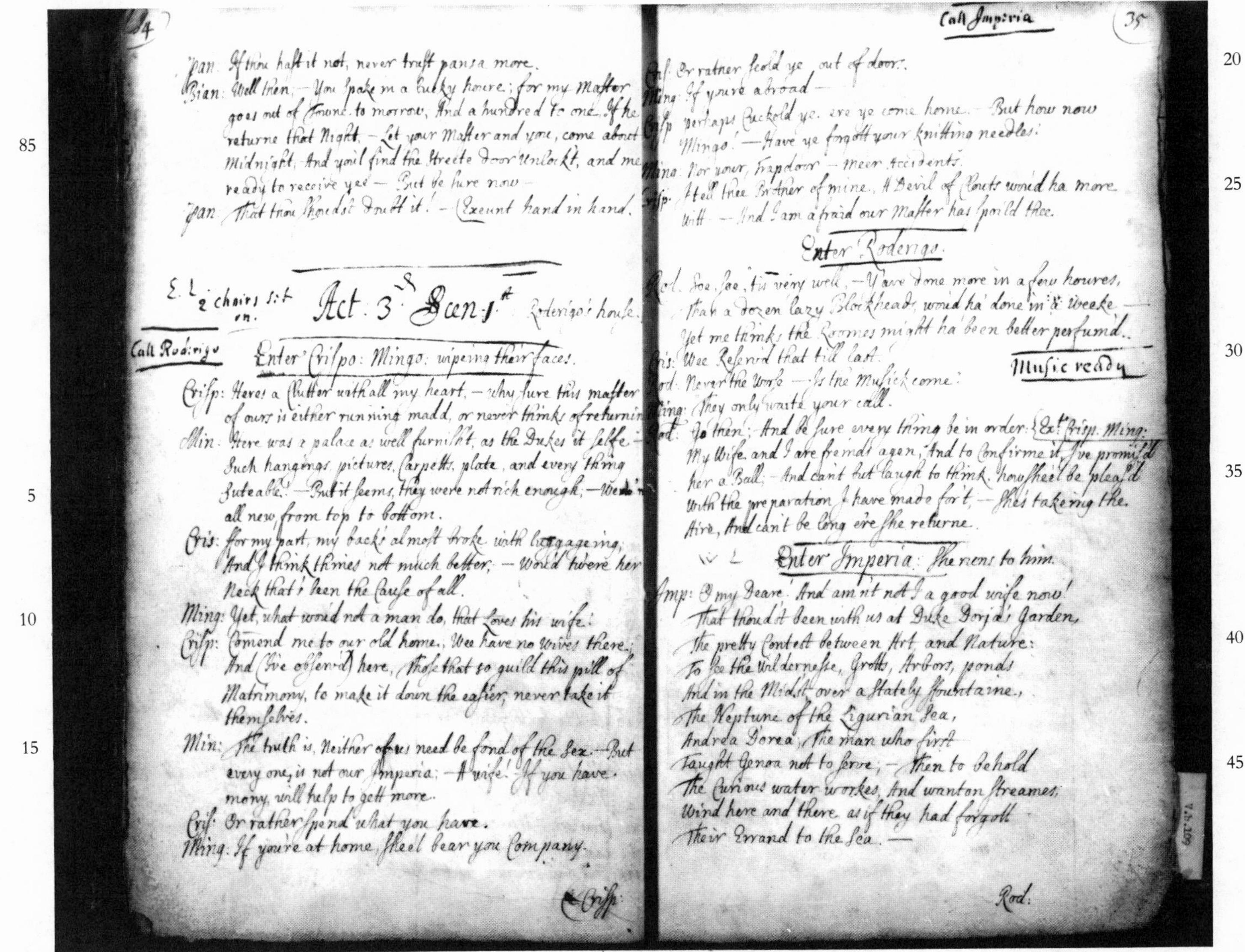

34

Pan: If thou hast it not, never trust Pansa more.

Bian: Well then; — You spake in a lucky houre; for my Master goes out of Towne to morrow, And a hundred to one, If he returne that Night. — Let your Master and you, come about Midnight, And you'l find the Streete doore Unlockt, and me ready to receive yee — But be sure now —

Pan: That thou should'st Doubt it! — Exeunt hand in hand.

E. L. 2 chairs set on.

Act. 3d Scen. 1st Roderigo's house.

Call Rodrigo

Enter Crispo: Mingo: wipeing their faces.

Crisp: Heres a Clutter with all my heart, — why sure this master of ours is either running madd, or never thinks of returnin[g]

Min: Here was a palace as well furnisht, as the Dukes it selfe — Such hangings, pictures, Carpetts, plate, and every thing suteable. — But it seems, they were not rich enough, — Wee'd all new from top to bottom.

Cris: for my part, my back's almost broke with luggageing; And I think thine's not much better; — Would t'were her Neck that's been the Cause of all.

Ming: Yet, what would not a man do, that Loves his wife!

Crisp: Comend me to our old home., Wee have no Wives there; And (I've observ'd) here, those that so guild this pill of Matrimony, to make it down the easier, never take it themselves.

Min: The truth is, Neither of us need be fond of the Sex. — But every one, is not our Imperia: — A wife! If you have mony, will help to gett more.

Cris: Or rather spend what you have.

Ming: If you're at home, sheel bear you Company.

Crisp:

Call Imperia 35

Cris: Or rather scold ye, out of door.

Ming: If you're abroad —

Crisp: perhaps Cuckold ye, ere ye come home. — But how now Mingo! — Have ye forgott your knitting needles:

Ming: Nor your Trapdoor — meer Accidents.

Crisp: I tell thee Brother of mine, A Devil of Clouts would ha more Witt — And I am afraid our Master has spoil'd thee.

Enter Roderigo.

Rod: Soe, soe, tis very well, — Y'are done more in a few houres, than a dozen lazy Blockheads would ha' done in a weeke — Yet me thinks the Roomes might ha been better perfumd.

Cris: Wee Reserv'd that till last.

Music ready

Rod: Never the worse — Is the Musick come:

Ming: They only waite your call.

Rod: Go then; And be sure every thing be in order. {Ext. Crisp. Ming:
My Wife and I are friends agen; And to Confirme it, I've promis'd
her a Ball; — And can't but laugh to think, how sheel be pleas'd
With the preparation I have made for't, — She's takeing the
Aire, And can't be long ere she returne.

W. L. Enter Imperia: she runs to him.

Imp: O my Deare! And am n't not I a good wife now!
That thou'd'st been with us at Duke Doria's Garden,
The pretty Contest between Art, and Nature:
To see the Wildernesse, Grotts, Arbors, ponds
And in the Midst, over a Stately fountaine,
The Neptune of the Ligurian Sea,
Andrea Dorea, The man who first
Taught Genoa not to serve, — Then to behold
The Curious water workes, And wanton Streames,
Wind here and there, as if they had forgott
Their Errand to the Sea. —

Rod:

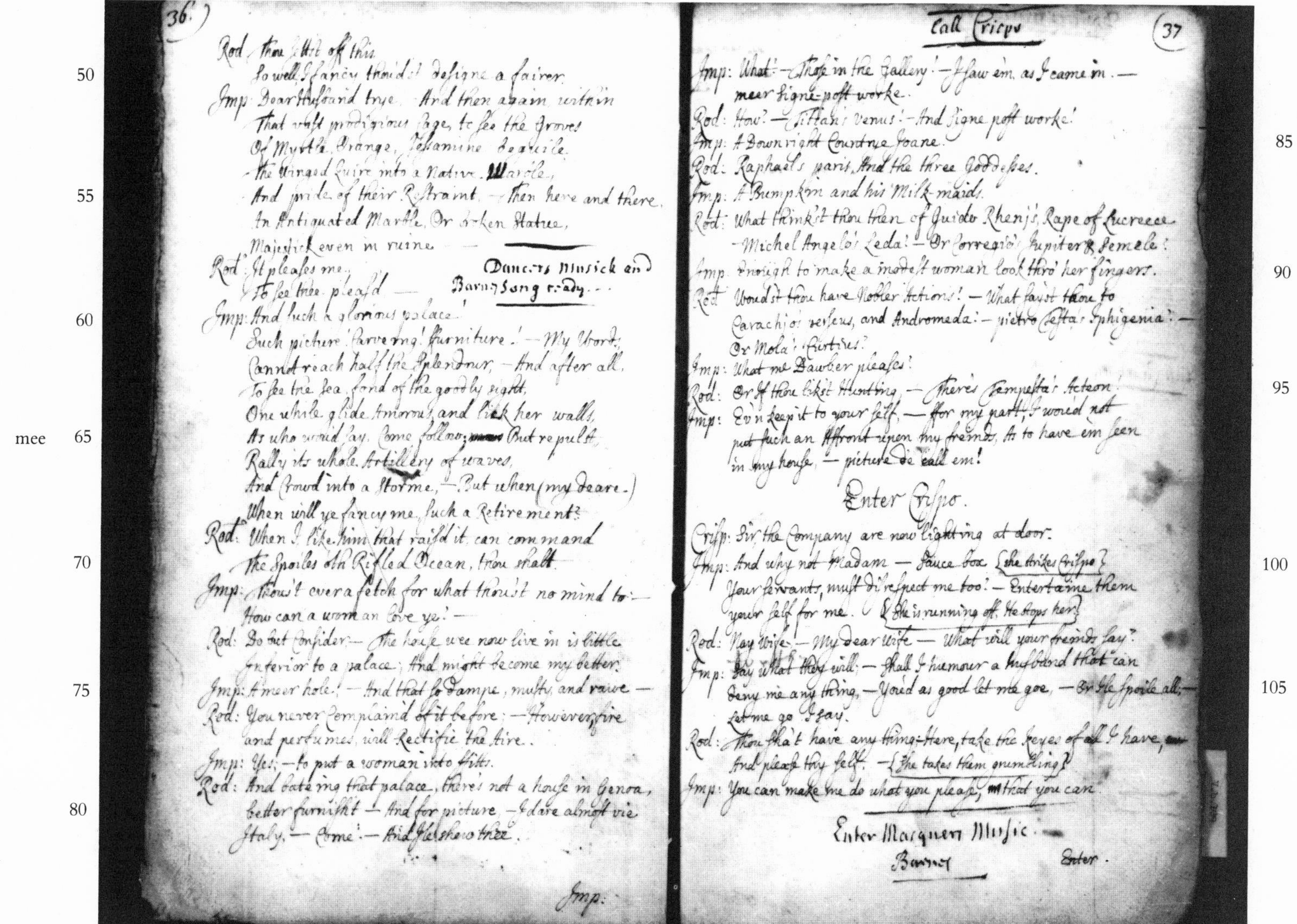

36

Rod, thou settst of this
So well, I fancy thou'dst designe a fairer.
Imp: Dear Husband trye. And then again within
That vast prodigious Page, to see the Groves
Of Myrtle, Orange, Jessamine & [illegible]
The Winged Quire into a Native Warble,
And pride of their Restraint. — then here and there
An Antiquated Marble, Or broken Statue,
Majestick even in ruine. —
Rod: It pleases me,
To see thee pleas'd — Dancers Musick and Barns Song ready.
Imp: And such a glorious palace!
Such picture! Carveing! Furniture! — My Word;
Cannot reach half the Splendour, — And after all,
To see the Sea, fond of the goodly sight,
One while glide Amorous, and lick her walls,
mee
As who would say, Come follow — But repulst,
Rally its whole Artillery of waves,
And Crowd into a Storme, — But when (my deare)
When will ye fancy me such a Retirement?
Rod: When I, like him that rais'd it, can command
The Spoiles o'th Rifled Ocean, thou shalt.
Imp: Thou'rt ever a fetch for what thou'st no mind to —
How can a woman love ye? —
Rod: Do but Consider — the house wee now live in is little
Inferior to a palace; And might become my better.
Imp: A meer hole! — And that so Dampe, musty, and rawe —
Rod: You never Complain'd of it before; — However, fire
and perfumes, will Rectifie the Aire.
Imp: Yes; — to put a woman into Fitts.
Rod: And bate me that palace, there's not a house in Genoa,
better furnisht — And for picture — I dare almost vie
Italy. — Come! — And I'le shew thee.
Imp:

Call Crispo 37

Imp: What! — Those in the Gallery! — I saw 'em, as I came in. —
meer Signe-post worke.
Rod: How? — Tittian's Venus! — And Signe post worke!
Imp: A Downright Countrie Joane.
Rod: Raphael's paris, And the three Goddesses.
Imp: A Bumpkin and his Milk-maids.
Rod: What think'st thou then of Guido Rhenis, Rape of Lucreece
— Michel Angelo's Leda! — Or Correggio's Jupiter & Semele!
Imp: Enough to make a modest woman look thro' her fingers.
Rod: Would'st thou have Nobler Actions! — What saist thou to
Caracchio's perseus, and Andromeda! — pietro Testa's Iphigenia! —
Or Mola's Histories?
Imp: What me Dauber pleases!
Rod: Or if thou likst Hunting, — there's Tempesta's Acteon.
Imp: Ev'n keep it to your self, — for my part, I would not
put such an Affront upon my friends, As to have 'em seen
in my house, — picture de call 'em!
Enter Crispo.
Crisp: Sir, the Company are now lighting at door.
Imp: And why not Madam — Sauce box [She strikes Crispo]
Your servants, must disrespect me too! — Entertaine them
your self for me. [She is running off, He stops her]
Rod: Nay Wife! — My dear Wife — What will your friends say?
Imp: Say what they will: — Shall I humour a husband that can
deny me any thing, — You'd as good let me goe, — Or I'le spoile all; —
let me go I say.
Rod: Thou sha't have any thing: Here, take the keyes of all I have,
And please thy self. [She takes them grumbling]
Imp: You can make me do what you please, that you can.
Enter Masquers Music.
Barns Enter.

they seate thems[elves]

a dance of all
They seate themselves
but Rod: & Imperia

of all but Rod. & Imperia—

The . . . ends . . . agen

Cherry

With

Whoo

you'd

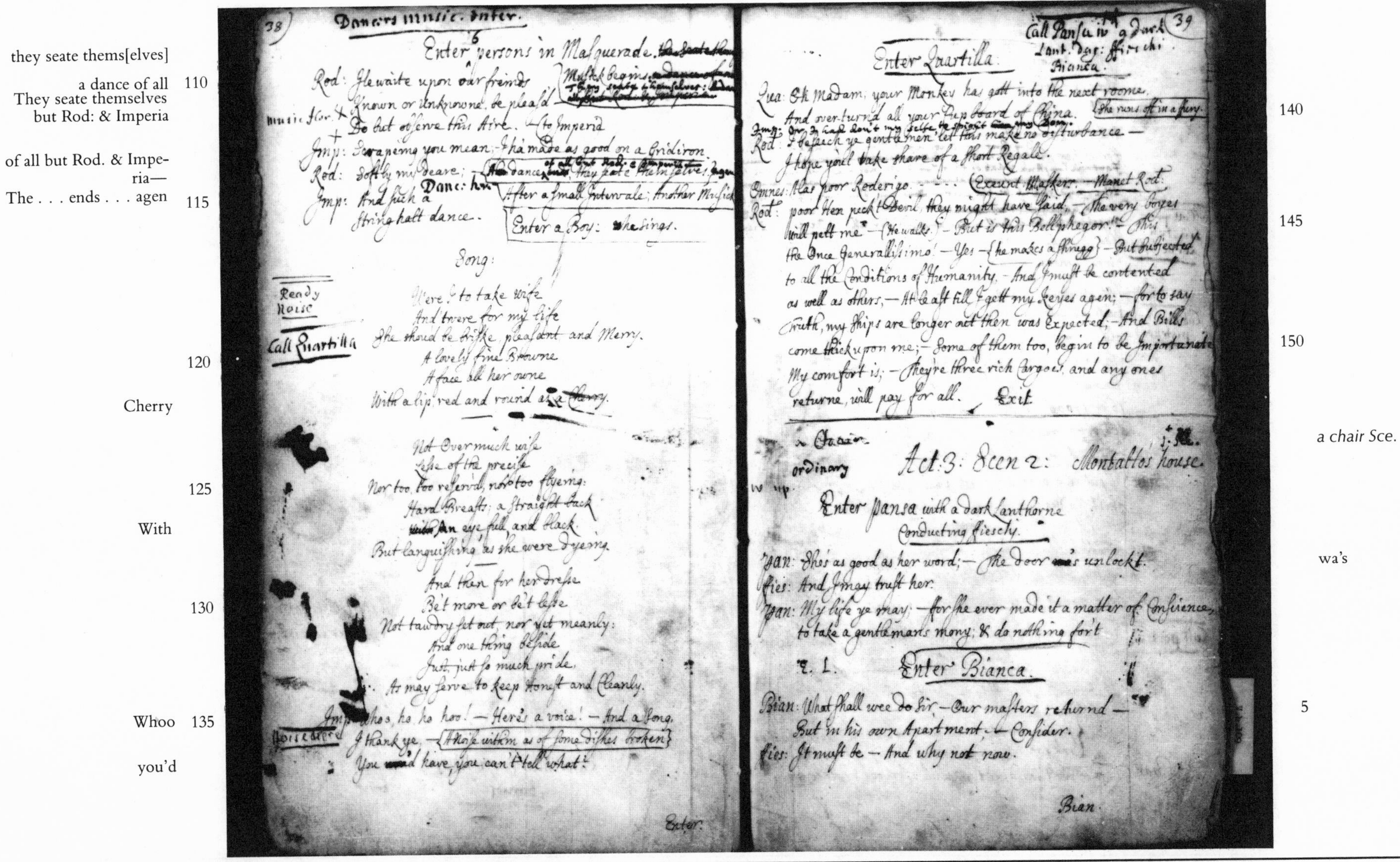
38 Dancers musick. enter.

Enter persons in Masquerade.

Rod: Ile waite upon our friends [Musick begins]
Known or unknowne, be pleas'd
Do but observe this Aire. — to Imperia
Imp: Scraping you mean: — I ha'made as good on a Gridiron
Rod: Softly my deare; — [A dance . . . they seate themselves: agen]
Imp: And such a String-halt dance. Dance: [After a small Intervale; Another Musick
Enter a Boy: who sings.]

Ready Noise

Call Quartilla

Song:

Were I to take wife
And were for my life
She should be briske pleasant and Merry.
A lovely fine Browne
A face all her owne
With a lip, red and round as a Cherry.

Not Overmuch wise
Nor of the precise
Nor too too refin'd, nor too flyeing:
Hard Breasts: a straight back
An eye full and black
But languishing as she were dyeing.

And then for her dresse
Be't more or be't lesse
Not tawdry set out, nor yet meanly:
And one thing beside
Just, just so much pride
As may serve to keep honest and cleanly.

Imp: Whoo, ho, ho hoo! — Here's a voice! — And a song.
I thank ye. — [Those within as of some dishes broken]
You woud have you can't tell what:

Enter.

Call Pansa w a dark Lant: Fiesci Bianca 39

Enter Quartilla.

Qua: Oh Madam: your Monkey has gott into the next roome
And over-turn'd all your Cup-board of China. [She runs off in a fury.
Imp: Or I had don't my selfe to spight my Don.
Rod: I beseech ye gentlemen let this make no disturbance. —
I hope you'l take share of a short Regale.
Omnes: Alas poor Roderigo. — [Exeunt Maskers. — Manet Rod.
Rod: poor Hen peckt Devil they might have said, — The very boyes will pelt me — (He walks.) — But is this Belphegor! — This the Once Generallissimo! — Yes — (he makes a shrugg) — But subjected to all the Conditions of Humanity. — And I must be contented as well as others, — At least till I gett my Leases agen; — for to say truth, my ships are longer out then was Expected; — And Bills come thick upon me; — Some of them too, begin to be Importunate My comfort is; — They're three rich Cargoes, and any ones returne, will pay for all. Exit.

a Chair ordinary

Act 3: Scen 2: Montalto's house.

Enter Pansa with a dark Lanthorne
Conducting Fiescly.

Pan: She's as good as her word; — The door was unlockt.
Fies: And I may trust her.
Pan: My life ye may; — for she ever made it a matter of Conscience, to take a gentleman's mony; & do nothing for't

Enter Bianca.

Bian: What shall wee do Sir, — Our masters returnd —
But in his own Apartment. — Consider.
Fies: It must be — And why not now.

Bian.

a chair Sce.

wa's

III, i, 140. The added line is: "Imp: Or I had don't my selfe, to spight ~~him~~ my Don."

III, ii, opening. Some of the notes are hard to decipher. The *ordinary* was the machinist's label for the setting to be used for Montalto's house. Why this is called the j^t. ~~Sce~~ (1st Scene) I do not understand, since that would refer back to the setting for Roderigo's house. Probably the whole note was supposed to be canceled.

call peer

Smeton

all

en[d]

Bia[nca]

Exit

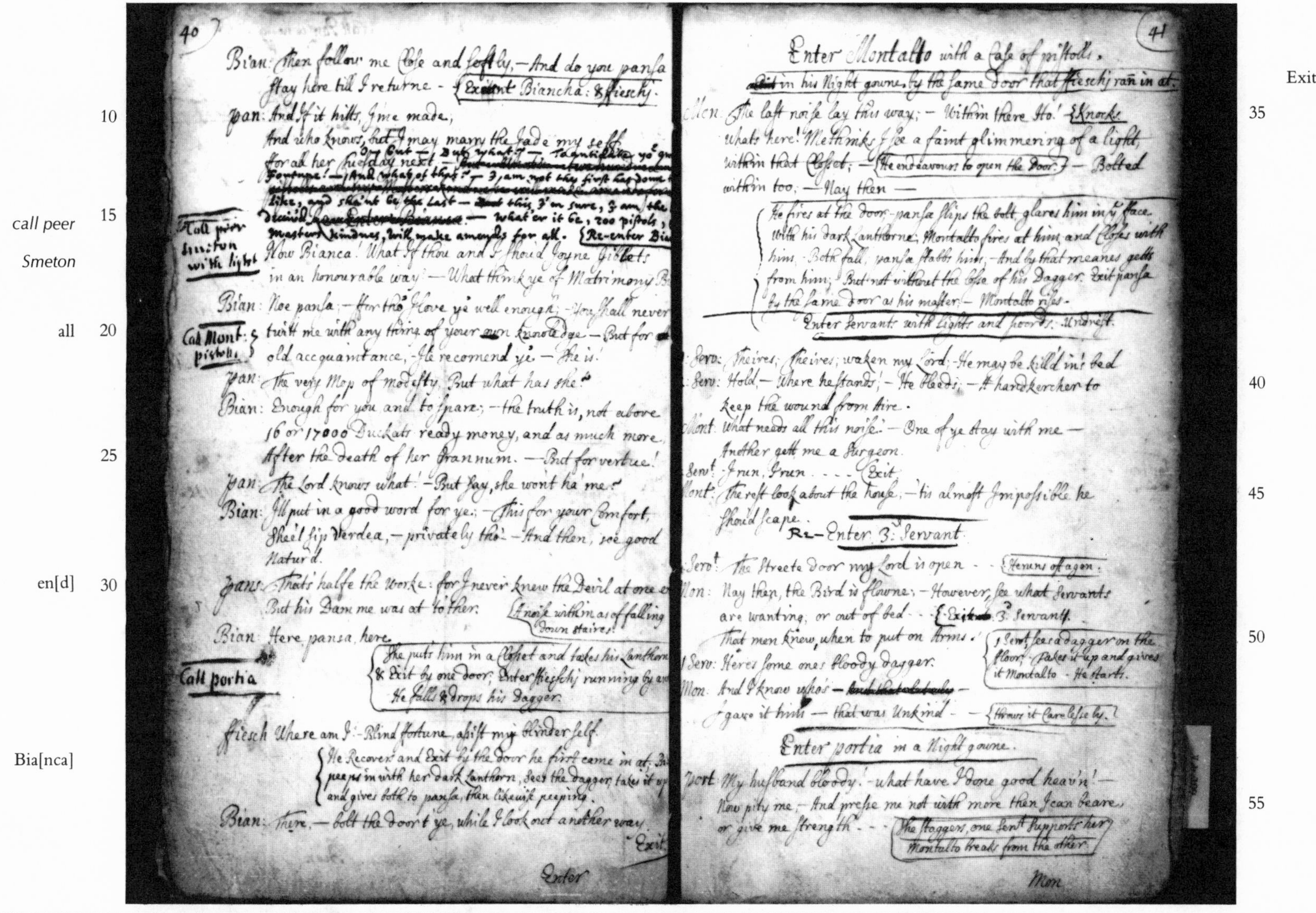
40

Bian: Then follow me close and softly, — And do you pansa
stay here till I returne — {Exeunt Bianca: & fieschy.
pan: And if it hitts, I'me made,
And who knows, but I may marry the Jade my selfe
for all her Holiday next — [deleted lines]
...
Now Bianca: What if thou and I should Joyne Giblets
in an honourable way — What think ye of Matrimony B
Bian: Noe pansa; — for tho' I love ye well enough; — You shall never
twitt me with any thing of your own knowledge — But for
old acquaintance, I'le recomend ye. — She is.
pan: The very Mop of modesty, But what has she?
Bian: Enough for you and to spare; — the truth is, not above
16 or 17000 Duckats ready money, and as much more,
After the death of her Grannum. — But for vertue!
pan: The Lord knows what! — But stay, she wont ha' me?
Bian: I'll put in a good word for ye; — This for your Comfort,
Shee'l sip Verdea, — privately tho' — And then, soe good
Natur'd.
pans: That's halfe the Worke: for I never knew the Devil at once e
But his Dam me was at t'other. {A noise within as of falling down staires.
Bian: Here pansa, here.
{She puts him in a Closet and takes his Lanthorn & Exit by one door; Enter fieschi running by an He falls & drops his Dagger.
fiesch: Where am I? — Blind fortune, shift my blinder selfe.
{He Recovers and Exit by the door he first came in at. Bi peeps in with her dark Lanthorn, sees the Dagger, takes it up and gives both to pansa, then likewise peeping.
Bian: there, — bolt the door t'ye, while I look out another way.
Exit
Enter

Call peer Smeton with light
Call Mont: & pistolls
Call portia

41

Enter Montalto with a case of pistolls.
in his Night gowne, by the same door that fieschi ran in at.
Mon: The last noise lay this way; — Within there Ho! {Knocks
whats here! Methinks I see a faint glimmering of a light,
within that Closet; — {He endeavours to open the Door.} — Bolted
within too; — Nay then —
{He fires at the door — pansa slips the bolt, glares him in ye face
With his dark Lanthorne; Montalto fires at him, and Closes with
him, Both fall, pansa stabbs him, — And by that meanes getts
from him; But not without the losse of his Dagger. Exit pansa
by the same door as his master. — Montalto rises.
Enter servants with Lights and swords. Undrest.
Serv: Theives; Theives; waken my Lord; He may be kill'd in's bed
Serv: Hold, — Where he stands; — He bleeds; — A handkercher to
keep the wound from Aire.
Mont: What needs all this noise. — One of ye stay with me —
Another gett me a Surgeon.
Serv: I run, I run . . . Exit
Mont: The rest look about the house; — tis almost Impossible he
should scape.
Re-Enter 3: Servant
Serv: The Streete door my Lord is open . . {Returns agen.
Mon: Nay then, the Bird is flowne; — However, see what Servants
are wanting, or out of bed . . {Exit 3: Servant.
That men knew, when to put on Arms.
1 Serv: Here's some ones bloody dagger. {1 Servt sees a dagger on the floor, Takes it up and gives it Montalto — He starts.
Mon: And I know who's — [illegible] —
I gave it him — that was Unkind — {Throws it Carelesly.
Enter portia in a Night gowne.
port: My husband bloody! — what have I done good heav'n! —
Now pity me; — And presse me not with more then I can beare,
or give me strength . . {She staggers, one Servt Supports her, Montalto treads from the other.
Mon

III, ii, between 11 and 16. Wilson deleted one and a half lines and a reentry stage direction for Bianca and substituted the following: "O—but—But what?—To antidate yo[r] own / Fortune!—And what of that?—I am not the first has done / like, and sha'nt be the Last—~~But~~ this I am sure, I am the / deceiv'd. —What'er it be, 200 pistols, [& my] / Masters kindnes, Will make amends for all. Re-enter Bian[ca]."

III, ii, following 46. Three servants were indicated by the author, but the warning shows that only two were used—played by the actors Peer and Smeton, who were warned at line 15.

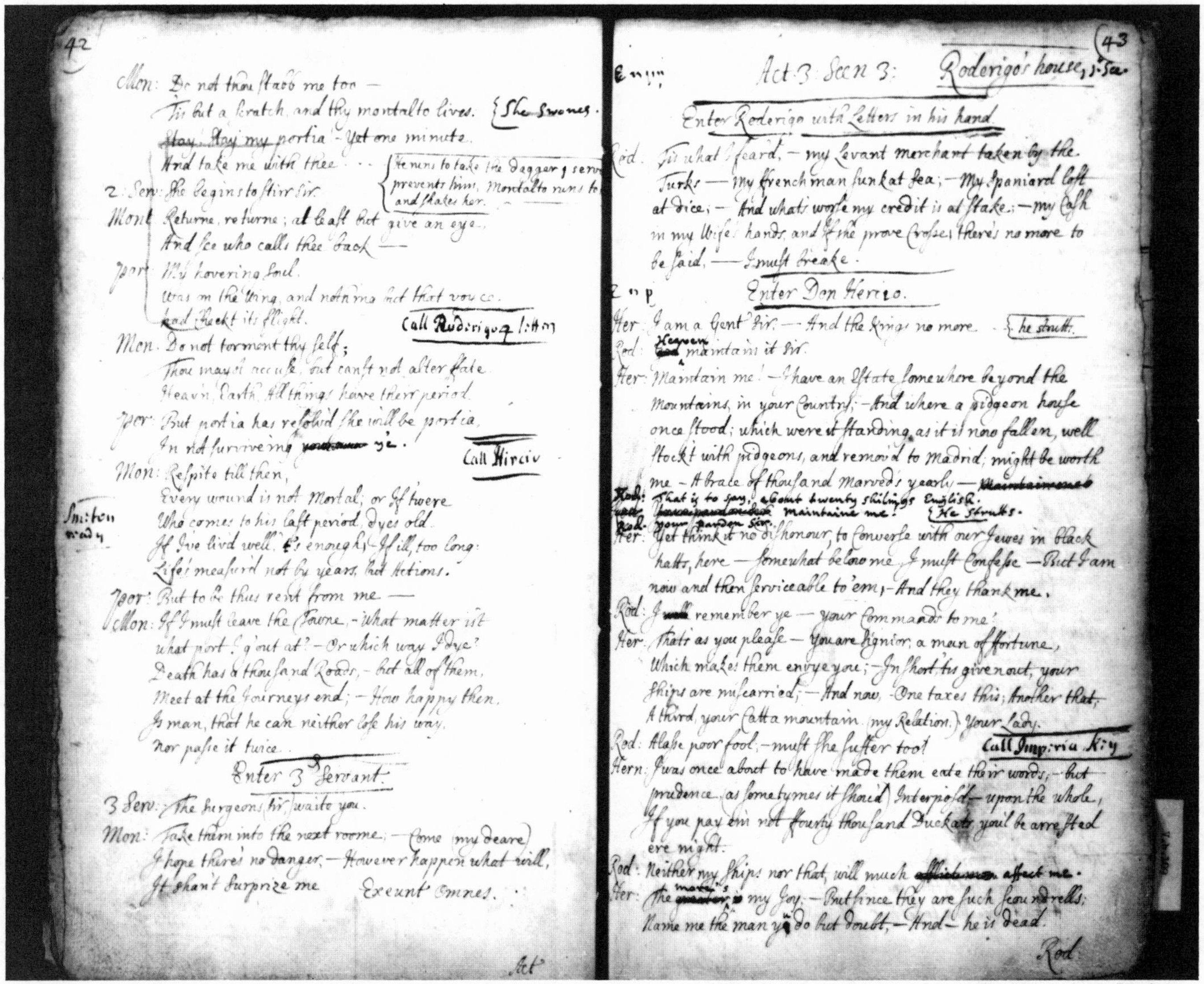

42

Mon: Do not thou stabb me too —
Tis but a scratch, and thy montalto lives. {She swones.
~~Stay, Stay my~~ portia - Yet one minute.
And take me with thee . . {He runs to take the dagger & serv prevents him, Montalto runs to and shakes her.
2 Serv: She begins to stirr Sir.
Mont: Returne, returne; at least but give an eye,
And see who calls thee back —
Por: My hovering soul.
Was on the wing, and nothing but that voyce.
had checkt its flight. Call Rodrigo & letters
Mon: Do not torment thy self;
Thou mayst accuse, but canst not alter fate
Heav'n, Earth, All things have their period.
Por: But portia has resolv'd she will be portia,
In not surviveing ye.
Call Hircio
Mon: Respite till then,
Every wound is not Mortal; or if twere
Who comes to his last period, dyes old.
If I've liv'd well, t's enough; If ill, too long:
Life's measur'd not by years, but Actions.
Smiton ready
Por: But to be thus rent from me —
Mon: If I must leave the Towne, - What matter is't
what port I go out at? - Or which way I dye?
Death has a thousand Roads, - but all of them,
Meet at the Journeys end; - How happy then
Is man, that he can neither lose his way,
Nor passe it twice.
Enter 3d Servant.
3 Serv: The surgeons, sir, waite you.
Mon: Take them into the next roome; — Come (my deare)
I hope there's no danger; — However happen what will,
It shan't surprize me Exeunt Omnes.
Act

43

Act 3 Scen 3: Roderigo's house, 1 Sce.
Enter Roderigo with Letters in his hand
Rod: Tis what I feard, — my Levant merchant taken by the Turks — My Frenchman sunk at sea; — My Spaniard lost at dice; — And what's worse my credit is at stake; — my Cash in my Wife's hands, and if she prove Crosse, there's no more to be said, — I must breake.
Enter Don Herrio.
Her: I am a Gent Sir. — And the King's no more. {he strutts.
Rod: Heaven maintain it Sir.
Her: Maintain me! — I have an Estate somewhere beyond the Mountains, in your Country; - And where a pidgeon house once stood; which were it standing, as it is now fallen, well stockt with pidgeons, and remov'd to Madrid; might be worth me - A brace of thousand Marvedi's yearly — ~~Maintaine me~~
Rod: That is to say, about twenty shillings English.
Her: Maintaine me! {He Strutts.
Rod: your pardon Sir.
Her: Yet think it no dishonour, to converse with our Jewes in black hatts, here — somewhat below me, I must Confesse — But I am now and then serviceable to 'em; - And they thank me.
Rod: I remember ye — your Commands to me!
Her: That's as you please — You are signior, a man of fortune, Which makes them envye you; - In short, tis given out, your ships are miscarried; — And now, - One taxes this; Another that; A third, your Catta mountain (my Relation,) Your Lady.
Rod: Alasse poor fool, - must she suffer too! Call Imperia Key
Hern: I was once about to have made them eate their words; - but prudence, (as sometymes it shou'd) Interpos'd — upon the whole, If you pay 'em not fourty thousand Duckats you'l be arrested ere night.
Rod: Neither my ships nor that, will much ~~afflict me~~ affect me.
Her: The ~~greater is~~ more's my Joy. - But since they are such scoundrells; Name me the man you do but doubt, — And — he is dead.
Rod

you

Heaven

Maintain me!

Rod: Your pardon Sir.

well

afflict me.
greater is

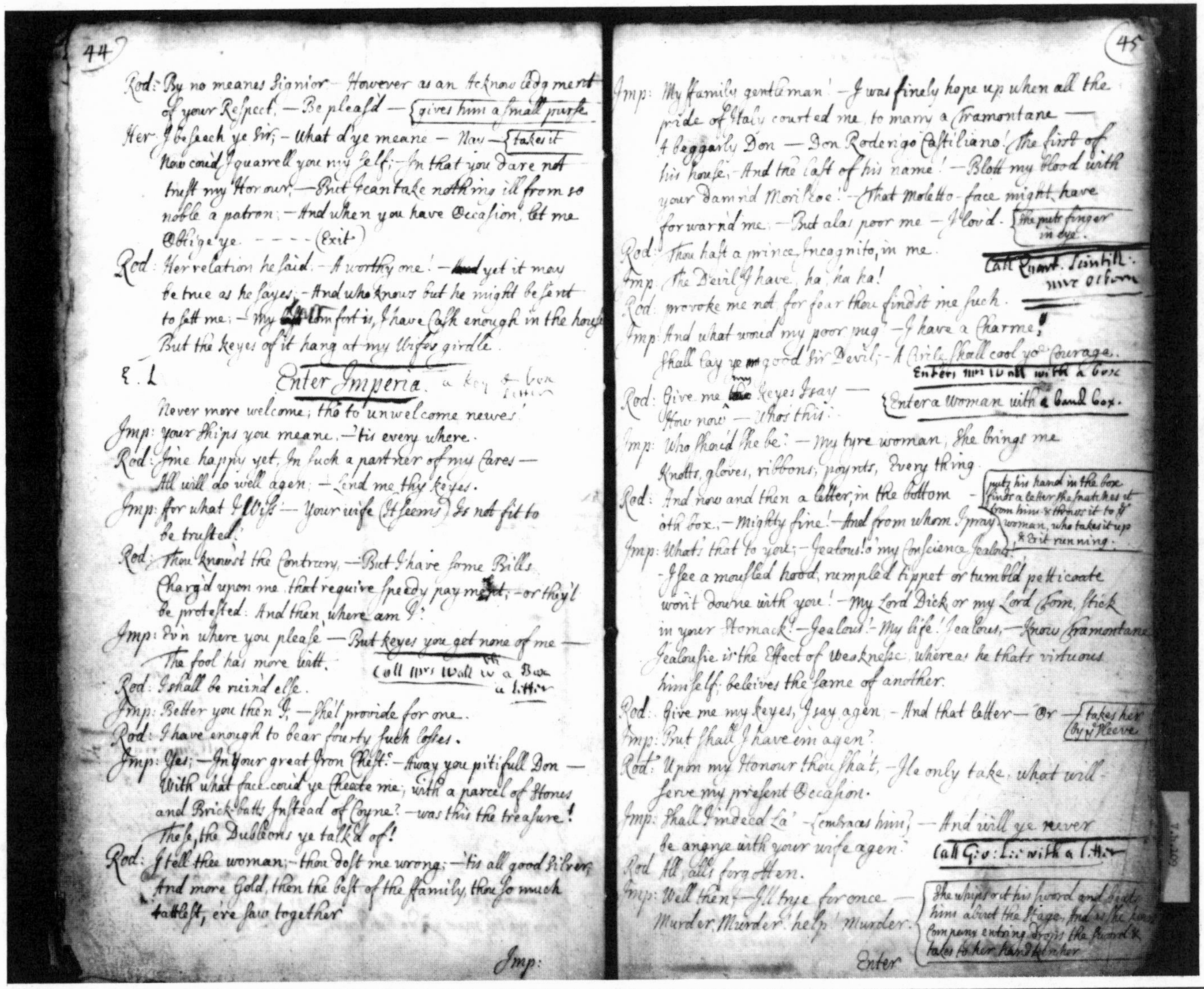

44

Rod: By no meanes Signior — However as an Acknowledgment of your Respect, — Be pleas'd — {gives him a small purse

Her: I beseech ye Sir; — What d'ye meane — Nay — {takes it

Now cou'd I quarrell you my selfe; — In that you dare not trust my Honour, — But I can take nothing ill from so noble a patron; — And when you have Occasion, let me Oblige ye. - - - - (Exit)

Rod: Her relation he said. — A worthy one! — And yet it may be true as he sayes; — And who knows but he might be sent to fett me; — My last comfort is, I have Cash enough in the house But the keyes of it hang at my Wifes girdle.

E. L Enter Imperia. a key & box letter

Never more welcome; tho to unwelcome newes!

Imp: Your Ships you meane. — tis every where.

Rod: I'me happy yet, In such a partner of my Cares — All will do well agen; — Lend me thy keyes.

Imp: for what I Wis — Your wife (It seems) Is not fit to be trusted.

Rod: Thou know'st the Contrary, — But I have some Bills Charg'd upon me that require speedy payment, — or they'l be protested: And then where am I?

Imp: Ev'n where you please — But keyes you get none of me — The fool has more witt. Call Mrs Wall wth a Box a letter

Rod: I shall be ruin'd else.

Imp: Better you then I, — she'l provide for one.

Rod: I have enough to bear fourty such losses.

Imp: Yes; — In your great Iron Chest. — Away you pitifull Don — With what face cou'd ye cheate me; with a parcel of Stones and Brick-batts; Instead of Coyne? — was this the treasure! These, the Dubloons ye talk'd of!

Rod: I tell thee woman; — thou dost me wrong; — tis all good Silver, And more Gold, then the best of thy family, thou so much talk'st, e're saw together

Imp:

45

Imp: My family gentleman! — I was finely hope up when all the pride of Italy courted me, to marry a Tramontane — A beggarly Don — Don Rodrigo Castiliano! The first of his house, — And the last of his name! — Blott my blood with your damn'd Morisco! — That Moletto-face might have forwarn'd me. — But alas poor me — I lov'd. {She puts finger in eye.

Rod: Thou hast a prince, Incognito, in me. Call Quart. Scintill: Mrs Osborn

Imp: The Devil I have, ha, ha ha!

Rod: provoke me not for fear thou find'st me such.

Imp: And what urged my poor mug — I have a Charme! shall lay ye good Sir Devil; — A Girdle shall cool yor Courage. Enter Mrs Wall with a box

Rod: Give me thy keyes I say — How now — Who's this! {Enter a Woman with a band box.

Imp: Who shou'd she be! — My tyre woman, she brings me Knotts, gloves, ribbons, poynts, Every thing

Rod: And now and then a letter, in the bottom oth' box. — Mighty fine! — And from whom I pray {puts his hand in the box finds a letter. she snatches it from him & throws it to ye woman, who takes it up & Exit running.

Imp: What's that to you; — Jealous! o my Conscience Jealous! — I see a mousled hood, rumpled tippet or tumbl'd petticoate won't downe with you! — My Lord Dick or my Lord Tom, stick in your stomack! — Jealous! — My life! Jealous, — Know Tramontane Jealousie is the Effect of Weakness; whereas he that's virtuous himself, beleives the same of another.

Rod: Give me my keyes, I say agen — And that letter — Or — {takes her by ye sleeve.

Imp: But shall I have em agen?

Rod: Upon my Honour thou sha't, — Ile only take what will serve my present Occasion.

Imp: Shall I indeed La! {embraces him} — And will ye never be angrye with your wife agen? Call Gio: L:: with a letter

Rod: All, all's forgotten.

Imp: Well then! — I'll trye for once — Murder, Murder. help! Murder. {She whips out his sword and beats him about the stage, and as the Company enters drops the sword & takes to her hand kercher

Enter

And

last (above canceled "last")

Call Mrs Wall wth a Box a letter

Call Quart. Scintill: Mrs Osborn

Mrs Wall
the

Quartilla

w. & E n[p]

Writ

studying

Read

voyce

Speak

h[eard]

ag' [the]

The best of 't is, I have not farr to goe.

brea[k]

you were. *But see who come here.*

Roder

Large . . . runn, shrink agt ye Wall & run

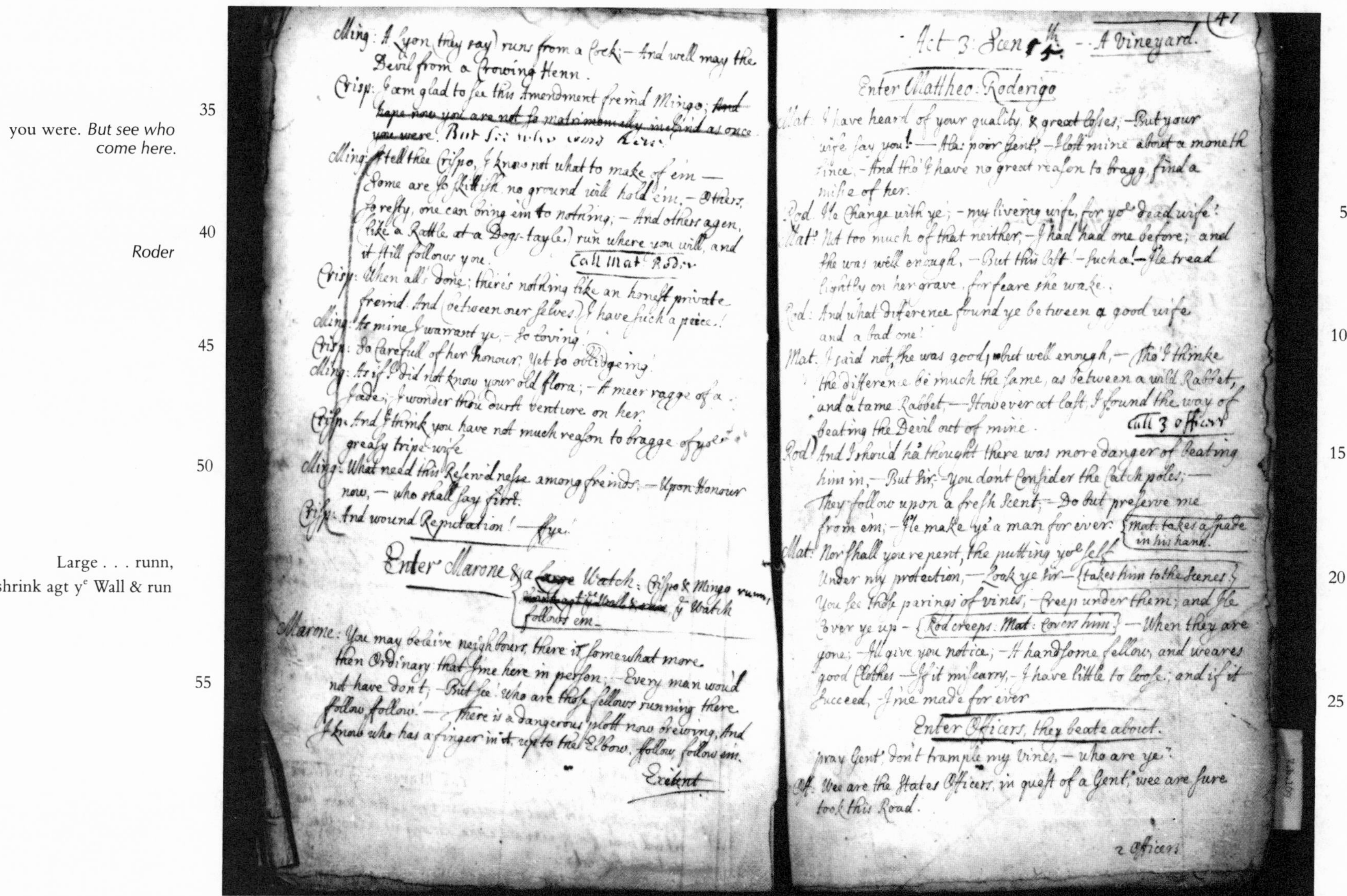

Ming: A Lyon (they say) runs from a Cock; — And well may the
Devil from a Crowing Henn.
Crisp: I am glad to see this Amendment freind Mingo; ~~And
hope now you are not so matrimonially inclin'd as once
you were.~~ But see who come here.
Ming: I tell thee Crispo, I know not what to make of em —
Some are so skittish no ground will hold em, — Others,
so resty, one can bring em to nothing; — And others agen,
(like a Rattle at a Dogs-tayle) run where you will, and
it still follows you. Call Mat: Rodr.
Crisp: When all's done; there's nothing like an honest private
freind. And (between our selves) I have such a peice.!
Ming: As mine I warrant ye, — so loving.
Crisp: So carefull of her honour, Yet so obliging.
Ming: As if I did not know your old flora; — A meer ragge of a
Jade; I wonder thou durst venture on her.
Crisp: And I think you have not much reason to bragge of yor
greasy tripe-wife
Ming: What need this Reserv'dnesse among freinds; — Upon Honour
now, — who shall say first.
Crisp: And wound Reputation! — fye.

Enter Marone & a ~~Large~~ Watch: Crispo & Mingo runn, ~~shrink agt ye Wall & runn~~ & Watch follows em.

Marone: You may beleive neighbours, there is somewhat more
then Ordinary that I'me here in person. — Every man wou'd
not have don't; — But see! who are those fellows running there.
follow, follow! — There is a dangerous plott now brewing, And
I know who has a finger in't, up to the Elbow. follow, follow em.
Exeunt

Act 3: Scen 4th — A Vineyard.

Enter Mattheo: Roderigo

Mat: I have heard of your quality & great losses; — But your
wife say you! — Alas: poor Gent; — I lost mine about a moneth
since; — And tho' I have no great reason to bragg, find a
misse of her.
Rod. I'le Change with ye; — my liveing wife, for yor dead wife!
Mat: Not too much of that neither; — I had had one before; and
she was well enough, — But this last! — such a! — I'le tread
lightly on her grave, for feare she wake.
Rod: And what difference found ye between a good wife
and a bad one!
Mat. I said not, she was good; but well enough, — Tho' I thinke
the difference be much the same, as between a wild Rabbet,
and a tame Rabbet, — However at last, I found the way of
beating the Devil out of mine. Call 3 officers
Rod. And I shou'd ha' thought there was more danger of beating
him in, — But sir, — You don't Consider the Catchpoles; —
They follow upon a fresh Scent; — Do but preserve me
from em; — I'le make ye a man for ever. {Mat. takes a spade in his hand.}
Mat: Nor shall you repent, the putting yor self
Under my protection, — Look ye sir — {takes him to the Scenes.}
You see those parings of vines; — Creep under them; and I'le
Cover ye up — {Rod creeps: Mat: Covers him} — When they are
gone; — I'll give you notice; — A handsome fellow, and weares
good Clothes — If it miscarry, — I have little to loose; and if it
succeed, — I'me made for ever

Enter Officers, they beate about.

pray Gent, don't trample my Vines, — who are ye?
Of. Wee are the States Officers, in quest of a Gent, wee are sure
took this Road.

2 Officers

III, iv, 35. The canceled line is: “hope you are not so matrimonially inclin’d as once.”

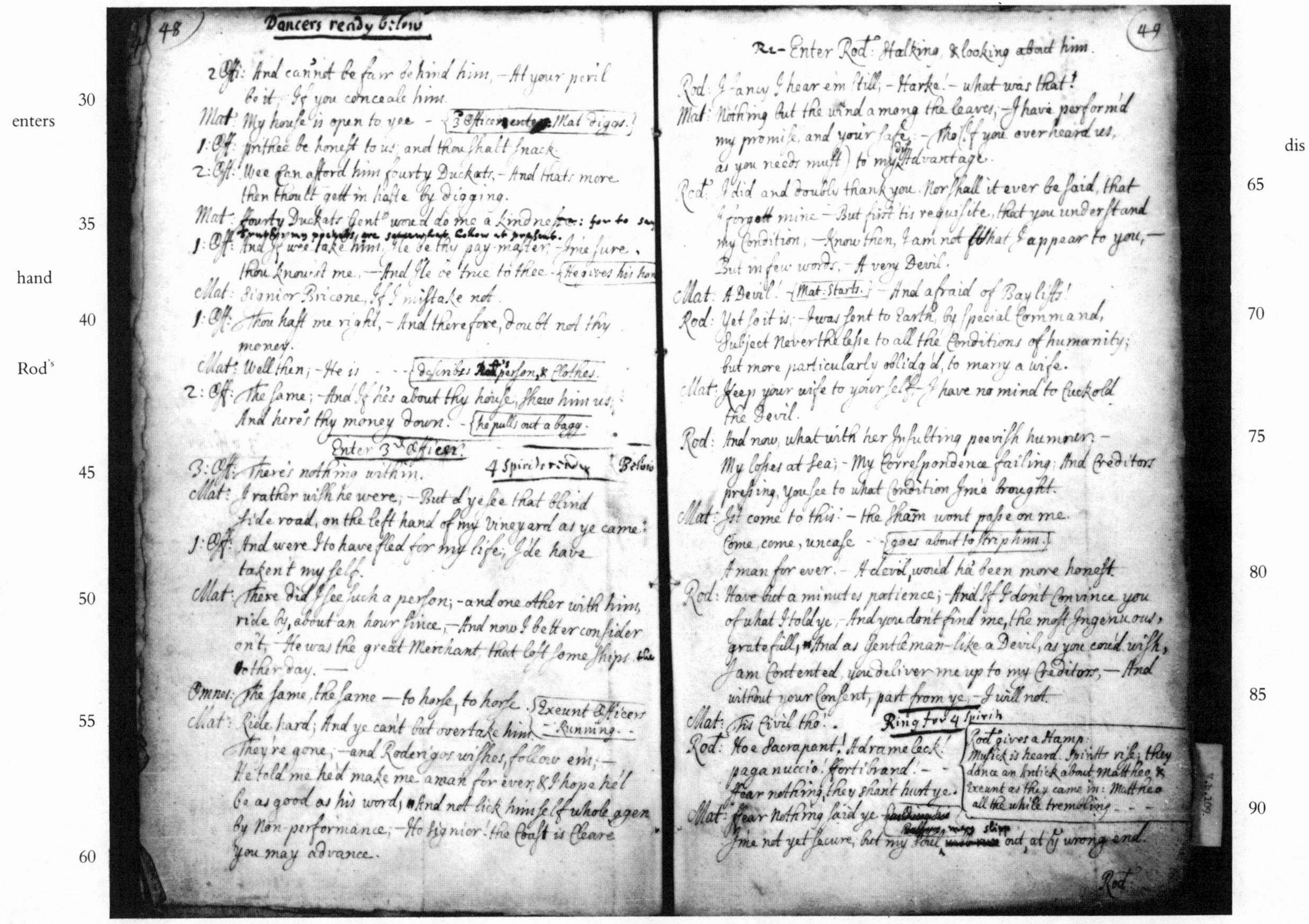

48

Dancers ready below

2 Off: And cannot be far behind him, — At your peril
be it, If you conceale him.
Mat: My house is open to yee — {3 Officer enters Mat diggs.}
1 Off: prithee be honest to us; and thou shalt snack
2 Off: Wee can afford him fourty Duckats, — And thats more
then thoult gett in haste by digging.
Mat: fourty Duckats Gent^o wou'd do me a kindness: for to say
Truth, my pockets are somewhat hollow at present.
1 Off: And if wee take him, Ile be thy pay-master, — Ime sure,
thou knowst me. — And Ile be true to thee. {He gives his hand
Mat: Signior Bricone, If I mistake not.
1 Off: thou hast me right, — And therefore, doubt not thy
money.
Mat: Well then; — He is — — {Describes Rod's person, & Clothes.
2 Off: The same; — And if he's about thy house, shew him us;
And here's thy money down. — {he pulls out a bagg.
Enter 3^d Officer.
4 Spirits ready Below
3 Off: There's nothing within.
Mat: I rather wish he were; — But d'ye see that blind
side road, on the left hand of my Vineyard as ye came:
1 Off: And were I to have fled for my life, I'de have
taken't my self.
Mat: There did I see such a person; — and one other with him,
ride by, about an hour since, — And now I better consider
on't, He was the great Merchant that lost some ships the
other day. —
Omnes: The same, the same — to horse, to horse. {Exeunt Officers
Running.
Mat: Ride hard; And ye can't but overtake him.
They're gone, — and Roderigo's wishes, follow em; —
He told me he'd make me a man for ever, & I hope he'l
be as good as his word, And not lick himself whole agen
by Non-performance, — Ho Signior! the Coast is Cleare
You may advance.

49

Re-Enter Rod: Stalking, & looking about him.

Rod: I fancy I hear em still; — Harke! — what was that!
Mat: Nothing but the wind among the leaves, — I have perform'd
my promise, and your safe; — (tho', If you overheard us,
as you needs must) to my disadvantage.
Rod: I did and doubly thank you. Nor shall it ever be said, that
I forgott mine — But first tis requisite, that you understand
my Condition, — Know then, I am not What I appear to you, —
But in few words, — A very Devil.
Mat: A Devil! {Mat: Starts.} — And afraid of Bayliffs!
Rod: Yet so it is; — I was sent to Earth, by special Command,
Subject Neverthelesse to all the Conditions of humanity;
but more particularly oblidg'd, to marry a wife.
Mat: Keep your wife to your self, — I have no mind to Cuckold
the Devil.
Rod: And now, what with her Insulting peevish humour, —
My losses at Sea; — My Correspondence failing; And Creditors
pressing, You see to what Condition I'me brought.
Mat: Is't come to this: — the Sham wont passe on me.
Come, come, uncase — — {goes about to strip him.}
A man for ever. — A devil, wou'd ha' been more honest.
Rod: Have but a minutes patience; — And if I dont Convince you
of what I told ye, — And you don't find me, the most Ingenuous,
gratefull, And as Gentleman-like a Devil, as you cou'd wish,
I am Contented, you deliver me up to my Creditors, — And
without your Consent, part from ye, — I will not.
Mat: Tis Civil tho'.
Ring for 4 Spirits
Rod: Hoe Sacrapant! Adrameleck!
paganuccio! Fortibrand! — —
Fear nothing, they shan't hurt ye.
{Rod gives a Stamp:
Musick is heard. Spirits rise; they
dance an Antick about Mattheo &
Exeunt as they came in: Mattheo
all the while trembling. — —
Mat: Fear Nothing said ye —
I'me not yet secure, but my Soul may slipp out, at ye wrong end.

Rod

III, v, 31. The stage direction for the entrance of the third officer may be an error, for he enters later at line 44.

III, v, 36. The replacement line is: "Truth, my pockets are somewhat hollow at present."

III, v, 45. The warning for the four spirits is superfluous; they were warned at line 28.1—where they were called dancers.

III, v, following 60. Roderick's entrance was not warned, but he seems never to have left the stage; at line 22 he was covered up with vines by Mattheo.

III, v, 90–91. The deleted word in line 90 is indecipherable; in line 91 "will run" is deleted and "may slipp" is added.

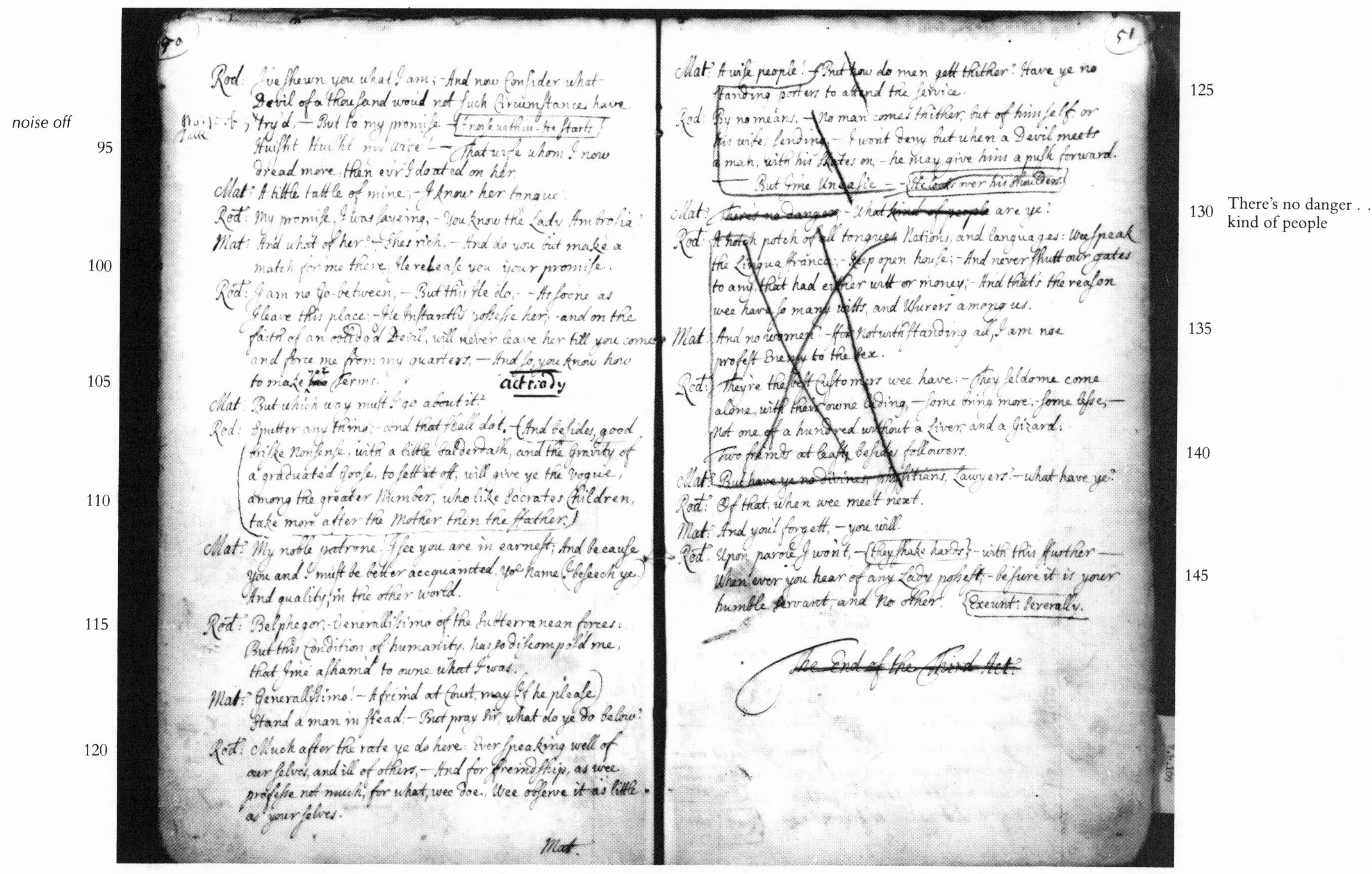

50

Rod: I've shewn you what I am; - And now Consider what Devil of a thousand wou'd not such Circumstances have try'd, — But to my promise. (He looks at him - he starts) Hush't Hush't my wife! — That wife whom I now dread more, then e'er I doated on her.

Mat: A tittle tattle of mine; - I know her tongue.

Rod: My promise, I was sayeing, - You know the Lady Ambrosia?

Mat: And what of her? - Shee's rich, - And do you but make a match for me there, Ile release you your promise.

Rod: I am no Go-between; - But this Ile do, - As soone as I leave this place; - Ile Instantly possesse her; - and on the faith of an outdo'd Devil, will never leave her till you come and force me from my quarters, — And so, you know how to make yor terms. actively [?]

Mat: But which way must I go about it?

Rod: Smutter any thing; - and that shall do't. - (And besides, good strike Nonsense, with a little balderdash, and the Gravity of a graduated Goose, to sett it of, will give ye the Vogue, among the greater Number, who like Socrates Children, take more after the Mother then the Father.)

Mat: My noble patrone! I see you are in earnest; And because You and I must be better acquainted. Yor Name (I beseech ye) And quality, in the other world.

Rod: Belphegor, - Generallissimo of the Subterranean forces: But this Condition of humanity, has so discompos'd me, that I'me asham'd to owne what I was.

Mat: Generallissimo! - A freind at Court, may (if he please) stand a man in stead; - But pray Sir, what do ye do below?

Rod: Much after the rate ye do here: Ever speaking well of our selves, and ill of others, - And for freindship, as wee professe not much; for what, wee doe. Wee observe it as little as your selves.

Mat.

51

Mat: A wise people! - But how do men gett thither? Have ye no standing porters to attend the service.

Rod: By no means, - No man comes thither, but of himselfe or his wife, sending, - I wont deny but when a Devil meets a man, with his skates on, - he may give him a push forward. — But I'me Uneasie — (He looks over his shoulders)

Mat: There's no danger. - What kind of people are ye?

Rod: A hotch potch of all tongues, Nations, and languages: Wee speak the Lingua franca; - keep open house; - And never shutt our gates to any, that had either witt or money; - And that's the reason wee have so many witts, and Usurers among us.

Mat: And no women? - For notwithstanding all, I am noe profest Enemy to the sex.

Rod: They're the best Customers wee have: - they seldome come alone, with their owne leading, - some bring more; - some lesse; - Not one of a hundred without a Liver, and a Gizard. Two friends at least, besides followers.

Mat: But have ye no divines, physitians, Lawyers? - what have ye?

Rod: Of that, when wee meet next.

Mat: And you'l forgett, - you will.

Rod: Upon parole I won't, - (they shake hands) - with this further — When ever you hear of any Lady possest, - be sure it is your humble servant, and no other. (Exeunt: severally.)

The End of the Third Act.

noise off

There's no danger . . . kind of people

III, v, 105. "yor" replaces "the."

52 a Letter. for Imperia

Act 4th Scen: 1. The first Scene.

E. a Letter

a Letter

Enter Imperia Quartilla: Scintilla.

Imp: Our Gentleman it seems, is gone to take the Aire. And I can look about me now without askeing leave.

Qua: He took so little with him; I wonder wee hear nothing of him his proud spirit will come down in tyme.

Scin: But to run away in such a hurry!

Imp: That last note I sent him, did the businesse.

Scin: What made a Gent of his wealth and Credit go off so soon?

Imp: I was privy to none of his Actions; — however so foresaw it as to secure his mony to my self.

mony

Scin: And (with yo Ladyships leave) are you not bound in Honour to set him up agen?

Qua: If I thought he might not be troublesome, I'de perswade my Lady, to take him home agen; And keep him in pocket-money, for her owne Credit.

Imp: No, no: — I'de better remove privately; — And secure what I have: And that the rather; — for if ever I heard any thing in my life, I heard his tread in my Chamber, last night.

Scin: So have I fancy'd a man in Bed with me. — But when all came to all, twas nothing but a Night mare. — However (madam;) Remove where you will: A man is some Credit to a house, — And ours methinks seems naked without him. Call Fieschi

Qua: These Girles never Consider, — wee should have him rummaging the next Band-box agen.

Imp: Oh thou remembrest me . . {She takes out a letter broken open and Reads — .} Terrachino! — The 1000 Crownes I formerly presented your Ladyship, emboldens me! — Ha, ha, ha! — My Lord Lackland! — There — {Throws away the Letter.} Tell her that brought it I have forgott the token. And he must send it again, or t'wont doe. {Quart: takes up the Letter.}

53

Qua: Now not upon him; — had he the Impudence to beleive other! — Noe (madam) You have it 7 yeares yet good, to take; And after that, — You may truck, Barter, or (at worst.) Give.

Enter Fieschi: — {Imperia beckens them off. Exeunt: Qua: Scin:}

Imp: Yo may keep within Call; — And now Fieschi, — wee have no more Excuses here? — And how? — Was my Sister complaisant? — Has good nature yet brought her about.

Fies: Judge of me, as you thinke I deserve: — I had found all open approaches, as troublesome as fruitlesse; — And therefore resolv'd on a Stratagem. — To this purpose I follow'd the hint you gave me; — And engag'd her woman to give me the opportunity of getting into her Apartment; — which (not many Nights since) I attempted. And tho' no one knew the house, better then my self. Yet being in the dark, It was my Misfortune to mistake his Apartment for herr; — Montalto heard me; & sprang out; — I (as well I might) fled; — And by another mistake, fell downe the staires; — He pursu'd, — I recover'd the fall, and gott off —

Imp: As to give ye your due; — You had ever the discretion to save one.

description

Fies: I thank Yo Ladyship, — In short, my servant endeavouring to make up with me, engag'd Montalto, wounded him, and gott off himself: And I know not by what Accident) is since taken; — Or you might have been sure, I'd waited on ye sooner. Call Bianca

Imp: Wou'd thou wert in his roome, — A pretty Story! — And I beleive't! — Noe, thou silly Nothing, — 'Twas thou that hir'dst thy servant, to kill Montalto, — to make roome for thy self; — You were there; — the same was I — I've heard the Story, — A meer Invention of your owne, t'excuse your self, and Choute me.

Fies: You do me wrong, — that my designe miscarry'd is not my fault!

Imp:

Admiration

(perhaps) a

Qua

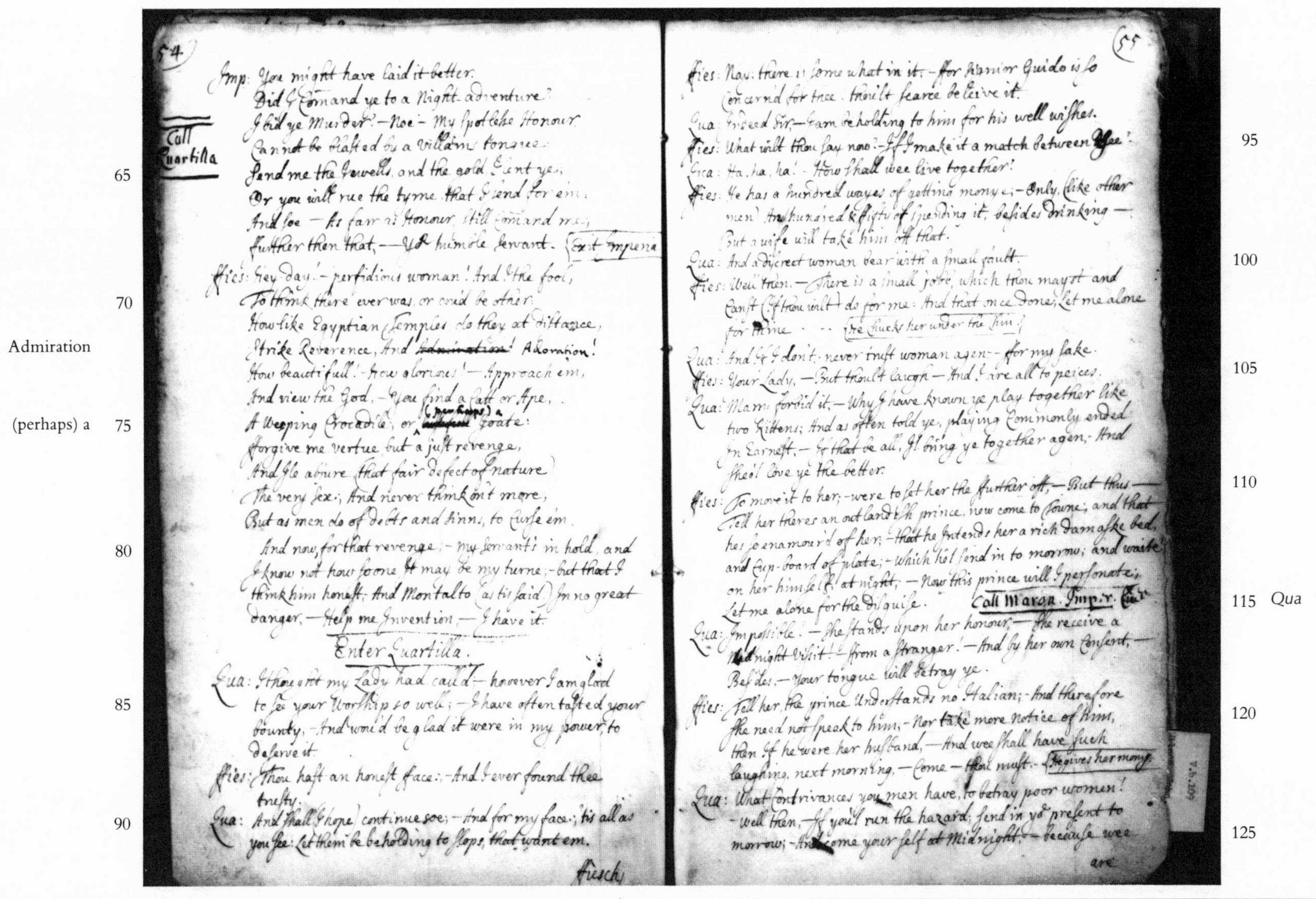
54

Imp: You might have laid it better.
Did I Command ye to a Night-adventure?
I bid ye Murder?—Noe— My spotlesse Honour
Cannot be blasted by a Villains tongue:
Send me the Jewells, and the gold I sent ye;
Or you will rue the tyme that I send for em:
And soe—As far as Honour, still Comand me;
further then that,—Yr humble servant. [Exit Imperia

Call Quartilla

Fies: Hey day!—perfidious woman! And I the fool,
To think there ever was, or could be other:
How like Egyptian Temples do they at distance,
Strike Reverence, And ~~Admiration~~! Adoration!
How beautifull!—How glorious!—Approach em,
And view the God,—You find a Catt or Ape,
A Weeping Crocadile; or ^(perhaps) a ~~[illegible]~~ Goate:
forgive me vertue but a just revenge,
And Ile abjure (that fair defect of nature)
The very sex:; And never think on't more,
But as men do of debts and sinns, to Curse em.
And now, for that revenge;—my servant's in hold, and
I know not how soone It may be my turne;—but that I
think him honest; And Montalto (as tis said) In no great
danger,—Help me Invention,—I have it.

Enter Quartilla.

Qua: I thought my Lady had call'd;—however I am glad
to see your Worship so well;—I have often tasted your
bounty,—And would be glad it were in my power, to
deserve it.
Fies: Thou hast an honest face:—And I ever found thee
trusty.
Qua: And shall (I hope) continue soe;—And for my face:; tis all as
you see: Let them be beholding to slops, that want em.

Fiesch

55

Fies: Nay: there is some what in it;—for Signior Guido is so
Concern'd for thee: thou'lt scarce believe it.
Qua: Indeed Sir,—I am beholding to him for his well wishes.
Fies: What wilt thou say now?—If I make it a match between ~~thee~~ Yee?
Qua: Ha, ha, ha!—How shall wee live together?
Fies: He has a hundred wayes of getting monye;—Only (like other
men) two hundred & fifty of spending it, besides drinking—
But a wife will take him off that.
Qua: And a discreet woman bear with a small fault.
Fies: Well then,—There is a small jobb, which thou mayst and
Canst (if thou wilt) do for me: And that once done; Let me alone
for thine . . . [He chucks her under the chin.]
Qua: And if I don't; never trust woman agen;—for my sake.
Fies: Your Lady,—But thou'lt laugh—And I are all to peices.
Qua: Marry forbid it,—Why I have known ye play together like
two Kittens; And as often told ye, playing Commonly ended
In Earnest,—If that be all, Il bring ye together agen,—And
shee'l love ye the better.
Fies: To move it to her;—were to set her the further off,—But thus—
Tell her theres an outlandish prince, new come to Towne; and that
hes so enamour'd of her;—that he Intends her a rich damaske bed,
and Cup-board of plate;—which hel send in to morrow; and waite
on her himself at night,—Now this prince will I personate;
Let me alone for the disguise. Call Maron. Imp. r. Qua
Qua: Impossible!—she stands upon her honour,—she receive a
Midnight Visit!—from a stranger!—And by her own Consent,—
Besides,—Your tongue will betray ye.
Fies: Tell her, the prince Understands no Italian;—And therefore
she need not speak to him,—Nor take more notice of him,
then If he were her husband,—And wee shall have such
laughing next morning,—Come—thou must.—[He gives her mony.
Qua: What Contrivances you men have, to betray poor women!
—well then,—If you'l run the hazard; send in yr present to
morrow;—And come your self at Midnight:—because wee
are

IV, i, 95. "thee" is altered to "Yee."

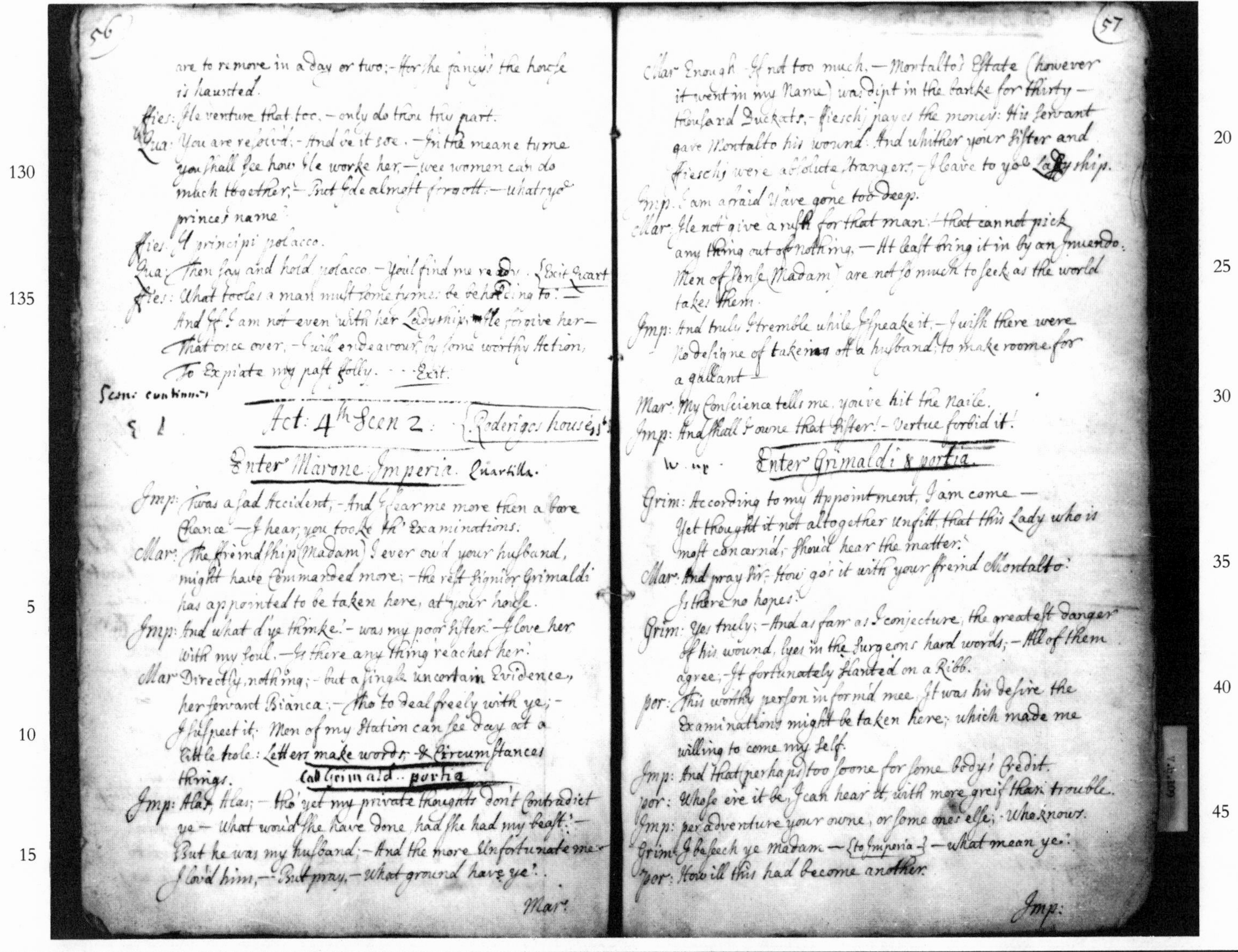

56

are to remove in a day or two;—For she fancys the house
is haunted.
Fies: Ile venture that too.—only do thou thy part.
Qua: You are resolv'd;—And be it soe.—In the meane tyme
you shall see how Ile worke her,—wee women can do
much together;—But Ide almost forgott;—what's yor
princes name?
Fies: Il principi polacco.
Qua: Then say and hold polacco.—You'l find me ready. {Exit Quart
Fies: What tooles a man must sometymes be beholding to:—
And If I am not even with her Ladyship, Ile forgive her—
That once over,—I will endeavour, by some worthy Action,
To Expiate my past folly. - - Exit.

Scene continues
& 1

Act: 4th Scen 2: {Roderigos house, 1^s^t

Enter Marone Imperia. Quartilla.

Imp: Twas a sad Accident,—And I fear me more then a bare
Chance—I hear, you tooke th' Examinations.
Mar: The freindship (Madam) I ever ow'd your husband,
might have Commanded more;—the rest Signior Grimaldi
has appointed to be taken here, at your house.
Imp: And what d'ye thinke?—was my poor sister?—I love her
with my soul.—Is there any thing reaches her?
Mar: Directly, nothing;—but a single uncertain Evidence,
her servant Bianca;—Tho to deal freely with ye;—
I suspect it: Men of my Station can see day at a
little hole: Letters make words,—& Circumstances
things. Call Grimaldi . . portia
Imp: Alas, Alas;—tho' yet my private thoughts don't Contradict
ye—What would she have done had she had my heart?—
But he was my husband;—And the more Unfortunate me—
I lov'd him,—But pray,—What ground have ye?
Mar:

57

Mar: Enough—If not too much.—Montalto's Estate (however
it went in my Name) was dipt in the banke for thirty—
thousand Duckats,—Fieschi payes the money: His servant
gave Montalto his wound: And whether your sister and
Fieschi were absolute strangers;—I leave to yor Ladyship.
Imp: I am afraid ha'ave gone too deep.
Mar: Ile not give a rush for that man: that cannot pick
any thing out of nothing,—At least bring it in by an Inuendo:
Men of Sense (Madam) are not so much to seek as the world
takes them.
Imp: And truly I tremble while I speake it,—I wish there were
no designe of takeing off a husband; to make roome for
a gallant—
Mar: My Conscience tells me, you've hit the Naile.
Imp: And shall I owne that sister!—Vertue forbid it!
w. up Enter Grimaldi & portia.
Grim: According to my Appointment, I am come—
Yet thought it not altogether unfitt, that this Lady who is
most concern'd, shou'd hear the matter:
Mar: And pray Sir;—How go's it with your freind Montalto?
Is there no hopes?
Grim: Yes truely;—And as farr as I conjecture, the greatest danger
of his wound, lyes in the Surgeons hard words;—All of them
agree;—It fortunately glanted on a Ribb.
por: This worthy person inform'd mee, It was his desire the
Examinations might be taken here; which made me
willing to come my self.
Imp: And that perhaps too soone for some body's Credit.
por: Whose ere it be, I can hear it, with more greif than trouble.
Imp: peradventure your owne, or some ones else;—Who knows.
Grim: I beseech ye Madam—{to Imperia}—what mean ye?
por: How ill this had become another.
Imp:

IV, ii, opening. *1^s^t* stands for "first scene," that is, Roderigo's house.

58 Call Bian: Smeton

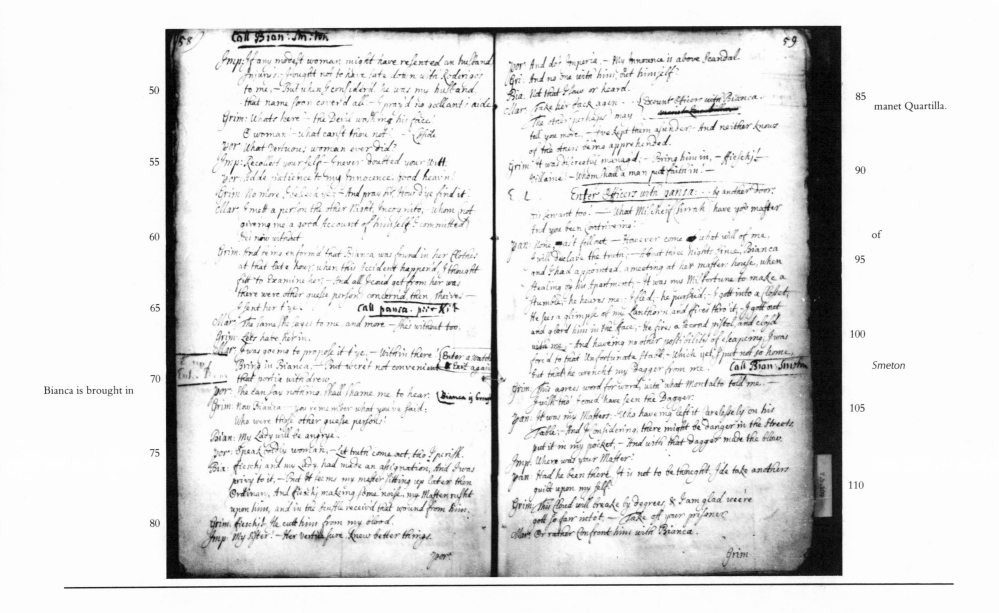

Imp: If any modest woman might have resented an husband,
Injuries, - I ought not to have sate down with Roderigo's
to me, - But when I consider'd, he was my husband,
that name soon cover'd all: - I pray'd no gallant's aide.
Grim: Whats here! - the Devil washing his face!
O woman! - what canst thou not! - Aside
Vor: What Vertuous woman ever did?
Imp: Recollect your selfe - I never doubted your Witt.
Vor: Adde patience to my Innocence, good heav'n!
Grim: No more I beseech ye; - And pray Sir, How d'ye find it.
Mar: I mett a person the other Night, Incognito, - whom (not
giveing me a good Account of himselfe) I committed.
He's now without
Grim: And being enform'd that Bianca was found in her Clothes
at that late hour, when this Accident happen'd, I thought
fitt to Examine her; - And all I could get from her was
there were other guesse persons concern'd, then theives -
I sent her t'ye. Call pansa. przr Kit
Mar: The same she sayes to me, and more - she's without too;
Grim: Lets have her in.
Mar: I was goeing to propose it t'ye, - Within there! Enter a Watch
Bring in Bianca, - But were't not convenient & Exit again
Ent. Bian. that portia withdrew
Vor: She can say nothing shall shame me to hear. Bianca is brought
Bianca is brought in
Grim: Now Bianca - you remember what you've said:
Who were those other guesse persons!
Bian: My Lady will be angrye.
Vor: Speak boldly woman; - Let truth come out, tho' I perish.
Bia: Fieschi and my Lady had made an assignation; And I was
privy to it, - But it seems my master sitting up later then
Ordinary, And Fieschi makeing some noise, my Master rusht
upon him, and in the scuffle receiv'd that wound from him.
Grim: Fieschi! - He cutt him from my blood.
Imp: My Sister! - Her Vertue sure knew better things.

Vor:

59

Vor: And do's Imperia. - My Innocence is above Scandal.
Gri: And no one with him, but himself?
Bia: Not that I saw or heard.
Mar: Take her back agen - Exeunt Officers with Bianca. manet Quartilla.
The other perhaps may ~~manet Quartilla~~
tell you more. - I've kept them asunder; - And neither knows
of the others being apprehended.
Grim: It was discreetly manag'd; - Bring him in, - Fieschi! -
Villaine! - Whom shall a man putt faith in! -

E. L. Enter Officers with pansa: - by another door.

His servant too! - What Mischeif (sirrah) have you master of
And you been Contriveing!
Pan: None, as't fell out. - However come what will of me,
I will declare the truth; - About three nights since, Bianca
and I had appointed a meeting at her masters house, when
stealing by his Apartment; - It was my Misfortune to make a
stumble; - he heares me; - I fled; - he pursu'd; - I gott into a Closet,
He sees a glimpse of my Lanthorn, and fires thro' it; - I gott out
and glar'd him in the face; - He fires a second pistol, and clos'd
with me; - And haveing no other possibility of escapeing, I was
forc'd to that Unfortunate stabb; - Which yet, I put not so home,
but that he wrencht my dagger from me. Call Bian: Smeton Smeton
Grim: This agrees word for word, with what Montalto told me. -
I wish tho' I could have seen the Dagger.
Pan: It was my Masters; - Who haveing left it Carelessely on his
Table; - And I Considering, there might be danger in the streets,
put it in my pocket, - And with that dagger made the blow.
Imp: Where was your Master?
Pan: Had he been there, It is not to be thought, I'de take anothers
guilt upon my self.
Grim: This Cloud will breake by degrees, & I am glad wee're
gott so farr into't, - Take off your prisoner.
Mar: Or rather Confront him with Bianca.

Grim

60

Grim: Well thought of.— Bring her in again.—

Enter Bianca brought in.

Call Imperia

You said ere while that Fieschi was alone—And Pansa says, 't his master, but himselfe; And that It was an Appointment between You two.

a Pan: By this token,—that the hearing the Noise, I put me into the Closet, and bad me bolt it on the Inside.— {Bianca stutters.

Bian: Y'ath a mind to hang thy self too.— Yes,—he was there,— And I beleive with a designe of robbing the house.

Grim: prithee speak truth:—who ever was there;—Did yo[r] Lady know any thing of it— {She stands confus'd at last kneels.

Bian: Good madam forgive me—you're Innocent. {She howls.

Grim: Take them away:—And keep them severally. {Exeunt Officers with the prisoners

Por: And now Sister—Judge favourably of me:
poor me, whom nothing but a quiet Conscience,
had kept from sinking.—This is the true Joy,
And this wee give our selves;—This makes us beare
A mind above our sex: fortune may cleare,
The visage, only this, can fill the Soul.

Mar: Your Servant Sir,—And as Occasion offers,—Ile waite on you.

Manet: Quartilla. {Ext. Grimaldi leading portia by one Door, Marone and Imperia by another.

Qua: And now when alls done Fieschi for my money,— He has scarce half gott rid of a Surfeit; And yet is ventring on the same dish agen.—He has a passion for her, that's certaine or otherwise, a Love-fitt at this tyme, were inexcusable— Well;—his present is sent in; and that so noble, I am afraid he do's not pretend to come often.

Enter Imperia.

Imp: What's all that luggage in the other roome.

Qua: A Damaske Bedd, with Maly fringe, and every thing suteable! besides a rich Cupboard of plate!—And no other name for't, but Luggage?—I wish yo[r] Lay had such another to morrow, Weed find it house roome.

Imp:

Call Matthe

61

Imp: I must Confesse it great.—But whence came it?

Qua: No Ferrachino.—I dare warrant ye.—It is the humble present of the out Landish prince, new come to towne; Il Xenior principi polacco — your Ladyship understands the rest.—But did ye know how I enhanc't th'affaire — Husband,—Relations,—Reputation—Honor—And to all this, your utter Averseness.—You'd say, I was no fool.

Call Grimaldi

Imp: Is he handsome?

Qua: What matters that: his presents is.—However to satisfie ye—He's as handsome a man, as the best of us need to lye board and board by—for my part I could sinke by his side.

Imp: When will he be here?

Qua: At Midnight,—And you'l be asleep.

Imp: But to a man I never saw:—How shall I look next morning?

Qua: Just as you did before.—Or you may If you think fitt, Crye out, your woman has betray'd ye;—No body will heare ye—tho yet If ye shou'd; He understands no Italian.

Imp: Thou that supply my place.—All petticoates are Sisters in the dark.

Qua: I would it were not to wrong your Ladyp—Come Madam, no more Words: Do you but leave him one side of your Bed, hee'l find the rest himself.

Imp: Well—Weel further Consider it within. Exeunt.

Act: 4th: Scen: 3: The Vineyard Scene.

Enter Mattheo: Solus. In a black velvet coate A tipt cane, turning up his Mustachoes strutting &c.

Mat: It is the same;—of a better Edition tho'—And truly (to give the Devil his due.) He has shewn himself much a gentleman;—Which is more then Ile say of every man;— I have already dislodg'd him, from two great Ladys.

And

IV, ii, above 115 and 116. The replacement lines are: "Fieschi was alone—And Pansa says, 't[was not] / his master, but himselfe."

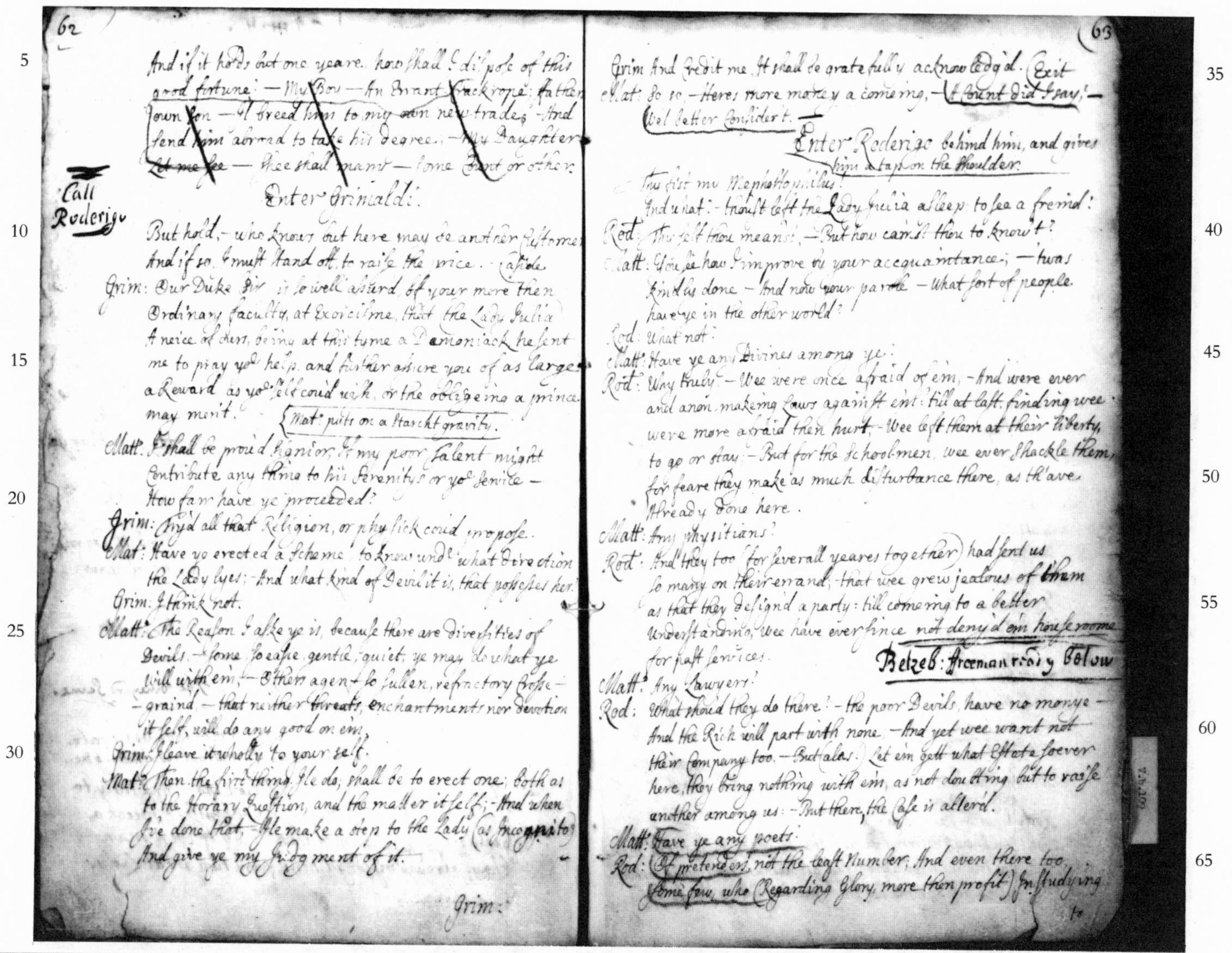

62

And if it holds but one yeare. how shall I dispose of this
good fortune: — My Boy — An Errant Crackrope: father
own son — I'l breed him to my own new trade; — And
send him abroad to take his degree. — My Daughter
Let me see — Shee shall marry — some Count or other.

Call Roderigo

Enter Grimaldi.

But hold, — who knows but here may be another Customer
And if so, I must stand off, to raise the price. — (aside

Grim: Our Duke Sir is so well assur'd of your more then
Ordinary faculty, at Exorcisme, that the Lady Julia
A neice of hers, being at this tyme a Dæmoniack he sent
me to pray yor help, and further assure you of as large
a Reward as yor selfe could wish, or the obligeing a prince
may merit. {Mat: puts on a starcht gravity.

Matt: I shall be proud Signior, if my poor Talent might
Contribute any thing to his Serenitys or yor Service —
How farr have ye proceeded?

Grim: Tryd all that Religion, or physick could propose.

Mat: Have ye erected a Scheme to know und^r what Direction
the Lady lyes: — And what kind of Devil it is, that possesses her.

Grim: I think not.

Matt: The Reason I aske ye is, because there are diversities of
Devils. — some so easie, gentle, quiet, ye may do what ye
will with em; — Others agen so sullen, refractory Crosse-
-graind, — that neither threats, enchantments nor devotion
it self, will do any good on em.

Grim: I leave it wholly to your self.

Mat: Then the first thing Ile do, shall be to erect one; both as
to the Horary Question, and the matter it self; — And when
I've done that, Ile make a step to the Lady (as Incognito)
And give ye my Judgment of it.

Grim:

63

Grim And Credit me, It shall be gratefully acknowledg'd. (Exit

Mat: So so, — Heres more money a comeing, — A Count did I say; —
Wel better Consider't. —

Enter Roderigo behind him, and gives
him a tap on the shoulder.

This is it my Mephostophilus!
And what: — thou'st left the Lady Julia asleep to see a freind:

Rod: Thy self thou meanst, — But how cam'st thou to know't?

Matt: You see how I improve by your acquaintance; — twas
kindly done — And now your parole — What sort of people
have ye in the other world?

Rod: What not:

Matt: Have ye any Divines among ye:

Rod: Why truly — Wee were once afraid of em, — And were ever
and anon makeing Laws against em: till at last, finding wee
were more afraid then hurt, — Wee left them at their liberty,
to go or stay; — But for the Schoolmen, wee ever shackle them,
for feare they make as much disturbance there, as th'ave
Already done here.

Matt: Any Physitians?

Rod: And they too (for severall yeares together) had sent us
so many on their errand, that wee grew jealous of them
as that they design'd a party: till comeing to a better
Understanding, wee have ever since not deny'd em house roome
for past services.

Belzeb: Freeman ready Below

Matt: Any Lawyers?

Rod: What shoud they do there? — the poor Devils, have no monye —
And the Rich will part with none, — And yet wee want not
their Company too. — But alas: Let em gett what Estate soever
here, they bring nothing with em, as not doubting but to raise
another among us: — But there, the Case is alterd.

Matt: Have ye any poets:

Rod: Of pretenders, not the least Number; And even there too,
Some few, who (Regarding Glory, more then profit) In studying

to

IV, iii, 13. Julia is presumably the "Ambrosia" referred to by Roderigo at III, v, 98. The prompter should have rectified this inconsistency.

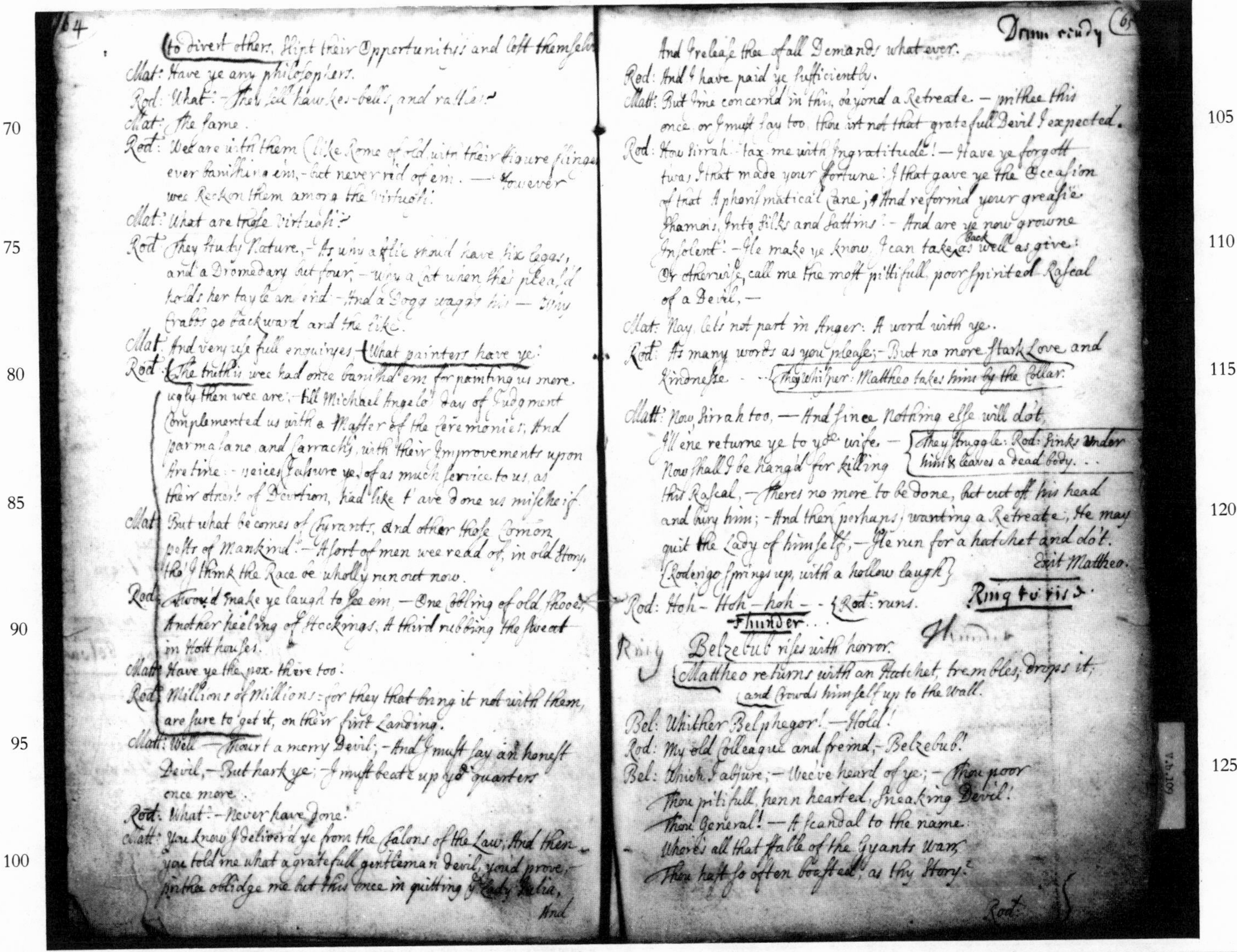

64

(to divert others, slipt their Opportunityes and left themselv[es]

Mat: Have ye any philosophers.

Rod: What: — These call hawkes-bells, and rattles?

Mat: The same.

Rod: Wee are with them (like Rome of old with their Figure flingers ever banishing em, — but never rid of em. — However wee Reckon them among the virtuosi.

Mat: What are those Virtuosi?

Rod: They study Nature, — As why a flie should have six leggs, and a Dromedary but four, — why a Cat when she's pleas'd holds her tayle an end — And a Dogg wagg's his — why Crabbs go backward and the like.

Mat: And very usefull enquiryes — What painters have ye:

Rod: The truth is wee had once banish'd em for painting us more ugly then wee are; — till Michael Angelo's day of Judgment Complemented us with a Master of the Ceremonies, And Parmalane and Carrachy, with their Improvements upon Aretine — voices I assure ye, of as much service to us, as their others of Devotion, had like t' ave done us mischeif.

Mat: But what becomes of Tyrants, and other those Common pests of Mankind? — A sort of men wee read of, in old Story, tho' I think the Race be wholly run out now.

Rod: Twou'd make ye laugh to see em, — One Cobling of old shooes, Another heeling of Stockings, A third rubbing the sweat in Hott houses.

Mat: Have ye the pox there too:

Rod: Millions of Millions: — for they that bring it not with them, are sure to get it, on their first Landing.

Matt: Well — Thou'rt a merry Devil; — And I must say an honest Devil, — But hark ye; I must beate up yor quarters once more.

Rod: What: — Never have done:

Matt: You know I deliver'd ye from the Talons of the Law; And then you told me what a gratefull gentleman devil, you'd prove, — prithee oblidge me but this once in quitting ye Lady Julia, And

Drum ready 65

And I release thee of all Demands whatever.

Rod: And I have paid ye sufficiently.

Matt: But I'me concern'd in this, beyond a Retreate. — prithee this once or I must say too, thou art not that gratefull Devil I expected.

Rod: How sirrah — tax me with Ingratitude! — Have ye forgott twas I that made your fortune: I that gave ye the Occasion of that Aphorismatical Cane; And reform'd your greasie Shamois, Into silks and sattins: — And are ye now growne Insolent: — Ile make ye know I can take back as well as give: Or otherwise, call me the most pittifull, poor spirited Rascal of a Devil, —

Mat: Nay, let's not part in Anger: A word with ye.

Rod: As many words as you please; — But no more stark Love and Kindnesse — — {They whisper: Mattheo takes him by the Collar.

Matt: Now sirrah too, — And since Nothing else will do't, I'll ene returne ye to yor wife. — {They struggle: Rod: sinks under him & leaves a dead body. . . Now shall I be hang'd for killing this Rascal, — Theres no more to be done, but cut off his head and bury him; — And then (perhaps) wanting a Retreate, He may quit the Lady of himselfe, — Ile run for a hatchet and do't.

Exit Mattheo.

{Roderigo springs up, with a hollow laugh}

Ring to rise.

Rod: Hoh — Hoh — hoh — — {Rod: runs.

Thunder . . .

Ring

Belzebub rises with horror.

{Mattheo returns with an Hatchet, trembles, drops it, and Crowds himselfe up to the Wall.

Bel: Whither Belphegor! — Hold!

Rod: My old Colleague and freind, — Belzebub!

Bel: Which I abjure; — Wee've heard of ye; — Thou poor Thou pitifull, henn hearted, sneaking Devil! Thou General! — A scandal to the name: Where's all that fable of the Gyants Warr, Thou hast so often boasted, as thy Story:

Rod:

V.b.109

IV, iii, 101. The unclear line is: "Prithee oblidge me but this once in quitting ye Lady Julia."

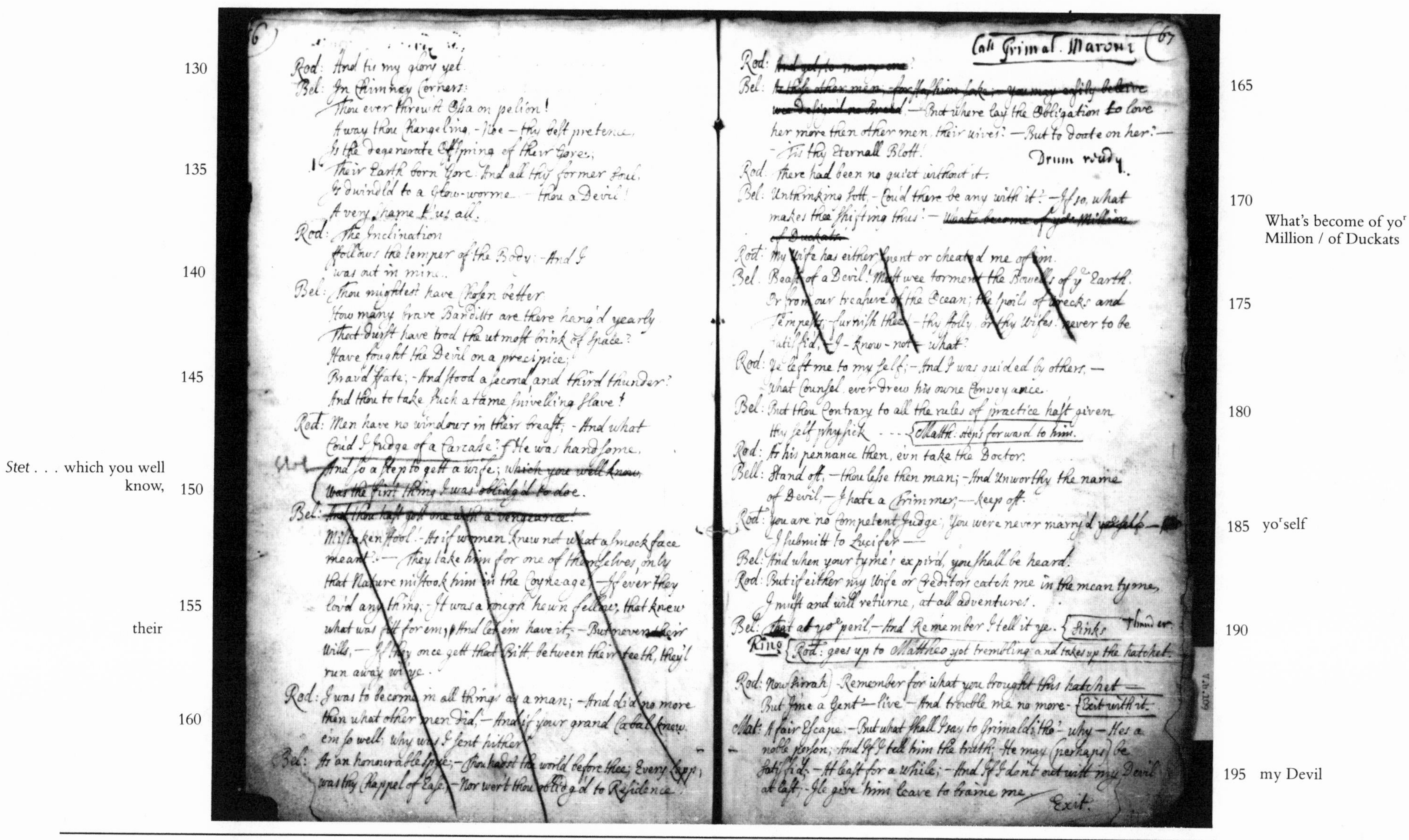

Rod: And tis my glory yet.
Bel: In Chimney Corners:
Thou ever threw'st Ossa on pelion!
Away thou Changeling, - Thee - thy best pretence
Is the degenerate Offspring of their Gore;
Their Earth born Gore. And all thy former Soul
Is dwindl'd to a Glow-worme - thou a Devil!
A very shame to us all.
Rod: The Inclination
ffollows the temper of the Body: - And I
was out in mine.
Bel: Thou mightest have chosen better
How many brave Bandits are there hang'd yearly
That durst have trod the utmost brink of Space?
Have fought the Devil on a precipice;
Brav'd ffate; - And stood a second and third thunder?
And thou to take such a tame sniveling slave?
Rod: Men have no windows in their breast; - And what
Cou'd I Judge of a Carcase: ffHe was handsome.
And so a step to gett a wife; which you well know
Was the first thing I was oblidg'd to doe.
Bel: And thou hast gott one with a vengeance!
Mistaken ffool! - As if women knew not what a smock face
meant: - They take him for one of themselves, only
that Nature mistook him in the Coyneage; - If ever they
lov'd any thing, - It was a rough hewn ffellow, that knew
what was fitt for em; And let em have it, - But never their
Wills, - If they once gett that Bitt between their teeth, they'l
run away wi' ye.
Rod: I was to become in all things as a man; - And did no more
than what other men did, - And if your grand Cabal knew
em so well: why was I sent hither?
Bel: Its an honourable side; - Thou hadst the world before thee; Every Lapp
was thy Chappel of Ease. - Nor wert thou oblig'd to Residence.

Call Grimal. Maroni
Rod: And yet, to marry one?
Bel: As those other men; for ffashion sake; you may easily beleive
wee design'd no Breed. - But where lay the Obligation to love
her more then other men their wives? - But to doate on her? -
- 'Tis thy Eternall Blott!
Drum ready
Rod: There had been no quiet without it.
Bel: Unthinking sott, - Cou'd there be any with it? - If so, what
makes thee shifting thus? - What's become of yo[r] Million
of Duckats
Rod: My Wife has either spent or cheated me of 'em.
Bel: Beast of a Devil! Must wee torment the Bowells of y[e] Earth,
Or from our treasure of the Ocean; the spoils of wrecks and
Tempests, furnish thee - thy ffolly, or thy Wifes. never to be
satisfied, - I - know - not - what?
Rod: Ye left me to my self; - And I was guided by others. -
What Counsel ever drew his owne Conveyance.
Bel: But thou contrary to all the rules of practice hast given
thy self physick ... {Matth: steps forward to him.
Rod: As his pennance then, ev'n take the Doctor.
Bell: Stand off, - thou less then man; - And unworthy the name
of Devil, - I hate a Trimmer, - keep off.
Rod: You are no Competent Judge; You were never marry'd yo[r]self -
I submitt to Lucifer -
Bel: And when your tyme's expir'd, you shall be heard.
Rod: But if either my Wife or Creditors catch me in the mean tyme,
I must and will returne, at all adventures.
Bel: At yo[r] peril. - And Remember I tell it ye. {Sinks Thunder.
Ring {Rod: goes up to Mattheo yet trembling and takes up the hatchet.
Rod: Now sirrah) Remember for what you brought this hatchet -
But fine a Gent - live - And trouble me no more - {Exit with it.
Mat: A fair Escape. - But what shall I say to Grimaldi tho' - why - Hes a
noble person; And If I tell him the truth; He may (perhaps) be
satisfied, - At least for a while; - And If I don't out with my Devil
at last; Ile give him leave to frame me. Exit.

Stet . . . which you well know,

their

What's become of yo[r] Million / of Duckats

yo[r]self

my Devil

IV, iii, 164–66. The canceled lines are: "And yet, to marry one / As those other men;—for ffashion sake; you may easily beleive / wee design'd no Breed."

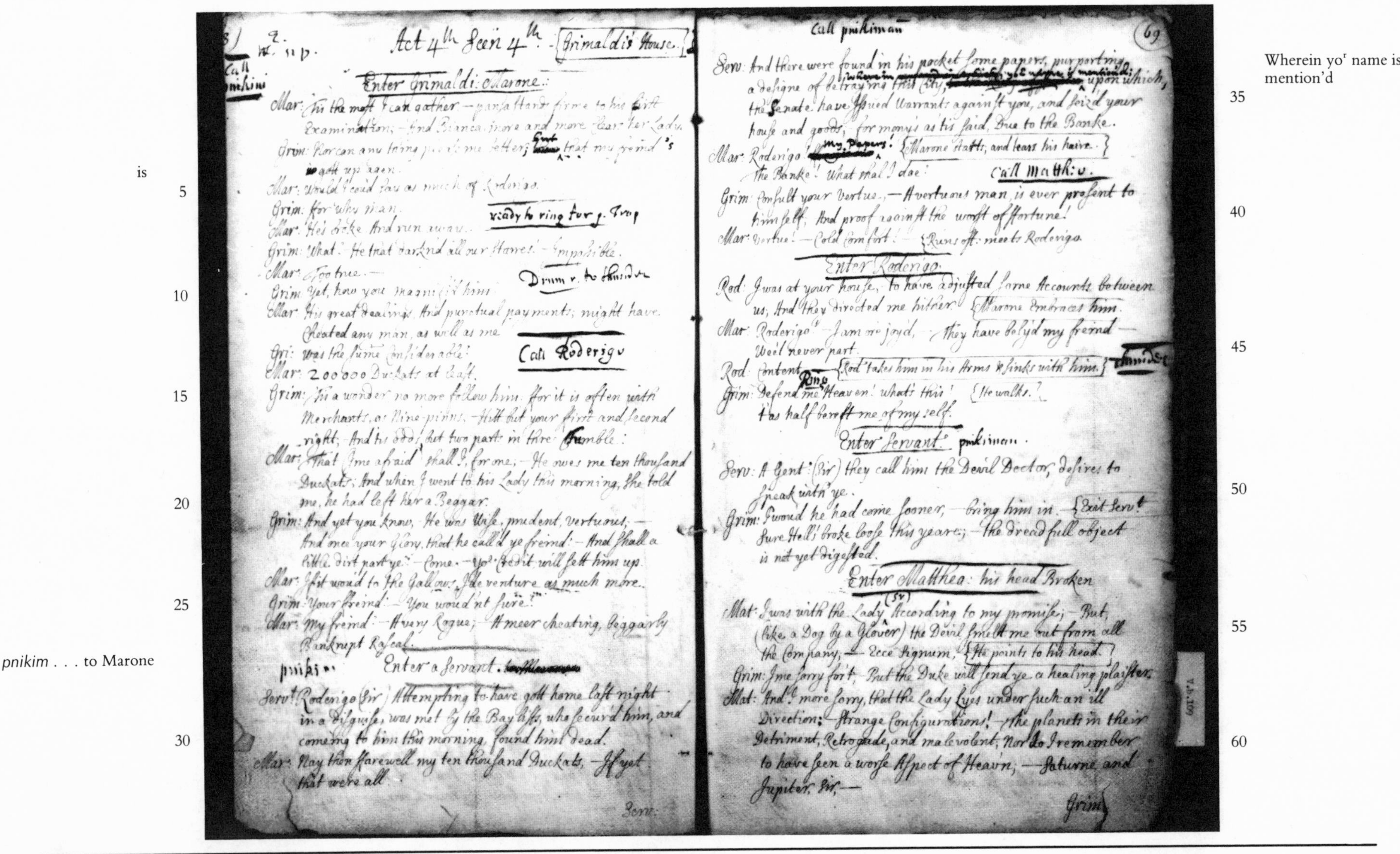
8) E. u p. Act 4th Scen 4th. {Grimaldi's House.}

Call pnikini

Enter Grimaldi: & Marone.:

Mar: Tis the most I can gather — [illegible] firme to his first Examination; — And Bianca more and more clear her Lady.

Grim: Nor can any thing [illegible] me better; Grit that my freind 's gott up agen.

Mar: Would I could say as much of Roderigo.

Grim: For why man.

Mar: He's broke And run away. ready to ring for g. Trap

Grim: What! He that bark'd all our Stores! Impossible.

Mar: Too true. — Drum r. to thunder

Grim: Yet, how you mean [illegible] him

Mar: His great dealings, And punctual payments; might have Cheated any man, as well as me. Call Roderigo

Gri: Was the sume considerable?

Mar: 200000 Duckats at least.

Grim: Tis a wonder no more follow him: for it is often with Merchants, as Nine-pinns; Hitt but your first and second right; And tis odds, but two parts in three Tumble:

Mar: That I'me afraid shall [illegible] for me; — He owes me ten thousand Duckats; And when I went to his Lady this morning, she told me, he had left her a Beggar.

Grim: And yet you know, He was Wise, prudent, vertuous, — And more your Glory, that he call'd ye freind: — And shall a little dirt part ye? — Come. — Yor Credit will sett him up.

Mar: If it would to the Gallows, I'de venture as much more.

Grim: Your freind! — You would'nt sure!

Mar: My freind! — A very Rogue; — A meer cheating, beggarly Bankrupt Rascal.

pnikin Enter a Servant.

Servt: Roderigo (Sir) Attempting to have gott home last night in a disguise, was met by the Bayliffs, who secur'd him, and coming to him this morning, found him dead.

Mar: Nay then farewell my ten thousand Duckats, — If yet that were all

Serv:

Call pnikiman (69)

Serv: And there were found in his pocket some papers, purporting a designe of betraying this City; [illegible] upon which, the Senate have issued Warrants against you, and seiz'd your house and goods; for mony's as tis said, Due to the Banke.

Mar: Roderigo! My Papers! {Marone starts, and tears his haire.} The Banke! What shall I doe! Call Matth: v.

Grim: Consult your Vertue; — A vertuous man, is ever present to himself; And proof against the worst of fortune!

Mar: Vertue! — Cold Comfort! — {Runs off: meets Roderigo.

Enter Roderigo.

Rod: I was at your house, to have adjusted some Accounts between us, And they directed me hither. {Marone embraces him.

Mar: Roderigo! I am overjoy'd, — they have bely'd my freind — Wee'l never part.

Rod: Content. Ring {Rod takes him in his Arms & sinks with him.} thunder

Grim: Defend me Heaven! what's this! {He walks.} T'as half bereft me of my self.

Enter Servant. pnikiman.

Serv: A Gent: (Sir) they call him the Devil Doctor, desires to speak with ye.

Grim: I would he had come sooner, — bring him in. — {Exit Servt. Sure Hell's broke loose this yeare; — the dreadfull object is not yet digested.

Enter Matthea: his head Broken

Mat: I was with the Lady (Sir) According to my promise; — But, (like a Dog by a Glover) the Devil smelt me out from all the Company; — Ecce Signum, {He points to his head.}

Grim: I'me sorry for't, But the Duke will send ye a healing plaister.

Mat: And I more sorry, that the Lady Lyes under such an ill Direction; — strange Configurations! — the planets in their Detriment, Retrograde, and malevolent; Nor do I remember to have seen a worse Aspect of Heavn; — Saturne and Jupiter. Sir, —

Grim

is

pnikim . . . to Marone

Wherein yor name is mention'd

IV, iv, opening. The prompter wrote *W. u p.* but then canceled the *W.* and replaced it with *E.* Below that he entered a call for *[P]nikini*—the actor William Pinkethman, whose name baffled the prompter elsewhere. Pinkethman had a considerable London career. In the right margin, going into the gutter, is: 2^d *Sce.* / ~~*Sce*~~

IV, iv, 6. *g Trap* means "great Trap."

IV, iv, following 27. The Servant, played by Pinkethman, is given an entrance but no exit; he presumably exits after line 36.

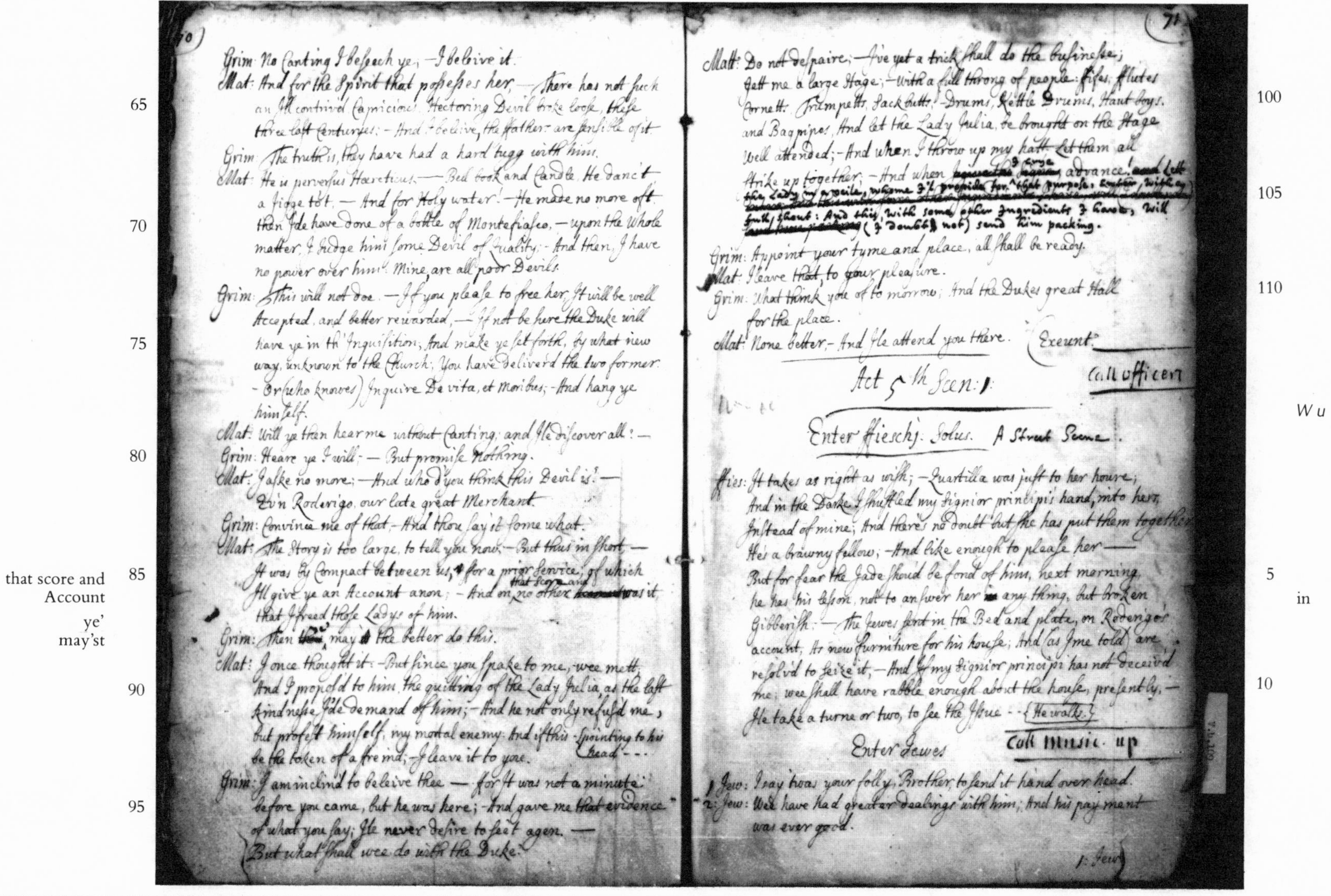
(70)

Grim: No Canting I beseech ye; —I beleive it.
Mat: And for the Spirit that possesses her, —There has not such an Ill contriv'd Capricious Hectoring Devil broke loose, these three last Centuryes; —And I beleive, the Fathers are sensible oft.
Grim: The truth is, they have had a hard tugg with him.
Mat: He is perverse Haereticus. —Bell book and Candle He danc't a figge to't. —And for Holy water! —He made no more oft then Ide have done of a bottle of Montefiasco, —upon the Whole matter, I Judge him some Devil of Quality; —And then, I have no power over him! Mine are all poor Devils.
Grim: This will not doe. —If you please to free her, It will be well Accepted, and better rewarded, —If not be here the Duke will have ye in th' Inquisition; And make ye set forth, by what new way, unknown to the Church; You have deliver'd the two former. —Or (who knows) Inquire De vita, et Moribus; —And hang ye himself.
Mat: Will ye then hear me without Canting; and Ile discover all: —
Grim: Heare ye I will: —But promise Nothing.
Mat: I aske no more; —And who d'you think this Devil is? — Ev'n Roderigo, our late great Merchant.
Grim: Convince me of that, —And thou say'st some what.
Mat: The Story is too large, to tell you now, —But thus in short, — It was by Compact between us, for a prior service; of which Ile give ye an Account anon; —And on that score and no other [illegible] was it that I freed these Ladys of him.
Grim: Then [illegible] may [illegible] the better do this.
Mat: I once thought it: —But since you spake to me, wee mett. And I propos'd to him, the quitting of the Lady Julia, as the last kindnesse Ide demand of him; —And he not only refus'd me, but profest himself, my mortal enemy: And if this —(pointing to his head) — be the token of a freind; —I leave it to you.
Grim: I am inclin'd to beleive thee —for It was not a minute before you came, but he was here; —And gave me that evidence of what you say; Ile never desire to feel agen. —
But what shall wee do with the Duke?

(71)

Matt: Do not despaire; —I've yet a trick shall do the businesse; Gett me a large Stage; —With a full throng of people: fifes, flutes Cornett, Trumpetts, Sackbutts, —Drums, Kettle Drums, Haut boys, and Bagpipes; And let the Lady Julia, be brought on the Stage well attended; —And when I throw up my hatt Let them all strike up together, —And when I crye advance! [illegible] (I doubt not) send him packing.
Grim: Appoint your tyme and place, all shall be ready.
Matt: I leave that, to your pleasure.
Grim: What think you of to morrow; And the Dukes great Hall for the place.
Mat: None better, —And Ile attend you there. (Exeunt.
Call officer
Act 5th Scen: 1
Enter Fieschi. Solus. A Street Scene.
Fies: It takes as right as wish; —Quartilla was just to her houre; And in the Darke I shuffled my Signior principi's hand, into hers, Instead of mine; And there's no doubt but she has put them together. He's a brawny fellow; —And like enough to please her — But for fear the Jade should be fond of him, next morning, he has his lesson, not to answer her in any thing, but broken Gibberish. —The Jewes sent in the Bed and plate, on Roderigo's account, & new furniture for his house; And (as I'me told) are resolv'd to seize it, —And if my Signior principi has not deceiv'd me; wee shall have rabble enough about the house, presently. — Ile take a turne or two, to see the Issue — (He walks.)
Call Music up
Enter Jewes
1 Jew: I say twas your folly, Brother, to lend it hand over head.
2 Jew: Wee have had greater dealings with him; And his payment was ever good.
1: Jew

that score and Account
ye'
may'st

Wu
in

IV, iv, 103–7. Wilson's lines are: "I crye . . . ~~and~~ Lett / the Lady in a veile, whome I'l provide for that purpose, Enter with a / full shout: And this, With some other Ingredients I have, Will / (I doubt not) send him packing."

V, i, opening. Fieschi was not warned; there is no act-ready warning near the end of Act IV.

V, i, following 11. The Jews were not warned.

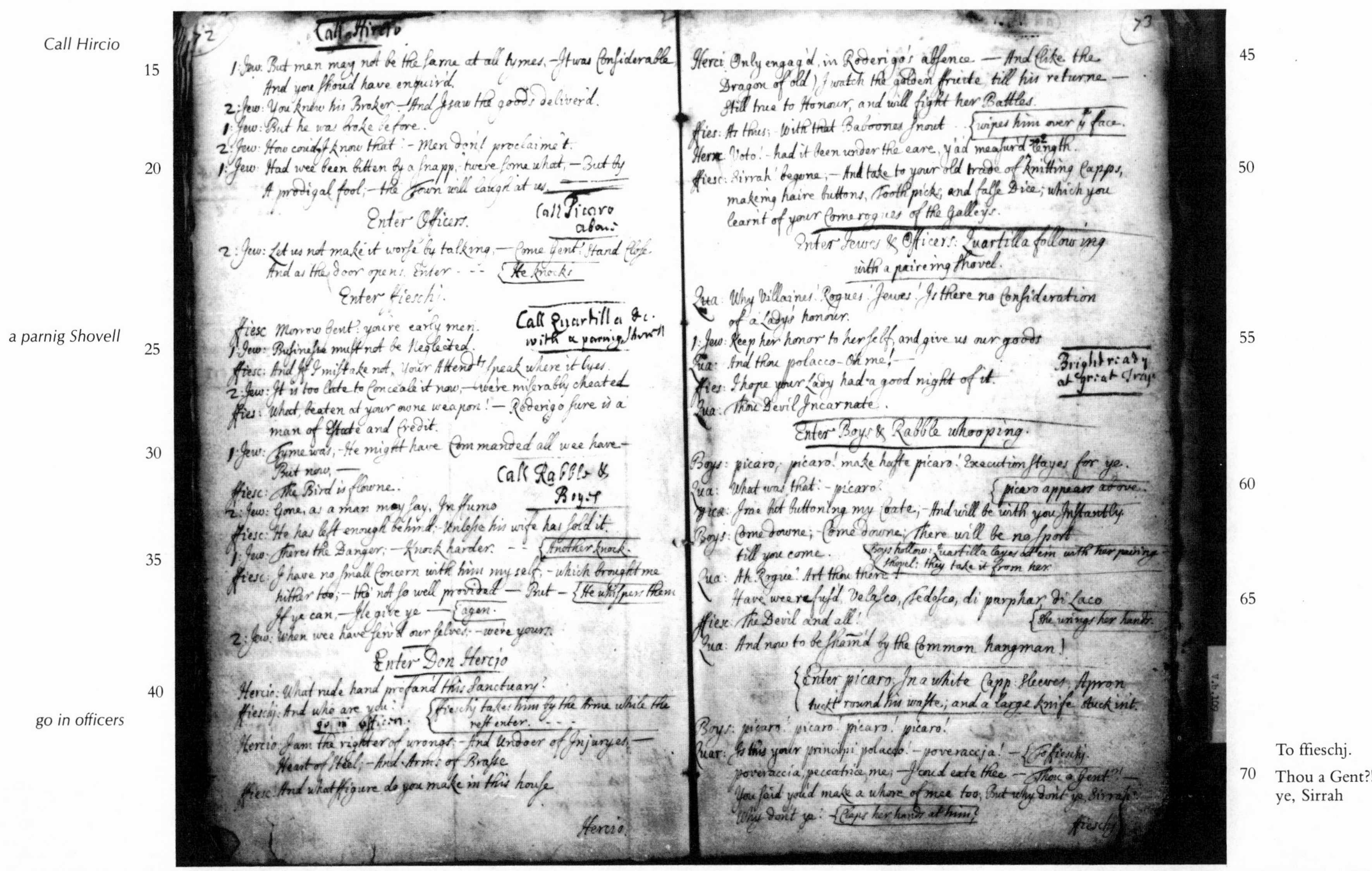

Call Hircio

1 Jew: But men may not be the same at all times, — It was Considerable
And you should have enquir'd.
2 Jew: You know his Broker — And I saw the goods deliver'd.
1 Jew: But he was broke before.
2 Jew: How could I know that: — Men don't proclaime't.
1 Jew: Had wee been bitten by a snapp, twere some what, — But by
A prodigal fool; — the Town will laugh at us.

Enter Officers. Call Picaro above

2 Jew: Let us not make it worse by talking. — Come Gent. Stand close.
And as the door opens: Enter — — {He knocks

Enter ffieschj.

Call Quartilla &c. with a parnig Showell

ffiesc: Morrow Gent: you're early men.
1 Jew: Business must not be neglected.
ffiesc: And If I mistake not, Your Attend^ts speak where it lyes.
2 Jew: It is too late to Conceale it now, — we're miserably cheated
ffies: What, beaten at your owne weapon! — Roderigo sure is a
man of State and Credit.
1 Jew: Tyme was, — He might have Commanded all wee have —
But now, —

Call Rabble & Boys

ffiesc: The Bird is flowne.
2 Jew: Gone, as a man may say, In fumo
ffiesc: He has left enough behind. Unlesse his wife has sold it.
1 Jew: There's the Danger; — Knock harder. — — {Another knock.
ffiesc: I have no small Concern with him my self, — which brought me
hither too; — tho' not so well provided — But — {He whispers them
If ye can, — Ile give ye — {agen.
2 Jew: When wee have seiz'd our selves: — were yours.

Enter Don Hercio

Hercio: What rude hand profan'd this Sanctuary?
ffieschj: And who are you: {ffieschj takes him by the Arme while the rest enter.
go in officers
Hercio: I am the righter of wrongs: — And Undoer of Injuryes, —
Heart of Steel; — And Arm: of Brasse.
ffiesc: And what figure do you make in this house

Hercio

Herci: Only engag'd, in Roderigo's absence — And (like the
Dragon of old) I watch the golden fruite till his returne —
Still true to Honour, and will fight her Battles.
ffies: Ah trues; With that Baboones snout — {wipes him over ye face.
Herm: Voto: — had it been under the eare, y'ad measur'd length.
ffiesc: Sirrah! begone; — And take to your old trade of Knitting Capps,
makeing haire buttons, Tooth picks, and false Dice; which you
learnt of your Come rogues of the Galleys.

Enter Jewes & Officers: Quartilla following
with a paireing shovel.

Qua: Why Villaines! Rogues! Jewes! Is there no Consideration
of a Lady's honour.
1 Jew: Keep her honor to her self, and give us our goods
Qua: And thou polacco — Oh me! — Bright ready at great Trap
ffies: I hope your Lady had a good night of it.
Qua: Thou Devil Incarnate.

Enter Boys & Rabble whooping.

Boys: picaro, picaro! make haste picaro! Execution stayes for ye.
Qua: What was that: — picaro? {picaro appears above.
pica: I'me but buttoning my Coate, — And will be with you Instantly.
Boys: Come downe; — Come downe; there will be no sport
till you come. {Boys hollow: Quartilla layes at em with her paireing shovel: they take it from her
Qua: Ah Rogue! Art thou there?
Have wee refus'd Velasco, Sedosca, di parphar, di Laco
ffiesc: The Devil and all! {She wrings her hands.
Qua: And now to be sham'd by the Common hangman!

{Enter picaro, In a white Capp: sleeves, Apron
tuckt round his waste; and a large knife stuck in't.

Boys: picaro. picaro. picaro. picaro!
Quar: Is this your principi polacco! — poveraccia! — {To ffieschj.
poveraccia, peccatrice me; — I cou'd eate thee — {Thou a Gent?!
You said you'd make a whore of mee too, But why don't ye, Sirrah?
Why don't ye: {Claps her hands at him.

ffieschj

Call Hircio

a parnig Shovell

go in officers

To ffieschj.

Thou a Gent?!
ye, Sirrah

V, i, following 23. The stage direction reads "Enter ffieschj," but he never left the stage.

V, i, 56. Bright must have been a stagehand working in the substage, for there is a separate entrance warning for the character of Marone, who is thrown up from below at line 97.

V, i, following 67. Picaro's entrance was not warned, though he just came down from an entrance on the balcony (presumably above a proscenium door), for which he was warned.

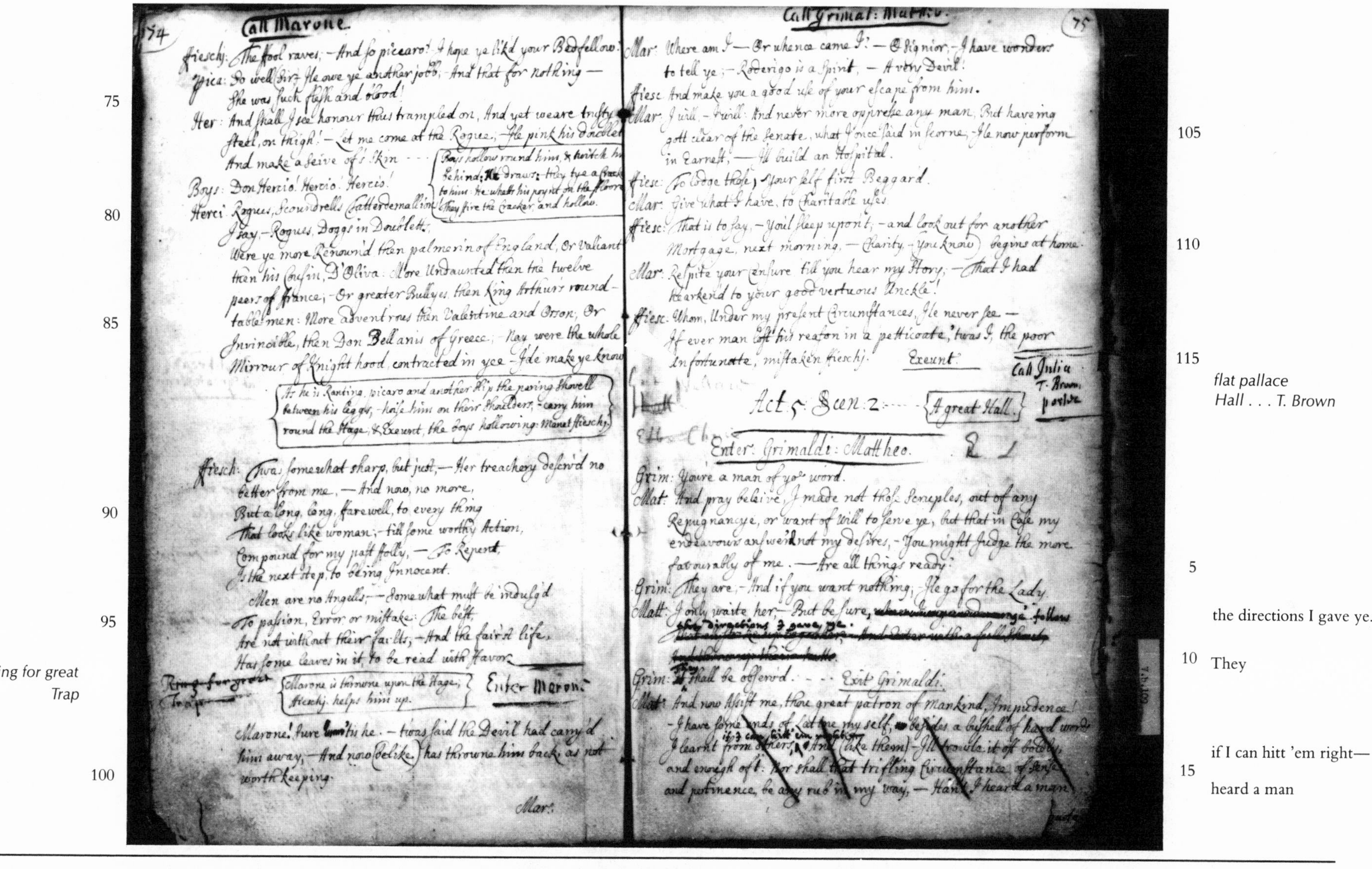

74

Call Marone

Fiesch: The fool raves; — And so picaro! I hope ye lik'd your Bedfellow:
Pica: So well Sir; Ile owe ye another jobb, And that for nothing —
She was such flesh and blood!
Her: And shall I see honour thus trampled on, And yet weare trusty steel, on thigh! — Let me come at the Rogues, — Ile pink his Doublet And make a seive of's skin - - -

Boys hollow round him, & twitch him behind; He draws: they tye a Cracker to him: he whetts his poynt on the floore. They fire the Cracker, and hollow.

Boys: Don Hercio! Hercio! Hercio!
Herci: Rogues, Scoundrells, Tatterdemallions, I say, — Rogues, Doggs in Doublets, Were ye more Renown'd then Palmerin of England, Or Valiant then his Cousin, D'Oliva: More Undaunted then the twelve peers of France; — Or greater Bullyes then King Arthur's round-table men: More adventrous then Valentine and Orson; Or Invincible, then Don Bellanis of Greece; — Nay were the whole Mirrour of Knighthood contracted in yee — Ide make ye know

As he is Ranting, picaro and another slip the paving shovell between his leggs, hoise him on their shoulders, carry him round the Stage, & Exeunt, the Boys hollowing: Manet Fiesch.

Fiesch: 'Twas somewhat sharp, but just; — Her treachery deserv'd no better from me, — And now, no more,
But a long, long, farewell, to every thing
That looks like woman; — till some worthy Action,
Compound for my past folly, — To Repent,
Is the next step, to being Innocent.
Men are no Angells; — Somewhat must be indulg'd
To passion, Error or mistake: The best,
Are not without their faults; — And the fair'st life,
Has some leaves in it, to be read with Favor.

~~Ring for great Trap~~

Marone is thrown upon the Stage; Fiesch helps him up.

Enter Marone

Marone! sure tis he. — twas said the Devil had carry'd him away, — And now belike, has throwne him back, as not worth keeping.

Mar:

75

Call Grimal: Mattheo

Mar: Where am I — Or whence came I? — O Signior, — I have wonders to tell ye; — Roderigo is a Spirit, — A very Devil!
Fiesc: And make you a good use of your escape from him.
Mar: I will, — I will: And never more oppresse any man, But haveing gott clear of the Senate, what I once said in scorne, Ile now perform in Earnest; — Ill build an Hospital.
Fiesc: To lodge those, your self first Beggard.
Mar: Give what I have, to Charitable uses
Fiesc: That is to say, — You'l sleep upon't, — and look out for another Mortgage, next morning. — Charity, — (you know) begins at home.
Mar: Respite your Censure till you hear my story, — That I had hearken'd to your good vertuous Unckle!
Fiesc: Whom, Under my present Circumstances, Ile never see — If ever man lost his reason in a petticoate, twas I, the poor Infortunate, mistaken Fieschi. Exeunt.

Call Julia T. Brown porter

Act 5. Scen 2. — A great Hall.

Enter: Grimaldi: Mattheo.

Grim: You're a man of yor word.
Mat: And pray believe, I made not those Scruples, out of any Repugnancye, or want of will to serve ye, but that in Case my endeavours answer'd not my desires, — You might Judge the more favourably of me. — Are all things ready?
Grim: They are; — And if you want nothing, Ile go for the Lady.
Matt: I only waite her; — But be sure, ~~the directions I gave ye.~~
Grim: It shall be observ'd. - - - Exit Grimaldi.
Matt: And now assist me, thou great patron of Mankind, Impudence! — I have some ends of Latine my self; besides a bushell of hard words I learnt from others, — And (like them) — Ile trouble it off boldly, and enough of't. Nor shall that trifling Circumstance of sense and pertinence, be any rub in my way, — Hark! I heard a man

Ring for great Trap

flat pallace
Hall . . . T. Brown

the directions I gave ye.

They

if I can hitt 'em right—

heard a man

V, ii, opening. T. Brown probably played an attendant. The second name I cannot make out, but it looks like *porter*. Clustered in the left margin are *flat pallace / Hall / Elbo Chair*. A setting called the "flat pallace" served for the "Great Hall" called for by the author. Some of the notes appear to be canceled, but those horizontal lines bled through from the verso of the page.

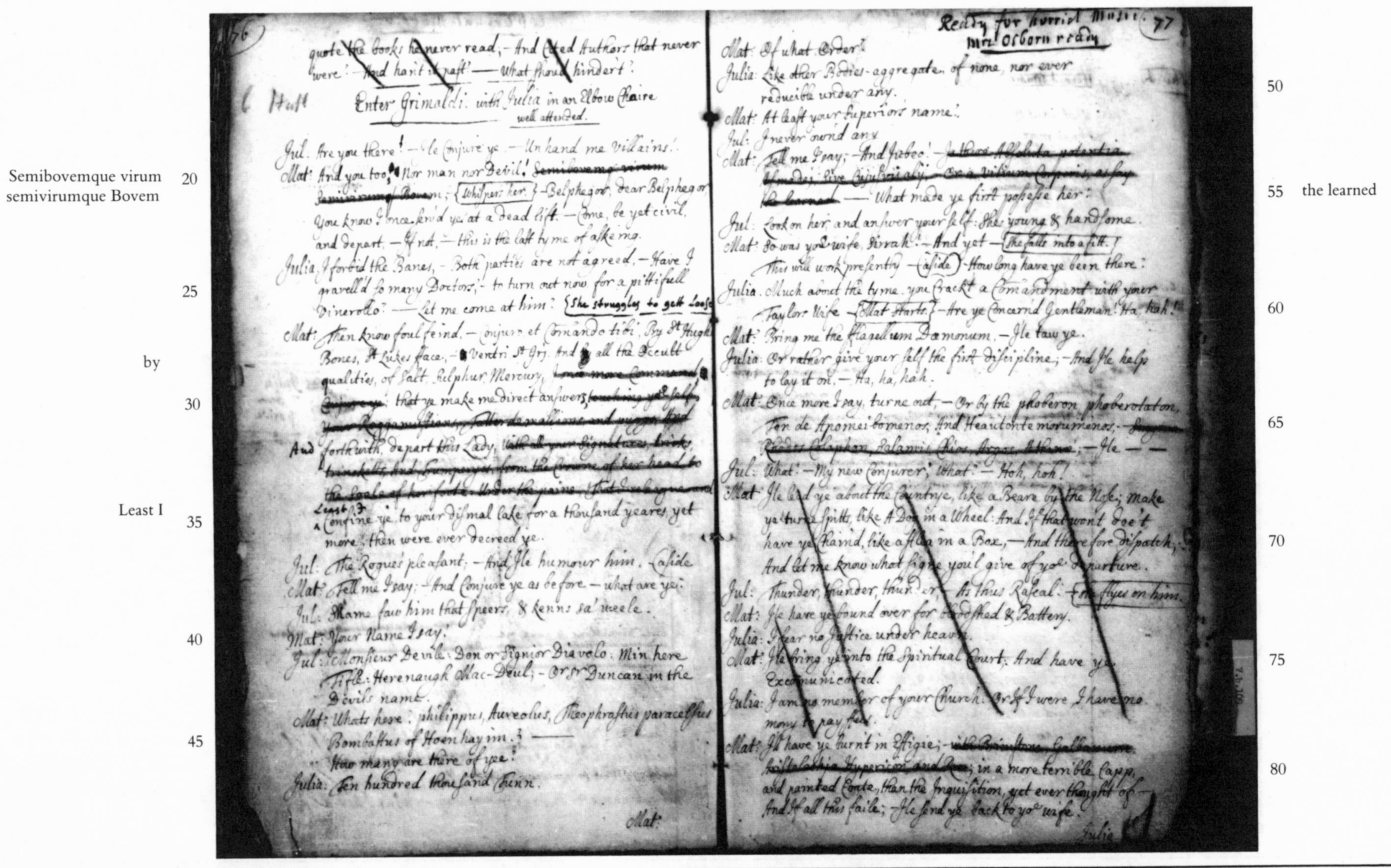

76
quote the books he never read, — And Cited Authors that never
were: — And han't it past? — What should hinder't:
G Hall Enter Grimaldi: with Julia in an Elbow Chaire
well attended.
Jul: Are you there! — Ile Conjure ye, — Unhand me Villains!
Mat: And you too; Nor man nor Devil!
Semibovemque virum semivirumque Bovem
m; {Whispers her.} — Belphegor, dear Belphegor,
You know I once serv'd ye at a dead lift. — Come, be yet civil,
and depart. — If not, — this is the last tyme of askeing.
Julia. I forbid the Banes, — Both parties are not agreed, — Have I
gravell'd so many Doctors, — to turn out now for a pittifull
Dinerollo? — Let me come at him: {She struggles to gett Loose}
Mat: Then know foul feind, — Conjuro et Comando tibi: By St Hughs
Bones, St Lukes face, — Ventri St Grj. And by all the Occult
by
qualities, of Salt, Sulphur, Mercury,
that ye make me direct answers,
And forthwith, depart this Lady,
Least I
Confine ye, to your dismal lake for a thousand yeares, yet
more; then were ever decreed ye.
Jul: The Rogue's pleasant; — And Ile humour him. (aside
Mat: Tell me I say; — And Conjure ye as before — what are ye:
Jul: Shame faw him that speers, & kenns sa' weele.
Mat: Your Name I say.
Jul: Monsieur Devile: Don or Signior Diavolo: Min here
Title: Herenaugh Mac-Deul; — Or Sr Duncan in the
Devils name.
Mat: Whats here: philippus, Aureolus, Theophrastus paracelsus
Bombastus of Hoenhayim.? ——
How many are there of yee?
Julia: Ten hundred thousand Chinn.
Mat:

Ready for horrid Musick. 77
Mrs Osborn ready
Mat: Of what Order?
Julia: Like other Bodies-aggregate, of none, nor ever
reducible under any.
Mat: At least your superiors name:
Jul: I never ownd any
Mat: Tell me I say; — And Jubeo! —
the learned
— What made ye first possesse her:
Jul: Look on her, and answer your self: She's young & handsome.
Mat: So was yor wife, Sirrah! — And yet — {She falls into a fitt.}
This will work presently — (aside) — How long have ye been there:
Julia. Much about the tyme, you crackt a Commandment with your
Taylors Wife — {Mat starts.} — Are ye Concern'd Gentleman! Ha, hah!
Mat: Bring me the flagellum Dæmonum, — Ile taw ye.
Julia: Or rather give your self the first discipline; — And Ile help
to lay it on, — Ha, ha, hah.
Mat: Once more I say, turne out, — Or by the phoberon phoberolaton,
Ton de Apomeibomenos, And Heautontemorumenos, —
; — Ile — —
Jul: What! — My new Conjurer; What! — Hoh, hoh!
Mat: Ile lead ye about the Countrye, like a Beare by the Nose; make
ye turne spitts, like A Dog in a Wheel: And if that won't doe't
have ye Chain'd, like a Flea in a Box, — And therefore dispatch;
And let me know what signe you'l give of yor departure.
Jul: Thunder, thunder, thunder, — As thus Rascal: {She flyes on him.
Mat: Ile have ye bound over for bloodshed & Battery.
Julia: I fear no Justice under heaven.
Mat: Ile bring ye into the Spiritual Court; And have ye
Excommunicated.
Julia: I am no member of your Church: Or if I were, I have no
mony to pay fees.
Mat: Ile have ye burnt in Effigie; —
; in a more terrible Capp,
and painted Coate, than the Inquisition, yet ever thought of —
And if all this faile; — Ile send ye back to yor wife.
Julia

V, ii, following 18. Grimaldi seems not to have been warned, though he just left the stage a few lines earlier; the prompter's practice seems to have been not to warn quick reentrances. The *G Hall* note suggests a scene shift, but the locale has not changed.

V, ii, 29–35. The deleted lines are: "I once more command, & / Conjure ye . . .touching yo[r] self, / [line 31 indecipherable] / With all your Signatures, tricks / [lines 33 and 34 indecipherable]."

V, ii, 65–66. The deleted words are: "Smyrna, / Rhodes Colophon, Salamis, Chios, Argos, Athenae."

V, ii, 79–80. The deleted words are: "with Brimstone, Galbanum, / Aristolochia, Hypericon, and Rue."

Call Montalto Marone Portia
Shout.. Horrid Music.

's in quest of ye', and

Julj. Tis she—Sh'as found me out.

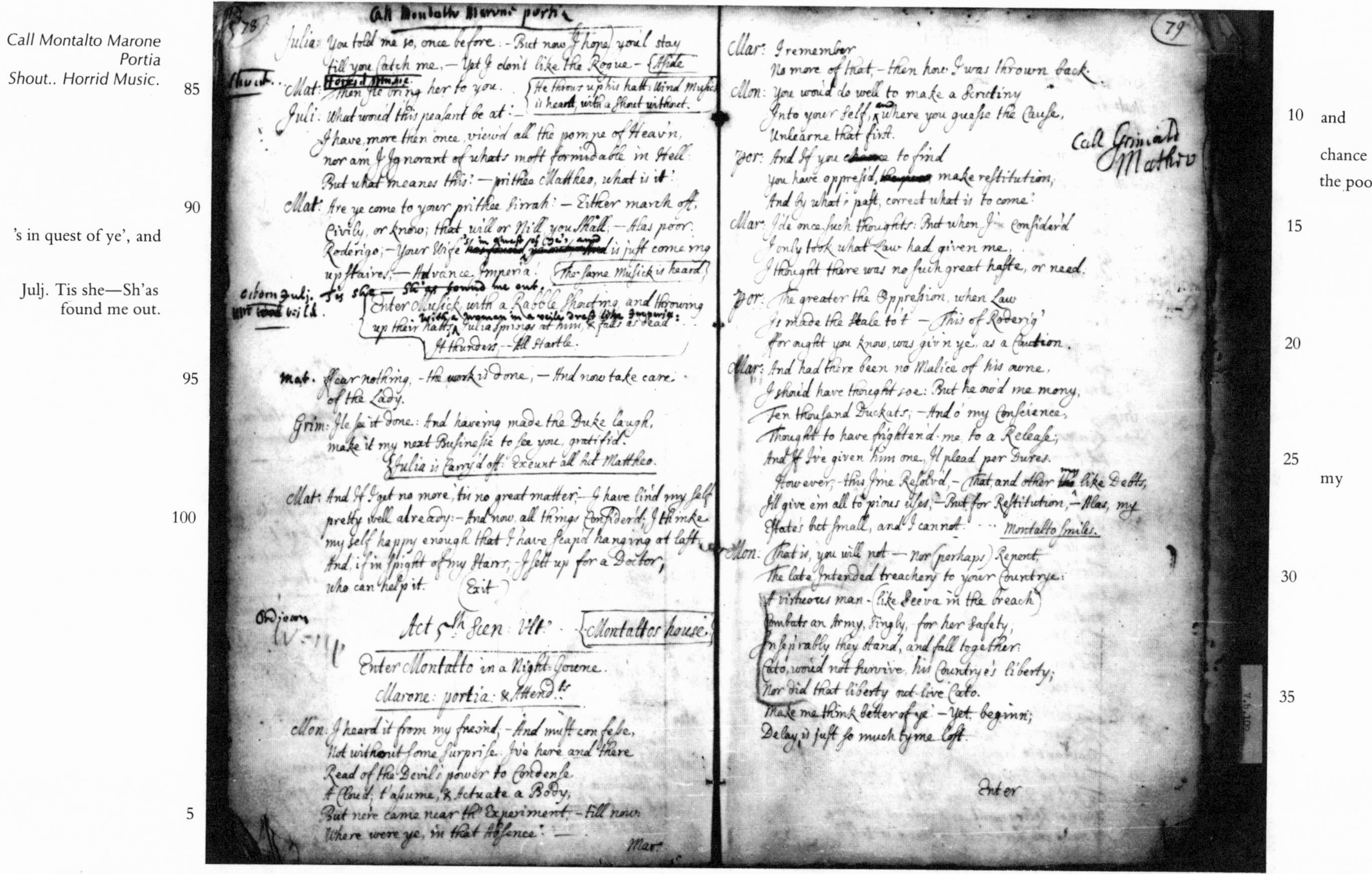
Call Montalto Marone portia

Julia: You told me so, once before. - But now I hope you'l stay
till you catch me, — Yet I don't like the Rogue — [Aside
Mat: Then Ile bring her to you. [He throws up his hatt. Wind Musick is heard, with a Shout without.
Juli: What would this peasant be at: —
I have, more then once, view'd all the pompe of Heav'n,
nor am I ignorant of whats most formidable in Hell.
But what meanes this? — prithee Mattheo, what is it?
Mat: Are ye come to your prithee sirrah? — Either march off,
Civily, or know; that, will or Nill you shall, — Alas poor
Roderigo; — Your Wife 's in quest of ye', and is just come up
staires, — Advance Imperia. [The same Musick is heard]
Julj. Tis she — Sh'as found me out.
Enter Musick with a Rabble shouting, and throwing
up their hatts, With a Woman in a veile drest like Imperia: Julia springs at him, & falls as dead:
It thunders. — All startle.
Mat. Fear nothing, - the work is done, — And now take care
of the Lady.
Grim: Ile see it done: And haveing made the Duke laugh,
make it my next Businesse to see you gratified.
Julia is carry'd off: Exeunt all but Mattheo.
Mat: And If I get no more, tis no great matter; — I have lin'd my self
pretty well already: — And now, all things consider'd, I thinke
my self happy enough that I have scap'd hanging at last,
And, if in spight of my Starr, I sett up for a Doctor,
who can help it. Exit
Act 5th Scen VIt. [Montaltos house.
Enter Montalto in a Night-Gowne.
Marone: portia: & Attend.ts
Mon: I heard it from my freind, — And must confesse,
Not without some surprise. I've here and there
Read of the Devil's power to Condense
A Cloud; t'assume, & Actuate a Body,
But ne're came near th' Experiment, — till now.
Where were ye, in that Absence? —
Mar.

79
Mar: I remember
No more of that, — then how I was thrown back.
Mon: You would do well to make a Scrutiny
Into your self, and where you guesse the Cause,
Unlearne that first.
Por: And If you chance to find
You have oppress'd, make restitution,
And by what's past, correct what is to come.
Mar: I'de once such thoughts: But when I consider'd
I only took what Law had given me,
I thought there was no such great haste, or need.
Por: The greater the Oppression, when Law
Is made the stale to't — This of Roderig'
For ought you know, was giv'n ye, as a Caution.
Mar: And had there been no Malice of his owne,
I should have thought soe: But he ow'd me mony,
Ten thousand Duckats; — And o' my Conscience,
Thought to have fright'end me, to a Release;
And If I've given him one, I'l plead per Dures.
However, this I'me Resolv'd, — that, and other my like Debts,
I'll give em all to pious uses, — But for Restitution, — Alas, my
Estate's but small, and I cannot · · · Montalto smiles.
Mon: That is, you will not — nor (perhaps) Repent
The late Intended treachery to your Countrye.
A virtuous man — (like Scaeva in the breach)
Combats an Army, singly, for her safety,
Inseparably they stand, and fall together.
Cato, would not survive his Countrye's liberty;
Nor did that liberty out live Cato.
Make me think better of ye — Yet, beginn;
Delay is just so much tyme Lost.
Enter

Call Grimaldi Mattheo

and

chance
the poor

my

V, ii, below 94. The new line is: "With a Woman in a veile drest like Imperia." In the left margin is: *Osborn / M[rs] ~~Wall~~ veild.*

And

80

Enter: Grimaldi: Mattheo.

Gri: My Doctor here; ~~And~~ has giv'n him a third remove.
Mat: And I hope there will be no Occasion of showing him round.
Grim: Hee'l tell ye the Story within; And not Unworth yor hearing.
In the meane, I cannot too often Congratulate yor Recovery.
Mon: Nor I, Acknowledge your Friendships.
Ile tell ye newes, — good newes (for there is nothing
Wee must not share) — methinks, I am become
Another man; — And this small quiet pleases,
Beyond the noise of Crowds, — Now I can see
The great ones heave like Moles, and at next turne,
Heave out themselves; Another, (Mushroome like)
Spring in a Night; — And Cropt ere Noon; A third,
Snatch at a Booty, which a fourth strikes from him,
And Unconcern'd my self.
Grim: True happinesse
Lyes not in greatnesse, but an honest mind,
Not fram'd of Accidents, nor Subject to em.
A Serene breast; And such a life as is not
~~Nor~~ Sham'd to live, Nor yet afraid to dye.
Por: And yet, how do's the World turmoile it self!
How do they play away their dayes! and trifle
Their tyme in parts, till they have slipt the whole!
One Businesse breeds another, Hope, desire;
And that, makes roome for more: How they afflict
Themselves, and envye others! Restlesse in War,
And ev'n in peace Unquiet! Compasse with Care,
What they possesse with more Anxiety!
Mon: To them that Love it, be't, — I neither like,
The Merchandise, nor the price — What is't to him
That can't dissemble? — Him that cannot flatter!
That's not Ambitious by Indignities,
To Rise to Dignities, and lose him self.
Whereas Retirement, as it costs us nothing,
Is much the shorter cut, to heav'n it self.
Enter

Call Imperia Quartilla

81

Enter Imperia: & Quartilla as distracted.

Imp: Help, help me Sister! — Can ye forgive me, — you can't,
you can't — Whither shall I run, — Hee'l ha'me hee'l ha mee.
Por: You never Injur'd me, or if you had, I have (as I ought)
forgot it.
Call Roderigo
Qua: Our house is more then haunted.
Imp: Sister — Sister, — I've marry'd the Devil — See where he stands!
Por: Blesse the poor miserable Woman, good Heav'n!
Qua: His eyes as bigg, as pumpkins, (she starts) — And a mouth like
any Bakers Oven; — Let me alone good Devil; — And take my
Lady, — she's younger flesh. — (she starts up and downe & shreeiks)
Imp: See, — see — the house cracks; — the walls are comeing together; —
That Beame was shott at me.
Qua: I'me your old servant Quartilla; — Good Devil!
Imp: There too, — The ground opens, — Ile at him tho — Dost thou
yet brave me, — Tyme was thou fear'dst me more —
Ile give ye back yor keyes, — Dost thou yet, — yet —
Por: I see nothing, Sister, — pray walk in with me — my Innocence
Dares speak to him.
Imp: There there, — the greater Devil, Fieschi!
Por: poor afflicted woman, — Her hurt Imagination, conceives
any thing — pray go in with me; Ile bear ye Company.
Imp: No, no, — Ile out at that window. (~~Imper carry'd off Portia follows.~~)
Enter Roderigo with horror.
(All are surpriz'd; — Imperia & Quartilla, shreike and run about
the Stage. — Rod. strikes into a Hayes with them; Imperia swoons
Quartilla runs of. — Roderigo makes up to Marone: He gets behind
Montalto: Montalto steps out. — Rod gives back. Imperia is carry'd off.
Portia follows)
Mon: Horror! — Be man or Devil! Ile know what thou art.
Rod: Thy vertue is beyond the powers of Hell — Be safe — And if
you have not heard my Story; — there's one — (points to Mattheo)
can tell it yee; — And now my Embassy is at an end, perforce.
Mat: And your Creditors may speak to ye, upon even terms.
(Exeunt Gabriel Montalto)
Rod.

Imper carry'd off
Portia follows.

V, iii, 56. "Nor" is canceled and replaced by "A."

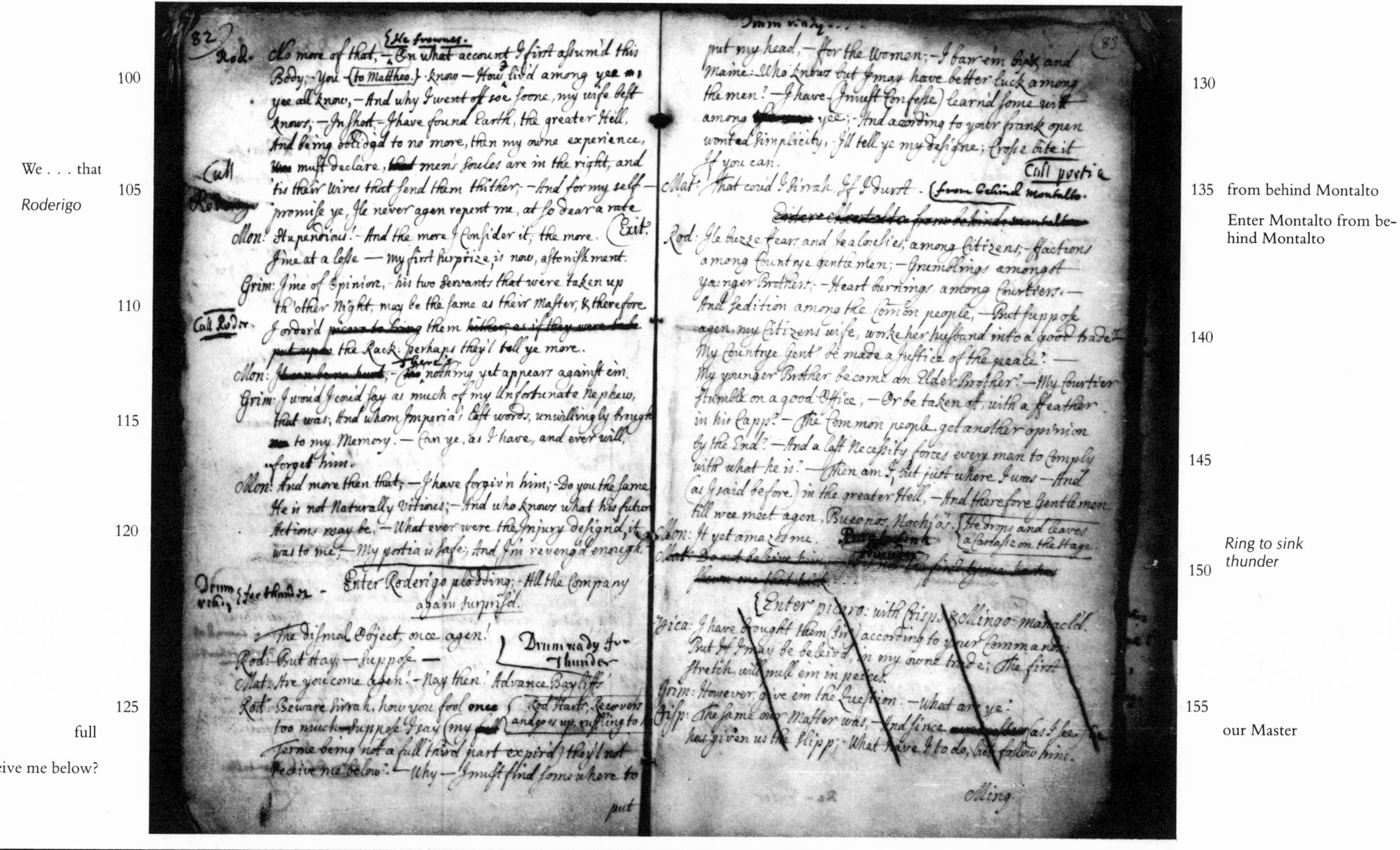

Rod. No more of that, — {He frownes.} On what account I first assum'd this Body; You {to Mattheo.} know — How I liv'd among yee all yee all know, — And why I went off soe soone, my wife best knows; — In short — I have found Earth, the greater Hell, And being oblidg'd to no more, then my owne experience, must declare, men's soules are in the right, and 'tis their wives that send them thither; — And for my self — promise ye, Ile never agen repent me, at so dear a rate

Mon: Stupendious! — And the more I consider it, the more. (Exit.) I'me at a losse — my first surprize is now, astonishment.

Grim: I'me of Opinion, his two Servants that were taken up th'other Night, may be the same as their Master, & therefore I order'd them the Rack: perhaps they'l tell ye more.

Mon: there's nothing yet appears against 'em.

Grim: I would I could say as much of my Unfortunate Nephew, that was; And whom Imperia's last words, unwillingly brought to my Memory. — Can ye, as I have, and ever will, forget him.

Mon: And more then that, — I have forgiv'n him; — Do you the same. He is not Naturally vitious; — And who knows what his future Actions may be. — What ever were the Injury design'd, it was to me; — My portia is safe; And I'm reveng'd ennough.

Enter Roderigo plodding: — All the Company again surpris'd.

— The dismal Object, once agen!

Rod: But stay, — suppose —

Mat: Are you come agen! — Nay then! Advance Bayliffs!

Rod: Beware sirrah, how you fool once (Rod starts, Recovers and goes up, ruffling to him) too much — suppose I say (my Terme being not a full third part expir'd) they'l not receive me below? — Why — I must find some where to put

put my head, — for the Women; — I bar 'em both and maine: Who knows but I may have better luck among the men? — I have (I must Confesse) learn'd some wit among yee; — And according to your frank open wonted simplicity, — I'll tell ye my designe; Crosse bite it If you can.

Mat: That could I sirrah If I durst. (from behind Montalto.)

Rod: Ile breed fears and Jealousies, among Citizens; — factions among Countrye gentlemen; — Grumblings amongst Younger Brothers; — Heart burnings among Courtiers. — And sedition among the Comon people. — But suppose agen, my Citizens wife, worke her husband into a good trade? My Countrye Gent' be made a Justice of the peace? — My younger Brother become an Elder Brother? — My Courtier stumble on a good Office; — Or be taken off, with a feather in his Capp? — The Common people get another opinion by the End? — And a last Necessity forces every man to Comply with what he is? — Then am I, but just where I was — And (as I said before) in the greater Hell, — And therefore Gentlemen till wee meet agen, Buonas Nochis. {He sinks and leaves a Carkasse on the Stage.}

Mon: It yet amazes me.

{Enter picaro: with Crisp & Mingo: manacl'd.

Pica: I have brought them (in) according to your Commands; But If I may be beleiv'd, in my owne trade; The first stretch will mill 'em in peices.

Grim: However, give 'em the Question. — What are ye?

Crisp: The same our Master was, — And since (as I see) has given us the slipp; What have I to do, but follow him.

Ming.

We . . . that

Roderigo

full

receive me below?

from behind Montalto

Enter Montalto from behind Montalto

Ring to sink thunder

our Master

V, iii, 111–13. The canceled words are: "Picaro to bring . . . hither, as if they were to be / put upon . . . / It can be no hurt;—Tho.'"

V, iii, 125 f. The blurred stage direction at the right is: "Rod starts, Recovers / and goes up, ruffling to [him]."

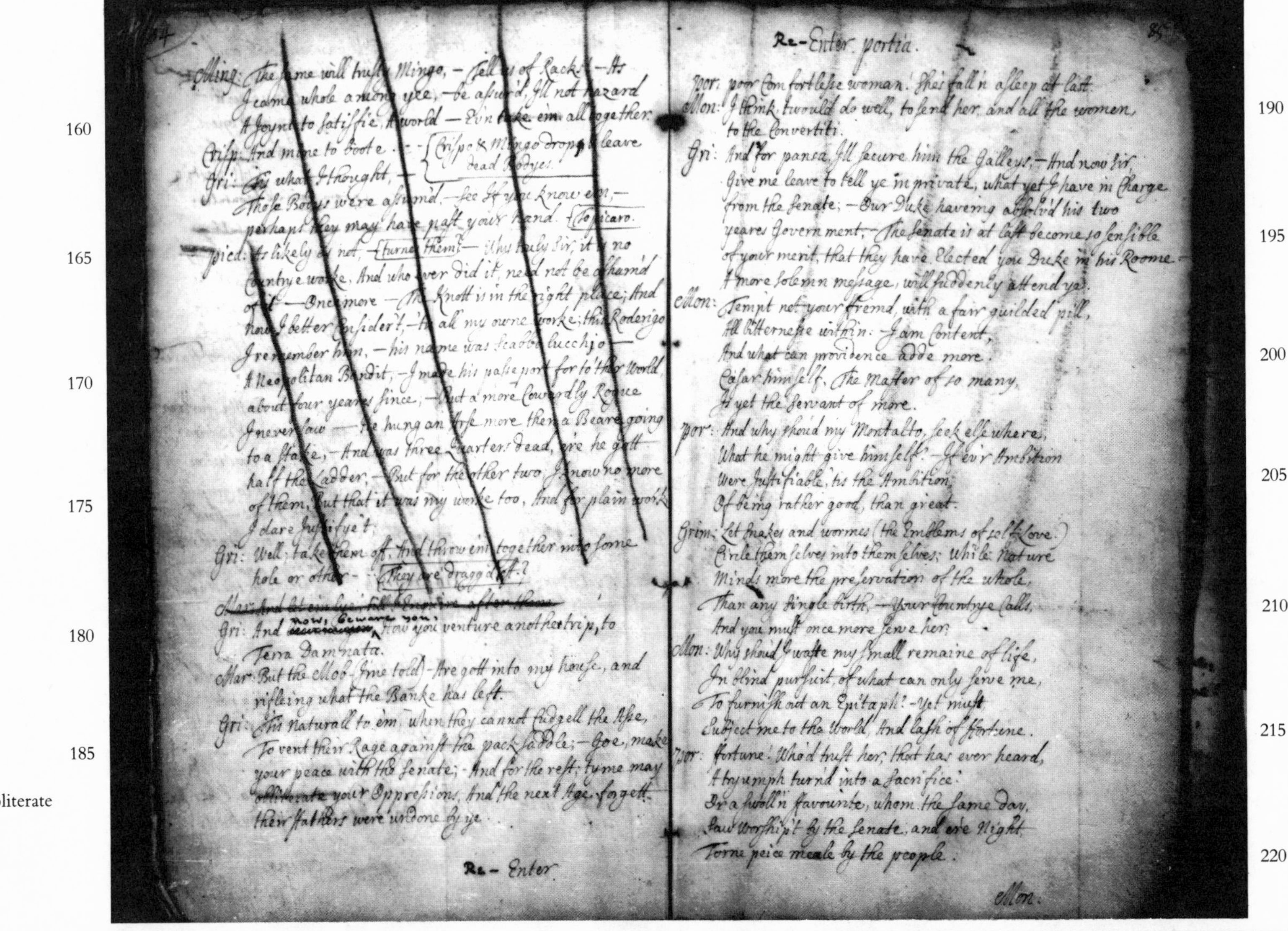

Ming: The same will trust Mingo, — tell us of Racks! — As
I came whole among yee, — be assured, I'll not hazard
A Joynt to satisfie the world — I'll take em all together.
Crisp: And mine to boote — {Crispo & Mingo drop & leave dead Bodyes.}
Gri: 'Tis what I thought, —
Those Bodys were assum'd, — see if you know em, —
perhaps they may have past your hand. {To Picaro.
Pic: As likely as not, — {turnes them} — this truly Sir, it is no
Countrye worke, And who ever did it, need not be asham'd
of it — One more — The Knott is in the right place; And
now I better Consider't, — 'tis all my owne worke; this Rodorigo
I remember him, — his name was Scarbo Lucchio —
A Neapolitan Bandit, — I made his passeport for to'ther World,
about four yeares since, — But a more Cowardly Rogue
I never saw — He hung an Arse more then a Beare going
to a stake, — And was three Quarters dead, ere he gott
half the Ladder, — But for the other two I know no more
of them, But that it was my worke too, And for plain worke
I dare justifye't.
Gri: Well; take them off, And throw em together into some
hole or other — {They are dragg'd off.}
~~Mar: And let e'm lye, till I Enquire after them~~
Gri: And ~~beware you~~ now, beware you, how you venture another trip, to
Terra Damnata.
Mar: But the Mob (I'me told) — Are gott into my house, and
rifleing what the Banke has left.
Gri: 'Tis naturall to em, when they cannot Cudgell the Asse,
To vent their Rage against the packsaddle; — Goe, make
your peace with the senate; — And for the rest; tyme may
obliterate your Oppressions, And the next Age forgett
their fathers were undone by ye.
Re-Enter

Re-Enter portia.
Por: poor Comfortlesse woman: shee's fall'n asleep at last.
Mon: I think, twould do well, to send her, and all the women,
to the Convertiti.
Gri: And for pansa, I'll secure him the Galleys; — And now Sir,
Give me leave to tell ye in private, what yet I have in Charge
from the Senate; — Our Duke haveing absolv'd his two
yeares Government; — The Senate is at last become so sensible
of your merit, that they have Elected you Duke in his Roome.
A more solemn message, will suddenly attend ye.
Mon: Tempt not your friend, with a fair guilded pill,
All bitternesse within: — I am Content,
And what can providence adde more.
Cæsar himselfe, The Master of so many,
Is yet the Servant of more.
Por: And why should my Montalto, seek elsewhere,
What he might give himselfe? — If ev'r Ambition
Were justifiable, tis the Ambition,
Of being rather good, than great.
Grim: Let snakes and wormes (the Emblems of selfe Love)
Circle themselves into themselves; While Nature
Minds more the preservation of the whole,
Than any single birth, — Your Countrye Calls,
And you must once more serve her.
Mon: Why should I waste my small remaine of life,
In blind pursuit, of what can only serve me,
To furnish out an Epitaph? — Yet must
Subject me to the World, And lash of fortune.
Por: Fortune: Who'd trust her, that has ever heard,
A tryumph turn'd into a sacrifice:
Or a swoll'n favourite, whom the same day,
Saw worship't by the senate, and ere Night
Torn peice meale by the people.
Mon.

obliterate

V, iii, 179–80. The canceled line is: "Mar: And let e'm lye, till I Enquire after them / beware you"—the last being replaced by "now, beware you."

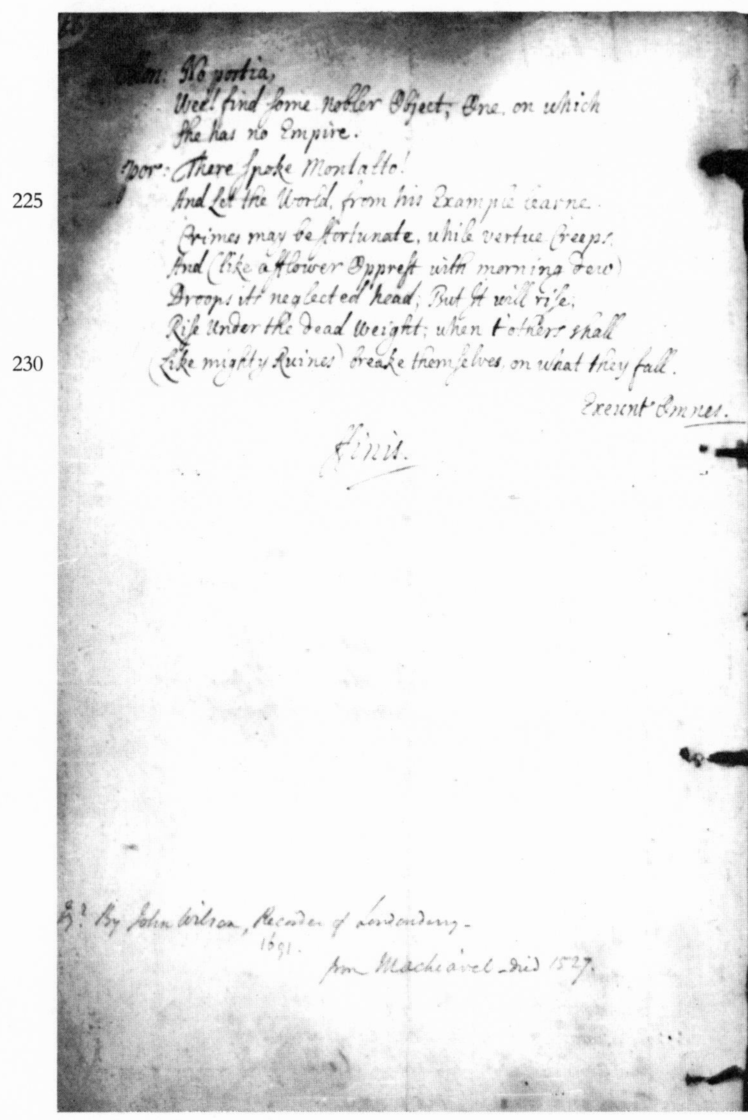

Mon: No portia,
Wee'l find some nobler Object; One, on which
she has no Empire.
Por: There spoke Montalto!
And Let the World, from his Example learne.
Crimes may be fortunate, while vertue Creeps;
And (like a flower Opprest with morning dew)
Droops its neglected head; But it will rise,
Rise Under the dead Weight; when t'others shall
(Like mighty Ruines) breake themselves, on what they fall.

Exeunt Omnes.

Finis.

By John Wilson, Recorder of Londonderry –
1691.
from Machiavel – died 1527.

NOTE. *The Belphegor* manuscript also contains a prologue and epilogue in Wilson's hand, but they were written for the London performances of the play in 1690 and are not related to the promptbook.

Appendix C

Some Pre-Restoration Promptbooks

Restoration prompters must have learned their trade from people familiar with backstage practices in the Jacobean and Caroline theatres. Sir Walter Greg in his splendid *Dramatic Documents from the Elizabethan Playhouses* described a number of early promptbooks, including several dating from the 1620s and 1630s: *The Two Noble Ladies* (1622–23?), *The Welsh Embassador* (c. 1623), *The Honest Man's Fortune* (c. 1624), Heywood's *The Captives* (1624), Massinger's *The Parliament of Love* (1624) and *Believe as You List* (c. 1631), W. M[ountfort's] *The Launching of the Mary* (c. 1633), and *The Lady Mother* (c. 1635). The Malone Society has published some of those as well as the promptbook for *The Wasp* (1630s).

Professor Evans in his *Shakespearean Prompt-Books* examined the books for *Measure for Measure*, *Macbeth*, and *The Winter's Tale* at the University Library at Padua and supposed them to have been connected with Sir Edward Dering's amateur players in the 1620s. He later found that the notes in those copies matched those in the promptbook for Shirley's *Love's Cruelty* at the National Library of Scotland, and the Shirley play was not printed until 1640. (Evans discussed the problem in *Studies in Bibliography*, 20 [1967], 239–42.) Though the dating of this group of promptbooks remains uncertain, they seem certainly to belong to the pre-Restoration period. They contain no mention of scenery but have textual emendations and warnings for actors. Actor entrances are usually marked with a marginal repeat of the characters' names, set between two horizontal lines.

The pre-Restoration promptbooks normally contain imperative warnings, such as "be ready," rather than the "call" that is found so frequently in Restoration books. But Restoration prompters clearly used procedures handed down from earlier generations. What distinguishes most Restoration promptbooks are the notes on scenery and scene changes.

Appendix D

Some Early Eighteenth-Century Promptbooks

There are several very full promptbooks dating after 1700, and since some of those from the first quarter of the new century may have been prepared by people trained during the Restoration period, I would like to cite some of the most interesting ones, along with a promptbook for an amateur production that may have taken place at one of the patent houses.

1. *Pastor Fido* by Elkanah Settle; British Library MS Egerton 2420. This manuscript promptbook was evidently prepared for an all-girl amateur production, perhaps at Dorset Garden Theatre on 30 October 1706, as Mollie Sands suggests in *Theatre Notebook*. The presence in the cast of a Miss "Preist" would argue that the girls may have been from Josias Priest's school in Chelsea, where Purcell's *Dido and Aeneas* was presented about 1689–90. I transcribed and discussed all the prompt notes in *Pastor Fido* in "Three Early Eighteenth Century Promptbooks." The manuscript contains careful actor warnings by characters, descriptions of settings, notes on sound effects and properties, and a cast list.

2. *The Force of Friendship* by Charles Johnson; Folger Shakespeare Library manuscript play (D. b. 62) with full manuscript prompt notes for the production at the Queen's Theatre in the Haymarket on 20 April 1710. Leo Hughes, in a note accompanying the manuscript, says that the copyist was probably James Wright, and the prompt notes were very likely written by the prompter Thomas Newman. This is a very neat and carefully prepared promptbook. In addition to descriptions of settings, the prompter provided a list of properties needed for each scene, indicated if a scene began with characters "discovered" (and, if so, named the actors), and signaled by asterisks all speeches containing cuts. The actor warnings are all by the names of the players, not the characters, so that both major and minor actors are cited (see illustration). All act endings except Act V have warnings, but ring cues for entr'acte activity are not used. Scene shifts at the beginning of each act are marked by the circle-and-dot symbol; all scene changes within acts are cued by double circle-and-dot symbols. Entrance doors and sides are marked as in *The Albion Queens*; here we find OP, MDPS, UDPS, MDOP, and LDOP. I do not think one should suppose that the use of the abbreviations for lower, middle, and upper should necessarily suggest that the Queen's Theatre had three entrance doors on each side of the forestage but rather three entranceways on each side—a door and wing passages.

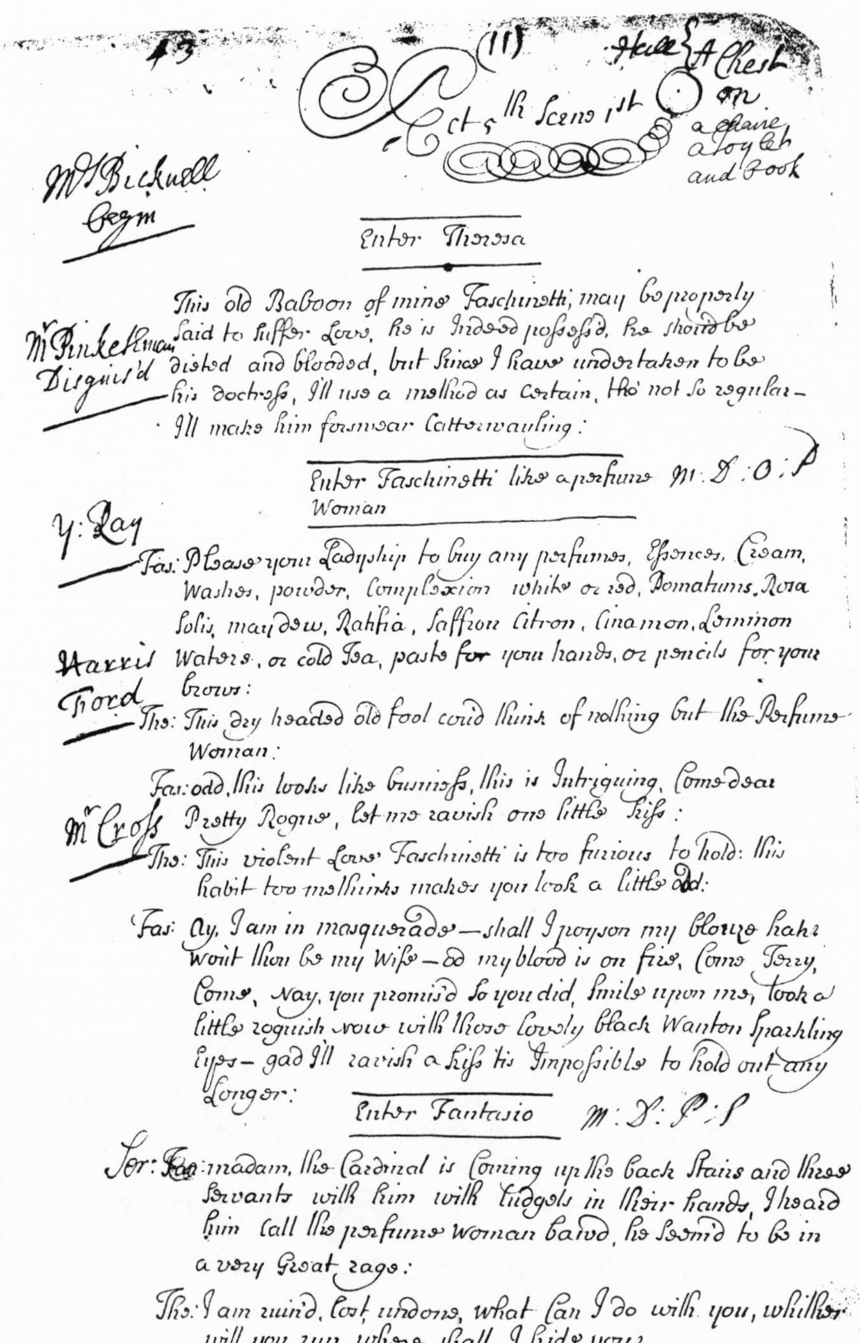

43 (11) Hall A Chest

Act 5th Scene 1st

on a chaire a Toylet and Book

Mrs Bicknell
Begin

Enter Theresa

This old Baboon of mine Faschinetti, may be properly said to suffer Love, he is Indeed possess'd, he should be dieted and blooded, but since I have undertaken to be his doctress, I'll use a method as certain, tho' not so regular — I'll make him forswear Caterwauling:

Mr Pinkethman Disguis'd

Enter Faschinetti like a perfume Woman M: D: O: P

Y: Lay

Fas: Please your Ladyship to buy any perfumes, Essences, Cream, Washes, powder, Complexion white or red, Pomatums, Rosa Solis, may dew, Rattifia, Saffron Citron, Cinamon, Cominon Waters, or cold Tea, paste for your hands, or pencils for your brows:

Harris
Ford

The: This dry headed old fool could think of nothing but the Perfume Woman:

Fas: odd, this looks like Business, this is Intriguing, Come dear Pretty Rogue, let me ravish one little kiss:

Mr Cross

The: This violent Love Faschinetti is too furious to hold: this habit too methinks makes you look a little odd:

Fas: Ay, I am in masquerade — shall I poyson my blowze hah? won't thou be my Wife — od my blood is on fire, Come Terry, Come, Nay, you promis'd so you did, Smile upon me, look a little roguish now with those Lovely black Wanton sparkling Eyes — gad I'll ravish a kiss tis Impossible to hold out any Longer:

Enter Fantasio M: D: P: P

Ser: Fan madam, the Cardinal is Coming up the back Stairs and three Servants with him with Cudgels in their hands, I heard him call the perfume woman bawd, he seem'd to be in a very Great rage:

The: I am ruin'd, lost, undone, what can I do with you, whither will you run, where shall I hide you?

From Johnson's *The Force of Friendship*. By kind permission of the Folger Shakespeare Library, Washington, D..C.

3. *The Mourning Bride* by William Congreve; Folger Shakespeare Library copy (Prompt M54) of the (1703) third quarto. The manuscript prompt notes and markings probably date after 1710, but for what theatre they were prepared I do not know. The circle-and-dot symbol for scene shifts, the ring cue for act endings, and the descriptions of settings are similar to notes found in many Restoration promptbooks. Missing are actor warnings and cross-hatch entrance cues, but the prompter used OP and PS to designate where entrances should be made. The circle-and-dot symbols vary in appearance; sometimes the circle has within it what looks like a W instead of a dot, and sometimes the dot becomes a squiggle or group of squiggles. The significance of the variations escapes me. The copy is heavily marked for cutting, but many planned cuts are marked for restoration. Though a performance might have been run from this book, it is quite messy in places, and the prompter may have transferred the final decisions on cuts and actor entrance sides to a cleaner and more complete copy.

4. *The Perfidious Brother* by Lewis Theobald; Bodleian Library manuscript play (Rawl. poet. 136) with full manuscript prompt notes for the production by John Rich's company at the new Lincoln's Inn Fields Theatre on 21 February 1716. The book was probably prepared by the prompter John Stede (or Steed) and his colleagues. I transcribed and discussed all of the prompt notes in this copy in "Three Early Eighteenth-Century Manuscript Promptbooks." Entranceways for actors are specified as LDPS, MDPS, UDPS, LDOP, MDOP, and UDOP. The promptbook contains a cast list, actor warnings by actor names, descriptions of settings, circle-and-dot scene-shift cues, notes on properties, and textual emendations.

5. *The Lady's Triumph* by Elkanah Settle; Bodleian Library manuscript play (Rawl. poet. 136) with full manuscript prompt notes for the production by John Rich's company at Lincoln's Inn Fields Theatre on 22 March 1718. The bulk of the play is in manuscript, but for the entertainments in the last act the prompter used pages from the printed edition. The promptbook was probably prepared by John Stede and his colleagues. I transcribed and discussed all of the notes in this copy in "Three Early Eighteenth-Century Manuscript Promptbooks." Entranceways for the actors are indicated by LDPS, MDPS, LDOP, MDOP, and sometimes just PS or OP; no UDPS or UDOP abbreviations are used. The promptbook contains actor warnings by actor names, descriptions of settings, notes on properties, and textual emen-

dations. Cue marks or symbols to catch the attention of the prompter also include #, X, *, ⊗, and the Mercury symbol ☿. The circled x has to do with the shifting of scenery, probably set pieces as opposed to wings. The Mercury symbol is used as a curtain cue. Dances have their own cue, a symbol that looks something like a linked ²4 or the Jupiter sign ♃. The circle-and-dot symbol for scene shifts is used, but infrequently. See illustration.

6. *The Rover* by Aphra Behn; 1677 first quarto with manuscript prompt notes and cuts, at the University of London Library. The promptbook may have been prepared by or under the supervision of W. R. Chetwood, the Drury Lane prompter in the 1720s, for a production during that decade. I transcribed and discussed all of the prompt notes in "Three Early Eighteenth Century Promptbooks." Entrances are specified as LDPS, MDPS, UDPS, LDOP, MDOP, and UDOP and sometimes just PS or OP. Actor warnings are by character names. A few properties are mentioned and a trap is used, but the notes provide no information on scenery or scene changes.

7. *Money the Mistress* by Thomas Southerne; Bodleian Library manuscript play (Rawl. poet. 136) with full manuscript prompt notes for the production by John Rich's company at Lincoln's Inn Fields Theatre on 19 February 1726. The promptbook was probably prepared by John Stede and his colleagues. I transcribed and discussed all of the prompt notes in this copy in "Three Early Eighteenth-Century Manuscript Promptbooks," and Daniel Alkofer suggested some new interpretations of the staging and the scenery symbols in *Restoration and 18th Century Theatre Research*. In the promptbook the entrances are specified as MDPS, LDOP, MDOP, PS, and OP only. The circle-and-dot symbol for scene shifts is used, sometimes singly and sometimes doubled and intertwined. Alkofer suggests that the double symbol may have indicated full shifts (wings *and* shutters—or, at that period, perhaps wings and drops) while a single symbol may have meant a partial shift: shutters *or* drops. But the promptbook for *The Force of Friendship* in 1710 shows two circle-and-dot symbols (not intertwined, however) for shifts within acts and single symbols for changes at act openings. The eighteenth-century promptbook for Otway's *Caius Marius* at the Folger Shakespeare Library contains double symbols for all shifts. In *Money the Mistress* the actor warnings are by the names of the characters, and one finds setting descriptions, notes on properties, the ²4 dance symbol, and textual emendations.

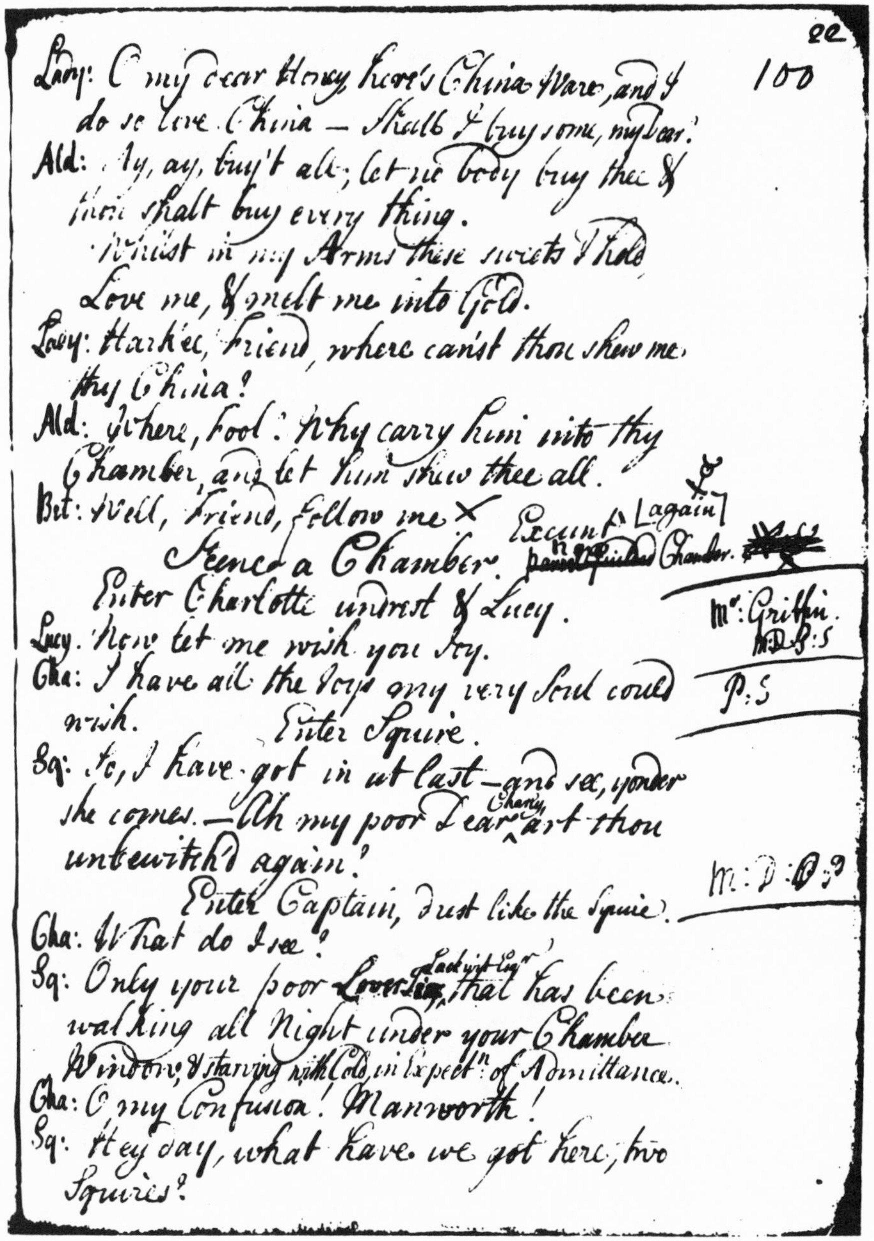

From *The Lady's Triumph*. By kind permission of the Bodleian Library, Oxford.

A comparison of the early eighteenth-century promptbooks with the richest of the Restoration books reveals a growing sophistication over the years. The theatres were getting larger and more elaborately equipped, and years of experience taught prompters and technicians the necessity of a fuller set of cue symbols. Restoration promptbooks contain nothing as precise as the entrance-door abbreviations that appear in several of the later books, and the complex system of cue symbols employed in *The Lady's Triumph* is far more advanced than anything found in Restoration promptbooks.

The information that Restoration books lacked—notes on stage movement, line interpretation, costumes, lighting—is also missing from the eighteenth-century books. That kind of information had yet to find a place in promptbooks, which, throughout the Restoration and early eighteenth century, were chiefly concerned with actor entrances, sound and special effects, dances, properties, stage settings, and scene shifts.

Appendix E

Trico's Part in *Ignoramus* by George Ruggle

The actor Matthew Medbourne's part for the character of Trico in Ferdinando Parkhurst's translation of George Ruggle's Latin play *Ignoramus* was prepared for the Duke's Company performance at court on 1 November 1662 but possibly not used. I know of no other actor's part (or "sides") from the Restoration period, and though we must be grateful for the survival of this one, it does not contain any notes by Medbourne that might show us just what Restoration actors did with their roles. The part was written out by Parkhurst himself and not the prompter, whose task that normally was. Parkhurst based the part on an early draft of the play and not the one used for the 1662 production. The reason it survived, one supposes, is precisely because it was not used by Medbourne after all. The part and the manuscripts of the play are at Harvard and were discussed by Edward F. J. Tucker in "The Harvard Manuscript of Parkhurst's *Ignoramus* and in my "Restoration Actor's Part."

Courtesy of the Harvard Theatre Collection, the following is a transcription of Act I, Scene v, the first scene in which Trico appears, with an accompanying transcription of the sides for that scene; the scene occupies the left column of the page, the sides the right column. The general format of Medbourne's part (see illustration) is similar to that used in Shakespeare's day, to partbooks of the eighteenth century, and, indeed, to sides still used in some professional playhouses today. Theatrical traditions die hard.

In the original manuscript interlinear corrections were made; these have been set in the transcription within pointed brackets immediately after the canceled words, thus: ~~follow after~~ ⟨not belong behind⟩.

SCEN: ~~6~~5	ACTUS PRIMUS, SCEN: 5.
Enter Antonius & Trico	
Ant: Now Trico all my hopes depend on thee, my time's almost expir'd, my life runs minuts.	——— life runs minutes
Tric: ffeare nothing Sir, both time & tide's preseru'd, giue me leaue to cleare your eyes, behold yon starr——	ffeare nothing Sir, both time & tide's preseru'd. giue me leaue to cleere your eyes — behold yon starr —

Ant: hah, my Rosabella, heaũes bless th' appearance.

Tric: approach not neere her sir, take my advice,
see you not that old woman?

Ant: what of her?

Tric: an old bitch sir, thou[gh] she has no teeth to bite
how er'e a barking curr may wake the Master,
but Ile stroak her gently, and make much of her
~~in the interim~~ while you discourse your mind to Rosabella
as the occasion offers; and heare you Sir,
you must be angry in a seeming way
to avoid suspition.

Ant: I like thy conncell.

Tric: saue you good woman — hah, I think shees deaf.

Sur: away, away, touch me not, keep of your hands.

Tric: precious, how feirce she is!?

Sur: out upon him he has hurt my hand. —
he shews me a ring ~~hee'd~~ hee'd be my sweetheart sure,
But Ile ~~haue none of him~~ ⟨not yeild at first⟩ Ile know him better
see how he folds his arms? p. 10

Tric: ahime——

Surd: how he sighs too?
because I am faire he thinkes I must be fond,
but he is mistaken.

Tric: ahime——

Surd: how thick he drawes his breath?
alackaday, hee's dying, I feare hee'l dy~~ing.~~

Tric: oh — her lips as white as milk,
her nose so purple pure
her skin like precious stones
oh — her breath I can't endure
Besides those amber-cheeks
and eyes like Turkey-eggs
and buttocks of pure brawne
oh — that Dee'l betweene her leggs.

——— appearance
approach not neer her Sir, take my aduice,
see you not that old woman?
——— what of her?
an old bitch Sir, though she haue no teeth to bite,
howe're a barking curr may wake the Master:
but ile stroak her gently, & make much of her,
while you discourse your mind to Rosabella
as the occasion offers; and heare you Sir,
you must be angry in a seeming way
to avoid suspition.
——— thy councell
saue you good woman — hah; I think shee's deaf.
——— your hands
Precious how feirce she is?
——— folds his armes
ahime——
——— mistaken
ahime——
——— feare hee'l dye.
oh — her lipps as white as milk
her nose so purple pure
her skin like precious stones
oh — her breath I can't endure.
Besides those amber cheeks
and eyes like turkey-eggs
and buttocks of pure brawne
oh — that Dee'l between her leggs.

Surd: alas the man's astonisht at my beauty,
that I could but heare my comendations now?
poore heart he weepes, what shall I do?
wo is me he swouns too, beare up thy heart
I loue thee, I tell thee I loue thee —

Ant: I can containe no longer; Dearest Lady
vouchsafe to cast your eyes upon an object
in whose countenance you may read the story
of a most faithfull and nnfortunate lover —

Ros: hah, my Antonius —

Ant: approach not (my Dearest) nor use one motion
may any wise discover our affections,
but striue to feigne (if possibly thou canst)
some pretty gentle passion of dislike daine

Sur: come haue a good heart, arrise, I tell thee I loue thee,
Ile not suffer any one to dye for me.

Tric: sayst thou so old wench, then thou'rt sure my owne,
what shall I do to forbeare laughing? ahime——

Sur: forbeare those sighs ⟨throbs,⟩ be confident I loue thee:
precious stones, yonders the young man come,
Mistress, shew him no countenance at all
but turne him with sowre looks and hee'l be gone.

Ros: Now Antonius I must feigne in earnest; p. 11
I heare you are preparing toward England.
I thought Id'e had more intrest in your loue
then to forsake me now, what oun't these men do?
oh heard hearted men——

Sur: de'e beat your breast, tis well, ah impudent

Tric: ahime——

Sur: oh how I am plung'd in loue,
euen like a waspe falne into an hony pott

Ant: thou knowst I'aue pledg'd my faith to none but thee,

Sur: ahime—— this loue

Tric: she sighs like a sow that has lost her first litter.

———— dye for me 55

Sayst thou so (old wench) then thour't sure mine owne:
what shall I do to forbeare laughing? ahime

———— impudent 67

ahime——

———— this loue 72

she sighs like a sow that has lost her first litter

Ant: thou art the sole comãndress of my thoughts,
not one escapes there.

Ros: Speake not beyond them,
dost think Antonius I can think he loues me
that can haue thoughts to leaue me?

Ant: pardon my fate
so wholy govern'd by my ffathers will
that neither sighs nor prayers can availe
tis forc'd obedience.

Ros: loue will not be forc'd
'twill slip aside, or find a thousand shifts,
thou dost not loue.

Ant: then let me perish ——

Ros: oh peace, for heauens sake and thine owne.

Sur: fye upon this loue

Ros: Ile rather question my feares that make the doubt
then summon new vowes to confirme a faith,
I am satisfyed; But deare Antonius now
the Tragick-scene begins to change on my part,
pardon the relation, and my innocence,
living in subjection to a cruell vncle

Sur: spitt in's face.

Ros: a merchant of Portugale to whose care
my ffather ~~comitted~~ ⟨left⟩ me, I am ⟨now⟩ become
as priz-goods ~~offred~~ ⟨tendred⟩ to sale at who giues more
and am ~~now~~ contracted for by Ignoramus,
who intends to come, or send his clerk anon
with th' contract mony and a private token.

Tric: know you what token 'tis?

Ros: not I, but there are ~~the~~ his conceited Verses. p. 12

Sur: she throwes away his letters, tis well
how he rages now? but I see thee my ~~Deare loue~~ joy

Tric: I may perchance fish something out of these

From Trico's part in Ruggle's *Ignoramus*, translated by Parkhurst. By kind permission of the Harvard Theatre Collection.

——— priuate token. 101 p. 2

know you what token it is?

——— thee my joy

I may perchance fish something out of these.

Ant:	oh Trico ——	———— oh Trico
Tric:	I haue it here shall do the work sir.	I haue it here shall do the work Sir.
Sur:	beat not thy head so, beleeue me I loue thee, I feare hee'l fall into a new convulsion.	———— convulsion
Tric:	alas for't (tender Monkey) I can hold no longer, ha, ha	alas for it (tender monkey) I can hold no longer ha, ha,
Sur:	does my loue laugh? then Ile laugh too, ha, ha	———— ha, ha, ha,
Tric:	hark how she neighs? Now sir you haue an oppertunity make use of it, away, Ile ~~follow after~~ ⟨not belong behind⟩ my Venus now is linkt in Vulcanes chaines.	hark how she neighs; Now sir you haue an oppertunity, make use of it, away, ile not be long behind, my Venus now is linkt in Vulcan's chaines.
Ant:	come my Deare soule, ⟨life⟩ let vs embrace the motion	
Ros:	as freely as life, but yet I feare——	
Ant:	lets banish feare that ~~hinders~~ ⟨frustrates⟩ our content so shall our joyes appeare more permanent. Exeunt Ant: Ros:	———— permanent
Tric:	phuh, away away, look not back on vs, shees safe enough while I can court her thus.	phuh away, away, look not back on us, shee's safe enough while I can court her thus.
Sur:	Now where's thy ring — sweet loue thy hand too — heauens prosper it	———— prosper it.
Tric:	that thou mayst perish.	that thou maist perish
Sur:	lets seale it with a kiss.	———— with a kiss.
Tric:	~~with all~~ ⟨euen from⟩ my heart out upont, how close she sticks? Judgme its enough to make water in a Mounsier's mouth.	euen from my heart — out upon't, how close she sticks? Judgme its enough to make water in a Mounsieurs mouth.
Sur:	eh, eh, eh I'm troubled with a little scurvy cough, eh, eh,	———— cough, eh, eh,
Tric:	up with those rotten intrailes.	up with those rotten intrailes
Sur:	come my little cock now lets be gone.	———— lets be gone
Tric:	but I shall leaue ~~you~~ ⟨thee⟩ to ~~your~~ ⟨thy⟩ selfe anon. Exeunt	but I shall leaue thee to thy selfe anon, Exn̄t { Tric Surd

Trico,

his part.

Mr Medburne p. 1

Appendix F

Related Documents

There are a number of copies of plays in manuscript or printed form that contain notes and markings that may or may not have originated in a London Restoration theatre. Below I have commented on a few of these to give the reader some indication of the kinds of materials that stand on the fringes of such a study as this. No item listed is a promptbook, yet any one might have served as the basis for a promptbook.

1. *The Whore of Babylon* by Thomas Dekker; 1607 first quarto at Worcester College Library, Oxford (Play. 3. 13) containing extensive cuts and emendations. The markings would appear to be theatrical in nature. Fredson Bowers in his edition of Dekker's *Dramatic Works* suggests that the notes may have been made about the time of the Popish plot in 1678, but *The London Stage* does not list any performances of the play between 1660 and 1700. Anthony Aston's supplement to Cibber's *Apology* (reprinted in Lowe's edition of that work) says that the actor Joe Haines set up "a Droll-Booth, and acted a new Droll, call'd *The Whore of Babylon, the Devil, and the Pope*" at Bartholomew Fair in 1685; perhaps the Worcester College copy of Dekker's play was marked in preparation for Haines's production.

2. *A Fine Companion* by Shackerley Marmion; 1633 first quarto at the British Library (82 c 25 [2]) containing a welter of manuscript cuts and emendations. I have not been able to date the marginalia, but three notes suggest the use of scenery: *[Sc]ene a Tavern* at the opening of IV, i; *a chamber* at the opening of IV, iv; and *ye street* at the opening of V, i. But the play is not known to have been performed during the Restoration period, and the copy contains no other notes or marks typical of promptbooks. The book is so littered with manuscript additions and corrections that a prompter could hardly have used it in performance. The notes certainly originated in a playhouse, but where? And when?

3. *A Faire Quarrell* by Thomas Middleton and William Rowley; 1622 second quarto at the National Library of Scotland, Edinburgh, containing manuscript cuts and emendations, possibly by a prompter or an actor or both and possibly for a Restoration production. No Restoration performances of the play are recorded, but in view of this copy, perhaps one was contemplated.

4. *Venice Preserv'd* by Thomas Otway; 1682 first quarto at the British Library (644 h 77) containing some prudish manuscript cuts and alterations on pages 71 and 72. There was a performance of the play by the Duke's Company at Dorset Garden Theatre on 9 February 1682, but there is no way of telling whether this copy is related to it, to some other, unrecorded, performance, or to some later production.

5. *The Duchess of Malfi* by John Webster; 1640 second quarto at the

National Library of Scotland, Edinburgh, containing some manuscript markings in acts I, II, and III. Several of the notes are corrections of typographical errors, some quite minor, and prompters usually did not bother themselves with such matters. Marginal brackets indicate possible cuts, and these may have been theatrical in origin.

6. *The Siege of Urbin* by William Killigrew; manuscript play at the Bodleian Library, Oxford (Rawl. poet. 29) containing manuscript emendations and a cast list. *The London Stage* reports the cast under the 1664–65 season. The emendations may have been made in preparation for a King's Company production at the Bridges Street Theatre that season, but the copy is not a promptbook. The play was published in 1666. Ivan Earle Taylor edited the manuscript in 1946.

7. *Comedies, and Tragedies* by Thomas Killigrew; 1664 folio at Worcester College Library, Oxford, containing manuscript emendations by the author. Killigrew was the manager of the King's Company and produced three of the plays in the volume: *Claricilla*, *The Princess*, and *The Parson's Wedding*. The manuscript notes show that he contemplated productions of *The Pilgrim*, *Cicilia and Clorinda*, *Thomaso*, and *Bellamira Her Dream*, and those works may also have been performed. Killigrew was certainly preparing his plays for performance, but he was editing, not working up promptbooks. William Van Lennep discussed the annotations in the *Joseph Quincy Adams Memorial Studies* and Albert Wertheim examined Killigrew's detailed stage directions in the first three plays cited above (which he did not annotate in the 1664 folio) in *Theatre Survey*.

8. *The Black Prince* by Roger Boyle, Earl of Orrery; 1669 folio (with *Tryphon*, in *Two New Tragedies*) at the New York Public Library (*KC 1669) containing extensive manuscript cuts and two manuscript casts for an amateur production (or productions?), possibly during the Restoration period. One of the two casts is all women, the other is mixed; among the names listed are Charles Blount, George Blount, June Blount, Lady Blount, William Hicks, Val Knightly, H. Hanford, Mrs. H. Hanford, and Mary More. There is only one certain prompt note in the copy—an entrance cue for an actress; the book could hardly have served a prompter in performance.

9. There are a few Shakespeare plays with manuscript notes and marks possibly related to London productions during our period:

a. A Huntington Library copy of the 1600 first quarto of *2 Henry IV* contains some manuscript entrance and exit notes.

b. At the University of Michigan is a *Merchant of Venice* from the 1632 second folio containing manuscript cuts. The markings cease near the beginning of Act III, and if a production was planned, it may have been abandoned before a complete promptbook was prepared. The play was assigned to the King's Company on 12 January 1669, but there are no records of its having been performed between then and the end of the century. Professor Evans will be dealing with this copy in a volume of his *Shakespearean Prompt-Books*.

c. At the Boston Public Library is a copy of the 1630 third quarto of *The Merry Wives of Windsor* containing manuscript entrance notes that sometimes repeat information in the printed stage directions and sometimes provide entrances where the text is missing them.

d. A copy of the 1600 quarto of *Much Ado about Nothing* in the Dyce collection at the Victoria and Albert Museum contains a number of manuscript marks. The most frequently repeated one is: Γ. It appears before many speech ascriptions, but whoever made the marks began giving up the rather pointless task about sixteen pages before the end of the play. Some entrances are marked with a horizontal line in the margin. The manuscript dramatis personae (no actors named) on the back of the title page appears to be in a late seventeenth-century hand.

e. At the University of Edinburgh Library is *A Midsummer Night's Dream* taken from a 1623 folio and marked with cuts and emendations, perhaps for a production planned at the Nursery (in the Barbican?) about 1672. Professor Evans has analyzed the copy in his *Shakespearean Prompt-Books* and concludes that the play never reached production. The copy is missing several pages, but Evans estimates that the full text may have had about 745 lines marked for deletion. Speech ascriptions for Robin are changed to Puck and a line is emended, but the copy contains none of the usual warnings and cues found in promptbooks.

f. At the Folger Shakespeare Library is a copy of *Twelfth Night*, from a 1632 folio, containing a number of prompt notes for a seventeenth-century production, possibly in London. Act warnings are in a hand similar to that in *The Wise-Woman of Hogsdon* and the actor warnings are in a hand similar to that in the Rhodes Company promptbooks. But *Twelfth Night* was a Duke's Company play, and the hands in the promptbook do not match those found in any Duke's Company books.

A related document of a different sort is the 1676 quarto of *Hamlet*, which I cited in the Introduction as containing playhouse omissions set within quotation marks. The edition, based on the 1637 quarto, must have been prepared with reference to the Duke's Company prompt-book.

Bibliography

Adams, Henry Hitch. "A Prompt Copy of Dryden's *Tyrannic Love.*" *Studies in Bibliography* 4 (1951–52): 170–74.

Alkofer, Daniel. "A Note on the Staging of *Money the Mistress* in 1726." *Restoration and 18th Century Theatre Research* 11 (May 1972): 31–32.

Ayres, Philip. "Production and Adaptation of William Sampson's *The Vow-Breaker* (1636) in the Restoration." *Theatre Notebook* 27 (Summer 1973): 145–49.

Bald, R. C. "Shakespeare on the Stage in Restoration Dublin." *PMLA* 56 (1941): 369–78.

Barlow, Graham. "Sir James Thornhill and the Theatre Royal, Drury Lane, 1705." In *The Eighteenth-Century English Stage*, edited by Kenneth Richards and Peter Thomson. London: Methuen, 1972.

Baur-Heinhold, Margarete. *Baroque Theatre*. London: Thames and Hudson, 1967.

Beaumont, Francis, and John Fletcher. *The Dramatic Works in the Beaumont and Fletcher Canon*. Edited by Fredson Bowers et al. Cambridge: Cambridge University Press, 1966–. (*The Scornful Lady*, ed. Cyrus Hoy, is in vol. 2.)

———. *The Works of Francis Beaumont and John Fletcher*. 10 vols. Edited by Arnold Glover and A. R. Waller. Cambridge: Cambridge University Press, 1906, 1907. (*The Spanish Curate* is in vol. 2, *The Loyal Subject* in vol. 3, and *A Wife for A Moneth* in vol. 5.)

Beaurline, L. A. *See* Suckling, Sir John.

Behn, Aphra. *The Rover*. Edited by Frederick Link. Lincoln: University of Nebraska Press, 1967.

———. *The Works of Aphra Behn*. 6 vols. Edited by Montague Summers. London: W. Heinemann, 1915. (*The Rover* is in vol. 1, *The City Heiress* in vol. 2, and *Sir Patient Fancy* in vol. 4.)

Bentley, Gerald E. *The Jacobean and Caroline Stage*. 7 vols. Oxford: Clarendon Press, 1941–68.

Bjurström, Per. *Giacomo Torelli and Baroque Stage Design*. Stockholm: Almquist and Wiksell, 1961.

Boas, Frederick S. "A Lost Restoration Play Restored." *Times Literary Supplement*, 28 September 1946, p. 468.

———. *See also* Howard, Edward.

Boswell, Eleanore. *The Restoration Court Stage*. Cambridge, Mass.: Harvard University Press, 1932.

Bowers, Fredson. *See* Dekker, Thomas.

Burner, Sandra. "A Provincial Strolling Company of the 1670's." *Theatre Notebook* 20 (Winter 1965/66): 74–78.

Byrne, Muriel St. Clare. "Prompt Book's Progress." *Theatre Notebook* 21 (Autumn 1966): 7–12.

Cameron, Kenneth. "Strolling With Coysh." *Theatre Notebook* 17 (Autumn 1962): 12–16.

Cartwright, William. *Plays and Poems.* Edited by G. Blakemore Evans. Madison: University of Wisconsin Press, 1951.

Cibber, Colley. *An Apology for the Life of Mr. Colley Cibber.* 2 vols. Edited by Robert W. Lowe. London: John C. Nimmo, 1889.

Clark, William Smith II. *The Early Irish Stage.* Oxford: Clarendon Press, 1955.

———. "Restoration Prompt Notes and Stage Practices." *Modern Language Notes* 51 (April 1936): 226–30).

———. *See also* Orrey, Roger Boyle, 1st Earl of.

A Comparison Between the Two Stages (1702) (by Charles Gildon?). Edited by Staring B. Wells. Princeton: Princeton University Press, 1942.

Congreve, William. *The Complete Plays.* Edited by Herbert Davis. Chicago: University of Chicago Press, 1967.

———. *The Complete Works of William Congreve.* 4 vols. Edited by Montague Summers. London: Nonesuch Press, 1923.

Crowne, John. *The Dramatic Works of John Crowne.* 4 vols. Edited by James Maidment and W. H. Logan. Edinburgh: W. Paterson, 1873–74. (*Juliana* is in vol. 1.)

Davenant, Sir William. *Davenant's Macbeth from the Yale Manuscript.* Edited by Christopher Spencer. New Haven: Yale University Press, 1961.

Dekker, Thomas. *The Dramatic Works of Thomas Dekker.* 4 vols. Edited by Fredson Bowers. Cambridge: Cambridge University Press, 1953–61. (*The Whore of Babylon* is in vol. 2.)

Devlin, James J. "The Dramatis Personae and the Dating of John Banks's 'The Albion Queens,'" *Notes and Queries* 208 (June 1963): 213–15.

Downes, John. *Roscius Anglicanus* (1708). Introduction by John Loftis. Los Angeles: William Andrews Clark Memorial Library, 1969.

———. *Roscius Anglicanus.* Edited by Montague Summers. London: Fortune Press, n.d. [1928].

Dryden, John. *Dryden: The Dramatic Works.* 6 vols. Edited by Montague Summers. London: Nonesuch Press, 1931–32. (*Tyrannick Love* is in vol. 2, *The Mistaken Husband* in vol. 4.)

———. *Works.* Edited by Edward Niles Hooker et al. Berkeley: University of California Press, 1956–. (*Tyrannick Love* is in vol. 10.)

D'Urfey, Thomas. *A Fool's Preferment.* In Robert Forsythe, *A Study of the Plays of Thomas D'Urfey,* q.v.

Evans, G. Blakemore. "The Douai Manuscript—Six Shakespearean Transcripts (1694–95)." *Philological Quarterly* 41 (January 1962): 158–72.

———. "New Evidence on the Provenance of the Padua Prompt-Books of Shakespeare's *Macbeth, Measure for Measure,* and *Winter's Tale.*" *Studies in Bibliography* 20 (1967): 239–42.

———. *Shakespearean Prompt-Books of the Seventeenth Century.* Charlottesville: Bibliographical Society of the University of Virginia, 1960–.

———. "Shakespeare's *Julius Caesar*—A Seventeenth-Century Manuscript." *Journal of English and Germanic Philology* 41 (October 1942): 401–17.

———. *See also* Cartwright, William.

Forsythe, Robert. *A Study of the Plays of Thomas D'Urfey.* Cleveland: Western Reserve University Press, 1916.

Gifford, William. *See* Shirley, James.

Gildon, Charles. *The Life of Mr. Thomas Betterton.* London: Robert Gosling, 1710.

———. *See also A Comparison Between the Two Stages.*

Greg, Walter W. *A Bibliography of English Printed Drama to the Restoration.* 4 vols. London: for the Bibliographical Society, 1939–59.

———. *Dramatic Documents from the Elizabethan Playhouses.* 2 vols. Oxford: Clarendon Press, 1931.

Harbage, Alfred, comp. *Annals of English Drama 975–1700.* Revised by S. Schoenbaum. London: Methuen, 1964.

———. "Elizabethan and Seventeenth-Century Play Manuscripts." *PMLA* 50 (1935): 687–99.

———. "Elizabethan-Restoration Palimpsest." *Modern Language Review* 35 (July 1940): 287–319.

Herbert, Henry. *The Dramatic Records of Sir Henry Herbert.* Edited by Joseph Quincy Adams. New Haven: Yale University Press, 1917.

Hewitt, Barnard, ed. *The Renaissance Stage Documents of Serlio, Sabbattini and Furttenbach.* Coral Gables: University of Miami Press, 1958.

Heywood, Thomas. *The Dramatic Works.* 6 vols. Edited by R. H. Shepherd. London: J. Pearson, 1874. (*The Wise-Woman of Hogsdon* is in vol. 5.)

Highfill, Philip H., Kalman A. Burnim, and Edward A. Langhans. *A Biographical Dictionary of Actors, Actresses, Musicians, Dancers, Managers, and Other Stage Personnel in London, 1660–1800.* Carbondale: Southern Illinois University Press, 1973–.

Hill, Aaron, and William Popple. *The Prompter.* Selections edited by William Appleton and Kalman A. Burnim. New York: Benjamin Blom, 1966.

Holland, Peter. *The Ornament of Action: Text and Performance in Restoration Comedy.* Cambridge: Cambridge University Press, 1979.

Hotson, Leslie. *The Commonwealth and Restoration Stage*. Cambridge, Mass.: Harvard University Press, 1928.

Howard, Edward. *The Change of Crownes*. Edited by Frederick S. Boas. London: for the Royal Society of Literature by Oxford University Press, 1949.

Hume, Robert D. "The Date of Mountfort's *The Life and Death of Doctor Faustus*." *Archiv für das Studium der neueren Sprachen und Literaturen* 213 (1976): 109–11.

———. *The Development of English Drama in the Late Seventeenth Century*. Oxford: Clarendon Press, 1976.

———. "The Dorset Garden Theatre: A Review of Facts and Problems." *Theatre Notebook* 33 (1979): 4–17.

———, ed. *The London Theatre World, 1660–1800*. Carbondale, Ill.: Southern Illinois University Press, 1980.

Jackson, Allan S. "Restoration Scenery 1656–1680." *Restoration and 18th Century Theatre Research* 3 (November 1964): 25–38.

Jones, Inigo. *Inigo Jones*. 2 vols. Edited by Stephen Orgel and Roy Strong. Berkeley: University of California Press, 1973.

Joseph, Bertram. "Stage-Directions in a 17th Cent. Copy of Shirley," *Theatre Notebook* 3 (1949): 66–67.

Killigrew, Thomas. *Comedies, and Tragedies*. London: Henry Herringman, 1664. (Worcester College, Oxford, copy.)

Killigrew, William. *An Edition of William Killigrew's Siege of Urbin*. Edited by Ivan Earle Taylor. Philadelphia: [University of Pennsylvania], 1946.

Lacy, John. *The Dramatic Works of John Lacy*. Edited by James Maidment and W. H. Logan. Edinburgh: W. Paterson, 1875.

Langhans, Edward A. "Betterton's Hamlet." American Educational Theatre Association 1971 Convention Preprint, 5 pp.

———. "A Conjectural Reconstruction of the Dorset Garden Theatre." *Theatre Survey* 13 (November 1972): 74–93.

———. "New Restoration Manuscript Casts." *Theatre Notebook* 27 (Summer 1973): 149–57.

———. "Notes on the Reconstruction of the Lincoln's Inn Fields Theatre." *Theatre Notebook* 10 (July–September 1956): 112–14.

———. "Research Opportunities in Early Promptbooks." *Educational Theatre Journal* 18 (March 1966): 74–76.

———. "A Restoration Actor's Part." *Harvard Library Bulletin* 23 (April 1975): 180–85.

———. "Restoration Manuscript Notes in Seventeenth Century Plays." *Restoration and 18th Century Theatre Research* 5 (May 1966): 30–39, and 5 (November 1966): 2–17.

———. "The Restoration Promptbook of Shirley's *The Sisters*." *The Theatre Annual* 14 (1956): 51–65.

———. *Staging Practices in the Restoration Theatres, 1660–1682*. Ph.D. dissertation, Yale University, 1955.

———. "Three Early Eighteenth-Century Manuscript Promptbooks." *Modern Philology* 65 (November 1967): 114–29.

———. "Three Early Eighteenth Century Promptbooks." *Theatre Notebook* 20 (Summer 1966): 142–50.

———. "Wren's Restoration Playhouse." *Theatre Notebook* 18 (Spring 1964): 91–100.

Lawrence, William J. "Early Prompt-Books and What They Reveal." In his *Pre-Restoration Stage Studies*, pp. 373–413. Cambridge, Mass.: Harvard University Press, 1927.

———. "The Prompter." In his *Old Theatre Days and Ways*. London: George G. Harrap, 1935.

———. "Sir William Killigrew's 'The Siege of Urbin.'" *Times Literary Supplement*, 18 October 1928, p. 755.

Lawrenson, T. E. *The French Stage in the XVIIth Century*. Manchester: Manchester University Press, 1957.

Leacroft, Richard. *The Development of the English Playhouse*. London: Eyre Methuen, 1973.

Lee, Nathaniel. *The Works of Nathaniel Lee*. 2 vols. Edited by Thomas B. Stroup and Arthur L. Cooke. New Brunswick, N.J.: Scarecrow Press, 1954–55. (*Constantine* and *Theodosius* are in vol. 2.)

Lesko, Kathleen Menzie, ed. *A Critical Old-Spelling Edition of the Plays of John Wilson (1626–1695?)*. Ph.D. dissertation, George Washington University, 1980.

McKinnen, Dana. "A Description of a Restoration Promptbook of Shirley's *The Ball*." *Restoration and 18th Century Theatre Research* 10 (May 1971): 25–28.

Mackintosh, Iain. "Inigo Jones–Theatre Architect." *Tabs* 31 (September 1973): 99–105.

McManaway, James G. "Additional Prompt-books of Shakespeare from the Smock Alley Theatre." *Modern Language Review* 45 (1950): 64–65.

———. "The Copy for *The Careless Lovers*." *Modern Language Notes* 46 (June 1931): 406–9.

———. "The Two Earliest Promptbooks of 'Hamlet.'" *Papers of the Bibliographical Society of America* 43 (1949): 288–320.

Mahelot, Laurent. *Le Mémoire de Mahelot.* Edited by Henry Carrington Lancaster. Paris: E. Champion, 1920.

Marmion, Shackerley. *The Dramatic Works of Shackerley Marmion.* Edited by James Maidment and W. H. Logan. Edinburgh: W. Paterson, 1875.

Martin, Lee J. "From Forestage to Proscenium: A Study of Restoration Staging Techniques." *Theatre Survey* 4 (1963): 3–28.

Middleton, Thomas, and William Rowley. *A Fair Quarrel.* Edited by R. V. Holdsworth. London: Ernest Benn, 1974.

———. *A Fair Quarrel.* Edited by George R. Price. Lincoln: University of Nebraska Press, 1976.

Milhous, Judith. "Thomas Betterton's Playwriting." *Bulletin of the New York Public Library* 77 (Summer 1974): 375–92.

Milhous, Judith, and Robert D. Hume. "Dating Play Premières from Publication Data, 1660–1700." *Harvard Library Bulletin* 22 (October 1974): 374–405.

———. "Lost English Plays, 1660–1700." *Harvard Library Bulletin* 25 (January 1977): 5–33.

Motta, Fabrizio Carini. *Trattato sopra la struttura de' teatre e scene.* Introduction by Edward A. Craig. Milan: Polifilo, 1972.

Mountfort, William. *The Life and Death of Doctor Faustus.* Introduction by Anthony Kaufman. Los Angeles: William Andrews Clark Memorial Library, 1973.

Mullin, Donald C. *The Development of the Playhouse.* Berkeley: University of California Press, 1970.

———. "The Theatre Royal, Bridges Street: A Conjectural Reconstruction." *Educational Theatre Journal* 19 (March 1967): 17–29.

———. "The Theatre Royal, Bridges Street: An Architectural Puzzle." *Theatre Notebook* 25 (Autumn 1970): 14–19.

Mullin, Donald C., and Bruce Koenig. "Christopher Wren's Theatre Royal." *Theatre Notebook* 21 (Summer 1967): 180–87.

Nagler, Alois M. *Sources of Theatrical History.* New York: Theatre Annual, 1952.

Nicoll, Allardyce. *The Development of the Theatre.* 5th ed. New York: Harcourt, Brace & World, 1966.

———. *A History of English Drama 1660–1900*, vol. 1: *Restoration Drama.* 4th ed. Cambridge: Cambridge University Press, 1952.

Novak, Maximillian. "The Closing of Lincoln's Inn Fields Theatre in 1695." *Restoration and 18th Century Theatre Research* 14 (May 1975): 51–52.

O'Donnell, James P. "Some Beaumont and Fletcher Prompt Annotations." *The Papers of the Bibliographical Society of America* 72 (1979), 334–37.

Orrell, John. "Inigo Jones at the Cockpit." In *Shakespeare Survey* 30, edited by Kenneth Muir. Cambridge: Cambridge University Press, 1977.

Orrery, Roger Boyle, 1st Earl of. *The Dramatic Works of Roger Boyle.* 2 vols. Edited by William Smith Clark II. Cambridge, Mass.: Harvard University Press, 1937. (*The Black Prince* and *Guzman* are in vol. 1.)

Otway, Thomas. *Venice Preserved.* Edited by Malcolm Kelsall. Lincoln: University of Nebraska Press, 1969.

———. *The Works of Thomas Otway.* 2 vols. Edited by J. C. Ghosh. Oxford: Clarendon Press, 1932. (*Venice Preserv'd* is in vol. 2.)

Parton, John. *Some Account of the Hospital and Parish of St. Giles in the Fields.* London: L. Hansard, 1822.

Pepys, Samuel. *The Diary of Samuel Pepys.* Edited by Robert Latham and William Matthews. Berkeley: University of California Press (with Bell of London), 1970–.

Pozzo, Andrea. *Rules and Examples of Perspective.* Translated by John James. London: Benjamin Motte, 1707.

Rochester, John Wilmot, 2nd Earl of. *Collected Works.* Edited by John Hayward. London: Nonesuch Press, 1926.

Rosenfeld, Sybil. *Strolling Players and Drama in the Provinces 1660–1765.* Cambridge: Cambridge University Press, 1939.

———. *The Theatre of the London Fairs in the 18th Century.* Cambridge: Cambridge University Press, 1960.

Sampson, William. *William Sampson's Vow-Breaker.* Edited by Hans Wallrath. Louvain: A. Uystpruyst, 1914.

Sands, Mollie. "*Il Pastor Fido* Promptbook," *Theatre Notebook* 21 (Winter 1966/67): 94.

Scanlan, Elizabeth. "Reconstruction of the Duke's Playhouse in Lincoln's Inn Fields, 1661–1671." *Theatre Notebook* 10 (January–March 1956): 48–50.

———. *Tennis-Court Theatres and the Duke's Playhouse, 1661–1671.* Ph.D. dissertation, Columbia University, 1952.

Sedley, Sir Charles. *The Poetical and Dramatic Works of Sir Charles Sedley.* 2 vols. Edited by V. de Sola Pinto. London: Constable, 1928. (*The Mulberry Garden* is in vol. 1.)

Settle, Elkanah. *The Empress of Morocco.* London: William Cademan, 1673.

Shadwell, Thomas. *The Complete Works of Thomas Shadwell.* 5 vols. Edited by Montague Summers. London: Fortune Press, 1927. (*The Woman Captain* is in vol. 4.)

Shakespeare, William. *The Arden Shakespeare.* London: Methuen, various dates.

———. *The New Shakespeare.* Cambridge: Cambridge University Press, various dates.

———. *A New Variorum Edition of Shakespeare.* Edited by Horace H. Furness. New York: American Scholar, various dates.

———. *The Tragedy of Hamlet Prince of Denmark.* London: Andrew Clark, 1676.

Shattuck, Charles H. "Shakespeare Promptbooks of the 17th and 18th Centuries." *Restoration and 18th Century Theatre Research* 3 (May 1964): 9–11.

———. *The Shakespeare Promptbooks.* Urbana: University of Illinois Press, 1965.

———. "The Shakespeare Promptbooks: First Supplement." *Theatre Notebook* 24 (Autumn 1969): 5–17.

Shirley, James. *The Dramatic Works of James Shirley.* 6 vols. Edited by William Gifford, completed by Alexander Dyce. London: J. Murray, 1833. (*The Maides Revenge* and *The Wittie Faire One* are in vol. 1, *Love's Cruelty* in vol. 2, *The Ball* in vol. 3, and *The Sisters* in vol. 5.)

Smith, Irwin. *Shakespeare's Blackfriars Playhouse.* New York: New York University Press, 1964.

Sorelius, Gunnar. *The Giant Race Before the Flood.* Uppsala: Almquist and Wiksells, 1966.

———. "The Smock Alley Prompt-Books of *1* and *2 Henry IV.*" *Shakespeare Quarterly* 22 (Spring 1971): 111–28.

Southern, Richard. *Changeable Scenery.* London: Faber and Faber, 1952.

———. *The Georgian Playhouse.* London: Pleiades Books, 1948.

———. "The Scene Plot of *The Change of Crownes.*" *Theatre Notebook* 4 (April–June 1950): 65–68.

———. "Theatres and actors." In *The Revels History of Drama in English*, vol. 5: *1660–1750*, by John Loftis, Richard Southern, Marion Jones, and A. H. Scouten. London: Methuen, 1976.

Spencer, Hazleton. *Shakespeare Improved.* Cambridge, Mass.: Harvard University Press, 1927.

Sprague, Arthur Colby. *Shakespeare and the Actors.* Cambridge, Mass.: Harvard University Press, 1944.

———. *Shakespearean Players and Performances.* Cambridge, Mass.: Harvard University Press, 1953.

———. *The Stage Business in Shakespeare's Plays: A Postscript.* London: for the Society for Theatre Research, 1954.

Spring, John R. "The Dorset Garden Theatre: Playhouse or Opera House?" *Theatre Notebook* 34 (1980): 60–69.

———. "Platforms and Picture Frames: A Conjectural Reconstruction of the Duke of York's Theatre, Dorset Garden, 1669–1709." *Theatre Notebook* 31 (1977): 6–19.

Stevenson, Allen. "The Case of the Decapitated Cast." *Shakespeare Quarterly* 6 (Summer 1955): 275–96.

Suckling, Sir John. *The Works of Sir John Suckling*, vol. 2, *The Plays*, ed. L. A. Beaurline. Oxford: Clarendon Press, 1971.

Summers, Montague. *The Playhouse of Pepys.* London: Kegan Paul, Trench, Trubner, 1935.

———. "A Restoration Prompt-Book." *Times Literary Supplement*, 24 June 1920, p. 400. Reprinted in his *Essays in Petto.* London: Fortune Press, n.d. [1928].

———. *The Restoration Theatre.* London: Kegan Paul, Trench, Trubner, 1934.

———. *See also* Congreve, William.

Survey of London, vol. 35: *The Theatre Royal Drury Lane and The Royal Opera House Covent Garden.* Edited by F. H. W. Sheppard. London: Athlone Press, 1970.

Taylor, Ivan Earle, ed. *An Edition of Sir William Killigrew's Siege of Urbin.* Philadelphia: n.p., 1946.

Theatre Architecture & Stage Machines: Engravings from the Encyclopedia . . . Edited by Denis Diderot and Jean le Rond d'Alembert (c. 1780). Reprint. New York: Benjamin Blom, 1969.

Troili, Giulio. *Paradossi per pratticare la prospettiva.* Bologna: Gioseffo Longhi, 1683.

Tucker, Edward F. J. "The Harvard Manuscript of Parkhurst's *Ignoramus.*" *Harvard Library Bulletin* 19 (January 1971): 5–24.

Van Lennep, William. "The Smock Alley Players of Dublin." *English Literary History* 13 (1946): 216–22.

———. "Thomas Killigrew Prepares his Plays for Production." In *Joseph Quincy Adams Memorial Studies*, pp. 803–8. Washington: Folger Shakespeare Library, 1948.

Van Lennep, William, ed., with Introduction by Emmett L. Avery and Arthur

H. Scouten. *The London Stage, Part 1: 1660–1700*. Carbondale: Southern Illinois University Press, 1965.

Visser, Colin. "The Anatomy of the Early Restoration Stage." *Theatre Notebook* 29 (1975): 56–67 and 114–19.

———. "John Dryden's *Amboyna* at Lincoln's Inn Fields, 1673." *Restoration and 18th Century Theatre Research* 15 (May 1976): 1–11.

Webster, John. *The Complete Works of John Webster*. 4 vols. Edited by F. L. Lucas. New York: Oxford University Press, 1937. (*The Duchess of Malfi* is in vol. 2.)

———. *The Duchess of Malfi*. Edited by Elizabeth Brennan. London: Ernest Benn, 1964.

———. *The Duchess of Malfi*. Edited by John Russell Brown. Cambridge, Mass.: Harvard University Press, 1964.

———. *The Duchess of Malfi*. Edited by Clive Hart. Edinburgh: Oliver and Boyd, 1972.

Wertheim, Albert. "*Production Notes for Three Plays by* Thomas Killigrew." *Theatre Survey* 10 (November 1969): 105–13.

Wilson, John. *The Cheats*. Edited by Milton C. Nahm. Oxford: B. Blackwell, 1935.

———. *The Dramatic Works of John Wilson*. Edited by James Maidment and W. H. Logan. Edinburgh: W. Paterson, 1874.

Wright, James. *The Humours and Conversations of the Town*. London, 1693. Reprint. Gainesville, Fla.: Scholar's Facsimiles & Reprints, 1961.

Index

Full indexing of promptbooks will be found under play titles, not authors.